CROWNS

TRILOGY OMNIBUS

NICOLA TYCHE

COLUMBIA RIVER
PUBLISHING

COLUMBIA RIVER PUBLISHING
Vancouver, WA 98685

First published in the United States by Nicola Tyche
Copyright © 2025 by Nicola Tyche

This omnibus edition includes the following previously published works:

North Queen © 2023 Nicola Tyche
Shadow Queen © 2023 Nicola Tyche
War Queen © 2023 Nicola Tyche
All rights reserved.

ISBN: PB: 978-1-959615-20-0; eBook: 978-1-959615-21-7

Cover design by Saint Jupiter Graphic

CROWNS
By Nicola Tyche
THE NORTH SEA
THE SOUND
MERCIA
Free Cities
Sandor
ALEON
Valour
ALEON EMPIRE
Praetoria
THE WILD
Elam
Persus
HORSEMEN TRIBES
Songs
Bahoul
Eilor
ATOLEAN SEA
LORYS
Tarsus
EMERALD OCEAN
Aviron
Choan
Tarao
OSAN
JAPHETH
Hetahl
NESTRANA
Cosar
Nayalour
Faulken
Odepeth
Ashan
KHARAV
Pryam
ANDAN OCEAN
AGED SEA
Iron Bay
ETREUS
RAEL
SERRA
Slaver's Bay
N

NORTH QUEEN

CHAPTER ONE

Consciousness came like a dream, bending the mind as dreams often do. Her eyelids fluttered under an icy weight, and she struggled to focus her vision against the blur that fell across her face.

Where was she?

She blinked back the cold of snow and drew a sharp breath as she made out the shapes of needled treetops against the sky. How did she get here?

Her pulse quickened as she sat up with a start to find herself in the middle of a winter forest. Trees rocked softly in slips of wind, and dry snowflakes danced through the air.

What was this place? Where was she?

The hair rose along the back of her neck as an icy trickle ran up her spine.

Who was she?

A rush of panic coursed through her veins. She tried to stand but stumbled as a throbbing pain inside her head caught her on the rise, threatening her fragile balance. She pressed her fingers against her temples. What had happened? As she breathed, the ache subsided. Her eyes cleared, but her mind didn't. Why couldn't she remember?

She glanced around. The eyes of the aspens stared back at her, watching; the wind swept whispers around her. Fear pushed back the cold. The rush of blood pulsed in her ears. Her body told her to run. But from what? And to where?

No. She couldn't let panic take over. Her mind would come back—she only needed to give it a moment.

She drew in a deep breath to calm herself as she surveyed the forest around her. Several inches of snow sat on the ground, but only a light dusting covered her. She hadn't been here long. Frozen tears stippled the corners of her eyes, but she was lost for their cause. She struggled for reason against her clouded mind.

"Calm down," she told herself. "You're a grown woman. Pull yourself together." But telling herself to calm and actually calming were two different things. Still, she managed to keep the second wave of panic at bay.

She brushed her long icy-blonde tresses back from her face and combed the trees as she turned her attention back to her surroundings. The snow held only her own footprints, and they ended abruptly a few steps away. How had she even gotten here? It was as if she'd been dropped from the sky. And she was alone. A pang of fear twisted in her stomach again, but she pushed it down. That wouldn't help.

Movement startled her, and she jumped to find a winter fox peering out from deeper within the trees.

"Hammel's hell," she said breathlessly. "You scared me."

His white coat blended with the snow, and his black-tipped ears flicked back and forth. A fascinating beauty with an unnatural pull hung about him, and his bright, golden eyes looked back at her with a deep curiosity. For a moment, she forgot about being lost—but only for a moment.

He gave a chitter and trotted off between the trees. *How peculiar.*

But her mind didn't stay with the fox for long; she had more pressing matters. She skimmed the trees as her pulse picked back up, and again, she resisted the urge to run. There was nothing to run from, and nowhere to run to, but that settled her only slightly.

She shifted her attention to herself. The cool blue of her dress, layered under a smoky-white cloak, matched the winter world around her. Her sleeves ran long over the backs of her hands. A delicate chain hung from her neck, and she reached up to feel a round pendant at her chest. She ran her fingertips over its braided edge as she looked closely at the raised image at its center: a winterhawk. Surely it meant something, but what?

Turning back to her surroundings, she spotted a break in the woods and headed toward it. When she reached it, she found herself looking out over the rolling hills of an open meadow, where clusters of trees sporadically broke the sea of white. The brightness of winter flashed harsh against her eyes, and she squinted.

She searched for signs of a village or town: a road, tracks in the snow, smoke against the sky—anything. But only winter lay as far as the eye could see.

A chitter sounded behind her, and she turned to see the fox again. He gave a small snort.

"You're back, are you?"

What did he want? He trotted off into the forest, as if beckoning her deeper into the trees, but then stopped to look back over his shoulder. He twitched his tail, seemingly in agitation.

"What are you doing?" she called. His presence gave a welcome distraction from the threatening panic over her situation. "Can't you see I have problems of my own?" She sighed, but as she eyed the animal, a small smile came to her lips. "Are you here to help me, little fox?"

He cocked his head at the sound of her voice and then flitted off again, light as the snowflakes around him.

Funny little thing. Did he want her to follow him? She shook her head. That was silly. She ran her eyes along the edge of the forest and then back to the meadow. The meadow seemed her best option; she'd have better visibility and possibly a better sense of direction.

She glanced back to see the fox again. He cocked his head to the side once more and flicked his ears.

"Do you want to come along?" she asked, nodding toward the meadow. "I'd appreciate the company." Gods knew this furry distraction was the only thing keeping her from losing her last sliver of calm.

He skirted back into an icy thicket at the base of a large tree, peering at her from within.

Talking to a fox was silly. Pretending the fox had a rational mind and understood her was silly. But he was cute, and she supposed she could allow herself a little silliness to help lighten her circumstance.

"Are you sure you don't want to come?"

He didn't move from the thicket.

She shrugged. "All right. Well, goodbye, little fox." She gave him one last smile and then stepped into the open winter.

Now, away from the forest and the shield of the trees, she shivered as the wind bit at her skin. She pulled up the thick hood of her cloak, but it did little to warm her. Her eyes stung, and her fingers ached from the cold.

Her pace slowed in the deeper snow of the open meadow. Twice she stumbled on hidden rocks. Perhaps following the tree line along the forest might have been better.

She couldn't control her shivering now, and she forced her eyes and mind on only her path ahead. The first cluster of trees wasn't much farther, and it would be a small reprieve from the gusts of icy air. Her legs burned as she pressed on. She reached the small grouping of trees and huddled against the rough bark, rubbing her arms underneath her cloak to spur some warmth. How had she managed to get herself in the middle of a frozen forest? Where had she come from? Her dress was well made; she seemed properly put together. Surely she hadn't been out long, which, she hoped, would mean someone would be looking for her and might soon find her.

"You look lost," a gravelly voice called.

She jumped and turned to see a burly man leaning against a knotted pine. He wore a frayed winter jacket lined in matted fur and a dagger belted around his waist. His unkempt hair fell unevenly over his grimy brow, and he gave a grin of rotting teeth. He rocked his weight off the tree and lumbered toward her.

A shiver ran down her spine. "Oh, I'm fine," she said, trying to hide her unease with a polite smile. Her mind raced for defenses. "I lost my horse on my morning ride, but I know my brothers are looking for me and will be along soon."

He scratched at the motley hair on his unshaven cheek and slid his gaze down and back up her body. His grin widened. "What a coincidence," he rasped. The snow crunched under the weight of his footfalls as he stepped closer. "My brothers should be along soon too. And they'd love to meet you."

Her heart pulsed faster. Escaping would be difficult in the open. She swallowed the panic rising in her throat. She needed to keep her wits about her.

"I'm sure they're lovely, but I should be on my way." She backed up slowly, positioning herself to flee, but he lurched forward and grabbed her wrist, stopping her escape.

"I can't let you do that."

"Get your hands off me!" she demanded, trying to pull away from him.

He gave a grisly chuckle.

She fought his hold, striking out with her free hand, but his thick layers thwarted her defense. He pulled her closer, and the putrid smell of his breath—a vile, rotting stench—filled her nostrils. She whipped her hand up and raked her nails across the exposed skin of his face. He reeled back, growling in pain, and she sank her teeth into the flesh of his fingers. He lost his grip, and she wrenched away.

Everything within her screamed to run—this time with reason.

She sprinted back toward the forest. Her heart raced, coursing energy through her and giving her a burst of speed. His raged curses rang heavily close behind, and she feared she might not make it to the trees. Her lungs stung with each icy inhale; her legs begged her to stop. But she pushed herself harder, coughing for breath as she ran.

His growling huffs grew fainter, and she finally dared to peek back. She had gained a bit of distance from him. He was fast for his size, but she was faster. Her body tired, slowing, but her fear kept her going. She couldn't feel her feet and worried about falling—she *needed* to make it to the forest. Almost there, she racked her mind with what to do next. The snow would give her position away. She would have to outrun him. She glanced back again and, to her horror, caught sight of not only her assailant but three more men a little way behind him.

Reaching the tree line, she charged into the wood. As she fled deeper into the forest, it grew quiet behind her. Had he stopped? Was he waiting for his friends? She looked around desperately. Her body couldn't run anymore, and the high-branched evergreens gave little opportunities to climb and hide. She couldn't see her pursuers, but the sound of their voices told her they had joined up at the edge of the forest.

She paused as she raced through her options. Suddenly, the small fox appeared again, sitting calmly on a fallen tree.

"You again," she said, panting as she looked around and tried to rationalize a plan. "Any help would be greatly appreciated," she added. His ears perked as he watched her.

Stupid, she scolded herself. Now wasn't the time to be talking to a fox.

She picked up her pace again, fleeing farther into the wood. Lighter snow made her trail less noticeable. She saw a ridge ahead and sprang toward it. A frozen stream lay below, sheltered from the snow by its banks. Her pulse raced as her chances of eluding her pursuers grew marginally better. She slid down onto the ice, trying not to disturb the snowy bank too much, and made her way along the frozen water, but it still didn't hide her. If they made it to the stream, they'd see her.

She noticed an alcove carved out along the stream's bank. Although it was small, it would conceal her. If she was lucky, she could wait until they moved on. She crept into the hollow, pulling her skirts tightly around her and trying to quiet her labored breath.

The forest stood quiet. She waited. No one came. She waited longer. Still, she heard nothing, but she knew better than to venture out.

A branch snapped nearby.

Her heart beat heavily in her chest. A wave of fear washed over her, and she cursed her choice to hide. She should have kept running. Now she could only wait and hope they wouldn't find her.

"Where are you, lovely?" a sickening voice called. "I know you hear me."

"Alke, we shouldn't be in here," a second voice replied. "It's not worth it. We should just leave her."

"Shut your face, you coward! I'm not leaving without that wench."

She bit back a cry rising in her throat.

"There's much worse than me in this forest," he called to her. "Be smart, come out."

His companion snickered.

The air grew quiet again. She strained her ears, but she heard nothing. Still, she waited. She wasn't foolish enough to think they'd gone. Her legs cramped in the tight confines, but she didn't dare move.

Suddenly, a hand reached down and grabbed her arm. She let out a scream as he dragged her from her hiding space.

"Gotcha," the brute wheezed, this time holding her at arm's length to stave off her defensive attack.

"Let me go!" she cried, twisting against him.

His companion, looking just as disheveled, chuckled beside him, but there was no sign of the other two. Where were they?

"We got her!" her captor bellowed over his shoulder, and she realized the others had stayed at the edge of the wood. They gave a few celebratory calls and urged their friends to hurry out as he dragged her back toward them.

"Let me go!" she shouted again as she struggled, desperately fighting against him, but she couldn't match his strength. He gave a raspy chuckle and pulled her along.

"Alke," the second man called from behind them, but her captor dragged her on, too enthralled with his catch.

"Alke!" The man's voice came more urgent now, enough to pull even her attention.

The man that held her looked over his shoulder with a snarling glare. "Shake off, man. Come on."

But something was wrong. His companion didn't move.

"Bullo, come on," her captor snapped, growing impatient.

But the man still didn't move. His lips trembled.

"Bullo?"

The man pulled a dagger from his belt with shaking hands and brought the blade to his own neck.

She paused in her fight to free herself as a creeping dread snaked through her.

Her captor's eyes widened. "Bullo, what are you doing?"

Bullo's face strained, his veins bulging at his temples. "Alke!" he cried to his friend in terror. "Help me—"

But the blade cut off his words as he sliced into his own flesh. She gave a terrified gasp but held back a scream. Bullo sputtered as he choked for air. Blood sprayed down the front of his matted furs, falling to the ground and coloring the surrounding snow. He staggered forward, then collapsed with a gurgle onto the forest floor.

"Bullo!" her captor shouted, and moved toward him. Then he stopped suddenly. He let go of her wrist, but she stood frozen, too terrified to run. He looked back at her as his face twisted, his eyes widening with fear. "Witch!" he snarled.

She stumbled back. He bared his rotting teeth as he pulled his own dagger from his belt. She took another step back, shaking her head. What was happening?

"Witch!" he bellowed.

His fellow men yelled to him from the tree line, their voices urgently calling him to get out of the forest, but they didn't enter. Why didn't they come?

He raised his dagger, and terror ran through her. He blamed her, and he was going to kill her.

"No, please!" she cried.

They both let out a scream as he swung the dagger inward on himself and plunged it into his own stomach. He fell to his knees, and she staggered backward.

"Witch!" he screamed, then he pulled the blade from his belly and swung it again, sinking it back into his gut. She covered her mouth and watched in horror as his screams died, and he fell forward onto the forest floor, soaked in his own blood.

"Alke!" the two men bellowed from the tree line. "Alke! Bullo!"

But they still didn't enter.

Her weeping breaths were uncontrollable now.

The air fell quiet. Had the others fled? The man named Bullo had been afraid—but of what? Whatever had killed these men would surely come for her next. She waited, her tears freezing on her face.

But nothing came. Quiet sat around her, broken only by the sound of her ragged breath.

A faint rustling made her jump, and she turned to see the fox sitting on a stump. He cocked his head.

A terrifying thought hit her. "Did you do that?" she whispered.

No. That was ridiculous. But if he didn't, what did? The animal flicked his tail, waiting.

She stood, shaking from the cold or from terror. Maybe both. As she stared at the dead men, her fear urged her to flee, but she was on her own, and she needed a weapon. Bullo's lifeless hand still clutched his bloody dagger. She approached cautiously, almost fearing he'd spring back to life. Sneaking forward, she grabbed the dagger by the blade so as not to touch him, and then scrambled backward in a hasty retreat. It was sticky with his blood, and her stomach turned. She wiped as much as she could on the frozen ground and then looked back at the fox.

"This is madness," she whispered shakily, "but I'm out of ideas. If you want me to follow, then lead on already. Take me away from here."

He leapt forward, finally happy at her compliance, and she followed after.

Chapter Two

She followed the fox north, breathing deep the winter air to calm herself, but calm wouldn't come. Blood still stained her hands. Fear still stained her mind. What had happened to the men in the forest would haunt her. But what *had* happened?

She eyed the fox warily. He had been there...

He trotted alongside her, stopping to pounce on anything that resembled something to play with, or a tasty snack.

"You seem to be taking this entire situation rather well." Her voice still shook slightly. "Better than I am."

He batted the tip of a stick above the snow with his paw and then skirted to the next.

"I mean, you didn't run away. You don't even seem... bothered, really."

Because he was a *fox*, with a twilight of memory, and he probably didn't even care. And yet...

She narrowed her eyes at him. "You can see how that might make one question... your involvement..."

The animal darted under a thicket at the base of a tree and shuffled around before barreling back out of it. He didn't even seem to remember she was still there, much less able to overpower the minds of her attackers and force them to kill themselves. It was a ridiculous notion, and she quickly pushed the thought from her mind. But if it wasn't the fox, what had come for those men? And why hadn't it come for her?

And now here she was, following this fox—admittedly not the wisest idea, but he was all she had at the moment. He was all she knew. And he helped settle her.

"If you're here to help me, perhaps you could do something useful? Maybe dig me a burrow to sleep in?"

He seemed oblivious to her now.

She gazed up at the fading afternoon sky. "A warm burrow, with a fire and fur blankets." She would need shelter soon. And food. "Maybe you could find me something to eat? Or lead me to a castle with a warm bath and a feast of roast and honeyed bread?"

He cocked his head. She would have smiled if she weren't trying so hard to quell the panic rising inside her.

"You're cute. But I'm beginning to think you're lost too." She scanned the trees around her. It didn't seem she would find shelter anytime soon, and she shivered as the cold sank into her core. She pulled the hood of her cloak up, covering her head for more warmth. "I'm ready for that burrow now."

The animal ignored her and sniffed around a large rock. She pursed her lips as she tried to not let desperation overwhelm her. It was foolish to have followed a fox. She wasn't any closer to improving her situation, and the day was fading. Fear crept back inside her, and tears threatened.

"Don't be so dramatic," she whispered to herself as she turned her attention to what to do next. The protection of the trees kept the wind at bay. She could build a fire for warmth, and she reminded herself people didn't starve to death right away. Her nerves started to settle.

Suddenly, the fox stopped. He crouched low, flicking his ears forward, then back. His nose tested the air, and her pulse quickened. He flattened his ears against his head with his hackles raised, let out a low growl, and then turned and raced back the way they'd come.

She clenched her stolen dagger tighter as her fear resurfaced. Two ill-intentioned men still lurked about. Had they returned? She stood frozen, listening and scouring the trees for any movement.

All was quiet.

She was alone.

She let out her breath. Flighty fox, she thought, feeling foolish to have believed he was leading her somewhere. She'd wasted precious time.

Just then, a sound caught her ear. She stopped, straining to hear from which direction it came. It echoed through the forest again—a rustling thud—closer now, and she peered through the trees. Spotting movement, her heart leapt to her throat. Her eyes narrowed, focusing.

An animal.

A horse.

A horse with a rider. A man. Drawing nearer.

She ducked low and sidled up to a large tree, but she wasn't exactly hidden. The best she could do was to not draw attention and let him pass unaware. She clutched the dagger tighter and praised herself for taking it.

The rider drew closer, and she slunk back out of sight and waited, listening to the hoofbeats of his horse. As they grew louder, she placed him only a few yards away. A little longer and he'd be past her. She backed around the tree to stay hidden, but her shoulder caught a small branch, and its echoing snap broke the quiet of the forest.

The hoofbeats stopped.

Her heart raced.

The sing of steel made her shudder as he pulled his sword from its scabbard, and she braced her back against the tree. Her mind screamed for her to run, but her body threatened to forfeit. She didn't have the energy; he would catch her.

With animals in the forest, the sound could have come from anything—if only he'd believe that. She prayed he'd move on. Waiting felt like an eternity.

She strained to listen, but she could barely hear over the hammering of her heart in her ears. Had he gone?

Slowly, she peered around the other side of the tree. Her heart stopped when she saw the horse.

It stood without its rider.

She made a hasty retreat backward but gasped as she collided with a figure behind her—a figure very firm. And very male. Whirling around, she stumbled, but he caught her. She wrenched herself away and whipped her dagger to his neck.

He didn't move to counter. Instead, he held his arms out, with his sword pointed down, yielding.

"I don't want any trouble." She tried to sound as fierce as she could.

His eyes widened as he drew in a breath. "Norah?" he whispered.

Did he call her a name? Was it *her* name? Her chest tightened. Did she know him?

She pulled back the hood of her cloak as she took a step back, with her arm still outstretched and threatening to use the dagger. They only stared at each other.

His blond hair was short, but not too short. His square jaw held the shadow of a beard as it tapered to his chin, although she could tell he was a man typically clean-shaven. He wore light armor over a thick jacket—he was a soldier of some sort. His fitted breeches met polished boots, and silver trimmed his scabbard. He wasn't like the men who had chased her before. And there was something about him...

He took a step closer, and she moved back, gripping the dagger. "That's far enough!" she warned.

His face twisted in confusion. "Norah?" he said again. He took another step toward her.

"Stop!" she demanded, holding the dagger in front of her. "Don't come any closer." He was already too close.

He looked at the blade and then back up at her. "Don't you recognize me? It's me, Alexander." His eyes held the glint of a tear. "Norah, it's me."

No recollection came as she studied him. She had no memory of his face, his concerned brow, his eyes. No memory of his name. Yet he seemed to know her...

Relief flooded her, but she clutched it back. She wasn't having the best of luck in meeting trustworthy strangers in the forest. He held his hand up in pause, then slid his sword back into its scabbard without taking his eyes off her. She softened her stance but didn't lower the blade. A handsome face didn't make one trustworthy.

"You know who I am?" she asked, still guarded.

"Of course," he said with a broken breath. "I'd know you anywhere."

"And who am I, exactly?" If he called her a witch, she'd stab him.

His brows drew together. "You don't know?"

If she knew, she wouldn't be asking, but she bit back the snap of words on her tongue. Emotion glazed his face, bringing a stir of her own. Her heart raced as she shook her head.

He hesitated but then asked, "And you don't know who I am?" His voice came even softer.

She shook her head again. "No."

He winced and then looked to the ground for a moment. Then he swallowed.

"Who am I?" she pressed.

His eyes found hers again, and they burned a brilliant blue. "You're Norah Andell... of Mercia, the Northern Kingdom."

Norah Andell. A name strangely familiar to her, yet not. Slowly, she lowered the dagger.

"I've been searching for you." He gazed down at her hands, and his brow creased. "You're bleeding. Are you hurt?"

Chained in her bewilderment, she didn't move as he swept forward and took her hands in his, but his touch made her jump. "Um, no," she said, pulling away. "It's not mine." He was so close to her now. Dangerously close. But he didn't feel dangerous. He felt safe, and...

No. She didn't know this man. Then something caught her eye. The breastplate of his armor bore a raised emblem—*a winterhawk*—the same as the pendant around her neck. She reached up to her chest and clasped her fingers around it. "Who are you?"

His brow dipped. He paused before saying, "I'm Alexander Rhemus, lord justice to the queen regent. Norah, she's been waiting for your return. We all have."

That didn't make sense. "The queen regent? Why?" Why would a queen regent be waiting for her?

"Because you're her granddaughter."

Her pulse quickened. Her granddaughter? She shook her head. "No, that can't be right." A granddaughter of a queen wouldn't be wandering alone in a forest. "That can't be right," she said again.

"I tell you the truth, but, Norah"—he glanced around them—"we should go. I can explain everything on the way, but right now, we need to get out of the Wild."

She took a step back. She wasn't going anywhere with him. Not yet. "How did I get here?"

He shook his head. "I don't know."

Her eyes narrowed. "Then how did you know where I was?"

"I didn't, exactly," he answered with a tilt of his head. "I've been searching for what I saw in a vision."

She raised a brow. "You saw a vision, and you just got on a horse and came to find me in the middle of a forest?" No rational person would do that.

"Not just any forest—the Wild. But yes."

She didn't know what that meant, but that was the least of what she needed answered. "That's madness."

"But... you're here," he countered. "And we really do need to go. It's not safe here."

She took another step back. "Why?" As far as she was concerned, the forest was keeping her safe from random strangers.

"The Wild isn't kind to those who trespass."

Was that what had happened to the two men earlier? Yet it hadn't done anything to her. Maybe this was a ploy to get her to go with him. If she was who he said, how had she come to be wandering alone in a forest, anyway? Perhaps she'd run away. Maybe she didn't want to go back. She bumped up against a tree behind her.

"How long have I been gone?" She couldn't have been out very long. Her dress wasn't too soiled, aside from her fall, and her hair hung untangled and neatly kept.

He pushed out a scant breath, baffled. "You remember nothing?"

She swallowed the lump rising in her throat. "No."

He stared at her. "You've been gone three years."

Her breath quivered, and she gripped the tree behind her to steady herself. "Three years?" She shook her head. That wasn't possible. How could one, especially the granddaughter of a queen regent, just disappear for three years?

He looked around them again. "Norah, please. We have to go." He reached out his hand. "Will you let me take you home? Your grandmother's at the castle."

Castle. She glanced around for her fox. Her thoughts had been in jest, but perhaps he really had been leading her to a castle. Better than a burrow.

"We won't arrive until tomorrow," Alexander told her. "But there's an old homestead we can reach before dark. It's not much, but it's shelter with a place for a fire."

She still fought the uncertainty, trying to take everything in and searching for clarity on her situation. But she did need shelter and a fire. And still, there was something about him...

"Norah," he pleaded, "you do know me. You may not remember yet, but I do. And your people do. They've been waiting for you a very long time."

Her people. She knew he meant it in reassurance, but it brought only more anxiousness. So much responsibility. If people were truly waiting for her, they'd expect something from her, need something from her, and what could she give if she couldn't remember?

And could she trust this man? She shifted, glancing at the winterhawk emblem on his breastplate again, then the gilded handle of his sword. He certainly wasn't the same as the foul-intentioned men before. It was almost nightfall, and it had started to snow. She couldn't see another choice. She'd have to trust this stranger—this stranger who knew her. Slowly, she nodded.

With a small exhale of relief, he led his horse in front of her and reached out his hand. "May I?"

She eyed him warily. "I can manage."

The corner of his lips turned up, and he gave an obliging nod.

She felt Alexander's eyes on her as she climbed onto the horse. Her dress made her efforts less elegant than she'd hoped, but she managed to settle sideways into the saddle, with the dagger still in her hand.

The animal, a trained warhorse, stood steady, but Alexander held it like he trusted nothing. He waited until she gave him a nod. Then, with a final look around, he led them back the way he'd come.

CHAPTER THREE

She didn't know him…

Alexander led his horse past the tree line, out of the thickly wooded forest, and north into the snow-covered hills. A small sense of relief filled him to step out of the Wild and away from its dangers, but it was short-lived. He'd rather face those dangers than accept the circumstance before him now.

Three years. Three years he'd waited for the day he would see her again, and she didn't even know him. A pain gripped his chest, but he fought to ignore it. Later. He'd deal with it later, after he got her to safety. After he got her home.

Leaving the forest, she pulled her cloak tighter around her and grew even smaller in the saddle of his giant destrier, like she was reluctant to leave. Her eyes swept warily across the open hills, as if she didn't know she was crossing into safety. As if she preferred to stay in the most dangerous place in the world.

Something had happened to her. The blood on her hands…

"Will you tell me what happened?" he asked.

Her lips parted, and she looked down at the dagger she held. Then she swallowed.

"Whenever you're ready," he added. It had obviously been traumatic for her. His chest tightened. He should have come sooner. If only he'd known.

At least she wasn't physically hurt. In fact, far from it. She looked well taken care of. Had she been in the Wild all this time? No—that was impossible. So where *had* she been, and how did she end up in the Wild?

He couldn't keep his eyes from wandering back to her as he led his destrier through the hills. He was so afraid it was all a dream, afraid none of it was real. When he glanced back to find her watching him, he forced his gaze forward again.

"How did I come to be lost?" she asked, finally breaking the silence.

He glanced back at her. He still couldn't believe he'd finally found her. Her question… He forced his mind to focus. Where to start? There was no easy answer, but he had told her he'd explain, and she was waiting. "We were at war," he said. "Your father took you away. Somewhere safe."

She straightened. "My father?"

"King Aamon." One of the greatest kings Mercia had ever known.

"You'll take me to him?"

His heart fell for her, and he stopped. "No, Norah." He'd been dreading the day she would learn of this. "He died in the war, shortly after you left, in the Battle of Bahoul."

She stilled, and her throat moved with a struggled swallow. She'd been close with her father. Perhaps it was merciful that she didn't remember right now. Despite that, there was no mistaking the sadness in her eyes.

"I'm sorry," he said softly. "He was a good man and a great king, and he loved you very much."

She cast her eyes down, but at nothing in particular. When she raised them, they were glistening. "And if my grandmother is queen regent, then my mother..." Her words trailed off.

"She died in childbirth. You never knew her."

She quieted. Anger coursed through him—how cruel fate was to give her loss before she'd even found herself. How cruel the gods.

Slowly, he started them forward again.

"How do we know each other?" she asked.

He wavered at her question, looking back at her from the corner of his eye. He couldn't yet accept being a stranger to her, but he forced himself to answer. "We've known each other since we were children. I'm the son of Beurnat Rhemus of Northridge—Beurnat the Bear—who was lord justice and right hand to your father. My family has served Mercia and the crown for twelve generations." He looked back at her. "It's in my blood to protect you and the realm."

That seemed to settle her slightly. He was glad he could give her some sense of comfort.

Their pace slowed in the deeper snow, but he pressed on with greater urgency. They needed to make it to the homestead by nightfall, before the darkness and true cold set in on them.

"Am I alone, other than my grandmother?" she asked.

"You have a cousin, although you don't know each other well. No other family."

He glanced back and caught the hint of a frown on her lips. "But you're not alone," he added. "There will be many to help you. Your grandmother's a strong woman who has great wisdom and the respect of the people. She'll guide you, along with the members of the Mercian Council. And"—he paused—"you'll have a lord justice."

Her brows drew together. "And what's a lord justice?"

Only his life's duty. But he gave a small smile. He wasn't offended. "A justice provides counsel and commands your armies. Executes your will. A justice is your right hand."

"Will that be you?"

He'd introduced himself with that title, but... "I'm justice to the queen regent, who holds Mercia in safekeeping until your return. After your coronation, you'll select a justice of your own choosing." And he wasn't so bold as to assume she'd choose him, especially not now.

The sun had set and only its fading light remained. A wave of relief filled him when he finally spotted the small house in the distance.

"Have you any family?" she asked.

A smile came to his lips. "I have a younger brother, Adrian. You'll see him at the castle again—or meet him, rather," he corrected himself. "He's missed you."

"It sounds like we were close?"

He nodded. "You were very much like a sister to him. He'll be incredibly happy to see you."

"I imagine it will be hard for him that I don't remember."

His steps slowed, and he swallowed. His own heart suffered the same. It *was* hard. The hardest. He pushed down the pain and forced a smile. "Even if you *did* remember him, you wouldn't recognize him. He's nineteen now, almost twenty, as tall as I am, and training for the guard."

"How old am I?"

"Twenty-five."

"And you?" She shifted in the saddle, as if suddenly feeling her questions too prying.

"Twenty-nine," he answered readily. He would tell her anything of himself, especially given that she knew everything about him already. Or she used to...

She pulled her lip between her teeth, the way she did when she was puzzling something. "Did you really believe I'd come back? After all this time?"

He shot her a look of surprise. "Why would I not?"

"Three years I've been gone. I could've been dead."

"But you weren't. And we didn't know it would be three years. Each time I searched for you, I thought I'd find you. But the days turned to months, and the months turned to years."

"You've searched for me this entire time?"

Alexander glanced back at her again. "Of course I have."

Their eyes caught, and he couldn't look away this time. Her mouth parted slightly, and she drew in a breath.

His heart beat faster. Did she remember something?

But she broke the hold and looked across the hills. "Why did my father take me away? You said we were at war?"

He didn't answer immediately. He'd tell her anything, but he feared some of it might be too much, too soon. "I know you have a lot of questions," he said over his shoulder. "But I should leave some of these answers to your grandmother. She'll want to share them with you herself." And it was better that way. Some things he didn't want to talk about—tried not to even think about.

It was near dark by the time they reached the homestead.

"It's no place for a princess," he admitted, "but it's shelter. We'll continue on at first light."

He brought the horse in front of the small stacked-stone house and turned to Norah, offering his hand. She accepted it and slid to the ground. He stared at her hand in his for a moment, holding it. The pause felt too long, but he couldn't let her go. Her fingers trembled, and he realized she was shivering. He needed to get her warmed.

He pulled her toward the house. "Let's get you inside."

The homestead was quaint, open, and bare beyond the necessary amenities. Alexander worked quickly to build a fire in the hearth on the far wall and motioned her closer. "Here. Come by the fire."

She neared, flexing her fingers that were still stained with blood. She'd said it wasn't hers. What had happened to her? He wanted to ask again, but he stopped himself. He'd let her settle more.

"I need to see to my horse," he said. "I'll be back in a moment." He didn't want to leave her, but the animal needed care. There was a small outbuilding behind the house that would provide shelter.

Alexander made quick work of it, putting the destrier in a stall and blanketing it with a cover that hung near the door. He broke the top layer of ice that had formed in the water barrel and tossed into the stall a half bale of hay that had been stacked in the corner. He'd leave some coins for the kind soul who kept the homestead stocked for travelers.

He returned to the house with his leather packs and a bucket of snow. When he entered, the sight of her stopped him in his tracks all over again. Norah sat by the fire, holding her hands out to catch its warmth. She glanced back at him. Her blue eyes danced with the light of the flame.

Alexander caught himself staring and pulled away, finally closing the door against the cold. He held up the bucket. "We can melt this," he told her. "It's not exactly a washbasin, but you can clean off your hands."

She gave him a small appreciative smile and worked on melting the snow while he put more wood on the fire. She didn't wait for it to warm before she plunged her hands in, rubbing them harshly to scrape off the blood and dirt.

Alexander watched her. "Where did you get that dagger?" he asked. Now able to see it better, he noted it wasn't a high-quality blade.

She scrubbed the last of the blood from her skin. "I took it from someone." She cut him a look that told him he'd be sorely mistaken if he expected her to give it up. He almost chuckled. He would never.

"A drifter?" he asked.

Her brow quirked in confusion.

"There are men who have no home," he explained, "but venture about, harassing people they run into and causing chaos. Their numbers have grown over the years. They've become quite a problem."

"Sounds about right," she mumbled.

"Is that where you were all this time?" he asked. "With drifters?"

She frowned. "Do I look like I've been with drifters?"

Was she offended? He shook his head quickly. "No. You look beau—not like you've been... No. No, you don't." It was a weird stumble of words, and heat rushed to his cheeks. She watched him as he watched her.

She flexed her fingers again against the heat of the flame. He was desperate to ask her more, but he didn't want to push her. Fortunately, he didn't have to.

"I came across a man, much like you described," she said. "He and three others chased me into the forest."

Alexander shifted his weight, and a fever of anger rippled over his skin. He couldn't help himself, and he asked, "What happened?"

She shook her head. "I'm not entirely sure. Two... um..." She struggled with the words as she clutched her hands together, and his heart lurched. What she must have gone through...

She rocked forward a little, then back. "Two, uh... they... killed themselves."

Killed themselves. In front of her. And she was still obviously shaken. He wanted to move closer, to take her hand, to comfort her, but he couldn't. He was a stranger to her—the best thing he could do right now was give her space.

"The other two ran off," she continued. "I can't explain it, but it was horrific. The most terrifying part was that... they didn't want to kill themselves, but it was like they had no control. One of them kept screaming that I was a witch."

She swallowed, shifting under his eye. "But I'm not a witch," she added quickly. Her voice dipped, betraying her lack of confidence in those words. She shook her head with an unsure shrug. "I don't know what happened. And I thought whatever killed them would come for me, too, but it didn't. So, I took the dagger because I had nothing else, and I was following a fox through the woods when you found me."

His brows drew together. "You were following a fox?"

"I'm not mad," she insisted.

"No, you're not mad," he assured her. "And I know you're not a witch. The Wild is home to the faeries, or spirits, whatever they are. It's said that they protect it with a kind of power, one that lets them take over the mind of anyone who enters, make them do things, harm themselves or others. Everyone knows the stories like the one you tell now."

"And you still came?" Her blue eyes stared back at him.

He was caught in the snare of her gaze again. "There's nowhere I wouldn't go for you, Norah," he said softly.

Her lips parted slightly, and her breath caught. He couldn't look away. Finally, she pulled back and broke the spell. "The fact we're talking about faeries at all is utter madness," she said.

He gave a small smile. "Then maybe you are a witch."

But his joke fell flat, and she only blinked.

"Forgive me," he said. "That was meant in jest."

"And it was funny. I'm just..." She let out a breath.

"You're tired, and you've been through a lot. You should eat." He reached over to his pack and pulled out some salted meat and bread, along with a wineskin, and handed them to her.

They sat on the floor by the burning logs, soaking in the warmth of the flames. He adjusted another log with his sword. "I'll hunt for us in the morning."

"It's fine, really. I'm appreciative just for this," she said, lifting the meat in gesture and then finishing it. He held out his bread roll, and a small smile escaped from her as she took it. He offered his meat as well, but she politely shook her head.

"I know you want it," he said.

"Thank you, but I'm full."

He knew she wasn't, but he didn't press. He watched her for a moment and smiled, then folded the meat back in the cloth instead of eating it and tucked it into his pack for her later.

"You shouldn't carry a drifter's dagger," he said as she finished the last of the bread. "Here." He pulled a knife from the sheath on his calf, tucked inside his boot, and held it out for her. "This suits you better."

She reached out and took it. The blade was shorter, and the hilt fit her hand better. It was his favorite knife, custom made and well taken care of, unlike the rusted drifter's dagger with open seams along its handle.

He pulled off his calf sheath and held it out to her as well. "Put this around your leg, inside your boot, with the knife where you can easily reach it."

She slipped the blade into the sheath and stared down at it in her hands. When she raised her eyes again, they locked with his. "Thank you," she whispered.

He shook his head. "No need to thank me. It's my duty."

Even in the dim light of the room, the storms of her blue eyes pulled him in, holding him. "We should get some rest," she said.

Yes. Rest. Alexander rose and pulled open the second pack. He shook out a rolled pad over the meager bed. "You sleep here. I can't promise comfort, but it's clean. I'll be by the door."

Norah gave a small nod. She settled in, creaking the bed frame with every movement. He pulled a chair to the door and sat with his sword unsheathed and resting across his knees.

But as she lay, she didn't close her eyes. She only stared at the ceiling. "What happened?" she asked finally. "I have to know. Why did my father take me away?"

He sat quiet. This wasn't a short story, and not one of the first he wanted to welcome her home with.

"Tell me," she pressed.

Alexander let out a long breath. "We were at war, and they were coming for you." He paused. "Your father feared your capture, and so he took you. Far. Somewhere safe."

"Who was coming for me?" she asked.

"These aren't stories to tell in the night. You're safe, Norah. There's so much to remember, to learn. There will be plenty of time." But he knew his answers only drew more questions. "Rest," he said. "There will be more tomorrow."

Finally, she closed her eyes. After a time, her breaths came longer and deeper. He relaxed in the chair, but he wouldn't sleep. Not until he safely got her home.

Chapter Four

Norah woke to the sound of a crackling fire. She pulled the blanket higher around her neck and nestled into its warmth. It smelled of pine and soft leather, comfort and refuge—a familiar smell, a smell she'd always loved. She smiled as she blinked her eyes open. But unfamiliar stone walls looked back at her, and her smile faded.

Where was she?

Memories of the day prior flooded back, and she sat up with a start. The blanket that covered her spilled down into her lap, and she saw it wasn't a blanket at all, but Alexander's cloak.

She glanced around the empty room. Where was he?

Sunlight poured in from the small window onto the bed and across the floor. Her racing heart slowed. She eyed the cloak again as she drew her fingers across it, all too aware of the sense it had given her.

The door opened, and Alexander stepped in with more firewood and something else in his hands. The smell made her stomach rumble. She pushed off the cloak and stood, straightening her dress and brushing her hair back from her face.

His eyes caught hers, and he paused, simply looking at her. His lips parted. "Good morning," he said finally.

Even though he'd spoken only two words, his voice held a strange familiarity.

"Good morning," she replied.

He broke from her gaze. "I hope you slept well. Are you hungry?" He held out a hand of freshly cooked meat with flatbread wrapped in linen. "There's water by the fire."

"That smells amazing, thank you," she said, taking the food. "And I slept surprisingly well."

Alexander refueled the fire and then sat on the edge of the hearth. He held his food in his hand but didn't eat it.

Norah tried to keep her eyes from him as she ate, wary of the lure of his gaze and of the stir it caused inside her. "Yesterday you said you saw me in a vision—what was it?" she asked, refocusing herself on getting more answers. "How did you know to come for me?"

He shifted back on the hearth. "It was the last vision seen of you, three years ago, right before you left. We didn't know what it meant at the time, but after you disappeared, we suspected it was a clue as to where you were. You were in the middle of a forest, with trees all around you, dressed as you are now." He paused. "And your hair was... bright, shining. As it is now."

She raised her eyes to his and found herself caught in the snare she had tried so hard to avoid.

"I've searched every forest this kingdom over," he said, "well into Aleon and south into the lands of the Horsemen tribes. The Wild was the only place I'd stayed clear of. Until now."

She gave him a small smile. "Because of the faeries?"

"Because men don't return from there."

Norah bit her lip, feeling her jest poorly placed.

"It was the last place I thought I'd find you," he added.

Well, it *was* the last place he found her, but she kept that joke to herself. This wasn't a joking matter. She'd seen firsthand the dangers of this land of no return. She pulled herself free of the shackles of his eyes and finished the last of her meal. "I still doubt that I'm the person you say."

He offered her his meat and bread.

She shook her head. "I've had enough, thank you. You eat." He hadn't eaten his food the evening prior. She suspected he'd saved it for her.

"You *are* Norah Andell. I wouldn't mistake you, no matter how much time had passed." He settled back, finally taking some of his own food. "Wait until you return home. You'll see."

Home. That word seemed so distant right now.

"Speaking of, we should go." He smiled. "Your grandmother has no idea she's going to see you today. And Catherine Andell is not an easy woman to surprise. I'm very much looking forward to it."

Norah couldn't help but smile at the sense of his genuine excitement. But inside, her stomach twisted at the thought of meeting her grandmother.

Catherine. The name held no recollection. Yes, she expected the woman to be surprised, but this might not be the surprise she was hoping for—her lost granddaughter with no memory of herself or those who knew her. Norah turned her thoughts to their arrival, and the weight grew heavier in her stomach. People had been waiting a long time for her return; she wouldn't be what any of them were expecting, and likely not what they hoped for. There would be people she'd be expected to know, expected to care about. People that cared about her.

They left the warmth of the homestead and continued on their way, with her riding and Alexander again leading the horse. They'd make better time both riding, but the suggestion seemed too forward, and she couldn't muster the courage. They traveled mostly without conversation, but he glanced back to check on her often, as he had the day before.

At midday, they stopped for a meal of salted meat and more bread. Norah looked over the powdered hills of snow and wondered how much farther until they reached the castle.

"Mercia is just beyond those hills," Alexander said, pointing in the distance, as if reading her mind. His eyes met hers, and he smiled. "It's beautiful."

Norah forced a smile, but her stomach sat heavy. She tried to imagine her arrival. What would she say when she saw her grandmother? Would she recognize the woman? Would Norah be a disappointment to her?

"Here," he said, handing her a wineskin. "This will help calm your nerves."

She raised a brow. "Is it that obvious?"

He tipped his head to the side with a smirk. "A little. But you should be excited. You'll be surrounded by people who love you and have waited for this day."

"Alexander," she said, looking into his eyes, "I'm trusting you." It wasn't a statement; it was a plea.

His face grew serious. "I'll be by your side," he promised. He offered his hand, and this time she took it. He lifted her to the saddle and then took up the reins and led the horse forward. They continued on, and Norah sipped from the wineskin as they went.

As they reached the final peak, she gasped. A large city sprawled from the base of the hills to the northern coast in the distance. On an island off the mainland, a castle stood with its turrets and spires sharp against the sun-filled sky.

"Mercia," Alexander said as he looked back at her, his eyes shining. "Home."

"It *is* beautiful," she whispered.

"People will know who you are the moment they see you. Are you ready?"

She was nowhere near ready. She shifted in the saddle. "Do I look ready? No dirt on my face or sticks in my hair?"

He smiled. "No dirt or sticks. You're beautiful."

She couldn't help but smile back.

Alexander led his horse down and through the city. People gathered along the sides of the streets as they saw them, murmuring to each other with increasing excitement. As she and Alexander passed, the crowd followed them. Shouts rang out, and Alexander looked back at her with his eyes bright.

People came in flocks now. She looked at all the faces; there were so many of them. Some were laughing, some were crying, some were merely watching in astonishment. A deep fear seeded itself inside her. She hadn't entirely believed Alexander before... but what if she really was the princess? It all seemed very... impossibly possible now...

Just then, a bell rang out from the castle.

"Now everyone knows you're here," Alexander said.

They made their way to the bridge that connected the mainland to the castle's island. Tall stone arches rose from the frozen waters, as if placed there by the gods. It was hard to believe this was the work of men. Streams of helmed soldiers poured out of the castle gates and lined either side of the bridge. Norah looked at them in awe as Alexander led her through and into the large courtyard inside the castle walls.

They stopped at an empty fountain in the center. He reached up to her, and she let him help her to the ground. A flash of white caught her eye, and she looked up to the banner of the winterhawk in the sky.

"White is the color of Mercia," he explained. "The winterhawk is your father's—your—sigil." His blue eyes danced with excitement. "Welcome home, Norah." He moved to lead her toward the castle.

"Alexander," she called, stopping him.

He paused. "Yes?"

"Be near." She needed him near.

"Always," he promised.

Throngs of people flooded the courtyard from the terraced buildings surrounding the castle on the isle. Alexander led her through, moving slowly to keep her close. He summoned more guards, who closed in around them. Norah reached for his hand but then stopped herself. The want came so naturally, and it surprised her. They reached the stairs to the entrance, and he halted abruptly, pulling her from the thought.

Norah looked up to see a woman approaching, flanked by her guard. She was older, elegant and regal in a dark navy gown. Brown furs lay bulked around her neck and lined the hood of her cloak, but there was no missing the striking white hair peeking out from underneath. She floated down the stairs with magnetic beauty.

Alexander stepped forward. "Queen Regent." He bowed. "I—"

But she moved past him, as if not seeing him, and not hearing him either. Her gaze was locked on Norah. She pulled back the hood of her cloak; the green pools of her eyes were filled with wisdom and the cautiousness of disbelief. She was slightly shorter than Norah but held a regal stature—the poise of power. Beauty graced her face with her high cheekbones, her bright eyes. Age respected this woman. She stared at Norah for a moment, her expression giving nothing away.

Norah bit the inside of her lip. Was this where everyone would discover she wasn't who they thought? Perhaps that was better, anyway—to get it out of the way early and save them all from embarrassment later.

But then the woman's lip trembled. "Norah," she breathed. "Oh, my dear. You've finally come home."

Or they would just continue with this insanity. Norah couldn't move.

The queen regent reached out, brushing a lock of Norah's hair with her fingertips, and tears sprang from her eyes. She let out a silent cry and embraced Norah, pulling her close.

Norah drew in a sharp breath. Her own eyes brimmed. Even though she was still lost to herself, this woman made her feel found. She let herself accept the warmth of the embrace, the warmth of love. Her fear, her anxiety, her worry, all stopped for a moment. She needed this embrace, and she let herself have it.

Stepping back, the regent's eyes darted over her, taking her in. "How long we've waited for you to come home."

Norah forced a smile, trying to quell her own emotion. She couldn't find the words to speak.

"Queen Regent," Alexander started again.

"You must be so tired," she said to Norah. "Come. Come inside."

"Catherine," he said again, stronger now, finally pulling her attention. He leaned in close to her and said in a low voice, "She has no memory."

The woman's brows drew together. "What?"

He shook his head. "She doesn't know herself, or you." He paused a moment before he said, "She doesn't know me."

The regent looked at Norah in shock. "How ever did you find her?" But she didn't give him time to respond. "No matter," she said as she took Norah's hand. "Come, child, let's get you inside. We'll figure it all out."

Norah looked at Alexander, and he gave her a nod as the regent pulled her toward the castle. The oversize doors swung open, and the woman swept through, with Norah following behind. As the doors closed, they drowned out the sound of the crowd.

Relief settled over her, now that she was away from the masses. She didn't like the attention, but she quickly forgot the crowd as they passed through an expansive hall and then several smaller hallways. She marveled at the polished stone of white and light and the intricately sculpted busts that sat between the arched windows. Everything around her was so... bright, as if made from the sun itself. She glanced behind her to see if Alexander still followed. And he did.

They reached a chamber and entered, startling a young maid inside.

"Rebecca," the regent called to her, "start a bath."

The woman stood for a moment, then her eyes widened. "Princess Norah!" she exclaimed, and bowed quickly.

The title still unsettled her, and Norah shifted under its weight. Rebecca beamed as she stared, then she caught herself and broke away to prepare a bath.

The regent turned to another servant. "Something to eat for the princess. And wine. And water."

Norah didn't think she could eat; her nerves had the best of her, and her stomach, but the servant left before she could refuse. She let her eyes comb over the room with its fine tapestries and ornate furniture. Light spilled through the tall windows on the west wall. It was beautiful and overwhelming. A castle, the finery, the servants—surely she didn't belong here. She glanced back at Alexander, who remained at the door, not stepping inside. He gave her a reassuring smile.

The queen regent stopped and took her hand. "Are you all right, child?"

She pushed out a breath, fighting an unexpected wave of emotion with all the strength she could muster. "I'm sorry. This is all a bit much," she managed to get out.

"I'm sure it is, but we'll sort everything out. It will come back to you."

Or it *wouldn't*. She didn't want to think about that possibility, though. Not right now.

"What do you remember?" Catherine asked.

Norah shook her head—what did she remember? "I woke in the forest, like this." She motioned to herself. "I was lost for a time." How much detail to share? She didn't have the energy and didn't want to relive it. "Then Alexander found me." She looked back at him.

"Of course he did," the queen regent said, letting her gaze rest on him with a warm smile.

He gave a bow. "I'll leave you, Queen Regent." To Norah he said, "Welcome home, Princess Norah." He was more formal now, and more serious. She didn't like it.

"Thank you," Norah said. "For everything. And don't tell me it's your duty."

He lingered a moment longer, a silent confession he didn't want to go, then he gave a small nod and left her to the queen regent.

"Lord Justice," the regent called, "one more thing." She swept out of the chamber and into the hall after him.

Norah heard their voices in the hall but couldn't make out what was being said. She stood, drawing her bottom lip between her teeth. Perhaps she should just wait, or...

The woman named Rebecca stepped back into the room from the side chamber. "Your bath is ready, Princess Norah."

A bath. A bath would be good. Her mind reeled with the increasingly likely possibility that she might truly be a princess—she just needed to focus her mind on one task to hold herself together. She turned toward the bath chamber.

"By the gods, child," her grandmother said as she came back into the room.

Norah paused and turned back to her.

"I know you must be tired, but let me look at you." She clasped Norah by the shoulders and gave a smile that trembled with emotion. "How I wish Aamon were here. You're the image of your mother." Then she caught sight of the pendant around Norah's neck, and her eyes welled. She brushed it with her fingertips. "He gave this to you on your last birthday that we celebrated. The winterhawk belongs to Kelos, god of protection and vanquisher of evil. It's the sigil of the Andell crown. Your crown."

Norah brought her hand to the pendant and glanced down as she tilted it between her thumb and forefinger. Perhaps it had been Kelos watching over her. Alexander had found her in the middle of a forest—seemingly unbelievable, without some divine intervention. And the matching winterhawk on his breastplate was the only reason she'd agreed to go with him.

Well, the *main* reason.

The other being... there was just something about him...

The woman let out an emotional breath, snapping Norah back to the present. "Let's get you washed," her grandmother said, "and then we'll see you fed." She and the maids shuffled Norah into the bath chamber.

Before Norah could protest, they stripped her of her cloak and dress. She barely had time to squirm from her undergarments as she was shooed into the tub. Despite the initial feeling of invasiveness, a strange familiarity at being bustled about hit her, and the warmth of the water washed any remaining objections away.

"Rebecca, Serene," the queen regent said to the maids, "I'll take it from here."

The two women curtsied and left as Catherine draped a robe over a settee and sat beside it. "I still can't believe you're home."

Norah couldn't either. Why couldn't she remember? How could twenty-five years of her life have been taken from her? Would her memories come back? A slight panic welled again at the thought of them not.

"Now that you're back, everything will be set right," Catherine said.

Norah didn't even know what that meant, but it sounded daunting and only added to her growing anxiety. "I don't even know what I'm doing here."

"That will pass, my dear. Your memories will return, but until they do, we have to take care. I want no one to know of your condition."

"Wait. What? Why?" She couldn't keep this a secret for long.

"Your circumstance is complicated enough. And we can't risk anything jeopardizing your path."

"What path?"

"Don't worry about it right now. We'll get you cleaned and rested and fed. Your memories will return, and we'll sort through everything."

How could this woman be so calm about this? "How are you so sure?" Something within her snapped. Norah shook her head. "I can't keep this a secret. I don't know anyone, I don't know myself, or how I should be or what I should say. I don't even know what to call you. I've woken up in this world with all these expectations, and everyone's going to quickly discover I'm a fraud." It was hot in the bath now. Too hot.

"Oh, child," the regent said as she clasped Norah's shoulder. "Somewhere inside, you have over twenty years of ladyship ground into you. I saw to it myself. And all young rulers know nothing. No one will think you're a fraud. You're Evanya's daughter, and my granddaughter. There's no doubt."

But Norah had a lot of doubt.

The woman picked up a jar of bath salts and scooped a handful into the water. "Let's start with simple solutions. You may call me *queen regent*, as is appropriate in public. My name is Catherine, as I'm sure you've gathered by now, which you may call me privately. Or you may call me *grandmother* if you're comfortable with that. I'll no longer be queen regent after your coronation—a day I look forward to very much. It's not right for a kingdom to be without a head for so long."

A knot formed in her stomach. "My coronation?"

"Of course. Now that you've returned, you'll be queen. I've only been queen regent in your absence."

Norah shook her head again. She couldn't be queen. She knew nothing of this place, of these people; she knew nothing of ruling. "I can't be queen," she said. No. *No*, she couldn't do this. She swallowed. The air was suffocating. "This can't be right. I shouldn't be here." She reached for the towel and moved to rise.

Catherine clasped her shoulders firmly, stopping her and forcing Norah to look at her. "Child, I know this is overwhelming, terrifying even. But you're strong. You always have been. And I'm by your side, and I'll guide your every step. For now, we'll take one thing at a time. You will get through this. Do you understand?"

Norah drew in a breath. The regent's words were firm, sharp even, but not uncaring. It was what Norah needed to stave off her panic. Ever so slightly, she nodded—not a nod of agreement, but a nod of settling.

The woman's hands softened, but still held her.

One thing at a time. She could do one thing at a time, with Catherine beside her. And Alexander. *One thing at a time.* "I think I'd like to call you grandmother."

Catherine smiled. "I'd like that."

Chapter Five

Inside his chamber, Alexander hung his belt and sword on the wall and pulled off his armor, but it wasn't the weight of the steel plating that had been sitting heavily on him.

He played it back in his mind—seeing her in the forest, calling her name. The sting of her not knowing him hurt more than any battle wound.

So many ways he'd imagined how their reunion might have gone. Mostly joyous. Sometimes he imagined her angry with him, perhaps still hurt, but in each dream, he'd held her in his arms again. But for her to feel nothing... He hadn't imagined that.

Perhaps it was better this way. Things could never be as they were before, but now it was as though he'd truly lost her, and he didn't think he could bear it.

Alexander lumbered toward his bed. His legs didn't feel like his own. He sank down with a grimace, then he covered his eyes with his hand. It had been a long time since he'd shed any tears, so long he couldn't remember when. But they flowed freely now, and he let them come.

He hadn't been able to keep his pain hidden from Catherine. She'd raised him; she knew him like her own blood. And while the queen regent loved him, he'd seen the warning in her eyes. No doubt she would see this as an opportunity for Norah to start new. She would try to convince him to do the same. But that wasn't possible.

And he'd have to find a way to support Catherine. She'd spent more than twenty years preparing Norah's free spirit for the obligations of the crown, but now everything was gone, and what had taken twenty-five years would need to be rebuilt in days—another feat he wasn't sure was possible.

A knock on the door pulled him back, and he straightened, collecting himself. Alexander ran his hand over his face, wiping away his emotion, and rose to answer. He opened the door to find the captain of the guard.

Caspian nodded in greeting but paused as their eyes met. Alexander suspected he saw the remnants of his sorrow, but the captain graciously offered no mention of it.

He stepped back into the room, leaving the door open for Caspian to enter. Alexander wasn't one to show emotion, and few men other than Caspian had seen him outside his calm and pensive nature. They'd fought together, bled together, won together, lost together. They were more than comrades, more than friends. They were like brothers. Still, Caspian wasn't one to pry, but he knew what Norah's return meant to Alexander, and he needed to know the situation.

"She doesn't remember," Alexander said, not entirely confident in his voice.

Caspian shifted back. "She doesn't remember what?"

"She has no memory, Caspian. She knows nothing. Not Mercia, not herself." He paused. "Not me."

Caspian's eyes widened.

But Alexander didn't want to linger on it. He couldn't without emotion threatening. "Brief her core guard," he said, "as well as her maids. They'll need to help her. The queen regent was clear—no one else can know. Not even the council. She's fought too hard to protect Norah's crown in her absence. We can't risk losing it now."

"That won't be easy. We'll have to keep the princess from them."

"I'll let the queen regent manage that," Alexander said. Then he frowned. They'd have to keep her from quite a few people. His mind turned to his brother. Adrian would want to see Norah as soon as he learned of her return, but he'd suspect something right away. Alexander would have to find a way to keep him from her for a while too.

"I've sent messengers to the outer reaches, calling all forces back," Caspian said. "Except for our men in Bahoul."

Alexander gave a small nod. The mountains—they'd need to keep men there to hold them. When the Shadowlands learned of Norah's return, it would only be a matter of time before they came for her. *Again.* "Send the Ninth to join them." Another thousand men in Bahoul would mean a thousand men less at the capital, but if the Shadow King attacked, Bahoul would be the first line of defense. Caspian nodded, and then he paused. "What about Aleon?"

The mention of their eastern ally made Alexander stiffen, but he pushed the twinge aside and took his belt and sword from the wall. "I'll send word to Aleon that the princess has returned. And then I'll go to the seer. Perhaps her return has brought new visions."

"I'll take care of the message to Aleon," Caspian told him. "You go see Samuel."

Caspian knew his struggle; he knew the bitterness that the thought of Aleon brought, and Alexander clasped his shoulder appreciatively. Then he buckled the belt of his sword and set his mind to the seer.

He didn't bother with a cloak as he passed through the castle and outside toward the gallery house. He'd made this walk many times over, each with the same hope. But today was different. Norah had returned.

Alexander strode over the cobblestone street to the gallery of the seer. While it was connected to the castle, it was only accessible from the outside. He pushed through the doors and sidestepped the paintings strewn throughout. It was growing more difficult to weave through to the back gallery where he knew the old man would be. As expected, he found Samuel at his easel, hunched over and working on his craft. Alexander's pulse quickened at seeing the seer at work. A vision must have come.

"A vision? You've had one?" he asked anxiously, not bothering with a greeting.

Samuel bobbed his balding head up in surprise. "Hmm?" In seeing Alexander, Samuel pushed his glasses back up the bridge of his nose. "Oh, it's you," he gruffed.

"You've had another?" he pressed the old man. "Of the princess?"

Samuel scowled, turning his attention back to his work. "Boy, you've been asking me that for years, and for years I've told you—"

"She's returned."

Samuel stopped, glancing back up at Alexander. "What did you say?"

"The princess. She's returned. Did you not hear the bells?"

Samuel wrinkled his nose and waved his brush. "Those damn bells ring all the time."

Alexander drew in a deep breath, trying to summon his patience. "Well, she's returned. Surely you can see something of her now."

The old man drew his brows together and shook his head, then set his brush down. "No. I've seen nothing of her."

Alexander sighed. The last painting of Norah was the image of her in the forest. It had come just before she had left, three years ago. When she'd disappeared, the visions of her stopped. Now that she'd returned, he hoped the visions had too. Samuel's gallery held only a few paintings of her, all of which had been completed before she'd disappeared. Alexander knew every detail, every brushstroke, especially of the painting that had made Norah's father take her away: the image of the enemy that would come for her—the Shadow King. The vision of her capture.

War. Death. That had been her fate, the fate her father changed by taking her to safety, wherever that might have been.

Then there were the images of himself. But those he put from his mind. "What are you painting then?" he asked Samuel.

The old man snorted. "Nothing you care to see."

Alexander moved around the easel to look over the old man's shoulder, and he sighed. *Not again.* "What is that?"

"What does it look like?" the seer asked with an edge of annoyance. "I've been painting long enough that I consider myself quite good at it."

Alexander stared at the painting on the easel. It was a village in flames. The dead littered the streets, the houses had been destroyed. And in its center stood Alexander. But his image didn't show fear. It was as though he relished the destruction. His image stared at him from the canvas with the want of war in his eyes, like the others Samuel had painted of him over the years.

Alexander sighed. Years ago, paintings like this had bothered him to obsession, but the visions of himself never came to be. He used to ponder every detail, trying to understand their meaning. Now they only served to annoy him. If it wasn't for the truth in the visions of others, he would have thought the old man a charlatan.

He looked closer and scowled at the black ink marking the skin on his neck in the painting. Dark patterns swirled just under his jaw. "Why must you always paint these markings?" he asked the seer.

"Boy, I've told you a hundred times, I only paint what I see," Samuel snapped. Then the old man snorted. "And is it only the markings that bother you? Not the wave of destruction you cause?"

"That's not me, Samuel," he said, irritated, but not *too* irritated. Samuel had stopped showing others the paintings of him, so he didn't have to keep defending himself.

"If it's not you, then why do you care if there are markings?"

Alexander let out a long breath and turned back toward the door, his interest waning. "You'll send word if you see her?"

The old man waved him off with his brush. "As I always say I will."

CHAPTER SIX

Norah stood by the window in her chamber, unsure if it was night or morning in the darkness. The winter sun didn't rise with the start of the day—it came later and set sooner. Despite the pristine white of her room, the linen and draperies of light and silver all looked black. She stared through the glass of the window, out into the abyss of more darkness. Much like her memories.

She had tried to sleep. Her body begged her for it, but her eyes couldn't close, her mind couldn't rest. Was this life really hers? It couldn't be. It felt... not right. None of it was right. But she couldn't shake the one thing that felt... a little less not right...

The one thing that felt familiar...

No—she couldn't let her mind fall into that trap, and she pushed Alexander from her thoughts.

Time passed slowly. She was almost contemplating attempting sleep again when Rebecca whisked into the room. The maid greeted her with a warm smile. "Oh, Princess Norah, you're already awake!"

The ring of the title in her ears made her wince, but she forced back a polite smile. "Yes, um, I was up early."

"The queen regent will be here soon, as will the dresses."

The dresses? Norah raised her brows in surprise. The fittings hadn't been finished until well into the evening prior. And there would be more than one? "So soon?"

"Yes, of course." The girl's smile grew broader. "The seamstresses have been working on them all night."

All night? How were the dresses so important they required midnight making? It seemed so... unnecessary.

"Are you hungry?" Rebecca asked.

Norah forgot the dresses. "Starved," she answered eagerly, a smile finally coming to her lips. The mere mention of food made her stomach rumble. Her maid's eyes widened. Was that not what she'd expected? Norah bit her lip. "I mean, just a little hungry. But not that much. Normal hungry. As one normally is in the morning." She pursed her lips between her teeth and scolded herself. *Stop.* But she couldn't. Everything came so awkwardly.

Rebecca fluttered back out of the room to get breakfast.

Norah made her way to the bath chamber but stopped when she caught sight of herself in the mirror. Her eyes, large and expansive, were the color of a stormy sea and stared back at her over the highs of her cheekbones. Her icy-blonde mane twisted wildly around her. When she'd seen her image the day before, it hadn't surprised her. She knew her face.

"You can't erase all of me," she whispered to whatever had stolen her memory.

The sound of voices and her chamber door opening pulled her attention.

"Norah?" Catherine's voice rang out.

Norah stepped out of the bath chamber to find the queen regent, followed by Rebecca, who was carrying a plate of fruit and cheeses.

"Grandmother," she greeted.

"How did you sleep, child?"

"Well, thank you," she lied.

"Wonderful. We've a busy day ahead of us. You'll be seeing the council today."

Norah nodded. Yes, *good*—her council. "And they'll help me figure out what to do until my memories—"

"No," Catherine said sharply.

No? "Wait, why not?" She was drowning merely in her thoughts of stepping into this life, into this world, and the reality would be so much harsher. She needed all the help she could get.

"I told you, no one must know of your condition."

Condition.

As if it were a sickness. Perhaps it was, but—

"We only have to present you," Catherine said, "and I'll make it as quick as possible."

Her heartbeat rose to her throat. Why didn't Catherine want the council to know? Alexander had said they would help her. Why couldn't they know?

Catherine set about the room, pulling out various drawers of dressers and chests and looking through them. "You probably won't even say more than a few words—"

"W-Wait," Norah stammered, "I can't meet the council like this. They'll discover me. I haven't even been back a full day yet. I have no idea what I'm doing."

"I'll take care of that," Catherine replied with a nod.

How? "You just want me to pretend?"

"Precisely," the queen regent answered back as she laid three necklaces on the vanity, eyeing them with a tilt of her head. The woman had clearly missed her sarcasm.

In her state of total astonishment, Norah almost laughed. "*How?* I literally know nothing—no people, no history. I barely remember the name of this place, and nothing of myself! You have to give me more here. I—I need to know my story, what's happened... just... something." *Anything.*

Catherine stopped. "And that's why I've come early." She took Norah's hand and led her to the settee, sitting them both down. "Listen to me. All of this will be very sudden for you. But we don't have much time, so you'll have to learn as quickly as possible."

Norah nodded. She could learn quickly. Hopefully. Her eyes caught sight of the plate Rebecca had brought in with cheeses and fruit. She'd kill for the pear looking back at her, but she forced her attention back on her grandmother.

Catherine drew in another breath, as if organizing her thoughts on where to start. Perhaps she did have time to get the pear.

"We are at war, Norah."

And Norah stopped.

Are.

Alexander had said *were*.

"We've been at war with the Shadowlands for ten years. The Great War, it's called. And we've been waiting for you to return, to end it."

Norah blinked. She hadn't heard correctly. "I'm sorry, what?"

Catherine folded her hands together. "You'll unite the kingdoms against the Shadowlands, and you'll end it. For good."

"Um… I didn't quite expect you to start with that. Um…" She stood. A *war*. She'd been anxious about the expectations of her before, but a war raised the stakes, and her pulse. She rounded the small table where Rebecca had set the plate, and she grabbed the pear. Not to eat—she wasn't hungry anymore with her mind on war—but she wanted to have something to hold in her hand, something to fiddle with, to calm her.

War.

She flexed her nails against the pear, but not hard enough to break its skin.

War.

Then she took a bite.

Catherine watched her, giving her a moment.

So… *war.* It would have been nice to start first with her mother and father, but she supposed they could start with the war. She swallowed the bite of pear. "Why are we at war?"

"This is not a short story."

"You said you came early."

Catherine sighed. "Mercia's been a longtime ally and friend of the Aleon Empire," she explained. "Aleon used to consist of six kingdoms ruled by the High King Horath. However, ten years ago, as Horath lay on his deathbed, he split the kingdoms of the empire between his three sons: Gregor, Phillip, and Aston."

Six kingdoms sounded like too much for any one man, anyway. And all this seemed perfectly reasonable, unless Norah was expected to remember all these names. She took another bite of her pear.

"But," Catherine continued, "Gregor, the eldest, although given the richest of the kingdoms, Japheth, felt robbed of his birthright. He killed his youngest brother, taking the second kingdom of Hetahl as well. He needed—and still needs—the remaining four kingdoms of Aleon from Phillip to restore the full empire. When he tried to take them, your father stood as Phillip's ally. This was the start of the Great War."

Norah struggled to swallow the pear as a sudden lump rose in her throat. That anyone could kill their family for power was a monstrous thing. Inhuman.

Rebecca whisked back into the room with a wine decanter and two chalices. Norah hadn't realized she'd even gone anywhere. The maid left them on the small side table beside the settee before seeing herself out of the room again.

Wine with breakfast... *odd*. Norah set her attention back to the conversation. "So, what do Aleon and Japheth, this war between Phillip and Gregor, have to do with the Shadowlands? And Mercia, and me?"

"Aleon and Mercia stood together, and so Gregor needed an ally," Catherine explained. "He joined together with the Shadowlands."

"So, it's Mercia and Aleon against Japheth and the Shadowlands?"

Catherine nodded. "Exactly. But Phillip will manage his brother Gregor. You must focus on the Shadowlands. The Shadow King is a greater evil, and he'll do everything in his power to see you dead."

Her stomach twisted. "Why?" It was a little extreme, to want someone dead.

"The visions have shown it. You'll take the Shadow throne, purging his darkness from this world."

Norah pulled her bottom lip between her teeth, not knowing what to make of her grandmother's words. She didn't want anyone's throne. She wasn't even sure if she wanted her own. "You sound so certain of this."

"I am. It was a powerful vision, Norah—seen by seers across the kingdoms. The Shadow King joined with Japheth soon after, with a vengeance. He'll stop at nothing to change his fate, and he almost did. Many times he's attacked, and many times your father drove him back, but three years ago, another vision came—a vision of your capture, and of the Shadowmen breaching our defenses, flooding into Mercia, and killing the council. That's when your father took you away, to keep you safe."

A chill ran down her spine, and Norah sat back on the settee beside her grandmother again. "But... they didn't end up breaching Mercia."

"Pay attention, child," Catherine said shortly.

Norah frowned. She was paying attention.

"It was a *vision*. It hadn't yet happened. But your father refused to take chances, and by taking you away, he changed your fate."

But that only raised more questions: Where had her father taken her? What place would have been safe if Mercia wasn't? And how had she lost her memories?

Catherine took her hand. "And while your father was successful in driving the Shadow King back deep into his hell, he still lives. It's why you must keep your course, Norah. You mustn't take chances either. You'll become queen and wed King Phillip of Aleon as planned, to keep the alliance strong."

Norah's heart stopped, and her head jerked up at her grandmother's words. Her nails pierced the skin of the remaining pear in her hand. "Wed? As in, marriage?"

Catherine pursed her lips. "That's what *wed* means, yes."

She knew what *wed* meant, but it couldn't mean that for her. "I can't be married." She didn't even know herself, much less know someone else enough to marry them. She struggled for words in the chaos overwhelming her mind. "I've never even met this Phillip. I don't love him. What if I don't even *like* him?"

"You *have* met him. Many times. And you do like him. But whether you like him doesn't matter. What matters is the future of Mercia and the strength of our kingdom. Only with Phillip can you defeat the Shadow King." Catherine paused. Then she said, "There are other things of which you must be aware. Mercia is in a dire position. We're still early into winter, and we've not enough food to sustain our people. Aleon sends provisions in goodwill, as they have for the past three years, but it won't be enough, and it won't continue without a marriage."

The weight in her stomach grew to a pit—a pit that her very being was falling into, flailing, and drowning.

Wine would be good now. Norah's hands shook as she dropped her pear on the tray, poured herself a chalice, and drank. Deeply. Everything she knew of life had been born in the last two days. She'd only just arrived in this strange kingdom she was to call home and was already a pawn in a game she didn't understand.

"And," Catherine continued, "with this marriage, you'll become queen of the new Aleon Empire."

"So, there's a new one now?" Of course. But she didn't want to be queen of the new Aleon Empire. She didn't want to be queen of Mercia. She didn't want to be a queen at all.

Catherine's frown deepened. "I know this is difficult for you, stepping into a life you don't remember, but it carries a great obligation, and I beg you to take it seriously."

Her grandmother's words sobered her. She swallowed as she set her chalice back on the table. "I do take it seriously. It's just very difficult to absorb everything, especially a surprise marriage."

"This marriage has been long in the making, with many marriages between Mercia and Aleon in our history. I myself am from the Aleon kingdom of Eilor. Your mother was from Songs."

Norah poured more wine into her chalice and took another drink.

"Mercia is a kingdom of honor," Catherine said, "and joins Aleon in cause. We share the same values, the same beliefs, the same language. An alliance between our two kingdoms is an essential one, for each fortifies the other. It's why Phillip has been so patient. But the council isn't patient and shoves the option of your cousin's hand at him at every turn. Now that you're back, they'll be eager to see you crowned and wed in short order."

Norah's head reeled. She suddenly didn't feel very well. Just then, the chamber door swung open, and ladies made their way in with dresses, fabrics, and trays of glittering accessories.

Catherine stood and pulled Norah to her feet. "It's a lot, I know, and as I said, you'll have to learn quickly. But you're strong, and I'll help you sort everything out."

The queen regent turned and worked through the array of dresses before she settled on one of her liking. Norah found herself amid a flurry of activity as servants rubbed her skin with scented oil, helped her into a deep-ruby gown, brushed out her hair, and powdered her face. But she barely registered what was happening.

Married. She was to be married. She could barely remember her own name and she was going to be married to... Wait—what was his name?

"So, we'll see the council this morning," Catherine told her. "There's no avoiding it, but you needn't worry. It's merely to present you and share your return."

"Will Alexander be there?" Alexander was... safe. And known. And she needed something safe and known. She wanted him by her side. Right now.

"You must use his proper title, Norah."

His title. She nodded blankly. What was his title? *Lord justice.*

Her grandmother sighed. "I can assure you that he'll never be far from you, but put the lord justice from your mind and focus on the council. I'm sure they'll have questions about where you've been, and we'll have to navigate through them carefully, but I'll keep it as short as possible. Just remember to..."

Catherine's words blurred into an echo inside her mind, and Norah's stomach knotted. She didn't want this: not the weight of it all, not the marriage, not the dress or the scented oil, and certainly not the necklace that her grandmother held up to her.

She stumbled backward and caught herself against the wall. The room swirled around her.

Catherine paused. She set the necklace down and took Norah's hand, steadying her. "Take a breath," the woman told her, and she did.

The room steadied, and so did she. Norah looked up to find Catherine staring back at her with a deep sadness in her eyes. Her grandmother pulled her closer and brought her hand to Norah's cheek. "I'm so sorry, my darling. I wish I had more time to prepare you for this. The weight of the world is on your shoulders, I know. Your life is not your own, and I understand how difficult it is to come to terms with that. But you must do exactly as I tell you. So much depends on it—you, your people, all of us. Do you understand?"

Her mind understood, but her heart still wavered.

"I'll be by your side every step of the way," Catherine said.

And Norah found herself nodding, just not exactly in agreement.

Nausea rippled through Norah as she stepped out of her chamber and into the large arched hall of white and light. Perhaps she'd had too much wine. Or not enough. The sun reflecting off the marble nearly blinded her, but she walked, unseeing, in more ways than one.

She envied the woman who had stood at the window in the dark only a few hours earlier, before she knew of this Shadow King that wanted her dead, before she knew she'd be wed to a stranger. As if waking up as heir to the crown and with no memory wasn't enough. Her grandmother walked briskly beside her, like this was all normal. Was this to be her normal? She looked back over her shoulder at the guard that followed close behind. Was this her life now?

As they turned a corner, she spotted a familiar face waiting at the end of the hall, and suddenly, the weight of it all seemed to lighten.

Alexander.

Their eyes locked as she approached. And his stare...

"Princess Norah," he greeted her with a bow once she reached him.

"Lord Justice," she replied. Using his title felt awkward to her, but he gave a small smile, and it settled her. "Am I overdone?" she asked sheepishly, glancing down at her gown. It was a rhetorical question. She was entirely overdone.

"Not at all," he assured her. "You look... very regal."

"I should. All this took an absurdly long time."

His smile widened.

"Good morning, Lord Justice," Catherine greeted him with a sternness in her voice.

Alexander snapped to with a quick bow, and Norah looked on in amusement as she suspected he hadn't even noticed her grandmother.

"Good morning, Queen Regent," he replied to Catherine. "I trust you've rested well."

"As well as all this excitement would permit."

"The council waits in the judisaept," he told them.

The queen regent looked at Norah. "Remember what I told you, and you'll fare just fine."

Norah's pulse quickened. Catherine had run through what to expect and how to respond to the council while Norah had been shoved into her dress and powdered like a ball of dough, but she still drew in a nervous breath. Remembering wasn't her strong suit at the moment. Catherine had told her to keep silent about her memory loss, but she still didn't understand why. Surely people would figure it out right away. She tried to push her fear from her mind and followed after her grandmother.

The judisaept was a smaller room than Norah had expected, given the stature of the castle she'd seen so far, but it was no less splendid. Carved beams ran along the walls and between the stone, reaching to the ceiling. In the center hung a large iron chandelier holding candles within delicately blown glass flutes. Underneath sat a rectangular table, with beautifully scrolled trestles. Large shields adorned the walls. They weren't made for decoration, as each of them bore the marks of battle.

Around the table stood four councilmen, who bowed as she entered.

"Princess Norah!" called the man to her right, coming forward. "Welcome home!"

Edward, maybe, based on Catherine's description. He was a shorter man, pale and balding, and about the same age as her grandmother. He was thin, except for a slightly protruding belly not entirely hidden by his council robes. His facial features were sharp—especially his nose and chin—but his face wasn't unkind. He reached out and took Norah's hand, which he promptly brought to his forehead as he bowed.

Her heart raced as she forced a smile and tried to appear calm. Could he feel her clammy hand shaking? He seemed oblivious. Everything her grandmother had told her evaded her mind, and all she could do was pretend normalcy.

"Councilman Edward," Catherine replied, "is she not the image of her mother?"

"Indeed, she is." He pulled Norah forward, extending his arm to the rest of the councilmen. "The gods smile upon us."

The councilmen all bowed again, clapping their hands, and Norah swallowed back the lump in her throat.

"And the gods favor upon the lord justice for bringing you back to us," he added with a nod to Alexander, who had taken a position on the side of the large table.

Alexander bowed his head stiffly, shifting under the attention. "As was my duty," he said. His eyes locked with hers again and held her. Was duty all it had been?

Edward turned back to her. "You must first tell us, Princess, where you've been all this time."

Norah's attention turned to his question, and her breath caught in her throat. Of course that would be their first question. Her heart beat faster.

"Councilman Edward," Catherine said, "there's so much to discuss, but I see Councilmen James and Elias aren't with us?"

"They're in Damask, and we expect their return in two days," Edward answered. "We'll assemble the state then."

The state? Norah didn't know what that meant, but it didn't sound like something she would look forward to.

"The princess's return is a serious matter," Catherine said firmly, "and requires our full council. We'll not discuss it without them."

Norah could already see the skill with which her grandmother handled these conversations. She couldn't imagine doing the same herself.

The councilman paused with a crease in his brow, but then he nodded. "Uh, yes, of course."

Norah let out a silent breath of relief.

"There will still be celebratory festivities, yes? To present her?" another councilman asked. He was about the same height as Edward, but double the width, and wore a thick cover of white, short-cropped hair. Norah couldn't match him to the names and descriptions her grandmother had run through. Henricus, maybe? "Everyone will be expecting to see her," he added.

Catherine gave a smooth smile. "Arrangements have already begun for tomorrow evening."

"Very good."

Edward turned back to Norah. "Well, there's much to discuss, Princess, but for now, welcome home once again. We look forward to our state and to hearing of your time away from us."

Before Norah could respond, Catherine put her hand on her arm. "Councilmen, if you'll excuse us, there's still much we have to tend to."

The men all gave respectful bows as Catherine pulled Norah toward the door. Norah glanced over her shoulder and caught Alexander's eyes, but a councilman called to him, pulling his attention from her.

"Marvelous, dear," her grandmother whispered as they stepped into the large hall and away from the judisaept. "You did better than I'd expected."

Norah frowned. "But I didn't say anything."

Catherine patted her hand. "Exactly."

Norah wasn't sure how she felt about that, but her mind was too consumed with other things to care much. "What's a state?" she asked.

"A state is a meeting of the council to work on resolutions for the challenges our kingdom faces. We discuss many things: matters of the purse, alliances, war, trade, pirates—"

"Pirates?"

"Yes, troublesome thieves. Any kingdom with a fleet suffers their raids. And Mercian fleets carry some of the most valuable trade in the world—Mercian steel."

So the council solved problems. Alexander had said the council would help her, so why didn't her grandmother want them to know of her circumstance? "How long will we keep my memory loss from them?" she asked.

"As long as we can," Catherine answered shortly.

"But that can't be long." Not long at all. The council's first question had left her stumbling.

Her grandmother eyed her sternly. "We can't risk anything that might delay your path to the crown or keep you from getting it at all."

That only raised more questions, but ones she knew she couldn't ask now, so openly. Her mind turned to other curiosities. "You said I have a cousin. Will I be seeing her soon?"

Catherine's gaze snapped back to her. "A second cousin," she said warily. "Evangeline. She'll present herself to you at the homecoming celebration, but you'll do well to keep her at a distance. There are those who would love to see her on your throne. Not everyone has been as patient for your return."

Evangeline on the throne? Perhaps that wasn't the worst idea. *Evangeline.* She'd likely be a better fit. The title even went better with her name. Queen Evangeline. It rhymed, as though planned. Queen Norah—it sounded like a vegetable when said fast enough.

"If she could do a better job..." Norah mumbled.

Catherine stopped and turned abruptly, making Norah almost run into her. She pulled Norah close, speaking in a hushed whisper. "Listen to me carefully. There are people who are hungry for power and will use whatever means necessary to get it. But this is *your* throne. *You* are the daughter of King Aamon, *you* are the rightful heir and the one who will unite the kingdoms and defeat the Shadowlands. Do you understand?"

What happened to one thing at a time? And what did she mean by *people who are hungry for power*? Within Mercia? Her heart pulsed. She didn't think she could manage another challenge.

"Now the council will push to have your coronation as quickly as possible," the regent continued. "I'll also insist on it."

"Wait, what?" Norah shook her head. "Why? You're obviously doing a wonderful job as queen regent." She hadn't even been able to wrap her mind around pretending to have her memories. This was all coming too soon. It was too much.

"The council will want to see you wed quickly to King Phillip, for which they'll want to crown you first. This works in our favor. Until then, you'll say nothing of your memories."

That sounded like a terrible idea. "I can't—"

"We'll not talk of it now." Catherine hushed her as Alexander emerged from the judisaept and made his way toward them.

Another objection sat on Norah's lips, but it slipped from her mind as her sight set on him.

Catherine sighed as she squeezed Norah's hand. "Don't worry, child. We'll get it all sorted. But right now, I must tend to some things. The guard will see you back."

"Queen Regent," Alexander called, coming up behind them. Catherine turned. His eyes, a deep cerulean, caught Norah's, and he gave a small bow of his head. Then he broke and turned to Catherine and said, "I'd like to introduce the princess to the captain and the rest of her guard. She needs to be familiar with them."

Catherine looked at Norah warily and pursed her lips. Then she sighed. "Very well. You'll see her directly to her chamber after."

He nodded.

"I mean it," Catherine pressed. "Don't linger about."

"Of course," he assured her.

He turned back to Norah.

And Norah smiled.

Chapter Seven

"This way, Your Highness," Alexander said. He extended his arm down the mainway.

She cringed inside. "Please don't call me that." She could bear it in public, but not here when it was just between them.

"Princess Norah."

She grimaced. "Not that either."

"I have to."

She was afraid he'd say that. "Always?"

"Not always," he assured her. Then the corners of his mouth turned up. "When you're queen, I'll call you *Your Elegance.*"

She shot him a heavy-browed eye of disbelief. "That can't seriously be a title."

He chuckled. "It is. And you thought it was ridiculous before too."

She stopped, desperate for the thoughts she'd had when she'd been herself. He'd known her. "Tell me more of what I thought before."

Alexander quieted. His eyes held a wisp of sadness, as if those old thoughts haunted him. Then the corners of his lips turned up, and the sadness disappeared. She wondered if she'd seen it at all. "You thought the king's title was better."

"Which was?"

"Regal High."

"That *is* better." Why didn't the queen get a powerful title?

"Would you rather be called *Regal High* when you're queen?"

"I'd rather not be called any of it."

He chuckled again, and she bit her lip. She should be more careful with her words. Catherine would be beside herself if she heard her say that.

"I know," he said.

How much did he know about her? He opened his hand and motioned them to continue, and they started again down the hall.

"My grandmother doesn't trust the council," she said as they walked. Why didn't she? They were her council, there to *counsel.*

"Your grandmother trusts no one."

Norah raised a brow. "She trusts you."

He shrugged with a smile. "Sometimes."

They turned down another hall, where several small groups congregated, and Norah slowed. The voices fell, and all eyes were on her. Her chest tightened, and her stomach puddled.

"Do I know these people?" she whispered. The threat of panic crept up her spine and tickled the back of her mind. Would they expect something of her, for her to do something, to say something?

"You know most of them. But no one will speak unless you speak to them first. So, we'll just walk through."

The men bowed, and the women curtsied as Norah and Alexander passed. Everyone was smiling. Not acknowledging them seemed pretentious, and Norah found herself nodding with genuine courtesy.

Alexander gave her a small smile as they left the hall. "People are going to love you."

She'd done absolutely nothing. "Why?" They turned down another hall, one that opened to the outside along a columned sidewalk.

"Because you see them."

How could she not? The acknowledgment felt strange, but Alexander didn't give her time to mull it over before he muttered something unintelligible and suddenly grabbed her arm.

"What..." she started, but couldn't finish her sentence. Wide-eyed, she let him hastily pull her back inside, down a hall, and into a small arched alcove of a doorway. He tested the door within its frame, but it was locked.

"I'm very sorry about this," he said in a hushed voice, "and it's highly inappropriate, I know." He waved the guards to keep walking, then he glanced out from their hiding place.

"What... what are you doing?" she asked.

"We just need to wait a moment," he whispered. He leaned over and cast another glance down the hall.

The alcove was small. Very small. He held her gently by her upper arms as they stood tucked in the tight space. She jerked her hand to his chest, as if that would put a barrier between them, but it only seemed to link them, to draw them closer.

"W-Why?" she stammered breathlessly.

"I know I said no one would speak to you unless you spoke to them first," he whispered, "but there are... a few in court who might not abide. And I'd like to avoid one of them right now."

"I thought I saw her!" a high-pitched voice called out.

Norah locked eyes with Alexander, and he tilted his head with a raised brow, as if his point had been proven. She didn't argue. To avoid people who knew her, people who might discover her, she was fine with hiding. She'd rather avoid everyone.

They stood, so close, waiting. He'd been carefully peering out from the side, but as he glanced down at her, he stopped. Her hand still sat against his chest, and she stared at it.

She should pull it off. *Off.* But she didn't. Underneath, his heart thrummed against her palm. It's rapid beating matched her own. So close they were. He stood still as a statue, but his warmth seeped into her, through her. It wrapped around her. It was the familiar warmth of a familiar body, the familiar beat of a familiar heart.

"I think it's clear now," he whispered.

He dropped his hands from her arms, and she pulled back her own hand, but still they made no move to leave. So many questions sat on her lips—questions she wasn't brave enough to ask. Finally, he stepped out from the alcove and back into the hall, breaking her from the invisible hold.

Norah smoothed her dress as she stepped out beside him, but her heart still raced. She glanced at him, and he looked as if nothing had happened. Had she imagined this connection between them? Or dreamed it, perhaps. Her cheeks flushed. Maybe there'd been nothing at all.

"This way, Princess," he said, motioning back down the hall and putting some distance between them, both physically and with his tone. Her cheeks grew hotter. She'd certainly imagined it.

They resumed their walk, back the way they'd come to the exterior doors and down the sidewalk. Alexander cast a wary eye as they went, watching for other inconvenient visitors. "I'm taking you to meet Caspian," he said, "the captain of the guard."

Excellent—something different to focus her mind on.

He paused for a moment and motioned behind her, where she once again found two men from her guard.

"This is Titus and Liaman—two of several men you'll see regularly." She hadn't realized they'd picked back up behind them. Had they seen her and Alexander duck into the alcove? Of course they had. *Not awkward at all.* "You have the best swordsmen in Mercia by your side," he told her.

She swallowed uncomfortably but followed Alexander's lead in pretending it didn't happen. "Then I feel very safe," she said with a nod to the soldiers. "Pleased to meet you."

"Your Highness," they said in unison, bowing their heads. She squirmed under the address. Liaman looked younger than she, almost boyish, but he moved with an aged grace. Titus was a large man, larger even than Alexander, and had certainly known a battle or two. His head was shaved, and he had a hint of a beard. A jagged scar lined his jaw, and one broke the arch of his right eyebrow.

Alexander continued, and she followed. As they made their way toward a gated building, a man stepped out to meet them with two soldiers at his flank. When he reached Alexander and Norah, he brought his fist to his chest in salute.

"Your Highness," Alexander said. "I present Captain Caspian Frey."

Caspian was handsome in an honest way. He was a kind-looking man with a generous smile and blond hair like many of the Northmen. He looked to be about the same age as Alexander.

"Captain Frey," she greeted him.

He smiled warmly as he bowed. "Your Highness." He then opened his arm to the men behind him. "Allow me to present Aaron and Daniel." Each man bowed his head as his name was called. "With Titus and Liaman, these men make up your core guard. You'll never be without at least one of them."

"Thank you," she replied, although it came out as more of a question.

"These men are all aware of your situation, and will help you acclimate," Alexander told her. "You can ask them anything."

Norah gave an appreciative nod. *That* she was truly thankful for, although she'd wait just a bit before she peppered them with questions.

Caspian gave her another bow. "We'll leave you to your business. Welcome home, Your Highness."

"Thank you... Captain." The titles still challenged her.

Caspian and the two soldiers left them to their walk.

Alexander turned to her. "I should get you back."

Right. She stifled a rising groan at the thought of returning to her chamber. "I suppose so." They started back toward the castle.

As they walked, her eye caught a large, majestic building with brightly hued stained glass threaded together with elegant tracery stretching to its peaks.

She stopped in her step. "What's that?"

"The library."

It was beautiful, sitting squarely and centered by a pointed arch over heavy wood doors. A vaulted walk with carved pillars lined its perimeter, and a tower in the back stretched toward the sky.

"It houses the largest collection of knowledge in the world," he told her. "History, philosophy, all modern works of science and study—it's all here. Everything about Mercia and beyond."

"It's beautiful." She smiled, forgetting everything else for a moment. "Can I see inside?"

Alexander hesitated, looking toward the castle, no doubt mulling over his promise to her grandmother to promptly return her.

"Just a look," she pressed.

He sighed. "I suppose a quick look won't hurt."

She grinned.

Alexander waved the guard to stay outside as they walked through the carved double doors.

Norah gasped as she looked around at the magnitude of books that lay shelved to the ceiling. "It's incredible!"

"When the visions foretold the Shadowmen would invade Mercia, your father ordered all the books and scrolls to be taken to Aleon for safekeeping. It took over ten thousand men."

The mention of Aleon made her stiffen. She wanted to ask him about the marriage, but that seemed too personal now. "Is Aleon safer than Mercia?" she asked instead.

"Not necessarily, but the Shadow King didn't have his destruction focused on Aleon."

No, it had been focused on her. Norah bit her lip and turned her eyes back to the shelved books.

"Your father had every intent to change the future, but he wasn't one to take risks. He always said knowledge was the most important thing in the world, besides you. After we took the mountains of Bahoul and drove the Shadow King back deep into the Shadowlands, only then did we know it was safe to bring everything home. And it was safe for you to come home."

She clasped the pendant around her neck, running her thumb over the winterhawk. "My grandmother said the Shadow King will still come for me."

His eyes burned a deep blue, then darkened like the ocean. "He'll try."

She swallowed. The thought of a dark foe coming for her rattled her. It more than rattled her—it scared her.

"But I won't let that happen," he assured her.

She nodded. She hoped so.

He caught her arm. "Hey"—he called her eyes to his—"I would never let anyone hurt you. Ever."

The promise in his voice... It was personal, beyond duty, beyond sworn loyalty.

He let go of her and continued walking through the library. "Thousands of years of work are kept within these walls. We spent many hours here when we were young, reading, studying." He stopped, growing somber, and touched a leather-bound book on the shelf. "This one you loved."

"What is it?"

"A story—told in a collection of poems." He pulled it from its place and held it for her. The darker dye of the leather had been worn through to the tanned softness underneath; the evidence of many readings. "It holds your favorite poem."

"Do you know which one?" Silly question—of course he wouldn't.

Alexander grew quiet, looking down at the book. Then he slowly opened its laced pages. He selected the passage, its final stanza, but his eyes found hers as he spoke the words.

"Sleep now, love, and wait for me
For in time, it will come to pass
That I will follow after, wrapped in rest beneath the earth—"

"Together, my darling, at last," she whispered, finishing. Emotion rippled through her—a familiar longing, an ache deep within. She knew it. She knew this, knew the words and the feeling and meaning. She knew the story.

Alexander stood frozen, staring. His lips parted. He stepped closer. "You remember?" he breathed.

She nodded with a shaky breath. "I know it."

"What else?" he asked, eager now. "Anything?"

But her excitement fizzled. *No.* Nothing else had come. No memories, not even the memory of actually reading the book, only the knowledge of it. Slowly, she shook her head.

He swallowed, straightening and stepping back, as if collecting his fallen hope. "It's all right," he said. "It will come."

"Unless it doesn't."

Now she could see it—the sorrow. But then he snatched it back quickly, hiding it behind a wall. "It will," he said with a face of perfect reassurance.

She looked through his words. What was he hiding behind that wall? Then she paused. "You know my favorite poem by memory?"

The countenance of perfection fell, and he swallowed. His lips parted, and his breath quickened. "Norah, I—"

The doors of the library swung open behind them, and she turned to see a man step inside. When his eyes found them, a large smile split across his lips, and he started toward them. His height, coupled with the shape of his face and jawline, gave him away almost immediately: Alexander's brother. Adrian.

Alexander had said they'd been close. Act close... smile, she told herself.

And she smiled.

"Norah!" he called with a hearty laugh. His pace didn't slow as he drew closer, and her heart beat faster. He moved to embrace her, but Alexander's hand snaked out and caught him with a friendly clasp on the shoulder, halting the young man under the guise of affection.

"Adrian," Alexander said as he pulled his brother closer to him and looked at Norah. It was a subtle effort to introduce him.

Adrian looked at Alexander, clearly confused. Then he found a bit of formality, no doubt from his brother's chastising eye. He smiled awkwardly as he bowed. "Princess Norah," he said with a slight stiffness.

She wasn't sure how to respond. "Lord Adrian."

Adrian's brow creased. Her words felt wrong as soon as they rolled off her lips. But he was a lord, wasn't he? Too formal, maybe? *Damn it.*

He gave a puzzled nod, but his smile quickly returned. "I almost didn't believe it when I heard. You're back."

"I am," she said. She was indeed back. And standing awkwardly. She glanced at Alexander.

Adrian's mouth opened to say more, but Alexander interjected. "Speaking of getting you back, we should go," he said to Norah as he returned the book to the shelf from where he'd taken it.

She sensed Alexander's unease with his brother, and Adrian's confusion. Catherine had been very pointed about keeping her memory loss a secret. It would be hard for her with people who knew her well, and she imagined it would be hard for Alexander to keep it from his brother too.

"Of course," she said, smiling politely at Adrian.

As they stepped out of the library, the wind brought a shudder, and Norah pulled up her cloak. The Northern Kingdom, Mercia was called. It felt very northern.

"I'm surprised my brother has you out in this cold," Adrian told her.

She smiled. "It's not Alexander's doing. I kept him out. The building was beautiful, and I had to see it."

His brows drew together, and Alexander winced.

"Just to see what might have changed," she added quickly.

Adrian chuckled. "A building that's stood for a thousand years won't have changed much in the past three."

"No, I know. I meant the books." She swallowed. "To make sure..." They'd been taken to Aleon for safekeeping and returned, hadn't they? "To make sure they were in the right place." What was wrong with her? She needed to stop talking.

Alexander shook his head faintly, and she knew. "I should probably get back," she said breathlessly.

"Yes, you should," Alexander said.

A servant approached. "Your Highness," he bowed politely to Norah and then turned to Alexander. "Lord Justice, the queen regent requires you."

Alexander looked at Norah, then back to the servant. "I'll come."

"She waits in her study," the servant said with a bow, and left.

His eyes found Norah's. "I have to go. Your guard will see you back."

"Where else would you like to go? I can take you," Adrian offered.

"You have your duties," Alexander cut in. He turned to Norah. "Titus and Liaman will see you back to your chamber."

"Can my duties not wait, brother?" Adrian asked. "Surely the princess—"

"No," Alexander cut him off firmly, taking Adrian aback and silencing him. "The princess needs to return to her chamber." He turned to Norah. "Your Highness," he said with a bow of his head. He gave Titus a nod and then left to find the regent.

Norah looked at Adrian apologetically as she started back toward the castle. He picked up alongside her.

He glanced at Norah. "Do you mind if I at least walk back with you?"

"Not at all," she said with a small smile. What else would she say?

"I still can't believe you've returned," he said as they walked. "Where have you been?"

"Adrian," Titus gruffed, and the young man glanced back at the guard in confusion.

Norah's pulse quickened. That was the question on everyone's mind. "It's complicated. I'm really just trying to get settled right now."

He nodded. "Of course."

Norah felt a pang of sympathy. He seemed kind and genuinely happy to see her. He just didn't understand, and neither did she.

They reached the castle and entered from a side door, and Norah found herself disoriented at the intersecting halls.

Adrian stopped. "I am glad you're back, Norah. There's so much I want to ask you—there are so many things to talk about, but"—he eyed Titus with a puzzled brow—"I guess that can wait for now. I can see you later, though?"

She swallowed and smiled. "Yes, of course."

This was where he clearly intended to part, but he lingered. His eyes narrowed. "Do you know where you're going?"

The question shook her. Of course she didn't know where she was going, but that would be a dead giveaway. "I was... just deciding if I might stop by the kitchen to get something to eat before I went back to my chamber."

The side of Adrian's mouth twitched. "Why would you go to the kitchen?"

Because that was where the food was. But... a princess wouldn't go get her own food. Norah bit the inside of her lip. *Damn it.*

"Liaman," Titus growled, "run ahead to the princess's chamber and have her maid fetch something to eat."

The younger guard hurried down the hall to her right, and Norah silently praised Titus's quick wit.

"Just looking for another reason to be out and walking, I suppose," she tried to explain. "But I guess I should get back. It's good to see you again, Adrian."

He gave a small bow of his head with a polite smile, but a line still stretched across his brow.

She turned down the hall that Liaman had chosen and tried not to exit too quickly as she felt Adrian's eyes still on her. When he was out of sight and earshot, she glanced back at Titus. "Thank you. That wasn't going well."

"Not well at all," he replied.

She frowned. He clearly wasn't the reassuring type.

CHAPTER EIGHT

The sun set and rose again before Norah felt like a day had even passed. Perhaps it was the overwhelming amount of information Catherine and Rebecca tirelessly pressed upon her—what names to remember, how to act, how not to act, what to say, what not to say, how to move. Perhaps it was because she was dreading the upcoming celebrations. She didn't feel like there was a reason to celebrate yet. The Mercian princess might have returned, but she wasn't herself.

Rebecca pulled the lacing of Norah's gown tight as Norah watched blankly in the mirror. Emerald silks edged in gold rippled around her.

"Are you all right, Your Highness?" her maid asked, finishing the lacing and smoothing the fabric.

Norah glanced at her maid in the reflection and forced a small smile. "Of course." But she wasn't all right. She was being stuffed into a dress again to show herself in front of people she didn't know and pretend to be someone she wasn't.

Rebecca fastened a matching emerald necklace around Norah's neck and added stringed jewels to her ears. "There. You're beautiful."

Norah found her reflection in the mirror again. Her loose tresses hung freely over her shoulders. Her high cheekbones were kissed with color under the bright blue of her eyes. She felt beautiful, and she couldn't help a small smile.

"Are you ready?" Rebecca asked her.

She wasn't ready, but she stepped out of the chamber and into the hall, where her guard was waiting. "Where's my grandmother?" she asked them.

"The queen regent is in the great hall," Titus said with a small bow of his head. "I'll take you to her."

"Is Alexander there?"

He briefly hesitated but nodded. "He is, Your Highness."

A heat tinged her cheeks at her question, realizing it was probably obvious that Alexander lingered on her mind, but that was quickly forgotten as her thoughts turned to seeing him again. She followed Titus through the halls, down the stairs, and past the throne room, to where the great hall brimmed with music. She slowed when she saw Catherine walking toward her.

"Oh, my dear," Catherine said with an approving smile, "you're beautiful. Come, come. Everyone's waiting. Now, this should ease you back into things. It's quite informal. I'll announce your arrival, and we'll take our places at the front of the hall. Throughout the evening, I'll announce any lords and ladies who wish to extend their congratulations so you can receive them. You may accept a dance, if invited. Don't bother with food; you'll need to speak. We'll dine privately later."

It seemed the opposite of informal, and Norah's stomach rumbled at the mention of something to eat. She was hungry, and a mouthful of food seemed a perfectly acceptable explanation for not speaking to people, but she turned her attention to the night ahead. Her heart raced as she tried to remember everything her grandmother had run through.

Catherine herded her to the heavy oaken doors, and Norah drew in an uneasy breath as the captain she'd met earlier pulled them open. Paneled tapestries stretched from the ceiling to the walls and draped down to the floor. Hundreds of candles flamed brightly in the tiered chandeliers and corner candelabras. People filled the room, dressed in fine gowns and jewelry. Yes, so *very* informal.

"Welcome home, our Princess!" Catherine's voice rang out, and it was met with deafening clapping. Norah followed Catherine's lead to the front of the hall, with her guard and captain close behind.

"Be ready, my dear," her grandmother whispered as they turned to face the room.

Almost immediately, an older man approached with a young woman beside him. He was the same height as Norah, with a moderate build and his graying-blond hair meticulously combed back. His embroidered doublet had cuffed shoulders, no doubt to augment his stature. Around his waist he wore a thin belt from which hung an even thinner sword. Norah wondered if the blade was even real. Her stomach knotted. Surely this was the worst part of being a princess—talking to people. People she didn't know.

"Lord Allan," Catherine greeted as he neared, "and Lady Evangeline."

Evangeline. Her second cousin, whom her grandmother had warned her about. Norah had pictured her... differently—not at all like the warm face smiling back at her, the rose-colored cheeks beaming, the blue eyes shining. She couldn't have been more than sixteen or seventeen. She curtsied as the man next to her—Lord Allan, her father—bowed.

"Princess Norah," he said, "we're so happy for your safe return."

She found herself doubting that, based on what her grandmother had told her and the stiffness radiating off him, which was very unlike his daughter beside him. The series of responses that Catherine had prepped her with evaded her mind. She glanced at her grandmother, who gave a prodding lift of her brow. "Um, thank you, Lord Allan. It's... so great to be home." She finished with a nod, hoping that was enough.

His lips smiled, but his eyes didn't. "We'll leave you to the evening. Welcome home, Princess Norah," he said. He looked at Catherine. "Queen Regent." He bowed again, and Evangeline curtsied beside him.

The exchange seemed mercifully short and surely more for onlooking eyes than anything else. Norah copied Catherine as she gave a nod. That was what she was supposed to do, right? Nod at a bow?

"Excellent," Catherine whispered to her as Lord Allan and Evangeline departed. "Now smile."

Norah forced her lips into a smile as her eyes swept the room. So many people, and not all of them happy about her return. And so many expectations. Her anxiousness grew.

"Here, have some wine," Catherine said as she handed her a glass provided by a servant.

Yes. Wine. Norah took a long drink from the glass, and it was promptly refilled. She took in a breath, feeling a little better, and then drank deeply again.

"But perhaps not all the wine," Catherine added as she pulled the glass from her hands. "And try to smile with your whole face, child."

She did her best to put on a cheerful face as another well-wisher came forward to greet her. The wine threatened to come back up, but she swallowed it down. She just needed to make it through this evening.

She stood through what felt like eternity—smiling, nodding, thanking the warm welcomes. One after another they came, and just when she didn't think she could bear it any longer, blue eyes met hers.

She stopped and smiled—a real smile this time.

"Queen Regent," Alexander smartly greeted Catherine first, and her grandmother nodded. Then he turned to Norah. "Princess Norah. You seem to be managing the evening quite easily."

That wasn't how she would describe it, but none of that mattered.

"Have you eaten?" he asked.

Catherine cast her a stiff glance.

"I'm really not hungry," she told him.

He stepped up beside her, turning and looking out across the hall. "Now, I know that's a lie," he said quietly, so only she could hear.

She held back a smile. It was a lie. She'd wreck a garden for something to eat right now.

"This is about the time you'd tell me you'd wreck a garden for something to eat right now."

Norah jerked her head to him, her eyes wide.

"Should I steal you something?" he asked, his eyes gleaming.

It was all she could do to keep from laughing.

"Norah," Catherine scolded.

Right. She was here with a purpose. "I'm sorry, I..."

Her words dropped as a poignant melody filled the hall, and she stopped. She knew this song. Norah turned and stared at the string orchestra as they played the familiar tune. A wave of nostalgia rippled through her, leaving her light-headed.

"Are you all right?" Alexander asked, stepping forward and ever so lightly catching her arm.

Her mind blurred.

"Norah?" Catherine asked. Her voice was distant.

"I know this song," she breathed. "I know this dance."

Alexander leaned closer. "You remember 'Allameade'?"

"Allameade." Yes, that's what it was called. She nodded and glanced at Catherine, who stared back at her, wide-eyed.

"Do you remember anything else?" he asked, eagerness growing in his voice.

She shook her head and closed her eyes, listening. "Just the dance, the music. I know it." She opened her eyes and smiled at him. Before Catherine could object, she grabbed his arm. "Come with me," she said breathlessly as she pulled him to the center of the hall amid others dancing, who readily made way.

They stood for a moment, facing each other. She bit her lip at his humble unease, trying to hold back a laugh, and then bowed, inviting him. He hesitated, then returned the bow, accepting.

They brought their right arms up together in a twist, but not touching. Their eyes met as they circled one another and then changed arms. For someone who seemed so reluctant, he knew the movements well, she mused. She did too.

He held his arm out to the side as she moved in a series of steps around him, through the story of the song. They carried themselves in the arrangement across the floor. He slipped behind her and curved his arm around her, but he was careful to keep ever the faintest of space between them. That was the challenge of this intricate dance: two people unable to touch, unable to truly be as one. She drew her arm across her chest between them, reaching back and stroking the air, down the length of his arm, then out to her side.

They moved in unison, losing themselves to the melody and in their closeness to each other. She turned in step to face him as he reached up and brought his palm so close to her cheek she could feel the warmth of his hand. Still, he didn't touch her. His eyes burned with a wild intensity and stirred something wild inside her.

The song ended, and their closeness left her breathless.

His lips parted—a question seemed to linger on them—but he didn't speak it. Instead, he took her hand and bowed, placing a gentle kiss on the back of her fingers.

"Well done, Your Highness. Thank you for that. It was a pleasant surprise." Then he straightened, his formality returning, and Norah realized all eyes in the room were on them. His voice came quieter now. "I should see you back to your grandmother."

Her head felt light as he swept her back to the company of the regent, who cast her a disapproving eye.

"Your Highness," Alexander said to Norah with another bow of his head. "I hope you enjoy the rest of your evening." He gave a small bow to Catherine. "Queen Regent." His eyes again locked with Norah's in a gaze that haunted the shadows of her mind. Then he took his leave to the other side of the hall.

"*When invited*, Norah," her grandmother chided in a harsh whisper. "You can't just go fluttering about and pulling men in to dance."

But Norah paid no mind to Catherine's chastisement. Her heart raced. She had been here before. Even though she had no memory, she knew the dance to "Allameade." She knew the bright light of Alexander's eyes.

Her heart beat even faster.

She knew the feel of his lips on her skin.

CHAPTER NINE

Alexander made his way toward James's chamber, taking the stairs two at a time. The councilman had been in Damask when Norah had returned, and it surprised Alexander he'd arrived back so quickly. Damask was two days' ride away. James had to have left as soon as the bird's message had arrived, then ridden through the night. Perhaps that shouldn't be a surprise. The entire kingdom had been waiting for Norah's return.

The seer had painted the vision of Norah in the forest before her father had taken her. Alexander hadn't known what it had meant then. He hadn't known she'd be lost to him. It was only after King Aamon had died, taking the secret of her location with him, that James thought the painting was a clue to finding her. More than that, James had believed it was part of Alexander's destiny to bring her home. Alexander had wanted to believe that, so much that he had dreamt about it night and day.

For three years, he'd searched the forests throughout the kingdom, and even those beyond Mercia's borders. For three years, he'd returned alone. Until he had ventured where no men dared to go, the land from which men did not return—the Wild. He should have gone sooner, but it was a place he truly hadn't expected to find her.

But he had.

A deep pride swelled within him as he walked the long hall. There had been so many times he'd doubted, so many times he'd feared failure and that Norah would be lost to him forever. And he'd feared disappointing James. No one could take the place of Alexander's father, the great Beurnat the Bear, but James had always been like a father—guiding him, coaching him, loving him, even.

Alexander caught himself and cast his pride aside. This wasn't his accomplishment. This was his duty, his obligation to both Norah and Mercia, his promise to his father and to James. He could be happy and grateful, but he couldn't be prideful.

He reached the councilman's chamber and knocked on the door.

"Enter!" James called.

All the councilmen of Mercia had servants, all except James, who viewed them as being excessive. He minded himself, dressed himself, and even upset the kitchen staff by making food at times. He was a selfless man, which made his counsel invaluable. Alexander desperately wanted that counsel now, but Catherine had been firm. No one, not even James, was to know about Norah's condition. It had even been difficult to convince her to share it with the guard, and even then, she'd limited it to the core guard. But he understood. The regent wouldn't risk anything that might keep Norah from the throne. Without her memories, Norah was even more vulnerable. Catherine was only trying to shield her granddaughter from those she didn't trust. And Catherine trusted no one.

It was a challenging balance between Catherine and the council—the council had given her the regency and had the power to take it away, yet Alexander's vows as justice were to the queen regent only.

As Alexander stepped inside the chamber, James emerged from his cabinet, washed from his ride in and donning a fresh councilman's robe.

"Ah, Alexander," he greeted. "I came as quickly as I could."

Alexander nodded. "I'm glad you're here."

"Is it true?" the councilman asked him. "Is it really her?"

"Yes." Alexander paused as the words caught thick in his throat—the words he'd feared he might never claim. "I found her, James. It's really her."

"Where?"

"In the Wild."

The older man reached out and clasped the side of Alexander's neck. "You've done it, my boy. You've done what I always knew you would."

Alexander's emotion brimmed, making it difficult to speak. He only nodded.

James took a deep breath and walked to the window, letting himself digest the news. "So, the time's finally come." He turned back to Alexander. "Where has she been?"

Alexander paused, then shook his head. "The queen regent has been waiting for you to return before answering that. There's much to catch up on, and she wants the full council present."

James humphed, almost to himself. "I want to see her."

"The queen regent is still getting her settled," he said quickly. Norah wasn't ready to meet James yet. Unlike the other councilmen, James had been close with King Aamon and Norah. He'd know she was different, that something was wrong, like Adrian already suspected, he was certain.

"I'm sure she'll wish to discuss her selection for lord justice once she catches her breath," Alexander told the councilman, hoping to move him past the effort to meet with Norah now. His statement was true. Norah would be expected to seek James's advice on her selection. Although Alexander had dreamed of the placement for himself, he didn't dare expect it. His father had groomed him for it, to follow in his footsteps, but the position of lord justice was one of great power. Only the queen and the combined council stood above it, and Alexander didn't presume himself worthy... or ready. There were others, great men who'd served King Aamon, men far wiser than he. The only reason Alexander held the position now was because of Catherine's distrust for everyone else.

"Has the coronation date been set?" James asked.

Alexander's head jerked up. "No. Not yet. Do you really mean for it to be so soon?"

"Of course. Her return sets everything in motion. Has word been sent to Aleon?"

Alexander's chest tightened. He nodded. Caspian had seen the message off. Within the next few days, the news would reach King Phillip, who would no doubt expect what had always been promised—the seal of their alliance. *A marriage.*

The council would be eager for this marriage, but first they'd see Norah crowned queen. Alexander had hoped she'd have some time. He had hoped *he'd* have some time.

"Good, good." James nodded. "I'd like to see her right away. I'll speak to the queen regent."

Alexander gave a respectful bow of his head. A lord justice didn't bow to councilmen, but James was different.

The councilman reached out and clasped Alexander's shoulder. "Well done, my boy. Your father would be proud."

The emotion returned with James's words. He certainly hoped his father would be proud and that he'd brought honor to their family. He wished his father were there now.

Alexander stepped from the councilman's chamber and headed to find Catherine. He'd need to inform her of James's intent to speak with Norah, so they'd both be prepared.

"How is James?" a voice called from a side hall as he passed.

A silent groan rolled in the back of his throat as he stopped and turned to find his brother. He'd been avoiding Adrian, and he was sure it hadn't gone unnoticed. Adrian's face didn't carry its usual grin. And Adrian didn't have the slightest interest in James, Alexander knew.

"Tired, but well," Alexander answered.

Alexander continued forward, and Adrian fell in step beside him.

"And how are you?" Adrian asked.

He pushed a long breath from his lungs. "The same." His brother could read him better than anyone. No matter how stoic Alexander's face, Adrian always knew how he felt. Now was no exception, especially not after the strange interaction with Norah, but he had neither the time nor the energy for Adrian's questions.

Adrian caught him by the arm, bringing them both to a halt. "You're not well. Why, brother?" His voice was soft and concerned.

"As I said, I'm tired." It wasn't entirely untruthful, although if he were to close his eyes, no sleep would come. It wasn't weariness that weighed on him.

"Why are things different?" Adrian pressed. "Why is she different?"

Alexander searched for the words that might appease him. "She's been gone three years. Of course she's going to be different." But Alexander knew that explained nothing. There were no words that would quell his brother's suspicions. Adrian was too smart for his own good sometimes.

"What about you?" Adrian asked. "Are you different now too? The way you speak to her, the way you act." He paused, looking around and dropping his voice low. "Like there was nothing."

A flash of anger ran through Alexander. Adrian was too free with his tongue. "Watch your words," he warned, but he knew his brother only questioned out of concern for him, out of love. He softened. "Things are different now. She'll be queen in a matter of days."

Adrian shook his head. "What aren't you telling me?"

Alexander clasped Adrian's shoulder. "I've told you all you need to know. Please, don't make my work harder."

Adrian's face fell. He conceded, nodding.

Alexander squeezed his brother's shoulder and then went to find the regent.

Chapter Ten

Darkness hung around her, but Norah wasn't afraid. Her lips pulled back into a smile as she slipped on her dress. The fabric clung to her damp skin. She grasped behind her to tie the lacing, but gentle hands took over, and she let them. Her heart pulsed warmth into her cheeks, and she reached up and swept her hair to the side, feeling the cool air tease the flesh of her neck. The last tie was made on her gown, but she lingered. A warm breath from behind her rolled over her shoulder. Her skin prickled. Then, ever so soft, lips brushed her skin. She let out a small gasp as her head fell to the side, and warmth pooled deep inside her stomach. She turned—

Norah blinked her eyes open as she lay under a wave of confusion. She sat up with a start, pushing back the thick quilts, and realized she was in her chamber. She'd been dreaming, although it didn't feel like a dream.

It was morning, but the sun hadn't yet risen. Rebecca would be in soon to wake her. She slipped out of bed, still breathless from her dream, and splashed water on her face from the basin. Her mind turned to the night before—the dance with Alexander, his nearness, his lips on her skin. Then she scolded herself. Alexander should be the last thing on her mind.

As expected, Rebecca swept into the room with a tray of biscuits and tea. "You're an early riser, Your Highness," she said with a smile. "I hope you slept well."

She hadn't, thinking of the dream, although she wouldn't be terribly upset if it were to happen again. Her cheeks flushed, even at her own private thoughts.

"The queen regent said she'll be in after midday meal," Rebecca told her as she pulled out a gown for Norah to wear.

Norah's brow tensed. That was a long way away. "What will I do until then?"

Her maid helped her into the gown and said, "There are several things I can bring you, Your Highness: drawing things, books, needlepoint."

Needlepoint? That sounded terrible. None of those things appealed to her. "Do I have to stay in my chamber?"

"Well"—Rebecca paused as she pulled the gown tight and fastened it—"the queen regent said she'd be here after midday meal."

Yes, she'd already said that. Norah wriggled inside her gown as Rebecca tightened it, situating herself as comfortably as she could, as if comfort were possible. Then she brushed her hair back from her face. "All right, I can be back before then."

Rebecca gave a small grimace. "I don't think the queen regent would be pleased." She pulled a brush through Norah's loose tresses and fastened the hair back from her face with floral pins.

Norah frowned. "Did she *say* I had to stay in my chamber?"

The maid wavered. "Not exactly."

Norah sighed. "I can't stay in here all the time, locked away."

Rebecca looked at her with sympathetic eyes.

"What about the library?" Norah asked her. The book of poems—she'd been wanting to return for it. She didn't need her maid's permission, but she recognized the value in an ally.

The maid hesitated but finally caved. "Then you can't take long. It wouldn't be good if she were to come and you weren't here."

Norah grinned. "I won't be long at all."

Rebecca grabbed a cloak and draped it over Norah's shoulders, and Norah slipped out into the hall.

Her guard shifted when he saw her, clearly not expecting her to go out anywhere.

"Your Highness," he said, "you should remain in your chamber."

"Good morning, Titus," she said, smiling sweetly. "I'm just going to the library to bring back some books." She turned on her heel before he could object again, knowing he'd have no choice but to follow.

She traced her way back down the halls from what she remembered. She wasn't too concerned with getting lost; Titus would help her if needed. As she stepped outside, she slowed. Where she expected to find the cold emptiness of early morning, she instead found people were already bustling about. For a moment, her confidence wavered.

Norah tucked her chin and kept forward, as if focused on important business. Alexander had said no one would address her unless she addressed them first, so she just wouldn't address them. *Easy enough.* But her self-assurance fell flat as she remembered that wouldn't work on everyone. She would just go to the library and back. Quickly.

But as she reached the end of the pillared walkway, a familiar face came around the corner.

Adrian. *Damn it.*

He was as tall as Alexander and carried himself with the same poise. Norah felt that he was older than his years, and she had to remind herself he was only nineteen.

"Princess Norah," he greeted her. His eyes were the same as his brother's, piercing, but more expressive.

"Adrian," she greeted him, smiling to hide her unease. He was just the kind of person she'd hoped to avoid. She was certain he already suspected something was off.

"How are you settling?" he asked.

She drew in a breath, pushing aside her anxiousness. "Well, thank you." He watched her curiously, and the silence pressured her to offer more. "I'm just going to pick up a few books."

He smiled politely.

She glanced back at Titus. He returned her gaze with a wary eye. She moved toward the library, looking for a natural break, and her pulse quickened as Adrian picked up alongside her.

"Is it strange to be back?" he asked.

"Yes, it is," she answered honestly. "Does it feel strange to have me back?"

"It does," he said, and Norah appreciated his honesty too. "But I'm sure in no time this will feel like home again."

It was hard to imagine Mercia feeling like home—a place that was so foreign now. "I'm sure," she mumbled.

"I imagine you'll—" He stopped as a small group of women walked by. One woman in the group locked eyes with Norah, and excitement flashed across her face, but she said nothing. Norah shifted her attention back to Adrian. What was he saying? Why had he stopped?

He glanced at Norah, then watched the group of women as they passed, before turning back to her. "Do you not want to say hello to Lady Jane?" he asked, his brows drawing together.

"Um"—the woman looking at her must have been Lady Jane, and Norah searched her mind for answers—"my grandmother asked that I settle in before catching up with anyone." She tried to give a jesting smile. "I probably shouldn't even be speaking with you."

Adrian smiled back, but his eyes burned an inquisitive, brilliant blue. "That's too bad. Jane's missed you, you know."

"And I, her." Norah swallowed back the choke of a lie in her throat. "It's been a long time."

He nodded, eyeing her closely. She shifted under his gaze.

"Her mother will be happy to see you too," he said.

"And... I look forward to seeing her as well."

He wasn't smiling anymore. "Except Jane doesn't have a mother."

Nine hells.

"You don't remember Jane?" he asked.

Norah fumbled for words. "I'm a little overwhelmed with everything. Of course I remember. I just wasn't thinking."

But his eyes told her he didn't believe her. "Why are you so different? And did you not know your way around the castle the other day?"

"Adrian," Titus warned from behind her.

Her heart raced in her chest. "Um..."

Titus stepped between them. "Enough."

Adrian wasn't swayed. "Do you not remember? Do you not know?" His voice came more urgently now.

Titus grabbed him by his tunic and pushed him backward.

"Why do you call me Adrian?" he called.

"Wait," Norah said to Titus, and the guard reluctantly paused. "Leave him be."

Titus released him, and Adrian drew nearer to Norah again. He swallowed. "Do you not remember me, Norah?"

This was why Alexander had wanted to keep him away. She couldn't hide her secret from the people who knew her well. It was too obvious. She cursed herself. She should have stayed in her chamber.

"You don't, do you?" he pressed. "You don't remember."

Her heartbeat pulsed in her ears. Titus stepped forward again, but she stopped him. "Leave him," she said. She looked back at Adrian. "You've discovered me." The admission took a weight off her shoulders—the weight of a lie, but it was short-lived. Now he knew, and she wasn't sure what to do about that.

He swallowed. "Do you remember my brother?"

Her silence answered for her.

"He said you were different."

She couldn't lie anymore. "I am different."

Adrian took a step back as the weight of the circumstance settled over him. "Do you remember anything?" he asked.

Titus shifted uneasily as she shook her head. "Alexander and my grandmother have advised me not to share my condition. Obviously, I'm doing a very poor job of that right now. I'd appreciate it if you would keep it to yourself."

"Of course." His voice came low and soft now. "But why don't you remember?"

That was the answer she was so desperate for. She let out a long breath. "I don't know. But I'm trying to find out. I'm reacquainting myself, seeing if anything stirs a memory, if anything might be familiar."

He nodded with a solemn frown. "Forgive me," he said softly. "It wasn't my place."

"There's nothing to forgive." She looked back at the castle. "I should get back." Then she paused. "Hey—what did I used to call you?"

He hesitated, and she wondered if he was reluctant now that she was a stranger to him.

"Adri," he said finally. "You always called me Adri."

His voice held a touch of sorrow. Her loss of memory was not only making it challenging for her but also hurting those she had been close to, those who cared about her.

"I'm sorry," she whispered. Her eyelids grew heavy under the sting of emotion. She turned back toward the castle.

"What about the library?" he asked.

"Another time," she said. She'd already done enough for today.

Chapter Eleven

Norah sat on the chaise in her chamber, a needlepoint canvas in her lap, but her eyes were on the gray skies outside the windows. She hadn't told Rebecca what had happened, about running into Adrian and that he'd discovered her.

Out of all things, her not remembering Alexander seemed to have upset him the most. There was a brief knock on the door. Rebecca moved to answer, but Catherine swept in before her maid reached it.

"Ah, there you are," her grandmother said when she saw Norah, as if she'd been looking everywhere.

"Here I am," she said, glancing at Rebecca to see if the maid would mention her outing. But Rebecca only smiled at her.

"Councilman James has requested to see you," Catherine told her as she picked up the hairbrush from the vanity and waved Norah over. "Rather persistently, I might add. He won't wait for the state. I can't hold him off any longer."

Norah sat at the vanity as Catherine dragged the brush through her hair. "Norah, of all the councilmen, James was closest to your father, and to you."

"Then he can help me manage whatever is going on with my memories. He can help me sort things out."

"No," Catherine said. "If he has concerns, he'll most certainly discuss them with the other members of the council, and we can't have that. Not yet. No, you must approach this with care. But don't worry, I'll be right by your side, and I'll help guide the conversation."

While Norah didn't like the idea of people speaking for her, she'd much rather have Catherine handle these conversations, and she took some reassurance in that. Nevertheless, apprehension grew in her core. She wasn't having the best of luck in maintaining appearances. Catherine raked the brush through another section of her hair, and Norah winced. She was beginning to think it didn't need brushing as much as her grandmother needed something to fill her hands.

"You must greet him warmly," Catherine told her. "You were very fond of him as a girl."

"All right, I can give him an embrace when I see him, and—"

"What?" Catherine grimaced. "That's exactly what you won't do."

Norah bit her lip, feeling sheepish.

"It's not proper. So no, you won't *embrace* him, but you will call him James. Others will see it as a slip, as will he, but it'll represent the relationship you had."

It seemed so odd, but Norah supposed she could understand that. Adrian hadn't used her title, and they had been close. And it wasn't lost on her that when they were alone, Alexander had called her by her name.

Catherine's voice brought her back. "As queen, you'll need to select a lord justice. And you'll need to do so quickly. No doubt James will raise it with you. You'll discuss three names with him: Lord Bosley, Lord Branton, and Lord Semaine."

Norah wanted to object to the coronation again, but the mention of choosing a lord justice drew her mind. "You don't think I should choose Alexander?"

Catherine's eyes met hers in the mirror's reflection with a fierceness. "You should not."

"Why?"

"You're a clever girl," Catherine said firmly, as if that answered her question. "But you must choose quickly. Seek James's council; it's what he'll expect, and it will hold his attention. Just make sure it's one of the three. Lord Branton should be your top choice, although the other two are satisfactory if James feels strongly."

Norah couldn't ignore the sinking feeling in her stomach. Why shouldn't she pick Alexander?

"Come," Catherine said, satisfied with Norah's hair, which looked no different than it had before. "James will be looking for your audience, and I can't delay him anymore."

She followed her grandmother as they made their way toward the throne room. Norah said the names of the lord justice candidates over in her mind. It wasn't the first time she'd heard them. Catherine had introduced her to each of them at her return celebration: Lord Bosley, Lord Branton, Lord...

Damn it.

Panic swelled inside of her. This was an important introduction, and she felt too rushed and ill prepared. James would see right through her.

James and Alexander were waiting when they arrived. Alexander stood fixed, but his gaze caught hers. She wondered if Adrian had told him about their conversation. She broke from his invisible hold and tried to push him from her mind to focus on the task ahead.

"Princess Norah," James greeted her, stepping forward and sweeping up her hand in his. He was tall and thin, balding on top, and old enough to be her father. His eyes held a deep affection. "Welcome home, my dear."

"James," she said, reaching for as genuine a smile as she could manage. She caught a glint of a tear in his eye, but he cleared his throat.

"Though years belated, let me express my sorrow for the loss of your father. He's greatly missed. As you've been."

Norah nodded, unable to speak. Her father had died in the war while she'd been gone. Was she expected to be mourning him? She wished she could remember him so that she could. But she did mourn everything she'd lost. "Thank you," she replied. "It's still difficult to speak of him." That was truthful enough.

James squeezed her hand in understanding. "There's so much to cover since you've been gone. And with your coronation fast approaching, I can understand that you might still be in shock of it all."

Norah let out a relieved breath. Finally, someone who seemed to understand, at least a sliver.

"You probably don't feel ready for this," he said.

If he only knew...

"Is anyone ever truly ready?" Catherine asked.

He gave a small nod, thinking. "Might we go for a walk?" he asked Norah.

"Um..." she said uneasily, looking back at her grandmother.

"James," Catherine said, trying to intervene. "Edward is looking to set up a state now that you've returned. You'll have ample opportunity—"

"Yes, I look forward to it," he said, giving her a bow of his head. "But I would like to speak to the princess now." He turned back to Norah. "Shall we?"

Norah glanced back at Catherine, who she knew couldn't do much more. "Of course," she replied uneasily. She tried to steady her breath as she walked with James out of the hall.

"All this must be quite overwhelming," he started.

She couldn't help a small smile. She appreciated his empathy. "It is," she admitted.

"Where have you been, Norah?"

She continued walking, trying to not let his directness intimidate her. The sun was setting over the castle, casting long shadows through the hall.

"I can't share that, at least not yet," she said, as confidently as she could manage.

"And why is that? Is there no longer trust between us?"

Her mind searched for words. She wished she'd been better prepared. "My father wished to keep it a secret. Secretly." Keep a secret secretly? *So stupid.* She cursed herself.

James's eyes narrowed as her heart beat in her ears. "Is that so?"

She shifted. "Yes."

"And when will you be able to share this *secret* secret?"

Norah cleared her throat. "Soon. I hope." And she did hope.

James nodded with a pondering frown. "It's interesting."

She frowned. "What is?"

"When you lie."

Her stomach tumbled.

He stopped and turned toward her, his eyes holding her captive. "You always seem to have a valiant reason, as I'm sure you do now. But you *are* lying."

Norah's breath caught in her throat, and she nearly choked as she swallowed. She couldn't bear his gaze, but she couldn't turn away.

"Will we leave it at that?" he asked. "Or will you tell me what's really going on? I care for you very much, Norah. Will you not let me help you?" He waited for an answer.

If Catherine was afraid he'd tell the rest of the council about her memory, he'd certainly tell them she was lying. She might as well come clean. And he did seem to care for her; she felt as though she could trust him.

"I don't know where I've been," she finally admitted. "Alexan—the lord justice found me in the Wild, where I'd been lost, but everything before that day is just... gone."

James's brow dipped, and his lips parted slightly before he drew them into a frown.

"Along with all my memories," she added, "of everything and everyone." She didn't know what else to say. Her heart raced.

"Hmm." His frown deepened.

Norah sighed with a small shrug. "Adrian discovered me as well. I'm finding I'm not very good at hiding anything."

"You never were. We'll figure out how to manage that."

Her heart skipped a beat, and a wave of hope ran through her. "You believe me? And you still support my coronation?"

She stood under his heavy gaze, feeling the threat of his condemnation, until he finally said, "An Andell with no memories is still better than a gullible teenage girl and Lord Allan's influence on the throne. Although, I'm not sure how many councilmen will share that view."

It wasn't quite the endorsement to bolster her confidence, but it was better than she'd feared.

He paused. "Who else knows?"

"Ummm... Adrian, Grandmother, and my guard. And Alexander, of course. Grandmother was adamant we tell no one else."

He nodded. "She's right. Listen to her, Norah. She knows how this game is played."

It didn't feel like a game, at least not a fun one.

"We'll have to move up your coronation," he said. "As soon as possible."

Her chest tightened. "Wait, no"—she shook her head—"now that you know, you can help me. We don't have to rush into this."

"On the contrary; time is of the essence now. It has to be before the state. The council, particularly Edward, will want to meet with you first, but there's absolutely no way you'll make it through a state meeting without revealing yourself and your situation."

Was that really so bad? "What would happen? Will they not support me as queen?"

James paused, mulling over her question, and then said cautiously, "I fear they won't if you give them a reason not to."

"Why?"

"Evangeline has a legitimate blood claim to the throne, and she'll do as she's advised." He locked his eyes with hers. "That's always been the concern with you, Norah."

Her eyes narrowed. "So, they'll look for a reason to give Evangeline the throne over me because they fear I won't do as I'm told?"

"That's not what I said."

"It sounded pretty close."

"Even so, who do you think will make the best decisions for a kingdom?" he asked sternly. "A young girl who knows nothing, or a council with the wisdom of generations?"

Norah stepped back, her mouth open, but no words would come out.

James's face was firm, and his mouth was pressed thin. "While we don't always agree, those on the council carry Mercia's best interests in their hearts. We make decisions for the good of our kingdom and the good of our people. Now, I will support you, Norah. I will help seat you on the throne, but you must *listen* and take it seriously. Do you understand?"

How else does one take a queenship if not seriously? She nodded, although she wasn't entirely sure what she was agreeing to. Was this a commitment in exchange for his support? She didn't know if she even wanted his support. Would Evangeline on the throne be such a bad thing? But she didn't have the time to ask him. Or the courage.

"What of your selection for lord justice?" he asked, pivoting the conversation. "The crown is heavy, and you'll tire with a kingdom on your shoulders. You must choose your lord justice wisely."

Yes, that's what she needed help with—a justice. "I was looking for you to help me with that. I wanted to discuss a few names with you: Lord Bosley, Lord Branton, and Lord... Seymour."

He raised a brow. "Lord Semaine?"

Norah cursed herself. At least he already knew her secret. Otherwise, that would have been yet another giveaway.

"Choose Alexander," he said firmly.

"W-Why?" she stammered in surprise.

"Why would you not?" he tossed back.

It was a fair question. One she had asked herself. He was justice now. Catherine had chosen him. Why shouldn't *she*? She gave a small shrug. "It's just a big decision, and it needs to be right."

"Do you feel it's not?"

"It's not that." She paused, searching for words. "I've only known him for a few days."

"My dear," James said with a rich warmth in his voice, "you've known him your entire life, and there's not a man alive more committed to his duty or more loyal." He paused. "You know, when Catherine selected him, the council worried he was too young and not ready. I worried that myself. But his father had prepared him for this role since he was a child, and over these past three years, he's done a damn fine job at it. He's kept this kingdom safe. His words are wise and true. He even manages to persuade Catherine at times, and that alone is a god's feat."

Norah couldn't help a small smile. That did seem like a god's feat. Her heart warmed. Alexander sounded exactly like the kind of man she should choose. "But what about the others?" she asked. "Like Lord Branton." She couldn't go back to her grandmother without at least one more name.

"No others. Choose Alexander, Norah. You asked my counsel, and I'm giving it."

It wasn't counsel that Catherine would be happy with.

"I guess I just need to think about it."

"You had better do it quickly."

Norah nodded, with a heavy stomach.

He paused again. "So... you remember nothing of your father?"

While she didn't feel the pain of his passing, the tragic void wasn't lost on her. She shook her head.

"It's a shame," he said sadly. "He was a great man."

"I want to remember him. I'm trying."

He nodded. "Then I suppose I'm not too insulted you hold no memory of me either." But deep lines of sorrow creased his brow. This was the hardest part—the pain of loss felt by the people who had cared about her. Suddenly, his eyes narrowed. "Did Catherine tell you to drop my title and just call me James?"

She pulled her lips between her teeth and winced.

"Oh, she's good," he said with a gruff. "Well, let's get back. I'm sure she's beside herself. Just do me a favor and wait until I'm gone before you tell her I know about you."

Norah couldn't help a small smile again. It lightened her spirit. They found her grandmother and Alexander in the throne room, and both turned abruptly as they entered, looking to see how the conversation fared, no doubt.

James turned to Norah. "Welcome home, Your Highness. Enjoy these last few days, for everything is about to change." He bowed to Catherine, then left the throne room.

Alexander followed James into the hall with a deep anxiousness in his stomach. The councilman had given no indication that Norah's secret had slipped, but he was a difficult man to read at times.

"No memories?" James said finally as they walked, eyeing Alexander with a raised brow.

Alexander snorted. *Of course.* "She told you." He shook his head. "She's not very good at secrets, is she?"

"I'm surprised by you, Alexander. Did you think I wouldn't find out?"

He expected this. "Of course not. But, James, I gave my word, and I'm committed."

"That you are." The old man pushed out a long breath. "Quite a mystery, though, isn't it?"

It was a mystery, one that Alexander was desperate to solve. But he also needed to focus on the future. "Will you help her, James?"

"I will, so long as it helps Mercia."

"Are they not one and the same?"

James turned to Alexander, a seriousness coming to him. "No, they're not."

Chapter Twelve

Norah followed Catherine to her chamber. She wasn't sure the woman could contain herself until they got there. She wasn't exactly looking forward to sharing that she'd told James about her memory loss, especially after Catherine had explicitly told her not to, and that Alexander was still her only consideration for lord justice. They reached the chamber too soon.

"How did James feel about Lord Branton?" Catherine asked as soon as the door closed.

Norah's heart raced. "He knows," she said with a frown. "He knows I'm not me, that I don't have my memories." It was best to get it out of the way.

"You told him?" Catherine asked, alarmed.

"He saw right away I was lying. There wasn't much I could do. But he's going to help me."

"Does he plan to tell the council?"

She bit the side of her cheek. That would have been a good question to ask. "I don't think so," she said slowly. "He asked me who all knew and said you were right: I shouldn't share it. He also told me to listen to you."

Catherine's eyes widened. "Did he now?" She straightened. That puffed her up a bit. "Let's hope he does the same," she added with an edge. "Norah, you have to be more careful."

How could she possibly be more careful? She'd have to not speak at all.

"Now, what did he say about Lord Branton?" her grandmother pressed again.

Norah's stomach knotted at the next wave of disappointment to deliver. "I have only Alexander to consider."

"You know that's not an option. You were supposed to discuss Branton."

"I did," she insisted. "I don't understand why Alexander's not an option. I don't know anyone else," she added, exasperated. "He wouldn't talk about any of the names you gave me. Branton, Bosley, Seymour—he didn't like any of them."

"Lord Semaine." Catherine sighed. "Oh, Norah, no wonder he discovered you."

"Well, he figured me out well before we even talked about names." And really, what did she expect?

"Don't worry, we'll solve this," her grandmother said flatly. "You'll choose someone else."

"Who? I just said I don't know anyone."

"There are many options. You'll settle on someone."

Norah felt a flash of frustration. Her grandmother wasn't listening. "All right, let's see, there's Adrian—"

Catherine snorted. "Don't be silly."

"Caspian." Norah counted the second name on her fingers.

"That's enough."

"These are literally all the people I know," she said. "Will a councilman do? Oh"—she brought a third finger—"there's a girl named Jane."

"Now you're just being ridiculous," Catherine snapped, but then she paused. "You saw Jane?"

"Um... kind of." She did *see* her.

Catherine's face turned an even paler shade of white. "What did she say? What did *you* say? Gods, that girl has a mouth on her. Just what we need."

Norah gave a smirk. "Actually, I didn't speak to her."

"Thank the gods," Catherine said with a sigh. "I'll have to set expectations better with the guard. We can't rely on courtesies for avoiding conversation."

"Oh, yes." *The guard.* "And add Titus to my list of people," Norah said as she held up four fingers. "And Liaman. There are more guards, but I forget the rest."

Catherine pursed her lips.

Norah looked at her grandmother squarely. "I'm not going to be able to keep this up for long. Adrian figured me out as well."

Catherine let out an exasperated huff. "Adrian knows? Norah! At this rate, the whole kingdom will know!"

"What do you expect?" Norah snapped back, her own desperation lashing out. "I'm not going to be able to fool everyone! These are smart people who've known me for a long time. They know something isn't right." Norah put her face in her hands, letting the cold of her fingers take away the heat from her cheeks. "I have to get my memories back. I have to find out what's blocking them."

Norah glanced up to find Catherine staring at her with an expression she didn't understand. Her eyes narrowed. "What?"

"I have an idea," the regent said.

Norah raised a brow, waiting. "Ummm... normally when people say something like that, they follow it up with the actual idea."

Catherine shook her head, breathless by whatever sudden thought had come to her. "Tonight. I have to do something first. I'll come back tonight."

Norah gaped at her, thoroughly confused. "Wait. What's your idea?"

"No time!" the regent said as she swept out of the room. "I'll see you this evening."

Norah snorted in disbelief.

Alexander sat in his study, looking through a stack of parchments, yet not reading them. He couldn't seem to keep hold of his mind. His thoughts kept returning to her—Norah.

He told himself what he always had: she had a path, one that would save Mercia, a path that he couldn't interfere with. But when she was near, it all came crashing back. The way she smiled, the way she laughed, the way she used to look at him. *Used to.*

"I thought I might find you here."

He looked up to see his brother.

Adrian smiled as he leaned against the doorframe. He stepped into the study and crossed the room. "You probably haven't eaten all day," he said as he put a plate with a pear and a biscuit in front of Alexander.

Alexander sighed, leaning back in his chair and giving a small smile at the pear. "Thank you," he said. Alexander loved his brother. They were very close; they had been ever since Adrian moved to the castle to be with him after their mother died. Adrian had been young, and her death had hit him hard. With their father busy with the duties of being lord justice, Alexander played the role of both parents and managed Adrian's studies while he himself trained. Where he fell short, there was always Catherine, who tended to them both as her own. In fact, Adrian took to her much like she were his own grandmother, as Alexander did as a child, although Adrian seemed to get away with more than Alexander ever could.

But now it was Adrian who often looked after Alexander. Adrian glanced around for a wine pitcher. "Do you want a drink?"

"No. Thank you." He could use some wine, but he had more work to do yet.

Adrian moved around and dropped into the wingback chair in front of the desk. "Are you all right?" he asked.

He couldn't answer that. "It's been a long day."

Adrian sighed, and Alexander knew he wasn't happy with his response. Adrian saw through him.

"Are you sure you're all right?" Adrian pressed.

Alexander closed a book that was open on the side of the desk. "Why do you keep asking me that?" He knew Adrian could see Norah was different. At least he didn't know—

"Because she doesn't remember you."

Alexander's eyes shot up, locking with his brother's. "What did you say?"

"Norah. She doesn't remember you. Or anyone else here."

The breath left his lungs. "She told you?"

Adrian bobbed his head to the side. "After I guessed." His voice softened. "Why didn't you tell me?"

Alexander sighed and rose from the desk. "The fewer people who know, the better."

"But I'm your brother," Adrian argued. "I can help you."

"You can help me by doing as you're told," Alexander said shortly.

"You should've told me. Why didn't you?"

"Catherine wouldn't permit it." He looked at the desk as he reached down and leaned his weight on it. "And I couldn't. You would... know what it meant, and I can't take another face looking at me... with pity."

They sat in silence.

Adrian finally broke the quiet. "To be fair, I have a much better pity face than Grandmother," he said, trying to lighten the air.

Alexander let out a snort, accepting his brother's effort. "Everyone has a better pity face than Catherine."

Adrian smiled.

They sat in the quiet, letting the ease return between them.

"Are you going to tell Norah?" Adrian asked.

Alexander sobered. "You can't call her that anymore. Things are different now. You must use her titles."

"Will you tell her?" he asked again.

Alexander shook his head slowly, staring at the three-candle holder on the desk. One candle had burned to the bottom, and as its flame died, a line of smoke trailed up until it disappeared into nothing.

"What if she remembers?"

Alexander shrugged. "What if she doesn't?" Then their story would be like the candle.

Adrian's eyes narrowed. "You don't want her to?"

He didn't want to talk about this. "It's not about what I want. It's about what's best for her right now. And what's best for Mercia."

"You should tell her," Adrian pressed.

"I don't have the right!" Alexander snapped, momentarily losing himself.

Adrian fell quiet.

Alexander drew in a long breath, calling his patience back. It was only because his brother loved him that he pushed as he did. He softened. "It's better if she forgets," he said quietly. "That part of her life, anyway. It's better if you forget too."

Adrian sighed. He stood and started toward the door, then he paused. "But will you be able to forget, brother?"

The answer haunted him.

Chapter Thirteen

Norah's silk shoes fell silently on the stone as she made her way through the halls from her chamber toward the dining room for dinner. She glanced over her shoulder at her guard behind her. They always felt closer than they were. Especially Titus. Underneath his serious brow, his stern eyes were always on her.

She shifted her focus back in front of her and paused in surprise as she saw Catherine hurrying toward her.

"Come, child," the queen regent said as she grabbed Norah's hand and pulled her back toward her chamber.

Confusion muddled her mind. "Are we not going to eat?"

"Later. You're tired now."

Except Norah wasn't tired. She was hungry. But Catherine's tone told her to go along, and she did. She glanced at Titus as Catherine practically dragged her along. He gave no reaction at all; he simply followed.

When they reached the chamber, Catherine closed the door behind them, leaving Titus and Aaron outside. "Get your cloak. We're going to meet someone."

Norah raised a brow. "Who?"

"Someone with a special gift." Catherine pulled Norah closer, lowering her voice to a whisper. "You know of seers? Those who can see visions of the future? Well, there are rare people, travelers, seers with a greater power—one that allows them to journey into the minds of others."

Norah's heart skipped a beat. "Can someone with this power help me remember?"

"I don't know. But if they can, wouldn't you want them to try?"

"Of course I would." It shouldn't have even been a question.

Catherine grasped Norah's hands. "It's important no one knows of this visit, not even Alexander."

"Why?" Norah was growing tired of secrets.

"Travelers are forbidden in Mercia. Many believe their power to go into one's mind is the work of great evil, of dark magic."

"Is that what Alexander thinks?"

Catherine snicked her tongue against the roof of her mouth. "Hardly. But he wouldn't approve of us flitting off in the night to meet an unlawful mind worker."

It amused Norah that her grandmother would worry about what Alexander did or did not approve of.

Catherine led Norah through the bath and into the cabinet chamber. "Where's your cloak?" she asked, but pulled it from a hanger before Norah had a chance to answer.

Norah wrapped the cloak around her, then took a second one that Catherine held out for her.

"Take this one for me," the queen regent said.

Her brows drew together in confusion, but she didn't have time to question her. Catherine pulled up the center rug and opened a hidden door beneath with a small staircase leading downward.

Norah's eyes widened in surprise. "What's that?" she gasped.

"A hidden passageway. All castles have them. It's how you snuck around when you were younger. You always had your guard on alert." She looked back at Norah. "And don't think that big bald one has forgotten."

Titus.

"Now, go to the bottom of the stairs and wait for me. I'll meet you there."

Catherine herded Norah down into the stairwell. Once Norah was clear of the door, her grandmother closed it again, then flopped the rug back over the top.

Norah turned back to the stairs, holding the railing carefully as she made her way down into the darkness. How strange to find herself here, but her lips curved into a smile. Catherine was showing herself to be quite the free spirit as well. Norah felt even closer to her.

She did as she was told and waited for her grandmother at the bottom of the stairs. It wasn't long before she saw the faint light of her grandmother's lantern approaching from a side tunnel. Once she reached Norah, she took the extra cloak and wrapped it around herself.

Without a word, Catherine led her through a series of cold, dark passageways, winding and weaving, before they finally emerged onto a cobblestone street.

"Stay close," Catherine said. "I'll not have you lost in the city."

The city. Norah felt a wave of excitement. She hadn't been able to explore the city yet, having been limited to only the castle on the isle.

"How will we get across the bridge?" she asked.

"We already are, my dear."

Norah's pulse quickened, and she looked around to get her bearings, but the connected buildings along the street limited her sight.

"This way," Catherine called, and swept forward under the cover of darkness. Adjoining houses lined the narrow streets, and they moved quietly so as not to draw attention. The queen regent was fast, floating through the streets, and Norah almost had to run to keep up with her. They turned down a side alleyway and followed the rowed homes until they finally came to a door. Her grandmother gave two knocks, and they waited.

The door creaked open. A woman, Catherine's age, looked out.

"Esther," Catherine greeted her.

"Catherine." The woman smiled and opened the door, inviting them in. Esther was taller than Norah's grandmother, and thin but with a round face. She wore a simple, green linen dress, and her long white hair fell over her shoulder in a thick braid.

Esther gave Norah a warm smile and bowed her head. "Princess," she greeted. Then she turned to Catherine. "I'll get Nemus."

Norah followed her grandmother in, pulling off her cloak and waiting patiently. She looked around. It was a modest home, made warm by the handmade quilts and candles.

A few moments later, Esther emerged from the back room with an older man, who Norah suspected was Esther's husband. He was tall, but the hunch in his back made him only slightly taller than his wife. His short, white hair matched his short-cut beard, and he wore a light brown tunic over his darker brown trousers.

"Catherine," Nemus greeted her warmly. "Princess Norah, we were so happy to hear of your return."

Norah gave a small nod, noticing their informality with her grandmother. They were friends.

"Nemus, we need your help," Catherine said. "We have a burden we share in the strictest of confidence."

"Of course," he answered, his white brows dipping together.

"While Norah has returned to us, her memories didn't come with her. We have to find a way to bring them back."

He looked at Norah in surprise. "No memories?"

Norah shook her head. It felt strange to be so open about it now.

Catherine let out a breath. "I thought you might be able to help."

He nodded. "I can try. Come."

Nemus ambled over to a small nook and took a seat cross-legged on a large woven floor pillow. He gave Norah a nod and motioned her to sit on a pillow across from him. She settled awkwardly in her dress.

He pulled a quill and penned ink markings down his forearms, his lips moving in silence as he drew circles, lines, and interwoven triangles, designs she'd never seen before. Then he reached out and poured wine into a small bowl and set it down in front of him. Nemus pricked his finger with the tip of a blade, letting a few drops of blood fall into the bowl. He breathed silent words over the mixture and held it out for her.

Norah raised a brow. Surely he didn't mean for her to drink it.

"Do you want me to see?" he asked at her hesitation.

She swallowed. *Perhaps not anymore.* But then, reluctantly, she nodded. "Yes."

"Then you must drink," he told her.

She glanced up at her grandmother, and Catherine gave her a reassuring nod.

Norah shuddered back her aversion and accepted the bowl, taking a deep breath before drinking. The wine was tart, and the thought of blood mixed within made her stomach queasy. She forced it down and handed the bowl back to Nemus.

"Close your eyes," he told her.

She complied, pushing out a breath and dropping her eyelids closed.

"Go inside your mind," he continued. "Imagine yourself sitting in a room."

She imagined herself as she was now, sitting on a floor cushion in Nemus's home.

"You must see it in your mind," he told her. "The room. Do you see it?"

Norah focused on the visual. "Yes," she said.

"Don't be alarmed," he told her.

Why would she be alarmed? There was a faint flutter around her, and suddenly she saw a man before her in her mind. Norah startled, and Nemus chuckled.

"Happens to everyone the first time." He was younger, much younger, and he gave her a small smile.

"Is this how you are in this world?" she asked him.

"I am however I want to be." His words were different now, not heard by her ears but from inside her head. "I project into your mind, and I can control how you see me."

"Are you able to be someone else?" she asked from inside.

Nemus frowned. "If I know the intricacies of their looks, yes. But I prefer being myself." He glanced around, noting that the room was his own. "This looks familiar," he told her, and she gave an awkward smile.

He reached out his hand. "Come," he said. "Let's walk around, shall we?"

She took his hand and stood, and suddenly the cushions they had been sitting on were gone. Norah looked around the room and noticed a series of doors. There were more than there had been before. He motioned to one, and they went to it. He pushed it open, and they stepped inside. It was her chamber in the castle.

Nemus turned, looking all around him. "It's been a long time since I've seen the castle, any part of it. This is your room today?"

She looked at the ornate bed and the west-facing windows. "Yes."

He nodded. "Let's try another." He led her back to the door they had come through, but instead of opening back up to the room in Nemus's home, it opened into the small homestead that she and Alexander had sheltered in before coming to Mercia, where she'd slept on the bed by the fire while Alexander kept watch by the door.

The walls fell away now, and she followed Nemus through what seemed to be stages of her memories. One after the other she saw: meeting her grandmother, meeting the council, Alexander taking her through the library.

Nemus shook his finger at the lord justice and sighed with a crease in his brow. "That boy is everywhere in here," he said as he looked around her memories.

Norah couldn't help the small giggle that escaped her. Nemus looked young, but he had the vexation of an old man.

"He's been a large part of my time back," she admitted.

"And in your long-term memories, judging by the clarity."

In her memories… Where?

He looked around again, and Norah noted a wall with another door. Nemus reached out to push it open but was met with resistance. A look of confusion flashed across his face, and he pushed on the door more firmly. It still didn't move.

"What's wrong?" she asked.

"It won't open."

Obviously. "Why won't it open?"

He looked at her. "It's *your* door. *You* put it there."

"What do you mean *I* put it there?"

"Mind workers can't put things into your mind like this, not permanently." He sighed. "Let's try together." They both reached out and put their weight against the door, but it wouldn't budge.

Suddenly, Nemus fell to his knees, as if something had struck him. He disappeared from her mind, and Norah opened her eyes. They were once again back in Nemus's home, sitting on the cushions.

Her eyes widened at the trickle of blood falling from his left nostril. "You're bleeding!"

"What happened?" Catherine gasped as Esther moved quickly to Nemus with a cloth.

He wiped his nose and took a moment before looking back up at Norah. "Nothing to worry about. I just used a little too much energy. I'll be fine."

"Are they there?" Catherine asked. "The memories?"

"Well, something's there, but it's blocked." He looked at Norah. "By her, I think."

Norah glanced at Catherine, then back to Nemus. "How do I unblock it?"

"I don't know," Nemus said as he wiped his nose again with the cloth. "I don't have enough power to help you."

Norah looked at her grandmother as a wave of disappointment washed over her.

"We understand," Catherine said. "Thank you for trying, Nemus."

"Wait," Norah said with a start. She wasn't leaving without getting as much information as she could. "You're a seer of visions too?"

"I see them, yes."

"Are you the one who saw me taking the Shadow throne?"

He shook his head. "No. Others have, but I have not. Seers may see the same visions, or they may not. No seer sees all visions."

Norah frowned and looked at her grandmother.

"But," he said, drawing Norah's eyes back to him, "I saw the vision of your capture. And the breach of Mercia. It was I who showed your father."

Norah's breath came in quick clips now. "Are you able to show them to me?"

"Norah, we've asked enough already," Catherine pressed her. "And these are old visions, changed visions—ones that will never come to be. Your father saw to that."

But that wasn't enough. "Still," she said to Nemus, "can you? Please?"

Nemus nodded. Norah heard Catherine sigh, but she ignored it.

They both closed their eyes again, returning to the room inside her mind. He motioned to the front door and led Norah outside into the darkness. But they were no longer in the city. Mercia was gone, and in its place lay shadows of rocky hills. Her mouth hung open as a large army passed silently through the night. Between their ranks rode an ominous figure on top of a destrier. He looked more wraith than man, floating through the darkness wearing a horned helm and bladed shoulder armor. Draped across his horse in front of him lay a lifeless young woman. Norah couldn't see her face, but her breath wavered at the long tendrils of snowy hair that fell down the side.

"Is that me?" she whispered.

Nemus gave a nod. He held his arm out, and the army fell away.

They stood inside the courtyard of the castle—the castle of Mercia. It was daylight now, but men cloaked in darkness surrounded them, with their faces covered. These weren't Northmen. In the center of the courtyard stood gallows, with three ropes hanging from the beam above. Three men were led toward them, and she recognized Councilman Edward among them.

Norah watched in horror as her councilmen were ushered up in single file, pushed along by a monster of a man. This man was different from the vision before but equally haunting. He wore nothing on his arms and torso, as if he were invincible. His skin bore dark ink patterns, and his face was covered in a wrap, from which only his eyes showed. Edward screamed words she couldn't hear, but she could see the terror in his face as the ropes were looped and tightened around the men's necks. The monster executioner nodded, and the floor fell out from underneath their feet. Norah covered her mouth to hold in her own scream. Two of the councilmen hung limply, their necks immediately broken, but Edward squirmed at the end of his rope.

Norah couldn't watch anymore, but she couldn't look away. She could only stand in horror. A cry escaped her lips. Finally, as if a sliver of mercy existed, the monster of a man pulled a dagger and ran Edward through with the blade. Then, he turned, and the dark pools of his eyes looked right at her. Seeing her.

Norah gasped and opened her eyes with a start, shaking and struggling for her breath. They were in Nemus's home again, sitting on the floor. Catherine was by her side, taking her hand and holding her steady.

"Are you all right, child?"

Norah swallowed back the fear in her chest, inhaling deeply to keep from vomiting. That was the breach Catherine had warned of—the Shadowmen taking her, taking Mercia, and bringing death to them all. Her eyes found Nemus again.

"That's why your father took you and hid you away from the world," he told her.

Norah waited a moment for her breath to come back to her. "And you can't see where he took me?"

"I cannot."

"Is there another like you? Someone with more power?" As she said the words, they sounded rude in her ears. She hoped he didn't take it that way.

"You'll find only seers in Mercia, not travelers. I know none like me." His voice held a hint of sorrow. "I'm sorry."

"So, my father, he changed the future?"

He nodded.

"Can you see what happens now?"

Nemus shook his head. "I have no control over what the Eye shows me, but there have been no visions of you since you left, by any seers, that I'm aware of. Perhaps there's a shield over you, like seers have, a shield that doesn't allow the Eye to see you or know where you are. I imagine this relates to your memory loss."

"Who could have put this shield there? Another seer?"

Nemus shook his head. "I don't know who would have that kind of power."

Chapter Fourteen

Catherine led them back through the streets toward the tunnels. Norah followed blindly, her mind racing. The vision of her councilmen would haunt her. And this shield—whatever blocked her from being seen in visions—who had put it there? Nemus had said he didn't know who would have that kind of power. If she could figure out how to remove it, would it bring her memories back?

They made their way quickly through the tunnels in the dark. Norah was amazed Catherine could remember the way. "How do you know all these passages?" she asked.

"I've been here a long time, my dear. And I've had many secrets to keep." They turned down another hall, and Catherine stopped. She felt the pockets of her gown.

"What is it?"

"Gods," Catherine muttered. "My key, the one for my own chamber. I've left it at Nemus's."

"Oh, that's all right, we can go back."

"No, no. I'll go. If you follow this walk two halls down, you'll see the stair on the right to your room."

"Wait." Absolutely not. No. *No.* "I can't go by myself."

"Oh, Norah, you'll be fine. I can't go back out through your chamber, anyway. The guard has already seen me leave. They think you're alone inside. Be sure to straighten the rug on the top after. I don't want anyone finding that door."

"What about *me* finding the door?" Walking through dark tunnels wasn't what she wanted to be doing. At all.

"Don't be dramatic. As I said, you're perfectly fine. No one knows of these tunnels but me." But she lingered for a moment. "I'm sorry about tonight, Norah," she said softly. "I really thought this would work."

Norah had hoped it would work too. She shrugged. "We'll keep trying."

Catherine patted her on the arm. "That we will. I'll see you in the morning, my dear."

With that, Catherine turned and disappeared into the darkness, leaving Norah holding the small lantern. She sighed and then turned down the tunnel toward her room.

It was difficult to see, even with the lantern, which barely lit the space in front of her. Fear rippled through her. Not from the dark—she wasn't afraid of the dark. She feared failure, disappointing those who cared about her and letting down her people and her kingdom. How could she be queen if she knew nothing? How could she make good decisions for her people when she didn't understand? And how could she fight an enemy she didn't know, especially an enemy like the one she saw tonight?

She paused when she noticed a hall, then cursed under her breath. She hadn't been paying attention. Did she already pass one, or was this the first? Surely she would have noticed if one had come up sooner. She kept going.

When she came to another hall, she turned and took it down to the end, where she found the stairwell. *Finally.* She held the rail as she climbed the stairs, but when she got to the top, the door wasn't above her head as before. It stood in front of her. She was at the wrong door.

Norah cursed under her breath. Maybe if she went back one hall? But what if she had passed two? She had walked quite a way while distracted by her thoughts. She glanced at the lantern. The candlewick was near its end. What she didn't want to do was get lost looking for a secret door with no lantern at all. She pursed her lips. Where was she now?

Her stomach knotted at the thought of returning to her chamber from the outside—where Titus stood. She supposed it wasn't the worst thing that could happen. It would be just like old times?

She turned the knob to the door as quietly as she could. It opened with no resistance, and she peeked through. A breath of relief escaped her. An empty room. She ducked out of what appeared to be a closet on the outside, then closed the door behind her. Everything was fine—she'd just figure out where she was and make her way back to her chamber.

Norah slipped out into the hall, appreciating the quiet of her silk shoes. It was late evening now, and she wasn't expecting anyone about, but she'd rather make it back to her chamber without anyone seeing her. There would be less to explain.

Light spilled out from a room ahead, and she slowed. She wasn't sure what room it was; she hadn't been in this hall before. When she reached the open door, she sidled along the edge of the frame, leaning forward just enough to peek inside. It was a study. Her heart beat faster.

Alexander sat at his desk, reading through several documents. The candle to his right dropped a trail of wax down its side—he'd been there for a while. He sighed as he put one parchment down and then picked up another.

She couldn't help herself. "What are you working on?" she asked.

He looked up in surprise, and a hint of a smile came to his lips. He rose from his chair. As his mind seemed to put things together, his brow creased. "Where did you come from?" he asked.

She stepped inside the study and shrugged. "Just walking."

His eyes ran over her cloak. "Outside?"

Hammel's hell. "Just around the castle. I... was cold." She bit her lip. That definitely sounded like a lie.

Alexander raised a brow.

She drew closer, and his eyes followed. She took a seat on the wingback chair in front of the desk, and he slowly sat back down. His face had a warm familiarity, and she struggled to separate whether it was the comfort of their new friendship, or something more. She spied a biscuit and pear on a plate on the corner of the desk, and her stomach grumbled. She hadn't eaten anything since Catherine had taken her to the seer. "Are you going to eat that?" she asked.

He glanced at the plate. "No. Are you hungry?" His brow dipped. "Have you not eaten?"

"I wasn't hungry earlier, but I just realized I am a little now." She grabbed the pear off the plate.

"I'll get you some food. Don't eat that. Adrian brought it hours ago." He moved to stand.

"No, it's all right," she said quickly. "The pear's fine."

He sighed and gave a small smile. "I'll have to make sure we do a better job taking care of our queen."

His words sat uncomfortably in her ears. *Queen.* She swallowed. She had no business being queen.

"Are you all right?" he asked. "Have I said something?"

She turned the pear in her hands, brushing her fingers over the smooth skin of the fruit. She wanted to tell him about the visit to the traveler, about seeing the visions, but Catherine had said not to. "My grandmother says that the council will push for my coronation right away." She drew her eyes back up, searching for confirmation.

He nodded. "It's true."

"How soon?"

"A few days."

A wave of panic washed through her. "A few days?" She wouldn't even know her way around the castle properly within a few days. How could she be ready to be queen and stand against a monster the likes of what she'd seen tonight?

"I know it seems soon," he tried to assure her, "but you'll figure things out. You always do."

Norah snorted in frustration. "I can't even figure out how to keep my memory loss a secret. Did you speak to Adrian?"

Alexander nodded calmly. "He told me."

"Talk about someone figuring things out. Well... he did. So did James. I hadn't even said three sentences, and James... told me I was lying. Which I was." She closed her eyes, silently cursing herself.

"Don't fault yourself for Adrian and James. I should have told them. There was no way they wouldn't have known something was wrong. They know you too well."

She shook her head. "It's more than just that. I can't do this."

Alexander leaned forward with his forearms on the edge of the desk. "Norah, you're going to be a great queen."

"You don't know that," she said, standing and bumping back the chair. "I have no idea what I'm doing."

Alexander moved to speak, but then stopped. The corner of his mouth curved into a slight smile. He rolled the documents in front of him into a leather binding and rose from the desk. "Come with me."

His sudden pivot in the conversation made her brow dip with suspicion. "Where?" she asked.

"I want to show you something."

She hoped it didn't involve navigating back through a series of dark tunnels. Her gaze met Alexander's. He offered his hand.

To hell if there were tunnels. She slipped her hand in his, and his skin warmed hers. It felt nice, and right.

He led her out of the study but paused in the hall. "Wait," he said. "Where's your guard?"

Norah twisted a little. "They... might... be back at my chamber door."

"Back at your door?" His brow furrowed. "You're alone? How did you slip out?"

She shrugged as she pursed her lips to the side. "Quietly?"

His jaw tightened, and the blue of his eyes burned brighter. Norah found herself not entirely annoyed at his concern. In fact, she wasn't annoyed at all.

"Never mind for now," he said. "Come on. We'll discuss this later."

She couldn't help a small smile.

Alexander led her through several halls, which were lit only by the dim glow of candles in chandeliers. Their shadows danced against the stone. It was the first time he'd taken her hand, but he held it so naturally, like it belonged to him.

They came upon a guarded door, and Alexander nodded to the soldier, who stepped aside. He pushed it open and looked back at her, giving her a reassuring smile.

Through the door was another long hallway that led to another structure of the castle. They walked through the arched stone, finally coming to the hallway's end. Ahead of them, the hall spilled into a vast, round chamber, with a glass ceiling dropping moonlight into the great room below.

"Watch your step," he told her as he started down a spiral staircase to the bottom. His fingers tightened around hers to offer support.

"What is this place?" she asked.

"You'll see."

As they reached the bottom, she noted large openings carved into the walls. Each opening held a stone sarcophagus. *Tombs.* They were tombs. And there were so many.

"Is this supposed to lift my spirits?" she asked, raising a brow. "I share how I feel woefully inadequate, and you bring me to a room full of tombs?"

Alexander chuckled. "No. I mean, yes, it is supposed to lift your spirits. Although now I can understand how this might seem very odd." He gave her hand a gentle pull. "But I want you to see something."

She let him pull her farther into the chamber.

"This place is called the Hall of Souls. It's the tomb of the kings of Mercia," Alexander told her. "And queens."

Despite being in the home of the dead in the darkness of night, there was a beauty to it. Intricate carvings lined the walls between the cists. In the center of the room were stairs to a small platform with a singular tomb that seemed to gleam under the rays of the moon. Inset in the stone were thick strips of wood engraved with scenes of battle triumphs.

"Here, look," he said, leading her up the center stairs to the sarcophagus in the middle of the chamber. "Only the kings and queens of Mercia have come here, with the occasional stealthy lord justice." His face held a smirk.

She smiled back.

He reached out and put his hand on the foot of the cist. "This is the tomb of King Hagen, the original great king of Mercia, who built this kingdom many generations before you. Put your hand here," he said, touching the engraving at the foot.

She reached out and felt the wood inset. It was smooth, almost polished.

"What do you feel?" he asked.

She shook her head. "Nothing. It's... smooth."

He took her hand and moved it further to the side. "And here?"

His touch was distracting, but she forced her mind to the carving. "Um... not as smooth?"

He nodded, his golden hair catching the moonlight from the windows above. "Think of how many men must have come here to ask King Hagen for strength, polishing this wood smooth with only the touch of their skin. How many hands does that take? How many touches?"

She moved her fingers back to the polished engraving, feeling its smoothness, to where her father must have touched and his father before him.

"See, Norah," he said softly, "you aren't the only one who's thought yourself lost."

The calm of reassurance settled her, and she looked at him. "Thank you," she whispered.

Alexander's lips parted to say more, but then he stopped. She glanced down at her hand, still in his. It fit so perfectly, warm, protected, and safe—the way he made her feel.

"I should get you back to your chamber," he said, finally breaking the spell.

Right. Her chamber. She felt a wave of disappointment, and it surprised her. She forced a nod, and he led her back the way they had come.

As they walked back to her chamber, she saw Titus's posture shift before they even reached him. Seeing her outside—he hadn't expected this.

"Sorry," she mouthed to the large guard as they reached the door. She turned back to Alexander.

"Good night, Your Highness," he told her. His formality had returned.

"Good night, Lord Justice." She turned back toward her chamber. "Sorry," she whispered again to Titus as she slipped past him and inside.

CHAPTER FIFTEEN

The door to Norah's chamber swung open. "Rise, child!" Catherine said as she swept in. "Quickly!"

Norah sat straight up in bed. Daylight shined through the window. Had she really slept until the sun had risen? She wiped her eyes. She'd slept—she'd actually slept. And it felt amazing.

"Quickly!" her grandmother pushed again as Rebecca hurried in with a dress.

Catherine's tone quashed Norah's restful satisfaction. Why quickly? "What's going on?"

"The council has called a state now that James and Elias have returned. I thought we'd have more time, both James and I pushed, but no. It's today."

Today. Her pulse picked up. Today—*no*. "I can't meet with the council today." She wasn't anywhere near ready for the state. She still didn't entirely know what that meant, only that they would ask questions—questions that she had no answers for. They'd want to know where she'd been, and while Catherine had come up with a response that she'd rehearsed a hundred times, it still didn't sound true. Because it wasn't. And then when they discovered her...

She didn't want to think about that. She *couldn't* think about that and keep control of her nerves.

"Don't worry, my dear," her grandmother said, seeming to read her mind. "I'm still queen regent. I'll lead us through. Everything will be fine."

But she didn't believe that. Even James wasn't confident she'd fool the council—he'd told her so directly.

Catherine practically ripped Norah's nightgown from her just as Rebecca swept around with a corset, tying it and pulling it tight before Norah could adjust for her breath. The gown came over her head, from her maid or her grandmother, she wasn't sure. Not that it mattered. She just needed it on. Panic flowed through her veins, and being rushed didn't help. She forced her mind back to the question the council would ask her first—where she'd been...

"Remember, you'll say you've been kept well by a secret ally, one that wishes to remain secret," Catherine said, as if reading her mind. "Instead of focusing on the past, I'll drive our conversation to the present and the future. We'll talk about your marriage to Phillip."

Norah stiffened. She'd rather tell the council about her memory loss.

Catherine tugged the fitted gown straight, then pushed Norah to the vanity and pressed her abruptly down in the chair. She pulled the brush from Rebecca's hand and raked it swiftly through Norah's hair. "By now, Phillip will know of your return."

Norah winced, more from his name than the speedy, aggressive hair brushing. This man she didn't know—the man she was expected to wed.

Her grandmother swept back the sides of Norah's hair with floral pins. "We'll hear from him soon, and it shouldn't be hard to occupy their attention with that—it's what's most important, anyway."

Norah's mind reeled. With every fiber of her being, she rejected the notion of this marriage. Her soul clawed against the obligations that chained her and against the path she couldn't choose for herself. Or perhaps she could choose, but there was the weight of so many looking to her—of so many lives depending on her. Turning her back to them would break her. And she found herself feeling the same as she had with James—there was nothing she could do but agree. Nothing she could do but follow. At least for now.

Catherine swept a cloak over Norah's shoulders and pulled her toward the chamber door, and she went. Her guard picked up behind them as they started down the hall, as if herding her toward her future. She swallowed even though her tongue sat dryly in her mouth. *Pretend.* Pretend to be the person she was before. Look the part. Play the part. *Pretend* the best she could.

They exited the castle through the double doors to the outside and walked along the courtyard toward the judisaept. The winter air was cold, and Norah shuddered, but she welcomed it. Anything to distract her spiraling mind.

Beside her, Catherine slowed, and Norah followed her gaze to something on the other side of the courtyard. She squinted against the icy air but couldn't make out what or who it was through the throngs of people gathering.

"What is it?" Norah asked her.

"I don't know," Catherine said, but she'd stopped. Castle guards broke from their posts and hurried toward the crowd.

Suddenly, a scream ripped through the growing masses. Norah's guard swept around her. Another scream sounded, but not one of fear—one of anguish. Norah started toward it.

Catherine caught her hand. "What are you doing?"

"Something's happened—I have to see!" And she pulled her arm from her grandmother's grasp.

"Your Highness," Titus called from behind her, but she ignored him and strode toward the crowd. He followed after with his sword in hand.

She drew closer. The crowd surrounded a large wagon, pulled by four horses caked with dried mud and dirt. The animals stood still, weary and spent from their journey. No one drove the wagon, but it was stacked high with what appeared to be grain sacks in the back, stained in browning crimson. One sat open on the ground, but she couldn't see what was inside. A woman was crying with her arms outstretched toward the wagon as a man pulled her away.

Suddenly, Alexander was in front of her. She jerked in surprise as his arm came out, halting her. "Norah," he said, low, "go back to the castle. I'll be there in a moment."

But she didn't want to go back. "What's in the sacks?"

"Norah." He clasped her arm, gently but firmly, and tried to move her back toward the castle.

"What's in the sacks?" she pressed again.

"Just go back. I'll be there in a moment, and I'll tell you then."

"You'll tell me now," she demanded. Her patience was waning, and she wouldn't leave until she knew what was going on.

His mouth tightened. "We expected the Shadow King to attempt to retake the mountains of Bahoul again, especially if he learned of your return. It's a critical stronghold that used to belong to the Shadowlands. I sent another thousand men for reinforcement."

That still didn't answer her question. "What's in the sacks?"

His lips thinned. "The men I sent. Their heads."

Nausea swept through her as she glanced back at the wagon and its horror-filled cargo. The heads of a thousand men. She wavered. His hand tightened around her arm.

"Go back inside," he said. "I'll come after I've dealt with this."

Titus stepped forward, offering his own arm, but she pulled away from both of them and turned back toward the castle, numb with shock.

Catherine stood just behind her with Edward, James, and two other members of the council.

"Lord Justice!" Edward called out, and hurried after Alexander. The other two councilmen bowed to Norah and followed after.

Catherine reached out and clasped Norah's hand. "It's all right. Everything will be all right."

Norah shook her head, her mouth hanging open. "No, it's not. None of this is all right." She felt James's eyes on her and cast him a desperate gaze. "Are we to discuss this today too?" As if the myriad of other topics weren't enough. As if she wasn't already near breaking. And still she had to face the council. In a matter of moments. She wasn't ready. She couldn't do this.

He shook his head. "No. The state's been postponed."

It was the smallest of mercies compared to everything else, but still the relief of it almost brought tears to her eyes.

"To prepare for your coronation," James added. "You'll be crowned tomorrow."

Norah's heart stopped, and her lungs turned to stone in her chest. She couldn't draw in a breath. "I can't be crowned tomorrow."

"This works in our favor," James said.

"Favor?" she stammered breathlessly.

"We don't have the luxury of time, and this puts pressure to pull the coronation forward before the state. Pressure we need. Things will move quickly now. You must be ready."

"Of course I'm not ready!"

Catherine hushed her and pulled her toward the castle. "Not here," she said sternly.

Not here, not in public. Not that it mattered, with everyone's attention on the wagon of severed heads. Her stomach threatened to rebel. She needed to get away from the courtyard, and she let Catherine pull her back toward her chamber.

No sooner had the door closed when her grandmother said, "Do you see now?"

Norah scoffed in astonishment. "*See*? I see that you'll have me slap a crown on my head so I can hurry and marry! And that's the only thing on all of your minds, not the thousand heads in our courtyard, the heads James says are in our favor!" Her voice came nearly at a scream now. "In what mad world would that be considered in our favor?"

"It helps secure the crown before your ignorance loses it," Catherine snapped back. "And perhaps now it will open your eyes! This is only a token of what the Shadow King has done, and what he will do. You don't want to marry? Well, I don't want a kingdom of severed heads!"

Her grandmother's words silenced her. She didn't want a kingdom of severed heads either.

"Norah, Aleon has the largest army in the world."

"To help me take a Shadow throne I don't want?" She shook her head. "I don't even want this one."

Her grandmother snatched her arm and pulled her close. "Don't ever say that again. Not ever. Not even behind closed doors. Do you hear me?"

Norah drew in an uneven breath, then another. Her desperation was talking for her, and she couldn't let it.

"It's not about wanting the Shadow throne," Catherine argued sharply. "It's about stopping a great evil. It's about saving yourself and your kingdom. And I don't mean evil in simply a vile sense, Norah. He's true evil incarnate. The Shadow King made a pact with Darkness, a pact that required his own heart."

Her eyes narrowed. "A man can't live without his heart."

"He's no longer a man. And out of his pact with Darkness, he was given a demon to command his armies. The blood of men gives this demon strength. It does the bidding of the Shadow King, and in return, it gains the souls of the fallen. And now, the Shadow King has the power to corrupt this entire world and bring death to us all."

Norah's skin prickled. And he was coming for her...

Catherine's hold on her hands softened. "I don't say these things to scare you, child."

It was a little too late for that. Norah swallowed.

"Come. I have to show you something." Still holding Norah's hand, Catherine pulled her out of the chamber and down the hall to a side door leading outside. Norah silently begged that they weren't headed back to the courtyard.

They weren't, and she let out a sigh of relief. She let Catherine lead her down a cobblestone side path to an adjoining stone building with no windows. Her grandmother pushed open the door without knocking, and Norah followed her inside.

They stood in the middle of what appeared to be a sitting room, but all around them were paintings. Hundreds of them. Panels of stretched canvas stood upright and were stacked against the wall, balanced on chairs, and piled high on a center table.

Norah maneuvered slowly through the images, following her grandmother. There were so many—mainly of war but some of celebration. Some were of individuals; there were countless faces.

"Samuel!" Catherine called as they worked their way back.

An older man with thick glasses dressed in a sand-colored tunic and matching trousers appeared in the doorway of an adjoining hall, leaning heavily on his cane. "Ah, Queen Regent," he greeted Catherine. When he saw Norah, he gave a wobbly bow of his head. "Princess Norah. A very unexpected but very welcome surprise."

"The painting," Catherine told him. As if there were only one.

"Ah. Yes, yes." He waved his cane for them to follow as he hobbled through a door and into a back room.

"Which painting?" Norah asked her.

"The only one that matters." Catherine started after the seer.

Norah followed them to the back room. It was much like the first and also had paintings stacked against the walls. This room had more furniture, which, like the room before, seemed to serve only to hold more paintings.

"Are all of these visions?" Norah asked.

"They are," he said as he made his way toward the back.

Norah let her eyes pass from painting to painting in the room of visions. She didn't know what to make of them. Images of death and carnage surrounded her: castle ruins, fallen men, blood pooling in the streets. And in every image of destruction, there was a dark, monstrous man with a horned helm—the Shadow King.

"There," her grandmother said, and she pointed to a large painting against the back wall.

Norah stopped and stared at herself. It was an image of her sitting on a throne of night, with a crown atop her head. She wore white, the color of Mercia, but this wasn't the throne of Mercia.

"It's the Shadow throne," Catherine told her. "Do you see now? You'll take it. You'll overthrow the Shadow King."

Norah could only stare. She almost didn't recognize herself; this woman looked strong. Powerful. Like a queen. It looked nothing like how she felt right now. Her soul still shook from the courtyard, and her mind was still foggy with the day's horror. This woman in the painting wasn't her.

"This can't be me," she breathed.

Catherine clenched Norah's hand tighter. "Of course it's you, my dear. It will be you. Fate's written it."

Chapter Sixteen

The day of Norah's coronation came with the sun, and Alexander sat in his chamber polishing his boots. He brushed them meticulously, trying to keep his mind from the thoughts that threatened to consume him. Today Norah would be crowned queen and would be one step closer to marrying King Phillip. They needed Aleon, but that didn't make supporting the marriage any easier.

A knock rattled the door. Before he could answer, Adrian stepped inside. Of course he'd come.

Adrian grinned. "Today's the day, brother."

Alexander raised a brow, but he knew what his brother was referring to. "You don't know that." Sometimes Adrian was too positive.

"What?" his brother scoffed. "Of course I do. You're going to be lord justice. Really this time."

Alexander shook his head as he wrapped the boot brush back in its cloth. "No. The decision hasn't yet been made, and there are others far more qualified than I."

"Like who?"

"Many." Catherine would have put forward a list of names. He suspected the decision would be Lord Branton. The Mercian lord had been a field general before he lost his sword arm in the war, and he'd been a trusted voice to the late King Aamon. His opinions sometimes differed from the council, which was a good thing. He was a good man, and Alexander could respect that decision. He pulled on one boot and then the other. "And even if she has decided, she most likely wouldn't announce it today."

"Councilman Edward said it's customary to name the lord justice on the day of the coronation."

"Councilman Edward has seen exactly one coronation. That hardly represents *customary*."

"Alec," his brother pressed, "get excited! This is real. It's going to happen. I *feel* it." He looked around. "Where's Jude?"

Alexander had sent his servant away. "I wanted to prepare alone."

Adrian shrugged. "I'll help you."

Alexander couldn't help a smile as he rose from the bed. Adrian picked up the polished breastplate from the table and lovingly gave it a wipe with his sleeve before positioning it on Alexander's chest and buckling the straps carefully. Alexander stood as Adrian finished, watching in the cheval mirror. This had been his father's armor. He remembered exactly how his father had looked wearing it. He looked very much like his father now.

Their eyes met in the reflection and Adrian smiled. "Father would be proud of you, Alec," he said, seeming to read his mind. "I am."

Alexander's eyes welled, and Adrian hugged him. Alexander held his brother close, treasuring the moment. Then he cleared his throat as he collected himself and clapped Adrian on the shoulder. "Thank you, brother."

Adrian handed him his sword, and Alexander buckled the belt around his waist.

"Are you ready?" his brother asked with a grin.

No, but he nodded, and they stepped out into the sunlit hallway.

They made their way through the crowded castle and toward the throne room. Well-wishers clapped him on the back as he walked through the crowd of people. The lords expected him to be named lord justice. He never considered himself an ambitious man, at least not the way most men were, but he had always hoped to follow in his father's footsteps one day. He'd hoped it was his destiny. Of all the visions Samuel had painted of him, none showed him as the lord justice. But then, they never showed someone else either.

Alexander left Adrian in the mainway and stepped into a side hall, finding the room where Norah was privately waiting. He paused for a moment, watching her. She was beautiful, as she always was, and she took his breath, like she always did. She was dressed in white, the color of Mercia. Ornate silver trim lined her gown, which was long with delicate beading. Her hair was pinned up, with loose curls swept back in twisted braids.

"Norah," he said softly. He should have bowed, but he couldn't take his eyes off her.

She turned and let out a breath. "Alexander. I'm so glad you're here. I'm a nervous wreck."

He couldn't help a small smile. "You needn't be. Remember, you only say two words. And I'm pretty sure you can say anything and it won't matter. In fact, your grandmother may speak for you."

The corner of her mouth turned up through her pursed lips. "So I'm just to stand there and look the part?"

"Well, you do look... very much a queen."

She glanced down at her gown. "I suppose that's the intent."

Time was slipping away from him. "Shortly, I'll be calling you Queen Norah."

"As long as it's not *Your Elegance*."

"Your Regal High," he said, and it finally pulled a real smile from her. Gods, he loved that smile.

"It isn't the ceremony I'm worried about," she said. "I'm not ready."

Neither was he. "No one ever is."

She let out a wavering breath.

"Norah," he said. She looked up at him. "It's not about remembering now. Leading people takes heart, and you've always been the heart of this kingdom. Follow yours, and you'll know what to do."

She pursed her lips into a fragile smile and nodded. "That's exactly what I needed to hear right now," she whispered.

He hoped he could give her some reassurance. If she could only see what he saw in her...

Her eyes moved past him and over his shoulder. He turned to see Catherine. "Queen Regent." He bowed. She gave him a nod, but her stern eye cued his leave. He looked back at Norah and gave her a reassuring nod. "When we speak again, you'll be queen." He gave her a small bow and slipped out of the room.

Norah's eyes trailed Alexander as he left to give her some privacy with her grandmother before the ceremony.

"Look at you," Catherine smiled, clasping her hand. "So much like your mother."

Her mother. *Evanya*. Had she felt the same when she'd married Norah's father? Had she been afraid? Unsure? Worried about disappointing everyone?

"Here," Catherine said, pulling out a velvet box. "I have something for you. You'll be crowned with this during the coronation, but I wanted you to see it first."

Norah removed the top, and her breath caught. Inside sat a gold crown. Carefully, she lifted it from the box. It was heavier than it looked. She ran her fingers over the smooth base, and then up the shaped floral-like edges.

"These represent lilies," Catherine told her, touching the top shapes of the crown. "They were your mother's favorite flowers. Your father would have them brought from Aleon for her." She smiled sadly. "She was taken from us before the crown was completed, but he had it finished, intending to one day give it to you. He would have loved to see this moment."

Norah's lip trembled. "It's beautiful," she breathed.

"Like its queen," her grandmother replied, with tears in her eyes.

Norah threw her arms around her grandmother, hugging her close.

Catherine squeezed her back. "They're with you now, child. And so am I."

Norah took a step back and nodded, unable to speak.

Her grandmother took the crown and put it back into the box. "Now, everything's ready. You needn't fret about anything. And tomorrow, we'll meet with the council and decide on your lord justice. Someone we trust implicitly."

Her stomach twisted. There was only one person she trusted implicitly.

Catherine smiled. "For now, one thing at a time, my dear."

But it was never one thing at a time. Norah swallowed down the lump rising in her throat. If she could just get through this ceremony...

Her heart raced. James had come earlier that morning, giving her the reassurance she had so desperately needed, guiding her toward what she already knew she needed to do. Still, it was hard, and she clenched her hands to keep them from shaking.

"Come now." Catherine smiled. "It's time."

Norah peeked through the double doors to the throne room and felt faint. So many people were inside, surely over a thousand. Her corset and stiff gown did little to help her catch her breath.

"All right, just as we rehearsed," Catherine directed, prodding her into place. "Yes. You'll stand out of sight as I enter. I'll walk to the end. They'll open the doors again, and then you'll come."

Norah nodded as she drew in a deep breath. She could do this, she told herself.

"Smile, my dear," her grandmother told her. "This will be the first time many have seen you. If it helps, keep your eyes on me as you walk."

Norah nodded again, and Catherine hugged her tightly. The doors opened, and she waited to the side as the queen regent walked regally down the center of the hall, toward the dais. The guards again closed the doors, and Norah positioned herself behind them. Servants ran quickly around her, adjusting her gown and making sure everything was in place. Time seemed to stop, and she wrung her hands nervously. How long could it possibly take for one to walk to the dais? Was Catherine stopping between each step?

Then the doors swung open, and she wished them closed again. Murmurs rippled through the crowd, and she swallowed as she tried to keep herself calm. Never had she seen so many people—it was more than she thought she'd seen just moments before.

"Your Highness," her captain, Caspian, murmured from the side. She glanced at him, and he nodded.

Walk. She was supposed to walk.

Slowly, she stepped forward. She took one step, then another. Down the center of the hall she walked—slowly, but all too fast. Her heart raced, and sweat beaded the back of her neck as she clenched together her frozen fingers. Norah looked for her grandmother, but there were too many people. She made her way between the masses on either side, focusing on the red floor runner in front of her.

Focusing.

Following.

Following the red. Dark red.

Dark red like the stained sacks in the back of the wagon in the courtyard. She walked the trail of blood.

Her mind roiled through the past several days, from waking in the forest to this moment. Waking from nothing. Into nothing. Remembering nothing.

Now she was about to be crowned queen. Then she'd wed a man she didn't know—a man, a mortal. She'd unite their armies of mortals. And then she'd face an enemy beyond mortal men.

And the painting. She knew Catherine had shown it to her to give her courage, but it didn't give her courage. It scared her. She didn't know that woman looking back at her—that woman who would take the Shadow throne. What if she couldn't be her? Perhaps the woman she used to be could have. But not *her*. Not *now*.

She slowed.

Everything was happening too fast, and the moment hit her. Hard. The throngs of people were so close. *Too close*. There were so many. *Too many*. The hall seemed to grow smaller. Each step she took came slower, yet faster—shorter, but longer.

She couldn't do this.

She couldn't breathe.

And she stopped.

Whispers breezed through the crowded hall. All eyes were on her—as were their expectations, their judgements. And she could only stand there. She combed the front for her grandmother, but she couldn't find her. She couldn't move.

Then she saw Alexander.

He stood just to the right of the dais, close to her chair. Near to her—where he promised he'd always be. He waited, straight and formal, but his smile was warm. He gave her a reassuring nod.

Air filled her lungs. She could breathe.

His hands were at his side. One flicked open. So subtle, but she saw it. And it called her to him.

She could do this, and she stepped forward again.

Her steps came easier.

His smile grew, and so did her courage.

As she reached the front, the high priest held out his hand, taking hers, and helped her step up. An ornate chair stood in the center of the dais where she turned and sat, just as she'd rehearsed, or rather, as she thought she'd rehearsed. She didn't know anymore. Every rational thought—every instruction she'd been given, every piece of advice—abandoned her now. She could only sit and hope it was right.

The priest held his arms high. "We assemble in the hall of our great kings, whose wisdom we call upon, and under the eyes of our gods, whose favor we seek, to crown Mercia's new queen."

Norah glanced at Alexander and found him staring back at her. He didn't move, but the air between them carried his strength to her—strength she drew in. Her eyes drifted to her grandmother, whose gaze sat firmly on Alexander. She prayed he didn't look to see the regent's daggered glare. But his eyes were only on her.

"You are charged with the protection of our people," the priest said, "of our lands, of our traditions, of the values that are the very foundations of our souls."

Her heartbeat drowned the rest of the priest's words. She was sure he said something about the gods, probably another responsibility as queen. A prayer, maybe. She couldn't focus.

The priest pulled her crown from the velvet box and stood before her, bringing her attention back to the ceremony. He placed it on her head. A servant held the sacred scepter, which the priest took and placed in her right hand.

"Rise," he told her.

Norah stood, holding the scepter tightly, and looked out across her people. *Her people.* The priest draped a long robe over her shoulders. Had that been part of the rehearsal? She wasn't sure. It didn't matter. She was cold, and it helped.

"Do you vow to govern the people of Mercia, to lead them, protect them, serve them, and deliver judgment and justice according to our laws and our customs?"

Her heart pulsed in her chest. Heat flushed through her. Hot. She was too hot now.

"I vow," she managed. She'd spoken the two words Alexander had mentioned only a few moments before. Of course, he expected no more.

"And so, you are named Queen Norah Elizabeth Andell, Regal High, and may the gods guide your hand for the strength of our people."

Regal High. A king's title. Her eyes shot to Alexander, and he winked at her. How had he...

Cheers rang out from the crowd, and she looked across the hall. There were so many smiling faces, so many people depending on her. So much responsibility.

And she wavered.

The responsibility—she was queen now.

She was *queen.*

Norah wanted to sit down again, but with all eyes on her, with the sacred scepter and the coronation robe, she could only stand and do her duty.

She had a responsibility—and she'd never been more certain. There was nothing James had told her that morning that she hadn't already known. Her eyes found the councilman in the front, not far from her grandmother. He gave a nod.

Norah raised her hand, bringing the people to silence. Her heart beat like it would break from her chest, but her voice came steady. "My first act as queen shall be to appoint my lord justice."

She breathed deeply, refusing to look at Catherine. She already knew the icy gaze she'd find. "Alexander Rhemus, come forward."

The priest gave a nod, extending out his hand for Alexander to approach. Alexander stepped in front of her. His eyes burned a brilliant blue.

"Kneel," she told him, following the sequence James had walked through with her.

Alexander dropped to his knees and held his hands out, palms up. His face was calm, but there was an exaggerated rise and fall to his chest. This was his moment, the day he followed the path of his father. The emotion pulsed from him.

"Alexander Rhemus," she said, "I appoint you lord justice of Mercia, high commander, proxy of the Queen, and protector of Mercia and her people."

Not a word had been forgotten. Norah had said it in her mind a thousand times, and what made it flow so easily was that she believed it. There was only one right decision, and it was Alexander. She dipped her fingers into the bowl of oil held by the priest. Slowly, she drew her fingertips along his palms. "May your hands be my hands."

She ran her thumb across his lips. "May your words be my words."

Then she reached and scribed a line on his breastplate with her fingers, just above the winterhawk. "May your heart be my heart."

Norah smiled down at him. "Rise, Lord Justice."

Alexander stood with emotion thick in his eyes. Then he took his place by her side, and cheers of approval deafened the hall.

Alexander was already in the great hall by the time Norah arrived. He watched as she stepped into the celebration, and cheers erupted. Several lords and their wives stopped by to offer their well-wishes to him, and he forced himself to peel his eyes from her long enough to extend his thanks. Then he turned his attention back to her.

She was beautiful. She captured the room the way she always did, filling the air with her light. He couldn't help but smile. He heard a faint call to his right, but it wasn't enough to pull him away.

"Alexander," the voice came again, more sharply now.

Catherine. Although not required now that she was no longer queen regent, he bowed his head. "You look stunning today," he greeted her.

She stood beside him with her eyes across the hall on Norah. "Flattery won't win my support."

Her words surprised him. Alexander looked at her. "Do you not support me as lord justice?"

She didn't answer, and it wounded him.

He pushed out a breath. "Did you not name me so yourself?"

"It's not that you won't make a fine lord justice, Alexander. The gods know you already do. But Norah wasn't here to cloud your mind before."

His pulse beat heavily in his ears. He looked out across the hall. "Do you question my commitment to my duty?"

Catherine put her hand on his arm, drawing him to look back at her. "Of course not. But it will only make the path harder. For both of you."

"My place is by her side. She's my queen."

"But she's not yours."

He knew this, but her words cut him. Still, he showed nothing. He admitted nothing.

Catherine sighed, looking back out across the hall. "But regardless of my worry and my attempts to keep you from it, you were always destined for this. I wish your father were here. He'd be so very proud of you."

He drew in a breath as he fought back a wave of emotion. "Are you?"

Catherine squeezed his arm as tears brimmed her eyes. "Of course I am." Then she stepped up on her toes and pulled him down, kissing him gently on his cheek. "Congratulations, my dear boy. There's no one more worthy. I only fear for you both." Then she squeezed his arm once again before leaving him to the celebration.

Her words hung heavy, reeling him into a mist of disquiet, that he almost didn't notice Norah approaching.

"Congratulations, Lord Justice," she said.

A smile crept back to his lips, and his worry was forgotten, as all worries were when she was near. "Congratulations, Queen Norah," he said with a bow.

"Please don't call me that," she said in a hushed voice. "I'm barely keeping it together between yesterday and today."

"Oh, I'm sorry. Your *Regal High*."

She laughed, and for that moment, he'd never been happier. He wanted to help take the burden away and make her forget—even if for only a moment—that the world hung on her shoulders.

"I feel like since the priest said it, it's proper now," she said.

"It *is* proper."

She shook her head, amazed. "How did you even manage that?"

"With my charm," he joked, and she laughed again.

To have her back, to have her laughing again... He hadn't dreamed it was possible. The deep pools of her eyes drew him in and held him. She was beautiful. And she was home.

He forced himself to break away and look back out across the hall, just as a familiar face approached.

His smile faded, and his chest tightened. He knew this was something he'd have to manage eventually, but he had hoped it wouldn't be tonight. Norah followed his gaze to the fair-haired woman. It was Ismene, the woman Catherine had been working so diligently to see him wed. He stood quietly as she approached.

As she drew close, Alexander forced a welcoming nod. "Queen Norah, may I present Ismene Dartan," he said.

Ismene gave a polite smile and curtsied.

"Ismene," Norah said. "A pleasure to meet you."

"The pleasure is mine, Queen Norah. Welcome home, and congratulations!"

Norah's eyes turned to Alexander, searching him for additional clues as to who this woman was.

Ismene looked at him for her introduction as well. Excitement danced across her face.

"Ismene is a friend," he said, avoiding eye contact with her. This wouldn't be the introduction she was hoping for.

Norah smiled at Ismene. Alexander knew her well enough to know it was forced.

"Well then," Norah said, "we shall be friends too."

"You're too kind, Your Elegance."

"Regal High," Alexander said. He knew Ismene wouldn't be the only one he'd correct. He only wished it didn't have to be here, like this, tonight. Ismene was a kind soul, and she had the best of intentions.

"Of course," Ismene said quickly, and curtsied to Norah. "Your Regal High." Then she turned to Alexander. "And congratulations as well, Lord Justice."

"Thank you, Ismene," he said, trying to keep the discomfort from his voice.

There was an awkward silence, and Ismene let out a breath. "I'll let you enjoy the evening. Congratulations again, Your Regal High," she said, giving another curtsy. "Lord Justice," she added.

Alexander gave a small bow as Ismene disappeared back into the crowd. He waited anxiously for Norah's reaction.

"She seems very nice," Norah said finally.

An easy compliment to agree with. "Yes, she is."

"And beautiful," she added.

Many men thought so, but Ismene's beauty held nothing for him. He shifted and then gave a stiff nod. He didn't want to talk about Ismene with Norah.

Norah's lips moved, as if to say something else, when James found them. Alexander let out a silent breath of relief.

"Queen Norah," the councilman said, taking her hand. "Congratulations. May the gods smile down on you."

Her smile widened, bright and warm. "Thank you, James," she said. She squeezed his hand. "I mean it. Thank you."

James patted the top of their clasped hands. "Of course, my dear. It's my duty and my joy." Then he turned to Alexander and grasped his shoulder. "Your destiny, my boy. Congratulations."

Alexander nodded as pride swelled within him. James had always believed in him, and it brought him joy that James was here to see him named lord justice. "Thank you, James."

The councilman smiled and gave a nod and a warm cuff on his shoulder, then left them to continue on.

When they were alone again, Norah turned back to Alexander. "Are you courting? You and Ismene?"

Alexander couldn't help the chuckle that escaped him at the forwardness he knew so well. He should have known she wouldn't let the conversation go that easily. But he had no secrets. "If your grandmother has her way."

"She's arranged you?" she asked, wide-eyed. "Are you to be wed?"

Another lord stepped forward with well-wishes for them both, and Alexander took the moment to collect his calm. While he'd answer anything Norah asked, it wasn't a comfortable topic.

The visiting lord bowed and departed, and they came together again.

"I'm sorry," she said. "That was rude of me, and intrusive."

"You're no intrusion," he said quickly. "And"—he brought his eyes to meet hers again—"I have no intention of marrying. It doesn't mean your grandmother won't try."

She gave a smile. "No, I suppose it doesn't."

At the mention of her grandmother, he glanced around the room and found Catherine looking back at him. He wondered how long she'd been watching, and how much she'd seen. His shoulders tightened.

Music picked up through the air. If he stayed, he'd ask her to dance. If he asked her to dance, he'd hold her hand in his, and if her skin touched his, he'd lose himself. So he couldn't stay.

"I'll say good night, though," he told her, "and not monopolize your time, as there are many who'd like to talk to you." Although there was no one who could want to talk to her more than he did.

A ripple of objection flashed in her eyes, but she didn't voice it. It was better that way. He gave a small bow. "Good evening, Regal High."

And she smiled a smile that he'd think about the rest of the night.

CHAPTER SEVENTEEN

"You're upset with me," Norah said.

Catherine sat in the side chair, petting a gray, long-haired cat in her lap as she watched Rebecca hold up dresses against Norah for approval.

"Disappointed," she replied. She flicked her hand, and Rebecca dropped the purple dress she was holding on to the bed and picked up a yellow one.

Norah bit the inside of her cheek. Catherine hadn't said but a few words to her since the coronation the day before, when Norah had named Alexander as her lord justice. "I know you didn't want me to choose him—"

"No, I didn't," she said sharply. "But it's not about that, Norah. We agreed we would meet with the council and decide."

Norah huffed a short breath, her frustration rising. "I didn't agree. I was told. But *I* am the one to choose my lord justice, and *I* chose Alexander. He was good enough when you chose him. He's clearly done a fine job, and he's the only one with James's support."

"The selection for lord justice doesn't require James's support."

"You say that now only because he didn't agree with you about Lord Branton."

Catherine's mouth fell open, but she didn't come back with another retort.

They sat in silence.

Finally, Catherine said, "I wish you would have told me that was your decision, instead of catching me by surprise."

Norah sighed, the fire inside her snuffed with guilt. "I do too," she admitted, her voice coming softer now. "I was just... afraid that you'd talk me out of it, and I didn't want to be talked out of it. I'd made up my mind. I know Alexander. I trust him. James trusts him."

"James doesn't know the implications."

"And what are the implications?" Norah asked, the heat returning. All this cryptic talk, she couldn't stand it anymore.

"Oh, Norah. Are you really so naive?"

And she certainly couldn't stand people continuing to talk to her like she was foolish. Even her grandmother. Her skin burned.

A knock on the door interrupted them, but Catherine's eyes didn't move from Norah. "Finish dressing. It's time to meet the council."

While Norah hadn't forgotten about the state, one benefit of being overwhelmed by the world was that it desensitized her to the crushing weight of other things sometimes. But her mind turned back to the meeting with the council, and her stomach twisted. It had been delayed to move up the coronation, but she had to face it now.

Catherine lowered the cat gently to the floor and stood. Then she moved for the door but paused and eyed the dresses. "Wear the blue. I'll see you in the judisaept."

Norah pushed out another breath, brimming with frustration as the door closed behind Catherine. She wanted to scream. Did Catherine think she could decide everything?

Rebecca reached for the blue gown.

"No," Norah told her. "I'll wear the green."

The council was already in the judisaept when Norah arrived, as were her grandmother and Alexander. She had thought her nerves had calmed as she had walked through the morning air, but the anxiousness came flooding back as soon as she saw them. The iron gaze of her grandmother didn't help. Perhaps she should have worn the blue dress. She felt childish now, which did nothing for her confidence.

While Catherine hadn't spoken to her much since the night before, she had worked to prepare her as much as possible for this meeting. Norah had her planned responses—her very vague and very short responses. They'd focus on the alliance with Aleon and *the marriage*. Norah would rather talk about anything else, but she reminded herself of the circumstances: the state of Mercia, the plight of their people, the threat of the Shadow King. She knew what she had accepted by taking the crown. It didn't make it easier, though.

The councilmen were so deep in a heated conversation that they barely noticed her entrance.

"Councilmen," Alexander called their attention when he saw her.

Edward turned. "Ah! Queen Norah." He bowed. "Forgive us. We were caught up in some disappointing news. But let's get started. I'd like to welcome you to your first state."

"What news?" she asked.

He paused in surprise but quickly recovered. "Nothing for you to worry about. These matters are why you have a council." His tone held an air of condescension that brought a heat to her cheeks. "Now, as Lady Catherine reminded me, you've not spent much time with the council, even before your... leaving. And it would be good to get reacquainted."

A small whisper of relief filled her lungs. That was very smart and very much appreciated. She glanced at Catherine, her earlier morning frustration forgotten, and her grandmother gave her the faintest of nods. But the mention of disappointing news still needled the back of her mind.

Edward motioned to each council member around the room. "Councilman Alastair, Henricus, Elias, Charles, and of course you know James."

Each councilman gave a respectful bow of his head as his name was said, and James smiled reassuringly. Catherine had walked through their descriptions with her before, and Norah felt solid on them now.

"We know you're stepping into a role that can be overwhelming for any person," Edward said. "And we'll guide you through each challenge."

They looked to her for a response. She had to say something, something that didn't sound like a woman completely in over her head. She clenched her hands together as she nodded. "Thank you, Councilman Edward." Her eyes rounded the table. She could feel her pulse in her palms. "Thanks to all of you. I only want to serve Mercia the best I can. I trust that, true to your titles, you'll counsel me in these matters of state to do what's right for our people."

The councilmen nodded, with smiles on their lips. They were pleased. *Good.* This was a good start. Her confidence grew... slightly.

Edward motioned to the chair at the head of the table. "Please, Queen Norah."

She took her chair, and the councilmen followed in seating themselves.

Edward nodded. "So, we'll start with—"

"The news," she said, now that they were past formalities. "Let's start with the news that came."

The room fell silent. It felt like the wrong thing to say, but why would it be wrong? News had come. She was queen. She should know.

"Ah," Edward said finally, clearly surprised again. "Very well." He wet his lips. "Word has come that a usurper has overthrown King Orrid, the king of Rael."

She wasn't familiar with the king of Rael, or his kingdom. Not that she was quick to assume this wasn't bad news, but she couldn't help but feel thankful it wasn't directly related to Mercia. Or was it? "Is the king of Rael a friend of Mercia?"

Edward puffed a small breath, seemingly amused at her inexperience, and her cheeks grew hotter.

"He's a godly man. It's a tragedy."

That was a yes, then? But before she could ask more questions, he pivoted the conversation.

"But let me once again convey how happy we are that you're with us. Now, to more pressing matters."

He was moving her on, and she didn't have the boldness yet to stop him. Not that she was keen to. She had enough to focus on in Mercia without worrying about another king in another kingdom.

"We're most eager to hear about your time away from us," he said.

All thoughts of the king of Rael fell from her mind, and she forced a dry swallow. She knew the planned response—she'd been with an undisclosed ally who wished to remain that way, and her father had committed her to secrecy. It was such an underwhelming answer. No one would buy it. She wouldn't, in their place. And if they didn't believe her, what would be her standing with them then? She needed their favor, and she was already off to a mediocre start at best.

Norah glanced at James. He nodded. She knew his position—there was little benefit to continuing to keep her condition from the council now that she was queen. They could do nothing against her. Perhaps they could actually help her, guide her. And she was desperate for just one weight off her shoulders. With everything she was facing, she couldn't waste energy holding a charade as well.

"Queen Norah?" Edward said.

She realized she'd just been sitting there. "I... um..." She glanced around the table at all the eyes looking back at her. "I, uh, actually don't know. I've lost my memories."

The councilmen shifted in their chairs and looked at one another.

As she said the words, she realized it sounded almost as unbelievable as a secret ally. At least it was the truth, and she could speak it confidently. She avoided her grandmother's eyes. It was another disappointment, she was sure. Add it to the list.

"Lost your memories?" Edward sputtered. "And you didn't think it important to inform this council before the coronation?"

The knot in her stomach grew. She had... but she didn't answer that.

Edward turned his lit eyes on Catherine. "You knew. You knew, and you didn't tell us."

"I made decisions for the good of Mercia," Catherine said flatly.

"The good of Mercia!" Edward exclaimed in a shrill voice.

Alastair spoke now, narrowing his eyes on Norah. "And how are we to know you're Queen Norah?"

"Oh, come now," James said angrily. "Don't be absurd. There's no doubt she's Queen Norah. There's no mistaking her. She's been gone for three years, not three decades."

Edward gaped at him. "You knew about this beforehand? And you said nothing?"

James flicked his hand through the air. "Because I knew you'd say ridiculous things like this."

Norah swallowed. She'd expected this conversation to go very differently. She had needed it to go differently. Could she get it back on track? Could she quiet them? She was queen.

But she found herself not needing to quiet them, as the room naturally fell silent.

Edward spoke first—of course he'd speak first. "Well, this adds a complicated element, especially considering the letter this morning."

What letter? A weight grew in her stomach. More news? Different news? She was trying to lessen the burdens on her shoulders, not add more.

"What letter?" she asked. Her eyes found Alexander's, where she hoped to find calm, but it wasn't calm she saw. Behind his stoic gaze, something bothered him. Her heart beat faster, and she swallowed the rising lump in her throat.

Edward's thin lips curved into a frustrated smile. "A letter from King Phillip of Aleon."

Heat rushed through her. Catherine had just been in her chamber. How could she not have said anything? She shot a glance at her grandmother but found only an equal look of surprise. She hadn't known either.

"He sends his elations at your return," Edward continued, "and he hopes he's not too forward in proposing that you suggest a date for the marriage."

That was too forward.

Edward gave a judgmental gaze. "He, of course, assumes the alliance between Mercia and Aleon still stands."

Did this condescending man always speak for the council? She stole a glance at Catherine, whose eyes told her to keep herself composed.

"Where's the letter?" she asked, hoping to buy herself time to pull her thoughts together.

Edward's lip twitched. "It was short, Your Elegance. But I would propose—"

"Regal High," Alexander interrupted, creating an awkward silence in the room. "And she asked for the letter."

"Edward," James said, lending his own voice.

Edward paused and swept his eyes around the room. "Of course," he said finally, and pulled a small envelope from his pocket. He rose and brought it to Norah, presenting it with a small bow of his head. "Your Regal High."

She took it, unfolding it and running her eyes down the parchment, but she made it no further than the first line—*Dearest Norah*—before the words blurred together. She had known this was the next step, what was expected of her, but... naming a date... It hadn't felt so real before.

Her eyes welled, simply from the weight of it all, and a wave of panic washed over her. The only thing worse than her council seeing her struggle with this conversation would be if they saw her become emotional.

"As I know Lady Catherine has explained," Edward continued as she pretended to read, "our provisions are nearing dangerously low levels and will be depleted well before winter's end."

"How much is there?" she managed to get out. "How long do we have?" How long did she have?

"Not long. But don't worry yourself about the numbers. We'll see to that. We need your attentions on Aleon, for King Phillip can provide what Mercia needs." He wanted her to focus on the marriage, not the issue. Anger sprouted in the depths of her mind and spread through her veins.

"Time is of the essence," he pressed. "You must think of our people." Of course she needed to think of the people. But was a marriage the only solution? She needed to think—and it was impossible under his guilting stare, under the pressure.

Her anger thickened, and her words came before she could stop them. "I won't be hasty to make a permanent solution for a temporary problem."

The councilmen shifted in their chairs, clearly unsettled by her response.

"Hasty?" Edward scoffed. "This is perhaps the longest anticipated marriage in the history of mankind. And it's not merely for today's problems. With this alliance comes the great army of Aleon, which we'll need to stand against the Shadow King."

She'd not forgotten. All eyes were on her, but no words would come. She had no rebuttal for these points, no defense. And it was impossible to think under Edward's smug gaze.

"Queen Norah knows what's necessary," James said, breaking the silence. "She'll fulfill her duty. We'll leave it to her and Lady Catherine to decide on a date."

James's response was certainly more diplomatic than the words forming in her head.

"That's enough for today, councilmen," James added.

But Norah stopped them. "There is one more thing," she said, glancing around the table. Her anger fueled her; her fear was gone. "From now on, any letters addressed to me will come directly to me."

Edward's eyes darkened, but he bowed. "Of course, Regal High."

The councilmen all bowed before shuffling out of the judisaept. James lingered as the room emptied.

"Thank you, James," she said when they'd gone.

He nodded. "I know this was a difficult meeting for you. But, Norah"—he paused until her eyes met his—"you will choose a date, and you'll seal our alliance with Aleon."

Her stomach twisted. Whatever hope she had of a different solution was quickly fading. James gave her a stiff nod before following the rest of the council out. Norah turned her gaze to Catherine, whose green eyes were aflame. Norah knew Catherine was angry about revealing her memory loss, but she couldn't deal with it. Not right now.

"I don't want to hear it," she said shortly.

Catherine's face was cold as stone. "Then I won't burden you." She strode from the judisaept, leaving Norah alone in the emptiness of the room.

She put her hands on the edge of the table and rested her weight forward. Her legs didn't feel like they'd hold her, but she couldn't sit down again. She couldn't argue with the situation, or even with the resolution. A marriage—it was very logical. It was just... sudden. And suffocating. The air in the room was heavy. She drew in a breath but couldn't breathe.

Norah turned and left the judisaept in a haze. Everything was getting away from her. She had no control, no choice. She felt like a... girl... a child. Her guard picked up behind her as she walked. She glanced back. It was Titus. She couldn't think with the sound of his steps in her ears. "Hammel's hell! Can you just stop following me for a moment!" she snapped.

He frowned. "I can't leave you, Regal High."

"Stop calling me that!"

"Titus," Alexander's voice called from behind them. "I'll see her back."

The guard gave a nod and left them in the empty hall.

Norah stood for a moment with Alexander. His presence brought a calm she so desperately needed, dissipating her anger, but the anger had been the only thing holding her emotion back. She bit into her bottom lip, trying to keep the tears at bay.

Alexander ambled forward, prompting her into a walk beside him. He didn't speak, only walked, and the silence was settling.

"They don't really see me as a queen, do they?" she asked finally. "Alastair challenged who I am, but it hardly seems to matter at all, so long as I wear the crown and marry. That's all they care about. I could be anyone, as long as I look the part and do what they say."

"But you aren't just anyone," he replied. His voice came softer. "Norah, this has been the plan for the past ten years. Mercia needs the alliance with Aleon. Of course they would be eager for it, now that you've returned."

Norah frowned. "So I should just marry?"

"That's not what I said."

She stopped, looking up at him. "What are you saying, then?"

His lips parted, but no words came.

"Would you have me do this?" she asked. "Would you have me wed King Phillip?"

The line of his jaw tightened. "There's been a lot said today. Put it from your mind for a while. When the emotion is gone, you'll be able to think more clearly."

"There's nothing I can do to put this from my mind."

Alexander's brow twitched, as though he'd had a thought.

"What is it?" she asked.

"I have an idea. Come on."

Her eyes narrowed.

"I promise it's not a tomb."

Chapter Eighteen

Norah raised a doubtful brow. "We're going in *there*?"

Alexander stood at the mouth of a cave that trailed deep into the darkness from the icy mountainside. She had followed him outside the castle, pulling her cloak over her face and tucking her hair inside to slip by undetected. He'd led her to the cliffs and to a small cleft large enough for them to step down into one at a time. Along the narrow walk they went, looking out over the sea of ice, and then carefully sidled along a ledge to where they stood now.

"A cave?" she asked.

"I'd normally allow a lady first as a gentlemanly courtesy, but you should follow me."

"Gladly," she said, waving him ahead. She followed him into the cave, and the light faded as they made their way deeper. A small rush of excitement ran through her.

Alexander paused, turning to her and holding out his hand. "It's going to get dark. Very dark. Just hold on to me, and I'll lead you. You needn't be afraid."

She had a number of feelings at the moment, but fear was not one of them. She smiled as she took his hand. They made their way farther into the cave, and it wasn't long before Norah couldn't see anything at all. "I didn't expect this today," she told him.

"I admit it's highly unconventional and certainly not endorsed by your grandmother. In fact, I'd appreciate if you would overlook it when next speaking to her."

She grinned into the darkness. "My lips are sealed."

They walked slowly, with Alexander giving her hand small reassuring squeezes as they went.

"How much farther?" she asked.

"Still a ways yet."

Her curiosity grew. "What's back here?"

"A magical place," he told her.

The cave grew colder, and darkness hung around them like a thick shroud. Norah found herself moving closer to him and taking his arm with her other hand.

She was about to ask another question when the darkness abated and she could make out Alexander's form and the walls of the cave around them. They kept to the left and curved through another tunnel that, suddenly, opened into a vast cavern with a large pool of turquoise water. Light poured in from somewhere ahead, past an island rock formation in the water.

Norah let out a breath in awe. "It's beautiful."

"Isn't it?"

"How did you find it?"

"*We* found it," he said. "You and I. When we were younger." He had stopped, but their hands were still together, and his eyes met hers. "This is where you liked to come when the weight of the world was too heavy. Just to get out from underneath it, if only for a moment."

Her chest tightened. The world was heavy now.

He stood close, so close, facing her with their fingers entwined, and suddenly the world felt very far away. The warmth from his hand spread up her arm and over her skin, pooling in her stomach. His gaze traveled over her face and down to her lips; they stayed on her lips. His mouth parted slightly as he leaned even closer. Her breath came faster. She wanted him closer still.

But he inhaled and stepped back, pulling his hand from hers and putting some space between them. Her mind tumbled, but she caught herself and straightened.

"The water is warm," he told her, looking out across the cavern. "The pool is fed from the hot springs in the rock."

"Is it really?" she asked, overly feigning interest. She was desperate for something—anything—to steer the conversation from where they'd been. She crouched down at the edge of the pool and dropped her hand to the water, but as her fingers touched its warmth, she stopped. Visions seemed to ripple in the pool. Not that she could see, but that she could feel. Something was here.

She scooped the water up and let it fall between her fingers. There was a yearning in her spirit, a freedom in the pool that called to her. And there was something... familiar. She knew this place, but the memory was just beyond her grasp. Yet it was close. So close. She scooped up another handful, listening as she closed her eyes. The sound of the drops as they hit the pool and echoed off the walls. The feel of the warmth between her fingers... The water called to her mind, called her back. There was a memory here.

"I want to go for a swim," she said breathlessly as she stood.

Alexander drew up a hand with a shake of his head. "I don't think that's a good idea."

But she didn't care. She reached back and pulled the ties loose on her dress.

"Queen Norah," he said uneasily, "you can't seriously take off all your clothes right now."

"I've got on at least three layers. I'll be decent enough."

Alexander shifted but quickly saw he didn't have a choice, and he turned his back as she pulled down her dress and wriggled out of it. She paused at her underskirts, looking up to make sure she remained unseen. He waited with his back to her, and she pulled them off, adding them to the pile of clothing. Then she slowly stepped into the water in her chemise and silk underwear.

The water felt incredible, and she leisurely sunk down to her chin. The tension seemed to flow out of her. She already knew she loved this place, even if she couldn't remember it.

"Are you coming?" she called to him. She'd feel silly if she were the only one. She'd make him share the awkwardness, at least.

He stood at the edge of the pool, seeming to wrestle with his proprieties.

"Come on," she called. "It's amazing!"

"I know it is," he called back with a chuckle. Finally, he relented, giving a small shake of his head as he shrugged off his cloak and jacket and pulled his shirt over his head. He kicked off his boots and tossed them next to his cloak.

She turned away as he pulled off his breeches, stripping down to his braies, but she turned back when she heard him splash in. The clear turquoise water did little to protect her modesty, but her undergarments covered her enough, and she wasn't feeling modest at the moment, anyway. She waited as Alexander waded deeper and moved toward her. For a moment, she forgot about the pull of the water on her mind.

They lingered in the beautiful silence, facing one another, circling. A warmth eddied in her stomach, a current that carried her to him. He moved closer, and her pulse quickened. Closer still, he came. She could reach out and touch him if she wanted.

And she wanted.

Her eyes were on his lips, the lips that had kissed the back of her hand, the lips she somehow knew. She could so easily imagine them against her own. Was she only imagining? Or was she remembering?

Norah pushed herself back, putting it from her mind. She dared not let her thoughts wander there for fear she might follow them.

With the hold between them broken, he pushed back as well, letting out an echoing breath. He swam toward the stone formation jutting from the center of the pool, and she followed. Norah reached the rock and gripped the damp surface. She softened her kick so as not to hit her knees against the jagged edges hidden underneath.

"Watch your knees," he warned.

She knew.

She looked up at the top of the rock formation reaching toward the ceiling of the cave, close to a ledge that protruded out over the pool. "Looks like that would be fun to jump from," she said.

"It is," he replied.

She gaped at him in surprise. "You've done it?"

"I have."

"No you haven't!"

Alexander grinned. "I'll do it now." He gripped the edge of the rock and hoisted himself from the pool.

She drew in a breath as his braies clung to his skin and the water rolled off his back. Perhaps she shouldn't watch him, but she wasn't caught up anymore in what she should or shouldn't do. Not here.

He reached high and climbed up the mass of rock, faster than she thought he might. Perhaps he *had* done this before. Still, it was high. He reached the top and stretched his leg to the ledge on the cave wall.

She cringed at the thought of him falling. "Be careful," she called.

But he moved to it easily. Then he flashed her a grin and jumped. She let out a squeal as he hit the water and a large splash rained over her. He broke the surface, laughing as he wiped the water from his face. "Did I get you?"

Of course he had tried. She splashed him back, and he laughed again.

"I don't know whether that was brave or foolish," she said.

"I've done many brave and foolish things here," he replied, serious now.

She stilled. She wanted to ask him. The question was on her lips, but her fear kept it inside. Had they both done brave and foolish things here? *Together?*

They quieted as they drew closer to each other. Was the water growing warmer? It felt warmer. Still, her skin prickled.

But he broke the silence as he pushed back. "This way," he said. "There's more to see."

The moment to ask had passed. She cursed her bashfulness.

He made his way around the rock formation. On the back side, the pool widened and curved to the left. They swam on, and around the corner, the cavern opened to the sky. Light hit the rippling water, and it sparkled in the sun.

She gasped in amazement. "It's incredible."

They waded for a long time, marveling at the natural beauty. Alexander's face held a rare grin, and it brought her a deep happiness with it. If only they could stay here, away from the weight of the world.

He moved to the side and took hold of the rock as he looked up at the sky. "It's beautiful in the moonlight," he told her. "With the stars above. You used to try to count them."

They used to swim here at night? She gripped the rock, edging beside him so she could still herself in the water.

"How many are there?" she asked.

He shook his head with an amused grin. "You'd come up with a different number each time."

Each time. As in, they'd been here under the stars more than once.

Their eyes found each other again, and they fell silent. He drifted closer to her, close enough again to touch. This time, she did. She reached out her hand, slowly, and pressed her palm flat against his chest. The racing of his heart matched her own.

He drifted even closer.

His eyes matched the sunlit pool, and water droplets glistened in the gold of his hair. He was beautiful. She moved her hand up his chest, over his shoulder, and behind the nape of his neck, pulling him ever so softly to her.

And he followed.

She leaned in, tipping her head slightly and bringing her cheek to his. They were so close. Not touching, but so close.

His breath dusted heat over her ear. She dropped her lips to his neck, not with a kiss—just the feather of a touch. The muscle across his shoulders tightened under her hand, and his breaths came faster now. So did hers. She trailed her lips up, still not kissing him, although she desperately wanted to. She traveled along his jaw and over his chin and paused a whisper away from his mouth.

They shouldn't be here, like this. Yet they lingered. He smelled like he was hers, and she breathed him in.

He ran his hand up the back of her neck and into her hair, and he parted his lips. His body pressed closer, and her breasts brushed against his chest through her chemise. She wanted him closer, still. His fingers gripped her tighter.

They couldn't be here.

He closed his eyes. An eternity passed in the quiet of their breaths. He swallowed. "We should go," he said, before opening his eyes again.

His words found the sanity of her mind, and she pushed back from him.

His face sobered. "I'm sorry," he said. "I shouldn't have brought you here." There was a sadness to his tone, a disappointment in himself. "We should go," he said again. He pulled back and away.

But it was as much her fault as it was his. "Alexander," she said.

He floated back the way they'd come, moving slowly to keep from splashing.

She sighed and followed.

They reached the point at which they'd started, and Norah found her footing in the shallows. Alexander had already exited the pool. He picked up his breeches and pulled them on.

Norah stepped out of the water and found her dress. And as if putting on undergarments with damp skin wasn't enough of a struggle, she found the back lacing was just beyond her grasp. Heat flushed across her cheeks. She hadn't thought things through when she'd stripped it off.

She glanced back to where he stood waiting for her. "Will you?" she called to him, and turned her back for him to help with the ties.

Her ask was met with silence, and she thought he might refuse. Then he stepped behind her. He was still for a moment before he reached out and pulled the lacing tight, closing the back of her dress and skillfully looping each fix.

Alexander shifted closer, and the warmth of his breath tickled her shoulder. A wave of familiarity rippled through her. *The dream.* It hadn't been just a dream.

She risked pushing him further away, but she couldn't help herself. "You've done this before," she said. "For me."

He didn't answer. But she knew. He was quick to put up walls, quick to put distance between them, but he seemed to forget sometimes, lapsing into a life that still called to her, a life she desperately wanted back.

"Are you ready?" he asked when he finished, stepping them back into the coldness of normalcy.

She gave a nod.

Alexander offered his hand, with his fingers politely together, for the walk back through the cave. She took it. He moved to start, but she pulled him to pause.

"Alexander. Thank you for giving this back to me. It did take my mind off things for a while."

His eyes gave a sad smile, and he nodded. Then he led her into the darkness, toward the castle and the pressures that waited.

Chapter Nineteen

The skirts were heavy but still allowed ease of movement. Norah pulled them on quickly, wondering what was in store for her. Alexander had knocked on her door early, instructing her maid to have her dress for the cold. She didn't like the cold much. Regardless, she was looking forward to whatever he had planned. Her mind drifted back to the day before, back to the cave, and a warmth pooled in her stomach. But she pushed it down. She couldn't allow herself those feelings. Not when she knew her future.

She stepped out into the hall, where Titus was waiting.

"The lord justice is just down the stairs," he told her.

"I'm sorry I snapped at you yesterday," she said back over her shoulder as she walked.

"You don't need to apologize."

That was what he was obliged to say.

"But I want to. I was having a bad day." She reached the stairs and started down.

"I know. I heard."

She frowned. "Do you hear everything?"

"Most everything."

Of course. What did she expect? She reached the bottom stair, where Alexander was waiting, and he gave her a low bow. She tried to ignore the stir in her stomach.

"Regal High," he greeted.

His tone and formality sat strangely with her, but she pushed the feeling down and gave him a small smile. "Lord Justice. You've captured my curiosity. Where are we headed?"

He turned and led her down the hall and outside into the courtyard. "It's not so much where we're headed as what we're doing," he said, piquing her curiosity further. He waved back to Titus, who fell farther behind. His voice dropped lower. "But first, I want to apologize. I shouldn't have taken you to the cave yesterday. Please, forgive me. I'd... like to forget it even happened."

While not intentional, his words stung. "I don't want to forget," she said, shaking her head. She'd forgotten enough.

"Norah," he said softly. "Please." His eyes were filled with an emotion she couldn't read. Sadness? Regret? It unsettled her, but she couldn't look away. He shifted his gaze, releasing her.

"Where are we going?" she asked, changing the subject.

He let out a sigh but seemed to accept her rejection of his completely foolish idea to forget the cave. She couldn't have it again, but she wouldn't forget.

"Where are we going?" she asked again.

The corner of his mouth curved up, but only for a moment. "You'll see," he said.

She followed him past the stables and around to the sparring field, where a boy was leaning weapons against the fence in preparation for the day's use. Alexander made several gestures with his hands, and the boy gestured back before bowing to Norah.

"What are you doing?" she asked him, puzzled.

"This is Cade. He works with the smith and sees after the sparring field. He's deaf and speaks with his hands."

She looked at the boy, amazed. He could speak with his hands? Then she realized she was staring and shifted. "Oh, um... how do I say hi?" she asked curiously.

Alexander chuckled and simply held up his hand. The boy smiled.

"I suppose that one's easy," she said sheepishly.

Cade drew a sword from the weapons' hold and held it out for her. She raised a brow at Alexander, and he nodded.

"Thank you," she said as she took it awkwardly. "How do I say thank you?"

Alexander cupped his fist and then extended his fingers. Norah copied it, and the boy gave her a large grin and then bowed. Alexander nodded to the boy, who bowed again and left them to the quiet of the morning. She watched him go, still impressed by his ability to adapt.

Alexander pulled his own sword from its scabbard.

"So... a lesson?" she asked with an uncertain smile.

His face grew serious, but there was excitement in his eyes. "Not exactly. You remembered the poem. And the dance." He paused, leaving out the cave. "And perhaps you've had glimpses of other things. I want to see if you remember the sword. If I'm right in my suspicion, you won't need a lesson."

Norah gave a skeptical smile as she took the sword, but once it was in her hand, she felt a comfort she hadn't expected. She rolled her wrist, getting familiar with its weight. She looked back at Alexander in surprise, and he gave her another nod.

Not giving her much time, he stepped forward with a swing, but she brought her blade up, countering and stepping to the side. She gripped the hilt tighter. The sword brought her power, confidence. Excitement swelled within her. She launched her own attack, cutting forward and driving him to step back. He spun to give himself more space to escape her. Their blades sang through the air, ringing into the morning.

Her ferocity grew with each strike, and she found the fight growing within her. But on a defensive turn, her boot slipped, and she stumbled. She tried to regain herself for a counter, but the tip of Alexander's blade met her chest.

She stilled, and he stepped back, letting her catch her breath. Norah let out a quiet laugh in surprise. "That was... unexpected," she finally managed to get out. "It seems I'm not terrible."

"Certainly not terrible," he said, out of breath himself. "A little out of practice, but even so, the better of many men."

"Out of practice?" she feigned offense. "You only got me because I slipped."

He grinned and took a ready stance again. She attacked this time with an arcing side swing, and he used his blade to deflect it. She pursed her lips. *Smooth.* Very smooth. He countered with a swing of his own. She tried to mirror him, but she didn't have his strength. He crossed his sword against hers and used it to push her backward and up against the fence near the weapons' hold.

He smiled, his face close to hers. Their blades were still crossed between them as he pinned her.

"Did you slip again?" he asked.

Her eyes narrowed. Was he really teasing her? She pushed against him, but he didn't let her free.

He winked. "Or did you forget how to defend yourself?"

He *was* teasing her. With her free hand, she whipped her knife from its sheath just inside her jacket and brought the tip to his chin. "Did you forget you gave this to me?"

His smile grew, and he gave a light chuckle. "No, but I did forget how good you are with it," he admitted, "and how quick you are to use it."

Norah grinned. "Does this mean I win?"

Their stares locked as they stilled.

"I think so," he said. Then, quieter, "Although I have to confess, I don't feel as though I've lost."

Warmth coursed through her, despite the cold. He only needed to lean a little closer, and she could meet his lips with hers.

No—they couldn't let themselves go there again.

As if he had the same thought, he pulled back, releasing her.

She drew in a breath, trying to regain her senses. "I've trained?" she asked, finding her words.

He shrugged. "Something like that." He held out his hand for her sword, and she gave it to him. He took it and pushed it back into the weapons' hold. "Sword training is not part of a princess's curriculum, but you wouldn't have that. So, growing up, every day you'd ask me to teach you what I had learned. We'd spend the evenings practicing in the back paddocks." He gave her a smirk. "I'd say I'm an excellent teacher."

She couldn't help a laugh. His eyes burned bright, and he smiled back at her.

Then his face sobered. "I have to go," he said.

"Oh." She bit the inside of her cheek to hide her disappointment. *Another wall*. It was for the best.

"Your grandmother has committed my presence," he explained.

A smile crept back to her face, and she nodded. That was better than a wall. "I understand. I should get back as well."

He delayed a moment, and she hoped he might find a reason to stay.

"Good day, Queen Norah," he said finally.

"Good day, Lord Justice."

He gave a small bow and took his leave.

Norah walked back to her chamber, surprised by the morning. She could fight—somewhat. That was good to know. She suddenly became aware of Titus behind her again. Had he seen her? Of course he had. "Did you know I could do that?" she asked.

He motioned to the break in his brow. "How do you think I got this scar?"

She stopped, and her mouth dropped open. "Are you serious?"

He chuckled and shook his head. "No," he said, and she scowled.

Back at her chamber, Norah opened the door to see Catherine waiting for her. "Grandmother," she said. They had spoken a little since the meeting with the council, enough to settle things between them. Mostly.

"Where were you?" Catherine asked.

"Just... out for a walk." She expected Catherine to press her more or find something else to chastise, like seeing Norah in her outerwear, but the woman had something else on her mind. Norah noticed she held a box in her hand.

"A gift has come for you. From Phillip."

Norah's stomach turned sour. She was afraid to ask. "What kind of gift?"

Catherine pulled the top from the box to reveal a stunning sapphire necklace. Smaller jewels plated the sides, and there was a large stone pendant in the center. "Isn't it beautiful?"

"It is," Norah replied. It was beautiful, but she didn't want jewelry. She wished King Phillip knew her better. Perhaps then he would have sent her a knife. She chuckled.

"What's so funny?" Catherine asked.

Norah pursed her lips and shook her head. "Nothing."

"Here, he sent this as well." Her grandmother handed her a small painted portraiture of the king.

She reluctantly took it. He wasn't much older than she was, and he had a strong, square jaw and bronzed-brown hair. His nose was straight, refined, but not feminine. His eyes were as blue as Alexander's. Well, not quite as blue. He was very handsome, she hated to admit, although she didn't like the mustache. "Do you think he really looks like this? Or maybe they just paint him favorably. He *is* king."

"I've laid eyes on him myself, as have you. He really does look this way."

She bit the side of her cheek. "Do you think he'd shave his face if I asked him to?"

"By the gods, Norah."

She shrugged with a frown.

"You should wear the necklace today."

Norah shifted, drawing her brows together. "I... don't think it will match." She looked at the small portraiture again and put her finger over his mustache. He had kind eyes. But she wouldn't wear his necklace.

"Norah, you haven't even chosen a dress yet."

"I have, in my mind. It doesn't match."

Catherine snapped closed the necklace box. "You are impossible sometimes." She sighed. "Get ready. I want you to attend worship with me today at the temple. It will be good for the people to see a pious queen. And it will do you some good to get out."

Norah felt quite the opposite, but she knew her grandmother was trying to give her something else to think about, and she smiled appreciatively as she went to decide on a dress.

Norah smiled as she and Catherine arrived at the temple and were heartily greeted by those walking in. She wasn't particularly interested in attending, but Catherine was right—it felt good to be out.

The temple was larger than Norah had expected, and as they entered, she noticed the rows of cushions on the floor, for kneeling. Her eyes caught the priest at the front, who motioned her forward, and she made her way toward him.

"Yes, yes, all the way forward," Catherine whispered behind her.

The priest smiled with a nod, motioning to the first row on the left, but as Norah looked around, she stopped. To her right, across the walkway, was Alexander, looking back at her. She was about to smile at him, but just as quickly, she saw Ismene, who had taken her place on the cushion beside him. Ismene gave a bow of her head, and Norah returned the nod, swallowing back her sudden swell of jealousy.

"Kneel on the cushion," her grandmother whispered from behind.

Norah turned her attention forward and found the cushion, dropping to her knees and sitting back on her heels. Catherine lowered herself beside her with a hand from the priest.

With everyone in attendance, the priest raised his arms, beginning the prayer. Norah couldn't rid herself of the fire building inside her. Alexander had said her grandmother committed his attendance.

She set this up.

Norah's cheeks burned with anger: at her grandmother's manipulation, at Ismene. She couldn't help herself and swept her eyes to where Alexander sat. A jolt ran through her as their stares locked. She tried to pull away, having been caught, but his gaze held her. It cupped her breath in her chest and seeded warmth across her skin. Her anger dissipated.

"Norah." Catherine's harsh whisper filled her ears, bringing her eyes forward again.

The morning wasn't as long as she had expected, and she found herself fueled by the silent exchanges with Alexander during the priest's prayer. As the worship ended, an older woman called Catherine's attention, and Norah rose with a start, seeing her chance.

Alexander was one step ahead of her, meeting her with a slight curve of his lips. "Queen Norah," he said.

"Lord Justice. I didn't know you were going to be here."

"Nor I, you, but—"

"Queen Norah," Ismene greeted as she approached them.

A flash of fire ran through her, but Norah forced a smile. "Lady Ismene, so good to see you again." The words were stiff on her lips, but she hoped they hadn't sounded so.

"And you, Regal High," the young woman said with a curtsy.

"I should be off," Norah said, looking for an opportunity to escape.

Her eyes locked with Alexander's again. His face was solemn, almost apologetic. Was he apologetic?

Alexander bowed, and she gave a nod in return before leaving them and making her way outside. She shouldn't have come.

She became all too aware of Catherine beside her as she walked. Norah glared at her grandmother. "Must you be so obvious?" she snapped, not bothering to disguise her irritation.

Catherine looked straight ahead, unbothered. "I don't know what you're talking about. And you've no concept of obvious."

Norah gave her a scowl and walked faster, stalking back toward the castle.

Chapter Twenty

Norah sat on a branch of the white oak tree as the sun set and the air turned colder with the fading light. It was an old tree with low boughs, one of the few trees on the rocky isle, and it sat thick and sprawling like a giant hand rising from the earth.

She fought the jealousy she knew she had no right to feel. Alexander was not hers, but she couldn't help the possessiveness clawing inside her. She bit her lip in broken concentration as she threaded the thin strands of leather through several tiny shells she'd found among the rocks. Her morning guard, Liaman, had shown her where to find them. He had told her that in summer the water came higher and teemed with life around the castle, then left the shells as it receded. Now they could be found in the crags underneath the snow. She tested the length around her wrist and added a few more.

Norah glanced up to see Alexander approaching. He waved off her guard, who left them and headed back toward the castle.

Alexander leaned against the tree, watching quietly as she finished the bracelet. She waited until she tied her knot before she looked up and forced a smile.

"Are you unhappy with me?" he asked.

She took in a breath and let it out slowly, then shook her head. "No," she said. Not with him.

"But you *are* unhappy?"

She looked out across the reach of the isle to the setting sun. She was unhappy, but she didn't have the right to be, at least not where Alexander was concerned. And she certainly couldn't share that with him.

"Here, let me see your hand," she said, changing the subject.

He held out his wrist for her. His skin was warm against her fingers as she tied the bracelet in place.

"There. Now you'll see it and think of me." As soon as she spoke the words, she regretted them. They sounded too possessive.

His eyes met hers. "I don't need a reminder for that," he said softly.

Norah's heart wavered in her chest. She might not have the memories, but there was no mistaking that there had been something between them. Something forgotten, but still there. Something buried far beneath the surface.

The words came out before she could stop herself. "Were we lovers?"

Her question sobered him, and he stepped back. She feared his answer but was desperate for it all the same.

Burden hung from his brow as the words sat silent on his tongue. "Our fathers never would have allowed us to be together," he said finally.

"That's not what I asked." She wondered if his heart was beating as heavily as hers.

"I would never dishonor you, Norah."

Her question remained unanswered, and it hung in the air.

"We should get back," he said, a formality returning. "Your grandmother will be wondering where you are."

But she didn't want to leave.

He offered his hand, and she took it, but as she slipped down from the tree, she stumbled, falling back against the trunk and pulling Alexander with her. He caught his balance on the bough and hooked his arm around her, steadying her. The closeness stilled them. A tremor ran through her, and Norah gasped as an image flashed in her mind. It was an old image, a memory.

"Are you all right?" he asked.

"We were here before," she breathed.

He froze, and his eyes burned. "You remember?"

"Yes. No." She shook her head but didn't take her eyes off him. "But I remember you. Here, like this." She reached her hand up and threaded her fingers through his golden locks. A wave of warmth washed through her despite the winter air. "Your hair was slightly longer," she whispered.

Norah drew her fingertips to his cheek, feeling the smoothness of his shaven face. The heat in her stomach grew, but the flash of the image was fading. Alexander's face. His golden locks. His eyes, young and mischievous. They were just moments, but she needed them. She needed to hold on to them.

She pulled him closer. "I know they're here."

His brow creased. "What's here?"

She searched his eyes, and the image reached out once more. Younger Alexander. The Alexander that smiled. She drew in a ragged breath, feeling a stitch in the canvas of her being.

"Norah?" His voice brought her back.

She shook her head. "No, no. They're here."

"What's here?" he asked.

"Stop talking."

She looked into his eyes again—the depths of their blue were drowning. It was Alexander. He was stirring her memories. Her breath quickened.

Summer lazed around them, and they lay on their backs under the tree, laughing. Alexander rolled to his side and caught a lock of her hair.

She smiled at him. "Where will we go?"

"Wherever your heart desires."

"By the sea," she said. "Where the water is warm, and we can lie in the light of the sun."

He leaned over, stroking her cheek with the back of his fingers. "You are the sun," he said, and kissed her tenderly.

The vision faded. She gripped him tighter, trying to draw more of the memory.

"What did you see?" he asked.

Familiarity flowed from where her skin touched his. Norah brought her other hand to his face and pulled him even closer. Her sight clouded. Before she could think of her actions, she lifted her chin and brought her lips to his. He stiffened but let her pull him in.

There was a sudden shattering, and the memory was as clear as the present.

Darkness sat around her as she waited at the tree for Alexander. Her heart raced, and she smiled to herself, pulling her bag closer. She'd brought only the things most important to her; this was all she was taking. There would be no more castles, no more life of privilege, but they would be together, and that was all that mattered.

A silhouette in the darkness made her jump, and she laughed as she recognized him, feeling silly. "You startled me," she said, reaching out and taking his hand. She could see his face in the moonlight.

He wasn't smiling back at her.

"Is everything all right?" She looked around him, noticing he wasn't holding anything: no supplies, no belongings. "Where's your pack?"

"There is no pack," he said, and she felt a strange pit in her stomach. "Norah, I can't take you from here. We can't go."

"What?" She shook her head. "What are you saying?"

"We can't go. You can't go."

Confusion flooded her. "I don't understand. We planned, we—"

"You're going to be queen, and if you leave now, you'd be abandoning your people."

"I don't want to be queen! I want to be with you! I love you, and this is the only way we can be together."

He pulled his hand from hers and stepped backward.

"Alexander," she pleaded, stepping forward to bridge the gap. "We love each other. We're going to be together."

"No," he said. "We can't."

A surge of desperation ran through her. "We can! We can go right now. You don't even need your pack. Let's just go!"

"Norah, we're not going," he said more firmly.

The heat of emotion sprang across her cheeks.

"We can't," he whispered.

"I don't accept that!" she cried.

His face hardened. "I don't love you!" he said sharply.

Her breath caught in her throat at the harshness of his words. "That's not true," she breathed. "That's not true."

"You're going to marry King Phillip. Everything you want, he can give it to you."

"I want you!"

Alexander shifted in the quiet. "That will pass. Go back to the castle, Norah." Then he pulled back, fading into the darkness.

She was alone.

Norah sank to the base of the tree as a sob escaped her.

She broke away from Alexander and stumbled back against the tree, touching her cheek, wet with tears. It was just one memory, but every emotion she had ever felt came flooding back: the love, the deep affliction of the heart, the agony of it breaking.

"You left me." Her voice didn't sound like her own.

"Norah—"

"Like I meant nothing to you." She shook her head as she bit back the bitterness of shame. How foolish she felt to have developed those affections for him all over again.

"Your grandmother discovered us," he told her. "She reminded me of my duty and told me what I should have told myself."

"Then why do you play with me now?" she cried.

He shook his head. "No. Norah, I—"

"I want to go back." She slipped past him and headed for the castle. She didn't want to hear what he had to say. It would hurt.

"Norah," he called after her.

But she didn't stop. She couldn't.

Norah lay in the bath, drawing in the heat from the water and desperately trying to focus on anything to take her mind away from the ache in her chest. She closed her eyes and leaned against the back of the tub, cursing her emotion. Catherine hadn't wanted her to name Alexander as her lord justice. Now she knew why. Perhaps she had always known but didn't want to see.

Regardless, as much as she hated to admit it, she wouldn't have chosen differently for her lord justice. Mercia needed Alexander. She still needed him.

The chamber door of the bedroom opened and closed, but she didn't sit up. She didn't open her eyes. There was only one who disregarded the social graces of her privacy.

"Norah," Catherine called.

She stayed, unmoving, not answering.

"Norah!" Her grandmother's voice came more urgently now.

Under the warmth of the water, a chill ran over her skin. Did Catherine know she had been with Alexander? Had he said something? Is that why she was here?

Catherine burst into the bath chamber. "By the gods, child! Did you not hear me calling you?" She didn't give Norah time to reply. "Samuel sends for us. A vision's come—of you! The first one since you left!" She disappeared into the side cabinet chamber.

Norah sat up in the tub, and her stomach knotted. "Of me?" Her mind drifted to the memory that had returned at the tree. Surely it wasn't a coincidence.

Catherine bustled back into the bath chamber with a gown and undergarments. "Why are you still in there? Get out! Quickly!"

Norah stood and stumbled out of the water. She wrapped a towel around her as her grandmother shoved the undergarments into her arms.

"Do you know what the vision is?" Norah asked.

"Not yet. Samuel only said to come. Gods, child." Catherine frowned. "Have you not a single thing on yet?"

Norah struggled with the clothing as it stuck to her damp skin, but she managed to wriggle into most of the items thrown at her. Catherine pulled tight the lacing on her corset before she had fully situated it, and it choked off her breath. The gown came over her head, and Norah thought she might fall over.

"Your hair is soaking wet," Catherine chided as she pushed the locks aside and fastened the gown up her back.

Norah frowned. "Well, I was... in the bath."

Dressed, Norah pushed her feet into her silk slippers. Catherine took a towel roughly to her head and then dragged a brush through her mane. Norah didn't mind the rush. It was better than primping, actually, but an anxiousness swelled inside her at what the vision showed. She wasn't sure she wanted to be in such a hurry to see it.

Norah looked in the mirror of the vanity. She looked normal enough.

"You look fine, my dear," the woman said, and herded her out of the chamber.

They hurried down the cobbled walkway outside, to Samuel's gallery. It wasn't far, but it would have been nice to have remembered her cloak. Her hair was still damp, and she shivered in the evening winter air.

"Would you like me to get a cover, Regal High?" Caspian asked from behind her.

She hadn't noticed the captain had joined her evening guard. She smiled back at him. "It's not much farther, but thank you."

They reached the seer's door, and Norah followed Catherine inside.

"Samuel!" Catherine called as they weaved through the paintings toward the back room.

"Queen Norah," Samuel greeted when he saw them. "Come, come." He waved them back. "It is not finished, but it is clear enough to see."

They stepped around the easel to discover a large and complex scene across the canvas. A battlefield. Norah's eyes were drawn to herself riding atop a black horse. Her hair was wild in the wind around her.

Bodies littered the ground, and the dirt was stained with blood. She recognized her own Northmen—fighting, dying. There were others battling beside Mercia, with colors of royal blue. Her gaze shifted to a man mounted on a destrier, charging the battle beside her. He wore a leafed crown on his full-faced helm and held his sword in the air. She almost touched the image, but remembered it was still wet. "Who is that?" she asked.

"That, my dear, is King Phillip," Catherine said proudly.

Norah leaned closer. His armor was a polished silver, and on his shield was the sigil of a lion encircled by four stars. She wished she could see his face and frowned in irritation as her eyes drifted across the rest of the image. Black figures saturated the left side of the painting.

"Shadowmen," her grandmother said.

A different army, of black and rusted red, caught her eye. "Who are they?"

Catherine shook her head. "I don't know."

It was impossible to tell who fought whom through the sea of death. Norah's stomach turned. How many kingdoms were in this battle?

"War is coming," Catherine said. "And not just any war, another Great War."

"Queen Norah," Samuel interrupted. "There's another."

Her head snapped up, and her eyes widened. "Another vision?"

He nodded.

Her stomach tightened as they followed him to a second easel where another painting sat. This one was smaller but just as haunting. It was an extension of the first. The battle raged on, and in the center of the painting fought a man clad in armor. But he wore no helm and his golden locks shined bright against the backdrop of war. *Alexander*. He wielded a sword above his head, with his teeth bared. His body twisted in attack on a man that had been knocked to the ground, a man with his arm outstretched against his fate. Norah's breath caught in her throat at the fated man, for on his head was a horned helm.

Catherine gasped. "By the gods!"

The Shadow King—the man her father had warred against, the man who sought to destroy her. He would fall in this war. Alexander would kill him.

Catherine clutched Norah's arm, almost pulling her over. "Norah! With Phillip by your side, we'll defeat the Shadow King!"

Well, Alexander would defeat him. But Mercia was joined with Aleon on the battlefield. Norah swallowed back the knot in her throat as she moved back to the first painting. She looked closely at Phillip on his chestnut stallion. This was the man she was expected to marry, the man that would feed her people and help win this war.

"Norah, you can't deny this," pressed Catherine from behind her. "Think about your people. You must do what is best for them. This winter rages on, and they look to you. And more than that, these visions are what await you. You need this marriage to Phillip, and soon."

Marriage. There it was again.

"Phillip is a good king," Catherine stressed further, seeming to read her mind. "You could come to love him in time."

Norah clenched her teeth. That wasn't how love worked. Perhaps she wished it did. She backed away from the easel. How helpless it felt to have no control, no choice. The images suffocated her. She stumbled numbly back through the sea of paintings and toward the door.

"Norah," Catherine called after her.

Norah pushed out into the winter, sucking in the icy air. It stung her lungs but felt good. It cleared her mind, helped her think. This wasn't about love. This was about helping Mercia and her people. They wouldn't survive the winter. And if this war was to come, she would need Phillip by her side, like in the painting. She would need his army.

Her grandmother was right, and she hated it. Catherine stepped out of the gallery, and they stood on the cobblestone walk. For once, her grandmother was silent.

"Will you help me write a letter?" Norah asked finally. "To this King Phillip of Aleon?"

Catherine let out a breath as she put her hand on Norah's arm. "Of course, my dear."

Chapter Twenty-One

Despite the eternity of night, the morning sun came too soon. Norah lay awake in bed, looking at the ceiling. Perhaps she'd acted too hastily, but it was too late now. She rose sluggishly as Rebecca opened the draperies and brought in her dress. The cold water woke her fully as she washed her face.

Catherine entered her room as Rebecca fastened the last of the clasps on the back of her dress, and Norah looked up at her in the reflection of the mirror.

Her grandmother gave her a sympathetic smile. "I won't pretend today will be an easy day for you."

Norah didn't respond. By now, the council was already aware of the new vision. She would go to them this morning and announce her acceptance of marriage to Phillip. In a week's time, she would travel to Aleon, where they would be wed. That would be her life.

Norah stepped out of her chamber and into the hall leading to the stair. She noticed the captain, Caspian, on guard with Titus, as he had been the evening before. *Odd.*

When they reached the judisaept, the council was waiting.

So was Alexander.

She tried to avoid him, but his gaze caught hers. She couldn't escape. There was a desperation in the storms of his eyes. And something else. But she couldn't think about that right now. She took her place at the head of the table, but she didn't sit. This wouldn't take long, and she couldn't bear to be there any longer than she needed to.

Norah swallowed, forcing an even tone. "As you're all aware, a new vision has come."

The council cast approving eyes on Alexander, clearly already feeling victorious over the Shadow King. Norah didn't. She wasn't sure if she could get the rest of the words out. "As queen, I can't see a clearer path than the one with Aleon. I've written to King Phillip, accepting his proposal of marriage, to continue the strong alliance between Mercia and Aleon."

The councilmen grinned and clapped, nodding in agreement and triumph. All except for Alexander.

"I'll leave in a week's time." She had more to add, but she couldn't speak it through the tears that threatened. She couldn't let them see her cry. "If you'll excuse me, councilmen," she said shakily. She turned and left before they could answer, stepping out into the hall and trying to catch her breath.

"Norah," her grandmother called from behind her.

But she couldn't face her. She couldn't face anyone. She hurried down the pillared walk and through the great hall, with only the sound of the captain's steps behind her. Of course he would follow.

When she reached the stairs leading up to her chamber, she paused, looking back. Catherine hadn't come after her. She glanced at Caspian, frustrated. There would be no getting rid of him. She turned and took a separate small hall toward a side drawing room. She wanted to be alone, as alone as she could be, and perhaps no one would look for her there.

The chill of the room would have normally pushed her from staying long, but she welcomed it now. It helped her stave off the tears that threatened. She'd do whatever was needed to help her kingdom and her people, but that didn't mean she'd resolved her emotion.

Norah stood by the window, looking out over the reach of the isle. The room had a view of the small sparring field on the west side, where she had tested swords with Alexander. Her mind moved to him. As if on cue, she heard footsteps behind her and turned to see him.

His presence forced more feelings that she was trying so hard to keep back. She turned to the window again, focusing on the sparring field outside and the men practicing on it.

Alexander drew close beside her. "Norah," he said softly. He waited until she looked at him. His face was etched in sadness, and it unleashed her own.

She closed her eyes against the overwhelming wave of emotion. Eternity spun around them in the silence.

"Norah," he said again, and she opened her eyes to him. "That night at the tree... it was the night before your father took you. It was the last time I saw you, and it's haunted me since. Had I known..."

He stopped himself and pushed out a long breath between his teeth.

Her eyes searched his. "What would you have done differently had you known?"

But he didn't answer.

She nodded. *Nothing.* She needed to accept this was what they were. She moved to leave, but he caught her hand.

"Norah."

His touch pulsed a warmth through her, and she stopped. Her eyes dropped to where his hand wrapped around her wrist. He loosened his hold but didn't let her go.

They stood as if they each feared the reaction of the other.

Alexander stepped closer. His fingers relaxed around her wrist, and ever so softly he grazed her palm as he ran his hand down over hers. His caress prickled her skin as he entwined his fingers between hers.

"Did you lie to me?" she whispered.

His breath clipped.

She lifted her eyes to his. "Did you lie when you said you didn't love me?"

His lips parted, but there were no words. She wanted to beg him to tell her he lied.

He leaned even closer as he lowered his head, with only a breath between them. If she raised her chin, their lips would meet. Her body betrayed her, rolling her upward.

"Norah," he breathed. "I—"

A tap on the doorframe by the captain broke the moment. She had forgotten he was there, and a flush came to her cheeks. But she didn't have time to mull over it. Someone was coming.

Alexander's jaw tightened as he pushed out a long breath. They couldn't be found like this. He pulled his hand from hers and stepped back, but their eyes stayed on each other's.

Catherine reached the room, drawing Norah's gaze as she entered. The woman stopped when she saw them. "Norah," she said. Her tone was stiff, a warning.

Norah glanced back up at Alexander. The words that she desperately needed to hear from him, they wouldn't come now. Perhaps it was better they were left unsaid. They would either further break her or make it that much harder to do what she must. Either way, no good would come of them. She swallowed back her need and moved around him to leave. She couldn't look at her grandmother as she stepped past her and out into the hall.

"Norah," Catherine said, but she didn't stop.

Caspian stood, waiting. He'd been the one to alert them. Had he seen them? She averted her eyes, heat creeping back to her cheeks, and quickened her pace toward her chamber as he fell in step behind her.

"Norah," Catherine called from behind.

She didn't want to hear whatever her grandmother had to say. She didn't want the judgment, the chastisement. She couldn't bear it on top of everything else.

"Norah," Catherine called again.

She paused.

Catherine caught up to her. Her eyes were shadowed in a cloud of sorrow that tempered her icy fire. "Norah, you mustn't make it harder than it already is. You're so close, child. Don't let yourself be distracted."

Norah let out a breath of disbelief. "Distracted?" The bitterness lay thick on her tongue. She couldn't hold herself back any longer. "No! I have agreed to everything that's been asked of me, everything thrust upon me. I wear a crown I don't want, I'll marry a man I don't know, and I'll go to war with an enemy for a cause I don't fully understand. And now you tell me to feel nothing?" She shook her head. "I won't pretend I don't. I can't."

"Norah! You'll watch your words in these halls!" Catherine shushed her as she glanced around them.

"Or what?" she snapped. With a glance of finality, Norah turned and strode back to her chamber.

Alexander looked out from the window of his chamber at the torchlit square down below. The alcohol stung his throat as he took another drink from his chalice. He could still feel the warmth of her hand in his, the way their wrists had touched, the brush of their arms as he had stepped closer. The nearness of her lingered on his skin, and her breath on his lips. She was so close, and yet beyond his reach, as she had always been.

She had asked him if he had lied. He'd hoped himself wiser and stronger now, solid in his decision that what he'd done was best for Mercia, best for Norah. The truth was, if faced with that decision now, he wasn't sure he was strong enough to make the same choice. The heartbreak in her eyes when he had left her at the tree—it had haunted him the last three years. Now to see it all over again, and to lose her again, he didn't think he could bear it. The pain twisted inside him—not the dull ache of wanting, but the kind of pain that makes a man fade to nothing.

A knock from the hall interrupted him. He set his glass on the small table by the side chair. When he pulled open the door, he wasn't surprised. *Catherine.* He opened the door wider, and she swept inside.

Alexander stood, waiting for the admonishment he knew he deserved.

But it didn't come.

Raising his eyes, he didn't find the anger he had expected, or the disappointment. There was no offense or rebuke. Only sadness hung between them, and it further opened his wound. He wanted her wrath, something that would take his mind from the pain. He needed it. Her sympathy would be the breaking point.

Catherine closed the gap between them, and her worry-worn eyes found his. "You've always known this would come."

His throat seized. He couldn't speak.

"You knew you couldn't love her," she said.

He knew. He'd always known. Yet he couldn't not. He drew in a breath and pushed it out, choking back the loss that threatened to break him.

Catherine sighed as she reached up and brought her hand to his cheek. "My dear boy," she said softly, "I feared this for you. For both of you. I've done everything in my power, but"—she ran her hand down to his chest and gave him a gentle pat—"you both have such stubborn hearts." She smiled sadly.

He feared his words wouldn't come without emotion, so he said nothing.

"I haven't come to chastise you," she said, smoothing the center trim of his doublet. "But I want to be sure you haven't forgotten yourself. You are the lord justice of Mercia."

Lord justice. A position he had aspired to his entire life, now a position that meant nothing when compared to losing Norah. However, his conditioned courtesies answered for him, and he felt himself nod.

Catherine gave him another pat and then stepped toward the door. As she opened it, she paused, turning back. "Alexander, when she leaves for Aleon, you won't go with her."

His head jerked up, and his eyes caught hers. "What?" he breathed, finally finding his voice. "She can't travel alone."

"You say that as though she's traveling half the world away. She'll be well within the safety of Mercian lands until she reaches Aleon. And she won't be alone. She'll have the captain and an army to escort her to the border, where King Phillip will meet her. In her absence, you're needed in Mercia with the rest of the council. That's your duty, Alexander."

Duty. He had given his life to duty. And it had ripped out his heart.

With a final gaze, Catherine stepped out, closing the door behind her.

Norah woke on the side chair where she'd fallen asleep, with her eyes still puffy from tears. It was dark outside. She stood as she reached up to push her hair back from her face. She opened her chamber door slowly to find Caspian and Liaman on watch.

"Queen Norah," Caspian greeted her.

"How long until morning?" she asked.

"Quite some time yet. Should I send for your maid?"

She shook her head. "No. Could I just get some water? And maybe something small to eat?"

"Of course." He nodded to Liaman, who left quickly for her requests.

Norah left the door open and sat down at the vanity, looking at herself in the mirror, but not seeing. Caspian stood in the doorway, facing outward. How awkward it felt with him now. "What you saw yesterday," she started, "what you heard—"

"I saw and heard nothing, Regal High."

"You would be a poor captain of the guard if that were true."

Liaman returned with some water, wine, and an assortment of food on a small plate. Caspian took it and excused him, leaving them to talk privately. He put the plate on the vanity in front of her and poured some water into a chalice. Norah eyed the wine, but she had spurred enough judgment for the moment, so she kept herself from reaching for it.

He gave her a sympathetic smile, as if reading her mind, and filled another cup with wine. "He wouldn't want you to hurt like this," he said softly.

Hurt was a good word. It did hurt. *And Caspian knew.* She shifted uncomfortably in her chair as she looked up at him. "What do you know of how he feels?"

His face sobered. "Forgive me," he said quickly. "It's not my place. I shouldn't have spoken."

"I don't want decorum. I want you to answer."

Caspian let out an uneasy breath. "I've known Alexander his entire life, and you've always been the center of it."

She swallowed. "He hasn't shared this with me."

"You mean he hasn't spoken the words that betray his duty? Because that's what he'd be doing." He paused. "It's not my place, but I urge you caution. He gets closer and closer to a danger I'm not sure you understand. If the council were to know, they would remove him."

"He's *my* lord justice," she argued. "*I* named him. *I* am queen."

Caspian frowned. "If the council thinks Alexander stands in the way of an alliance with Aleon, even you won't be able to save him."

Norah's heart beat heavy in her chest as a fear seeded itself within. What did *that* mean? She looked back at her chalice. "Is that why you've taken to guard work? Am I so obvious now it requires a captain's attention?"

"It requires a friend's attention," he said. "Discreet attention."

Her cheeks flushed with embarrassment.

"You must take care to not show your feelings in front of anyone else," he told her. "And trust your grandmother. She loves you both, and she works to protect you *and* the lord justice."

Chapter Twenty-Two

Preparing to depart Mercia felt surreal. Norah had only known it as home for a short time, but it was strange to leave. She knew nothing else. Her grandmother would continue in the role of regent in Norah's absence, with the council's support. Perhaps it was better. Norah hadn't exactly mastered being queen.

Packing everything had been time-consuming. It would take a week to travel southeast through Mercia to the border of Praetoria, the first kingdom of the Aleon empire, where Phillip would meet her. Weather permitting, they'd reach the imperial capital of Valour in another week. The army gathered across the bridge on the mainland, readying the horses.

In the castle, Norah said goodbye to her grandmother. "Are you sure you'll be all right?" she asked. While Catherine would travel to attend the wedding, policies prevented them from traveling together, so her grandmother would follow separately.

Catherine clasped Norah's hands. "Child, don't worry about me. I'll join you in Aleon in time for the wedding."

The wedding. The mention of it made her stomach turn, but she forced a smile and kissed her grandmother's cheek. She turned as Alexander entered. He paused when he saw her, then seeming to remember himself, he said, "The army is ready."

Norah glanced back at Catherine and then followed him out into the courtyard.

Caspian held her horse for her, and she mounted as gracefully as she could manage, knowing all eyes were on her, although the only eyes that mattered were Alexander's.

And his stare nearly broke her.

He reached out and gripped Caspian's breastplate, clutching him in a silent plea.

"With my life," the captain assured him.

Alexander's gaze met hers again, the storms in his eyes haunting her. Would she see him again? He looked back to Caspian and clasped the captain's shoulder tightly. "With the gods' speed, brother."

Caspian nodded and mounted his own horse, and Alexander's eyes locked back on Norah.

"I know Mercia's safe in your hands," she told him.

"Do you still have the blade I gave you?" he asked.

She did—strapped to her calf inside her boot. She nodded.

"Keep yourself well, Norah."

"Goodbye, Alexander," she whispered, and gave herself one last look of his face before she turned and urged her mount across the bridge.

Travel was slow with a large army; the first week felt like a year. Normally they'd have reached the border by now, but Alexander had increased the guard from one hundred to five hundred men, slowing their pace. It was hardly necessary, as Mercia bordered Aleon, and Norah wouldn't be leaving the safety of the kingdoms, but the council hadn't argued, so neither had she.

Inside her tent, she pulled off her dusty riding skirts as Rebecca laid a fresh riding dress out for her. Today had been especially long, and Norah's muscles ached from the ride. She thought about opting for the carriage in the morning, but the boredom of sitting in a cramped box for hours didn't appeal to her.

Thoughts of Alexander had filled her mind through the long hours of the day and well into the night. She wondered if he was thinking about her. She hoped he was, but then again, she hoped he wasn't. The longing was a curse she didn't wish for anyone.

Norah sighed. Two more days until they reached the first Aleon kingdom of Praetoria. And Phillip. She shifted uncomfortably in her saddle at the thought of seeing him. Or meeting him, rather, since she didn't have any memory of him at all. She'd decided to tell him of her memory loss right away. Her heart picked up a little. Perhaps he'd reconsider the wedding. But she pushed the hope away as quickly as it came. No. If he'd waited three years for her to return, it was because he was committed to the alliance with Mercia, memory loss or no.

She turned her attention back to the journey. She should enjoy the quiet while she could. Her life would be very different once she was wed to Phillip. She already missed the castle. She even missed Titus, but he'd arrive with her grandmother a week after Norah reached Aleon.

Rebecca ducked outside and returned with a basin and a pitcher of warm water.

"Would you like me to bring you some stew, Regal High? There's fresh venison tonight. It's delicious."

Norah smiled as her stomach grumbled at the thought. "That does sound good, but I think I'll get it myself. I'd like to sit by the fire for a little while, anyway."

"Of course, Regal High," her maid replied, and then ducked out of the tent.

Norah poured some water into the basin and washed her hands. They were so dry from the ride, and the water felt good. She longed for a hot bath. That would be the first thing she did when she reached Aleon, she promised herself. She dampened a cloth and cleaned her face and neck, letting the warmth refresh her. After re-braiding her hair and pulling on the clean, pale-blue riding dress, she felt almost a new woman, and she went to find the venison stew.

Caspian stood by the main fire, laughing at a story a soldier was recounting. Seeing her approach, he straightened and motioned to the men nearby for a bowl of stew. One was quickly delivered, and he handed it to her. "Be careful, it's hot."

She smiled, taking it from him. "Thank you." Rebecca was right—it was delicious. "Compliments to the chef," she said.

Caspian stretched out his hand toward the soldier he'd been talking to. "That would be Anderson."

Anderson bowed his head with a wide grin, and she raised her bowl to him in salute. Then she made her way closer to the fire to soak in the warmth. The air was crisp, but the heat from the flame danced across her face. Tiredness seeped into her body and pervaded her mind, but her spirit smiled. Despite the circumstance, there was freedom away from Mercia, away from the castle and eyes of judgment and expectation.

"It's a clear night," Caspian said, coming up behind her. She looked up at the stars. Surely there were millions. She ran her hand over her face, feeling the transfer of heat from her cheeks to her palms.

"I've sent a bird to the lord justice," he added, "to let him know we're in good health and two days from Praetoria."

The mention of Alexander drew her mind back to the hopelessness of her situation, but she forced a nod. "Good."

A fire went up in the distance, a perimeter check. It was quickly extinguished, and another continued the pattern. Each post took its turn, signaling all was well.

"How long has it been since you've stepped on unfrozen earth?" she asked him, dragging her boot through the dirt.

"I spent last summer on the isle, so it would have been the summer before," he answered.

She felt born of the winter, not able to recall anything else.

"They say Aleon has winters like our summers," he said. "I should very much like to see that."

Summer. Norah liked the thought. "Me too," she said. She drank the last of the savory liquid from the bowl. A wind rustled through the camp, and she shuddered. "Thank you for the company. I think I'll retire now," she said. "I'll see you in the morning."

But he didn't answer. His attention was to the south.

"Captain?"

"Wait." His voice came low, making her skin prickle.

She followed the direction of his gaze but saw only darkness. "What is it?"

"No signal."

She looked back into the night, straining her eyes to see. "What does that mean?"

"Something's not right," Caspian mumbled. He turned back to Norah. "I think returning to your tent is a good idea."

Norah's pulse quickened. It was probably nothing, she told herself, but she couldn't shake the unease.

The captain turned to the soldier closest to them. "I want to know why there's no signal. Go!"

But as the soldier turned, a wisp of an arrow cut through the dark and hit him in the chest, dropping him to the ground. Then a flurry of whistling darts came, and chaos filled the night.

It took Norah a moment to understand what was happening. Hands pulled her back, and she looked to see Liaman beside her. Soldiers scrambled for their shields and raised them overhead, coming together and forming a defensive circle around her. Her army was spread through the darkness; she couldn't see them all. A scream sounded in the distance, then it was brutally cut short. Her stomach turned.

They were under attack. Her heart raced.

An agonizing pause came, and she forced herself to push the panic down. She looked to Caspian as he and Liaman stood together with more of her soldiers in front of her. They'd keep her safe.

A second onslaught of arrows came, with the groans of dying men, and then there was another pause. Her men fell on either side of her. Another wave of her soldiers tried to join in her defense but were downed as quickly as they came. Those remaining kicked back the bodies of the dead and circled closer, their shields up and swords ready, and the panic she was trying desperately to keep at bay surged through her.

Shadows moved around them, but the enemy was invisible, and her men fell one by one. All she could see was darkness. It was enough to set fear into the bravest of hearts, but her men stood fiercely.

"Hold!" Caspian ordered.

She heard the *sip* of an arrow into flesh, and Liaman stumbled back, bumping against her. In the firelight, an arrow protruded from his chest.

"Liaman!" she screamed.

He waved her back as he forced himself to stand and pull his shield back up. But she knew it wouldn't be enough. And her panic turned to anger.

Another onslaught of arrows came, and two more men fell. Anger erupted into fury. She had to do something. Her men were dying all around her. How many remained? She couldn't lose another.

"Enough!" she raged. She ducked out from behind her men, screaming into the night. "Show yourselves, cowards!"

"Norah! Get behind me!" Caspian bellowed.

A haunting call reverberated through the night, and an eerie silence settled around them. Her remaining soldiers pulled tight around her with their arrows fixed on the darkness as Caspian pulled her back again.

A shadow loomed into view—a mounted fiend, larger than any man. His destrier, the color of night against night and plated in dark metal, snorted and screamed like a hell horse of Hammel as it pulled at the bit. The rider sat cloaked in darkness, broad shouldered and armored in shadows and chain. His horned helm was silhouetted against the moonlight.

She recognized the helm—the helm from Nemus's vision, the helm from Samuel's paintings.

"The Shadow King," Caspian said.

"I know who he is," she seethed. The tension of bowstrings sung around her as her remaining soldiers aimed at the king. But she called out, "Hold!"

His army was there; she could feel them. Ever so slowly, she made out the dark, shadowed shapes. Then Norah's breath caught as she realized they were surrounded by them. Hundreds, or more, of them, barely visible from behind the black of their shields.

"Demons," Liaman whispered beside her. He'd somehow managed to stay on his feet.

"If they were demons, they wouldn't be carrying shields," she said between her teeth. She looked back at the mounted man, forcing as much strength as she could into her voice. "You're who they call the Shadow King?"

Even in the night, she felt the Shadow King's eyes upon her, and the hair on the back of her neck stood on end.

"North Queen," he responded, his voice thick and haunting.

She stepped forward again. She wouldn't let him see her fear. "You attack the Mercian queen on Mercian lands. Do you mean to provoke a war?"

"We've been at war for a long time."

She squirmed under his unseen stare, but she didn't dare turn away. Her fury built. "Stop hiding and fight like honorable men!"

A low rumble came from him. A laugh. "I am not an honorable man," the Shadow King said.

The whir of another arrow came, and the soldier to her right fell. Two of her archers loosed arrows into the darkness, and a counterstrike of arrows hit them in return, killing both. Another arrow hit Liaman, and he sank to the ground. This time, he didn't get up.

"No!" she cried, but Caspian clutched her tightly behind him.

It was only Caspian with her now. A dark shape rushed toward him, and her captain swung to meet their attacker. The clash of their weapons echoed in the night, and Caspian kicked him back. Another Shadowman came from the side, and Caspian turned to defend, but he was hit from behind by a third.

Caspian tried to counter but was met by a fourth who swung and cut into his sword arm, making him drop his blade to the ground. He stumbled back, stunned.

"Caspian!" she screamed.

The Shadowman attacked again, and, without a sword, Caspian was easily overpowered and knocked to his knees. The Shadowman grabbed a fistful of his hair and held him before the king.

"Go," the king growled to Caspian from atop his beast. "Go tell the Bear I have your queen."

The Bear? She didn't know who that was, but she didn't have time to mull over it.

In one final effort, Caspian whipped a blade from its sheath at his side and delivered a quick stab to his captor's leg, who fell back, releasing him. Caspian let out a cry as he then hurled the blade toward the king, but he'd thrown it with his left hand, and the dagger missed its mark, burying itself into a tree.

Norah jumped forward and grabbed Caspian's sword from the ground and moved in front of him to meet her enemies. She let her fury drive out the fear. If they didn't expect a fight, they were mistaken.

"Take her," the Shadow King growled.

"Norah!" Caspian yelled.

A soldier rushed her with a sword, but she met the attack fiercely, driving him aside and ripping her blade through the soldier's leathers. Another jumped at her, trying to knock her to the ground, but she sidestepped him and sank her blade into a third attacker. The Shadow King dismounted, drawing his own sword. She inhaled deeply, calculating and focusing her anger. Committing, she attacked with every ounce of strength she had.

But the force of his strike knocked the sword from her hands, dislocated her shoulder, and made her cry out. She gritted her teeth against the nauseating pain and looked desperately for another weapon.

He caught her from behind and picked her up by the waist. She flailed back with her good arm, catching the chin of his helm with her elbow and flinging it from his head. She couldn't see his face, but her fingers met his flesh, and she clawed at him with her nails. He caught her hand and twisted it down, pinning it beside her. She struggled, but the pain in her shoulder took the breath from her, and she felt her consciousness fading.

"No!" Caspian's bellow came from behind her.

This was it, she thought. She wasn't afraid. No one escaped death. She just hadn't expected it so soon.

Hands gripped her, and she drew in a ragged breath. Pain shot through her chest and down her arm, but she wouldn't cry out again. She was pulled upward, and it was too much. The pain crept into her mind, and everything grew dark.

The army marched silently through the night as the king carried his prize—a snow-haired queen cloaked in pale blue under the light of the moon.

Chapter Twenty-Three

Norah woke in a tent, on her side, lying across a bedroll with a thick fur that had been dropped over her. The bedroll gave little cushion to the hard ground, and her joints protested as she stirred. Clinking metal and voices outside swirled in the fog in her mind. It took a moment for her senses to come, and then she bolted upright, remembering. An ache shot across her chest and down her arm.

Her shoulder.

She moved it gingerly. It had been reset, but it was still sore. At least she could move it.

She still wore her riding dress, and even her boots were on. Remembering her knife, she fumbled desperately under the bottom of her skirt and swore under her breath. They'd taken it; only the empty sheath remained strapped around her calf. A tremor ran up her spine as she thought of the Shadowmen searching her, touching her. She bit back the emotion threatening to surface—she couldn't be emotional now.

She had to focus on the positive—anything that could give her strength.

She was alive and seemingly unmolested. That should bring some relief, but there was little relief to be had. So many of her men were dead. How many had been captured? How many might have escaped? Liaman had fallen.

Caspian. A crushing weight fell on her. He couldn't have survived either. She covered her face in her hands, emotion shuddering through her.

Norah tried to swallow back her sorrow. She needed to assess her situation and figure out what to do. She looked around. The tent was bare save for her bedroll and the fur. She was alone. Daylight spilled in through the heavy canvas, and the continued sound of men outside drew her attention. She rose and crept toward the front flap of the tent, listening closely. Her heart beat wildly in her chest. She'd been captured, but she wasn't restrained.

She gathered her nerves and stepped out to face her fate.

A guard standing outside stepped back from her in surprise, clearly not expecting her to so boldly emerge. A head wrap covered his head and face—all but his eyes. He wore fitted, black breeches, armored at the knee and tucked into a high boot. Looking closer, she realized that what she'd thought was a shirt under his cloak wasn't clothing at all, but inked markings covering his bare skin.

He gripped his spear tighter, and she stiffened, anticipating a fight, but he made no move to keep her inside the tent. She took a step forward and garnered some confidence as he took another step back. Perhaps he wasn't permitted to engage her, and her courage grew.

Norah looked around. Shadow soldiers were busy at work, sharpening weapons and tending horses, but when they noticed her, a quiet fell over the camp. She shifted uneasily. The army was massive, with men as far as she could see. Her eyes widened in surprise. There were men *and* women. They all wore wraps over their faces and were clothed in black and covered in ink markings. However, the women wore breasted plating that was feminine, but threatening all the same. She'd never seen a woman soldier in Mercia.

All eyes were on her, but no one moved to challenge her. She grew bolder still.

Norah let her gaze roll over the masses, taking everything in, when she saw him.

The Shadow King.

He stood beside a tent nearby, fully armored and crowned with his horned helm, just as she had remembered. Another man stepped into view, and Norah's breath caught in her throat. She recognized the monster from Nemus's vision of the future her father had stopped, the one of a fallen Mercia. This was the brute who had killed Edward and the councilmen in the vision—the demon commander, *the Destroyer*. She had almost snickered at the title when she'd first heard it, but she wasn't snickering now. He was even larger than the king, which didn't seem possible, and looked very much like he enjoyed destroying anything he could touch.

She swallowed. Don't show fear, she told herself. As if that were possible.

Norah stepped toward them. A tension rippled through the air, but no one moved. She continued toward the Shadow King. As she drew closer, the sound of blades drawn from their scabbards cut the air.

The king held up his hand to steady his army and let her come nearer still. She couldn't see his face, but she imagined something wicked underneath. The chest plating of his armor was dark and battled, but polished. His arms were covered in a light armor of small overlapping scales for fluid range of motion. She made mental notes to think on later. He waited, letting her inspect him. *Arrogant.*

"Where are my men?" she demanded.

His voice came as it had before, dark and haunting. "What men?"

Her pulse raced. He had to have taken some of them captive. "I had an army."

Another deep chuckle vibrated in his chest. "*Had,*" he replied. "And five hundred men do not make an army."

Her chest tightened. Were they all dead? "What happened to them?" she asked between her teeth.

"Dead. All except one to deliver a message. I only hope he doesn't die before he reaches the North. Perhaps I should send birds after just in case." His eyes smiled from under his helm. "I regret you missed it. I lined them up on their knees and slit their throats, one at a time. You can be proud, though. No one begged me for their life, like so many do."

Her body shook. Caspian. Liaman. Aaron. Daniel. Tears threatened. "What about my maid?" she seethed, her voice quaking.

"She took her own life," he replied. "That wasn't my doing."

Her lip trembled. *Rebecca.* "Everything is your doing!"

He chuckled again. "I suppose it is."

"Every soldier of Mercia will come for me," she spat.

The Shadow King gave another dark, rumbling chuckle. "Good. I'm counting on it."

Alexander stood in the watchtower, looking blankly out over the horizon. It had been five days since the last message had arrived, two days longer than expected. A deep worry grew in his core. Caspian wouldn't have carelessly forgotten, knowing Alexander would be waiting on the messages. *Every* message.

Footsteps came behind him, but he didn't turn around. He knew who it was.

"Still no word?" Catherine asked.

He gave a small shake of his head. "Something's wrong."

She stood beside him, looking out across the bridge to the mainland. "We don't know that yet. Sometimes birds are lost or delayed. Let's wait to see if another will come."

"That's another day," he snapped, sharper than he had intended. He pushed out a breath. "If something's happened, I can't wait another day to discover it. I can travel quickly with only a few men."

Catherine frowned. "And do what? She has an army of five hundred with her. What will you accomplish with only a few more?"

Alexander wiped his face with his hand, pushing back the desperation mounting inside him.

Catherine put her hand on his arm. "My dear, I'm as sick with worry as you are, but you must think about this rationally. Another bird's due tomorrow. Let's see what comes."

Just then, a flurry on the horizon caught his attention, and he narrowed his eyes.

"What on earth is that?" Catherine asked, seeing it as well.

But Alexander didn't answer. His pulse quickened as he drew in a ragged breath. Messenger birds. *An entire flock.* He spun and raced down the spiral staircase of the watchtower.

"Wait!" she called after him.

He couldn't.

Alexander reached the bottom of the stair and broke into a run across the courtyard to the library with a crushing weight in his chest. He tore through the front doors to the staircase of the avian tower.

"Rector!" he shouted as he bounded up the stairs, three at a time, and threw open the door at the top. Rector Tusten stood by the window, holding a bird in his arm that had just landed. He looked up at Alexander in confusion and held out his hand. Alexander, out of breath, took the small piece of parchment. His body shuddered. It held no message, only a dark earthen stain.

"What is it?" the rector asked.

He ran his finger over the rippled parchment. "Blood," he breathed.

The rector's hands trembled as he released the bird onto the table. "What does it mean?" he asked.

Alexander looked to see a pile of similarly stained parchments on the corner of the rector's desk. More birds were still landing. Whoever had sent them, had sent them *all*, and their message would all be the same.

The capital bells sounded, and Alexander pushed by the rector to look out the window. A rider on horseback crossed the bridge, into the courtyard. Alexander clenched the parchment in his hand as he spun around and made his way quickly back down the stairs.

Catherine had just reached the library by the time he was coming out. "What's going on?" she demanded.

Alexander paid her no mind. Panic rose in his chest as he saw the rider, slouching over and clinging to his horse. Guards pulled the blood-covered man down, and Alexander's breath caught in his throat as he recognized Caspian. The captain's right arm hung limply.

"Where is she?" he roared, grabbing him by the breastplate.

"Gone," Caspian said hoarsely. "He took her."

Alexander's voice shook. "Who?"

"The Shadow King."

A deep and aching horror rippled through him, followed by a rush of rage. He turned and bared his teeth with a roar. "Ready the army!" he thundered. "We march tonight!"

"Wait!" Catherine cried. "Wait! This is obviously a trap. You can't blindly rush in! We need a plan."

Alexander ignored her.

"The council will override you," she said, breathless.

He whirled toward her with a fire under his skin. "That would take the *collective* council. Henricus and James are in Damask. They cannot assemble in time to stop me."

"Alexander," Catherine cried as she grabbed him by the arm. "Think about what you're doing!"

He ripped his arm from her hold and strode out to meet his army.

Chapter Twenty-Four

The Shadowmen were silent travelers. Norah didn't find herself particularly keen on conversation, but she wanted information. However, the day passed without words, and at night she slept again in the quiet cold of darkness. She took comfort in the thought that Alexander would come for her with the full force of the Mercian army. She wondered where the Shadow King planned to meet them. They weren't headed northwest, toward Mercia, but instead they rode south along the rocky hills of the midlands.

They stopped midafternoon and watered their horses at a small stream. Norah wished it were larger so that she might throw herself in it and float away. She crouched down and scooped the water to her lips. It was cold as ice and stung her fingers, but she drank her fill.

She felt the king's dark presence behind her, and she looked back over her shoulder.

"Eat," he ordered as he tossed a small pouch of bread and dried meat on the ground beside her.

She glanced at it but didn't move to pick it up. She wanted to eat. Her stomach begged for it, but she had no intention of taking food from the Shadowmen. She rose, leaving it, and said nothing.

His eyes narrowed underneath his helm. "Starve then."

But Norah didn't plan to be in his hold long enough for it to matter.

The next day passed much like the one before. Despite the move south, the winter was merciless. The wind stung her cheeks, and she couldn't help the shivers that ran through her. She buried her hands in her horse's mane, trying to warm them.

As the afternoon waned, energy picked up through the army. Something was coming—something that excited them. As they made their way through the hills, she caught sight of mountain peaks and knew immediately where they were going.

Bahoul.

It's where the unit of her Northmen had been heading—the unit whose heads the Shadow King had sent back to Mercia. She shuddered at the memory.

Catherine had told her about Bahoul—a walled stronghold across the rocky mountains separating the Shadowlands from Mercia's southern reaches. It had once belonged to the Shadowmen, but her father had driven the Shadow King back and took it. Mercian forces occupied the stronghold now. The Shadowmen had tried to reclaim Bahoul several times, but Alexander led defenses that had held the mountains. The fortress was near impenetrable, and even a small resident army could defend against a much larger foe, so long as they stayed within the stronghold.

Her pulse quickened. Was he going to try to retake it now?

They made their way through the rocky hills and along a small ridge, but as they started down the other side, Norah's breath caught in her throat.

Another massive army of Shadowmen waited between the hills, just out of sight from the stronghold. Her heart beat faster. The Shadow King reined up his horse and looked back at her. "Are you ready, North Queen?" he asked with a haunting snarl. "Tomorrow, I take back what's mine. Then the Bear will bring your army, and I'll take them too."

The Bear. He'd said that name before. Beurnat the Bear—Alexander's father? He'd died in the war. But she said nothing.

The king's eyes were still on her. "I'll kill them all," he said. "This time I'll make sure you watch." He was trying to get a reaction from her, but she kept her gaze forward and remained silent. She wouldn't give him the satisfaction.

Norah lay awake in the darkness. It was morning. She had been given no tent that night, only a thin bedroll and a fur, and she was surrounded by Shadowmen. But that wasn't why she hadn't slept.

Her stomach turned. The Shadow King would use her to get her Northmen to hand over the stronghold, and then bait Alexander and her army into battle. If the Shadowmen succeeded in taking the stronghold now, the Mercian army would be at a severe disadvantage when they arrived.

As the faintest light of morning chased back the darkness, she pushed herself up to sit. A blanket of mist lay around them. A low chuckle reverberated through the fog. Her skin prickled.

"A perfect morning for battle," the king's voice came.

She couldn't tell from which direction, and she shuddered. Her heart beat faster. It was a terrible morning for battle. The mist would cover the Shadow army. Mercia had the best archers in the world, but they could do nothing if they couldn't see.

Then, through the mist, she saw him as he stepped in front of her.

"Are you ready, North Queen?"

The king's demon appeared to her right, and she jumped. He grabbed her.

"What are you doing? Let me go!" She twisted against him, but he squeezed his arms around her until she couldn't breathe, then bound her wrists with the long rope.

He dragged her to where his destrier stood, and mounted. Then he pulled up a spear, as if he needed another weapon in addition to the sword on his back and the massive battle-axe resting across his thighs. He urged his mount forward, jerking the rope—and her—toward what she surmised was the base of the mountain stronghold.

Norah's mind raced. The commander had touched her and held her tight as he bound her hands. She'd felt not the body of a demon, but a body of flesh and bone. He was a man, a brute of a man, but a man nonetheless. *And men bleed.*

Her skin flushed with the heat of fight.

She tried to work loose the rope around her wrist as he pulled her along, but it was hopeless without a blade. A *crack* under her heel caught her attention, and she glanced down to see a partially buried skull in the ground. She jumped sideways in surprise. Her eyes widened as she realized they were the scattered remains and timeworn fragments of weapons from battles past. They covered the ground. Were these Northmen she walked across, or Shadowmen? She shuddered. The commander pulled her along, and she stumbled forward.

They stopped at the base of the mountain stronghold, but the mist still covered them.

"Northmen!" the brute boomed in a deep, resounding thunder. "I have your queen! Come and claim her!"

He was trying to draw them out.

"They aren't fools!" she spat at him.

He gave a low chuckle. "Your screams will make them come." Then he jerked the rope, pulling her toward him. Her anger surged. She fought back, but she was no match for his strength and only stumbled forward.

But Norah had no intention of allowing herself to be used against her army. In a split decision, she lunged toward him, running and sliding under his horse. She gave the animal a sharp blow to the underbelly as she skirted out and then reeled back, pulling the slack of the rope tight against its hind legs. The animal reared, and she threw her weight against the rope, making the beast lose its balance and crash to the ground atop the brute. She pulled the rope free, twisting clear of the animal's kicks as it tried to right itself.

The destrier rolled off the commander, who stirred and gasped for breath. As the animal staggered back to its feet, she jumped up and struggled onto it. Her window of opportunity would be short, and the Shadow army was near. Her bound hands made movement difficult, but she spurred the beast forward. Under her thigh, a short sword had been stowed in the saddle. She thanked the gods and slipped the hilt up, sliding her bound wrists up the blade and freeing herself.

Norah stretched forward to give the destrier his head to run. She'd lost her direction in the mist, and she prayed she was headed toward the stronghold.

And then she was falling.

She hit the ground with a force that knocked the wind from her. Rolling to her side and struggling for breath, she looked back in horror to see the horse had been downed with a spear. The beast struggled to rise, and thrashed for a moment, but then gave up and lay in silent agony. Behind, she could only make out the commander's form in the mist, on his knees, still not fully recovered. But he had recovered enough to spear the horse—he could have hit her.

Norah gasped as her lungs gave her air again, and she stumbled up to her feet.

The commander rose, pulling up his axe and moving toward her.

She raced back to the horse and pulled the short sword from the saddle and stood to meet her enemy. The king's brute lumbered closer, and she backed away. He reached the animal, swinging his axe and plunging it into its neck to give it peace.

And then she heard them—all around her in the mist.

She couldn't see them, but she knew they were there. *The Shadow army.* The king appeared on her left and swung down from his horse, pulling his own sword. A soldier beside him tossed him a spear as well.

Norah clutched her sword firmly in her hand, widening her stance for more control and settling her breath. She praised her younger self that she had learned how to fight, and cursed her current self that she hadn't practiced more in Mercia, but she knew she was dangerous with a blade. Her shoulder still ached, but she pushed it off and braced for the king's rage.

He took long strides toward her, with his sword in one hand and spear in the other. She was no match for his strikes; she'd have to be quicker. Her stomach twisted. She hadn't been quick enough when he'd taken her before—it had been like she wasn't even fighting, like she was nothing.

Fear coursed through her, but she couldn't let that take over. Still, her body shook at the thought of countering the thunderous blow of his strikes with her own.

The king swept the body of the spear at her, attempting to knock her off her feet, but she darted back. He swung again, harder this time, his patience waning, and she twisted sideways, dodging the blow. He wasn't trying to kill her, but the strength of his swings could seriously hurt her. Not that he cared.

He swung again, and she jumped back but collided with the fortress wall behind her. Her head struck the stone, and a pain cracked through her skull, darkening her vision.

And then he was on her.

He grabbed her by the throat, pressing her hard against the wall. Norah dropped her sword and clawed at his hand, but it held.

"Do not test me, North Queen," he snarled.

But Norah wasn't testing him; this wasn't facetious rebellion. She needed to get away, she needed to be free. Her life depended on it. Mercia depended on it. So she fought. With everything she had, she fought.

Her fingers grazed the hilt of a dagger at his waist, and she snatched it, ripping it across the unarmored forearm of his spear hand. He snarled again as he dropped the spear and tried to catch the knife, but in a final effort, she drove it between the break in his armor on the side of his breastplate. Her angle was off, and the hit wasn't true, but he roared in pain. Then she threw up an elbow and caught him at the base of his throat, just under his helm. She just needed to get him off...

He crushed her against the wall, leveraging his weight to overpower her. She couldn't breathe. As he recovered, he pulled her to him, tight. She was no match for his strength, and, with no more weapons, no more energy, she stilled.

Norah panted between her teeth as she waited for his wrath. He had warned her, and no doubt she'd suffer his anger now. But it wasn't anger that she saw in his eyes underneath his helm. Surprise, perhaps? Disbelief?

"Hold her," he growled. His brute commander stepped forward and seized her arms, not gently.

The king gathered himself for a moment and then pulled the blade from his side with a grunt. Then he stepped toward her with the blood-covered blade in his hand. Terror rippled up her spine. What was he going to do?

A horn sounded from the mist behind them, and he stopped and turned. From behind her, the brute let out a low whistle.

Just then, a soldier on horseback stepped through the mist. He called to the king in the Shadow tongue. The king straightened and looked at his brute.

News.

He growled something unintelligible back to the messenger, who only gave a nod. Then he looked at her with eyes of night under his horned helm and shifted.

News that bothered him.

The king snapped an order to a soldier, who brought him a leather cord. He stepped forward and caught her wrists, clenching them tightly and tying her hands. Then he jerked her from the commander and pushed her toward the army. She didn't fight. There was no chance for her now, but seeing the brute commander limp back to another horse brought her a wave of satisfaction.

The king pushed her in front of him as they walked. His presence behind her made her skin crawl, but she focused her eyes ahead and kept walking. She stumbled over a sliver of a spear protruding from the frozen ground but caught herself—she'd almost forgotten the field of death they were walking across. She kept her eyes on the ground to watch her step. Just then, she spotted a sheath belt, half-covered in frozen mud, with what appeared to be a knife inside it. Or maybe it wasn't a knife at all. But if it was...

She faked another stumble and dropped to her knee over it, quickly grabbing at the hilt. Her heart leapt. It was a knife—a rusted knife, but a knife nonetheless. The king grabbed her arm and pulled her back to her feet, and she tucked the blade up her jacket sleeve the best she could manage with her hands tied.

A soldier brought a horse, a smaller palfrey—no doubt a less energetic mount, and the king dragged her toward it. She struggled against him. "I can manage myself," she hissed.

He shoved her forward. "Get on."

She grabbed the pommel, careful to keep her knife hidden in her sleeve, and mounted the palfrey. The binding cut into her wrists, but she gritted through it. She glared back at the king as he mounted his destrier beside her.

Wait. Was that it? Were they leaving?

"What about the mountains?"

"Change of plans," he said shortly. "The Bear comes for you."

She swallowed. Did he mean *Alexander*? Had he confused him with his father?

"He brings your entire army. Just as I expected."

"Well, if it's a change of plans, it's not *exactly* as you expected," she cut back.

His eyes burned into her. "Your army will meet their fate all the same. And you can watch, before you join them."

He was trying to scare her. It was working.

Taking one last look at the stronghold, he gave a frustrated snarl and led them away.

She shifted uncomfortably as they rode. She knew he wanted the stronghold of Bahoul. What had been the news? What had changed? He had expected her army, and they were coming. What was different?

"Where are we going?" she asked.

The king ignored her, and hot anger flushed her cheeks.

They rode all day, until the darkness of night came. She had managed to slide her stolen knife undetected into the empty sheath in her boot. At least now she had a weapon.

The ache in her shoulder crept up her neck and made her head throb. The fight, the fear, the struggle—it had drained her. When they finally stopped, she thought she might fall from her horse in exhaustion.

The king dismounted. "We'll camp here."

The army started their work, tethering their horses and erecting their tents. The king grasped her arm, pulling her from her horse and dragging her through the tasked soldiers.

"Let me go!" She struggled against him. "I can walk myself."

He gripped her arm tightly as a warning but finally released her and kept walking. She followed. She struggled to keep up. The army had no fires burning, and she wasn't used to maneuvering through the darkness.

"Where are we going?" she asked him again, and again he didn't answer. Anger flashed through her. "If you think you can best my army, you're mistaken. They've beaten you back before, and they'll do it again."

He whirled around and grabbed her, pulling her close. "They had Aleon." There was a deep irritation in his voice. "But now they come with nothing. And your men are archers and peace wishers. My army is skilled in true battle, and we do it often. The Northmen march to their end."

He released her and kept walking.

He was right. Phillip wouldn't yet know of her capture to send forces to join them, and without Aleon, they weren't strong enough to defeat the Shadow army. This nightmare was only just beginning.

They came to a large tent in the darkness. He pushed her inside and stepped in after her. It was dimly lit by a small candle. Dread rippled under her skin with him so close.

He reached to pull off his helm, and she looked away, afraid to see what it would reveal, but she couldn't help herself, and her eyes found their way back to him. A wave of surprise hit her. He was younger than she'd thought, aged by battle, but perhaps only a few years older than she was. His shoulder-length hair was tied back and was black as his cloak. The bruises and scrapes from her fight during her capture were bold on his face. *Good*—he deserved it. An old scar ran from his brow to his cheek. Apparently, she wasn't the only one who disliked him.

But this wasn't the man she'd thought he was. "You're not the Shadow King," she said coldly.

"You were expecting something else?" he asked. "A monster, perhaps?"

She scoffed. "Stories, meant to scare people."

He ambled toward her, the darks of his eyes almost drowning her, but she stood firm.

"You're flesh and blood," she said coldly. "Like your brute. You're men. And I'm not afraid of men."

"You should be," he said hauntingly.

Her eyes narrowed at him. "My father battled the Shadow King. You're not him. Where is he?"

His face darkened, and he shifted uneasily. She had struck something within him.

"You'll sleep here," he growled. Without another word, he ducked out of the tent and nodded to the soldier outside.

Was that it? Was that all he would tell her? She snorted in frustration and jerked the tent flap closed, but she did take a small comfort in being alone. A *small* comfort.

She blew out the candle and struggled for clearer vision in the darkness, then felt for the stolen dagger against her calf inside her boot. They still didn't know she had it. It brought a calmness to her. She wanted to run, but they would be expecting her to, and she didn't want to think about what would happen if she was caught trying to escape again. She struggled against the binding. She could cut it off, but then they would know she had the knife. No, she needed to wait.

Norah curled up on the bedroll. Her mind was filled with thought after thought, thoughts that sowed fear deep inside her, but she tried to push them out. She needed sleep.

She shuffled awkwardly to reach her bound hands down to her boot and curled her fingers around the knife. It wasn't Alexander's knife, but it would do. She held it as if it were his hand. And finally, sleep came.

Chapter Twenty-Five

The tent provided little warmth, and Norah shivered in the early morning chill. She lay long after waking, wishing for a fire. The Shadow army built no fires. She clenched her hands together; they ached with stiffness. Hearing voices outside her tent, she recognized one as the king's and quickly stumbled up from the bedroll.

He ducked into her tent but paused when their eyes met. "We leave now," he said.

She stood and eyed him coldly. She knew she'd dealt him a painful injury with the dagger, but it didn't show. He stepped closer to her, but she stood her ground. He reached out and grabbed her wrists, inspecting the binding.

She twisted away. "As you left me," she said sharply.

He towered over her, but she narrowed her eyes and faced him squarely. His face hardened, and he turned, leaving her alone once again.

Norah paused but then followed him out to find the palfrey from the day before saddled for her. She mounted as gracefully as one could manage with bound hands. The king mounted his destrier and reined up beside her. He held out a wrap of salted meat. She only shot him a daggered gaze in response.

"Eat," he said irritably.

She didn't want to accept food from him, but she was incredibly hungry. She needed to keep her strength, she told herself. Reluctantly, she took the meat.

He eyed her with a bitter smile. "Tell me, why come out now? Why come out freely after hiding for so long, where it was so easy for me to take you?"

Norah refused to answer him. She looked out across the hills as she bit the inside of her cheek, silently cursing. She'd been foolish for thinking the journey to Aleon would be an easy one, even if it was through Mercian lands. She'd been foolish for leaving the safety of the castle when the Shadow King wanted her dead, and for thinking he hadn't yet known of her return. Now he had her.

They rode most of the day in silence. The sun was out, but it did little to provide warmth from the winter air.

The king's voice pulled her from her thoughts.

"Who taught you to fight?" he asked.

She looked at him, her eyes narrowing. "Do you have some tips for me?"

He seemed surprised but surprised her back when he moved his horse closer to answer. "You let me get too close to you," he told her. "Your advantage is speed. You need to protect it with distance."

She scoffed. "Since you're free with your advice right now, how might I get this distance?"

"You won't," he said darkly. "You won't escape me, North Queen."

"Who are you?" she asked.

"You don't believe I'm salar of Kharav?"

Salar of Kharav? "I don't believe you fought my father in the Battle of Bahoul."

"I did not. Kings die. You should know this."

Norah paused as the realization hit her. "You're his son?"

He looked forward, ignoring her question. "Where have you been all these years?"

In turn, she didn't answer.

"Why did you wait so long to wed the Aleon king?" he asked.

"I wasn't sure if I liked him," she said flippantly. "Where did your brute commander come from?"

He shifted in agitation.

"Are you the Shadow King's son?" she asked again, not willing to give him information without receiving any in return.

"I am the Shadow King," he snapped.

There was a long silence between them. Finally, he spoke. "I am Mikael Ratha Shal, salar of Kharav, or the Shadowlands, as you call it."

"Salar?"

"Yes. *King*. I'm the son of Rhalstad Ratha Shal, who's the man your father fought in the Battle of Bahoul. Now, tell me where you've been."

It was no longer a question.

"My lord justice taught me to fight," she said, not willing to answer any of his other questions.

He didn't press her for more, which was good, because he wouldn't get more.

In her tent that evening, Norah's mind raced with the events of the day. If Alexander came for her, he'd be walking into a trap. She had to get away before they took her farther.

She strained to hear any sounds around her, but it was eerily quiet. How was an army of that size so quiet? She reached down and slid her dagger from her calf strap and worked quickly to cut off the binding from around her wrists. Except, the blade was rusted and dull, and her movements weren't *that* quick. Finally, with her hands free, she reached out to touch the back of the tent. *Cloth*. She worked patiently, cutting upward. She'd give anything to have Alexander's knife again. She could chew an opening faster, she mused.

Once an opening was big enough to look through, she peered out to check for guards. She'd hoped there would be no soldiers behind the tent, and she breathed a sigh of relief to find none. Norah continued cutting, creating an opening large enough to fit through. She pushed the fearful sickness down as she gathered her courage. Once again looking out, she snuck through the opening and crept away, crouching close to the ground and not daring to breathe. There was nothing to hide her, and she cursed her light-colored clothing as she hurried through the darkness.

Norah made out the shape of a large tree in front of her, and she sidled up behind it to catch her breath, her hands shaking. Where was she? She needed to head north, back to Bahoul where her Northmen were, back to safety.

She darted from her brief cover to continue on, but a hand snaked out in the darkness and grabbed her from behind. She stifled a scream and sliced at her captor with her dagger. The blade hit something, but she wasn't sure what—his arm, his side? Had she gotten him at all? Maybe it had only grazed his leathers. She lashed out again, but he gripped her tight, thwarting her attack. Struggling desperately, she dropped her head to the hand on her shoulder and sank her teeth into the flesh, but he didn't release her. She tried to catch him with a butt back from her head, but he was a large man, and she hit only his chest. He clutched her tighter.

With her free left arm, she clawed back, reaching for his eyes. He twisted his head, and she caught only the flesh of his cheek and his lip through the wrap on his face. Norah ripped her arm upward and caught him on the brow with the heel of her palm. It sent a jolt of pain to the core of her bone, but it would be worse for him.

A blow to her stomach knocked the wind from her, and he pulled her close from behind. The warmth of blood dripped from his face and onto her shoulder as he wrestled her hands down. He squeezed her so tightly she could hardly breathe, and bile rose in her throat. *The brute.* She wrenched her body against him, only incenting his arms tighter. She feared her ribs might crack. Unable to breathe and with her energy depleted, she stopped struggling, and he pulled her back toward the tent.

"Let go of me!" she snapped at him.

When they reached the tent, the king was waiting for her. Norah tried to sheath the dagger in the sleeve of her jacket. She hoped the brute hadn't noticed it since she wasn't entirely sure whether she'd actually cut him in the darkness. Her wrist throbbed, and she prayed she hadn't broken it.

The commander released her in front of the king and called out in the Shadow tongue. She looked back at him in irritation, cursing him under her breath. The king stepped forward, grabbing her arm, and pulled the dagger from her sleeve. Not letting her go, he dragged her into his tent.

"You have more weapons?" he growled.

"No," she said stiffly. Like she'd have told him...

"Show me."

"I don't have anything else," she insisted.

"Undress," he commanded.

The audacity. The heat of anger rushed to her cheeks. "I will not!"

He grabbed her hand and pulled her to him. It was her injured wrist, and a pain shot through her. She tried to jerk away, but his grip was tight, and she cried out. He snaked a hand around her waist, feeling for another dagger. She twisted, throwing the elbow of her free arm up and catching him in the cheekbone. The strike hit hard, and he stumbled slightly. She used the momentum and twisted again, driving her shoulder into him, and they fell onto the bedroll.

Norah tried to roll away, but he still had hold of her wrist and jerked her back, scooping her underneath him. Using his body weight, he held her down. She fought to keep her arms at her chest as he tried to pull them above her head. She struggled with all the strength she had, but she couldn't move. In a final effort, she cracked her head forward, butting his face. It briefly stunned him, and his body weight crushed the breath from her.

Recovering, he forced her arms above her head and crossed them, scooping a fistful of her hair and completely immobilizing her. Repositioning his weight, he straddled her, holding himself above her and allowing her to breathe again.

"Stop making this harder!" he snapped.

"You mean stop fighting you?" she hissed. "Does it make you feel strong? Is this what you meant when you told me I should fear men?"

"You should fear a king!"

"Kings die," she seethed, quoting him.

His face sobered. A gash spanned across the bridge of his nose where she'd hit him, and blood ran down his face. His lip was split, and she couldn't remember if it was an old wound from their previous tussle or a new one. He ignored both. Slowly, he moved his free hand down her stomach, feeling around her waist. She tensed but couldn't move.

She struggled again as he unbuttoned her jacket, but he continued to hold her. Her breath quickened as he ran his hands up her hips and sides. She looked away, shaking with rage, and waited. He used the back of his hand to touch her, a move that felt strangely considerate, but it only fueled her frustration.

Moving down, he ran his hand over her outer thighs and pulled her knee up to reach around her calves through her boots. He finished but didn't let her go. They lay in silence, the king above her. The dark pools of his eyes didn't hold the bitter hostility they once had. While he certainly wasn't gentle, he wasn't trying to hurt her, and despite his hold, her anger started to dissipate.

The king released her, standing up and straightening his clothing. He wiped the blood from the bridge of his nose and flicked his tongue over his lip.

She sprang to her feet, her heart pounding as he watched her. He swallowed and shifted. Her fury dampened slightly as she tried to make sense of him. He seemed at war in his mind, but then he pulled another leather cord from his packs and approached her again.

"Must I do this forcefully as well?" he asked.

She stewed in her anger but held out her hands to be bound. The skin was raw, and she grimaced as he pulled the cord tight around her wrists. His eyes locked with hers as he finished—they were almost apologetic, but only for a moment.

He called for another bedroll, and her stomach turned at the realization she'd be sleeping in the same tent as him. A bedroll was brought quickly, and she eyed it irritably before settling onto it.

Norah turned her back to the Shadow King and tried to imagine herself alone. She didn't hear him behind her, and it made her uneasy, but she didn't dare look back at him. Tears threatened. She bit her lip sharply, forcing an even breath. She couldn't allow herself to cry.

Despite the circumstance, and the binding, she did sleep. In her dreams, she saw Caspian's face. She saw her men falling, one after another, and all she could do was watch.

Chapter Twenty-Six

Norah woke to an empty tent. The king was gone. She combed her fingers through her hair, re-braiding the locks and tucking wayward strands behind her ear as best as her bound hands could manage. What had they done with her things when they captured her? She found a basin of water, which she hoped was fresh, and washed her face and hands. Then she stepped outside. The sun hadn't yet come up, but light seeped over the hills. Crisp air chilled the dampness that remained on her skin. She shivered.

The massive Shadow army had started assembling, but there was no sign of the king. She turned and, almost colliding with a soldier, jumped. It wasn't a soldier, she quickly realized, but the king's brute. She couldn't see his face with the wrap on his head, only his eyes, which were like the king's—dark pools of night. There was something unnatural about him, and she swallowed back her fear. He wasn't really a demon, she told herself. She had hurt him.

He held a horse for her, remaining silent.

"Where's the king?" she asked, taking the reins and being careful not to touch his hand.

He didn't respond as he turned and mounted his own horse.

"I know you can speak," she muttered, and settled onto her own mount.

"Don't try to escape," he warned.

"I'll take your request into consideration."

The brute looked back over his shoulder, his impatience with her obvious. "Don't try to escape, or I'll walk you naked behind me with a rope around your neck like a dog."

Norah swallowed back her horror at the thought. She suspected he was just trying to frighten her, but she decided it was better not to test him. She'd made a spectacle of him the day prior, and he seemed like he would enjoy humiliating her if he could.

"Well, lead on," she mumbled.

They headed west, breaking away and leaving the army behind. Frost covered the ground, and the wind stung her cheeks. They'd hit snow before the day's end. She wished she had her belongings—the thicker gloves, the warmer clothing.

They rode in silence. She resisted the urge to ask questions. She knew he wouldn't answer. The army fell farther behind them as they rode. She wanted to turn back. It wasn't that she wanted to be back with the army but rather that she didn't want to be alone with the brute.

Time passed, and she grew more uneasy. Where were they going? Where was the king? Was the commander planning to kill her? Why else would they have left the army? Why else would they be alone?

The smell of smoke interrupted her thoughts. As they reached the top of the hill, she gasped at the sight. A small walled city lay in ruin before them. They drew closer, and the magnitude of destruction hit her.

Impaled heads lined the front gates, a grotesque message for anyone who passed. Her stomach turned, and she looked away, but there was nowhere to look that didn't show the horrors that had happened. Charred bodies littered the ground, and buildings smoldered. Her horse snorted nervously. A child's shoe lay in the mud, and Norah's breath quivered. What had happened here?

The king met them at the collapsing town center, waiting atop his horse of night, and she looked at him in horror.

"How could you…" Norah couldn't finish.

"This isn't my hand," he said.

"Then who?"

"That's a question for you, North Queen."

Confusion needled her. "What?"

"These are lands protected by Mercia, and this isn't a normal attack."

Norah swallowed back the bile in her throat. "That doesn't mean this was an attack against Mercia."

"Perhaps not." He paused. "Or perhaps it does."

Norah looked at the city, overwhelmed by the death around her—the death of all these innocent people. Anger rose inside her.

"Do you really not know who might have done this?" he asked.

"Mercia has only one enemy," she said bitterly. And she was staring right at him.

"No one has just one enemy." His eyes, dark and strangling, locked with hers. "And there are men worse than I, North Queen. You'll do well to remember that."

Who could be worse than the Shadow King? The thought struck Norah hard, and she swallowed the sickness rising in her throat.

He turned to the two soldiers that accompanied him. "We're done here."

Her brow furrowed. "That's it? We're going back?"

The king urged his mount forward. "Would you rather stay here?" he called over his shoulder.

She would rather not have come here at all. Norah bit her trembling lip. She couldn't bear it anymore; she was sick in her mind and her heart. But what could she do? Nothing. She could do nothing but follow behind.

The ride returning to the army was as silent as it had been with the brute. Norah tried to push the images from the village out of her mind. How could someone cause such devastation? And why?

The winter days were short, and darkness set in on them early. Norah trusted her horse to follow when she lost sight of the king in front of her. She nodded off as they rode, wishing she were back in the tent, warm in her bedroll.

Suddenly, she woke to being pulled off her horse. A hand covered her mouth before she could scream.

"Quiet," the Shadow King whispered in her ear.

Norah struggled against him.

"Quiet!" he hissed.

Her heart pounded, coursing alarm through her veins.

He pulled her through the darkness to a cover of brush, and they peered through to see a group of men sitting round a fire. There were eight, maybe nine—more than the number of soldiers with the king. They spoke in a language she didn't recognize.

"Drifters," he said quietly.

Norah's stomach turned, remembering her encounter in the Wild.

"Stay here, and stay down," he whispered, then disappeared.

Norah crouched low, listening and trying not to breathe. She struggled against the binding around her wrists, wishing for her dagger again, as she watched the men around the campfire.

Suddenly, one man straightened and looked out into the darkness, opposite her direction. He called to the others, who quieted and drew their swords. They left their fire to investigate, and Norah strained to see them as they disappeared into the night.

The darkness was quiet around her. Where had the horses gone? Where was the Shadow King and his brute? Where were the drifters now? Her heart beat in her throat. She was alone. She crouched lower.

Suddenly, the sound of a fight rang out. Weapons sang together in the night. She couldn't see them, but she could hear them from a distance away.

Her heart skipped. She was alone...

Was this the moment? Could she escape?

Before she could talk herself out of it, she turned and stumbled down the hill behind her. The binding around her hands made it difficult to run. Bushes tore at her clothing. A thin branch from an unseen tree caught her in the face and cut into her cheek, but she didn't slow. She didn't stop. Her legs burned, and her lungs felt like they were going to explode. She tripped on something and fell to the ground, stifling a cry as a jolt of pain ran up her arm, but she gritted her teeth and pulled herself back up. She had to keep going.

Norah knew she needed distance, and she fled farther into the night. She came upon a steep bank and thought she might not reach the top, but she pushed herself up and stumbled down the other side. Through the trees, then through the open, she ran. At some point, she stumbled through a stream, breaking the thin layer of ice on top and soaking the bottom of her riding dress. Still, she ran. When she couldn't go any farther, she let her legs slow. They shook with fatigue, and she steadied herself against a tree. Her breath echoed through the darkness, and she tried to calm it so she could listen.

Quiet. There was quiet all around her. Her wrists were raw. She needed to get the binding off. The moon provided little light, just enough to show the trees around her.

Which way?

Norah took a deep breath and decided to keep in the direction she was headed, but a shadow loomed in front of her and grabbed her. She screamed, and a sharp blow caught her across the face. She fell backward onto the hardness of the cold ground, knocking the wind from her lungs. A cackle escaped from another man to her right. He called something to her attacker she didn't understand. She struggled for a breath, but the man was suddenly on top of her, pinning her down. He yelled at her with a clipped accent, and there was no wrap around his face. These weren't Shadowmen.

He forced her bound arms above her head and held them there. The rope ate into her wrists as she desperately fought to pull them free. She screamed, but another blow to her face stunned her.

More men called out, encouraging him on. Another set of hands grabbed her, helping her captor hold her. She fought harder. The man on top of her pulled at her breeches underneath her riding dress, but he couldn't get them loose.

"No!" she screamed, struggling against them. The cold blade of a knife cut up the leg of her breeches under her riding dress.

Norah bucked frantically, panic setting in. The man on top of her forced his hips between her legs and reached down to release himself. The curve of his shoulder hit her chin and she bit into it. Hard. He grunted and delivered another blow to her face.

This couldn't be happening. She kicked, but she was no match for him. He gripped her thigh to hold her.

Just then, another shadow swept over her, and a fountain of warmth sprayed across her face. *Blood.* Her attacker's weight came off her, and his hands released her. She was free. She scrambled backward, but her arms were still bound.

The sound of steel meeting flesh hissed through the night, and the silhouettes of bodies dropped to the ground as they were cut down. She stood shakily. Her legs didn't feel like they could carry her. She pushed herself away from the sound of death, stumbling through the trees. She stifled her cries, her fear helping her focus on one thing: escaping.

But hands grabbed her again, and she screamed.

"Let me go!" she cried, trying to wrench away.

"Stop," a voice rumbled.

But she wouldn't. She couldn't. She needed to be free.

"North Queen," he said, holding her as she lashed out at him with her bound fists. She couldn't help the sobs as desperation closed in around her. He pulled her close, holding her tightly—not the hold of capture.

"North Queen," he said again.

The Shadow King.

Her fight weakened as the realization came, and a wave of relief washed over her, but still, she couldn't hold her emotion.

"Calm yourself," he said quietly.

A blade slipped between her wrists, cutting loose the binding, and he peeled it away. It was sticky with her blood, and stung as he pulled it from her skin. She stood shaking as he knelt and cut her tattered breeches from her leg. The warmth of his cloak came around her, and she didn't fight as he scooped her up in his arms.

The sound of horses drew near, but he didn't put her down. Surprisingly, he swung up on his destrier while holding her. She was relieved; she didn't think she could stand.

They rode slowly. She tried to fight the helplessness that wrecked her, but she couldn't. There was no fight left in her. His arms tightened around her as he carried her, and she turned her face into his chest as the tears came.

Chapter Twenty-Seven

Norah and the king reached the Shadow army camp and arrived at his tent. He slipped off his horse and set her down. She was a little unsteady on her feet, but she caught herself. Feeling the chill against her bare legs, she drew the cloak tighter around herself and ducked inside.

A few moments later, the king entered. Without his helm and armor, he didn't seem like such a monster now. He put a clean cloth and small washbasin by her bedroll. "I'll be outside," he told her.

He turned to go, then stopped. He pulled his shirt over his head and draped it by the basin. "You can wear this until we find you something else."

With that, he left her in the dim candlelight. Her hands shook as she slowly pulled off the cloak. Her jacket was dirty but still serviceable, and she peeled it off her arms. The riding dress, on the other hand, was torn up the side. She wouldn't be able to salvage it. She pulled off her chemise. It was only torn at the bottom. If a shirt and breeches could be found, she might be able to pull herself back together somewhat.

Norah trembled as she soaked the cloth in the water and scrubbed her skin. Her eyes welled, and she blinked the tears away. The feeling of helplessness, of violation, returned. A sob escaped her. She scrubbed her stomach, her legs, everywhere she had been touched. Her skin stung under the cold-water scouring. She'd never feel clean again. She put her chemise back on and pulled the king's shirt over her head. It was large on her and covered her past mid-thigh.

She reached up to re-braid her hair and felt the swelling from the blows she had received. There was still blood on her face. She needed clean water, but she couldn't bring herself to ask. She rolled her torn clothes into a ball and dropped them beside the bed. As she crawled under the blanket, her body shook uncontrollably. She reached out and pulled the cloak over her as well, rolling to her side and drawing her knees up, defeated.

After a time, the king cautiously entered the tent, eyeing the blood-tinted water and Norah, curled up and watching him from underneath his cloak. He took the basin out and returned with fresh water and another cloth. He lowered himself to the ground beside her and submersed the cloth. "Your face," he said as he wrung the water out.

Slowly, she sat up, but she couldn't look him in the eye. She reached for the cloth, but he pulled back, meaning to tend to her himself. She didn't have the will to fight him.

Norah looked away as he brought the cloth to her brow just below the temple. It was where the first strike had caught her. She flinched at the memory. He drew the cloth over her skin with unexpected gentleness, sponging away the dried blood. She tensed as he touched her chin, turning her face toward him. He surveyed her right cheek and the split on her lip, then cleaned around them as well.

"I suppose we look the same now," he said.

"Why are you being kind to me?" she snapped. She couldn't bear his pity on top of it all.

"I respect my enemies."

Anger flashed through her. "Really? Respect?" she hissed, meeting his eyes. "The North Queen—captured, humiliated, beaten..." She couldn't help the shaking in her voice.

His nostrils flared, and he looked away. Turning back to her, he said, "I take no pleasure in seeing you this way."

It surprised her that she believed him.

He dropped the cloth into the water and stood up. She watched him, still wary, but felt herself start to calm. Her eye trailed down to his thigh, where blood seeped through his breeches. Had he been wounded? She bit back the words that almost came out; she refused to show concern for this man. This was his fault. He was the cause of all of this.

Norah curled back on the bedroll, pulling the blanket and cloak over her again, and waited for sleep that wouldn't come.

Mikael was angry. More than angry. He looked over the North Queen as she lay curled on the bedroll underneath his cloak. She'd run. If she'd stayed hidden, she wouldn't have been caught and this wouldn't have happened. He'd told her to stay put. She didn't listen.

He stooped to pick up the washbasin and ducked out of the tent.

"Salar," a soldier called to him, and offered to take the basin, but Mikael shook his head.

"I'll take care of it," he replied.

He tossed the water out and walked down to the nearby stream to get more. His leg ached, but he welcomed the pain. It distracted him from the embarrassment of his failure. She was fast. Even with her hands bound, it had taken quite some time to catch up with her. He remembered how he'd heard her scream and how it had cut off suddenly. He'd raced toward the sound, his heart pounding.

Her attackers were Horsemen. He'd seen them in the darkness; he'd seen the man on top of her. Mikael remembered the rage he'd felt when he ripped the man's head back and dragged his blade across his neck. It was too kind a death.

When he'd pulled the body from her and killed the second man holding her, she'd struggled to get away. She was like a wounded animal, trying to flee, to fight, to stay alive. He and his commander killed the rest of the Horsemen, but not before one caught him in the thigh with a blade.

He shook his head, remembering her ferocity at the base of the stronghold. She was good in a fight. *Too good.* She may have actually defended herself if she hadn't been tied. Why had he tied her? He'd been angry that she'd tried to escape again, but it was something he would have done in her place.

This queen surprised him. He rolled his shoulder and winced at the stretch of the stitches under his arm where she'd stabbed him with his dagger. She was strong. Bold. Not at all what he'd imagined her to be. He almost regretted what he would do to her. He would try to make it painless.

When he returned to the tent, she lay as he'd left her, under the blanket and his cloak. Her eyes were closed, but he doubted she was asleep. His men had found a small shirt and some extra breeches from an accompanying weapons boy, and he laid them beside her.

Mikael stood over his own bedroll and pulled off his leathers, boots, and breeches. He eyed the gash in his thigh. It was deeper than he'd thought, and he grimaced as he bound it with linen strips. He hoped the blade hadn't been poisoned, but knowing the Horsemen, with their mixes and tonics, he wasn't confident. No matter. He was a large man, and strong. It wouldn't be the first time he'd taken a poison blade. It might make the next few days particularly painful, but he could manage pain.

Blowing out the candle, he settled onto the mat, looking up into the darkness. It took a long time for the tiredness to set in as he replayed the events over and over in his mind. When sleep did come, it came lightly, and he found himself drifting awake again. In the quiet of the night, he listened to the sound of her breathing. Her breaths were clipped and irregular—silent cries. His chest tightened. It stung him more than the Horseman's blade.

Chapter Twenty-Eight

Mikael rose before dawn. He quietly gathered his leathers and boots. The queen was still asleep and wearing his shirt; he'd have to get another.

His body moved stiffly. The wound to his thigh made it difficult to walk, but as he stepped out into the morning, the cold air seemed to bring back his strength. Fresh clothing was waiting for him outside, and he pulled it on.

One of his captains approached and looked at him with a raised brow. Mikael supposed it did seem odd that he'd be dressing outside his tent.

"Salar," the captain greeted.

"Katya," he replied as he pulled on his boots. "What did you find out about the city?"

Katya shook her head. "We've found nothing."

Mikael paused. "Nothing?"

"No, Salar."

The king shook his head. "That was a walled city with armored, fighting men. It would have taken an army to destroy it."

"Well, it's as though they've disappeared," she told him.

"The same is said of us. Find them. And what of the drifters we caught last night?" They'd had some spoils. Obviously, they looted the city after it had been destroyed. "Find out if they saw anything."

Katya shook her head. "They're all dead, Salar."

Mikael's brow furrowed. His men had brought four of them back to the camp alive. "What?"

She motioned to the bodies nearby. "It appears one killed the others, then himself."

"Why?"

She shook her head again. "Maybe they feared the death you might choose for them. Or maybe they knew something they didn't want us to find out."

"Now what could that be?" Mikael asked under his breath. He'd have to think on it later.

"Are you well, Salar?" the captain asked, a slight concern across her brow.

"I'm well enough," he said. "Have two horses readied."

"What should we do with the bodies?"

Mikael glanced back at the drifters. "Leave them for the birds."

Katya gave a nod. "Yes, Salar."

"North Queen."

Norah woke to the king calling her, and she turned to see him standing by the front flap of the tent. She sat up, briefly confused, but then the memory of the night before came back to her. His cloak still lay over top of her, and she clutched it in her fists.

"I want to show you something. Get dressed. Come with me." He ducked out, giving her privacy.

She was still in his shirt, but she spied the fresh clothing by the bedroll and rose quickly to pull it on, along with her jacket and boots. Her mind swirled with the events of the night before and the king's strange kindness. Then she pushed it away. She wasn't sure what had happened, but nothing had changed. She was still a prisoner, and her army was marching to wage a war she knew they couldn't win.

Norah emerged from the tent. While she'd salvaged her jacket, she still shivered in the morning chill. She was surprised to see the king standing with two horses saddled.

"Where are we going?" she asked.

He didn't answer, and she felt a flash of annoyance. Could no one answer a question?

He held out a cloak for her. Her irritation faded, but only slightly. She slipped the cloak around her shoulders, thankful for its warmth. Her horse pawed the frozen ground as she mounted, sensing its rider's anxiousness.

Norah paused when she saw the bodies of the drifters. She knew they were dead, but she felt a pang of fear twist through her as she thought back to the night before.

Beside her, the king mounted his destrier.

"Are they the men who..." she couldn't finish.

"No. Your attackers were Horsemen. These are some of the drifters from around the fire we saw on our way back from the village."

Horsemen? Were they close to the Tribelands? That would put them well south of Mercia.

She looked back at the drifters. Their skin was a waxy blue, and the eyes of one man were still open. Norah swallowed back her nausea. There was a strange marking centered on one's forehead. It was dark. Dried blood, perhaps. She pulled her gaze away and turned back to the king, who was waiting.

"Are we leaving the army again?" she asked. That couldn't be good.

"We'll catch up to them."

He urged his horse forward, and she followed. They parted from the army and rode up a hill to a wooded area. The bitter wind brought tears to her eyes and froze them on her cheeks. She urged her horse to keep up with the king's destrier as they rode through the trees. Bramble crept out onto the trail, but she could tell it once had been a well-worn path. An uneasiness sat in her stomach as she wondered where he was taking her. She didn't think she could handle the sight of another destroyed city.

She watched him as they rode. He wore his armor but not his helm. Without it, he seemed less of a monster. The events of the night prior confused her. Apparently, she was a responsibility of his, but why had he tried to comfort her? Why did he care? She didn't understand, but she couldn't mistake his brief kindness for the safety of trusting him. He wanted the North. He wanted her dead.

Her mind turned to Mercia. She envied who she'd been a week ago, before she knew the horrors of this war, before she knew her helplessness. The lingering winter was the least of her concerns now. She knew Alexander would bring the whole of the Mercian army for her, and if they were decimated, there would be nothing left to protect Mercia. The Shadow King would destroy them all. She needed to escape and get her army back to Mercia to protect her people.

They came to the edge of the wood, and rolling hills opened in front of them. She saw an abandoned country manor in the distance and sighed in relief. There were no torches or impaled heads—that was a good sign.

The king reined up for a moment. He looked down at the house and then scouted the tree line. She watched him, noticing something was off. He was pale. Sweat beaded on his brow despite the cold. She opened her mouth to say something, but the mountains in the far distance to the north caught her eye. *Bahoul.* Her pulse quickened. Alone with the king, she felt her freedom close.

The king scanned the land with a careful eye. Seemingly satisfied that there was no immediate threat, he spurred his destrier forward, and she followed behind. As they got closer, she looked over the manor. It was close to collapsing.

The king slowed his horse, taking in the scene around him. "I haven't been here for a long time," he said.

"What is this place?" she asked.

He didn't answer, and she pursed her lips in frustration.

He looked around a little longer. "His name is Soren," he said finally.

Norah's brows drew together. "Who?"

"My lord commander. My *brute*, as you say. You asked where he came from. This was his family's home. My father charged him with this land. It stretches over the mountains to the north."

"To Bahoul? The mountains that Mercia holds?"

"The mountains you stole from us," he said with an edge of anger in his voice.

"After you attacked us," she threw back defensively.

"Because you'll take my throne."

"I don't want your throne!"

He stilled, and quieted.

Norah looked back over the failing manor. A calm returned. "What happened to them—his family?" she asked.

"Murdered. By the North." His words were like steel, and they cut her.

She swallowed the sickness in her mouth. She couldn't bring herself to ask how, but she didn't have to.

He took an unusually strained breath and continued. "We had set a camp here for our wounded. When my father's armies retreated back to Kharav, the North followed but not just to the border. They flanked them all the way back to the mountains and beyond, destroying villages, farms... farmers."

Norah bit her chapped lips, watching him.

He continued. "We were here, and they came upon us. They murdered everyone: Soren's mother, his brother, his sister. Everyone."

Norah forced herself to breathe.

"We fought," the king said, "but it wasn't enough. My father fell. I was injured. Severely." His eyes glazed as he stared at the manor. He straightened, and his voice came only slightly stronger. "Soren's father had been captain of the Crest, a great warrior, before he became lord of Bahoul. He told Soren to get me back to Kharav, to protect me. And then he took his sword and ran to hold off the Northmen while we fled. That's the last we saw of him."

Norah couldn't speak. She'd only heard of the triumphs of the Great War, not the tragedies.

"We traveled for days, until we came to Aviron, a small kingdom along the borderlands. We thought they would help us, but they knew who I was the moment they saw me. They captured me, they..." His voice trailed off. "Soren found a way to free us, and we fled again. We finally reached the canyons and were able to make it to Kharav. He was going to return to his home, but I told him, 'There's nothing left for you anymore. We're brothers now, and you'll stay with me.'"

Norah looked back over the farm in horror, swallowing the emotion in her throat. "That's why he hates me so much," she said softly.

The Shadow King gave a weak snort. "And you killed his horse," he added.

"*He* killed his horse," she corrected.

"Letting you escape wasn't an option," he snapped back defensively, then paused. "There's nothing he wouldn't sacrifice for me, for my cause." His voice came softer. "Even that which he holds most dear."

Norah wasn't sure she believed the brute capable of holding something dear. She looked back at the falling manor. She didn't want to believe her father would cause such devastation either.

The king gave a thick cough, and she glanced back at him. He was looking down at his hand. His lips were tinged with blood. He swayed in his saddle and started to slump forward.

"Are you all right?" she called to him.

He didn't respond.

She urged her horse beside him, warily leaning closer. "King Mikael, are you all right?"

Something was wrong. His breaths came short and shallow, and his movement was lethargic.

"Are you unwell?" she asked.

"I'm well enough," he struggled. "We should get back." He shifted his weight to rein his horse around but started to fall.

She reached out and caught him, gripping him tightly. "What's happening?"

He blinked and grabbed her arm. "I'm fine, just help me to my horse."

"You're on your horse! What's wrong with you?"

His senses seemed to return somewhat. "The blade," he said. "It's the poison."

She shook her head as confusion hit her. "The blade? What blade?" Then she remembered the night before. "Are you talking about the wound on your leg? Were you stabbed? That was yesterday! By now..." Her words fell. By now, it would have spread through his body.

She stopped. She had a horse. Her eyes found the mountains in the distance, and they called to her. The mountains where she'd find her Northmen. They could take her back to Mercia. *Back to Alexander.*

She turned back to the king. Surely his commander didn't know they were here. She looked back at the mountains. Even if she wanted to save him, it was unlikely. She couldn't stop poison.

He wavered, and she gripped him tighter to keep him upright, struggling as the horses moved.

"Hammel's hell," she cursed, deciding. She really hated herself right now.

Norah urged her mount closer and awkwardly climbed onto the king's destrier behind him. She put her arms around him and reined the horse back toward the tree line.

"If you fall off, there's no way I'll get you back on," she told him. "I'll leave you here!"

He gave a weak snort.

Where were the soldiers when she needed them?

Norah urged the destrier forward. She cursed again as anger welled inside her—anger at herself, at the situation, at the king. "How did you even get stabbed with all this armor?" she snapped. "And why didn't you get help earlier? Are all men so daft?"

Her flurry of scolding fell on unconscious ears, and she clenched her teeth in frustration. She eyed the tree line for the path to return, but it seemed to have disappeared. Norah struggled with the weight of the king as she swept the base of the trees. Her search yielded nothing. She pulled the horse up, feeling she had gone too far, then turned the destrier around. The king's weight shifted to her left, and she clung to him to keep him from falling. She cursed again under her breath, with fear that she might not be able to get him back seeding inside her. Just then, she spotted the path between two oversize trees, and she breathed words of thanks to whichever gods were listening.

The ride from the army to the manor hadn't seemed far, but the way back along the path felt like a year. Her arms burned as she struggled to keep the king upright. She breathed a sigh of relief when they broke through the trees, and she saw the army marching in the distance.

"Soren!" she cried at the top of her lungs.

Movement rippled through the ranks as they looked to see what was happening.

"Soren!" she cried out again.

A large man mounted on a horse broke away from the army, galloping toward them, and she knew it was him. When he reached them, he reined up beside her, his horse rearing and exciting the king's destrier, almost making her lose her grip on the Shadow King.

"What happened?" the commander thundered.

"He said something about a poison."

The commander barked out an order to the men who were running toward them, and others broke from the ranks as well. Despite the cover on his face, she could see the alarm in his eyes. He snarled out another blast of commands and then spurred his horse away.

Soldiers surrounded the king's mount, and Norah slid off as they pulled him down and carried him to a tent being erected close by. They looked at her warily but left her alone, and she followed them inside as they laid the king down on the bedroll. She watched as they stripped him of his armor, feeling lost to help. Did they have the means to save him?

"Where's your healer?" she asked.

As if on cue, another man ducked inside with a small pack. He flung a sharp gaze at her as she edged closer to see better, but quickly turned his attention back to the Shadow King. Blood soaked the king's breeches, and the man used a dagger to cut the fabric. Then he peeled the dripping bandages from around the king's leg to inspect the wound.

Norah swallowed nervously. By now, it should have scabbed over. It hadn't. "It's not clotting," she mumbled, and looked at the soldier. "Is it because of the poison?"

He gave her a sharp glance but didn't answer.

"Do you people not speak?" She wiped the hair from her face with her forearm in frustration.

The soldier pulled a needle from his pack and threaded a thin strand through it. Horsehair, perhaps? She didn't bother asking. He set to work on the wound, pouring a cleansing mixture over it and then bringing the skin together, carefully closing the flesh. Blood seeped out while he worked. When he finished, he pulled out strips of bandages and wrapped them tightly around the king's thigh. It was too tight, she thought, but she stayed quiet. He pinned it closed.

"What now?" she asked as he covered the king with a blanket.

The soldier eyed her darkly. He didn't answer.

"We wait," a feminine voice said.

Norah looked up with a start and saw a woman standing in the corner of the tent. She hadn't noticed her there before.

The woman clipped out commands in the Shadow tongue, and the other men ducked out of the tent until only she remained with Norah and the king.

Norah watched her, fascinated. Not only was this woman a soldier, but clearly, she held a position of power. She wore a wrap over her head and face, like the men, showing only her eyes. What revealed her sex, aside from her smaller frame, was her breastplate, which was sculpted of a woman's body, in every detail. Its brazenness almost made Norah flush.

She caught Norah's gaze on her armor, and the woman's dark eyes hinted at a sinister smile. "Do you like it?" she asked, her voice provocative and taunting.

Norah knew the woman was enjoying her discomfort, and a flash of irritation rose in her cheeks. "Does the Shadow King make all women wear such things?" she asked shortly.

The woman raised a brow. "Make us?" She laughed. "I designed it," she sneered. "We want our enemies to know who they fight in battle. We want them to know our women can gut them."

Norah swallowed back a patronizing reply. The woman's statement was a powerful one, and it struck her deep within. Her irritation faded. Mercia could learn a thing or two from these people. "Fair," she mumbled.

The woman shifted, clearly surprised at how the conversation had turned.

Norah drew her gaze around the tent, unsure of what to do. Then she looked down at her hands, which were stained with the king's blood. She wrung them together.

The woman called out again in the Shadow tongue, and within a few moments, a soldier entered with a basin of fresh water.

Norah glanced at her, appreciating the small kindness. She wasn't sure how to respond in these situations, still being held against her will and with war on the horizon, and she bit back the thanks on her tongue. She submerged her hands into the basin, and the water turned pink as she washed the blood from her skin. "What's your name?" she asked.

The woman's eyes narrowed, and Norah bit the inside of her cheek, feeling foolish. Of course, she wouldn't answer.

"Katya," the woman replied, surprising her. "Captain Katya Sator."

Norah's eyes widened. *Captain.* She pursed back her smile, trying to keep it to herself. Yes, there was much Mercia could learn.

Her eyes moved to the king again, and worry rippled through her. Blood dripped from his left nostril.

"Oh no," she breathed as she scrambled beside him. She turned his head toward her, and a small trail of blood trickled from his ear. She looked at Katya in alarm, and the woman called out to the others.

The soldier who had stitched the wound ducked back into the tent, and Norah backed up as he checked the king by moving his head and eyeing the trail of blood.

"What does it mean?" Norah asked him, her fear growing. "What's happening?"

The soldier looked back at Katya and spoke to her in words Norah didn't understand. But the captain's eyes revealed her own dismay.

The sound of horses outside caught their attention, and suddenly, the brute commander pushed through the front of the tent, leading a man behind him: a Horseman. It had been Horsemen who had attacked her. Bile rose in her throat, and Norah shuddered bitterly.

The commander motioned the man closer, and Norah backed up quickly to give space. The Horseman tipped the king's head to the side and saw the blood run from his ear, then quickly searched a small pack strapped to his waist. He pulled out a vial of liquid and poured it into the king's mouth, holding his head for the antidote to run down. More blood ran from the king's nose and ear.

The Horseman looked at the commander nervously. Norah's heart beat heavy in her chest; she understood that look. The outcome was bleak.

The commander growled out orders in the Shadow tongue, and everyone cleared out, including Katya and the Horseman. He eyed Norah darkly but let her be. Then he sat on a trunk not far from the king and waited.

He pulled the wrap from his head, and she realized it was the first time she'd seen him without it. Mikael had told her they were the same age, which had been hard to believe with his face covered, but she saw it now. The sharp line of his jaw tapered squarely to his chin, and his nose fell straight and symmetrical under his dark brow. He held a similar look as the king. It was a handsome face, she loathed to admit. Everything else about him was as she had imagined, though. His thick, black hair was tied back, and the hair on his face was cut short, almost to the skin.

She spotted the marks down his cheek, from where she had caught him with her nails, and the bruising around the stitched split in his brow. She held back the smile of pride in her work.

He looked up to see her watching him. His eyes were black. Murderous.

Norah pulled her gaze away. The sun was setting, and her body ached. "What if it's too late?" she asked, putting her own hatred aside. "How long before we know if the antidote is working?"

"What do you care?" he snarled.

"I brought him back, didn't I?" she snapped.

There was a silent rage about him. He wore his hatred on his skin. Norah let out a long breath. She didn't have the energy to fight with him. She pushed herself back to a bedroll on the other side of the tent.

"You won't stay here with him," he said shortly.

"By all means, appoint me another keeper," she challenged.

Anger flashed across his face. She knew he wouldn't risk trusting another to watch her. "If you try anything—"

"Obviously," she said, cutting him off.

His nostrils flared in anger, but he didn't say anything else.

Norah lay down on her back. She needed sleep. She pulled the furs over her, trying to get comfortable, and closed her eyes.

Chapter Twenty-Nine

She woke to the cold. It was still night, but dim candlelight kept the tent from total darkness. Norah didn't stir, trying to keep the warmth trapped under the furs, but she opened her eyes to see the commander sitting beside the king. She watched him.

His hand was on the king's chest and his head hung with emotion. His brow sat heavy with worry. Despite his callousness, his pain touched her. And something more caught her attention.

He whispered to the king in the Shadow tongue as he gently pushed the hair back from his brow. He let his thumb graze the sleeping king's cheek and brush over his lips. His eyes held a longing sorrow she'd seen before—in Alexander's eyes. She didn't have to understand the words to understand the meaning. *He loved him.*

Mikael had told her the commander was like a brother. Soren had saved him during the war, brought him home. Of course they cared for each other. But this care seemed beyond the love of a brother.

Norah pinched her eyes closed tight again and steadied her breath. She saw nothing, she told herself. She wouldn't give the brute another reason to want her dead.

When she opened her eyes again, it was morning. Surprisingly, she'd slept. The tent was empty, except for the king, who was still asleep. Where was the commander?

Her mind turned to Mikael. Slowly, she pushed off the blankets and moved to his side. His breaths were deep and steady. Gently, she took his head in her hands and turned it to the side. No blood came from his ear—a good sign. His color seemed to be returning—also a good sign.

She pushed the blanket back from his leg to check the dressing. No blood had soaked through. "That's good too," she found herself whispering. What was wrong with her? She scolded herself. She should have left him; she should have escaped. But a stinging disappointment needled her—she knew if given the choice again, she'd choose the same.

Norah reached to pull the blanket back over him but paused, letting her eyes trail up the exposed skin of his side. His body was well muscled. Even in his state, he had a strength about him. She ran her fingertips over the ripple at his hip, but then caught herself and quickly pulled the blanket back over him, tucking it under his side.

She noticed a scar that ran half the length of his collarbone and then curved sharply over his chest. The price of his pact with evil, her grandmother had said, was *his heart*. She reached out and drew her fingers across it. Then she spread her hand wide, feeling the rise and fall of his breath. Under her palm, his heart beat slow and rhythmic. She smiled to herself. How funny the human mind could be, what it could imagine and what it could believe. Her eyes traveled over the inked markings across his chest and torso: bold lines in intricate patterns. She traced her fingertips over them. His skin was smooth. And warm.

A scabbed wound on the inside of his arm, just above his wrist, caught her eye. It was where she'd cut him in their fight at the base of Bahoul. She brushed over it; it was healing quickly. His hand turned upward on its own, offering more of his forearm and startling her. She drew her gaze up, and it locked with his.

His eyes pierced her, and her heart rose in her throat. How long had he been watching her? The intensity of his stare was paralyzing.

"Is there water?" he asked.

She let out a breath of relief as his words broke his hold on her, and she could pull her eyes away. She nodded and retrieved a cup by the front of the tent. Kneeling beside him, she held it to his mouth, and he drank deeply. "Careful," she told him.

He lay back when he was finished, looking up at her. "You're still here," he said weakly.

"I'm trying to remedy that," she mumbled.

He stirred, trying to get up, but Norah put her hand firmly on his chest, pushing him back down. "No. You need to rest."

The corner of his lips turned up ever so slightly, and she cursed herself. She didn't care if he needed rest. She didn't... she didn't care.

"What happened?" he asked.

"It was the poison. It almost took you."

His brow dipped as the memory came back to him. "We were at the manor."

Norah nodded.

"And you brought me back?" he asked.

"I don't really want to talk about it."

He gave a small snort. "You could have run, escaped."

Heat rushed to her cheeks. "I said I don't want to talk about it," she snapped. She was frustrated, at him, at herself.

He paused for a moment, then asked softly, "Tell me, why didn't you let me die?"

"Because I don't want you dead!" she replied angrily. "Why is everyone so intent on killing one another? All everyone talks about is war. What about peace?" She pushed out a breath as she shook her head, exasperated.

The king's brows drew together in an expression that was hard for her to read.

Just then, the commander returned. He looked at the king, surprised to see him awake. Relief flashed across his face. Then he looked at Norah, and his eyes darkened. He spoke low and in the Shadow tongue. Mikael responded, and she could feel the commander's anger. Whatever the king had told him displeased him. He cast Norah another dark look and then ducked back out of the tent.

"Get ready to travel," Mikael told her. "We can't stay here."

"Where are we going?" she asked.

"To friends."

"What friends?"

He gave a labored chuckle. "You won't like them."

Her stomach felt heavy.

Outside, Norah found the commander readying his horse. It wasn't as large as the previous destrier, but she watched him as he tightened the cinch of the saddle and then patted the beast's shoulder. He paused when he heard her approach, but he didn't turn to look at her. He was still without his head wrap, seeming even more like a man.

"I'm sure you're relieved," she said. "He's going to be all right."

He looped the horse's reins back over its neck.

"Soren," she started, "Mikael told me about your family. I didn't realize—"

He spun and caught her by the neck, almost pulling her off her feet. "He is *Salar*," he snarled, "and I am *Lord Commander*. Don't make the mistake of thinking you know me—I am not a friend. I'll use you to draw the Bear, then I'll till our fields with the burnt bodies of your armies and savor a harvest grown in Mercia's destruction. It's this alone that keeps me from choking the life from you right now."

Norah struggled for air, frightened by his sudden aggression. "I'm under the king's protection," she gasped.

He gave her a wicked smile. "He told you our story, yes? Then believe me when I say there is nothing I can do that Salar would not forgive."

He pulled her closer, bringing his lips to her ear. "*Nothing*."

Norah's eyes widened, and she struggled against him. He released her, and she sank forward, gasping for breath.

His nostrils flared, and he gave her a merciless scowl. "Good day, North Queen," he said stiffly, and left her in the cold of fear.

Norah sat on her horse, watching as the Shadowmen carefully laid their king into a makeshift haul. She knew exactly where they were going. A group of Horsemen waited as the army prepared to move. More than anything now, she needed to make her escape. But under the watchful eye of the commander, that would be impossible. Her hands weren't bound anymore, but he'd tied the lead of her horse to his saddle. As the army moved out, they fell in behind the haul, where the king's brute could keep his eye on the king and on her.

It was a long ride, and one that probably would force another change of plans, she expected. Her anxiousness grew at the thought of Alexander gaining ground on them. While meeting the Shadow army with the king down was the optimal time, she couldn't say she hoped for it.

When they arrived at the Horsemen tribe, it was larger than Norah thought it would be. Adobe houses sat in large groupings around a central town square. They brought the king to a center house of mudstone and thatch, where they laid him on a large bed. Norah was quiet, watching all the activity as he was made comfortable—blankets were rolled out, food was brought in. Weakness slowed his movements, along with weariness from the travel. But his tired eyes found her.

"Eat," he said.

"Why are we here?" she demanded. "Are these not the people who assaulted me and tried to kill you?"

"They didn't know who they were attacking. The Horsemen tribes are friends of Kharav." He paused, taking another labored breath. "And it wasn't safe to camp where we were. Abilash will keep us until I can travel. Now eat."

"I'm not hungry." It was a total lie. She was near starved.

"You'll need your strength."

Norah scowled at him. Fine. She'd eat, but she'd be angry about it. She took a loaf of bread and a small cut of meat. "Who's Abilash?"

He gave her a mischievous look. "A Horseman king. I think he'll take a liking to you." He smiled, and she could tell he was teasing her. "He's looking for a wife."

Norah gave a repulsed laugh. "I'm not to be had."

"Because you're betrothed to the Aleon king?"

His reminder of her marriage needled her. "Because I'll marry who I deem worthy," she snapped.

He shrugged. "Abilash is a king."

"Then he should find a woman who thinks that's good enough."

She saw the corners of his mouth turn up in amusement. He watched her, thoughtful. "What makes the Aleon king worthy?" he asked.

Norah didn't answer. She wasn't sure he was. What made any man worthy? His kingdom? His wealth? None of that mattered to her, especially now. Her chances of escaping lessened each day. There was fight still inside her, but she knew she would likely never make it to Aleon, or back to Mercia.

The day passed slowly, with the king drifting in and out of sleep. Norah watched him as he moved about restlessly in his sleep. What haunted his dreams? She knew what haunted hers. She was still lost, failing to simply remember. She was failing as queen. Failing her kingdom and her people. Failing Alexander. All she could picture was Alexander walking into a trap. If anything happened to him...

As night fell, she looked out across the village, seeing the houses filled with firelight. How wonderful it must be, she thought, to be with loved ones in the comfort of a simple home. Where there was no pressure of the crown, no vengeful enemies. How wonderful it must be to choose a life of the heart—these were the things she longed for.

"You didn't answer my question," the king's voice came from behind her. She turned to see him sitting up in the bed.

She raised a brow. "There are many questions you haven't answered for me."

"Ask one, then. I'll answer."

She eyed him suspiciously.

"Truthfully," he added. "I'll answer truthfully." His breathing was uneven. His strength was returning, but it still took energy for him to hold himself up.

"All right, then," she said, biting. "What have you planned for me? Is it to kill me?"

He cast his eyes around the room, molding his response, then his gaze locked back on hers. "I have planned for you to die, yes."

Norah let out a long breath. She'd thought she'd fear the answer, but it wasn't fear that ran through her now, just sadness. A sadness she'd let down her kingdom, her grandmother. Alexander.

"Now my answer," he commanded.

Norah's mind was a blur. What did he want from her? "What is your question?"

"Why is the Aleon king worthy?"

Confusion flooded her. "Of all the questions you could ask me, that's the one you choose?"

His eyes bore into hers. "Tell me why."

Norah felt a heat come to her cheeks. This question felt most personal to her, most invasive. "You only have one," she warned, a bitterness rising in her.

"What is it about him?" he asked again.

There was nothing about him. Norah remembered nothing, so she knew absolutely *nothing* about him.

"Why do you want to marry him?" he pressed.

"I don't!" she snapped. She let out an emotional breath. She shouldn't have said that.

"Then why are you?" he asked.

"Because he has what I need," she said, relenting.

He gave a wry smile. "An army? To fight against me?"

"You're out of questions."

He snorted. "No matter. I already know the answer. I know what you need."

"You don't know anything about me," she cut back. No one did. Not even her. A cold calm returned. She turned back to the window to take her peace in the dream of village firelight.

Chapter Thirty

A noise stirred Norah from her dreams. It was light outside, early morning. She lifted her head to see the king. He was still asleep. She heard faint cries from a distance and rose quietly to the window. At the edge of the houses in the Horsemen's village, she spotted a high-walled corral with a group of men trying to settle a frenzied horse. She glanced back at the king, who lay silent in his slumber.

Quietly, Norah slipped outside the house, looking curiously toward the corral. Shouts echoed from the men; there was alarm in their voices. She briefly forgot about the Shadow King and hurriedly walked over to see the commotion. A guard by the door made no move to stop her, but he followed close behind.

As she reached the corral, she slowed, her eyes wide. Men held ropes around a horse's neck, and they fought to bring it under control. The animal lashed her head about, and a series of screams pierced through the air. Norah quickened her pace. She reached the enclosure and leaned against the thick beams, fascinated.

The mare pulled back against her restraints, and the men quickly drew together in front to hold her. A man approached her from the side, with a halter in his hand. When the horse spotted it, she tried to rear again. The man looked back at his teammates with a grin.

Norah became aware of a presence beside her. She didn't need to look to know it was the commander, and she kept her sight on the men in the corral, ignoring him.

The mare tossed her head again and pulled back against the ropes. Norah felt the beast's will to fight. Freedom was precious. Suddenly, the mare charged. She tore through the small group of men, knocking two of them to the ground and beating them with her front legs. Hooves met flesh with a sickening thud. The other men scrambled back, each pulling his rope, but they didn't have the power to control her. The mare reared, whipping herself free from them, and set her sights on another man to her right. She rushed at him, shouldering him into the wall of the paddock, and whirled to find her next victim.

Norah gasped, stepping back. Her worry shifted to the men in the corral. Two of the men staggered to the edge and slipped through the railing, but one still lay in the center.

Men yelled at the mare to draw her attention as others tried to approach the man, but the mare charged them again, pushing them back.

The man on the ground in the middle of the paddock stirred, reaching up an arm and calling out to his companions. His pleas angered the mare, and she attacked again, beating him viciously with her hooves.

"Why aren't they helping him?" Norah said, gasping, to the commander, putting her contention aside. "Will they do nothing?"

He snorted. "And what would they do? That mare is more valuable than all their lives together."

His words confused her. How could a horse be more important than men?

The mare let out an angry scream and pummeled the man again. He cried out once more and then fell silent.

"Help him!" she pleaded.

He chuckled. "There's no helping him."

Norah felt sick. If no one would help him, the man would die. She couldn't just stand there and do nothing. Before she could talk herself out of it, she slipped between the railings of the high-walled corral. Shouts rang out, and the mare reared, screaming into the air. Men yelled what she surmised to be warnings at her, but she ignored them.

"Get out of there!" the commander boomed behind her.

She ignored him too.

"Get out of there!" he roared again as he started to climb the railing. He was too large to fit in between.

Norah looked at the mare across the paddock. The horse had backed away from her victim, intrigued by Norah's presence, but stomped her hooves agitatedly.

The commander barked out an order to the Horsemen and, although the language was foreign, she could hear the vexation in his voice. Men climbed the railing of the paddock, standing tall with ropes in their hands.

"No!" Norah called to them. She looked back over her shoulder at the commander. "Tell them to stand down. They're only making it worse."

"Back up slowly and get out of there," he told her.

"I have to help him!" she insisted. She stepped toward the man on the ground, and the mare snorted but warily stayed.

"North Queen!" the commander growled. The mare reared again as the commander swung himself over the top of the corral.

"Wait!" Norah cried, making him pause. "Just wait." Slowly, she inched toward the man and knelt beside him, keeping her eyes on the mare. He lay crumpled on his side. She touched his face, but he didn't respond. Blood ran from a deep gash on the side of his head. Slowly, she rolled him onto his back. He was alive, but his breath was faint. He needed help. Norah rose slowly, looking at the horse. The mare shook her head, tossing her mane. This was no ordinary horse. The beast called to her.

The mare was snowy silver with a dark face and matching legs. As Norah drew closer, she could make out the dapple in her coat. Her beauty was intoxicating, but what caught

Norah's attention was the brilliant fire in her eyes. She'd seen eyes like these before. And it dawned on her—they were the same as the fox in the Wild, where Alexander had first found her. They had to be connected somehow.

"Don't!" the commander called to her, but she ignored him.

The animal's wild eyes looked at Norah through her thick mane, and her nostrils flared nervously. Norah clicked her tongue, drawing the mare's ears forward. She stepped closer and reached out her hand. "It's all right," she said softly.

The animal tossed her head again but finally stretched out her neck to nose Norah's hand. Norah waited patiently.

"You're all right," she whispered. Slowly, she moved to scratch the mare's chin, and then ran her hand up the animal's jaw. The horse threw her head up, but Norah paused, and the animal calmed.

"Easy, you're all right," she soothed. Slowly, Norah reached out again. She ran her hand down the horse's neck and chest, patting her. She loosened the ropes and pulled them away.

"That's better, yes?" she said to the animal. "Will you let him go? Death's not the answer."

The mare snorted, but Norah felt her yield.

"Collect your man," she called back to the Horsemen. The commander echoed her in a foreign tongue, with a few additional words she was sure, and they hurried warily to gather their man.

The mare flicked her ears and pawed the ground but stayed. Norah drew her hand along the animal's neck and shoulder, still working to calm her.

"North Queen!" the Shadow King's voice boomed from behind, and she looked to see him making his way toward the enclosure. The commander straddled the top of the corral with a spear in hand, and a man she assumed to be King Abilash stood below. Her stomach turned at being the center of their attention.

"I'll get you out of here," she whispered to the mare and then turned to face the ire of her own captors.

She strode to the edge of the corral and slipped out between the railing. The commander dropped to the ground from the top and stood beside the King Abilash. Both looked astonished.

"What is this power you have over the Wild?" Abilash asked. "How do you do this?"

But there was a fury inside her heart. "She doesn't belong to you. Why do you have her?" she demanded.

Her offense caught Abilash by surprise. Then he noticed the Shadow King approaching and gave a bow. "Salar, I'm glad to see you're recovering, my friend," he said, in an effort to change the subject.

Anger rose within her at being dismissed. "No thanks to your men," she said shortly. "Is that how you treat your *friends*? Attacking those under their protection and then poisoning them?"

Abilash, his face heavy with dishonor, looked at Mikael. "My men didn't know who they were attacking, and we suffer great shame. We offer you our deepest apology and whatever you require to mend the bond between Kharav and our people."

Mikael didn't appear to be in a forgiving state. "The North Queen's attackers. I want their families. Ten years' servitude in Kharav as restitution for their crimes."

Abilash nodded reluctantly.

Norah gasped. "Their families?" Mikael's eyes found hers, and they held a warning, but she couldn't help herself. "Sins of the father are not sins of the son," she said, objecting. "You punish innocents."

His face gave away nothing, but she knew she was pushing him for clemency he wasn't accustomed to.

"There must be recompense," he said.

"One fitting of the crime!"

His eyes blazed. "And what do you think is fitting of assaulting a queen?"

It wasn't lost on her that he called for restitution only for her grievance, not his own. Norah felt like the men guilty had already paid the ultimate penalty, but he wouldn't leave with nothing. "What about the mare?" Norah asked, and Abilash's eyes widened. She knew the horse was valuable if they would let men die over it. "We'll take the mare instead."

A tension rippled through the air, one that Norah didn't understand. The commander's face darkened—he was perhaps offended by her audacity to bargain as a prisoner.

Mikael looked at her with reluctance in his eyes, but then he turned to Abilash and surprised them all. "I'll have the mare," he said.

Abilash's face hardened, but he gave a stiff nod. "Our friendship with Kharav is very dear to us. If the North Queen can ride the beast, it's hers."

Norah sensed Abilash doubted she could ride the mare. She doubted it herself. Mikael shifted uncomfortably, and she feared he would interfere.

"I accept," she blurted, and turned back to the enclosure before he could stop her.

Norah approached the mare again, and the horse shook her head. "Easy," she whispered, reaching out her hand. The mare allowed her touch, but Norah wasn't sure about riding her. "I told you I'd get you out of here, but you have to trust me. Can you do that?"

The mare snorted.

"I'm going to trust you too," she said. "I'm going to trust that you won't maim me or make a fool of me. We can help each other."

Ever so carefully, she stepped to the side of the mare, who snorted again and turned to watch her. Norah reached over her back and slowly put weight on the animal. The mare waited. Summoning her courage, Norah gathered a fist of mane in her hand and jumped up, rocking her weight forward over the horse's back. Mounting a horse with no saddle wasn't the most elegant of actions—it was certainly not how she pictured herself doing it in her mind, and she struggled a bit before she swung her leg awkwardly over. Her heart pounded in her chest as she waited for either acceptance or a quick throw. But fortune was with her, and the mare moved quietly underneath her. Norah urged her forward and toward the gate. "Open it," she called.

The men looked at each other in astonishment and swung the gate open wide, watching in awe as Norah rode through.

The commander gave a beat to the ground with his spear as she passed. "Don't get any ideas," he threatened.

She frowned. He'd already struck a horse from underneath her, and she knew he'd do it again. Away from the enclosure, she slid off the horse, sure the mare would immediately bolt, but she didn't. Norah reached out and ran her hand under the thick mane, reveling in the warmth. "You'd be crazy to stay," she said, "but I could really use a friend right now."

The mare gave a snort and shook her head but seemed even-tempered and calm. Norah gave her a pat, leaving her there and making the short distance back to Mikael and King Abilash.

Mikael's eyes had a look that she didn't understand, but he turned to Abilash with a nod. "I forgive the transgressions of your people. Restitution has been paid."

"We look forward to your return," Abilash told him. Then he gave another stiff nod and turned back to his waiting Horsemen.

"I'll ready the men," the commander told Mikael as they walked toward the center house.

"What?" She didn't understand. "Are we leaving?"

"We are."

So soon? "We can't leave. You can barely walk. You're not fit to travel." She followed Mikael into the house.

He paused, gripping the back of a chair and leaning against it to rest a moment.

"Why the hurry?" she asked.

"We need to get back to the army before Abilash changes his mind and thinks about the fact that his men outnumber the few of us here."

Norah shook her head, still in a cloud of confusion. "Why would he change his mind? You showed mercy on all those innocent families."

"You required his most prized possession," he snapped.

"Are his people not what he cares for most?"

"No," he growled with a fury that shook her. "That is a horse of the Wild, and his mastery over it can make him a very powerful man among the tribes. I shouldn't have taken it from him."

"If you're so angry about it, then why did you?" she cut back.

"Because you asked it of me!"

Norah's breath faltered. He looked just as surprised by his words as she was to hear them.

Mikael pulled his eyes away and picked up his cloak. "Get what you need," he said, pulling it over his shoulder. "We leave now."

Chapter Thirty-One

The dark was fading; it was almost morning. They'd traveled in haste the day before. She'd ridden a small packhorse, not being trusted with an energetic mount, but the mare had followed along behind her. Tension still hung around her, with the commander's hatred for her seeming to grow with each passing hour.

Her whole body was sore, but she readied quickly after waking. Outside came the sounds of metal and leather packs: men preparing to leave. She pulled her hair back from her face and tied it behind and then slipped into her boots and jacket. Snow fell from the sky as she ducked out of the tent. There wasn't enough to coat the ground but it was enough to warn of the coming storm. The sound of the Shadow King and his commander in a heated conversation made her pause.

They stopped when they saw her emerge, and the king broke away toward her. "A storm is coming," he said as he neared. "You'll go with the lord commander."

She didn't like the idea of that at all. "Where are you going?"

Mikael paused with hesitation on his face. Then he said, "Gregor brings the Japheth army to join me against your army. I'm going to meet him."

The fact he'd answered her question surprised her, but the mention of his allied forces more than surprised her—it filled her with a sickening horror. Mercia wouldn't have Aleon with them, not yet. She didn't even know if Phillip was aware she'd been taken. The Shadowlands and Japheth against Mercia alone—her army would be decimated.

His eyes burned into hers. "This is my one opportunity. Did you think I wouldn't come with everything I had?"

There was nothing she could do, and the weight of the threatening devastation crushed her. "So, you've planned a slaughter? There's no honor in that."

"I told you, I'm not an honorable man."

No, he certainly wasn't.

"You'll go with the lord commander," he told her. "And I'll meet you in three days' time." He looked at the horse of the Wild. "He has orders to spear the mare should you try to ride her."

Norah wasn't sure why riding the mare would be such a concern, but his threat only fueled more fire inside her. "After you've risked so much to give her to me?" she asked angrily.

"Don't make that risk be in vain," he warned.

Norah's cheeks burned with fury. She pursed her lips and looked out into the frost of the morning. There was nothing she could do to help her army—nothing she could do to even warn them. And she didn't want to go with the commander. Her chances of escaping him were slim, and he'd surely see her dead.

"North Queen," the king said, seeming to read her mind. "You'll be safe with the lord commander. You have my word."

"What good is your word if you're not an honorable man?" she asked coldly.

Norah and the commander rode in silence as snow continued to fall. The mare followed behind without a lead. It was so peculiar. It was as if the animal knew her.

She watched the large, fluffy flakes as they landed on her arms and melted into her jacket. Wet snow was dangerous, and she pulled her cloak tighter around her. "How much farther?" she called.

He didn't respond. Naturally.

"Did you not hear me?" she pressed.

"Before nightfall," he clipped shortly.

Norah pursed her lips in agitation. His answer brought little comfort. Nightfall was still a far way off. Despite her cloak, the wetness had begun working its way into her layers, and she started to shiver. As they rode on, the wind picked up and the air felt colder. The snow began to layer on her arms and legs. The winter wind burned her face, and she buried her chin into the fur collar of her jacket. Time passed slowly, and Norah found just breathing to be difficult.

She couldn't bear it any longer. "We need to stop," she called to the commander. "We should build a fire."

"We can't stop."

They continued into the late afternoon. Norah couldn't control her shaking. The cold stabbed the inside of her chest, and she couldn't draw a breath.

They trudged on, with their horses starting to struggle in the snow. The reins slipped from her frozen fingers. She couldn't make her hands work to get them, but her horse followed his. Her teeth chattered, and she bit her tongue but didn't feel the pain. Sleep called to her.

The commander looked back at her and mumbled what she assumed to be a slew of curses. He reined back beside her and pulled her from her horse, sitting her in front of him. She would have rather frozen to death, but she didn't have the strength to fight him. He wrapped his cloak around them both and urged his destrier forward again.

The temperature dropped quickly as nightfall drew near. The commander held her close as they rode, trying to build warmth between them. Norah could barely hold her head up. Her body was so cold that it no longer shivered.

"Stay awake," he said, but she couldn't keep her eyes from closing. "North Queen," he snarled, "you need to stay awake."

But she couldn't help but let the darkness consume her.

Norah's eyes fluttered open, and she found herself tangled in Alexander as they lay in a wheaten field under the summer sun.

"Alexander?"

He smiled down at her, his blue eyes shining.

She'd missed him. "Am I dreaming?" She put her hand on his chest and spread her fingers against his skin.

"North Queen," he said.

"Why do you call me that?" she whispered. His body felt good close to hers, and she burrowed into him. "I'm cold, Alexander. I'm so cold."

He wrapped his arms around her and held her close. His warmth was inebriating, and she smiled as she nestled deeper. Norah let her lips graze his chest and felt a surge of heat inside her. She kissed the smooth warmth of his skin and let herself rest blissfully in his arms.

She opened her eyes again, and confusion rained over her as dark markings sprung from his skin. Ink bled into ominous patterns, patterns she'd seen before. The summerscape fell away, and she was inside a stone room. The darkness of night was held at bay by candlelight and a crackling fire behind her.

But her eyes were on the markings.

Panic flooded her. She sat up quickly and gasped as she saw the commander lying on the bed, looking back at her. The covers fell away, revealing her near nakedness underneath, and she grasped desperately at the blankets, pulling them to cover her chemise.

He chuckled in amusement as he rose from the bed, and her breath shook in horror at seeing his nakedness as well.

"Now you're not dreaming," he jeered with an evil smile. He walked around the bed and crouched in front of the flame, putting another log on the fire and stirring the embers with his sword.

"Don't worry yourself," he said, although he seemed to relish her panic. "I wasn't improper with you."

Heat radiated from her face. "What do you consider improper if not forcing a woman naked into bed?"

"You cannot imagine," he said in a low, disturbing voice. "But you're not entirely naked. And I didn't force you. You were merely an unwitting participant."

"Of which I'm sure you enjoyed," she snapped.

"Quite the opposite. I like a good fight," he said wickedly. "Actually, I would have preferred to leave you to die in the storm, although it would have been too kind a death."

She found his words as chilling as the winter air. What was to be her death then? She couldn't think of that right now.

"Why are we both without clothes?" she demanded.

"They were wet, and you needed to be warmed skin to skin. Do you not know how to survive a north storm, *North* Queen?" he taunted her.

Norah snorted, astounded at his brazenness.

The commander stood, again not bothering to cover himself. She averted her eyes, pulling the blanket up higher. He walked over to her shirt on the floor, picking it up and dropping it on the bed.

She grabbed it and pulled it quickly over her head, trying to keep herself covered with the blanket. Her underwear was still on, she noted, appreciative of the small assurance that he hadn't been entirely free with her.

"I want my breeches," she said.

He nodded to them lying across a chair by the fire, along with his own clothes. "They're not dry. You'll have to wait."

The commander sat on the edge of the bed, and she pulled her feet away from him, tucking her knees up to her chest and wrapping her arms around her legs. He gazed at her hands and then reached out and grabbed one. Norah tried to jerk it back, but he held it firmly. She struck him in his face with her other hand and he let out a growl. She tried to strike him again, but he caught her wrist and pulled her closer. Redness rose on his cheek from her blow.

"Let go of me!" she spat.

He ignored her and pulled her hands up, looking closely at her fingertips.

"What are you doing?" she hissed.

He grasped her face as she tried to bat him away, but he pulled her closer, looking carefully over her.

"The winter didn't eat your skin," he said. "You're lucky."

"That's the opposite of what I would consider myself right now," she said shortly, finally beating him back.

He released her. "You should be thanking me you're alive."

She snorted in disbelief. "I should be thanking you for saving me from a situation you put me in to begin with? And only to kill me later?"

Irritation flashed across his face, and he turned away from her. "Who is Alexander?" he asked.

Her eyes darted up to him, and her pulse quickened. "Why do you ask this?"

"Because it's what you called me... before you kissed me." He gave a cruel grin in satisfaction at the horror on her face.

"I did not!" she hissed.

He chuckled. "You were on your way to marry the Aleon king, but you love another. A secret love?" he taunted.

"Like your love for the king?" she spat back.

The commander jerked his head up in surprise. His smile faded. "Of course, I love Salar," he said. "As any warrior should."

"Except your love is different," she challenged.

His jaw tensed, and he shot her a look she hadn't expected—fear. It confirmed what she had only suspected. He was in love with the king. A love he hid, a twin to her own tragedy. She felt a pang of sympathy for him, but that sympathy was short-lived.

"Does he know?" she needled, still angry at his impudence. "I imagine that might change things between you two."

He lunged forward, pinning her to the bed with a fiery rage. His skin burned with the heat of fight, and his hand clenched her at the base of her neck with a force that made her struggle to breathe.

"Is this where you remind me how you can kill me?" she said through her teeth.

He ran his hand higher around her neck.

"Do it," she seethed. What did it matter anymore? If death was to come, better not to wait in fear.

The commander's lip quivered in fury as he bared his teeth. Then, suddenly, he released her and pushed himself off and away from the bed. "You won't speak of this again," he snarled.

"And you won't speak of Alexander," she countered.

A pact sealed in animosity. Surprisingly, he seemed to settle. He pulled out a flask and some wrapped meat and dropped it on the bed beside her.

Just then, Norah heard a shuffle outside the room. "What was that?" she asked.

"The horses."

"Inside?"

He shrugged. "No one to care."

She wasn't sure what he meant by that, but she found herself looking around the room. They weren't in a simple house.

She picked up the flask and brought it to her lips, surprised to find whiskey instead of water. She suppressed a cough as she swallowed, then drank again. Her stomach grumbled as she bit into the meat. She hadn't realized how hungry she was.

The commander stood watching her as she took another drink.

"When will the king be here?" she asked.

"Two days."

"What about the storm?"

"The army will keep him well."

Norah finished the meat and took another drink. The warmth of the alcohol spread under her skin, and her shivering calmed.

The commander rose to put another log on the fire. He still walked with a slight limp from when his horse had fallen on top of him at the stronghold. *Good.* She hoped it still hurt. Her eyes stopped on a freshly healing cut on his side, and a smirk pulled at her lips that she *had* managed to get him with her knife when he'd caught her trying to escape. Served him right. She hoped that still hurt too.

Norah let herself look at him. His body was thick and muscled from fighting. Ink patterned his chest and shoulders, running down his arms. His skin was smooth and hairless, and she followed the lines of his form lower. Unlike the king, the commander bore the markings over his thighs as well.

He looked at her, and she quickly turned away.

"Are you just going to stand naked by the fire until your clothes dry?" she asked irritably.

"Would you rather me come to bed with you?"

"Don't be ridiculous," she hissed.

He chuckled, entertained by her anger.

They sat in silence for a while. The commander sat by the fireplace and leaned back against the wall. She turned her back to him and pulled the blankets tighter around her. She needed rest; escaping took a lot from the body. She listened for the steady rhythm of the commander's breath to tell her he was asleep, but it never came.

Norah woke to the commander still sitting by the fire. It was morning. "Do you ever sleep?" she asked shortly.

He gave her an annoyed look but didn't respond.

She rolled her eyes. "They say no sleep will make a man go mad."

"Perhaps I'm not a man."

"Or perhaps you're already mad." She found herself thinking of the king, wondering how he was faring through the storm. "If the king dies, will you kill me?" she asked him.

"He won't."

"What if he does?"

"I said he won't," he said sharply. "But yes, I'll kill you."

His words no longer scared her. "How?"

He smiled. "I'll let you choose, so long as it's slow."

She lay back on the bed and looked up at the ceiling of stone. Perhaps this was to be her death: a death of despair with an intolerable brute.

The hours passed. Waiting was tiresome, and the time passed painfully slow. The commander stepped out often, leaving her alone, which she was thankful for. His nearness made her skin prickle.

A shuffle sounded outside the door of the room. It was the horses, she told herself, but her curiosity grew. Norah opened the door to what she thought was a hallway, but she found a great hall instead. They were in a castle. It hadn't seen people for some time. Had it been abandoned?

Their horses stood in the center of the hall, and Norah clicked her tongue as she approached. The mare nickered. Norah looked around as she patted her, running her hands up the animal's neck and under the warmth of her mane. Bales of hay sat in a corner with a large tub of water. As she moved her fingers under the mare's long, draping hair, she noticed it had been brushed, as had the other horses'. It surprised her that the commander had cared. What surprised her even more was that the mare had let him.

The hall was cold. Most of the windows were broken, letting the winter wind blow through the walls. Something outside caught her eye. She made her way to the large wooden doors and pushed them open, stepping out into the winter.

Norah gasped as she looked around. The old ruins of a city lay around her. It was a large city, and the quiet of long-abandoned lives made her uneasy. She heard the commander behind her and turned. "What happened here? Where are all the people?" she asked.

"Dead," he said, with a faint curve at the corner of his mouth.

"What happened to them?"

He gave a rumbling chuckle. "Me."

Norah gaped at him in horror. "You did this?" she breathed. "Why?"

His eyes, thick pools of black that choked out her breath, turned on her. "Why not?" he sneered.

Chapter Thirty-Two

When Norah woke the next morning, she found herself alone. The fire burned with fresh wood. The commander wouldn't be far. But she couldn't spend another day in this room; she had to do something. She opened the door to the great hall. It was empty. There was no sign of the brute, or the horses. He must have taken them out. She made her way across the hall and started up the staircase, her curiosity getting the better of her.

Norah passed from room to room, exploring what remained of the battle-torn castle. Heavily dusted and broken furniture lay strewn across the floors, with shattered busts in various corners and torn tapestries on the walls—remnants of those who had lived here. She passed a room that made her pause and pushed the door open wider before stepping inside. It was a girl's room, with pastel palettes and floral side panels. Someone had put thought and care into this room, someone who had loved its occupant—a mother, perhaps, or a grandmother. She imagined it in its former glory and smiled sadly. The ripped bedding matched what was left of the draperies. Her heart hurt. Was this all she would find now? The ruins of happiness past? Everything destroyed by darkness and death? A hopelessness washed over her. Glancing around, she caught her reflection in a three-paneled vanity mirror.

Norah walked slowly toward it. She hardly recognized herself. Her left cheek was bruised just under her eye, and the cut on her lip marred the softness of her mouth. Her eyes welled. The feeling of hopelessness turned to anger, and she cried out in rage as she slammed the side panel closed, shattering the mirror and dropping shards of glass all around her.

She broke down, sinking into the chair with a sob. All felt lost. Alexander was marching toward a force that would decimate the armies of Mercia, and she had no way to stop it. She should have never allowed herself to be brought here, never allowed herself to be taken. She should have never left the castle isle.

A large piece of glass on the floor caught her eye, and a calmness returned as she slowly picked it up. She would die soon. She wondered how they would kill her. Her hand curled around the glass; she shouldn't give them the satisfaction.

Norah rose and walked to the double doors leading out to a balcony, pushing them open and stepping outside. Looking down to the ground far below, she didn't remember climbing so many stairs. She wondered if it would hurt—death from falling—and she looked back at the shard of glass she clenched in her hand. Perhaps it was a better way to depart than cutting herself.

If she were to die, would it end it all? She'd no longer be a threat to the Shadow King. He'd have no reason to pursue the attack against Mercia. She would no longer be used as bait for her army.

Norah leaned forward against the railing.

She *was* going to die, she told herself; the Shadow King had told her. It was better for it to be by her own hand, on her own terms. She wished she could have seen Alexander again. She closed her eyes, imagining him, imagining his smile.

She leaned farther, inhaling deeply.

Suddenly, a hand grabbed her arm, pulling her backward and spinning her around.

Norah gasped.

The Shadow King. His gaze pierced her, seeming to see everything of her. Did he see her anger, her disappointment at her failure? The shame of her defeat?

There was a sadness in his eyes, remorse in his triumph. And something more. She felt a wave of confusion. She expected him to be angry, but he wasn't angry. He was *afraid*.

"North Queen," he breathed.

He let go of her arm, but still clasped her wrist. She could feel the stickiness of blood as she clutched the shard of glass in her fist.

"Do you find me unbearable?" he asked.

"I find this entire situation unbearable," she said coldly.

He brushed her closed fingers gently, and she found herself opening her hand, yielding her weapon. He carefully pulled the blood-covered glass from her palm and tossed it away from them.

"Perhaps you regret not leaving me to the Horseman's poison."

Frustration coursed through her. "Why would you say something like that? Why can't you believe I don't want you dead?"

"Because all my enemies want me dead, especially the North."

"I'm not your enemy!"

His nostrils flared. "You were on your way to build an alliance with Aleon. For power, for their army—"

"For food!" she cried. "You want to know what makes Aleon worthy? What I need? It's food! My people will starve without provisions for the winter!"

Mikael shifted in surprise, and then his face softened. She turned away to hide her emotion.

"And yes," she continued, "Aleon brings the strength of unity—arms, soldiers, protection against a threatening kingdom, specifically *you*. I won't pretend I don't want that strength, because I do. I know the stories. I've seen the destruction you've caused. I want Mercia to stand tall against any foe." She paused, and her voice came softer now.

"But that doesn't mean I want a foe to stand against. I want to protect my people. That's why I accepted the marriage."

The air settled between them.

"But you don't want to marry the Aleon king," he said.

She gave a defeated shrug. "What does it matter?"

"It matters if you would want to take my throne."

Norah let out an exasperated breath. "I don't want your throne!"

"As *my* queen," he added.

Her head jerked up, and her eyes widened. "What?" she breathed.

"You want to save your people. You want to avoid war between our kingdoms."

Norah shook her head. "I don't understand."

"What don't you understand? You're betrothed to the Aleon king. I offer my own hand instead."

"Why would you do that?"

He shrugged. "I break your alliance with Aleon. There is no war; I change fate."

Change fate. How much did he know of his fate?

"Not only do I double my army," he added, "but I gain the best archers in the world, access to Mercian steel, and a renowned fleet of ships. Kharav becomes a force even Aleon won't challenge. And"—his voice came softer—"I wed a queen worthy in her own right. You'd be my salara."

Norah felt light-headed. She wasn't sure if she was hearing him correctly. "Why would I marry you?"

"So long as you align yourself with an enemy of Kharav, you'll also be an enemy. You want to avoid a war? Only *I* can give that to you. And..." he paused, waiting for her to look up at him, "you'll still have whatever you require for the North—food, provisions, horses. My army, should you need it."

"All this just so I won't wed King Phillip? Why not just kill me to save yourself the trouble?"

He stepped closer. "Because I don't want you dead either, North Queen."

Her breaths came shallower now. "But I thought that was your plan."

He pulled out a handkerchief and wrapped it around the cut on her palm, closing her fist inside his and holding it tightly. "That plan expired well before I even told you of it."

She didn't know why his saying that affected her so. She swallowed. "Is that all? We just marry, and all's well with the world?"

"Yes. And..." He paused as her eyes found his. "The Bear is mine."

Norah shifted uneasily as a weight grew in her stomach. "Beurnat the Bear has been dead a long time now."

The king shook his head. "No. I saw the Bear just a year ago when I tried to retake Bahoul." His eyes darkened. "And I saw him again, recently, in the vision of my fall."

Norah's heart beat faster. It was Alexander that defended Bahoul. And it was Alexander in the vision, striking down the Shadow King.

And the king had seen it. It's why he wanted Alexander. Not just to change fate but to change *his* fate.

Then she froze. He'd said *seen.*

He had a traveler seer, someone who could show him the visions. How powerful was this seer?

"So, we'll be wed," the king said, "and the Bear will be mine."

She forgot about the seer as a flash of anger ran through her, and she pulled away from him. "Alexander will never be yours."

"Alexander," he said thickly, letting the name roll over his tongue. "Is that his name? *Alexander.*" Then he snorted, frustrated by her answer. "He's but one man."

"Then he should mean nothing to you," she cut back.

"I will have the Bear," he said, his anger rising. "Think of it as the price of peace."

"Then you'll have nothing!"

His face hardened. "So will you," he snarled.

In a single movement of fury, she wrenched away from his loose hold and grasped the hilt of his sword, pulling it free from its scabbard. He moved after her, but she brought the blade up, halting him. "So be it," she said as she backed against the railing of the balcony. She already had nothing else to lose. She stepped back toward the rail.

He held up his hand. "No!"

She stopped.

"No," he said, his breath coming quicker. "Don't."

Neither of them moved. His eyes held an intensity that unsettled her, but she stood firm. Then his face softened slightly. Still, she didn't move.

"Those are your terms?" he asked finally.

Norah's breath caught in her chest. Was she setting terms? Was she seriously considering marrying the Shadow King? She lowered the sword but took another step back. She didn't feel herself standing before him. Perhaps it was all another dream, a terrifying dream. Suddenly, the image of her on the Shadow throne came crashing back. She swallowed. Was this what she had seen? Perhaps the vision hadn't meant that she'd take the Shadowlands by force. Perhaps this had been her fate all along.

She took a deep breath and looked around. Fate or no, she couldn't live like this, with death and destruction. She couldn't marry a man who did these things for pleasure.

"Before I answer that—what is this place?" she asked him. "What happened here?"

The king paused, letting his eyes wander. He grimaced, as if there was pain for him here. "This is what's left of Aviron."

"Where you were captured when you fled Bahoul?"

He nodded. "They sympathized with Aleon. They were enamored by the charm of the empire and Aleon's riches. Their king, Jaiah, planned to send his daughter with the offer of marriage, along with the gift of my heart cut from my body."

Her skin prickled.

"They cut open my chest..." His words drifted as he looked out across the hills from the balcony. "But they underestimated Soren." He paused. "I don't remember how we made it out. I don't remember fleeing to the canyons. Only that he got us out and brought me home."

Her breaths came unsteadily.

"After my coronation," he continued, "I appointed Soren as my lord commander, and he gave me my first gift as salar—the kingdom of those who'd sought my death."

Norah remembered the story her grandmother had told her about the destruction of Aviron. If only Mercia knew what had really happened. She turned away, trying to gather her thoughts. Vengeance was never a defense of one's actions, but things weren't always as they seemed. These stories she'd been told, the stories that drove fear into so many, they weren't the truth. At least, not entirely. And she had the power to change everything.

But regardless of the circumstance, she couldn't condone this devastation. "If we're to wed, I'll defend only," she heard herself say, looking back at him. "Mercia won't invade another kingdom for you. I won't have this... all this destruction."

He gave a slight nod.

"My people will have food and horses and weapons," she added.

He stepped closer to her. "All that is mine will be yours. Everything and everyone." There was a weight to his tone, one of assurance. He was committing to her. "And all that is yours will be mine," he added.

"Except Alexander," she said firmly.

He sighed, yielding. "I accept these terms."

Norah's heart beat in her throat.

"Are we betrothed then?" he asked.

The circumstances were suddenly very real.

"I suppose we are," she replied, as the weight of sadness shrouded her heart.

Chapter Thirty-Three

The journey toward Kharav seemed endless. Mikael let her ride the mare of the Wild freely, to her surprise. She followed the king as they made their way through the rocky hills. The commander was quiet, somber. No doubt the news of their marriage weighed on his mind. Norah almost felt sympathy for him.

As the sun climbed higher in the sky, something felt off. "We're heading west?" she asked.

"Your army draws closer," he told her. "We go to meet them."

"They're not behind us?"

"No. They didn't march for Bahoul. They will come directly through the Tribelands."

The realization hit her. He had relented too easily in trying to take back Bahoul. Now she understood. He had discovered her army wasn't headed there. That had been his change in plans.

Her heart raced in her chest. Alexander was close. She wasn't sure she believed the king's promise not to take him, not to harm him. There was nothing at all that prevented a battle, only the words spoken between them.

"What will happen when we meet them?" she asked nervously.

He looked at her calmly. "Announce our marriage and send them home."

"Right," she breathed, feeling the slightest of reassurance. But her mind wandered to Alexander again, and her anxiousness returned. She didn't know how she'd tell him she was marrying the Shadow King. Would he understand? Would her people understand?

"How is it you can ride her?" the king asked, bringing her mind back to him. "How can you ride a horse of the Wild?" His question caught the commander's attention as well.

Norah looked down at the animal and shook her head. "I don't know. I think she understands me somehow." It was a mystery to her as well, but there was something different about the mare—they had a connection... like she'd had with the fox when she was lost in the forest.

He raised a brow and looked at the commander, and they rode on. Norah still didn't understand the significance of the mare. Her mind had been so consumed with Alexander and her army that she hadn't given it enough reflection. This was a special animal. Perhaps if she had her memories, she'd know why.

The journey was quiet, and Norah found the time blurred as she lost herself in her thoughts. They were tormenting thoughts—Alexander's face when she'd tell him she was to wed the Shadow King, how she'd leave him to return to the Shadowlands. Each hour weakened her resolve.

She shivered against the winter air and pulled the hood of her cloak forward, trying to find some warmth. Just then, in the distance, Norah spotted movement. She squinted her eyes against the wind.

Horses.

Riders.

Moving quickly toward them.

They drew closer, and her pulse raced. A sword gleamed in the air, held high by the lead rider. They were attacking.

"Mikael!" she called, pulling the mare back.

Norah's chest tightened. She didn't even have a weapon. The Shadow King sat quietly on his horse in front of her. He raised his fingers slightly to calm her, but she couldn't take her eyes off the advancing Horsemen, feeling panic well within her. But Mikael seemed indifferent, and Norah forced herself calm. While she considered herself to be ill fated in marrying him, she did trust he'd keep her safe.

The commander slid off his mount and pulled out his axe. She looked at the other soldiers and noted that they hadn't taken up their arms. But the commander stood, wielding his axe, and waited.

A shrill scream sounded from the lead Horseman, and Norah realized it was a woman. The woman's horse bore down on the commander with a thunder. Just before she reached him, she leapt from her mount and met his blade with her own. The clash rang through the air as she hit the ground and tucked into a roll, leaping up and turning to meet him again. The rest of the Horsemen fanned out to either side, surrounding them.

The woman fought him back with a fury, and Norah was mesmerized. She was clothed in soft leather and furs, fitted to her form. Her dark auburn hair was pulled back in braids, and black markings lined her eyes. She bared her teeth as she exchanged blows with the commander, but there was a hint of a devilish smile—she was enjoying the fight.

She swung high, and he met her blade with his axe, striking it down with a force and pushing her backward. The woman pulled her sword back quickly, slicing into the flesh of his arm and drawing blood. She moved to attack again, but he spun and delivered a blow to her side. She countered with an elbow and caught him on the brow. The commander reached out and grabbed her, sweeping his leg under her and taking her to the ground. She loosed another elbow to his shoulder, and he winced. Pinning her with his weight, he looked at her to yield. Instead, she ripped down the wrap from his face and drew him down into a deep kiss.

Norah gasped, not fully understanding what was happening. The commander broke away in surprise and disgust, releasing the woman. She flashed a fiendish smile and rose, pulling her sword from the ground. "You're losing your edge, Soren," she goaded him, eyeing his arm. She stepped forward, looking closer at him. "Or perhaps you're still recovering from whoever gave you that look." She grinned, nodding at the bruising on his face.

The commander shot Norah a glance, and the woman followed his gaze. It was as if she hadn't realized they were there.

"Tahla," Mikael greeted her.

"Salar," she replied with a nod, a formality coming to her. Then her eyes widened as they found Norah. "Savantahla?" she gasped. Tahla drew closer to them as though she were looking at a ghost.

Norah didn't understand, but she remained still, keeping the hood of her cloak pulled down low. It took her a moment to realize the woman was looking at the mare, not her.

Tahla glanced at the commander and then back to the horse, stepping even closer. The commander's axe came up, halting the woman. She scowled at him but then turned her attention back to Norah.

"How is this possible?" she asked. "How do you ride with Savantahla?"

Norah still didn't understand.

And Mikael didn't answer her question. "We seek accommodations for the night, as my armies pass through. We go to meet the Northmen at the far Canyonlands."

"The Northmen?" she said with surprise, lifting her brow. Then her face hardened slightly. "You go to battle the North Queen?" she asked, glancing at him for a moment but then looking back at the mare. "You call us to go with you?"

"No." Looking at Norah with a slight curve in his lip, he opened his hand and gave a nod. She pushed the hood of her cloak back, showing herself. "This is the North Queen," he said.

The woman drew in a bewildered breath, speechless. "The North Queen commands Savantahla?" she asked finally. "And rides with you?"

"We go to announce our marriage," Mikael said. "The union of Kharav and the North."

"Sol!" Tahla exclaimed, which Norah assumed to be an expression of disbelief. "Marriage?" the woman asked, looking at the commander, not seeming to believe the king. "Kharav and the North?"

A smile came across Tahla's face, and her brows raised in astonishment. "That's unexpected. I don't know what to say." She paused, shaking her head. "But the Uru would be honored to host you this evening. And to host Savantahla." She swung onto her horse with a big grin and waved them to follow.

Norah urged her mare close to Mikael as they rode after the Horsemen toward their village.

"I don't understand. Who's that?" she asked Mikael quietly.

"Tahla Otay of the Uru. Her father is chief." He paused. "When Soren and I escaped Aviron, I was near death. Tahla and her father helped me, healed me, and saw us through the canyons and back home."

It was all coming together for her now. Bahoul. Aviron.

"The Uru are the largest of the Horsemen tribes," he told her. "And they're friends. They're keepers of the western Canyonlands, one of the only two entryways into Kharav."

Norah had heard of the Canyonlands but didn't fully appreciate their magnificence until they came into view. Massive cliffs of black rock rose from the ground, as if split by the gods, creating thin passages in their crevices with an eerie darkness at their base. As they wove deeper into the dark labyrinth, she urged her mare closer to Mikael's mount.

The ground beneath them held patches of ice, but as they rode farther, she noticed small trails of running water. Deeper into the canyons, the water ran faster. They moved to the banks, and at the end of the canyons, the water poured into a large river.

They followed it around until the earth broke and Norah heard the sound of waterfalls. A path emerged and narrowed, and the descent became steeper. She fell back, behind Mikael, as they rode single file. The trail turned sharply and then climbed back up. They rounded another corner, and a massive village sprawled out in front of them. Small structures were carved into the hillside, revealing hundreds, perhaps thous, of families and stone homes.

The sight took Norah's breath away. "It's beautiful," she said.

Tahla glanced back at her and smiled.

As they approached the village, people gathered at the edge. There were many, but as they drew near, Norah spotted a man with a regal stature. He wore a wrap beautifully twisted around his head and adorned with beaded overlays, and in his right hand was an intricately carved wooden staff.

Tahla called to him in Urun tongue, and he looked wide-eyed at Norah and her mare. He replied and bowed his head low. Norah shifted uncomfortably as the Uru people dropped to their knees, bowing as well.

"My father says it's a great honor to host Savantahla," Tahla said. "We give thanks to Savan for this blessing."

Norah glanced at Mikael. He gave her a small smirk, amused by her confusion, and slid off his horse. She watched as he made his way to the chief and bowed low to the old man, his reverence unmistakable. The chief reached out and put his hand on Mikael's shoulder and then pulled him into an embrace. Norah was surprised at the emotion that touched her, and she swallowed it back with a smile.

The army set camp outside the city. Norah left the mare with other horses by the river and followed Mikael to a large fire with people gathered in a circle around it.

"Why is Abilash a king and... this man... a chief?" she asked him.

"Coca Otay is his name. The Uru are one tribe, and Coca Otay leads them. Abilash has taken many tribes. He is a chief of other chiefs."

"Is Abilash chief of Coca Otay?"

"I would never allow that," he told her.

Strange, Norah thought, that Mikael had such influence on the Horsemen tribes. She watched as the Uru welcomed him, bowing, smiling, and giving him small gifts. They respected him here, loved him even.

A hefty Urun woman offered Norah a hot drink and motioned for her to sit. She took a seat on a large stone and watched the celebration around her. They were happier about her marriage than she was, but Norah had to admit she wasn't *unhappy*. Everything was so different from what she had expected. Even Mikael. Especially Mikael. Nothing was as it seemed, nothing was as she'd imagined. What else was hiding in this strange, special world?

Chapter Thirty-Four

The fire blazed brightly in the late afternoon's dying sun, and the sound of celebration rang through the Urun city. Norah sat quietly, soaking up the warmth and enjoying the first feeling of ease since her capture. She watched the flames of the fire reach into the night as dancing Horsemen celebrated around it. Pulsing, twisting, turning, they moved their bodies to the sound of the drums—like spirits not bound to the earth.

She sensed eyes on her and looked over to see Tahla watching her.

The chief's daughter moved to the large rock beside her and gave her a friendly smile. "I'm sorry, I don't mean to stare," Tahla told her. "I just didn't believe the stories. But now you're here."

"What stories?" Norah asked, puzzled.

"The North Queen with winter hair. I couldn't even picture you. Can I touch it?"

Norah smiled awkwardly. "My hair?"

Tahla grinned with a nod.

Strange. Norah shrugged. "Sure."

Tahla reached out and combed her fingers through the blonde locks. "I don't know what I was expecting. I imagined ice in some form." She smiled sheepishly. "It feels like normal hair."

"It is normal hair," Norah said, and both women laughed.

"Do all people in the North have light hair?"

Norah nodded. "Most of them, although not as light as mine. Many are more golden haired."

Tahla's mouth opened in surprise. "Even the men?"

"Yes."

"That sounds beautiful," the chief's daughter said with a smile.

Norah thought of Alexander. "It is," she said, and they laughed again.

Tahla quieted, but still radiated a burning curiosity. "How do you command Savantahla?"

Norah didn't know how to answer. "I'm not even sure what that is. Do you mean the horse?"

"Savantahla means the spirit of the Wild," she explained. "Animals from the land of the Wild, they're all Savantahla. Horses, birds, wolves, foxes. Savan is in all of them."

"Foxes?" Norah asked in surprise. Her mind drifted back to the fox in the Wild. Now she was certain they were connected. But how were they connected to *her*?

"Any animal of the Wild. You know them by their compulsive beauty, and their eyes."

Norah thought about the mare. She was beautiful. Her mane was thick and long, and even without the sun, her dappled coat shined. Norah knew that compulsive beauty, and she knew the eyes: a hypnotizing gold. "I don't command her," Norah told her. "I only ask of her."

Tahla paused. "They say only witches can speak to Savantahla."

Norah raised a brow and rocked her head to the side. "I'm not a witch, although I have been accused of being one."

"How did you capture her?"

"I didn't. King Mikael took her from a man named Abilash as recompense... for a transgression."

Tahla's eyes widened. "King Abilash? Salar took Savantahla from King Abilash?"

"The king didn't seem very happy about it, but Abilash gave the horse willingly. We parted on good terms."

"I can assure you that you didn't part on as good of terms as you think. But he dares not defy Salar. Not alone anyway, unless he wants his tribes to starve. And he was probably scared of you and your witchery." She smiled. "Horsemen are extremely superstitious people."

Norah realized that the Shadow King must help the Horsemen with provisions through the winter, too, and she smiled at the witchery jest. "The king said the mare was quite valuable to them."

Tahla nodded. "Tribes of the Horsemen compete for land and power. If Abilash had Savantahla, he could rally more tribes to follow him."

"Over a horse?"

"The animals of Savantahla are not ordinary animals. You cannot track them. They speak to the earth, and the earth speaks back. You can't tame them unless they want to be tamed. They have great power, and anyone who controls Savantahla has great power too."

Norah looked back at the horse, which was grazing by the others along the river. She wasn't sure what this great power could be.

Tahla smiled. "I was named after Savantahla. *Tahla*."

"Ah," Norah said, "I hear it."

"My mother died in childbirth. I should have died too. But I didn't. My father said I was so wild out of the womb that the spirit must be within me. It's a strong name." She looked at the horse with a smile. "Few have seen Savantahla. Your visit is a great honor."

The warmth of gratitude filled her. "Do you want to see her?" she asked. "Touch her?"

Tahla let out a gasp. "Surely she wouldn't let me."

Norah shrugged. "We can see."

The chief's daughter jumped up eagerly, making Norah laugh, and the women made their way toward the river. The other grazing horses took little notice of them as they approached, but the mare tossed her head and snorted.

"Easy," Norah called to her. "I bring a friend who wants to meet you."

The mare shook her head again but let them draw near. Norah scratched her neck under the thick mane and gave her a gentle pat. Turning back to Tahla, she held out her hand. "Come here."

Speechless, Tahla stepped closer, and Norah brought their hands together to the creature's silver coat. Tahla let out an emotional breath, running her hand down the mare's neck. Norah smiled at the love and respect the chief's daughter had for the animal. This horse was special. Norah just wished she knew what her connection was to it.

Norah grabbed a fistful of mane and pulled herself onto the mare's back. "I think she likes you," Norah said, reaching down. "Do you want to try a ride?"

"What?" Tahla breathed in disbelief.

"Come on."

Tahla patted the mare gently, unsure, but she grasped Norah's hand. Norah pulled her up and behind her. The mare danced anxiously but seemed amenable.

"Good?" Norah asked.

"Beyond!" Tahla exclaimed. "I've only dreamed of such things!"

"Let's go!" Norah whispered to the mare, and the beast kicked into a gallop along the river. The rippling water caught the last rays of sun, and the curve of the earth rose to meet them. Tahla let out a squeal of joy, spreading her arms wide, as if in flight, and Norah laughed. Norah urged the mare faster, and they flew over the banks of the river. The wind whipped through their hair, and tears stung Norah's eyes. Finally, she slowed the mare to a walk, breathless.

"I can't believe this is happening!" Tahla squealed.

Norah smiled back at her.

"It feels like we've left the earth behind." The chief's daughter laughed, looking into the purple sunset. "And now we ride among the heavens."

It was heavenly. Beauty lay all around them, but the weight of her circumstance pulled her spirit back. "I suppose we should return." Norah sighed. "The king will have noticed my absence and fear my escape."

"Your escape?" Tahla asked. Then she paused as the realization came to her. "You don't want to marry him?"

Norah's silence answered for her.

"Look," Tahla told her, pointing behind them. Norah slowed the mare to a stop and looked behind them. There were no tracks along the muddy bank of the river, no trail of their ride. Norah's breath caught in her throat.

"See?" the chief's daughter said. "The power of Savantahla."

Norah let out a shaky breath, realizing her chance.

"You could go," Tahla said softly. "If this isn't what you want, if you don't want to marry him."

Norah wanted to run. She closed her eyes and breathed in the pull of freedom. "Why would you help me?" she asked Tahla. "Is Kharav not your ally? Your friend?"

Tahla paused for a moment, and then let out a breath. "Six years ago, my father forced me to marry. And on my wedding night, when I didn't want to give myself to him, my husband beat me, then took me anyway."

"Oh, Tahla. I'm so sorry."

"Don't be. I got my revenge."

Norah's stomach turned. Was that her future?

"Salar's a good man," Tahla said, seeming to read her mind. "And he'll be a good husband. But I'll not be idle for a woman marrying against her will. Ride two days west, past the ruins of Choan, and then turn north. You'll find yourself deep into the Tribelands, but with Savantahla, any tribe will give you shelter, safety, provisions."

Norah's heart beat wildly in her chest. The mare pranced underneath them, feeling her energy. Norah reached a hand down to calm her. She turned back toward Tahla, smiling sadly. "You don't know how much your kindness means to me. And it's true I don't want to marry him. But this marriage will end ten years of war. My Northmen are marching as we speak. Battle is imminent; thousands will die. And Mercia needs help. The winter drags on, and my people are desperate. We have no food. This marriage seems to solve everything. I have to do it."

"You're a strong queen for your people."

"I want to be."

Tahla smiled and put a warm hand on her arm. "Then we'll return. But always remember it's your choice."

Norah smiled and urged the mare back the way they had come. The sun had set, and the sky grew darker. "You spoke of the ruins of Choan," she prompted. "The border kingdom the Shadowlands destroyed?"

Tahla snorted. "That sounds like a Northern way to describe it, but yes, I suppose."

"How would you describe it?"

"It was a kingdom that almost wiped out the Uru. They wanted our land along the river. They attacked our villages, took our horses, slaughtered our people."

A wave of horror washed through her. "What happened?"

"Salar came. He drove Choan back. But after the battle, after Salar returned to Kharav, they attacked again despite his warning not to. So, he did what he had to."

He'd protected them. Norah swallowed. "He told me the Uru helped him after he fled Aviron, that you saved him."

"Death was coming for him. We gave our best crops and furs to the spirits, and we prayed for six days. On the sixth day, his fever broke. Then we showed them through the canyons and home."

Relief filled her. The king hadn't destroyed Choan for fun. He'd been protecting them. He'd been protecting the people who'd helped him in his time of need—people who'd sacrificed for him, who cared for him.

How different everything was than what she'd thought she'd known. But still... all this death.

"Is your husband dead?" she asked. Then she chided herself. It was too personal a question, too prying.

"Publicly—who knows? Privately, in the most beautifully horrible way."

Norah's stomach twisted, but she couldn't muster sympathy for such a man. "What happened?"

"Soren."

Tahla didn't need to say more. Norah could imagine. She noted that Tahla called the commander by his name. "You two are close?"

"I've known Soren since he was a boy. Now he's all grown up and thinks he's a fancy lord, but I never let him forget I can always get him with a blade."

Norah smiled. Tahla was a beautiful spirit.

When Norah and Tahla arrived back at the village, a crowd of children surrounded them, cheering at Tahla, who grinned back at them. The woman slid down, and Norah returned the mare to the other horses beside the river.

The chief was waiting. "You rode Savantahla?" he asked Tahla incredulously.

"By Savan's grace, and Salara's," she said, smiling back at Norah.

Tahla's use of the Shadow title surprised Norah, but it felt... nice. She pushed the feeling down. She didn't want to like it. She didn't want to be salara, *the Shadow Queen*.

Norah's eyes found Mikael's. He looked shaken—he'd feared she'd left. She gave him a small reassuring smile before Tahla pulled her attention back.

"Come!" the chief's daughter said. "I have something for you I think you'll like."

Norah glanced back at the king and then let Tahla pull her away again. She followed the Urun woman up a path, through the rock, and down a trail that curved around, revealing a large waterfall with a pool at the bottom. Torches circled the pool, chasing back the night.

"This place is amazing," Norah said.

"Come on!" Tahla said excitedly as she pulled off her clothes.

Norah laughed in surprise, and she looked around shyly.

"Don't worry. It's private for us," Tahla assured her.

Getting naked and jumping in a waterfall in the middle of winter after getting betrothed to the Shadow King was not what she'd expected herself to be doing right now. But Tahla's spirit made her happy, so she pulled off her boots and wriggled out of her clothes.

Tahla dove into the pool, disappearing underneath and then rising back to the surface. She grinned at Norah, waiting.

"What are you waiting for?" she asked.

Norah took a deep breath and jumped, prepared for the sting of the cold. But to her surprise, the water was warm, and she let it carry away her burdens in its current. She came to the surface and breathed, finding Tahla. "It's warm!" she exclaimed.

"It's fed from a hot spring in the falls," Tahla told her.

Like the cave. Norah paused, reliving the memory. She thought of Alexander. He was marching on Kharav right now, ready for war. He was coming for her.

"Are you all right?" Tahla asked.

"It just... reminds me... of a place back home. I was thinking of it."

"Do you miss the North?"

Norah nodded. "Parts of it. Mainly the people."

"You'll see it again, though. Right?"

Norah forced a smile. *Maybe.*

"Come on," Tahla called to her, swimming toward the falls. "Come over here."

Norah followed and found herself under a shower of hot water. After the long days of riding, it felt incredible.

Tahla reached into a basket that had been placed by the falls. "Here," she called, holding something out in her hand.

"What is it?"

"Corian. It's a soap root. Smell it."

Norah brought it to her nose and breathed in its sweet fragrance. "Smells incredible."

"Wash your hair with it. You'll breathe its scent all night."

Norah grinned as she lathered the paste into her hair and rinsed it in the falls. She took a deep breath. She finally felt clean. Clean from the journey. From the fear. From the pressure. Clean from the sorrow and the heartbreak. She knew it was temporary, but for now, she would relish it.

A stack of folded garments lay by the pool as they made their way out of the water.

"Here," Tahla said to Norah, handing the clothes to her. "Put these on."

Norah shrugged into a long-sleeved dress, and Tahla tied it behind her. They laughed as they combed out their hair, and for a short while, the weight of the world felt a little lighter.

"Thank you for this," Norah told her. "Your kindness—"

"Don't." Tahla smiled, grabbing her hands. "We're sisters now."

Norah smiled and then nodded, feeling a little emotional. In this moment, everything was perfect.

Tahla and Norah made their way back to the celebration and sat by the fire, enjoying cups of warm, sweet wine.

"He has his eye on you," Tahla told her, "and I don't think it's for worry of your escape."

Norah looked across the fire to see the Shadow King gazing back at her.

"Do you not like handsome, powerful men who change the fate of kingdoms for you?" Tahla asked.

Norah smiled but then grew serious. "He changed it for himself. And there are many incentives in this marriage for him. I'd be foolish to believe he had feelings for me or to let myself have feelings for him."

"I don't know about that." Tahla smiled back toward the king. "That look doesn't say, 'Hooray! I'm getting archers and steel and rocks!' or whatever you have in the North."

Norah smiled at her. "I appreciate your effort to scheme a love affair into my situation, but I don't want to hope for that. It's better I accept this for what it is—an arrangement that will help both our kingdoms. I believe he and I could be friends, allies. That's what I hope for."

"Fine, I understand," Tahla whispered with a mischievous smile.

The evening wore on, and Norah mingled freely through the warm acceptance of the Uru. It surprised her how much she enjoyed herself. She'd been desperate for the freedom to be out and to breathe and to be herself, even in Mercia. Why was she able to feel this freedom only now, after being captured by her enemy?

She saw the king on the other side of the fire, still gazing back at her, and she gave a small smile. She hadn't spoken to him since they'd arrived, having been spirited away by Tahla. Norah gathered her courage and made her way around the fire to him.

His eyes shifted over the dress Tahla had given her as she approached.

She raised a brow. "Do you like it?"

He stared at her a moment, and she thought he might not answer. Then he said, "I do." His voice was thick, a different tone than the light jest she'd expected. Alexander would have politely complimented her, but the king's gaze held more than a compliment.

He stood and stepped closer. Too close. Norah pulled the outer wrap tighter around her shoulders; he still unsettled her. He grasped a lock of her hair and brought it near his face, smelling the corian. Her skin prickled, and she pulled away.

The king's brow furrowed, and his lip twitched. "Do you not want me to like it, North Queen?" he asked.

She didn't know how to answer. Did she?

He stepped closer again, his voice low. "Will you come to me tonight?"

She puffed a small breath of surprise with a sting of offense. To his *bed*? "Why would I?" she asked, taken aback.

Confusion flashed across his face. "Because you're to be my wife."

"But I'm not yet your wife," she snapped.

His words came choppy. "Then why do you fashion yourself... with scent in your hair?"

"Because I like to be clean and feel beautiful and smell... not like I've been battling and riding for weeks. Not everything is about pleasing a man, you know. Women like to do things for themselves!"

Mikael took a step back, clearly not expecting her response. He'd mistaken her self-attention, and she could tell she'd hurt his pride.

He gave a stiff nod. "Of course," he said. "I'll leave you, then."

A wave of regret ran through her, but she wasn't sure of the reason. She had no intention of being intimate with the king, yet she found herself not wanting him to go. But she pushed it down. She felt nothing for him.

He paused, turning back to her. "North Queen," he said, his eyes piercing into her. "You do... look beautiful."

She felt nothing for him, she reminded herself.

CHAPTER THIRTY-FIVE

The morning sun spilled over the horizon as the Shadowmen prepared to leave. Tahla approached with a smile as Norah readied her mare.

"I brought you something to take back with you," Tahla said, holding a satchel out.

Norah took it and peeked under the flap. Inside were small jars and wraps of oils, balms, and soaps. She'd already felt a deep appreciation for the extra clothes that Tahla had provided. She smiled. "I know I've only been here a short while, but I want to thank you. Not only for your hospitality, but for your friendship. It was very much needed and so appreciated."

"I'm glad we're not going to war, Salara. Riding Savantahla is a moment I'll never forget. Remember, we're sisters now. Whatever you need, say the word." Tahla cocked her head and looked over Norah's shoulder at the horse. "Take care of her, yes?" she called out.

The mare snorted, and both women laughed. Norah turned and swung up into the saddle, then looked down. "Goodbye, Tahla," she said.

"Goodbye, Salara," the chief's daughter replied.

The king sat on his destrier, waiting patiently. When she was ready, they started out into the morning. He brought his horse up along hers, glancing at her.

"What?" she asked without turning.

"You said something yesterday that made me question."

She finally looked at him, waiting.

"Have you lain with a man before?" he asked.

Norah snorted in surprise, offended. "Do you question my honor?"

His brow creased. "What does virginity have to do with honor?" he asked.

Norah didn't know what to say. "If it doesn't matter, then why are you asking?"

"It's good I know," he said. "For our wedding night."

A pit grew in Norah's stomach as she tried to swallow the tightness in her throat. "Well, if we make it to our wedding night, we'll talk about it then." She urged her mare ahead, leaving the king and the conversation, and tried to push the subject from her mind.

The Shadowmen camped at the top of the canyons for two days before the Mercian army arrived. War horns sounded, and Norah wondered what Alexander must be feeling as he readied for war, coming for her. She was desperate to see him, but she wasn't sure she could face him.

She stood quietly, looking down from the cliffs at the legions organizing in the distance. The Mercian horns sounded again in anticipation of battle. And she was suddenly aware of the Shadow King beside her.

"They're preparing for an attack," she said.

"Then how happy they'll be when they learn they won't die today," he replied.

"What of the Bear?" the commander called, coming up behind them.

Norah's pulse quickened. "What of him?" she said shortly, looking at Mikael. "Do you forget our agreement?"

The commander's eyes were on Mikael, ignoring her. He waited for his king's response.

Mikael looked back at him with a ruthless calm. "The Bear's not to be harmed."

The commander snorted in anger. "He will engage."

"I said he's not to be harmed. Make sure every warrior is aware. I'll have the head of any man who raises a hand to him."

The corners of the commander's eyes tightened, but he turned back toward the army. Despite Mikael's words, Norah's concern for Alexander rose. She glanced at him warily.

His nostrils flared, and he slipped his helm back on. "Why is this man so important to you?"

Norah's heart threatened to beat itself out of her chest. She was certain he could hear it. "Is your lord commander not important to you?" she challenged. "Would you so freely give me his head if I asked for it?"

Mikael looked out at the Mercian army in the distance, but he didn't press her further. "As I've said, he's safe. But he's to return with your army to the North."

Norah nodded. That's what she wanted—her army back in Mercia and Alexander safe. She hoped it would be that simple.

The commander returned, followed by a small group of soldiers with covered carts. She looked at Mikael, puzzled, and he pulled back a tarp, showing bags of rice and dried goods underneath.

"For your army," he said. "Our scouts have reported they're low on provisions. When you return to me, I'll send more." He stepped closer to her. "I'm sincere in my commitment, and I trust you are as well."

She hadn't expected offerings from him in good faith. The gesture left her speechless as she stared at the wagons.

"North Queen," Mikael said, drawing her to look back at him. "You'll send the Bear—this Alexander—back to the North."

The commander's head jerked up in surprise. He recognized the name. Her stomach dropped as the fiery rage of his eyes burned into her, and she clenched her hands to keep from shaking. To her astonishment, he said nothing, but she knew it wouldn't be a detail he would dismiss.

She forced a nod to Mikael.

"You'll have until tomorrow with your army, then you'll come back to me," he told her.

Norah nodded again. "Tomorrow."

She mounted her horse, and the mare stirred anxiously underneath her. The commander mounted beside her, and she snapped her head toward Mikael in surprise. "He's not necessary," she said.

"He's most necessary," Mikael replied stiffly, and he clapped a hand on the neck of the commander's horse. "He's yours to command, but he'll not leave your side."

Norah severely doubted that Soren—no, not Soren, *the lord commander*—would follow anything she commanded of him. She shot him a steely gaze. With one last look at the king, she urged her mare forward, down the narrow path leading to the trenches of the canyon.

"Your Alexander is the Bear," he snarled when they were out of earshot.

"We agreed not to speak of it again," she said over her shoulder.

"That was before I knew who he was." The path widened, and he brought his horse alongside hers. His eyes burned into her, but she refused to look at him.

"The Bear is your lover," he pressed.

"No." She shook her head. "Whatever was between us, it was a long time ago." A time she couldn't even remember.

They rode down farther, passing into the shadows of the canyons.

"Will you weep when I kill him?" he asked.

The question sent a tremor down her spine and caught her breath in her chest. A rage rippled through her. She snapped her head to catch his stare, her teeth bared and eyes blazing. "If he dies, so does this marriage, and my alliance with Aleon will be certain. Will your king forgive you for that?"

He grabbed her arm, jerking her close as he pulled them to a stop. "I don't give a fuck about Aleon. It's the Bear that brings Salar's fate, and I'll take his head no matter the consequence." His eyes smiled cruelly. "Perhaps it won't be today." He paused. "Or perhaps it will. But make no mistake, I am going to kill him."

"Take your hands off me," she said between her teeth.

The commander snarled, but for the first time did as she'd told him and released his hold. He pushed his mount forward again, continuing through the dark labyrinth of the canyon walls.

She had no choice but to follow. Panic swelled inside her. He'd come to kill Alexander, and there was nothing she could do. The Shadow army watched from the top of the canyon, and Japheth waited just to the east. If her men killed the commander, the Shadowmen and Japheth would attack the Mercian army and easily overwhelm them. If the commander killed Alexander, her army would counter, leading to the same end. She needed to keep the peace, keep the commander from Alexander, and send her Northmen back home.

Light returned as they neared the end of the canyon's break, and the commander paused and looked back at her. His eyes brimmed with dark fire through the split in his head wrap. He sat larger than a fully armored man, yet he wore no armor, save the pauldron on the shoulder of his sword arm and the black poleyns above his boots. He'd forgone his winter tunic, showing off the inked markings across his chest and arms, and carried his massive battle-axe. His horse wore crested armor, and red war paint ran down the beast's chest like blood. She rolled her eyes at the display. No doubt her army would be uneasy, though.

They emerged from the depths of the canyon, toward her army waiting beyond.

A cry rang out: "The Queen!"

They drew closer to the Mercian army, and she knew Alexander would have recognized her by now. While she wore Horsemen clothes from Tahla, there was no mistaking her hair, especially in contrast to the darkness of the commander beside her. She combed the ranks for him, and then she stopped.

A large mounted man waited at the front of the army, with the crown head of a white Northern bear as a pauldron on his shoulder. *The Bear.* His helm gleamed under the sun, and his horse pawed the earth at his rider's impatience. *Alexander.*

She cast the commander a stern look. "Will you really be the cause of a war your king works to avoid?"

He gave a malicious chuckle. "Are you sure *I* will be the cause?"

She glanced back to see Alexander break from the Mercian army, racing toward her with a cavalry behind him. Her heart leapt to her throat. He wasn't coming simply to meet them—he was coming to free her.

He was attacking.

Surely his eyes deceived him. Alexander stared with his heart racing, watching as two riders emerged from the canyons and rode toward the Mercian army.

He knew them instantly.

Norah. His hand tightened around the hilt of his sword. *And the Destroyer.*

His enemy was taunting him. He didn't know what nefarious plan was at work, but he had come for Norah, to save her. And that is what he'd do, no matter the consequence. No matter the sacrifice.

His archers along the front line drew back their bows. They were the best in the world, and right now, they had one target. At this range, they wouldn't miss the Destroyer, but Norah was too close.

"Hold!" he called. He scanned the top of the canyons where the Shadow army looked down at them. What was this trickery? No doubt the Shadow King was using her to draw the Mercian army closer, to draw Alexander closer.

But it didn't matter if it was a trap. He'd come.

He looked at Titus to his right. "We go fast and hard. I'll take the Destroyer. You get the queen and ride for Aleon. Do not stop. After this, there will be no Mercian army. Only King Phillip will be able to protect her. Get her to him. At all costs."

The giant of a soldier nodded. "Yes, my lord."

Alexander swept his gaze across his cavalry and tightened his grip on his sword. His destrier pawed the earth and trembled underneath him, feeling the charge building. "With me!" he roared. He hit the face cover of his helm into place with his blade and spurred his destrier forward. His eyes locked on Norah and the Destroyer. He pushed everything else out. Nothing else mattered except getting her to safety.

A battle horn sounded from the Shadowmen at the top of the canyons, and Alexander pushed his mount faster. The Shadowmen would sweep down and overwhelm his army quickly, but not before he reached Norah, not before Titus got her away.

The Destroyer pulled up his massive battle-axe—a weapon Alexander had fought before, held by a monster he'd fought before.

Ten years of war. And this was the beginning of the end.

But just before Alexander reached them, Norah spun her horse in front of the Destroyer, putting herself between them. "Stop!" she cried out.

Alexander's destrier came to a grinding halt, and the rest of the mounted soldiers swept around them in a circle. What was she doing? Confusion flooded him. "Norah! What's the meaning of this?"

"Put down your sword!"

Alexander raised it higher, and his horse reared.

"Put down your sword!" she demanded again.

He pulled his destrier back in bewilderment, looking at Norah and then back to the Destroyer. He gave a quick glance at Titus, who sat ready to snatch her but paused in his own bewilderment.

"The lord commander comes under treaty," she said, loud enough for everyone to hear. "He's with me." She shot the Destroyer a warning look, and he lowered his axe.

With her? "How?" Alexander seethed. He glanced back at the Shadow army on the ridge, then back to Norah.

"It's not for us to discuss here."

What did that mean? He looked at the carts behind her and pointed his sword at them. "What's that?"

"Provisions," she said, "for our soldiers. Let's return to the army, and I'll explain."

"You negotiate with the Destroyer?" he asked icily. He pointed his sword at the monster. "Get off your horse," he ordered him.

"He'll do no such thing," Norah snapped, taking him aback. "I'm queen, and I said put down your weapons. I won't be made to explain myself as I suffer to avoid war. Draw back, Lord Justice, and let him pass!"

Her ferocity stunned him, and Alexander pulled his destrier back. Norah urged her horse toward the Mercian army with the Destroyer beside her. Alexander gave another look to Titus, who stared back at him wide-eyed, and he pressed his destrier to follow.

The Mercian archers still had their bows drawn. The Destroyer's horse reared and let out a ghostly scream, but Norah called out to the army to stand down.

The Northmen looked at each other, as equally confused as Alexander, but they obeyed and parted for the carts and the Shadowmen delivering them. The Shadowmen pulled the carts to a stop and stood, waiting for their next command. Did Norah really command them?

"We'll take them from here," she said. "You can return." The Shadowmen left to rejoin their army as the Northmen, including Alexander, watched in shock.

"What about him?" Alexander called, pointing his sword at the Destroyer.

She glanced at the monster, who sat silently, but he didn't fool Alexander. There was still an evil within.

"He stays with me," she said.

Alexander could only gape at her and grip his sword tighter.

They rode to the back of the army, up a small hill where a tent already stood, and dismounted. Alexander's eyes searched Norah for answers. What was going on?

"There will be no battle," she said abruptly. "Tell the men to rest and make camp."

No battle? Rest? "It's early still," Alexander argued. "And what do you mean, there will be no battle?"

"I'll stay here with you until tomorrow," she replied. "And then you'll return to Mercia."

Return to Mercia? What?

She ducked into the tent, where the Northmen soldiers scrambled to arrange things for their queen. The Destroyer followed her in and stood to the side. Alexander stepped in behind them, glaring. He still couldn't believe it—the commander of their greatest enemy stood mere steps away, and Norah acted as though he were a friend.

Alexander dropped his voice low. "Norah, are you going to tell me what's going on?"

"Leave us," she said to the other soldiers inside, and they emptied the tent.

He glared at the Destroyer. "She said *leave us.*"

Norah shook her head. "He won't go."

"I'll make him go." Alexander stepped toward him.

She reached out and clasped his arm, stopping him. "No. He's been ordered to stay."

Ordered? "By whom?"

She swallowed. "By the Shadow King... to whom I am betrothed."

Her words cut his heart from his chest. He couldn't breathe. *Betrothed.* "Betrothed?" His shallow breaths came faster but still starved his lungs for air. "But you're to marry the king of Aleon."

"I've changed my mind." Her voice cracked as she spoke.

Alexander stepped backward. No. *No.* "You were to unite our kingdoms." His eyes cut back to the Destroyer. "He's the monster we're fighting. You betray Mercia!"

"I am saving Mercia! Now there will be no war. No more death. The winter carries on, but our people will have food."

"Aleon will give us the provisions we need."

"But the Shadowlands will give us peace! Yes, Aleon can help us, but Phillip will bring another Great War with him." She shook her head. "I have to do what is best for Mercia."

"They will destroy us!" he seethed, with tears of rage in his eyes.

"They don't want war."

Alexander shook as he stepped in front of the Destroyer. "No? This one lusts for it," he said between his teeth.

The monster eyed him from underneath the wrap around his face. Alexander bared his teeth. This was a beast of a man, but he wasn't afraid. Only a coward would cover his face.

Norah stepped between them. "I need to write a letter to my grandmother," she said. "And it will take me some time. Distribute the food to the army. There will be more tomorrow."

"The army won't eat food from the Shadowlands."

"They will if you tell them to. Prepare for the journey back to Mercia." Her voice broke again, and it threatened to break him as well. She didn't want this. He had to find a way to stop it.

"Go," she said.

But he couldn't leave her. Not with this monster.

"Go!"

His face tightened in overwhelming bitterness, and it crushed him, but he obeyed and stormed out of the tent. He stopped just outside, pausing to suck in a deep breath and swallow back the bile rising in his throat.

Norah was to marry the Shadow King? *No.* That wasn't going to happen.

He wouldn't let it.

A low chuckle vibrated from the commander as he pulled the wrap down from his face and lowered the head of his battle-axe to rest on the ground.

Norah glared at him. "I'm sure you find this all very amusing."

"Some of it," he answered with a smirk.

"Ah, you found your tongue."

She turned from him, but he caught her arm. "Return to Salar today."

"What?" She pulled her arm away. "Why would I do that?"

"I know a desperate man when I see one."

"Alexander's not desperate," she cut back. "He's thinking about what this means for Mercia."

"He's thinking about you in his enemy's bed."

She slapped him sharply across the face.

He bared his teeth against the sting, but his eyes blazed back at her. "He's making stupid mistakes. He should have marched through Bahoul. That would have been the smart choice."

Norah swallowed. That's why the Shadow King had taken her to Bahoul. They had expected Alexander to go there. It had been *the smart choice.*

"But instead, he marched straight through the Tribelands," he told her. "And he drove your army much faster than he should have. Look at your men. They're tired, spent." He paused, with a slight curve of his lips. "His emotion controls him. And that makes him easily beaten."

He leaned closer to her. "Would you like to make a wager, North Queen? If you stay here tonight, there will be war. You give him time—time to think, to plot, to plan, for the madness to take hold—and he won't let you go." He smiled. "And I'll kill him."

Norah's pulse quickened again. She wasn't confident Alexander could stand against the king's brute. If she went back now, the commander would go with her, keeping Alexander safe.

"And if I return today?" she asked. "You won't harm him?"

His eyes burned with an unsatisfied fire, but finally, he gave a single nod.

Tears stung her eyes, threatening to fall. "Let me write my letter, then. And I'll go."

Norah folded her penned letter, pouring the wax and stamping it slowly. This wasn't a letter of good news, but her grandmother would be relieved at her safety, and Norah was sure she would understand. This marriage changed everything, for everyone.

Alexander stepped into the tent and eyed the commander, finding him as he had left him, with the head of his axe resting at his feet and his hand on the handle. Then his gaze found Norah. She stood and stepped close to him. He was silent, hesitant to speak in front of the commander, but his eyes bore into hers, and she could see the sadness inside him.

"So this is why they call you the Bear," she whispered, touching the crown head of the beast on his shoulder.

His voice came in barely a breath. "I was so afraid I wouldn't see you again."

Her lip trembled, and he stepped closer. She couldn't stop herself—she swept forward and threw her arms around him. He wrapped his arms around her and held her tightly. Tears fell as she breathed him in. If this was the last she'd see of him, she wanted to remember everything about him—how he felt, how he smelled. She only wished she could kiss him. She wished she could tell him she loved him. But that wouldn't help either of them now. Especially not with the commander so near.

The commander.

Remembering his presence, she pulled back, wiping her cheeks and inhaling deeply. "I'm going back today," she told Alexander.

His breath quickened, and he shook his head. "No, stay. You said you would stay until tomorrow."

She swallowed the lump in her throat and held the letter out to him. "For my grandmother."

He reached out and took the letter. "Norah, you can't."

"Will you tell her I'm well?"

Alexander reached up and gently brushed the bruise that still marred her cheek. His eyes were thick with emotion. She'd forgotten about her face. It had healed mostly, but there was still evidence of a fight. How difficult it must be for him to see her this way.

"What have they done to you?" he breathed. His gaze shifted back to the commander.

"This isn't their doing."

"All of this is their doing." He shook his head and dropped his voice. "Norah. You can't do this. You can't go." His words broke. "I can't let you go this time."

"Don't you see? It's the only way."

"What about Aleon?"

"If I wed Phillip, there will still be war," she argued. "Yes, Aleon gives us the means to fight, but we still have to. You saw the vision. With Phillip by my side, this war carries on. Thousands will die."

His brow dipped. "You think Phillip won't bring a war if you marry the Shadow King?"

"With what? He can't fight Japheth and the Shadowlands and Mercia. He won't be happy, but there's nothing he can do. Alexander, an alliance with the Shadowlands is the only alliance that can bring peace."

"Norah, please," he begged.

Norah put her hand on his cheek and shook her head softly. "It's too late," she whispered through her own tears. "I made a promise, and I can't break it now. Look around us. These men, they'll all die. You'll die. I have to do what's best for Mercia." And what was best for *him*.

"This isn't it," he said hoarsely. "You can't marry him."

Norah's heart broke. "I'm sorry."

She stood up on her toes and brought her lips to his cheek, kissing him a longing goodbye. Then she pulled away and stepped out of the tent and into the winter.

Chapter Thirty-Six

Norah and the commander rode in silence back up the pass to the Shadow army camp where the king met them with surprise. Mikael called out in the Shadow tongue and the commander responded in kind.

The king reached out to help her as she slid down from the mare. She could tell he was at a loss for words over their early return. "You said you would send more provisions," she reminded him, forcing her voice steady.

"That I will," he assured her.

She gave a small nod and walked past him, toward the large tent. She was starting to fall apart and needed a place to be alone. The king let her go. Tears streamed down her face by the time she ducked inside, and she fell onto the bed and wept.

It was daylight when she woke to the sound of the king's voice outside the tent. She wiped her eyes and sat up, surprised she had fallen asleep, and even more surprised it was morning. A thick fur had been draped over her. She heard the king enter and looked up to see him holding a bowl of steaming soup and a wineskin.

He held the bowl out for her. Norah took it and drank down the savory broth. Her stomach grumbled. She'd eaten nothing the day prior, and she was famished. She finished the bowl quickly.

He held out his hand for the bowl, and she slowly gave it back to him.

"Do you want another?" he asked.

Yes. "No."

The corners of his mouth turned up. He moved to the flap of the tent and extended the bowl to a soldier outside. "Another," he said.

He held out the wineskin, and she took it, eyeing him.

"Why did you return?" he asked.

She took a drink of the wine. A deep one. It was good, and she hated it. "Because I said I would. Did you not expect me to?"

He didn't answer.

The realization came to her. "That's why you sent the commander with me, wasn't it? To kill me if I tried to leave?"

"He was to kill the Bear."

Her heart quickened. "We agreed—"

"It was only if you would have broken our agreement," he interrupted her.

Anger pulsed inside her. "But I didn't."

"And the Bear is still alive."

"Stop calling him that," she snapped. "He's my lord justice."

She pushed a breath out to slow her heart. The name didn't even bother her. She just needed to be angry at something—at him. She needed the anger. It was the only thing holding her together. A soldier returned with another bowl of soup, and Mikael held it out to her.

Her eyes welled, and she took it.

"Do you want some bread?" he asked.

A tear rolled down her cheek, and she shook her head.

He gave a gentle smile and sat down beside her. Then he held out a bread roll.

Another tear fell as she took it, but there was a warmth about him that surprised her, and settled her.

He sat in silence with her as she ate the bread and drained the second helping of soup. She could have downed a third, but she didn't dare say it. When she'd finished, he said, "My kingdom has good food." The corner of his mouth turned up. "That's important to you, yes?"

She wiped her lips and held her empty bowl. "What?"

He shrugged. "You eat a lot."

"What's that supposed to mean?"

He shrugged again. "That you eat a lot."

She stared at him. Was that a bad thing? She ate like a perfectly normal person. Yes, Alexander may have occasionally teased her...

She jerked. *Alexander.* They'd be heading back to Mercia. She set the bowl down. "Have they departed?"

"They're preparing now. Go to the cliff. You'll see them."

Norah rose quickly from the bed. As she pulled on her cloak, the fastening caught in her hair. She tried to pull it free, but it held in the braid. Heat rushed to her cheeks as she fumbled with it in front of him. He rose and stepped forward, stopping her. Gently, he untangled the locks from the clasp and straightened the cloak over her shoulders.

She wavered for a moment. "Thank you," she breathed. Their gazes caught each other, and they stilled. The darks of his eyes held her, quieted her.

Alexander, she remembered.

She peeled herself away, and then she ducked out of the tent, hurrying toward the cliff and freeing her tresses from the disheveled braid as she went. She reached the edge, out of breath. The wind blew her hair wildly around her as she looked down at her army. She saw the horses and the wagons of food the Shadow army had delivered.

And she saw Alexander.

He was already mounted on his horse, conferring with his soldiers. One pointed up at her and he spun to see her.

The army started their march. The cold of the wind burned her skin, but she stayed and watched them leave. Alexander waited for the last soldier to depart, still looking up at her. He raised his sword to her—a silent vow. With a last longing look, he turned to join the army back to Mercia.

Norah made her way to her tent. She expected another rush of emotion to come. But it didn't. Perhaps the weight of everything had taken all the emotion. Maybe she had nothing left. She reached the tent where the king still waited inside.

"We'll depart shortly," he told her.

"I'd like to change, if that's all right." Tahla had given her a leather-and-linen layered dress to meet her army, and like Mercian dresses, it wasn't made with comfort in mind. She'd rather wear the riding dress for the journey to the Shadowlands.

"Of course," he said with a small nod, and stepped out to tend his army.

She stripped off the heavy dress and stood for a moment, naked, letting the chill of the air clear her mind and quiet her soul. Then she put on her breeches and boots and pulled the riding dress over her head. She cursed under her breath as she found she could only tie it loosely behind. Why must all dresses have fastenings in the back? She reached behind awkwardly, trying to pull the leather lacing tighter, tempted to don the weapon boy's clothing once more instead.

Mikael entered, startling her, and she quickly turned her back to him, flushing.

"I'm sorry. I thought I'd allowed enough time," he said.

Norah turned her head, looking at him out of the corner of her eye. She paused for a moment, gathering her courage, then asked, "Can you help me?"

He stepped toward her slowly.

She reached up and pulled her hair away, waiting.

"Would you like it tighter?" he asked.

"Please."

He pulled the hastily tied bow undone and paused, letting his fingers skim the skin between the edging. Her skin prickled.

"I want to see you," he said, his voice low and thick. "Would that imperil your honor?"

She looked back over her shoulder. His brazenness astonished her. "No, but it doesn't mean I'll let you."

He chuckled and fixed the lacing tighter. Then he stepped closer, and she felt his breath in her ear. "Are you unmoved by a man's suffering? You'd make a decent torturer."

A flush crept up her skin. She knew it was a jest, but there was an underlying message of desire. What bothered her more was that she liked it. She turned around, eyeing him boldly. "You'd make a decent lady-in-waiting," she said, then ducked out of the tent to prepare for their departure.

The Shadowlands were well suited to their name. They rode between the canyon cliffs that towered over them and held back the light—they were dark and foreboding, like the men they homed. It took a full day to reach the end of the labyrinth, where the trail opened and the rocky darkness fell away to reveal the beauty of terraced mountains, even in their winter slumber.

Norah's eyes widened. It was like stepping into another world.

Mikael nodded out over the terraces. "In the spring and summer, this will all be lush and green. It will be beautiful."

"It's already beautiful," she said. She hadn't imagined a place of such dark renown could be so lovely. She noticed the paddy fields. "The Shadowlands grow rice? Is that your trade?"

"Our main one, yes."

"Is that what you trade with the Horsemen?" That must be how he'd become so close to the tribes.

"It's what we trade *through* the Horsemen, with everyone," he told her. "Including the North."

Norah's brows creased. "Mercia doesn't get their rice from the Shadowlands."

He chuckled. "The whole world gets their rice from us. They just don't know it."

Norah shook her head, amazed. "The Horsemen take it to market for you?" she asked. She thought longer. "Do you feed them as well? Is that what Tahla meant when she said Abilash dare not defy you, unless they want to starve?"

He didn't answer, but his smirk told her it was.

"Do you control all the Horsemen tribes?" she asked, her curiosity growing.

"Most. Not all."

She thought about their departure from King Abilash and what Tahla had told her. "Do you think there will be consequences with Abilash now?"

"If so, I'll deal with them, but they're of no matter." He looked at her. "I have what I want."

A wave rolled through her stomach, stirring feelings that confused her. Despite their history and start, he had been kind to her, protected her, this Shadow King with his destroyer of men. "Tahla told me what happened at Choan, how you saved the Uru."

He shifted uncomfortably in his saddle. "You believe her?"

"I have no reason not to."

He pulled up his horse and looked at her with a steely gaze. "Don't."

Her brow creased in confusion. "Don't believe her?"

"Don't mistake me for a good man, North Queen," he warned. "You'll be sorely disappointed."

Norah's chest tightened, surprised at his sharpness, and they continued on in silence. The terraced mountains gave way again to the black rock of the Shadowlands. Her pulse quickened as an enormous castle loomed in the distance against the skyline. It was like nothing she'd ever seen. "Even your castle is black," she said, more to herself than to him.

"It's made from the black mortite under our earth," he told her. "It's also why the canyons are so dark. It would have been a greater feat to build a castle any color other than black."

As they neared the castle, it was even larger than she'd originally thought, larger than Mercia's castle and with an even larger city sprawling out from its walls. The gates, adorned with gold scripts, were as ornate as they were strong, and she marveled at them as they passed through. The expansive courtyard was packed with people craning to see the king and the strange woman he'd brought back with him. They brought their horses to a stop, and Mikael dismounted.

She slid off her mare, and murmurs rumbled through the crowds as they recognized her. She immediately became self-conscious remembering the beating to her face and pulled the hood of her cloak over her. The throngs of people parted as Mikael led the way, and they cheered their king as he passed.

They reached the polished stairs and intricately sculpted doors, and Mikael led the procession inside. As the great doors closed behind him, he turned and called back to her, "Come."

Then he and the commander started through the castle. Did he think she was a dog? Norah rolled her eyes but reluctantly followed. They turned down a large hall, larger than the great hall in Mercia but just as beautiful. Dark, polished tile patterned the floor and sprang up the walls to the arched ceilings overhead. Symmetrical geometries created intricate designs, weaving complex patterns that drew the eye to every corner of the room.

At the end of the hall, a woman stood, regal and majestic. Silver kissed the long hair that had once been a brilliant black. She looked at Mikael with warmth and affection as he walked toward her.

"Mother," he greeted her, kissing her cheek and bringing her hands to his lips.

Norah immediately felt a wave of anxiousness in anticipation of being presented to the king's mother. It would have been nice to have cleaned up first.

The woman's brow dipped as she grazed his beard with her fingertips. "What happened to your face, and your hand?" she asked as she reached out and touched his arm in horror. She turned to the commander with a scowl, clearly annoyed at his poor keeping of the king, but her eyes widened in seeing his wounds and accompanying limp. "From the Northmen?" she asked.

"Not the Northmen," Mikael said, stepping back and turning to Norah. "The North Queen."

It was not the introduction Norah had been hoping for.

The king's mother looked at her incredulously, her eyes darting from Norah to the lord commander and then back to Mikael again. She drew closer and looked over Norah in astonishment.

"Your Majesty," she said to Norah, with a cold steel in her voice. While her eyes were rimmed in loathing, she held her etiquette, much as Norah expected Catherine might do. The woman looked at her son, searching for direction, but he gave none.

Apparently, Norah's arrival was as unexpected to his mother as it was to her.

The king's mother turned back to Norah. "We'll see you comfortable during your stay here," she said stiffly. "I'll take you to your chamber." She looked back at Mikael with displeasure and then turned toward a side hall. "Come," she called to Norah.

Norah pursed her lips. She was beginning to see the resemblance.

The woman led her down the hall to a large staircase. At the top of the stairs and at the end of another hall, they came to an open chamber.

"You're surprised I'm here," Norah said, breaking the silence.

"I'm surprised you're alive," the king's mother said bluntly. "And yes, that you're here." The woman turned and looked at Norah more closely, disappointment brimming in her eyes. "But I am sorry for your condition. It doesn't please me you've been handled in this manner. It's not right for a queen."

Norah realized she was referring to the bruising and cut on her face. "This wasn't your son's fault." The woman seemed as surprised at Norah's defense of him as she was herself. "I mean, most things are," she added, "but not my appearance."

The king's mother was quiet. Her lips parted slightly, but no words came out.

Maids filled a tub with steaming water and draped a linen gown over a side chair.

"We'll find you an appropriate gown for the evening," the woman said stiffly. She gave Norah a small nod. "Your Majesty," she said, and left her to the bath.

Norah waited as they all made their way out and closed the doors behind them. She looked around the room. It was ornately decorated with dark, heavy furnishings and tapestries of black and gold. The windows in the room were tall tri-sets of thin glass panels, separated by iron staves like a beautiful cage. Even if she was no longer a prisoner, she still felt like one.

Norah sighed and peeled off her soiled clothing. She welcomed the chance to feel clean again. The water burned her skin as she stepped into the bath, but she didn't care. She wanted to burn off everything that had happened since she'd left Mercia. If only she could wash away this situation. She closed her eyes and sank underneath the surface, relishing the sting of the water over her body and face. When she could hold her breath no longer, she pushed herself up, gasping for air.

Norah worked the soap into a rich lather and rubbed it into her skin. It smelled like springtime. She hated that she liked it. The water changed color as the soil came off, and she was surprised at how dirty she'd been.

She wanted to stay in the bath, soaking in its warmth, but she didn't want the king's mother to return with her unready. Quickly, she finished washing and climbed out, drying off and slipping into the linen gown. She shivered. Castles were cold. Especially enemy castles.

Chapter Thirty-Seven

The sun set on her first day in the Shadowlands, and Norah fought to keep control of her emotions. Her duty had been to free Mercia from the darkness of the Shadow King, but here she was, marrying him and joining their kingdoms together. Her stomach turned at the thought of her grandmother receiving her letter. She'd understand. She'd see this was what was best for Mercia and her people. Wouldn't she?

But Norah couldn't escape the nagging fear that wasn't how her marriage would be seen, and she would be doing all this for nothing. The thought threatened to break her. She forced her mind to focus on one task at a time. Bathe. Dress. Breathe.

There was a knock on her chamber door and the king's mother swept into the room before she could answer, with a maid close behind. Very Catherinesque. A pang of homesickness struck her. What she wouldn't give to see her grandmother right now.

"I've brought several dresses," the woman told her. "We should find at least one that fits for this evening."

Without a word, the maid shuffled Norah in front of the mirror and lifted a yellow dress against her form.

The king's mother looked at it in the mirror's reflection. "No," she said, and the maid laid it aside on the bed.

The maid held a green dress, and the woman again shook her head. Norah swallowed. She would have been fine with either of the dresses.

The maid held up a third dress—burgundy with heavy embroidery down the center. "That will do," she said.

Despite the woman's coldness, the marked reminder of Catherine brought emotion to Norah's eyes. She forced it back.

The maid helped her into the dress. "It fits well," she said as she moved to Norah's back and tied the straps. "Your being the same size as the princess makes it easier."

Norah glanced up at the king's mother. "You have a daughter?" Her heart leapt at the thought of another young woman in the castle—perhaps someone like her.

The woman glared at the maid, who continued working in silence. "I did," she said shortly.

Norah's heart broke for her. The woman had lost a daughter. She didn't know what to say, or whether to offer her condolences. "I'm sorry," she said softly.

The room was silent. That made it worse.

"What should I call you?" Norah asked her, changing the subject. "Do you have a title here in the Shadowlands?"

The woman looked at her with eyes of black sapphire. For a moment, Norah thought she wouldn't answer.

"My name is Analil. In Kharavian tongue, as this is Kharav, not *the Shadowlands*, I am called Salara-Mae, if you wish."

It wasn't her intent to so quickly offend her future mother-in-law. She gave a small nod. "Forgive me, Salara-Mae. And thank you for your counsel. Kharav it is."

After dressing, Norah followed Salara-Mae down the stairs, through the great hall, and into a large dining room, and her eyes widened at the expansive table. The king sat at the end, with the commander seated to his left. The king looked up as she entered, pausing in his conversation, and straightened. Their eyes locked. He'd washed too. His hair was tied back, and his beard trimmed short, almost to the skin. Without his armor, he wore a sleeveless tunic, prominently displaying the ink markings down his arms and just below his neck. Heat flushed across her cheeks. He looked... very nice.

She realized the commander looked different as well. He'd forgone his wrap and was openly showing his head and face. His hair was tied back like the king's. He wore a tunic similar to Mikael's, which was better than his normal form of none at all. At first glance, he looked very much like the king, although he was certainly *not* like the king. And he looked... *not* nice.

A chilling snarl came from her right, and Norah gasped as two beasts crouched low, ready to attack. Their heads and frames were like enormous wolves, but they weren't wolves. Their necks and chests were thick and maned in dark fur, but their backs sloped to a smaller, thick-muscled hind, like they were built for fighting.

Salara-Mae glared at Mikael. "Control your dogs," she snapped angrily.

The king's eyes drifted to his lord commander, who called over his shoulder, "Cusco. Cavaatsa." The beasts settled back to lie on the floor.

"Forgive us," Salara-Mae said to Norah, eyeing the commander sharply. "We've had very few guests for some of us to hone our manners. But as you *are* our guest, please," and she waved Norah to the end of the table, opposite Mikael.

Norah glanced at him, uncomfortable with his mother's unawareness of their betrothal, but she gave a nod and sat gracefully. When would he tell her?

A young woman pulled fruit and meat from the platters and filled her plate. Norah watched her, noting her soft brown hair. She was different from the people in Kharav. Catherine had told her Kharav took people as slaves. Was this woman a slave?

"Must he drink that filth in front of me?" Salara-Mae's voice cut through the air.

Norah glanced around the table to see what had upset her. The king's brute held a chalice in his hand and was cheekily taking another drink before setting it on the table. She wondered what was inside it. He seemed to hold Salara-Mae's contempt. She wouldn't even speak directly to him, which was surprising. And somewhat entertaining.

"Well, we didn't know you'd be joining us for dinner this evening, Mother," Mikael answered in his commander's defense.

Salara-Mae scowled at her son, who took a bite of food and chewed it slowly, unfazed. Then she straightened her shoulders and turned to Norah. "I take my dinner in my chamber, as I prefer an early meal. I'm sure you'll prefer to do the same during your visit."

Visit.

Norah held a grape in her fingers. It was the largest grape she'd ever seen, and she popped it in her mouth. Salara-Mae looked at her as though she expected her to respond. *Nope.* Norah pushed in two more grapes. Then her eyes found Mikael, who was looking back at her.

She stopped mid-chew.

"It's more than a visit, Mother. The North Queen and I are to be married," he announced, rather abruptly.

Norah forced herself to swallow her mouthful of half-chewed grapes and frowned. Perhaps he could have waited for just a little better timing and maybe had a softer approach or a bit of a buildup? But there it was—out.

A coldness swept through the room. Norah's heart raced in her chest.

Salara-Mae carefully put down her glass and smoothed out the cloth on the table in front of her. "If this is your attempt at humor, it's ill spun."

Norah shoved another set of grapes into her mouth. She wouldn't be available to speak for this engagement.

"This isn't a humorous matter," he replied. "I will wed the North Queen."

"You'll do no such thing!"

Norah pushed in another two grapes without having chewed the others.

"You speak to your salar," he reminded his mother.

"What would your father say?" she hissed.

His voice was as sharp as steel. "My father's dead."

Norah swallowed her grapes and took a deep drink from her chalice. It wasn't exactly how she'd hoped this conversation would go. She wondered if it would have been different in Mercia. Probably not. She was starting to appreciate that she'd only had to write a letter to Catherine and the council.

"I would speak with you alone," Salara-Mae said to her son.

Norah would be perfectly fine with them speaking alone.

"No need," he said stiffly. "My decision's final."

Norah thought the lump in her throat might choke her. She focused on controlling the shake in her breath.

Salara-Mae moved her icy gaze to Norah and then to the commander. Surely a fire burned inside him in violent agreement with the king's mother, regardless of the bitterness that sat between them, but he gave no support to her protest.

The room was ghostly quiet. Mikael took a drink from his chalice. Norah took a bite of the marinated meat. Mikael was right. The food was good here. And it was the only thing helping her get through this conversation.

"I think I'll retire," Salara-Mae said, pushing back her chair and rising.

"You haven't eaten," Mikael said.

"I'm not feeling well. I'll take something later, in my room, if my appetite returns."

"I trust you'll be better tomorrow after you've rested."

She looked at him coldly. "I seriously doubt it." Despite her abhorrence to the idea of their marriage, she wasn't without etiquette, and she gave a small bow to Norah. "Your Majesty."

Norah struggled to swallow the meat and gave a nod back. "Salara-Mae."

The woman turned and left with two guards at her flank.

The king's brute took another drink from his chalice, and Norah saw the color on his lips: a dark iron red. *Blood*. Blood filled his chalice. His eyes locked with hers, and the hair on the back of her neck stood on end as her stomach twisted in revulsion.

"We'll announce our marriage tomorrow and celebrate," Mikael told her, as if everything were perfectly normal. Was drinking blood normal? "Then we'll begin preparations for a wedding that will happen in a few weeks' time."

Wedding? Right. She peeled her eyes from the commander. Another topic that threatened to empty her stomach: she was to be married.

Norah drew her bottom lip between her teeth. "When will I be able to return to Mercia?" If she could just get home, she could... pretend, perhaps, that this was not as terrible as it seemed.

The king paused in lifting his chalice, stilling for a moment as he looked at her. "You won't."

What? Her pulse quickened. "Not even to visit?"

"You'll be salara," he said, and then took a drink of wine. "Your place is in Kharav."

Norah's chest tightened. She couldn't breathe. She hadn't expected to return right away to Mercia, but she'd hoped at some point she would. Even in going to Aleon, she would have traveled back and forth between the two kingdoms.

His words made everything real for the first time. This was her home now. She might never see Mercia again. Or her grandmother. Or Alexander. The weight of everything threatened to crush her. She needed out. She rose abruptly, gripping the edge of the table for support.

"Excuse me," she managed to utter before she made her escape from the room. She didn't wait for acknowledgment. Her mind was a haze as she wound through the maze of halls, toward her room. Her panic grew with each step, and she was desperate to find her chamber before she fell apart. But each hall, each door, looked the same. The sound of a guard so close behind, following her disoriented course, further overwhelmed her. She couldn't hold herself together anymore. She stopped, backing against a wall to catch her breath, and covered her face with her hands. Her cheeks burned with embarrassment, which only fueled her emotion.

A soft touch on her elbow startled her, and she looked up to see one of her guardsmen. He moved his hand, motioning her back the way they had come. She wiped her cheeks and stepped forward slowly, allowing him to lead. They wound back through the halls, and she tried to regain her composure. Relief filled her when he stopped at the door of her chamber.

"Thank you," she whispered through her shaking breaths, and then slipped inside.

Chapter Thirty-Eight

Norah sat at the small table in her chamber in the fading darkness of morning, a heavy weight in her chest. The king had issued an announcement of their marriage, and tonight there would be a celebration, but she didn't feel like celebrating. She should, she told herself. She was avoiding war. Her kingdom was safe. Alexander was safe.

A small knock rattled her door, and a servant entered, carrying a gown over her arm and a small tray of bread and fruit. The young woman was the same one from the dining hall—fair skinned with soft hazel eyes and brown hair. Norah wanted to ask if she was a free woman, but that seemed rude. So she didn't. The maid avoided Norah's eyes as she set the tray on the table and then draped the gown over the side chair. She gave a small bow and left the chamber without a word.

Norah stared at the tray, then picked up a strawberry half the size of her palm. She closed her eyes as she bit into it, letting its sweetness fill her senses, and imagined herself somewhere very far from the kingdom of Shadows.

But she only gave herself a moment. She needed to dress. Gods only knew what was in store for her today. Quickly, she rose and shucked off her nightgown before pulling on the dress that lay over the side chair. She breathed a few words of thanks that it had front lacing. Salara-Mae hadn't offered her a maid, and she wasn't going to ask for one. She'd manage herself. She pulled her hair back into a braid and washed her face in the basin. The cold water made her shiver.

Dressed, she waited. She wasn't sure what for. Was she expected to stay in her chamber, or—

A hard knock on the door startled her. She wasn't expecting anyone so soon. In fact, she wasn't expecting anyone at all. She opened the door slowly to find the lord commander looking back at her.

"I would speak with you in the hall," he said shortly.

"No, thank you," she replied and moved to close the door, but he caught it with his hand. "Please," he said between his teeth, with more bite than request.

Norah sighed. He wouldn't leave until he accomplished whatever he was burdened to do. Reluctantly, she stepped into the hall and was surprised to find a group of soldiers with him.

The commander turned his gaze on the closest man. "This is Captain Artem. He leads the Crest, the protectors of the royal family, and now apparently you."

Apparently. The ring of distaste in his words wasn't lost on her. She drew her eyes over the captain, who didn't bow at his presentation and didn't speak. His mouth was a hard line as he stared back at her.

He was different from the other Kharavian soldiers, and different from the lord commander. He wore armor, something she hadn't seen much of in the Shadowlands, aside from the king. Older than the commander, in his fifties perhaps, he wore no wrap on his head. Gray touched the temples of his black hair above his angular face that held a peppered shadow of a short beard. But it was his eyes—his eyes told her of an evil within. She shuddered.

"You'll have at least two men with you at all times, four if you step outside the castle walls," the commander said.

"That's really unnecessary," she said.

"It's not negotiable," he growled back, and her face flushed with the heat of anger. "You'll always have at least one guardsman who speaks the Northern tongue." He held his hand out, and four of the dozen men stepped forward. With their faces covered, they all looked the same, except she thought she recognized one's eyes as the soldier who'd helped her find her chamber the day before. She gave a nod back, with a small sense of comfort that at least one of her guardsmen could be kind.

"You'll never be without your guard," he said. "Am I clear?"

Norah pursed her lips together. "Perfectly." Just like at home.

But this wasn't home.

The morning passed slowly, and Norah felt awkwardly confined to her room. Not that it mattered, she told herself. She didn't have an appetite to see the castle right now. So she waited and tried to pretend, if only for a moment, she wasn't trapped in the darkness of the Shadowlands. *Kharav,* she reminded herself.

She lay across the bed, looking up at the great beams along the ceiling. Then she let her eyes close as she thought of Alexander—his face, his eyes, the warmth of his hands. She could almost feel them around hers. A tear fell from the corner of her eye to her soft locks underneath.

A knock on the door pulled her from her thoughts, and she sat up as she wiped her face. Would this be how she spent her time—constantly answering her door? She opened it to see her guard. Not the nice one.

"We will escort you down to the celebration."

Her brows drew together in confusion. "So soon? It's barely midday."

"Yes, but it's already started."

"Oh." She felt a wave of anxiousness. She wasn't one for social celebrations, especially ones celebrating her, especially ones celebrating her unfortunate marriage. "Will it last all day?" she asked.

"Of course."

"Wonderful," she mumbled to herself. "Give me a moment."

She closed her door and leaned back against it, inhaling deep breaths. Celebrations were better than war, she told herself. That's why she was doing this. This was best for Mercia.

Not for her.

But she couldn't think about herself. Not just because she couldn't be selfish, but she had to control her emotion. Maybe she could pretend it was someone else's marriage. Yes, *someone else's*. She went to the vanity, wiping her face and tucking a few wayward locks behind her ear.

"Someone else's marriage," she said to her reflection. "I'm very happy for them. May they have a long life, much happiness, many children"—wait, no—"*No children.*"

Then she let out a breath and opened the door, waving the guard to lead her.

People filled the hall from end to end, and her eyes widened as she entered. The magnitude of it all was overwhelming. Everyone grew quiet with her arrival, and all eyes fell on her. *Someone else's marriage.* She forced herself forward.

Her wandering gaze found the king seated at the large center table at the front of the hall, and he stood when he saw her. He picked up his chalice and held it high, and the room erupted in clapping as the crowd parted for her. She made her way toward him.

His eyes smiled. "Please," he said, motioning to the chair beside him.

A servant pulled out the chair as she took her seat.

He sat down beside her. "I'm happy to see you, North Queen."

"Good," she said smartly, but gave him a small smile.

His eyes lingered on her. "I thought you might be angry with me for how we left our conversation last evening."

She looked down at her hands. The thought of not being able to return to Mercia still tore her heart from her. "More... sad."

He shifted in his chair, and his mouth opened to speak, but he said nothing. He looked out across the celebrating hall, then back to her. His brows drew together. "You're sad?" He leaned back in his chair. "But you'll be salara."

As if the two weren't the same.

He let out an unsettled breath. "You'll return to the North again. I promise you this."

She straightened in her chair. *When?*

"But tonight, I want you to enjoy yourself," he told her, looking out across the great hall. "Celebrate. We're to be married."

Did he have to remind her? Norah noticed the king's mother was absent from the festivities. She wondered how long she'd have to endure before she could excuse herself.

Could she excuse herself from her own wedding celebration? She glanced around—was there at least some food?

Three women approached. They lined up before the king and gave a low bow. They were beautiful, hair like black silk, and large brown eyes. Sisters, maybe? Her gaze moved over the ornate embroidery of their dresses, the gold around their wrists, and the adornments in their hair. Women of status.

"Salara," Mikael told them, introducing her.

The women smiled politely at her, giving another low bow.

"Myral, Rasha, and Heta," he said to Norah. "They'll be with you in the villa, where you'll stay once we're wed."

Royals maintaining separate spaces wasn't surprising; it was customary in Mercia as well. Forced friends—odd—but Norah liked the idea of not being entirely alone. "We'll be good friends, then," she told them, giving a polite smile.

The women bowed again and then left as gracefully as they had come.

A string of music caught her ear, and she glanced up to see a dancer in the center of the hall. Norah took in a breath of astonishment at her clothing, or rather, her lack of clothing. The woman wore only braided weaves of richly patterned cloth around her hips and small bells that jingled with each movement. Beaded bracelets wrapped her wrists, and she shook them in unison to the rhythm of the music. Heavily beaded adornments covered her neck, with intricately woven strands cascading over her chest. The nipples of her bare breasts were pierced with small golden rings.

Norah's eyes widened as the woman moved her hips to the fluted song. She'd never seen anything so brazen. Such entertainment in Mercia would be the ruin of a good name. Her cheeks flushed with embarrassment, but she couldn't look away. The dancer had lighter hair, blonde, like her Northmen. Norah wondered where she was from.

"She's beautiful, yes?" Mikael said as he watched the dancer.

"Um..." She swallowed, unsure how to answer. Despite her discomfort, she was mesmerized. The dancer flowed with the music, her body rolling like the waves of the sea. She was light on her feet, as if she weren't held by the pull of the earth. Her eyes locked with Norah's. She was close enough for Norah to see their emerald depths. The woman smiled.

The dancer spun, and Norah finally broke from her hold. She glanced at Mikael, only to find him watching her.

"You like her?" he asked. His eyes flashed with amusement.

Norah's cheeks flushed, like she'd been caught. She swallowed back her embarrassment. "I've just never seen anything like her."

"She's all the way from Elam, given as a gift to Japheth's King Gregor, but I won her from him in a bet." He smiled, smugly pleased with himself.

Disgust knotted in her stomach. She found nothing pleasing about gifting or betting human beings. Bitterness rippled across her tongue. "Do people's lives mean nothing to you?" she said before she could stop herself.

His smile faded. "She's a slave."

"She's a person," Norah snapped.

Anger flashed across his face at her rebuke; he was clearly unaccustomed to being chastised, but he didn't respond. He only sat for a moment, then gave a small wave of his hand. The music died. He called out in the Shadow tongue, and the dancer stopped. She looked at Norah with a troubled face.

"What are you doing?" Norah asked him.

The dancer bowed low and quickly left the hall.

"What's going to happen to her?" she asked, her alarm growing.

"Whatever you decide. She's yours now."

She sat back in her chair. "What?" Was he serious? *No*—he couldn't be. Was he? "I don't want her."

"Then you'll have to figure out what to do with her."

Gods, he was serious. Norah scoffed in frustration as she looked back out across the hall. She knew she'd offended him, but she didn't really care. He was offensive. The Shadowlands were offensive, with their slaves and their bloodlust. This was a mistake; she couldn't marry this man. She had to get out of here. She had to... escape... somehow. Get back to Mercia...

And prepare for war. Because that's what she would cause: *war*.

Norah sighed. She couldn't leave. She had to make this work. But she vowed to herself that she would change things.

The celebration wore on through an endless evening. Mikael settled. She felt his eyes on her, often, but didn't look at him. Finally, she bid her parting and, thankfully, slipped away. As she walked to her chamber, her mind spun around her. She had to find a way to live here, despite her abhorrence of the idea. She had to learn how to live as queen of the Shadowlands.

Norah opened her chamber door and jumped at the figure inside. "Hammel's hell," she breathed as she recognized the woman—the green-eyed dancer.

The woman bowed low. "I'm sorry, Your Majesty. I didn't mean to startle you."

She gripped the side chair close by, her heart still racing. "What are you doing here?"

"I'm yours now," she said quickly.

Norah drew in a sharp breath and clipped it out again. "No, you're not mine. That's not... *no*."

Panic flashed across the woman's face. "Do you not find me pleasing?"

"I don't," Norah said shortly. "You have to go. No one can see you here."

The woman fell on her knees in front of Norah. "Your Majesty! I'm sorry I displease you. But I beg of you, please don't send me away! Let me try again."

Norah shook her head as she swallowed back the awkwardness of the situation. "There's nothing to try again, I don't want"—she waved her hand—"whatever it is you do."

"I'm most discreet. And trained in pleasure for both men and women."

Norah's cheeks flushed hotter. "That's exactly what I don't want," she insisted. "Please, go."

"Do you have a need for a maid?" she pleaded.

"No, I—" Norah paused. She did need a maid. She thought she'd be given one, but that seemed unlikely now. She eyed the woman doubtfully. "Are you trained as such?"

"I've been in Kharavian court for three years. I know the ways of Kharav, and I know what proper maids don't." Her deep-emerald eyes sparkled, begging. "I can help you."

But Norah pushed the idea from her mind. "No," she said. "I can't have you as my maid."

The dancer bowed low on her knees. "Please, Your Majesty! I can't stay at court if you won't have me."

Why would she want to? "You don't need to stay at court. Go. I free you."

"But I can't live freely in Kharav as an outsider. They won't allow it. I'll be killed."

Norah let out an exasperated breath. "Why don't you go home?"

"I can't return home. I was a gift to King Gregor. Nor can I return to Japheth. If I can't stay at court, I have nowhere. Please, Your Majesty."

Norah felt a twinge of guilt. What was she to do with this woman?

The dancer's emerald eyes found hers. "Your Majesty, I know what it's like to be a stranger in a strange land, to not trust anyone or anything around you. Please, let me serve you in whatever capacity you see fit."

Norah pushed out a long sigh. She did need a maid, and this woman might be able to help her in other ways she hadn't anticipated. "What's your name?"

"Vitalia, Your Majesty."

"Do you have clothes, Vitalia? Appropriate clothes?"

The woman gave a breathless smile. "Yes. Yes, Your Majesty."

"Very well," Norah relented. "We'll try it out. Fetch your things. Take the side room, and I'll see you in the morning."

Vitalia jumped up, smiling and bowing. "Yes, Your Majesty. Thank you! Thank you!" She bowed again and fluttered from the room.

Chapter Thirty-Nine

Norah made her way down to the dining room for breakfast with her new maid close behind. She hoped no one would recognize the dancer in a more conservative dress.

Mikael's gaze locked on her as she entered. He straightened, and his mouth opened slightly, but he didn't speak. He only stared at her, and a flush came to her cheeks.

Salara-Mae rose from her seat and stood, as proper courtesy dictated, then gave her a stiff nod and sat after Norah did, returning quietly to her breakfast.

Norah wondered if breakfast in the dining hall was a routine for Salara-Mae. She also noted the commander's absence.

"I trust you slept well?" Mikael asked. His tone seemed unsure, if the Shadow King could be such.

"I did."

Just then, his eye caught the sight of her maid standing in the wing, and he looked back at Norah in surprise.

"Is everything all right?" she asked him, feigning ignorance to what pulled his attention.

He looked at his mother, who took a bite of her biscuit, clearly unaware and indifferent to their conversation. "Perfectly," he said with some amusement.

"Does the lord commander not take breakfast here?" Not that she missed him.

The question was enough to catch Salara-Mae's ear. "No, he does not," she said sharply. "Breakfast is my time."

Norah smiled to herself. She felt a kinship with this woman who disliked the commander as much as she did.

After they finished eating, Salara-Mae excused herself, and the king rose from the table. Norah turned to leave.

"North Queen," Mikael called, stopping her. "Will you walk with me?"

Walk where? But his voice had come gently, and she gave a small nod.

He offered his arm, and she paused. It was the first time he'd extended a public physical connection toward her. A courtesy, she told herself. She swallowed, but then looped her hand under, accepting. His skin was warm, and he covered her hand with his own.

Damn the gods. She didn't hate it.

He led her through the halls. "I see you found yourself a maid."

"I needed one," she said. "So, I've put her to use. But"—she met his eye—"she's no longer a slave."

"Will you be freeing all my slaves around the castle?" he asked, a slight irritation in his voice.

She didn't care. "Probably."

His nostrils flared, but he didn't reply. His skin warmed, perhaps from his anger returning. She stiffened. Let it. Slavery wasn't something she'd pretend to be okay with. He glanced down at her, his eyes ablaze, but she only returned his glare.

Unexpectedly, he seemed to calm again. And so did she.

He was an interesting man, crafted of fire and war, quick to anger, quick to fight. But as he looked at her, she noticed that he was also quick to yield.

She felt it too. She didn't want to fight him either. "Where are we going?" she asked, changing the subject.

They walked a little longer, and then he paused in front of a hall with a single door. "As I said before, after we're wed, you'll stay in the villa, but this will be your sanctuary away from everything. It's for you alone."

He led her down the hall and opened the door to reveal a sprawling suite. A bed sat centered against the wall with abundant pillows and furs, and there was a plush settee by two windowed doors that opened out onto a balcony.

She walked to the balcony.

"It faces north," he said, his voice softer, "so you can look to your home sky."

The notion brought a wave of emotion she wasn't expecting, and she bit her cheek to hold it back. She looked over the rest of the room. There was a small bath chamber off the side, and a vanity against the far wall.

"No one will visit or disturb you here," he said. "Your guard will stop at the end of the hall, not outside your door. No one will enter without your invitation. Not your guard, not your maid,"—he paused—"not even me. It's here you may come when you want to be alone and be left alone."

Warmth rolled through her. "I don't know what to say."

"Say nothing. You'll be salara and above all others." His eyes were dark, but kind. "This is your home now. This castle is yours, and you can do in it what you'd like."

"Thank you," she said with a faint smile.

"Good day, North Queen." He gave her a small nod and left her to her sanctuary.

Norah let out a breath and looked around again. A sanctuary. Unlike her room, it was whitewashed and bright. She opened the doors to the balcony and breathed in the winter. It didn't seem quite so cold.

She made her way out of the chamber and back down the hall to where her guard and new maid waited. It was the kind guard—*Kiran*, she'd learned from Vitalia. Another guard stood with him; one she didn't recognize. She decided to take the king up on his statement. She could do what she liked, and she'd like to look around. "I want to see the castle," she told Vitalia. "Can you show me around?"

"Of course, Your Majesty," the maid said with a nod. "You'll love it. And just wait until you see Ashan."

"Ashan?"

"The city. Right outside the castle."

There *was* a city, Norah remembered. She wondered when she'd be able to explore it. The commander had told her she needed four guards to leave the castle, but she didn't take that as open permission. That she felt she needed permission irked her, but she decided she'd take one thing at a time.

Norah made her way around, with Vitalia quietly answering her questions as they went. The maid's knowledge surprised her, and she listened closely. The castle was beautiful, with its arched halls and intricately designed tilework, and she found herself admiring everything around her.

A large hanging portrait in the hall caught her eye and drew her closer in curiosity. Right away, she recognized Salara-Mae, and although it looked like Mikael beside her, it wasn't.

"Salar's father," Vitalia told her. "Rhalstad Ratha Shal."

Norah looked carefully at the intricate painting. The detail was so incredibly fine that it almost seemed real. Mikael's resemblance to his father was undeniable, but the senior king wore his hair cropped short and his beard longer. On the side of his head ran a large scar, starting at his temple and stretching backward.

Norah let her eyes move to Salara-Mae, except she was Salara then, who looked quite young but still had an elegant sharpness to her face. She was beautiful, Norah mused. "Do you think they were happy together?" she asked.

"Who wouldn't be happy serving their king?" a voice boomed from behind, and Norah spun to see the lord commander. He wasn't wearing his wrap, and she wasn't sure if she preferred to see his face or not. Well, she'd prefer not to see him at all. His two dogs followed obediently at his heel, their heads low, as though prowling on a hunt. They looked menacing. Like their master.

"What are you doing here?" he asked stiffly.

"I'm looking around the castle, as I was invited to," she cut back. "If you have a problem with that, go talk to your king."

His eyes darkened, then he said, "I have no problems with that. In fact, I'll join you."

Norah fumed. Of course, he knew exactly how to control her. "No need," she said sharply. "I was just finishing."

The corners of his lips turned up in a satisfied smirk, and Norah raged even more inside. She turned toward the hall to her left, not knowing where she was going, but she'd sort it out once she got away from him.

"Do you seek my bedchamber?" he asked cheekily, halting her step. "Because that's all you'll find that way."

Norah's face flushed with heat, and she glared at him as she turned and headed back the way she had come. Her steps quickened as her irritation grew to anger. She hated how he could get to her.

"Is he always so maddening?" she hissed at her guard when they were out of earshot.

"No, Your Majesty," Kiran answered.

Norah puffed a breath in frustration. "That's what you're compelled to say, I suppose. And does he always have those wretched creatures?"

"Cusco and Cavaatsa? Yes, Your Majesty. He's raised them from pups."

Norah found it hard to imagine the lord commander raising and caring for anything. "What are they? Hunting dogs?" she asked.

"Hunters of men," Vitalia mumbled.

Norah didn't doubt it. She slowed as the hall turned to the left and brightened into a glass ambulatory. Her irritation dissipated as she marveled at the large white flowers lining the outside of the glass and casting whimsical shadows from the sun onto the stone floor. She knelt by the glass, amazed. "Flowers in the winter?" she breathed.

"Rhines," Kiran told her. "Aren't they beautiful?"

"I've never seen anything like them, let alone in the winter."

"You've never seen flowers?" Vitalia asked.

She stilled. She'd seen flowers before. Small blooms of purple and yellow speckled across the Mercian mountains flashed in her mind. They weren't something she remembered seeing, yet they were something she still knew. If she saw them again, would they bring more memories? An ache grew in her stomach. If she couldn't return to Mercia, she wouldn't be able to find out. And how could she hope to gain her memories in the Shadowlands, a place so foreign to her, with nothing of her old life, nothing of who she once was?

"Do you like them?" Kiran asked, bringing her attention back.

She drew in a breath to clear her mind and smiled. "Very much."

His eyes smiled. "I know a place you'd love to see, then."

Norah followed him through the castle and outside. They curved around to the south side, and she grinned when she saw where he was taking her. Beautiful greens patterned the ground in a large garden. They made their way down the small pebble walk as she marveled at its beauty. "It all grows in the winter?" she asked, amazed.

"Some of it. These are all evergreens. They stay green like this all year. Some flowers you'll see on the winter plants..."

Kiran's words continued, but she didn't hear them. The sound of a horse had caught her attention, and she looked over her shoulder toward a grand building offset from the castle. Behind it were circled paddocks, some with horses.

"Is that the stable?" she asked.

Kiran paused in his flower tour. "Yes, Your Majesty."

"Is my horse there?" She desperately wanted to see the mare again. She had a connection to the animal. Maybe it was a connection to her old self. And she was fond of the mare—a friend in a place where she had very few.

"I would assume so," he answered. "But we should get back, Your Majesty. The lord commander will check that you've returned to your chamber, and Captain Artem, too, no doubt. And forgive me, I've led you outside the castle with only two guardsmen."

"I don't answer to the lord commander," she answered shortly. "Or the captain."

"Please, Your Majesty," he said softly. "I do."

Norah sighed. She didn't want any trouble for those who were kind to her. She gave a relenting nod, casting one last glance toward the stable, and they headed back the way they'd come.

Chapter Forty

Each day passed slowly. Norah struggled to find her place in it all. She was a queen, but she still felt more prisoner than queen in the kingdom of Shadows. Would that change when she became salara?

She pulled back the draperies on the windows, letting the morning light pour in. Vitalia had gone early to the dressmaker, but Norah spotted the tray of breakfast she'd left on the table. She smiled. Biscuits and honey. She loved honey, although she couldn't remember the last time she'd had it.

Norah dropped down and curled into the cushioned chair at the table, crossing her legs up under her and into the warmth of her nightgown, then scooted the tray closer. Perhaps she was letting this honey draw too much excitement, but she was alone, and she'd let herself have this small joy.

She broke the biscuit in half to pour the honey across but then pushed it back; she really didn't care about the biscuit, and instead scooped her fingertip into the small jar of gold. She gave barely enough time for the drip to break before she brought it to her mouth.

And it was the most amazing thing she'd ever tasted. There were hints of lavender mixed in the sweetness; it was rich and thick on her tongue. She wanted to drink it from the jar. There was no spoon to spread it, no knife. It was meant to be poured on the biscuit. She didn't care, and she dipped in her finger again.

Norah heard movement in the hall—Vitalia, back with her dresses. She grinned and moved to the door. She was going to tell her she was the best maid ever and beg her for more honey. But when she opened the door, it wasn't Vitalia.

It was Mikael, poised to knock.

Norah stood, her nightgown loose over her shoulder, holding her jar of gold with a honey-coated fingertip. Not exactly how she wanted anyone to see her. Not how she wanted *him* to see her.

His gaze traveled down her length and back up. "North Queen," he said.

"Um…" She shifted. "Hello." She winced. The right way to address him still escaped her.

They stared at each other for a moment. "I'm"—his brow dipped as he glanced at her honey-coated finger—"sorry to disturb you."

She felt she might die a little.

His gaze rose to her face again. "I just... wanted you to know that I have to tend some things in the south. But I'll return tomorrow. Late."

She nodded, trying to act normal. "I'll... be here." She cursed herself. Where else would she be?

He nodded back. That seemed the end of his message, but he didn't move to leave. His eyes shifted down to her hands again.

"Do you... want some honey?" She cursed herself again. *Stupid*. Of course he didn't want honey. She bit her lip to keep from cringing. Gods help her.

He didn't answer, and it only made it worse. But then he stepped closer. His eyes said he wanted *something*. She swallowed but didn't move.

Slowly, he reached out and took her hand with the honey-dipped finger. She froze. Her breath stopped, and her pulse thrummed heavily in her ears. His eyes melded into hers as he brought her finger up and wrapped his lips around it.

His mouth was cool against the flame of her skin. The flick of his tongue, the graze of his teeth, sent prickles rippling across her body. Every hair stood on end. It was so brazen of him. And of her to let him. It was shameful, even though it wasn't shame she felt.

She should stop him.

But she didn't want to. So she didn't.

Finally, he drew her finger from his mouth—slow, tortuous—and lowered her hand, releasing it.

Norah stood breathless.

The corner of his mouth turned up ever so slightly. "I'll see you tomorrow, North Queen."

She could only nod.

He turned and left, and she closed the door behind him, leaning back against it. Her heart still thundered. She could still feel his mouth, his tongue. The thoughts sent heat pooling to her stomach. This man. She didn't know what to do about him, didn't know what to think.

He knew no boundaries, no restraint. Alexander would never—

Alexander—she pushed him from her mind. She couldn't think about Alexander right now.

She needed air. A walk. Something. She couldn't wait for Vitalia to get back with the dresses. She pulled a green front-laced gown from the side dressing room and shuffled it on. Grabbing her cloak, she slipped on her shoes and then swept out of the chamber and down the hall.

Her guard picked up behind her, and she fastened her cloak around her shoulders as she walked.

"Do you plan to go outside, North Queen?" a guard asked from behind. *Sonal.* With Vitalia's help, she was learning to tell the guards apart. She didn't like Sonal. He wasn't accommodating like Kiran, and she didn't like the way he called her North Queen.

She kept walking.

"You've only two guards," came his voice again.

"Then you'd better find two more before I reach the door." She walked quickly, hoping to avoid anyone who might stop her, like the lord commander, or the captain. As she reached the entry hall, two more guards fell instep behind her.

That wasn't as difficult as she'd expected.

"Where are you going?" Sonal asked.

She didn't answer, giving the guard a taste of their own medicine. But the corners of her mouth drew up. She knew exactly where she was going. The mare.

Outside, the air was chilly, and she pulled the hood of her cloak up but inhaled deeply. It felt good to get out of the castle—to set her mind on something other than Mikael and the morning's happening. The brief thought again brought a heat to her lower stomach, and she pushed it away.

The castle grounds were expansive, easily double the size of her castle in Mercia, and beautiful. The main courtyard had three fountains and a wide cobblestone path for daily markets and activities. Meticulously kept hedges surrounded the outer edges, and the long side garden that Kiran showed her before held even more topiaries. She lengthened her stride toward the stable.

The inside of the stable was almost as grand as the inside of the castle, with stacked stone lifting the ceiling high to let in the light and beautiful dark-wood stalls lining both sides. Most of the stalls were empty and large enough to fit at least three horses. Then she reached one that was occupied and realized perhaps they weren't—she'd forgotten how massive the destriers were.

A knicker sounded from an end stall, and she immediately knew it was the mare. She smiled and hurried toward it. When she reached it, she looked through the top bars, and her smile widened. The mare tossed her head and let out a squeal, as if just as happy to see her.

The stall doors were split in half, with most top doors open for the horses to hang their heads out, but the mare's was closed. Norah reached for the latch.

A gravelly voice, foreign and angry, called out from her right.

She turned as what appeared to be a stable hand approached. He didn't wear a head wrap. That practice seemed reserved for soldiers.

"He says this one will take a piece out of you," Sonal said from behind her. "This mare won't let anyone touch her."

Norah glanced back at the mare, who wore a stable blanket and had clearly been brushed. Obviously, someone was able to touch her. She looked well cared for, and Norah was appreciative of that.

The stable hand spoke again. "You'd do well to let her alone," Sonal translated.

She pulled back the hood of her cloak, and the man stilled. His eyes traveled to the guard behind her, and he took a wary step back. He hadn't realized who he was speaking to.

Norah pulled back the latch of the top door and swung it open, and the mare knickered again and stretched her head out to her. She smiled and gave the animal a hearty scratch on the cheek. The mare snorted. Norah scratched her forehead before running her hand to the soft flesh of her nose. The horse nuzzled her fingers. Her smile widened, and she looked up at the stable hand. "Tell him to leave her top door open, so she can see out."

Sonal translated. The man's eyes told her he didn't approve, but he gave a stiff nod. Then he glanced once more at her guard and left them alone.

Norah turned her attention back to the mare, giving her another round of affectionate scratches, to which the mare arched her neck and leaned out farther against the bottom door. She wished she could go for a ride, but she felt she was already pushing her luck with the visit.

"I just came to say hello, friend, to see how you're doing. And you look well." She pulled the mare's head closer and gave her a peck on the face. "I'll come back later and see if we can get out of here for a little while. Maybe a ride sometime." The mare snorted again, and Norah patted her neck. "Don't hurt anyone, at least not the ones that care for you." She lowered her voice to a whisper. "All others are fair game."

The animal shook her head, and Norah gave a small laugh.

She should get back, she knew. "All right, goodbye, friend. I'll be back." She gave the mare one last scratch and reluctantly headed out of the stable and back toward the castle.

As she made her way back, she let herself admire the gardens. Norah loved gardens. Mercia's felt so quaint when compared to those of the Shadowlands, but still they were beautiful. She missed them.

She noticed a man on his knees digging a line of small holes. He was an older man; his dark hair was streaked with gray, and his skin had been weathered by the seasons.

"What are you doing?" she asked him.

He looked up with a start and rose to his feet when he recognized her. "Salara," he said, bowing low. His voice held the warmth of welcome, and his eyes smiled like summertime. "How can I be of service?"

That he spoke the Northern tongue surprised her. "What are you doing?" she asked again.

"I am planting isarium, Salara. While they're dormant."

"North Queen," Sonal said, "we should return to the castle and leave this man to do his work."

She ignored him. "What's your name?" she asked the man. One of her soldiers broke away and headed toward the castle. If only the rest would leave her too.

"My name is Bremhad, Salara."

He was such a gentle soul. He reminded her of Kiran.

"Bremhad," she repeated. "Can I plant one?"

His eyes widened in surprise—he looked a little worried even. "This isn't work for Salara."

"I'll decide that," she said, picking up a root ball waiting to be planted and looking closely at it. "Do I just put it in the ground?"

"Here," he said, crouching down, "I'll show you." Bremhad scooped some loose soil and put it at the bottom of the hole he'd already dug. Then he waved her to set it inside. She placed the root into the center, and he filled in the sides with the soil, leveling it off with a layer on top.

She smiled, looking at the row of holes. "I want to do another." She moved to the next, scooping the loose soil to the bottom as Bremhad had done, and then setting the root ball on top. She filled in the sides and added a top layer. The dirt felt good between her fingers, and the smell of earth was familiar somehow. She smiled, feeling pleased with herself.

"So, you speak the Northern tongue?" she asked.

"Common tongue? Yes, of course."

Sonal interrupted the man with sharp words in the Shadow tongue. The man's smile fell, and Norah knew he'd been warned. She shot a look at Sonal, giving him a warning of her own.

"Does everyone speak the Northern tongue?" she asked.

The old man was silent, and his eyes darted to her guard. Footfalls came behind her, and she looked back to see the lord commander approaching, followed by Captain Artem and more soldiers. Had the commander not gone with the king? She groaned inside.

"What are you doing?" he demanded.

It was none of his business. She pursed her lips. "I'm planting flowers."

"North Queen, you can't be out here digging in the dirt."

"Bremhad has already done the digging," she said flippantly. "I'm planting the flowers."

Agitation rolled off his brow. "You can't be out here *planting flowers.*"

"Why not? What am I to do? Sit in my room all day?"

"Something more proper for a queen."

"You should let the queen decide what's proper for queens," Norah said shortly. "I'll go back inside once I'm finished here." She could feel the heat from his anger, but she focused on her next root ball.

The lord commander gave an order in the Shadow tongue, and each soldier quickly picked up a root bundle and dropped them into the holes lining the walkway, covering the roots with dirt.

"You're finished now," he told her.

Norah gritted her teeth, anger swelling inside her. She stood, glaring at the lord commander. His eyes returned her stare like pools of hell. But what could she do?

She turned to the old man. "Thank you, Bremhad. Perhaps I might come again? I'd like to see how things are coming along."

"Of course, Salara. I'm here every day and would be honored."

She gave the lord commander and the captain another scowl and then turned back toward the castle.

Four guards. Four guards now stood on duty as she stepped out into the hall from her chamber—no doubt a punitive response to the day prior. But she wouldn't give the lord commander the upper hand.

She smiled at them. "Oh, perfect. I was headed outside for another walk, so we're all ready." And she started down the hall. They fell in step behind her. Close. Too close. Suffocating. She tried to brush it off as she passed the dining hall—where she'd originally intended to go. Petty rebellion was much more important than breakfast.

Her stomach grumbled in protest. She ignored it. She'd eaten a hefty dinner the night before, taken in her chamber. Nine hells before she'd eat alone with the lord commander. And being out for a walk wasn't for naught. She hadn't properly explored the castle grounds. She wished she'd thought to bring Vitalia.

The beauty of the Shadowlands was hard to deny. In every recess of the castle sat a garden area, meticulously kept. The walls and stonework were well maintained, and even the cobblestone walks appeared to have been scrubbed clean. Tall iron posts lined common walkways, holding oil lanterns for the night.

She turned the corner of the castle, and the walk opened to a broad green space. Within a short distance were structured activity fields, each filled with training soldiers. The fields were much larger than in Mercia, and on first observation, the training was much more aggressive. Where her Northmen practiced in an organized fashion, the Shadow fields could easily be mistaken for battlefields.

Norah stopped and watched, wide-eyed. With no reservation and no restraint, the Shadow warriors fought—lethal strikes with real weapons and devastating consequences. How were they not killing one another? Her pulse quickened. Even if they were Shadowmen, she didn't want anyone hurt...

Suddenly, her eyes found Captain Artem. *Except him.* He could hurt himself all day. And so could the lord commander—wherever he was. The captain stood in the center of the far-right field as he scanned the soldiers, calling out commands of gods only knew what. And then, as if he sensed her gaze, he turned. The hair stood on the back of her neck, and she broke away to keep walking.

He'd seen her. But she didn't dare look back to see if he would come after her. She focused her eyes ahead. And then she slowed.

The king was walking toward her. A surprise—he'd said he wouldn't be back until late. It wasn't an unwelcome surprise, though. Beside him strode the lord commander. *He* was unwelcome.

Thankfully, the commander forked away and headed toward the training fields, though not before casting her a dark eye. *Good riddance.* She turned her attention back to the king. The corners of her mouth turned up, and she pursed it back. But she certainly wasn't unhappy to see him.

His own mouth held the hint of a smile, and her eyes moved to his lips. She hadn't forgotten how they felt. She swallowed and tried to shake the path from where her mind was beginning to wander.

"North Queen," he greeted her.

"Salar Mikael," she greeted back, trying out the Kharavian title. It felt very... unnatural. She wasn't sure why.

He tilted his head. "It's not customary to use both names."

She didn't want to call him Salar—a name so... distant. "All right. Mikael." That felt natural. She wasn't sure if he'd be fine with her calling him by his name, but she caught the hint of a smile, and she smiled back. "You're back sooner than I'd expected."

"I had something to get back to."

"Battle planning?" she jested. Something else dark and nefarious, no doubt.

"You."

She paused. Why did she like that? She bit her lip. "Worried I might make my escape?" It was a jest. Mostly.

But he shook his head. "No. I wanted to see you again."

She liked that even more. Had their last interaction stayed in his mind, as it had in hers?

"I heard you had the Crest working in the gardens yesterday," he said as they started toward the castle.

She glanced out at the practice fields to where the commander had picked up inspection of the soldiers. "No, that was the lord commander's doing," she said irritably. "I was planting flowers."

"A queen shouldn't be laboring in the dirt."

"It wasn't laboring," she argued. "I actually quite enjoyed it." She needed to be out of the castle and doing something. "And even if I was, I'll do what pleases me. The lord commander oversteps, and it's unacceptable."

He slowed. "I know he's not a man of gentle nature, but the lord commander looks out for my interests, and now yours."

She scoffed. "Not *my* interests."

"You judge him too harshly." His tone held an edge of defense, and she quieted. He put his absolute trust in his brute, loved him as a brother, and would defend him fiercely, even to her. The commander could divide them, and that's the last thing she wanted. She had to be careful.

Silence hung between them as they walked, then he said, "Labor in the dirt if it makes you happy. I just ask you to refrain when your people arrive for the marriage. I don't want them to think I took their queen for slave labor."

It was a jest to bridge them back to a good place. He was trying. And it was an acceptable compromise. Norah couldn't help her smile. "Yes, I can see my grandmother having heart palpitations."

Mikael's brow creased. "Surely your grandmother won't come."

His assumption surprised her. "She'd planned to travel to Aleon. Of course she'll come. Why wouldn't she?"

Mikael raised an eyebrow but didn't answer.

"This alliance is important, and I'm her granddaughter," she insisted. "I'm getting married, and I need her. She'll come."

"Of course," he replied, but doubt lingered on his face.

There would be tension between their kingdoms, understandably, and it would take time to adjust, but her grandmother wouldn't deny her. Mikael didn't know Catherine. He'd see.

"I'm sure you've already eaten," he said, "but will you join me for some breakfast?"

Her smile returned. "I'd love to."

Norah strode outside into the daylight with a spring in her step. Breakfast with Mikael had left her in high spirits. He was... different... than she'd expected. She liked it.

She decided to visit the mare again and stop by the garden and say hello to Bremhad along the way. Vitalia followed close behind, as did Norah's guard. She was disappointed to have Sonal in her service again today, but she wouldn't let him dampen her spirits.

Norah made her way along the manicured topiaries and combed the gardens for the greenskeeper, but he was nowhere to be found. Norah spotted another man by the laurels, and she approached. He bowed low when he saw her.

"Is Bremhad here?" she asked.

The man said nothing and remained bowing.

"A man named Bremhad," she said again. "Is he here?"

Still, the man said nothing.

Vitalia spoke to him in the Shadow tongue. He answered, and she looked back to Norah. "He says there's no man that works in the gardens by that name."

Norah shook her head, her brows drawing together. "That's not right. He was here yesterday. He said he's here every day."

Vitalia spoke to the man again, and then she looked at Norah with her lips pursed and shook her head.

Something wasn't right. Norah turned to Sonal. "Where's the man who was here yesterday?"

Sonal gave a frown and then shook his head. "I don't remember what he looked like."

Her eyes narrowed. *Liar.* "You know exactly what he looked like," she countered, a weight growing in her stomach. "His name was Bremhad. Has something happened to him?"

Sonal shrugged. "I don't remember him."

Anger crept across her skin. But what could she do here? She turned and strode back toward the castle. She needed to find him.

Behind closed doors and away from her guard, Norah paced the room.

"Do you think they did something?" she asked her maid. "Do you think something's happened to him?"

"Don't you see?" Vitalia whispered. "The lord commander sends you a message."

A lump rose in her throat. That was exactly the kind of message the lord commander would send. "Do you think Bremhad is all right?"

"I don't know, but if the lord commander was involved..." Her words trailed off.

Norah's heart raced. This was her fault. She had to help him. "Where would they take him? What would they do?"

Vitalia shook her head. "I don't know. Will you go to Salar?"

"I can't go to him on suspicion alone. He already thinks I judge the commander too hastily. And the brute would deny it." Then Bremhad might disappear forever.

"I have many friends in the castle, Your Majesty. I can try to find out what happened."

Norah prayed she could.

Chapter Forty-One

"Please don't be angry," Vitalia said in a hushed voice. The setting sun cast long shadows across the hall as they walked.

"Why would I be angry?" Norah followed her maid toward her sanctuary. She hadn't visited it since Mikael had given it to her. It was for when she wanted to be alone, and to be left alone, he'd told her. Aside from her suffocating guard, she hadn't felt that way.

Vitalia didn't answer.

Had she found out what had happened to Bremhad? Norah didn't dare ask within earshot of her guard, who'd likely helped in whatever devious plan the commander had.

The guard stopped at the end of the hall, as they weren't permitted within it, and Norah and her maid continued to the sanctuary. Vitalia's breath came faster now, nervously. It made Norah's quicken as well. What news did she have?

They stepped inside, and Vitalia closed the door behind them.

Norah couldn't wait any longer. "Did you find out what happened to Bremhad?"

Vitalia clenched her hands, wringing them nervously. Then her eyes darted over Norah's shoulder. Norah turned, and she startled at the man standing in the doorway of the side bath chamber.

"Who are you?" she demanded of the man. "What are you doing here?" No one was allowed in the sanctuary.

"It's Kiran, Your Majesty," Vitalia said quickly. "I brought him. I'm sorry. This is the only place I could think of that was private enough."

Norah hadn't recognized the guard without his head wrap; she'd only ever seen his eyes. She looked closer. Yes, she knew those eyes. They were kind eyes. But now, troubled.

He was different from how she'd imagined him. Older—perhaps a couple years older than she was. A trenched scar ran from just under the inside of his right eye and down over his cheek to his jaw. A second scar claimed the space over his left eye and channeled back into his shoulder-length black hair that was tied from behind. Perhaps they'd been from the same injury. Unlucky. Or lucky, depending on how one looked at the situation.

"Bremhad is his father," Vitalia said.

Norah let out a breath. She saw it now—the resemblance.

Kiran shifted uneasily, the muscle tightening underneath his inked skin. This was a secret—a secret he protected.

"Bremhad has been thrown in the dungeon," her maid added.

"There's a dungeon?" As it rolled off her lips, she knew it was a stupid question. Even Mercia had a dungeon.

Kindly, Vitalia only nodded. "Kiran's planning to break him out."

He shot her maid an angry glare. "You said you wouldn't tell her that."

"You can trust her," her maid pressed.

Norah gaped at him. "Break him out of the dungeon? You can't do that."

"I'm a warrior of the Crest. I can." His courtesies were gone. But she didn't fault him. Anger and fear drove him now. And he was right, he probably could get his father out, with some planning. He was an elite member of the Crest, skilled beyond any prison guard.

"No, Kiran, listen to me. This isn't the way. If you break him out, you won't be able to stay here. You'll have to leave, to flee. You'll both be hunted."

He shook his head. "It doesn't matter. I can't do nothing. And once they know he's my father, they'll know my papers are fake. I'll be thrown in there with him."

She quieted as her mind raced. He'd faked his status to be eligible for the army. She clutched her own hands. This complicated things. "Regardless, you can't break him out."

How quickly the kindness in his eyes changed to aggression. "I won't let him die down there because he made a mistake."

Confusion filled her. "What mistake?"

Kiran hesitated, then he said, "Speaking to you in the Northern tongue."

"Why would that be a mistake?" She knew the answer before she'd even finished the question. She scoffed in frustration. "Because the commander wants me to think that only a few can understand me. Better to spy on me, I see."

Kiran didn't confirm it. But he didn't deny it.

"Let me take care of this," she said. "I'll have your father released."

Kiran straightened, but he cast his gaze to the side with his lips tight and drew in a cynical breath.

"Do you not believe me?"

He looked back at her. "I believe you'll try." He didn't think she could.

"Kiran, please. Let me help you before you do something rash. Do you not love your life here?"

"I love my father more," he said.

Emotion swelled within her. Had she loved her own father this strongly? She reached out and clasped his arm. "Kiran, please. I promise you I'll get him out."

The silence was long and agonizing. But Kiran sighed, relenting. He gave a short nod.

She pursed her lips into a reassuring smile.

"Wait until we've gone," Vitalia told him. "We'll take the guard with us, and you can leave unseen."

He gave a small nod. "Thank you."

Morning couldn't come soon enough. Captain Artem had been on a task outside the city, and Norah had to wait for his return. Her stomach twisted at the thought of having to talk to him, but she didn't dare take the matter to the commander. She'd never see Bremhad again.

She strode toward the stables with her guard close behind. Kiran was among them. Her heart hurt for him. Surely it was all he could do to act unaffected, as no one knew Bremhad was his father. His nearness didn't help her own anxiousness.

She found Artem walking out just as she was approaching. He held his helm under his arm and his gloves neatly in his hand. Her brow stitched down. He didn't even appear to have traveled; his armor was still clean.

"North Queen," he greeted.

But she didn't care for his greeting, and she didn't care to offer one back. "You'll release the greenskeeper," she said firmly.

The captain of the Crest frowned. "I'm not sure what greenskeeper you speak of."

Were they all liars? "The greenskeeper that was with me when you harassed me in the gardens with the lord commander," she said shortly. "The greenskeeper that's been thrown in the dungeon. I want him released. Now."

He gave a dip of his brow, feigning concern. "I'm not familiar with the situation, but even so, only the lord commander or salar can grant pardon."

"Pardon?" she asked angrily. "He's done nothing wrong! What's his crime?"

He shook his head, frowning through the cruel smile underneath. "As I said, I'm not familiar with the situation. You should talk to the lord commander."

Yes, rely on the man who'd *caused* her grievance to *fix* her grievance. Hardly.

"I think I'll talk to the king," she replied sharply.

"As you wish."

Norah hated this man just as much as the lord commander. She cursed herself. They were probably the best of friends. She gritted her teeth and breathed deep to keep herself calm, then spun on her heel, heading back toward the castle.

The morning was still early. She'd find Mikael before breakfast—before Artem could tell the commander what she was trying to do. She cursed herself for not going straight to Mikael, but Artem was a captain, and she was queen. Even if not the queen of the Shadowlands yet, she expected his compliance. She *would* be his queen. And she fully rejected the idea he couldn't free Bremhad.

She hated the idea of going to Mikael. He already felt she was too biased against his commander, and she was bringing yet another grievance. And she was queen in her own right—it diminished her authority. But she'd do it for Bremhad. Time was of the essence. She'd sort the rest out later.

Norah found the king stepping out of his study. "North Queen," he greeted when he saw her. "This is a surprise."

"I have a pressing matter I need to discuss with you."

His brow creased, and he gave her a small nod. "Of course."

"The greenskeeper," she said.

His brow creased further. "The greenskeeper?"

"Yes, the greenskeeper, the old man I was planting flowers with in the garden. The lord commander put him in your dungeon. I want him released."

"The greenskeeper?" he asked again.

She resisted the urge to tell him to pay attention. Now she felt like Catherine.

"What's he done?" he asked.

"He talked to me in Northern tongue. Tell me, is that a crime?"

The line of his mouth thinned. "Of course it's not."

"The commander—"

"The lord commander wouldn't condemn a man for no reason."

Norah scoffed. "The lord commander would knife a man for breathing."

Mikael stopped and stiffened, and the pools of his eyes grew darker. She wasn't winning him over to her cause—she needed a different approach. As much as she hated to appeal to his mercy, she would. For Bremhad and for Kiran.

She put her hand on his arm. "Mikael, please. He's my friend."

"A greenskeeper is your friend?"

She drew in a breath as she collected herself; cheekiness and sarcasm wouldn't help her now. "I enjoy the garden here. It's a place in which I hope to spend more time. Will you not have him released? He's done nothing wrong." Norah held her breath. He'd given her a horse worth losing an alliance. Would he not give her a greenskeeper?

He sighed. "I'll see that there's no greenskeeper in my dungeon."

It wasn't exactly complete assurance, but she couldn't push him more. She gave his arm a warm squeeze. "Thank you." She glanced down the way toward the dining hall. "Are you going to breakfast?"

"No. I'm headed to Basrah, just west. I'll be back tonight."

She hated that he was leaving again, but she nodded. "I'll see you when you return."

By evening, Bremhad had still not arrived home, and Norah felt a pit growing in her stomach. Why was it taking so long to release him? Was he even going to be released? Perhaps Mikael hadn't addressed it with the commander before he'd left.

He said he'd address it, she told herself. She should trust him to do so. But the truth was, Mikael held the lord commander with a long leash, if with a leash at all. The brute had told her there was nothing he could do that the king wouldn't forgive. And she believed him.

Mikael hadn't returned by dinner, and Norah took her meal in her chamber. Her worry grew as she ate. What if she had been wrong? What if she couldn't get Bremhad out?

Chapter Forty-Two

"Your Majesty!" Vitalia's excited voice woke Norah from her sleep. She sat up quickly, not sure if she'd slept at all. She'd been restless much of the night. "Was Bremhad released?" she asked before her awareness had even come to her.

Vitalia paused, shaking her head. "I haven't heard, Your Majesty, but you'll want to rise quickly. Northmen have arrived!"

Vitalia's words woke her instantly. "Northmen?" Her heart leapt.

"Soldiers," her maid explained. "They say they're part of the Mercian royal guard. They've come to be in your service. The man that speaks for them, his name is Titus."

Norah tried to quell her disappointment. Of course it wouldn't be Alexander, and she shouldn't want it to be Alexander, as much as her heart wished otherwise. It wasn't safe for him here. It would make sense he would send her guardsmen, or what remained of them, and it would be good to see Titus.

She slipped down off the bed. "I'm glad they've come. Where are they?"

"They're settling in the soldiers' barracks. They'll meet you in the throne room."

Norah dressed quickly. It would be nice to have her own soldiers on her guard, men she could trust. Thinking of trust, her mind wandered back to Kiran, and her stomach sank.

She opened her chamber door to Kiran and Sonal standing guard. She didn't dare ask for news with Sonal so close, but Kiran gave the faintest shake of his head, and his eyes told her his father hadn't returned home.

Her feet felt like weights as she walked. She'd promised Kiran, and she'd been so sure of herself. It hurt. She'd let him down. She let Bremhad down. And it hurt she hadn't been able to move Mikael. The lord commander had sent his message, and the king's lack of action showed his decision. What power did she have here if she couldn't free an innocent greenskeeper from the dungeon? The answer scared her.

Mikael stood in his chamber in front of a large cheval mirror while servant tailors bustled about to his mother's demands. She scrutinized every detail, requiring perfection in everything. It was late morning. He'd already missed breakfast with the North Queen, and that had put him in an unfavorable mood. But this was a hard transition for his mother. The least he could do was give her the morning.

He watched the tailors in the reflection—measuring, taping, and pinning the fabric of the garb he was to wear for the wedding ceremony. The effort was unnecessary, having three like it already in his cabinet chamber. He'd prefer his armor; that seemed to be more fitting of his salara, anyway. Mikael caught his smile in the mirror and quickly stifled it.

Just then, the door swung open with a boom as Soren pushed inside. Everyone stopped abruptly, and his mother turned to him with a scowl. "Has he no restraint?" she seethed.

Mikael looked at Soren with a disapproving eye, but he knew his commander wouldn't interrupt without reason. "Leave us," he told the tailors, which no doubt would run afoul with his mother.

"You can't be serious," she argued. "You're right in the middle of a fitting."

"I'll finish it later."

His mother cut Soren a daggered look, and then she stormed from the room, followed by the cluster of tailors.

"The Northmen have come," Soren said as the door closed behind them, completely unfazed by his mother's annoyance.

Mikael pulled off the half-pinned swath of fabric and laid it over the side chair before donning his sleeveless tunic again. "As we expected," he said, and he tucked his tunic back into his breeches. This news wasn't worth his mother's ire. He did wish for Soren to try harder to please her sometimes.

"The—"

Mikael cut him off. "Have you dealt with the old man?"

Soren stopped and gave a stiff nod.

"I don't expect that to happen again," he warned. "You've offended the queen."

Soren snorted.

"You've offended me," Mikael said angrily, and Soren stiffened.

His commander said nothing. He struggled personally with the North Queen, and Mikael sympathized, but he couldn't tolerate this behavior toward his salara.

Mikael moved to leave, but Soren caught his arm. "Salar, the Northmen—the Bear will be with them."

Mikael stopped. Now this he hadn't expected. His chest tightened. "You've seen him?"

Soren shook his head. "No, but I know he's here."

He let out a long breath with a clenched jaw. Having the Bear in Kharav would be problematic. "Where?"

"They're unloading their wagons and settling into the soldiers' quarters now. Then they go to present themselves to the queen in the throne room."

Mikael slammed his fist on the desk, spilling a bottle of ink.

"I'll take the Crest and head them off," Soren told him. "I'll bring him to you."

"No," Mikael said stiffly.

His commander let out an angry breath. "His charge was to return to the North. The agreement's been broken. Let me take him."

"Does she know he's here?" Mikael asked.

"The North Queen?" Soren shook his head. "I don't know. He's not revealed himself."

"But you're sure he's come? Because that would be very foolish of him."

Soren's eyes blazed. "I'm certain."

Mikael pulsed with the want for blood. "Then let's go to the throne room."

His sword slid smoothly out of its scabbard as he checked it. He might need it. Alexander had found it easier than expected to slip into the Shadowlands hidden among the Northmen. Perhaps he shouldn't be too surprised. Few knew what he looked like out of his signature armor. That worked in his favor. Alexander doubted he'd have made it a single step past the border had the enemy known who he was. They'd have had his head if they'd known he'd been the one to kill so many when they'd tried to retake the mountains of Bahoul the year prior. He'd left a scar on the face of their king, and he'd be the one to kill him.

He *would* kill the Shadow King.

Maybe he'd been foolish to come, but he couldn't not. Not when Norah was here, unprotected. Adrian had wanted to come, too, but it was too dangerous. With the Shadowmen, anyone Alexander loved would be a target. Especially his brother.

Alexander didn't fear his own death in the Shadowlands, at least not until he fulfilled the vision, but he still came under the guise of a regular Mercian soldier. He didn't want to be deterred or taken before he could see Norah and make sure she was all right.

He'd come as quickly as he could after returning the army to Mercia. He'd broken off from the travel company with a smaller group to go even faster. Caspian followed with more of Norah's belongings and more men—things that would hopefully bring her comfort in the hold of their enemy until he could get her out.

"Are you ready?" Titus asked him.

Alexander smiled at the seasoned guard and pulled on his helm. "Lead the way." And he followed Titus as a normal soldier would.

Norah was surprised to find the king and his brute in the throne room when she arrived. Mikael stood, armored—which seemed a little excessive. The commander's face was covered. She'd gotten used to seeing him around the castle without his wrap and had almost forgotten how monstrous he looked with only his eyes showing. He was dressed for battle in usual Shadow form—nothing covering the markings on his chest and torso except his weapons' strappings, and he wore only light armor over his breeches on his knees and the shins of his boots.

She desperately wanted to ask Mikael about Bremhad, but she didn't dare with an audience and with whatever was happening here with this display.

The ranks of the Crest guards lined the sides of the room, and the commander stood beside the king's chair, his axe in hand. It was quite a strong response to several Northmen, she mused.

The king greeted her with a small bow of his head. "North Queen," he said, holding his hand out to the throne beside his. "Please."

She hadn't expected to sit on the queen's throne before she was crowned salara, but she took her seat beside him.

He looked at her with an expression she couldn't understand. "We've not said our vows yet, but you are my salara. You still make this commitment to me, yes?"

What an odd question. He seemed to be deciding something in his mind. "Of course," she told him, and he gave her a small nod.

The doors swung open, and a small army of her Northmen entered the hall. Norah couldn't help the smile that came to her face when she recognized the bald head in the front.

"Titus!" she said, standing and stepping forward. "I'm so glad you've come."

He bowed. "Queen Norah. I'm glad to see you well."

"How was the journey?"

"It was uneventful—the best kind. And everyone is well, as I hope you are."

Her smile widened. "I am, and very glad to see a familiar face."

"Not just one familiar face, Regal High," he said as he stepped to the side. Another large soldier came forward, removing his helm.

Norah let out a gasp, and the world stood still as blue eyes smiled back at her—eyes that were never far from her mind.

Alexander.

But the happiness lasted only a moment, then came the fear—a crippling, sickening fear. "What are you doing here?" she breathed.

"Norah," he said softly.

She felt Mikael behind her. His voice came low and cold. "You have a guest."

She glanced back to see he'd risen from his chair and had his hand on the hilt of his sword, with the commander beside him.

"Yes," she said shakily, desperately searching her mind for how to keep the calm. "I'd like to present—"

"I know who he is," he cut her off as he stepped beside her. His eyes locked on Alexander. "My lord commander told me you'd be foolish enough to come," he snarled at Alexander. "I almost didn't believe him."

Alexander didn't answer. And he didn't bow. He only stood with an icy fire in his eyes. The Shadowmen drew closer from their position around the room. Norah's heart raced faster, and her stomach turned. Things were escalating, quickly. The commander spoke to the king in the Shadow tongue, and she heard weapons being readied. Titus stepped to Alexander's side, and the Northmen pulled their swords defensively.

Mikael gripped his own sword, moving forward, and panic surged through her. She had to stop this. She clasped Mikael's arm, stepping in front of him and looking earnestly into his eyes. "Please," she whispered softly.

He paused as his gaze shifted to her. When he stopped, everyone stopped. And they waited. His eyes moved back and forth between hers. The eternity of the quiet weakened her, but she held his arm tighter. Mikael looked at Alexander, then back to her. Finally, he growled a command, and the Shadowmen drew back.

Norah let herself breathe, but she couldn't shake the wave of nausea that twisted in her stomach. Tension still hung thick in the air.

"Lord Justice," Mikael said to Alexander, using his title for the first time, "we expected you to return to the North."

Alexander ignored the king, looking only at Norah. "I did return, but I had to see your guard back to you, or rather, what's left of them. I'm relieved to find you well."

"How else did you expect to find her?" Mikael asked, his voice edged in anger.

Alexander's eyes met the king's, and he made no attempt to hide his disdain. "Perhaps similar to how I last saw her: assaulted and ill treated."

Rage radiated from Mikael, and she squeezed his arm again—her silent plea for restraint. "As you can see, I'm quite well." She grasped at how she might redirect the conversation. "What news do you have from Mercia?" She wanted to hear of home.

Alexander eyed Mikael before answering. "All is well," Alexander said finally. "The army returned in good health. I departed after with your guard. Caspian follows shortly with additional men and more of your belongings."

"Caspian! He lives?" She almost couldn't believe it.

Alexander cast a hard glance back at Mikael. "He's still healing, but he's well and eager to lead the guard back in your service."

The backs of her eyes stung with relief. Caspian was all right.

"She already has a guard," Mikael said.

"She needs a guard she can trust," Alexander cut back.

The lord commander gave a low chuckle. "Because the North has kept her so safe?"

"Please," Norah interjected, hoping they would settle, if only for her sake. A silence returned.

The line of Alexander's jaw tightened and then relaxed again. "Your maid Serene comes as well," he said, picking back up the conversation.

She smiled. "With Grandmother?"

Alexander's lips parted, but he hesitated before he said, "No."

"No?" Her smile fell.

He glanced at the king and then back to Norah. "It's a great risk for her to come now."

"Too great a risk for the queen and regent to both be in enemy hands, he means," the lord commander said.

"We're no longer enemies," Norah said, her eyes on Alexander.

Alexander was silent for a moment. He lowered his voice. "Try to understand. It's difficult for her to accept things as they are now."

"Difficult to accept things as they are?" she said angrily. "Is that not what she's had me do from the moment I returned?" Norah swallowed back her emotion, forcing composure. The king still didn't know of her memory loss. She wasn't sure why she hadn't told him yet. She'd have to eventually, but not now. "Does she send a letter?" she asked.

He shook his head slowly.

A weight crushed her. She'd asked her grandmother to come, and Catherine had refused without even a letter. Her cheeks flushed in embarrassment at her naivete. She hadn't even doubted. The heat of tears stung the corners of her eyes as her emotion swelled. *Not here*, she told herself. She couldn't get caught up in the frivolity of feelings as she stood between Alexander and Mikael.

"You should settle the men," she told Alexander. "We'll speak more after." She needed to get him away, out of the hall and far from Mikael and the commander.

He gave a nod. "Of course." He bowed. Then, with an icy glance back at the king, he turned from the hall and reluctantly left with the Northmen behind him.

Norah pushed out a shaking breath and swallowed back the knot rising in her throat. She turned to Mikael, but where she expected eyes of storming rage, she found none. Instead, his face had softened. Worry scored his forehead.

"I'm sorry about your grandmother," he said, his voice gentle. His unexpected tenderness unleashed the emotion she had been trying so hard to keep inside, and a tear spilled down her cheek. He reached up and brushed it with his thumb. "You should take a walk through the gardens. I think it will make you feel better."

Why would that make her feel better?

Her mind tumbled as her heart quickened. Was he saying what she thought he was saying? She nodded, suddenly breathless.

With the faintest smile, he turned and strode from the throne room with the commander close behind.

Norah forgot everything else as she hurried through the halls toward the gardens. Mikael's touch still lingered on her cheek. Her being upset had bothered him—bothered him more than Alexander's being in Kharav.

By the time she reached the courtyard, she was practically running. Her guard had to move quickly to keep up with her. Her silk shoes on the pea gravel sounded like rain as she ran past the fountains and out into the gardens.

She stopped suddenly as her breath caught in her throat.

Tears sprang to her eyes when she saw the old man by the hedges. "Bremhad!" she exclaimed.

When he heard her, he turned. "Salara," he said as he bowed his head.

Norah was speechless, and it took her a moment to gather her wits. She thought of poor Kiran behind her, forced to contain himself and act detached.

"Are you all right?" she managed to get out.

"Most kind of you to ask, Salara. I'd taken ill for a few days, but I'm quite well now. I'm able to return to my work, which I am very thankful for."

No doubt his excuse was for the benefit of her guard. She nodded, blinking back the tears in her eyes. "I'm glad," she breathed. She was so very glad.

Norah tried to keep her eyes on the hall ahead of her, but they kept drifting back to Alexander as he walked beside her. She still couldn't believe he was here. If she closed her eyes for a moment, would she find it had all been a dream when she opened them? Maybe she wished it were a dream. As much as she wanted him with her, as happy as she was to see him, she couldn't think past the clawing fear that she could lose him forever to the forces that so badly wanted him dead.

Her voice came unsteadily. "Why did you come? It's not safe for you here." She needed to send him back, only she couldn't bring herself to say the words.

His eyes burned a bright blue. "I would never leave you to face hardships on your own. Wherever you go, I'll follow."

"If anything happens to you—"

"Nothing will happen to me," he assured her.

She shook her head. "You don't know that."

"Of course, I do. I have a destiny."

Norah glanced back at the Crest guards in alarm. They were far enough back and didn't seem to have heard, but by the gods, if she wasn't going to have a panic attack. She grabbed his arm and dragged him down the hall into her sanctuary, away from listening ears.

"Those are words that will get you killed!" she said in a harsh whisper as the door closed behind them.

"No, Norah. I don't die here. I do have a destiny."

"A destiny Mikael will do everything in his power to change!" A destiny she found herself wanting to change.

He didn't argue.

Norah straightened, bringing her hand to her forehead and forcing herself calm. She needed to send him home, both to see him safe and to help her manage her grandmother and the council. With Catherine refusing to come to Kharav, they'd obviously taken the news of the alliance more poorly than she'd hoped.

"What did my grandmother say?" she asked.

He sighed. "She's having a difficult time, as you can imagine."

A difficult time? Anger flashed inside her. What did her grandmother expect *she* was going through? "What did she say?" she asked again.

His brow dipped, and his mouth turned down. "This isn't your path, Norah. You can't marry the Shadow King."

"Does she not see this is the only way to bring our people peace?"

"You side with darkness."

"I side against war!" she argued.

"The council feels it's a righteous war."

"Is that what you think?" she asked angrily. She turned away, but he caught her hand, drawing her back.

"Norah, I don't want any more men to die. Ten years we've been at war, and I would give almost anything to bring its end." He glanced down at her hand in his. "Anything but you."

Her fingers laced through his, and the threat of tears stung her eyes. "My decision brings peace. It might not be the path any of us want, but it's what's best for our people. Does that not matter?"

He didn't answer as they stood in the painful quiet. Then he pulled her closer. He dropped his head and rested his forehead on hers, and she let his warmth settle her. His arms moved around her and pulled her even closer.

Norah reached up and brought her hand to his face, and he turned his head into her palm to brush his lips against her thumb.

"Norah," he begged her with cerulean eyes. "Let me take you away from here. We'll leave. Tonight."

"Where?" She shook her head. "Back to Mercia with nothing? To Aleon for another husband and war?"

"No," he said hoarsely. "To the sea. Where the water is warm, and we can lie in the sun."

Tears sprang from her own eyes now. The memory. Their plans. She wanted that more than anything.

But that life was gone.

"There is no sun," she whispered.

He pulled her tighter and nestled into the fold of her neck. She wished they could stay like that forever. But they couldn't. Her heart was breaking, and she couldn't bear it. "You should go."

His breath came uneven against her skin, then he stepped back and collected himself. "Yes, I'm sure the men are wondering where I am."

"I meant back to Mercia."

His brow creased, and he shook his head. "I won't leave you."

"It's not safe for you here."

"If this is the path you've chosen, it's the path I follow." He took her hand and brought it to his lips. Then he released her, leaving her broken in the center of her sanctuary.

Chapter Forty-Three

Norah was already awake when Vitalia entered. This was the day she'd feared, the day she'd so desperately wished would never come—the day of her marriage.

Her Mercian maid, Serene, followed Vitalia in. She'd arrived with the rest of the Northern company a few days after Alexander had. Vitalia was excited at the thought of another friend, and Norah was happy to have her, although she couldn't muster feelings of happiness for long.

Her maids busied themselves around her, chatting excitedly, but Norah couldn't hear them. Her heart beat heavily in her chest. *Peace,* she thought to herself. This was what peace looked like—no impending battle; her people were fed; Mercia stood strong. She drew in a deep breath and let it out slowly. Her grandmother would come to realize this was best, as would the rest of Mercia.

Salara-Mae had overseen the making of her gown and additional details in the days before. She'd walked Norah through everything: the ceremony, the binding vow, the celebration after, and the expectations. All except the Witness. *The Witness*—the ceremony in the bedchamber that ensured the marriage was consummated, fully executed, and acknowledged by both sides. It was odd Salara-Mae said nothing of it, but Norah didn't mind. She didn't want to talk about it either. It was what she was most anxious about. To have an officiator observe such a private act between husband and wife—she didn't think she could do it. Even when Catherine had explained the ceremony in preparation for her marriage to Aleon, the thought had overwhelmed her. Now, with the Shadow King... She tried to force it from her mind. She didn't have a choice.

Norah didn't know how the morning passed so quickly. Before she realized it, she was in her dress in front of the mirror, staring at a woman she barely recognized. Her white gown boasted the color of Mercia, as she'd wanted it to, or rather, as she thought was appropriate. Strands of shimmering silver were embroidered into the fabric, starting mid-skirt and running to the ground. It looked as though she had walked through a river of crystal. Norah wasn't one for ornate adornments, but even she couldn't deny the gown's beauty. She had wanted simplicity, which she got, yet Salara-Mae had still made her look like a queen. Even Catherine would have approved. A sadness rippled through her at the thought of her grandmother, who wouldn't be here to see her married.

She forced her attention back to the mirror, fearing her emotion would get the better of her. Diamonds studded her neck. It was a common stone, but she liked how they caught the light and was insistent on them over others more expensive. Her hair fell in loose waves around her, and a silver crown sat atop her head. She wished she had her mother's crown, but she'd lost it when she was captured.

"You're ready, Your Majesty," Vitalia told her, smiling and looking at her reflection.

But she wasn't ready.

Vitalia took her hands, pulling Norah to look at her. "This is it. This is where you become queen of both Mercia and Kharav and bring peace to your people. You'll take your vows and complete the ceremony just as you rehearsed. And then you'll be salara."

Norah swallowed. Yes, just as she'd rehearsed. Then she'd be salara. She gave a nervous nod, and her maid held her hand as she led her to the great hall.

"Thank you," she whispered to Vitalia. Her maid smiled and gave her hand another reassuring squeeze, then stole away to prepare.

Norah forced one foot in front of the other. She'd had plenty of time to accept this, she told herself, yet somehow, her mind was still in denial. Her thoughts shifted to Mikael. He wasn't as she'd expected, and she wasn't entirely appalled at the idea of him being her husband. He roused feelings in her that she had struggled to ignore—feelings that might be right for a wife to have for her husband.

But those thoughts came to a halt when she rounded the corner and saw Alexander.

His eyes moved down her dress and then back up. He looked at the crown on her head, and his lips parted, but he didn't speak.

She reached up and touched the crown. "Salara-Mae had it made," she started to explain. "I..." She didn't know what to say. She what? Hoped he liked it?

Her gaze caught his, but he couldn't hold it. He glanced at the ground before he drew in a breath and raised his eyes once more. "You look like a Mercian queen."

She gave a sad smile.

Alexander looked back over his shoulder to where Caspian stood waiting. Norah had been so thankful to see the captain again when he'd arrived, and she was thankful he was with her now. Caspian nodded to her but didn't draw closer, clearly intending to give her and Alexander privacy.

Alexander turned back to her, and his eyes glistened. "Norah," he breathed.

"Don't," she said. She'd fall apart. And she couldn't fall apart. She pulled her eyes from him, unable to look at him anymore. If she did, she wouldn't go through with it.

She kept her eyes down.

"Caspian and I will be right behind you," he told her.

She nodded.

Vitalia came sweeping back, with Serene right behind. "Everything's ready," she said breathlessly as they both worked to straighten her gown. "Salar is at the front. Just walk straight to him."

She could do that, she told herself.

The doors opened, and Norah gave a small gasp at the magnitude of people. Had she really just thought she could do this?

The crowd was overwhelming, larger than her coronation in Mercia. Her eyes found Mikael at the front, with the lord commander behind him. When he saw her, the corners of his lips curved upward ever so slightly. She stepped forward, making her way through the throngs of people lining the great hall.

Norah didn't need to look back to know that Alexander was behind her. She could feel him.

She kept her gaze forward, on Mikael. It wasn't hard to do. His garb was... not what she'd expected. He wore nothing over his upper half—the Kharavian battle form—leaving visible all the markings on his skin. Around his waist he wore a dark wrap tied like loose-fitting trousers, tapered to just below the knee, showing the ink on his calves and his feet. While a seemingly simple garb, it was anything but, with its heavy embroidery and beading. His hair hung loose, a way she hadn't seen, and it was beautiful.

Still, she wavered.

When she reached him, he offered his hand. Norah moved to look back at Alexander, but then stopped. If she met his eyes...

He'd see her struggle. He'd see her on the cusp of breaking. She needed to stay strong. She forced herself to look back at Mikael and took his hand.

The prefect spoke in the Shadow tongue, but Norah knew what he said from what Salara-Mae had explained. He held a woven strip of silk in his hand, a strip of silk Mikael would loop round her waist that would signify her bond to him.

Mikael took the woven silk from the priest and looked at Norah, stepping closer to put it around her.

But she reached out and caught his arm, making him pause. "Wait," she said under his questioning eyes. She'd thought about this for a long time after she'd learned of the practice, and she pulled a silver braided ribbon from the folds of her gown. "If I'm to be bound to you, then you'll also be bound to me."

Murmurs rippled through the masses, and then all was quiet as they waited for the king's reaction.

She couldn't read his face, and her pulse quickened. What if he refused her? But she waited, not shying from the silence.

Finally, he raised his arms slightly, giving her leave to slip the ribbon around his waist. She tried to hide her relief as she reached around him. Her hands grazed the warm skin of his torso, and she flushed but looped the ribbon into a loose knot.

The king made his own tie, pulling it tight around her waist as he looked down at her. His eyes were curious, and she gave him a small smile. She watched him during the prefect's words. There was a gentleness to him, a softness in the way he held her hand.

The people who filled the hall started clapping, and Norah turned and looked out across the crowd.

It was done. They were wed.

Her eyes met Alexander's, and she saw the glisten of his emotion. A deep, snaking pain crept around her heart, wrapping itself and squeezing tightly. She couldn't breathe.

Mikael pulled her hand over his arm, as they'd rehearsed, and he led the processional through the cheering crowd and to the dining hall for their celebration. She struggled to keep herself together. The double doors to the adjacent rooms had been opened, making the hall seem vastly larger. At the front was a table, and he led her to their places.

"An interesting addition to the ceremony," he said as they sat.

She tried to make sense of his words through the fog of her torment. "I thought it was appropriate."

He didn't answer, but the corner of his mouth turned up in amusement.

People entered, filling the tables. As expected, lords made their way to offer their well-wishes. For once, Norah welcomed the distraction, hoping it would free her of the image of Alexander's eyes still in her mind. But their congratulations reminded her that...

Mikael. He was her husband now, and she, his wife.

He clenched his jaw so tightly he thought his teeth might crack. He couldn't peel his eyes from Norah's hand in the Shadow King's during the wedding ceremony. She'd almost looked at Alexander before she took it but stopped herself. Why had she stopped herself? He knew... she tried to hide her torment, but he knew. And it gutted him.

And when the Shadow King tied the rope around her waist... like he owned her... Instinctively, Alexander's hand moved to his sword. But Caspian stepped slightly forward, bumping a shoulder in front of him and discreetly pushing him back.

Still, fight rippled under his skin. Why wait for battle? Why not kill the Shadow King now? If he waited, Norah would suffer. This man was a monster. Alexander swallowed, but the knot in his throat threatened to choke him. This king wouldn't be kind. He wouldn't be gentle. He wouldn't take care of her the way that she needed.

His pulse thrummed faster as his hand tightened around his sword. The Shadow King wouldn't hold her as Alexander would. He wouldn't kiss her softly. Alexander's breath shook. This man wouldn't love her.

Suddenly, the hall erupted in cheers, jolting him. He caught Norah's gaze for the briefest of moments. Her lips parted as she sucked in a breath. Then she pulled away, and the king led her down the center and toward the celebration feast.

Alexander followed. Caspian walked in front of him, Titus at his side. It wasn't their proper places, but it was their necessary places.

He sat at the table reserved for the Northmen—a table of honor that had been positioned close to Norah and the king. It wasn't close enough. He barely noticed Caspian waving off servants who offered wine and ale as he kept his eyes focused on Norah. She avoided meeting his gaze, but she knew he was there.

Well-wishers lined up to congratulate them, and with each conversation, Norah's forced smile staled even more. She rolled the edges of the tablecloth between her fingertips, keeping her hands busy as she often did when she was anxious... and when she was afraid and trying not to show it. Was she afraid now?

Alexander was afraid. For her. And for tonight. As of earlier that morning, the Mercian priest hadn't yet heard when the Witness would be held. But it wasn't uncommon to wait a day or two after the ceremony. He wasn't sure if it was a blessing or a curse that he didn't know when. Regardless, it consumed him.

The line of well-wishers was too long and too short. When they were finished, and the Shadow King stood and pulled Norah up with him to leave, Alexander would have given anything for more time. The hall rose to their feet, and Alexander rose with them.

Norah's eyes stared down in front of her. He silently begged her to look at him, to let him know she was all right. She'd avoided his gaze for the whole celebration. If she would just look at him...

And then she did.

Eyes, the deepest blue. Eyes, afraid.

The Shadow King pulled her hand, but she didn't move as their stares remained locked. Her lip trembled, and pain—a ripping, clawing, burning—cracked through his chest. He couldn't let her go. Alexander stepped forward, but firm hands held him.

She turned and let the Shadow King take her away.

All too soon, the celebration ended, and Norah found herself being led back to Mikael's chamber. Alexander's eyes haunted her mind, and her heart. She'd tried not to look at him. She'd made her decision, and more than anything, she hoped it was the right one, but she couldn't escape the fear seeding inside her that maybe this wasn't right at all.

Except... walking now, with her arm looped through Mikael's, it didn't feel entirely wrong.

Then her mind shifted to what was to come, and the fear came rushing back.

The room was dimly lit, and Norah forced back the nervous sickness in her stomach as she stepped inside. He followed, closing the doors behind them without taking his eyes from her. The pulsing of her heartbeat in her ears was deafening.

But the room was empty.

"Where is everyone?" she asked, her voice barely a whisper.

Mikael glanced around the room. His brows drew together. "Why would anyone be here?"

"For the Witness."

"The witness of what?"

Was he really going to make her say it? "Of our union, to ensure it's consummated. To complete the contract."

His mouth moved to speak, but no words came. He tilted his head. "But you're here. You'll know what has been done."

"It's not for us. It's so our kingdoms can be assured." She couldn't believe she was defending the Witness. Not defending, she told herself—explaining.

"Is your word not enough?" Mikael gave a small snort of amusement. "What a strange place the North is. That is normal?"

As she said it out loud, it didn't seem normal at all. "I think so? It was expected when I was to marry in Aleon. The council will require confirmation. I think."

He drew closer. "Tell your old men if they question our contract, they can come discuss it with me personally."

Norah couldn't deny the wave of relief that washed over her. Perhaps the evening might be almost bearable now, but a deep reservation still brewed in her stomach.

The darks of his eyes held a reservation of his own. The line on his jaw tightened and smoothed again. "I don't expect you to love me, Salara. In fact, I fear the opposite. But I do believe you can have a comfortable life here, and after we have an heir, I won't... require anything from you, if it's not what you want."

An heir. Her stomach turned again. She hadn't thought of a child, and now she felt extremely foolish. Of course he'd expect an heir, but if she dwelled on that, her courage would leave her.

She turned her attention to the room, trying to redirect her mind from the panic creeping in. It was an expansive space with few furnishings. Centered on the back wall was the largest bed she'd ever seen. Beside it sat a chair and a side table, with a standing mirror nestled in the opposite corner. Despite its size, the room seemed minimal. There were no paintings on the walls, no draperies, no personal oddities or tokens.

All right, then. The sooner they started, the sooner this could all be over. She stepped closer to the ornately carved bed and drew her hand across the black silk cascading over its edge. Must everything be made of shadows? Dark and ominous, the bed threatened to swallow her, drown her in its depths. Her heart raced. She glanced back at Mikael, and he watched her with a hesitation of his own.

He approached her slowly, stiff with restraint, but with a wanton look in his eye. Her breath quickened as she pressed back against the corner column of the bed.

"I won't take you against your will," he said.

"Well, I suppose that's a good start to any marriage," she replied dryly.

He stepped closer. "Will you allow me, Salara?"

She reminded herself why she was here. This marriage was for Mercia, for her people. She swallowed and gave a reluctant nod.

"Take off your dress," he said.

Her heart pounded in her chest. "You first," she countered. Not that there was much—he would pull off the garb around his waist and then watch her strip multiple layers of dress. Still, it made her feel slightly better.

Surprise flashed across his face. He didn't move. Their eyes locked, unblinking, each waiting for the other to break.

Finally, Mikael relaxed his shoulders, submitting. He reached down and loosened the embroidered belt from around his waist and dropped it to the floor. Slowly he untied his trousers, and she was surprised to see him pull it off as a singular wrap of cloth.

He stood only in short braies now, and she let her eyes roll over his body. Again, she noted the scar across his chest, a stark contrast against the smoothness of his skin.

She stepped closer, close enough to touch him.

He only waited.

Feeling bolder, she reached up and brushed her fingertips over the raised line of the scar. "They say you cut your heart from your chest to make a pact with Darkness."

The corners of his mouth curved up ever so slightly, watching her. "I haven't heard that story."

She raised her eyes back to his. "This pact gave you a demon commander to do your bidding. They say he collects the souls of the fallen."

"That part is probably true," he said in rare jest, and she found herself smiling. "Did you believe I was a man without a heart?" he asked. "Before I told you my story?"

"No," she whispered. She flattened her palm against the scar. "I felt your heart beat in Bahoul."

It beat now. Fast. Was he nervous? His face didn't show it. She traced her thumb down the center of his chest, and the depression underneath. His skin was smooth and warm.

"Take everything off," she told him.

He waited a moment, seeming to contemplate her authority, but then complied. She watched him with an unashamed curiosity—a curiosity he seemed to enjoy. His nakedness captivated her. She drew her hand over his shoulder as she stepped around behind him.

"Why do you mark your skin?" she asked, tracing the inked patterns that ran from his chest, over his upper arms, and to his back.

"It's my story," he said.

Behind him, she moved her hand down, her thumb along the trench of his spine. Slowly, softly, she trailed the round of his buttocks. Moving higher now, she lingered briefly at the muscled arc at his side and then drew her hand up around his other shoulder. She followed her touch, stepping back around in front of him, and ran her fingers over his body once more—feeling, testing, exploring. He stood silently for her, letting her discover him.

She let her eyes drop to his lower body, and a wave rolled in her stomach. She wanted to touch him, but a sudden shyness overcame her.

A wry smile stretched across his lips. "Am I to your satisfaction?" he asked with a slight hint of impatience.

Norah looked back down. Feeling bolder, she reached below his waist and wrapped her hand around him. A rumble escaped him, and he moved forward. She put her other hand on his chest, quietly bringing him to a stop. A vibration rumbled through him, but he stayed. Turning her attention back to his flesh, she was surprised how he could be so hard and yet so soft, and her pulse quickened at the thought of him inside her. She let her fingertips explore his anatomy underneath, and he shifted. The fire in his eyes could burn her.

His hunger sent a flash of heat across her skin, and she suddenly wanted out of her gown. She turned her back to him, pulling her hair to the side and looking over her shoulder at him.

Not needing further prompting, he reached out and pulled at the lacing on her dress. "Gently," she insisted.

A complaining rumble came from his chest, but he slowed. Her dress fell open, revealing her corset, and he pulled loose the lacing on it too. She turned to face him and let the gown and corset drop to the floor. She stood in her chemise but then pulled it from her shoulders, letting it fall. Prickles rippled across her skin as she stood in her underwear. Summoning her courage, she hooked her thumbs in the sides and slid them to the floor before stepping out of them.

His breath quickened at the sight of her, and she flushed to see him grow even larger in his arousal. Norah stepped forward, slowly, and took his hand. She spread her fingers and measured her palm against his. His hand dwarfed her own.

Mikael moved forward, using his body to walk her backward toward the bed. She kept a firm hand on his chest to control his pace. When the backs of her thighs brushed against the edge, she paused. And so did he. Then she crept back into the sea of black.

He followed with a hunting prowl, moving between her legs and covering her body with his own. His mouth found hers, and it was hard and wanting. She clasped the base of his jaw, pushing him back to slow his storm. But she wasn't sure she still had control.

She trembled underneath him.

He pulled back. His eyes moved back and forth between hers, dark and questioning. "Are you afraid?" he whispered.

Her voice came in barely a breath. "A little."

Mikael's face softened. "You don't ever need to be afraid of me."

She believed him.

Slowly, he brought his mouth back to hers—probing, asking. He pulled back to look at her, seeking her approval before he bent to kiss her again. The kiss was soft, cautious. Something changed in him, an added tenderness, and she kissed him back. A warmth pooled inside her. Her kiss grew hungry, and he answered with a leashed hunger of his own.

Mikael drew his fingers across her shoulder and down. She trembled again, but not from fear. He swirled his touch around each breast, and she writhed, wanting more. Everything fell away—the circumstance, her worry, her mind. All that mattered was the touch of his skin against hers.

He trailed his hand lower, over her stomach and down between her thighs. She gasped, and his eyes burned darker. He slipped a finger between the lips of her sex, and she writhed against him. As he found the center of her heat, she clutched him tighter.

He made her body answer to his call. Tension built in her stomach, pulsing into her thighs and tightening every fiber in her body. Her hips rocked to her need as her breaths came faster. He took his time, watching her, waiting.

Then she shattered. Release quaked through her, making her cry out. She arched against him, but he held her tight, not letting her escape his touch.

As her body came back to her, she stilled, panting. He covered her mouth in his and captured the last of the fading release on her lips. When he pulled back, she looked up at him, and her face grew hotter. She hadn't imagined he'd be able to make her feel this way, to pull the desire from her, expose her, make her bare herself.

He moved between her thighs again, and her breath shook as he positioned himself. Their eyes met as he rolled his hips forward to meet her. He paused, waiting. She shifted slightly and opened her thighs wider for him.

"Forgive me," he whispered.

He let out a growl and pushed into her. The pain was sharp, and she sucked in a breath, balling the sheets in her fists. The second thrust put him deep within her and she couldn't help the cry that escaped. He trembled under the effort of control.

"Wait," she begged.

He buried his head into her neck, and they lay in the dark quiet of their union.

"Just wait," she whispered.

He did.

Norah brought her hand to the nape of his neck and then threaded her fingers into his hair.

Mikael drew back, pulling her eyes to him. "Are you all right?"

He made it all right, and she nodded.

Her body relaxed, and slowly, he began to move inside her. It wasn't long before the burn subsided to an ache, and the want returned. Feeling him inside her, filling her, brought a new wave of sensations. She rocked her hips, and he moved faster. His breaths quickened, and she watched him. Her fingers moved along the lines of his body—feeling him, learning him.

Intimacy with Mikael was not as she'd imagined; *he* was not as she'd imagined. She tightened her thighs to slow him and moved her hips to push him faster. Where she led him, he followed. She needed control, and he gave it to her. He gave her power. And she gave herself back to him, because what she wanted in that moment *was* him.

The muscle under his skin hardened as he reached his own release, and he buried himself deep within her. She took him; she wanted him, all of him—his body, his being. Everything else fell away.

They lay unmoving as the air quieted around them. Norah closed her eyes and waited for her body to come back. His frame engulfed her, holding her, keeping her safe, and then, ever so gently, he pulled himself from her.

She winced, and he nuzzled the side of her cheek, his breath warm against her ear. "I'm sorry," he whispered. "Are you all right?"

She couldn't answer. Was it all right that she didn't want this time with him to be over? That he'd made her forget everything else, and she didn't want to leave him? That she wanted to kiss him again? A longing stirred deep within her. Was it all right she wanted more than an alliance between them?

"Salara?"

Norah opened her eyes to find large pools of black brimmed with concern staring back at her.

"Say something," he pleaded.

"How long before you can do that again?" she whispered.

The corners of his lips turned upward. He slipped his arms underneath her and laid his head between her breasts. "What are you doing to me?"

A smile crept across her lips, and she drifted into the sweet arms of sleep.

Chapter Forty-Four

Norah woke with the morning sun, her eyes hazy with sleep. She stretched languidly and sat up, alone in the bed. It had been the most restful night she'd had since arriving in Kharav. The warmth of Mikael's body next to hers lulled her into dreaming; his skin brought the sweet scent of comfort.

Vitalia swept in. "You look like you had a very good night," her maid said with a grin as she piled the mix of clothes together that had been cast to the floor.

Heat flashed across her cheeks. It was strange to think of it as a good night. But it felt good between them, her and Mikael. More than good.

Vitalia poured a cup of water, set it on the side table, and laid out a new dress across the bed.

"Where is he?" Norah asked.

"He left early to go see the lord commander. He said to let you sleep a while longer."

The windows let the sun pour in, and Norah smiled under its beams. Everything felt in its place.

"How long will you stay here before you move to the wives' villa?" Vitalia asked.

Norah jerked her head up. "The what?"

"The villa, where the king's wives are."

Her heart stopped in her chest.

"What wives?" *What wives?*

Vitalia looked at her in surprise and then backed up slightly.

"What wives?" Norah asked again, her voice shaking.

Her maid swallowed. "Salar's wives."

Horror flooded her. This couldn't be true. "He has other wives?"

"Forgive me, Salara," Vitalia said quickly. "I thought you knew. You saw them at the betrothal celebration."

Then she realized. The women. What were their names again? Rasha. Myral. Heta. They weren't sisters. They weren't meant to keep her company.

They were his wives.

It hadn't even occurred to her. Norah stumbled up from the bed, her mind reeling. She shook her head, unable to speak.

"It's normal for Salar to have many wives," Vitalia told her.

Normal? "So, I'm just one of many?" she asked, trying to hold back the flood of emotion overwhelming her.

"Only you are salara," Vitalia explained. "You assume the highest status of them all."

Norah bristled. "I don't want to be the highest. I want to be the *only*! How is this *normal?*" Her heart felt it would burst from her chest. Shame flooded her.

"Salar's father had seven wives. His father before, five."

"How many are there?" she demanded.

"Only three."

Only three. Norah drew in a shaky breath as an anger grew inside her. She'd foolishly believed the king felt something for her, something he hadn't felt before. But he had married before, brought a woman to his bed before. Three times before. *At least.*

Her eyes welled. What she and Mikael had wasn't special. She bit back the pain. She wouldn't let herself be another woman to him. She was a queen, and now she was salara.

"Find him," she said with bitterness thick on her tongue. "Now."

Norah sat silently on the edge of the bed, waiting. The heat of embarrassment flushed her cheeks.

She hadn't even realized. How could she not have realized?

Mikael stepped into the chamber, and she rose. When he saw her, he paused. "I don't think I've ever been summoned before," he said as he draped his cloak on the side chair by the window. While his words came in jest, there was a slight edge to them. He was offended, perhaps.

But she didn't care.

He let out a long sigh. "I'm told you're displeased about my wives."

"That's an understatement," she said icily. "Why didn't you tell me?"

His head tilted slightly, and his eyes narrowed. "I presented them to you."

"Not as your wives!"

"Who did you think they were?"

True, she could have asked who they were, but it wasn't a question she'd even considered. Just then, her stomach clenched. *We shall be good friends*, she'd told them. The embarrassment was unbearable. She wanted to crawl under the quilts of the bed and never come out. But not this bed. Not his bed, not ever again.

"And kings have many wives," he added. His tone carried an air of dismissal.

"Mercian kings don't!"

"I'm not a Mercian king."

"I'm a Mercian queen, and you're my husband!" she snapped.

He snorted, and she could see his own anger rising. He wasn't used to being challenged. "Fine," he said cheekily as he lumbered toward her. "I won't marry any more."

She let out a quaking breath. "That's not good enough."

Mikael used his size to back her against the edge of the bed, where the fire in his eyes intensified. "It'll have to be."

Anger radiated through every fiber of her being. "It's not. And you'll fix it," she demanded.

"What do you expect me to do?" His voice came edgier now. "The marriages simply are. There's no pretending they didn't happen."

"You'll annul them."

His nostrils flared. "How am I to do that?"

"You'll figure it out, or you won't be married to me."

"You can't unwed me," he scoffed. "It's done. We've consummated it." His eyes burned into her. "I know you now. Would that not bring dishonor in the North?"

He seemed to be mocking her, and it hurt.

"You don't know me," she hissed back. "And I won't recognize you as my husband unless I'm your *only* wife."

"So, this is the benefit of a Witness?" he cut back. "I'd thought it was a Northern perversion, but perhaps I'll require one now. I'll make the whole world watch."

A flash of fury swept through her, and she delivered a sharp slap across his face. He bared his teeth with a growl against the sting. She tried to strike him again, but he caught her hand.

"Is it a fight you want?" he snarled.

Norah wrenched against him, but he held her. She fought harder, making them both stagger sideways. As she flailed out, her hand knocked the water basin on a table close by. She grabbed it and swung with all her strength, hitting him squarely in the temple. The force of the blow broke the basin, and he lost his grip on her as he stumbled backward and crashed to the ground.

"Curse it, woman!" he roared as he brought his hand to the side of his face. A deep gash poured blood into his eye and down his cheek.

She gasped in concern, but only for a moment. Her fury swelled back, pushing her concern aside, and she turned and fled the chamber.

"Salara!" he bellowed.

Norah escaped out into the hall to see her Crest guard, wide-eyed and debating whether to follow her or answer the king's thunder.

"Are you not *my* guard?" she snapped, and they fell into place behind her as she hurried to her sanctuary.

His bellows echoed through the halls, and her pulse raced. Her fingers fumbled to latch the door, although there was no way it would hold him out. She sank down into the chair by her vanity, gripping the back until her knuckles turned white.

"Salara!" His roar shook her to her core. He was coming.

She forced herself to breathe, struggling for calm. He'd said she never needed to fear him, but that was before she'd hit him with a water basin and threatened to deny their marriage. Would he hurt her? Her mind raced for how to temper his anger. Perhaps if she apologized... *No.* She'd done nothing wrong. And she'd meant it when she said she'd be his only wife. If he thought he'd force her otherwise, she had another water basin waiting.

"Salara!" he bellowed, nearer now. He sounded near the end of the hall; he'd be at the door in a moment.

She gripped the chair tighter, crouching slightly, and braced herself.

"Come out, woman!"

Oddly, his voice sounded the same distance away.

"Salara!"

She swallowed. Had he stopped at the end of the hall? He'd told her that was the boundary, but surely in his anger he wouldn't confine himself to a mere verbal threshold.

"Come out!"

She most certainly would *not* be coming out.

"You can't claim sanctuary from me in the room that I gave you out of my goodwill!"

That was exactly what she intended to do.

"Come out!"

She stared at the door, not daring to move.

The hall grew silent.

She waited.

Had he gone? It remained silent.

Her breaths calmed as the moments passed, but her body still shook. He could have forced her out. Why hadn't he? She turned slowly to the vanity. Her hands trembled as she brushed back her hair from her face. What was she going to do now?

Mikael showed no intent of dissolving his other marriages. Mercia wouldn't recognize a marriage where she wasn't the only wife, and neither would she. What was worse, she'd already given herself to him. She'd naively thought she meant something to him. Tears threatened, but she clenched her teeth. She wouldn't let him reduce her to this.

Chapter Forty-Five

Mikael sat at the table and took a long drink of wine. It had been two days since the wedding, and there was only one thing on his mind, one thing that tormented him. He looked at Salara's empty chair.

"I thought she might come this evening," he confessed. He shifted his eyes to Soren, who stabbed a chunk of meat with his knife and put it in his mouth.

Soren snorted.

Mikael rested his elbows on the edge of the table and ran his fingers over the scabbed stitching along his brow. "How long do you think she'll stay angry?"

Soren shrugged as he chewed his food. "As long as you have wives." He chuckled as he took a drink from his blood bowl. "Let her."

Mikael's anger stirred. Soren was of little help in these matters. "She said she refuses to acknowledge our marriage."

Soren snorted again. "Did she not see the thousands there to witness it?"

His irritation grew. He wasn't in the mood for Soren's sarcasm. "If she denies me, so will the North, marriage or no."

His commander gave a wry smile. "What's really lost, though? You still hold the queen within your walls. Better now—you have the Bear."

"I don't want the Bear!" Mikael snapped as he slammed his fist down onto the table, rattling the plates.

Soren's face sobered.

Mikael's words surprised even himself. They weren't entirely true. He did want the Bear. He wanted his head. He wanted to gaze into his dead eyes and spit into the face of fate. But there was something he wanted more now.

He sat back in his chair. He had to do something. "I could make her my only wife."

Soren straightened, and the line along his jaw tightened. "Careful, brother," he warned. "You'd offend three of the most powerful lords in your kingdom. That wouldn't be without consequence."

But how likely would they be to act?

Soren leaned toward him, his eyes dark and serious. "Don't do something stupid."

Mikael sighed. Soren was right. That would be stupid. "Have you heard anything from Salara?" he asked the servant who poured him more wine.

The servant bowed his head. "She said she's not hungry this evening."

Mikael swore. He knew that was a lie; that woman ate more than he did.

"She'll need to eat eventually," Soren rumbled.

Mikael ignored him. "Have meals left outside her door," he told the servant.

Soren cut him an annoyed glance. "That only aids her in hiding away."

Mikael looked at the servant. "Do as I say."

"Yes, Salar," the servant said with a bow.

Mikael crossed his arms and brought the knuckles of his fist to his lips. What was he going to do?

"She'll get over it," his commander told him. "She just needs time to learn how things are here."

Perhaps. Perhaps not.

Norah woke on the settee in her sanctuary to the sound of a knock on the door. Her book had fallen to the floor. She was surprised she'd drifted to sleep. The knock came again, stronger this time. There was a man behind it, and she shuddered. Mikael had finally come, but she still wasn't ready to face him.

The knock came louder, forceful now. "North Queen," a voice snarled.

It wasn't Mikael. Her pulse quickened. It was his brute. Mikael might have shown restraint, but the lord commander had none. She rose and walked to the door but didn't open it.

"I know you hear me," his voice rumbled.

She *did* hear him, and his hatred. And she knew he wouldn't leave simply because she didn't answer.

"You doubt I'll break down this door?"

She most certainly didn't. Norah lifted the latch and pulled the door open a small crack. His eyes met hers with smoldering animosity. "What do you want?" she asked coldly.

"I suggest you very quickly get over this foolishness. Salar has no time for these games."

"This isn't a game," she snapped.

"I caution you. It's unwise for you to press this, North Queen. You're held deep within Kharav." He paused, and then added, "As is your Bear."

Prickles rose over her skin. He was threatening her.

"It would be a shame if someone were to get hurt," he said.

"Mikael wouldn't do that."

"Wouldn't he?" he challenged. "You have no idea who he is, or what he'll do. There's only one will, and that's the will of Salar. You're a fool to think you have any power over him. And you'll be done with this nonsense, now."

With that, the commander turned and left her to the lingering warning of his words.

She didn't want to believe him, but now she wasn't so sure. She didn't know Mikael as well as she thought she had. Did he see all this as nonsense? How long would he let her avoid him? She couldn't stay in the sanctuary forever.

Her thoughts turned to Alexander. He wasn't safe in Kharav. As much as she wanted to hide away from the world, she couldn't leave him to the consequence of her fallout with the king. She had to see him and make sure he was all right. Although her stomach dipped at the thought of facing him now. She hadn't spoken to him since the wedding. Since...

Her chest tightened. It had been two days. He'd be sick with worry. She should have gone to him sooner, to let him know she was okay. Except she wasn't okay. It didn't matter; she had to see him. She unlatched the door and slipped out into the hall.

Norah paused to see a small tray of food by the door. The commander certainly hadn't left it. Vitalia must have dropped it off. And even though it called to her hungry stomach, she'd eat later. She had more important things to tend to.

Norah moved cautiously, wary of seeing the commander again, but as she neared the end of the hall, a broad smile broke across her face.

Titus and another Northman guard stood on duty. When they saw her, they gave small bows of their heads. But her smile fell as she got a closer look. Titus bore a cut on the side of his cheek and under his chin. His left eye seemed slightly swollen, with bruising over his brow. Blood stained the left shoulder of his tunic, but she wasn't sure if it was his or someone else's. The Northman beside him held similar injuries, and a glance at the Crest guards standing on the opposite side showed they weren't better off. A hallway brawl?

Wonderful. Something else to manage.

When she reached them, Vitalia jumped up from a side chair she'd been sitting in.

"Salara!"

"Hello, Vitalia," she said, pulling her eyes from the guards. She was glad to see her maid, but Vitalia knew about her ignorance of the marriages, and Norah still felt the shame of it.

"I'm so sorry I haven't come," her maid told her. "They wouldn't let me disturb you in your sanctuary, even to see if you needed anything."

Norah forced a small smile. "That's perfectly all right. I appreciate you bringing a tray by, though."

"I'm happy to take the thanks, but that wasn't me. Salar ordered food to be brought to you for every meal."

Well, that was... kind.

"Are you going to see the Northmen off?"

Norah didn't know what she meant. "For what?"

"Salar's given them provisions to take to the North. He's also arranged horses in the valley from the Tribelands. He's given your captain men to help, and they leave later today."

"Oh," Norah said. She'd never expected... Of course these allowances had been a part of their marriage arrangement—but it was an arrangement she'd threatened to not acknowledge. A seed of hope sprouted in her chest. "That's good news," she said.

"It is. Oh, and Serene has already moved to the villa. Would you like her to come here?"

Her stomach soured. If Serene was in the villa, that meant she knew about the wives. Norah wondered how long it would be before her grandmother knew. "No, she can tend to things there." One less person to bear her shame in front of. "Could you bring a few more dresses, though? There's only a couple in the sanctuary, and I'll be staying there a while."

"Yes, Salara. I'll get those right away." Vitalia started off and then stopped. "May I have your permission to wait on you there? In the sanctuary?"

"Of course," Norah told her. "I'd like that."

Vitalia gave a small smile with a bow and went to get Norah's dresses from the villa.

Then Norah set her mind on her original intention: to find Alexander. She started down the hall, and Titus moved in behind her. The slide of steel came as a warning, and she spun to look back at the guards. The Crest guard stood coiled, daggers and spears in hand with their eyes on her Northmen, and Titus had his hand on the hilt of his sword.

"Northmen with me," she said. Her Mercian guard fell instep close behind her, and although the Crest guard gave some space, she gritted her teeth as they followed behind. Yes, she'd have to do something about this. Now wasn't the time to discuss her guardsmen's assignments with Mikael or the lord commander, but she also didn't want a guard of both Northmen and the Crest with a small battle brewing behind her everywhere she went.

She pushed out a breath. One thing at a time. First, Alexander.

He paced his chamber, ready to topple this castle to the ground. It had been two days since the wedding, two days since he'd seen Norah or heard anything from her, and Alexander couldn't wait any longer. He'd tried to focus on his work—communications with the council, seeing to his men, and assigning their stations to protect her as much as he could deep in an enemy kingdom—but a dark madness kept clawing into his mind, threatening his control. What had the Shadow King done with her? What had he done *to* her? For two days...

Caspian tried to take on more and give him space to calm and sort his mind. But there would be no calm until Alexander could see her.

A knock sounded on the door, and he nearly tore it off its hinges as he swung it open. One more Shadowman who—

He froze as blue eyes stared back at him. His nostrils flared and he forced a swallow. He couldn't hold himself—he swept her into an embrace.

Norah clutched his tunic, sinking into him. He brought a hand to her head and held her to his chest. Just the scent of her settled him. She was here. In his arms. Safe. Unharmed. Or so he assumed. He quickly pulled back and cupped her face in his hands.

"Are you all right?" he asked.

"I'm fine," she replied. But she didn't sound fine.

He held her tighter. "You're not." Her lip trembled. She was wed to the Shadow King. She wasn't fine. He cursed under his breath as he pulled her back to him, forgetting all proprieties and kissing the top of her head. "I'm here," he murmured.

He'd figure out a way to get her out and back to Mercia. It didn't matter if she was wed if he could get her out before...

"The Witness?" he asked. "When will it be held?"

She didn't answer, and his blood ran cold. His heart stopped. Was it too late? A crippling nausea rolled through him. He forced himself to pull back from her; he needed her to answer him. "Norah?"

Her lips parted, and his stomach twisted. She swallowed, then said, "There will be no Witness."

Alexander let out a quaking breath. *There would be no Witness*. Had the Shadow King intended this marriage to be in name only? His eyes stung as he pulled her back to him, and he breathed his undying thanks to the gods. All he could do was hold her and breathe her in.

When he found his voice again, it came hoarse and thick with emotion. "I couldn't bear it, Norah. My mind's been filled with madness these past days." He held her tighter. Now he could breathe again, focus again. And he only needed to focus on getting her home.

"I'm all right," she whispered, but there was a strangeness to her voice, something not all right.

He pulled back again and clasped the side of her neck, brushing her cheek with his thumb and looking over her.

"I am," she said, her voice a little stronger now. "I just had to come to make sure you were too."

"I don't want you to worry about me. You have enough to deal with."

Her lip still trembled. Was there something else? Something she wasn't telling him?

"Are you returning to Mercia with Caspian?" she asked.

He narrowed his eyes. Was she really all right? Or was she changing the subject?

He shook his head. "No, but I do need to leave very soon to investigate a situation." He hesitated, not wanted to put more burden on her, but she needed to know. "Mercian villages, and others under Mercia's protection, are being attacked."

Her brow dipped. "Again?"

What did she mean *again*? "You know about this?"

She pushed out a breath. "After I was taken, we came upon a town that had been destroyed, but there was no sign of who had done it. Do you know?"

He shook his head again. "Not yet. But I don't want you to trouble yourself with it now. I'll find who it was and put a stop to it."

"How long will you be gone?"

"Not long. I'm going only to the southern reaches, so a couple weeks perhaps." He clasped her hands and brought them to his chest. "But I won't leave yet. Not right now. I need to make sure you're okay."

"I am," she assured him. "And honestly, it would make me feel better if I knew you were out of harm's way until things have settled. You should go. I'm fine. Really."

"Titus and the rest of the guard will be here with you."

She shifted. "About that—send them to help Caspian."

"And leave you alone?" *Absolutely not.*

"Alexander. Please. You can look out in that hall and see I'm most certainly not alone. I don't have command over the Crest, and until I work things out with Mikael, there will be duplicate guard and the threat of battle between them at every hall. I can't deal with that right now, I can't. Alexander, please—"

"All right," he said, yielding. As much as he hated the idea, he couldn't resolve it for her now, and it was obviously yet one more overwhelming burden.

"It will only be a couple of weeks," she said. "That's a short time."

It was an eternity away from her.

She gave a weak smile. "Go," she said. "I'll be here."

He pulled her hands to his lips. "I'll return as soon as I can." Then he'd find a way to bring her home.

Chapter Forty-Six

Two more evenings passed and Mikael still found himself without Salara. He sat in the dining hall again, brooding over her empty chair. By now, she'd have moved into the villa. Perhaps she'd see it wasn't as she'd expected. The villa had every comfort, every luxury.

"You still let the North Queen worry you," Soren said, interrupting his thoughts.

Mikael let out a deep sigh. "She still doesn't come. She's still unhappy."

Soren shrugged. "What will she do? Leave?"

"She's not a prisoner."

Soren's face grew serious. "But you know we can't let her go."

Mikael knew this. So long as he held the North Queen, he kept her from Aleon. If he kept her from Aleon, he denied his fate. But he didn't want to hold her. He wanted her to want to stay.

"Go to the villa," he told a servant. "Tell her I... I wish for her to come. It's not required, but I wish for her to want to come. If she should find herself wanting to, wanting to eat. With me."

Soren snorted and raised a brow.

Mikael glared at him and cursed under his breath. He sounded like a rambling fool, but he worried for her.

"She's not in the villa, Salar," the servant said. "She still remains in the sanctuary."

Mikael flung his chalice across the hall, frustration coursing through him.

"Would you like me to deliver the message to her there?" the servant asked.

"No," he rasped, tempering his fire. "She's not to be disturbed there."

A banging on the door of the sanctuary made her jump, and Norah pushed her breath through her teeth. She already knew who it was: the one person for whom Mikael's rules didn't apply. She debated not opening it, but it wasn't as though he would go away.

"North Queen," he growled through the door.

Norah pursed her lips as she put her book down, and she rose to answer. She opened the door to find the commander's shadowed eyes looking back at her. Behind him prowled his dogs, as menacing as their master.

"What do you want?" she asked, not bothering to hide the iciness in her own voice.

"I came to suggest you might dine with Salar tonight. Each day only brings greater discord." It wasn't a friendly request.

Her eyes narrowed. "I didn't know you were so eager to see me again."

"I'm not," he snarled. "But his waiting for you is even more disturbing than your presence. At least pretend to settle your grievance."

"If he wants amends, then he shouldn't send his dogs!" She moved to close the door, but he jarred it with his foot and flung it back open, and she stumbled back into the room.

"I come on my own accord."

She bared her teeth. "You're not allowed here."

"There is nothing I'm not allowed!" he raged. "You'll do well to remember that."

And yet he didn't step inside.

"This is *my* sanctuary," she snapped.

"And you have it by Salar's grace! How much longer do you think that will last? It's by that grace you live here in comfort, and by that grace your Bear's still alive."

"Leave!" she seethed, her anger casting aside any fear.

Fury dripped from his skin, but she drew closer in challenge. He couldn't scare her. Alexander had left; there was nothing he could do.

Finally, he relented, storming back down the hall the way he'd come. Norah shut the door behind him and sank onto her bed, breathing deeply to calm her shaking.

She couldn't let him get to her. Despite everything that had happened between them, she didn't believe Mikael would hurt her. She didn't believe he'd let his commander hurt her. And with Alexander gone, she had time to work on a solution. But what was the solution? What could she do if nothing changed?

Outside her door, a tray rattled with a slight clattering of dishes—another meal being delivered. Her stomach reminded her she hadn't eaten.

Norah opened the door and moved to take the tray from the small table that had been set up by the wall. She stopped. On the tray sat a bowl, and inside were three small, rolled parchments.

She pulled open one of the parchments, and her heart thrummed in her chest. Then she quickly glanced over the rest. Her hands trembled.

There were three.

Three annulments.

For three wives.

And they bore the king's seal.

Her silk shoes fell silent on the stone floors as Norah hurried through the castle with Vitalia close behind her. Her heart raced as she went. The king had annulled his marriages, which she'd doubted he'd do. Despite his coarseness, he cared. And what surprised her more was that *she* cared. The commander was wrong. She *did* know him.

They reached the throne room, but the king wasn't without company. Norah paused in the wing, watching out of sight.

Mikael sat on his throne, listening to a man in an emerald-green cloak. An embroidered golden crest on the chest of the man's jacket caught the light as he moved, but she wasn't able to make it out fully. He wore his hair cropped short but his beard long.

"An envoy from Serra," Vitalia whispered. Her breath came shallow. "Perhaps it would be better to speak to Salar later."

Vitalia was afraid. But of what?

"Who is that—Serra?"

"It's the slavers' kingdom. South. Across the Aged Sea."

Norah swallowed. The kingdom that dealt in slave trade. Her own revulsion swelled. She watched them. Norah understood the man's words as he spoke to the king. "They speak the Northern tongue?"

"The Northern tongue is the Common tongue. Almost all kingdoms use it for trade and relations."

That meant everyone spoke the Northern tongue. After what had happened with Bremhad, she'd known it was that way in Kharav, but she hadn't realized it was a common language across kingdoms. A bitter taste crept over the back of her tongue and down her throat as she thought about the lord commander. And as if thoughts made him appear, her eyes found him. He stood to the right of the king's throne, looking murderous, as always.

"King disagrees," the envoy told Mikael as Norah started to listen in. "He proposes a reduction of Serra's share by one third, or an increase in provisions from Kharav."

"They talk of trade?" Norah whispered to Vitalia.

Vitalia nodded, visibly upset. "Kharav trades slaves with Serra and provides provisions to support them."

"Go back to the sanctuary," Norah told her. "I'll return after I've spoken to the king."

"Are you sure?"

"Yes," Norah whispered. "Go."

Vitalia left her standing in the wing, and Norah turned her attention back to Mikael.

"He awaits your answer," the envoy said.

"I've already given it," Mikael replied. His face didn't show the anger that Norah heard in his voice.

"King Milar says this is unacceptable."

Mikael rose from his throne. He walked down the stairs, calm and composed. Then, in a single movement, he pulled his sword from his scabbard and cut down the Serran guard beside the envoy. Norah's heart leapt to her throat, and she clasped her hand over her mouth to stifle a cry.

Mikael grabbed the envoy by his jacket and forced him to his knees as he swept the tip of the blade to the man's neck.

"No!" Norah called out, stepping forward from the shadows of the wing.

They all turned at the sound of her voice. Mikael's eyes met hers, and he stopped.

"What are you doing?" she cried.

He looked back at the envoy, and his face darkened again. "Sending my answer to King Milar."

"Don't harm him," she said. "Please."

Mikael paused for a moment, looking back at the envoy. He angled the tip of his sword against the man's throat. "Salara asks for mercy," he said finally. "Your gods smile on you today." He released the envoy, and the man scrambled backward and to his feet.

But Norah didn't feel relief. She stared at the dead guard on the floor. Blood pooled around him and veined out along the grooves where the patterned stone joined together to form its image.

"Leave us," Mikael said to the room. The Serran guards collected their dead companion and ushered their lord out and away from the loosely leashed danger. The Kharavian soldiers followed, clearing the room and leaving only Mikael and Norah.

And the lord commander, of course.

Norah peeled her eyes from the smeared blood on the stone.

"I'll have it cleaned," Mikael told her.

Is that what he thought she cared about? "Will you bring back the life you took?" The life he'd taken so easily, like it had been nothing.

Her words silenced him for a moment. "These are not good men, Salara," he said finally.

As if that justified murder.

Mikael glanced at the parchments in her hand. His eyes met hers again, and his expression shifted. "You read them?" he asked.

Norah looked down at her clenched hand. She'd forgotten she was holding the marriage annulments.

"This is what you wanted, yes?" he said, his voice softer now.

Yes, but no. None of this was what she wanted.

The lord commander stepped forward, the line between his brow creasing. "What have you done?" he asked the king.

Was he serious? This man was truly unbelievable. Norah glared at him, finally finding her voice. "You're fine with him killing a man but not absolving a marriage?"

But he did not respond to her reproach. His eyes stayed on the king. "Salar?"

"Leave us," Mikael told him.

The commander's eyes shifted to Norah, and she could see the swelling rage within. But he said nothing, only turned and left them in silence.

"Walk with me?" Mikael asked, only he didn't wait for her to answer before moving them forward and out of the throne room.

"Do you kill all your trade envoys?" she questioned as they walked.

"Not all of them."

She wasn't sure if he was being cheeky or serious. Anger touched her cheeks either way. She didn't like this Mikael—the dark Mikael. He drifted closer to her as they walked, close enough to touch her. He'd better not dare.

They reached the great hall, and he slowed. From the corner of her eye, she saw him looking at her. "I spared him."

"Because I asked you to. Not because you had mercy in your heart."

They stopped and stared at each other.

"Has it come already?" he asked. "Your loathing for me?"

Did she loathe him now? She wanted to.

"Not that I thought it would take long," he added. His voice came fainter, as if he were speaking more to himself than to her, as if he were regretful, even. "I just hadn't expected it so soon." His face fell, and his eyes softened. "What would you have me change?"

His question wasn't what she had anticipated. What would she have him change? His kingdom? Their values, their culture, their way of life? Anything she could ask for was too much or not enough. Or both. She stayed quiet.

He shifted his gaze forward again and let out a long breath. "The villa is yours alone now. Will you be moving there?"

Her mind was still on the man that had just been killed; she couldn't think about the villa, other than that she would most certainly not be moving there.

"You don't want the villa?" He paused a moment. "Have you seen it?"

No. She didn't need to see it. She didn't *want* to see it. She didn't want to stay where there had been wives before her, women he had known in such an intimate way. But she didn't want to argue about the villa right now. "I'm sure it has everything I need," she managed finally, hoping to put the subject to rest for now.

"But you don't want to stay there," he pressed.

Fine. "No," she admitted. "I don't want to stay there. I'm fine with the sanctuary." The sanctuary was hers. Kind of.

He stepped in front of her. His voice dropped low. "I've been with no other since I've met you, no other woman. I want you to know this. If it's important."

Her breath hitched in her throat. And her heart... "It is," she whispered. He was trying. Could she try? "Thank you for telling me."

He nodded, and they continued walking.

She swallowed. "What did you do with your wives?"

He shifted his weight back. "They returned to their homes, to their families."

So, no violent ends. That was good. "You'll see them provided for?"

He looked at her curiously. "I've allowed them to keep the Provision Promise moneys. It's a substantial amount."

She wasn't sure what that meant. Perhaps something like a dowry or a bride price. She bit the inside of her lip. That didn't seem enough.

"Is there something more you'd have me do?" he asked.

"I don't want them to be dishonored. They come from noble families?"

He shifted uncomfortably. "They do."

"You should give them more. Land, perhaps."

He nodded.

"You'll see them taken care of, then?" She wanted confirmation.

"I will."

She paused. "Do you have any children?"

He fell silent, then said, "No."

His answer surprised her and relieved her at the same time. They stood awkwardly in the silence.

"I should retire," she said. It was enough for now.

"Can I walk you back?" he asked, drawing closer.

No. But she found herself giving the faintest of nods. He offered her his arm. She wavered a moment, but then slipped her hand under and let him take them forward. He put his hand over hers, locking her to him. Her skin tingled under his touch, but she couldn't let herself forget so easily. He'd just killed a man, like it had been nothing. He would've killed another had she not stopped him, all while discussing the trade of people's lives as if they were bags of grain.

Could she bear this, the price of peace? She'd known who she'd married. Maybe it had been foolish of her to expect change quickly. Maybe over time...

She needed to try.

When they reached the door to her sanctuary, he stopped but didn't release her hand. Nor did she pull it away. His eyes churned like the tempest of a storm. They were dangerous—she could get lost in them. A want tugged at something within. Did she want to get lost in them? *No.* She couldn't trust this man. He moved closer, and she leaned back against the door.

"I'm glad you've come out," he said softly. "I'd like to see you out more often. If you want to return to the gardens, or even go for a ride, or if you'd like to simply come dine with me, I'd like that."

He moved his hand to brush her cheek, a brush that left her skin all too quickly. "Good night, Salara."

"Good night," she breathed, and slipped inside her sanctuary.

CHAPTER FORTY-SEVEN

Her mind swirled around her. Norah sat at her vanity in her sanctuary, reeling in a mix of emotions. She would continue to struggle in the kingdom of Shadows, this kingdom of blood and battle. And what could she do? Could she change this world?

Maybe when Mikael let her closer. She wanted him to. She wanted to be closer.

Was she letting *him* closer? She still hadn't told him of her memories; she wasn't sure why. Maybe telling Mikael meant letting her old self go, and she didn't want to let go. With Mikael... she feared she would lose herself more, in this dark world. This world wouldn't help her find herself. She had nothing of who she was before to remind her, except Alexander. And if he could, Mikael would take Alexander from her. But Alexander was hers. She needed to protect him, to protect the person she used to be.

But still she wanted to tell him. She wanted Mikael closer. The divide between them tore at her. She chastised herself for hinging her happiness on her relationship with the king, but these feelings were complicated. This marriage wasn't for love, she reminded herself. This was a marriage that would protect her people. She should be happy if she could achieve civility with a solid alliance. Why wasn't she happy? Mikael was working to mend things between them. Why wasn't it enough?

Why was her heart asking for more?

Norah decided a ride would help clear her head. She'd slipped into the stables to visit the mare a few times now, but the animal needed to go out beyond the stall and the paddocks. And Norah had been hiding away in her sanctuary too long; she needed out too. Mikael had suggested a ride, and it was a good idea, although he probably meant the two of them together. She'd overlook that. She felt bolder now that Mikael was trying to resolve the distance between them, bold enough to go by herself. To her surprise, her guard didn't object. Perhaps Mikael had leashed his commander.

Norah found the mare happy to see her, and she smiled. She saddled the horse herself before mounting and breathing deep the air of near freedom. "Let's go," she told the mare, and urged her from the back gates of the castle and into the hills. The Crest followed close behind. She was glad the Mercian guard had gone with Caspian and that she didn't have them both to contend with.

The mare didn't need encouragement and stretched out into a gallop. They took the south side out of the castle to keep out of the city and headed to open lands.

They rode well into the late morning, and Norah felt a strength returning. Despite the winter cold, the freedom warmed her. It was the first time she'd been outside the castle grounds, her first time away from the king and the commander.

At the top of a hill, Norah slowed the mare, smiling back and waiting for her guard to catch up.

"Salara, please," Kiran called to her. "Will you not keep closer to us?"

"I'm sorry." She grinned. "It just feels so good to be out."

His eyes smiled back from underneath his wrap. "I know what you mean."

Suddenly his face changed as his gaze shifted to something in the distance, and Norah followed it to see rising smoke against the sky.

"What's that?" she asked.

"Likely a camp. Outsiders. Not Kharavian."

"Who then?"

He shook his head. "I don't know. But let's get you back, and I'll send forces to investigate."

Norah had no intention of being stuffed back into the castle. "I'm not going back." She gave a cheeky smile. "This is my kingdom now. I want to know who visits me."

"Salara," he protested.

"Come on!" And she urged the mare forward.

They covered the distance quickly but slowed as they reached the last hill, making their way up with care. When they reached a view of the camp, Norah's curiosity grew.

Five young men sat around a campfire. Norah put them close to Adrian's age. She heard their laughter and smiled, appreciating their fun. Then annoyance flashed within her. Who were they, and what were they doing here? They were too young and foolish to be wary of danger approaching. She needed to send them on their way.

"Salara," Kiran cautioned.

"Come on, Kiran," she said over her shoulder. "They're only boys."

They made their way down the hill, and the young men stood quickly when they sighted them approaching. The Crest guard circled them, and the men held out their hands, showing no weapons.

"Who are you?" Norah called to them.

"Who wants to know?" one of the men cut back. His accent told her he wasn't from Kharav, as Kiran had surmised.

"Salara wants to know," Kiran snapped at them.

The man's eyes widened, and he looked at his friends.

"Who are you?" Norah asked him again.

"Ando," he replied quickly. Norah could hear the fear in his voice. He glanced at his friends again.

"Where are you from?" she asked.

"We've made a mistake, Your Majesty," another man said quickly. "Please."

"They're from Osan," Kiran told her.

Norah hadn't realized they were so close to the neighboring kingdom.

"They're forbidden to cross the border," he added.

"Please, Your Majesty," Ando said. "We mean no harm. We'll be on our way."

"Why are you here?" she asked.

They looked at each other hesitantly.

"Well?" she prodded.

"We lost a bet," Ando admitted. "We are indebted to spend a night in the Shadowlands. We didn't think anyone would be here. Please, Your Majesty."

She turned to Kiran. "Let them go."

"The lord commander would never let them live," he told her.

"Well, the lord commander isn't here." *Thank the gods.* She looked at the young men with a scowl. "This isn't a place for games. Go back home and consider yourselves lucky."

"Yes, Your Majesty. Thank you! Thank you!"

They bowed appreciatively, and Norah waited while they collected their things. They gave one last bow before they clambered onto their horses and spurred them off over the next hill. Norah smiled after them. *Boys.*

"We should return to the castle now," Kiran called.

"Let's wait a bit and then ride to the top of the next hill. I want to make sure they're off." She took a moment to drink water and rest. "I think we should make this a regular event," she told Kiran. "I like it out here."

"Thank you for the warning," he said wryly.

She chuckled. "All right, let's see if they've gone."

They rode up the hill to check on the young men, but as she reached the top and looked down, her pulse quickened. A small group of soldiers had stopped them. *Kharavian soldiers.* And in the center, she saw the commander.

"This isn't good, Salara," Kiran said. "You should go back. You don't want to be out here."

But Norah wasn't thinking about going back now. She urged the mare down the hill, with her guard following close behind her. She reached the bottom as the men were being pushed to their knees.

"Lord Commander!" she called out, breathless.

He stood by the young men and turned when he heard her. His eyes narrowed. "You shouldn't be out here," he said darkly. "Return to the castle."

"I won't! What are you doing?"

"Your Majesty!" Ando called to her. "We told him you released us."

"Ride on or watch them die," the commander snarled at her.

The threat made Norah shudder. "No, these boys are returning home. I'm salara. You'll release them!" she demanded.

A wicked smile came to his eyes. "Where the security of the kingdom is concerned, I act on behalf of Salar. You have no authority here."

"They're just boys!"

"They're men. Not that it matters."

Norah slid off her horse and stepped close to the commander so no one else could hear her. "If you're angry at me, then let's resolve that, just you and me. But I beg you, let them go."

"I would never act in anger against Salar's wife," he said in a tone that chilled her more than any winter.

"Anything you ask," she begged. "Please!"

He paused. "The Bear. Give him to me, and I'll let them go."

Bile rose in her throat. "You ask for what you know I can't give."

Before she could react, the commander ran Ando through with his sword, and the young man fell forward onto the ground.

"No!" Norah screamed as he turned and dropped another. She begged of Kiran, "Make him stop!"

The Crest guard gripped his sword handle but didn't move. "We can't do that, Salara."

The commander cut down another man—so casually, so easily. Then he stepped toward the next. Norah clasped her hand over her mouth, stifling another scream, feeling completely helpless.

"Wait!" the man cried as the commander stepped toward him. "Wait! I'm the prince! Prince Jeord. If restitution is required, it can be paid! Just let us go. We'll leave right now!"

The commander paused, and his eyes held a haunting smile. "Prince Jeord. I didn't recognize you." He leaned closer to the young man. "I have a message for your father. Restitution *is* required. Tell him to bring his army and pay in blood."

Jeord gaped in horror. "You want war?"

The commander looked at Norah. "It's been said I lust for it."

Jeord stood, shakily backing away.

"Run along," the commander said. The other two young men scrambled up with Jeord, but before they could run, the commander dropped them both with his sword.

Norah let out a short scream. This couldn't be happening.

The commander eyed the prince, who stumbled back with a cry in his throat.

"Just you," the commander said as he stooped down and wiped his sword on one of the dead men's clothes. "Go."

Jeord whimpered, backing away. Then he turned and ran, stumbling but catching himself again.

The commander watched him until he was out of sight. "Stake the bodies by the border," he told the Crest. "Bring the horses." Norah staggered back in shock, and the commander turned to her. "Let's go."

"I'm not going anywhere with you!" she seethed.

His eyes grew darker. "Get on your horse, or I'll drag you back."

She knew he meant it. Still shaking and filled with horror, she climbed back on the mare.

Mikael sat in his study, poring over the deeds of his lands. He looked for more to give his ex-wives, as Salara had asked of him. It surprised him she'd asked this, but then, she was always surprising him.

He knew it wasn't easy for her in Kharav. Could she see how much he was trying? Soren was furious with him, and understandably so. There would be consequences with the lords, he knew. But he was willing to suffer the cost.

Footsteps echoed in the halls, and the door to his study slammed open against the wall.

"I hope you're proud!" Salara seethed as she stormed in.

He rose from his desk in alarm. What was going on?

Her eyes blazed with a fire he hadn't seen before, not even when she'd been upset about his wives.

"How better to show your strength than by killing boys!" she spat at him.

Mikael darted his eyes to Soren, who had walked in behind her.

"What's the meaning of this?" Mikael asked.

"A group of boys crossed the border, and I sent them back," she told him. "But they ran into your brute along the way, and he slaughtered them!"

"They weren't boys," Soren countered. "They were nearing twenty."

"Boys!" she cried.

"Old enough to battle," Soren argued. "And from Osan."

She gave the commander an appalled look and shook her head in disgust. "What's wrong with you? And what does it matter where they're from?" She turned back to Mikael. "He does this in your name! The prince was with them, and your monster sent him back with a threat to his father—he openly invites war!"

Anger flared within him. She didn't understand the ways of Kharav, and Soren was certainly ensuring her introduction to them was most unpleasant. He'd deal with him later. "Salara," he tried to calm her. "You'll come to understand we must do necessary evils to keep Kharav safe."

She shook her head again. "No. Don't pass this off as a necessary thing! Any competent man would've seen they weren't a threat."

He looked at Soren, who waited quietly, unfazed. Mikael gritted his teeth. Heat veined under his skin at his commander's indifference to her upset. But she would need to understand that Kharav was a kingdom of war. He turned back to her. "We defend our borders most savagely. This is known to our enemies with certainty, and it's this certainty that keeps us safe."

Her face twisted. "That's your answer? Safety?" She backed away from him as she shook her head in disgust. "Well then, enjoy your safety thinking of slaughtered boys!" She turned and stormed from the study.

Mikael pushed out a breath as he slowly rolled the parchments and wrapped the leather cord around them. His fury built from deep within, and it took every ounce of strength he had to control it. He waited until she was out of earshot before he cast a sharp eye at Soren. "Have you no sense?"

Soren's brow hung darker. "You would have done the same," he argued.

"Not in front of Salara! She thinks we thirst for violence." The harming of innocents—it bothered her. Deeply. "She doesn't understand our ways. She isn't hardened to them."

Soren sighed. "I let Jeord live. His father will see it as a mercy. They dare not bring war against us, and that piss prince will think before he crosses our border again."

"You fail me."

Soren shifted back. Mikael had never uttered those words to him before. "I told her to leave. What else was I to do?"

Mikael's frustration grew. "You should have let them go. Her loathing is already upon me, and you push her further away!"

"Is it not better now than later, brother?"

Mikael slammed his fist on his desk. "I'm not your brother—I am salar!" he thundered. "And so help you if I lose her."

Soren stepped backward, clearly taken aback by Mikael's rage toward him. His eyes flashed with his own anger, but he bowed his head in submission, and Mikael pushed past him and out of the room.

Norah stood in the library. She stared at the books on the shelves, but she didn't see them. She couldn't stay here any longer; she couldn't be here. Her heart longed for Mercia—its grace, its refinement, its civility. Kharav... Kharav was a kingdom of monsters.

She drew in a deep breath. With this marriage, she kept these monsters from Mercia, she reminded herself. But how much more could she bear?

Norah squeezed her eyes shut and gritted her teeth. She would endure as much as she had to.

The doors opened behind her, and she turned to see Mikael. She cursed herself for lingering too long.

"Salara," he greeted as he neared. "I'm glad I found you here."

Norah stepped around a large table, putting it between them. She wasn't so glad. She didn't reply.

"Talk to me," he said.

Fine. "Would you have killed those boys?"

He paused. His hesitation answered for him. She knew he wanted to move her past it, but she couldn't. These weren't things she could turn a blind eye to.

"I would have released them," he said. "If you'd asked me to."

"And if I wasn't there to ask?"

Mikael walked slowly around the side of the table. "Will you judge the man in front of you, instead of the one in your mind?"

"Because the one in front of me is so much better?" she cut back, moving so the table stayed between them.

Mikael's brow creased, and then he sighed. "I don't want things to be like this between us. I do care for you, Salara."

The fire of her fury died down ever so slightly, but she didn't want it to die. She told herself she'd change things—she had to change things. And it would start by the lord commander being held accountable. "What will you do about him?" she asked. "What will you do about your commander?"

"I've spoken to him."

"That's not enough."

He looked down, and then nodded. "All right."

She hadn't expected him to agree. Was he agreeing? "You'll deal with him?" she asked.

"I will. These things won't happen again."

But relief didn't come. She didn't entirely believe him.

"Are you on your way out?" he asked.

She looked down at the books in her hand and then toward the door. She knew what he would ask if she said yes.

But he didn't wait for her reply. "Can I walk you?"

He moved to the end of the table where she stood, and he held his arm for her. He was trying, she told herself. She did want him to try.

And she had to try too, for Mercia.

Slowly, she slipped her arm under his. He put his hand over hers and started them toward her sanctuary. They walked in silence, but there was a calm in his touch, a warmth. It wasn't the touch of a monster. She felt his eyes on her. Her breaths quickened, but she kept her eyes forward.

When they reached the hall to her sanctuary—the boundary—he stopped, turning and looking down at her. "Will you dine with me tomorrow?" he asked.

He was trying. And she would try. Slowly, she nodded.

"Good night, Salara," he said softly. Then he released her and left her to the quiet of her sanctuary.

As evening came the following day, Norah arrived in the dining room to find Mikael alone. He stood when she entered. "Salara," he greeted.

She slowed as she approached the table, looking around. "Where is the lord commander?" He always ate his dinners with the king.

"He won't be joining us anymore," he said.

Norah paused in surprise. For the commander to be sent from the king would be a heavy blow to him, but she couldn't muster any sympathy, and she couldn't deny the relief of his absence. They both took their seats at opposite ends of the table, and servants set plates of food before them.

"And I've told him he's to obey your commands as my own," he added.

She didn't know what to say. He'd given her control over the most powerful man in his kingdom, a man he loved as a brother. He'd told her he would deal with the commander. And he had. Whether the commander obeyed her—that was a different matter. But this was a good start. "Thank you," she said finally.

They ate in silence, with their eyes catching each other occasionally. The tumbling in her stomach returned, and Norah couldn't help the small smile on her lips. When they were finished, they stood.

"Can I walk you?" he asked as he moved to her end of the table and offered his arm. She slipped hers underneath, and he covered her hand in his, leading her toward her sanctuary. She was starting to like this walk.

When they reached the hall, he stopped, but he didn't let her go. "Can I take you to your door?"

A nervous flutter hit her stomach. Why was she nervous? She *did* want to bridge this gap between them, for them to be closer... She nodded.

When they reached her sanctuary door, she moved to pull her hand from his arm, but he tightened his hold, and they both stilled. His dark eyes flickered between hers, and his lips parted slightly. Then they closed, as if he were nervous too. Was he nervous? Her stomach fluttered more.

"Can I kiss you, Salara?" he asked ever so softly. He lowered his head to hers, but paused, waiting for her answer.

Her breath hitched in her chest. She wanted him to kiss her. So why couldn't she say yes? This was a harsh kingdom, and he was a harsh king. The memory of him killing the Serran envoy's guard filled her mind. He could be ruthless, and cruel. Although he wasn't cruel to her.

But that wasn't enough.

He'd given her control over the commander, she reminded herself. He'd asked her what he needed to change. For her...

His lips were so close. Her body threatened to betray her warring mind, conspiring with the gravities of the earth to pull her closer. She only needed to lift her chin.

He drew in a breath as he gave a small nod and pulled back. She'd hesitated too long, and her stomach dropped. She could still tell him yes—

"Good night, then," he said, his voice polite.

She could still tell him... "Good night," she whispered.

He turned and walked back the way they'd come.

CHAPTER FORTY-EIGHT

The ink dried slowly on the parchment as she wrote, and Norah blew the letters dry. It had been hard to write a letter to her grandmother. She'd started over many times and still wondered if she should start again. She folded it, stamped her seal, and watched the wax harden.

The door opened, and Vitalia entered, carrying a plate of dried fruit and bread. She smiled at Norah. "Is that a letter you're sending?"

She looked at the folded parchment in her fingers. "To my grandmother." She wondered what Catherine was doing at that moment.

"Do you miss her?"

Norah did. "Salara-Mae reminds me of her."

Vitalia frowned. "So, no?"

Norah couldn't help the laugh that escaped her. It pushed the sadness away, if only for a moment. The quiet returned. "I do miss her. I wish she understood." She inhaled, trying to breathe energy back into herself and shift her mind to lighter thoughts. "I want to do something different today." She thought for a moment. "Do you think we could go to the market?"

"I doubt the lord commander would approve of that."

Norah shrugged. "The lord commander has no say." There was a freedom to the words. "And I'll take a proper guard."

"That does sound amazing." Vitalia grinned. "I'll fetch your cloak."

Norah stepped out of the castle and breathed in the winter morning. It felt good. She decided to walk through the gardens on her way to the front gates, and she smiled when she saw Bremhad tending a tall set of shrubs.

"Salara," he greeted her with a bow as she approached.

"Good morning, Bremhad."

She gazed over at the rows of small shoots that had been planted a few weeks prior. They seemed to be coming along. "I was wondering about the planter boxes under the windows outside the great hall. In my sanctuary, there's a balcony. Could you put the same there?"

"Of course, Salara. I would be happy to."

She smiled. "Thank you."

Norah's step had a new spring of life. She grinned at Vitalia as they left the walls of the castle and wandered into the busy market of the city. *Finally.* The feeling of freedom was one she'd hungered for—one that had escaped her, even in Mercia. But not any longer. She glanced over her shoulder at her guard behind her and saw Kiran didn't share her same glee. She couldn't help but be amused. Beside him was Bhastian. She didn't see him as much as the others in the Crest. A close man of the lord commander, he took duties for the brute often, no doubt spying on her for him.

Norah strolled through the market stalls, looking over the handiworks and art. She hadn't expected to garner so much attention, but all eyes were on her. Many bowed as she passed, and some smiled. No one was unkind.

"Here, taste this," Vitalia said as she held out a small red treat.

Norah put it in her mouth and laughed at the burst of sweetness. "What *is* that?" she asked.

"They're candies made from mountain berries."

"They're delicious!"

"Here." Vitalia dumped a pile into Norah's hand.

Norah laughed as they walked on. Just then, a child ran across the cobbled street, but stopped abruptly when he saw her. He stared at her, wide-eyed. She smiled and held out one of the sweets for him, but he only stood frozen. Just when she thought he might not take it, he grabbed it from her hand and ran away. She looked at Vitalia with amusement and laughed again.

A few moments later, a cluster of children came, eager to see the North Queen who was handing out treats. Bhastian scolded them, and they scampered off, but not without leaving her empty of sweets.

"I see you're already gaining favor," Vitalia told her with a grin.

Across the way, in a larger market stall, Norah noticed a beautiful sheer fabric and wandered toward it. "What is this?" she asked the woman in the stall as she ran her fingers over it. The woman answered in Kharavian tongue.

"Butterfly silk," Vitalia told her.

"From butterflies?" Norah asked incredulously.

"From the valley."

"How do I buy some?" she asked her maid in a hushed voice. "Do I need to go get money?"

"No, Salara. They'll charge the castle. Just take what you like."

The woman smiled, folding the rolls of silk and chattering excitedly. Norah didn't even know what she'd use it for, but she'd figure something out. Perhaps as a gift for her grandmother. Suddenly, Vitalia's face fell, and Norah turned, following her gaze to Captain Artem approaching.

"You can't be out here," Artem said when he reached her.

"That's not your call."

"I'm charged with your safety."

Nice try. "The lord commander is to take my words as Salar's. You can tell him I'll return when I'm ready."

"I don't answer to the lord commander. I answer directly to Salar."

Wait, Artem didn't answer to the commander?

"Your maid will collect your things," the captain said. "You'll return to the castle now."

"I'll decide what I do," Norah told him, an anger swelling inside her. If he thought he could control her like the lord commander had tried, he was mistaken.

"See her back to the castle," he ordered the guard, ignoring her.

"I'll go back when I'm ready," she snapped, sending a ripple of tension through the air.

"Salara," Kiran said softly from behind her. "I must obey."

She pushed out a breath, shaking with anger. But what could she do? "Vitalia, get the silk. It looks like we're finished shopping for today." Then she spun on her heel and turned back toward the castle, stewing in rage as she walked. She wouldn't live like this. She was salara, and she would go where she pleased.

Norah stormed through the castle and found Mikael in the library.

He stood from his chair with a concerned brow as she entered. "Are you all right?"

"You have to choose another captain," she demanded. "Or better yet, I'll use mine."

He stiffened. "I've already dealt with my lord commander. Now you ask me to remove my captain of the Crest?"

"Am I prisoner here?"

His brow dipped. "Of course not."

"Yet I'm still under constant watch and command."

"For your protection."

"No." She shook her head. This wasn't about protection with the captain and lord commander. It was about control. "I've accepted the stipulation of a proper guard. If I'm a prisoner, then tell me I'm a prisoner. But if I'm salara, I'll go where I please; I'll do as I please." She held the fire of her gaze firmly with Mikael's. "Am I your prisoner? Or am I salara?"

Mikael's brow dipped in concern, and he drew closer. "You're salara. I'll speak to Artem."

Norah narrowed her eyes.

"I'll speak to him," he said again. "With a proper guard, you'll go where you want and do as you please."

"Including going to the market?"

He paused but gave her a nod. "Including going to the market."

But rage still burned on her skin.

Mikael stepped in front of her. He took her hand and pulled her closer, gently, like he feared the fragility between them.

As he should.

But as his warmth danced across her skin, she feared what was between them wasn't fragile enough.

He pulled her hand to his lips and kissed the back of her fingers softly. Something stirred inside her. He was doing more than just trying for civility, more than simply fostering an alliance. Norah forgot about the market.

"Where are you going now?" he asked.

Where was she going?

"Can I walk you?"

She nodded.

Instead of offering it this time, he simply pulled her hand under the fold of his arm and covered it with his own. Then they stepped out into the hall.

Her mind seemed to return as they walked. "I'd like to discuss my men's assignment when they return from Mercia," she said.

"Your man, Titus?"

It surprised her that he remembered his name. "Yes, and others."

"I'll see your guardsmen are named to the Crest."

"Thank you," she breathed, feeling a swell of relief. "Oh, and Caspian is a captain." She'd see him assigned appropriately for his rank.

He nodded. "We will discuss him when he's healed."

This was progress.

"I hear the Bear—your lord justice—is investigating more attacks on North towns."

"Mercian towns and those under Mercia's protection. The same as the town we saw." She pursed her lips in frustration. "We still don't know who's responsible."

Mikael frowned, and she wondered what he was thinking. "You'll let me know what he finds?" he asked.

"I will."

The muscle along his jaw tightened. "Will you send him back to the North after he returns?"

She nodded reluctantly. "I do intend to," she said.

"Good." His tone held an edge of irritation, but his face lightened as their eyes met again.

They walked the rest of the way quietly, but it wasn't an uneasy quiet; it was the quiet of comfort returning. He set a slow pace, seeming to enjoy the moment, as she was. When they reached the hall, he paused. "To the door?"

"Of course."

But that distance only gave her the blink of an eye longer with him. At the door, he turned to her. His eyes seemed brighter than they usually were—lighter, almost brown.

"I must admit, when I gave you this sanctuary, I didn't expect it to be where you'd stay. I fear I regret it now."

Her pulse quickened as a worry balled in her stomach. Would he take it away from her?

"It's a place I can't follow after you, a place I can't visit without your invitation." He paused. "I want you to know I think of you... inviting me in. Often."

Her pulse raced with each of his words. She wanted to invite him in, but when she opened her mouth, the words wouldn't come. Perhaps it felt too forward, too bold, and too soon. She didn't know.

"Can I not stay with you, just a while longer?" he asked.

It wasn't a wise idea, she told herself, but she wasn't ready to part from him yet. "Just a while longer," she found herself saying.

The corners of his lips turned up.

It certainly wasn't a wise idea. She chastised herself as she opened the sanctuary door and led him in. Now she wouldn't be able to get him out. Did she want him out?

Norah poured herself a chalice of wine and drank deeply. The wine would help.

Mikael looked around the sanctuary. He smiled as he stepped closer. "What do you do in here?" he asked.

She thought about going home, thought about Alexander, thought about *him*.

"Read," she replied.

He stepped closer—close enough to touch her. His eyes moved back and forth between hers, looking deep inside her. She set the chalice down. The wine wasn't helping.

Mikael reached up and brushed a lock of hair behind her ear. She didn't pull away. His brow creased. "Salara," he said softly. "I don't know what to do. I don't know what you need from me."

His vulnerability stunned her. She swallowed and looked at the settee. "Maybe we can just sit for a while?"

Mikael let out a breath and nodded. He stepped back and sat on the lounge, and she sat beside him. A quiet hung in the air, but she felt no need to fill it. He rested his arm between them, with his hand open and palm up. An invitation.

Norah placed her hand on top of his, and he closed his fingers around it. He was asking her for closeness. She settled against him and laid her head on his shoulder—her silent reply.

Chapter Forty-Nine

Norah woke under the rays of the morning sun, lying against Mikael with his arms around her. They were still on the settee. It was late afternoon when they'd come to the sanctuary. Had they really slept through the evening and night?

She let herself nestle into the warmth of his body. He smelled like belonging—something she hadn't felt since... ever. Anywhere.

Mikael stirred, wrapping his arms tighter around her and pulling her close. "I didn't expect myself so lucky as to wake up next to you," he said.

"I didn't expect it either," she admitted. "When did you wake?"

"The middle of the night."

She pushed herself up abruptly. He'd been awake since the middle of the night?

"I didn't want to wake you. I didn't want..." His eyes were bright. "I didn't want to leave."

Her stomach fluttered. "I wouldn't have made you leave."

He smiled as he brushed a lock of her hair back over her shoulder and drew his fingers over her cheek. "But it's morning now, and I have to go for a few days to settle trade with some of the Horsemen tribes. When I return, I'd like to... talk more. Spend more time together."

"I'd like that." She needed that.

"The lord commander will be coming with me," he told her. "So he won't be a bother to you."

There was no hiding her relief. "I'm glad to hear."

"Salara, I know he's a hard man to understand. But I hope you can come to. Eventually."

She understood the commander perfectly.

He cupped her face in his hand. "I trust him above all others. He knows you're important to me, and he's loyal. I know you don't believe this, but he'll be loyal to you as well."

He was right—she didn't believe that. "I'll keep busy while you're gone," she said, changing the topic from the commander.

He smiled. Then his brow creased faintly.

"What?"

"I have something for you," he said. "Come with me."

He pulled her up from the settee and led her out of the sanctuary toward the back of the castle.

"Where are we going?" she asked.

"A place I think you'll like." He took her through several halls, outside the back of the castle, waving the Crest guard to stay inside. She couldn't help the flutter of excitement in her stomach. She let him lead her, hand in hand, down a small embankment and toward a stone building. Mikael pushed open the carved wooden door and led her inside, and Norah's breath caught in her chest.

It wasn't a simple stone building. Once through the door, the room opened into a garden conservatory. The morning sun spilled through the wall of windows on the opposite side, kissing the greenery that filled it.

In awe, Norah clasped her hands together, walking slowly into the center of the conservatory. "What is this place?" she whispered.

"My grandmother was from Japheth. But when she came to Kharav, she was overcome with the longing sickness. My grandfather built this for her."

"The longing sickness?"

"The sickness in wanting for one's home," he answered. "We were at war back then. She couldn't return. My grandfather built this place to house the green of Japheth's Colored Valley. He and a few of his best soldiers snuck into Japheth and stole greens from the royal gardens to bring here."

"That's incredible," she breathed.

"Yes, it is." He gave a small smile.

"Did it take the longing sickness away?" she asked.

"Probably not entirely, but she had a great love for it, and she was happy."

Norah breathed in deeply, closing her eyes and letting the scents and light take her away.

"Do you have the longing sickness?" he asked softly.

She missed Mercia, but longing? It wasn't that deep. Norah's stomach knotted, and guilt tugged at her heart. She still hadn't told him she'd lost her memories. She hadn't told him when he'd asked her where she had been the years she was gone. And he hadn't pressed her more. Perhaps he felt she didn't want to tell him.

"I can't bring you the North—its cliffs, its rocks, its winter," he said as he plucked a flower from the small bush beside her and stepped closer, "but this place isn't Kharav." He held the flower out for her. "And perhaps you might look to come here instead of your sanctuary. Here, where I would be able to visit you."

Norah felt a wave of emotion at his tenderness. She took the blossom from his hand and breathed in its sweet fragrance. "It's beautiful," she said.

He smiled. "So are you."

"Mikael, there's something I need to tell you." She spun the small flower between her fingers. "You once asked me where I'd been those years that I was gone from Mercia."

He stood quietly, waiting.

"The truth is, I don't know. My memories were taken in the time I was lost. I, um... I'm still trying to figure out who I am."

His brow dipped, and his lips parted. But he didn't speak.

The words just tumbled out of her. "I don't know what happened. The only thing I remember is waking in the Wild. By some miracle I was found, but then I became queen of Mercia, betrothed to King Phillip, and was expected to war against an enemy—*you*—all of whom I didn't know."

He remained silent, and her pulse quickened. She should have told him sooner. She wanted to make this marriage work—not just the marriage, but whatever it was that was growing between them—and she didn't want secrets.

"Everyone expected all these things from me. There are expectations still." She took a breath. "But I don't know what to do. I don't know what I want. I'm just trying to figure things out as I go. And all I have is how I feel."

He only stared at her, and she shrunk inside, silently begging him to say something. Anything.

He let out a long breath and took her hand. Her heart beat faster.

"Maybe that's all you need," he said finally, and gave a small smile. "Salara, the woman I see knows exactly who she is and what she wants."

His words surprised her. "You're not upset I didn't tell you?"

Mikael shook his head. "I'm realizing my luck. If you hadn't lost your memories, I seriously doubt you would have wed me."

The realization hit her that he might be right. "All this time, I thought it was a curse. But now, I wonder if it's been a blessing, to help me see past emotions that would've otherwise clouded my judgment." She raised her eyes to his. "I don't want secrets between us. Not when I feel for you the way I do now."

He pulled her closer as he reached up and brushed her face, gazing down at her. "And how is it you feel?" he asked.

Norah swallowed. Why couldn't she say it?

"I hope it's the same as I feel for you," he said softly.

"You can kiss me now," she whispered.

He smiled and brought his lips to hers.

The sun cast a deceptive warmth through the windows as Soren walked through the side hall of the castle, toward the king's chamber. He'd expected Mikael at daybreak at the stable. They were to ride to the smaller Horsemen tribes of the Shoen to renew their agreements, but Mikael hadn't come.

When he reached the king's room, he was surprised to find it empty, with only Mikael's servant.

"Where is Salar?" he asked.

Vimal gave a small bow. "He joined Salara last night in her sanctuary, my lord. He's not yet returned."

Soren bristled. He turned and strode back out of the chamber, down the hall, and through the castle, toward the North Queen's sanctuary. As he turned the corner, nearing her hall, only a sentry guard stood watch, not her Crest guard. He slowed his pace; she wasn't there.

He lingered in the cross section a moment, then he turned and left the way he'd come. He wondered where he might find Salar now. Mikael had already left the queen and the sanctuary, but he hadn't headed back to his chamber.

As he crossed the center of the castle and headed toward the dining hall, something caught his eye. Two soldiers of the queen's Crest guard stood at the end of a hallway at the back of the castle, by a door leading outside. Why would the queen be outside? And without her guard? He strode toward them. "Where is the North Queen?" he called.

"In the conservatory," Bhastian answered.

"Without you?" he asked angrily but didn't give them an opportunity to answer as he pushed through the doors and stepped outside. He stalked the short way to the conservatory, but as he reached the front step, he stopped. Through the side windowpane, he saw the North Queen. *And Mikael.*

The queen stood with her back against the stone wall. Mikael held her face in his hands, cradling her as his mouth covered hers.

A chilling burn crept under his skin and to his chest, then sank like a weight into his stomach. It wasn't the kiss. It was what the kiss meant.

He slipped around the outside corner of the castle, out of sight from the conservatory, and leaned back against the stone exterior.

Soren drew in a slow breath and forced it out. He'd seen the king with other women, with his previous wives, but those marriages had been motivated by political gain and meant very little. Mikael had never loved anyone. Until now. And that was dangerous—loving the North Queen. The one threat to him. Mikael welcomed his fate.

Soren wanted blood so badly he could taste it on his tongue. He put his hand on his dagger again, curling his fingers around the hilt to settle his fury. But there was no settling.

"I don't want to leave you," Mikael said softly as he drew back from Norah's lips. "But I've kept the lord commander waiting long enough."

Norah didn't want him to leave either, but she understood. She gave him a smile. "Go on, then."

"I'll return in four days."

She nodded.

"Goodbye, Salara," he whispered, and kissed her once more. Then he stepped out the door and headed toward the castle, leaving her alone in the quiet.

Norah waited a moment, her mind in a fog. She brought her fingers to her lips. She had never imagined this life. Mikael had woken a feeling inside her she struggled to accept. It was no longer just a marriage for an alliance. She wanted to be with him. Norah smiled to herself as she stepped out of the conservatory, heading back toward the castle.

She almost didn't feel the blade as it plunged into her belly.

The second stab came in an instant, spilling a trail of blood to the ground. *Her* blood. She clutched her stomach as the red warmth saturated the front of her dress.

Norah stumbled back. What was happening? Her legs felt like they weren't her own, and they folded under her weight. She tried to catch herself as she fell, but she couldn't feel her arms. She lay on the ground, looking up at the sky. It was so gray. No clouds, just gray. She blinked as it grew darker.

"Where's the light?" she asked the hands that grabbed her.

But there came only darkness.

Chapter Fifty

Soren heard the door to the conservatory open and peered around the wall to see Mikael stepping out, leaving the queen inside and heading toward the stables. He leaned back against the stone in the recess and waited. The king would be looking for him now.

He gripped the dagger at his side. Blood settled him. Blood created fear, and fear gave him control. But he wasn't in control now, and no amount of blood would solve that.

His skin burned with hate. The Battle of Bahoul felt like a lifetime ago, but when he thought of everything he'd lost, everything the Northmen had taken from him, it was as if it had happened yesterday. His mother, his brother, his sister. His father. His land. Now to have the North Queen in Kharav, as his salara... this he couldn't accept. And Salar had changed. He saw it—Mikael's love for her.

But Mikael refused to see this madness. Even with the visions that foretold his fall, he chose the North Queen. And he gave her everything she asked, everything he thought she wanted. He even protected the Bear, the man that would bring his own end, all because she asked it of him.

He watched his breath in the winter air. When he heard the conservatory door open again, he knew it was the queen. He delayed, waiting for her to go back into the castle. He'd rather not face her either. But it wasn't the sound of the castle doors he heard as he waited for the queen to go inside. Footsteps rang out—someone running. He peered around the corner again and saw a man fleeing around the conservatory and into the thick of trees behind.

Then he saw the queen.

Something was wrong.

She stood, looking down. From her stomach, blood spilled down the fabric of her gown to the ground below. She stared at her hands, swaying. Then she staggered forward and collapsed.

"Bhastian!" Soren thundered as he raced to her side. He dropped to his knees beside her, covering her stomach with his hands to stop the bleeding. Bhastian and another Crest guard tore through the doors at his call and looked at him in alarm.

"A man!" he barked at them. "He's gone into the wood. Go!"

They raced after.

"North Queen," he said, his worry rising. "North Queen!" But she didn't respond. He pulled her into his arms and carried her into the castle. "Healer!" he bellowed, drawing another wave of guards. "Get the healer! And Salar!"

He carried the queen down the hall and up the stairs, toward her sanctuary. The queen's maid met him halfway down and gasped when she saw them. Then she spun around and ran ahead to prepare the room.

Soren made his way into the chamber, carefully bringing her through the door, and laid her on the bed. Her blood covered him, running down his stomach and soaking into his breeches, which now stuck to his skin. He pressed his hands back over her stomach to slow the flow.

"North Queen!" he called to her again. He held pressure on her wounds with one hand as he checked her pulse with the other. Her heart still beat, but faintly. He pressed the wound tighter. Never had he thought he'd wish the North Queen to live.

It seemed to take an eternity for the healer to arrive. He was breathless from the run and started looking over the queen's body, measuring the extent of her injuries.

"Are you blind?" Soren snapped. Fuck the four kingdoms—this healer would need a healer of his own if he didn't get to it.

"I see it, I see it," the healer said quickly, and pulled some shears from his bag. He quickly cut away the gown.

Mikael thundered into the room, his eyes wide and his face etched in horror. In seeing the queen, his face twisted in anger, and his eyes burned. He rushed to her side. "What happened?" he raged.

"She was attacked," Soren told him. "Outside the conservatory."

"Who was it?"

Soren shook his head, still holding pressure to the queen's stomach. "I didn't see. Bhastian and the Crest are after him."

The healer stepped beside Soren and motioned him to loosen his hold. Soren eyed him skeptically, then raised his hands and stepped back. Blood seeped from the wounds again, and the healer quickly covered them and reapplied pressure. He mumbled some unintelligible words to his assistant, who dug in his pack for more tools. Soren's agitation grew. If this healer let her die...

"What of it?" Mikael urged the old man from the other side of the bed. "How bad is it?"

The healer shook his head. "Wounds to the abdomen are extremely dangerous. I can stitch her, but I have no way of knowing the damage inside."

"Will she live?"

"I don't know," the old man replied.

Mikael's nostrils flared. "She'd better, or you'll join her." He sank down beside the North Queen as the healer worked, his fingers on her cheek. He looked up at Soren, his eyes rimmed red. "Brother," he said hoarsely. "Bring me the man who did this."

Mikael's emotion for this woman knifed him. But he gave a stiff nod and turned to his mission. There was a man in Kharav that thought he could take what belonged to Salar. And Soren would see him dead.

CHAPTER FIFTY-ONE

The thunder of galloping horses shook the ground as Alexander rode through the gates of the dark castle of the Shadowlands, surrounded by Shadow soldiers. He'd pushed the pace hard in returning. They slowed only to rest their horses and sleep for a short stretch each night, but Alexander hadn't slept. When the Shadow soldiers had found him, they'd said only that Norah had been injured, nothing more. It was this unknown that pushed him harder.

Part of him wondered if Norah might not be injured at all. Perhaps it was a ploy to draw him back into the hold of his enemy. It didn't matter. He would come.

He drove his mount beyond the courtyard and up the stairs to the iron-barred doors, not waiting until his horse stopped before sliding to the ground. Shadow soldiers left their mounts in the courtyard but tailed after him as he tore into the castle and raced up the stairs toward Norah's sanctuary. When he reached the alcove of the door, a sword rose to meet him, its point hitting just above his breastplate at his throat, stopping him in his tracks.

At its hilt—the Destroyer.

The dark-eyed beast of a man pushed him back into the hall with the tip of the blade.

"I want to see her," Alexander demanded.

A deep vibration came from the Destroyer's chest—a chuckle. "I'm sure you do." His face was covered, but his eyes burned with hate. "I knew you'd come."

Alexander stepped back and put his hand on the hilt of his own sword. For a moment, he dared to feel the slightest hope—perhaps it was a trap, and Norah wasn't hurt. "Where is she?"

"Let him enter," the Shadow King's voice called from inside her sanctuary.

The Destroyer's eyes darkened through the slit of his wrap. He dropped the tip of his sword and took a reluctant step back.

Alexander's breath quaked. This wasn't a ploy of the Destroyer, and now he wished more than anything it had been. Norah had been hurt. Was she inside her chamber? Why wasn't it her voice that called him?

Alexander pushed past him and pressed into the room, where the king stood at the foot of the bed. In its center, Norah lay as pale as the moon. Her cheeks lacked the color of her spirit—they lacked the color of life.

Fear gripped him. His heart dropped like a rock in his chest. He forgot about the king; he forgot about the Shadowlands. They didn't matter anymore. If Norah was gone, nothing mattered anymore.

Alexander moved to the edge of the bed, his soul cold, desperation writhing within him. His hand trembled as he reached out and grazed the bottom of her cheek. He turned her face toward him. The faintest of breaths whispered across his palm, and it flooded him with emotion.

She was alive.

He blinked back the tears welling in his eyes as he dropped down beside her. "Norah," he whispered. But she didn't answer. "I'm here." He cupped his hand against her cheek, silently begging for her to open her eyes. But she only lay on the cusp of death underneath his touch. "Norah," he whispered again through his teeth. His breath shook and his eyes brimmed. "Come back to me." He pulled her hand to his lips and kissed her fingers.

Her skin burned with the fire of fever, and her brow was damp; a cloth and basin rested on a small table beside the bed. He drew his hand back to her face and let his thumb graze her lips. A light salve covered them, keeping the skin from chapping. Her hair was clean and brushed, and a blanket lay over her. She was cared for. But it wasn't enough.

He was suddenly aware of the king's eyes on him. He had revealed himself—his heart—but he was too angry to care.

If Norah died...

The king's gaze was still on him. Alexander straightened and stood, and his anger grew to a fury. An all-consuming fury. He'd kill this king—for everything he'd done, but especially for this. He'd kill him.

Now.

Alexander ripped his sword free. The Destroyer lunged forward, but with a blind rage, Alexander kicked him back against the door. Then he went for the Shadow King. The king was without a sword, but he blocked Alexander's attack with the armor of his forearm. Alexander knocked him back against the wall and swept his sword to his neck, but in turn, Alexander felt the tip of the king's dagger at his own. They both stood with their blades to each other's throats.

"You were supposed to keep her safe!" Alexander seethed. "This is your kingdom. She's in your care. This is your doing!"

In the darkness of the Shadow King's eyes swirled emotion that Alexander couldn't read. Sadness? Guilt? Shame? He should feel all those things. And now he'd feel death. But before Alexander killed him, he had to know. "What happened?" he demanded.

Still, the king didn't answer.

Alexander bared his teeth, his rage growing. "What happened?" he demanded.

"Alexander," came a faint whisper behind him. He jerked his head back to Norah, forgetting the king.

Her head moved weakly, but her eyes remained closed. She inhaled deeply, wincing.

Alexander released the king and was back to her side in an instant, taking her hand and pulling it to his cheek. "I'm here," he said.

The Shadow King moved to her other side.

Her eyelids fluttered open, weakly. Then she saw Alexander. "You're back," she said with the faintest of breaths. Her face held only the whisper of a smile, but it lit the room.

He nodded. "I came as soon as I heard."

She blinked slowly. "What happened?"

"You were attacked," the Shadow King told her.

Attacked. Alexander's rage returned, but Norah's voice stopped him before he spoke.

"Is there water?" she asked.

The king's eyes moved past Alexander, and Alexander turned to see a back table in the room, behind the Destroyer, where a pitcher and glass sat. The beast of a man still stood with his sword in hand, ready for a fight. Finally, he turned with a protesting rumble and poured the water. He eyed Alexander with dark contempt before reluctantly stepping to him and handing him the glass.

The king put an arm behind Norah and helped her sit up, sending a ripple of fire through Alexander. But he knelt beside her and held the water to her lips. She took a few gulps, coughing in between and wincing again in pain.

"Easy," Alexander told her.

She took a few more sips, more careful this time. When she'd had her fill, the king laid her back against the pillows on the bed. Alexander held the glass back out to the Destroyer, who scowled at him murderously underneath his wrap. But he took the glass and set it back on the table.

"Who did this?" Alexander asked the king. He would kill them too.

The king was silent.

"Do you even have him?" he asked angrily. "The man responsible?"

"Of course we have him," the king said defensively, finally speaking.

"Who is it?" he asked again.

"The brother of one of my previous wives."

Previous wives? How does one have previous wives? His eyes blazed at the king.

"Avenging her honor, no doubt," Norah said weakly. "Her family's honor. They've been humiliated with the annulments."

Annulments? The king had had other marriages? Alexander glared at him with an indicting fury. All of this was his fault—everything that had happened. He looked back to Norah. Her sympathy, her compassion, her understanding—they had always amazed him, even now, as she lay near death. But he couldn't find compassion within himself for the attacker or this king.

"I want to speak to him," she said. Her voice came at barely a whisper, yet it still managed to take them all aback.

"That's not a wise idea," the king said to her.

"He tried to kill you," Alexander added to the argument. "What is there to say?"

Norah turned her head to the king. "I want to speak to him," she said again.

"Your fever hasn't even broken," the king replied. "You need to rest and heal before you do anything." As much as he hated it, Alexander nodded his agreement with him.

She swallowed, struggling with her words. "Promise me you'll let me speak to him, that you won't kill him."

The Shadow King's face remained hard and disapproving. "Rest," he said, "and I give you my word I won't kill him before you speak to him."

Norah nodded faintly and leaned back, closing her eyes to sleep again.

Days fell away, and Norah finally found herself able to sit up without assistance. She didn't remember the attack, and for once, she was appreciative. Her skin was healing, but an internal ache still lingered. She forewent the drink of herbs offered by the healer to relieve it. There was something between Alexander and the king, a new animosity, and she didn't want the fog of pain medicines as she tried to understand what was happening.

Mikael sat with her often, not saying much, but his presence calmed her. He brought her books and anything else he could think of that might help her pass the time.

The cool air of morning hung around her as she sat in bed for yet another day. Vitalia brought a tray of breakfast as Mikael took what had become his regular place in the bedside chair.

"How is Salara-Mae?" she asked him.

He rocked his head back in slight surprise. "She's been worried about you."

Norah tried not to move as a chuckle escaped her.

"I think she's secretly starting to like you," he said.

"She likes me more than she likes the lord commander."

He nodded. "That she does."

"Why does she dislike him so much?" That was a silly question, perhaps. There were no redeeming qualities about the brute. Quite the opposite. But the commander was fiercely loyal to the king—had saved him, protected him—how could a mother not appreciate that?

"I don't know. She always has. From the moment she saw him."

A knock rattled the door and Alexander stepped inside. Mikael stiffened.

"Lord Justice," she greeted. His presence in Kharav brought a thick tension, but she still couldn't help her happiness each time she saw him.

"Queen Norah." He didn't acknowledge the king. "I came to see if you needed anything. Or if you wanted to write a letter. I'm sending word back to Mercia with news of your health."

"Yes, I'd like to write a letter." She moved with a start. "I completely forgot. What about the towns you went to investigate? Did you find anything? Who attacked them?"

Alexander shook his head. "We found nothing. Only the aftermath. Whoever it was, it's like they had disappeared."

His words drew Mikael's interest. "Where was this?" the king asked.

Alexander eyed him as if loathing the thought of speaking words to him. "East of Bahoul."

Mikael looked at Norah. "Not far from the town we saw destroyed. Same offenders, no doubt."

Norah felt her stomach turn, remembering.

"You found nothing?" Mikael asked Alexander.

"Same as you, I believe," he replied coolly, but there was a knife to it.

The king sat calmly, but his nostrils flared. "Did you really expect me to properly investigate an attack against the North as I launched my own?"

"What about now that you're wed to Mercia's queen?" Alexander's voice held an icy air. "Do you care? Or is your protection of Mercia the same as your protection of her queen?"

Mikael bristled and moved to stand.

"I'm ready to speak to him," Norah said, drawing their attention away from the argument, and from each other. "The man who attacked me. I want to see him."

Both men stared at her.

Mikael rose. "I'm going to execute him."

Alexander's gaze snapped to the king with the same surprise as Norah's, although he didn't object.

But that wasn't what Mikael had promised. "You said I could speak to him," she said, frustrated.

"Which is why I haven't taken his head yet."

"He attacked *me*, and it's *me* he should answer to."

"But will you make him answer?" Mikael asked, his eyes burning. "Will you punish him, Salara?"

Norah looked down at the lining of the blanket as she pleated it between her fingers. Punishing someone would be difficult for her, regardless of the crime. "When can I see him?"

"As soon as you're well enough."

"I'm well enough now."

Mikael's lips thinned, then he gave a reluctant nod. "Then you can see him in the courtyard, before he's executed."

He would force her hand. She glanced at Alexander, but there was still no objection in his face.

The knot in Norah's stomach grew. She needed to see her attacker, look into his eyes, hear his defense if he bothered to give one. She wasn't sure if she could execute him, but if she didn't, Mikael would. Would he think her weak? What about the people of Kharav?

And what would she think of herself?

Bhastian pushed Norah in a wheeled chair outside to the courtyard. Vitalia walked beside her, followed by the rest of Norah's guard. Mikael required more of them now—an army everywhere she went. They were suffocating, but this wasn't the time to complain about her guard. Things would return to normal eventually.

The sun sat low, close to the horizon, spilling colors of blood across the sky. Fitting. A crowd had gathered ahead in the courtyard, and it unsettled her stomach. "Stop here," she said.

Bhastian brought the chair to a halt. "Is everything all right?"

"Help me up," she said to Vitalia. "I want to walk the rest of the way."

"Salara," her maid protested. "You're still healing."

"I said help me up."

Her maid sighed disapprovingly but stepped to help her as she was bid.

"Let me," Bhastian said, coming forward and gently scooping his hands under her arms to help her stand. She didn't want his help. He was loyal to the commander, was someone the brute trusted, which meant she couldn't trust *him*. But she did need the help.

Norah winced in pain, forcing herself to inhale and exhale until it subsided to an ache.

"Salara," he said as he stepped around the chair to her side, trying to encourage her to abandon her effort.

"Just give me your arm," she panted.

Bhastian looked around, clearly unhappy with her decision, but he held out his arm for support. She looped her hand through it, steadying herself.

Carefully, they continued forward, arms locked, unhurried.

The crowd parted as they drew near. She spotted Alexander. His face was full of disapproval. He started forward to meet her, but she shook her head to stop him. Mikael shot her an objecting look as well, but he said nothing. Out of anyone, he knew the importance of the perception of strength with power.

Her attacker was on his knees, his arms bound behind him. What she didn't expect to see were others with him—a woman, a boy, and an older couple. The younger woman wept. Norah looked at her closer. She knew this woman.

It was one of Mikael's previous wives.

Norah had seen her at the celebration when she first arrived in Kharav, only Norah hadn't known who she was then. She suspected the older man and woman to be their parents, and the boy a younger brother perhaps. They all knelt, bound, with their heads down. Why were they here?

Norah looked at Mikael in dismay. "What's the meaning of this?" she demanded.

He said nothing, but his eyes were dark, his intentions written on every crease of his face. He was going to execute them *all*. A wave of horror flooded her.

"North Queen," her attacker called out to her. "I beg you. Please spare my family! Myral. My mother, my father, my brother. They had no part in my doing. I acted alone. Please!"

Norah found herself clutching on to Bhastian as she gaped at them. *Myral.* Yes. That was the woman's name.

"North Queen," Myral cried. "I've spoken harsh words against you. But my parents and younger brother are innocent." The woman swallowed back a sob. "Please, spare them!"

Norah could only stare at the woman. The knot in her throat choked her voice. Norah had required the annulments. She was the outsider who'd come and turned the wives away from a life they had known, a life of status and privilege. How could she fault this woman just for speaking against her?

"Please, North Queen," her attacker begged, and she turned her eyes back to him.

Mikael stepped forward, seeming to grow even larger as he readied to give his judgment. Her heart hammered in her chest. He was going to kill them.

She let go of Bhastian's arm and willed herself to stand on her own. "I'm not the North Queen," she called out. "I am Salara."

Mikael stopped, and she felt his attention on her.

Her attacker nodded desperately. "Yes, of course, Salara."

"What's your name?" she asked him.

"Amet, Salara," he said quickly.

"And you sought to avenge your sister?"

Amet fought back the tears and nodded his head. "Yes, Salara," he said. "To avenge my family's dishonor."

"It's you who dishonor your family, by attacking your salara, and without the decency of a challenge." She paused, unable to say the words, unable to speak his fate. But she had to. "I can't let you live," she managed to get out.

The man nodded, weeping.

Quickly, she told herself. She needed to be quick to save the rest of them. Her eyes moved back to Myral. "But you. I forgive your words, and I won't seek further justice, against you or your family."

Amet and his sister gasped in relief, crying in appreciation.

Norah glanced back at Mikael, and rage rippled across his brow. His lips parted, flashing his teeth. She'd pardoned them publicly. Would he overrule her with his own judgment?

Urgency clawed at her. "Remove them," she ordered the guards. She didn't want Amet's family to see his fate, and if she could get them away before Mikael acted on the threat in his eyes...

The guards grabbed the family and dragged them from the courtyard. Myral let out a cry but didn't resist. *Gentler*, Norah wanted to call out, but Mikael's fury grew with each passing moment, and she just wanted them gone. Away.

Mikael watched as they were dragged from the courtyard. He didn't stop them, but his need for retribution hung heavy in the air. She gave into it, nodding to the punisher.

Amet resigned himself to his fate as the steel blade came for his life. Blood sprayed across the cobblestone. Even though she knew it was coming, she couldn't help but flinch.

A sickening calm settled over the courtyard.

Norah clutched her stomach tightly. Her lip trembled, but not from the crippling pain she gritted her teeth against. She had to get away from the death, away from this place, away from Mikael. She moved back toward her chair with as much calm as she could muster, but she thought she might not make it.

"Salara," Bhastian's voice came behind her. "Let me carry you. You can't walk."

She shook her head. "No," she breathed through the pain, "just help me back."

He took her arm and walked her back, and she sank thankfully into the chair when she reached it. Then he pushed her back to the castle.

Back in her chamber, Norah let Bhastian and Vitalia help her into the bed, where the healer busied himself with checking her wounds.

Mikael entered, standing back and waiting as Norah was tended to. She refused to look at him. He was angry, she knew. But she was angry too. He would kill an entire family...

The healer gave a nod when he was finished. "The wounds are fine," he told her. "But you need to be more careful until you're healed."

The healer and Vitalia gave a bow and left her to Mikael. She could feel the burn of his gaze, but she still couldn't look at him. "Those people were innocent," she said. She couldn't keep her voice from shaking. "They didn't need to die."

"They did," he replied with cold gravel in his voice. "They did so that everyone would know what happens to those who threaten you. *You* could have died."

She snapped her gaze to his. "But I didn't!"

"But now they know you're weak."

"Mercy isn't weakness!" she spat back.

"Fear is!" His nostrils flared, and his brow dropped low. "You didn't spare them with mercy! You spared them because you couldn't stomach their blood." He drew back. "And I'm weak for letting you."

He left her alone in the wake of his anger.

Chapter Fifty-Two

"Is the pain gone?" Alexander eyed her as they sat at the small table in her sanctuary.

Norah drew in a long breath and nodded. "For the most part." It wasn't exactly a lie. Two weeks had passed since she'd been stabbed outside the conservatory behind the castle. Her flesh had healed over, and the physical pain was gone. It was her heart that hadn't yet healed. While Mikael no longer seemed angry, things were different between them. They still hadn't reconciled.

Vitalia set a tray of tea and fruits in front of them. This was how they had started taking breakfast—with Alexander stopping by each morning and sitting with Norah as the sun poured through the windows. She liked him near. While tension remained high, his presence kept Mikael at a distance, something she needed, or thought she needed.

So easily the king killed, without thought and without regret. That scared her.

He scared her.

And yet... something seemed missing without him. And his absence spiraled her further into self-loathing. Who was she if she could look past this darkness? And what would she be for her people if she couldn't?

Alexander waited until she finished before taking anything to eat for himself, as he usually did. She left the dried figs, as she usually did. She knew they were his favorite.

"This came for you this morning," he said, breaking the quiet as she chased down the last bite of her biscuit with a drink of tea. He pulled a letter from inside his coat and set it on the table. Norah froze. The folded parchment held a silver seal. Catherine's seal.

She only stared at it, unmoving. It was the first letter her grandmother had sent. "What does it say?"

Alexander shook his head. "I don't know."

Norah leaned back in her chair. She had prayed her grandmother would write. Letter after letter she'd sent with nothing in return. But now, now that she was full of self-doubt, her grandmother was the last person she wanted a letter from. Catherine abhorred her marriage to the Shadow King, seeing him as the great evil. Maybe she looked to remind Norah of that now, to tell her how this wouldn't work. And maybe she was right.

"Will you not read it?" he asked.

"So she can shame me? Tell me I've made a terrible mistake and how this will all fail?" She couldn't take it. Not when she truly felt like she was failing.

"She wouldn't do that."

Norah cast him an unbelieving eye.

"I've been keeping her informed of your health. I'm sure she's sick with worry for you." He waited for her eyes to meet his. "Read it, Norah."

She picked up the letter, feeling the heavy parchment between her fingers. "I will. Just not right now." She stood and stepped to the vanity and slipped it inside the small wooden letter box on top. "How is your brother? Have you heard from him?"

He snorted. "Yes. About how unfair it is I won't let him come to the Shadowlands." She smiled.

"He asks of you. I've told him you're well."

She nodded. It wasn't exactly untrue. "If I write him a letter, will you make sure it gets to him?"

"Of course." He paused for a moment, then said, "There is something else. I have a task from the council. I need to leave for a while."

She frowned as she sat back down at the table. "What kind of task?"

"Nothing I want to bother you with. You have enough on your mind. I shouldn't delay, but I'll wait until Caspian and Titus have returned."

She supposed she should be thankful for the opportunity to send him away from the Shadowlands for a while. The tension between him and Mikael had only grown since her attack. She should have sent him home to Mercia, but she couldn't. Perhaps this task was what she needed to force herself into action. He needed to go. But he wouldn't leave if he feared for her.

"I have an entire army guarding me now," she told him. It was the closest she could get in assuring him to leave.

He snorted. "Of Shadowmen."

"There are good men here, Alexander." She thought of Kiran. If not any others, at least one of them was good.

"Regardless, I don't want to leave you again."

She didn't want him to leave either. He'd just returned a short time ago from investigating the attacks on Mercian towns. "I'll be here when you return."

Finally, he nodded.

"How long will you be gone?"

"Only a couple weeks."

Too long. She nodded sadly and took another drink of her tea.

Norah made her way down the long hall of the castle to the library in the far wing, with an entourage of guards behind her. While her stomach wounds had healed over, the lengthy walk brought an aching stitch deep within. At least she didn't have to go out into the winter to a separate building like in Mercia.

As she walked, she looked out through the windows at a narrow garden area with a thin pool in the center. It had wintered over, and its greenery had been cut back to the ground, but it would be beautiful when it came to life in the spring. On the other side of the garden ran another windowed hall, parallel to her own, and she stopped when she saw Mikael. He was speaking to an older man from his Circle, Kharav's council. The man noticed her, and Mikael turned, with his eyes now on her. They stood a moment, their stares caught through the windows until she broke away and started forward again.

From the corner of her eye, she saw the king part from his councilman and walk down his own hall, keeping pace with her. Norah cursed under her breath. She would see him around the corner, where the halls met and became one. She could turn back—an appealing option. But she continued.

She came to the end of the windows and paused against the stone before turning the corner. She could still turn back...

And awkwardly shuffle through the army behind her...

And make it even more difficult when she next saw the king.

No. She pushed out a breath and turned the corner.

Mikael stood waiting where the halls joined before stretching to the library. "Salara," he greeted her when she reached him. "I almost thought you'd turned back."

"I thought about it," she confessed.

His head gave a slight nod, and his eyes grazed the ground. "Are you going to the library?"

There was no denying it. The library spanned the entire wing; there was no other reason she'd be there. "I am."

"As am I."

She tilted her head in feigned amusement. "How coincidental."

They walked side by side under the arched hall. Columns of stone rose to meet at the center above their heads and bounced the light with a majestic air. No matter how many times she walked this hall, she never grew tired of its beauty.

"It's good to see you out," he said.

It was good to be out, but she said nothing.

They reached the carved doors of the library—another sight that always overwhelmed her. Mikael could stand a man on his shoulders, and they still wouldn't touch the top. But Mikael wasn't looking at the doors; he was looking at her.

She shifted uncomfortably, searching her mind for how to part. "Did you have something to find here?" she asked, prompting him on his way.

But he gave a small frown. "No."

She could only stare at him. "Then why did you come?"

"To be with you."

Norah's breath faltered. These were the moments that made her want him near, that made her forget about everything else.

He stepped closer. Her hand hung at her side, and he brushed it softly with his own, testing. The warmth of his touch seeped into her skin, creeping its way up her arm and through her body. So little time they'd spent alone the past several days. Her anger had been driving her mind, almost making her forget his effect. Almost.

She didn't pull away.

"I don't like how things have been between us," he said. "Tell me how to fix it."

He wanted to fix it? But she didn't know how. They came from completely different worlds.

"Please, Salara. Tell me."

She shook her head. "I can't live like this, with this violence. Or with you thinking I'm weak because I value human life."

His eyes moved back and forth between hers. "I don't think you're weak."

"But that's what you said."

"I was afraid."

She stilled.

He drew closer. "I was afraid because I'd been so close to losing you." Ever so gently, he pulled her hand up to his face, cupping her fingers against his cheek and kissing her palm. "I can't lose you."

In front of the world, he was cold and dark, threatening. He was the Shadow King. Impossible to love. But with her, the darkness fell away. He was Mikael. Impossible to hate.

She shook her head. "Don't do that."

He frowned. "Don't do what?"

"Don't make me stop being angry at you. I need to be angry." If she wasn't angry, then she would be accepting of the darkness, and she couldn't be accepting.

A low rumble came from his chest. "Have you not been angry long enough?"

"No!" Him trivializing her emotion only brought it to the surface again. These things were serious. People's lives were serious.

His brow bent. "Will it be forever?" His words came at barely a whisper. It wasn't patronizing but a question steeped in longing and worry. And it disarmed her.

"Just longer" was all she could manage to get out. Except there was no *longer*. Any anger she'd struggled to hang on to slipped from her grasp.

"All right," he whispered.

She let out a breath, and an ease came between them again. There was a rawness about him now, a vulnerability. And he was still so close. His warmth permeated her barriers and pulled her in. She found herself leaning in, and he dropped his head to hers.

But she put a firm hand on his chest. "No."

He stopped. His lips were so close to hers, but they didn't touch. Then he nodded, relenting.

"I can't trust you," she whispered. "It makes me afraid."

And while she told herself she was afraid of him, it wasn't just him. She feared herself. This wasn't about who Mikael was. This was about who she was—something that still escaped her. Could she be who she wanted and still feel for this man?

His mouth opened to speak, but no words came. His eyes searched hers. "I'm salar. These aren't easy decisions for me."

His brow stitched, and she leaned back. "Really? Because they seem to come quite easily. And I'm salara. They're my decisions too." She paused, trying to slow the sudden rush of frustration. "You don't rule alone."

He quieted again.

"You have to talk to me," she told him, "before you act. We decide together."

He nodded again. "I can do that."

He could do that. She softened. That wouldn't solve all their problems, but if he talked to her...

A calm returned, and her spirits rose. She'd missed him, and to be near him again, to have gained some understanding between them, relieved her. They continued through the library.

Mikael followed her, holding her selection of books as she pulled them from the shelves.

"Do you need all these?" he asked. "You can always come back for more."

She gave a small shrug of her shoulders. "Then I'd have to come back every day."

"I wouldn't mind." He took her hand, stopping her and shifting to a more serious note between them. "I want to see you every day. I want to be near you. Every day."

She swallowed back the words on her tongue, the words that would have said she wanted the same. Because she did. "I'm finished," she said softly.

Mikael waved her guard back and away as they stepped out into the hall. They walked toward her sanctuary—slowly, quietly—with him at her side, carrying her books. She couldn't deny she preferred Mikael to her army entourage.

"Your lord justice left this morning," he said, picking back up their conversation.

Norah bit the inside of her cheek. "You keep a close eye on him."

"His every move."

His tone chilled her. She silently praised the Mercian council for whatever task they had for Alexander—anything to get him away from Kharav for a while. She cursed her selfishness in keeping him near. When he returned, she'd have to send him back to Mercia.

Norah glanced outside, across the courtyard, and saw the man Mikael had been speaking to earlier still standing in the parallel hall. "Is he waiting for you?"

"Yes. But he can wait a little longer."

"You should go," she said. "I'm sure there are many important things for you to tend to."

"Nothing is more important than being here with you, right now."

She couldn't help a small smile to herself.

They reached the hall to her sanctuary, and she took her books from him.

"Thank you," she said softly.

"Of course." He brought her hand to his lips and pressed a gentle kiss against her fingers. Then he left to return to his waiting Circle.

Chapter Fifty-Three

Mikael was waiting in the dining room when Norah arrived. Instead of at the end of the table opposite her, his plate and chalice sat to the left of her own. She raised a brow and bit back her smile. She liked that he threw out rules and proprieties to be near to her.

He pulled her chair out for her and waited.

Norah couldn't hold the hint of a smile any longer. "Thank you," she said as she took her seat.

Mikael took his own chair and set to work moving food to their plates from a large center platter.

"The king plays the servant this evening?" she asked.

"Every evening if you want, so long as you're here." The corner of his mouth turned up. "Does it win me favor?"

"Maybe a little," she admitted with a wry smile. But then her smile fell, and her seriousness returned. "But it's not what I want, you know."

His face grew solemn. "I know." He poured wine into their chalices and raised his to his lips but didn't drink. He set it back down. "I'll continue to disappoint you, Salara. We're very different, you and I."

She stared at him for a moment. "Or maybe we're two imperfect people in an imperfect world, fighting for the good of our kingdoms."

His eyes met hers. "Can we fight for each other?" he asked softly.

Fight for each other. Not just for an alliance, but *for each other.* She felt the soft knocking at her heart.

They ate quietly, exchanging reassuring glances. When they were finished, he stood and offered his arm, as she expected. She took it and let him walk her back to the sanctuary. The returning ease between them brought back a comfort she'd missed.

When they reached the alcove, she stopped and turned to him. Mikael pulled her closer, threading his fingers in hers. He smelled of smoky earth and lemon thyme, and she breathed him in. His touch, his warmth... "Stay," she found herself saying.

His lips parted in surprise, and he nodded.

Norah led him inside the sanctuary, where he waited for her cue. She wavered. "I didn't mean... intimately."

He nodded again.

She wondered if he could hear the lie on her lips, but she couldn't allow herself that tonight. Not yet. Her mind wandered back to what she'd once told Tahla—that she'd only hoped for friendship with Mikael, to be strong allies.

That wasn't true.

She wanted more between them.

But she hadn't given herself to him since their wedding, and they seemed to be different people now. Different people who needed to make this step forward again, as if it were the first time. But before that could happen, she needed them fully well, and for that, she needed more time, with him. She needed them to be closer.

They stood in the candlelit silence.

"Can I simply sleep beside you tonight?" he asked.

Sleep. She needed sleep. But she didn't know if she trusted him. She didn't know if she trusted herself.

But she wanted him to stay, and she nodded.

He reached back, between his shoulders, and pulled his shirt over his head and then sloughed off his boots. Then he lay on the bed under the quilts with his arm stretched out to his side.

She glanced down at her dress. A nightgown would be more comfortable, but she had absolutely no intention of changing clothes with him so close, even in the side bath chamber.

Norah sat on the edge of the bed and then shuffled back and under the quilts. She laid her head on his outstretched arm, and he pulled her close to him. The heat from his body seeped into her, quieting her shiver. She let his nearness calm her, and she closed her eyes in the warmth of his being.

Then she drifted into dreams.

When Norah opened her eyes again, it was morning. Mikael lay beside her, his breaths long and rhythmic. She'd slept deeply, feeling safe, feeling right. Was this right?

She shifted back, careful not to wake him, and propped her head on her elbow. He lay on his back, and she gazed over the patterned skin of his chest and torso. It wasn't often she was free to simply look at him, to study him. Close and unhurried.

At the base of his throat, shoulder to shoulder, spanned a thick collar of inked design. Overlapping shapes like plated spears edged the top, with hanging banners like the night sky. The color of his skin created an image against the black, resembling the peaked arches of the kingdom's architecture. She reached out and drew her fingertips across it. She liked this one. He bore the only one like it. The other designs were the same as those of the lord commander—the braided motif on his right chest and the banding that ran to his right shoulder around a ring of mountains centered by a sun against a black circle. This one she didn't like. Without thinking, she scratched at it with her fingernail.

"They don't come off," he said, his eyes still closed.

She bit her lip.

"You don't like my markings?"

"Not this one," she admitted. "It's the same as the lord commander's."

He opened his eyes and turned his head toward her, inhaling a waking breath. "It's when we fled Bahoul," he said.

She ran her fingernail over the ring of mountains.

"To Kharav," he added to his story as she made her way along the design. Her fingers grazed the sun. "And I became salar. It's Soren's story too. It's why he bears the same."

"He has a black sun. Yours is the color of your skin against a black circle."

"Because I'm salar. My skin is the sun."

Norah drew her brows together. "Why a sun?"

"That's what *salar* means."

She almost laughed. "The Shadow King is called the Sun?"

"Yes," he said, giving a small smile. "As are you. *Salara.*"

She drew her hand back to the design across the top of his chest.

"It's called a khlavik," he said. "The mark of salar."

She traced the patterned bands circling down his arm, admiring the intricate detail. "What do these mean?"

"Histories of our people, duties, my purpose," he said.

She brushed a bare space on his left chest. "There's nothing here."

"It's not finished." He was quiet for a moment. "I'd saved it for Mercia's defeat, but instead it will be the story of you becoming my salara. I haven't gotten it yet because I was waiting for the right time. I wanted you to be there."

"To get the marking?"

He nodded.

This was important to him, she knew. And what was important to her was that he was letting her in. It was more than just his words now, more than just his touch. He was building her into his story, giving her a piece of him.

"Are you sure that's what you want?" she asked. "I mean, maybe you should think about it more." She tilted her head slightly as the corner of her mouth turned up. "It doesn't come off."

He chuckled as he rolled to his side. "I've been thinking about it ever since you agreed to wed me in Aviron." His eyes shone brightly in the light of the morning. "Will you come with me, Salara?"

"I'll come," she said softly.

He smiled.

"What will it look like?" Norah asked as they walked past the gardens and toward a large temple. It had been two days since he'd told her he wanted to write their story in ink, and that was where they were headed now.

"I don't know. We go to Salta Tau, and the Gift will show her the story and give her the image for my body."

"Salta Tau?"

"Mastera of the ink." He stopped and took her hand. "This is very special. It's a ceremony, a long one. Soren will be there, and my mother."

She nodded. She could tolerate the lord commander for a time, so long as she didn't have to speak to him. Or look at him. Or acknowledge his presence.

They reached the temple, and he led her through a series of halls back to a large open chamber. As he'd said, Salara-Mae was there, as was the lord commander. They stood on opposite sides of the chamber from each other. In the center of the room stood an old woman. She wore a simple, light linen gown, with her long white hair pulled back into a thick braid behind her.

The woman bowed. "Salar. Salara."

"Salta Tau," Mikael greeted back, bowing his head.

Watching him, Norah did the same.

The old woman spoke in the Kharavian tongue, but Mikael answered so that Norah could understand. "I come for the story of my salara," he said.

Salta Tau rolled her lips together with a bob of her head and held out her hands. Mikael took one and then took Norah's. Then he nodded for Norah to take the other.

Norah reached out, taking Salta Tau's hand and completing the circle.

Salta Tau closed her eyes and spoke what sounded like a spell into the air. She rocked slightly, forward and back, forward and back, with her eyes closed as she silently mouthed the words over and over.

Norah glanced at Mikael, but he only watched the old woman intently.

Salta Tau stopped. "I see," she said, her eyes still closed. She dropped their hands, but Mikael still held on to Norah's.

"Battle. Blade. Blood. Crown." The old woman spoke in the Northern tongue now, her accent thick and choppy.

The corners of Mikael's mouth turned up, but Norah frowned at her words. Surely it didn't take a special gift to see what could describe most every story in Kharav.

Mikael released her hand. Servants in long linen tunics stepped forward and stripped him of his clothing. Norah squirmed, still uncomfortable with the unabashed Kharavian ways, although she wasn't offended. She kept her eyes on his face.

They spread a mixture of herbs across his chest, letting it sit a moment before sponging it away.

"To clean the skin and numb it," Salara-Mae explained. Norah hadn't realized Mikael's mother had stepped beside her, and the woman's voice startled her.

"Does it hurt?"

"Not much," Mikael assured her.

"It hurts a great deal," Salara-Mae said. Mikael scowled at her.

Norah swallowed.

"Sit beside me," he told her. Then he lowered himself onto the heavily embroidered mat on the floor and lay on his back, waiting.

Norah took a seat on the floor cushion to his right, and Salara-Mae took the additional cushion just behind.

Salta Tau sat on Mikael's left side. The woman picked up a long tool with what appeared to be barbed bone at the end. She dipped it into a bowl of ink and set the edge against the skin of Mikael's chest. Then she struck it with a small mallet. Blood sprang from around the edge of the tool, but the woman wiped it away and continued.

The inking felt like eternity. The constant tapping of the mallet, the bleeding—Norah felt it pained her more than Mikael, who lay motionless. She could barely make out the design forming under Salta Tau's hands—a patterned circle of some sort.

Finally, as the sun started to set, Salta Tau stopped. Mikael's chest was a mix of blood with ink, and Salta Tau spread a thick mixture of herbs over it. Then she covered it with her hands and spoke again in the Kharavian tongue. Norah bit the inside of her cheek to quell her impatience. She wanted to see the finished image. Even though it seemed somewhat unoriginal, as she had gathered through Salta Tau's words—swords, blood, something with a crown—this was their story, and she wanted to see it.

She cast her eyes around the room as they waited. Salara-Mae sat expressionless. Norah looked up at the commander to find him staring back at her, his eyes dark and cold. They hadn't spoken since her attack. Mikael told her Soren had been the one to find her, the one who'd saved her. She wondered if he would add that to his own inked stories. Under *Tales of Regret*.

Salta Tau wiped away the herb mixture from Mikael's chest, catching Norah's eye and calling back her attention. Mikael watched her as she leaned over him to see.

His skin was still raw and swollen, but very clearly now appeared the image of two crowns, mirrored against each other along a spear in the center, and bordered with layered blades to create a circle. On the top sat Norah's Kharavian crown, or rather, a representation of it in the geometric patterns of their marking style.

Then she gasped.

She hadn't recognized it at first because it was inverted, but on the bottom was her Mercian crown—her mother's crown. It wasn't a patterned interpretation like Kharavian ink images, but instead bore the crown's exact likeness.

"How did you see this?" she breathed. "Where is it?"

Mikael looked down at his chest. "What?"

Norah's lip trembled. She looked back up at Salta Tau. "Can you tell me where it is?"

Mikael pushed himself up to sit and caught her hand. "Where what is?"

"My mother's crown. I lost it." She paused, her eyes welling. "I lost it when you took me as I was on my way to Aleon." She looked back up at Salta Tau, her desperation surfacing. "How can you see it? Do you know where it is?"

"That's not how the Gift works, Salara," Mikael said softly.

"No." She pleaded Salta Tau. "If you saw it, maybe you can see what was around it. It could help me find it."

But the old woman shook her head.

And the disappointment came as heavily as the original loss. Norah let out a breath, trying to regain control of her sudden emotion.

The servants spread another mixture of herbs across Mikael's skin, and he shifted for them to wrap it. When they finished, he donned his clothing again. Then he reached out his hand and helped her to her feet.

He didn't release her after she stood. Instead, he pulled her closer. "I'm sorry, Salara."

She shook her head. "You've done nothing wrong." Her voice came in barely a whisper.

He seemed to waver on his words. "Does it bother you?" His eyes searched hers. "Does it bother you that it's on my body?"

He was worried about how she felt about it. His concern quieted the churning inside her. It calmed her mind. "No." She looked at his chest, now covered in bandaging and his tunic. "At least I have an image of it now."

He raised a brow. "Do you always do this?"

"Do what?"

"Look for the best in everything?"

She struggled for words. What else was she to do?

He gave a gentle smile as he offered his arm, and she slipped her hand into its warmth.

Norah stood in her sanctuary, looking at Catherine's letter—the letter Alexander had given her a week ago—still unopened. She should read it. But not yet. She didn't know what was keeping her, but just... not yet.

The door of the chamber opened behind her. "Salara," Vitalia said, and Norah turned. She held out a folded parchment, a wide smile on her face.

"What's this?" Norah asked as she opened it. When she saw the image, she gasped. The image of her mother's crown.

"I thought you'd want it," Vitalia said.

"Where did you get this?"

"The lord commander sent a detachment out this morning. Each soldier holds a copy. They're tasked with finding it."

Norah's eyes widened.

"There's even a reward for citizens," Vitalia added.

"The lord commander?"

Her maid raised a brow with a shrug. "I know."

This man continued to confuse her. Norah couldn't believe she was about to do this, but she took the parchment and left to find the commander.

He sat in his study, finishing a letter. Norah had never been in the room before. It looked much like Alexander's in Mercia—a large desk covered in parchments, cabinets full of books and records. When he saw her, he didn't rise. She bit the inside of her cheek. He was always testing her, always trying to show her she didn't have complete power.

She would overlook it, partly because she didn't have the energy to argue with him and partly because she was here to thank him. She was already rethinking the latter. But maybe this could be the start of a civil relationship. He was lord commander of the Kharavian army, and she was salara. They couldn't hate each other forever.

"Do you need something, North Queen?" His voice was rough and unwelcoming.

He didn't call her Salara, something she had yet to correct him on. She didn't know why she hadn't. Each time he used it, she felt she lost more ground to demand it of him. She hated it. But she still couldn't bring herself to correct him, even now. Especially now. She looked down at the folded parchment in her hand, reminding herself why she was here.

"Yes, um, I..." Why was this so hard? "I heard you sent a detachment out this morning and—"

"I do as I'm bid," he said gruffly, cutting her off.

Of course. Her cheeks flushed with embarrassment at her assumption the kindness had come from him. Of course it had been Mikael. And here she was, making a fool of herself, giving him more power. Her embarrassment turned to anger. "You know, a gracious person would just allow someone to say thank you. Maybe politely credit another."

His brow furrowed. "Do you take me for a gracious person?" He almost seemed offended. "And did you really want to thank me?"

"I *did*," she answered, her voice rising. "But I obviously don't now."

"Well, you're welcome for that, then."

She snorted. This man was unbelievable. "You're an asshole."

He raised a brow. "Is that all?"

Norah wasn't sure if he was dismissing her or prompting her for more insults. Her breath shook, and she had to keep from crumpling the parchment in her hand. Forcing back the words on the tip of her tongue, she pursed her lips in festering rage and spun on her heel, leaving him in her wake of frustration.

She stormed down into the great hall, gritting her teeth. To think she went in there to thank him—never again. They *could* hate each other forever.

"Salara," Mikael's voice called her.

She stopped and turned to see him walking toward her.

"Are you all right?" he asked.

"Yes," she managed, trying to calm herself. This was where her thanks were owed, and she didn't want to start by criticizing his beloved commander, his asshole brother-in-arms.

"Yes," she said again, swallowing back her frustration and trying to put the commander from her mind. "I was actually just looking for you."

"Were you?"

She nodded. "I heard about the detachment sent out this morning to look for my crown. I just wanted to let you know that... it was more than I ever would have expected, and... I wanted to thank you."

The corners of his lips turned up. "It's unlikely we'll find it, but now that we have its image, it's possible. When Soren suggested it, I admit I felt a bit of a fool. I should have thought of it myself."

Wait. It *was* the lord commander's idea?

He reached out and touched her arm. "The men will start where I took you. Let's see what we find."

She nodded, her mind still spinning. Then she stopped. "My Northmen might not take kindly to Kharavian warriors in the outer reaches." She couldn't even get her grandmother and the council to accept her marriage. She certainly wasn't going to get them to accommodate Shadowmen within the borders.

He smiled. "They won't even know we're there."

Like they'd been there before...

CHAPTER FIFTY-FOUR

The afternoon sun waned as Norah walked along the windowed hall, looking out into the courtyard. The sky was alive with colors of purple and orange. It was beautiful. A smile crept across her lips. Sometimes it was easy to believe a good life could be made here, if she let it.

Her mind still churned with everything that had happened. She could let herself dwell on the hardships and the despair, everything she had lost. Or she could look to the good: Mercia was safe and fed, and the threat of war between their kingdoms was gone. Mostly. And marriage to Mikael was not as she'd expected. Maybe she *could* be happy here.

She turned back toward her sanctuary, but her smile quickly faded when she looked up to see Mikael and the lord commander walking toward her, with Artem just behind. Mikael's stride was one of purpose. One of anger.

"What business do you send your lord justice on?" he called before he even reached her.

It took her a moment to understand what he'd asked. "It's a task for the council. Why?"

"What kind of task?" he pressed sharply. His tone made her own defenses raise.

She paused, trying to remember her conversation with Alexander. "I don't know, he didn't say. It's insignificant."

"Is it, now?"

Why was he so bothered? "What's this about?"

"He rides for Aleon," the lord commander snarled.

Norah gaped at Mikael in surprise. "What? That's not true." It didn't make sense.

"Our scouts confirmed it," Mikael told her.

"He wouldn't go to Aleon without telling me," she insisted.

"Well it appears you're wrong," the commander said.

Mikael's eyes shifted to his brute, warning him. He turned back to Norah. "You didn't know of this?"

She shook her head. "No, there must be some mistake. But even if he *is* going to Aleon, I'm sure there's a perfectly rational explanation."

"What could be a rational explanation for meeting with our enemy?" Mikael asked.

"Aleon isn't an enemy," she countered. "They've been friends and allies for generations."

"Of the *North*," Mikael stressed. "And let me remind you, that was with the promise of your hand."

She felt the tension escalating. "Let's not jump to conclusions. I'll speak to him when he returns and sort everything out."

"I'm eager to hear," Mikael said stiffly.

The commander's face flashed with anger, clearly offended by Mikael's tolerance. Artem stood behind them, smug and hostile.

Norah's stomach turned. What was the council doing? Just as things were seeming to settle, this jeopardized everything.

Norah paced the winter gardens with Vitalia and Serene in tow. She sucked in the chilled air to clear her mind. Why would the council have sent Alexander to Aleon? And why had Alexander not told her? He'd said he hadn't wanted to burden her more. Perhaps he'd gone to mend the relationship between their kingdoms. The news of her betrothal to the Kharavian king hadn't been received well by Aleon, understandably. She felt a pang of guilt when she thought of Phillip. He'd have seen her decision as an insult. And he'd done nothing wrong, nothing to break their alliance. She'd just changed her mind. Mikael was the only one who could give her peace.

"Try not to worry, Regal High," Serene's voice came from behind. The Mercian title fell strangely on her ears still. Her Kharavian title felt more natural now. "Mercia and Aleon have been friends for a long time, and business between them isn't uncommon. It could be something rather trivial."

She looked back at Serene and forced a smile, appreciating her maid's effort to ease her heart. "That's what I keep telling myself, but trivial things don't require a lord justice."

Norah paced the garden until she could no longer feel her fingers, then she headed back to the castle. She walked the long hall, and when she reached her sanctuary, she froze. Inside stood Captain Artem. And in his hand—Catherine's letter.

"What are you doing in here?" she demanded.

He didn't answer.

"This is my sanctuary. You're not allowed here!" Her eyes moved to the parchment in Artem's hand. "That's my letter!"

He stood, unbothered by her anger. "Why would a letter come from the regent?" he asked. "Telling you to return home urgently?"

"You read my letter?" she seethed. She held out her hand. "Give it to me!"

But he only looked at her with an icy gaze. "All while the Bear meets with Aleon."

"Give it to me!" she demanded again.

Kiran stepped inside from behind her, his hand on the hilt of his sword.

Artem shifted his gaze to Kiran, and his eyes darkened. "Do you forget your place, warrior?"

"You forget yours," Norah snapped. "Give me my letter, and get out! You're never to set foot in here again."

Artem gave an amused snort. Then he tossed the opened letter on the vanity before leaving, giving Kiran a daggered glare as he shouldered by.

Norah stood, still in shock.

"Are you all right, Salara?" Kiran asked her after Artem had gone.

She only nodded, unable to speak.

"We'll take our post. Call if you need anything." Then he and two other members of the Crest saw their way out, closing the door behind them and leaving Norah to her rage.

Vitalia and Serene said nothing but shifted closer to her.

Norah's hands shook as she picked up the letter from the vanity and sat on the chair at the small table. For the first time, she read its words.

Dearest Norah,

This letter comes without excuse for the time it's taken me to write you. Indeed, I should have sent it earlier. Much earlier.

The lord justice sent news of your attack. Times such as these fill one's mind with everything they wished to have done differently, everything they wished to have said. There's much to say, Norah.

I pray this letter finds you safe, but safety is not enough. I need to see your face, my child, to see you well. And Mercia needs her queen.

Come home, if only for a short time. Return to Mercia. Urgently.

You have my love,

Catherine

Norah's mind raced. At first glance, the letter seemed a heartfelt realization by her grandmother that she'd almost died, with a plea to return home. Understandable. Except, Catherine had said *urgently*.

The letter had arrived with Alexander's order to visit Aleon. Surely the two were related. He'd told her he didn't know what the letter said. Did he know Catherine wanted her to return home? What was really going on?

Norah found Mikael in his study, with the lord commander and Captain Artem. Of course. They turned as she entered. The cold of the room made her skin prickle. Her stomach knotted, but she forced herself steady.

Mikael's eyes followed her in. "Do you know what the North is planning?" he asked her.

Now didn't seem the right time to air her grievance about the captain's intrusion in her sanctuary. Mikael obviously knew about the letter; he had to know how it had been found. Did he care? She tried to pull her mind from it—she needed to focus on settling things down. "You don't know if anyone is planning anything. It's purely speculation at this point."

"The Bear rides for Aleon," the brute snarled at her. "And the regent calls for your immediate return."

Yes, it was damning, but she needed to keep things from escalating until she could figure out what was going on. "I was attacked," she countered. "My *grandmother* is worried. She wants me to return home."

"Urgently," he added.

Norah glared at him. "She fears for my safety. Can you blame her?"

The brute snorted. "You're not in *urgent* danger." But his stormy glare swore otherwise.

Her eyes narrowed. "She doesn't know that, and frankly, neither do I."

"She sends the Bear to Aleon."

"The council sends him," she argued back.

"It's the same," Mikael said, stepping into the argument. His face was calm, but his voice brimmed with anger. And something else... Sadness? "As regent, your grandmother would be involved, even if she didn't order it herself."

No, her grandmother wouldn't do that. Would she?

His eyes were still on her, seeking answers. "Do you know what the North plans?"

"Mikael. Just give me some time to understand what's happening."

He stepped closer and cupped her face in his hands, quieting her. "Do you really not know?" he whispered. "Salara."

Again, she shook her head, but she could see his doubt.

"Salara," he said again, more faint this time.

She realized it wasn't Mercia he focused on—it was her, and what *she* knew. He was more concerned with her than Mercia. And his eyes were filled with more than doubt. All she could do was look back at him. She had no words. She didn't know how else to assure him.

Slowly, he bent his head and brought his lips to hers. It wasn't a kiss of passion, or of longing. It was a confession of fear. It said what his words couldn't. He was begging her not to betray him. He pulled back slowly, his eyes searching her.

"Do you still wish to escape me?" he whispered.

Not escape... but she did wish to go back to Mercia, to the people who loved her, to the only people who could help her find herself. "Would you let me leave?"

His brow dipped, and pain flashed in his eyes. "Would you not stay with me of your own free will?"

If she had the choice to leave... "Mikael." Her voice cracked.

His nostrils flared, and his brow dipped lower. He saw her hesitation. Her truth.

"Mikael," she said again. Yes, she wanted to leave. But that didn't mean she wouldn't return. Did it?

He straightened and looked to the lord commander. "We leave now." The commander handed him a belted sword.

Norah's pulse quickened as he fastened it around his waist. "What are you doing? Where are you going?" she asked. Fear flashed through her. *After Alexander.* She caught his arm. "Mikael, wait."

"I have to go to the seer," he said. "I'll be back in three days' time."

Her heart steadied a little with the relief he wasn't riding after Alexander, but she didn't understand. "The seer?"

"I have to see if the Bear plans to bring Aleon against me." His voice was cold now, and he backed just out of the reach of her touch.

The knot in her stomach twisted until it ached. "What about me?"

He paused. "I can't let you go." To the seer or to Mercia? A dark storm eddied in his eyes, and her heart dropped. *Neither.* "I'll return in three days," he said.

"Take me with you," she pleaded. If there were new visions of what was to come...

"Only Kharavian royal blood can visit the temple of the seer," the commander said.

And apparently the commander, Norah added to herself in frustration. She pursed her lips. Rules didn't apply to him.

Mikael frowned. "You'll stay here," he told her. He cast an eye toward Artem, then he and the commander strode out, leaving her with only the captain.

And just like that, she was a prisoner again.

Chapter Fifty-Five

Norah woke to Vitalia calling her in a panicked voice.

"Salara! Salara!" her maid cried. "You have to wake up. Something terrible has happened!"

Norah sat up with alarm, blinking the sleep from her eyes and trying to focus her mind. "What? What's happened?"

"It's Bremhad!"

What? "What about Bremhad?"

"He didn't come home last night. Kiran found him on the workmen's stairs, just outside the kitchens."

Vitalia's words came too quickly, and Norah was having trouble following. "Wait, but... is he all right? Where is he now?"

Her maid paused, swallowing, and then shook her head. "He's dead, Salara."

Norah clenched her quilts in her fists. A weight crushed her chest. She couldn't breathe. *Dead?* Her mind swirled around her. She stumbled from the bed and let Vitalia help her with a dress. "Where's Kiran?" she asked, her voice trembling.

"At the public mortium."

The mortium. She felt as though a dagger had been thrust into her chest. "W-What happened?" she stammered as Vitalia quickly finished the lacing on her dress and ran to get her cloak.

"The prefect is saying Bremhad fell on the stairs and hit his head, that it was an accident."

Norah swept out of her sanctuary with Vitalia beside her.

"But it makes no sense," her maid continued. "Bremhad doesn't even come into the castle, except to tend to the greens on your balcony when you're out. He wouldn't have been on the stairs last night."

Vitalia led the way to the public mortium, a large stone building where Bremhad's body had been taken. Norah followed her inside. The halls were poorly lit, and the smell of death hung heavy in the air. Vitalia led her down a long hall, past a series of open chambers. Pale bodies lay atop wooden tables. Norah pulled her cloak tighter. They reached a chamber at the end of the hall. Inside, a woman was weeping. Norah entered to see Kiran and an older woman, presumably his mother. They were cleaning the body of his father, who lay on a table in the center of the room.

Bremhad.

And it hit her.

This was her fault. Her eyes stung. It was another message from the lord commander. He was punishing her by hurting those around her, those she cared about.

The older woman wept as she worked, sponging Bremhad's head and gently smoothing his silver hair. Kiran looked up when he heard them enter, and his tear-stricken eyes widened in surprise. "Salara," he said as he stepped toward her. "You didn't have to come here, to this place."

"Of course, I did! Kiran, I'm so sorry," she cried, tears streaming down her own cheeks.

Suddenly, Kiran's eyes moved over her shoulder to someone behind her, and she turned to see Captain Artem.

Kiran bared his teeth with a ragged breath of wrath. "You did this!"

He rushed the captain but was caught by two of her Crest guards.

"You did this!" he thundered at Artem. "I know you did this!"

"Kiran!" Norah cried as her guardsmen dragged him from the room and down the hall. What was happening? She could only stand in horror as Kiran's bellows echoed through the mortium. She gaped back at Artem. "Did you really do this?"

"The prefect has ruled it an accident," he answered calmly.

That didn't answer her question, and horror struck her. Kiran's roars still echoed from the hall. "Where are they taking him?" she demanded.

The captain looked at her with gloating eyes. He didn't answer. Then he turned and left the chamber.

Norah stumbled backward in disbelief but caught herself against the wall. Vitalia stepped forward and clasped her arm. "Are you all right, Salara?"

She'd forgotten her maid was even there. She looked back at Kiran's mother, who stood frozen, still grieving her husband and frightened for her son.

The woman swallowed back her emotion to give a small nod of her head, and whispered, "Salara."

Norah's heart burst into pieces. Everything inside her hurt. "I'm so sorry," she whispered. She looked at her maid. "Vitalia, please, stay here. Help her."

"Of course."

"Anything she needs—help preparing the body, money. Anything."

Vitalia nodded. "Yes, Salara."

"I have to make sure Kiran's all right." She cast one last apologetic look at the woman. "I'm so sorry," she breathed again, then she turned and left the chamber.

It was everything she could do to not fall apart as she stepped out of the mortium. Bremhad's death was no accident. She wanted to blame the commander—it seemed fitting. But the commander was with Mikael. That didn't necessarily absolve him. He could have ordered it.

Kiran had accused Artem. Maybe it was only his grief lashing out. Or perhaps he was right. Maybe Artem was punishing her. Did he know Bremhad was Kiran's father? Perhaps Artem was punishing Kiran for his defiance in her sanctuary.

She scanned the grounds for the captain, but he was nowhere to be seen.

"Where is Artem?" she snapped back at the Crest following behind her.

"He may be in the forces office," her guardsman Sonal told her.

"Take me there. Now."

She followed him to a building beside the soldiers' barracks. Inside, Artem stood with another soldier. The soldier bowed and left as she entered.

"North Queen," Artem greeted her coldly.

"It's Salara," she cut back. She wasn't going to let *two* assholes get away with that. "Where's Kiran?" she demanded.

"He's been detained."

"Where?"

He cast her an annoyed eye. "Where we detain men."

In the dungeon. "He's a member of the Crest!"

Artem snorted. "No longer. He falsified his documents and attacked his superior."

Superior. Artem was anything but. "You can't do that!"

"I'm captain of the Crest. I can."

His cool tone infuriated her. She'd thought she couldn't loathe anyone more than the lord commander. She'd been wrong. "I order you to release him." She may be a prisoner, but she was still queen.

The corners of his mouth turned up in amusement. "I answer to Salar."

He was such a smug bastard, so confident that Mikael's attention was focused on the threat with Aleon and that it would bode unfavorably for her. She was starting to understand the want for blood. If she had a dagger in her hand...

She wouldn't let him get away with this. Without a reply, she turned and stormed from the office and back to the castle.

Night passed, and another day came, but Norah couldn't sleep. Her body was tired, but her mind couldn't rest. Vitalia had stayed with Kiran's mother, and Serene had spent the night in the sanctuary with her.

Her maid helped her dress, carefully fastening the clasps of the gown and straightening the lacing. "You look like you haven't slept a wink, Regal High."

She let out an exhausted breath. "I haven't."

"You might find it more comfortable in the villa," Serene suggested. "It's nice there."

Norah sat down at the vanity with a stoic face as the maid brushed her hair. "I don't want to talk about the villa again," she said. "Ever." If she could, she'd burn it to the ground. She'd burn everything. She hated this wretched place—it was breaking her.

"Yes, Regal High," Serene said quietly. Norah watched her maid in the mirror as she gathered the linens from the bed and swept them into a basket. She left the room just as Vitalia entered with breakfast.

"Salara," Vitalia said breathlessly. "Good news! Kiran was released. Just this morning."

Norah spun around in her chair. That was good news.

"The Crest is unhappy with his treatment. I fear Artem's mercy is temporary, just to appease them. Hopefully Salar returns soon."

Yes, Norah was desperate for his return. But for now, she was relieved that Kiran was at least free. "Where is he now?"

"Back with his mother, preparing. The burial will be this afternoon."

Norah rose from her chair. "I have to go." She had to be there.

"Salara, it would be... unconventional for you to be there. Bremhad was a servant. Only those who have died a warrior's death would be seen into the ground by salar. Or salara."

To hell with conventions. "I don't care." She paused. "Unless... Kiran doesn't want me there?" After all, this was her fault.

"Of course he'd want you there. It would be a great honor."

"Then I'll go."

Vitalia gave her a sad smile.

"Help me get ready."

The wet, muddy ground was soft beneath her feet.

Outside the city, Norah walked with Vitalia up the hill to the large public burial ground. She wished she'd left her jacket in the carriage. The sun sat high in the sky. Even though it was still winter, it was as hot as a summer day.

They gathered in a large circle around a hole in the earth, with Bremhad's body wrapped in linen beside it. It seemed such a strange thing, to bury the body of a loved one in the dirt. In Mercia, bodies were burned to free the soul so it could travel to the gods, except the bodies of the kings and queens. Their souls remained tethered to this world, watching over the people, guiding their hands to the will of the gods.

The Kharavian people didn't believe in gods or souls. They believed bodies should be returned to the earth from which they came. Norah didn't know what she believed. Neither made her feel differently about death, neither took away the pain.

More people had come than she'd expected; many were servants, and some were dressed in finer clothing. She was surprised to see so many soldiers of the Crest—perhaps all the members of the Crest—nearly an army.

"I didn't know the Crest knew Bremhad," she whispered to Vitalia. "Or knew that he was Kiran's father."

"They didn't. They only found out yesterday. But they came to support Kiran."

Her eyes combed the people to find him, and she did—standing beside his mother. He spotted her and started toward her.

Vitalia slipped away as he approached, giving them space.

"Salara," Kiran said as he reached her. "You honor us."

"It was the least I could do." She watched as he pressed his lips together tightly to hold back his emotion. It only prompted her own. "It's warmer than usual," she said, breaking the weight of the air.

Kiran's breath steadied. "It's what greenskeepers call alhilat—the great trick, a false spring." His lips held a weak smile. "My father hated it. It lasts just long enough for the blooms to start, then the ice returns and kills them all." He looked at the skies. "We'll soon be in winter again."

Kiran's face hardened, and Norah followed his gaze to see Artem at the edge of the grounds.

"Ignore him, Kiran," she told him. "Focus on your father."

"I'll see that man dead."

She couldn't object. "You really think he did this?"

"He ordered it. He wouldn't do it himself, fucking coward." He glanced at Norah. "Forgive my words, Salara."

Norah watched Artem as he watched them. He did look like a fucking coward. He was the only man who wore full armor, aside from Mikael. He probably viewed himself of equally deserved status. He wasn't.

"Are men loyal to him?" she asked.

Kiran snorted. "A few. Not many."

"How is he captain, then?"

"He was captain of the Crest for Salar's father. He'll stay captain until he's promoted. Or dies."

"Maybe that's why he wears all that armor. The latter's more likely."

Kiran snorted again. He turned and looked at her. "If you ever need anything, Salara, I'm still in service to you. I took my oath for life. I'm still a soldier of the Crest."

"Thank you, Kiran."

He gave her a small bow of his head and went back to join his mother by the body of his father. She wished Mikael would return sooner, to right this wrong. But how could it be righted? And what would he do? Now there was this distance between them, and she was a prisoner. *Again.* Maybe that's what she'd been all along. Maybe she'd only been fooling herself. Maybe what she'd felt, what she'd thought she'd felt...

Vitalia took the vacated place by Norah's side.

"I can't stay here any longer," Norah said. "I can't bear it, Vitalia. I have to find a way to get home." She watched as men lowered Bremhad's body into the earth. No more—she was leaving. Today. Tonight. She turned her eyes to Vitalia. "You know this castle. You can sneak us out."

Her maid nodded. "I could get you as far as the burial ground. Then I could return and keep them unknowing a while longer for you to get away."

Norah grabbed her arm. "No. You're coming with me. And Serene. I'm not leaving you to these monsters."

Vitalia stared at her for a moment.

"Do you not want to go?"

"No. I mean, yes, I-I do," Vitalia stammered. "I just didn't think you would... think about me."

"You're my friend," Norah said firmly. "You're coming with me. You and Serene."

Her maid gave her a teary-eyed nod. "All right. We'll go." She paused. "Wait. Even if we get out of Ashan, we still have to get through the Canyonlands."

Norah couldn't help a small smile. "I know someone who will help us."

Tahla.

Chapter Fifty-Six

Darkness hung over them. A successful slip-away plan put Norah and Vitalia outside the blacksmith forge, just across the way from the stables. They hid by the walls of the forge. It surprised Norah how easy it had been to climb out of the bath-chamber window in her sanctuary, down the trellis, and to the ground below.

Serene had stayed in the sanctuary and was tasked with making occasional noises—talking, laughing—to confirm occupancy. After the guard change, she was to take a tray of half-eaten dinner down to the kitchen, *tidying up*. No other staff would be in the kitchen at this hour. She'd slip out the side hall and down the stairs to where Norah and Vitalia would be waiting with horses.

Time passed at a snail's pace. Norah's heart raced in her chest. She prayed everything would go to plan. They only needed to get the horses and meet Serene outside the kitchen.

She and Vitalia slipped along the wall of the smith's forge and silently crossed the cobblestone street toward the stables. But before they reached the side doors, a soldier stepped out in front of them. Norah stopped suddenly, and Vitalia grabbed her arm. The soldier held a spear in his hand—he was a member of the Crest. Norah sucked in a breath. Then she recognized him.

Bhastian.

"You need to get back to the castle, Salara," he told her. "The captain's looking for you."

"Well he can keep looking," she said sharply.

"Salara." There was something in his voice that made her skin prickle. "You'll want to go back."

But she didn't want to go back. She couldn't live like this anymore. "No." She shook her head. "I won't."

"Salar and the lord commander will be returning soon."

All the more reason she had to go now. "I'm leaving. Step aside."

But he only blocked her way. She couldn't fight him—she was no match for a warrior of the Crest. And even if she could get away, she'd lose Vitalia, and Serene. She had to try a different approach. "Bhastian. Please. I'm begging you." Was Kiran the only one with compassion?

He hesitated, but then shook his head. "I can't, Salara. I have to take you back."

"Bhastian," she pleaded. "Help me."

He motioned her back toward the castle. Fight flooded her mind, but she couldn't, she reminded herself. And, since Bhastian was here, they'd likely found Serene. She wouldn't be outside the kitchen waiting, and Norah couldn't leave without her.

Defeated, she headed back. As they walked, he waved off the guard that came running, and continued toward her sanctuary. They entered the west wing, but as they reached the main hall, Bhastian halted.

Artem stepped out from the shadows, and Norah's stomach dropped.

Bhastian struck the ground with his spear in salute and stood at attention.

"I would have thought you'd be more careful with yourself now, Salara," Artem said with a chilling tone. "All the problems you've caused, the people you've hurt."

"You mean the people you've hurt," she snapped.

"You forced my hand." Artem scoffed. "I initially took you for a sharp woman, but you still fail to grasp your situation."

Her situation. He didn't view her as queen. He didn't recognize her authority. No one did.

"Mikael won't stand for this." She didn't know if she believed her own words, though.

"I think that depends on what he sees in Odepeth."

Odepeth. Where the seer was, where Mikael had gone.

"You're so confident it will go poorly," she said.

"Because it's known—you cannot change fate. Salar will see nothing different."

This was the first she had heard that. Her father had changed fate. Hadn't he? His words scared her. What would Mikael do if he thought his fate remained?

He eyed her for a moment. "Where were you just now?"

She didn't answer, and he looked at Bhastian. Norah's heart beat heavily in her chest.

"She was in the library," Bhastian answered.

Her heart leapt in relief, but Norah pursed her lips in feigned anger.

Artem's eyes narrowed. "You said you searched the library."

"Not well enough," Bhastian answered.

He tilted his head, looking back at Norah. "A little late for a library visit."

"I couldn't sleep."

"Strange you would slip your guard for that. And I would have thought your maid would have given me that answer—a place so innocent."

Norah's stomach knotted. *Serene.* "She didn't know."

"So she said."

He'd caught Serene. He'd questioned her. "If you touched her—"

The corner of his mouth turned up, and he looked at Bhastian. "Take her back. And take your new post."

Norah stepped around him with a fury and stalked back to her sanctuary, the panic building inside her with each step. When she reached the door, she swung it open and let out a ragged breath.

Serene sat on the edge of the bed, trembling as blood ran from her brow and lip. Her face was swollen from crying.

"Serene," Norah gasped, rushing to her. "What happened?"

Her maid let out an uneven breath but shook her head. She couldn't speak.

Norah sank down beside her and pulled her close. "I'm here now," she said, stroking her hair.

"It was the captain," Serene managed to get out, her voice shaking. "I hadn't even left yet. He came looking for you. I told him I didn't know where you were. He didn't believe me."

Rage surged through her.

Serene glanced over Norah's shoulder and grew quiet. Norah realized Bhastian hadn't stopped at the end of the hall but had come into the sanctuary. "Get out," she hissed at him.

"I can't do that, Salara. The captain has ordered a post in your room. You're to have a guard always." Norah let out an enraged breath, but Bhastian spoke with a softer voice. "I'll take the shift until Salar and the lord commander return. They'll be back soon, and neither will stand for this."

"You can't be serious. This is all the lord commander stands for!"

The guardsman sighed and stepped to the door, turning his back to give the desolate women privacy.

Norah trembled in a maddening rage, but the only thing she could do was wait for Mikael to return. She and Vitalia pulled Serene into the bed and lay in the dark, trying to hold back the tears.

"Salara."

Norah woke to Bhastian calling her. She blinked the sleep from her eyes and sat up, careful not to wake Serene and Vitalia lying beside her.

"Is it morning?" she whispered.

"Yes, early morning. Salar and the lord commander have just returned."

"Oh," Norah breathed as she slipped out of the bed.

He hesitated. "But, Salara, it's not a good sign. The lord commander has gone straight to his study, where he's to be left alone."

That wasn't entirely indicative of something bad. If the lord commander was unhappy, it could be the seer had spoken in her favor.

She hoped.

Norah padded into the bath chamber and ran her fingers through her hair. She splashed water onto her face from the basin and took a deep breath. Mikael would listen. Things between them weren't completely broken. She just needed to talk to him.

She stepped back out into her chamber and slipped on her shoes. "Where is he?" she asked Bhastian.

"I imagine he'll be reaching the castle from the stables any moment."

Norah left her sanctuary and made her way through the castle with Bhastian close behind. What had the seer told Mikael? Would it break things more between them? She feared the answer.

She waited by the stair, pacing circles around the inlaid image of a sun on the stone floor. Her mind raced, and her stomach threatened to upheave the contents of her last meal. But she had to stay calm. She walked through the conversation in her mind. She'd tell him what Artem had done, about Bremhad and Kiran. She would tell him about Serene. She'd have to admit her effort to escape. He would understand. Or he might become more suspicious.

Her heart thrummed faster.

The front doors of the castle swung open, and Mikael strode through. He stopped when he saw her.

He looked weary. Dried mud covered the greaves of his armor. He held his helm in his hand by a single horn. He didn't speak.

Every intelligent sentence in her mind left her, every word. The silence was overwhelming between them as she searched his face for clues.

He silently walked to her, and she didn't move.

Ever so slowly, he brought his hand to her face. He brushed her cheek with his fingertips and grazed his thumb over the line of her lips. His eyes trailed his somber touch—mournful even.

Mikael pulled back, still without a word, and then turned for the stairs.

"What did the seer tell you?" she asked.

He didn't answer. He didn't want to talk about it—not a good sign, but she needed to talk to him.

She followed him up the stairs. "Mikael, I need to speak with you. About Captain Artem."

He paused. "I can't speak about this right now."

She couldn't accept that. "I'm sure you're tired and want to rest, but it's important," she pressed. "I can't tolerate him any longer. He—"

"Don't ask any more of me," he said, turning back to her. His voice was tinged with exasperation and hints of anger. "Not now."

She stepped back in surprise. She hadn't expected his reaction.

"I won't hear it," he said, and he started back up the stairs.

A heat rose in her cheeks at his dismissal. She trailed behind him, a fury growing in her core. "You will hear it!" she snapped.

He whirled back to face her. "Have I not given you everything?" he raged.

Norah stumbled back but caught herself against the railing.

His voice came low, but it chilled her soul. "I've required nothing of the North, put no demands upon you. I've given everything you've asked—peace, mercy, tolerance. I give provisions for your people. I give your army horses and weapons. Men." His face grew darker. "And I let you keep the one threat to my crown. The man who is to strike me down rides unchallenged through my kingdom, through my castle. Even now he goes freely to my enemy. Still, I do nothing."

He looked at her with defeat in his eyes. "I wed you to change my fate. But I've only brought it closer." He steadied his weight against the railing. "I won't hear it." Then he turned and continued up the stairs.

Norah took a deep breath, tempering her fury. He was speaking from fear, she told herself. And meeting that fear with anger wouldn't help either of them.

She followed him up the staircase and down the hall to his study. He said nothing as he unfastened his sword belt from around his hips and leaned the blade against the wall.

"What did the seer tell you?" she asked again.

Mikael waved his servant away, and Vimal left them to the quiet of the crackling fireplace. He pulled off his breastplate, dropping it onto the floor by his desk. He started with his left pauldron but fumbled with the small clasps and gave up. Norah watched as he gripped the corners of the desk and leaned his weight against it. He breathed heavily through his mouth.

She moved to his side. "What did the seer tell you?" she asked again, softly.

He breathed in a long breath and let it out slowly. "I die at the hand of the Bear."

She needed to walk him back from this. "That's an old vision."

"No. There will be another Great War. A powerful event. There are many visions of it now: North flags throughout the Tribelands, Aleon forces in Bahoul." He paused, his eyes burning. "You. Beside the Aleon king."

Samuel's paintings flooded her mind. But she knew things weren't always as they seemed. "Mikael, these are but interpretations of what the seer has seen. They lack context, all the detail. You can't necessarily rely on his translation."

"I saw it with my own eyes!" he snapped back.

Norah stopped as her breath hitched in her throat. *Of course.* She felt so stupid—how could she have forgotten? Mikael had a traveler, someone who could enter his mind and show him these visions. She needed to see them. "How powerful is this seer?" she asked.

"The most powerful of the four kingdoms."

Was he powerful enough to see what happened to her memories? Was he powerful enough to unlock them?

Mikael stood with a somber weight curving his shoulders. There was something more.

"He showed Soren a vision," he added quietly, "one that Soren won't speak of, even to me. It's his own demise, I'm sure." He paused, drawing in a devastated breath. "I haven't changed my fate. I've brought it to my door. And I've cursed those closest to me."

He struggled again with the clasps of his armor. She moved forward to help him, but he caught her wrist, pulling back from her touch.

The storms of his eyes eddied. "Leave me, North Queen."

Chapter Fifty-Seven

Mikael's anguish from the night before weighed heavily on Norah. And there was nothing she could do. Morning brought a new day, but not a new hope. This place, this kingdom of darkness that decayed the mind and heart, was breaking her.

She decided to try for a ride. She needed fresh air, and sun. How far had she fallen from Mikael's grace? Would she be denied the little freedom she'd had before?

Norah stepped out of her sanctuary to see Captain Artem personally waiting for her.

"Salara," he greeted her coldly.

His nearness made the hair on the back of her neck stand on end. Of course there'd been no retribution for his cruelty, and his smug presence enraged her. She hated this man. She praised herself for sending Vitalia and Serene to stay with Kiran and his mother—they were hidden, and safe.

"Captain Artem, what a surprise," she said, not bothering to hide her disgust.

His eyes moved over her clothing. "We're going riding, I see."

Norah pursed her lips. He was attempting to keep her in. She wouldn't let him. "Try to keep up," she quipped.

His eyes darkened.

They rode out into the morning; Norah on the mare with Artem and a small group of his soldiers behind.

Norah took them far. Her spirits rose under the sun. Artem couldn't hurt her, this she was certain. It's why he hurt people around her. And Vitalia and Serene were hidden away, protected. All he could do now was harass her directly. And she would make it very tiresome for him.

They reached Hava Lake—a deep pool below a cliff overlook. Against the dark and rocky terrain, the water sparkled a brilliant blue. Kiran had shown her this place. *The bluest water in the world*, he'd said, from the minerals in the springs that fed it.

Artem pulled off his helmet and wiped the sweat from his brow before putting it back on. He didn't wear a wrap on his head, like the other soldiers, but rather a helm that looked more decorative than functional. And like everything else in Kharav, the metal of his armor was dark, almost black, soaking in the sun. His head was likely baking in it. *Good*. She smiled to herself.

Norah looked up at the rocky overlook above, and her smile grew to a grin. She urged the mare to the water's edge and dismounted, using her hand to block the sun as she looked upward at the rock face. "A nice day for a walk," she called pleasantly. An even better day to require an overheated captain of the Crest to hike up a steep mountainside.

"You can't be serious," Artem scoffed.

She shrugged. "Stay here, then," she replied, and started up the narrow path.

Artem's annoyed grunt sang sweetly in her ears as he dismounted and followed with his guard. Petty pleasure, she scolded herself. And Artem would probably find a way to make her pay for it later. But for now, she'd give herself this small joy. It was all she had left.

It was a long climb, and despite leaving her jacket back with the mare, she found herself perspiring. Delight rippled through her as she thought of how Artem must be faring.

They were all breathless by the time they reached the top. Her legs burned, and a deep stitch clenched her side, but it was worth it. She closed her eyes, breathing in the sky and drawing life back into her body. This was exactly what she had needed. In a short while, she'd be back in the castle of shadows. She needed to remember this place—how the wind felt, how the sun hit her face. She needed it to endure the dark.

Everything was lost.

Yet something still pulled at her heart. Something small but strong.

Not everything, it said. Not yet.

Norah stood in the sun and looked down to the sparkling blue of the water below. The light danced across its surface. Its magic smiled at her. The wind swirled around her, whispering into her ears, breathing strength into her mind. It told her to remember—remember what she was here for.

And a new strength came.

She'd almost lost herself again. She had almost resigned herself. But she couldn't. She owed it to her people. And those she loved. She owed it to herself.

Norah turned around to see Artem standing a distance away from her. He watched her with his dark and despicable eyes, no doubt thinking dark and despicable thoughts.

She raised her arms, feeling the wind underneath them. Artem's mouth opened slightly, and he took a step toward her.

Her lips peeled back into a wry smile.

And she let herself fall backward, over the edge.

"No!" he bellowed as he charged forward. But he was too far away. He couldn't catch her.

The fall was a fall into freedom.

Norah hit the water, and its chill sent a shock through her body. It took her a moment to recover, and she kicked feverishly back to the surface. She gasped for air as she battled the tangle of skirts around her legs, and her teeth chattered as she got her bearings. Looking up, she saw Artem at the top of the overlook, gaping at her but not daring to jump. She let out a triumphant laugh.

The lord commander would have jumped in after her.

But Kiran was right. This man was a coward.

Norah made her way to the bank and let out a low whistle, calling the mare. The horse found her quickly, and she sprang onto her back. Giving one last look to Artem, she urged the animal forward into a gallop.

North.

She rode until she was out of sight before she let the mare slow. It would take Artem some time to get back down to his horse, and she'd be well ahead of him. He'd never track her with Savantahla, a horse of the Wild. Norah brought the mare to a stop and looked around. Her teeth chattered in her wet dress under the wind, but she was thankful for alhilat—the break in winter. If Bremhad were there, perhaps he might not hate it so much now.

She shifted her mind to what she needed to do next. Artem had watched her ride north, toward the Canyonlands and Mercia. She smiled as she turned the mare east.

To Odepeth. And the seer.

SHADOW QUEEN

Chapter One

Time was of the essence now. Collective footsteps echoed through the halls of the Kharavian castle. The sun hadn't yet reached its peak, but Soren worried the day was too far gone. The queen had fled, and every moment counted in recovering her.

He strode quickly, and his men followed in unison. Artem strode beside him, like an equal.

But he was not.

Soren waved his men and Artem to wait as he turned into the alcove of Mikael's study, and he paused as he took in a deep breath before letting it out slowly. He had never felt anxious about delivering bad news. But today was different. This was different. Mikael was different now.

He pushed open the ash-wood door and found the king at his desk, mulling over a letter. Mikael lifted his head on hearing him enter, and leaned back in his chair, tossing the letter to the edge of the desk for Soren to see. "Aleon has sent additional forces to their borders. Nearer to Japheth, and nearer to us."

Aleon had long been the North's ally. Now, with an alliance between the North and Kharav, the North Queen would have Mikael believe Aleon was a friend. But Kharav was still allies with the Aleon king's brother, the king of Japheth, and the conflict between the brothers would be resolved only when one of them was dead. Aleon would never be a friend.

Soren picked up the letter and read through it. His uneasiness grew. The Bear was in Aleon now. It was as they feared. The Bear was bringing Aleon against them.

The king sighed, unsettled. "They're preparing. But whether it's with intention of—"

"The North Queen is gone," Soren interrupted him. No sense delaying.

Mikael stopped in his words and looked up in surprise. "Gone where?" he asked as he rose from his desk. "What happened?"

"She went riding this morning and"—Soren paused—"went through great lengths to escape the Crest. This isn't a coincidence."

Mikael rested the knuckles of his closed fists on the smooth hardwood of his desk as he stood, and he leaned his weight forward. "If the North plots against me, she's promised she has no part in it."

Soren's jaw tightened as he fought his irritation. The king's love for this woman blinded him to reality.

Mikael moved to the window and looked out across the city. "Was Artem with her?"

The mere mention of the Crest captain's name irritated him. "He was."

"Where is he?"

Soren sighed. He'd already gotten the details from Artem and needed to leave now to catch the queen. This was a waste of time. "He's in the hall."

Mikael drew in a breath of what Soren knew was forced composure. "Bring him in."

Soren opened the door and summoned the captain, and Artem strode in, bowing low. "Salar," he said with a smooth but needling voice.

A quiet growl rumbled in the back of Soren's throat as he tried to not show his annoyance. Artem—always seeking to be at the top, yet always over the top.

Mikael stepped back to his desk. "I'm told Salara's gone. Evaded you."

"Yes, Salar. She rides for the North."

Mikael nodded. He calmly stacked the parchments on his desk, but Soren knew the storm below the surface. "Tell me, how is it possible for her to slip the elite soldiers of the Crest and their captain?"

Artem shifted uncomfortably. "Salar, this is the same woman who stole the lord commander's horse from under him at the base of Bahoul."

Soren bristled. Artem was a pisspot coward who did whatever he needed to do to deflect from himself. Soren's father, Tyrhar Nazim, had once been captain of the Crest, and Artem defiled the honor of the position. Artem had taken over as captain under Mikael's father when the former king charged Tyrhar to look after Bahoul. Artem had no principles, and Soren couldn't stand a man with no principles.

"She led us to the overlook at Hava Lake," the captain continued. "When we reached the top, a madness took hold of her, and she jumped."

Mikael shifted back in surprise. "Into the water?"

Artem gave a nod. "Yes, Salar. She swam to shore, and by the time we got back to the horses, she was gone."

Mikael stood silently for a moment. He reached down and moved the bottle of ink in line with the parchments. "Madness, you say?"

"Yes, Salar."

"And you didn't jump in after her, Captain?"

Artem hesitated before shaking his head. "No, Salar."

The corner of Mikael's mouth twitched. "Then she's not mad. She's clever."

The captain gave a reluctant tilt of his head. "Perhaps, Salar."

Mikael swept the top of his desk in a rage, flinging the items on top to the floor. "Not *perhaps!*" he roared. He gripped the corners tightly—no doubt to keep from flipping it over. His cold calm returned. "Yesterday, she told me she needed to speak to me, that she could no longer tolerate you." He straightened and walked around his desk to stand in front of Artem. "Tell me, Captain, why would she find you intolerable?"

Artem's breath came unevenly. The captain was nervous. He should be.

"She wants to do as she pleases, without restriction," the captain answered.

Mikael lunged out and grabbed the captain by his breastplate, slamming him backward, up against the wall. "She is *salara*!" he said from between his bared teeth. "She *will* do as she pleases, without restriction. You are the captain of the Crest! You keep her protected *as she does as she pleases, without restriction*!"

"Yes, Salar," Artem said quickly. "I understand."

The king's nostrils flared with rage. "You no longer answer to me, you answer to Salara. When you find her, you'll swear your sword and beg her forgiveness. You'll keep your position if she sees you fit." Mikael released him.

"Of course, Salar," Artem said, bowing low again and not daring to look up from the floor.

"Get out of my sight."

Artem bowed even lower before quickly leaving the room.

Soren didn't find moments of joy often, but he did now. Perhaps this wasn't a waste of time after all.

Mikael turned back to him. "Find her. I want her here. I want her safe."

His silent joy evaporated. He gave a stiff nod and turned to leave, but Mikael stopped him.

"Has her captain returned from the North? Caspian is his name."

Soren didn't like where this was going. "I believe this morning."

"Take him with you. He may be of help."

A Northman wouldn't be of help, but Soren forced another obedient nod.

The king gave a regretful grimace. "I wouldn't hear her," he said bitterly. "I was so seized by the visions that I couldn't even speak to her. Now she's out there alone."

Anger rippled under Soren's skin. Mikael couldn't see it, even when it was right in front of him. "The Bear is bringing Aleon against you. The North Queen—"

Mikael's eyes flashed. "I urge you caution if you have an accusation," he warned.

"You would have me do you a disservice? Who else can make you see?" Soren pressed.

"Careful, brother."

But Soren wasn't one for care. "She goes to meet her original betrothed."

Mikael ripped his sword from its scabbard with a shaking fury and swept it to Soren's neck, his nostrils flared.

Soren stood, unmoving. He saw Mikael's offense, but this was what he feared. Mikael was blinded to the danger he welcomed. He was turning a deaf ear to those who loved him, those who would give everything for him. The North Queen would bring his end, and Mikael harbored her, defended her, bent to her, even in the face of her betrayal.

Slowly, Mikael lowered his sword, but his warning was clear. Without another word, Soren took his leave.

Vitalia sat quietly at a small table in a stone, terraced home, mending a pair of her gloves as Serene read a book. For their own safety from Captain Artem, Salara had sent her maids to the house of the Crest guard Kiran, which he shared with his mother. Vitalia wished she could have stayed with the queen to help her. Salara carried the weight of the world on her shoulders.

"Do you think she'll return?" Serene asked quietly. The queen was obviously on her mind as well.

Vitalia looked up from her sewing and smiled reassuringly. "Of course she will. She wouldn't leave us alone here."

"What if something happened to her?"

It was a question Vitalia asked herself over and over—with the answer she feared most—but she forced a smile. "If there's one thing I know about Salara, it's that she can take care of herself." She nodded to the book Serene was holding. "What are you reading?"

"It's a book of poems, a favorite from home. It always brings me comfort." Serene held it out for her. "Would you like to read it?"

Vitalia swallowed. She felt so inadequate as a queen's maid sometimes. She didn't have a proper education, as the Mercian maid had. "I'm not able to read," she said with a flush of embarrassment in her cheeks. She would forever be indebted to Salara for giving her the opportunity for a better life, in a respected position, and for treating her as more than a slave. She only wished she could do everything expected of a maid, all that Salara needed of her, all that Serene was able to do.

"Oh," Serene said softly. Then she gave a warm smile. "Would you like me to read it to you? I could even teach you, with time."

Vitalia let out an unexpecting breath, and she smiled. "I would like that very much."

Serene opened the book again, but a banging outside made them stop.

"Open the door!" a man's voice called from the street below.

Serene looked at Vitalia with her eyes wide. With Salara's disappearance, they knew they'd be sought for questioning. And likely worse things.

"Guards," Vitalia whispered, hurrying to the large armoire against the wall. "Get in. Hurry!"

Serene ducked inside, and Vitalia followed in after. They pulled the doors closed. Unable to stand fully, they crouched, holding hands. It was difficult to hear over the sound of their nervous breaths.

They waited.

Time stood still.

Outside fell quiet. Had the guards gone?

The front door of the home opened and closed, and footsteps traveled up the stairs to where they crouched in hiding. Serene clutched Vitalia's hand until it hurt. Vitalia ignored it. They peered through the misalignment at the bottom of the doors but could see only the legs of the table where they had been sitting. A man entered the room; just the black of his breeches and boots were visible. He picked up Serene's book that she'd dropped on the chair, and Vitalia cursed under her breath.

He turned toward the armoire and stood in front of it for a moment, then pulled open the doors, making Serene gasp.

A breath of relief escaped her when she saw it was only Sonal. "You scared the piss out of us," Vitalia said to Salara's Crest guard.

"A book from the North. You can't leave things like this around," he told Serene, tossing it at her.

"I know, I'm sorry," the Mercian maid said as she fumbled to catch it. "We just heard the guards, and I guess I panicked."

They moved to the window and looked across the street to Kiran's home, watching guards depart. Salara had sent Vitalia and Serene to stay with Kiran's mother before Sonal moved them across the street to his own grandmother's house.

"I knew they'd come for you," he told them. "It's not safe to return to Kiran's. Stay here. They're leaving now, but they might come back. He's ordered a search for you."

"Salar?" Vitalia asked.

"No. Artem."

The thought made Vitalia's stomach turn.

CHAPTER TWO

Alhilat. That's what Kiran had called the sudden wave of warmth. The earth's great trick, a false spring. Norah was grateful for it. Its warmth in the harsh of winter had given her the break she needed, the opportunity to escape Artem—an opportunity she'd been desperate for—but it would last only a few days. She had to find this seer, this mind traveler. If he truly was the most powerful in the four kingdoms, maybe he could help her get her memories back.

And she needed to see the visions. She'd seen the images painted by the Mercian seer; she knew the vision Mikael spoke of—Alexander killing him on the battlefield. But everything should have changed when they wed. The vision *had* to have changed. A marriage meant no war, which meant Mikael should be safe.

She wanted him safe, this man who had once been her enemy, whose kingdom had warred against hers for ten years. This man who had captured her, and a piece of her heart—she *needed* him safe.

Yet he wasn't.

And if he wasn't safe, Alexander wasn't safe.

Alexander. What was he doing? She was barely holding peace between their kingdoms, and he'd traveled to Aleon without telling her. Of course Mikael would see it as a plot against him. She needed to find this seer and figure things out before Alexander returned to Kharav. If it was true the vision hadn't changed, she needed to figure out how to change it. She needed to see this traveler, not just for herself, but to save both the men in her heart.

Her mare of the Wild carried her east, toward Odepeth. Norah knew nothing of the city, only the name and a general direction based on poorly remembered maps she'd seen in Mikael's study. At least she hoped she was riding in the right direction. It certainly wasn't the most thought-out plan, but then again, she hadn't really planned this.

Norah rode until her legs were numb and her hips stiff. Finally, when she came upon a small stream, she slowed the mare to give them both a rest. Not that the mare needed it—a horse of the Wild was no ordinary animal. Norah still wasn't sure what her connection was to the horse, but for now—especially now—she was grateful for it. Captain Artem would be unable to find her, unable to track the mare, and she inhaled a rich breath of freedom. However, her relief was short-lived as she turned her thoughts to the challenge ahead. She couldn't trust anyone to help her. In fact, quite the opposite. If she was discovered, they might return her to the lord commander or, worse, Captain Artem. She shook her head. She'd figure it out, she told herself. She just needed to rest for a moment and gather her wits.

She slid from the mare's back and let the animal drink her fill at the creek's edge as Norah scooped the cold water to her own lips. It tasted good, and she drank deeply. She closed her eyes and let her mind settle. When she opened them again, she saw a young man standing a small distance away, looking back at her. He'd startled her, yet he didn't look startling.

Norah put him at sixteen or seventeen, not quite a boy, not yet a man. His hair was short and black like his clothing. A sword hung at his side, but his look wasn't that of a soldier's.

"Hello," Norah called out to him, rising to her feet. "Who are you?"

He didn't answer.

"Who are *you?*" a voice said behind her, and Norah whirled around to see a young woman between two trees. She was dressed like the boy, only she carried a bow instead of a sword. Her dark hair was pulled back into a thick braid, and her face closely resembled his—likely his sister—but a little older. She had a fierceness to her, one that Norah liked.

"Why are you here?" the girl pressed. "What do you want?"

"I'm just passing through."

"Outsiders don't just pass through Kharav. Where are you going?"

Norah paused. She had told herself she couldn't trust anyone, but they might point her in the right direction if they were eager for her to move on. On the other hand, they'd also be able to divulge where she was headed to anyone who happened along behind her. But merely knowing the name of her destination wouldn't get her there, and time wasn't a luxury she had. She needed help. She had to take the risk. "Odepeth," she said cautiously.

"You speak the common tongue," the girl said. "Where are you from?"

A benefit to the Northern language being the common trade tongue between kingdoms—it didn't immediately give her away. The girl obviously didn't recognize her, and Norah wanted to keep it that way. "Very far," she said. "It would be a great kindness if you could point me in the right direction, and I'll gladly be on my way."

The girl eyed her skeptically, then looked over Norah's shoulder to her brother. She made a small motion with her hand by her cheek. Norah turned to look at him as he gave a small hand motion back to his sister.

"You talk to him with your hands," Norah said. "Can he not speak?"

The girl's eyes darted to Norah with an intense defensiveness. "What of it? He's not stupid, if that's what you're thinking."

"Of course not. I have a friend who's deaf," she said, thinking of the young boy that worked in the sparring field back in Mercia. "I've never met another like him, that's all."

The girl's face softened. "Can you speak with your hands?"

Norah shook her head. "No, I can only say hi," she said, trying to remember what she'd been shown so long ago and holding up her hand. "And thank you," she added, cupping her fist and then extending her fingers.

"Hi is the same," the girl told her, holding up her hand, "but thank you is"—she brought her fingers to her lips and made an arc downward. "But Cohen can read your lips, in both the common and Kharavian tongue."

"That's amazing." *Cohen*. It didn't sound like a Kharavian name, not that Norah was an expert in Kharavian names.

The girl smiled. "I'm Calla," she offered, her defensiveness forgotten. "Short for Callamine."

That also didn't seem like a Kharavian name. Norah smiled back. "I'm Norah."

"You should keep east for Odepeth," Calla told her, pointing to her left, "but you won't make it there tonight."

"Oh," Norah said with a sigh. *Damn*. "Well, that's all right. I'll see how far I can get."

"Come to our house. You can rest there tonight and leave for Odepeth in the morning."

That was the opposite of what she should probably do. Norah could name more than one person who'd chide her for trusting strangers, including herself. She eyed the girl. Hells—she knew a good spirit when she met one. "I think I'll actually take you up on that offer. It's incredibly kind, thank you."

Calla smiled again. "This way," she said as she started down a trail through the trees, waving for her brother to join.

Norah followed Calla and Cohen down a trail that opened into a meadow. A small homestead sat in the sunset. She smiled at the cobbled farmhouse as they approached. It was humble but well cared for, with boxes of thick-stemmed flowers hanging under the windows. Evergreen shrubs lined the graveled walkway to the front door, and dark flagstone on the side led to a large garden. "Do you and Cohen live here by yourselves?" she asked.

"With our grandparents," the girl answered.

"How will they feel about a visitor?"

"I don't know," Calla replied. "We never have visitors."

That was a good sign. She should be able to keep to herself if she wasn't on a path well traveled.

"You can hobble your horse on the side if you'd like."

"That's all right," Norah said, pulling the saddle from the mare. "She won't go anywhere."

Calla gave her a doubtful look. "She's really pretty. Would be a shame to lose her."

"It would be, but she's fine."

Calla shrugged. "C'mon," she said, tipping her head toward the garden.

"Apah! Amah!" Calla called as she walked.

A head rose from between the thick rows of green and yellow, and a man stepped out into the pathway. He was an older man, his long hair tied back and grayed by time, but there was no mistaking the evidence of a warrior. The inked skin on his arms told her he'd seen his share of battles—he still looked like he could manage a few more, but a heavy limp slowed his walk. He carried a small bucket and tossed a handful of pulled weeds into it, not yet aware of Norah. He replied to Calla in the Kharavian tongue, brushing his hand on his apron.

"Apah," Calla called again for his attention. "We have a visitor."

The man looked up and stopped. He stared at Norah as he slowly set down his bucket. He was darker than the children, and the lines on his skin told his years. His eyes moved to Calla and then Cohen. He looked at the mare, then back to Norah. She could feel his unease.

"I don't mean to impose," Norah tried to assure him. "I'm only passing through."

"Marta," he called over his shoulder.

A woman stepped out of the flora to join him, equally wary of their visitor. Norah looked over her with curiosity. Her skin was light, like her own. And despite the gray of her hair, it hadn't been black in her youth. This woman wasn't from Kharav.

"We don't have many visitors, but you're welcome here," the man said.

"Thank you. I mean to stay for only the night, and then I'll be on my way in the morning."

He eyed the mare again, distracted, but then pulled his gaze back to Norah. He glanced around. "You're traveling alone?"

She supposed it did seem odd that a lone woman would be traveling across a foreign kingdom. She hoped that was the only thing that seemed odd to him. "Yes."

He looked at his wife, quiet, but then gave Norah a nod. "I'm Hamed," he said, then gesturing to the woman, "and this is my wife, Marta. Come. Let's go inside."

Marta placed her basket full of leafy greens on a preparation table, and Calla started washing them in a large bowl of water.

Norah watched, fascinated, as everyone busied themselves with dinner. "You have a full garden in winter?" she asked, trying for polite conversation.

"While it's cold, it doesn't freeze here in the valley," Hamed said. "We can get away with a good variety of winter vegetables. It's one of the many reasons we like it here."

Cohen quickly set bowls on the table and then went to fetch water in a pitcher. Hamed stirred the coals on the fire, fueling the heat under the pot that hung from above. Calla added her chopped vegetables and smiled at her grandfather as he held the lid for her.

"So, you just live out here by yourselves?" Norah asked.

Hamed gave a nod. "We lead a simple life, but it's ours." He looked over and smiled at Marta lovingly.

Norah's heart warmed. They seemed content. Happy. She wondered how they came to be together.

"Japheth," Marta said.

"What?" she asked.

"It's what you are wondering, yes? Where I'm from?"

Norah looked at her in surprise. "No. I mean, yes. You don't look like you're from Kharav." Then she eyed Hamed with a raised brow. "Well, you do, obviously. But I was mostly wondering how you two came to be together."

"Apah was a warrior," Calla said proudly. "He saved Amah's life, fell instantly in love with her, and then wooed her with his charm."

A warrior. Her eyes traveled back to the markings on his arms. Yes, he had definitely been a warrior.

The old man gave a chuckle.

"All true," Marta told Norah. "I was taken by Japheth soldiers and brought to their camp for entertainment. Fortunately, this was at the border of where Japheth and Kharav meet. Hamed saw from his border post and intervened. Can you imagine? A Kharavian soldier taking a Japheth woman from the Japheth army on Japheth land? This was back when Japheth was still part of the Aleon Empire, before being allied with Kharav. Almost started a war in the process." She smiled at her husband. "I couldn't return after that, so he brought me to his mother, who took me in."

Calla grinned. "Then he discovered she liked flowers and wove a bracelet of white lacies for her every day until she agreed to marry him."

Hamed grunted. "I suppose I was charming."

"Still are," Marta said with a smile.

Norah laughed. She would be fortunate to have a life like this.

Marta took the bowls and filled them with stew from the hearth. Calla carried them to the table as Cohen poured cups of water. Hamed motioned for her to sit, and they all took their places. He poured some tea from the pot Marta placed in front of him and calmly took a drink.

"Forgive me," he said, "but I can't help but ask the most troublesome question of why you're traveling on your own, in such a state. Are you fleeing? Do you need help?"

Norah shifted uncomfortably, looking around the table. How would she explain her situation? "I'm not fleeing," she replied, then mumbled to herself, "although I'm sure Artem thinks otherwise."

Hamed raised his brow. "Captain Artem?"

Norah stopped and cursed herself, realizing her mistake. A weight grew in her stomach. Hamed had been a warrior. Of course he'd know who the captain of the Crest was.

He stirred his stew in his bowl, silent.

Norah's heart pulsed in her throat. "You know him?" she asked, trying to hide the disquiet in her voice.

Hamed sat back in his chair. But he didn't answer.

"Artem thinks my brother's an abomination," Calla spoke up angrily. "Like being deaf makes him not fit to live."

Norah's eyes widened as she shifted her attention to the girl—it wasn't the response to Artem she'd been expecting, but neither was it surprising.

"Calla," Hamed scolded, trying to restrain her, but the girl ignored him.

"He wanted my father to leave Cohen at an orphanage, to throw him away, like he was nothing. Well, my brother wields a sword better than anyone in the Crest, including Captain Artem!"

"Calla," Hamed warned, stronger this time.

Cohen looked at his sister and gave her a small smile.

Calla gave him a wink. "If they'd had a warrior like Cohen, maybe Kharav would've already taken back Bahoul from those Northern cowards."

"Callamine!" Hamed snapped.

Calla's head jerked toward her grandfather in confusion. "Apah! You know—"

"Hold your tongue!" He looked at Norah with an uneasy eye. "She doesn't know what she says."

He feared for his granddaughter. Norah's pulse quickened.

"Why would you say that?" Calla persisted.

A silence fell over them.

Norah's heart hammered against her ribs. "Because he knows who I am," she said. She didn't take her eyes from Hamed. "Don't you?"

The old man shifted in his chair. "Yes, Salara," he said finally.

She was pleasantly surprised that he didn't call her the North Queen like so many others. Calla and Cohen gaped at her in astonishment.

"How did you know?" she asked. "Did Artem give it away?"

"You're clearly not from Kharav. I've heard of the North Queen with winter hair, and"—Hamed paused—"your horse, the Wild one. I've seen only one other like it before, ridden by the North King."

Norah's heart leapt into her throat. "My father rode a horse of the Wild? You saw him?"

Hamed nodded, taking Marta's hand. "Years ago. In battle. The day my son died"—his eyes moved to Calla and Cohen—"and their mother."

Norah's heart fell. Calla and Cohen's parents had both been warriors, and both died in the war. It had claimed so much from so many on both sides. She suddenly became aware that perhaps her presence brought them pain. Her father had led forces against them in war. "You don't have to offer the Mercian king's daughter your hospitality," she said softly. "I understand the pain I must cause you."

"I offer my hospitality to my salara. You honor us, and our home."

Norah forced a smile as her eyes brimmed with tears. How could people continue to be so kind after suffering such loss?

"So, if you're not fleeing, what are you doing? What's in Odepeth?" Calla asked her.

Hamed cast his granddaughter a look of disapproval, but Norah found herself appreciating the girl's boldness.

"There's a man there. A seer. I'm hoping he can help me."

"You want to see the future?" Calla asked.

And the past, but Norah would keep that to herself. She only nodded.

"Going by yourself—that seems like a lot to go through just to see a vision," Hamed said.

It *was* a lot to go through. "There are so many things that don't make sense. I'm just trying to find answers." She hoped that was enough of an explanation. It was all she could give. "Anyway, I just need to get there."

"We could go with you, Cohen and I," the girl offered. She turned to her grandfather. "We could help her."

"Your kindness has helped me more than you can imagine," Norah said quickly, already feeling indebted to them. "But it's probably best if I go alone."

"You can't really think that," Calla challenged. "The North Queen, traveling without protection." The girl quieted, then shrugged apologetically. "Salara, I mean."

Hamed nodded. "Lone travel isn't safe for an outsider, even you, Salara. I can't ride to see you there myself with my ailment, but you'll find Calla savvy of the city, good with a bow, and Cohen skilled with a sword. I've trained them myself."

"You've given enough already," Norah said. "And I worry about attention coming to your family for your part in my transgressions."

"You're salara, you have no transgressions," Hamed said, surprising her. "And to be a member of the Crest is a great honor for a soldier. It would bring great honor to our family to serve in their stead."

This family amazed her. "How can I refuse?" she said finally.

They all let out a laugh. Even Cohen was grinning. Norah's heart was full and grateful.

Chapter Three

Caspian stretched his travel-worn muscles as he rode. He had just returned to Kharav from his journey to Mercia, and had been back only a couple of hours before he found himself thrust into a journey to find Queen Norah. It was a situation he'd never imagined—tracking his queen in partnership with the Destroyer through the Shadowlands—yet he couldn't say he was entirely surprised. Nothing surprised him when it came to Norah. He just wondered what she was up to.

The captain of the Crest joined them, Captain Artem. He wasn't the kind of man Caspian could relate to, or the kind of man he could imagine leading the Crest to protect Norah at all costs. He was the kind of man Caspian knew to watch.

And then there was the Shadow commander, the Destroyer. This was the man Caspian needed to be the most wary of, be the most cautious of. Regardless of whether the stories of the Destroyer were all true, he was certainly the most dangerous—he moved with an unnatural power and had eyes that saw right through a man, into his soul. He fed off fear, and he knew how to make people afraid. And he seemed in a particularly foul mood.

But regardless of the company, Caspian was appreciative to be part of the search. He'd rather be doing something than simply waiting for the queen's return, although he wasn't keen on the thought of bringing Norah back to the Shadow King if her intent had been to leave. He told himself he'd find her and take her wherever she wished to go.

"She rode north," Artem said as they passed through the gates and out of the capital city of Ashan. "We can head toward the Canyonlands and hope to pick up her tracks there."

"You can't track a horse from the Wild," the commander said. His voice held an edge of annoyance. "But we'll start there, with the Uru."

Caspian didn't know what he meant by *a horse from the Wild,* but he was more focused on the icy air between the captain and the commander. This was going to be interesting.

They spurred their horses northwest, riding in silence. Caspian found himself curious about the western pass and the Horsemen tribe that watched over it. Previously, he'd only traveled the eastern pass, taking the route through Bahoul.

Kharav fascinated him. For a kingdom viewed as being so evil in the eyes of men, it seemed to hold the gods' favor. It was protected by the earth itself, with its mazed canyons on the north side and sharp cliffs on the south and eastern sea sides. With the addition of their Urun friends, who stretched from the north canyons and partway down the western borders, the Shadowlands were positioned favorably. It was a kingdom not easily breached.

Aleon had once tried to take the Shadowlands. King Mathias, King Phillip's grandfather, had moved against them when he overtook the eastern kingdoms to form the great empire of Aleon. It was an infamous battle, but in the end, the Shadowlands stood strong. Caspian had never imagined himself within its borders. Now that he was, he had to give it due respect.

Despite the unpleasant company, they moved fast, and time passed quickly. The Destroyer pushed on mercilessly, not allowing them to slow. The sun set as they rode, and they continued on. As darkness fell, the moon sat full in the sky, and they easily found their way in its light.

Finally, the ridges of the canyons loomed dark against the moonlit sky, and they slowed their mounts. The night lay quiet, save for the chitters of wildlife in the distance.

"Is there a village?" Caspian asked. "Where are these Uru?"

The commander didn't answer, but Artem gave a dark chuckle. Caspian couldn't help the tension growing in his shoulders, and he kept his hand on the hilt of his sword.

They reached the base of the canyons, and all lay still around them. As they rode into the shadows of the narrow slot canyon, the pit in his stomach grew heavier. The commander pulled up his mount and slid down.

"Why are we stopping?" Caspian asked as he swung down from his own horse.

"We're here," Artem said.

Caspian was just about to ask more when a movement behind him made him spin and draw his sword. Shadows shifted around them—a man, Caspian realized. Then more. Many more.

The commander spoke in the Shadow tongue, and the man answered. Their exchange was brief, but there was no mistaking his respect for the commander. The mysterious man barked orders into the night around them, and he gave a low whistle with a chitter into the dark of the canyons. Caspian realized it hadn't been animals he'd heard.

They followed the Uru farther into the canyons, deep into the narrow slots of earth. Caspian knew the dangers of these mazes, where a man could easily lose himself. But the commander knew his way, and Caspian followed. The narrow canyon opened back up to the sky, and he was thankful to again have a little more sight.

They rounded a corner, and a village appeared. Houses of rock, stacked and layered, sprawled wide. He paused and momentarily stared in amazement at its sheer size. He was no stranger to Horsemen tribes—they spanned the vast lands beyond Mercia's outer reaches—but he'd never seen one this large.

They continued. The hour was late, and few fires remained, although a large central fire still blazed bright. As they drew closer to the light, Caspian could better see the man they'd been following. The Horseman was covered in twisted strips of leather and fabric, with ghostly coloring spread over his face and the bare-skin areas of his chest and back.

As they reached the central fire, a woman emerged from the darkness. She had long dark hair, interwoven with braids and feathers, and beautifully wild. Black paint striped her brow and cheeks. Her eyes burned fiercely. There was a strength about her. Caspian had never seen anything like her, and it was as if he'd been struck.

"Soren," she greeted as she approached. Interesting that she would address the Destroyer by his name. Caspian realized he hadn't even known his name. She gave a wry smile. "I wish I had known you were coming. I would have come to meet you properly."

"Tahla," the commander said with a nod.

Tahla. Her name was Tahla.

"Aleon places additional forces along the borders," Soren told her.

Caspian glanced at him. King Phillip was moving forces south along the border? He hadn't known that information. It unsettled him further, with Norah out alone.

The Horsewoman nodded pensively. "Salar sent word, but we've seen nothing. Regardless, we've called our men in the hills back to the canyons. We'll spread them east for more eyes."

"Good," he replied.

Tahla eyed Caspian suspiciously. "You ride with a Northman? Surprising."

"Is it?" the commander replied. "Our kingdoms are joined. It should be no surprise our forces are joined as well."

"You command him?" she asked the Destroyer, not taking her eyes from Caspian.

"The commander leads," Caspian cut in. "But I answer to my queen."

"What about your salar?" she challenged.

Caspian knew he was being tested. "Queen Norah would expect my obedience to him, and so I give it."

Tahla looked him over, seeming not to have made up her mind about him, but her eyes were curious, and he waited patiently as they explored him. "How is Salara?" she asked. "I trust you're keeping my sister safe."

Caspian noted her fondness for the queen, and that she obviously hadn't seen her. "Keeping her safe is what I've dedicated my life to," he replied honestly.

"Good." She turned back to the commander. "Stay. We'll see you rested and fed."

"We need to keep going," the commander replied, "but we're in need of food and fresh horses."

"Of course." Tahla nodded as she turned and motioned them around the large fire.

"You didn't tell her about the North Queen," the commander said to Caspian, low so that only he could hear.

"She obviously hasn't seen her. And the fewer people who know of a lone queen roaming the open, the better."

The Shadow commander gave the slightest tilt of his head. "You surprise me."

"In that you agree with me?"

"In that you seem like a smart Northman. A rarity."

Caspian gave an amused puff of breath at the complimentary insult. And he didn't so much think himself smart as just... not stupid.

It was quiet at the late hour, but people emerged from their stone houses to eagerly greet the commander. They seemed not only to respect the formidable Shadowman, but also to genuinely like him. *Quite peculiar.*

A large woman handed Caspian a bowl of soup and a loaf of bread. "Thank you," he said as he accepted it.

He took a seat on a rock not far from Tahla and watched her in the firelight. She laughed as she talked to a man beside her, and Caspian sat, fixated on her beauty. The paint on her face did little to hide her high, chiseled cheekbones or the slender slope of her nose. This was a dangerous woman, he could tell right away, but it made no difference. He saw only her eyes, the shape of her face, the graceful way she moved in the flickering light of the flames.

And then her eyes found him. They burned brightly, seeing into him. Through him. His skin prickled over his arms, across his neck, and down his back. Inside, he twisted and fought the strange hold taking over.

The commander kicked his boot, bringing Caspian back.

"What has you?" the Shadowman asked with a hint of annoyance. "Finish and get a horse. We've a long ride still ahead."

Caspian forced his senses back. "Where?" he asked. "Did you get an idea of where she might be?"

"I know she's not here. And she didn't come this way. Perhaps she flees to Aleon through the eastern pass." The commander let out an irritated sigh.

Flee? "She wouldn't flee, not now," Caspian said. "She doesn't just give up; she's too intent on bringing peace. Knowing Norah, she's probably searching for answers, or a way to solve whatever problem is in front of her. And Aleon is the last place she would go."

The commander looked at him with a skeptical eye.

"Aleon's forces must be quite worrisome if this calls for a joint effort," Tahla called out to the commander from where she stood by the fire. "Maybe I should go with you? Or send warriors?"

"I'll take you up on a couple men," the commander said.

"Will more men not slow us down?" Caspian asked him quietly.

The Shadowman shrugged. "If I said no, she'd just come herself. We'll cut them loose when we're clear from the canyons."

Caspian suppressed a chuckle. "Just like the queen. There's no telling her not to do something."

The Shadowman stopped. He stared at Caspian with a strange stillness in his eyes.

"Commander?"

"If she's not fleeing, then I think I know where she's headed."

Caspian furrowed his brow. "Where?"

"Get your horse."

Caspian's pulse quickened as he saddled a horse from the Uru. It was a larger beast than he was used to, and he couldn't help but admire the quality of the stock. He gave the animal a light pat on the shoulder and turned, nearly colliding with Tahla right behind him.

The corners of her mouth turned up in amusement. "You're a long way from home, Northman."

Her voice held a smokiness, and it lingered in his ear. His mind told him to step back from her, to put space between them, but his body refused. She held him with a force unseen to the eye. He had a task at hand, but he could no longer recall it. What was this power?

"Are you an enchantress?" he asked her.

Tahla laughed, leaning closer. "Do you find yourself enchanted?"

"Enchanted, bewitched," he said. "What other explanation?"

"Do you wish to be free?" she asked in a low voice.

He didn't answer, gripped by her nearness.

Tahla's smile softened. "Can I ask something of you?"

"Anything." He meant it.

She held out a soft leather sachet of scented gifts. "Will you give this to Salara, with my well-wishes?"

The mention of the queen brought him back, and he let out a breath, freed temporarily from the trance. "That seems like hardly an ask at all," he said. "But I'll deliver it to her hands myself."

Tahla smiled. He couldn't get enough.

She cast a wary eye toward the commander and then back to him. "You should be on your way. Soren won't be too keen on me giving a handsome Northman my attention."

Caspian leaned back, glancing at the commander, then back to her. Of course she'd be taken, a woman like this. "My apologies. I, uh... I didn't know you two were..."

Tahla laughed as she shook her head. "No. We're not. But Soren is protector of the Uru, and our family."

Strange to think the Destroyer protective over anyone, but his pulse quickened, and he gave an encouraged nod. "Well... did I hear correctly that you found me handsome?" Then he cursed himself silently. *Stupid thing to say.* This shouldn't be the topic on his mind, but how easy it was for her to pull his attention, to make him forget even his name.

"Hair of the sun. How can I not?"

He smiled. "Then I can't let you meet another Northman."

She let out another laugh. Then, growing more serious, she asked, "Will I see you again?"

"I'll make certain of it," he promised. And he meant it.

Chapter Four

His destrier moved anxiously underneath him with an uneven gait, as it did just before the charge into battle. No doubt it felt the tension in its rider, and Alexander was indeed in the midst of a battle, a battle of mind and heart.

He dropped his hand to the thick neck of the beast, patting it underneath the silk of its white mane to settle it, or maybe to settle himself. It had been a difficult journey to Aleon, in more ways than one, and while he wasn't eager to return to the Shadowlands, he was eager to return to Norah. He ignored the beauty of Aleon's capital city, Valour, with its manicured gardens and fountains that wound through the silver-stone structures that seemed to reach to the sky, its patinaed domes that covered the hills in additional layers of green. None of it mattered.

What mattered was that Norah would be safe here.

And out of the clutches of their enemy.

He urged his mount down the mainway, under the blue banners of the lion. Once past the front gates and posted city guard, he turned and headed south, back to the Shadowlands.

Alexander hadn't wanted to come to Aleon, but the council's task had been clear, and one he couldn't refuse. Not just because of the council's authority. He knew he had to come.

Norah wanted peace so badly—enough to sacrifice herself for it. But he wouldn't let her. It was only a matter of time before the alliance fell apart, and he wouldn't let her fall with it. It wasn't easy choosing between what she wanted and what she needed, what was best for her and what was best for Mercia. But he'd made a vow. He'd sworn himself. And more than that—he loved her, and there was nothing he wouldn't do for her, nothing he wouldn't give, even if it broke him. It was already breaking him, over and over again, as Norah was taken from him. He'd lost her, and he kept losing her. Over and over again.

He would bear it, and continue to bear it, so long as she was safe.

But she wasn't safe now. He cast a last look over his shoulder at the Aleon capital as he rode out. He would do what he had to. No matter the cost.

Chapter Five

The journey was long but relatively peaceful, save for Calla's continuous conversation. Norah didn't mind. She found herself growing quite fond of the girl, who was confident, proud, and fiercely loyal. She noticed Cohen's smile as he watched his sister talk, and his admiration for her.

By the end of the day, Odepeth loomed into view. The city stood like an ancient oasis, a stark contrast to the barren high desert around it. Stacked stone formed the foundations, but it wasn't dark like Ashan, Kharav's capital city. It was bright, golden even, and it glistened in the sun. Not at all like she'd expected.

Calla pointed to the temple in the center. "That's where the seer is."

Norah frowned. "That's it? He just spends his days in the center of a small city in the middle of nowhere?"

Calla shrugged. "Pretty much. How are you going to get in? Only Kharavian royal blood may enter the temple."

"Well..." She hadn't thought it through entirely. "I was just going to walk in."

For once, the girl was speechless.

"What does the seer look like?" Norah asked.

"I don't know. I've never seen him." Calla wrinkled her face. "Old, I bet. What are you going to do about the guards? They won't let you in, even if they know you're salara."

Norah puffed a breath through her lips. She really should have thought this through. "What do you propose?"

Calla was silent for a moment. "I can distract them in the front by trying to enter there. I'm good at making a spectacle." She grinned mischievously. "And you and Cohen can slip inside from the back. But I've never been inside, so I can't tell you what you'll find there. More guards, likely."

Norah moved her hand to the hilt of the sword at her side. She was thankful that Hamed had lent it to her. She looked at Cohen. "How good are you with a sword? Really?"

He shrugged and gave a flat wave of his hand.

That wasn't comforting. And she wasn't entirely sure how good *she* was with a sword. She supposed she'd find out on both accounts.

They left their horses in an inconspicuous hitching area. Norah worried the mare might draw attention, but there wasn't much she could do about it. It wasn't easy to hide a horse. They split up, Calla curving around and making her way through the streets to the temple from the front, and Norah and Cohen approaching from the back. Although small, the city was dense, with the buildings mostly connected to one another. The structural faces of the houses varied, making it easy for Norah and Cohen to slip stealthily from corner to corner. They reached the point where the structures ended, and a long sweep of stairs started to the temple. Two guards stood at the top. Norah looked at Cohen from his hiding place across the walk, and they waited.

True to Calla's plan, her exaggerated attempted entry from the front of the temple pulled the attention of even the rear guards, and they left their posts to aid their fellow guardsmen. Norah and Cohen moved quickly, racing to the top of the stairs. They paused outside a set of large double doors.

Norah struggled to listen over the pulse of her heart pounding in her ears. This was it. She had risked a lot to come here. And what if they couldn't find the seer? What if the seer refused to see her? Worse, what if she was caught and turned back over to Artem and the Crest?

Cohen put his hand on her arm. While he was deaf, he seemed to *see* everything. He gave her an encouraging nod. He wasn't asking her if she was all right—he was telling her. All without words. And her strength returned.

They pulled open one of the oaken doors and slipped inside, finding themselves in a hall that ran along the perimeter of the temple's base. High arches made up the inside wall that opened to a large center, filled with delicately carved stone pillars. Norah followed it around, with Cohen close beside her.

The temple seemed empty. They turned a corner, and a man surprised them. A guard. He wore a crimson robe and was armed with a bladed staff. "Halt," he said to them.

"I've come to speak to the seer," she told him, as confidently as she could muster.

"You're forbidden," he answered angrily. "Leave this place."

She pulled back the hood of her cloak. "I'm salara," she said firmly. "I'll leave after I speak to the seer."

"You'll leave now," he answered.

Norah bit the inside of her lip. She really had imagined this differently.

The guard pulled up his bladed staff. "Do not make me remove you."

Barbs of anger prickled along her back. "You can try," she challenged as she pulled her sword from its scabbard. Then she cursed herself—probably not the wisest reply, as she was pretty sure he *could* remove her. *Easily.*

Cohen stepped forward with his own blade in hand.

The guard started toward them, and she cursed again under her breath. She had hoped for a more tactful approach, but she wasn't faring well.

The guard rushed Cohen with an overhand swing, and for a moment, fear flashed through her. The guard was twice as large as Cohen and surely doubly as skilled. But the boy used the arc of the guard's swing to his advantage, stepping left and delivering a blow that steered the man's momentum to the side. Cohen spun and swung outward in a move that hooked the guard's helm and flung it from his head. Then he lunged, whipping up his elbow and catching the man under his chin. The guard dropped to the floor.

Norah stood, shocked at the extraordinarily short fight she just witnessed. Then her eyes narrowed at the young man. "Cohen, I don't think you've been entirely honest with me."

He gave a sheepish smile.

Footsteps sounded behind her, and she turned to see three more guards running their way. *Great.* Norah readied her own sword. She glanced at Cohen, and he nodded.

Norah clenched the handle of her sword, calling to it, and it answered with familiarity. The first guard thrust his staff forward, and she spun along it, bringing her blade down and cleaving it in two. He tumbled forward, off balance, and she sliced her blade into his thigh. *Not bad,* she pepped herself.

Norah met another guard with a counter swing as he lunged at her. The sound of steel rang in the air. To her left, she heard Cohen's sword working, but she couldn't peel her eyes to look. The temple guard lunged forward again. She swept up her sword to respond, but the power of his strikes beat her back. She wavered. He was too close. Dangerously close. Mikael's words came back to her. Her strength was speed, and she needed to protect it with distance. But she had no distance. She stumbled backward, but the temple wall stopped her retreat. The guard grabbed her sword arm. She tried to push him off, but she wasn't strong enough.

It had been a terrible idea to come here.

Just then, the guard's head bounced forward from a blow from behind. He released her and crumpled to the ground. Behind him stood Cohen.

Norah's eyes darted around the hall. There were more than four wounded guards that lay on the ground. She hadn't even realized two more had come. And Cohen had managed them.

She feigned a scowl. "Now that's just bragging."

The corner of his mouth turned up, but it was too early to celebrate a victory. He grabbed her hand and pulled her down the hall.

When they rounded another corner, they skidded to a stop.

In front of them stood more guards, twenty at least. Footsteps rang behind them, and Norah jerked her head to see more. A lot more.

Her spark of hope was quickly snuffed. There were too many guards, even with Cohen's skill. This was definitely a terrible idea. Now they were caught. She was caught. No doubt she'd be in Captain Artem's hands again by nightfall, with nothing to show for it. In fact, she'd be in a more precarious situation than before.

Her heart hurt. She'd gotten Cohen into quite a mess, and Calla too. She wondered where the girl was. She couldn't let them get hurt. They had only been helping her.

The guards closed in around them, and Norah reached back and clasped Cohen's arm, stilling him.

It was over.

"Let them be," a voice called, bringing them all to a pause.

Norah jerked her head to see from where it came. The guards parted, and an elderly man walked through. "It's not very often I'm surprised," he told her.

Norah looked at the guards. They reluctantly withdrew a few paces but watched her closely. She turned back to the man. "You're the seer?"

He gave a single nod. Calla had been right, he *was* old. He wore a simple brown robe, modest and unpretentious, not at all what she had imagined of the head of a highly guarded temple. His head was shaved bare, or perhaps he grew no hair, but his white beard hung long and straight.

"I'm sorry," she started. "I don't mean to intrude... or cause such a mess... but it's very important I speak with you." She needed to see these visions he'd shown Mikael. Maybe she could make better sense of them. And if he could unlock her memories...

"It must be important if it brings the North Queen to my temple," he said.

"You know who I am?"

"It's also not very often I meet the subjects of my visions," he told her.

"Your visions are why I'm here. I need to see them."

He frowned. "You want me to tell you of them?"

"No, I want you to show me."

He shifted back in surprise. "I do not conjure them in the air," he said stiffly.

"But you're a traveler, are you not?"

The briefest look of surprise flashed across his face. "How do you know such things?"

"You are, then."

He didn't answer; he only turned and started deeper into the temple. "Follow me," he said over his shoulder. "The boy waits outside."

Norah turned back to Cohen. "He's agreed to see me," she told him. He hadn't seen the seer's lips to read them. "But he asks that you stay outside."

Cohen gave a reluctant nod, sheathing his sword.

"Thank you, friend," she mouthed, then turned back to the seer.

Norah followed him through the pillared room, to a door, and down a narrow hall that opened into a smaller room. Lit candles stood in each corner, with sitting mats in the center.

"So, the North Queen returns," he said. "How did you escape my sight for so many years? What power do you have?"

Norah shook her head. "I don't have power. And I don't know."

His aged eyes narrowed.

"I tell you the truth. In fact, it's part of the reason I'm here. My memories were taken from me, or locked away, rather. I was hoping you could help me get them back."

She took a seat on one of the pillows in the center of the room and waited. He stood for a moment before he finally took his seat on the pillow across from her. He eyed her skeptically.

Norah still waited, resisting the want to urge him along.

The seer reached to a thin mat near his cushion and took a cup in his hand. Ink markings trailed his forearms to the rolled cuffs of his sleeves. These were different from the patterned markings the Shadowmen bore. Their dark bands with rune images in between looked more like a written language.

Norah leaned forward. Nemus, the Mercian traveler seer, had similar markings, but he had penned them on. The markings of this seer were permanent, like Mikael's markings. The thought of Mikael brought a twinge to her stomach. He'd know now she was gone. Did he think she'd betrayed him? The pain in his eyes when he saw that she wanted to leave...

She couldn't think about that right now, and she forced the hurt in her heart down, turning her attention back to the seer. "You've permanently inked the spells onto your skin?" she asked.

The seer pulled back. "Easier than drawing them on each time. And they're not spells."

"What are they?"

The seer pursed his lips.

She leaned back, giving him space as he poured wine into the cup. "What's your name?" she asked.

He paused, and for a moment she thought he might not answer. "Bhasim," he said finally. "But I've not been called that for a long time."

The lord commander had said only those with Kharavian royal blood were permitted in the temple. Was Bhasim all alone? Besides his guards, was there no one else who spoke to him?

Bhasim sat with a cup of wine in his hand. "They're not spells, they're staves," he said.

"What are staves?"

He eyed her warily, obviously not used to conversation about his power, or perhaps not used to conversation at all. "The power of the Gift is not easy to wield. It can consume the body. One must protect himself, and the staves give this protection. The more powerful the Gift, the more protection required."

Bhasim bore more markings than Nemus, which meant he was a more powerful traveler than the Mercian seer. Mikael had said he was the most powerful seer in the four kingdoms—which four kingdoms, she wasn't certain. But her excitement grew. He might be able to help her where Nemus couldn't.

Bhasim breathed a silent spell into the air.

"Why do you need the blood?" she interrupted. She didn't think his lips could get any thinner, but they did. Was he annoyed?

"You seem to already know quite a bit about seers." But where she expected a dismissive reply, he only asked, "Do you know of the Eye?"

She searched her mind of her visit with Nemus in Mercia, but he'd only mentioned that he had no control of what the Eye showed him. "It's what shows you the future?"

He frowned, as if somewhat disappointed in her awareness. "To get to the Eye, one must step into the Aether, the place through which all energy flows. The Aether connects us all, but it's a place of chaos. It is easy to find the Eye, but to *travel* to others, we need the blood spell to find our way, and to connect. Our blood calls us and lets us in." He paused, eyeing her. "May I continue now?"

She swallowed and nodded.

He breathed his spell again. Then he pricked his finger and squeezed a small drop of blood into the goblet and held the cup for Norah.

She took it and drank it, then closed her eyes and tried to relax. Even though she knew what to expect, she still jumped with a start when he came to her. Bhasim kept his current form, unlike Nemus, who'd shown his younger self.

In her mind, they stood in the same temple, only it was dark, with long cloths that draped from an endless sky, creating rooms of memories between them. She turned, seeing all around her, almost overwhelmed by it all. With Nemus, there had been almost nothing.

They walked slowly, in silence, from memory to memory: seeing her grandmother for the first time, Alexander showing her through the castle, meeting with her council, talking to Adrian.

Norah paused.

A pain gripped her heart.

In front of her was the moment when Alexander found her in the forest. She watched him realize who she was. Now she understood the emotion in his face: the elation, the fear, the sting of her not knowing him. She wished she could touch him now, but he was only an image.

Another memory pulled her attention from Alexander.

Mikael.

The day of their wedding. His eyes were on her. Always, his eyes were on her. She smiled sadly and was surprised at the longing that pulled deep inside. She suddenly remembered she wasn't alone. "I'm sorry," she said, turning back to the seer.

He looked at her curiously, and they continued through the memories.

Suddenly, Bhasim stopped. "So, this is how you know of travelers."

She turned to see the image of her with Nemus.

He lingered at the memory, looking at it intently. "I've never seen another," he said quietly.

"Another traveler?"

He nodded. "Those of us with the Gift of sight have a shield—a shield that protects us from others with the Gift. It hides us from visions. I cannot see others, and they cannot see me. But to see in a memory..." He smiled. "I'd never thought of that."

"It must be very lonely," she said softly.

His eyes met hers, surprised. "It is."

"His name is Nemus," she said, realizing the significance to him.

"Nemus," he repeated back to himself.

Just then, something drew Norah's eye. Her pulse quickened.

The door—the door that had been locked and that Nemus couldn't open.

This was what she had come for. This was it. Nemus hadn't been strong enough to help her, but Bhasim could be.

Norah left Bhasim and moved to it, her heart racing. She reached out and grasped the knob, giving it a turn.

It clicked open.

It was so unexpected that it almost made her jump.

That was it? So easy now? Without even a struggle? Her breath shook as emotion swelled within her. To have her memories back, to have everything back—she couldn't even imagine.

She pushed it open. So easily.

And stepped inside.

The first memory she saw was one she was already familiar with—her and Alexander lying on their backs on the hill, in the summer sun. Where they'd made their plans. Where they'd dreamed.

And then the memory that had broken her—them under the tree before her father had taken her away, and Alexander telling her goodbye. It still tore her heart. Tears threatened, but she pushed them back. She wasn't here for this memory. She was here for the others.

Except there weren't others.

Norah stepped forward, but only darkness hung in front of her. "Where are they?" she breathed. "Where are the others?"

"There are no others," Bhasim said from beside her.

She shook her head. "No," she said, her voice shaking. "They have to be here. This is the door that wouldn't open. They're here. They have to be."

"There's nothing more here," he said.

Norah turned and ran back into the stone-columned hall of memories. Maybe she'd been mistaken. Maybe it had been another door that had been locked. "There has to be another." She charged the hall, searching, praying, pleading. There had to be another door.

"North Queen," Bhasim said, "there's nowhere in your mind I cannot see. There's nothing else of your past here."

That couldn't be. There couldn't be nothing. *No.* She felt the threads of desperation weaving their way into her being—growing, spreading, taking over. But she stopped and swallowed back the hopelessness. This wasn't defeat. This wasn't the end. It couldn't be.

He wasn't powerful enough, she told herself. She would find a way to get her memories back, just not here. She forced her mind to calm—she'd find another way. She told herself that over again. It was the only thing keeping her from the edge of complete defeat.

Then, an image caught her eye, and she stepped toward it. It was her, sitting on a bench in a garden. She didn't recognize the place. It wasn't Kharav, or Mercia, and it wasn't a memory, she was sure. "What is this?" she asked.

"Sometime in the future," Bhasim said. "Not all visions are of significance. Some are beautiful. Quiet. Peaceful. These are my favorites."

Norah watched herself as she sat on the bench. Her image held out her hand, and a butterfly landed on her palm. She smiled as she studied it, then she let it flutter into the air.

It brought her back to a place of calm, and she appreciated his showing it to her, but she shifted her attention back to the present, to visions that *were* of significance. "Will you show me what you showed the king?"

Bhasim gave a nod, and the image of her in the garden faded. The rooms fell into darkness. After a moment, a faint light came from one, and she drew closer to it. Something moved in the distance and started toward her. Norah squinted her eyes against the light.

A horse.

Horses.

Horses galloping toward her.

Norah stumbled back as a wave of mounted soldiers flooded past her. Their numbers were in the thousands. Blue—the color of Aleon. The soldiers held their weapons high in attack. She whirled around to see them clash against a sea of green—Japheth.

The scene changed. The same battle? A different battle? White mixed with blue, Mercia joined with Aleon. To her right, Kharavian forces battled another army she didn't recognize.

Norah turned back against the tide of war and saw herself. Riding beside her—the Aleon king. *Phillip.* They rode side by side, battled side by side.

Her heart beat in her throat as she staggered backward. She'd seen this image before. She knew what accompanied it. She spun around, her eyes combing the clash of death. She searched for him. *Alexander.*

And she found him. *No.* Norah ran toward him.

He slid off his black warhorse, his sword in his hand. But something was different about him, there were things she hadn't noticed when she'd first seen the painting of the vision in Mercia. His hair was cut short, his golden locks gone. Malice dripped from his skin. His black leather-plated armor was trimmed with the color of old blood, and on his shoulder, bladed pauldrons—not the head of the great Northern bear.

This wasn't right. This couldn't be Alexander.

His eyes were locked on the figure of a man downed by an arrow in front of him—a large, armored man in a horned helm. *Mikael.* Alexander stalked toward him as Mikael tried to pull himself backward and away. Mikael held his sword in his hand, but he didn't lift it. He didn't even try to fight—why wasn't he trying?

"Get up!" she cried. Why wasn't he fighting? "Mikael! Get up!"

Alexander swung his sword above his head.

"Alexander, no!" she screamed, but he couldn't hear her. "No!" she screamed again as he brought the blade down, severing the helmed head from the king's body. A cry ripped through her throat; the feeling of loss as real as if it had truly just happened.

The image faded and fell away, and Norah dropped to her knees on the marble floor with a sob. This couldn't be the future. It should have changed when they wed. This couldn't be Mikael's fate.

She wouldn't let it.

"How do I change it? Please," she begged, "tell me how to change it."

The seer shook his head. "You cannot change fate."

"Of course you can! My father saw me captured by the Shadow King and hid me away."

"Yet you were still captured," he said.

A chill rippled through her. How had she not realized it before? Her father hadn't seen the senior Shadow King capturing her. He'd seen Mikael. Her father took her away for fear of a danger that wouldn't come until years later.

He'd changed nothing.

What if she could change nothing?

Her emotion threatened again. What had she done to warrant a fate so cruel? Did the gods hate her? Did they even exist?

Well, damn the gods. Damn Hammel himself. They could curse her. They could take from her, but if they thought they could break her, they were wrong. If they thought she wouldn't fight, they were wrong.

Norah forced the despair-filled air from her lungs. She needed to pull herself together and figure out what to do next. She gathered her strength and stood.

"Thank you for seeing me, Bhasim," she whispered.

He gave a small bow of his head.

She turned to go, then paused. "What did you show the lord commander?" Mikael had said the commander wouldn't speak of it, even to him.

The seer hesitated. "That you must ask him."

How strange he'd share what he had shown Mikael, but not the commander. She didn't have the strength to press him for it, though.

She left the temple feeling like the air's weight would crush her. The vision of Mikael's fate seared her mind. It haunted her.

Calla ran to her as she stepped outside, with Cohen right behind her, and Norah was relieved to see them both safe.

"What happened?" the girl asked. "Did he refuse you?"

Norah shook her head.

"Then you saw? The visions? Did you get your answers?"

Norah shook her head again, the despair returning. Suddenly, her breath caught in her chest. The lord commander stood at the bottom of the temple stairs, axe in hand.

Waiting for her.

The sunlight hurt her eyes. Norah walked slowly down the stairs of the temple of the seer. The lord commander stood at the bottom, waiting. Her stomach churned. How had he found her? Behind him stood Captain Artem and four other soldiers: two of Artem's men and Bhastian and Javed from her own Crest guard. She hadn't expected to see Caspian, but he was a welcome surprise.

Cohen stepped in front of Norah and Calla and drew his sword.

"You don't want to do that, boy," the commander said from under the wrap hiding his face. He fixed his grip on his axe in warning.

But Cohen didn't move.

"I'll tell you only once to step aside," the commander warned.

"He can't hear you," Norah said as she put a hand on Cohen's shoulder to settle him. "And they're in my service, seeing me safe."

The lord commander snorted. "You put your safety in the hands of children instead of your captain? All for a seer who won't see you." He was so smug. *Ass.*

"The captain cares nothing for my safety, and you know it," she snapped. The commander looked over his shoulder at Artem. There was a strangeness between them, as if the commander were waiting for something. But no matter. "Have you come to escort me back, Lord Commander?" No point avoiding the obvious.

"You're most perceptive," he said with an icy edge in his voice.

The bitterness of disgust wormed its way up her throat. She had almost forgotten how much she hated this man. But as her eyes found Caspian, she managed a small nod. At least there was one man she could trust here. "Caspian," she greeted him.

He bowed with his fist to his chest as she drew nearer to him. "Queen Norah, I'm relieved to see you safe." He stepped closer, dropping his voice so that only she could hear. "While I've come on this mission to find you, it's not my intention to take you back if that's not what you want."

She didn't want to be taken back, but there was no avoiding it now. She would only endanger those she cared about. "Thank you, Caspian. But I have to go back. I need to repair things with the king." And she needed to find a way to change the vision.

Her mind turned back to Mikael, and guilt bubbled up inside her again. She wasn't sure what she would say when she saw him.

She turned to Calla. "I suppose this is where we part. I'm so thankful to you, and to Cohen and your grandparents. I wouldn't have made it here without you, and I'm in your debt."

Calla smiled. "It's been our greatest honor serving you, Salara. I only hope we have the fortune to see you again."

Norah reached out and hugged her tightly. "You will. I can promise you that."

She turned to Cohen, and he gave her an awkward bow. She handed him Hamed's sword and pulled him into a hug too. Then she stepped back so he could read her lips. "Thank you, master swordsman. You honor yourself and your family. Your father would be proud."

He gave an emotional smile.

"Take them back to their home," Soren said to the soldiers. Javed stepped forward.

"Caspian," Norah called, and he gave a nod. "I want you to go with Javed and see that Calla and Cohen return home safely." She didn't trust anyone else. Not after what happened to Bremhad, the greenskeeper and Kiran's father.

He started to object. "Queen Norah—"

"Please," she said softly. "They're very important to me. You know I'll make it back to the castle just fine."

Caspian sighed, giving a reluctant nod. "I'll see them safely home."

"And then I'll see you back at the castle." With one last look back at Calla and Cohen, Norah mounted her mare and turned toward Ashan.

The commander led the way, and Artem followed with his two soldiers and Bhastian. She rode between them. An anxious ache rolled in her stomach. Artem would find a way to punish her for slipping him. The commander would too. Had it been worth it? She had no more answers than when she'd started.

The lord commander set a fast pace, no doubt eager to get back. They traveled against the wind, and Norah had to hold the front of her hood while riding to keep it from blowing back. Her arm grew tired, and she let it go. It wasn't like she was trying to hide herself anymore. She'd been captured.

Hours passed, and a stitch grew deep in her stomach. She pressed her hand against the scar to allay the cramp. Finally, she could go no longer. They reached a small stream, and Norah slowed her mare to a halt. She slid to the ground. It felt good to stand again.

"We'll take a moment here," the commander called to the men as he reined his destrier nearer to her and dismounted, probably wary of another escape attempt. He pulled a skin of water from his saddlebag and held it out for her.

Norah eyed it. She would rather drink from the stream, even if it was a muddy stream, but she took it. She was thirsty, and as much as she hated to admit it, it was good. She drank her fill and handed it back to him, and he pulled down his wrap and took a drink as well.

"You were wrong, you know," she told him. "He did see me. The seer."

The commander stilled. His face darkened as he put the stop back on the waterskin. "What did he show you?"

"Everything."

A silence hung between them, and Norah could feel the rage under his calm—a rising, fearful rage. Whatever the seer had shown him—whatever he was hiding—he was afraid of it.

He looked over his shoulder at the men and then back at her. "What did he show you?" he asked again. There was a threat in his tone.

She moved to step past him, but he grabbed her arm, pulling her close with a tightness that hurt.

"Let me go!"

"What did he show you?" he hissed.

"What are you so afraid of?" she cut back.

His shoulders relaxed, and he released her arm. She could see it in his eyes—his relief. He knew she didn't know, and she cursed herself for speaking too quickly.

Norah couldn't help the frustration, the hopelessness that suddenly washed over her. She found a large rock to sit on and gazed blankly out at the uneven terrain. She came all this way, and for what? She'd married the Shadow King, and for what? The visions still held. While there was peace, it could break at any moment. She held the title of salara, but she could do nothing.

The commander looked at the sky. "Winter's returning, and a storm's coming. We need to go."

Let it come. She didn't care anymore. The hopelessness was overwhelming.

"North Queen," he called to her again.

She sat, not letting him push her to leave. "Why do you still call me that?"

"Are you not the North Queen?"

The hopelessness gave way to anger, and something snapped inside. "Am I not your salara?" she knifed back.

A rumble came from his chest. "Of course, *Salara*," he corrected himself, his voice thick with agitation.

She stood and faced him, all care gone, all caution gone. "That's what you'll call me from now on."

He snorted. "Surely you don't seek to quarrel now."

"What quarrel should I have with *my* commander?" she snapped. "You're *mine!*" Norah stepped forward, drawing close enough to touch him. A shaking fury rippled through her. "I'm salara! And Salar has committed to me everything of Kharav. Everything and *everyone.* He said you're a loyal man. Does he lie? Because all I've seen is your opposition to his promise at every turn. You *and* your men." She shot a daggered glance at Artem.

Black pools eddied in his eyes, but she refused to let them drown her. She returned his gaze with a dark intensity of her own. She had nothing more to lose.

"I am loyal to my salara," he said slowly, "as are the rest of my men."

Norah didn't believe him. She snapped out her hand, snatching the dagger from his belt and whipping the cold steel to his neck.

He didn't move.

Artem and his two soldiers behind him drew their swords. "Release him," Artem demanded.

Her Crest guard Bhastian stood unmoving, his eyes on the commander. He looked at Artem and then drew his sword slowly. That hurt her. She had started to think he was one of the few she could trust.

Norah tilted her head, bringing her eyes back to the commander. "Ah, yes. I see they're so very loyal to me."

His face twitched in a burning fury. Slowly, he reached up and curled his hand around the dagger in her hand. She wouldn't kill him, and he knew it. Defeat tethered her spirit. She let him pull it from her fingers, and he stepped backward, toward his men.

Her strength left her.

She wasn't salara.

She wasn't queen.

She was a prisoner.

But then the commander turned, letting out a growl, and drove the dagger into the soldier to his left. Bhastian swung his sword out, slicing open the throat of Artem's other man. The commander recoiled, then grabbed Artem by his breastplate and pushed him to his knees, onto the ground. "You fail Salar," he seethed.

"My lord!" Artem cried out, but he wasn't able to finish his plea before the commander pushed the point of the dagger into the front of his neck and through to the back.

Norah stumbled backward in shock and gulped a startled breath.

The commander pulled the blade out slowly and held Artem by the hair, watching the dying captain choke on his own blood. Artem flailed his arms, grasping for life as it left him. When his struggling gurgles stopped, the commander let his body drop to the ground.

Norah gaped at him, wide-eyed and speechless.

The commander turned back to her, stepping forward and sinking to his knees. He held the dagger by its bloodied blade, offering it to her. "If you doubt me." But his voice still betrayed his hatred.

Of course she doubted him. Did he think this would absolve him? Her breath shook, but she forced it quiet. She could no longer let him go unchallenged. "Killing your men doesn't remove my doubt."

"Only one man here is mine, and he still stands."

Bhastian.

"The others were not," he added. "They take up arms against you and are traitors to the crown. Let me share their fate if you judge me the same."

She took the dagger slowly. The commander pulled down his wrap farther and let his head fall back slightly, exposing his neck. She clutched the handle tightly. It was warm from his grip, and she pressed it against his skin at the base of his throat. He sat motionless, except for the rise and fall of his chest.

She wanted to kill him, or rather, she wanted to want to kill him. She wanted to rid herself of him. But she couldn't. That wasn't what strength was to her. She sighed, lowering the knife. "You already know I won't kill you. But just because I won't doesn't mean I'm weak."

His voice came low. "I've never thought you were weak."

"Why do you hate me?"

He clenched his jaw with a twitch of irritation. "Because you'll be the end of Salar. You'll be the end of all of us."

"You really believe that?"

"It doesn't matter what I believe," he seethed. "I told you I'm loyal, and I am."

"Hate pours off you. Is that really loyalty?"

"I am, nonetheless. I have been, ever since Salar wanted you for his salara. In Aviron, he made me swear myself to you, even after he's gone."

Norah stopped and swallowed. *Even after death*? Why would Mikael do that? She eyed him warily. He said he was loyal. How could she believe a man she knew hated her? Yet, for some ungodly reason, she did. "Get up."

He rose.

"If he dies, what does it matter to you, then?"

His eyes burned into her. "Because I made him a promise."

And he loved the king. Norah let out a deep sigh. She let her eyes drift back to Artem's body.

"Bhastian told me what happened, all that he's done," Soren said.

Norah glanced at Bhastian in surprise. The guardsman gave her a small nod. She wanted to hug him.

"It's important you know those things weren't on my orders," the commander added, "nor were they done with my knowledge."

Her eyes narrowed. "If you had known, would you really have done anything?"

"I would have," he said angrily, as if offended.

Freezing droplets of rain hit her cheek, and she looked to the sky. "The storm," she said.

"There's a hillside house," he told her. "We'll take shelter there and continue to Ashan in the morning."

The thought of staying with the lord commander even longer soured her stomach, but she supposed she didn't have a choice. She looked at the bodies of the fallen men.

"Leave them," the commander called back to Bhastian. "Bring only the horses."

Mounted again, Norah followed the commander, with Bhastian behind. She shivered as the freezing rain soaked through her layers. They hurried their horses, but the biting wind made Norah want to slow.

She followed the commander down a trail and through the crag of a mountain. The rain fell harder, and the trail became slick.

"Careful," he called back to her.

Around a turn, the crag narrowed with barely enough room for their horses to pass through. It didn't seem like a path to shelter. They wound upward until the crag opened wider, revealing a hillside looking out over the mountains. Norah straightened in surprise. A quaint house sat carved into the side stone.

Soren dismounted and led his horse to cover under a recess in the rock, and Norah slipped down, off the mare. They were drenched by the time they reached the door.

"Does anyone live here?" she asked through her chattering teeth.

"No. Almost no one knows it exists. This is a royal safe house, and it's stocked." He led them inside and motioned down a small hallway. "There's an armoire in the back room. You'll find clothes there."

She turned toward the back room but paused. "I'm sorry about Artem."

"He didn't deserve mercy," he said angrily. "Or your sympathy." He turned toward the fireplace. "I've wanted to kill him for a long time."

Norah had wanted him dead for a long time. Well, days. But it felt like a long time. Now that he was, she carried a twinge of regret. Not that she felt sympathy for Artem, but the end of any man's life held a great sadness.

She took to the back room to see what clothes might be available and was surprised to find the armoire filled with a variety of options: riding gowns, sleepwear, underclothes. And beside garments for her hung those for Mikael. She reached out and drew her fingers across them. In a way, she was glad to be returning to Ashan. She'd missed him, but her stomach turned at the thought of facing him again. She'd said straight to his face that she wouldn't betray him, yet she'd left. Would he understand?

She settled on a navy, front-fastening riding dress, the only one she could manage herself. There was no denying it was good to get into dry clothes again, although her body still shook with cold.

When she returned to the front sitting room, she found the commander tending the fire. His cloak hung nearby to dry, but he still wore his damp breeches. As usual, he was without a shirt, wearing only his weapons strappings, and she watched the inked flesh of his arms work as he fostered the growing flames. It was silly he hadn't worn his heavy tunic, given the return of winter. She hoped he was cold. Very cold.

"Where's Bhastian?" she asked.

"Outside. He's not permitted in. No one is."

She pursed her lips. "Except *you*."

"I'm permitted everywhere."

"You're not *wanted* everywhere," she cut back, sharper than she'd intended.

He paused. "Do you want me to leave?"

She gritted her teeth. She did want him to leave, but she also wanted him to tend the fire. Norah saw a wine bottle on a small side table, and she walked over and poured herself a cup.

"I know you hate me," he said.

She took a drink and closed her eyes, savoring the sweet taste of berries on her tongue as she sank into an armchair by the fire. She was tired, tired of the constant fight. Her shivering stopped, but she wasn't sure if it was from the flames of the fire or the warmth of the alcohol.

"That's what you want, isn't it?" she asked. "You try to intimidate me. You stand against me on everything."

"I say what needs to be said."

Norah sighed. She couldn't win this argument with him, not with his hatred running so deep. She swirled her wine in her chalice. "Why would Mikael have you swear yourself to me?"

He shifted the wood on the fire with his sword. "To keep the peace. That's what you want. And as with everything else you want, he gives it to you." There was a hint of bitterness in his voice.

"But you don't want peace," she said. It wasn't a question.

"It doesn't matter what I want."

Norah felt a small sadness, not in the way he yearned for war, but in the way he cast all his desires aside, how he gave without expectation. He really did love the king. She sighed, thinking. "Surely the army wouldn't follow you and continue to be allied with Mercia if the king fell."

His brow dipped. "They would," he said, taking offense. "They would follow me anywhere." He leaned his sword against the stone of the fireplace. "It's the nobles that wouldn't. That's why you need an heir."

An heir—it was a topic she dreaded. Mikael hadn't brought it up again since their wedding night, but she had expected it would surface eventually. She just hadn't expected it from the commander. Norah took another drink of her wine. "What would the nobles do if I didn't have an heir?"

"Try to take the throne."

"What would you do, then?"

Soren stood and stepped back from the growing fire, taking a chalice and pouring wine for himself. "Kill them," he said blankly. Then he brought the cup to his lips.

Norah frowned. So much death. "Is that what you were worried about when Mikael absolved his marriages? The nobles? Did you think they'd do something?"

"They did. And they still might."

She hadn't forgotten the attempt on her life. A knot tugged in her stomach—it might not be settled still.

"Salar needs to satisfy the nobles to keep his crown," he said. "You do *nothing* to help him."

She wanted to. She wasn't sure she was ready for a child yet, but she wanted to help Mikael. She cupped her chalice in both hands, letting the brim rest on her lips. The alcohol warmed her cheeks. "Do you have any children?"

He snorted. "No."

"Have you been with a woman before?" she asked, surprising even herself. Her cheeks grew hot. Why had she asked that?

"Of course I have." He balked at her question, insult heavy in his voice.

"Oh," she said awkwardly. She had just thought with his preference... What was his preference? It was none of her business, that's what it was. She pursed her lips and then mumbled, "That was rude. I'm sorry."

"Don't apologize," he said irritably. "You're salara, you don't apologize."

That hardly seemed the criteria for whether an apology was owed. Norah took another drink of her wine. "Do you have anyone? A lover?" she asked. Yet another question that surprised her. What was wrong with her?

"You said you wouldn't speak of this again."

Their pact... "This is different." *Kind of.* And here she was again, deep into not-her-business territory.

His eyes seared into her. She forced back another apology that sat on the tip of her tongue. Another intrusive question. She should stop drinking the wine.

He surprised her when he actually answered. "If I let myself care about another, my enemies will hurt them to hurt me. To pull me away from Salar."

"You mean that's what *you* would do."

"It's what any cunning foe would do," he said sharply. A tension hung in the air, and he exhaled. "No one can take me from Salar. No one, save for you, as he's made me promise."

"And here I was hoping it was because you were starting to like me," she mumbled sarcastically.

"I *don't* like you."

She pursed her lips. *Yes. Precisely.* And she took another drink of wine as he went outside to spend the night on guard with Bhastian.

CHAPTER SEVEN

The storm was a long one, and the commander finally yielded to Norah's demands that he and Bhastian take refuge inside the house. They set their post just inside the door while she took the back room to sleep.

She woke occasionally through the night to the sound of the fireplace in her room being tended. She knew it was the commander. Part of her stiffened under the quilts in annoyance that he would come into her room so freely. Closed doors meant nothing to him. The other part of her secretly appreciated she didn't have to tend the fire herself.

When the morning came, they continued on their way. The commander set a slower pace, seeming to have found some compassion, but he sent Bhastian ahead to inform the king of their arrival. The air was easier between them now, the quiet not so intimidating.

"What did you name her?" the commander asked, breaking the silence.

Norah frowned. "What?"

His eyes twitched in annoyance at having to repeat himself. "The mare. What did you name her?"

Strange. "Oh, um... she has a name. Savantahla."

The skin between his eyebrows wrinkled. "Savantahla's not her name. It's what she is."

She hadn't thought of it like that. Norah tilted her head and brushed her fingers through the mare's mane. "All right, I think I'll call her... um, Cloud... no... Spirit."

The commander rolled his eyes.

"What? You don't like it?"

"It's a terrible name."

Was he serious? "What would you name her then?" Not that she cared what he thought.

He looked straight ahead as he rode, absolutely no help. She should have known. He didn't have anything less terrible. A terrible person, he'd only have terrible names to offer.

"Sephir," he said finally.

And she paused the mutterings in her mind. She silently rolled the name along her tongue. *Se-FEER.* "What does it mean?"

"It's just a name," he replied, annoyed.

She hated that it wasn't a terrible name. Norah bit the inside of her cheek in annoyance. It was actually a nice name. She might call the mare Sephir.

It wasn't long before Ashan loomed in the distance. Norah grew more anxious as they neared the capital city. How would Mikael react with her return? It had hurt him when he thought she wanted to leave, and surely it had hurt him when she actually did. Would he be angry? Would he mistrust her now?

"Your cover," Soren called to her as they got closer. "Put it on. Conceal your hair."

They'd hidden her disappearance, she realized. She'd expected the entire kingdom to be looking for her, but of course, the king had put his faith in his commander. She tempered her irritation. The king had trusted him, and again he delivered. He'd tracked her like a hound, even though she'd been on a horse of the Wild.

The guards let the commander through without a word, and they rode to the stables. After leaving their horses, he didn't take her through the front of the castle. Instead, he led her into a small stone building. She followed him out the back and into a small side street, then through a maze of alleys. They entered another small structure, and inside found a stairway leading downward.

He led the way through narrow halls and back up a small staircase with a door at the top. The door opened into a sitting room. She made mental notes, trying to remember as much as possible. The doors to the sitting room led to another hall, and then she knew where she was. They were making their way to Mikael's study. Her heart beat heavily in her chest. She couldn't escape the feeling of being captured once again.

They entered the room, and her breath came unevenly at the sight of Mikael. His armor was piled on a side chair, as if he'd taken up residence in the study. His hair hung loose around his shoulders. He rose slowly from the desk when he saw her.

The commander stepped forward with a bow of his head. "Has Bhastian made it to you?" he asked.

"Yes." Mikael's eyes were locked on Norah. "Leave us."

The commander glanced back at her before leaving the study, then closed the doors behind him.

Mikael's eyes pierced hers, and she waited, her mind tumbling for what to say. But the anger she expected from him didn't come. She searched his face, not sure of the emotion behind it. Hurt? Concern?

"You didn't flee to the North," he said. His voice was soft, uncertain almost.

She shook her head weakly. "No."

"Or to Aleon."

"Why would I go to Aleon?"

"Why would you go to Odepeth?"

Really? For the same reason he went to Odepeth. "Because I wanted answers."

"Did you get them?"

Not as many as she wanted. "I discovered my father rode a horse of the Wild, the same as I do."

Mikael shifted back in surprise. "How? What does this mean?"

She wished she knew. "I don't know."

"The seer told you this?"

Norah shook her head. "No, someone else I met along the way." She frowned. "The seer couldn't help me."

"We told you he wouldn't see you."

Patronizing. "Well, he did see me," she cut back, and his eyes widened. "I saw the visions. Bhasim showed me everything."

"Bhasim?"

She narrowed her eyes. "You go to this seer, and you don't even know his name?"

He didn't have an answer for her.

Now who was being patronizing, she chided herself. She looked to the ground, drawing in a deep breath and letting it out slowly. "I asked if he could unlock my memories."

He stilled, so still it seemed unnatural. Like he wasn't even breathing. Was he afraid of her getting her memories back?

"He couldn't," she said.

Mikael's shoulders loosened. But his face... it held... a disappointment. A sadness. Was he sad for her that she didn't get what she was searching for, even though he was afraid of it? Her chest tightened. At least now he knew she hadn't fled back to Mercia—she hadn't just left him.

"But he showed me the visions," she told him. And now it was her turn to feel sadness for him. "I won't deny that they're... terrifying. I understand what you fear. And to be honest, I fear it too. But Mikael, something's wrong. That isn't Alexander." She shook her head. "I don't know who that man is, but it isn't him."

He didn't speak; he only stepped closer.

Her eyes welled, and she cursed herself. Why was she getting so emotional? Maybe it was the exhaustion, the frustration, the fear that she wouldn't get her memories back. Maybe it was the fear that the vision of Mikael would be true. But she knew in her heart it couldn't be.

He lifted her chin so that her eyes met his. "After the seer, where would you have gone? Back to the North?"

She didn't know where she would have gone, but she knew she couldn't run. She wanted to go back to Mercia, but if she returned in flight, she risked war. She couldn't do that. And if she was completely honest with herself, she didn't want to leave Mikael. Slowly, she shook her head.

"Why?"

"For the same reason you swore the commander to me." To protect the peace.

His brows drew together. "He told you this?"

She nodded. "He said you made him promise in Aviron, when you wanted to make me salara."

The corner of his mouth twitched.

"What?" she asked.

"I wanted you for salara well before Aviron."

She drew her brows together.

He pulled open his shirt, revealing the crown marking from the ink mastera, Salta Tau, on his chest. "Battle. Blade. Blood. Crown."

She hadn't understood when they'd gone to Salta Tau, and she didn't understand now. What did that even mean?

He reached and curled his hand around hers, and her heart beat faster.

"It was the day you cost me Bahoul. The day you threw my commander from his horse, cut my spear from my hand, and stabbed me with my own dagger."

So much had happened that day she could barely recall it, but she couldn't help the smile that came to her lips. "That sounds more magnificent than I remember."

Mikael pulled her even closer. "You are magnificent." He took her hand and pressed it over the marking on his chest. The nearness of him...

And then she knew—this was for more than peace now. It was for more than her people, or Mercia. It was for her. He had to see it—the power he had over her, not as an ally, not as a king. Just as himself.

His voice dropped to a whisper. "I'm sorry I didn't listen to you. I'm sorry I wouldn't hear you when you tried to speak to me. I wasn't there when you needed me."

She shook her head. "I know what compelled you. But you have to know I wouldn't betray you, Mikael. I know words are just words, but I—"

Her voice fell as he lifted her chin and covered her lips with his own. His tongue tasted of want and fire, but it was tempered. Most of all, he tasted of remorse. Of safety. Of promise.

He pulled back and looked at her. "I believe you and your words. Let's find the truth then. You can start with your lord justice when he returns from Aleon."

The thought made her stomach knot, but she nodded.

The afternoon sun hung high, and Norah wrung her hands as she walked quickly back to her sanctuary from Mikael's study. Worry writhed in her stomach, twisting and thickening, eating up the space for her heart to beat and her lungs to breathe. Alexander's business with Aleon could be dangerous for everyone.

She pushed open the door of the sanctuary and gasped when she saw her maids, Serene and Vitalia. Her gasp turned to an emotional laugh as she rushed forward, hugging them both. "Thank the gods, you're safe!" she breathed. While she'd sent them into hiding, Artem was cunning, and she'd still feared for them.

"And you!" Serene exclaimed. "Queen Norah, we were so worried."

"I was worried about you both! You're supposed to be with Kiran. What are you doing here?"

"Bhastian came and told us you returned just this morning," Vitalia told her. "He brought us here."

Serene nodded. "Artem's soldiers were looking for us when you left. Sonal told Kiran they were going to search Kiran's house, and he brought us to stay with his grandmother."

"Sonal?" Norah felt her eyes well as she nodded. He was one of her less favored Crest guards. Perhaps she'd judged him too harshly. There were good men in this place.

"And"—Serene paused—"Bhastian told us Captain Artem was dead. But all he said was treason."

Norah nodded, hesitant at first. "I threatened the lord commander, and Artem and his soldiers pulled their swords on me."

Serene gasped. "What did you do?"

"I didn't do anything. The lord commander and Bhastian killed them."

Vitalia raised a surprised brow and shook her head. "Well, despite my loathing for him, he does seem to have his priorities in order."

Norah sighed. "Maybe." He was a difficult man to understand.

"How did you even get away from Captain Artem to begin with?" Serene asked.

She hesitated. She didn't really want to recount her overly dramatic escape. "I just found an opportunity to slip from sight, and then he couldn't follow me on Sephir."

"Sephir?" Vitalia asked.

"Oh, I named the mare. Apparently Savantahla's not her actual name."

"You gave her a Kharavian name?" Vitalia grinned at Serene. "It means *spirit*. It's so perfect."

Norah paused. Sephir meant *spirit*? But the commander—

"Where were you?" Vitalia asked her, not giving her an opportunity to mull over the difficult man.

Norah pushed out a breath. "I went to Odepeth, to the seer. He showed me the visions. In every way it appears Alexander kills Mikael, but there's something not right about it."

"Why not?" her Mercian maid asked. "He's been battling the Shadow King for years, trying to kill him. Mercia feels Kharav is still a threat. And, if I may be so bold"—Serene shifted uncomfortably—"the lord justice obviously cares for you a great deal, and he's very unhappy with this current arrangement."

Norah felt a flash of anger at her maid's words, but how could she be angry at the truth? She pushed it down and gave them both a small nod. "I know." Serene was right, but she knew the visions weren't.

"You'll figure it out," Vitalia said. "You'll find the truth."

Their eyes were on him. Even in the darkness of night, he could feel them watching. Alexander strode from the stables toward the castle, keenly aware of the Shadowmen who stalked his every move. And the Destroyer was there—unseen, but Alexander knew he was there. No doubt the Shadow commander knew the moment he'd crossed back into the Shadowlands. Did the commander know where he'd been? It was possible. His chest tightened. Alexander needed to find Norah and give her the news himself.

He expected word of his return had spread to her quickly, and that she'd be looking for him. It wouldn't be good for her to meet him outside under prying eyes, and prying ears. He crossed the threshold inside. Alone, he settled slightly.

The hour was late, and the castle, quiet. The torchlit halls were wrapped in shadows. As he strode the long corridor, a shift of light came around the corner, and he slowed.

Norah stood like a flame, bright against the night, against the darkness that surrounded her—the darkness that always surrounded her now.

"Lord Justice," she said when she saw him. There was a weight to her voice. A hesitation. A worry.

She knew.

His chest tightened, his heart feeling the pressure as he continued toward her. "Norah."

Even in the dimly lit hall, the blues of her eyes pierced through him. "Where have you been?" she asked softly, but it wasn't meant softly.

He heard it, her fear, and he stepped closer. "On a task. From the council."

"What kind of task?"

His mouth moved to speak, but he paused. She would see this as a betrayal. She wanted peace so badly, it blinded her. But Alexander knew—more than anyone—wanting something couldn't make it so.

When this all fell apart, and it *would* fall apart, she would need options. "A task of building options," he said.

"What does that mean? Where have you been?" Her voice begged him not to say it.

He could hear the silent plea for her suspicions to be wrong, and it clawed at his heart. But she needed a way out of this world that was breaking her. It *was* breaking her. More than that—when this alliance crumbled, it would kill her. And wasn't this his duty—to protect Mercia? Protect her? To save her, even if she didn't know she needed to be saved? "Aleon," he said finally.

She let out a shaky breath. "Why didn't you tell me you were going to Aleon?"

"I wanted to fully understand the situation." And come to terms with it himself.

"No," she said sharply. "You didn't tell me because you knew I wouldn't let you go." She was upset.

So was he. It had been a hard journey—traveling to the man who still had intentions for Norah, the Aleon king. It had been torturous to look at his face and negotiate her hand. "The offer for marriage still stands."

Shock stopped the obvious argument on her tongue. "What?" she breathed.

He could barely get it out the first time, the second cut even deeper. "Phillip's offer for marriage still stands."

Norah shook her head, her brows stitching in confusion. "I'm already married. *To Mikael.*"

"For how long? Even if this all doesn't come crashing down, there are many who seek his fall."

She shook her head again. "Mercia stands with him."

"Norah, the council will never support the Shadow King." He hadn't intended to be so direct, but she needed to understand.

"He's *their* king! I wed him!"

"In name only!"

She stopped. But it wasn't the stop that suddenly gripped his heart. It wasn't the abrupt quiet. It was the small catch of her breath—so faint that it was barely noticeable.

But he noticed.

The catch of breath she gave when she was caught...

"Welcome back, Lord Justice," the Shadow King's voice called from behind them.

Alexander spun to see the king and the Destroyer step out from the shadows. How much had they heard? He almost didn't care, his mind was still on Norah's reaction.

"Interesting news from Aleon," the king said calmly. "Does it come with a proposal of how to be rid of me?"

The scraping of the Destroyer's giant axe on the stone floor as he stepped toward Alexander made Norah step closer to him, but that was the opposite of what he wanted her to do. He needed to get her away from here, away from the danger of this situation, and away from this king.

"There were no such discussions," Alexander said stiffly. His mind replayed the catch in her breath, and heat rippled over his skin.

"Then a little premature for a marriage conversation. Don't you agree?" the king asked.

Alexander didn't agree, but he said nothing. His pulse thrummed deafeningly in his ears.

The king pulled his sword, and Alexander put his hand on his hilt.

"Alexander," Norah pleaded. In normal circumstances, he might have listened.

His mind swirled—the catch in her breath...

He pulled his sword.

Her head jerked to the Shadow King. "Mikael, wait." She was trying to calm the tension, but there would be no calming. She looked back desperately at Alexander. "Go to your chamber."

He wouldn't need his chamber after this.

"If I didn't know better"—the Shadow King took another step toward him—"I'd think you were a man of Aleon."

Insult to injury.

The catch in her breath...

"I'm a man who will see your end," Alexander bit back.

The Destroyer let out a roar and raged forward, swinging his axe with a fury.

"No!" Norah cried as Alexander charged forward to meet him. The clash of their weapons echoed through the halls. Footfalls sounded, soldiers fast approaching. They swarmed into the hall and surrounded them.

"Don't!" the Destroyer snarled at the Shadowmen warriors. His eyes of night found Alexander. "He's mine." And he attacked again.

Alexander fought him back with equal skill.

"Mikael, stop this!" Norah cried, but the king wasn't listening. None of them were.

Alexander's own fire of rage burned. He broke from the Destroyer once again, and they circled each other, each looking for an opening.

Suddenly, Norah rushed forward between them and grabbed Alexander, forcing him to look at her.

"You'll stop!" she cried. "Stop this!"

He gaped at her in surprise, and the commander saw the opportunity for distraction. He swung with a forceful blow, barreling by Norah and striking the sword from Alexander's hand.

The king called to her, but she was too entangled in the attack. The Destroyer delivered a lunging kick, taking the wind from Alexander and dropping him to his knees. Then he raised his axe to deliver the fatal blow and brought it down with all his weight.

"No!" Norah screamed as she threw herself forward, wrapping herself around Alexander to shield him.

Too quickly for him to stop her.

A loud clang rang through the hall as the Shadow King's sword met the Destroyer's axe, sending the commander stumbling back. He caught his balance, stunned, and looked in shock at his king.

The king staggered back, his eyes on Norah.

Tears streamed down her face as she clutched Alexander.

Alexander reached up and threaded his fingers into her hair, pushing her back to look at him. All was quiet. "Why would you do such a stupid thing?" he said between his teeth, not able to keep the anger from his voice, not able to hide the fear, the horror of what had almost just happened. "Do you know what you could have done?"

"I can't let you die," she cried softly, shaking her head. "I can't."

He brushed her cheek with his thumb, his emotion too thick for him to speak. If anything happened to her...

Norah looked up to see the king, who held his sword low. Their eyes locked, and the king grimaced.

And Alexander realized. She'd revealed herself, her heart.

"Out," the Shadow King ordered the soldiers, and they quickly filed out the way they had come. He looked at the commander. "You too."

"You can't mean for me to leave you here," the Destroyer hissed.

"Go," the king said sternly.

The commander's eyes tightened with a bitter rage, and he reluctantly drew back with his axe, disappearing into the shadows.

The king looked back at Norah with an expression Alexander knew all too well.

"Mikael," she started.

But he shook his head. Then he turned and followed after the commander.

"Mikael!"

Norah followed after, leaving Alexander alone.

His body shook. He'd lost himself and endangered Norah. He'd lost control. And he wasn't sure if he could get it back again, as his mind reeled back to...

The catch in her breath.

Chapter Eight

Norah sat on the bench in the conservatory, grasping the quill tightly in her hand and looking at the page of blank parchment. Words wouldn't come. There was so much she wanted to say, but she struggled for a way to say it. Every sentence she tried sounded ridiculous. Maybe what she wanted to say was ridiculous. Maybe trying to say anything was ridiculous.

"I didn't think I'd find you here." Mikael's voice startled her.

For two days, she hadn't seen him, not since what had happened with Alexander. Her breath knotted in her throat, and she stood quickly. Had he not wanted to find her here? Did he not want her in the conservatory anymore? It was a place that was special to him, meant only for people who were special to him. She wasn't sure she was considered so anymore.

He eyed the quill and parchment.

"I'm just writing a letter," she said. *Or trying to.*

"To?"

Norah looked down at the blank parchment. She wasn't sure her voice would come. "You," she said finally. "I... wanted to explain myself in a way that made sense, but"—she paused—"I'm having difficulty starting."

"What's there to explain?" he asked, strangely calm.

His composure scared her. Had she lost him? Norah opened her mouth, but she still couldn't find the words. Her chest tightened, wringing the air from her lungs. "So much" was all she could manage.

A long silence sat between them. He only waited, watching her. She had to say something. *Anything.* But nothing came.

She had nothing.

Except for how she felt. She focused on that. "If I'd tried to guess my future when I woke in the forest of the Wild," she started, "I would never have imagined this for myself."

It felt like an understatement. *Never in the wildest of dreams*, she should have said.

"So haphazardly life seems to have been thrown at me," she continued, "like the gods cared nothing, planned nothing." How could the gods have planned this path? She couldn't even call it a path. "I doubted there even were gods."

Mikael only watched her.

She sucked in an uneven breath. She couldn't hold back the tears now. "But now there's no doubt. This path isn't haphazard, it's purposeful. The gods are there, and they're angry with me, and they're cruel. And the more I care for you, the more they use that to hurt me too." They knew how to hurt her the most. *Damn them. Damn them all.*

Norah looked down at the stone floor. Mikael stepped to her and drew her face up to look at him. But she couldn't read his eyes. She couldn't understand his face.

"How much?" His voice came barely above a whisper. His hands clasped her arms just below her shoulders. "How much do you care for me? Am I in your heart?"

"Do you not see it?" She knew it wasn't enough. Why couldn't she say the words?

But he nodded. "Yes," he said hoarsely. "But I see there is also another. And not just any other."

She had no excuses. She couldn't deny it. She wouldn't lie.

He brushed her hair softly from her face. "It's important you speak the truth to me," he said in a low voice. He hesitated, seeming to fear his words. "He stays in my kingdom. Have you been to his bed?"

"What?" Did he really think—

"Please," he said, his voice softer. "These past two days, I—" He shook his head. "My mind is weak. I need to hear you say it."

She wanted to be offended, but she knew how easily the frenzy of jealousy could poison the mind. She shook her head, looking into his eyes. "No. I've not been to his bed."

He closed his eyes, seeming to calm before opening them again. "But you love him." It wasn't a question. "It's why you wouldn't give him to me."

She said nothing. She couldn't deny it. Now he knew why she protected Alexander so fiercely. What would he do?

Alexander was still in Kharav.

What would he do?

His face held no emotion now, no hint of his thoughts or of his intentions. He dropped his head beside hers, and his breath danced across her ear. Alexander's fate lay on his lips, and she feared it—more than feared it. Terror trembled through her. Surely he wouldn't let him live now.

But instead, he whispered, "Tell me the heart is not finite. Must you love one less to make room for another?"

Norah's heart raced. Was he telling her he would do nothing? A tear fell down her cheek. She whispered the only thing she could. "The heart is not finite."

He nodded, taking the parchment and quill from her hand, and dropped them to the ground. Then he pulled her close. "You don't need to explain anything else," he said softly.

They stood in the light of the morning sun. Everything should have felt perfect, but there was still something that lingered, something that weighed heavily on her mind. She had to ask him. "When you asked me to marry you, did you really believe it would change your fate?"

"I wanted to believe."

She pulled back and looked up at him. "Did you, though?"

He shook his head. "Not truly, no."

Her heart hurt. "But you still married me. Why?"

"Because I needed you." He threaded his hand back into her hair. "I still need you."

His words caught her in the most beautiful way. Her lip trembled. "And I need you."

"Then we need each other, and we'll have each other."

She smiled as she sniffed.

"Can I walk you back?" he asked.

"Of course," she whispered. "I'd like that." There was nothing she wanted more in that moment.

He pulled her arm through his and led her from the conservatory, back toward the castle. "You still stay in the sanctuary," he said as they entered the castle and walked through the high-arched halls.

This conversation again. "It's comfortable."

"But not fit for the quarters of salara."

"It has everything I need." Would he press her to stay in the villa? She couldn't stay there. She *couldn't*. "I like the sanctuary, really," she tried to assure him. "And it looks north."

"As does my own chamber," he said, stopping as he turned to her. He reached up and ran a lock of her hair through his fingers. "Maybe you'd like to stay there from now on?"

"In your chamber?" she asked in surprise. "Where would you stay?"

"With you."

Oh. "I see," she breathed, feeling foolish. Of course with her.

She looked down the hall, toward her sanctuary, and then back toward a hall that led to the king's chamber. He pulled her hand gently, asking.

Should she give him what he asked? No—not what he asked, but what she wanted. She did want to stay with him, be close to him. He was her husband, who—surprising even herself—was stealing her heart.

Norah threaded her fingers between his, giving her answer. He smiled and led her back toward his hall. They walked slowly. When they reached his chamber, Mikael stopped in the doorway. "If there's anything you'd have differently, you only need to say it," he told her.

"I've seen your chamber, and it's perfectly fine."

"Not just the chamber. Anything."

She knew.

He stepped forward and caught her in a kiss, and she kissed him back. His lips were soft, yet firm.

Claiming.

He reached behind her and opened the door to the room, using the frame of his body to push her backward and inside without breaking their kiss, then swung it closed behind them. His hunger—she could feel it in him, loosely leashed. He made no effort to hide his want. There was no reserve, no mask. And she loved it.

The scent of him was intoxicating, and she breathed him in. All of him. He moved her backward, toward the bed, the hunt in his eyes and his intentions clear. She could stop him, slow him, she knew. But she didn't want to.

He laid her back on the bed, as gently as the storm inside him would allow, then he stepped back and away. She watched him as he reached over his shoulders and pulled his shirt over his head. The muscle rippled under his skin in forced restraint, and a warmth pooled in her stomach. His need fueled hers. He kicked off his boots and unbuckled his belt, pushing his breeches down and off, and stood naked in front of her.

Norah drew her bottom lip in between her teeth. She loved his body. She'd always considered herself a somewhat modest woman, but just the look of him made her want every inch of his flesh. And she'd have him. She brought out her foot from underneath her dress and held it for him. He reached out and slipped off one shoe, then the other. Her heart beat faster.

She pushed herself up, onto her knees, and turned around, her back to him. A shiver ran up her spine as he stepped closer. He pulled her jacket from her shoulders and tossed it to the side, then set his attention on the fastenings down her gown, so many fastenings. He pushed apart the backing and pulled loose the lacing from the corset underneath. Then she turned back to face him.

The thought of inviting him back to her bed before was always *just* beyond the reach of her confidence. Perhaps it was the shyness of convention, or the pervasive voice in the back of her mind telling her she couldn't love this man, she shouldn't want this man. But she did want him. He'd said he thought of her inviting him into her sanctuary, often. She did too. But only in the darkest corners of her mind did she let herself think of his touch, and of his body. But tonight, she wouldn't let herself be confined to only thoughts.

Slowly, Mikael pulled the gown from her shoulders and down. They both paused for a moment, breathless. Then he pushed the fabric down farther, over her hips, sweeping her undergarments with it, and she rocked to the side as he stripped it down her legs and pulled the dress free. Her skin prickled, but not from the cold.

Mikael pushed her onto the bed, prowling over her, and drew her back into a kiss. He wrapped his arm around her and pulled her to the pillows as he drank from her lips. She could taste his want and responded with her own. He nipped along her jaw as she let her head fall back, giving him her throat. He trailed hungry kisses down her neck and bared his teeth against her shoulder. She wouldn't have minded if he'd bitten her; she wanted to bite him.

Mikael followed the line from her shoulder to the base of her throat, letting her feel the warmth of his breath across her skin. She knew his breath, his mouth, his touch, and she needed it all. He brushed his lips over the side of her breast, and she arched her back, wanting more.

Norah pulled him up, opening her thighs, begging him to come to her, and she felt his body respond. Mikael loved with a strength, not one that overpowered her but one that fueled her, made her stronger.

He positioned himself and moved slowly. But she needed him now. She rocked forward, taking him inside her and joining them together. Deeper, then deeper still. The full length of him, until he filled her completely. The pleasure that rippled through her stole her breath.

He groaned as she moved her hips against him, bringing him almost all the way out and then sheathing him fully again. Pressure built within her core, and she quickened her pace.

Mikael gripped her waist, slowing her. Every fiber of her body protested—she needed him. She needed them to be one, not just in body, but in mind and heart. They had to be one to overcome the world against them, their own kingdoms against them, the gods against them. Mikael was hers, and no one would take him from her. He was hers, she told herself again as she gave in to her own desires. And he let her. There was no reservation with Mikael, no shame. Only freedom.

Norah pulled his hand down between her legs and guided him to touch her. She angled herself to feel him more, to take him deeper, and he gave himself to her. She let the fire build within until she thought she would burn, and then they both writhed in the inferno of their release.

As they descended, he collapsed, dropping to his elbows over her and panting. Slowly, he calmed, nuzzling into the warmth of her neck. She loved his tenderness—something so many thought he was incapable of. But she knew him.

"Mikael," she breathed. There was no reason. She just needed his name on her tongue.

He drew up to look at her. "You're the only one who calls me that."

She bit her lip. "Do you not like it?"

He smiled. "When you say it, it's the most beautiful sound in the world."

She smiled back, and he brought his mouth to hers.

Chapter Nine

Norah woke to Mikael sitting in the chair by the window and pulling on his boots. He'd already donned his clothes. His black hair fell loose on his shoulders, a way she didn't often see. She loved his hair, thick with a silky curl. He noticed her watching him, and he stopped and smiled.

"What are you doing awake so early?" she asked as she propped her head up on her elbow. "And where are you going?"

"I have to go find the lord commander," he said.

Of course.

"I won't be long, though," he added.

She bit her smile in her teeth. "I suppose I should take a bath, anyway."

"Vimal will draw you one and fetch you some breakfast."

She nodded.

Mikael rose from the chair and stood beside the bed. She pulled the sheets around herself and sat up on her knees, and he pulled her close as he leaned down to kiss her. "I'll return soon," he said.

When he'd gone, Mikael's servant, Vimal, stepped inside the chamber, careful to avert his eyes. "Salara, a bath is ready for you. I'll get breakfast and have your maid bring a new dress."

"Thank you," she said appreciatively.

Vimal left, and Norah padded into the bath chamber. She slipped into the tub. The heat from the water made her skin tingle as she submersed herself. It felt wonderful. Vimal had put salts in the water, and she closed her eyes as she breathed in their scent.

This was what happiness felt like. *Finally.* Things were right between them. For the first time in a long time, she felt like she could persevere—more than persevere, she could make a life. She could love this life.

Remembering Vimal would return soon with breakfast, Norah quickly finished washing. She wrapped a towel around herself and stepped out of the tub. Through the hanging panels, she found the dressing room. Surely there would be a robe she could put on. But the dressing room had only Mikael's clothes: shirts, breeches, boots, and a wide variety of leathers and armor. She reached out and touched a shoulder shield. It was thin, smooth, light, but strong. Its polish hadn't removed the wear of war. How many battles had it seen? Battles against Mercia?

Suddenly, the hair on the back of her neck stood on end. She felt a presence from behind, and she spun around as the commander plunged through the panels with his sword ready.

Norah gasped and stumbled back a few steps before catching herself. "Hammel's hell! What are you doing?" she asked angrily.

His eyes widened in surprise. He pulled back, slowly lowering his sword.

"What's wrong with you?" she snapped. "I could have been Mikael, or a servant!"

"Salar's sword isn't here," he said between his teeth, "and Vimal's in the kitchen."

Norah sighed, shifting uncomfortably under his eye. Her near nakedness didn't seem to bother him. But her presence did. It didn't matter—she had no fear of him now.

"Why are you here?" he challenged.

"I live here," she spat back.

"You know what I mean."

"My answer's the same. I'm to stay here now, in the king's chamber."

His nostrils flared. "You were in his bed last night?"

"No, I just run about random rooms with no clothes on." She rolled her eyes. "Obviously I stayed here last night."

He made no effort to hide the fury inside him.

"Can you at least give me my dress, by the bed?" She would put on her old dress until Vitalia came with a new one.

"There is no dress," he said coldly. "Otherwise, I would've known it was you."

She pursed her lips. Vimal must have taken it. "You mean otherwise you wouldn't have hesitated before running me through," she mumbled under her breath.

The commander reached out and pulled one of Mikael's shirts from its hanger. He threw it at her, and not kindly. She clenched it in anger, wanting to throw it back at him. But she didn't. It was better than a bath towel.

She scowled at him. "Can I have some privacy?"

He walked out to the bedchamber, and Norah pulled the shirt over herself. It was large, more of a short gown.

"Where's Salar?" he called from the bedchamber.

"Looking for you."

"I'll wait here for him."

"Of course you will," she muttered. There really was no getting rid of him.

Norah raked her fingers through her damp hair, trying to look as regal as a woman could in an oversize man's shirt and without a hairbrush. Then she walked back out to the bedchamber.

The commander had sheathed his sword back in its scabbard and stood by the window.

She forced herself calm. She couldn't fault him for his anger. Undoubtedly, the seer's vision of Mikael's death haunted him, as it did her, and her defense of Alexander on his return from Aleon would still be fresh in his mind. But she didn't want things to be like this between them. "I understand your concern—"

"My concern?" he snarled as he spun to face her. "You don't. Because it's more than concern. You lead Salar toward death, but I won't let that happen."

"You think that I would? I care for him!"

"Then you'd give me the Bear!" he raged. "Or at least send him back to the North. If you cared for him, you'd protect him!"

Just then, Mikael entered. There was no mistaking the high tension in the room, and he looked at his commander with a warning eye. "Wait for me outside," he said stiffly.

The commander gave Norah one last glare and left the room without a word, closing the door behind him.

Mikael's eyes moved back to her, and he softened. He stepped forward, reaching out and pulling her close to him. "I'm sorry. I meant to tell him first. That was my intention this morning. But I'll deal with him."

She sighed as she swept her locks behind her ear. "Don't be angry with him," she said. "He worries for you. He doesn't understand, after all that's happened. And my being here caught him by surprise."

He looked down at her, and the faintest smile touched his lips.

"What?" she asked.

"You defend him."

Then he looked down at his shirt on her.

"Sorry," she said, glancing down at the shirt and shrugging. "I don't have a dress yet."

Mikael brushed her hair back from her shoulder. "I was just remembering what I felt the last time I saw you in my shirt."

Norah swallowed, remembering the night he had saved her from the Horsemen's attack. "What did you feel?" she whispered.

His eyes moved back and forth between hers. "I wanted to hold you. I wanted to put my arms around you." He pulled her closer. "I was already falling for you."

She remembered that night well. Too well. It still haunted her—what had almost happened. She covered the emotional scar with jest. "Took you long enough."

He smiled, dropping his head, and caught her in a kiss. She needed his kiss. She opened her mouth to him, and his body responded. He picked her up and carried her back to the bed.

But as much as she wanted to continue, the commander was angry enough with her. "The lord commander's waiting for you," she reminded him as he laid her on the bed and nipped at her breasts through the linen shirt.

He growled in protest before rising and pulling her back to her feet.

There was a small knock on the door, and Vitalia appeared. She held a dress and a tray of cheese and fruit.

Norah smiled at him as she shimmied her shoulders. "Perhaps I'll put it on for you again this evening."

"I'd prefer to see you taking it off," he said. Then he kissed her once more and left to join the commander.

Mikael found Soren in the hall. His commander watched him approach with a steely gaze. They had much to talk about.

Soren's nostrils flared. "You're a fool. You welcome your death."

"Watch yourself," he warned.

Soren snorted. "Are you just going to ignore what happened with the Bear? What you've seen? What you've heard?"

Mikael's anger grew. "We talked about it. The matter's over."

"You mean your rutting has bewitched you."

Mikael grabbed Soren by his weapons strap and slammed him against the wall. "Be very careful of your next words," he said between his teeth. "I have no more tolerance for you, brother."

Soren shook with fury but yielded, quieting.

"Salara's joined me in my chamber," Mikael told him. "She is my wife and rules by my side, and you'll respect her as such."

"And what of the Bear?" Soren demanded.

"I've committed to her his safety."

Soren's eyes blazed. "He plots against you!"

"If you engage him, there will be consequences." Although, when had Soren ever cared for consequences? "Severe ones," he added.

Mikael released him, then turned and walked away. But he didn't head back to his chamber. He had another matter to address.

He had promised Salara the Bear's safety, but he couldn't tolerate treason.

Mikael found the lord justice with the Mercian captain and several Northmen outside by the forge, looking curiously over the hearth. No doubt they found it far less advanced than the forges of the North that produced Mercian steel. Mercian steel would advance his army to near invincible heights, and it was something Mikael needed to speak to Salara about. He should have bargained it as part of their marriage arrangement, but he hadn't, because the only thing he'd been focused on getting was *her*. He'd deal with it later. He had more pressing things to focus on now.

The Northmen stiffened when they saw him. "Northmen," Caspian called, and led them away for Mikael and the justice to speak alone.

Mikael watched them leave, noting the captain lingering a distance away should he be needed. He didn't mind. Caspian struck him as a man that would equally stop the Bear from doing something stupid as much as he'd give his life to save him. He was a respectable man, and Mikael had no intentions of doing unrespectable things. Not yet, anyway.

Mikael spoke first. "Let's not bother with courtesies," he said as he eyed the Bear.

The justice puffed a small breath in amusement, clearly never having intended to.

"You're not welcome in Kharav. I tolerate you because it's Salara's wish, but this is my realm, and regardless of whether you see me as your king, I am. And there will be rules."

The Bear snorted.

Mikael used every ounce of his strength to temper his rising anger. "You think my rules don't apply to you? Well, they apply to everyone, and if you wish to discuss it with your queen, you'll find her in my chamber where she's taken residence."

The Bear showed no emotion, but Mikael knew he'd wounded him.

"You'll cease your work of division. Kharav and Mercia are united. *Salara and I* are united. If you seek to divide us again, there will be no one to save you, not even Salara. If you engage my lord commander again, there will be consequences, and as I've told him, they'll be severe. While you're in my realm, you're subject to *my* rule. You are *mine*."

Then he turned and left the justice in the wake of his anger.

CHAPTER TEN

"Another!" Alexander bellowed as a Mercian soldier picked himself up off the ground of the sparring field. He didn't usually participate as the army practiced their drills, but he desperately needed an outlet for his anger. It had been two days since his confrontation with the Shadow King, but time had done nothing to temper his frustration, his disappointment in himself. He was failing. Failing himself and Norah.

And his challenge with the Destroyer had almost killed her. He'd been blinded by his emotion, the fear that her marriage to the Shadow King wasn't in name only.

And the king had practically confirmed it.

He waited for another soldier to step from the ranks. He had lost count of how many men he'd tested this morning on the field. His body was tiring, but he'd take a few more to help ease his troubled mind.

Another Northman stepped forward with his shield and sword.

But Alexander's mind swirled—the Shadow King had said she resided in his chamber. Did she do so willingly? It was beyond his comprehension. Did she want this marriage to be more than in name only? And worse—what turned his stomach and haunted his dreams—had she given herself to him?

He pulled up his sword again, and let the soldier make the first attack. The Northman lunged forward with an overhead swing, and Alexander met it with an upstroke of his blade. The steel echoed through the early morning. Alexander pivoted, throwing his shoulder against the chest of his opponent, and sent the man stumbling backward.

His thoughts drifted. This alliance would fail. He could understand her logic that a marriage to the Shadow King would stop the war between their kingdoms. And it had temporarily, but it wouldn't last forever. Successful alliances were formed by those who shared common goals, held common values. But the Shadowlands warred against everything Mercia stood for, against everything they believed in. And if her marriage to the Shadow King truly was complete, it would be hard to exercise any other options in the wake of a fall.

The Mercian soldier launched another attack, and Alexander found himself having to focus to counter against the well-coordinated maneuvers. His soldiers' training was coming along nicely in the Shadowlands. His men made good use of the advanced practice stations, and they had learned a few things from watching the Shadowmen run their drills. He felt both pleased and irritated, but he forced his irritation aside—if his men were improving, it was a good thing.

As the Mercian soldier broke from his attack, Alexander's mind shifted back to Norah. Did the Shadow King require her to share his chamber? Despite his loathing for the man, the king did seem to genuinely care for her. He didn't deserve the benefit of the doubt, but Alexander had seen him yield to her. If what the Shadow King said was true, if they now shared a bed, he couldn't get past the thought that this was Norah's decision. And he would want it to be her decision, yet...

His Northman launched another assault, driving him back a few paces. Alexander's body begged for rest, but his mind begged for distraction. He charged forward and locked his grip on the soldier, giving his arms a reprieve from the swing of the sword. Then he shoved the soldier back.

Had she come to have feelings for this man? He'd watched how she looked at the Shadow King—not with contempt or disdain, but he hadn't taken it for love. However, one action lingered on his mind—the way she took the king's arm. Most of the time it was the proper way, her arm scooped under his with her hand resting on his forearm. But then, sometimes, she'd curl around and clasp his upper arm, as if wanting to hold him close to her—the way she used to hold Alexander's. Before he'd lost her.

The Mercian soldier stopped and straightened, halting their bout, and Alexander followed his gaze to see the Destroyer approaching with his own warriors. The Shadow commander came in his usual fashion—darkness and depravity personified. Alexander hated that he couldn't see his face.

"Enjoying our amenities, Bear?" the Destroyer rumbled as he approached.

Alexander didn't answer. The Shadowmen invested in death; of course their practice stations were superior to those of the North.

"A friendly spar?" the Shadow commander asked, pulling his sword.

Alexander knew the invitation was anything but friendly, but he had to fight the desire to accept it with every fiber of his being. His blood burned with the want to sink his sword into the Destroyer, to cut limb and life from him. Yet it wasn't the king's warning that made him pause. He cared nothing about the king's orders, or his threats. But Norah needed more from him. Expected more. He was already failing her.

He flicked his gaze over his men. "We're done here," he said, giving them a slight nod to leave the field. "To your duties." His men pulled up and stowed their weapons and turned to leave.

"Well, isn't that just like the North," the Shadow commander growled out. "Avoiding the fight. And you wonder why your men are so poor at it."

Alexander paused. The Destroyer was goading him, he knew, and he sent back a daggered insult of his own. "Were we so poor at it during the Battle of Bahoul? When we took the mountains from you?"

If a shadow could grow darker...

"You had Aleon," the commander snarled. "Now you're alone. And do you forget, Little Bear, it was your father who helped the North King take Bahoul. You think you're half the warrior he was? You think you're worthy to wear his armor?"

Alexander's chest quaked under the taunt that hit at his core. But he couldn't let the Destroyer see. "Yet you still fear me," he cut back. "So obsessed you are with trying to kill me."

The Shadowman gave a dark chuckle. "Fear? It's *you* who runs away at a mere suggestion of a spar. Does your queen know her commander is a coward? Does she really believe you can protect her?"

His blood heated to near boiling. Alexander cast aside the protest of his weary muscles and tightened his grip on the hilt of his sword. A spar, then, to show this Shadow beast his place.

The commander's eyes smiled as he read Alexander's acceptance, and he advanced, delivering a few basic blows.

They were easy enough for Alexander to deflect, but there was a force behind them, and he knew the commander was playing with him, testing. Their men backed up to give them more space.

The Destroyer launched another attack, and Alexander countered. Their swords came together with a force that shook Alexander up his arms and to his shoulders. While the Shadow commander stood only half a head taller than him, he carried a muscled frame almost twice his size. Alexander wasn't a small man, but damn it if he didn't feel small in the wake of this giant. Their blades cross-caught as they each pitted their weight forward, but Alexander was no match in strength, and the commander pressed him backward. Their eyes locked, their faces close.

The commander chuckled.

"Show your face, coward," Alexander spat.

"What will my face show you that my sword won't?"

Alexander shoved him back and away. They circled one another, each looking for an opportunity to strike. Alexander's body moved numbly from exhaustion, but anger fueled him and kept him on his feet.

The Destroyer lunged forward, and their weapons came together in a deafening clang. They locked again, and he drove Alexander back all the way to the fence along the weapons' hold. The Shadowman used his weight as he crushed Alexander against the railing.

"But I don't think it's my face that bothers you," the commander sneered quietly so that only Alexander could hear. "I think it's your queen in Salar's bed."

The Destroyer's eyes smiled. Rage rippled through Alexander, searing the need for blood inside his heart and lighting a burn across his skin. He ripped his dagger from his belt and plunged it into the side of the Shadow commander. But his range was limited, and it wasn't a fatal strike. Regrettably.

The Destroyer stumbled backward, his eyes dropping to his side as he held his hand to the wound that now streamed blood over his hip and down his thigh. The morning came alive with the sound of swords pulled from scabbards. The Shadow commander's eyes blazed, and a snarl ripped from his throat as he charged Alexander again.

And hell broke loose onto the field.

The days came easier with Mikael's love, and Norah found herself loving in return. She could be happy here, she knew, and she started to dream about it. But with that dream came the darkness of fear, and of worry. The vision of Mikael's death haunted her. The search for the truth—and to change fate—had become even more important to her, and not just for Alexander's sake, but for her own and for Mikael's.

She walked solemnly through the main hall, but her thoughts were interrupted by a sight out the window—two soldiers helping the lord commander up from the field, shouldering his weight between them. Blood poured from a gash in his side.

Norah ran outside to meet them. "What happened?"

"I just caught a blade—it'll be fine," he said between his teeth.

Norah followed them to the healer's workroom.

"I said it's fine," the commander snapped as the healer poked at him.

Blood still poured from it. It didn't look fine. It didn't look fine at all. "How did this happen?" she pressed. "Who did this?"

"Your Bear," he snarled.

No, she didn't believe that. "Alexander did this? I don't understand. What happened? Where is he?"

He eyed her darkly.

If Alexander had been harmed... "Where is he?" she demanded, anger swelling inside her.

"Salar has him."

Norah's breath caught in her throat. *No.* She spun for the door.

She raced through the castle, outside, and toward the courtyard. Panic filled her. There would be no wounding the commander without consequence. She stumbled but didn't slow. When she reached the courtyard, a wave of horror washed over her. Two soldiers dragged Alexander toward one of two posts erected in the center. His hands were bound.

Mikael looked on, with a crowd growing around to see the commotion.

She raced toward him. "What's going on?" she demanded as she reached him.

"Salara, go back inside," Mikael told her.

She shook her head. Did he really think she would leave? "I won't! What are you doing? Release him!"

"Bring the lord commander," he bellowed as he waved to the second post beside the one Alexander was being tied against.

"Wait. What?" She reached out and clutched Mikael's arm. "He's injured! He's with the healer!"

"It won't keep him from punishment," he said, his voice solemn.

Her fear grew to desperation. "What punishment? What's going on?"

Mikael turned to another guard. "The lash," he said in a low voice.

"No!" she cried. "No!" She ran to Alexander and struggled with the rope around his wrists.

"Norah, stop," Alexander said. "There's nothing you can do. Go. Please."

"Take Salara inside," Mikael ordered.

The guards tried to take her gently, but she twisted away from them.

"Don't touch me!" she spat.

"Norah," Alexander pleaded again. His voice stopped her, and her desperate eyes found his. "Go," he said. "I don't want you to see this."

"Whatever this is, it's not going to happen!" she seethed through her tears. She wouldn't let it.

"Norah," he said again. "Please. Go."

The commander was brought out and bound to the post beside Alexander. The wound to his side was wrapped, but the blood had already started seeping through.

"No." She gritted her teeth, rising up to Mikael. "They're the heads of our armies!"

"That's why they are getting my lenience."

"*For what?*" He called this lenience?

He frowned. "They started a fight between our men."

Was that all? "Men fight all the time!"

He looked at Norah with a fury she hadn't yet seen. "They drove dissent within our armies. We lost twelve men—North and Kharavian men. I've already warned them, and I've promised severe consequences."

"The lord commander isn't fit for punishment!" she argued. "Look at him!"

Again, the king glanced at the guards. "Take her inside."

"Wait!" She reached forward and clutched Mikael's arm, her mind racing for anything else to stop him. "Mercy! I beg you, mercy!" She looked up at him, pleading. "Husband, please. I'll do anything for your mercy."

He grimaced. "This is my mercy."

The guards took her by the arms, but she wrenched away. "I said don't touch me! I'm not leaving!"

Mikael nodded to the guards and then looked at her with sadness in his eyes. "Leave her, then."

"Queen Norah," came Caspian's voice behind her, and she turned with a start.

"Caspian! You have to stop this!"

But he shook his head. "Queen Norah. I can't."

"You have to! This can't happen!"

Caspian caught her arms, pulling her still. She looked on in horror as the punisher walked toward Alexander and Soren with the lash in his hand. Their shirts had been pulled off, and their bare backs were exposed.

"Courage," Mikael called to them.

The punisher struck Alexander first, who grunted at the lash, but held fast. Again he drew the lash across Alexander's back. Purple welts sprung up across the skin. On the next strike, Alexander cried out, pulling against the rope.

"Stop!" Norah screamed, but Caspian held her tightly. She clasped her hand over her mouth to hold back a sob. That she could be married to a man who could do this—no, not a man—a monster.

Again, the lash hit across Alexander's back, and he twisted. Lash after lash. Norah didn't know how many. Alexander's legs gave way, and he lost consciousness. She sobbed as his body swayed on the post.

The punisher looked at the king, and Mikael gave a nod. Then he turned, delivering a stinging lash to the commander, who flinched but let his body hang against the post. The commander was still, almost lifeless, only tensing when the whip hit. Another lash opened the skin, and blood spilled down his back. Another lash made him cry out, and finally, after a sickening number, unconsciousness came for him too.

Norah wept with fury as the two men hung from the posts. Mikael motioned the finish and for the soldiers to collect them. Caspian released her, and she ran to Alexander. He hung limply by the binding around his wrists.

"Help me!" she cried. Caspian and another Mercian guardsman stepped forward to cut the rope.

"Careful!" She looked back at the commander. "And him."

Kharavian soldiers stepped in to help, pulling him off the post.

"Take them to my sanctuary," she said, her voice shaking.

Mikael stood, watching her. She stopped and glared at him, tears streaming down her cheeks and rage seeping from every pore.

"Salara—"

"Don't speak to me," she hissed, and she turned and followed the beaten men into the castle.

Serene met them in the room.

"Lay them both across the bed on their stomachs," Norah ordered the soldiers. "And get another bed for the commander. They won't be happy if they wake beside each other. Where's the healer?"

"He's on his way," Serene said.

The soldiers brought in another bed and set it up along the opposite wall. They moved the commander to it.

The healer came and mixed a salve while Norah washed their backs. The cleansing would be painful, and she wanted to do it while they were still unconscious. When she was finished, she took the mixture from the healer and sat on the bed next to Alexander. She bit her lip as she spread the salve across his broken skin. She'd never forgive Mikael for this.

Alexander stirred.

"Be still," she said softly. "I have only a little more to apply."

He tried to turn his head back to look at her.

"I said *be still*."

"I'm sorry," he said faintly.

She drew in a shaking breath. "I'm sorry I couldn't stop it."

"Twelve men died because of me, some of them our own Northmen." His voice cracked with guilt.

She set the bowl of salve down on the small bedside table. Men had died today. North and Kharavian men. All her men. "What caused this?"

His eyes settled on the commander on the other bed. "Only words, and they're best left unsaid."

"What words?"

He inhaled and let his breath out slowly. "I have to ask you—do you share the Shadow King's bed now, Norah? Do you love this man?"

She tried to swallow, but her throat was dry. She couldn't love a man who would do this. Because what did that make her?

The healer returned with a bowl of milky liquid. "Poppy," he told her as he offered it. "This will take away the pain and make him... unaware. Sleepy."

She took the bowl. "Drink this," she said as she held it to his lips.

Alexander drank and lay his head back down on the bed.

"Rest now," she whispered as she brushed her fingers through his golden locks. This man... If anything happened to him, if he was hurt—

She stopped. Something *had* happened to him, and he *was* hurt. Gods help Mikael when she left this room...

Within a few moments, she could see the fog roll into his eyes. They closed, and he fell into a deep sleep.

The commander was just waking as she walked over to him. The healer had almost finished coating the bleeding welts with the salve.

"I'll do the rest," she said, taking the bowl.

The healer motioned to another bowl on the table. "The poppy."

She nodded. She looked back at the commander and stared at him for a moment, before cautiously taking a seat on the side of the bed. He said nothing. He didn't snarl at her, and his eyes didn't seem to will death in her direction. Had this broken him as it had her? Did he feel betrayed, as she did?

He lay in silence as she spread the mixture over the rest of his wounds. His skin was hot to the touch. "Your side required stitches," she told him, "so don't move about." When she finished with the salve, she held the bowl of poppy for him, but he turned his head away.

"It'll help with the pain," she said.

"I want a clear head."

"Well, you're beyond that," she snapped. Then she bit her lip. She'd wanted to take a different approach with him—a kinder approach. Maybe she shouldn't care; he didn't respond to kindness.

The commander snorted in irritation.

"What happened?"

A deep rumble came from his chest. "Send the Bear back to the North."

"Why?"

"You know why," he snapped. "He shouldn't be here. And I can't trust him with Salar."

"Alexander wouldn't hurt the king. He knows I stand with Mikael."

His eyes blazed. "Have you lost your mind?"

She sighed. She didn't want to fight with him. He was as loyal to Mikael as Alexander was to her. But he didn't understand. "I need him," she whispered.

"Why?"

Filled with sadness, she looked out the window and swallowed back the threatening tears.

"Salar didn't want to do this," the commander said. "We left him no choice."

Anger flashed inside her. "How can you say that?"

"He would never choose to hurt me."

Norah scoffed. "You can't believe that. He made a choice—this choice!"

"What else should he have done? I should lose my head, and so should the Bear. Our soldiers need to see accountability. But Salar—he loves me. And he loves you. So he gave us pain over death, and I'm grateful."

Grateful? Norah didn't know what to feel, but she certainly wasn't grateful. She couldn't imagine a world where pain like that was necessary.

"Why did you defend me?" he asked.

Norah stared at him for a moment. Why *had* she defended him? "It's a character flaw," she mumbled.

She finished with his wounds and wiped the salve from her fingers, but she didn't move to stand. Their conversation wasn't over, and she gave it time.

"I'll serve you," he said finally. "Send the Bear home. You know it's best. And I'll serve you as I serve Salar."

It wasn't about service, and it was hard for her to think of being without Alexander. She needed him. She loved him. But the commander was right. It *was* best. She needed to send Alexander back to Mercia—he wasn't safe in Kharav.

And Mikael wasn't safe.

She took a deep breath, trying to quell the emotion. "Drink the poppy," she said, holding the bowl out, "and it will be done."

The commander drank deeply and let sleep come.

Chapter Eleven

Whispers all around her—a voice that flowed not through her ears, but directly into her being.

She knew this voice.

Alexander's voice, but words she couldn't understand.

Then she saw him.

He stood over a weathered trestle table layered in parchments. Maps. He spoke as he marked paths with a pen, as if to people around him, yet he was alone. Who was he talking to?

His golden locks were gone, shaved off. He was dressed in a loose black tunic and leather breeches.

"Alexander," she called.

He stopped.

He looked up from the table, but the eyes looking back at her were not the brilliant blues she knew so well. They were dark sapphire, and angry.

They locked with hers, and his lips peeled back in a chilling smile.

Norah woke with a start to Vitalia gently nudging her. She sucked in a breath and stumbled up from the chair she'd been sitting in.

"Are you all right, Salara?" Vitalia asked.

Her racing heart slowed as she realized she'd fallen asleep watching over Alexander and Soren in the sanctuary.

Slowly, she nodded. She looked at the men. Thanks to the poppy, they were still asleep, their chests rising and falling slowly with their breaths.

"You should go wash and get some rest," Vitalia whispered. "I can stay with them until you return."

Norah looked down at her dress, with its golden fabric crusted in browning blood. She wasn't sure if she could go back to sleep, but she did need to wash. Norah brushed her hair out of her face. She could trust the men to Vitalia's care for a time.

She walked stiffly to the chamber she shared with Mikael. He wouldn't be there, not after what had happened. He was most likely in his study. She caught her reflection in the hall mirror and noticed a dried smear over her temple. Alexander's blood.

Would she accept this? She thought she knew herself, but she could barely recognize the woman looking back at her. Her hands shook as she pushed open the chamber door. The image of Alexander stung her over and over, and she couldn't breathe. Her stomach twisted at the memory of his beaten body hanging limply from the post.

As she stepped inside, she stopped. Mikael's sheathed sword leaned against the wall. He was here.

A madness swept around her, crawling up her body and searing itself into her mind. She reached down and wrapped her hand around its hilt and then pulled it from the scabbard. Her skin burned with a fury, and her vision tunneled as she moved around the linen panels.

As Mikael stepped out of the bath chamber, she met him with his blade to his neck. He stopped abruptly. Norah pressed the point of the sword against his throat and walked him backward to the wall. Her arms shook—whether from her rage or the weight of the weapon, she didn't know. She dug the tip of the blade farther into his skin. Could she really hurt him? She wanted to.

"Salara," he breathed.

Did he expect her mercy? When he had none? She gritted her teeth as her eyes welled. Slowly, Mikael reached up and curled his hand around the blade.

But still she held him. She could make him pay. Except her body wouldn't let her. She couldn't move.

Mikael guided the tip away from his neck and then pulled the sword toward him. She trembled as she surrendered and let it slip from her hands.

And she hated herself—she hated that she couldn't hurt him, like he had hurt her. She hated that he could see her weakness for him.

He stepped closer, his eyes burning into her. She couldn't meet them. He reached up to touch her cheek, but she turned her face. He pulled her closer still. "I know you'll bring death to me, but it won't be today," he whispered before he kissed her head somberly. Then he moved to the door and left her to her heartache.

Mikael found the Mercian captain on the wall, and the captain straightened as he neared. Mikael leaned forward against the stone, looking out over the city. He was curious about this man. Caspian—the only Northman that Soren didn't seem to completely despise, and who held the Bear's trust. A rare combination. Perhaps the rarest. He was also the man who managed to contain Salara as Mikael punished the commanders.

"I believe her heart's filled with hatred for me now," Mikael shared in a burst of openness.

"It's very possible," the captain answered honestly.

Mikael could see why Soren tolerated him. His commander valued candidness, no matter how brutal. He did too. "I knew it would come," he said somberly. "But I didn't think she'd try to take my head. She threatened me with my own sword. But then, I'm not sure I'd expect anything less."

Caspian's eyes widened, and he shifted in surprise.

Mikael sighed. As painful as her rage toward him was, he couldn't even muster anger over it. "She loves so fiercely." He had hoped he had won some of that fervor. But after today, he was sure that anything he'd won in her heart had been lost.

The captain was quiet.

"Perhaps you can reason with her," Mikael said. "She seems to listen to you."

Caspian hesitated. "I'm not sure she'd see that as my place. And I'm not sure she'd hear me. Not on this."

Mikael nodded again—it was as he'd feared. "Is it beyond repair?"

Caspian gave a reluctant tilt of his head. "I don't know."

Mikael crossed his arms and brought his fist to his lips. "I can't lose her."

"Give it time, then, Salar. I won't say that she'll forgive, but I don't think she can lose you either."

Mikael looked at the captain curiously. "Why aren't you angry with me, Northman? Why don't you hate me? For what I've done to you, your men, your kingdom. And now to your justice, whom I can see you're close with."

He watched as the captain drew in a deep breath and let it out slowly. "I have been angry. Sometimes I still am. But I know war makes men no longer men. And we've warred for so long that none of us should recognize ourselves, including me. I don't like your decisions. They wouldn't have been my own, but I don't wear the burden of the crown."

"I don't know what to think of you, Captain," Mikael admitted. He looked out over the wall at the city. "I have to travel to the Horsemen tribes of Caan. I won't be gone long, but perhaps long enough that Salara may settle a bit. Will you tell her, tell her that I'll be eager to return to her?"

Caspian nodded. "Of course."

Mikael gave him a nod in thanks and left the wall.

Washed but not rested, Norah made her way back to the sanctuary. She worried Alexander and Soren would try to kill each other again, or disappear to tend to themselves. But in peeking through the door, she saw them still resting on their beds.

She tried to enter quietly, but Soren was awake and turned his head toward her. She glanced over at Alexander, who was still asleep.

"You're still here," she said softly, drawing close to the commander.

He gave an annoyed snort. "I thought you might see me lashed again if I left."

She couldn't help a small smile. Norah picked up the bowl of salve on the table and sat carefully on the bed beside him. She touched his back gently, testing the wounds. The lacerations had started to scab over, but they still needed care. She dipped her fingertips into the healing mixture and spread it across the torn skin.

"You don't have to tend me," he said.

She shrugged. "Well, I'm here, you're here, and you need it, so that's how this works."

Norah finished applying the salve and wiped her hands on a cloth. She picked up a rolled strip of clean linen. "Can you sit up?"

He pushed himself up, wincing.

She held the end of the linen roll against his chest, and he raised his arms, letting her wrap it around him. She looped the wrap over his shoulder and pinned it, then picked up another.

"You'll send him back to the North?" Soren asked as she worked.

She knew he would press her to send Alexander back. It was the right thing to do. It was what she should do, and she had agreed. Why was she struggling so much with it?

He grabbed her hand, stopping her. "You'll send him back?"

Reluctantly, she nodded. She pinned the second wrap, then pulled some fresh clothing for him from a side chair.

Soren rose gingerly from the bed. He pulled on his breeches but eyed the shirt she held for him.

"You should keep covered while you heal, and not let the wounds dry out," she said, stepping close. "Let me help."

But he pulled away. "I don't need help to dress myself," he said sharply.

She knew he felt vulnerable, and that it unsettled him. "I know you don't," she said back, with her own sharpness, trying to keep from sounding too caring. "But I don't want you messing up my bandaging."

He stood a moment, then yielded grudgingly, letting her pull the back of the shirt down as he pushed his arms through one at a time. Then he put on his boots. Dressed, he stopped and looked at her quietly. Silence—his means of thanks.

"Go on." She nodded to the door. "And have that bandage changed daily."

He gave an obliging nod and then glanced over at Alexander, who still slept, before letting himself out of the room.

Norah sighed heavily and made her way to Alexander. His eyes were closed and his face peaceful, but his back still bore the harshness of the day before. She sat on the bed beside him and brushed her fingers along the curve of his shoulder and down his arm.

His eyes opened at her touch, and he gave a small smile. She reached and swept the blond locks from his forehead. "How do you feel?" she asked.

"Sore, but better than I expected."

Norah checked the scabbed welts. She spread salve over his wounds again, as she had for Soren. He grimaced as she touched a particularly nasty abrasion.

"Sorry," she whispered. Her heart hurt. This was her fault. She should have sent him home sooner.

He watched her from the corner of his eye as she finished and wiped her hands on a clean cloth. He waited patiently, always so patiently. She reached her hand out and ran her fingers through his hair. He closed his eyes again under the feel of her touch.

"Do you miss Mercia?" she asked.

He opened his eyes and gingerly rolled onto his side to look at her. "All the time."

"Me too."

Alexander winced as he sat up.

"Easy," she told him. His eyes burned a brilliant blue. They were beautiful, and they brought a wave of emotion she hadn't expected.

"Hey, hey," he whispered as he took her hand. "What's the matter?"

Everything was the matter. She shook her head. "You have to go back. To Mercia."

He balked slightly, his brow creasing in objection. "I'm not leaving you."

"You have to," she insisted.

"You need me."

"I'm a queen with two kingdoms now, and both my military heads are here. Mercia needs you. Grandmother needs you."

"I can send Caspian," he argued.

"Alexander, I'm sending you."

His face twisted. "I dishonored you, I know, but—"

"I'm not sending you back because you dishonored me!" She couldn't fight the tears that threatened. "You could have been killed. So long as you remain in Kharav, it's my constant fear. Simply being here puts you in danger, and it puts the king in danger."

"I swear to you, Norah, I swear to you I won't bring harm to the king. You have my word."

And she believed him, but—

"It's not enough," she whispered. She stood and picked up a strip of linen. She pressed the end against his chest, but he reached up and covered her hand in his, making her pause.

"Norah," he said softly, looking up at her. "Come with me." His eyes bore into hers, begging.

Norah's heart ached. *Go with him*—how she wanted to. She brought her hand to his face and grazed his cheek with her fingertips. She felt her eyes well as she gave a sad smile. "You know I can't," she said. "Plus, I left things... harshly with the king. I..." She paused. "He'll be back before the moon wanes. I need to stay and settle the division of our kingdoms."

"He left?"

"He had to meet with a Horsemen tribe." Norah bit the inside of her cheek. "You need to leave before he returns."

Just the thought of his absence left her with a gaping hole. To not be able to hear his voice, to not see his smile, to not feel the warmth of his touch or to have his nearness. It stole her peace and crushed her heart. But she needed him to leave. To keep him safe. To send him away from this Shadow King—this Shadow King she loved.

The cold morning air gave away the unsteady emotion of her breath. Norah watched as the Northmen finished preparations for the journey to Mercia. Caspian would escort them back and return with a new unit of soldiers. Only her Mercian guardsman Titus would remain with her.

She stood in the courtyard to see them off. Alexander mounted his white destrier, and she stepped close, running her hand up the animal's neck and under the warmth of its thick mane. She looked up at him and gave a sad smile.

"How long?" he asked her. "How long will you let yourself be kept here?"

She didn't answer. She didn't know. She might not ever be able to leave, but she couldn't think about that now. It would break her. The thought of not seeing him again—it was already breaking her. She needed him to leave before she couldn't let him go. "Goodbye, Alexander." She gave his mount a soft pat and stepped back.

His jaw tightened as he gave her a longing look of goodbye, then he reined his destrier around and urged it forward with his men following behind.

She walked back to the castle and found Soren waiting for her out front. Her heartache turned to bitterness. "I hope this satisfies you."

"Salar will be obsessed with your forgiveness when he returns."

"It's not to be had." She pushed past him and continued toward the castle. It was all she could do to make it back to the privacy of her bedchamber before the tears came. Alone, she sank to the cold stone floor and let the sadness take over.

Chapter Twelve

The Northmen set a quick pace en route to Mercia, and Caspian could feel the army's spirits lifting as they set their thoughts on home. But an uneasiness sat in his stomach. They would ride through the western Canyonlands instead of east and through Bahoul as they normally traveled. While it was a faster route, it wasn't preferred. The route through Bahoul passed through the allied outreaches of Aleon. Safer lands—at least, they used to be safer.

With Mercia and Kharav now united, they would travel through Kharav's allies, mostly the Horsemen. The first test would be the Uru.

But Caspian was looking forward to one thing—seeing Tahla again.

It took almost three days to reach the Canyonlands. The army traveled much slower than Caspian and the lord commander had traveled before. He found himself growing impatient, but his frustration fell away as his attention shifted to his friend riding beside him.

Alexander rode lethargically, but not from his wounds. Caspian knew the justice was not looking forward to returning to his cherished Mercia, for he had left his heart in Kharav. They hadn't talked about what had happened—the lashing—and they wouldn't. Pain of the flesh was temporary. Caspian worried more about Alexander's spirit, which seemed to die more with each step farther from Kharav, each step farther from Norah.

"She worries for you," Caspian told him, breaking the silence in unusual form. "That's why she sends you back."

Alexander shifted from his thoughts. "She shouldn't."

"Yes, she should," he corrected him. Alexander wasn't thinking straight. "You don't generally threaten the life of a king like she did with no consequence. Especially the Shadow King."

Alexander's head jerked up and his brow furrowed. "What?"

Caspian gaped at him in surprise. Alexander hadn't known. "I'm sorry. I thought you knew."

"Norah threatened the king?"

Caspian nodded. "That's what he said, threatened him with his own sword."

Alarm grew in his eyes. "And what does he plan to do?"

He shook his head. "Nothing. He seeks her forgiveness."

Alexander looked back at him in disbelief. "Her forgiveness?"

It had dumbfounded Caspian too. But he saw something in the Shadow King he hadn't thought possible—he loved the queen. Surely that was the only reason Alexander was still alive and permitted to come and go from the Shadowlands as he did. Alexander was the Shadow King's greatest threat, yet he remained untouched. But for how long?

"She needs to take care," Caspian warned his friend. "And you do too."

It was almost dark when the canyons came into view. Caspian knew the unease that rippled through the army, the same unease he'd felt when he had come before. He'd be lying if he said he didn't feel it again. While he didn't think Tahla and the Uru would attack them, he wasn't sure they'd welcome them either. Not like the Shadowmen.

"Where are these Uru?" Alexander asked him. "And the village?"

"They are watching us, I'm sure," Caspian said as they reached the base. "They'll show themselves soon. Our men should wait here. Let us go to meet them."

Alexander cast a skeptical eye. He bid the men to stay at the base, and he and Caspian set into the canyons on foot.

Darkness layered the canyons, and Caspian found the footing difficult. He heard Alexander struggling as well. How did the Kharavian soldiers find their way so effortlessly in the night?

"It doesn't appear these Uru are going to show," Alexander said after a time.

Caspian looked up into the darkness. "They're here. I know it."

"Then what do they wait for?" Alexander asked. "Let's make camp with the men. We'll find our way through in the morning."

"We won't find our way through the canyons without their help."

"Then we'll go to the eastern pass and go through Bahoul."

That would take even longer than originally going the route through Bahoul. No. The Uru were here. "Tahla!" he called.

But there was no response.

Caspian combed the peaks of the canyons against the starlit sky, looking for movement. But all was still.

"Tahla!" he bellowed again.

Again, silence.

Alexander gave him a hearty pat on the shoulder and turned back the way they had come. Caspian sighed and finally followed.

But a woman's voice stopped them. "Is the North so bold to assume the Uru friends now?"

Caspian spun to see a shadow drawing close.

"Queen Norah would think so." He knew it was Tahla, and although he couldn't see her face, he knew she was smiling.

A torch was lit, and Caspian stepped back in seeing the Uru had surrounded them. Alexander put his hand on his sword, but Caspian held out his arm to settle him. Then he looked back at her, and his heart raced. She was just as he remembered, perhaps even more beautiful.

"How is my sister?" Tahla asked.

"She's well. She sends us back to Mercia for an exchange of men and goods. We hoped"—he hoped—"that you would see us through the canyons."

"I might be persuaded." Her lips curved into a sly smile. Then her eyes found Alexander. "Who's this?"

"The Mercian lord justice."

She drew closer to Alexander, and Caspian gave him a small nod of reassurance. "This is Tahla. Daughter of the Urun chief. The Uru are close friends of Salar and Kharav," he explained.

"And Salara," Tahla added, and Caspian smiled.

"And Salara," he echoed.

"Tahla." Alexander gave a respectful bow of his head.

"The Mercian lord justice," Tahla said curiously. "That sounds important. Are you an important man, Lord Justice?"

"He is the queen's right hand," Caspian told her. "Her commander."

Tahla exhaled a breath of realization. "The Bear." A smile peeled across her lips. She stepped closer. "I never thought I'd actually meet you." Tahla took a torch from the Urun warrior next to her and moved even closer to Alexander. She circled him, running her eyes over him, studying him. "You don't look like a bear."

The corners of Alexander's mouth turned up. "I hope I don't disappoint."

Her smile returned. "Not at all."

A pang of jealousy coursed through Caspian, but he leashed it. He wasn't blind to seeing Alexander was an attractive man and drew the eyes of many women, but Tahla seemed mostly curious. And who wouldn't be curious about the famed Mercian justice?

"Have your men make camp where they are," she told them. "In the morning we'll provide passage. But you both, we'll host you this evening."

"We can stay with the army," Alexander said.

But she cut him a sharp eye. "I said we'll host you."

"We would be honored," Caspian interjected, and Tahla gave him a wry smile.

They made their way back to the small army and had the men set camp, while the Uru waited just inside the canyon.

Alexander eyed him warily. "Are you sure about this?"

"I'm not sure of anything," he replied.

After their men were settled, Alexander and Caspian followed Tahla through the narrow slot canyons until they opened up to the sky, then around to where the village appeared, just as he remembered.

People gathered as they approached.

"My father's away," Tahla said. "He's visiting another tribe. He'll be very disappointed to have missed you."

Caspian knew she was talking to Alexander. Of course the chief would want to meet him. Everyone always wanted to meet Alexander, but Alexander was a man who kept to himself, and didn't particularly enjoy the attention. Caspian wouldn't have either in his place. The life of the justice was one he didn't envy.

When they reached the village, Tahla waved toward a small house and looked at Caspian. "You'll find your quarters there," she told him. Then she turned back to Alexander. "Bear, you'll come with me." And she led the lord justice toward the center of the village.

Caspian looked at the small house, then back to Alexander and Tahla disappearing around a corner behind a row of small houses. He sighed, disappointed. His return hadn't been as he had expected. But what had he expected? He chastised himself. He shouldn't have expected anything. He'd had only the briefest of exchanges with Tahla. She'd already forgotten, as he should.

Caspian made his way to the house provided to him and stepped inside. It was comfortable, with a prepared bed and a fire. He pulled off his sword and armor, laying them by a small table, and sat on the edge of the bed. His body ached, but he wouldn't complain. The queen was cared for. Alexander was leaving Kharav with his life and on his way back to the safety of Mercia. The Shadow King seemed committed to the peace the queen sought. War no longer loomed over the kingdoms. With this, he would be content.

A knock on the door pulled him from his thoughts, and he rose to answer. He opened it and then stepped back in surprise.

Tahla stood with a small plate of food. "May I?" she asked.

She didn't even need to ask. "Of course," he said as he swept the door wider and motioned her in.

"You delivered on your promise, Northman," she said as she put the plate down on the table.

He hoped his nervousness didn't show. "And what promise was that?"

She turned back toward him with a slight smirk. "That I would see you again."

She had remembered. His pulse quickened. "Were you looking forward to it?" he asked.

"Perhaps I was." She drew closer to him. "I wondered if, perhaps, you were looking forward to it too."

Caspian swallowed. He didn't find himself a particularly shy man, but with this woman, he couldn't think—not enough to trust his words. "Perhaps," he answered back finally.

"Is that all?" she prodded.

He stepped closer to her. She was playing with him. "You would ask a man to bare his soul?"

"Among other things," she said mischievously. She closed the gap between them, looking up, her dark brown eyes drawing him in. "Is that all?" she asked again.

In a move that surprised even himself, Caspian reached up and pushed a lock of hair back over her shoulder. How did she have such power over him? He would give her whatever she asked. "Perhaps I thought of you every day since I last saw you," he admitted. "Perhaps on the journey here, I was consumed with the thought of being able to see you again. Is that enough?"

She raised a brow with a wry smile. "If it were true." She didn't know how true it was.

"Do you think it's not? Enchantress?" He lowered his head closer to hers.

Tahla lifted her chin, bringing her lips to where they almost touched his. "Do you want to kiss me, Northman?"

"You don't even know me. You shouldn't let me kiss you."

She grinned. "I know you well enough. And that doesn't answer my question." She put her hand on his chest. "Do you?"

Was it an invitation? He brought a hand to her cheek, threading his fingers around to the nape of her neck and pulling her closer.

Just then, an Urun warrior called to Tahla from outside, interrupting them.

She answered, then gave Caspian a mischievous smile. "You're a dangerous one, Northman."

But Caspian knew he was the one in danger.

She slipped away and stepped toward the door. "Will you be returning?" she asked him.

He straightened, pulling himself back together. "Yes, I'll be returning to Kharav with a new unit from Mercia."

"Then I'll expect you to return through the canyons."

With certainty.

"And you owe me a kiss," she added.

Caspian's pulse thrummed in his throat, and he gave a shy smile. "On my return, then."

"Rest well, Northman," she said.

Caspian let out a breath as he watched her go.

Chapter Thirteen

True to Caspian's message, Mikael wasn't gone long. Only a week had passed, and the horns signaled his return. When he'd left, Norah thought it would be hard to face him again, but as she stood looking out the window of the chamber they shared, the flutter in her stomach surprised her. She pushed it down quickly. This wasn't a man she could let herself love. She'd move back into the sanctuary tonight.

Norah checked herself in the mirror and headed down to the courtyard. She walked into the square and took her place next to the lord commander.

"I didn't think you'd come," he said without turning his head.

She'd surprised them both, then. "I didn't think I would either."

The returning soldiers brought with them a new herd of horses, and Norah watched as they drove the animals toward the corrals behind the stables. These weren't the normal working horses that she often saw around the castle and city. They were giant beasts—destriers—like Soren's. Like Mikael's.

Mikael rode through the gates. Her heart pulsed painfully in her chest. She shouldn't have come, but she'd missed him. She hated herself for it.

He looked up at the castle, to her sanctuary window, expecting her to be there instead of in the courtyard. She wished she could see him underneath his helm. As if hearing her wishes and answering, he pulled it off. His gaze moved to her sanctuary window again. But she wasn't there. Melancholy hung from his face. Her heart hurt more. His eyes moved through the crowd until he found Soren, and he gave a nod.

Then his eyes locked on her.

Norah almost smiled at him but stopped. She couldn't let herself forget. The thought of Alexander being beaten brought back the wave of anger.

He urged his mount nearer to them, not taking his eyes from her. When he reached her, he swung his leg forward and over, and slid to the ground.

She stood, unmoving.

"Salara," he said softly.

"Salar," she replied. She'd never used his title, and it felt strange on her lips.

He closed the space between them but didn't touch her. "Have you been well?" he asked.

That was a relative term in this kingdom. She hadn't died. "Well enough. And you?"

"Not well enough," he said, even softer.

His words thrummed a chord within her, but she quieted the song that called. She couldn't be so quick to forgive him. He offered her his arm, and she stared at it. Had they been in the castle, in a more private setting, she would have refused it. But in the courtyard, in front of everyone, the slight would be noticed. He would deserve it, she told herself.

He didn't press her. He only stood, waiting.

She yielded. But instead of sliding her hand underneath and taking it, she simply laid her hand atop his vambrace, letting him feel her distance.

He led her through the throngs of people who had come to greet their salar, and into the castle. Behind the latch of the heavy wooden doors, she dropped her hand as they made their way through the great hall.

Mikael glanced at Soren. "We'll meet later. There's something I have to tend to," he said, shifting his gaze to Norah.

He meant her. So much for avoiding him. She led the way to their chamber, hoping to reach it before he said anything. Confrontations in front of others unnerved her, and she'd need all her strength for this. They swept inside, and he closed the door behind them.

He unfastened his belt and leaned his sword against the wall. He would be smart to leave it on, she thought to herself.

"You're still angry," he started.

She'd never stop being angry.

He stepped closer. "You hate me now, then?"

"I hate you," she jabbed. The words slipped out before she could stop them. They weren't entirely true; she hated herself more. She hated that she wanted to forgive him.

He stiffened. She'd wounded him. Good. He'd wounded her.

"I knew it was only a matter of time," he told her, his voice low.

"How astute," she knifed back, "that you can expect me to hate a monster."

His jaw tightened and anger flashed in his eyes. "I had no choice."

"You always have a choice!"

Heat radiated from him now as his own fury grew. "You're right," he snarled. "I should have killed him. If this is what it cost me, I should have killed him."

She struck him across the face, a stinging slap that hurt her too. She tried to strike him again, but he caught her hand. Norah twisted sideways, almost breaking his hold, but he spun around behind her, caging her with his arms and holding her close.

"I should have killed him, and I should have done it sooner," he hissed in her ear. She sank her teeth into his wrist, stunning him enough to wriggle loose and catch him with her elbow. He grunted and pulled her tighter, using his size to overpower her. "I should have taken his head when he first arrived," he said through his teeth. "When I was stronger. When your hate might have been bearable."

"Get off of me!" she cried. She struggled against him.

"But I was a fool," he said, "and I let myself love you. The seer showed me my fate, and I gave not the slightest resistance. The Bear will take everything from me. Even you. He doesn't even acknowledge me, in my own realm, so smug he is under your protection! He refuses my rule, refuses even to present himself at my return!"

"He's not here!" she screamed through the tears that had started to fall. "I sent him back!"

He stopped. He loosened his hold but did not release her. "What?"

"I sent him back to Mercia," she said between uneven breaths. Norah wept as he turned her to face him. She tried to shake him off, but he still held her. "I couldn't look at him. To see the wounds *you* gave him!" She hit his chest with her fist. He didn't bother defending against the blow.

She stilled, spent with emotion. "I sent him away because I can't protect him." She took another sobbing breath. "And because I love you, and I can't face him." Those were words she hadn't intended to speak.

The heat of his fury faded. They stood in the quiet, him watching her. She put her face in her hands. Mikael pulled her to him and held her. His touch was gentle now, and it only brought more tears from her. She cursed her emotion.

Mikael lifted her up and carried her to the bed, where he laid her down atop the cover of black silk. Then he crept up and lay beside her. He waited for her to calm, then he spoke. "Is it possible?" he asked softly. "For you to love me?"

Norah drew in a ragged breath of emotion. "It's impossible for me not to," she whispered. She hadn't wanted to admit it, but it had been true for a long time. That scared her. Regardless of what he'd done—and perhaps more frightening, what he might do—she loved him.

He moved over her, covering her body with his. The dark pools of his searching stare swept over her face, as if not quite believing. But she'd meant what she said.

And he saw it. The faint flicker in his eyes—she knew he saw it. He bent his head to hers, but she reached up and gripped him at the base of his jaw, making him pause. "But if you touch him again..."

Mikael's face grew serious. "I know," he said softly.

And she pulled him down to seal her promise with a kiss.

Chapter Fourteen

Cheers rang through Mercia as the Northmen crossed the bridge and entered the courtyard of the castle. Families met their loved ones with hugs and tears. Alexander should have been happy to return, yet he wasn't. He doubted happiness would find him again. Regardless, he covered himself with a smile as he nodded to the throngs of people who had come to greet them.

He dismounted and turned his horse over to a stable hand, then strode up the stairs of the castle judisaept to where he knew the council awaited him. As he made his way through the great hall, he stopped.

Catherine stood, alone in the hall, waiting, for news of Norah, no doubt. While she was regent in Norah's absence and concerned with the health of the queen, she was also Norah's grandmother, and she feared as a grandmother would.

He walked to her.

"Does she not come?" she asked when he reached her, her eyes brimmed with worry.

He shook his head. Norah hadn't come. She *wouldn't* come.

"Grandmother," he said softly. He didn't know what made him call her by the name he had used for her as a child, or what brought the crushing heaviness of emotion down on him, but it came suddenly and without warning. He couldn't say any more.

"Oh, my dear boy," she breathed, and pulled him into a tight embrace.

He clung to her and gave himself a moment—a moment to suffer his loss, to grieve, to feel the weight of hopelessness and defeat. So many feelings he denied himself, but he let them come this once.

And then the moment was over. He collected himself and pulled back.

"How is she?" she whispered.

"She's all right," he told her.

Catherine let out a long breath as she clutched her chest. She seemed to find the relief that escaped him.

It was true Norah was safe, but for how long? He'd been forced to leave her alone in the kingdom of a false ally, unable to see her, to protect her. Every day he faced the risk of losing her. Forever.

Catherine searched his face. "Why doesn't she come home?" She clutched at the ruffled collar of her gown as she stepped back and cast her gaze to the floor around her. "Did she not read my letter?"

It was a rhetorical question, and one he didn't answer. He wasn't sure he could answer. He hadn't seen Norah read it, but surely she wouldn't have ignored a letter from her grandmother. He had placed it in her hands almost two months prior, seemingly a lifetime ago.

"I told her to come urgently. She must come home." Catherine looked out the windows of the hall as she wrung her hands. "Why doesn't she come?"

He offered the only explanation he could. "The peace between Mercia and the Shadowlands hangs in a delicate balance. She stays and works to sustain it."

"She can't sustain it! Foolish girl. The council won't stand for this." Catherine's breaths became labored from her worry. "Phillip amasses troops at Aleon's southern borders. He intends to advance. She can't be there. She needs to come home, where she's safe. I told her to come urgently." She wavered slightly.

He grabbed her arm to steady her, but his mind reeled and his pulse quickened. "Phillip intends to advance against the Shadowlands?" With Norah there...

"No, against Japheth."

Alexander settled, but only slightly. If Phillip moved against his brother, the Shadow King's ally, the Shadowlands would join. No doubt that was the intent.

Catherine gripped his hand tightly, catching herself, then she released him. "We must go to the judisaept," she said, straightening. "The council awaits."

The council remained a governing body in the queen's absence, even though Catherine was regent. If they had a unanimous decision on a matter, they could override her, and even Alexander. Alexander didn't detest the council as Catherine did, but there were only a couple he deeply trusted, primarily James, who was more like a father to him.

Alexander strode alongside her to the judisaept, where the council was indeed waiting.

"Welcome home, Lord Justice," Edward greeted him as he stepped inside.

He bowed his head. "Thank you, Councilman." He almost added that it was good to be home, but he'd be lying.

The councilmen looked past him, then at each other.

"Where is the queen?" James asked.

Alexander swallowed. "She didn't come."

Edward looked at Catherine. "You were to convince her to return home in the letter."

"I tried, but she doesn't understand there's a larger plan at work."

Plan. Alexander stiffened. There was a difference between knowing Phillip would move against Japheth and planning with him. Planning with him would be... treason. Alexander curled his hand around the hilt of his sword. That, he wouldn't allow.

"You didn't tell her?" Edward asked.

Catherine scoffed. "I wouldn't put such words into enemy hands!"

Alexander's heart thundered as he realized—he'd helped them. He was also guilty, but his intentions were to make sure Norah had options. That she wasn't forced to stay in a situation that wasn't her choosing.

But this... She wasn't choosing this...

His eyes met James's, Mercia's most loyal adviser. Norah's father had trusted him. Alexander's father had trusted him. Alexander trusted him. James wouldn't tolerate treason, and James's eyes told him to settle.

"Our priority is keeping Queen Norah safe," James said, not taking his gaze from Alexander. "Protecting her and protecting Mercia."

Was it treason when they worked to protect her? And Catherine—for years she'd worked relentlessly to hold Norah's throne, in the face of uncertainty and doubt. She'd never betray her blood. Alexander settled, dropping his hand from his sword.

"We have to proceed cautiously," James said. "If the Shadow King discovers—"

"The Shadow King knows," Alexander said. "He knows I went to Aleon. He knows of Phillip's offer."

Catherine put a hand over her mouth, and the councilmen looked at each other in fearful surprise.

"They have eyes everywhere," Alexander said. "Tensions are escalating. It's why the queen bid my return." He left off the lashing. That wouldn't help the circumstance.

"Is she in danger?" Catherine asked, her voice barely a whisper.

"She's always in danger there," he cut back, sharper than he'd intended. He softened his tone. "But the Shadow King"—he paused—"he seems to... have a great affection for her."

"We could use that," Henricus said.

"Time is against us," Edward stressed. "Whatever we do, we must do it now, while her marriage remains unconsummated."

Alexander's chest tightened. He stayed silent. He wouldn't speak of what he suspected, what he feared. He wouldn't say that Norah returned the king's affections. That she now shared his bed. As far as the council was concerned, the marriage contract had not been fully executed. An alliance to Aleon was still an option—one that he would let them believe if it helped get her back to safety. But his skin still rippled with unease. They walked a fine line here.

"Tell us of the attack, the stabbing," Catherine said. "Who's to blame?"

Alexander's mind reeled back to the attack on Norah, and he stiffened. But he chose his words carefully. "A disgruntled citizen, offended by the marriage." The topic of the king's previous wives would only fuel the fires, and despite Alexander's desire to build a wall between Mercia and the Shadowlands, and between the Shadow King and Norah, he found himself pulling back.

"We need to get her out of there," Catherine breathed. She turned to James. "What do we do now?"

Edward looked at Alexander. "We must find a way to get you back to the Shadowlands."

"He can't return," Catherine argued. "It's too dangerous for him there, now that our efforts are known. And the vision of the Shadow King's fall shows the lord justice on the battlefield with Aleon, who is not yet by our side. We must trust the gods and wait. You can't force the hand of fate."

"I lean the same," James said.

Edward pursed his lips. "Send word to Aleon, then. Phillip must know the queen is still there, and to hold. We wait—for the Shadow King to be drawn from his shadows."

Alexander's hand rested on the hilt of his sword again.

His feet fell heavy through the hall as he made his way to his chamber. Alexander's mind was chaos, warring with his heart. The comfort of home should come as consolation, but it didn't. He found himself wishing he were back in the Shadowlands, with Norah. He would follow her anywhere, even into the fires of hell.

Jude came quickly as Alexander stepped into the chamber. "My lord." He bowed. "It's good to have you home."

"Good to see you, Jude." He greeted his servant with a friendly nod. Jude had worked for him for well over twenty years, and Alexander was fond of him. "I hope you've been well."

"I have, my lord."

"How's my brother?"

Jude raised his brows. "Asks the council about you incessantly, but he's well."

Alexander couldn't help a smile. "Send for him"—he held up his fingers—"actually, let me wash first."

"Of course, my lord." Jude heated water for the tub in the side bath chamber as Alexander sat in a chair and pushed off his boots by the heel.

He stood and pulled off his travel-worn clothes and then stepped wearily to the tub and into the bath.

Suddenly, Jude stepped back in alarm.

Alexander had almost forgotten—his back. It was a few weeks healed now, the pain gone, but no doubt still evidenced on his skin. "Not a word," he said as he sank into the steaming water. His servant nodded obediently and left him to wash.

Alexander bathed quickly. He wanted to see how Adrian fared. His body ached, but he'd have to muster the strength to spar as well. His brother loved showing him his progress with the sword. He had become quite good, rivaling even Alexander. Any day now he might overtake him. That would be a proud day.

He stepped from the bath, drying quickly, and pulled on the clean breeches Jude had laid out for him. The water seemed to have returned some of his energy. He stretched his arms out, enjoying the prickle across his skin from the chilled air. Then he pulled the clean linen shirt from the hook on the wall and stepped out of the bath chamber and back into his room to the vanity.

"Jude, I—"

"Gods' mercy!" Catherine's voice rang out.

He stopped, and his chest tightened. She'd seen his back. He turned to face her. Her lip trembled in horror.

Alexander glanced at Jude in the corner of the room, who shook his head fervently that he hadn't betrayed him. "You may go," he told him, and Jude slipped out of the room.

"You've been tortured," Catherine breathed.

It wasn't entirely different from how he expected she might react. "I wasn't tortured. I was punished. By the king."

"For what cause?" she demanded.

"I'd prefer not to discuss it." But he knew that wouldn't be the end of it.

"And what makes him think he has the right to punish the lord justice of Mercia in such a way?"

"He's the king of Mercia," he snapped. As much as he hated to say it, it was true. He took a breath, drawing back his patience. It was out of concern she was reacting in this way, he told himself.

"You'll tell me what happened," she pressed.

"I said I don't want to talk about it."

"You'll tell me, or I'll convene the council to address the matter of your torture."

His nostrils flared. He didn't think she would take it that far. And the council was already walking a line he wasn't comfortable with. "I said I was punished. Not tortured."

Catherine stepped to him, her cheeks shaking. There was real fear in her eyes, and it sobered him. He calmed himself. Slowly, she moved around him. There was no use trying to hide it from her. He stood silently. Her breath hitched behind him, but she said nothing. Then, slowly, she came back around to face him. Her eyes were large and rimmed red.

"You'll tell me what happened," she insisted.

"A crime against the crown," he said finally. "I engaged with the Destroyer. It created chaos in the ranks, and twelve men died, Northmen included. It's my punishment."

Catherine shook her head. "How could Norah allow such a thing?"

"Did you not hear what I just said?" he asked, his voice sharp and angry now. "I was guilty. The Destroyer was charged the same, and he bears the same marks I do."

"Norah should have stopped it!" she said through her tears.

"She tried!" he thundered back. "She begged him for mercy. But we'd already been given mercy in keeping our heads. Caspian had to hold her."

Catherine gaped at him in horror.

"She threatened his life that night," he continued. "She threatened the Shadow King."

"What?" Catherine's voice shook.

There was no hiding his rage now. "If she'd have done that to a Mercian king, she would have been guilty of high treason and her fate much worse, even as queen. I'm sure it's the same in the Shadowlands, except... the Shadow King loves her." He forced an icy calm back to his voice. "So, no, she didn't *allow* this to happen."

Rage steamed from his skin. "It's so easy for you and the council to judge her, to question her. But you have no idea the sacrifices she makes. She bears the burden of our people the best she can, this burden you like to remind her of so frequently." Alexander's anger left him breathless. "And you've abandoned her in it. Everyone has. And now she's all alone."

Catherine stood, speechless, whether by his words or by her regret, he didn't care. He pulled on his shirt and boots and left her to the afternoon.

Chapter Fifteen

The morning air hung cold and wet, heavy enough to drown a person, but it didn't matter. Nothing could dampen her spirits. Norah pulled on her gloves and mounted Sephir, looking back at the soldiers who were preparing to depart. It seemed the entire Crest was to travel with her, but she wasn't going to complain. It had taken a great amount of convincing for Mikael to allow her to visit Hamed and Marta and their grandchildren who'd helped her to the seer, and even more convincing to do so without him escorting her. It didn't require a king to see her visit friends. Apparently, it did require the commander of the entire Kharavian army, who had nothing more important to do. Soren insisted on going, and of course Mikael had agreed. At least her Mercian guardsman Titus was accompanying her as well—not all her travel companions would make her want to jump off another cliff.

Mikael stood in the courtyard to see her off. He eyed the large wagon that accompanied them. "What is all that?" he asked.

She smiled down at him from atop Sephir. "Gifts. And I'm very excited to give them."

He raised an amused brow and nodded. "Here," he said, pulling a purse of coins from his belt and holding it out. "Add this."

She leaned over and pulled him close. "Who is this kind soul?" she teased him.

"This family took care of my salara," he replied. "I'm in their debt."

She smiled and kissed him. "I'll return tomorrow."

"I'll do my best not to come out after you before then."

She feigned a scowl. Then she straightened and urged Sephir out from the courtyard, starting her way through the hills and toward the valley.

The journey was quiet but enjoyable, and Norah let the daydream of seeing the small family again entertain her mind. She wondered what Calla kept herself busy with, and how Cohen fared. She hoped Hamed and Marta's garden was coming along nicely, and she was excited for them to see the gifts she had brought.

Titus rode alongside her.

"I'm glad you've come along," she told him.

"Are you expecting things to run afoul?"

"No, of course not." She smiled. "I'm excited for you to meet Calla and Cohen. More than anything, I want to take Calla to Mercia—her skill with a bow…" She smiled again. "And Cohen, he's an incredible swordsman, and at such a young age. I think it will be good for them to see Mercia and Kharav's greatest warriors: you, Bhastian, Kiran, the others."

"Do they not have anyone?"

"They have their grandparents. Their grandfather trained them. Their parents died in battle, fighting for Kharav."

"So, they're generational soldiers," he said with an approving nod. "Like me."

"Your father was in the army?"

Titus nodded again. "Yes, and his father, and his father, and on a long line before. Almost as long as the lord justice's family."

So much pride in family commitment. She could understand that. "Will you have any children of your own, Titus?" she asked him with a small smile. "To carry on the line?"

The seasoned guard grew quiet for a moment. "Regal High, I…" his voice fell low, keeping his words private. "This isn't where I would normally make such a request, but when I return to Mercia, it's my intention to find a wife. With your permission."

Norah gasped. "Of course you have my permission! I'm so happy for you!"

He smiled bashfully. She almost thought she saw some pink in his cheeks.

"Well, first let's see if a woman will have me," he said.

"You're a handsome man, Titus, and honorably stationed. I'm sure you'll have no trouble."

He gave an objecting snort, but she could tell he was happy.

The afternoon sun rose high with Norah's spirits.

"Why are you smiling?" Soren asked, bringing his horse beside hers.

"Oh. There you are. I'd almost forgotten you had come along to suck the joy out of me."

"You've been grinning ever since we left Ashan."

"Only you can make that sound like a bad thing," she said. Then she sighed. Was this how the entire journey would be with him? "I'm just looking forward to this visit," she explained in an attempt at civility. "These people are important to me. Let me be happy about it."

To her surprise, he didn't goad her further.

By late afternoon, the homestead appeared in the distance, and Norah felt a surge of excitement. She urged Sephir forward.

As they approached, Calla emerged from the house, with Cohen close behind her holding his sword. When she saw Norah, a grin came to the girl's face, and she bounded off the porch to meet them. "Salara!" she cried as Norah slid down from the mare.

"Calla." Norah smiled as she embraced the girl warmly. She looked over Calla's shoulder at the boy. *Hi*, she signed. Cohen smiled shyly and gave a bow, signing back to her.

"He said he's happy to see you, Salara. So am I!"

"I'm happy to see you both too! Where are Hamed and Marta?"

"In the garden, of course. I'll get them!" And the girl ran to fetch her grandparents.

Hamed and Marta came from around the side of the house, wiping their hands on their garden aprons.

"Salara!" Hamed said, bowing. "Quite unexpected, but we're most happy to see you again."

Norah clasped his hands with a broad smile. "And I'm happy to be here again." She looked at Marta, and the woman took her hands with a warm squeeze.

"Salara," Marta said in a heartfelt welcome.

Hamed stopped suddenly as his eyes found Soren. "Lord Commander," he said as he straightened as much as he could, then bowed.

Soren returned a reverent nod, something Norah hadn't expected. They didn't seem to know each other, but she didn't ask. Soren wouldn't want her to do so publicly.

"I've come on a proper visit this time," Norah told them, drawing the conversation back. "I wanted to thank you for all of your help. It meant the world to me."

"You've come all this way to thank us?" Marta asked.

"Yes, and I've brought a gift for you."

"Oh, Salara." Marta gasped. "You're too kind."

"It's the least I could do." Norah led them around the wagon and pulled back the cover. "Rice, grain, flour, dried meats. But perhaps most precious of all"—she pulled out a small, wrapped package from beside the bags of food and handed it to Marta—"clippings and roots for your garden."

The woman unwrapped it carefully and her eyes widened.

Norah pulled more wrapped packages, and Marta's eyes welled as she looked in each one. "Tresantha, oleiden, serium, and many more."

"Where did you get these?" Marta breathed. "They're only found in Japheth."

"They're clippings from the private garden and conservatory in the castle." Norah grinned. Mikael's grandfather had retrieved them for his Japheth bride, in efforts to give her a piece of home in Kharav.

Marta smiled, teary-eyed, as she looked at Hamed, and he put an arm around her.

Norah felt her own eyes brim with emotion. "I just worry that the winter probably won't allow them in the ground now."

"We'll start them inside. Then we'll move them out in the spring. Oh, Salara, thank you." Marta smiled through her tears. "Come inside. Surely the ride's been long. Let's get you in and fed."

The Crest made quick work of the supplies in the wagon and then set their attention on a small camp for the evening. Cohen was happy to help them while Calla made up a bed in the house for Norah. With the plant cuttings tended to, Marta busied herself with dinner. Norah found herself in the kitchen, looking for an opportunity to be useful. "What can I do to help?" she asked as Marta kneaded dough.

"Please make yourself comfortable. Dinner will take no time at all."

Norah smiled as she picked up the basket of vegetables and started washing them in the basin. "I'm not going to sit here while everyone else works."

"Isn't that what salaras do?" Calla joked as she joined them.

"Callamine! You'll show respect!" Marta scolded, but Norah laughed out loud.

"Amah, it was only a joke," Calla said quickly.

"And a very funny one." Norah laughed again.

Calla smiled, pulling out a cutting board and knife, and started to cut the vegetables as Norah washed them.

"Oh my," Marta shook her head. "I can't believe I have Salara cooking in my kitchen."

Soren and Hamed entered from the outside, followed by Cohen. They all froze, astonished, at the sight of Norah in the kitchen.

"Salara," Soren said slowly.

"Say a word and you'll be cutting potatoes," she warned.

Soren looked at Hamed and then Cohen, and the boy shrugged with a smile.

Cohen went quickly to fetch more water, while Hamed positioned the cast-iron pot over the fire. Calla scooped the chopped vegetables into the pot, gave a happy sigh, and sank down into a chair by the table as everything cooked.

"Calla, Cohen," Norah said, "might I have a private word with your grandparents before dinner?"

"Of course," Calla said, and Cohen followed her outside.

Norah glanced at Soren, then widened her eyes to silently urge him along.

"I'll check on the horses," he grumbled, before seeing himself out.

After the door closed, Norah turned back to Hamed and Marta. "There is something else," she started. "I wanted to invite you back to Ashan with me. Both of you, and Calla and Cohen. It would be an easy life, and the children could study and train. They could make a future for themselves."

Hamed looked at Marta and she smiled sadly.

The woman turned her eyes back to Norah. "I'm not from Kharav," she said. "A life in Ashan would not be an easy one for us, with me as an outsider. It's one of the reasons we live out here."

"I'm an outsider too," Norah told her. "But Ashan is beautiful. And I'll see you're taken care of."

"With all due respect, you're salara. Any other outsider in Kharav is a slave, and treated as such, even with a queen's support." She looked back at Hamed. "And we're happy here."

"What of the children?" Hamed asked his wife gently. "We can't keep them here forever. Augustan and Misa would have wanted a life for them, more than we can give them."

"They'd have challenges too," she said. "With their names. And Cohen being deaf."

Hamed shrugged. "The lord commander doesn't have a Kharavian name."

Marta scoffed. "He's the lord commander!"

Soren wasn't a Kharavian name? "Who are Augustan and Misa?" Norah asked instead.

Hamed smiled sadly. "Augustan was our son, and Misa, his wife."

Marta's eyes welled as she stared at her hands clasped on the table.

Norah felt a pang of guilt. "I'm sorry," she said. "It wasn't my intention to bring back painful memories, or ask you to part with the children. Forgive me."

"We're extremely grateful for your kindness," Hamed said, "and for the offer. It's one"—he looked at Marta—"that we should most seriously consider."

Norah smiled apologetically. "I don't want to pressure you. Think about it. I'll be happy with whatever you decide."

Dinner was delicious, and Norah found herself accepting a second helping after Hamed offered. She looked around the table at the smiling eyes and the sound of laughter, and her heart was full. This little family felt like her own. She loved this place, and she loved these people.

After they ate, Calla and Cohen took hearty bowls of food outside to Soren and the soldiers. Norah smiled at Marta as she helped the woman clear the table.

"Could they visit us?" Marta asked suddenly. "If they went to Ashan."

Norah put down the plate she had just picked up and took Marta's hand. "Of course," she breathed. "Regularly. I would come myself at times, if that's all right."

Slowly, the old woman nodded. "All right. They should go. They should go with you. And they should return when you visit."

Norah smiled through her tears and hugged Marta.

The winter wind was cold, but Norah found warmth in the energy between Calla and Cohen as they excitedly journeyed back to Ashan. Calla's face held a wide grin, pulling a smile from her brother. Norah loved Cohen's smile. It was shy and sweet and full of heart. He wore his father's sword across his back, and Norah couldn't look at him for more than a moment without getting a little emotional. She wished their parents could see how beautiful their children had turned out to be.

She fell back, closer to Soren, and let Calla and Cohen ride ahead. The commander had been scowling at her all morning since finding out the siblings would be returning with them. Might as well get the argument over with.

His low voice cut through the beauty of the morning. "What are we going to do with children at the castle?"

She shrugged. "They'll study, and train. I promised their grandparents."

"You can't be serious. A mute and a farm girl?"

"He's not mute, he's deaf," Norah cut back. "And, yes, keen observation. Calla is a girl."

"They don't meet eligibility standards for the Kharavian army. Who will train them?"

She hadn't thought of that, but she refused his scorn. "Titus," she said. From the corner of her eye, she saw her Northman look at her.

Soren sighed through his teeth. "Surely they don't meet Northern standards either."

"We're not in Mercia."

Soren looked at Titus, who offered no support to Soren's objection.

"Did you know Hamed?" she asked him, changing the subject.

"No. Why?"

She shrugged. "When you saw him, you just seemed to respect him, that's all. It made me think you knew him."

"He is a man to be respected. His markings tell he was a great warrior. He's had many kills."

Norah shifted uncomfortably. "How could you tell? He wore a long-sleeved tunic." It was hard to imagine Hamed killing anyone.

The lines in the corners of his eyes deepened. He really didn't like explaining things to her, but it didn't intimidate her anymore. She found it rather amusing now.

"Kill markings are the only ones to reach the outside wrist," he shared finally. He extended his own arm out from underneath his cloak, showing her the patterns along his skin. "They start at the elbow, a lined triangle for every three kills—a solid for every ten. If one has markings to his wrist, he's a man to be respected."

Norah's eyes stayed on his skin. Geometric patterns formed larger images, deceivingly beautiful. Some swirled like currents of the sea, some were chained like mountains. She hadn't realized they were all made of triangles before. From his elbow to his wrist. So many triangles. So many deaths. And Hamed had them too.

"Mikael doesn't wear marks like that," she said. Surely it wasn't for lack of accomplishment. But she found herself happy for it—she didn't want to be reminded.

"Because he's salar." His eyes betrayed his snarky smirk underneath his wrap. "But if he did, he'd have more than I do."

She wasn't sure she believed him, but it was enough to drown the gratefulness she'd felt only moments prior. She pushed her disquiet down. This was what Soren liked to do to her. She wouldn't let him. "Well, if Hamed was a great warrior, his grandchildren will be great warriors too." Preferably without scoring their arms with triangles.

Soren snorted his annoyance. Then his brow changed, and his eyes narrowed as he looked out across the hills. "You keep on with the Crest," he told her. "I'll catch up." And he urged his horse northwest, away from the group.

What had he seen that he was going to check out? She didn't really care. She was happy to be rid of him for a while. Norah continued with Titus beside her.

Titus urged his mount closer. "Will you really have me train them?" he asked her as he looked at Calla and Cohen up ahead.

"I'll have someone train them. It'll likely not be you, though." She smiled at the relief on his face. "Maybe Caspian, but don't tell him."

He chuckled.

They reached Ashan just before dark, and Norah saw Calla and Cohen to a temporary room in the castle until she could sort a permanent place for them. With them settled, she headed toward her own chamber.

Mikael was waiting for her. Norah had passed Soren in the hall on her way, so he'd have already informed the king of her new wards.

"Salara," Mikael greeted her with a kiss and pulled her close. "I almost rode out to find you."

She pulled back to look up at him and snaked her brow in mock disapproval. "I said I'd return today, and I did."

"Today. *Day*. It's night."

"I had to see Calla and Cohen taken care of. I've put them in the east quarters. I know they're for royal guests, but I'll have them out once I've found suitable accommodation for them tomorrow."

"Who?" he asked.

"Calla and Cohen, children from the family who helped me. I've brought them to study here in Ashan. Did the lord commander not tell you?"

He shook his head. "No, but no matter. Whatever you desire." He pulled her close again and kissed the top of her head.

Strange that Soren hadn't mentioned it. She had expected some kind of resistance, and smiled appreciatively in finding none.

They readied for bed. Norah climbed under the quilts and nestled against Mikael's warmth. He wrapped his arms around her, but his mind was elsewhere.

"Are you all right?" she asked.

"I am now that you're here." He tightened his arms around her. "I have to tend to something in the morning with the lord commander. I'll be gone before you wake, but I should return in time for breakfast."

"What are you going to do?" she asked.

He shifted and moved on top of her. "Right now, I'm going to make love to my wife."

Norah smiled as he lowered his lips to hers.

Chapter Sixteen

Norah woke with a chill. Her eyes fluttered open, and she reached across the empty bed beside her. She knew Mikael wasn't there. He had mentioned he'd be leaving early with Soren, but it wasn't his absence that disturbed her. Something unsettling hung in the air. She sat up. And gasped.

A strange man sat in the corner chair.

He wore fitted clothes, dark. Black. His head was covered with a formfitting cloth that showed only his eyes, similar to the Kharavian head wrap. But it wasn't a Kharavian wrap. And he wasn't Kharavian.

He waited quietly, watching her.

"Who are you?" she demanded. "And what are you doing here?"

He let out a low chuckle.

"Guards!" she cried. But the room was quiet. "Guards!"

"There is no one else," he said, then there was a sickening lull. "Only you and me."

Mikael stood with Soren around the remains of a small campfire in the hills, deeply bothered. They'd traveled out after Soren had spotted it on his return to Ashan. There were intruders in Kharav. He studied the campfire. It had aged a day or two, with very few clues around. Salara had just traveled through the area close by. The intruders had been near her, and the thought unsettled him.

"Large enough that it's more than one man," Soren said as he kicked over a charred limb in the ash. "And no sign of horses. They have to be on foot to leave no trace."

"They're bold to build a fire."

"They're bold to be in Kharav," Soren replied. "Do you think they're in the city by now?"

The thought seeded Mikael's anger. "Quite possibly."

There were only three ways to enter Kharav. One was through the labyrinth of one of the two canyon passes, under the watchful eyes of the Uru to the west and Kharavian forces to the east. Another was by sea, but cliffs lined Kharav's coasts and were violent with waves. A man could neither land a boat nor swim ashore. Kharav held only two ports safe for a ship's entry, and they were heavily guarded. The last option was crossing the river from the southwest kingdom of Osan, but since the incident with the Osan prince, where Soren had killed the group of trespassing young men, Mikael had increased forces along the border.

A man would have to be incredibly skilled to enter undetected. For several men, it was near impossible. Yet they were here. How?

"Find them. I want to know who these men are."

"What do you want?" Norah asked angrily, slowly sitting up more and getting her legs underneath her. She cursed her long nightgown. It would encumber her in a fight if there were to be one. And there would definitely be one.

Although his face was covered, she could see the wicked smile in his eyes. He stood slowly and then stepped toward the bed. He wasn't a large man, but the ease of his movement told her he was dangerous.

"Don't come any closer," she warned, backing toward the opposite edge. Almost quicker than she could react, he leaned forward to grab her. She narrowly escaped his reach, slipping off the bed and bolting for the door.

But he was fast and he caught her arm, twisting her back toward him. She fought against his hold, and the dagger at his hip brushed her stomach. Norah whipped it from its sheath and plunged it into his side, just under his armpit. A solid hit. She wasn't sure if it had reached his heart, but it would steal his breath.

The man grunted, releasing her, and stepped back in surprise. He looked down at the blade as the wound poured blood down his side, and he struggled to inhale. Then he fell to his knees and forward onto the stone floor as his strength left him. A hit to the heart. She'd been lucky.

But there was no time for relief. She threw open her chamber door and froze at the sight of the empty guard post. Blood streaked the wall and puddled on the floor. Whose blood was that? Who had been on guard? She fought back her panic and dashed out, but another man with a covered face stood in the middle of the hall.

"Impressive," he said. "You surprise me, Queen Norah." His accent wasn't entirely foreign.

Confusion hit her as she glanced back toward the bedchamber. Had he seen her stab the first man? But that would be impossible.

"Who are you?" she seethed.

"Let's say, a very old friend."

"Friends don't kill each other," she snapped.

"No, I suppose that's what family's for."

Again, his words confused her. "What do you want?"

"Is it not obvious?" he said as he stalked toward her. "You."

She bared her teeth. "Well, then, I'll have to disappoint."

He drew his sword as Norah stepped back, trying to devise a plan. She didn't have a weapon, but there was the downed man's dagger in her chamber. She spun and ran back toward the room, and he chased after her.

What had happened to her guard? She reached the chamber in only a few steps, but he was close behind. She tried to swing the door closed behind her, but he was already in the doorway. He bellowed as it caught his arm. Norah threw her weight behind it, but he surged forward, forcing her back. She lunged toward the dead man and pulled the dagger from him, then spun to face her attacker.

He swung his sword, and she jumped back. His blade caught the fabric of her gown and sliced it open. He swung again, high this time, and she ducked. It hit the post of the bed and lodged itself into the wood—a mistake. She jumped forward, slicing the dagger into his forearm. He released the hilt and staggered back, and she was ready. She jerked the sword free and advanced her attack. He wore no armor or leathers—cocky bastard—leaving his only defense to avoid her swings. She brought the sword down hard. He reached up to shield himself and the blade cut into his arm, partly severing it. He bellowed again as she whipped forward with the dagger in her other hand and plunged it into his gut. Then she arced the sword in a final blow, slicing open his neck. He fell back against the wall, spilling blood in fading pulses onto the stone floor.

Norah fled the chamber, trying to keep the fear from taking over. That had been close. Too close. It was by luck she had escaped them. They hadn't known her skill with a blade, and she'd caught them by surprise. The dagger and the sword were sticky in her hands, but she clutched them tightly. She passed a side hall. And froze.

Titus lay crumpled on the floor.

"Titus!" she screamed as she ran to him. She dropped the blades and pulled his face to look at her. But he didn't move. Norah let out a sob. "No! Titus!" she cried as she held his head.

She needed to find help. She stood shakily, grabbing her sword and dagger again, and using the wall for support as she staggered back into the main hall. She'd almost reached its end when two men turned the corner. *More attackers.* Where were they coming from? How were there so many? And where was her guard?

"You keep surprising me," one said, as if continuing the conversation.

"Who are you?" she screamed in rage.

"As I said, an old friend. But not a friendly one."

Norah shook her head, trying to catch her breath through her tears and steady her mind. It was as if they were all the same man. And they were here to kill her.

The man to her left attacked first, cutting his sword upward. She jumped back and swung down, meeting it with her own. Then she turned and broke past, fleeing down the staircase. The men were fast, and one caught her at the bottom. She wrenched free but didn't run again. She couldn't escape them, and she clenched her blades as she faced them.

One of the men charged forward, and she turned just in time to escape his intent, but as he reeled past, it put her in between them. One chuckled, and they both backed up a couple of steps, giving space, taunting her.

Norah stood with her back toward the wall, looking left and right to keep her eyes on both. Panic threatened. Where was Bhastian? Sonal? Javed? Anyone? Was she all alone?

"*Salara*," the man to her right taunted. "Not queen of Aleon. Even I didn't realize the vision of you on the Shadow throne meant a marriage to the Shadow King."

How did he know about the vision? And what did he care? "You're from Aleon?" she asked between her teeth. "You're here for revenge?"

"I'm most certainly here for revenge," said the man to her left. "But I'm not from Aleon."

She was confident now that only one man was speaking to her. "How are you doing that?"

He was playing with her. Her skin burned in anger, and she attacked, driving him backward with her sudden onslaught. He wasn't quick enough, and she sliced her sword across his side. He fell to his knees, but it wasn't a fatal wound. She spun to meet the second man, and their swords clanged as she was forced back, toward the dining hall.

Norah paused. No one called Mikael the Shadow King in Kharav. And no one called the lord justice Alexander. These weren't men from Kharav. They weren't from Aleon. And whoever was talking to her knew Alexander well enough to call him by his name.

"Why?" she asked. "Why have you come?"

"They'll suffer, as I have suffered. The Shadow King. Alexander. *Especially Alexander.*" His wrap couldn't hide the quaking breath of his anger. "Where is he?" he demanded. "Where is Alexander?"

Norah bared her teeth with an angry satisfaction. "You won't find him here. He's gone." She smiled when she saw the rage flash in his eyes.

"He's here!" the assassin barked back at her. "His blood touched your skin not even a fortnight ago."

From the lashing. How did he know that? She didn't have time to think about it. The second man was on his feet again and moved together with his partner assassin toward her. But Norah's fear was gone. Fury surged through her, and she lunged forward. She threw her dagger at the wounded man, hitting him squarely in the shoulder, and she swung her sword with full force at her other opponent. He met her with his own blade, and they twisted together in a dance of death.

He was larger than the other men, and their blades hit with a force that shot pain into her hands and up her arms. He was strong and quick, and she was tiring. She was desperate for help. He heaved another swing, and she dodged, knocking his shoulder and using his momentum to drive him sideways. She took her chance and bolted toward the dining hall.

Norah pushed through the doors and cried out to the servant who was carefully setting the table for breakfast. He spun around, knocking everything on the side of the table to the ground with a noisy clatter. The assassin laughed as he mercilessly cut him down.

She stumbled backward, turning to flee, but he caught her from behind again. She tried to swing her sword, but he was too close, and he tore it from her hands.

He flung her to the ground and straddled her, grasping her neck and squeezing the air from her. Norah clawed at his hands and beat at his arms, but his eyes smiled down at her. Darkness started closing in, and she struggled against it. She felt herself slipping away.

Then her fingers found something to grasp at her side—a fallen candle iron. She swung it up with as much force as she could muster, hitting her attacker on the side of the head and knocking him off her. She scrambled to her feet, gasping for breath, and fled from the dining hall, toward the throne room.

But the other assassin blocked her path. She backed up, her mind racing on where to run.

She heard a chuckle to her left as the attacker that had choked her walked slowly toward her from the dining hall. There was a split above his eye from the candle iron, with blood flowing freely. It hadn't been enough to take him down, though. A hopelessness washed over her. She had no fight left in her. She turned and darted down the side hall. Her last resort for help might kill her, but she was already a dead woman.

Mikael slid off his horse in the courtyard and stormed into the castle, followed by Soren. "I want increased guard around the castle," he said as he made his way toward the dining hall.

"And I'll bring in more men to sweep the hills," Soren said.

Mikael gave a nod, then he pushed open the dining hall door, where he expected to find Salara. They both stopped.

Before him lay an empty room with a dead servant surrounded by scattered table settings on the floor.

Mikeal's pulse picked up in his chest. He stood only a moment before he broke with a start and raced toward his chamber, with Soren close behind him. He bounded up the stairs two at a time, his sword ready. They reached the upper hall and wound around but paused at the side hall where the body of the large Northman lay.

His pulse raced faster. Had these intruders made it to Salara? He charged toward the bedchamber. As he rounded the corner, he stopped for half a heartbeat. Blood scored the wall at the end of the hall where the guards should be, and his heart hammered in his throat. The door to their chamber was partway open.

Mikael exploded into the room, flames of fury licking his skin, ready to rain his fire on any soul that dared to touch her.

But all was quiet.

The body of an assassin lay on the floor. He seethed with rage as he swept his eyes over the room and saw another assassin, dead on the floor as well. There had been a struggle, but there was no sign of Salara.

Soren brushed past the bodies to the bath chamber. "She's not here," he called back.

Mikael cursed under his breath, and they moved out quickly, down the stairs and back toward the dining hall.

Where would she have gone from there? And where were all the guards?

"Salar," Soren called, stopping him in his step. He motioned down the side hall.

Mikael looked down the hall toward the painting of his mother and late father, the painting before the hall to Soren's chamber. Just to the left of it—a smear of blood.

They darted forward and thundered down the hall. As they neared Soren's chamber, his heart pulsed battle fury through his body. The door was closed, but blood marked the frame. He let the rage take over.

Mikael burst through the door.

Cusco lay lazily in the center of the floor, and Norah sat beside him, stoically stroking the giant dog's back softly with her fingernails. A dead assassin lay on the floor. Nearer to the wall, Cavaatsa pulled entrails from another assassin's stomach with her razor-sharp teeth, eating eagerly as Norah watched her in a trance. She couldn't think, she couldn't speak. All she could do was sit with the dogs. And breathe. Breathe to keep the panic from taking over.

The door to the chamber crashed open, and it sent Cavaatsa backward with a threatening snarl. Cusco got his legs underneath him, prepared to attack.

"Cusco! Cavaatsa!" Soren's voice settled them. Norah didn't get up, but she let out a sobbing breath of relief as Mikael and Soren thundered into the room.

Mikael rushed to her side, pulling her up and wrapping his arms around her, almost suffocating her in his hold. He breathed heavily into the top of her hair, and just held her. She needed his arms as her tears came. Normally, she cursed her emotion, but now she let it come. Death had been close. She hadn't thought herself afraid of death before, when faced with it on her own terms, but this was different. Killing the first two assassins had been sheer luck, but the second two had played with her like a mouse—taunting her. What scared her more—while she might have been their target, they'd come to hurt Alexander and Mikael. And they could have.

Mikael pushed her back slightly, moving his hands around her face, cupping it, looking her over with fearful eyes. He asked her a question, but his words didn't register. His hands moved down her arms and body as he carefully looked over the bloodstained nightgown for any signs of injury.

"Are you hurt?" he asked her. Perhaps that was what he had asked her before.

Slowly, she shook her head, and he pulled her close to him again. They stood for a moment. Then Mikael pushed her back and made her meet his eyes. "You used the dogs?" he asked. "They could have killed you."

"Cusco and Cavaatsa would never harm Salara," Soren told him.

"I was already dead," she said as her voice came back to her. "They were all I had left." Her eyes welled again as a sob escaped her. "Titus," she said as the tears started again.

Mikael gave a sorrowful nod. "I saw."

"Sonal and Javed too," Soren said quietly. "They were on guard this morning. And likely a number of others, given that these halls are empty."

A wave of panic hit Norah. "Where's Vitalia? Serene? And Calla and Cohen?" If anything had happened to them...

"The girl and the mute were outside when we returned this morning," Soren told her. "They're fine."

A painful breath of relief escaped her. They were in her care, and her stomach roiled thinking of what could have happened. But she still didn't know how Vitalia and Serene fared. Had they been in the castle?

"We'll find your maids," Mikael promised. "First, let's get you to the sanctuary."

"No." She shook her head, letting her hand find Cusco by her side. "I want to stay here." She'd previously thought Soren's chamber was the darkest place in the castle, a place to be feared—the most dangerous place. Instead, she found it was dangerous for those against her. She couldn't leave. Not yet. "Please, just find them. Vitalia and Serene. Find them."

"I'll return with more of the Crest," Soren told Mikael. "Stay here with Salara until then."

Mikael brushed Norah's cheek. He paused, looking at the bodies. "Please. Salara, let me take you away from this."

But she shook her head again. "No. I want to stay here." She felt safe here. And she needed to feel safe.

Mikael nodded. He pulled Norah close once more and kissed the top of her head.

Cusco sat at her feet. The animal's shoulder was warm against her thigh. Norah dropped her hand back to his head, finding comfort in the fanged beasts—Soren's hunters of men.

CHAPTER SEVENTEEN

Despite Mikael's attempts to get her to go to her sanctuary and away from the bloody room, Norah didn't want to move. She'd found the place where she could let her mind come back to her, let herself settle, and she wanted to stay as long as she could.

Within moments, Soren had summoned an army to his chamber—the remainder of the Crest who had been on duty, and those off, as well as others. Norah was relieved to see Bhastian was all right.

With an army now by her side, surrounded by those she trusted, she felt her courage start to return. She managed to convince Mikael she was all right and that he should go see what Soren had found out. The Crest cleared the assassin's bodies from the room, but blood still smeared the floor. She didn't mind. She needed to see their blood.

They'd been here to kill her. No—not *they.*

He. One man.

He'd been here to kill her. But who was *he?* This man scared her. More than any other.

A woman's voice caught her ear. "Let me through!"

"Vitalia!" Norah cried, and she stumbled to her feet from where she sat in the side chair. Bhastian pulled the door open for her, and her maid ran to her, throwing her arms around her.

"I was so worried for you," Vitalia breathed. "Are you all right?"

Serene was right behind her, and Norah pulled her close too. "I'm so glad you're safe!"

"We were at the seamstress's this morning," Vitalia explained. "When we returned, the castle was in chaos. The lord commander found us, told us that you'd been attacked, but you were safe."

"We've taken Calla and Cohen back to their chamber, until things are settled," Serene added.

Norah clung to her maids' hands, thankful those she cared about were unharmed. Well, not all of them. Her eyes welled as she looked at Serene. "Titus" was all she could manage to say.

"He's alive!" Serene assured her.

Nora's heart faltered. "What?" He was *alive?*

"He's alive, and they've taken him to the soldiers' infirmary."

Norah reached out and clutched Bhastian's arm. "You have to take me to him!"

"You should stay here," he told her. "The Crest is here. I'll see how he is and bring you news."

"I want to see him," she demanded. "Right now."

Bhastian glanced at the other soldiers of the Crest in the room, then reluctantly nodded.

Serene ran to get a dress. Then she and Vitalia helped Norah hastily change from her torn and bloodstained nightgown in the side bath chamber.

After, Bhastian led Norah and her maids through the castle, outside, and toward the soldiers' infirmary, with the Crest close after. They entered from the side. The building was mostly empty, with all warriors actively sweeping the castle for any remaining threats.

They made their way through what appeared to be a large dormitory hall. Beds lined the walls. Some were empty, some held wounded men. At the end stood a small cluster of soldiers. She saw the concern in the men's eyes. Titus was a man of strength and had built respect from the Kharavian ranks, much like Caspian. The healer was at the foot of a bed, wiping his hands with a clean cloth. His face was solemn—not a face of good news.

Norah's heart raced as she drew closer. Titus's massive frame lay the length of the bed, and a clean blanket had been draped over him. His eyes were closed.

"He's still in grave danger, Salara," the healer told her. "He's lost a lot of blood. I've done all I can. Now we wait to see if he wakes."

If he wakes. He had to wake. Titus had been with her from the beginning, before even she could remember. She couldn't lose him now. This couldn't be his death—handed to him by some faceless bastard.

The healer left, and she stepped closer to the bed. His face looked so peaceful, not at all like he was on the brink of eternal sleep.

Norah sank onto the bed beside him. She laid her hand on his arm. "His family has served mine for generations," she said to the small cluster of warriors around her, not taking her eyes from him. She felt her emotion rising. "He deserves so much more than this."

The men all stood quietly. A deep sadness hung in the air.

"They found four more bodies of assassins in another hall," Bhastian said gently from behind her. "We think he killed them before he was overtaken."

"Mighty Titus," she whispered through her tears. "If there had been four more of them, I would have been dead for sure." She leaned forward and kissed his forehead. "Thank you."

Norah wiped her cheeks and stood. "Where did they take the bodies?"

"Salar wouldn't want you there," Bhastian told her.

She didn't care. "Take me."

Norah followed Bhastian with a small army of the Crest behind her. They wove down and underneath the castle, to the dungeon hall, and reached a large room where the bodies of the assassins had been taken and laid atop tables under the torchlight.

Mikael and Soren stood, their backs to her, looking at the dead men with a small group of warriors. Norah felt a pit in her stomach. "Who are they?" she asked as she came up behind them.

The men turned, surprised at her sudden appearance. Mikael's objection showed on his face, but he didn't voice it. "We don't know," he said.

Norah looked at the dead men, and a shudder ran through her. These were the men who had tried to kill her. But it wasn't these men she still feared, it was the one who sent them.

"I want to know who they are and what they want," Mikael said.

Norah knew what they wanted. "He seeks revenge," she said, her eyes on the dead man closest to her.

He followed her gaze. "This one?"

"All of them," she said. "They're him. One man."

"There is obviously more than one man," Soren said.

Anger stirred inside her. "It's one man that embodied them."

Soren raised a brow and glanced at Mikael. "She's in shock."

"I am not in shock!" she said angrily. "And don't speak about me like I can't hear you. I know how it sounds, and I don't understand it myself, but he spoke to me through each man, as if he possessed them. He sees through them, he speaks through them, but none of them are actually him."

"It's a trick," Soren told her.

Norah pushed out a frustrated breath. She didn't have the energy to deal with him, and instead turned her attention to the assassins. They didn't share a common skin color. Two were darker, like men from Kharav. Perhaps even darker. Several were white, like her. But they all wore their hair trimmed short. Then something caught her eye. On each of their foreheads was a small smear of rusty brown. She hadn't noticed it during the attack; it had been hidden under their face coverings.

"I've seen this before," she said, drawing closer. She reached and touched it, then pulled back, eyeing the substance closely as she rubbed it between her fingers. Blood, maybe? "On one of the drifters. Near the village that had been destroyed after we left Bahoul. The night..." her voice trailed off. The night she had been attacked by the Horsemen. Even after all this time, the memory still made her stomach turn.

"These men aren't drifters," Soren said gruffly.

Clearly not. But... "They're linked somehow," she insisted. "And the lord justice is his target. He attacked me to get to him." She looked up at Mikael. "He was angry when he discovered Alexander wasn't here."

Mikael's breath shook in anger. "Well, whatever he is, if he jumps to another body when you kill him, then he's still out there."

"Only if you believe this nonsense," Soren muttered.

"I do," Mikael said gruffly, and the commander's eyes darkened.

"Then the solution is easy," Soren said matter-of-factly. "We kill the Bear."

That was his solution to everything. "You won't touch him," she warned.

"If his only cause to come after you is to hurt the Bear, then we should eliminate the Bear to eliminate the cause," he argued.

"How convenient a solution for you," she seethed. "Will you kill your king as well?" She looked back at Mikael. The assassin had wanted to hurt both Alexander *and* Mikael. "This man wasn't a supporter of yours either."

Mikael stewed in anger. "I want to know who he is."

Norah sighed. "He wouldn't tell me his name, and his accent..." She paused. His accent was similar to her own, yet different. "Not Mercian, but close. And he called the lord justice *Alexander*, and you *the Shadow King*."

"Similar to the North, and now wanting revenge. Sounds like Aleon," Soren said, looking at her darkly.

"But he's not from Aleon," Norah cut in. "That much he said."

Soren tilted his head, as if mocking her. "And you believe him?"

She eyed him, irritated. "Yes."

Norah looked back at the bodies. Who were these men? And where were they from? This was personal, driven by a deep hatred. This was an enemy of Alexander, an enemy of Mikael, and they had no idea who it was.

The night was eerily quiet, and Norah woke in a cold sweat. She sat up abruptly, not able to shake the feeling of someone watching her. She and Mikael had moved to her sanctuary, out of their bed chamber that still made her jump at every turn.

Mikael sat up beside her and reached out, putting his hand on her arm. "No one's here," he told her.

"He is."

Mikael called out in the Shadow tongue, and a guardsman quickly entered. "Have the Crest sweep the castle, every hall, every stair," he told him. "Recheck the perimeter."

"Yes, Salar." The guardsman bowed and left quickly, closing the door behind him.

Mikael rose from the bed and looked through the bath chamber, then checked the balcony to make sure the doors were latched. He sank into the quilts beside Norah and held his arm for her to come to him. She slowly lay back, pulling the quilts up and trying to calm her breath.

"Don't be afraid," he told her. "You've never been one to be afraid."

"But this... I don't understand. This man, whatever he is, he has unnatural powers. He's able to speak through other men, see through other men. He passed through what's supposed to be an impenetrable kingdom, into the city, into the castle. He knew you were away with the lord commander. He knew I was alone."

"He didn't know your justice had returned to the North."

She paused. No, he hadn't.

"And he underestimated you, like all other men," he said softly. He pulled her close. "It's he who should be afraid."

Norah drew in a long breath and let it out slowly, nestling against Mikael and soaking in his warmth. But the feeling of safety still escaped her.

Morning brought the sun, and Norah rose without having slept. Vitalia entered and dressed her as Mikael pulled on his leathers. Norah watched her reflection in the mirror as Vitalia tied her lacings. She looked unwell. Dark circles pooled under her eyes, stark against her skin that seemed paler than normal.

"Do you want me to stay with you today?" Mikael asked her softly.

She shook her head. "No. You've got things to tend, and I'm well looked after. Go."

He squeezed her hand and kissed her forehead.

Norah spent the day in the calm of her sanctuary, reading quietly with her maids and trying to settle herself. Kiran had taken Calla and Cohen to look after them and had started them on a training plan, easing at least one thing from her mind. Mikael checked in on her frequently, and she continued to remind him of the army that surrounded her. In the late afternoon, she tried to rest, but rest wouldn't come. She didn't feel like herself anymore—easily startled, anxious, uneasy.

She sat by the windowed doors to the balcony, drinking the tea that Vitalia had made, as the afternoon waned. A little brown bird landed on the railing, and she smiled. The bird looked at her, strangely interested, cocking its head back and forth.

Suddenly, her pulse quickened, and her smile fell.

On its head was a small smear of red. Blood. *The same that had been on the assassins.*

"Salara, are you all right?" Vitalia asked, seeming to notice a change.

"He's watching me," Norah breathed.

Vitalia looked out to the balcony and gave a small laugh. "He does seem to be fascinated by you. Cute little thing."

"No," Norah said, standing from her chair and stepping backward. "It's *him*. He's watching me!" She flung her cup against the window, shattering it and the pane of glass, and making the bird flutter off.

Hearing the commotion, Bhastian pushed open the door. "Salara, are you all right?"

"No!" she cried. "He's here!"

Bhastian and three other soldiers swept inside, pushing the doors to the balcony open and looking around.

"Where did you see him? The man?" he asked.

"It wasn't a man, it was a… a bird." She knew her words sounded like lunacy as she said them.

"A bird?" Bhastian asked.

She shook her head, her eyes welling. "I swear. It's him!"

Bhastian nodded. "Of course, Salara."

But she could see the disbelief in his eyes. She clutched her skirts in her fist. "Leave me."

Bhastian gave a reluctant bow. "We'll walk the perimeter again," he assured her, and then he and the other soldiers stepped out into the hall.

"Close the draperies," she ordered Vitalia, and her maid quickly pulled the heavy fabrics closed. She sank into the chair in the corner and drew up a quilt around her. What was happening? She bit at her nails until they hurt. Was she losing her mind? Was she imagining it? No, it was real. *He* was real.

There was a knock on the door, and Soren stepped into the room without waiting for an answer. Norah bit her lip as she turned away. Of course he'd come. No doubt he took joy in seeing her weak and afraid. That's what he relished.

Cusco and Cavaatsa trailed in after, following their master, but she didn't object. She found comfort in the dogs now.

He glared at Vitalia. "Get out."

Vitalia looked at Norah, and she nodded. The fewer people to see the commander poke at her, the better. Vitalia gave a wary glance at the commander and then slipped out of the room.

"You think you're being watched?" he asked after her maid had left. He pulled back the drapery from the window and looked outside.

Norah pursed her lips. "I am," she insisted.

"By a bird?"

Her cheeks grew hot. "Have you come to mock me, Lord Commander? You think I'm mad?"

He turned back to her. "No. I think your mind plays tricks on you because you're afraid." He stepped closer to her. "He's made you afraid." His voice held a scornful tone.

"Of course he's made me afraid!" she cried as she stood abruptly from her chair, spilling her quilt to the floor. "He almost killed me! And he's still out there. He's watching me!" She couldn't believe she had to defend her fear.

"But why are you afraid?" he snapped.

"Why do you care? And why are you so angry?"

"Because *I* bow to you!" he thundered. "You'll fear *no one*!" Rage seeped from his skin. He stepped closer to her, his voice dropping to a growling whisper. "He watches you? Let him. Open your windows. Beg him to come. You're salara, the Shadow Queen. You'll kill him again. And again. And again."

Norah swallowed and stepped back in surprise.

He reached out and gripped her arm tightly and pulled her forward. "Coward fuck doesn't even come himself. You will *not* be afraid of him, do you understand?"

She couldn't speak.

"Do you understand?" he snarled as he gripped her tighter.

She forced a nod.

He released her, but his eyes still blazed. "I'll put their heads on our gates. You'll send him a message—show him how the Shadow Queen welcomes him."

He turned to leave, but paused, snapping at Cusco and Cavaatsa in the Shadow tongue. The dogs jumped on Norah's bed, making themselves at home and consigning themselves to a new master.

The commander cast her another dark gaze before leaving her to her chamber.

CHAPTER EIGHTEEN

Weary and spent. The months of constant travel had left Caspian weary and spent. He had reached Mercia with Alexander, only to assemble a fresh unit of forces and start the journey back to Kharav and Queen Norah. But when the Northern army reached the Canyonlands, surprisingly Caspian felt like he was coming home.

The sun set, dipping into the earth, and the air grew colder around him. But a warmth stirred within when he saw the figures of the watchful Uru on top of the canyons, against the brilliant sky. It had been a long journey, made even longer by his eagerness to see Tahla again. He had always told himself he'd never be distracted by a woman. Duty first. But now it seemed he was constantly distracted, and by nothing of substance. He had merely promised a kiss—a promise that Tahla likely had already forgotten about, and surely would no longer care about. Still, he couldn't stop the pull inside him.

The Urun warriors rode down to meet them, circling around. As before, the Northern army set camp outside the sprawling village, but the Uru hosted Caspian in their company. He looked for Tahla as he entered the village and was shown accommodation, but she was nowhere in sight.

"Is Tahla here?" he asked his escort.

"She is in the hills, with the chief."

Caspian sighed quietly, and disappointment washed over him—he'd miss seeing her. But he knew it was best. He gave a polite nod and stepped into the small stone house.

He pulled off his shirt and washed his face and hands in the basin provided, appreciating the hospitality of the Uru. Cleanliness brought comfort, and despite his disappointment, he would sleep well.

He took a small cornmeal cake from the plate of food on the table. It was different from the staples of meat and rice of Mercia, which were coincidentally common in Kharav, with the addition of potatoes. He liked the cake. It was different in a good way. Like Tahla.

"Is it to your liking, Northman?" a voice called from behind him, and he turned to see Tahla in the door. She wore a fitted dress—more of a tunic—short, above the knee. Her hair hung loose, not braided now, falling past her elbows. He hadn't realized how long it truly was.

Caspian stared at her for a moment. She really was the most beautiful creature he'd ever seen. He couldn't help his smile. "It is now."

She smiled back.

"They told me you weren't here," he said.

"I had just returned and was cleaning up when I heard that Northmen had arrived. I knew it was you."

"I didn't think I would see you."

She pulled her bottom lip between her teeth as her smile widened. "Did that disappoint you?"

"It did," he answered honestly.

"I worry about you, Northman," she said with a sly smirk, moving inside and closing the door behind her.

He gave a jesting frown. "Do you?"

She raised her brows and nodded. "Kharav's not a place for a man like you."

"Well, I don't draw attention. I'm fortunate enough to be... insignificant."

Tahla stepped closer. "You're anything but insignificant." She lifted her chin and looked up at him. "And I believe you owe me a kiss."

Owe. He almost chuckled. One kiss from this woman would leave him forever in *her* debt. He reached up and brushed a lock of hair from her shoulder, something he had done before and had played over and over again in his head. He let his fingers linger on her shoulder. Never had he touched a woman with want, but everything about her seized him. He dropped his head lower; his lips were so close to hers. Tahla put her hand over his, and she smiled as she guided it to her breast.

Her nipple hardened through the cloth, and Caspian paused. He drew in a breath, calling back his senses, and dropped his hand as he took a step back. "Forgive me."

Her brows drew together in amusement. "What's there to forgive?"

He didn't respond, and her eyes widened.

"Have you never been with a woman before?" she asked.

The directness of her question caught him off guard, and his mind stumbled. Finally, he managed, "I've never been married."

"That's not what I asked."

He drew in a quick breath. This woman. "Where I'm from, intimacy comes only with marriage."

"Just because a kingdom claims values doesn't mean men follow them."

"I believe in Mercia's values."

Tahla looked at him curiously. "And if I don't share these values?"

Was she looking for his acceptance of the difference? Or was she testing if he would pass judgment? He wasn't sure, and he didn't answer.

Her eyes narrowed. She stepped closer again. "What if I've taken men to my bed?"

"I wouldn't like it," he admitted.

"Would you think me ruined?" she asked, her voice sharper.

The fire in her eyes could warm him in a winter storm. "Of course not," he said. A woman like Tahla could never be ruined. "But I don't like thinking of you taking pleasure with another man."

The hint of a smile came to her eyes. "Would you rather I take my pleasure with you?"

Caspian shifted, unable to hide his discomfort.

"Do you think about me?" she asked, seeming to enjoy his uneasiness. "My body?"

She had no restraint. It excited him and scared him at the same time. "Do you not know the answer?"

"I want to hear it," she whispered.

He reached up and gently touched her face. "I think about your eyes," he said as he brushed her temple. He drew his fingers down her cheek to her neck. "Your voice. Your laugh. Your hair, your lips."

She leaned even closer, bringing her face upward. "Is that all?"

He gave a slow shake of his head, letting his fingertips linger at the base of her neck. "I think about your skin against mine. How you would feel. How much I want you. I do want you, Tahla."

Her breath came shallower now.

"So don't speak again of being with another," he told her. "It's not for thought of ruin, but for the deep jealousy that eats me. The bitterness knowing that another man's possessed what I so desperately want to be mine."

She put her hand on his chest and ran it over the curve of the muscle. "I could be yours tonight," she whispered.

He smiled sadly. "But you wouldn't really be mine, would you?"

"I'm no one's." Tahla ran her hand up and over his shoulder. Her eyes followed her touch. She seemed to like his body, want it even, and it fueled the burn inside him hotter. She drew her fingers down his arm. The graze of her fingertips ignited a fire over his skin.

Tahla took his hand and pulled it down, turning his palm upward and slowly bringing his fingers between her thighs. She wore nothing underneath her dress, no barrier to her skin. He was dangerously close to losing himself. She guided his fingers between her folds and let out a small gasp under his touch. Then she lifted her chin to his. "I'll take that kiss now."

But a kiss would be his undoing. He pulled his hand from her, but gripped her arms and dropped his head to rest his forehead against hers. He breathed deeply and prayed for control.

"Do I not please you, Northman?" she asked.

"Quite the opposite," he panted. "Too much so."

"But you would deny yourself?" she asked.

Much more and he wouldn't be able to.

She let out a breath. "If you want me to go, I'll go." She pulled back from him, but he didn't release his hold.

"I don't want you to go," he said. "Please. Stay." He struggled through his words. "Not lost in our flesh, but just... stay with me."

The corners of her mouth turned up.

He sank down onto the bed and lay back, leaving a space for her. Tahla crept in beside him and lay on her side, facing him. He wrapped his arms around her and pulled her close. "Tell me what you dream about, Tahla."

"This is what you want to do in bed with me?"

He threaded his fingers through her hair. "I want to know you. Everything about you."

"You're a strange man, Northman," she whispered.

He lay with Tahla in his arms, soaking in the warmth of her body. They talked deep into the night. She told him about the Uru, their love and respect for the earth, about her childhood, and the Uru's friendship with Kharav. The story of her meeting Norah drew a chuckle from him. Then Tahla told him about her own failed marriage, which drew anger. The need to protect her overwhelmed him, but he knew she didn't need his protection. Or want it.

In turn, he told her of Mercia, the beauty of the capital city and the North. She asked questions of the people and their customs, of their gods, deeply curious. It made him happy to share it with her.

Morning came too soon. Tahla had drifted into slumber sometime in the dark hours of the morning. Caspian didn't sleep, but as the sun peeked over the horizon, he felt more rested than he had in a long time.

The time came to depart. He drew his fingertips over the skin of her shoulder to wake her. She opened her eyes with a smile.

"This isn't how I expected the night with you to go, Northman," she said softly.

He brushed her bottom lip with his thumb. "I'm sorry I didn't give you your kiss."

She pushed herself up on her elbow. "I think I'll keep the debt so that you have to return." She leaned in and brought her lips to his ear. "I do want you to return," she whispered.

"Then I'll have to," he answered.

Tahla let her lips graze his cheek as she pulled away, and she rose from the bed and straightened her clothing. "Goodbye, Northman," she said, and with one last smile, she disappeared into the morning.

Chapter Nineteen

Norah stood on the wall, looking out across the city to the north. Despite the chill, the sun was warm on her face, and the wind lifted her hair like a flickering flame behind her. Spring was almost upon them. It had already arrived in the valley, and crops were abundant. Shipments of food had been sent to Mercia.

Caspian had returned weeks ago and, to her shock and complete joy, was appointed captain of the Crest. Of course the commander denied his hand in it, but Mikael had shifted Crest responsibilities underneath the commander after Artem's death. Kiran had rejoined the guard as well, after he was given proper exception papers. Titus, although still recovering, had taken over Calla and Cohen's training. Norah still needed to figure out something long term for them after Titus was able to rejoin the guard, but it was working well, and the sibling pair were making progress. Things almost felt complete. *Almost.*

She should be happy, but she wasn't. She didn't want to admit it, but she was still afraid. It had been over a month since the assassins had come, and still she was no nearer to understanding who wanted to kill her, or why. Her stomach twisted in thinking how close they'd come. How had men gotten through the Canyonlands and into the castle, especially so many of them? Caspian wanted to send for more Northmen, but that wasn't the answer.

Cusco sat beside her and nudged her leg for attention. She smiled and dropped a hand to the large dog's head. It hadn't been long since the commander had given her the animals, but she'd become quite attached to them. Cusco was always near, always seeking attention from her. Cavaatsa stayed to herself, just out of reach, avoiding touch, but she trailed Norah wherever she went and slept at the foot of the bed.

Norah looked across the horizon, to the north sky—her home sky. Alexander had gone back to Mercia, back to what felt like the other side of the world. But the emptiness hadn't stayed empty. The pain hadn't been quite as sharp as she'd once thought it would be without him. Yes, she loved Alexander, but in her heart there now stood another.

Mikael. This man, opposite of everything she thought she stood for, confounded her. Yet he brought a level of clarity she failed to find anywhere else. Her memories still eluded her, but with him, she felt... herself. Free to be herself, whoever she wanted that to be.

Still, she found her mind wandering back to Alexander. Especially on days with clear blue skies, like today, while she stood on the balcony looking northward, as she was now. As if her thoughts were playing tricks on her mind, she could almost see the Mercian army on the horizon—as if he were returning to her. She gave a sad smile. They were only tricks.

Then she stopped.

Her heart beat faster.

There *was* movement on the horizon. It wasn't real, she told herself.

The horn of arrival startled her, and she leaned forward, gripping the wall tightly. Her heart thrummed in her ears as she squinted against the light to see. It was an army unit, and against the sky, *the Mercian flag*. She knew it was Alexander. Happiness mixed with dismay, and a cry rose in her throat.

Norah caught a sound behind her and turned to see Mikael. She sucked in a breath and looked back out at the approaching army. If Alexander had returned, how would Mikael react? Certainly not well.

The power of his body came behind her, and his arm curved around the front of her shoulders. He spread his hand wide over her chest, running it up to the base of her neck, and he pulled her firmly back against him. He saw them too. She struggled to calm her breath. Surely he could feel her heart racing. Norah closed her eyes as the possessiveness rippled through him.

He dropped his head beside hers, drew a deep inhale, and let it out slowly. She didn't move. The heat of his anger singed her ear, and she braced for the storm to come.

But he only whispered, "Go." She turned in surprise. Did he know Alexander would be with them? His eyes brimmed with darkness, and the muscle underneath his skin tremored with restraint. Of course he knew. "Go meet them," he said, and he nodded.

He knew. And he told her to go. She cupped his face in her hands, pulling him down, and kissed him. Deeply. Then she gave him a reassuring smile and gathered her skirts as she hurried down to the courtyard.

The size of the arriving Mercian army was a significant one. Soldiers parted the way for her, and she greeted them hurriedly as she sought out Alexander. But in the sea of men, she couldn't find him. Where was he? A weight pulled her heart to her stomach. Had he not come? She'd ordered him back to the North; perhaps he'd stayed.

As he should have.

It was better this way, she told herself, and she stowed her disappointment. She wanted him to have stayed; she needed him to have stayed and to not have her heart wishing him back at every turn. She loved Mikael. Things had changed. *She'd* changed.

Then she heard her name.

"Norah."

She spun to see him walking toward her, and her breath seized on her lips. Alexander pulled off his helm, and the sun caught the gold in his hair. And suddenly she was afraid that nothing had changed at all.

He stopped when he reached her, his blue eyes sparkling. The corners of his mouth turned up. "Hello, Norah."

She couldn't stop the rush of happiness to see him, and she threw her arms around him. To have him back, to have him near, to be able to see him and touch him. The return of something lost, of *someone* lost.

They stood in the center of the courtyard, surrounded by her arriving Northmen.

And then she remembered herself, remembered Mikael on the wall, and she pulled back. A sudden flash of anger twisted inside her as a pain needled into her heart. "You shouldn't have come back." She needed him to not have come back.

"I had to as soon as I heard of the attempt on your life." He stepped closer, and she couldn't breathe. "It's the second time, Norah. I couldn't not come."

She couldn't have this argument with him now. She stepped back to put some space between them. "You brought all of Mercia with you, I see." She struggled to get ahold of her mind as she swept her eyes around them. This was the most Northmen that had ever come to Kharav.

He nodded. "Caspian will need more men."

"He has plenty of men. All the Crest are at his call. Hundreds."

"Now he has thousands." He gave her a small smile, that smile that pulled at her heart. "I've missed you, Norah," he said softly. She didn't dare to speak her own heart. His eyes moved to someone behind her, and she followed his gaze to a familiar face.

"Adrian!" She grinned as he made his way to them. "I can't believe you've come!" He seemed to have grown even taller, and she stood on her toes as she pulled him into a hug.

"Yeah, well Alec's been trying to send me back since he found out I came along." He shot a smile back at his brother. "But he can't keep me away forever. I wanted to see the Shadowlands, now that they're our allies."

"Kharav," she corrected him gently. "It's called Kharav here."

His smile widened. "Kharav, then."

"It's a beautiful place." And she meant it.

"Is the Destroyer here?" he asked.

Alexander frowned. "What do you care about the Destroyer?"

"What do I care about seeing the most famed man of war?" Adrian asked cheekily. "Have you seen him?"

Alexander's eyes drew together in irritation. "He's just a man. You'll be sorely disappointed. And of course I've seen him."

"Is he here?"

"Don't mind the Destroyer. Your queen's here. You forget yourself."

Adrian grinned sheepishly and bowed his head. "Apologies, Queen Norah."

Norah smiled with a small laugh. "It's good to see you, Adrian." She nodded toward the castle. "Come on. I'll show you around."

As they left the courtyard, her eyes shifted up to the wall, where Mikael stood, watching her.

The door to the bedchamber stood slightly ajar, and Norah pushed it open curiously. She smiled. Mikael stood patiently while two tailors worked to correct the sleeve length on a jacket that looked quite uncomfortable for him. She glanced at the bed where Vitalia had laid a fresh gown for her. The joys of social gatherings. But she didn't want to think about the evening's activities at the moment.

"Leave us," she called. Mikael turned in surprise.

The tailors and Vitalia bowed and saw their way out of the room, closing the door behind them.

"I thought you wanted me to wear a proper jacket this evening," he said.

She couldn't help but smile again. She had asked him not to come to the welcome social in his battle attire. He'd taken it upon himself to select the jacket, no doubt feeling pressured in comparison to the elegant, more conservative style of Mercia. But she had other things on her mind.

"I don't really care about a jacket right now." She took his hand, carefully making sure the needles on the cuff wouldn't prick him. Then she pushed it off over his shoulders and laid it across the bench at the foot of the bed.

He stepped away from the mirror and sank into the chair by the window.

Norah sighed. She knew Alexander was on his mind. She stepped quietly over to him, climbing on top of him and straddling him in the chair. Running her fingers into his hair, she pulled his face up to look at her. "I know his return upsets you." She brought her lips close to his. "But, Mikael, I love you. You alone."

"Don't say things that aren't true."

She frowned. It hurt her heart for him to have insecurity. "You're my husband. I'm committed to you—*you alone*. I'm faithful to you. I love you." She brushed the backs of her fingers along his jaw.

The hard lines on his face softened. He needed reassurance, and she'd wholeheartedly give it to him. She might not have loved him when she'd chosen him, but she loved him now. And she chose him now, all over again.

She brought her lips to his and kissed him deeply. And he kissed her back. His body hardened underneath her. She loved how he responded to her touch—wanting, needing—and her body answered in kind.

Norah ruffled up her skirts and reached below, loosening his breeches and freeing his flesh. He was ready, and she was too.

And then the urgency came.

She struggled to hook her fingers on the hips of her underwear in the chaos of her skirts. She couldn't get them off fast enough. His hands found her flesh under her gown, and the silk of her undergarments tightened and bit against her skin as he tore it away. He moved his hips upward, grasping her tightly and pulling her down to join them together, and she gasped as he sheathed himself inside her. They stilled for a moment, their foreheads together, but only for a moment. The calm before the storm. Then she began to rock against him. His head fell back as her pace quickened. She felt his need growing. As she moved faster, he pitched forward and lifted her from the chair, and she wrapped her legs around him.

Mikael carried her to the bed and laid her down without breaking their union. He tore the top of her dress and chemise down below her breasts and kneaded the milky flesh with thick desire. She writhed underneath him. He buried himself in her, possessing every part of her, and she let him take her.

Mikael clasped her shoulder firmly, pinning her down, and a wave of heat rushed through her. She pulled him closer, urged him harder, and surrendered as he took what he needed. The fiend inside him tore at her—claiming her, consuming her—and her own need answered back. He brought his hand to her face, looping his thumb into her mouth, and she bared her teeth against his skin and bit him. His chest rumbled, and he thrust harder, gripping her tighter. Norah pulled him deeper—deeper into her body, and into her mind. She gave herself—she gave all of herself. She cried out as release came, and pleasure rippled through her. He followed. His body shook as he thundered to his finish, and he collapsed on top of her.

After, they lay in each other's arms, panting, sweat beading across their skin. Finally, Mikael pulled himself from her and rolled onto his back. Norah turned on her side in sweet exhaustion and reached out her hand to trail it down his chest.

He drew in a breath and turned to face her. "I'm sorry," he said as he brushed his fingertips across the marks he'd left on her shoulder and along her sides. "I should have been gentler."

She smiled and whispered, "Sometimes a woman likes a good ravaging."

A deep rumble came from him again, and he pulled her back to kiss him.

Music filled the halls. Mikael felt surprisingly settled going into the evening's social. Despite his loathing for the Northmen, they seemed allied with Kharav against this unknown threat to his queen, and he couldn't deny he appreciated the additional men. Anything to keep her safe, even if it meant tolerating the Bear.

He shifted his shoulders uncomfortably in his crimson jacket. Salara had been pressing him away from the usual battle dress, and his dark linen and leather. She was beautiful, in a gold gown with beaded patterns on the bodice. He walked with her on his arm and couldn't keep his eyes from her. As they reached the great hall, she paused.

"Salara-Mae has come," she said.

His mother rarely attended social events. "How did you manage that?"

She shook her head. "It's not my doing, but I'm going to go greet her."

"Of course," he said, and watched her make her way across the room. She really was beautiful.

Soren stepped in beside him, and his mind shifted.

"Where is he?" Mikael asked, and followed Soren's eyes to where the Bear stood with a small group of Northmen.

Mikael and Soren approached, and the surrounding men took their leave to give them space but kept a wary eye over their justice from a distance.

"Shadow King," the Bear greeted him coldly.

Mikael stood casually, watching Norah across the way. "I see you found your way back," he said, not taking his eyes from her.

"I needed to ensure the well-being of my queen, as is my duty."

"As you can see, she's quite well." Mikael cast him a sideways glance. "You can return to your place back in the North."

The Bear scoffed. "My place is by her side."

"I don't believe Salara shares your view. Has she not sent you back to the North twice already?"

The justice cut him a glance with a sharp brow. "She sends me away because our closeness disturbs you. But it's not what she wants, and I know you know that."

Mikael bristled at the Bear's boldness—at the audacity he would hint at Salara's affections for him so directly. His skin burned with the heat of war. Any other man he'd force to his knees and cut his tongue from his mouth. Any other man he'd split his neck with his bare fingers and pull out his throat. But this wasn't any other man, and Mikael attacked the only way he could. "Oh, I'm not disturbed," he said. "I find your visit a pleasant surprise."

The Bear gave an unbelieving chuckle.

Both men kept their eyes on Norah, but Mikael leaned in closer. "I enjoy what your visit brings. You see, when you're here, our lovemaking isn't how it normally is—gentle and passionate. It's raw. She comes to our bed with a wildness to her."

The justice inhaled sharply as the fake smile fell from his face.

Mikael's eyes burned cruelly. "I feel it when I'm inside her," he taunted. "Her body begs me to take it. And I do. Most violently."

The Bear's nostrils flared.

"Salar," Soren said as he stepped forward, putting himself between them.

Mikael broke from his attack, gathering himself and pulling back his shoulders. He stepped out onto the floor and looked back at the Bear with a smile. "So, Lord Justice, stay as long as you'd like." Then he turned toward Salara with the hunt in his veins. He clapped twice as the quartet finished their song to start a new one—the song of his choice.

Salara turned and saw him approaching, and her smile turned into a grin. She was the most beautiful woman on the earth. And she was his.

"I love this song," she said.

"I know." He moved behind her, slipping an arm around her waist, and bared his teeth against the smooth skin of her neck. She let her head fall back against his shoulder and closed her eyes as he led her through the dance.

CHAPTER TWENTY

It was late evening, and Norah found Soren in his study, sitting at his desk and looking closely at a map as he scribbled notes to the side. He sat without his wrap, his dark hair tied back, seeming almost... normal. He was a handsome man, more so than she cared to admit. He had a strong jaw, like Mikael, and a straight and proportionate nose, like Mikael. He could be desirable, like Mikael, if he weren't such an ass.

"Lord Commander," she greeted him, pulling his attention. "I have a favor to ask."

He glanced up and eyed her, annoyed. "Not to kill the Bear?"

Norah sighed. "All right, two favors," she said irritably. "There's a young man from Mercia, Adrian. He's very eager to meet you."

He took a drink from the chalice sitting to his right, and then set it down, suspicious. "Why would he be eager to meet me?"

"You would better understand the fascination with war idols," she replied, more elbowed than she'd intended. She inhaled deeply and gathered herself. "Please, I'm very fond of him, and it would mean a great deal."

"What's the favor you ask? You're salara. You don't need my permission to present him to me."

"No, but I want you to make it meaningful. And"—she paused—"he's the lord justice's brother."

He stilled. The commander's nostrils flared, and he sat back in his chair. "You want me to show a kindness to the brother of the Bear?"

Why did it sound so abhorrent when he said it? "Yes."

He snorted. "Then the Bear should ask me himself."

"Alexander will be looking to send Adrian back to Mercia at the first opportunity, preferably without seeing you."

The corner of his lip turned upward. "Then I would love to meet him."

"Yes, I suspected that would be the case with such context. But I'd also ask for your discretion. Alexander wouldn't be pleased."

The commander's lip twitched slightly. "Then what would I get from this if not the Bear's ire?"

"That's why it's called a favor," she said sweetly.

The lord commander leaned heavily into the arm of his chair. "Is this a favor I can call upon?"

Norah sighed. Of course he would be difficult. "Fine," she said stiffly. She was sure she'd regret it later.

He gave a small smile. "Then I suppose I can't refuse my salara," he said.

Despite her annoyance, she couldn't help a small smile. "I'll bring him to the stable tomorrow morning."

Morning came slowly with her excitement. Norah tried to chase the small wave of guilt back. Alexander would be upset if he found out what she had planned, but this wasn't about Alexander. Adrian was eager to see Kharav and to meet the commander. He embodied what she wanted of her kingdom and her men—genuine curiosity and appreciation for the other side. Men like Adrian could help her bring both sides together.

Norah found Adrian with several other Mercian soldiers near the barracks, already sparring. They all stopped and bowed when they saw her.

"Northmen," she greeted them. "Adrian, is the lord justice here?"

"No, but I'll fetch him."

"No," she said quickly, stopping him. "That's not necessary. I've actually come for you."

He lifted a brow. "For me?"

"Yes." She smiled. "I have something for you. Come with me."

He grinned and stepped promptly through the men.

She led him toward the stable, looking back at him. "How long are you staying?"

"As long as Alec allows, which probably isn't very long."

"No, I imagine it's not." Alexander, wanting to protect him, wouldn't be happy with him in Kharav.

He looked at her with a flash of hope. "Maybe you could talk to him?"

"I don't think I should cause any more aggravation with your brother."

He frowned. "What do you mean by *more*? Why would he ever be aggravated with you?"

They walked into the stable, and she waved her hand toward a shadow within. He followed her motion with his gaze, and his eyes grew wide. Soren stepped forward into view.

"The Destroyer," Adrian breathed.

"You'll address him as Lord Commander," she said. "His proper title."

"Yes, of course. Lord Commander." Adrian bowed. "I mean no disrespect, I'm honored."

The commander looked down at Adrian with a gaze that silenced him. "What's your name, boy?" he rumbled.

"Adrian," he managed to get out.

"How old are you?

"Just turned twenty, my lord."

Norah hadn't realized he'd had a birthday. The time was passing quickly in Kharav.

"What's your hand?" Soren asked.

"Uh," Adrian stumbled, "a bow." He shook his head. "I mean, a sword."

The commander frowned. "Well, which is it? A bow or a sword?"

Norah scowled. She'd asked the commander to make it meaningful, not intimidating.

"I'm keen with a bow, my lord," Adrian answered. "But much better with a sword."

The commander's eyes narrowed. "Much?" He turned and pulled two swords from a side weapons wall.

Norah looked at him with uncertainty. She hadn't expected this exchange.

The commander handed him a sword and then walked out of the stable. Adrian followed excitedly. Out in the paddock, they squared off and circled each other. Adrian seemed timid at first and gripped the blade tightly.

The commander made the first move and swung, testing. Adrian jumped back, his nerves getting the better of him. Soren took a step back, swinging his sword wide and bringing it back to ready. Adrian moved forward. He settled his stance in preparation for the next move. Soren advanced again, but this time Adrian hit his blade away and spun, swinging a counter. The commander deflected it easily, striking the sword from Adrian's hand.

Norah stepped forward, but Soren put his hand up, stopping her. He nodded to Adrian, who picked up his sword and readied himself again. Her stomach twisted. The only thing worse than Alexander finding out about this was Alexander finding out with his brother in pieces. Perhaps this hadn't been the best idea.

The commander swung hard this time, and Adrian darted away. Adrian launched his own attack. The commander met it with a counter of his own, and Adrian danced away. Soren cut his sword upward, again pushing him back, but Adrian was quick and struck his blade to the side in its arc. He spun and brought his sword down, grazing the pauldron of the commander's shoulder.

Adrian gripped his sword tightly for the next attack, but the commander straightened. His eyes hinted a genuine smile, something Norah hadn't seen before.

"You're not bad," Soren said.

Adrian grinned and looked at Norah, and she smiled back in her own surprise.

"Keep practicing," the commander said.

"Yes, my lord," Adrian said breathlessly. "Thank you!" He looked back at Norah. She didn't think she'd ever seen anyone so happy.

"That's all," she told him. "You can go now."

He gave an excited bow of his head. If the lord commander hadn't been there, she knew he would have hugged her. "Thank you, Norah!" he said. Then he turned to Soren. "Lord Commander." He bowed again, then turned and trotted back toward the barracks.

Norah smiled. "Thank you," she told Soren after Adrian left.

He gave a small grunt.

"If I didn't know better," she added, "I might think you enjoyed yourself."

"Well, it wasn't terrible," he said with mild irritation.

She pursed her lips to keep her smile from growing. "Again, thank you."

He shifted uncomfortably but gave a nod.

It was late afternoon as Norah made her way through the great hall and toward the conservatory, with the dogs at her side. She looked forward to spending some time in the gardens. Movement caught her eye, and she turned to see Alexander walking toward her.

"You took Adrian to meet the Destroyer," he said angrily as he drew near.

Cusco growled in warning, and she reached down to calm the animal. He had become quite protective of her, even growling at Mikael, which had given her a good laugh. "They were both out this morning," she said, "so I introduced them."

"How kind of you," he said shortly.

"Alexander," she pleaded. "Adrian was ecstatic."

"About meeting the man who's killed thousands of our people?"

"About meeting the greatest warrior of our time!"

Alexander took a step back, visibly insulted, and she instantly regretted her words. "I didn't mean it like that."

"That man is a monster," he said bitterly, "and I don't want Adrian near him. I don't even want you near him."

Anger rose in her cheeks. "Our fathers created that monster! Do you forget?"

Alexander gave a disgusted grimace. "You defend him?"

"He extended a kindness to the son of the man who led the forces that killed his own family! His father, his mother, his sister, his brother. Kharav has suffered at the hands of the North, and the lord commander has lost just as much as anyone else!"

Alexander's eyes burned in troubled astonishment.

Norah sighed. She didn't want to argue, especially not with Alexander over a man like the commander. She stepped closer to him. "Put aside your own bitterness. Allow your brother this small joy."

He snorted and looked away.

She reached out and took his hand. "Alexander."

He brought his gaze back to her.

She gave a small smile. "It *is* small. You know, if Adrian could choose to be like anyone, it would be you. He idolizes you."

Alexander looked down at their hands clasped together and sighed, conceding.

"And I wish you'd try to understand the commander." She glanced down at the dogs. "He's not always what you think."

But that, she knew, he'd never do.

Chapter Twenty-One

Norah stood in the doorway of Mikael's study, watching him. He sat at his desk, his eyes on a letter but not reading it.

"What troubles you?" she asked.

He looked up at her in surprise, and she gave a reassuring smile.

Mikael drew in a breath as he sat back against his chair. He seemed reluctant to answer as he folded the letter back and set it on the desk. "Gregor," he said finally. "He arrives in two days' time."

"Japheth's king? Why is he coming?" Norah knew a little history from what her grandmother had shared with her.

Japheth had once been part of the greater Aleon Empire ruled by Phillip's father, but upon his death, the empire was split between his three sons. Feeling robbed of his birthright as the eldest, Gregor had killed his youngest brother, Aston, and absorbed Aston's kingdom of Hetahl under Japheth. When he rose against Phillip to take the remaining Aleon kingdoms, Mercia stood as Phillip's ally, prompting Gregor to seek an alliance with Kharav. Kharav, already motivated to go to war with Mercia, was quick to agree. This had been the start of the Great War.

Now that Norah and Mikael were wed, and Mercia and Kharav united, this no doubt left both their previous allies uneasy. She was surprised that Gregor would visit, especially with her presence at the castle.

Mikael gave a grumbled sigh, clearly annoyed by the news himself. "He comes to set new trade terms."

"Trade terms you're not pleased with?"

He cast her a hesitant eye. When it came to ruling Kharav, he still kept her at a distance. The ways of Kharav still bothered her—the harshness, the violence—and it was his way of sheltering her from them. But she didn't want to be sheltered. She wanted him to share his burdens with her. She drew closer and reached out, putting her hand on his cheek. "Will you not tell me?" she asked softly.

He looked at her for a moment. "I'm not pleased," he said finally. "I suspect he's allied himself with another." He stood. "His demands are outrageous. Something makes him bold."

"Who could he join who is greater than you? Greater than Mercia and Aleon?"

Mikael shook his head. "I don't know."

"Maybe it's a bluff."

Mikael snorted. "Gregor's a coward. He wouldn't take the risk."

"So, what are you going to do?"

He sighed. "I don't know. I can agree to his demands and appear weak."

"Or?"

"I can kill him."

Norah frowned. She wasn't sure why she'd expected anything different. "I'm glad to see we've covered options at both extreme ends of the spectrum." She pushed out a breath. "What about something in between?"

"There is nothing in between."

Her brow stitched down. "How about just refusing?"

"If Gregor leaves without an accord, it means he leaves as a potential enemy. And I can't have another enemy. Not with the North and Aleon both poised against me."

Her heart hardened. How could he say that? And to her... "Mercia is not against you."

He snorted. "Even your lord justice confirms your council won't stand with me. I need Japheth more than ever."

"Phillip waits for the moment to avenge his youngest brother and kill Gregor. Japheth needs *you*."

"He clearly doesn't!" he snapped. "And if he's not with me, he's against me, and then I have to remove him." She took a step back, and his shoulders fell. "I don't expect you to understand how any of this works," he said shortly.

Norah raised a brow, a flash of anger coming to her cheeks. "Fine. Since *you* know how this all works, I'll leave you to continue planning how you'll lose *all* of your allies and the support of your nobles. You have a good start. Don't let me stop you." And she turned and left in frustration.

The great hall was loud with celebration when she entered. Norah moved gracefully through the bowing nobleman to the table where Mikael sat. He stood when he saw her, and she took her place beside him. Unlike in the dining hall, the table sat longways, facing the festivities, with chairs lined on only one side and Mikael and Norah at the center. She was glad for it—to be beside him, to be able to touch him.

He cast her an unsettled look, seemingly wanting to break the icy wall between them, but the doors swung open before they had a chance to speak.

An overly extravagant procession swept through the great hall, and in its center—Gregor, king of Japheth.

"I thought he'd already presented himself to you," Norah said quietly, unamused. Gregor had arrived earlier that morning.

Mikael sighed. "He did."

"Then why the show?"

"To present himself to you, I'm sure. Appearances are not for friends."

Not for friends.

The Japheth king was not as Norah had imagined. He was tall and thin, gaunt almost, with a fragile walk, albeit a cocky one. His cheekbones sat high and sharp, stretching the skin taut, and the bronze of his hair was speckled with gray. He had a prominent brow that shadowed his eyes, hollowing them. Norah thought back to the portraiture of Phillip she had seen. The only thing he seemed to have in common with his brother was the mustache. And Gregor looked much more than fourteen years Phillip's senior.

"Salar," he greeted Mikael, with no nod and no bow. Kings did not bow to kings, although they generally gave a dip of their head in greeting—a sign of respect. But there was no respect here, and anger rippled through her. She tempered it, though. If she felt the flame of anger, Mikael certainly had, and while she didn't like this Japheth king, bloodshed was not the answer. Not yet.

Gregor's eyes fell on Norah. "North Queen," he said in a gravelly voice. He didn't hold the Japheth accent, being from Aleon.

"King Gregor," Norah said. "Welcome to Kharav."

He gave a forced smile, clearly not liking a welcome to Kharav from the Mercian queen.

"King Gregor." Mikael's voice echoed through the hall, stiff and forced as well. "Tonight we celebrate, to welcome Japheth, our friend and ally. Please," he said, motioning to the chair to his right at the long dining table.

They all took their seats, with Gregor on the opposite side of Mikael from Norah, and music picked up in the air.

"How long will you keep me waiting on my proposal?" Gregor asked Mikael as he eyed the food placed in front of him. Norah lifted her chalice to her lips but willed her breathing quiet to listen.

"As I said, tonight we celebrate," Mikael answered. "Tomorrow we'll speak of trade."

Gregor let out a small chuckle. "So, you don't like my proposal." *Brazen persistence.*

Norah couldn't tell if the heat in the room was from her anger or Mikael's. She placed a hand on his thigh under the table, settling them both.

Gregor leaned forward and looked past Mikael at her. "Tell me, North Queen. Now that you're wed to Kharav, does Mercia consider herself friends of Japheth?"

The Japheth king *was* bold, and it bothered her even more. A few more moments and she might be asking for the sword to end Gregor herself. "I suppose we'll see," she said calmly, then took a bite of lamb from her plate.

"See what?" he pressed.

Norah took her time to chew and swallow her food before answering. He would wait for her. "If Japheth is worthy of our friendship."

Gregor snorted. "You insult Salar and I both."

"My husband's ego is not so fragile," she said sweetly. She met Gregor's eyes and smiled when she saw his offense. Under her hand, she felt the faint vibration of a near chuckle from Mikael, and he seemed to relax. These restrictions he forced himself to in the name of an alliance with Japheth—they didn't apply to her. "You should try the lamb," she told Gregor. "It's delicious."

With the festivities over, Norah and Mikael bid their goodnights and took to their chamber.

Norah let out a liberating breath as Vitalia pulled the heavily adorned gown from her and helped her into her nightgown. "That man is insufferable," she said to Mikael as she pulled down her hair.

He waved off Vimal as his servant moved to take off his attire. "Leave us."

Vitalia gave Norah a curtsy and followed Vimal from the room.

Norah looked at Mikael with a raised brow. "What's the matter?"

He shook his head.

"Tell me," she pressed.

He reached out and pulled her close. "The only thing the matter is the way I spoke to you before about Gregor."

A small smile came to her lips, and she let him wrap his arms around her. "I accept your apology, if that's what it was supposed to be."

"It was. It *is*. I'm sorry."

"I thought you might be angry with me for goading him."

He shook his head and held her tighter. "You say things I can't. And, I'll admit, it does allow me greater leverage when you hint the threat of the North against him, if I appear the advocate on his behalf."

"Well, I'm glad to be in service to my salar."

He smiled, and his eyes grew darker. "Say that again."

Her lips peeled back to reveal her own smile. "I'm glad to be in service to my salar."

And he picked her up and carried her to the bed.

Water puddled on the cobblestone streets. A billow of gray hung over the city. Alexander pulled his hood farther over his brow as he stepped out into the rain. He was appreciative of the weather for once, as a hooded man wouldn't draw attention. But as he made his way toward the castle, he was acutely aware he was being followed. He stepped into a side street, intending to cut through to another walkway, when a man stepped into the path in front of him. Alexander stopped and looked behind him, where the other man who had been following him cut off his retreat.

"The Mercian lord justice," the man in front of him called out. "I heard you were here." He had a chopped cadence to his accent—he was a man from Japheth.

"Good day, gentlemen," Alexander said, then he moved to continue walking.

But the man in front of him stepped into his path, and two more men appeared.

"What's your intention?" Alexander asked them. "I'm expected at the castle."

The man in front of him smiled. "Be a shame if you didn't make it there. An accident, perhaps?"

Alexander put his hand on his sword's hilt. "An unlikely accident."

He heard the draw of a sword behind him and looked back out of the corner of his eye. The men were closing in. In a singular motion, he pulled his sword from its scabbard and spun with a blow to the closest opponent behind him. The man fell backward, onto the cobblestone street. He followed with an upswing at the man on his right, who met his attack with his own blade. Alexander fought him back before turning his attention to the advancing man to his left. But a blow to the back of his head dropped him to his knees. He tried to stand but was met with a swift knee to the chin, sending him spiraling backward.

Alexander rolled to his side and staggered to his feet, but he had dropped his sword. A man rushed him with a short sword, and he ducked, pushing the man to the side and bracing for another attack. A sword swung wide, and he leapt back. It sliced through the fabric of his shirt but didn't reach his skin. But he couldn't escape the second swing that bit into his thigh.

He stumbled backward, losing his balance and again falling to his knees. There was no time to react to the blade that came for his head.

But a small battle-axe hit his attacker in the chest, killing him and dropping him to the ground. Alexander swayed on his knees as the Shadow commander walked by him, killing two more men with shots from his double crossbow. The commander turned back toward the fourth man, who was picking himself up off the ground.

"Are you mad?" the man yelled as he looked at his fallen companion with an axe in his chest. "That was King Gregor's nephew!"

The lord commander paused, and the man took the opportunity to run away. He turned back to Alexander. "Get back to the castle and don't leave," he snarled. Then he pulled his axe from the king's dead nephew and disappeared into the rain.

Norah found Mikael with Soren in Mikael's study. He stood, gripping the sides of his desk and leaning over it with a stoic look on his face. Soren stood across from him, his eyes dark.

"The lord justice told me what happened," she said breathlessly as she entered. Her pulse beat in her throat. Alexander's recount had her running to find Mikael before he'd even finished his words.

"Your justice is exactly the problem," Mikael snarled. "If he wasn't here, this wouldn't have happened."

"W-What?" Norah stammered, caught off guard by the direction of the conversation. "Those men attacked him! This isn't his fault!"

"No? It's not his fault that he works to align the North with Aleon? It's not his fault that he provokes hostility from my ally, and my lord commander is forced by duty to aid him?"

"*Mercia* is your ally!"

Mikael swept his books from the desk, and they scattered to the stone floor. "And will they join me when the Aleon king invades to build his new empire?"

"Gregor won't stand by and let his brother build his empire around him," she snapped back.

"Will the North stand with me against Aleon?" he pressed again.

Norah looked at him, speechless. They both knew the answer to that question.

"That's what I thought," he said. "And now you force me to break with my ally if I can't resolve this."

"Give me to him," Soren said to Mikael. "He'll punish me, but he won't kill me. You know he's wanted me for his army for some time now."

"I won't do that, brother," Mikael told him.

"If you lose the alliance with Japheth, you'll lose the support of the nobles," Soren said.

But Norah knew Mikael would never give up Soren, even in the face of losing everything. "You aren't going to lose your alliance with Japheth," she said, trying to reassure him. "We'll figure something out."

"*I* will figure something out," Mikael snapped at her. "You've done enough."

She stepped back in surprise, but Mikael didn't give her time to react. He turned and left the study. The commander gave her a cold eye before following after.

Gregor burst through the doors of the throne room, where they waited. Norah sat to Mikael's left, beside him on her own throne. Soren stood to his right, just off the dais.

She hadn't tried to talk to Mikael again before they'd gone to face Gregor. She'd wanted to, given the stress written over his face, and the challenge of how to fix this. Losing the alliance would bear severe consequences, some from which he might not recover.

The question was—how far was he willing to go to mend things before severing the alliance—and Gregor's head with it?

"I want his head!" Gregor bellowed. This stupid man truly didn't know how much danger he was in.

Mikael rose, poised, calm, not showing any of the signs of worry he'd had just moments before. But Norah knew what lay below the surface.

The king of Japheth glared at Soren, who stood silently while he waited for the determination of his fate. "You'll give me his head!" he seethed at Mikael.

"You don't want his head," Mikael replied coolly.

Gregor trembled with all the rage a frail man could muster. "I want justice! Give him to me, and I'll take him to Japheth to decide reparation."

"And what would that be?" Mikael asked.

"I'll let the boy's mother choose."

Mikael's voice was calm and steady. "We both know that's not a solution. Let's come to an appropriate punishment and it will be done here. Today."

Punishment. A tremor rolled up Norah's spine. Would he really punish Soren? And how?

"We're speaking of my nephew! The son of my wife's sister."

She frowned. There was a woman who could stand to be married to this man?

"A mere lashing won't be sufficient," Gregor spat.

"There's nothing *mere* about a lashing," Mikael said, his voice getting edgier.

Norah's skin prickled. Soren would *not* be getting a lashing.

"You'll give him to me," Gregor demanded. *Demanded.* He had the nerve to demand.

"I can't do that," Mikael told him.

"What do you mean you *can't*?" Gregor spewed each word with venom. "You mean you *won't*?"

While Mikael stood calmly, he was on the verge of blood rage, which wouldn't end well for anyone. Norah stood. "He means the lord commander is no longer his to give," she cut in, a sharp edge to her tone. She shot a steely glance at Mikael. "*Or* to punish."

All heads turned toward her, and she heard several audible surprises. Even Soren's head snapped up. Mikael stood motionless. He said nothing, but his eyes were fixed on her.

"He's *mine*, sworn to *me*," she said firmly, stepping down the stairs toward Gregor. "And I most *certainly* won't be giving him to *you*."

"You seek war?" he challenged.

"Your nephew waged an attack against the highest command of the Mercian army, which in itself is the very act of war!" Norah spat back, letting her rage cut through the hall. "The lord commander, now the servant of Mercia, was compelled to act on this threat. *As am I.*"

The king of Japheth took a step back at the ferocity of her words.

Norah calmed, but still pressed toward him. "However," she continued, "my husband has tried to tell me that this was merely the foolishness of a young man, for which he's unfortunately paid with his life. And so Salar has asked for compassion, that I not take this as an intentional threat, and that I not rouse our combined forces and *allies* on such a misunderstanding."

Norah stepped directly in front of Gregor and stared at him with an icy fire. There was no question of her reference to allies. *Aleon.* And it hung heavy in the air. "So, I ask," she said, "is this a misunderstanding? Or does Japheth seek war against the queen of Mercia and salara of Kharav?"

Gregor stood, speechless. An eerie quiet hung in the hall as all eyes waited for the Japheth king's response. No single alliance could be stronger than the forces of Mercia, Kharav, and Aleon together. *If* they were together. Norah knew her threat, if believed, turned the tables. And it showed this pitiful excuse of a king that Mikael was the only thing that stood between him and a crushing war.

Finally, Gregor gave a slight nod, acquiescing. "Forgive me, Salara, for I neither knew the commander was sworn to you, nor the circumstance by which my poor nephew suffered his fate. I ask your pardon, and your understanding, as sometimes young men make poor choices without thought of consequence."

She gave a pursed smile and looked back at Mikael. "I'm just thankful to Salar, otherwise I may have acted in haste. But his friendship with Japheth is of importance to him." To *him*, not to *her*. She hoped she'd made that clear. And this king should grovel at Mikael's feet to keep him.

"It was wise counsel," Gregor replied, "and Kharav is of great importance to Japheth." He dipped his head low, toward Mikael.

As he should. *Grovel.*

"Then I'll let you both get on with your negotiations, keeping that importance in mind," she said with a warning smile.

Gregor gave a final nod and left them, his entourage following him out.

Norah swallowed back the bile that was building in her throat. Her knees shook, and she was thankful for her layered skirts.

Mikael stepped close behind her. "You risk another Great War," he said.

She turned to face him. "Japheth against three of the most powerful kingdoms in the world would not be a Great War."

Mikael cast his gaze to the side before bringing it back to her. "Is this to mean that you've negotiated Aleon as your ally?" he asked.

"Aleon doesn't have to be an ally to join me against Japheth in war. Phillip wants Gregor's head above all else. Everyone knows this."

She turned to leave, but Mikael caught her arm. "I'm beginning to think you know exactly how all of this works."

"I was waiting for you to figure it out."

The corners of his lips curved ever so slightly.

"Did you really intend to lash Soren?" she asked.

He frowned. "If it would get us an accord and save the alliance, yes. And he would have gladly accepted it."

"I wouldn't have," she said firmly.

He leaned back on his heel.

"I meant what I said." Her stare locked with his. "Soren's mine."

Clouds covered the sky. Winter had lost its power, giving way to the rains. The wind blew cold, but the ground was no longer frozen. Having left Mikael to work things through with Gregor, Norah wriggled her toes in her boots against the mud under her feet as she watched men in the corrals working the new herd of horses that had come in. They were beautiful beasts, giants. They looked like mounts of the gods. When they ran in unison, their hoofbeats shook the earth.

Another giant moved to stand beside her, and she didn't need to look to know it was Soren. They stood quietly, watching the horses.

Unexpectedly, Soren reached out, holding a dagger in front of her.

Alexander's dagger—the dagger that had been taken from her when she was captured by Mikael as she traveled to Aleon. She hadn't expected to ever see it again, and she stared at it.

He held it by the blade, and, very slowly, she reached up and curled her fingers around its hilt. He released it, all without taking his eyes from the corral. His thanks.

Soren said nothing.

And Norah said nothing.

But the nothing felt like friendship. And that was nice.

Chapter Twenty-Two

Sun poured through the paneled crystalline windows of the great Kharavian library and spilled across the mosaic floor; it was quite heavenly for the kingdom of Shadows. Norah sat at the black ash-wood table, with books strewn about her.

King Gregor's entourage was in the courtyard, preparing to depart back to Japheth, but she didn't join Mikael to see them off. She'd done enough—to help or to hurt, she wasn't sure.

But despite the tension-riddled weeks, between Alexander's return to Kharav and Gregor's visit, Norah found herself grateful for the distractions. While she was still wary, her fear of the mysterious enemy who had tried to kill her had mostly dissipated. She wasn't continuously looking over her shoulder or jumping at sudden noises. Now she was able to think more clearly, more rationally, about who'd sent the assassins, and she set her thoughts to action.

They'd found no additional clues on the assassins' bodies, no threats had been received, no sign of more intruders. It was as if he'd given up.

She knew he hadn't given up. An effort such as the one he'd made was not taken on by a man who gave up easily. But still, the question hung over her—who wanted to kill her? Who wanted to hurt both Alexander and Mikael?

If only she had her memories—something else that still evaded her—surely she'd have a few more clues.

She leafed through the pages of yet another book. She didn't know what she was looking for in the aged archives—histories of tenuous or soured political relationships, forgotten rifts? Not that she really expected to find anything, but she might uncover a history she didn't know before. She frowned. At this point, any history would be something she didn't know before.

In front of her lay open a historical account of the Great War. It was written in a combination of Kharavian and Northern tongue and contained a number of drawings. As she flipped through, one image in particular caught her attention, and she looked at it for a long time. It was the battle between what appeared to be the senior Kharavian king and her father. The title was faded but she could still read it—"Clash of Kings."

She eyed the image of her father closely, but it was only a simple drawing. She ran her fingers over him, and over his horse. Was this the horse of the Wild? Would the witness to it be recorded in the words of this book? She wished she could read the rest of it. While she was becoming more familiar with Kharavian words in conversation, written words were still entirely foreign. She sat back in the chair with a sigh.

"I thought I'd find you here," a voice came from behind, and she turned to see Alexander. He wore a warm smile on his face, and she couldn't help but smile back.

"Am I that predictable?"

He chuckled. "Tell me one other thing predictable about your life. I'll wait."

Her smile widened. He was right. Predictable her life was *not*.

He took the chair beside her, and the air grew quiet between them. He cast his gaze down. "Are you angry with me?"

She rolled her bottom lip between her teeth, but then let out a long breath and shook her head. "No. I don't blame you for what happened with Gregor."

He sat back in his chair, and his lips thinned. "Perhaps you should."

Her brow dipped. "Why would you say that?"

"Norah, we both know I haven't made this easy for you."

"It's not been easy for anyone," she countered.

"But especially not for you, and I haven't helped that."

"You're doing the best you can."

His nostrils flared. "I went to Aleon against your will."

"It was a task from the council."

"Stop defending me!"

She quieted.

He turned to her and reached out, cupping his hands around hers. His eyes held the weight of a mountain. "You have so few you can trust, so few you can lean on. But you can trust me, Norah. I won't ever give you another reason to doubt me. Whatever you ask of me..." He shook his head and dropped his gaze again. "And if you tell me to go..." He pulled her hands to his lips but stopped short of kissing the backs of her fingers. "Please don't tell me to go." He clasped her hands tighter. "But if you do... I'll go."

He needed to go. She needed to tell him to go, for the complications that his presence brought, for his own safety and Mikael's. So why couldn't she tell him? The brilliant blues of his eyes glistened with emotion. They begged her.

Their fingers laced together. She knew he would do anything for her. And the world felt right with him by her side, right enough to face any challenge. And she *did* trust him. He said he wouldn't harm Mikael, and she believed him.

She would tell him to go. But not right now.

As if he could read her mind, the corners of his mouth drew up ever so slightly, although his eyes still reflected a sadness. And they settled.

As things eased more between them, Alexander sat back in his chair. He glanced at the books strewn around her on the table. "What are you doing in here?" he asked.

Her heart skipped a beat. She'd completely forgotten to tell him her discovery about her father and his horse from the Wild. "Hamed, Calla and Cohen's grandfather, fought in a battle against Mercia. When I first met him, he figured out who I was by my hair and because I rode a horse of the Wild—*like my father*."

Alexander shifted. His brow creased, and his lips parted.

She could tell from his expression this was news to him too.

"I never saw your father on a horse of the Wild," he said. "When was this?"

"I don't know. I should have asked. Calla and Cohen's parents were both killed, so it would have been a battle with heavy losses for Kharav."

"The first Battle of Bahoul, maybe." Alexander hadn't fought in the original Battle of Bahoul, the battle that had claimed her father's life. His eyes shifted back and forth in thought.

"What?" she asked.

"If your father rode a horse of the Wild, it's not a coincidence that you do too."

Her thoughts exactly.

"And the Wild protected you from the drifters," he added.

"I don't know about *protected*. It killed trespassing men."

"But not you."

These were all things that had swirled in her mind.

"Norah, the Wild is known to mess with the minds of men. Again, this can't be a coincidence. What if we can find answers there? What if you can get back your memories?"

She stilled. Was he proposing they go there? "But the Wild is a dangerous place."

"Not for you. And, Norah, if you could get back your memories…" He leaned forward, holding her hand tighter. "If you could remember."

If she could *remember*… she'd have her whole life back, everything that she was, everyone that she loved. Perhaps she'd be another step closer to finding out this unknown enemy.

"I could take you," he said. He reached across the table and pushed through the books to one that had a loose map parting the pages. He spread it wide and drew his finger from Kharav along a path north, stopping when he reached an unlabeled area just southwest of Mercia. "Here. I could take you back to where I found you."

She bit along her bottom lip. "Alexander, that's a long journey. And it's not that simple."

"Why not? If there are answers there—"

"No. I can't just leave."

His brow dipped. "But you would come back. I'd bring you back. You'd only be gone a few weeks."

"It's not that. I mean, it is a little, but it's not that I don't trust you to bring me back. It's…" It was complicated.

His face hardened. "The Shadow King."

A silence came between them.

"He wants you to forget," he said.

"No, he doesn't want me to forget."

"But he doesn't want you to remember."

She shook her head. "He's never said that. But Alexander..." Her stomach twisted, and her voice dropped to a near whisper. "What if it makes things harder?"

He stilled, and the muscle along his jaw tightened. "Do *you* not want your memories back?"

"Of course I do. How can you say that?"

He quickly drew in a breath and shook his head. "I'm sorry."

She leaned forward and took his hands again. "I think about getting them back all the time, about *needing* them back. But it's also a little scary, I guess. What if the person I was isn't the same as the person I am now? I know that sounds silly—"

"It's not silly." He sighed, looking down at his hands covering hers. "Norah, this is your decision. Not mine, not the Shadow King's. Whatever you choose, I will support you. But if you do want your memories back, I think there are answers in the Wild, and I would gladly take you. Just think about it." He moved to release her, but she held him, pulling his attention back.

"Alexander. Thank you."

He nodded, giving her fingers a gentle squeeze, then stood and left her to the quiet of the library.

Norah pushed out a breath, trying to keep her mind from tumbling into chaos. Of course she wanted her memories back; there was still a desperation to unlock them. So why was she hesitating about the Wild? Because it was a dangerous place, she reminded herself. And they were only drawing conclusions of her ties to it. What if the Wild hadn't been keeping her safe from the drifters? Maybe it just hadn't noticed her. It didn't mean she'd be welcomed back.

But hope sprouted along the cracks of doubt. What if there were answers for her in the Wild? If she wanted to go, would Mikael understand? He'd once said her memory loss might have helped them come together, that she might not have wed him otherwise. And if that was true, how would he feel about her getting them back now?

As if thoughts summoned him, the library doors opened, and she turned to see Mikael walking toward her. Had he seen Alexander departing? His demeanor suggested he hadn't. Yet his stride wasn't an easy one.

There was a strangeness between them, but she couldn't quite place it. They hadn't talked much since her handling of King Gregor the day before, and since her bold claim on Soren.

Mikael had come to their bed late into the night and left before she woke to continue his discussions with Gregor. Midmorning, she'd joined them both for a formal breakfast. While Gregor didn't look at her, Mikael's eyes never left her. He seemed settled, calm, but there was a hook to his gaze, and she couldn't shake it. And the look in his eyes... not anger, but... a challenge? *No*—not a challenge. But what?

She had forced herself to stay composed—unshaken—copying the mask Mikael wore so often, until she could deal with him later.

And that later time would be now, she told herself as he strode toward her to address this strangeness between them. She stood as he neared.

"Gregor's just departed," he told her.

"So, you've reached an accord?"

He tipped his head slightly. "For now."

The king of Japheth had been scheduled to stay another day, but she wasn't surprised by his earlier departure announcement. "I'm sure he was eager to be on his way."

"I'm sure," Mikael said, his voice low. "After seeing a side of the North Queen he wasn't expecting. A side I wasn't expecting either."

This was the root of what lay between them. She'd overstepped, she knew. Both on Soren and Gregor. "I know I've probably made things more difficult..."

He stepped nearer, quieting her. "Perhaps it's a side you'll let me see more often." His eyes burned down into hers, the same as they had at breakfast.

And it hit her. It wasn't the fire of challenge his eyes held.

He stepped closer but didn't touch her, and his voice came in a raspy whisper. "And perhaps I like difficult."

He had liked her control—more than *liked* it. A smile poked at her lips, but she didn't let herself show it. She only stared back at him with the same solid calm she'd given him that morning.

Mikael swallowed, and his eyes darkened until the outer ring was as black as the inside. Hunger pulsed off him. He wanted that control from her now, as if he'd been waiting, as if he couldn't wait any longer.

Her own pulse quickened. The thought of obliging him... It was all she could do to keep her breath from quivering.

Then the words came before she could stop them. "Get on your knees," she told him. But then her mind raced. What was she going to do with him? He wanted from her what she wasn't accustomed to doing—taking.

His nostrils flared as a tremor rolled over his skin, and he sank to his knees. But as he looked up at her—hungry, waiting—her own desire flared, and she knew exactly what she wanted from him.

She pulled the corner of her gown up, raising it slowly. "Kiss me."

A smile peeled across his lips, and his mouth opened slightly, flashing his teeth like he might bite her as well. Heat pooled in her stomach. She might like that.

He slipped a hand under her gown and pushed it up to her right knee, then he bent and brushed his lips across the skin of her upper calf. It was all she could do to keep from trembling under his touch, but there was no hiding the prickles that sprang across her skin.

And he worked his way up, slowly, savoring each spot, teasing her. He reached her thigh, letting her feel his teeth now, and she shuddered. He chuckled darkly—now who was in control? She ran her hands into his hair, mussing it from its tie and weaving her fingers through, then she clenched tight and stopped him. He raised his eyes to hers, his mouth still open, his bottom lip on the inside of her thigh. He would listen to her. She would make him. She clutched him tighter, then she pulled him farther upward, and he followed.

Mikael nipped the sensitive skin inside her upper thigh, too eager, and she clenched him tighter to hold him. She moved a hand from his hair to the side of his face, curving her fingers down underneath the line of his jaw, and tightened her grip—a warning—and he followed with soft kisses. She shifted her leg out to give him more access.

His breath warmed the joining between her thighs, and Norah let her head fall back as anticipation rippled through her. She didn't want to wait any longer—she couldn't—and she hooked her fingers in the silk that covered the most sensitive part of her and pulled it to the side.

And he kissed her.

He kissed her like he did when he took her mouth—his tongue tormenting, his lips worshiping, consuming her. Her spine arched back, and it was all she could do to keep on her feet.

He unleashed the darkness within him that she'd summoned, and she reveled in it. She wanted to drown in it, and she *was* drowning. But still, she needed more, and she'd have it.

Norah pushed him down to the floor, on his back. He reached down and tore at his breeches, but she grabbed his arm, gripping him tightly and stopping him.

"Do not," she hissed.

He would do what *she* wanted. *When* she wanted. The corners of his open mouth flicked upward slightly, and he panted as he yielded.

She didn't know this woman—this woman who moved herself up over him, who was on her knees, straddling his chest. She didn't know this woman who moved up farther, bringing her body back to his mouth. But she liked this woman. She liked the power inside her. The power he gave her—*no*—the power she took. And she liked the feeling of the Shadow King beneath her.

Still, she needed more. Norah moved quickly, impatiently, sliding back down and ripping his breeches open. She released his length and slid down onto him before he was completely free, still fighting to get their clothing out of the way. He was ready, more than ready. He hardened to near bursting inside her, but she gripped him under his jaw and held him. "You'll wait for me."

Everything within him surged under the force of restraint, the struggle of it, and it was enough to send her over. She broke.

As she shattered around him, he found his own release, growling as his body quaked. She clutched him with her thighs—holding him, taking him, absorbing him into the very essence of herself. And as the waves of complete abandon washed over her, she collapsed on top of his chest.

They lay in the silence, still as one, simply breathing. When her senses returned, when her body calmed, she raised her head and propped herself on her elbow, looking at him.

He brushed the tresses of her hair back over her shoulder, and a quiet chuckle rumbled through him. A sudden bashfulness came over her, and heat rose to her cheeks. "What?" she asked him, but she knew she'd gotten carried away.

His eyes moved back and forth between hers, and his lips held a satisfied smile. "If you ever look at me and I seem to get weak, know that I'm thinking of this moment, and how you made me get on my knees for you."

The bashfulness fell away, and his words made her want to do it all over again. She pulled her bottom lip in between her teeth and bit into the soft flesh to stop herself.

They didn't have time to play all day. Unfortunately.

Norah pushed herself off him and rose, re-situating her clothing. The silk of her underwear was slick against her skin—from them both—and it stirred a dip in her stomach again. He watched her as he tied his breeches. Could he see the lust still behind her eyes? Heat rushed to her face again, and she scolded herself. What was wrong with her? He'd done... quite enough. Yet she felt like she couldn't get enough of him.

And suddenly, it dawned on her—they were in the library. She'd been so caught up she hadn't even cared.

"What's wrong?" he asked.

She swallowed as heat rushed to her cheeks. "We just... in the *library*."

His smile widened as he reached out and pulled her close to him. "What's wrong with the library?"

"Someone could have seen us." *Alexander* could have seen them, and her stomach twisted.

He brushed the line along her jaw with the back of his fingers and pulled her attention back to him. "Then they'd see how their salar loves their salara." He bent to kiss her cheeks. "How he worships her." He trailed his mouth back to her lips. "How he sees to her every need."

This man. "You're going to get us on the floor again," she warned, and his eyes darkened with new intent. She put a hand on his chest to contain him.

He chuckled as his eyes drifted to the table and the books scattered around. "What are you even doing in here?" Then his eyes fell on the map, the map Alexander had been walking through with her not even an hour earlier... in the same place she'd told Mikael to get on his knees.

Guilt flooded her.

She shook her head, trying to push back the overwhelming shame filling her to the brim. "Nothing, Alexander was just—"

"He was here with you?"

Her breath seized in her chest. She hadn't meant to say that. Not that she was trying to hide it, but the timing... "Mikael, we were only talking—"

"I'm not upset."

She swallowed. "You're not?"

"Salara, I'm fairly confident that when you think of this library now, you won't be thinking of your justice."

A deep heat flushed across her cheeks, and he smiled. Then his eyes trailed to the table and the map spread wide on top of it. His smile faded.

"It appears one of us still thinks about my justice," she said.

His eyes met hers. A silence hung over them. He didn't ask her what she had talked about with Alexander. She knew he wouldn't, even though he clearly wanted to know.

She wouldn't make him wonder. "He thinks there may be answers for me in the Wild, possibly a way to get back my memories."

Mikael shifted. "Why would he think this?"

"My father was seen riding a horse of the Wild, as I can now."

"Yes, you've told me this, but it doesn't mean the Wild has answers for you. This one connection—"

"It's more than one connection—it's both me *and* my father. And don't forget, I was found in the Wild. Still, it's more than that. Before I was found, I was attacked by drifters."

Mikael stiffened.

"But when they tried to harm me, something intervened and made them kill themselves. It might be a stretch to think this something saved me, but now, with my being able to ride a horse of the Wild, the same as my father..." She shook her head, wiping her face as she pieced it all together for him. "Stories are told about the Wild taking over the minds of men, and my memory loss is a problem of the mind. It can't *all* be a coincidence. And I do wonder—what if there *are* answers there? What if I can get my memories back?"

He said nothing.

She frowned. "Do you not want me to get them back?"

He took her hand. "It's not that." His eyes were dark, but soft. Worried. "It's selfish, I know," he said quietly. "But I fear it. What if remembering everything changes who you are today?"

She slipped her arms around him and leaned against his warmth, breathing him in. They stood in the quiet. Then she said, "I feared that too. But one thing I know for sure—I love you. I know you, who you are." Her voice dropped to almost a whisper. "I just really want to know myself. I want to know my father, and my childhood. Memories are a place where the things you lost aren't fully lost. And maybe I'd discover things that could help us face today's challenges."

He pulled back from her, enough to look at her, and cupped her face in his hands. His eyes moved between hers. "Then you should go."

Her brow dipped, and she sucked in a breath. "Really?"

Mikael nodded. "I'll take you myself."

"Are you mad?" Soren's voice echoed out of Mikael's study and into the halls, making Norah jump.

Alexander stepped closer to her.

"Calm, brother," Mikael said.

"You want to go to the Wild?" The vein on the side of the commander's temple pulsed.

"That's what I said," Mikael said coolly.

"This isn't an enemy you can fight. And you're needed here in Kharav."

"I don't plan to fight. And the Circle will manage things until I return."

Norah had almost forgotten about his council—they could look after things for a short time.

Soren snorted in frustration. "It's too dangerous."

Norah glanced at Alexander, knowing all too well the dangers of the Wild, and she tried to swallow back her building worry. Ever since Mikael had agreed to go, she'd been second-guessing herself. What if they traveled all the way there and found nothing? Worse, what if she'd assumed wrong and there wasn't a connection? What if the same thing that happened to the drifters happened to them? What if someone was hurt? What if Mikael was hurt? "Maybe the lord commander is right," she interjected. "The Wild is a dangerous place. And I've already been there. If there's something or someone there that could help me, why wouldn't they have done so then?"

Mikael shifted his gaze to her. "Maybe because you weren't asking them to." He turned his head back to the commander. "We'll go."

Soren crossed his arms and let out a snarling sigh. "Then I'll take her. This is a suicidal journey."

"*I'll* take her," Alexander said, his eyes fixed on Mikael. "I can take her back to where I found her. It's the best place to start."

Mikael's face darkened. "Then you'll lead the way. But I'm going with you."

"As am I," Soren added, his glare at Alexander matching the daggers in his voice.

Alexander sighed. "Fine."

"Fine," Mikael echoed.

Soren grunted. "Fine."

A fog of quiet rolled in.

Norah swallowed. "Well, then," she said uneasily. "Looks like we're *all* going." She drew in a breath, trying to calm her nerves, then nodded slowly. "I'm sure it will be...*fine*. All of us. Together. Going to the Wild."

Just fine.

Chapter Twenty-Three

Norah breathed in the cold air of morning, but her excitement warmed her. Or maybe it was her fear. Fear of the Wild and—she looked at the men riding with her—fear that if tempers ran afoul, they might not even make it there.

They rode north. Their route would take them through the Canyonlands of the Uru, through more Horsemen tribes, and then northwest, to the Wild. She looked forward to seeing Tahla again. A smile came to her face as she thought of the Horseman chief's daughter.

Despite Soren's and Alexander's vehement objections—the first time she'd seen them agree on anything—they journeyed without an army or even the Crest. Mikael felt they'd travel more safely without attracting attention, although Norah suspected that Soren and Mikael drew as much attention as any army. Caspian came with them, and he and Alexander rode ahead. Mikael rode beside her, and Soren followed behind.

The journey was quiet. They reached the clefts of the canyons on the second day, with everyone still alive and somewhat civil. Now if only they could repeat that for ten more days or so.

As expected, the Uru swarmed in welcome.

"Salar," Tahla greeted Mikael as she reached them. She grinned at Norah. "Salara." She slid off her horse.

Norah did the same, and they embraced warmly. "Hello, Tahla."

"This is a happy surprise." The chief's daughter laughed. "What brings you?"

Norah looked back at Mikael.

"We travel to the Wild," he said.

"Sol!" Tahla exclaimed. She stared at Mikael for a moment before looking at Soren, then to Alexander, then back to Norah. "All of you?" she asked. "Together?"

Norah pursed her lips and nodded. "Yep," she said stiffly. She held back the jest of whether they'd even make it there.

"Why would you go there?" Tahla asked.

"We think it holds answers to questions I have," Norah told her. "Answers that I desperately need." Tahla didn't know about her memory loss, or the assassins, and neither were something Norah wanted to explain, at least not right now. Luckily, Tahla didn't push her for more.

Tahla's brow furrowed as she clutched Norah's hand and looked at Mikael and Soren with a concerned eye. "But the Wild isn't a welcoming place."

Soren grunted. "We don't like to be welcomed."

Tahla rolled her eyes. "Come," she told them. "Come get something to eat, and rest before you're off again."

They made their way to the settlement on the river that glowed against the evening's setting sun. Mikael broke off to give his respects to Chief Coca Otay, and Tahla showed Norah to her room.

"I can see you're worried," Norah said as they stepped inside, and she put her pack on a chair.

Tahla nodded. "The Wild is a dangerous place, Salara. You hold Savan's favor, but Salar and Soren don't. I fear even for your Northmen. Promise me you'll take care of them. That you won't let them be harmed."

"I promise," Norah whispered.

Tahla gave a warm smile. "It's good to see you, sister."

"And you. Maybe on our return, we can spend more time."

"I'd like that." The chief's daughter gave another smile with her hand on the door. "Salar should be along soon. I'll let you rest now."

Caspian smiled as he pulled off his jacket. He wasn't facing the door, but he knew she was there. He laid his jacket on the chair and turned. By the gods, she was beautiful. But she wasn't smiling.

Tahla stepped inside, closing the door behind her. "How did you do it?" she asked him. Her tone was almost angry.

His brows drew together. "Do what?"

"Make me think about you every day, every moment that you were gone? It's a cruel thing."

He almost smiled again, but he couldn't tell if she was truly angry. "I would never be cruel to you."

Tahla crossed the space between them, and his pulse quickened. Her nearness both freed his spirit and captured him at the same time. She reached up and grazed her fingertips against his chest before spreading her palm flat. Even through his shirt, her touch ignited a fire across his skin. His body came alive. As much as he tried to conceal it, he knew she felt his energy when the corners of her mouth turned up.

"Have you suffered this cruelty too?" she asked.

The cruelty of wanting—he knew it well. But he didn't answer.

"I'll be taking that kiss now," she said as she lifted herself onto her toes.

Instinctively, he dropped his head to hers so that their lips were almost touching, but his mind screamed restraint. He had known temptation would come with seeing her again, but he hadn't expected it so quickly. He'd almost forgotten the power she had over him, and how strong it was. It took every ounce of self-control.

"Tahla," he breathed.

She clutched his shirt in her fist and pulled him closer. "Kiss me, Northman."

It was enough to push him over. His body betrayed him and moved before his mind could stop him. He swept his arm around her and covered her mouth with his. Tahla kissed him back with a hunger that drove a frenzy within. Her body moved against him, demanding more than a kiss. She pulled up his shirt, and he broke from her lips long enough to let her take it from him. Then they collided again.

While he'd never touched a woman, he wasn't ignorant in ways of the flesh. Primal desire whispered in his ear, instinctively telling his body exactly what to do. He ran his hands over her hips, down the backs of her thighs, and lifted her against him. She wrapped her legs around his waist.

Caspian walked her to the bed as she peeled her dress off over the top of her head. She wore nothing underneath, and the feel of her skin against his drove an animalistic desperation to escape the rest of his clothing. He laid her back onto the bed, not knowing quite how he managed to shuck off his boots and breeches and find himself naked over her. Not that he cared for how. The warmth of her body was intoxicating, and he was rapt in it.

He moved between her thighs, but as she positioned him to slip inside her, he paused.

"What's the matter?" she panted.

He shook his head softly. "Nothing," he whispered, trying to temper his need. "I just want to look at you for a moment."

Her large brown eyes moved back and forth between his. How could any man not be swallowed into their depths? Everything about her was perfect, even her imperfections. Caspian had never thought he'd be pulled from the values he'd held all his life, but it didn't feel like he was acting against them. Something more than temptation called to him now.

Slowly, he brought his mouth back to hers. He slipped his hand behind the nape of her neck and—gently, tenderly—held her to him. He let his lips bare his heart. When he pulled back again, her eyes held a look he didn't understand.

"That's a lover's way to kiss a woman," she whispered.

"Then I've revealed myself."

She shook her head slowly. "Don't say things like that."

"I don't want to just madly take you like this, Tahla."

She raised a brow. "Is this where you deny yourself pleasures of the flesh again, and we spend the night drunk on each other's words?"

"No," he whispered, "this is where I decide I'm yours." He had been since the moment he first laid eyes on her. "But I want to give myself to you, not lose myself in you."

She reached up and brushed his cheek with the back of her fingers. "I told you not to say things like that. I can't love you, Northman. I cannot be yours." Her voice held a twinge of regret.

"I know," he said sadly, and bent his head to kiss her again. It didn't stop him from being hers.

She kissed him back, and he tightened his arms around her. Tahla reached down to guide him back to her, and he sank inside her. They both gasped and lay still in the silence. His body begged to move, to thrust, to fill his need, but he stayed. He wanted to feel her, to know every part of her.

Slowly, she started to rock her hips against him, and he matched her rhythm. They moved together as one. Never had he felt so close to someone. He pushed himself deeper. His need for her was beyond the want of the flesh, beyond desire. He loved this woman.

They alternated between love and desire—between moments of feverish build and the slow of relishing one another.

As they moved, he felt her hunger for him grow. She shifted and rolled them so she could take the top, and she straddled him with her hands spread wide against his chest. Her breaths came faster now, and the thrust of her hips more fervent. He worried he might not last until her peak, but as her body clenched and bucked around him, he let his own climax come.

He was no stranger to the pleasure of release, but with Tahla it came deeper, richer, etching her mark into his innermost self. The fall of a thousand rains stippled across his skin, and the hold of a thousand chains bound him to her.

She collapsed on top of him, and they both lay panting. Caspian wrapped his arms around her and mouthed gentle kisses along her shoulder. He could stay like this, with her, forever.

Tahla pushed herself up to sit but didn't pull free. Her warmth still surrounded him. She brushed a lock of hair from his brow.

So many things he wanted to tell her, but most were confessions of his heart—things he couldn't ask from her in return.

"I fear for you going to the Wild," she said.

She feared for him. He smiled. "Don't. I've lived a life to be envied, and I'm grateful. I accept my fate whenever it may come."

"I don't accept it," she told him. "Come back to me, Northman." And she leaned forward to kiss him again.

Chapter Twenty-Four

The journey to the Wild felt endless. It took longer than what it would have taken to reach Mercia. The flatlands of the Horsemen tribes gave way to rocky hills, slowing their pace. Norah found herself looking northeast, knowing Mercia wasn't far beyond the horizon. Her heart longed to change her course, ride to her grandmother, her kingdom, her home. But they journeyed on.

The Wild came into view as any other forest, ordinary and unremarkable. Norah knew it was anything but. They stopped at the edge of the tree line and dismounted. Sephir tossed her head, and Norah put a hand on the mare's neck to calm her.

"I forgot this is home for you," she told the animal, smiling sadly. She knew what she needed to do. She loosened the girth on the saddle and pulled it from the mare's back. Then she took off the pad underneath. Sephir tossed her head again, feeling her freedom, and bolted into the forest.

Norah stood, holding the saddle pad in surprise. She sheepishly looked back at the men. "That wasn't exactly how I had imagined it," she admitted. "I thought I'd at least get some kind of goodbye."

Alexander gave her a sympathetic smile.

The men dismounted and hobbled their horses. Norah raised a brow as they situated their weapons. Soren wore a crossbow on his back along with his short sword, and a dagger and axe at his waist. He held his massive battle-axe in his hand. It seemed excessive, but had she expected anything else?

They left their horses at the boundary and continued into the trees. Norah wasn't sure what she was expecting, but she found breaching the edge of the Wild to be somewhat anticlimactic. Everything about the forest seemed like a forest should be—filled with natural beauty. Serene. Peaceful.

They walked deeper into the Wild, but nothing was unusual about the needled trees, the wood-spiced air, or the mossy ground. Spring hadn't fully come to the northern lands, but the rage of winter had passed and given way to a sprouting of small greens.

Her eyes combed the trees. She didn't even know what she was looking for—a random animal? The fox friend she'd met when she first found herself lost in the Wild? Norah started to feel foolish. What if this was all for nothing? She chided herself for expecting a white fox to show up and lead her to a magical faerie that would restore her memory. What if they found nothing here?

"I'll scout ahead," Alexander said, and picked up his pace, splitting away from the small group.

"I'll go with him," Caspian added, and followed.

She didn't like the idea of them breaking off, but she didn't stop them. They were likely safer away from Mikael and Soren, anyway.

"We're wasting our time," Soren muttered as Alexander and Caspian disappeared into the trees.

"We keep going," Mikael pushed.

Deeper into the forest they went. Norah let her hands skim the trees as she walked by them. The rough bark against her skin was strangely comforting. There was a beauty to this place that felt like home.

"There's nothing here," Soren growled, thumping the head of his axe on the ground in agitation.

No sooner than he'd spoken, a strange feeling rippled through her, and the forest became suddenly silent. Too silent. Norah scoured the trees around them. They weren't alone. "Something *is* here," she breathed. Prickles rose across her skin.

"Salar," Soren called out. Norah looked back to see the commander stopped. He bared his teeth in pain.

Mikael paused and looked back. "What is it?"

"Run!" Soren shouted as he dropped his axe and pulled the crossbow from his back.

Mikael glanced around them, looking for the danger. Norah did the same, but she saw nothing.

"Run!" the commander begged.

Then Norah realized what was happening. Terror flooded her, but before she could react, the commander released a bolt from the crossbow at Mikael. The arrow hit him squarely in the shoulder with a force that twisted him back.

"No!" Norah screamed.

"Run!" Soren pleaded.

"He has no control!" Norah cried. "Mikael, run!"

But Mikael couldn't. He clasped onto a nearby tree for support, gripping his shoulder as blood poured between his fingers. "Soren!" he called back. "You're stronger than this!"

Soren shook his head, raging through his clenched jaw in the agony of helplessness. A second bolt still sat in the double crossbow, and he wept as he took aim again. "Run!" he pleaded.

"No!" Norah screamed again as she jumped in front of Mikael.

"Salara, get out of the way!" Mikael bellowed.

"Soren, stop!" she called to the possessed commander. "Look at me. You're not going to hurt me."

Just then, Alexander burst through the trees with his bow and took aim at the commander. Caspian was ready beside him with his sword drawn. "Drop the bow!" Alexander roared.

"End me!" Soren begged.

"Norah, get out of the way!" Alexander yelled.

"Don't shoot him!" she cried back.

"Bear!" Soren begged again. "Kill me!"

"Alexander! No!"

"Salara!" Mikael yelled from behind her.

Soren strained against the unseen force. "Bear—do it!"

"I said no!" Norah screamed back.

Alexander snarled through his teeth, but he held firm.

No arrow pierced the air. From either of them. A quiet came again.

Caspian put himself between Soren and Norah, and as Alexander moved closer to the lord commander, his bow still drawn, the force released him. The crossbow fell from Soren's hands, and he dropped to his knees. His head hung low as he gasped for breath.

Norah turned and ran to Mikael, helping support him as he sank to the floor of the forest. She gasped at all the blood. "Are you all right?"

He grabbed her arm and pulled her close. "Why would you do that?" he hissed through clenched teeth. He held her tightly, his eyes glistening in a raging fear. "You'll be the death of me before any arrow!" He released her arm and reached up to clasp her cheek. "You can't ever do that again. You can't risk your life for mine."

But she couldn't promise that. "Are you all right?" she asked again.

He groaned as he pulled the arrow from his flesh and held his shoulder tightly. "I think so," he panted. "How did you make it release him? How did you make it stop?"

"I don't know, but I think I'm safe here."

"Safe from what?"

"From you," a voice answered him, startling all of them.

A woman stepped out from behind a tree. She was small, but not a child. Her dark hair hung long, with a few tendrils braided with forest greens. She wore earth-toned fitted layers, delicately woven with beautiful but subtle embroidery. Norah had seen this before—on her dress when she woke in the Wild. But she didn't have time to reflect on it, for what she found most shocking were the small, elegantly curved horns that sat atop the woman's head.

"Princess Norah," the creature said.

Did she know her? "Who are you?"

"Why do you protect the Shadow King? And what power do you bring here?" There was a sharpness to her tone.

"Are you the Wild?" Norah asked her.

"All around you is the Wild." The woman tilted her head curiously. "This is unexpected, Princess."

"Queen," Norah corrected her. "Queen Norah."

The woman's eyes widened, and she pursed the slightest of smiles. "We knew you had made it home."

To Mercia? Norah didn't know how to respond to that. Surely, a longer conversation would follow. In the meantime, she looked back at the men. "They're with me," she told the creature.

"They're not welcome here!" a voice called from Norah's right, and she turned as another woman emerged from the forest. She was slightly taller than Norah and looked as if she had been formed from the earth, with a soft hue of green to her skin. More striking were the thin roots that grew from her head, weaving back into the mane of flowers and ferns that fell heavily around her shoulders. She was beautiful, and she moved with grace, making no noise as she drew closer. But there was a pain in her eyes and a rage in her tone.

She brought her hand up as if clutching the air. Roots sprung from the earth and seized Mikael.

"No!" Norah screamed.

Alexander released the arrow from his bow at the Wild women.

"Naavi!" the horned creature cried to the woman, and knocked the arrow from its path. Naavi stepped back in surprise, and a third Wild woman leapt from a tree to join her. She was similar to the green woman called Naavi, but her skin shone a shimmering bronze. Above her cheeks and around her temples grew wisps of branches twisted back into the hair woven high atop her head.

A wave of power surged through the air, but it seemed to only pass through them. Alexander released another arrow, unfazed, and this time it found its mark. Naavi cried out in pain, grasping the protruding shaft in her side. The Wild women stumbled backward, and Norah gasped.

Soren leapt forward to Mikael, axe in hand, bringing down the blade and freeing him from the clutches of the forest.

"I can't control them, sister," Naavi cried. "There's a shield!"

Norah's mind swirled, trying to understand what was happening. Then the realization hit her—the women couldn't get inside their minds.

Alexander pulled another arrow into his bow as he advanced closer.

But Norah didn't come here for this. "Stop!" she cried, stilling everyone. Alexander paused but held his stance, his bow ready.

"Please," Norah called, "we mean no ill will."

Naavi pulled the arrow from her side, and Norah watched in astonishment as tiny threads of roots braided themselves over the wound, closing it. "Then why do you bring these monsters here?" the woman demanded. "Norah, how can you protect them?"

Norah's heart stopped in her chest. "You know me?" she breathed.

Naavi looked back at the other woman, the one she called her sister.

"Please," Norah begged. "I've come for your help."

"We'll never help the Shadowmen," Naavi said bitterly.

"I said *I* need your help."

"And what makes you think we'll help you?" the sister asked coldly. "You made your choice."

What did *that* mean?

Naavi straightened, recovering from the arrow's wound as if it had never pierced her. "What is it you seek?" she asked.

The bronze woman cut Naavi a sharp eye, and Naavi seemed to withdraw under her sister's gaze.

"My memories," Norah said.

The Wild women looked at one another again in surprise. "You cannot help her," the bronze woman hissed to Naavi. "Not now. But we can rid her of this wickedness that surrounds her."

The sisters looked at the Shadowmen with bitterness, seemingly contemplating their end. But Alexander pulled up his bow again and stepped in front of Mikael and Soren. "I can't let you do that."

"Sana," Naavi called back to her sister, "do you feel it? It's *him*." She stepped toward Alexander, and he fixed his aim on her again.

"I feel it," Sana said between her teeth. The bronze woman cast a daggered glare at Norah. "You say you want our help, but you come with the means to fight?" She looked at Alexander. "I feel your power, seer," she seethed. "But I don't need to take your mind to kill you."

What?

Alexander glanced at Norah and back to the Wild woman. "I'm no seer."

"Then what are you?" Naavi demanded.

"I'm the lord justice of Mercia."

"*What*, not who," Sana said icily.

Confusion flashed across his face, matching Norah's, and he shook his head. "I'm but a simple man."

"And a liar," Sana snapped. "You serve the Shadows?"

Alexander bristled, deeply insulted. "I'm not a liar, and I serve Mercia's queen."

"If you're not a seer, what are you?" she demanded.

Norah's mind spun. Alexander wasn't a seer. He had no powers. But what were the sisters sensing? He glanced back at her, and she could see he had no idea how to answer.

"If you truly come with no ill will, you'll let us look inside him," Sana said to Norah.

Alexander tightened his stance, his bow ready. But Norah hadn't come for violence. She'd come for answers. She needed their help, and she realized she needed to make the first move of trust.

"Alexander," Norah called to him. "Put down your bow."

He hesitated a moment, then reluctantly, he lowered it.

Sana nodded to Naavi, and the green-hued woman moved toward Alexander. She reached out to touch him, but he stepped back. The Wild woman looked at Norah.

Norah couldn't deny her own curiosity. What power did they think Alexander had? "Let her touch you," she told him.

Alexander stilled as Naavi reached out again. She put her palm against his chest. Norah glanced at Mikael and Soren, then at Caspian. They all watched with equal curiosity. The forest was silent as they stood, waiting.

Naavi's eyes widened, and she looked back at her sister. Something unspoken passed between them, but Norah wasn't sure what.

"What are you?" Sana asked Alexander again. "What is this power?"

"I told you, I'm but a man."

Naavi took a step back, giving some space between them. "You serve Mercia but ally yourself with the Shadow King?" she asked him.

"I serve Norah Andell, Queen of Mercia *and* the Shadowlands."

Both sisters jerked their heads toward Norah in surprise. "How is this possible?" Naavi breathed.

"The most obvious way," Mikael said shortly. "We're wed."

Naavi's face twisted. "Norah, this cannot be true."

"It's true," she confirmed. Although she didn't want to talk about her marriage, she wanted to understand what had happened with Alexander. But she didn't get a chance.

"We cannot help you," Sana said firmly.

Cannot or *will not*? "But I've been helped here before," Norah pressed. "It was you, wasn't it?" she asked Naavi, the green-hued sister she felt the most connection to. "You helped me escape the drifters."

Sana scowled at Naavi, who didn't answer, but Norah could see she was right.

"I came here riding a horse of the Wild," Norah continued, "and I've been told my father's ridden the same. Whatever this bond, whatever this connection, I beg you, can you help me? I have no memories, and I'm desperate to get them back."

But Naavi shook her head sadly. "No."

"Who can?" Norah pressed.

"No one," Sana said. "Once memories die, they're gone."

"No," Norah breathed, shaking her head. "That's not true! Pieces have come back. I just need to find out how to get the rest."

Naavi's eyes widened in surprise, and she looked back at Sana. "This cannot be. Perhaps I missed something."

Missed something?

"Naavi," Sana hissed to quiet her.

Norah gaped at her in horror. "You took them?"

The pain in Naavi's eyes answered for her.

Norah let out a quivering breath. "Why?"

The Wild woman shook her head. "That's not an easy question to answer."

"Try!" Norah pleaded, her eyes welling.

Sana glared at Mikael and the commander. "Enough of this foolishness," she told Naavi angrily. "Be done with them."

"Please!" Norah begged.

"Sister," Naavi said softly to Sana, "if this is possible—"

"It's not."

"We must make certain. And"—she looked at Alexander—"do you not want answers about him? We should take them to the pool. The water will show us."

Sana eyed Alexander, then Norah.

"Sana," Naavi pleaded.

Clearly, Sana held more power. Was Sana queen of the Wild? Was there such a thing? Why didn't she want to help?

Sana sighed, relenting. "Only for answers," she said sharply.

Naavi let out a breath and turned back to Norah. "Come. There is much to talk about."

Norah's relief brought a wave of emotion, but she swallowed it back.

"But not them," Naavi said, looking back to Mikael and Soren.

"Please," Norah asked softly. "They mean no harm, and they brought me all this way."

Naavi looked at Sana, and Sana looked at Mikael and Soren. Then Sana said, "I won't kill the Shadow King and his fiend so long as they don't remind me they're here."

The commander snorted, and Norah shot him a daggered look. Mikael grimaced as he stood upright.

The sisters turned and started along a small path.

Norah let out a breath. Whatever drove the hate for the Shadowmen ran deep here. She clutched Mikael as he started forward, and they followed the sisters farther into the forest, and deeper into the Wild.

Chapter Twenty-Five

The Wild was hauntingly beautiful, with long tendrils of earthy binds falling from the trees and into the shadowy mist of the forest floor.

A movement to her right caught Norah's attention, and she looked to see a fox, a white fox. She smiled. "It's you," she called incredulously.

"He's missed you," the small, horned woman said.

Her comment confused Norah, but before she could ask more, they came to a large tree with reptilian roots wound thick at its base. A knotty cleft sat in its center, and Sana climbed gracefully upward and slipped through. Naavi followed. Norah stepped into the cleft of the tree and looked back at the men—they'd have trouble getting through. Alexander was already pulling off his breastplate. He gave her a nod, and she turned back to the tree and slipped through the gap.

As she stepped into the darkness, she caught her breath as it opened into a grand cathedral. Tall trees lined the sides like pillared walls, coming to an arched peak, with medallions of stained glass set deep into the woven branches, like windows. Lights hung like stars strung from above, filling the hall with an enchanted glow.

Norah looked back to see how the men were faring. Alexander and Caspian had made it through, but both were without their armor. And then Mikael showed, surprisingly.

"Where's the lord commander?" she asked.

"He's coming," Alexander said with a wry smile.

Soren finally emerged from the passage, stripped of his weapons strappings, his guard covers, and even his winter tunic to fit through. Blood smeared his chest from the scrapes of skin. But in his hand, he still managed to pull through his axe.

Of course.

They followed the sisters through the cathedral and down a hall leading to two ornately arched doors. The doors opened as they approached, and Norah saw they were as thick as the walls. As they walked through, she looked around the room in wonder. Moss and trailing ferns covered the stacked stone. In the center was a crystal-blue pool, lit with floating flowers and vining lights from above.

"It's beautiful," she breathed.

"It is a place of great power," Naavi said. She stepped into the pool and waded to its center. Sana followed.

"Come," Naavi said.

Norah stepped forward, but Sana stopped her.

"Him first," she said, pointing to Alexander.

But Alexander shook his head. "No. I'll give you whatever you ask, but only after you give Norah the help she came for."

Norah's heart swelled.

"We never said she would get her memories back," Sana said.

"You said you would look to see if it's possible," he pressed.

"We will," Naavi said.

"Then you will do that first," he insisted.

Sana pursed her lips, then nodded reluctantly.

Norah wondered what they wanted so badly from Alexander that they would comply.

He nodded to her, and she pulled off her boots and stepped slowly into the water. It was cool, but not uncomfortably so. She waded toward the Wild women, feeling the water move upward, past her thighs and through her clothing. When she reached Naavi, she stopped, waiting.

But Naavi looked at her apprehensively.

"Why do you hesitate, sister?" Sana asked.

Naavi was quiet for a moment. "What if they are back?"

"They are not."

"But what if they are?"

Sana softened. "Then you will see him."

"Who?" Norah asked.

The Wild women paused. Norah didn't understand the reluctance.

"Your father," Naavi answered finally.

Why would the Wild woman care about seeing her father? But Norah didn't have time to think about it before Naavi reached out and took her face in her hands.

Norah closed her eyes and felt herself fall into a glowing darkness, her memories swirling around her. Unlike with the traveler seers, there was no blood spell. She couldn't see Naavi beside her, only her memories being searched before her like the turning pages of a book. Most flew by quickly as Naavi sorted through, but Norah noticed the Wild woman lingering on memories with Alexander, seemingly looking for information. She found the memory of the kiss in Mercia under the tree and watched it slowly—from the initial spark of memory to the kiss. Naavi drew it back and watched it once more. Norah flushed, but she noticed Naavi moving deeper to the memory from within. Then came the memory of Norah at the tree, waiting for Alexander. The vision expanded and shrank as Naavi looked through each detail.

The pages of her memories turned quickly again as Naavi sifted through her mind. Through Mercia, through her time there, through the castle itself. Naavi stopped in the hall to the throne room. On its wall was a painting of her father, King Aamon. Naavi looked at it for a long time.

The Wild woman finally let the image go and began looking once again through the memories. She shifted to Norah's capture, through the journey back to Kharav, her journey to Odepeth, her time with Mikael. She slowed for a moment on the vision of them lying together in her sanctuary, Mikael holding her close. Norah's cheeks flushed again. She could hide nothing.

Naavi pulled up from the memories and flipped back to the beginning—when Norah first woke in the Wild. She seemed already familiar with the drifters, spending little time on them. But suddenly Naavi slowed, seeing Norah come upon Alexander in the forest. She watched him with seemingly great interest.

Suddenly, her images blurred forward to the temple in Odepeth, quickly pulling the vision of Alexander shown by the traveler seer, comparing it with the image of Alexander in the Wild. Then everything went dark, but Norah still felt her moving, searching through time.

And then she was released. Norah opened her eyes to find herself back in the pool with Naavi.

"I have nothing for you," Naavi said sadly.

Norah's eyes welled. "There must be another who can try," she said.

The Wild woman shook her head. "It does not work that way. We sever them, and they die. You cannot bring them back."

"So, you didn't hide them?" Norah's voice broke. "You just destroyed them?"

Naavi sighed sadly and nodded.

"Why would you do that?"

"For your protection. We severed your link to the Aether. It was the only way we could hide you. As a result, your memories were lost."

Norah shook her head. "I know they're not gone. Something triggers their return!"

"No, it isn't possible to bring them back."

"No!" Norah cried. "If it's not possible, then I wouldn't have gotten any memories back. But I did!" She turned to Alexander. "When you kissed me in Mercia, I saw you, I saw your face. Us, together. We were lying in the fields under the sun, and you loved me. I remembered." A new thought struck her, and she looked at Alexander. "Maybe *you* can bring them back. Maybe you do have power, you just don't understand it."

Alexander shook his head, but Norah's breath shook as she thought aloud. "We were at the tree. Perhaps it's what gave you strength. This pool is a sacred place, a place of magic. Maybe you can use it?"

"Norah, I've spoken the truth," he said. "I'm only a man. I don't have this ability. I don't have any power."

"There's a great power within you," Naavi countered. She turned to her sister. "I saw it. He is the one who found her. But his shield hid him from us. It covered her too. It's why she disappeared from our sight." Naavi paused as she shook her head. "But I don't understand. The vision from the traveler clearly shows his face. How can the traveler see when we cannot?"

"How do you know there's a power?" Norah asked. "What is it you feel?"

Sana didn't answer, visibly reluctant to share, but Naavi explained, "It's not so much the feeling of his power, but rather the interruption of our power. Seers are protected from the sight of others by their shield. It creates a void. We've never seen a shield strong enough to cover others, but," she paused and nodded at Alexander, "his does. It's why you seemed to disappear from us when he first found you. And why we didn't sense you in the forest today until he distanced himself from you."

When Alexander had gone to scout ahead.

"I told you I'm not a seer," Alexander said, growing short of patience.

"Where there is a shield, then there must be sight," Naavi insisted. "And with a shield as strong as yours, then a very great sight."

"If he had sight that powerful, he would know," Norah said.

"Unless he's not telling the truth," Sana replied.

"I speak only the truth," Alexander said agitatedly. He turned to Norah. "I swear to you."

Naavi looked perplexed. "Then how does he have a shield? And how can the traveler see him when we cannot? None of this should be possible."

Soren snorted. "How long will you keep saying things are not possible when they are obviously so?"

Sana shot him a warning look. "You were not to remind us of your presence," she snapped.

"What must you do to try to help her?" Mikael asked Alexander directly.

"I don't have power," Alexander stressed.

"You will try!" Mikael snapped.

Alexander sighed in resignation and looked at the sisters. "Tell me what to do, and I'll do it."

But Sana shook her head. "You're talking about a power that we don't know. We only guess at this point."

"You said the memories came when you touched him?" Naavi asked Norah.

Norah nodded uncomfortably. "When I kissed him." Mikael's face darkened.

Naavi waved Alexander to the pool. "Come."

Slowly, he pulled off his boots and stepped into the water.

"Think of a memory that is important to you," Naavi told him. "One that you share with her, one that is strong within your being."

Alexander took Norah's hands and closed his eyes. His hands were warm around hers. Norah watched him as he drew in a deep breath and exhaled slowly. She wondered which memory he'd choose. Would she see it as hers? Or from his perspective? She closed her eyes too. And waited.

But nothing came.

Norah opened her eyes again. She glanced at Naavi, then back to Alexander, who still stood immersed in his mind.

"You must push against your shield, beyond it," Naavi told him. "Dig into your being. If you love her, use it."

Alexander broke from his memory, straightening. Norah bit her lip. He would never admit such a thing so openly.

Yet he didn't deny it. He glanced at Naavi, then back to Norah. He stepped closer.

Norah's heart raced in her chest.

He brought his hands to her face and brushed her cheeks with his thumbs. Then he pulled her even closer as he lowered his head to hers.

Her breaths came quicker now.

"If this doesn't work," he whispered, "forgive me."

Alexander and Norah stood in the pool of the Wild. A memory that was important to him, the Wild woman had told him. There was such a memory. There were many—ones he thought about often. But one in particular filled his mind. It wasn't a great event, or one that many would think was significant, but those weren't the memories that fueled his love. The memories most important to him were the smaller things—Norah's smile, the way her eyes gave away every emotion, the way she laughed.

Slowly, he brought his lips to hers and kissed her, deeply. He willed her mind to come back to her. And he focused.

Alexander walked through the kitchen of the castle, searching for something sweet to eat. He grinned as he spied a fig and pulled his knife from his belt, grabbing it and cutting it in half. Just then, Norah sprang through the door, laughing in surprise at seeing him.

"What are you doing?" he asked her with a grin as he slipped his knife back in its sheath.

"Hiding from Grandmother!" she smiled breathlessly. "Don't tell her you saw me."

He chuckled and shook his head. "I'll not lie to your grandmother."

"Alec!" she pleaded.

"She'll know."

They heard voices in the hall, and Norah looked at him wide-eyed, but he shook his head again.

"You're intolerable!" she exclaimed as she grabbed his arm and pulled him along with her. "You're coming with me, then." She ran down the back hall and into a small supply room, pulling him in and closing the door behind them. They stood together closely in the cramped space, facing each other.

"Why are you hiding?" he asked her.

"Quiet," she hushed him, and covered his mouth with her hand. "Seriously, Alec, you've no concept of whispering whatsoever."

He grinned under her palm. But they both froze as the voices echoed through the hall and drew nearer to the door.

"Where has that girl gone?" he heard Catherine say. "Victoria, check the stables."

Alexander's heart beat faster, and he knew Norah felt it. She drew her hand down to his chest and looked up at him with smiling eyes. Her nearness intoxicated him, and she seemed to like it. He still had half the fig in his right hand, and he brought it up toward her mouth.

"Fig?" he breathed.

She smiled and cupped his hand with hers, bringing it to her mouth and taking a bite. He let his fingertips graze her cheek, and his thumb line her lips. He dipped his head and brought his mouth to hers, drinking in the sweet taste of fig and the honey of her being. She pulled him closer and kissed him back.

She gently broke their kiss, looking into his eyes. "Do you love me, Alec?" she whispered.

"I've always loved you," he told her. "Surely you know this." Then he bent his head to kiss her again.

When he pulled away, they were standing in the pool again.

"Did you see?" Alexander asked her, still holding her face in his hands.

Norah stood with her eyes closed, her mind swirling. A tear fell down her cheek, but not from the memory.

From failure.

She had felt nothing. Seen nothing. Remembered nothing. They'd come all this way, braving the dangers of the Wild. And for nothing. She'd lost them, her memories. They were gone.

She shook her head, opening her eyes.

"I'm sorry," he said softly.

A trickle of blood ran from his nose, and she quickly forgot her sorrow. "Alexander," she said, alarmed.

He moved to step back, but his legs gave out and he sank to his knees, nearly falling forward. His eyes closed as his consciousness faded.

"Alexander!" she cried, and grabbed him, keeping his head above the water. "Help me!"

Naavi and Sana grasped his arms and pulled him to the edge of the pool. Caspian grabbed him, dragged him out, and rolled him onto his back.

Fear surged through her. "What's happening?" she cried.

Naavi pursed her lips together. "His shield is very strong. When he works against it, it's too much for his body."

"Why didn't you say something?"

"We told you we don't know what his power is!" Sana snapped. "We don't understand it. We don't know why he has a shield but not the sight. We don't know how some of your memories came back, or how to bring back the rest. We certainly don't know the consequences if we try!"

"Sana," Naavi whispered, trying to calm her sister.

"Do you know if he'll be all right?" Norah asked through her tears.

A heaviness hung in the air. "He should regain his strength with rest," Naavi told her. Norah knelt beside him, brushing the wet locks from his face.

"Try to look inside him now," Sana told her sister, "while his strength is gone."

"I don't know if I like that," Norah said.

"We've kept our part," Sana said. "He promised us."

She was right. Alexander had promised. And maybe they could learn more about this strange power Alexander had. Reluctantly, Norah nodded.

Naavi knelt over Alexander, putting her hands on his chest, and she closed her eyes. Shifting her shoulders, she bowed her head. A frown formed on her lips. She paused, opening her eyes briefly and looking at her sister, and then ran her hands to Alexander's head before trying again.

Finally, she stopped, shaking her head. "It's too strong, sister. It protects him even now. I can see nothing. Not his memories, not his dreams. I can't even feel his mind. I don't know what he is. But if I can't see him, others can't either."

"Well, you're wrong," Soren cut in. "We saw the visions of him with our own eyes."

"There is no power escaping this shield. Whatever creates those visions, it's not here."

"Or it is, and you can't see that either," he said gruffly.

Sana's eyes burned. "I'll see you cut out your own tongue."

"Please," Norah begged for civility. She fought to hold back her tears of disappointment, the upset. She would never get her memories back, but if she focused on that right now, she'd fall apart. She turned her mind back to Alexander. "We'll stay until he wakes, and then we'll be on our way."

There was a darkness to Sana's eyes, but she said nothing.

"Bring him this way," Naavi told them, turning down a long corridor.

Caspian looped one of Alexander's arms over his shoulders, but Alexander was a larger man, and Caspian struggled to rise.

Norah looked pleadingly at Soren, and he clenched his jaw as he grudgingly pushed Caspian aside, picked up Alexander over his shoulder, and carried him after the woman.

Naavi led them to a chamber with a small bed and soft woven blankets. Soren dropped Alexander onto it less gently than Norah would have liked, and she glared at him.

Norah straightened his head on the pillows and brushed his hair from his face. With his eyes closed, he looked so peaceful.

"Rest now," she whispered to him as she clutched his hand.

Chapter Twenty-Six

Naavi offered Norah a cup of hot tea as she sat down in a side chair. "Sana's gone to the library to search the manuscripts, to see if there's anything that can be found."

Norah gave a nod as she took the tea. "All I keep thinking is that there was the tree in Mercia."

"There's no tree in this world with magic more powerful than the Wild, and the greatest of our powers is in the pool. If there was magic that could give you what you wanted, it would be the water."

"Then it has to be Alexander," Norah said.

"Or it's you," Soren interrupted.

Norah looked up with a start. "What?"

He shrugged. "Maybe it's not that you're bringing memories back to life. Maybe you just didn't let them die. Not all of them." He nodded to Alexander. "At least not of him. And then maybe you uncovered only the pieces still there."

"No," Naavi shook her head. "I broke the bond."

He grunted in annoyance. "Only a fool would believe they could."

The room fell silent. Mikael sank onto a bench by the wall, his face stoic. Even Caspian shifted uncomfortably in his place near the doors.

Her heart sank with the thought that maybe Soren was right. When she'd seen the traveler in Mercia, there was a door that wouldn't open to her. Then the kiss with Alexander brought back the memory of them at the tree. With Bhasim, the traveler in Odepeth, that same door had been opened, that memory inside, but nothing else. He'd told her there was nothing else, but she hadn't believed him. She believed him now.

"So that's it then," Norah said softly, breaking the quiet. "The rest of them are gone." She felt the tears on her face and wiped them away. Anger suddenly welled inside her, and the cup of tea shook in her hand. She looked up at Naavi. "What a cruel thing," she said. "Those memories were mine, and you took them!"

Naavi sighed. "It wasn't meant to be cruel. It was meant to save you."

Norah stood abruptly, dropping her cup to the floor. It shattered against the stone. "But you didn't save me, did you? I was still taken by the Shadow King, and as if that weren't enough, everything I loved was stripped from me. My home, my family—you took everything from me."

Sana stepped into the room and came quickly to the defense of her sister. "Your father saw the vision of the Shadow King taking you, your lifeless body carried away by a monster." She glared at Mikael with a bitterness in her eyes, then looked back at Norah. "He brought you here, begged Naavi to protect you. He knew what would happen, but he begged her anyway. And she did as he asked."

Naavi's eyes were filled with tears. "It was the hardest thing I've ever done," she said, recalling. "Your father didn't want this for you, but he was desperate." She looked at the unconscious justice. "To hide you from the Eye, I had to break the bond to the Aether. When you could no longer cry out for those you loved, I stopped. And you disappeared from the eyes of this world."

Those she loved...

Mikael stood. He didn't meet Norah's gaze as he stepped through the side door into an adjoining chamber.

Norah glanced at Soren, and he cut her a dark scowl. What did he want from her? She had nothing left to give.

"I'm sorry, Norah," Naavi said. "If there were more I could do for you, I would." Then she and Sana slipped out of the room, leaving Norah to her despair.

Norah put her head in her hands. Cruel, cruel fate. She let out a defeated breath. She had lost everything. Then she stopped.

Not everything.

She stepped through the side doorway, into what she had thought was an adjoining chamber, but it was a large outdoor hall with a small fountain in the center. Mikael stood beside it, gazing into its waters.

"Mikael," she said softly.

He stirred slightly, hearing her, but he didn't answer.

She came to his side, letting herself take in the calming sound of the fountain. "I said things I didn't mean," she said.

"You did mean them, but they're things I already knew to be true."

"I'm sorry," she whispered. "I know this is hard. But, Mikael, I love you."

He shook his head. "You wouldn't if you could remember." He looked blankly at the fountain. "So strong it was, your love for him, that even the Wild couldn't take it all from you. It's but a shell now, a fragment of what it once was, yet... I still not dare ask you to choose."

She brought her hand to his face. "Mikael," she breathed. "I—"

But he clasped her hand gently and pulled it down. "Please, Salara. Leave me for a while. Just a while."

She didn't want to leave him. She wanted to take back what she said. But it was too late for that. He thought she didn't love him, at least not as she loved Alexander, but he was wrong. She would make him see that. But for now, she squeezed his hand before leaving him to the quiet.

Norah returned to the room with Alexander and sat in the chair beside the bed, at a loss for what to do or what to say.

Soren watched her with his same menacing scowl.

"I know you're angry with me," she told him.

"We should never have come here."

"Do you really believe that?" she asked.

"So, you had one question answered. At what cost?" he said bitterly. "Salar almost died today. Your Bear lies unconscious. All so you can live in the past. What about your future? What about all of our futures? Is that not enough?" He turned and left, walking back toward the great cathedral, where they first entered.

Her gaze found Caspian's. His eyes weren't unkind.

"Was I selfish to come here?" she asked.

He shook his head. "No. I don't think so. It seemed... very possible before... that you could get your answers here. All of us wanted that for you. And we all knew the Wild was a dangerous place."

She nodded, but inside she felt herself about to fall apart, and she swallowed it back. Soren was right. They should have never come. She'd known the Wild was dangerous. Why had she let them?

She moved to sit beside Alexander on the bed. Caspian gave a small bow and excused himself from the room. Alone with Alexander now, she brushed her fingers through his golden locks just above his brow. What had he tried to show her in the pool? Perhaps it was best he couldn't. A tear fell down her cheek.

"These Northmen aren't easy on the heart, are they?" a voice called behind her, and she turned to see Naavi. The Wild woman had seen everything, knew everything, Norah remembered.

"You loved my father," Norah said.

Naavi nodded. "Very much."

"It's why you helped me before."

The woman took a deep breath in and let it out slowly. "It's why I've done everything that I have."

"How did you come to love him?"

Naavi sat down in the chair nearby, pausing a moment in silence. "It was perhaps a year or two after your mother died. Your father would ride out for days at a time, wandering, thinking, wanting to be alone. That's when he found himself lost in our wood. So many trespassing souls we've taken, death for all who enter. But something was different about him. A... sadness."

Naavi closed her eyes, seeming to remember. She continued, "I don't know what made me do it, but I allowed him to see me. He stopped, got off his horse, and came to me, as if he knew my power, as if begging for the mercy of an end to his pain. I asked him about this sadness inside him, but he couldn't talk about it. It was too great. So, I looked through his mind, and I saw your mother. I saw you. I asked him if he wanted me to take her away, take away the memories. But he didn't. He said, 'How will I tell my daughter of her beautiful mother if I can't remember her?'"

Norah's eyes welled.

"We sat for a long time," Naavi continued. "He told me about you, how you had hair like the brightest rays of the sun, and how you smiled." She paused. "That's when I fell in love with him. That's when I fell in love with you."

Naavi let out an emotional breath. "I sent him away, home, but he was all I could think of—his eyes, his sad smile. When he returned several weeks later, I knew he thought of me too. He came many times over the years, our love growing stronger each visit." Her face fell. "But when he came in the night, with you, with war on the horizon—I can't see visions of the future, but I knew it was the last time I would see him." She reached out and clasped Norah's hand. "I'm so sorry. But I did what I thought was right."

"I don't fault you," Norah said softly. "And I'm sorry for my words. I understand that without your protection, I would've been visible to the seers. Had I been found by the senior Shadow King, as opposed to his son, this would have been a very different story."

Naavi nodded, and they rose. Norah followed her to the window, and they stood quietly in the soft glow of the setting sun.

"Was I here all this time?" Norah asked.

"Yes," Naavi told her. "I loved you like my daughter."

"Is that how I was able to ride the mare? Did she know me?"

Naavi smiled. "All the Wild knows you."

"And you gave the horse to my father, the one he rode in battle?"

Naavi nodded. "My own stallion, Lethos. But Lethos returned to me, alone, after the battle with the Shadow King." The woman looked away, unable to hold her emotion.

That's why Naavi so hated the Shadowlands. Norah waited until her own emotion passed, then she asked, "Did I know my story when I lived here?"

"I told you pieces, enough that you decided you had to return. We rode to the edge of the Wild, where we said goodbye. Kiku was to lead you back to Mercia."

Kiku? Norah smiled. The fox.

"But you didn't follow him, not at first." Naavi pursed her lips. "I should have known that would happen. You've never been one for signs. I hope fate has learned to be very direct with you."

They both let out a small laugh.

But then Naavi grew serious. "I did intervene, to save you from those men. You were so scared. I wanted to come to you, comfort you, but you no longer knew me." She seemed wounded by the memory. Then she straightened. "You followed Kiku after, though, and I let you go. But then he returned before nightfall, much too soon. He said a man had found you, taken you away. But we couldn't see this man. We couldn't see what had happened to you. I... I almost left the Wild to find you." She took a breath. "But the wind brought us whispers that the Mercian princess had returned. And I knew you were safe."

"Why did you take the memory of this place from me too? The memory of you?" Norah asked her.

"You made the decision to leave and return to Mercia. We must protect the Wild, and the secrets here. That is why Sana wouldn't let you keep the memories."

"You let my father keep his."

"She shouldn't have," Sana's voice called from behind her. Norah turned with a start. Sana's eyes locked with Naavi's. "Knowledge of the Wild cannot be trusted with men, with their greed and their need to destroy things." Her gaze shifted to Norah. "And we cannot let you keep what you have seen here."

Norah's heart dropped. Not that she had uncovered many answers, but she had more than she had before, and the thought of losing them again crushed her.

"Do you understand?" Sana asked.

As devastating as it was, she nodded. She did understand.

"And it's why the seer can't return with you."

Norah sucked in a breath. "What?"

Naavi sighed, her eyes pleading Norah to understand. "We can't let Alexander go, Norah."

"He's not a seer!"

"Regardless, he knows too much, and we're unable to take it from him."

Norah shook her head. "No. I'm not leaving without him."

Sana's voice came cold as death. "Then none of you will leave."

Chapter Twenty-Seven

Norah sat in the darkness in the room where Alexander lay, trying to quell the threatening panic. Her hands shook as she tried to think of what to do. She wouldn't leave Alexander. Mikael had returned, and he sat with her on a stone bench. Silence hung around them like a thick fog.

Alexander stirred, and Norah moved to his side. His eyes opened, and he stared at her for a moment. Then his brow creased. "Where am I?" he asked. "What happened?"

"We're still in the Wild," she told him. "You exerted yourself too much."

He lay still, his eyes hazed, but then she saw the memory flood back to him. Alexander tried to sit up, but he was still weak. He caught sight of the commander and Mikael, and then Caspian against the far wall, and he looked back at her. "What aren't you telling me? Are we being held here?"

"Not exactly," Soren spoke out. "We leave at dawn. Well, all except you. They're unable to erase your mind, protect their secret, so you stay."

Norah struggled to swallow through the tightness in her throat.

"Well, I suppose we were already down a horse," Alexander joked in rare form.

Soren let out a chuckle, but Norah wasn't amused.

"I'm not leaving without you," she said adamantly.

"You're not staying here," he told her.

"You can't make me go."

"I trust the Destroyer to do what needs to be done to get you away from this place," he said as he settled back and let his eyes close again.

Norah glanced at Soren with a flash of anger, daring him to respond. He refrained, but his look told her he would.

Just then, the chamber door opened, and Norah spun around.

Naavi stepped inside. "Hurry," she said in a hushed voice. "We don't have much time."

"What?" Norah asked, her eyes wide. "Where are we going?"

"Hurry! You're leaving. All of you." She eyed Alexander. "Even him. But you must come quickly."

"Help me!" Norah called to Soren as she tried to pull Alexander to stand. Soren's chest rumbled in objection, but he handed his axe to Caspian and stepped forward. He put a shoulder under Alexander's arm and supported his weight with his own frame.

Naavi led them through the doors and into a narrow hallway. "Stay close," the Wild woman said, setting a fast pace. "His shield covers us, but he's still weak. We have to stay together."

Naavi clasped Norah's hand and pulled her along faster. They wound through a series of halls before reaching a door and emerging into the forest. The cold wind hit Norah's face, and she shuddered.

"We couldn't have entered from this way?" Soren muttered.

"Quickly," Naavi said as she pulled Norah through the trees. Mikael and Caspian followed, with Soren behind them, supporting Alexander.

"We're almost to the tree line," Naavi told them. "Hurry!"

The flight out of the Wild seemed shorter than their journey in. Norah's mind reeled. The magic of this place confused her. They reached the edge of the trees where their horses were waiting for them. All but Sephir.

Soren pushed Alexander onto his destrier, but the justice wavered. He wouldn't be able to stay atop a horse by himself.

"Norah," Naavi said, pulling her to a pause. "I give you your Northman, but"—she looked at the commander and Mikael—"I can't let the Shadowmen go knowing all they've seen. They can't remember the pool, and how to find us. I have to take their memories."

"Take them," Mikael said, surprising Norah. "Take everything of this place." He looked at Norah with a pain that shook her. "And you'll be very cautious of what you tell me."

Norah's eyes welled.

"He must go," Naavi said of Alexander. "I need him to leave so I can use my power."

Norah looked to Caspian. "Take him. We'll catch up to you."

Caspian started to object, but Norah stopped him. "Go," she pressed.

He reluctantly mounted behind Alexander and urged the horse into the darkness.

Naavi looked at Mikael. "Step between the trees."

They could flee, Norah knew. The Wild woman held no power over them beyond the forest. But Mikael stepped between the trees, and Soren begrudgingly followed.

Naavi approached the commander first. "I'll leave you with one memory—just how close your king was to his end. And if you return, there will be no mercy." He grunted as an invisible force took hold of him. She reached up and brought her fingers to his temples, closing her eyes. His body twisted, and he let out a growl as she worked into his mind. She dug deeper, and his growl grew to a roar. Every fiber of his body strained against her, but she held him still.

"What's happening?" Norah asked, her worry rising. "Stop! You're hurting him!"

"It's because he fights," Naavi told her. "It makes it painful."

A cry ripped from his throat as she took the last of the memories from him. Finally, his body grew limp, and his head fell forward.

Norah's breath faltered. She knew she would have fought for her memories. This was her past as well. The commander dropped to his knees, upright, his eyes closed.

"Careful when waking him," Naavi warned her. "There's still a fight inside."

Norah trembled as the Wild woman stepped in front of Mikael. She didn't think she could watch.

But Naavi paused. "I see you, Shadow King. And you're not what I thought you were." She reached out and spread her hand over his bloodied shoulder from where the arrow had struck him. He winced, but then stilled. When she pulled her hand away, the hole in his flesh was fused with thin forest threads.

He looked at her in surprise as he tested his arm.

She nodded. "It will be sore for a few days. This is the only grace I give you, enemy of Aamon. You're not to enter this forest again. And same as your Destroyer, you'll remember the consequences." Then she reached up and put her hands on either side of his face to take his memories.

"Please," Norah begged. "Please don't hurt him."

Naavi closed her eyes, but all was quiet. Mikael made no sound.

"Is it not working?" Norah asked.

"It's working," Naavi said softly, her eyes still closed, "he just doesn't resist."

Finally, Naavi stepped back from Mikael and lowered him to his knees. "Remember," she said, "take care in waking them." She paused. "I'm sorry, Norah," she said, with tears in her eyes. "I'm sorry for everything."

Norah shook her head and caught her in a warm embrace. "I'm alive because of you. Thank you for keeping me safe. Thank you for saving me from the drifters. And for tonight. But most of all, thank you for bringing my father happiness again."

Naavi hugged her tightly. "You'll always be in my heart, and any creature of the Wild will serve you as my daughter. I love you, Norah."

Norah wiped the tears from her cheeks as Naavi disappeared into the darkness of the wood. She turned back to Mikael, and kneeling in front of him, she pulled his face to hers and kissed his eyelids softly. They fluttered underneath her lips, and she trailed her kisses to his cheeks.

"Wake, husband," she whispered.

His hands came up to her arms, and he pushed her back slightly as he opened his eyes to look at her. Confusion flashed across his face in the moonlight, but his emotional pain was gone. Suddenly, he reached up and felt his shoulder. "What happened?" he asked, looking around.

"I thought I lost you," she whispered.

"I'm here," he said softly.

She smiled and kissed him again. But then the urgency returned. She wanted to get away before Sana found them missing. "We have to go. We have to leave now. Will you help me wake him?" she asked, looking at Soren.

His eyes found Soren, who was kneeling and slumped in an unnatural sleep. Mikael stood, shaky at first, but found his footing. He looked at her for a moment, then back to the commander, still trying to make sense of what had happened. She knew he still had the memory of being shot, but now wasn't the time to catch him up on the rest.

"We have to hurry," Norah pressed.

Mikael walked to the commander and put a hand on his shoulder. "Soren," he called.

The lord commander twitched, but he didn't wake.

Norah felt a deep unease in her stomach. "Careful," she warned.

"Soren," Mikael called again, leaning closer.

Suddenly, Soren's hand flew up, grabbing Mikael and pulling him to the ground. He clutched Mikael by the base of his throat, a fury pouring out of him.

"No, stop!" Norah cried.

Her voice made him pause, and he glanced around in confusion.

"Brother," Mikael grunted, and Soren released him, stumbling back from his attack as he recognized his victim. He gripped his head, and Norah suspected some lingering effects. "What happened?" he growled.

"Now's not the time," she said quickly. "We have to go."

"Where's the Bear?" Soren demanded. "And my axe? And my sword?"

"And my armor," Mikael added.

"The justice has ridden ahead. We'll meet up with him soon," she explained. She looked at Soren. "Your axe is by your horse. Forget about everything else. We have to go." Norah reached out and took Mikael's hand. "Please," she said softly. "Trust me." She could see his uncertainty.

Mikael let out a troubled breath, yielding. Then he mounted his horse as Norah climbed onto Caspian's, and they rode into the night.

They journeyed south with a thick silence between them. Mikael glanced at her as they rode, no doubt with questions heavy on his tongue. But he asked none, and she didn't know where to start, or what to even begin to share.

They caught up with Caspian and Alexander, who had set a small camp. Alexander lay against a rock by the fire, still weak. Caspian cooked a small rabbit over the flame.

"Put out that fire," Soren said angrily. "You tell the world we're here."

"We need warmth, and food," Norah argued.

"Leave it," Mikael told the commander.

Soren grumbled under his breath. "What happened to him?" he said as he looked at Alexander.

Mikael slid off his horse and caught Norah by the hand. He pulled her close and spoke for only her to hear. "Why did you think you lost me?" he asked her. Then he glanced at Soren. "I was shot?"

She took a breath in and nodded.

"And I've been healed, yet I don't remember. Tell me what happened."

Where should she start? Naavi trusted her to keep the secrets of the Wild safe, and she would, but she wouldn't deny Mikael an explanation. A real one.

"Did you get them? Your memories?" he asked.

She shook her head. "No," she whispered. "They're gone. Forever."

His brows drew together. "But you weren't made to forget again?" Like he was.

"No," she said again.

He looked at Alexander. "Was he?"

She didn't want this to be about Alexander. "It's complicated. My father had a deep friendship with the Wild. It's where he took me to protect me during the war. It's where I was all those years, and it's why I don't remember. My memories were lost when I was hidden from the seers."

His eyes drifted back to Alexander. She kept silent about Alexander's power, whatever it may be. There was already enough mistrust for him.

"They blame Kharav for my father's death," she continued. "There's still a lot of animosity." She took his hand. "But they saw you differently than they had before and gave a small mercy and healed you."

He thumbed the mended injury to his shoulder.

"Although," she added, "if you return, they'll kill you. So I... wouldn't recommend that."

He smiled sadly as he cupped her cheek in his hand. "I'm sorry," he said softly.

"Thank you for bringing me. It was... a significant risk for all of you. And while I don't have what I came for, I do have *some* answers. And I'm incredibly grateful for that."

He kissed her. "It was worth it then." He turned and pulled a roll from his saddle and laid it near the fire. "Sleep," he told her. "We've a long journey back." Then he left to tend his horse.

Norah sat on the bedroll, but she didn't lie down. She couldn't sleep. Caspian offered her the rabbit, and she ate it slowly as she watched Mikael, who now stood off in the distance, almost blending into the darkness.

Soren came to the fire and dropped down on a large rock nearby. She still felt his scowl upon her. She'd tell him more when he wasn't so angry, which would be a while.

Mikael drifted back toward the fire, but as he moved to sit by Norah, they were interrupted by a sound in the night. They jumped to their feet, and Mikael and Caspian pulled their swords. Soren drew up his axe, and even Alexander staggered to his feet.

Norah looked around, but she couldn't see in the darkness. Her pulse quickened. They should have put out the fire. What else lurked about in the shadows, unseen? She was tired of the constant battle, the constant threat of danger. She wanted to be home. She wanted to feel safe.

A shadow stepped out of the darkness.

Norah let out a breath as she grinned.

Sephir.

The mare had returned. The horse tossed her head with a nicker, and Norah ran to her, throwing her arms around the animal's neck.

"I didn't think I'd see you again," she told her as she exhaled a sigh of relief. "And I also thought you might have been a monster."

Caspian chuckled, a little embarrassed as well. "That horse is not what I was expecting either."

Norah couldn't help but laugh herself. Even Soren gave an amused snort. For once, there was a good surprise.

CHAPTER TWENTY-EIGHT

The Uru welcomed them back in celebration, and Tahla's relief at their safety was palpable. Norah smiled, grateful for friends who cared so deeply.

Caspian followed Norah to the large central fire, where she sat on a large elongated rock. Tahla took a seat beside her.

"I'm so happy to have you back safely," Tahla said. "Tell me of it. Tell me of the Wild."

Of course she'd be curious about it—home of the spirits they had so much reverence for. But Norah had been trusted with its secrets, and she would keep them. Still, it was harmless to share some things. "It's a magical place," Norah told her, remembering its beauty. "But dangerous. And as you said—unwelcoming, even to Northmen. Once you step into the trees, you're at their mercy, and they have little of it."

Tahla leaned closer, captivated.

"The spirits within are powerful," Norah continued. "They embody not only the animals, but the earth, the trees, the wind."

"The wind?" Tahla breathed.

Norah nodded. "But it's not a place for men. And we shouldn't have gone there. We were lucky to leave, all of us."

Norah could see more questions on Tahla's lips, but the chief's daughter seemed to sense her hesitation, and she didn't ask them. She was a good friend. She only asked, "Did you find what you were seeking?"

Norah shook her head sadly.

Tahla reached out and clasped Norah's hand, squeezing it warmly. "Well, I'm grateful you've returned safely."

Norah smiled as she looked around the village. She noted there were quite a few Horsemen, and they looked different from the Uru.

"Who are these men?" she asked Tahla.

"They're Kartan, a neighboring tribe. They're friends."

An Urun woman came and held a bowl of broth out to Norah, and she took it appreciatively. It was delicious, and she tried not to gulp it down too quickly. Caspian accepted a bowl as well, taking a seat nearby.

Chief Coca Otay came and took a seat on a thick log beside Tahla. He said a few words to her that Norah didn't understand, and Tahla responded back—an argument of some sort.

"What's the matter?" Norah asked Tahla quietly as she warmed her hands against the large fire.

Tahla shook her head. "My father's been attempting to convince me I should wed again."

Norah raised a brow and looked at the chief.

"You must look to the future," the chief said. "This would be a good match. Boshtok would make a fine husband for a chieftess."

Tahla mouthed his name at Norah with an annoyed look, clearly disliking it, then she turned back to her father with a smile. "That he would. For some other chieftess."

"Who is this Boshtok?" Norah asked her.

Tahla nodded her head at a man a short distance away who was standing with a group of other Horsemen. "Son of Totekah, chief of the Kartan."

The man she had pointed out was tall. He was lean and muscular, with long, black hair braided back. Norah shrugged. "He's handsome, at least."

Tahla smiled. "That he is."

"And taken with you," the chief prompted further.

Caspian shifted uncomfortably, and Norah smiled. Marriage made some men so uneasy. But she supposed she couldn't blame them, thinking back to how she originally felt about her own.

"Let me prepare you, Father," Tahla said. "There will be no more wedding ceremonies for me."

The old man snorted and poked at the fire. "Foolish woman. An alliance with another tribe will bring strength."

Tahla wrinkled her nose. "I'm strong enough."

"What of an heir?" Coca Otay asked.

She shrugged. "If I want an heir, then I'll have a child."

"Without a husband?" Norah asked in surprise.

Tahla's eyebrows drew together. "Besides the means to make a child, what will a man bring that I don't already have?"

Norah dipped her head to one side, then the other. She couldn't argue with that. Caspian shifted again, to her amusement. Her Northmen would have to accept the more liberal ideals of other peoples, eventually. There were much worse things than a child out of wedlock.

Coca Otay pointed at the lord commander as he approached. "At least be wise enough to choose a powerful father for a child. Soren perhaps."

The commander stopped midstep, realizing he'd entered a conversation he had no interest taking part in. He backed away and slipped into the night. Norah couldn't help the laugh that escaped her.

Caspian rose abruptly, and Norah looked up at him. "I think I'll go check everything before you turn in for the evening," he said, giving her a small bow of his head.

"Of course. Thank you, Caspian." She watched him curiously as he disappeared into the darkness.

But her attention was pulled back to Tahla, who stood and took her father's hand. "I know that you mean well, Father, but these decisions are ones I must make for myself." Norah felt her words all too deeply.

Tahla leaned down and kissed him on the cheek. "Sleep well." She turned to Norah. "Goodnight, Salara."

"See you in the morning," she replied.

Coca Otay gave Norah a respectful nod goodnight and followed after his daughter.

Alexander took Tahla's place on the rock next to her. She was hoping she'd get the chance to talk to him.

"How do you feel?" she asked.

He nodded. "Better. Almost normal."

"But you're not normal, are you?" She watched him for a moment. "Are we going to talk about what happened in the Wild?"

He shook his head. "Norah, there's nothing to talk about. I don't have the gift of sight."

"Why couldn't Naavi control your mind?" she asked. "Why couldn't she see you?"

"I don't know. But I can be seen. You've seen the paintings. The seers *have* seen me." Norah's stomach knotted as the vision of Mikael's end came to her mind.

Yes, they had.

Caspian sat at a small table in the one-room home he'd been given. He cursed himself. He couldn't think of Tahla as his. She'd been very clear with him, and he'd agreed. At least in his mind.

He cursed again. Of course there would be expectations of her. She was the daughter of the chief. What had he hoped for? That she would marry *him*? He was a simple captain of the Kharavian Crest and Mercian Royal Guard. He had no true wealth, nothing to offer her. In fact, their marriage would dishonor her. He hung his head; he had already dishonored her.

There was a knock on the door, and Tahla stepped inside. Caspian rose to his feet. He hadn't expected she would come to him. She hadn't so much as cast him a gaze since they had returned, and after the conversation around the fire...

They stood, their gazes locked on one another. Then she moved to him. Still, he waited. The silence between them ate at his strength.

Tahla reached up and clasped the side of his neck at the base of his jaw. Not hard, but not gently. "I worried for you, Northman." She pushed herself up on her toes as she pulled him to her. "More than I should have." And she kissed him.

It was a move he hadn't anticipated, like many things with Tahla.

Caspian's body responded, as only she could make it, and he caved to his need. He pushed her back against the wall with their mouths together, and cupped the bare skin of her buttocks underneath her leather sarong. Tahla pulled at the ties of his breeches and freed him, and he lifted her as she wrapped her legs around him. They both shuddered as he sank inside her.

They paused for a moment, and then she shifted to take him deeper. The warmth of her body called to him, and he pulsed with a growing fire, giving in to his want. He moved more fervently.

Suddenly, her thighs tightened around him, almost crushing him. He let out a painful growl as he stopped and strained against her hold.

Tahla smiled and drew her lip between her teeth. "Slow, Northman."

He stilled as he waited for his panting breaths to calm. She was right. He was losing himself.

Caspian carried her to the bed and laid her down on it, without breaking their bond. They peeled off their clothes, somewhat awkwardly, and she laughed as he twisted to shake off his breeches. Then they lay still, looking at one another. Gods, he loved this woman.

He pushed himself deeper, joining their bodies and their souls. He buried himself in the essence of her, but it wasn't enough. "I need you, Tahla," he breathed. "I need you to be mine like I am yours."

A line wrinkled over her brow, and her eyes dipped in sadness. He immediately regretted his words.

"Caspian," she started, "I—"

"Don't answer," he whispered as he cupped her face in his hand. He shook his head. "Don't answer." Then he covered her mouth with his to keep silent the words he most feared—that he would have to let her go.

Chapter Twenty-Nine

It had been several weeks since Alec and Norah had returned from the Wild, and Adrian's mind still spun, wondering what had happened. Norah had shared only that she couldn't get her memories back, that they were gone for good, but no one would actually speak of what had transpired. Not Norah, not Caspian, and certainly not Alec.

He made his way along a cobbled road veining out from the castle. Perhaps he'd ask the lord commander. But that would make Alec furious, as would knowing Adrian had been outside the castle and exploring the city. Anger rose in his cheeks, and he snatched up a rock and flung it behind him, high into the air, toward the wall of the castle. Everyone treated him like a boy still, but he wasn't a boy. He was twenty now, and better than most men with a sword. He picked up another rock and flung it even farther.

Voices caught his attention, and he focused his gaze ahead of him, where a young woman walked with three men around her. She was perhaps his age, her dark hair pulled back and up, although he couldn't see her face from behind. One of the men put his arm around her shoulders, but she shoved it off. She spoke firmly in the Shadow tongue, her words sharp with objection. Laughter rang out from the men, but she wasn't laughing.

Adrian watched closely as he trailed behind, quickening his pace. Another man snaked his hand around her hips and pulled her to him. She tried to twist away, but he held a firm grip, taunting her. Adrian couldn't understand the words, but he knew the message. The man sneered something into her ear, and she twisted back, giving him a sharp slap to his cheek. She had spirit.

The man grabbed her wrist and pulled her closer, and she cried out.

"Leave her alone!" Adrian shouted.

The men paused their noxious play and turned in surprise. On seeing Adrian, one gave a low chuckle. "This doesn't concern you, Northman."

"Yet here I am, concerned," Adrian cut back as he caught up to them. He looked at the young woman. "Are you all right?"

She gave a small nod, but the fear in her umber eyes told him otherwise.

"You see?" the man nearest to him said. "She's perfectly all right with things. Be on your way."

Adrian gave a challenging smile. "But *you* see, *I'm* not perfectly all right with things." He looked at the young woman. "Can I accompany you to where you're headed?"

"How noble of you," the man that held her retorted. "But she's not going anywhere."

Adrian dropped the forced smile. "Release her."

The man pulled the girl closer to him. "If you want her, come get her."

Adrian cursed himself for not having his sword, but he was never one to refuse a fight, and this would certainly be a fight.

As if on cue, the man nearest to him charged with a balled fist for his stomach. Adrian curled forward with his elbows down and together, blocking the attack. He spun and delivered a sharp blow to the man's back as he passed, knocking him to the ground. The second man leapt forward, arcing his fist in the air and bringing it down. Adrian knocked it aside, countering with his own. The first man was back on his feet, and he delivered a steel punch to his ribs. Adrian doubled in pain as he stumbled to the side. The man advanced with a second attack, but Adrian blocked, saving himself from another hit to the side. He threw his elbow up, catching the man under the chin and sending him backward.

The second man grabbed him from behind, pulling him into a choke hold. His first attacker jumped forward, delivering a blow to the stomach that knocked the wind from him, followed by a hit to the side of his face. Adrian coughed and gasped for his breath as blood ran down his cheek. Another blow to his stomach made him drop to his knees.

Adrian fell forward, struggling to draw his breath. The man who held the girl pushed her to the side and drew a dagger from his belt. He grabbed a fistful of Adrian's hair and pulled his head back.

"Would you rather lose your tongue or an eye, hero?" he asked with a grin.

"Fuck you, coward!" Adrian spat.

The man's grin fell, and his breath quivered in anger. He brought the tip of the dagger to Adrian's eye. "I'll take them both, then."

But the tip of a sword touched the man's neck, stopping him.

"Release him," a familiar voice ordered.

The man let him go, and Adrian sank forward, coughing. When he looked up, he was surprised to see the lord commander.

The three men stood obediently at attention and bowed.

Adrian gritted his teeth through the pain as he rose and bowed as well. "My lord," he said, grimacing.

The lord commander looked at the young woman. "See her home," he said to Adrian.

Adrian felt a wave of appreciation—whether for being saved from losing an eye or for the opportunity to walk the woman home, he wasn't sure. "Yes, my lord."

The woman gave a small bow of her head. "Thank you, Lord Commander." She stepped forward, waiting for Adrian to reach her side, then started down the cobbled street.

Adrian looked back over his shoulder as they walked away, but the lord commander stood watching him, presumably waiting until they left to deal with the others. He wondered what the commander might do.

They reached a corner street, and the woman turned and started across the burial grounds.

"This is the way to your home?" he asked.

"It's shorter than going through the city. And generally safer."

He eyed the burial grounds. "You call this safe?"

She shrugged. "Dead people are safer than live ones."

Very true. But he paused at the ground's edge. He'd heard about how the Shadowmen buried their dead, chaining their spirits to this world. The grounds lay covered in marked stones—hundreds of bodies were buried here. Hundreds of souls. What would they think about being walked on? Did they haunt those who disturbed them?

Her brows drew together. "Are you scared?"

He snorted. "Of course I'm not." Still, he lingered.

Her eyes narrowed. "You'll provoke three men and almost get yourself killed, but you won't walk across burial grounds?"

"To be fair, I did see that going differently back there."

She frowned a smile. "How so?"

He didn't want to brag, but... "I'm actually pretty good, I just, uh... I didn't have my sword."

"Oh, I see." She nodded slowly. "Right."

"No, really, I am."

Her smile widened. "Okay."

He couldn't help but laugh. Blood trickled from his eye and down his cheek, and he wiped it away.

"Let me see," she said, and stepped to him.

He dropped his head lower as she examined him with a grimace.

"You've got a pretty nasty gash there." She pulled a handkerchief from her pocket and pressed it against his brow. He winced.

"Sorry," she said, her voice soft.

"What's your name?" he asked as they awkwardly stood and waited for the pressure to stop the bleeding.

"Sevina."

"Sevina," he repeated as he looked at her.

She had large, expressive eyes, but they weren't dark like the eyes of the Shadowmen. They shined of burnt umber, like Mercian summer fields, and light danced in them like each was its own world, with its own sun. She had dark, short-cut locks that fell over her forehead, and longer hair swept back and up, with a few strands loose on the sides. The round of her face curved down to the small point of her chin, and her full lips parted slightly as she held the handkerchief to his head.

"Yours?" she asked.

His brow creased in confusion. "Mine?"

She gave a small laugh. "Your name?"

"Oh, right. I, uh... Adrian," he stumbled over his words. "My name is Adrian."

She bit the bottom of her smile and folded the handkerchief over itself. "You should keep holding this, I think. The cut is deep."

"Right," he said, taking hold of the cloth against his brow.

She started across the burial grounds, and this time, he followed.

"You're from Mercia?" she asked as they walked.

He gave her a smile. "What gave it away?"

"Are you in the army?"

"Not exactly."

"Do you serve the queen?"

"Yes. Well, kind of. I mean, I'm not on the guard yet. I will be, though."

She glanced at him, questioning. "Why are you here in Kharav, then?"

"My brother's here. And I wanted to come see the notorious Shadowlands. Kharav, I mean," he corrected himself. "And meet the lord commander."

"Why?"

Adrian looked at her in surprise. "Because he's a great warrior. And your kingdom is famed."

"As is the North. And you have the Bear. He's supposed to be a great warrior too."

Adrian grinned. He hadn't liked that they called Alec *the Bear* initially, but he'd come to like it. It was a name said with awe, and sometimes a little fear. "He is," he said proudly. "The greatest."

They reached the end of the burial grounds and came to a cobbled road, then took it until it joined another. Rows of houses stood tall against the late-afternoon sky. The homes were quite grand, grander than what was typically found in Mercia, even for nobles.

Sevina stopped in front of a large house with iron gates at the walk. "I'm glad you're here, Adrian," she said. Then she stepped up on her toes and gave him a kiss on the cheek. "Thank you for walking me home."

He grinned. "You're welcome."

She unlocked the gate and stepped inside, then closed it behind her.

"Sevina," he said, making her pause. "Can I see you again?"

She looked back at the house hesitantly, then smiled. "I plan to go to my cousin's tomorrow at midday, if you'd like to walk me."

He'd walk across a hundred burial grounds to do that. "I'll be here."

"All right," she said in a half whisper.

Adrian watched her as she walked to the house and slipped inside. Then he made his way back toward the castle, smiling to himself. He'd seen many women since coming to Kharav, and none were as he had expected. The army had female warriors, powerful women. Sevina was different. Not that he would have minded if she were a warrior—she would have been able to fend for herself, certainly, which Adrian would have liked. But Sevina was delicate and soft, and he liked that too.

When he reached the gates of the castle, the lord commander was waiting. "Lord Commander," he said in surprise.

"Is she home?"

"Yes, my lord."

The commander reached out and clasped his chin, turning Adrian's head and judging the cut above his eye. "That'll need stitches. Come on."

It was worth it.

They walked across the courtyard, but Adrian slowed in seeing Alec striding toward them. His stomach knotted. He'd promised his brother he'd keep out of trouble, which was the opposite of what he'd been doing.

"What is this? What happened?" Alec asked when he reached them.

"It's nothing," Adrian said quickly.

Alec was calm, but his eyes blazed. He was angry. "Did you do this?" he asked the lord commander.

"No!" Adrian said quickly. "There were these men—"

"You got in a fight?"

"He'll need stitches," the lord commander said.

Alec's voice came low, composed—the voice that Adrian hated the most: the voice of disappointment. "You dishonor me, Adrian; you dishonor your queen."

The lord commander snorted. "Seems to me that honor is what he was brawling about."

"You know nothing of honor," Alec cut back.

The commander's eyes darkened.

"What's going on?" Norah interrupted from behind, and all three turned in surprise. "Adrian! Your face!" she exclaimed.

"It looks worse than it is," he assured her.

"How did this happen?"

"Foolishness not to be repeated," Alec promised.

"It was for a woman's fancy, so it probably will be repeated," the commander said with an amused smirk on his brow.

Adrian felt his brother's eyes on him, but he couldn't meet them.

"Are you all right?" Norah asked him.

"Yes, thanks to the lord commander."

The commander moved to leave, but not before pausing in front of Norah. "That's three favors now," he said to her. "Is this another I can call upon?"

Adrian wondered what he meant.

She sighed. "I almost had a positive sentiment about you. Must you ruin everything?"

He shrugged and left them to Alec's disappointment.

Chapter Thirty

Norah lay awake in the blissful light of morning, staring out the window. Mikael was sprawled sideways across the bed, his head on her hip. It was a rare moment, relaxing together in the calm, not rushing to duties or responsibility.

Things had settled since they had returned from the Wild. Even the contempt between Mikael, Soren, and Alexander had seemed to die down somewhat. *Somewhat.* But she couldn't shake her guilt. She'd asked a lot from Mikael, and he gave her everything. What had she given him?

"Why haven't you asked me to return the mountains of Bahoul?" she said, breaking the silence.

Mikael drew in a long breath, clearly not expecting this subject. He rolled to his side, looking up at her.

"You want it, yes?" she asked.

He swallowed. "Surely you know the answer."

She bit her bottom lip. "I'm sorry I haven't thought to discuss it with you until now. But... why haven't you asked me for it?"

He turned his head and looked out the window. "I should have negotiated it with our marriage agreement, but the truth is I wasn't even thinking of it at the time." He paused. "Soren pressed me to discuss it with you after. But, as the days passed, the harder it became." He grew silent for a time before continuing. "I feared the answer, that you wouldn't give it to me. Not that I'm so desperate to get it back now, but... are you unable to deny me... the way I'm unable to deny you? I... don't think I want to know."

Norah reached down and ran her fingers through his hair before resting her hand on his cheek. "It's yours, husband."

His eyes grew thick with emotion, and he put his hand over hers, bringing it to his lips and kissing her palm.

They lay naked together in the beautiful quiet.

"There's something else I've been reluctant to press you for," he said. He ran his hand over the skin of her stomach, swirling his fingertips so that prickles rose on her skin, and then he widened his palm against her flesh again. "A child."

Norah's pulse quickened. They certainly hadn't been trying *not* to have a child, but they never spoke of it, never made it an intentional effort. And she wasn't sure how she felt. She wanted children, eventually, but was she ready? She still didn't feel in control of her own life enough to now be responsible for another. But with a husband who loved her, and whom she loved in return, she started to feel a stirring for something more. A child between them sounded less and less of an obligation, and more of a beautiful life.

Norah put her hand over Mikael's on her stomach.

He shifted and moved up, rising over her and covering her with his body. "It's now the most important thing, Salara. I need an heir to settle the nobles. Unrest will build as time goes on. And"—he paused—"it's what will keep you safe when I'm gone."

His words rippled through her. When he was dead, he meant. She shook her head. "Don't talk like that."

"We need to talk about these things. The nobles won't follow the North Queen alone. But an heir will keep you on the Kharavian throne, even after I'm dead. An heir will keep the peace, keep the alliance. It will keep you safe, even if the North turns against you."

"Mikael, stop," she said, her eyes welling.

"Kharav needs an heir. We need an heir." He bent to kiss her lips. "And I want a son, a child, with you." His eyes brightened. "I would be a good father, Salara. I would love him."

Norah had never imagined Mikael as a father. She had never tried. She wasn't sure why. There was no doubt that Mikael would be a good father. The thought made her smile. It made her happy. Then why was she hesitant?

She wasn't.

She threaded her fingers back into his hair and nodded.

Mikael grew serious. "Do you mean it?" he breathed. "We'll have a child then?"

The thought filled her with an unexpected joy. She caressed his cheek with her hand. "Well, it's not exactly like we haven't been trying." She raised a teasing brow. "Do you not know how children are made, husband?"

He smiled. "I meant, isn't there planning—a specific time?"

"Mmm..." she moaned as she pulled him closer. "How about all the time?"

"That's an excellent plan," he rumbled as he covered her mouth with his. He moved between her thighs and slipped his arm underneath her, running his hand down and lifting her hips to him.

Norah gasped as he sank inside her. She didn't think it was possible to need someone the way she needed Mikael, with a deep and desperate hunger. He consumed her—her body, her mind, her spirit. And still, she needed more.

They moved together, as one. Mikael wove his fingers into hers and pushed her hands above her head. She let him take what he needed, because their needs were one and the same.

Norah wrapped her legs around him, pulling him deeper, begging him with her body. The rush was sudden and fierce, and it took her breath. She bucked against him as she lost herself.

Mikael's body hardened as he neared, and Norah settled to just watch him. She pulled her hands from his grasp and ran them down his chest, feeling the muscle tighten under his skin. He was beautiful, every piece of him. She drew her hands up to his face and pulled him down into a kiss, but he was too taken to kiss her back. She smiled as she caught his bottom lip between her teeth. A rumble built in his chest, and it grew to a thunder. Mikael came with a growl as he buried himself inside her. He dropped his head beside hers, and she could feel his panting breath on her cheek, in her ear. His whole body shook, and she savored it.

He nuzzled her neck as his body calmed. "When I'm inside you, nothing else matters," he breathed. "Nothing." He stayed a moment longer. Then he pulled himself from her and shifted his weight to the side, resting his head on her breast.

"I want you again," he said, with his eyes closed and his breaths still heavy with fatigue.

Norah gave a small laugh. "You don't have the energy." She looked at him as she brushed her fingers through his hair. She loved this man. How could anyone not? If they didn't, it was because they didn't know him.

"Let's go to Mercia," she whispered.

His eyes opened. "This is what you think of right now?"

She drew his face back up for his eyes to meet hers. "Let's go to Mercia, Mikael. You're not who they think you are. They need to know you. Once they do, they'll love you like I do. I know they will."

The quiet answered for him.

"Please?" she asked.

His face creased with sadness. "I can't."

Norah blinked back emotion. "Will I never see my home again?"

Mikael pushed himself up and lay over her again, bringing his hand to her face. "Go," he said softly.

Norah's eyes widened. "What?"

"Go. See your grandmother. See your people. Then come back to me."

She let out a shaky breath, not sure if she was understanding. He was trusting her to do this? "Go to Mercia?"

He nodded. "I only ask that you take the lord commander, and that you leave your justice there."

She drew in a shocked breath, nodding.

He dropped his head down closer. "Now, as I said, I want you again." And he covered her mouth with his.

Adrian paid no attention to the morning cold seeping through his clothes as he sat on the stone wall of the courtyard. He was too focused on carefully crimping the small metal cuffs to the woven leather necklace in his hands. He smiled as he worked, seeing it come along better than he had imagined. It was soft and delicate, like Sevina.

"What are you working on?" a voice called.

He jerked his head up in surprise. "Queen Norah!" He curled the necklace in his hand and stashed it down, giving a small shake of his head. "It's nothing."

Her eyes narrowed. "Let me see."

Slowly, he pulled up his hand and opened his fingers, sheepishly showing her the necklace.

She let out a small breath as she picked it up. "Adrian, this is beautiful!" She inspected it closely. "How did you get the leather to sparkle like this?"

Her admiration brought a smile to his lips. "I crushed peoly shells and made a mix, soaked the strips in it."

She handed it back to him. "Is it for someone special? Perhaps a beautiful girl with large brown eyes?"

Adrian shrugged bashfully. Of course Norah had picked up on things, having seen him with Sevina a couple times now. "Uh," he started as he stared down at the necklace.

"She'll love it." Norah smiled, saving him from words.

Adrian had been wavering all morning on whether to give it to Sevina, wondering if she'd even like it or if she'd find it silly. But Norah's reaction fueled his confidence, and his excitement grew.

"Where's your brother?" she asked.

"In the sparring field, last I saw."

She nodded, but paused, lingering a moment. "I'm going back to Mercia, Adrian."

A grin spread across his face. "That's great news! Your grandmother will be so happy to see you." But then he felt a weight in his stomach as he looked down at the necklace in his hands. If Norah was going back to Mercia, that would mean he would be too. "When?" he asked.

"A few days, maybe?"

He nodded as he rolled the soft leather between his fingers. He looked up at her, and she gave him a sad smile. But he swallowed his emotion. Norah's return was exactly what Mercia needed right now. He smiled back at her. "I'll start to prepare."

She squeezed his arm and then went to find Alec.

Norah found Alexander in the sparring field, as Adrian had told her. She thought it mildly entertaining how the Kharavian soldiers and the Northmen would watch one another, each progressively growing more aggressive in their sparring to impress the other. But her presence on the field drew a pause, and Alexander handed his sword and shield to another soldier as she approached.

"Queen Norah," he greeted.

"Lord Justice," she said, trying to keep the bubbling joy from her face. "Will you walk with me?"

She waited until they cleared the field, and the ears of the men on it. "I'm returning to Mercia."

Alexander stopped. A smile came to his lips.

"I don't know for how long, probably *not* long," she added quickly. "But I need to see my grandmother and the council, and how everything is there."

"And the king?" he asked.

"Will stay here."

He nodded, unable to hide the relief on his face.

"Mikael's supportive, but he's asked me to take the lord commander. And I've agreed."

Alexander's smile fell. "What? You can't allow the Destroyer into Mercia."

She sighed. "Alexander, stop calling him that like he's a demon of destruction. He's a foul-tempered man with a questionable conscience."

"Questionable?" he scoffed. "Are you serious?"

Norah swept her eyes around them. "I didn't come here to talk about the lord commander. I only meant to share the news, the good news, that we'll be returning to Mercia. We'll leave in a few days, if you'll ready the men. I want to take them all home. I also want to bring the Crest. I think it would be good for them to see Mercia."

He eyed her skeptically.

"They're good men, Alexander."

He looked out toward the sparring field. "Caspian has said as much."

"Let's go home."

Excitement rippled through the ranks as they marched out of Ashan and toward the canyons to Mercia, home. But despite this excitement, tension hung in the air. The Mercian units marched with the Kharavian commander, who traveled in his signature style. Even though the Northmen had seen him as a man, and had grown somewhat accustomed to his presence, his weapon-laden battle dress and the scream of his armored destrier still unsettled them.

Caspian's heart beat heavily in his chest as they drew closer to the Canyonlands, his mind on Tahla. Never had he imagined himself with a woman, or hiding it from those closest to him, but Tahla made him feel ways he had never imagined, ways he never understood. She would break him, eventually, he was sure of it. But it didn't stop his need for her.

They arrived in the Urun camp, and his eyes combed the Horsemen warriors, but there was no sign of Tahla. Caspian worked to settle the army quickly. As was the normal Urun custom, they were welcomed to eat by the large center fire. Caspian took a seat on a rock, and Alexander sat on the log that lay beside it.

Caspian stared into the hypnotic flames of the fire. Through its dance, the eyes he so often dreamed about stared back at him. He straightened as he realized Tahla watched him from the opposite side.

"It feels strange to be going home with the Destroyer," Alexander said.

Caspian pulled himself from Tahla's gaze and tried his best to focus his attention on Alexander.

The justice took a drink from his bowl. "It feels strange to be going home with Norah. I... wasn't sure this day would come."

While Caspian understood, he didn't feel quite the same. Mainly, he didn't feel the queen had been lost, as Alexander did, merely by her being in Kharav. And Kharav had come to feel like home, too, now. But that was something he could never share with Alexander.

Caspian tried his best to stay attentive to Alexander's words, but his eyes and his mind found their way back to Tahla, who flashed him a mischievous smile, seeming to enjoy his suffering. Finally, when he could bear it no longer, he excused himself to his quarters. He lingered a moment, looking for Tahla, but she seemed to have disappeared. Caspian started back toward the houses, hoping she would come to him.

As he cut between the houses, a hand snaked out, bringing a blade to his neck. "Did you think you could just slip away from me, Northman?" came the voice, and the corners of his lips turned up into a wry smile.

"You shouldn't threaten a man with a knife unless you intend to use it," he said.

Tahla stepped out in front of him, still holding the blade to his neck. "Who says I don't?"

Blood coursed through his veins. This woman woke something inside him.

But Caspian hadn't become captain without merit. Before Tahla could react, he threw up his arm and knocked the blade away. Catching Tahla's wrist, he pulled her to him, forcing her along a sidewall and pushing her back up against it. She moved her body against his suggestively. This game was new. And it excited him.

She grinned. "Unexpected, Northman." Her body relaxed, but as soon as he loosened his hold, she snapped up a knee against his thigh, almost dropping him, and ducked to slip past him. But he caught her and spun her around, pressing her against the wall again. Her back was to him this time, and he leaned against her, his mouth to her ear.

"I am generally not a man who enjoys a fight, but—"

A hand grabbed him from behind and threw him back against the opposite wall. The commander snarled at him with a deep rage, swinging his axe in attack. Caspian dodged the blade, and it hit the stacked stone behind him.

"I thought I knew you better, Northman!" the lord commander seethed.

"Soren, no!" Tahla cried, but he was focused on Caspian. He swung again, just missing, but the axe gave a skin-prickling sound as its tip scraped Caspian's armor. Caspian scrambled back, but the walls of the joined houses gave him no escape. The commander coiled back for a final blow.

"Soren, stop! Stop!" Tahla cried. "I love him!"

The lord commander paused his assault, and both he and Caspian gaped at her in surprise.

"I love him!" she said again, breathless. "We're together."

The commander shifted his gaze from Tahla back to Caspian with an angry trench in his brow. He was quiet for a moment. "A *Northman*?" he asked Tahla, with a tinge of disgust in his voice.

She nodded.

His rage faded, but his anger remained. He glared at Caspian. "Who knows about this?"

"No one, my lord," Caspian admitted, looking at the ground in shame. "But I'll tell the queen."

"You won't," Soren growled.

Caspian's eyes widened, and he jerked his head up. "What?"

"You won't," the commander said again. "She has a weak heart, and she'll release you to be together."

Caspian looked at Tahla. While he would never choose to leave the queen's service, the thought of being with Tahla, together, always, was a pull he didn't expect.

The commander grabbed him by the breastplate and pushed him back against the wall. "Salara needs you," he said between his teeth. "If you leave her, I'll kill you."

Caspian knew he meant it, but he had no intention of leaving the queen's service.

"Soren," Tahla gasped.

"I'm sworn to Salara!" the commander snapped. "Don't make me choose."

His statement surprised Caspian.

"What do you mean you're sworn to her?" a voice called out behind them. *Alexander.* Caspian prayed he hadn't overheard the exchange about Tahla. He didn't want him to find out this way.

The commander let out a long breath, baring his teeth. "It's not your concern, Bear."

Alexander looked at Caspian. "It is my concern. I'm her lord justice. And that is my captain."

Soren chuckled. "And I'm her lord commander."

"That means nothing," Alexander said.

The beast of a Shadowman turned. "Does it not? I command the armies."

Alexander shook his head. "Not the Northmen."

Soren frowned with a shrug, as if allowing Alexander a small victory. "Not *all*, that's true."

"None," Alexander stressed.

"I lead the Crest. That makes Caspian my captain. And now I command Bahoul." His eyes smiled wickedly. "More will come. Give me time, Bear."

"Bahoul?" Alexander repeated.

This was the first Caspian had heard of this as well. The queen had given the mountains back to Kharav? To the Destroyer?

"Perhaps you should talk to Salara," the commander said, before casting a warning gaze at Caspian and leaving.

Alexander found Norah in a large stone house in the village's center. His skin burned in anger. "You gave Bahoul back to the Shadowlands?" he asked when he saw her.

Norah turned. He saw her anger in response to his own, but he didn't care.

"I gave Bahoul back to Kharav, where it rightfully belongs," she said with an edge in her voice.

Surely, she didn't know what she had done. "Your father died for those mountains."

"No, my father died for a war fueled by fear and hatred."

He stepped back in surprise. How could she say that? "The Destroyer says he is sworn to you."

She hesitated before replying. "He is."

Had she not wanted him to know?

"Norah, you can't accept his oath. He can't truly swear himself to you."

Her eyes narrowed defensively. "Why not?"

He couldn't believe he had to explain this. "He's the Destroyer. Oaths are for men who know loyalty!"

"There's no man more loyal than the lord commander," she snapped back.

Her words struck him. He couldn't reply.

She closed her eyes momentarily. "I didn't mean it like that. Of course I don't consider you in that statement. You know how I feel about you."

He wasn't so sure anymore. He took another step back, then turned and left her to the evening.

CHAPTER THIRTY-ONE

The glory of Mercia shone brightly on the horizon, and Norah felt a spring of joy in her heart. *Home.*

Adrian rode beside her, and he wore a lopsided smile. He was happy to be returning too. She'd wanted to bring Calla and Cohen, but she wasn't sure if Hamed and Marta would approve of their grandchildren traveling across the continent to a kingdom that used to be their enemy—to the kingdom that had claimed the siblings' parents. So she'd had them stay. Soren had just put them into a training regimen and assigned tutors for their studies, without Norah even asking. He'd likely cite it as another favor to call upon, but for the moment, she was grateful. They'd be looked after until she returned to Kharav.

Norah turned her attention back to Mercia. She shot Adrian a grin. "How fast is your horse?"

"Faster than Sephir," he challenged.

"Salara," Soren called out in warning behind her.

She glanced back over her shoulder, knowing that his large destrier didn't have the speed. "Am I hearing you want to race too, Lord Commander?"

"Don't break away from the army," he gruffed.

Don't break away from him, he meant. "Then they need to keep up," she said with a smirk, and urged the Wild mare into a gallop toward Mercia.

The gates of Mercia opened wide as the bells rang out. Norah and Adrian rode through the city, across the bridge, and into the courtyard, followed closely by Alexander and Caspian. Norah brought her mare to a stop in front of the grand entry to the castle.

At the top of the stair stood Catherine. Norah didn't take her eyes from her as she slid off Sephir to the ground. She hadn't exchanged words with Catherine since receiving her letter in Kharav, urging Norah to return home.

Now she *was* home.

Catherine stepped down the stairs slowly. Cautiously even. Norah's heart hurt. Did her grandmother think of her as the enemy now?

When they reached each other, they stopped. Catherine's face was difficult to read, but then her eyes welled. She reached out and pulled Norah to her, holding her tightly. "My dear child," she breathed. "I wasn't sure I would ever see you again."

Norah tried to blink back the tears in her own eyes. "I wasn't sure if I would see you either."

Catherine pulled back and gave an emotional smile. "I'm so glad you're home." Then she stiffened. A cold fell over her face as she looked past Norah to the arriving company. Norah followed her gaze to see the lord commander with the Crest. All eyes were on him.

His destrier let out a ghostly scream. Soren slid from his mount like thunder to the ground and strode toward them.

Mercian soldiers parted warily.

"Grandmother, may I present—"

"How dare you bring this monster here!" Catherine spat bitterly. "Do you not think of your people, Norah? How many Northmen has he killed, and you waltz him in as our guest?"

Norah took a step back, surprised. "I know that this is difficult," she started, "but—"

"Take him!" Catherine commanded the guards. The Northmen pulled their bows, and the sound of steel rang out as Soren drew his sword.

"Stand down!" Norah shouted, backing up to him with her arms raised.

"I didn't believe it when it was said to me," Catherine said, her voice shaking. "You side with the Destroyer?"

"I'm queen of Mercia *and* Kharav, and the lord commander serves me, under my protection. Anyone who defies this will answer to me," she stressed, loud enough for everyone to hear.

Her Northmen lowered their bows, and she looked back at the commander, who sheathed his sword.

"Then put him in the tower," Catherine seethed. "If he must be here, then I want him out of my sight."

"No, he'll stay in a royal guest chamber, as is right for his position," Norah said firmly.

"Are you mad?"

"I'm getting close," Norah said shortly.

Catherine's face darkened as she stepped back. "He's here to guard his king's interest, isn't he? The Shadow King has made you a prisoner, even in your own castle."

Norah glanced back at Soren. It was an easy assumption to make, but it wasn't true. Not now. Mikael trusted Soren. She trusted Soren. And she was glad he'd come.

Catherine puffed a breath of disgust, then turned and strode into the castle, but the Northmen were still on high alert.

Norah turned to Soren. "Caspian will show you the stables, and you can see to your horse. Then he'll take you around the castle."

Caspian stepped forward. "Of course, Regal High." He nodded to the commander. "Lord Commander."

But Soren didn't move, clearly disliking the thought of leaving her.

She spoke low, pleading. "You'll see me again after Caspian has shown you around." But his face told her he wasn't interested. "You are quite literally moments from starting a battle in this very courtyard." She dropped her voice to a whisper. "Please."

Reluctantly, he gave a nod, deciding to cooperate, and then turned and let Caspian lead him to the stables.

Norah watched them go, praying no further drama would follow. She knew it was wishful thinking. Soren was the symbol of the Shadowlands, and to Mercia he was the symbol of evil, everything they'd warred against for the past ten years. Mending these perceptions would take time.

She turned toward the castle and made her way to the drawing room, where she knew she'd find her grandmother. As she reached the alcove of the door, she paused and took a deep breath before entering. She needed her grandmother's support, especially if Norah hoped to win over the council. She pushed open the door and stepped inside.

Catherine stood by the window on the far wall, looking across the courtyard below. "This wasn't the return I was expecting. Or hoping for."

A pang of hurt needled her heart. "Would you rather I not have returned at all?"

Catherine puffed a breath. "Don't be ridiculous."

"Why didn't you come to the wedding?" It still crushed her.

Her grandmother's brow dropped. "You know why."

Norah's eyes welled. "I needed you!"

Catherine's eyes cut back with an icy stare. "You didn't need me when you made this decision, all on your own."

Norah scoffed as she shook her head. "I don't expect this to be easy, nor do I claim it a perfect solution, but I'm queen, and I've made my decision. I didn't ask for this responsibility, but I have done—and will always do—what I think is best and right."

They stood for a moment in the silence.

Slowly, Catherine softened. "I know," she said finally. "I know you do what you believe is right."

Norah crossed the distance between them and reached out and took her hand. "I still need you," she whispered.

Catherine looked at her with emotion in her eyes. "And you have me, my dear girl."

Norah let out a long breath, giving her a warm smile. She pulled her grandmother to a side table that held a hot pot of tea, and they both sat. Norah poured them both a cup.

"So other than my marrying the king of all things evil and breaking the prophecy to unite Mercia and Aleon, ending the world, how has everything been?"

"Oh, Norah, for gods' sakes."

Norah wrinkled her nose. Too soon for humor, she supposed. "Fine. But really, how are things?"

Catherine sighed. "It both pleases me and pains me to say, somewhat better. Our people are fed, only a couple more months are expected of the winter, and we don't have a war looming on the horizon."

Norah wanted to smile, but she knew better.

"But"—Catherine took a sip of her tea and then set the cup back down on the saucer—"Mercian villages are still under attack. Drifters seem to grow in number, and now that our ships are sailing with trade again, they're being targeted by pirates."

Norah's brow creased with worry. "Still?" Alexander had told her about the pirates. Pirates had always been a challenge, but in times of desperation, such as the lingering winter, their attacks became increasingly bolder. But she'd thought their ships had been faring better.

Catherine nodded. "We just lost another twenty-eight men and a quarter haul of steel. The council will want to hold a state session, and soon, to hear from you on the matter."

Norah bit her lip. She didn't even have a fully formed thought around these challenges, let alone a solution.

Catherine squeezed her hand. "Don't worry, my dear, we'll figure it out. I'm just glad you're home."

Norah made her way toward the great hall, not quite with a destination in mind, but simply trying to sort her thoughts. She ran her hand through her hair, pushing the wayward strands out of her eyes. She hadn't expected things to be easy in returning to Mercia, and she couldn't shake the sinking feeling that her grandmother's sour welcome was only the beginning.

The sun had started to set. She glanced out of the window-lined hall toward the purple sky and spotted Caspian in the courtyard, still with Soren. He was explaining something with his hands and motioning westward.

She followed the hall to the side door and took it outside. "Do you have a plan of attack scoped out yet?" she asked as she came up behind them.

Caspian turned. "Queen Norah."

Soren raised a questioning brow through the eye opening of his head wrap.

"That's what people will wonder," she told the commander. "Do you know how you'll attack?"

Caspian gave an uncomfortable chuckle at her joke.

Soren frowned. "We've been trying to assess the North for years. I doubt I'll have a plan after only an afternoon."

Norah eyed Caspian in amusement, realizing Soren hadn't understood she'd asked him in jest.

"But," the commander said, "I'd start with your mainland city. They lack defenses. You should be building houses of stone. You certainly have enough of it. Stone doesn't burn."

"You would burn the city?" Caspian asked.

"To draw the army out."

"They wouldn't come," Caspian said. "They'd stay on the isle to protect the queen."

Soren shook his head. "No. One Northman at a time—their screams in the air as I peel the flesh from their body. One after another. Then the army would come." Soren nodded at Norah with a dark eye. "*She* would send them."

Norah swallowed the bile building in her throat. He was a master at his craft. "Thank you, Captain," she said, turning to Caspian and breaking the unease. "I can show the lord commander to his chamber."

Caspian stood for a moment, disturbed. "Regal High," he finally bowed. "Lord Commander."

Soren watched him leave.

She scowled at him. "Was that necessary?"

"It was what you were really asking, yes? My perception of your weakness?"

"I congratulate you for finding it—my compassion for human life," she said irritably.

"And there's your other," he said, and she followed his gaze to Alexander, who was leaving the stables with Adrian. She saw Adrian smiling, and Alexander gripped his shoulder warmly. It made her happy to see them as brothers, and she lingered a moment before turning back to Soren.

"I'll show you to your chamber," she said with a sigh, resigned.

He followed her through several hallways, to a room looking out at the temple. "You'll sleep here," she told him.

"By the temple?"

"You need prayers," she said shortly. "Many prayers."

"It's too far from your quarters."

Composure, she reminded herself. "Do you not see my struggle? I'm in my own home. You don't have to sit outside my door or make it more difficult than it already is."

So much for composure, she thought to herself.

There was a deep rumble in his chest, but he gave a small nod in acceptance. "Fine."

She moved to leave but paused. "Oh, for the rest of today, I would ask that you stay here. Out of sight."

"Be confined to my chamber?"

"I just want things to settle, to let tensions calm."

"Should I wear chains? Would that make your men feel better?"

She looked at him with a sigh, absent of any energy, and turned wearily from the doorway.

"I'll stay," he called after her. She paused and looked back, surprised by his compliance.

"Thank you," she said.

Norah made her way toward the dining hall, and a wave of guilt rippled through her. Despite how she loathed him sometimes, Soren was a good commander and not a completely reprehensible man.

A servant passed her in the hall, stopping first to bow.

"Will you take something to eat to the lord commander?" she asked.

"Yes, Regal High."

She paused and thought for a moment. "Add a plate for me as well. And tell my grandmother that I'm tired and will be taking dinner privately this evening."

"Yes, Regal High."

The servant hurried to the kitchen, and Norah made her way back to the commander's chamber.

His face flashed with surprise when he opened the door and saw her.

"I thought I would join you in confinement," she said. "At least for dinner."

"I don't need your pity. I'm well suited alone." His voice was edged with annoyance.

"Well, maybe I'm not yet suited to face the continued judgments of my grandmother and my council." Or Alexander, who was no doubt still stewing over Bahoul and her decision to bring Soren to Mercia. "So, will you bear my company?"

He relented and opened the door wider, and she stepped inside.

A servant whisked in behind her with a tray of food and set it on the table. The maid set down two goblets and a carafe of wine and gave Norah a bow before slipping out of the chamber and closing the door behind her.

Soren motioned her to the table. Norah pursed a smile and sat, and he took the chair across from her. He pulled off his wrap, and she let her eyes travel over him. She saw his face often; he didn't cover himself inside the castle in Kharav, but somehow, he looked different here. Sharper. Unsettling.

"No blood bowl?" he asked as he looked at the food.

Norah filled her wineglass and handed him the carafe. "I thought it might be a little too much. At least in the beginning, until everyone's acquainted with you." She wrinkled her nose. "Because asking for blood is... weird... and creepy."

He let out a small snort as he filled his own cup. "I wasn't serious. I'll manage."

She couldn't help a smile. He was always serious. Her curiosity couldn't be contained. "Why do you drink it? Blood."

"It makes me strong."

She raised a brow. "So does food and water."

"I like it," he answered shortly.

Norah brought her cup to her lips to fill the tensioned silence.

Soren leaned back in his chair. "When Salar and I escaped Bahoul after the North overran us, we traveled for days. I protected him. I hunted. We ate the food raw because we couldn't build a fire." He picked up his chalice and took a drink. "I remember the blood on my tongue. And when I drink it now, it reminds me of who I am."

Norah had never imagined herself feeling emotional over a story about drinking blood, but she felt that way now. Soren drank from a blood bowl because it reminded him of when he had been strong. It made him feel strong. And she could understand that.

"I'll hunt," he told her.

"Hunting sounds perfect. I'm sure Adrian would love to take you."

He paused, then said, "I would like that."

Norah took a bite of the dauo root and rice on her plate. She watched him as he made an effort of the karo fish. He grimaced, and she realized he likely had never eaten fish from the North Sea. Its taste wasn't for everyone. She couldn't help a smile. They sat quietly for a moment.

"There's something I would ask your help with," she started again. "Something I need a fresh perspective to resolve."

He didn't answer, but his eyes met hers and his face grew even more serious.

"Pirates," she told him.

"Pirates?"

"Mercia and other seafaring kingdoms have always been plagued by the threat of pirates. One of our ships was attacked last week, and we lost twenty-eight men. Alexander is increasing forces and weapons to defend our shipments, but that spreads our ranks thin and takes up valuable trade space."

"I know nothing of the sea."

"But you know war. You know how to deal with threats. The *Evanya* sails in a week's time, and she'll have our largest trade of steel this year. I have to find a solution."

"The *Evanya*?"

Norah gave a smile. "The ship named for my mother. They're all named after Mercian queens."

"Do you have one?" he asked.

She nodded. "The *Norah*." She sighed, thinking. "I have to find a way to keep my men safe. I can't tolerate it anymore." She paused. "I don't need a lord justice. I need the Destroyer."

He seemed surprised but nodded. "Let me look into it. I'll see what there is to be done."

"Thank you."

They ate quietly, and Norah's heart was light. He was dropping his guard with her. "There is something else I've been wanting to ask you," she said.

Soren looked up from his plate in curiosity. She waited, and he gave an urging nod.

"What did the seer show you? In Odepeth?"

His face grew dark, and he sat back in his chair. He looked away, his mind obviously drawn back to the memory.

"Tell me," she pleaded. "Is it Mikael? Is it you? What did you see?"

"Put it out of your mind," he said in a low voice.

"I can't. Why didn't you tell Mikael?"

He set his fork on his plate. "I think it's best if you leave now."

Norah stood, leaning over the table. "Have you not told me the worst I might imagine about Alexander? About Mikael? What else is there?"

"Leave me," he growled, rising from his own chair. He moved toward her and used his size to push her back toward the door.

"Whatever it is, you can tell me—"

"I kill you!" he thundered.

Norah's breath caught in her throat as she stumbled back against the wall.

"You want to know what the seer showed me? It's your death." He boxed her in against the doorframe with his arms, bringing his face inches from hers. "I kill you," he said in a fierce whisper, "willingly." His eyes were cruel, and they hurt her. Surprisingly, they hurt her.

He reached and opened the chamber door, and she stumbled backward, out of the room. Their eyes locked again as she stood, trying to get her breath, and he closed the door between them.

Chapter Thirty-Two

Norah stared at herself in the mirror while Serene laced the back of her dress. All the while in Kharav, she had dreamed of returning to Mercia, but now that she was here, it didn't feel as she'd expected. It didn't feel right, just as Soren's words the night before hadn't felt right. She wasn't sure she believed him.

She wondered how he felt, finally in the kingdom he had worked so hard to invade—the kingdom he had tried so hard to destroy.

"Has the lord commander risen?" she asked.

Serene nodded. "He already left, Regal High."

She met her maid's eyes in the reflection. "What?"

"Early this morning. Lord Adrian went with him."

Norah shifted uneasily. They must have gone hunting. She *had* proposed that he take Adrian hunting, but she'd thought she'd have more time to warm Alexander up to the idea.

"Is everything all right?" Serene asked.

"Um, yes, of course. Just let me know when they return." Until then, she'd try her best to avoid Alexander.

Norah chewed her sausage slowly. It had been too big of a bite.

Her grandmother watched her between her own bites. "You've barely said a word all morning."

She swallowed and wished she had more sausage. It was better than talking. "Oh, um... I'm just thinking about the upcoming state session with the council, and other things..." She let her voice trail off. She didn't mention Soren's threat, or her current worry of Adrian's whereabouts, or that he was with the lord commander. She suspected Catherine would be beside herself, and Alexander would send a full army to recover him. That wasn't the situation she cared to deal with at the moment.

"The lord justice was looking for you earlier. Did you speak to him?"

Norah quickly put a large bite of bread in her mouth and shook her head. It was shocking that he hadn't been able to find her while she so actively avoided him.

"What will you do about the demon?" Catherine asked. "Is he to wander Mercia as he pleases, assessing our weaknesses, devising his plans?"

Norah swallowed the piece of bread she had over-chewed. "You *do* know he's not a demon, right?"

"Flesh and blood or no, there's evil in him."

Norah took a drink of her tea and tilted her head. "Yes, everyone seems to have that impression. Is it the eyes, you think?"

"The gods' mercy." Catherine sighed. "Norah, this is not a joke."

"It almost is!" she said with a slight smile that garnered her grandmother's scowl. "He's a grudging, resentful, angry man, rather large, slightly scary-looking, who's managed to frighten entire kingdoms." Norah shook her head. "I think he just doesn't like people." Then, a little quieter, she added, "You should understand that."

Catherine let out a breath of offense. "Are you really comparing me to the Destroyer?"

"No, of course not. I just think you'd get along. Well." She shrugged, looking at the cat lounging on a pillowed bed against the wall. "He's an animal lover, you know."

Catherine's face was dark for one so pale. She dropped her napkin on her plate and rose from the table, leaving without a word.

Norah sighed. She hadn't meant to upset her grandmother or be disrespectful, but she was frustrated. It seemed there was no reasoning, no logic, only hate and intolerance. She knew she wasn't dealing with it well, but she didn't know how to, and in these moments, her emotions seemed to choose her words for her.

Alexander's voice behind her made her cringe, but Norah turned with a forced smile.

"Queen Norah, I've been looking for you everywhere."

"Oh. Really?"

He raised a brow, and she cursed herself quietly. Why was she so obvious?

"I don't mean to disturb you at breakfast, but have you seen Adrian?" he asked.

"I haven't," she said. *Not this morning.*

His eyes narrowed, and her pulse quickened.

"I wanted to go over what will likely be discussed in the state session tomorrow," she said, changing the topic. "Grandmother has let me know there are a few challenges. With the pirates."

"I'll handle them," he assured her.

"Alexander, you can't take this all on yourself. It's a challenge for more than one person."

"I said I'll handle it."

Norah wanted to suggest help from the lord commander, but for once her mind controlled her tongue, and she was quiet.

Evening came, and Norah was relieved to be back in her chamber, away from the eyes of judgment. She'd left Vitalia back in Kharav, and she missed her desperately. She could use a bit of sarcasm and support right now. Her Mercian maid Serene was happy to be back, Norah could tell. The girl dashed around the castle in high spirits. Norah felt a pang of guilt. The Shadowlands were too harsh a place for her. She would leave her here in Mercia when she returned to Kharav.

"Did you hear about Titus?" Serene asked as she pulled down the coverlet on the bed.

"What about him?"

"He's found himself a wife. Well, not a wife yet, but they're to be married."

Norah's eyes widened. "Already? He hasn't even been back long enough to put his horse away from the journey."

Serene laughed. "He's a high-ranked soldier of the queen's guard, of good lineage. And handsome. He had his pick as soon as word was out that he was looking."

Yes, she supposed that was how marriages worked around here. "Well, good for him." If Titus was happy, and his bride was happy, then she was happy for them.

"Any word of the lord commander?" Norah asked as the maid busied herself drawing a bath.

"No, Regal High."

Norah felt an anxiousness creeping in. Hunting wouldn't be as it was in Kharav. She knew they'd have to ride far, but not a whole day, and it was unlike the commander to be away from her for so long.

"The lord justice still looks for Lord Adrian as well," Serene added. "He's getting worried."

Norah's stomach knotted. "You... didn't mention anything, did you?"

"No, Regal High," Serene assured her.

She nodded as she let out an uneasy breath and prayed they'd return soon. She stripped off her dress, but as she stepped out of her undergarments, her eye caught the spotting of blood on the fabric. Her stomach dropped. Not that she was expecting to be with child, but it occupied her mind occasionally, and she found herself hoping. Daydreaming, even.

"Are you all right, Regal High?" Serene asked.

She nodded, pushing out a breath. "Of course, I just started my bleed and don't feel very well."

Serene scooped up her clothes. "Why don't you get into the bath? I'll go fetch you some tea. That will make you feel better." The girl gave her a warm smile and swept out of the room.

Norah stepped into the steaming water and sank down to the bottom of the tub. At that moment, everything flooded her at once: Mercia being home but not home, challenges for which she had no solutions, the fact that her memories were gone forever, the continued tension between Mercia and Kharav, the weight of her kingdom's disappointment at her every decision... and now there was no child.

And she missed Mikael.

She covered her face in her hands and let the tears come.

CHAPTER THIRTY-THREE

A knock on the door pulled Norah from her thoughts. She had skipped breakfast with her grandmother. Her stomach knotted enough at the thought of meeting with the council; she wasn't sure she could bear another conversation with Catherine prior to it.

She groaned as she rose from the settee—this was probably Catherine coming to chastise her now.

But Caspian was at the door when she opened it. "Queen Norah." He bowed. "The lord commander has returned. He asks you to come."

Thank the gods, he was back, but... "Now? I'm about to go meet the council."

Caspian's lips formed a thin line. "You should come."

She'd thought it wasn't possible to feel any more anxious. She'd been wrong.

Norah quickly followed Caspian to the stables with a looming sense of dread. When she saw Soren and Adrian, she let out a breath of relief. But her relief quickly turned to anger. "Where have you been?" she demanded before she even reached them. She looked at Adrian. "I've been avoiding your brother like the Cold Death." Turning her attention to the commander, she said, "When I mentioned that you should go hunting, I didn't mean immediately. And what took you so long in returning?"

"We didn't go hunting," Adrian said.

She paused, her eyes bouncing between the two of them. "Then where have you been?"

"Doing as you requested," Soren answered. "Finding a solution."

Norah felt a weight in her stomach. "For what?"

"Your pirates," he said, and motioned to a group of boys in one of the horse stalls awaiting their fates.

She raised a brow. "Those aren't pirates."

"No," Soren said, "they're the sons of pirate captains. And while in our care, the North's ships will no longer be attacked."

Norah looked at him, bewildered. Her bewilderment turned to a sickness rising up in her throat. "Where did you get these children?"

"The inlet port city," he said matter-of-factly.

Norah shook her head, a horror swelling inside her. "They're hostages?" she stammered.

He shrugged. "Wards," he suggested.

She brought a hand to her head, trying to calm her breath and think. "Wait, there are many more pirates than just those out of the port city."

"All you need is a few," he told her. "They'll keep the others away."

She shook her head again. "What happens if a Mercian ship is attacked?"

The commander frowned. "Salara, you knew my methods wouldn't be favored, yet you asked me regardless."

She huffed a small breath. "I didn't mean—"

"You said you needed the Destroyer. I've provided you a near guaranteed solution with no lives lost."

"Unless a ship is attacked!"

He shrugged. "I doubt that will happen. But if it does, then yes, and only one will be required to send a message."

"We won't harm a child!" she snapped.

"Then how many men are you willing to lose? Is one pirate boy worth the lives of twenty-eight soldiers? Is he worth all the men you lost before, or those you've yet to lose?"

"I can't answer a question like that," she whispered.

"You need to do what's necessary. That's the worst case. It's most likely these boys will be kept safely as wards of the crown, as their fathers won't seek to put their lives in danger, and then they'll be exchanged in a few years."

Norah looked at the boys with a heavy weight in her chest. "I can't do that."

"Is that not why I'm here?" he growled. "Consider this situation resolved."

Norah forced out a breath. "You will not, under any circumstances, harm a child. *Ever.* Pirate or no." She turned to Caspian. "Have the men see them fed and placed somewhere safe, *not* a horse stall, until I can figure out what to do with them." Then to Adrian, "I would advise you not to announce your part in this to your brother."

Adrian nodded. "I kind of figured."

Norah pushed down the sickness in her throat as she turned and made her way toward the judisaept. Soren followed behind her. She almost told him to return to his chamber, but if she was completely honest with herself, she needed someone with her who was on her side. Despite what Soren said and did, and despite his threats, he was on her side. And if his position were recognized properly, he should be part of the council, as Alexander was. Of course, the council themselves wouldn't agree. Well, she told herself, if there was to be a battle over her decisions, might as well make it a war.

"What is he doing here?" Edward called as she entered, without so much as a greeting.

As expected. "He's attending our state," she replied. "Good morning, Councilman Edward," she added as she took her seat at the head of the table.

All eyes were on Soren.

"He cannot be here," Alastair argued.

Norah looked at James to find his gaze upon her, dark and disappointed. But he said nothing.

"Where's the lord justice?" Catherine asked.

"On his way, I'm sure," Norah answered.

"This is a private meeting," Henricus voiced, "not one that should be privy to our enemies. He must go."

"He won't," she snapped. "He'll attend what's appropriate for his station. He's lord commander of my army in Kharav, and he commands the forces in Bahoul."

There was an audible gasp from the council and her grandmother.

"You've given Bahoul to the Shadowmen?" Edward asked, astonished.

"I've given my husband what is rightfully his," she cut back. "It will continue to be a base for soldiers of both Kharav and Mercia."

"The army won't have this," Edward said angrily. "They'll rebel."

Norah looked at him with a cool calm. "I've found the army will support that which their leaders support, and rebel when inspired to do so. Are you saying you'd inspire them to rebel, Councilman?"

Soren stepped closer to the table, and Norah realized he still carried his battle-axe.

"Of course not," Edward stammered.

For once, she appreciated the commander's intimidation. "We agree, then," she said. "On the next topic—"

Alexander thundered into the room, making them all rise. All except Norah.

"So, we're taking hostages and slaughtering children now?" he started angrily. Just then, he caught sight of Soren. "This is your doing," he seethed.

"What are you talking about?" Catherine asked, alarmed.

"Word through the docks." Alexander glared at Soren. "Apparently, the Destroyer seeks to solve our pirate problem by taking their children and threatening to kill them."

The council gasped again in horror. Norah had a feeling she'd be hearing them gasp a lot.

"Take your brutality back to the Shadowlands," Alexander snarled at Soren. "No one asked you—"

"I asked him," Norah said.

All eyes shifted to her. Alexander paused, and the color drained from his face. "You asked him? You would kill these children?"

"It won't come to that," she said. She wouldn't let it.

"And what if it does?" James asked. "Is this what we've become?"

Norah stood. "We lost twenty-eight soldiers on the *Celeste*, eleven on the *Anne*, and sixteen on the *Mary*. I'll not lose another man."

"But you can stand to lose your soul," Alexander cut back.

"Lord Justice," she warned him, "enough."

"And who will do the deed?" he said, throwing his hands up as his eyes burned into the commander. To Soren, he said, "Ah, the Destroyer. Or better, my brother? You seem to have quite the appetite for pulling him into your vices." He turned back to Norah in his rage. "Will you watch as they die?"

The commander stepped forward. "Caution, Bear, you speak to your queen." His defense of her caught everyone by surprise.

But Alexander ignored him and looked at Norah. "Yes, I appreciate the reminder, for I barely recognize who's in front of me." He sighed, dropping his voice and taking a softer approach. "You can't seriously be thinking of this as a solution. I told you I'd handle it."

"I've been letting you handle it, and our ships are still being attacked, our trade stolen. Mercians are dying!"

Alexander's nostrils flared, and he looked at Catherine, exasperated.

Edward shook his head in disgust. "So, is the *Evanya* to sail on the blood of children? Your mother would be heartbroken to see her ship leave harbor under this circumstance."

"Then send the *Norah*," she replied.

Waves crashed high on the bow of the *Norah* as the Mercian ship cut through the water. The worst of winter had passed, but large chunks of ice still floated atop the icy blue of the sea, thundering into the hull as she sailed. But her captain, Theander, wasn't worried. This is what their ships were built for; they were strong with Mercian steel, able to withstand the best the sea could throw. No ship of the North had ever been sunk. But this strength came at a cost. The fleet was slow, which made them easy targets for pirate attacks.

The *Norah* was smaller and faster than the other Mercian ships, fitting of her namesake. But she still couldn't outrun a pirate's ketch, and Theander had the largest trade of Mercian steel this year. The queen had felt confident in fewer arms and men to make room for more trade. He felt a little less so.

On the horizon, another ship came into view. Theander looked through his scope and felt his pulse quicken.

His first mate stood beside him. "Pirates?" Austus asked.

Theander nodded.

Chapter Thirty-Four

The table was quiet as Norah and Catherine ate their breakfast in the chill of the morning. Her grandmother had hardly spoken to her since the state meeting, and Norah didn't blame her. She knew she was disappointing them—Alexander, her grandmother, the council. But she wouldn't have made decisions differently. Perhaps that's why she couldn't shake the guilt.

The doors opened, and Alexander strode in with a letter in his hand. He looked pale and uneasy.

"What is it?" she asked him.

"News," he said, holding it for her. "From the *Norah*."

News from the ship. Her stomach knotted, and she swallowed back the bile building in her throat. Her hands shook as she broke the seal and opened it. She covered her mouth with her hand.

"What is it?" Catherine asked.

"They've reached port," she breathed. "They encountered a pirate ship but were left alone."

Catherine let out a breath and leaned back against her chair.

Alexander's eyes were cold and calm. "Congratulations on your victory."

Norah forced herself to draw air into her lungs. Her racing heart slowed to a heavy pulse.

"But don't mistake this for a bluff well played," he added. "The only reason they believe the Destroyer will kill their children is because he will. And he has. Killed children, that is."

Norah knocked on Soren's chamber door and waited restlessly for him to answer. He opened it and, seeing her, swung the door wider, inviting her in. She held out the letter with the news of the *Norah* for him, and he took it, unfolding it and reading it calmly as he stepped back into the room. He looked back up at her and gave a small nod, handing the letter back.

"Alexander called it a victory, but he didn't mean it," she said quietly. "And if I'm honest, it doesn't feel like a victory."

He shrugged. "Your trade made it to market. Your men are safe. That's a victory."

She nodded reluctantly as he buckled his weapons strap across his chest.

"What are you doing?" she asked.

"I'm going out to look at more of the city," he said as he pulled the strap tight.

"You're not going to battle. It's perfectly safe."

"It's safe for you—but I'm the enemy."

Norah paused, realizing that he was alone in a strange land and surrounded by longtime adversaries, just as she had been in Kharav. She knew this loneliness. It was hard, surely even for the Destroyer.

He pushed the end of the final strap through its buckle and picked up his head wrap. She sighed. Not seeing his face added to her men's suspicion, but she wouldn't be able to talk him out of it. The only time he didn't wear the wrap out was when he was in the castle in Kharav.

He reached for his axe, and she shook her head, drawing the line. "No. Not the axe. I don't want you scaring people." His eyes showed his objection, but she stood firm. "No."

He gave a deep protesting rumble in his chest but left the axe leaning against the wall.

"Come on, I'll walk with you," she said.

The morning air was chilly.

"These are your people, too, now," she told him.

He snorted. "The North will never see me as one of their own."

As they reached the stables, a boy came careening around the corner, colliding with Soren's legs and falling backward into the dirt. He wasn't more than seven or eight years old.

"Oh!" Norah exclaimed, rushing forward. "Are you all right?"

The boy scrambled to his feet, shaken. He stared at Soren with wide eyes. In the dirt lay a makeshift axe that had been refashioned from a wooden toy sword.

Norah looked at the lord commander. His eyes showed no emotion. She turned back to the boy. "Hello there," she said. "What's your name?"

The boy didn't answer.

"Do you not have a name?" she asked.

The boy looked at her, then back at Soren. "Thomas," he said finally.

"Do you know who I am?"

He nodded. "You're Queen Norah."

She smiled. "Do you know who this is?" she asked, waving a hand at the commander.

"The Destroyer," the boy said, his eyes still on the lord commander.

Norah looked back at Soren and scowled at his formidable posture. He shifted, reaching down and picking up the wooden axe from the ground.

"You have an axe?" Soren asked him.

"I made it myself," the boy said, a boldness coming to him.

"Why not a sword, or a bow?"

"Everyone has a sword," the boy said. "And I don't want to stand and shoot arrows. I want to fight!"

Norah thought she saw a hint of a smile in Soren's eyes. He held the wooden axe back out to the boy.

"I'm going to make a bigger one, like yours," Thomas said.

"There's no skill in a big axe," Soren told him. "And it's not an easy battle weapon. Smaller is better for quick work."

"Why do you have a big one?"

He shrugged. "More blood when I kill someone."

"Lord Commander," Norah scolded, but the boy grinned.

Soren reached behind and pulled a smaller battle-axe from a sheath belted around his waist and flung it at a nearby railing, burying the head into the wood. Thomas let out a small laugh in amazement.

Soren walked to the railing column and pulled the axe free, then returned to the boy. "Try it," he said, holding out the weapon.

Thomas's eyes grew even larger, and he took the axe, positioning himself toward the column. He moved his arm to swing.

"Arm up, boy, not out. You want it to fly straight and not arc sideways."

Thomas raised his arm upward and flung the axe toward the column. It fell short, clanging on the cobbled walk. The boy looked back at Soren, waiting for his reaction.

"Don't expect a hit on your first try," the commander nodded. "Go fetch it."

Thomas ran and grabbed the axe off the ground and brought it back, holding it out.

"Do it again."

The boy flung it harder this time, and it hit the column but bounced back, onto the ground. Soren nodded again, and the boy ran to fetch it. When he came back, he held the axe out to Soren.

The commander paused. "Keep it," he said. "Practice."

"Yes, Lord Destroyer," Thomas exclaimed, grinning and holding the axe tightly. Surely it was now his most prized possession.

"Soren," Norah said softly, "I hardly think this is an appropriate gift for a child."

He looked at her for a moment, seemingly surprised. Then he shrugged, turning back to Thomas. "Don't go throwing it at your friends. It's a weapon. You'll kill someone."

"I won't kill anyone," the boy grinned. "At least not my friends."

Norah raised an eyebrow.

"One more thing," Soren said. He pulled off the belt with the axe sheath, holding it wide and eyeing its size. "It's big, but..." he stopped. "Hang on," he said as he drew his dagger and used the tip to cut notches down the length of the belt. Then he looped it around Thomas's waist and fastened it. "A little thick, but you'll grow into it."

Thomas beamed.

"Run along now," Soren told him.

"Thank you, Lord Destroyer!" the boy said with a clumsy bow, then darted away, into the sun.

The commander chuckled, a genuine chuckle, a sound she hadn't heard from him before. "He forgot about you," he told Norah.

She let out a laugh. "He forgot about the world, I think. That was very kind. You made for a very happy little boy, but... let's not give any more weapons to children."

Soren shrugged with a smirk, and for a moment, it was hard for Norah to believe he could hurt anyone. Especially a child.

Chapter Thirty-Five

Norah stepped carefully as she made her way through the darkness of the cave. It had been a long time since Alexander had shown her the hidden hot springs. She realized now that perhaps it wasn't the best idea to be traipsing into the darkness and down a path she vaguely remembered, and also having not told anyone where she was going. But the wine she had finished off just a short while ago had been very convincing of the adventure, and away from the bustle of the castle and the weight of the crown, she already felt her energy returning. She just needed to escape for a while.

The wet walls seeped cold into her fingers as she felt her way deeper into the darkness. She stayed to the left, following her touch. The cave was longer than she remembered, and for a moment, she feared she might find herself lost. But she calmed. She'd followed a singular wall, and she could merely turn around and feel her way back out at any time. She continued.

Her persistence paid off as the darkness started to fade. She could make out the walls of the cave now—she was almost there. Just as she remembered, she turned a small corner, and the tunnel opened into a massive cavern. It had been day when she had last come with Alexander, with the large opening at the top spilling in the sun. She had thought it was the most beautiful place she had ever seen. Now, moonlight lit the cavern, and it was even more magical than before. She smiled as she saw the pools of water. In the sun, they'd shimmered a beautiful turquoise. Not tonight. In the night, they were pools of darkness. But she liked the darkness now.

Her teeth chattered as she pulled off her shoes and wriggled out of her gown. She paused at her undergarments, but then chided herself for being silly. She was alone, and she stripped everything off. She rolled her clothes and put them beside a large rock, then walked to the edge of the pool and dipped her toes in the water. Its warmth made her grin, and she stepped out farther, letting herself sink down into its abyss. The rush of heat surrounded her body, and she breathed out her worry as it enveloped her.

Norah swam out farther, past the rock formation in the center and around to where the cave opened to the starry heavens. Rolling onto her back, she floated in peaceful bliss under the light of the night sky. She closed her eyes and breathed in a new energy.

How wonderful it would be to stay in this magical place, away from everything and everyone. She smiled, remembering Alexander telling her that no one came to the cave for fear of monsters lurking in the deep. She rolled and let her body sink down so only her eyes and nose rested above the surface. The edge of the water softly lapped against her lips, caressing them like a lover's kiss. Perhaps the pool wanted her to stay. She could be its monster.

She glided quietly through the night like a serpent of the sea. Each stroke through the water brought her strength. Its power flowed through her—her power now—queen of the dark and the deep.

A disturbance in the air pulled her from her peace. Norah stilled, listening.

There it was again.

It had only been a stir, but she was one with this cavern now, and she felt it like thunder. Someone was here.

She swam silently back to the center rock formation to investigate.

A man stood waist deep in the water, his back to her, and a wave of intrusion washed over her. If she were a monster, he'd be her first victim. She imagined it—slipping through the darkness under the still of the surface, coming up behind him, then reaching up and taking hold. She'd pull him down into her depths, and into the clutches of death. That's how she'd welcome those who disturbed her.

She pulled her mind back from its murderous thoughts and scolded herself. She was spending too much time with Soren.

Norah watched this intruder from the shadows. But as she looked closer, her pulse quickened. She knew this man, and a smile came to her lips. *Alexander.* What was he doing here? Did he come often? He obviously hadn't seen her clothing rolled up by the large rock to the side.

She slipped closer. The warm water rolled over her skin as she moved, and she felt every bit a prowling monster of the deep. It made her bolder.

Norah bit her lip, feeling mischievous. "Who disturbs my waters?" she called in a low voice.

He looked around with a start. Her voice had echoed through the chamber, not revealing her position. She watched him comb the cavern for her, but he couldn't see her from her place among the shadows.

"Only another seeking the calm," he called back. He turned, still searching, his back to her again.

She held her voice deeper, husky; her best serpent voice. "These are my waters."

"I've not seen you here before," he answered.

She grinned. He hadn't recognized her voice. She moved from behind the rock formation, silently drawing closer. "Are you sure about that?" she called.

He spun to face her. She hung deep in the water, showing only her head. It took him a moment, but his eyes softened, and she flashed him a smile.

"Queen Norah?"

"No," she said. "There's no queen here." Only a serpent of the deep. She came closer as he stepped farther into the water.

His eyes locked with hers. "Are you a phantom, then?" he asked. His voice was smooth and warm, like the water.

She rolled her lips together to hold her smile. "Perhaps I'm only in your mind."

"You're always in my mind," he confessed, and a quiet settled around them. His admission sobered her.

This wasn't a game.

"Are you still angry with me?" she asked, now more serious. They hadn't spoken much in the past couple weeks. She'd felt a distance between them, a distance that grew with her every decision, her every action. And now, after the meeting with the council, and her employment of Soren to help solve the situation with the pirates, it felt like they were further than they'd ever been before.

He stepped farther into the water, not taking his eyes from her. Norah circled him. Was he wearing only his skin, like her? The thought stirred a heat in her stomach, but she pushed it down. She needed to leave.

"I could never stay angry with you. Surely you know this."

She thought she did, but lately she wasn't so certain.

He drifted closer, close enough for her to touch him. His nearness called to her, and before she could stop herself, she reached out and brushed his chest with her fingertips. Quickly realizing her mistake, she moved to pull back, but he caught her, covering her hand over his chest with his own.

Norah's breath faltered.

Alexander reached up and clasped the nape of her neck, pulling her to him. He dropped his head and caught her mouth with his. His kiss was deep and possessive as he pushed her back against the rock and snaked his arm around her. The smoothness of his skin against hers stole her resistance, if she even had any.

Norah tasted the sweetness of berry on his lips, with the faint scent of wine on his breath. She realized the wine had gotten the better of them both, and she pulled back. "You're not yourself," she whispered. Neither was she.

He paused, seeming to call back his senses, and his face sobered. "Forgive me."

But he didn't release her, nor did she pull herself from him. But they couldn't be here, not like this.

Norah pulled him down and brought her lips to his ear. "You need to leave. Now." Any longer and she wouldn't let him go. Then she slipped from his arms and drew back into the depths of the darkness.

Alexander stayed for a moment, lingering in the silence. Then he waded slowly to the edge of the pool. Norah watched him, the smooth round of his buttocks, the curve of his thighs, as he rose from the water. She couldn't take her eyes from him.

She moved slowly, stalking him from the darkness. She felt every bit a monster lurking in the shadows, wanting to call him back to her. And he would come. She knew he would come.

Alexander picked up his clothes and disappeared into the darkness of the cave, and Norah let out a long, shaking breath, begging her senses to come back to her.

Norah stood in the library by a towering shelf that stretched to the ceiling. She focused her eyes on the pages of an open book in her hands, but found herself unable to read it, or even see it. Every time her mind wandered, it took her back to the cave, back to Alexander.

She cursed herself, angry at what she had done, for what she had almost done. He still held a piece of her, and she loathed herself for it.

The doors opened, and she turned to see Catherine sweeping toward her, clearly upset about something. *Perfect.* Norah needed a good berating to take her mind away. She wondered what she had done—or maybe what Soren had done—to warrant the deep scowl her grandmother wore, although she didn't really care. She'd appreciate a scolding for just about anything right now—anything to keep her thoughts from the cave.

"What did you say to him?" Catherine demanded when she reached her.

What? "To who?"

"To Alexander."

Norah's blood ran cold, and she swallowed as her stomach knotted. She had been hoping to be chastised for something different, something very different. Surely there was a myriad of other things for Catherine to be angry about. "Why?" she asked, with a crack in her voice that made her cringe inside.

"Weeks ago, he finally accepted a marriage with Ismene, but this morning, he came to advise me he'd changed his mind."

Norah's chest tightened. *Ismene?* The young woman Catherine had worked to match him with so long ago? Were they courting? For how long? Why hadn't he told her?

"What did you say to him?" Catherine demanded again. "I can only assume you've had an influence on his decision."

"I didn't even know he was betrothed!" Norah looked around. She needed to sit down, but there was no chair. Alexander had agreed to marry Ismene? The heat of jealousy flooded her, but she knew it was a jealousy she had no right to feel.

"He'd already asked her father's permission, and Lord Dartan has given it. Rescinding his marriage offer now would be a disgrace."

Was her grandmother really blaming her? "Then you shouldn't have forced it on him!" Catherine *had* forced him. He hadn't wanted to. *Right?*

"This is what is best for him," her grandmother said angrily.

"How?"

"That girl loves him!" Catherine snapped back. "Selfish child! Look what you do to him. When you were captured, a madness took him. He marched to war without listening to reason. When he returned with the news of your marriage, all he could think about was getting back to you. And when he did, you sent him home beaten and broken. And still, wherever you go, he longs to follow. Is this what you want for him? You have to let him go!"

Her emotion spoke for her. "If he wants to be free, then I free him."

"He would never want to be free from you." Her grandmother's eyes burned into her. "But you let him love you, Norah. You're responsible for his pain, and his disgrace."

Norah's lip trembled, and her eyes welled. Deep in her heart, she knew this was best for him, and she couldn't push down the rising guilt—perhaps she'd just ruined it.

Catherine turned and left, and Norah leaned back against the wall of the library as the wave of emotion washed over her.

The sun rose slowly, eating back the frost on the ground. She sat on a bench in the garden in the chilled air of morning, but she didn't feel the cold. Norah hadn't slept, and she wouldn't. She didn't deserve rest—the peace it brought, the renewal.

Heavy footfalls came behind her, and she turned to see Soren approaching. She quickly wiped the tears from her cheeks.

"Your maid told me you were here," he said when he reached her. "That you wanted to be alone."

"Which apparently means nothing to you," she said shortly.

He snorted in amusement and took his post by the bench, standing with his axe between his feet and his hands resting on the wood of the handle.

"And where have you been?" she snapped angrily. She needed to be angry, to hold her other emotions at bay. "I looked everywhere for you yesterday."

He stiffened and dropped a shoulder as he leaned back on his heel. "I took the boy hunting," he said. Adrian, he meant. "Why? Did something happen? Did you need me?"

She folded her arms and rocked gently as she stifled a sob, but there was no holding back the emotion now. "I'm messing everything up. I shouldn't have come back." She buried her face in her hands.

Soren shifted again. "What happened?"

She drew in an uneven breath. "I ruined his marriage."

He stepped around closer to her. "Whose?"

"Alexander's!"

His brows drew together. "The Bear would never wed."

"It was arranged by my grandmother. He'd agreed." Her voice shook. "But I ruined it."

The bench shifted as he sat down beside her.

"You're the Destroyer," she cried. "You're supposed to be the corruption, the darkness. But it isn't you, is it? It's me." She sucked in another sob. "What have I done?"

Soren turned and grasped her arm. "Salara," he said in a low voice—a steely voice rich with warning. His eyes were dark and intense. "Did you lay with him?"

She paused through her tears, but then shook her head.

He dropped his head as a small breath escaped him.

"But I kissed him," she said. "I swam naked in a pool with him. Is that not practically the same thing?"

"No, it's not." But a deep, angry line folded between his brows. "Not exactly."

"What will I tell Mikael?" she breathed.

The shadow under his brow darkened, and he tightened his hold. "You'll consider this your confession, and never speak of it again. Ever."

His eyes demanded an answer, and shakily, she nodded. He let go of her arm, and they sat on the bench until the sun rose enough for its rays to reach them.

"I want to go back," she whispered.

"Then we'll go."

"To Kharav."

"I knew what you meant," he said.

Chapter Thirty-Six

Norah chewed her dinner slowly as she watched her grandmother stir her tea. Her eyes wandered to Alexander, only to find him looking back at her. Her stomach turned. It would only get worse the longer she waited, she knew.

"I'm returning to Kharav," she said before taking another bite of potato and looking back at her grandmother.

Catherine's head snapped up.

Norah clenched her dress in her fist underneath the table and avoided Alexander's eyes. She chewed her potato methodically, trying to appear calm.

"You've only just gotten here," Catherine said.

"I've been here a month," she replied. "And the lord commander is needed back in Kharav."

"Well, he's free to go," Alexander said with an edge to his voice.

Norah still couldn't look at him. She took a drink of wine and shifted in her chair. "I need to go with him. He's the only one the king trusts to see me safe in my travels." Norah felt guilty about using Soren as an excuse to leave, but what other reason could she give? That she couldn't let Alexander go so long as he was near? That she couldn't bear the shame? That she needed to leave? Perhaps what would be the most offensive to them—she wanted to go back to Kharav. She wanted to go back to Mikael.

She pulled a small piece of bread from the loaf by her plate, but she worried that she might not be able to swallow it if she put it in her mouth.

"What has he to worry?" Alexander asked. "The Shadowmen are the only ones who would attack the queen of Mercia as she travels."

"And the drifters?" Norah shot back at him.

"I'll see your return to the Shadowlands," he said. "The drifters are pockets of rogues, and they can be managed by any capable army."

"Mercia needs you here," she told him.

"Mercia needs her queen."

Norah banged down her goblet with a force that splashed wine onto the table. "I won't argue this. I'm returning to Kharav. Tomorrow."

She stood abruptly and left the dining hall. As she reached the stair, she heard Alexander's voice behind her.

"Norah," he called, following her.

She kept walking.

"Norah! Please!"

She paused, then turned, forcing herself to look at him. Pain etched across his brow, and she thought she might come undone.

"Why? Tell me why," he begged. His voice dropped to a whisper. "Is it because of me? Because of us? Because of what's between us?"

"There is no us! There's nothing between us." Her words shook as she cried them, and his breath shook as he heard them. "And I don't belong here," she whispered. "I shouldn't be here." And it completely broke her.

Footfalls sounded behind him, but Alexander didn't need to turn to see who it was. He knew.

Adrian.

It was only a matter of time before his brother heard about him calling off the marriage to Ismene, a marriage Adrian had tried so hard to talk him out of accepting to begin with. Why had he accepted it? He had no interest in marrying, he had no interest in Ismene.

But Adrian didn't say anything about the marriage. They sat in the quiet.

"She's leaving," Alexander said finally. "Norah's returning to the Shadowlands."

"Grandmother told me."

Of course she had. Had Catherine also told Adrian to come talk to him? To get Alexander to convince Norah to stay? As if he could. Or perhaps... to make sure Alexander stayed. If only she knew how little choice he had. Norah would go back to the Shadowlands alone.

She would continue to struggle against the world, alone.

Alexander stilled. She didn't have to be completely alone... "You'll go with her."

Adrian's eyes widened. "Me?"

"I can't go." He gripped Adrian's shoulder. "Please. Brother. If things go poorly in the Shadowlands, I need you to get her out. I need you to protect her."

Adrian's mouth opened slightly, with words that wouldn't come, then he said finally, "Of course. Of course, I'll go. But she'll also have Caspian."

Alexander gripped him tighter. "She needs you too. *I* need you with her." Caspian couldn't protect her alone. Adrian was still young, but his skill with a sword rivaled the best of Mercia, and Adrian knew what Norah meant beyond her role as queen. Adrian knew what she meant to Alexander. He would keep her safe.

Norah made her way to the courtyard where the lord commander waited. The Crest sat ready on their mounts, with a new unit of Northern soldiers prepared to march as well. Soren had even arranged for the pirate wards to come with them, not trusting Mercia to retain them.

Alexander walked with Adrian to his horse. She'd been most surprised that Alexander had allowed him to come. She wondered how Adrian had talked him into it.

Alexander clasped arms with his brother, saying words she couldn't hear, then he pulled him into a tight embrace. Norah's heart hurt. She felt like she was taking everything from him.

She stood quietly as he approached her. The blue of his eyes was dull and somber. For a moment, she didn't think she could leave. She wasn't sure when she would see him again, or even if she would see him again. She had no intentions of returning to Mercia, and...

"You can't return to Kharav again," she whispered. Her throat wouldn't give her the voice.

He nodded.

She wanted to hug him one last time, to put her arms around him, but she didn't. "Goodbye, Alexander." She thought she might choke on the words.

"Goodbye, Norah." So cold, with finality.

She mounted Sephir, then looked at her grandmother, who stood at the top of the stair. Catherine had embraced her stiffly inside. It was everything Norah could do to not break. Did everyone she loved hate her now?

The remnants of her heart barely beat in her chest, and she urged Sephir on and away.

Outside the city, Norah stopped and gave one last look to Mercia as Soren pulled his horse up beside her.

"Can it be now?" she whispered.

"Can what be now?"

She turned to him with tears in her eyes. "The vision the seer showed you. If it's to be, let it be now."

The army moved relatively quickly, and Norah was glad for it. She was desperate to get back to Kharav. She traveled with a new unit of Northmen, absent Titus, who she'd left back in Mercia with his new wife.

Norah rode in silent sorrow. It was hard to imagine a life without Alexander. And her guilt ate her. She hadn't let him love someone else, and she'd ruined his hope for happiness. Norah added the weight of the council's disappointment, her grandmother's disappointment, and the hidden enemies she was no closer to finding and no closer to stopping. And now returning to Mikael with no happiness in her heart and no child, she couldn't hold the tears that ran down her cheeks.

Soren moved his mount beside her, drawing close, but still looking ahead. "You bring the young bear back with you. It's unexpected."

Adrian.

She nodded. "I know. I'm surprised Alexander let him come. But I'm glad."

He held out a small cloth, still not looking at her. "And you have your captain. And the mute and the girl are waiting for you back in Kharav. Salar waits for you."

She took the cloth. She knew what he was doing, this destroyer of men. He was trying to make her feel better. And he did. She watched him, sitting on his destrier like a foul-tempered seraph, and she felt the smallest of smiles through her tears.

He eyed her irritably. "Wipe your face. Tahla can't see you like this."

The cool air chilled the beaded sweat on his skin. His panting slowed, and Caspian's body came back to him again. He brushed his fingers along the length of Tahla's bare back as she lay nestled against him on a blanket by the river. They'd slipped away from the village as the sun set, away from the music and the ears and eyes of others.

He'd last left her after she'd confessed her love for him—something he'd never expected to hear. Every day, her words ran through his mind again and brought a smile to his face. And now he was back in her arms, his heart was full.

She propped herself on her elbow and swirled a finger over the curve of his chest. "I've missed you, Northman."

And he'd missed her, more than anything.

She rolled back down, laying her head on his shoulder, and looked up to the sky. "Sometimes I feel like we're Hakah and Umai."

"Who are they?"

She turned her head slightly toward the horizon and pointed to where the sun had already set. Only the fading twilight remained. "See how Hakah stretches his light, even after he's been pulled under the earth? He's trying to catch a glimpse of Umai." Her gaze moved to the eastern sky, searching. She found the faintest outline of the moon starting to appear. "There," she said, pointing. "There's Umai."

She smiled sadly.

"Their paths don't allow them to be together," she continued. "Saddened that he couldn't be with Umai, Hakah's heart broke into thousands of pieces. He scattered them across the sky to create the stars so that when Umai wakes, she can see how much he loves her."

Caspian watched as the sky grew darker and the moon fully emerged with the stars all around.

Tahla nestled against his shoulder again. "But then I remember that Hakah can never hold Umai in his arms. He can't kiss her or touch her. They can't be one." She tipped her face up to his. "Hakah and Umai wish they could be Caspian and Tahla." She stretched her neck to bring her lips closer. "Kiss me, Northman."

And he did.

Chapter Thirty-Seven

Kharav welcomed her return. The breeze kissed her cheeks and lovingly brushed through her hair. The sweet scent of the gardens embraced her. Norah was finally home.

When she reached the courtyard, Mikael was waiting for her. She stopped when she saw him. Nearly two months had passed since she left—two months they'd been apart. Too long. She slid off Sephir, her body stiff and aching. It had been a long journey, a seemingly endless one. But she was finally back where she belonged.

Norah knew how this was supposed to go: she would bow her head in greeting, he would bow in return, then he would offer his arm and she would accept, and he'd lead her into the castle. This was the general way of royal things, not unlike Mercia.

But unlike Mercia, none of that mattered too much to Mikael, and when she reached him, she threw her arms around his neck. He picked her up and held her tightly, and she clung to him.

He pulled back to look at her and cupped her face in his hand. "Are you well, Salara?"

She wasn't well, but he was making it better. All she could do was nod.

"Let's get you inside." With his arm around her, he practically carried her into the castle. She didn't mind. She was almost too tired to carry herself.

Mikael waved everyone off as they reached the great hall. When they were alone, he stopped and turned her to him. "Let me look at you," he said softly. His eyes moved over her face. "You've been gone too long but returned sooner than I'd expected. I"—he brushed her cheek as he paused—"I worried you might not return at all."

"I had to."

His face changed, and he brought his hand to her stomach with asking eyes.

Norah swallowed, then shook her head. The hope on his face gave way to disappointment. Disappointment that there was no child. A deeper sadness seeped into her. "I had to return because Kharav is my home," she told him. "And you're here."

A small smile came to his lips.

Her words weren't just to lift his spirits. They were true.

"And the Bear remains in Mercia?" he asked.

"He won't return."

His smile grew. "Let's get you settled."

Mikael followed her up to their chamber, where Vitalia met her with an unconventional squeal and hug and then went to draw her a much-needed bath. Norah pulled off her overcoat and draped it over the bench at the foot of the bed.

"I've missed you, Salara," he told her as he sat down in the side chair and watched her loosen the lacing on the back of her dress.

Norah stepped in front of him and took his face in her hands. She had missed him too. His skin was warm, and she liked the way his short-cropped beard tickled under her nails.

"I'm hungry," he said, gazing up at her.

She reached up and pulled her hair free from its tie and unraveled the braid with her fingers. "You should call for some food," she said as she stepped toward the bath chamber. "Eat something. I'll just get cleaned up and join you after."

He caught her wrist and pulled her back to him. "It's not food I'm hungry for," he said in a low voice.

Norah couldn't help her smile. She loved his want for her and that he didn't hide it. "You should let me bathe. I'm terribly dirty."

"I like a dirty woman," he argued.

She laughed. "I'll make better love if I'm a clean woman."

His jaw tightened, and a protest rumbled in his chest, but he released her. "Go on then. I'll wait. But not long."

When the water was ready, Vitalia helped her peel off her dress, and she climbed into the tub, relishing its warmth. Vitalia soaped up her hair and poured pitchers of water to rinse it. Years seemed to wash away, and their heaviness with it.

After her hair was clean, she leaned her head back against the tub and closed her eyes. She was tired, but she knew sleep wouldn't come.

"You can go," Mikael's voice came, directed at Vitalia. "I'll take care of my wife tonight."

The door shut behind her.

Norah kept her eyes closed, but a smile crept across her lips. Finally, she opened them to see him leaning against the wall of the bath chamber and watching her.

"So, you missed me, husband?" she asked.

"I did," he replied as he kicked off his boots. He pulled his shirt over his head, and her smile grew.

"What are you doing?" she asked him.

"I'm getting ready."

She raised a brow. "Getting ready for what?"

"For when you say you're clean."

Norah laughed. She'd certainly missed him.

Mikael shucked off his breeches and braies and leaned back against the wall, naked. She turned in the tub so she could lay against the side and see him. The lines of his body stirred something inside her, and suddenly she didn't seem quite as tired.

"Are you clean now?" he asked.

She shook her head with a smile. "No, not yet."

He snorted impatiently. "Hurry up or I'm going to drag you from that tub."

Norah bit her lip to keep from grinning. She'd love to be dragged from the bathtub. She stifled her smile as she pulled a small round of corian root from the dish on the small table beside the tub. She dipped it into the water and worked it into a lather. Rolling her head back, she rubbed it over her neck and her shoulders, taking her time and working it deep, as if soothing her muscles.

A rumble vibrated from him again. She liked this game. How long would he wait? Slowly, she rubbed the soap down her breasts and swirled the sweet-scented lather around her nipples. Then she paused to look back at him.

Mikael was visibly roused for her now, but he kept his place against the wall, patient—too patient for her taste. Norah ran her hands down over her stomach and raised a leg from the water, lathering one, then the other.

Still, he waited.

Her eyes narrowed. She brought her hand down between her thighs, under the water, and gave a small moan. She rolled her head to look at him again, and finally, he surged forward with a growl.

Norah screamed a laugh as he clambered into the tub with her, spilling water over the sides.

"I still have soap on me!" she protested as he moved to carry her out.

"It's a root. I'll eat it off."

"Mikael!" she screamed.

Relenting, he hurriedly splashed her in a quick rinse as she laughed, and then he settled for a moment. "Are you done now, Salara?" he asked her.

She bit her lip and nodded.

His face was serious now. The game was over. Mikael lifted her up and stepped out of the tub. He carried her to the bed and dropped her onto the silken sheets of darkness before prowling over her. Her skin prickled—from the air against her wet skin or his hunting gaze, she wasn't sure.

His body held a different hunger now. No more playfulness in his eyes or sweetness on his lips. He stretched his hand across her chest and held her firmly as he moved between her thighs. She realized this wasn't a taking of passion or of lust, but a taking of need. He claimed her. She was his.

Norah understood this need. She angled her hips to meet him, yielding, and he buried himself inside her. He drove hard, and deep.

She let his madness consume her, knowing it wouldn't last long. Mikael rolled his body as he bared his teeth, pushing himself even deeper. She didn't reach up to touch him, she didn't try to tame him. She let him fill his need, and he did, shuddering to an end.

Mikael held his weight on his elbows as he recovered, panting into her ear. Only then did she dare to touch him. She ran her fingers up his arms and over his shoulders, to the nape of his neck and into his hair. He pulsed inside her, but his body calmed.

He pushed himself up and looked into her eyes.

"Are you back now?" she asked him.

He nodded. Concern marred his brow. "Did I hurt you?"

She shook her head but tightened her grip in his hair. "No," she whispered. "But I'll hurt you if you think you're finished."

A smile came to his lips, and he lowered himself to kiss her.

Chapter Thirty-Eight

Weeks fell to months. Norah wanted to believe she'd settled into a new normal, but the hole in her heart still lingered. She wondered how her grandmother was faring, and Alexander. She'd received two letters with reports of the kingdom, but that's all they'd contained—reports.

She passed the sparring fields on her morning walk and smiled when she saw Cohen. The boy was coming along nicely in his training. He'd been doing well ever since coming to the capital with his sister, Calla.

Cohen was matched with a young Kharavian soldier, and their blades sang through the afternoon sky as they practiced their skill. She stopped and leaned against the fence to watch them.

"He's unbeaten, out of all the earlies. Even second years," Calla said proudly as she came up beside Norah, beaming at her brother.

Norah's eyes widened. "That's impressive."

Earlies were men in the army who showed special promise. They were pulled from the normal regimen and put on an accelerated training plan with the hope they might make the Crest. Even so, less than half of all earlies made it to the Crest. Norah knew all this since Soren regularly told her Calla and Cohen didn't deserve to train with them. Yet, he still had them train with the earlies, the same as he had done with Adrian.

"He'll be a soldier of the Crest one day," Calla said. "The best swordsman in Kharav."

Norah smiled at the girl. Calla was a strong spirit, who loved with the same fervor as she fought, and her loyalty to her brother made Norah emotional sometimes. "I'm sure he'll be amazing."

"He'll never be in the Crest," Soren's voice called behind them.

Norah sighed as she rolled her eyes. *Destroyer of hopes and dreams.* "Way to inspire, Lord Commander," she said.

"False hopes will see you starved in the winter," he said dryly.

Calla scoffed. "But he's the best swordsman on the field!"

Soren cut the girl a daggered look. No one questioned him among the soldiers, and Calla brought a new test he wasn't accustomed to.

He leaned close, using his size. "He can't hear, so he can't control his sound. He's deaf, but he doesn't know what silence is. He can't talk, so he can't command. And at any moment, I could come behind him and slit his throat."

Calla's eyes blazed, and her hand clenched the dagger at her waist.

"Calla," Norah said, breaking the girl from a rash reaction. "Get your brother and go on to your studies."

The girl fumed for a moment before she slipped out from under the commander's force and went to fetch Cohen from his match.

Norah looked at Soren and shook her head.

"What?" he growled. "I'm just being truthful."

"No," she said, shaking her head again. "Sometimes you're just mean."

Norah and Adrian walked through the courtyard as the afternoon waned. They were spending more and more time together, and Norah had started to think of him as her own brother. His playful candor, his cheeky teases, his easy laugh—he made the distance of family seem not so far.

"Anything new from your brother?" she asked him.

"I got a letter from him yesterday, but nothing new. He mainly just asks about me, and if I'm seeing to all my duties." He chuckled.

Norah smiled sadly. "I hope you write him regularly. I'm sure he misses you. You're the only family he's ever had, other than your parents, and now you're gone."

Adrian glanced at her. His mouth opened slightly, but he hesitated before saying, "We had another brother. Did you not know?"

Norah stopped, stunned. She shook her head. How had she not known this?

"He died."

"Oh, Adrian," she breathed. "I'm so sorry. I had no idea. No one's ever talked about him."

"No, I know. And it's all right. It was a long time ago, before I was born. I never knew him. But he and Alexander were close." He started forward again, and they continued walking. "Lucien was his name."

So many questions flooded her mind, but all seemed prying and intrusive. What does one say in times like these, other than *Sorry*?

"And I did send a letter," he said, turning the conversation back to Alexander. "I let him know you were well."

Norah smiled appreciatively. She didn't think it appropriate for her to write him just to tell him how she fared, but he would worry for her, and she did want him to know she was doing all right. "How's Sevina?" she asked.

A bashful grin came to his face, and he looked down at his feet. "She's well. I, uh... I've been meaning to talk to you... about her."

She smiled at his nervousness.

"I, um... I plan to ask for her hand."

Norah's eyes widened as she searched for words. "Adrian, that's exciting and... unexpected!" She paused. "Are you sure?"

"Of course I'm sure. I know I'm young, but I can still know what I want."

She didn't disagree, but it was such a big decision. "Have you thought about asking Alexander's advice?"

Adrian quieted, then he said, "No, he wouldn't approve of a Kharavian wife."

Norah's heart hurt that Adrian would keep something from Alexander, and something so significant. "But he's going to find out eventually," she said. "And that would make things very hard between the two of you."

He bit his bottom lip but didn't answer.

"I'm not saying to ask his permission," she said. "Of course you can make your own decisions. But you should still talk to him. Just think about it, okay?"

He nodded.

As they drew nearer to the castle, Norah slowed. Two wagons sat by the fountain, with Mikael beside them reading a letter in his hand. His face was dark and fixed, and Norah knew him well enough to know something bothered him.

"I'll catch up with you later," she told Adrian.

"Of course," he said, and headed back toward the sparring field.

"Is something wrong?" she called to Mikael as she approached.

He looked up from the letter and folded it before slipping it inside his jacket. "Nothing you need trouble yourself with," he said.

She raised a brow. "That wasn't condescending at all."

He sighed. "I'm sorry." Then he offered her his arm, and they walked toward the castle. "Gregor only sends a quarter of his due trade," he told her. "He says he's suffered a failed crop, and it's all he can part with."

Norah pursed her lips as a weight sunk in her stomach. "Do you believe him?"

Mikael shook his head. "No. Our own crops have fared well. Japheth has some of the most fertile lands in the world, and I've not heard of any news of pests or disease. And the herbs he doesn't send—they're medicinal ones, those that can be found only in the Colored Valley. They're the most valuable to us."

"So you think he does this intentionally?"

Mikael stopped. "I don't know what to think. If it's intentional, it confirms what I feared. He's built an alliance with another." The line of his jaw rippled as he looked back at the wagons. "We have shipments of rice and grain to be sent within a few weeks' time. If I send them, it's a statement that I accept his excuse. If I don't, I essentially call him a liar and force his next move."

"What will you do?"

He shook his head. "I haven't decided."

Quiet filled the room as they ate their evening meal. Since returning from Mercia, Soren had resumed eating with them, and even Salara-Mae had taken to joining. But the king's mother still made no attempt to hide her disdain for the lord commander.

Cusco and Cavaatsa lay at Norah's feet, and she shuffled her toes under Cusco's warm belly. She watched Mikael as he sat without eating, only drinking from his chalice. Japheth and the trade dilemma were still heavy on his mind.

Salara-Mae dropped a small chunk of meat to the ground for Cusco, and the large dog swallowed it without chewing. Soren looked at her in surprise, but she avoided his eyes. "The beasts have become quite tolerable," she said to Norah, "now that you've been seeing to them."

Norah smiled but swallowed it back when Soren turned his offended eyes to her. She'd done nothing different with the dogs, other than allow them some additional poor behaviors. She shrugged at Soren apologetically. He set his attention back on his meal, and Norah's lips curved upward again. But her amusement was short-lived. Mikael smoothed his short-cut beard on his chin, gazing out the side windows, and it drew her thoughts back to his worry.

"You haven't gone hunting in a while," Norah said, pulling his attention back to the present.

He drew in a long breath and let it out as he set his chalice on the table. Then he nodded. "That's a good idea. I think I'll go tomorrow."

"Will you take Adrian?" she asked. Not surprisingly, neither Mikael nor the commander balked at the idea. Adrian was doing well in Kharav. He was smart, learned quickly, and could handle his own on the field. He was already growing on them, and—she smiled—they didn't even realize it.

"Have you decided what you'll do about King Gregor?" she asked, and Soren sat back in his chair, also curious.

Mikael's eyes met hers, but he didn't answer.

"Send me to collect the rest of the trade," Soren told him.

Send him to intimidate him was more like it. "That's the opposite of what you should do," Norah said, drawing an annoyed look from the commander. "You should talk to him."

"You would have me call him out as a liar?" Mikael said.

"I'd have you talk to him like a rational human being—I think it's okay if he knows that you're unhappy with this situation, that it raises suspicion. But I wouldn't so boldly threaten him."

Soren snorted, "Like *you* did when he was here last?"

She pursed her lips at him. "Let me remind you that was to save *your* skin, which I assumed was more important than a partial shipment of herbs." Her eyes narrowed. "I do wonder if it was the right decision sometimes." She looked back to Mikael. "Either talk to him or send your shipment due."

"He tests me," Mikael said.

"You should be sure that Gregor's leaning away from his alliance with you before you act. Buy yourself some time to discover more, or time to prepare if there *is* to be a confrontation."

"He'll think me weak."

"Which is why you should send me," Soren insisted.

Norah disagreed. "You should respond in a way that shows less paranoia and more confidence. Just send your shipment. It gives you time, it makes it easier if you ever come to your senses and actually decide to talk to him, and it shows you aren't worried. Act as though: Who of any intelligence would dare break an agreement with Salar of Kharav?"

Mikael sat, mulling. He took a drink from his chalice as she and Soren watched him. Then he turned to Soren. "Send the shipment."

The commander glared at Norah with anger thick across his brow, but he gave a forced nod to his king. Still, she knew this situation was anything but resolved.

"Did you know Alexander had another brother?"

Caspian's head snapped up. "Where did you hear this?"

They stood in the library, and Norah pushed the book in her hand back onto its place on the shelf. "Did you know?" she asked again.

He nodded with a long exhale. "I did." His eyes grew somber. "Lucien."

"Why has no one talked about him? No one told me."

He gave an apologetic tilt of his head. "It was a long time ago."

"Still, it seems important."

"It was," he admitted. "*Is.*"

"Will you tell me about him? What happened?"

Caspian glanced down uncomfortably. She knew he didn't like speaking about others, especially their private lives, and especially Alexander's.

"If I were in Mercia, I'd ask Alexander himself," she added. "But I can't, and it's not something I'd write him about."

He still seemed to mull over her ask.

"Would he not tell me?" she asked.

"Of course he would." He glanced around them to ensure their conversation stayed private, before giving a relenting sigh. "They were very young when Lucien died. Seven, eight. They were very close."

Norah waited for him to continue, but he didn't say anything else. It was as if he thought that were enough. "How did he die?" she pressed.

"A sickness took him."

And? Caspian was the worst storyteller. "Is that when Alexander came to stay at the castle?" she prompted. "When did Adrian come? And what happened to their mother?"

Caspian sighed again, not pleased at all with her questions. "After Lucien died, their mother went mad with grief. She would have nightmares and couldn't sleep. She would hear him." He paused again, but continued before Norah asked another question. "She became confused and would lock everyone out of the house. Massey would find Alexander forced outside almost every time she stopped by."

Norah's heart hurt. "Who's Massey?"

"She ran the kitchen in the castle. Still does. Lady Catherine had Massey take meals to Alexander's mother because her mind was too far gone to look after herself. One day, Massey came back and said Alexander was forced outside again—it was the dead of winter—and Lady Catherine went and got him and brought him back to the castle."

"My grandmother?"

He nodded. "She does have a heart, Regal High."

"What happened to his mother?"

"She went through a period where she seemed to get better. But it wasn't long after Adrian was born that she started to deteriorate again. Things were rough for a long time, and she ended up taking her own life. That's when Adrian came to the castle."

"Oh," Norah breathed. That was so much more terrible than she'd thought. She was actually relieved she hadn't asked Alexander about his mother. She'd come close several times. Surely it would have been hard for him to have told her this story. Her mind turned to Caspian. He'd been close with Alexander growing up. He obviously knew everything about him, even the most private of details.

"Did you live in the castle?" she asked him.

He shook his head. "No, but I was always there, it seemed. My father was a field captain, gone a lot, and my mother taught the nobles' children there. She even helped tutor you."

Norah smiled. "Were you and I close as children?"

Caspian shook his head again. "No. We didn't know each other, really. Alexander and I studied and practiced together, but you had private schooling." He chuckled. "But I know Alexander taught you the sword. I used to ask him all the time if he wanted to spar, and he would tell me he wasn't up to it. Then I'd see you both in the field behind the stables with your swords. That's how he got so good, you know. He wasn't sparring with other boys; he was sparring with you."

They both let out a laugh. An easy quiet returned between them.

"Thank you for sharing all of this with me, Caspian," she said softly.

CHAPTER THIRTY-NINE

Norah sat on the edge of the bathtub, holding her wadded nightgown in her hands. Inside it were the few spots of blood that told her there was still no child. The months had fallen away, and still there was nothing. She had consulted with fertility wisewomen, charting her cycles and meticulously planning. She had talked to the healer, and even Salara-Mae, who had put her on a regimented diet of disgustingly healthy food. And yet, nothing.

Mikael still wrestled with the foretelling of his own end, and with the nobles growing more restless without an heir, she could feel his increasing desperation with each passing month. They needed a child. As each month came and went, she felt like she was failing him.

Norah put her hand on her stomach, wondering what it would be like to have a child. *A baby*. How strange it would feel to have something inside—living, growing, kicking.

She spread her fingers against her skin. What if she couldn't bear a child? No, she couldn't think like that. She breathed deeply and tried to channel positive thoughts. She imagined herself already pregnant. But her mind drifted to other worries. Would Kharav love him? A half Northman. Would Mercia accept him?

She still needed something more positive, she told herself. What would she name him? What would she lovingly call him? She wondered if he would look like Mikael, or like her. Surely he would look like his father, and she smiled.

"Salara," Mikael's voice called softly, and she looked up to see him in the doorway. His breaths came short and uneven in seeing her, his eyes hopeful.

Her smile fell. He had misread her. Emotion swept through her. All she could do was shake her head.

Mikael let out a long exhale but came to her, pulling her up and holding her close. This was their monthly ritual, their monthly curse.

He kissed the top of her head. "Don't worry yourself," he whispered.

"The summer is beautiful," Salara-Mae said as she cut a lemon in half and squeezed it into her cup of tea. "It will be gone too soon."

"It will," Norah said quietly. It was late summer in Kharav and more stunning than she had ever imagined. The earth was green with life, flowers of every color covered the ground, glowing brilliantly against the black of the mortite rock.

They finished their breakfast and walked through the doors and into the sun. Since learning about Norah's efforts to become pregnant, Salara-Mae insisted that she get regular exercise. Norah didn't mind. It felt good to be out and stretch her legs. They'd made a habit of walking the castle grounds after eating, soaking in the light and clipping colors from the gardens. Norah had come to care for Salara-Mae. She reminded her of her grandmother—cheekily foul and unintentionally amusing.

As they walked, Salara-Mae pulled out a small sachet and held it out for her.

Norah looked at her curiously and then took it. "What's this?"

"For the child," she said. "Torith root, from Lorys. My cousin has written to tell me how effective it's proven with women trying to conceive."

"Your cousin's in Lorys?"

"No, no. Of course not. She's in Etreus, but after I wrote to her, she wrote her sister-in-law in Pryam, who said that her own wisewoman, who is from Lorys, recommended it. Eat it directly. But she warns, it's bitter."

Norah pursed her lips. Salara-Mae meant well, but at this rate, the entire world would know her plight. She could see it now: her grandmother receiving a message from a port merchant that she was trying to get pregnant with the Shadow King. And failing.

"Don't worry, I didn't mention your condition," Salara-Mae said, seeming to read her mind. "I merely asked."

This woman was as inconspicuous as Catherine. "And who will they think you're asking for?" Norah scoffed back. "Not yourself."

"Regardless, it's already obvious. You've been married quite some time now, and anyone can count the months and know there's a challenge."

A wave of emotion took her by surprise. Perhaps it was the pressure, the constant disappointment, or maybe the desperation. She bit the inside of her cheek to hold it back. She shoved the sachet in her pocket and noticed Caspian approaching.

His face told her he brought news—bad news, likely. Whatever it was, it couldn't be as bad as the conversation now.

"Queen Norah," he greeted as he drew near. "I need to speak with you. Urgently."

She was relieved to slip away from the conversation with Salara-Mae, but a weight grew in her stomach at what Caspian brought. She nodded to Salara-Mae, who gave a small bow of her head in return, and she followed Caspian back toward the castle.

"News just arrived," he told her as they walked. "Aleon has taken Tarsus."

"What?" That *was* news. "King Phillip has taken Tarsus?"

He nodded.

The island kingdom of Tarsus was small but extremely wealthy. It was a premier trading port, where merchants paid high royalties for inclusion, but collected wealth in the sale of their goods many times over. Only goods of exceptional quality were sold in Tarsus, and it was common for luxury merchants to deal only in trade that had been exchanged there, as demanded by their buyers. Mercia sold most of her steel goods there.

Few had ever dared to attack the trading nation. The island was known for their fierce warriors, who savagely protected their harbors.

Norah's brows drew together. "Why would he take Tarsus?"

Caspian shrugged. "To accomplish what his grandfather couldn't, perhaps? But Queen Norah, this will surely make Salar nervous. If Phillip is trying to succeed where his grandfather failed, he could set his sights on Kharav."

Aleon had once tried to take Kharav.

Norah shook her head. "No. That doesn't make sense. Phillip doesn't have the power to war against Kharav and Mercia and Japheth."

"But does Mercia really stand with Kharav? The council's already been in contact with Phillip. You know this. You have a standing offer of marriage. And it's rumored that Kharav and Japheth's alliance is failing."

"Where did you hear that?"

He frowned. "Most everywhere."

Norah's stomach twisted. This would put Mikael on edge.

Caspian held out a letter. "And this arrived for you."

Norah's breath caught in her throat. The letter bore Alexander's seal. She nodded to her captain, excusing him. "Thank you, Caspian."

She paused for a moment and sat down on a bench at the edge of the garden, holding the letter in her hands, desperate to open it but afraid. They hadn't written to each other since she left Mercia. She imagined what its words held.

Norah ran her fingers over the seal, a steely blue wax that shimmered in the sunlight—the seal Alexander had poured and stamped with his own hand. Gathering her courage, she pulled the paper apart, careful not to crack the wax bear embossment.

But as she read the words, her heart sank. Then she rose, turning to the castle to find Mikael.

The king stood with the lord commander in his study, his face stoic and overly calm—the face that worried her.

"You've heard the news then?" he asked when he saw her enter.

She nodded. "Caspian's just informed me."

He frowned. "The Aleon Empire grows."

"Why would he want Tarsus?" she asked.

"Who doesn't want Tarsus?" Soren rumbled.

"It just doesn't make sense that he would do it now."

"Of course it makes sense," Soren said. "This Aleon king is just like his grandfather."

"But while he's on the brink of war with Japheth?"

"It boosts Gregor's confidence, I'm sure," Mikael said. "To know his brother is occupied."

He wasn't seeing her point. Norah sighed. She didn't come to debate Aleon. She held up the parchment from Alexander. "A letter's come from Mercia."

"From the Bear?" Soren asked.

She nodded. "The outlying villages of Mercia are still being attacked. The lord justice has stretched our forces across the kingdom, and it's still not enough. He asks for men."

Soren's brow dipped in irritation. "We can't send men to Mercia. Not while Aleon advances, and Japheth plays games."

"Aleon does not *advance*," Norah argued. "Tarsus is in the opposite direction of Kharav."

"You know his plans?" Soren asked.

"No, but it just doesn't make sense that Phillip would march on Kharav, not right now."

"Whether it makes sense to Salara, the threat is still there," Soren argued to Mikael. "We need all men in Kharav."

Mikael moved to Norah and eyed the letter. She offered it to him, and he took it and read it quietly. "It's so formal," he said.

Norah swallowed. It was. He hadn't even asked how she was. She guiltily pushed down the emotion. She shouldn't want him to. She should want him to not think of her, as she tried not to think about him.

Mikael refolded it, and looked at the seal for a moment before handing it back to her and glancing at Soren. "Send two thousand men."

Norah's eyes met his in surprise. He was giving her men?

Soren pushed out a breath between his teeth in anger, but he didn't speak his objection.

She nodded. "Thank you."

Mikael reached up and brushed her cheek with his fingers. "Of course."

Chapter Forty

Alexander sat back in the chair at his desk and let out a weary sigh. He stacked the army's status reports and shuffled them into a leather cover before standing and sliding it into the cabinet behind him. It was late morning, and he'd worked all night—preparing updates for the council, issuing directives, reviewing grievances, approving payments—anything to keep his mind occupied.

To keep his mind from her.

Norah.

He'd written her out of desperation, to the horror of the council. They didn't want help from the Shadowlands, but they were out of options. Alexander had put it off as long as he could—partly at the council's urging, partly because he couldn't form the words that he knew Norah would be reading from his pen. He'd started his letter a hundred times, and the fireplace in his study had burned bright with his discarded pages. He wanted to know how she was, if she was well, if she was happy. Did he really want to know if she was happy?

Happy with *the Shadow King.*

He could still feel her kiss on his lips, see her smile when he closed his eyes, hear her voice in his mind. But he wrote none of this, at least not in the letter he sent.

Did she think of him? *No.* She cared for him deeply, he knew, but he didn't have her heart. Not anymore. Not in the way he used to.

But he did want her to be happy. Even if it wasn't with him. Even if it was with... he put the thought from his mind. He settled with the hope that she was simply happy.

He wondered how Adrian fared. He surprised even himself when he had sent his brother to Kharav. But Norah needed loyal men, trusted men, good men, and his brother was as good as they came. Adrian would hold the Mercian values and remind her who she was. He wouldn't let her drown in the darkness of the shadows. Alexander needed him, but Norah needed him more.

The bells rang out, and he headed to the courtyard. His eyes widened at the army of Shadowmen approaching. It was larger than he'd expected, a pleasant surprise, and he strode out to meet them.

James and Edward stood at the top of the castle stair. Edward shook with disgust, and Alexander followed his eyes to the Shadowman leading the army.

Not Shadow*man*.

Shadow *woman*.

A wrap covered her face, as with all Shadowmen, but she wore a fitted breastplate molded to her shape. Her *every* shape. He peeled his eyes from the steel breasts and swallowed back his discomfort as she slid from her horse.

She cast a cold eye around the courtyard. "I'm here for the Bear," she called.

"Have you come to serve?" Alexander asked.

She stepped in front of him. "Call him."

"He doesn't come to your call."

In a flash, she ripped her short sword from the sheath on her back and had it at his throat. Around him, his Northmen pulled their swords, and the whole of the Kharavian unit followed suit.

"I'm not here to play games, Northman," she seethed. "I've been sent by the lord commander to aid your failing Bear."

That certainly sounded like the lord commander. "Then perhaps you might lower your blade from his neck."

Her eyes narrowed. "You're the Bear?"

He gave an ever so slight nod of his head.

"You don't look like a bear."

"So I've been told."

She eyed him suspiciously as she needled the tip of her blade into his skin.

"Do you mean to draw blood?" he asked her.

Her eyes smiled. "Consider it a proper Kharavian greeting." Slowly, she withdrew the blade and took a step back, still eyeing him as if deciding whether to obey her orders or kill him.

"I knew this was a mistake," Edward called from behind them. "We don't need the help of heathens! Send them back."

They did need the help, heathens or no, but were the Shadowmen really here to help them? Alexander supposed he'd find out.

Alexander stood in his bath chamber. He leaned forward and tilted his head in the mirror, eyeing the mark still on his skin from the Shadow woman's blade. She'd cut him. It was a small break in the skin, but she'd actually cut him—in the middle of his own courtyard, surrounded by his own men. He pulled on a shirt over his head and tucked it into his breeches, but then he couldn't help but be drawn back to the mirror and the mark on his neck. She'd *actually* cut him.

Of course the lord commander would send her—a woman like that. No doubt she'd give him more than a small cut if he wasn't careful. Perhaps he might want to sleep with one eye open. He pushed out a breath and finished dressing. The best he could do was resolve whoever was attacking the Mercian villages, and send her and the Shadow army back to the Shadowlands.

He walked out to the barracks and a tented station beyond where the Shadow soldiers were settling. Two thousand men were a lot to house, but it was only for the evening, until he dispersed them out to their assignments. Now to find this woman...

It didn't prove difficult. As he reached the Shadow army, she stepped out to meet him. Her eyes were large and dark and steeped in distrust. "Have you come with your orders, Bear?" she asked with daggers in her voice. She didn't want to be here any more than he wanted her here. Good—she'd be motivated to help him find out who was attacking the villages, end it, and leave.

"What's your name?" he asked her.

"Captain Katya Sator."

Captain? Interesting. "Can I call you Katya?"

"No."

This was going to be challenging. "Very well, *Captain.*" His gaze traveled down until it met the molded full breasts on her breastplate, and he glanced away.

"You can look," she taunted. "I worked hard to make it exactly the same." She stepped closer to him, enjoying his unease.

He met her stare but didn't let his gaze wander again.

Her eyes smiled. "You don't like it?"

He didn't answer.

"I hear Northmen don't allow themselves pleasures of the flesh if they're not married. Is this true?" She was purely seeking his discomfort now, trying to get a rise out of him.

And it was working.

She stepped closer. "What's wrong, Bear? Worried I might corrupt you?"

As if she could. "I'm worried you might like it here and decide to stay," he quipped back.

She snorted, and her eyes laughed. "If you Northmen are as bad in bed as you are with a sword, you needn't worry about that."

He drew in a breath as he leaned back on his heel, and she gave him a cruel wink and stepped around him.

CHAPTER FORTY-ONE

Norah breathed in the crisp autumn air, trying to appreciate it while she could. She urged Sephir back to the stables and slid to the ground. It felt good to be outside, to feel the wind on her face and to spend time with the mare. She held some carrot pieces in the palm of her hand and gave a small laugh as the horse lipped them up.

She waved at the stable boy, who took Sephir for a brush down, and she set her thoughts on the rest of the day. But she turned when she heard Adrian's voice.

"Queen Norah," he greeted her, and she smiled.

"Adrian."

"Uh, I was hoping, uh..." He shifted with troubled eyes. "Can I speak to you?"

Her brows drew together. "Of course. Is everything all right?"

Adrian wrung his hands nervously as he took a breath. "Sevina's with child," he blurted.

Her breath caught in her throat. "What?" she breathed.

He opened his mouth, but no words came. He only nodded.

"Oh, Adrian. I... I don't know what to say." She paused. "How is she?"

He shook his head. "I, uh..." He shuffled as he drew a breath. "I, uh, asked her father for her hand."

"Oh!" she said, nodding. This was good then.

"He said no."

"Oh," she breathed again. This was bad.

"He doesn't know, though, about the baby, but"—Adrian licked his lips—"she's scared now." He paused again. "I am too. I... I don't know what to do."

Norah nodded, taking it all in. "Why did her father say no?"

He shrugged, and she could see his frustration. "Because it's customary for nobles to make a Provision Promise, a large payment that can be put aside to sustain a woman—well, their children—if her husband dies."

"Oh, Adrian," she said, letting out a breath of relief with a small smile. "I can help you with money, if that's all you need."

He shook his head. "Alec would kill me. It would dishonor him for the crown to pay for what's my responsibility. And it's more than just the money. I'm a Northman and brother to the Mercian lord justice, who does *not* hold favor here. Understandably."

Norah sighed sadly. "You should write to Alexander."

"And tell him I got a woman from the Shadowlands pregnant out of wedlock?" He shook his head. "I'd rather face her father." He swallowed, shifting nervously again. He was worried, and her heart hurt for him. This should be the best of news, not the worst of news.

"I have to go," he said. "The lord commander's expecting me."

She nodded. "Hey," she said, making him pause. "We'll figure this out. There are options, just let me think on it. Let's talk later, okay?"

He nodded somberly.

Norah needed air. Adrian's news brought complex emotions. She tried to put on a brave face, but she had no idea what they would do about Sevina. Returning to the castle wouldn't bring answers, and she decided to follow Adrian to the sparring fields. She leaned against the fence and watched the earlies—those soldiers hopeful of one day being on the Crest—testing their skills.

Adrian fought with them, although he wasn't one of them. The lord commander had explicitly told him he wasn't considered an early, yet he insisted Adrian be at every training. The same with Calla and Cohen. At first, Norah had thought he was purposefully making it as difficult as he could for them, hoping they would fail, trying to *make* them fail. But then she caught him occasionally offering genuine guidance—correcting their stance, adjusting their hold on the weapons, and even nodding approvingly when they did something right.

Adrian squared off on the field, sparring with a young man quite a bit larger than he was. Not that Adrian was a small man, by any means. He was a full head's height taller than Norah, like Alexander. Adrian's opponent attacked with powerful swings of his sword, but Adrian was fast and maneuvered around him easily.

"Shield up!" a voice boomed.

She turned to see Soren walking toward the men.

Adrian quickly brought his shield up as he continued to spar, but just as quickly forgot and dropped it back down as he darted around his rival.

"Shield up!" Soren bellowed again.

Adrian jerked it back up, continuing to work his opponent, but as he cut behind the early, he dropped it low again for more range of his sword arm.

Soren stalked out to the field and grabbed the early by his practice armor, shoving him back and pulling his own sword. He launched a swinging blow at Adrian. Adrian darted to the side, but Soren pivoted with a surprising grace. The commander sliced through the air and poured down blows on Adrian with a fury. The attack threw the Northman back, and he shouldered his shield as he crouched low behind it. Wood splintered from the shield as Adrian stumbled farther back. Each blow from Soren had the power of death behind it. Norah's breath caught in her throat. Soren drove Adrian against the railing, cornering him and raining a storm down over him.

"Soren!" Norah cried.

The lord commander paused and drew back.

Adrian straightened slowly, holding his shield high, breathless with the exertion of defense.

The commander grabbed Adrian's shield and pulled it down, using it to slam him up against the railing. "*That* is what battle's like," he snarled. "The enemy doesn't dance around. He attacks with everything he has because it's you or him. Your speed will help you, but your shield will save your life. *Keep. It. Up!*" Soren shoved him back and then walked to where Norah was standing. "Again!" he called back over his shoulder, and the men came together for another round.

Norah tried to steady her breath. "Was that really necessary?" she hissed. "You could have seriously hurt him!"

"He has to learn," he rumbled as he watched the sparring.

Or lose a limb, Norah thought to herself. More likely lose a limb. "You don't have to be that hard on him."

He pulled his eyes from the men and glared at her. "I do." Then he looked back out to the field. "I can't be soft with him. He's going to be a commander one day. A great one."

Norah stared at him. This man confounded her. He obviously cared, in his own strange Soren-like way, but she wasn't sure if it was a blessing or a curse. She hoped it a blessing because she needed his help now.

"Regarding Adrian," she said, "there's something I want to talk to you about."

"You're not sending him back," he said firmly.

"No, um," she paused, puzzled by his concern with that. "I'm not. No. Something else. Um…" Why was this so hard? "What if Adrian had his eye on someone, a woman, that he wanted to wed?"

"The doe?" he asked without looking at her, his eyes still on the men in the field.

Soren's description of the girl felt… strangely accurate. Any other time Norah would have been amused. "Sevina, yes. What if he wanted to marry her?"

"Her family's one of the oldest noble families in Kharav. Getting her hand won't be an easy task. The Bear needs to speak to her father. He's the head of the family, yes?"

"Yes, but… Well, obviously he isn't here, and even if he were, your entire army thinks he's the enemy of Kharav, so I don't imagine that would go well."

He chuckled darkly. "Probably not," he said, still not taking his eyes from the earlies.

Not helpful at all. "Then what should Adrian do?" she pressed.

He looked at her, his annoyance etched on his face. "He should find another woman," he said shortly. "Or better yet, no woman at all. I want him focused on his study." Then he turned his eyes back to the field.

Norah huffed a frustrated breath as she shook her head. This man was impossible. But she needed his help. Adrian needed his help.

"Sevina's with child," she said abruptly. She pursed her lips together and pulled them in between her teeth. Her stomach twisted as she waited for a reaction.

He didn't look at her, but neither did he look at the field. His brows came together, but he didn't speak. Concern? Anger?

"He told you this?" he asked finally.

"Yes. He asked for her hand, and Sevina's father denied it. Something about a Provision Promise and how he's a Northman and brother to the lord justice."

Soren was silent for a moment, then he said, "He needs to tell his brother. It will be the Bear's responsibility."

She shook her head. "I don't think I can get him to do that. He fears Alexander's disappointment too much."

Soren gave her an irritated scowl and then pushed himself off the railing with a rumble in his chest. "Spears!" he bellowed out over the field and left to rejoin his earlies.

Norah sighed in frustration. She didn't know what she had expected—certainly not compassion—but she'd hoped he might offer some options, a recommendation, even a sliver of advice. But he gave nothing, perhaps because there was nothing. She wasn't willing to accept that yet. She had to figure something out, and she turned and headed back to the castle.

Chapter Forty-Two

Norah sat on the bed, clutching her knees to her chest. Her blood cycle had come again. Still, there was no child. She tried to shake her growing obsession, but it was all she could think about. While Mikael showed kindness with each month's disappointment, she knew the burden weighed heavily on him. And it killed her. She couldn't bear telling him again. She sent her maids away and waited in the dim candlelight.

Norah heard Mikael's voice outside the chamber, and she quickly wiped the tears from her face. The chamber door opened.

"... send word to Lord..." His voice quieted. There was a pause, then he said, "We'll discuss it tomorrow." The chamber door closed. His footsteps were slow to bring him around the hanging panels.

He saw her and sighed, unfastening his sword belt and leaning it against the wall.

She stood as she searched for the words she'd said so many times before. "Mikael. I—"

"You needn't say it."

He stepped close and pulled her in, as he always did, holding her tight and kissing the top of her head, as he always did.

"Nineteen," she whispered.

"What?"

"Nineteen months we've been together. Nineteen months with no child." She couldn't stop the tears now. "Mikael, we need to come to terms with the fact that I may not be able to give you one." She pulled away from him and sat on the bed and covered her face with her hands.

"Stop," he said as he sat beside her, running his hands nervously over his thighs.

"No," she said through her tears. "We have to be honest about this." She shook her head through her tears. "I'm failing you."

His face twisted. He reached out and caught her hands and pulled them to his lips. He kissed her palms, breathing in deeply. "Or maybe it's me," he said finally.

Her brows drew together in confusion. "What?"

He stood and ran his hand across his face. "By the time my father was my age, he had four daughters between his other wives and concubines, and my mother became pregnant with me within the first few months of their marriage. I had three wives, and... others... but I haven't borne a single child—with anyone."

Norah swallowed, trying to make sense of his words. She shook her head. Mikael's inability to produce an heir was just as haunting. What would they do? What would the nobles do? And they didn't need an heir just for Kharav. She wanted a child. She wanted to be a mother.

Her heart beat with the weight of defeat. "That's it, then? We can't have a child?"

His eyes glistened with sadness.

She looked down as she gathered her gown in her fists. After everything she'd been through, the gods still cursed her.

Mikael ran his hands through his hair. "But we need an heir, Salara. You need a child." He pulled her chin to look at him. "You need to take another," he said softly.

"What?" she gasped as she stumbled up from the bed and backed away from him.

His voice came hoarsely. "You have to take another. It's the only way."

She pulled back farther, and her face wrinkled in disgust. He couldn't possibly be considering such a revolting idea.

"You think I suggest this lightly?" he asked.

"We can keep trying!" she cried.

He stood, moving toward her as she retreated. "And keep doing this? Month after month, year after year? Until I'm dead?" He grasped her arm to stop her retreat. "I *am* going to die, Salara. We've both seen my fall."

A sob ripped from her throat, but he didn't relent.

"And then you'll be overthrown," he said. "Whether by the Kharavian nobles or the North, you won't keep the throne without a child."

"Soren won't let that happen!"

"Soren is one man! And he'll die too. He won't tell me, but I know he's seen his death. I know that's what the seer showed him."

Her lip trembled. She knew what the seer had shown Soren, and it wasn't his own death. It was hers, by his hand. That's why he hadn't told Mikael, and she wouldn't tell him either.

Norah shook her head. "I can't..." She felt sick, and she ripped her arm free from him and took another step back. "I'll go to war first." Her emotion came thicker now; a deep hurt spiked her heart. "And that you would even think..." She couldn't finish through her tears.

"Salara—"

"No," she said as she took another step back. Her hurt turned to anger. "How can you even ask that of me? To whore myself?"

He stopped, and pain snaked across his brow. "That's not... Salara, I didn't mean..." He reached out and pulled her back to him, wrapping his arms around her. "I'm sorry," he whispered. "Forgive me. I should have never said it. I should have never thought it." He squeezed her tightly. "I'm sorry."

Sun poured through the windowed halls giving the impression of warmth, deceivingly so. Outside, the air was frigid. Norah walked deep in thought. When her emotion had subsided, her anger toward Mikael faded. She had spoken harshly to him. When he had suggested... she'd felt so betrayed. But his words weren't an act of betrayal; they came out of desperation—desperation for her.

They needed a child. She wanted a child. But a child would require a pregnancy and a pregnancy would require... another. An overwhelming shame came with the thought—the shame of sharing something so private, the shame of defeat. And there was no one she trusted with that shame. Even if she could, who could be trusted with a secret that could break a kingdom?

Norah turned the corner and almost collided with another, breaking her abruptly from her thoughts.

Soren reached out and caught her. "Salara."

"Lord Commander," she said, shaken. He always seemed to catch her off guard at the worst times.

"Where's the boy?" he asked.

She shook her head, trying to get her wits about her. "What?"

"Where is the boy?"

"Um, Adrian? I don't know," she said, looking around. "The field, or the stables, maybe?"

"He's not on the field. Come on." He turned on his heel and headed toward the stables.

Norah let out a breath of confusion. She wasn't sure what was going on, but she followed. She almost had to run to keep up. "What's going on?"

"How quickly can you manage a wedding?"

"What? What do you mean?"

"How quickly can you manage a wedding?" he asked again.

She rolled her eyes. "When I ask you for more, you can't use the same words." She grabbed him, pulling him to a stop. "Soren! What wedding?"

"Where is the boy?"

She pursed her lips in frustration. "Stop answering a question with a question—" She stopped. Her eyes widened. "Did you get Sevina's father's blessing? Is Adrian to marry her?"

The lord commander pushed out a breath. He wasn't wearing his wrap, and his annoyance was written all over his face. "What other wedding would I be referring to?"

Norah drew her brows together. "You're a terrible communicator."

His jaw tightened and his nostrils flared.

"There!" she pointed to the end of the stable. "There he is."

"Boy!" the commander thundered.

Adrian came quickly to the commander's call. "Yes, my lord," he said when he reached them.

"Go get your doe, get ready."

"What?" Adrian asked.

The commander snorted his frustration at all the questions. "You're getting married."

Adrian looked at Norah with the same shocked expression that she was sure she'd had only moments before. Then he looked back at Soren. "I don't understand. What about her father? He denied me—"

"I've managed it," the commander told him.

"How?" Adrian breathed.

"You needn't worry about that. Go see to your preparations."

Adrian grinned, almost in tears. He rushed forward and hugged Soren, catching the commander by surprise. Soren stood stiffly, his wince giving away his distaste for affection. Norah bit her lip to hold back her own emotion. Then Adrian hugged Norah and ran off to find Sevina.

She looked at Soren incredulously. "What did you say to her father to make him change his mind?"

Irritation rippled over his brow. "Am I not a persuasive man?"

Norah smiled.

The wedding was relatively small, but beautifully arranged, given that it was done in two days' time. A surprising number of soldiers attended. Norah hadn't realized all the friendships Adrian had formed, especially among the Kharavian army.

Serene and Vitalia had hung strings of flowers from a private hall in the castle, and Calla braided winter blossoms into Sevina's hair. The girl was beautiful, and she beamed at Adrian as he ceremoniously looped the silk ribbon around her waist and tied it.

Norah remembered her own wedding as she watched. She slipped her hand into Mikael's, squeezing it tightly. Was he feeling nostalgic too?

He put his arm around her and pulled her close. "Do you remember when you pulled out your own ribbon at our wedding?" he whispered. "Of course I already knew I wanted to marry you, obviously, since I was in the middle of doing so. But that is when I doubly knew."

She smiled.

After the ceremony, they hosted a dinner in the dining hall, and laughter rippled through the air. Norah's heart was full. Everything was perfect.

She walked around the mingling guests, and found Aman Arvedi, Sevina's father.

He bowed his head as she approached. "Salara," he greeted.

"Lord Aman," she greeted back. "This marriage has made Adrian extremely happy. He's going to be a wonderful husband. He loves your daughter. Very much."

Aman nodded, obligingly.

"May I ask, what made you change your mind? I know Adrian asked for her hand prior."

"A Provision Promise by the lord commander is not one to be refused," he said.

What? Norah's mouth fell open. "The lord commander made the Provision Promise for Adrian?"

He nodded. "Not just the payment, but he endorsed the Northman under his own seal, in his own name. It's an honorable marriage now."

Norah gaped across the hall at Soren, who stood near the wall begrudgingly watching the evening's festivities, with a chalice of wine in his hand and a slight scowl on his face.

"Congratulations, and I hope you enjoy the rest of the evening," Norah said as she gave Aman a parting nod.

He bowed. "Thank you, Salara."

Norah made her way to the commander. He didn't look at her as she stepped beside him.

"You made Lord Aman a Provision Promise for Adrian?" she asked. "And endorsed the marriage with your own seal?" She had planned to ramp up to the question, but it just poured from her lips.

Soren shifted in surprise, but he didn't answer.

"Why would you do that?" she asked. "That's a big obligation."

"It's what was required," Soren said absently.

She frowned. "This will upset Alexander. He'll see this as his responsibility. Incentive for you, I'm sure."

"It *is* his responsibility," he growled back. "But the Bear doesn't need to know. Even the boy doesn't know."

Her eyes widened. "You should have told him."

"No," he said firmly.

"Why not?"

His nostrils flared as he glowered at her. "Because no matter how much he loves that girl, no matter how much trouble he's facing, he'll put his brother's feelings first."

Norah sighed, and her stomach knotted. "If Alexander finds out—"

"He won't," he snapped. "But if he does, then you'll say you didn't know."

Norah sat quietly as Vitalia brushed the braids out of her hair. She looked at herself in the vanity mirror, at her tired eyes and her worry-worn face. "I think I should like to be alone for a while," she whispered.

"Yes, Salara," Vitalia said, giving her a small smile and setting the hairbrush on the vanity. Then she bowed her head and left the chamber.

Norah gathered her hair to the side and gently pulled the brush through it. It fell in winding ripples from the press of the braids. Her eyes moved over her reflection. How pale she was in comparison to the people of Kharav. Perhaps even more pale with what weighed on her mind.

The chamber door opened and then closed. She waited.

Mikael stepped around the linen panels, coming up behind her. He traced his fingers over the bareness of her neck, prickling her skin.

She put the brush down. "There's only one," she said faintly.

His puzzled gaze caught hers in the mirror. "Only one of what?"

"Only one who can be trusted with a secret that could break a kingdom."

He paused a moment, then spread his hand across her skin and gripped her shoulder. "What are you saying?"

"You know what I'm saying. Only one can be trusted. And would a son of Soren not pass for your own? Are you not like brothers—large build and black hair, the shape of your face?"

"Salara," Mikael whispered. "No."

She felt the breath leave her lungs, and she struggled to draw it in again. She hadn't yet said it aloud, and it struck her like a blow to the stomach.

Mikael turned her in the chair toward him and dropped to his knees, bringing them eye to eye. He clasped her hands and brought them to his lips. "It was wrong of me to ask this of you," he said.

She cupped his face in her hand. "You need an heir. *We* need an heir." She looked into his eyes. "We need a child."

Emotion etched across his face. He bared his teeth against her hands, silent. He shook his head again. "It doesn't have to be Soren." He paused, then his voice came hoarse as he grimaced. "The Bear?"

She saw the pain in his eyes as he looked up to her, and she caressed his face with her hand. "No. A child between us, as your son, it would destroy him. And you. Let alone a fair-haired child would raise questions. It has to be Soren."

"And that would destroy you," he said softly.

"No." She shook her head. "I'm not the one he desires, and he wouldn't take pleasure in our desperation."

He leaned back slightly. "What do you know of his desire?"

Norah's eyes darted back and forth between his, and she cursed her carelessness. She shook her head again. "Nothing, I only meant he wouldn't take advantage."

"What do you know of Soren's desire?" he said again, his voice quiet but forceful.

Norah swallowed.

She couldn't answer.

She couldn't say Soren's secret out loud.

His brows creased. "You know. You know it's me. He told you?"

Her heart raced. He *knew*.

"Not willingly," she whispered. "He thinks you don't know."

"Of course I do." His voice held a deep sadness. "It makes it all the harder for me to ask this of him. But I'll speak to him tomorrow."

She nodded as a weight crushed her heart.

Chapter Forty-Three

Mikael knocked on Soren's chamber at first light. It was quiet, and his resolve threatened to leave him. He almost turned away, but then a shuffle came from inside, and the door opened.

"Salar," Soren greeted him.

He wasn't sure he had the strength for this conversation. "I have a taste for archery this morning," he said. "Let's go."

Soren flashed a rare smile and collected his bow.

Mikael clenched his own bow tightly as they made their way through the castle, outside, past the stables, and to the archery field. The walk was the longest he'd ever known. He was thankful his friendship with Soren consisted of few words, and the silence brought no awkwardness between them. But he would have to speak, eventually.

Just not yet.

When they reached the field, Mikael breathed in the cold morning air, trying to inhale courage as well. With his exhale, the fog of his breath came unevenly, and he worried it might give him away. Soren could sense fear. Surely he sensed it from him now. But if his commander did, he gave no indication.

A light dust of snow covered the ground. It was beautiful, but he couldn't appreciate beauty now. The barrels had been stocked with a fresh batch of arrows, and he pulled one for his bow.

"There's something on your mind, brother?" Soren started.

There it was. Soren knew something was wrong. Still, his prompt for conversation took him by surprise. Mikael wasn't ready.

"There's a lot on my mind," he said as he nocked the arrow onto the string. Mikael pulled up his bow, exhaling completely as he aimed, and released. The arrow whispered down the field and buried itself in the outer ring of the target.

"Must be serious if your aim's that off," Soren joked as he released an arrow of his own, finding the bullseye.

He had no idea how serious.

Mikael let loose another arrow, hitting the target only slightly better than the first. "Very serious," he said.

Soren's smile fell, and he handed Mikael another arrow instead of taking his own turn again.

The air seemed to turn colder. Still, Mikael could feel the sweat on his back. He nocked another arrow but didn't draw it back. "We've failed again for a child," he said. Then he raised the bow and released, and the arrow missed the target completely.

Soren stared at the target, with his face fixed. "You need more time," he said.

Time wasn't what he needed. Even if it was, he didn't have time.

Soren pulled another arrow from the barrel and held it for him, silent.

But he didn't take it. "I need you."

Soren's head snapped toward him. "Me?" His brows came together.

Mikael lowered the end of his bow to the ground and leaned on it like a staff. He needed its support. "I can't give her a child." He paused—an agonizing, gutting pause. "I need you to give her your seed." Then he waited—an agonizing, gutting wait—giving Soren a moment to think about what he was asking.

Perhaps it was only a moment, but it felt like eternity. Then Soren shook his head, stepping backward. "No," he said. "No, I can't. She'll not have me."

"She will. We've discussed it. You're the only one I trust... with this, with my kingdom..." Mikael's voice cracked, and his eyes filled with emotion. "With my wife." He sank to his knees. "I know what I ask of you, but I beg you."

Soren lunged forward, grabbing him and pulling him back up. "No, get up. Get up!" Mikael got to his feet, and Soren let him go before leaning his own frame up against the arrow barrels.

They stood in silence for a long time. Too long. Worry sprouted in the pit of Mikael's stomach. He had been confident Soren would agree, but this was the most personal thing he'd ever asked from him. Had he reached Soren's limit?

Soren rubbed his face roughly with his hand. "She agrees to this?"

Relief flooded him, but it was short-lived. Nothing about this situation brought relief. Mikael couldn't speak, but he nodded.

Soren forced out a breath. He gritted his teeth as he broke an arrow. "I'll do whatever you ask of me," he said finally.

Mikael sighed heavily. He had been certain of it, but the words still brought a wave of emotion. He gave it a moment to pass. "I haven't thought through all the—"

"I don't want to talk about it," Soren cut him off. "Just tell me where to be, and when."

Mikael was grateful. He didn't want to talk about it either. He nodded.

They looked over the field as an icy breeze blew through. Soren held out another arrow.

Norah shoved a slice of marinated meat into her mouth, overly fixating on her food. Salara-Mae sat to her left, closer to her than Mikael, and across the table from Soren, who positioned himself more in the center. At the opposite end of the long table sat Mikael. This was their normal way of things, but dinner was anything except normal now.

Mikael had told her Soren had agreed. She cursed herself for not thinking of waiting to ask until the time of need. Now came the agonizing awkwardness of having to look at him, having to speak to him, knowing he knew what was to come.

Soren sat quietly, as he normally did, but it was a different kind of quiet—a troubled quiet. And he avoided looking at her, as he normally did, but it was a different kind of avoidance. He drained his blood bowl in large swallows. She almost wanted to offer him more if it would make him feel better. Would it make him feel better? Perhaps she might try it. Then the retching and upheaving would take her mind off things for a while.

She focused her attention on the plate in front of her, trying not to think about any of it. She wasn't sure how many dinners like this she could endure. And surely after, it would only be worse. She wouldn't be able to face him. Her cheeks burned at the thought of *after*—the shame threatened to melt her in her chair.

A servant stepped into the dining hall and quickly moved to Mikael, holding a letter in his hand. "This just arrived, Salar."

A small breath escaped her. Thank the gods there was something else to occupy her attention.

Mikael took it from him, and the servant departed. He glanced at Norah before he broke the seal and opened it. She didn't recognize the seal—bright yellow with a symbol she couldn't make out from the opposite side of the long table.

The line on his brow deepened as he read it. "From Surat in Kolkar," he said.

Norah had no idea who or where that was.

"He sends news that the kingdom of Rael has overthrown Serra." He tossed the letter to Soren.

Serra, Norah knew—that was the slavers' kingdom. Good riddance. But Rael... where had she heard of Rael? She searched her mind. It had been quite some time... "Wait, the usurper?" she asked. Her council had been upset the king of Rael had been usurped, if she remembered correctly.

The faintest hint of amusement came to Mikael's face. "Where did you hear that?"

She shrugged. "Mercia, some time ago, I think. Is it correct?"

Soren grunted but didn't say anything.

"It doesn't surprise me that the North looks at the Raelean king as a usurper," Mikael replied. "Rael's old king converted to the religion of the North, converted most of his kingdom, actually."

"So, of course, the North loved him," Soren added.

"But he was a cruel king," Mikael said. "He had men slay each other for entertainment, among other things you don't want to know about. I suppose you could call the new king a usurper, but he put an end to a lot of their savagery."

She supposed there could be good usurpers. "Who is this new king?"

Mikael frowned as he shook his head. "They call him Cyrus. Other than that, I don't know."

"So, this man usurped the Raelean throne, and now he's overthrown the kingdom of Serra? The slavers' kingdom?" she asked.

Mikael nodded. "And apparently, he's set all the slaves free."

Salara-Mae's eyes widened. "All of them? The entire kingdom?" She looked at Norah with a raised brow. "He should like Kharav, then, given that Salara has freed all our slaves," she added sarcastically.

Norah had freed *some* slaves, primarily those around the castle who stayed now as paid servants, much to Salara-Mae's horror and protest. But she hadn't freed as many as she would have liked, certainly not all across the kingdom. Kharav had thousands of slaves. It would require a significant change in Kharavian culture to do away with slavery all together, one that she didn't have the power to drive. Not yet, anyway. Mikael was already pressed with unhappy nobles. He wouldn't risk giving them yet another grievance, and one that would affect their economies on top of that.

But perhaps this usurper might bring a conversation on the idea. And action started with conversation. "Sounds like a rather decent man," Norah said, then popped a small potato into her mouth and smiled innocently at Salara-Mae.

Soren snorted. "Depends on what you consider decent. Impaling all the slavers on their ships and anchoring them in the harbors for all to see? Flaying them alive? Then yes, he sounds decent."

Ah, there was the Soren she knew—the Soren she kind of missed. "Is that what it says in the letter?"

"And other things," he answered.

"Don't read it," Mikael said to her, purely intending to shield her from its contents.

"What does all this mean?" she asked. "Should we be worried about anything?"

"Why would we be?" Mikael said, and took another drink from his chalice.

That didn't comfort her.

CHAPTER FORTY-FOUR

Mikael sucked in the cool morning air. He normally savored this time of day. Early mornings brought a peace with them. But not today. A weight sat heavy in his stomach, and a pain daggered his chest. Nothing could bring peace to him now for what lay ahead.

He found Soren in the stable, as he suspected he might. The commander's destrier stood in the mainway with leads fastened from its halter to the wall on either side, keeping the animal still as Soren replaced its shoes.

"We've farriers for that," Mikael said, even though he knew Soren preferred doing it himself. He needed something to say, words to speak, something to fill the suffocating air.

"I prefer to do it myself," his commander replied, not looking up.

Mikael waited for him to drive the last nail and release the hoof—an agonizing wait, but a wait that wasn't long enough.

Soren stood when he finished and patted the beast on the shoulder. When their eyes met, he stopped. He shifted back slightly as his face sobered. He knew.

"It's time, brother," Mikael said quietly. "She's at the safe house, on the hillside." He couldn't manage anything else.

Soren stood, silent and unmoving, and for a moment Mikael thought he might refuse—now that he'd had time to think, and now that the time was upon him. But he only nodded solemnly and then pulled off the leather apron and stalled the horse before heading toward the castle.

Soren arrived at the hillside house, his chest tight, his throat dry. Salara's mare stood out front. Alone. There were no guards. They couldn't risk suspicion. Mikael had personally brought her, then departed, but Soren knew he wouldn't have gone far.

His heart pulsed heavily in his ears. He felt calmer in battle, he mused. But then, he wasn't afraid of battle.

Tension gripped his shoulders. He hoped she would find him… tolerable. He'd washed and trimmed his beard short like Mikael's. He swore under his breath—he should have worn a shirt. He knew she didn't like his markings, and everything they stood for. It was too late now. He wished he would have thought of it sooner.

Soren let himself into the house, looking for Salara. All was quiet. He ventured into the sitting room and saw her at the window. She was looking out across the cliffs. She wore a simple riding dress—a gray split-front gown with breeches underneath. The creak of the floor under his weight made her jump, and she turned to face him. He hadn't meant to startle her.

They stared at each other in silence. Soren moved slowly, not sure how to engage her. He noted the knife sheathed at her waist, the one he had returned to her.

"In case you need to fend me off?" he asked.

Her brow tensed as her eyes grew wider, and her lips parted with silent dismay.

His attempt at humor had failed. "The knife," he tried to explain.

"Oh." She looked down and stared at it for a moment, then looked back at him, seeming to wait for what he would do next.

But he didn't know what to do next, or what to say. "Are you sure you want to do this?" he asked. Then he cursed himself. Why would he ask her that? She obviously didn't want to do this.

"Need we undress fully?" she asked, avoiding his question.

He shook his head. "No. Of course not." He hadn't expected it. He didn't know what he expected. He had tried not to think of it. "If you want to go to the bedchamber, I'll give you a few moments."

She stood frozen, as if contemplating fleeing or fighting. He felt like fleeing himself, if he was honest. But she nodded stiffly and turned down the hall to the back room.

Soren pulled off his cloak, and his fingers struggled with the buckles of his weapon's strap and spaulder. He wasn't sure why he had even worn them. He wasn't going to battle. Habit, perhaps, or comfort. But comfort still escaped him.

He wasn't sure how much time to give her, or how much time he should spend with her. He didn't want to draw it out, but he didn't want to be callously swift. The tension in his shoulders grew. He rubbed his hand over his face, trying to calm his own nerves. Soren had been with women before, but this was different. Mikael loved her and entrusted him with her care.

Soren walked down the hall and gave a small knock on the door before opening it slowly. Salara stood, still in her dress, but the small pile of clothes on the chair suggested she had removed her undergarments. The knife lay on top of them, and he was appreciative of that. He still suspected he might not leave without another battle scar. He almost wanted one—this would wound her, and it only seemed fair he suffered the same.

She waited by the bed, and he stepped inside and closed the door behind him. Every sound rang loud in his ears—the latch of the door, his footfalls, even his own heartbeat. So loud. And she watched him warily.

Soren supposed he should initiate; she certainly wasn't going to take what she needed from him. He moved toward her, slowly unfastening his belt and untying his breeches. She backed toward the bed, and he followed. But as he reached for her, she shrank back, bumping up against the carved corner post.

"I don't want to do this," she blurted. She sucked in a breath and shook her head. "I don't want to do this."

He stopped. Did she mean for him to stop? It sounded like he should stop. Should he try to reassure her? Talk her into continuing? That didn't feel right. But not wanting to do something and not *actually* doing something were two different things. He didn't want to be here, yet here he was. That argument didn't sound right either. He looked around the room, searching for what to do next, but there was nothing *to* do.

So he just nodded. "All right."

She let out a shaky breath. "I'm sorry. I thought I could, but I can't."

"All right," he said again. He looked around the room again. Clearly, she didn't find him tolerable. He cursed himself. He should have covered his markings. Should he go?

"I'll... I'll go," he said.

He moved back toward the door, but as she sank onto the bed and buried her face in her hands, he stopped. Crying had never bothered Soren before. He found it annoying more than anything else.

But he didn't like Salara crying.

Worry sat heavy in his chest. He had never wanted to be gentle. Kind. Safe. Not until now. Curse this wretched woman for making him feel things.

"Are... are you all right?" he asked her.

She pulled her face from her hands and gaped at him, as if surprised he was speaking to her kindly. As she should be, he supposed. When had he ever been kind to her?

He moved to the bed and sat down beside her. He didn't look at her, but he knew her eyes were still on him.

And they sat.

"I'm sorry," he said finally, breaking the silence. "If you could have chosen, this might have been easier for you."

She looked down at her hands clasped in her lap. "I did choose. And I chose you."

His eyes darted to her as he turned. That couldn't be true. "Why would you do that?"

"Because you love Mikael, you'll protect him and Kharav, protect this secret." She swallowed and sucked in an uneven breath. "And you won't guilt me with the shame of our sin." She put her face back in her hands. "I can't believe I even considered this, though."

He sighed. "Desperation makes men do things they wouldn't otherwise dream of. And there are many sins of men, but wanting for a child isn't one of them." He looked up at the ceiling. He hadn't made it easy for her. Guilt had never afflicted him, but he felt it now—guilt for his harshness and his cruelty, and despite that cruelty, she chose him still. For Mikael, and for Kharav.

"Am I a terrible person that I'd rather fight for the throne?" she whispered.

He shook his head. "It appears I'm the terrible person, that you'd rather go to war than take me to bed."

She laughed through her tears and looked at him, and he was glad his jest lightened the air. Things settled between them. Thoughts and words came easier now.

"It's not just that," she said. "I imagine it wouldn't be... too terrible to lie with you. Now that I know you."

Not too terrible. He certainly hadn't expected her lusting after him, but he had hoped himself a little more than not too terrible. But he deserved that, he supposed.

"And you look"—she tilted her head slightly as she eyed him—"quite nice. Now. Different from how you usually do."

There was a compliment in there somewhere, he was sure.

"Anyway," she continued, "there are many women who would readily take you to bed... or"—her brows drew together—"many not women, I mean, people other than women... if that's what you wanted... you know what I'm trying to say, maybe. And it's not that I couldn't be with you. I trust you. You probably know that. I think. Maybe I told you"—she looked down at her hands again—"or maybe I didn't, because you're mean sometimes."

As much as rambling annoyed him, he didn't mind Salara's rambling. He found this rambling amusing, with her under the same strain of awkwardness that had plagued him only moments ago.

Her face sobered again as she paused, and she drew her gaze back to his. "But I don't just want any child. I want Mikael's child. I love him."

He grew serious again, too, and nodded. "I know." There was no doubt in him.

She rose, and he did as well. He turned to go.

"Soren," she said, stopping him. "Thank you. For not making me feel wrong, or humiliated."

"I would never humiliate you, Salara," he said. "And I'll tell you when you're wrong."

She smiled as she wiped her cheeks again. "Would it be weird to hug you?" she asked.

"Yes—"

"I'm going to anyway," she said as she stepped forward and snaked her arms around him.

He stiffened. This was the second embrace he'd endured lately, but surprisingly it was... nice. Not natural, or something that he'd want again, but warm and real and right. This vile creature—worming her way into his heart. He rumbled his protest, but slowly brought his arm around her and hugged her back.

They broke, and he straightened. She smiled up at him.

He hesitated before asking, "Should I wait here with you?" Why she would want that, he didn't know, but it seemed to be what he should say.

She shook her head. She just wanted him gone, and he understood. So he nodded and left her to the quiet.

Norah lay under the bed coverlet in the hillside house, winding strands of hair around her finger. She had come here filled with shame and guilt, but Soren didn't make her feel either of those things. He made her feel strong. And right again.

The door of the chamber opened and closed.

Mikael climbed into bed beside her and slipped his arm underneath her, sidling up and pulling her close. "Are you all right?" he asked softly.

She nodded. "Yes." She was all right. More than all right.

He let out an uneasy breath. "Soren told me..." His words dropped off.

She turned to face him. "I'm so sorry," she whispered. "I couldn't, I—"

"Don't. You've nothing to be sorry about. Never have I been so relieved." His fingers curled around the nape of her neck, and he pulled her closer. "I should have never..."

A silence sat between them, then he asked, "Was he... unkind?"

She shook her head. "No, not at all." *Not at all.* "In fact, he makes me feel safe where I struggle to manage my own morality. But Mikael, I couldn't. I just couldn't."

"And I'm grateful for it," he breathed as he wrapped his arms around her.

But what would they do now?

CHAPTER FORTY-FIVE

The small group of soldiers made their way through the foothills of Moray, a Mercian township in the outer reach of the kingdom. Word had come that it had been attacked, and they traveled to investigate. Alexander looked back at the men following behind him—about fifty. How strange to lead a group of Shadowmen through Mercia. He'd been sent two thousand Shadow warriors, much more than he had expected, yet still not enough to keep the North protected. But he couldn't ask for more.

The Shadow captain rode ahead of him, and he watched her. Two months she'd been in Mercia. She hadn't tried to kill him yet—at least, not that he knew of. But her eyes occasionally threatened it. Her words had lost some of their harshness, though, he noticed. Perhaps her hate had cooled a bit.

She'd shown herself to be smart, quick, strong, and decisive—a good captain. A good captain for the lord commander, he reminded himself, which would make her a bad captain for Mercia. Still, perhaps his own hate had cooled a bit too.

"Another one," the Shadow captain called to him, and he shifted his attention back. He followed her motion to the ground, where he saw a downed winterhawk. They'd found one of them shot already, and two more the day before.

"Someone doesn't like hawks," she said as she gazed at the dead animal on the ground. The Shadow woman slid off her mount and kicked over the carcass of the bird, then she bent down and pulled an arrow from its chest. She looked at it closely and shook her head. "I don't recognize it," she said, holding out the arrow for Alexander.

Alexander took it, eying the tip. It was smooth, sharp, well fashioned, and barbed on the edges for maximum damage. Wings at the base prevented it from being easily pulled from flesh. These were dangerous arrows, and they came from dangerous men.

"Inventive, though," she said, her eyes smiling. "I think I'd like to meet these men."

Alexander wondered what she looked like under her head wrap, what all the Shadowmen looked like. It felt strange not to know the faces of those whose company he kept so often lately. But he knew the captain's eyes—large and dark. Powerful.

He shifted his focus back to the arrow.

"Smoke," a soldier called out, and they looked to see a dark plume rising just south over the hills.

They reached the village of Moray, and it stood as the others did—in smoldering ruins. Bodies hung from bars above the gates, the victims' faces swollen and blue. The dead littered the streets. The captain called out in the Shadow tongue, and the men set to work, pulling the bodies down and dragging them to a pyre. Mercian bodies needed to be burned to pass to the next world—all except kings and queens, whose spirits were bound to watch over their realm. The Shadowmen buried their dead, but they respected Mercian customs and lent their help. Alexander was grateful.

He slid off his mount and surveyed the damage. He felt a deep fury building inside. The attacks were worsening, and he had no idea who was responsible.

Moray still had a few buildings standing, and he waved the men to look around. As he walked through the ruins, he noticed there had already been looting. *Drifters.* They always seemed to appear and fill their pockets before his soldiers arrived. He checked the bodies as he went, looking for anyone still alive. But there were none. Everyone was dead. This enemy was savage.

"Anything?" Alexander asked as the men came back together. They shook their heads. He looked at the captain.

"We can send half the men here to the two villages we passed along the way, and the other half to the lower hills," she suggested. "I can pull more men back from the west as well."

"We haven't enough men to cover them all," Alexander said.

"Will you write for more?" she asked.

He let out a long breath. "I can't. Two thousand men is more than generous. And I've already drawn the council's concern with the number of Shadowmen in our ranks." He paused. "I mean no offense."

Her eyes smiled. She looked around once more. "What do you want to do?"

"Send out your men. You and I will return to Mercia. I'll pull more from the castle, and from Bahoul."

Then they turned their mounts north and spurred them back toward the castle.

The judisaept felt colder than usual. Perhaps it was the winter, perhaps it was the disapproval that hung in the air from Alexander's acceptance and deployment of the Shadowmen—of the Shadow *woman*. But that weighed little on his mind now.

A letter had come from Eilor, the most southern kingdom of the Aleon Empire. Alexander handed the letter to James as he addressed the council. "News from Eilor. The usurper of Rael has met with Japheth's king."

Edward grunted. "Perhaps he intends to join Japheth and the Shadowlands against us?"

"The Shadowlands are our ally," Alexander said, as much as it pained him to do so. Edward scoffed, and Alexander shot him a warning gaze. "I advise you use caution," he added, and Edward quieted.

"And it's rumored the usurper holds no favor for the Shadowlands," James said. "The Shadow King supported the slavers' kingdom, which the usurper has recently taken."

Councilman Alastair gave an amused frown. "So perhaps this usurper has a redeeming quality after all."

A few of the councilmen chuckled. Alexander didn't. An enemy of the Shadow King was an enemy of Norah. And an enemy of Norah was an enemy of Mercia—an enemy of Alexander.

"For some time we have suspected the Shadow King might be at risk of losing his alliance," Councilman Henricus said. "Especially after the attack on the lord justice and Queen Norah's intervention."

Alexander frowned at the memory of the attack that resulted in the Destroyer coming to his aid, and Norah's subsequent confrontation with the king of Japheth.

"But it wouldn't make sense for Japheth to abandon an ally, *any* ally," James said, "given that Aleon waits for an opportunity to strike."

Henricus frowned. "Perhaps this usurper is a more powerful ally than the Shadowlands."

"Ridiculous," Edward said. "Even with the combined armies of both Rael and Serra, this usurper's power is mediocre at best."

Alexander's worry grew. Neither an additional ally joining Japheth and the Shadowlands nor the alliance between Japheth and the Shadowlands crumbling boded well for Norah.

"Have you heard anything from the Shadowmen on this, Lord Justice?" James asked him.

Alexander shook his head. "No. They haven't heard."

"Or they have and they're not saying," Edward said.

Alexander didn't believe that.

"When will we send them back?" Edward asked.

"I've no intention of sending them back," Alexander replied. "At least not yet. I need them to protect the villages in the outer reaches."

Edward snorted. "Can we not pull more men from Bahoul? Perhaps two thousand?"

"There was barely two thousand before, and I called the majority back just yesterday, leaving only a hundred there now."

"Only a hundred men hold the mountains?" Alastair asked in surprise.

"No, three thousand men hold Bahoul, but only a hundred are Northmen."

"Might as well bring the rest of them home," Edward said angrily. "We lost Bahoul when Queen Norah gave it back to the Shadowlands."

Just what he needed—men who knew nothing of war telling him where to place his army. "I can't pull them all. I need to keep men on the inside, to give our forces access should we need it."

An ache ran through Alexander's temples, and he realized he had been clenching his jaw. The gods were truly testing him.

The Shadow captain was waiting for Alexander as he stormed from the judisaept. "It didn't go well, I take it," she said, with a hint of amusement in her voice. "Do they want more men from Salar?"

"No, they want to send you and the rest of your men back to the Shadowlands."

"Ah, so the strategy of abandoning logic."

He couldn't help a small smile. Sometimes he almost liked this woman.

They reached his study, and he shut the door behind him. "Do you know anything about the usurper meeting with the king of Japheth?" he asked directly.

She straightened, her eyes narrowing. "Cyrus has met with Gregor?"

Katya was good at evading him when she didn't want to answer him, when she had something to hide. She wasn't hiding anything now, as he'd expected. Despite the tension between the Shadowlands and Mercia, he didn't believe the Shadowlands plotted against them. He couldn't say the same for Mercia.

He sighed as he sat down at his desk and pulled out a blank parchment. He wrote quickly, keeping his message short, pointed. Then he wrote a second, less short, less sharp. Katya waited patiently as he folded them and affixed his seal to both. He held them for her. "See the first gets to your Destroyer. The second, to the queen."

"You freely give the lord commander this information?"

"I give him what he needs to know to protect my queen."

She paused, studying him. "He will, you know. He will protect her."

He did know.

Now how to protect Mercia—Alexander stood and pulled the army records from his cabinet. Where to draw more forces...

"The council wants me to pull the last of the Northmen from Bahoul to help defend the villages," he said, freer with information than he would normally be.

"I won't argue with that," she said. "But then you'd be stupid. To Kharav's benefit, though, so by all means, listen to your old men."

He tightened his lips to keep from smiling. He could use a captain like Katya, especially with Caspian gone. He ran his eyes down the records and through the soldier counts and placements. "This is a cunning foe, whoever he is, is he not?" he said as he leafed through the pages of numbers. "Mercia has a large army, but he forces me to spread them across the kingdom, so in effect, I have nothing."

"He's a clever opponent," she said, nodding. "But then, Bear, so are you."

He lifted his gaze from the records to find her looking back at him. Her eyes smiled. Dark, but bright.

Captivating.

No. He caught himself. Just dark.

Chapter Forty-Six

The sun hung high in the cloudless hues of blue. Soren leaned against the rail of the sparring field, watching the earlies as they practiced. He was pleased with this group. Their movements were fluid, their weapons' work accurate and deadly. Several of them would make the Crest. He needed more of them, but he wouldn't take those who didn't meet his standard. He couldn't sacrifice quality, not when it came to Salara's safety.

Adrian caught his eye, and he watched him. The boy had skill, and he was clever—sometimes too clever. Soren had wanted to loathe him, this brother of the Bear, but there was nothing to loathe about him, aside from having to admit the Bear had trained him well. He was born of natural talent, he worked hard, his loyalty was absolute, and his spirit unbreakable. He was an excellent soldier.

And Soren could make him even better.

The Bear would call for his return eventually, and Soren would send him back the greatest warrior of both kingdoms.

"Boy!" he called.

Adrian turned mid-practice; he knew when Soren called him. He pulled off his helm and trotted up to him, breathlessly giving a quick bow of his head. "Yes, Lord Commander."

Soren eyed him for a moment. "Have you written to your brother?"

Adrian looked to the ground. "Uh, not yet," he answered. "But I will."

Soren shot him a steely gaze. It was one of the boy's rare faults—the fear of disappointing his brother. He still hadn't shared the news of his marriage. No doubt, the news would upset the Bear, but not telling him would cause a greater conflict between them. Soren didn't want that for him.

"You're a man now. You make your own decisions, but you must also own them."

Adrian nodded. "I'll do it tonight."

"You'll do it now."

The boy looked back out to the field. "But what about practice?"

"I said you'll do it now," Soren growled.

Adrian swallowed and then gave another bow. "Yes, my lord." Then he trotted off to do as he was bid.

Soren sighed. He hoped this wouldn't cause the Bear to call the boy back. There was so much potential in him, but he still needed a lot of work. He needed more experience—experience only Soren could provide. He needed at least two years. Soren would have to accelerate his training.

He turned back to the sparring field and caught sight of Salara beside the far railing. She must be out for a walk; she liked to occasionally take the route by the sparring field to see how Adrian and the sibling pair were doing.

Soren waited for her to see him and give him her usual stupid smirk, but when her eyes found him, she quickly looked back to the earlies, then abruptly turned and headed back toward the castle.

Why didn't she smirk at him? Or smile, or something?

A voice sounded beside him, but he paid it no mind.

Had she not seen him?

No—she'd seen him.

"Lord Commander," came the voice again, and he looked over to find his training captain, Vasil.

"What?" he rasped.

"Should I start the spear circuits?"

Spear circuits? Soren glanced across the earlies, who were finishing their sword rounds. *Spear circuits.* "Fine."

Vasil bellowed out to the earlies, and Soren looked back to find Salara. But she was gone.

"Gods, that's hot!" Norah exclaimed, and tried to soothe her scorched tongue against the roof of her mouth.

"I'm so sorry, Salara," Vitalia said quickly, rushing over. "I made it too hot."

Norah set the cup of tea back on its saucer. "No, it's my fault. I wasn't paying attention." Her mind had been... far away.

"Are you all right?"

"I'm perfectly fine." And she was fine... physically.

Mikael hadn't come to their bed last night. He'd said he had work to tend, but he always had work to tend, and he'd always slept in their bed. And now three nights in a row she had slept alone—the three nights since she had returned from the hillside house. Was he disappointed with her? He'd said he was relieved she hadn't taken Soren, but perhaps now the gravity of her decision sat with him, as it did her. There would be no child.

Or perhaps now that they'd reached acceptance and were beyond desperations, he found himself regretting they'd even taken the option into consideration, like she did.

She closed her eyes and gritted her teeth against the shame. Although brief, she *had* been willing. She'd chosen Soren, and Soren knew she'd chosen him. Now she couldn't even look at him.

And Mikael couldn't look at her.

"Here, I'll get you some wine to temper it," Vitalia said as she reached for the decanter.

Norah snapped back to the present. "No, it's all right. I should actually get out and start the day." She had let too much of the morning pass.

Vitalia smiled warmly. "Of course, Salara. I'll just set to tidying up, then."

Norah forced a smile back and rose from the small table by the windows. She slipped on her silk shoes and moved to the chamber door, but when she opened it, she jumped.

Soren stared back at her.

"Hammel's hell, you scared me," she said as her pulse slowed.

"Are you avoiding me?"

"No," she replied defensively. She was just trying to not talk to him. Or see him. She glanced back at Vitalia. "Leave us, please."

Her maid bobbed her head and left them to privacy.

His eyes narrowed between the slit in his wrap as he stepped inside the chamber. "You saw me in the field yesterday and didn't smirk at me."

"I thought you didn't like when I smirked at you."

"I don't."

"Then why are you angry that I didn't?"

"I'm not angry," he said, with angry eyes.

"Well, I'm not avoiding you," she lied.

He shifted back on his heel. "At dinner you didn't speak."

"*You* never speak at dinner."

"But you do," he said. "And you usually say at least one cheeky comment to me. But you didn't."

She stopped. She'd thought he never paid her any mind at all.

His voice came softer now. "I thought when we parted... at the hillside house... we were well."

"We are well. It's not that. I mean, it *is* that, but..." Why was this so hard to talk about?

"Then why do you avoid me?" he asked.

"Because I'm ashamed!"

He quieted and stood awkwardly. Or maybe it was she who was awkward. This whole situation was awkward.

"Why are you ashamed?" he asked. "You've done nothing. We did nothing."

"No, but I had decided to. Mikael had resigned to leave it alone, and it was *I* who brought it up again. *I* chose you." She rubbed her forehead with stiff fingers. "I obviously thought about everything, thought about being with you. So, to have thought about it, to have those intentions, and now to walk around trying to pretend like nothing ever happened..." She shook her head as she gave a self-scoffing laugh to keep herself from growing emotional. "But now you know. And Mikael knows. And he's barely looked at me these past few days. He doesn't come to our bed. So what's left to feel but shame?"

Soren sighed and pulled down his wrap as he looked around the room. He moved slowly to the windows and looked out over the courtyard.

Norah waited. But he said nothing. Was he just going to stand there?

"You asked me what the seer showed me," he said finally. "In Odepeth. You asked me what I kept hidden. It wasn't your death." His breath came uneasy now. "It was... of me... with a lover."

Oh. She tried to form words with her mouth, but none would come. Her heart raced faster, and she swallowed. "Who?"

He shook his head. "I don't know. I've never seen him before."

"Hammel's hell," she breathed, and let out a laugh.

He looked back at her with his brows drawn together. "Why do you laugh?"

"Because I thought you were going to say *me*."

His face twisted. "Why would you think it was *you*?"

She laughed again. "You don't have to act so disgusted."

"*You* were the one who wouldn't bed *me*."

Fair, but... "Well, you told me the vision was of you killing me, and if it wasn't killing me, then my mind just thought it was something else having to do with me. And we just, almost, you know..." She stopped and narrowed her eyes. "Wait, this entire time you were okay with letting me think you were going to kill me?"

He let out a long breath but didn't answer.

"That was an asshole thing to do, you know."

Soren glanced down. "I know. But it was the only thing that came to mind in the moment."

"Really?" she asked angrily.

"You kept pressing me. What else could I say?"

"You could have said 'nothing'! Or just 'mind your business'?"

"I know you," he argued back. "When have you ever minded your business?"

She rolled her eyes. "I didn't believe you, anyway."

"You didn't believe I'd kill you?"

She pursed her lips as she looked back at him. "I know you too."

They quieted again.

"Why are you telling me this now?" she asked.

He looked out the window again. "Because you tell me you feel shame, for your thoughts, your intentions. I know shame too."

"Why are you ashamed?"

"Because I think about him. Often."

"Oh, Soren. You can't be ashamed of that."

"Neither can you, of wanting a child. At least your thoughts were driven with purpose. Mine are only for my own... selfishness."

She stepped closer to him. "I don't think you're selfish at all."

They stood, and their eyes quietly locked. She gave a small smile.

He stiffened. "Don't hug me again."

"I wasn't going to," she lied.

He snorted, obviously knowing her better, then he pulled up his wrap and covered his face again. "Now are we well?"

She couldn't help another smile, and she nodded. "If I can just fix things with Mikael."

"If he can't look at you, it's not you. It's because he feels his own shame. You have to help him past it."

She nodded again. "Thank you."

Mikael sat alone in his study. Parchments covered the table: maps, letters, updates from his scouts and his army. And a letter from Japheth, again telling him Gregor wasn't satisfied with the terms of their trade and sought to renegotiate. The king of Japheth puzzled him. He had resumed his normal trade shipments, to Mikael's surprise. Now, Gregor invited him to Japheth, to resume negotiations of their contract.

Mikael had been to Japheth many times; it wasn't an unusual invitation. And no doubt Gregor wanted to avoid returning to Kharav, to the North Queen who had served him his manhood on a platter. But the words on the parchment held a different air, and Mikael wondered if Gregor's intention was truly to negotiate.

His eyes moved to the letter that had brought news of Aleon taking Tarsus—the island kingdom in the southern waters of the Atolean Sea. The ports of Tarsus hosted premier trading, where it never wintered, never stormed, and where only merchants of great merit were permitted. Tarsus was a wealthy kingdom, perhaps one of the wealthiest in the world. It was also fierce. Tarsen soldiers were renowned fighters, and they defended their island ruthlessly, drawing even Mikael's respect. As large an empire as Aleon had become, it still surprised him they were able to take the island. And it worried him. Phillip's grandfather had tried to claim Tarsus before and failed, but Phillip was forging ahead. Surely it was only a matter of time before he turned his eyes to Kharav, another kingdom that had eluded the empire's grasp.

And a continued worry still plagued him—he and Salara remained without a child. He couldn't deny the relief that came with Salara refusing Soren. He'd never been more grateful for anything in his life. He wouldn't have been able to look at Soren after, tolerate his presence, although his commander wouldn't have done anything wrong. Soren would have done what had been asked of him, and *only* what had been asked of him. Guilt riddled him at the jealousy that reared itself with just the thought, and at his relief it hadn't happened. It was a selfish relief. They needed a child. Without one, the nobles wouldn't support Salara on the throne alone—not a queen of the North. Soren would protect her, but he was one man. He wouldn't be able to keep her safe. Not completely. Of all Mikael's burdens, this one was the heaviest. He gripped his forehead in his hand, leaning heavily on his elbow over his ash-wood desk. The candlelight flickered beside him.

"It's late," Salara's voice said. He hadn't heard her come in. He looked up to see her leaning against the doorframe. "Are you coming to bed soon?" she asked.

Bed. He longed for it and avoided it all the same. Why, he didn't know. Perhaps because he felt like he was failing her. He wasn't worthy of her. "I still have some things to do yet," he said, turning his attention back to the work in front of him.

Norah reached up and loosened the ties of her nightgown, pulling it over her shoulders and letting it fall to the floor. She stood naked and let his eyes run over her body. She was beautiful.

She stepped around the desk and stopped in front of him as he gazed up at her. She took his face in her hands. "I won't wait any longer," she whispered.

And he wouldn't make her. "I'll come to bed then," he said softly. He moved to pile his parchments together.

But she stopped him, pulling his face back to her. "You don't hear me. I won't wait any longer." She pushed him back and climbed on top of him in the chair, her knees on either side.

Mikael watched her as she reached down and unbuckled his belt and breeches and pulled him free. She brought her lips to his, seeking, searching, wanting. She teased him with her fingers, asking him with her touch, and his body responded.

Salara shifted forward, positioning them, and slowly took him inside her. They sat a moment in the quiet of the candlelit night, their bodies and breaths together. She leaned forward and kissed his forehead, then drew her lips over his brow and down to each eye, kissing one and then the other. She moved down his cheek to his mouth. He kissed her back.

She moved slowly at first, containing the fire he felt inside her. He let her fill his senses: the taste of her tongue, the sound of her breath, the scent of her need. She rocked her hips, bringing them into a rhythm and making him rise to meet her. She ran her hand around the back of his neck and twisted her fingers into his hair, pulling his head back and biting his bottom lip. He growled and snaked his arm around her waist. But she caught his hands in hers and pushed them against the arms of his chair, holding him down.

She quickened her pace. He bent his head and bared his teeth against her shoulder, and she began to fall apart. She rocked forward, panting. Her body twisted against him, but he held her, not letting her free.

With a final cry, she collapsed on top of him, burying her face in his neck.

Mikael lifted her up, still keeping them joined together. He swept his hand across his desk, pushing everything to the floor—his letters, his parchments, his maps. They didn't matter anymore. He laid her down and felt her skin prickle against the polished wood of the desk.

Mikael pushed himself deeper. There was no control in him now. He gripped her shoulder and pulled her against him, letting his own desire take over. She raised a hunger in him that would never be satiated. It was more than the wants of the flesh.

She knew him.

She loved him.

She needed him.

He growled as he shuddered to a finish, clutching her tightly and holding her close. He filled her with everything of himself—his love, his worries, his insecurities—and she took him. All of him. Under the weight of the crown, he was cracking, but she bonded those cracks with gold, and made him whole.

CHAPTER FORTY-SEVEN

A knock on the door interrupted Norah from her letter, and Vitalia moved to answer it. Norah smiled when she saw the girl enter. "Calla."

But the girl didn't smile back. "Salara, you need to come to the sparring field. It's Adrian." Her tone told Norah not to delay.

She rose quickly and followed Calla through the castle halls and out through the courtyard, toward the fields. "What's going on?" she asked.

"Three of the earlies earned their sword entitlements today. Adrian was denied because he's not actually an early. He challenged the lord commander on it, saying he was just as good as every man there." She looked at Norah as they walked quickly. "He is, Salara! He's better!"

Norah's pulse quickened as she picked up her pace. "And what did the lord commander do?"

"He said Adrian could have his entitlement, if he defeated them. *All*."

"All?" she repeated with her eyes wide. "That's ridiculous."

"I know." Calla shrugged breathlessly. "But when has being ridiculous ever stopped any of them?"

Norah frowned. That was true.

They reached the sparring field, where Adrian was engaged against an early. He moved with the grace of the Shadowmen, every strike calculated yet natural. He wore the black army breeches and boots, with no shirt, only a weapon's strapping. His hair was longer now, and he tied it back like the Kharavian men, sporting a close-cut beard to match. Aside from the stark difference of his fair complexion and no markings on his body, he looked very much like one of them.

The men exchanged brutal blows, each looking to overwhelm the other. Norah's heart pulsed in her throat. This wasn't a practice sparring; this wasn't a friendly match. Adrian was fighting for honor—a purpose the North took as serious as life.

The early launched another attack, driving toward Adrian and swinging his sword high. But Adrian met him with a counter, turtling under his shield and hurling his weight forward. He hit the man's legs with a force that knocked the early off balance, making him fall forward, onto Adrian's shield. Adrian used his momentum to lift the man over and slam him to the ground. He pivoted, his sword ready, bringing his blade to the felled early's neck, and taking the match. The man raised his arm, yielding.

But it wasn't yet a victory. Adrian spun to find his next opponent. The man was a little more cautious in his approach than the first, testing, looking for weakness. He moved with elegance and poise, despite his size. In practices before, Norah would marvel at the grace of the men as they sparred, appreciating their skill and strength. But today she only worried. She worried this early had too much skill, too much strength.

Adrian made the first strike. He beat the man back with both his sword and his shield, using them fluidly as though they were parts of his own body. But the early moved with the same agility, and on a strike where Adrian's shield came down, the man caught him with an elbow to the face. Adrian stumbled backward, and Norah gasped.

A low, rumbling chuckle to her right startled her, and she glanced to see the lord commander. She hadn't realized he was there. "Why are you doing this?" she hissed. "This is how someone gets hurt!"

"This is how a man makes his rise," he said without taking his eyes from the bout.

Adrian suffered another hit to his face. Blood came from both his nose and his brow now.

Soren let out another chuckle. "If he remembers to keep that shield up."

"He's not even wearing a helm," she said through her teeth.

"All the more thrilling."

"This is a game to you?" she snapped.

He shot her a gaze of icy fire, serious now. "This is most certainly not a game."

They watched as the men fought on. The early beat Adrian back with a brutal attack. But on a downward swing, he opened his shield arm. Adrian twisted and caught it with his own shield, knocking the man's arm out and exposing his front. Adrian was ready. He barreled forward with his shoulder, sending the man sprawling to the ground. Adrian leapt atop him, pressing him down against the earth with the edge of his shield and sweeping the tip of the blade to the early's neck. The man held his hands open, conceding.

But Norah didn't have time to feel happiness for him. Another swordsman stepped forward, and her anxiousness rose. Adrian was tired. These weren't general soldiers that one might find in everyday battle. These opponents were earlies. Many would be men of the Crest, and besting them took an immense amount of skill and energy. She questioned if he'd be able to withstand another bout.

The early charged forward in a fresh attack, and Adrian defended, but he was slowing. Their swords rang through the air and fell upon each other's shields in fatal blows. Adrian moved in a side swing, but his rebalance was slow, and his opponent delivered a hit with the edge of his shield, knocking Adrian to the ground.

"Soren," she breathed, her alarm growing. "Please."

The opponent sprang forward in a subsequent attack, but Adrian rolled away, stumbling back to his feet. The early saw Adrian's strength waning, and he attacked again. Their shields clashed together, and Adrian fell back with the man on top of him. But

Adrian used the force in the fall, kicking the early up and over his head. With both men now on the ground, Adrian rolled to his stomach and reached forward. In a single motion, he grabbed a fistful of the early's hair, pulling his head back toward him and bringing his blade to his throat. They held until, reluctantly, the man yielded. Both men lay on the ground, taking a moment to regain their breath.

Then Adrian rolled and staggered to his feet, and a wry smile came to his lips with his triumph.

"I said all," Soren growled, and the men around the field looked at one another in surprise.

"You can't be serious!" Norah exclaimed. "He just beat three earlies! That's what you asked of him."

He looked at her with a scowl. "I said *all,*" he repeated.

Another soldier stepped forward. Adrian's right eye had swelled shut, and blood trickled into his left. He wiped it away with the back of his hand. The early charged forward. Adrian moved to meet him, but he was slow, and the man spun with a blow, knocking him to the ground with his shield. He rained lethal strikes at the downed Northman, but Adrian rolled away and stumbled back to his feet. The early charged again.

"There's got to be a hundred men here," Norah said angrily. "You ask the impossible!"

The lord commander didn't respond. He only watched as Adrian suffered blow after blow, fall after fall. But Adrian didn't stop. He rose again and again. Beaten and bloody, he still welcomed the battle.

The early charged him again. Adrian sidestepped, but he caught the man's arm as he passed, pulling him back. With a sheer force of will and strength, he swept his blade to the early's armpit, threatening a thrust to the heart. The man stopped, his wrist in Adrian's grip, and he nodded his submission. Adrian swayed on his feet, but he stayed upright, waiting for his next opponent.

The next soldier stepped forward, and he looked at the lord commander hesitantly.

"Soren," Norah pleaded again, but the commander nodded, prompting the man to continue.

The soldier stepped forward, first to attack. Adrian deflected his first blow with his shield, but the early knocked it to the side with his own and delivered a kick that sent Adrian sprawling backward, to the ground. Before Adrian could fully recover, the early swung his shield again, catching Adrian in the chest and knocking him down again.

But the man didn't spring on his advantage.

Adrian struggled to his feet once more, but he could barely lift his shield. The early advanced again, throwing an elbow and catching him in the chin. Miraculously, Adrian stayed on his feet, but he didn't have the strength to defend against another blow.

Norah couldn't stand it any longer and stepped forward, but Soren caught her arm. "Don't dishonor him," he warned, his voice low.

She was about to argue when a soldier within the ranks of the watching earlies started to beat his shield with his sword—a slow and persistent drumming. Another soldier joined him, then another. And another. The circle of men all around them joined the rhythm.

Even the soldier facing Adrian beat his shield.

Norah looked at Soren in utter confusion. The commander stood for a moment, then he turned to the training captain, who handed him a sword. Her heart raced as Soren stepped out onto the field. Even as the shadow of the lord commander loomed over him, Adrian stood, bloody and bold, determined to fight on.

But Soren didn't attack. He only faced the Northman in silence. Then he gripped the sword by the blade and held it for Adrian to take. Adrian dropped his own sword to the ground and reached for the one offered to him. The beating of shields grew to a deafening thunder.

Norah glanced at Calla by her side, still not fully understanding.

The girl grinned. "He got it. He earned the entitlement. He's an early now."

Norah looked back out to the field as Soren returned to where she stood.

His eyes blazed a dark fire, ardent and fierce. "You just saw the best warriors of the Kharavian army call for a Northman to receive a position of status and a most coveted entitlement." He paused, almost seeming proud. "He rises."

Norah sat in the throne room, nearly suffocating from the tension of the air. Mikael sat beside her, facing his nobles who filled the room in front of them.

This was her doing.

At her insistence, Mikael had declined Gregor's invitation to visit Japheth. Surely it had been a trap. His words were too kind, too flattering, very unlike what he had shown in Kharav. He was wooing Mikael to come. And she didn't trust him. In response to the offense, Gregor stopped all trade—to wait until they discussed it in person, he said. Of course, this reached the nobles, who demanded an audience.

The relationship between the royals and nobles was different in Kharav than in Mercia. They held more power here; and the nobles weren't happy with Mikael. They didn't approve of his marriage to her, especially after he annulled his marriages to several of their daughters and executed a member of a noble family. And they most certainly didn't approve of his jeopardizing the alliance with Japheth.

They blamed her. Of course a marriage between Kharav and Mercia would offend Japheth. Mikael had told her Gregor had been upset that they hadn't attacked the Mercian army right after her capture. It was a prime opportunity—perhaps the only opportunity—to defeat her army and leave Phillip without an ally by his side. Alexander had driven her army across the Tribelands, and they were weak and vulnerable. She remembered the army of Japheth had been ready to unite with Mikael and attack, only for Mikael to send Mercia home to safety.

Then came the incident that killed King Gregor's nephew, which they blamed the North for, followed by Norah's confrontation with Gregor in protecting Soren. In their eyes, Norah was threatening the alliance between Japheth and Kharav, and Mikael was letting her.

"Your actions weaken us," one of the nobles said to Mikael sharply. Narsing was his name, and Mikael's previous wife Heta was his daughter. Norah had seen him only a few times before, but she knew him enough to know she didn't like him, and enough to fear him. He was one of the more powerful lords, and his lands stretched a good portion of the border between Kharav and Japheth.

"We give the North provisions, men, horses," he said. Then he looked at Norah. "And what does she give in return? Nothing, no steel goods—although they readily sell them in Tarsus. They don't even allow us the ability to forge what we need if we were to buy it ourselves. It doesn't feel like an alliance. The North Queen doesn't even give an heir."

Mikael rose abruptly, and Soren moved forward from where he stood beside the king. Fear flashed through her. They had enough to face from outside threats. They didn't need a battle within as well.

Norah rose from her throne, and all eyes turned to her. "I understand your frustrations, Lord Narsing. But I assure you, Mercia is Kharav's ally."

"You don't act as one," he challenged.

Anger heated her blood. "I've returned Bahoul."

"So you gave us what was already ours," he countered. "Is this all the strength Salar has?"

Narsing was faulting Mikael—judging him—for what they saw as her shortcomings, and giving ever so subtly the threat of what his failure could bring. Regardless of how subtle, that threat brought her blood to a boil.

"I gave you what Mercia took from you, and what I can take again," she snapped back. She was not a weak queen to be bullied, and Mercia wasn't a weak kingdom. They would do well to remember that. But she didn't care for what they thought of her, more that they supported Mikael. They needed to believe in their king.

"Salar has also spoken to me of shipments of steel trade," she said. "to which I have agreed."

Murmurs rippled across the nobles in approval. Mercian steel would be of great importance to them. Mikael hadn't discussed this with her, but she knew it was on his mind and that he wanted it. He needed it now, and he would have it.

"That's a start," Narsing said as he looked back at Mikael. "When can we expect the first shipment?"

"I only await word from my council on mining status." Her stomach twisted as she thought of her council. They would never agree.

She needed to make them.

CHAPTER FORTY-EIGHT

Alexander stood over his desk, resting his weight on his palms on the corners. He stretched his neck to one side, then the other; he'd been sitting all day.

"You've not moved since I saw you this morning," came a voice, and he looked up to see the Kharavian captain in the doorway.

"I'm standing this time."

Her eyes smiled. "Barely." She tossed an apple at him, and he caught it. "So many papers. Now I see why you Northmen can't fight. You spend all your time doing this kind of work."

He chuckled. "I don't know about that—we've done a pretty good job fighting back you lot over the past ten years."

"Luck."

He chuckled again. But if he was honest with himself, he'd certainly had luck on his side. The Shadowlands were the fiercest of kingdoms, and it had taken everything he'd had to hold the mountains. In truth, he wasn't sure how much longer he could have sustained.

The Shadowmen. For so long, he'd known them as enemies. But he didn't truly know them. He looked at Katya, and he couldn't deny the questions needling him. He wanted to know them more. He wanted to know her more.

"Why do Shadowmen not show their faces?" he asked.

"Because we're to be recognized by our achievements only." She extended her arms, showing her markings. They ran from her shoulders to her wrists.

He set the book down on the desk and slowly stepped around it, closer to her. Unabashedly, he traveled his gaze down her arms. Geometric patterns formed larger images across her skin—they were really quite beautiful. But they held a darker meaning, he knew. Accomplishments for the Shadowmen meant death.

His eyes drifted up to hers. "Are you not allowed to show your face?"

"I'm allowed to do anything I want." Her eyes taunted him.

Alexander felt the pulse of his heart against his chest. "Would you *want* to show me your face?" he asked quietly. "Because I would very much like to see it."

Her eyes narrowed. "Come look then, if you're bold enough," she challenged.

Alexander stepped closer. Slowly, he reached up and brought his fingers to her cheek, where the cloth met her skin. Ever so carefully, he pulled it down, revealing her smile underneath. Her nose, straight and masterfully sculpted, sat just above the full arches of her lips. The line of her jaw ran as sharp as her wit to the elegant curve of her chin.

The warmth of her skin against his fingers sparked a heat through him. He dropped his hand, remembering himself.

"Am I not a match for Northern beauty?" she asked with a wry smile.

He hesitated a moment before saying softly, "You're beyond."

His admission quieted them both. Then she smiled again. Not a challenging, smirking smile that her eyes so often showed, but a smile of one unsure. A curious smile. She stepped nearer to him.

"Do you want to kiss me, Bear?" she asked.

He did want to kiss her, but he made no move, and no comment. Not when he loved another—another, he reminded himself, that couldn't love him back. Another that he could never be with. Norah was a dream, but Katya... Katya was real, and everything he told himself he'd never find in a woman. And Katya made him want to forget about dreams, if that was possible. Was it possible? Was *this* possible?

Katya pushed herself up on her toes and raised her chin, but she stopped just short of his lips. The sweet scent of her nearness dared him to come the rest of the way.

And he did.

He dropped his head and met her lips with his. The heat of her mouth stirred a burn inside him, and he pulled her closer, drinking her in. She tasted like the dew of summer, and he wanted more. But his mind caught up with him and pulled him back, and he broke their kiss.

They both stood breathless.

"I'm sorry," he said.

Her brows knitted together. "For what? Do you think you've offended me?"

He couldn't help an uneasy chuckle as he shifted his gaze down. "Have I offended you?"

She waited for his eyes to meet hers again, then she shook her head. "Not at all."

Words sat jumbled on his tongue. "Good," he said finally. *Good?* He cursed himself silently. A stupid thing to say.

She smiled again, this time a mocking one, and his cheeks grew hot. She stepped closer. "I like you pale Northmen," she teased him.

"Why is that?"

She stepped even closer. "Because your skin betrays you. Do I make you uncomfortable, Bear?"

"I think you know exactly how you make me feel."

Her smile widened, and she rocked onto her toes, lifting her lips. He dropped his head to meet her again, but before their lips touched, she pulled away. And smiled.

"Yes, I do," she said smartly, and left him in his study.

Ashan was a beautiful city. Norah stood on the wall of the castle, looking out. This was her city. Her kingdom. She was salara.

A noise behind her made her turn, and she smiled when she saw Adrian. It had been several days since his entitlement challenge, and his face had finally started to heal.

"I can almost recognize you again," she teased him. He grinned, and Norah noticed there was an air of excitement around him. Her eyes narrowed. "Why are you grinning like a derpy hound?"

He laughed. Then he pulled up his sleeve with a breathless smile, revealing the inked marking of a Kharavian warrior. Overlapping patterns circled his arm just below his elbow, and on the inside of his forearm he bore the image of a sword. "I got a sword marking," he said proudly.

It was beautiful, but a weight grew in her stomach. Mercian customs and beliefs kept the Northmen from marking their skin, and her mind turned to Alexander. "I'm so proud of you, Adrian," she told him. "You've done what no Northman has. You've gained the respect of Kharav." She paused, searching for how to handle her worry delicately. It wasn't as though he could change his mind now. "Have you shared any of this with Alexander? The sword entitlement, your plan to get the marking?"

The smile fell from his face, and she could tell he hadn't even thought about it. His brow creased with the beginnings of worry. "Do you think he'll be upset?"

She hesitated. "I think he might not understand. He won't know what it means, its importance."

Adrian gazed down at his arm solemnly, realizing what she was saying. "He's going to be angry. He's going to think I turned my back on Mercia."

"No, he won't," she said quickly as she shook her head. "You just need to talk to him. I think he'll be very proud of you and what you've accomplished here."

He nodded, but she could see she had given him little assurance. It saddened her. Adrian had so much to be proud of. Alexander had so much to be proud of.

"Have you told him about Sevina?" she asked.

"Uh, I wrote him about the marriage."

"And of the child?" she pressed.

He sucked in a breath and let it out slowly. "Not yet. I'm going to. Today, I suppose. I just wanted to give it some time... since my last letter."

She understood. He didn't want Alexander to connect that he had gotten Sevina pregnant out of wedlock. Not that she blamed him. "You might want to wait on the marking," she suggested. "I mean, it's not urgent. Maybe let him come to terms with the child first."

He nodded. "I'll do that."

Norah forced a smile. She wished Adrian weren't the only one with the announcement of a child. She'd give anything for the anxiousness of sharing such news. But that wasn't her future, and she'd come to terms with it. Instead, she'd be content with the blessing she'd been given as she looked out across her beautiful city.

The days felt like eternity, but the months passed quickly. Months—seven of them. It had been seven months since Norah had left and taken Adrian with her. Alexander sat at his desk, clutching the parchment in his hand.

"News?" Katya said from the doorway. "From the looks of you, not good."

He pulled open the side drawer and dropped the letter into it, then pushed it closed. This wasn't something he could speak about. Not right now.

He still felt her eyes on him, but he didn't look up.

"Are you really not going to tell me?" she asked.

He said nothing.

"Bear—"

"I don't owe you an explanation," he said sharply, cutting her off.

She rocked back on her heel. She said nothing, but her eyes betrayed her surprise.

He sighed. "I'm sorry. I'm upset. I don't mean to take it out on you."

Katya only stood. Waiting.

"My brother's wed," he said finally.

She stepped into the room and made her way around the wing chair in front of his desk and sat down in it. She waited until he looked at her, then raised a brow. "This isn't good news?"

"No, it's not."

"I thought that's what you Northmen liked, to be married off so you're not breaking your vows, or whatever keeps you from being normal men."

She had a playful tone, but he wasn't in the mood for play. "I didn't send him to the Shadowlands to be distracted by a woman," he said angrily.

"You make it sound as if that's a woman's intention. You mean you didn't send him to go distract a woman?"

He sat back in his chair and paused before nodding. "The fault's with him, not this woman."

"Why must there be fault at all?"

"He has his duties," he argued.

"He still has them. Can a woman and a man not find happiness in one another and still be loyal to their duties?"

Her words caught him, and they sat quietly.

"Can I see?" she asked, holding her hand out.

He sighed, relenting, and pulled the letter back out of the drawer before handing it to her.

Her eyes widened as she read it. "Sevina Arvedi?" She chuckled. "How did he manage to win *her* hand?"

Alexander drew his brows together. "Adrian's a high noble of Mercia, son of the previous lord justice, brother of the current."

"The Arvedi family is one of the wealthiest noble families in Kharav." She shook her head. "Status in the North wouldn't have won him her hand, even if he's as beautiful as you."

He snorted.

"He must be doing well in Kharav. He'd need the lord commander's support. This means he represents you well and brings honor to your family. You should be proud."

Proud. He looked down at the letter. He hadn't felt proud before, but an honorable marriage was something to be proud of, especially if it meant Adrian was proving himself and had won favor in the Shadowlands. Alexander could certainly be proud of that.

She stood to go and stepped toward the door.

"Katya," he called, and she stopped. "Thank you."

CHAPTER FORTY-NINE

Mikael folded his letter and poured the wax before affixing his seal. He stamped it hastily, leaving only half his mark, but he didn't care. It was still recognizable. No one else used a black seal.

Soren stepped inside. "Salar," he greeted.

Things were normal between them now, and he was thankful for it. The nonsensical jealousy he'd felt before had passed. He knew what he had always known—Soren loved him and would give everything for him. Even himself.

"News from the Bear," Soren said. "Gregor has met with the Raelean king."

Mikael straightened. "Cyrus?" he said in surprise. He leaned back as he crossed his arms and brought his fist to his lips, pondering. "What business would Gregor have with Cyrus?"

"The Bear warns that Cyrus holds ill will against Kharav, for our part in supporting Serra and their slave trade."

Mikael snorted. "I wouldn't call giving our defeated enemies to Serra and trading provisions *support*." He hadn't liked Serra's previous king, King Milar. In fact, he'd almost returned his envoy's head when he attempted to renegotiate their contract. Salara had intervened, and he smiled slightly, remembering. But this new king Cyrus was beginning to irritate him as well.

"Let them talk, and let him come," Mikael said, annoyed. "If he seeks to make enemies of those involved with slave trade, it'll be a long list." His chest rumbled as he stood. "How much of a threat could they be? Even with the forces of Serra and Rael combined, Cyrus's army is but a mound of fleas."

"It's rumored that all the slaves who were freed from Serra have joined his army. If that's true, he'll have strength in numbers. And he has hundreds of blood sport fighters from Rael, if not thousands. No telling how many were kept in the arenas."

Mikael leaned against his desk. "So, Gregor meets with a known usurper who holds ill will toward Kharav. You think Gregor plots against me?" He frowned. That didn't make sense. Gregor needed all the help he could get against his brother, Phillip.

"Your marriage to the North Queen threatens him. If he took Kharav, he would take revenge on those who humiliated him. Not to mention, if he does align himself with Cyrus and the kingdoms of Serra and Rael, Kharav would be a valuable stronghold to move their armies north, closer to Aleon."

Mikael sighed. "We're making assumptions on rumor alone, none of which may be true. Gregor might still be an ally, with merely a disagreement on trade between us."

Soren's face told him he didn't believe that. Mikael wasn't sure if he did either.

"There's too much we don't know," Soren said. "Aleon may see us as a target as well, for Kharav would be a powerful stronghold in a position against Japheth, helping Phillip surround his brother. We need to pull back our forces. We need all men in Kharav, including the unit in the North."

Mikael shook his head. "Salara's using those men to protect her villages. And"—he rubbed his temples with stiff fingers—"did the Bear not send us this warning? In thanks, I turn and pull our forces when he still needs them?"

"Kharav needs them more," Soren pressed. "And you have no choice. You can't give Narsing and the nobles another reason to doubt you."

Mikael gripped his temple. This wouldn't sit well with Salara, but Soren was right. The threats were too great, and even if he could spare men to the North, he was already on the cusp of losing his nobles' support. He sighed, then nodded. "Call them back."

Soren gave a single nod. "I'll also send a message to the Uru, for them to draw back into the canyons and send half their warriors to the western pass."

"Call back our men from Bahoul as well," Mikael said.

His commander shifted his weight back. "What?"

Mikael knew Soren wouldn't agree, but the Bear could keep Bahoul for now. Some solace for the North, surely. "How many men do we have there?" he asked. "Three thousand? Bring them back."

"That will only leave Northern forces in Bahoul," Soren argued.

"How many?"

"Two thousand Northmen."

Two thousand men was enough to protect the stronghold, even it they *were* Northmen. "Do it."

Soren scoffed in anger. "We're giving it back to them?"

Mikael couldn't fight all threats at the same time. He'd have to worry about the risk with the North later. "I need your attention focused on Kharav."

Soren's face darkened, but he nodded stiffly and left to see to his orders.

Mikael sank back into his chair and rubbed his face again in his hands. Not only did this news weigh on his shoulders, but Mercia still hadn't sent their steel goods, and the nobles were growing restless. He knew Salara's intentions were true, but the North's council wasn't cooperating.

How quickly everything could fall apart.

Norah found Mikael and the lord commander in the army's planning office with several of their generals. She'd received Alexander's letter at the same time she'd learned of Mikael's decision to pull his warriors in Mercia back to Kharav. Heat of anger pulsed off her skin.

"You pull back your men from Mercia?" she asked as she stormed in.

Mikael nodded to his soldiers, who bowed and left. "I have no choice," he said when they were gone. "Aleon dreams of war, and Japheth is an unknown threat. Kharav would be a prize for either one of them. I've pulled my forces back from Bahoul as well. This should please the Bear."

Norah gaped at him. "Why would you do that, and why would it please Alexander?" Her voice betrayed her worry. "It means he can't pull men from Bahoul if he needs them, which, if you recall the Kharavian units back from Mercia, he will." She looked at Soren, desperate. "Surely you see this."

But the commander said nothing.

"He needs your help!" she said angrily.

"I need the North's help," he snapped back. "It's only a matter of time before Aleon has his eyes on Kharav, if he doesn't already, and Japheth schemes with a new ally who holds ill will against me. The North does *nothing* to show they stand with me."

She could feel the anger radiating off him, but her own anger stripped her of her patience for it. "Aleon is not planning an attack on Kharav," she argued. "It doesn't even make sense that Phillip's attention would be on you. The only thing he cares about is Gregor."

"I don't believe that," he said, his voice rising with his anger. "If all he cares about is his brother, why did he take Tarsus? And if he were to take Kharav, he would further surround his brother. I need to show him we're not an easy target."

"So you'll make Mercia one?" she cut back.

"I need to show my strength with the North behind me!" he boomed with fury. "I've not asked you for men, but I need them. And where's the steel? Your council still refuses to send it."

"I'll write them again."

"We're supposed to be allies," he bellowed, his anger now raging. "This is why I wed you. This is what an alliance is!"

Norah stopped. Even though his words were true, they still hurt her. "So, what would you have me do?" she asked coldly. "Will you have me let Mercia fall, to give you more forces in Kharav?"

"Your kingdom won't fall to drifters. You don't face a real enemy."

Her own fury grew with his words. "I don't face a real enemy? You know the attacks on our villages aren't from drifters. I have an enemy not only at my door, but in my home as well. Have you forgotten the attempt on my life? Do you forget someone wants me dead, wants my lord justice dead?"

"I want your justice dead!" he thundered.

Silence fell between them.

Norah couldn't think through her anger. "I'm sorry our alliance is failing you. I'm sorry our *marriage* is failing you." She turned and headed toward her sanctuary.

"Salara," he called.

But she didn't turn back.

Alexander walked down the main hall of the Mercian castle toward his study, lost in his mind. He didn't see the servant until the man appeared abruptly in front of him.

"A letter, my lord," the servant said with a small bow.

Alexander took it and turned it over, and his own seal looked back at him. The image of the bear had been his father's seal. Now it was synonymous with the seal of the lord justice—the seal Beurnat the Bear had used when he was justice, the seal Alexander now used. But really, the seal meant family. *Adrian*. He smiled.

He waited until the servant disappeared around a corner before opening it. And when the words found him, he stopped. He read them again to be sure and leaned against the wall.

A child.

Adrian was expecting a child.

A sudden wave of emotion hit him, and he wiped his face. He'd never thought about children in the family. He'd always pictured himself and Adrian as the only two of their name. But now... now there would be a child. He'd be an uncle. His eyes welled, and he smiled.

He was going to be an uncle.

His lip trembled through his smile.

He was going to be an uncle.

He gave himself the moment of joy, then turned back the way he'd come. As he stepped into the courtyard, he spotted Katya walking toward him. He couldn't help the grin that came to his lips before he reached her.

Her brows drew together. "This can't be good. What are you grinning about?"

He handed her the letter but couldn't wait for her to read the words. "I'm going to be an uncle."

He couldn't see her face, but he knew her mouth dropped open underneath her wrap, and her eyes smiled back at him. "Congratulations, that's beautiful news. So much to be happy about."

He nodded, still smiling as she handed the letter back to him. But there was something in her eyes—something not right. "Are you all right?" he asked.

She nodded. "Of course."

They stood for a moment, a long pause between them. Katya reached up and pulled down her wrap, and she held out her own letter. "I'm to return to Kharav."

What? She was being called back? But she couldn't be called back. "You can't return, I still need the Shadowmen. I still need..."

He needed her. To stay.

"Kharav needs me. We depart tomorrow." Her words were firm, and he understood. Where duty called, one went. There was no other decision to be considered, despite racking his mind for one. Her eyes were on him, and he swallowed. Did she see how much it bothered him?

She smiled sadly. "I think your fears have proven true."

He shook his head. "What fears?"

"That I've decided I like it here, and I want to stay." She smiled again to hide the glistening in her eyes. "I hope I haven't corrupted you too much."

He looked at the ground. *Corrupted.* The truth was, he'd never felt so right.

"This won't be the last we see of each other," she said.

"No, it won't," he promised.

The weeks passed, slow and full of tension. Mikael tried to right his words, and Norah appreciated that, but things still felt unsettled between them. She knew she was also to blame. The council still denied her the trade she sought for Kharav, though not directly, the cowards they were. They undermined her efforts through *misunderstandings* and delays. They gave mining times that sounded too long, but she didn't know enough to question it. She wished Alexander were with her. Perhaps she needed to go to Mercia herself to resolve it.

No additional news came of Japheth, or of this usurper, or of Alecn looking to invade Kharav. Yet Alexander's letters came with increasing concerns. He didn't have enough men to stretch across the kingdom, and the attacks were continuing. He had to leave the outer reaches undefended. The council didn't understand why Kharav had recalled their men. Strange, Norah mused, because they had been actively working to send them back. But of course, Mikael pulling his forces from Mercia signaled to them he was preparing for something, and she was sure they would assume it was something dark and ill-intentioned.

She searched for ways to help Alexander. He could only encourage villagers in the outer realm to fall back to the central lands for safety. Norah resorted to sending all the Northmen in Kharav back to Mercia. Only Adrian and Caspian stayed with her.

Norah sat at the dining table. The meal was quiet, as they had become lately, strained under the pressures of the crown. She watched Mikael as he ate. He looked up to see her gaze, and he gave a small smile, but it was forced, she knew.

The doors opened and Caspian entered, followed by another Northman. "Queen Norah," he said, bowing, "there's news from Bahoul."

Norah's pulse quickened. The Northman that had entered with Caspian bowed to her. "Queen Norah, I come with an urgent message. Aleon now occupies Bahoul."

Mikael and Soren stood abruptly, and Norah rose as well.

"What?" she breathed.

"When did they attack?" Soren asked.

The Northman eyed the lord commander warily, but he answered. "They didn't attack. They came in peace, but with a vast army. We had no choice."

Soren's face shook with a growing fury. "So, you just let them in? You let them take Bahoul?"

"What were we to do with a hundred men? King Phillip came with tens of thousands."

"What do you mean a hundred men?" Soren asked. "There are two thousand Northmen at the stronghold."

The soldier shook his head. "No. The lord justice had to call them back to Mercia. They left about a week before your Shadowmen did."

Soren jerked his gaze to Mikael, who leaned his weight on his fisted knuckles against the edge of the table.

Norah's stomach twisted as the realization set in on her too—both Alexander and Mikael had withdrawn forces from Bahoul, not knowing the other was doing the same.

"The Aleon king is there?" Mikael growled. "At Bahoul?"

The Northman nodded. "He sends a letter," he said, pulling it from inside his jacket.

Mikael held out his hand. "Bring it."

"For Queen Norah," the Northman said, and presented it to her. "I am to see this directly to your hand," he told her.

She took the letter, her heart racing. It bore the blue seal of Aleon, the seal of Phillip. She nodded to the messenger. "Thank you. You may go for now."

He bowed and left.

Norah shakily broke the wax and read the letter's contents. "He says he bids us tidings of friendship," she started.

Soren snorted. Mikael drew closer as she skimmed her eyes over the parchment.

"He asks if he might set a stronghold in Bahoul, to better surround Japheth," she said.

"To be closer to Kharav, he means," Soren interjected.

"He offers whatever we ask in exchange." Norah handed the letter to Mikael to let him read it.

Soren fumed in anger. "Is he accustomed to doing as he pleases before asking?"

"Is that not what you all do?" Norah cut back. "At least Phillip has the courtesy to send a civilized letter."

"Not *we*," Mikael said, his eyes still on the letter.

"What?" she asked.

"He doesn't offer whatever *we* ask. He offers whatever *you* ask."

Norah pursed her lips. "You read too much into it. Plus, I can ask for the both of us."

Mikael's brow creased. "You aren't seriously considering this."

She knew he wouldn't like it. "Of course I am. How can I not? How am I to remove him? And I can't hold Bahoul on my own and defend Mercia. I need more men. Mercia needs more men. If Phillip will give them in exchange for a stronghold against his brother, I'll give it to him."

"Bahoul is mine," Mikael snarled.

"And you left it!" she snapped. Soren's eyes blazed with anger, but she couldn't let him sway her. She couldn't see another way. "Mikael," she said, softer now. "We can ask for help for Kharav as well."

"Are you mad?" he scoffed. "We would welcome an enemy inside our walls to move against our ally? We would allow him to divide us and take us one by one."

"Aleon's eyes aren't on Kharav. And you and I both know Japheth is not an ally." She stood firmly, her patience gone. "Those are my men in Bahoul, no matter how few. It is my kingdom that is *actually* under attack, and Phillip's letter is addressed to *me*. I will consider it."

Finding the lord commander had been more difficult than she thought. Norah had checked the sparring fields, the stables, his study, Mikael's study. Nothing. She bit the inside of her cheek in frustration. He had always seemed to be everywhere—perhaps that was only when he wasn't wanted. Finally, she knocked on his chamber door. She was just about to turn away when he opened it. In seeing her, he shifted back in surprise.

"Um," she started, wringing her hands. She'd had plenty of time to assemble her thoughts before, yet here she stood without the words. "Can I come in?" she asked.

He stepped back into the room, leaving the door ajar.

Not exactly inviting, she mused as she stepped inside.

"I know you're angry about Bahoul, and with me," she said. "But I don't know what to do, about Mikael, or about Aleon and Mercia. I need your help."

The stiffness in his shoulders eased ever so slightly. She wasn't placating him for amends. She had never faced the challenges she did now. Mikael leaned on Soren to help him make decisions for the good of Kharav. She needed that same help.

"I can't tell Phillip no," she continued. "I have no way of forcing him out of Bahoul. I have to make the most of it."

He said nothing, which was fine. Just to talk through her thoughts aloud with him was enough—he'd tell her if she was erring. This she knew for certain.

"I know Phillip's first priority will be Japheth," she said, "and his brother's head. A stronghold in Bahoul puts him in position to strike. Of course he would want to be there. And I could get more men for Mercia, which I desperately need."

Soren folded his arms. He spoke sooner than she had expected him to. "You assume Gregor intends to move against us. If he does *not* have this intention, then we would be helping to destroy our ally, against a foe who will turn on us next."

Norah shook her head. She'd seen the look in Gregor's eyes when she'd threatened him. She'd seen the hate that brewed inside. She'd read the words of his letter to Mikael, sickeningly complimentary in welcoming him to Japheth. Lies. Japheth was no ally.

"Who do you think is most likely to attack Kharav—Aleon or Japheth?" she asked pointedly.

Soren's eyes held a dark intensity, and his reluctance to respond answered for him. He finally broke the lock of their gaze, turning away from her. "It would be a bold move," he said, "to support Aleon in attacking Japheth—striking first before Gregor moves against us."

She noticed that the conversation had shifted from *if* to *when*. He believed Japheth was against them. "So, you agree?" she asked.

He looked back at her. "I don't disagree."

It wasn't the same, but she didn't have time on her side to appreciate the difference. "It's what I need to do, then."

"But, Salara," he warned, "don't be naive to think Aleon won't try to take Kharav. If we support Japheth's fall, you need to ensure we can stand against Aleon after."

"The council would never support a war against Aleon," she admitted. "Especially as we fight an unknown foe on our own soil."

"The Bear would. If you asked him. Your army follows him, not your council, and he comes to your call."

No. Norah shook her head. "Alexander's loyal to Mercia."

"He's loyal to his *queen*," he countered.

Silence hung between them.

Soren stepped nearer to her. "If you accept the Aleon king's proposal, you must be willing to protect Kharav. You must be willing to bring the Bear."

How quickly things had turned—from Soren feverishly working to get Alexander out of Kharav to now calling for him back. But he was right. She would need Alexander to bring her army if Aleon turned against them. Norah swallowed. That would mean she would defy her own council and ask Alexander to do the same—to turn his back on Mercia. But she didn't think it would come to that.

"Will you do that, Salara? Will you bring the Bear?"

Norah drew her bottom lip between her teeth. She would. "If Aleon tries to take Kharav, I'll call Alexander."

He nodded. "Then ask Aleon for men to help you."

Norah thought about her plan for a long time. Despite it sounding the best option, and even after her conversation with Soren, it still twisted her stomach. It was a gamble, for sure.

Now to do what twisted her stomach even more—tell Mikael.

She found him in his study with Soren, poring over maps and plans. He stopped and looked up when she entered. She wondered if Soren might have already told him.

"I've decided to accept King Phillip's request to base his forces in Bahoul," she announced. "In exchange, I'll ask him to send men to Mercia to help me with the attacks on my villages."

Mikael's face hardened. Soren hadn't told him. "So you'll allow him to position himself to march against our ally?" he asked. There was already an edge of anger in his voice. She'd known he wouldn't be happy about her decision.

"Is that really what you think Gregor is?" she asked.

"I don't know what he is," he said sharply. She could see his anger growing. He nodded, but it wasn't a nod of acceptance. "So you've decided, on your own, that you will divide Kharav and Japheth. This is a move I won't be able to recover with him. You would do this to me?"

"Mikael, he's not an ally," she insisted.

"You don't know that!" He leaned over his desk, gripping its sides. "Then what?" he asked. "I'm to stand alone against Aleon?"

"Of course not," she replied, forcing a calm back to her voice. "You'll have my lord justice, and the Mercian army."

He scoffed in disbelief. "You would call him back? He would fight against me, not for me."

"He'll fight for me," she insisted.

"Do you not see what you do? You set in motion the war in the vision. The four kingdoms on the battlefield! And you call back the man who will end me."

"We're not fighting! We're letting Aleon wage a war that benefits us both."

"You're a fool if you believe that. You know nothing about war."

"Soren does," she cut back.

Mikael shook his head in bewilderment and turned to Soren. "You agree with this?"

"I'm not in disagreement," he said. "If Salara can influence Aleon to remove a threat against Kharav, she should."

The king's brows dipped as if the words had hurt him. "And after, when Aleon rises against us? You put your faith in the Bear?"

Soren looked at Norah with eyes of shackled storms. "I put my faith in Salara."

Chapter Fifty

The air of Ashan hung thick with apprehension. Aleon's forces in Bahoul, so close to Kharav, made the Kharavian legions uneasy, even with the Canyonlands between them. Messages traveled quickly now, with Phillip so near, and Norah had already received a response to the letter she had sent eight days prior. She had written accepting his request to occupy Bahoul, provided Mercian and Kharavian armies could use it as a shared base. Of course, she knew Mikael wouldn't station Kharavian forces there, wary of an easy escalation to war.

She had asked Phillip to lend his men in return, to help identify Mercia's enemies and stop them. And she had asked if Aleon still truly considered themselves friends of Mercia. It was a painful question to ask, after refusing Phillip's hand for marriage in favor of an ally of his enemy.

Norah held his response in her hand, unopened. She brushed her fingertips over the seal, her heart racing at what the words inside might say. She wondered if she should wait for Mikael before she read it. He hadn't yet returned from the Canyonlands, where he'd gone to ensure the Uru and their border forces were prepared. He could have sent Soren—it was the commander's job after all—but he'd gone himself. Alone. He was upset with them. Both of them. But they didn't have a choice. He just needed some time to calm, and he'd see things more clearly, she was sure. He'd see.

She broke the seal and opened the letter.

Dearest Norah.

Phillip's words had a personal feel. Too personal.

I found no sleep after I sent my last letter, unsure of how you'd respond, or if you'd respond at all. How different these circumstances are from what was planned so long ago. The hand of fate is cruel, isn't it? Twisting and surprising even the most assured of men. That was my lesson. I was too proud, too confident, and the gods sought to humble me.

And they have.

When I received your reply, I knew it was a sign of their returned favor.

In response to your first question, of course Aleon still looks to Mercia with deep affection and friendship. Were our fathers and grandfathers not bonded in the blood of battle? Were they not fused together in the kiln fires of war? These ties aren't easily broken. And your acceptance of my request to remain in Bahoul shows me these intentions still remain.

Your request for my help in protecting Mercia shouldn't even be a question. As I write these words, I've already ordered ten thousand men to flush out this unknown enemy of both Mercia and Aleon.

Norah paused, forcing herself to breathe. He was sending men—ten thousand of them. Why would he be so generous? She turned her eyes back to the words.

I've thought many times on the circumstance by which we'll meet again. I look forward to seeing you, Norah. We have much to discuss.

Most sincerely, I am,

Phillip

Norah refolded the letter with shaking hands. It felt as though he had whispered the words into her ear, like he knew her. Catherine had told her they'd met several times before she'd disappeared. Perhaps they'd been friends. But things had changed now. Why and when did he expect to see her again? It sounded soon. Why did it sound so soon?

She pulled a small wooden letter box from her vanity to place it inside, but when she opened the lid, she stopped. A small handheld portraiture sat between the stack of folded parchments, and she pulled it out. It was the small portraiture of Phillip that had been sent to Mercia, with the talks of marriage that felt so long ago. She looked at his face and his tousled hair of bronze, his smiling lips and kind eyes. He looked the way his letter sounded.

A knock on her door made her jump, and she turned to see Soren enter.

"Hammel's hell," she breathed, scowling at him. He never waited for a response to his knock. It merely served as a warning. Soren's peculiar friendship came with the dearth of privacy, a product of his absent self-awareness, or perhaps his absence of care.

"They said a letter's come," he said impatiently.

She nodded, clutching it in her hand, her stomach knotting. Then she held it out for him.

He took it, reading the words quickly, and then folded it back. But his face didn't reveal the anger she'd expected. "He sends the men you requested, and more than I expected," he said with a nod. "Much more. Good."

"Good?" she asked, raising a brow. "Did you not read the rest of the letter?"

His forehead creased. "What of it?" he asked.

She gave a small breath of disbelief laced with amusement at his lack of awareness. "He speaks as though our kingdoms are still united, Mercia and Aleon. Perhaps as though *we'll* still be united."

"Good." He nodded.

"Wait, no, it's not good," she argued.

His brow creased. "I do take you for smarter sometimes."

She pursed her lips as a flash of anger brought heat to her cheeks.

"Salara, you're trying to influence a kingdom that's not your ally to fight your war."

"It's *his* war," she argued.

"No," he said, shaking his head. "He only thinks it's his war. And he'll attack Japheth on his own time, unless you make it your time. You can't force him, as he's shown you with Bahoul. You must incent him. And if he is incented by the thought of the North and Aleon together, you'll use it."

"Soren, manipulation isn't the answer to everything. I actually do want a good relationship with Aleon. I want trust between us. We could be strong friends, allies."

Soren stepped closer, his eyes dark. "You can't be allies. If you ride beside the Aleon king, you bring Salar's end."

The thought of the vision hit her like a blow to the stomach, like it always did. She felt sick.

The horns sounded.

"Salar's returned," he said. He held the letter over a candle, lighting it afire.

"No!" she cried, reaching for it.

But he pulled it back. "Why would you keep it?"

"I keep all my letters."

He shook his head. "That's a stupid mistake. You'll not keep this one," he said as he tossed it into the fireplace, letting the flames consume the rest. "Now go meet your husband."

Norah walked quickly to the courtyard to meet Mikael, overwhelmed by the vision that she tried so hard to push from her mind. Would a pact with Aleon really put them on the path toward his death?

When she saw him ride in, she smiled. He had only been gone a few days, but she missed him. She had missed him before he'd even left. There was a distance between them now, one that left a crushing weight on her heart, one she didn't know how to fix. He felt alone. She needed to show him she was by his side.

His eyes searched for her, and when he saw her, he moved toward her. She waited until he reached her and dismounted before she stepped to greet him.

"Husband," she said softly.

"Are you well?" he asked.

She nodded with a small smile, but he didn't smile back. Worry still etched his brow. "I'm glad you're home," she said. Norah stood on her toes and kissed his cheek. "Come inside." She curled her arm around his, and they started up the stairs.

"Did you get your men?" he asked as they stepped inside, and the large doors closed behind them.

Norah didn't want to speak of Aleon, not now. She only nodded.

"How many?" he asked.

"Let's talk about this later. I just want—"

"How many?" he asked again.

Norah swallowed back the unease rising in her throat. She had hoped to ease things between them before venturing into this topic again. But not answering him would only fuel his anxiousness about it, she knew. "Ten thousand," she said finally.

His face held no expression, hiding the emotion behind it. "I should have given you the men."

She hated that he faulted himself. "You need them for Kharav," she tried to assure him.

"And I shouldn't have pulled them from Bahoul. Soren told me not to."

"You didn't know the Mercian forces had been stripped back as well. Mikael, you can't blame yourself."

"I'm salar," he snapped. "There's no one to blame but me." He rubbed his hand over his face, and his calm returned. "Forgive me. I'm tired. I'm going to clean up."

She squeezed his arm lovingly. "I'll send for some food, and I'll be right there."

He nodded and turned toward their chamber.

Soren came up beside her as the king took the stairs. "Don't speak to him of an alliance with Aleon," he said with a warning gaze. "And have an answer ready on why your council still hasn't sent the steel."

She nodded.

"Go to him," he told her. "I'll send Vimal with a meal."

Norah nodded again appreciatively and followed after Mikael. Now that he was back, she needed to show him she was with him, beside him. She understood his fears, the pressures closing in around him. They were pressures she felt too. They needed each other.

She reached the chamber and stepped inside, but stopped when she saw him. He stood by her vanity, oddly still and not yet stripped of his armor, his back to her.

"What are you doing?" she asked, giving him a curious smile. But her smile fell as he turned, and she saw the portraiture of Phillip in his hand. She cursed herself. Her earlier conversation with Soren had distracted her, and she'd forgotten to put it away.

"Why do you have this?" he said softly, but she could hear the upset inside him.

Norah forced a casual tone. "I was going through some old letters today. I was interrupted, and I forgot to put them away." She silently praised Soren for having the good sense to burn Phillip's latest letter. She felt like such a fool.

"Why do you have this?" he asked again. His words were slow, enunciated.

"I have everything. Every letter that's ever been written to me, by anyone." She nodded to the small wooden box. "It's all there. You're welcome to read them." She paused—not all would please him, but that wasn't the point. "I suppose I just feel like I have so little of my life. I try to hold on to everything. I don't want to forget."

"You want to hold on to *this*?" he asked as he clutched the portraiture in his hand.

"It's not like that."

His nostrils flared. "Does he have a portrait of you?"

"My grandmother sent one," she replied with a calm nod, "as is customary in conversations of marriage. I doubt he still has it, for I'm sure he's quite moved on."

"And you haven't?"

"That's not what I meant."

A coldness seemed to settle over him, and it frightened her a little. "He still remains unwed," he said.

"I haven't followed his marriage prospects. Nor do I think about them."

"Has the Bear not kept you apprised?" he asked. "It wasn't so long ago he brought the news of the Aleon's standing offer. And I doubt your council's diligence in solidifying an alliance has waned. Have you thought about that?"

"Don't be ridiculous," she breathed. She could see his anger reaching dangerous levels, but she didn't know how to pull him back.

Mikael shook as he crumpled the portrait in his fist and hurled it into the fireplace. Then he stopped—something caught his eye. He stepped closer to the hearth and knelt down to scratch at the melted wax that had hardened on the stone.

Norah's heart pounded in her chest. The royal blue wax of Aleon.

"You burned a letter from Aleon?"

Well, Soren had burned a letter from Aleon, but she wouldn't implicate him in this madness. "It was nothing," she insisted. Her pulse thrummed in her ears. "I've told you everything he's offered, and everything I've accepted."

"Yet you don't keep his letter, as you do with all your other letters. What do you hide from me?"

She shook her head. "Your mind's running away with you. Listen to yourself. I'm your wife."

"Then act like it!" he thundered.

Norah stepped back, speechless, and he brushed by her as he stormed from the room. She let herself sink down onto the side chair, out of breath and out of ideas about what to do. How could she get through to him? How was she going to fix this?

Chapter Fifty-One

Soren walked briskly toward the stables, where he found Mikael leading out his horse. His pulse quickened. He'd heard Salar was preparing to ride out, and it surprised him he'd leave without saying anything, and after he'd just returned.

"Where are you going?" he demanded.

"Odepeth," Mikael said coldly.

Soren sighed. The seer. What did he expect to see? "I'll go with you," he said, starting toward the stable to get his own horse.

"You'll stay here," Mikael said sharply as he mounted his destrier.

Soren stopped in surprise. Perhaps it shouldn't have been a surprise; Soren had felt the distance between them growing. But they'd always gone to the seer together, faced the future together. Not now. "Are you angry with me, brother?"

"I don't know what I am," Mikael spat back, looking down from his horse. "You ask for the return of the Bear. The man who's to take my head. You would so quickly call him back?"

Soren shook his head. "Of course not, but I would have him bring the North forces if Aleon turned against you, to help keep your throne."

"They would join Aleon against me!" the king snarled back. "And what about keeping my queen? You encourage her treaty with Aleon?"

"She has no choice!"

"You do!" Mikael raged. He pulled up his reins and turned his destrier east. "I'll return in three days. If you're truly my brother, you'll help me stop this."

Tension cramped her shoulders, and anxiousness turned her stomach. Norah paced the length of her chamber, then back. She wasn't angry with Mikael. He had the weight of the world on his shoulders—crumbling alliances, mounting enemies and ambiguous threats, displeased nobles, no heir to solidify the hold of the throne, and uncertainty in his marriage. She'd hoped to alleviate at least one of those for him. He loved her, wholly, and she needed to assure him that he also held her heart. Only she struggled with how to show him. And something had to give—she couldn't take one more setback, one more worry.

The door to her chamber swung open. "Salara!" Vitalia called.

Norah jerked her head up at the urgency in her maid's voice.

"The child—it's coming!"

The child? Adrian and Sevina's child? *No*—it wasn't due for another month, *more* than a month. It was too early.

"The midwife is with them, and the healer," Vitalia said breathlessly. "But I thought you'd want to come too."

She most certainly did. Norah grabbed her cloak and followed her maid quickly down the halls and out of the castle. The Crest fell in step behind her, but she paid them no mind, she only went faster. If this baby was lost...

It was a long walk from the castle to the stately Arvedi home and was made even longer by her worry. She should have taken a horse. By the time she arrived, she was breathless. A servant opened the door to her, and she quickly stepped inside, ignoring the burn of the muscles in her legs.

Aman, Sevina's father, met her promptly in the foyer. "Salara," he said in surprise, and gave her a bow.

"Lord Aman. I'm so sorry for the disruption, but I had to come. How is the child?"

"Norah," came Adrian's voice, and she looked to the top of the stairs, where he stood by the overlook railing.

He moved quickly down them.

"Adrian," she said, "I don't mean to impose, but I had to come see if the baby is okay, if you and Sevina are okay."

He reached the bottom of the stairs and moved to her in three additional steps, catching her in a warm embrace. "You're here," he said. Then he stepped back to look at her. His lips formed a smile, but the crease along his forehead was deep with worry. "Thank you for being here. I'm sorry I didn't send word. He came so quickly."

He. The child had already been delivered.

"No, it's perfectly fine. How is he?"

He gave a jerky nod. "All right, for now."

"How is Sevina?"

He swallowed and nodded again. "She's well. It wasn't a difficult birth, but it's too early. The midwife and healer are both with them. They said we'll know over the next couple days"—he paused and swallowed again—"if the child will make it."

If the child will make it. His words hit her like a blow to the stomach. "Is there anything I can do? Anything you need?"

He shook his head. "Only prayers. His fate is with the gods now."

Norah clutched his hands tightly.

"Do you want to see him?" he asked.

More than anything. "I don't want to impose, I only—"

"You're not imposing. I would..." He paused when his voice cracked. "I would love for you to meet my son."

A tear escaped the corner of her eye, and she nodded. She let Adrian lead her up the stairs, down a wide hall, and to a large chamber in the back of the house. Inside, Sevina sat in the center of the bed, propped up with a small, wrapped bundle in her arms. A woman Norah assumed to be Sevina's mother stood to the side and curtsied as Norah entered. The midwife was cleaning up, while the healer had set to packing away his tools. Norah looked over her shoulder at Adrian, who smiled encouragingly.

She drew nearer to the bed. Sevina was beautiful. Aside from the sweat across her brow, she looked far from having just delivered a child. She smiled at Norah.

"Salara, you honor us by coming."

"I had to. How is he?"

Sevina looked down at the bundle in her arms. "He's well, only sleeping." She pushed back the blanket from the child's face, and Norah could see his black hair peeking out from underneath. She smiled.

"We've named him Theisen," Adrian said from behind her.

Norah glanced back at him in surprise. "A Mercian name?"

"As soon as I heard it, I knew it was the one," Sevina said. "Theisen Arvedi Rhemus. It's a strong name, for a strong boy."

"That he is," Norah agreed, "if he's anything like his father."

Sevina's smile widened.

Norah glanced around at the small family. Aman stood in the door. They were welcoming, but she knew she should give them space. "I should go," she said. "I only meant to see how you were. Please keep me updated."

"Of course, we will." Sevina still wore her smile, but Norah could see her worry underneath—the worry of a mother as she waited to see if her child would live.

The ride to Odepeth was long. It was warmer in the valley, and it brought a sweat to Mikael's brow. He coveted the cool walls of the seer's temple that channeled the breeze like funneled lips of the earth's breath. But the fear of what he might discover there sat heavy in his chest, and it suffocated him.

Still, he reached Odepeth too soon. He slid from his wearied destrier and walked the steps of the temple with a growing anxiousness. He thought about the gift of the seer often, a blessing and a curse. He questioned himself—if he had the ability to go back and not see his fate, would he? For the agony that came with knowing how little time he had left was maddening, and it made a man maniacal and obsessive. Visions fueled wars; they grew anger like crops in fields of suspicion and haunted even the best of intention. Yet, knowing this, he couldn't keep himself from returning. He supposed that answered his question.

The guards bowed their heads as he passed. They were keepers of the seer. Some kingdoms had several seers; Kharav had one. One was enough in Mikael's opinion. He knew that seers didn't all see the same visions, and he had no desire to have another purveyor of obsession.

As usual, the seer greeted him in the center of the temple, surrounded by the intricately carved columns of stacked stone. "Salar." The old man bowed his head respectfully.

Mikael paused under the gravity of the moment. He would know today—he would see if there was a different future for him now. "I've come to see my fate," he said.

The seer gave a long breath of regret. "But I have shown you your fate."

The seer's words cut into his chest like a blade of battle, stopping his heart, taking his breath, and draining his life force.

"So, I've not changed my future?" he asked.

"You do not change fate, Salar."

"You don't know that," Mikael snapped. "Perhaps you don't see. I wed the North Queen! I broke her marriage to Aleon, yet when I last came, you told me nothing had changed." He shifted his tone to be softer, hoping, pleading. "Perhaps you don't see?"

"Nothing has changed, Salar."

Mikael let out a shaking breath. This was the strongest seer in the four kingdoms. As much as he hated to admit it, if there was a change to his fate, he was sure the old man would have seen it.

"There are other visions, though," the seer told him.

Other visions. These he had to see. "Show me."

The seer led him down the narrow hall to the back room that Mikael knew well, and the king took his place on a floor pillow in the center. Mikael waited as the old man gathered his things and sat on the floor across from him. The seer poured wine into a small bowl and pricked his finger with a gemmed dagger, letting the droplets of blood mix with the sweet juice of fermented fruit. Then he breathed the words of the blood spell and held the bowl out to the king. Mikael accepted it and drank.

As he swallowed the last of the wine, he waited for the seer to enter his mind. As all the times before, they sat in the temple of draperied shadows.

Mikael rose, standing in the temple of his mind, with visions all around him. The seer waved him to follow, and he did. They walked in the darkness, with no light on their path, and then stopped at a room hidden by a thick drapery. The seer pulled back the curtain, revealing a room so bright that Mikael squinted against the light.

They stepped into it, outside and into the center of a sprawling city. He didn't recognize it, with its large buildings of marble and glass and patina copper domes. But his eyes caught the flags that lined the center mainway, leading to a large, opulent citadel.

Blue flags with a golden lion. The flags of Aleon.

His heart beat faster as he looked down the mainway to figures approaching on horseback.

Salara. Smiling. Crowds gathered on either side of the mainway, throwing rose petals. His blood chilled. Beside her rode Soren. Why would she go to Aleon? Why would Soren? So willingly, like Aleon was a friend. He felt the delirium of suspicion returning, but he forced it down. There had to be a reason—a completely rational reason, he told himself—for them to travel so freely to his enemy and to be received so warmly.

"Is this all you've seen?" he asked.

The seer hesitated, but answered. "It is all you want to see."

Mikael knew this moment well—the moment where he could choose the path of peaceful ignorance or the path of haunting knowledge. But then he asked himself, had it ever been a choice?

"Show me," he told the seer. "Show me all of it."

Mikael turned and stalked the dark hallways, not waiting for the seer to lead him, but searching on his own. He wandered through the visions he had already seen, those that were already etched into his mind. He wasn't interested in those, but one caught his eye—the image of Salara's capture. It seemed like yesterday, yet so long ago. He paused at the room, remembering. He watched himself as he carried her, her unconscious body draped across his thighs as he rode his destrier through the night. He remembered how she'd felt—small and fragile, warm and soft. She'd smelled like fresh-hewn adda trees, intoxicatingly sweet. It had lingered on him even after she was no longer in his arms. The pull she'd had, even when he'd hated her...

And now, now that he didn't hate her, now that he loved her...

Mikael let out a long breath. He ached for her now. He cursed himself. He had so little time left with her, and instead of spending it near her, with her, inside her, he had ridden to the ends of the earth, away from her. He needed to go back. He needed to leave this madness and get back to her. Ignorance—he chose it now. He didn't want to see. He turned to leave. And then stopped.

Norah sat on her knees at the edge of a bed in her nightgown. She looked at him, but not *at* him. He wanted to reach out, to touch her, to pull her to him, but he knew she was only a vision.

Her hair glowed bright in the moonlight, like she was the moon herself. He looked around her. Mikael didn't know this place. Another castle, perhaps, but not one he'd seen before. A cloaked man stepped past him from behind. Mikael's pulse quickened as he watched Norah slip off the bed. She spoke words he couldn't hear.

"What is she saying?" he asked, but he already knew the seer couldn't tell him. There was no sound in a vision.

She didn't seem to fear him as she stepped closer. Too close. Mikael gripped the hilt of his sword, but there was nothing he could do.

Faster than he thought human, she snatched her dagger to the man's neck. Mikael panted a breath as pride rippled through him. His salara.

But the man didn't counter. He only reached up slowly, showing his empty hands, and pulled back the cloak of his hood. Mikael felt his breath leave his body, and the heat of rage hit him like a battle charge.

The Bear.

Kill him. But Mikael knew she would never.

She dropped her dagger to the floor. Her mouth formed unheard words as she hitched a step back. He'd give anything to know what she said.

Norah reached out and put her hand on the Bear's chest but made no move to push him away. Instead, she spread her fingers wide. Emotion filled her eyes as she looked up at him. Her gaze moved to his face, his lips. She trembled. Again, her mouth moved in silent words. The Bear stepped closer and brought his hand to her face.

Mikael gripped his sword tighter. If only he could strike that hand from its arm. But he could do nothing.

She leaned into his touch, only for a moment... before she surged forward and threw her arms around him. Mikael had seen her embrace the Bear before, but the way she clung to him—like she'd missed him, like she needed him. She held him like she couldn't let him go.

Mikael shook with fury. He couldn't stand to watch but he couldn't look away. At last they broke, and Salara stepped back.

Then the Bear brought his hand up to her cheek again. That hand—he would lose that hand. And just when Mikael thought that was the end, the Bear pulled her closer and dropped his head to kiss her.

And what was most gutting—she let him.

Mikael pushed out a breath through his teeth. There was no containing his rage. In the room where she slept, in the night, the Bear would come to her. And she would take him.

The vision faded to dark, a small mercy, and they stood in the emptiness once again.

"When?" Mikael breathed to the seer, who stood behind him. "When does this happen?"

"When she is still young and beautiful."

Mikael was quiet for a moment, taking in all the seer had shown him. "Are there any more?" he asked.

"Not new."

Mikael opened his eyes, and he was in the daylit temple of Odepeth once more. He stood, forcing his breath to calm and trying to harden his heart. "The other visions of the Bear... of my fate?" he asked.

The seer drew his brows together in regret. "As it always is, and always will be. Unchanged."

So that was it. The Bear would take his head.

Still.

And his wife.

"Salar," the seer said. "Salara has asked that I send word if I receive another vision."

"You won't," he said, and the seer bowed his head. Then he left the way he had come.

Norah came down the stairs just as Mikael stepped inside the double doors of the castle. It was late, and she hadn't heard his arrival. Soren had told her he'd gone to the seer, and she was desperate for news.

"Husband," she said as she crossed the floor to him. She wanted to tell him about Adrian's son and that she'd received the good news that they expected the boy to survive. But she could see torment on his face, silencing any news. The weight in her stomach grew. "Are you well?" He didn't look well.

He didn't answer.

"What did the seer show you?" she asked.

He still didn't answer, and that scared her. It hadn't been good news. She forced out an even breath. He would need her. He would need her reassurance. They walked toward their chamber in silence. She tried to stretch the tension out of her neck as she walked, but she knew nothing could take that away.

Suddenly, he stopped, turning and looming over her. "Has the Bear come to you in the night?" he asked.

His question came unexpectedly. "What?"

"Have you taken him to your bed?"

Where was this coming from? "Of course not!"

"Then it's still to come."

She shook her head. "I wouldn't do that."

"I saw you," he seethed.

"Mikael," she breathed, "this is madness."

He grimaced as he reached up and ran his fingers along her cheek. Then in a startling move, he clasped the base of her jaw and forced her still to look at him. Not painfully, but with an unnecessary strength. "Have you kissed him since we've been wed?"

Norah's heart raced. She'd kissed Alexander in the Wild, but the memory had been taken from Mikael. He wouldn't understand the circumstance now. But the greater weight on her heart—she'd kissed Alexander in Mercia in the cave. Guilt riddled her, but she couldn't tell him. It would only add to his mania.

"No," she whispered.

Tears filled his eyes. "You lie to me," he breathed.

A sob rose in her throat. She couldn't speak.

His face twisted. "If he had been here, would you really not have chosen him for a child? He's who you want, yes?"

"Mikael, stop," she cried.

"And you'll go to Aleon. I saw it. Freely you'll go, under a marriage alliance, I'm sure. A rose petal welcome. Will the Aleon king be as tolerant a husband as I am, I wonder?" he seethed. "Will he protect your lover? Will he be patient, as I have been? Not make you choose?"

"Mikael, stop it!"

He pushed her back against the wall. "No longer. Now you must choose." He bared his teeth with a trembling fury, pulsing fear through her. "You want me to send men to the North? I'll send them." His eyes were dark and full of hate. "And they'll bring me back his head."

No. Norah clawed at his hand to release her, but he held her firm.

"I'm going to kill him, Salara. I'm going to kill the Bear."

Chapter Fifty-Two

Soren sat in his study with his arms crossed, leaning forward onto his desk. He stared at the parchments in front of him, unseeing. He should have been present for Mikael's return from the seer. He wanted to know what Salar had seen. But it was better, he figured, that he hadn't been there. Better to let Salara calm him, reassure him. Soren might be able to better mend Mikael's anger against him after.

Just then, Bhastian tore into his study, and Soren jerked his head.

"Lord Commander!" the guardsman called urgently. "Salara's gone!"

"What?" he said, rising.

"She took her mare directly from the field. By the time the men got to the stables for horses to follow, she was gone."

What had happened with Salar? But more concerning, Salara was gone. "She's alone?"

"We think Cohen followed her."

Rage rippled through him. "So a mute can follow after her, but not the Crest?"

"It's a failure, my lord," Bhastian admitted.

Soren forced out an exhale. "Where did she go?"

Bhastian shook his head. "We don't know, but the men said she was upset."

Soren cursed himself. He knew Mikael was troubled. Why had he let her meet him alone?

"Should I ready the horses?" Bhastian asked. "We could catch up to her before she even reaches the Canyonlands."

The Canyonlands? No. She wouldn't flee to the North. It would unravel everything she had fought so hard to keep together. Soren forced himself to think. Where would she go? Somewhere safe, somewhere she could get her mind back, figure things out—he knew a place. "Tell them to prepare my horse. I'll go alone, after I tell Salar."

Bhastian bowed and left to his charge.

Soren walked quickly to the royal chamber, where he found Mikael stripping off his armor. "What did you do to Salara?" he asked without greeting. "What did you say to her?"

Mikael glanced at him. "She stays in the sanctuary. That should answer your question enough."

"She's not in her sanctuary," he snapped angrily. "She's gone. Left the castle."

Mikael took a step back. The thought seemed to strike something deep within him—a fear, a sadness. "Then she goes to warn him," he said quietly.

"Who?" Soren asked.

"The Bear."

Soren's chest tightened. The last thing Kharav needed was the threat of war against yet another kingdom, especially the North. Why would he think she'd ride to warn the Bear? "What did you say to her?" he asked again.

Mikael didn't answer. He stripped off his breastplate. "She's chosen. And now she rides for the North."

"They would respond to their queen fleeing Kharav with certain war. They're waiting for a reason. She wouldn't do that."

"She would for him."

Soren didn't recognize this man before him—was he giving up? "I'm going after her," he said.

"You won't find her if she's on Savantahla."

"Cohen's with her."

"The mute?"

"He's not mute, he's deaf," Soren snapped.

Mikael's nostrils flared at the small defiance, and his anger shifted to Soren. "I didn't think that when I made you swear to her, you'd so easily turn on me." His words cut like knives.

"You question my loyalty to you?"

Mikael bared his teeth. "You stand with Salara while she accepts a treaty with Aleon."

"I don't stand against you," Soren argued. "She doesn't oppose you!"

"She opposes me now!" Mikael bellowed. "And she must choose! Me or the Bear, and that's how I know she rides for the North." His eyes blazed. "And now you must choose, brother. Perhaps I should be especially grateful you didn't seed her with your child. Then I might have none of your loyalty left."

Soren grabbed Mikael by the throat and shoved him against the wall. "If you speak those words again, I'll cut them from your mouth," he snarled. He glanced over his shoulder to make sure the door to the chamber was closed and Mikael hadn't been overheard. Then he tightened his grip and leaned close so that their foreheads were almost touching. "That's how you lose your salara and your kingdom. It's how you lose everything. Do you understand?"

Mikael's body slackened under Soren's grip. Soren had never seen him this way. He pulled Mikael to him in a tight embrace, as the king shuddered under the weight of his burdens.

"She rides for the North," Mikael said hoarsely. "I know it."

"She wouldn't betray you. Not even for the Bear. I'll find her, brother," Soren assured him, "and show you this is madness."

A heavy thunder of hooves rang through the night as Soren drove his destrier east. Salara had fled the castle on her mare of the Wild faster than her guard could follow, but he knew where he might find her. She wouldn't be headed to the North. She wouldn't betray Mikael. Not even in his madness. Not even for the Bear.

When he reached the hillside house, he wasn't surprised to see a second horse standing with Salara's mare in the night. Both were without saddles, having been taken in haste. Cohen *had* been able to follow her. He wasn't surprised. Cohen's abilities didn't surprise him anymore. He had put the boy and his sister to train with the Crest. If they were going to be around Salara, they would have the best training of the Kharavian army. He hadn't expected them to perform so well.

While they hadn't picked up all the skills of a well-rounded soldier of the Crest, they both excelled in their specialty—the girl with her bow and the boy with his sword. Cohen was perhaps even better than Adrian, who Soren considered one of the best. He only cursed the boy being deaf. His disability created too much risk—too much weakness—to put him in the ranks of the Crest. But it was moments like this Soren questioned that decision.

He pushed the door of the hillside house open and stepped inside, where he was quickly greeted by the tip of a sword to his neck. He couldn't help a wry smile as he turned his head to find the raven-haired boy with his arm outstretched, the blade like an extension of his hand. What pleased Soren most was that he had no doubt the boy could kill him.

He pulled down the wrap from his face so Cohen could read his words. "Salara can shake the Crest, but not you?" he said. "I'm impressed, boy, as usual. Where is she?"

"What do you want?" she answered as she stepped into the foyer in front of him. She nodded to the boy, and he lowered his sword. "He sent you?" she asked, looking back to Soren.

He shook his head. "No. But he knows I've come."

Her face hardened. She looked ready for a fight. "So, you've come to drag me back?" she asked, her voice sharp and challenging.

Soren eyed her for a moment. He wouldn't dare. "You forget I serve *you.*"

That seemed to pacify her, and she turned and stepped into the side sitting room. He followed. She took a seat in the chair by the fire, where it appeared she'd been sitting before he'd arrived, and she picked up a mug of steaming tea from the small side table.

"Salar thinks you've ridden for the North," he told her.

She took a drink of her tea.

He let out a breath as he sank into the chair on the opposite side of the fireplace. "This isn't him, Salara. This man isn't him."

"I can't live like this, Soren."

A pit seeded itself in his stomach. "Are you thinking of leaving?"

She took another drink of tea from her cup. Her silence worried him.

"Have you ever wondered what it would be like to live a life in a place where no one knew your name?" she asked finally. "Where no one wanted anything from you. No expectations, no burdens. Where you could simply love and be loved."

"No," he said. He had never wanted any other life than the one he had now.

She smiled sadly. "I envy you," she whispered.

"Are you going back to the North?" he pressed.

She stared into the flames of the fire.

The pit in his stomach grew. She couldn't leave. She couldn't go back to the North. It would destroy Mikael.

But she shook her head. "No, but I think I'll stay here awhile."

He let out a long breath. That, perhaps, was a wise idea. The hillside house was quiet, and safe. And it was not the North.

"Will you tell Mikael?" she asked.

He nodded.

"And have my maids come tomorrow? I'd like some company." She bit her bottom lip, thinking. "No guards."

"Salara," he objected. "I can't leave you in a house alone in the countryside, even if it is a safe house."

"I have Cohen."

That was true, and the boy was as good as two or three soldiers. But that still wasn't enough. "Let me send Adrian and the girl."

She pursed her lips together. "Fine."

"And Bhastian," he added.

"No one else."

"Kiran?"

"I don't need a whole army," she argued.

He snorted. "They're hardly the whole army."

"I'll think about it," she said as she stood and turned toward the hall. "But for now, I'll get some rest." She looked back at him. "Are you staying through the night?"

He shook his head. He didn't like the idea of leaving her alone, but he had to return to Mikael as soon as possible, and Cohen would keep her safe until he sent others. "No, I have to return to Salar tonight."

"By the time you get back, it will be morning."

"Already too long."

She pursed her lips. "Don't send an army."

"No army," he assured her. An army was thousands of men. He wouldn't send thousands.

Chapter Fifty-Three

Mikael stood, leaning his weight over the desk in his study. He gripped the edges until he could no longer feel his fingers. Spread in front of him were the letters from his scouts, warning him Cyrus was moving his forces across Japheth. Gregor had found his new ally, and war was on the horizon.

His eyes were fixed forward, but unfocused. Sleep had escaped him through the night. He felt the darkness of madness taking him, closing in over his head. He could smell it as it filled his lungs, taste it in his throat as it drowned him. But he couldn't stop it.

He was losing everything—his alliance, his power, his mind. It was only a matter of time before he lost his kingdom.

And he was losing *her*. Salara. It was his own doing. He felt himself pushing her away. He could hear it as he raged, but he couldn't stop.

And then there was the Bear. Mikael knew he wouldn't kill him. He wanted to, more than anything. Not because the Bear would bring his end, but because the justice held a piece of Salara's heart—enough of it to pull her back to the North to save him. And now Mikael would know what he feared the most—she loved the Bear more.

Soren had said she wouldn't go to the North. He believed that once, but not anymore. She'd have to still love him to stay, and he'd destroyed that love, he was certain. Perhaps it was best. She'd be safe in the North. With Gregor and Cyrus now more than just a threat, he didn't want her in Kharav.

The door opened, and he turned to see Soren enter, alone. He swallowed. That was his answer, then. Slowly, he looked back at his desk.

"You were wrong, brother," Soren said.

Mikael snapped his head back to him. Wrong? He couldn't mean...

"She didn't ride for the North."

His chest seized. She had stayed? "Where is she?" His voice broke as he spoke.

"The hillside house. She just needed some time."

The hillside house. So near, yet so far. He needed to see her. "Should I go to her?"

"I've only committed that I wouldn't send the army."

Mikael let out a breath of relief. Would she see him, though?

"You can get her to come back," Soren told him, as if reading his mind, "but you can't be as you were—thinking crazed things, spewing madness."

"I know. The seer—"

"I'm going to kill that fucking seer. Go to her. She loves you."

He nodded.

Soren bobbed his head toward the door. "Go," he pressed angrily.

Mikael reached out, clasped the nape of Soren's neck, and brought their foreheads together. He didn't deserve this man.

Then he turned and stepped into the sunlit hall to go get his salara.

The afternoon sun waned, fading under gray skies of rain before it dipped below the horizon. Norah looked out the windows over the mountains. She expected Soren to return soon with a full legion, completely ignoring her insistence for no army. It was unfortunate, as they wouldn't all fit in the house and they'd be unable to make a camp to keep them from the rain. Perhaps she should just go back. It would be selfish to keep them all here, just so she could be away from the castle—away from Mikael and his delusions. She had her sanctuary, and if she was honest with herself, it was a bit dramatic that she'd insisted on being completely away.

She'd go back.

Norah pulled her cloak from the hook on the wall and stepped toward the door. She should be able to make it back before nightfall, although she'd have to travel in the rain. She didn't mind. Water never bothered her. She had to find Cohen; he wouldn't be far. He'd spent his time constantly scouting the area around the house. But when she opened the door, it wasn't Cohen looking back at her.

Her breath caught as Mikael's dark eyes stared into hers. He stood, wet, in front of her. She glanced around him; he was alone. Not even Soren had come with him. Her heart beat heavier in her chest. Had he come to drag her back himself? Was he still angry?

He didn't look angry.

"Salara," he said softly, finally breaking the silence. He didn't sound angry.

She couldn't leave him standing there. Norah stepped backward and opened the door wider, inviting him in, and he followed. He shut the door behind him, then stood silently.

"I didn't expect you," she said.

"Are you upset I've come?"

She shook her head slowly. She'd never be upset about him coming to her.

He breathed out, as if relieved. "Would you be upset if I stayed?" he asked.

How quickly he could make her forgive him. She shook her head again.

He stepped nearer and slowly reached out his hand to take hers. Despite him being drenched by the rain, his skin was warm, and it felt good. She let him pull her closer to him.

"I'm sorry, Salara," he breathed. His nearness made the world fall away. He pulled her even closer. "Would you be upset if I kissed you?" he asked.

She would be upset if he didn't. She lifted her chin to him.

His kiss wasn't the hungry force it usually was. He kissed her softly, as if unsure—asking, searching, seeking her forgiveness.

And she gave it to him. She sought forgiveness herself. He wasn't the only one among them with fault.

"You were right to be angry," she said as she broke from their kiss. "I'm sorry I lied. Two times I've kissed Alexander, and both bring deep regret. It's not something I want to talk about, but I will if you ask me. And yes, I didn't want you to read Phillip's letter. His tone toward me is not one you'd take kindly to, and it worried me. But I'll recite it word for word; the worry has burned it into my mind. I just... I don't want secrets between us. And I want to rid you of this doubt."

Norah reached up and ran her fingertips through the short crop of his beard. "And I want you to let me in. I want you to tell me what worries you." She pulled his lips back to hers. "Will you talk to me?" she whispered, then kissed him softly with her own plea for forgiveness.

She pulled back and looked up at the darkness of his eyes. Slowly, he nodded. She dropped her cloak on a chair by the door.

"Come, then," she said, taking his hand and leading him to the bedchamber. Inside, she turned to him. She pulled his wet cloak from his shoulders. He stood as she took her time draping it over a chair and turning her attention back to him. He was soaked through, and needed dry clothing.

"What did the seer show you?" she asked as she pulled his shirt out from his breeches, one side and then the other.

"I've failed," he said. "I've failed to change my fate."

She swallowed as she drew his shirt up. He bowed his head and lifted his arms, letting her take it from him.

Norah dropped down, pulling at the heel of his boot, and he let her take them, the left and then right. She rose again, and their gazes locked as she pulled loose the ties of his breeches. "How does the seer know?"

"Because fate can't be changed. But I already knew this."

She pulled down his breeches, then stooped as he stepped out of them. "Then why did you go?" Rising back up, she met his eyes again.

"It's the curse of the seer—to draw a man into obsession."

Norah stepped to the armoire and pulled out a clean linen tunic and breeches. "What else did you see?" she asked as she moved back to him. She knew he'd seen Alexander. He'd already told her so.

He hesitated. "I saw the Bear." His eyes were filled with sorrow. "He came to your bed in the night, and you took him."

She said nothing but cursed the seers in the depths of her soul. She cursed the visions. They did nothing but cause pain, and for what? She unfolded the clean breeches, and he took them and stepped into them. He drew them up, around his waist, and she pulled tight the ties, slowly looping them closed.

"Many things are not as they seem in these visions," she said finally. "You know this."

"Some things aren't. Yet some things are exactly as they seem."

She shook out the folded tunic and raised it, and he complied, bowing his head for her to put it on him. She swallowed again. "I don't know how else to show you that I choose you," she whispered. "That I love you and that I'm beside you. I would never betray you."

She spread her hand over the fabric of the tunic against his chest. His warmth permeated through it.

He reached up and put his hand over hers. "I know." He brought her chin up so that their gaze met again. "I know you choose me, Salara."

She gave him a small smile through the wave of emotion. That was what she desperately needed to hear. She did choose him, and she needed him to know it, to feel it, to believe it.

"While I'm still here, you choose me," he added. "But it's not betrayal when I'm gone. And this has made me realize I must help you prepare."

A sickening fear seeded in her stomach, vining up into her heart. "For what?" she breathed.

He brought up his other hand and brushed her cheek. "To rule without me."

"No." She shook her head, denial rippling through her. "Don't say that."

"I have to. You have to be ready."

"No!" She tried to pull her hand away from under his, but he held it.

"Salara," he said as she fought against him.

"I won't hear it!" Talk of defeat meant he accepted his fate, but she didn't. She fought harder.

He gripped her sternly. "Norah, stop!"

Her struggles weakened.

"You'll listen to me," he said, softer now. "When I'm gone, you need the alliance with Aleon. You'll take his offer of marriage. Then, with Soren and the Bear beside you, and the power of the empire, no one can stand against you."

She would never do that. "Stop!"

"I'll stop when you acknowledge it. I *will* die, Salara. And soon."

She shook her head again, and a cry escaped her.

"You'll have Soren and the Bear by your side, regardless of what happens to Kharav. They bring with them the loyalty of both our armies, and I know they'll do whatever's necessary to keep you safe. As I must do. It's why I'm sending you back to the North."

Norah's mouth dropped open, and she pulled back again. "What?"

"Cyrus grows a vast army, which he's already moved into Japheth. If it's Gregor's intention to march against me, which I'm certain it is, I don't want you here."

He couldn't possibly be sending her away. Her place was by his side. "I can't leave you!"

He brushed her cheek again. "Salara, you have to go. Go to the North, where you're protected. And if I should fall, you won't be alone. You'll have the Bear. And Aleon will stand beside you."

He was right in that Phillip would be hesitant to come to her aid in Kharav, but he would readily join her in Mercia to march against anyone who opposed her, especially if the opposition was Japheth. But she would never wed the king of Aleon. And she wouldn't leave Mikael. She hadn't weathered this madness only to lose him again.

"I'm not leaving you," she insisted.

"Salara, you have more power in the North. You'll be able to help me more there."

Yes, she would have more power in person than trying to influence her council from afar, but that wasn't enough to pull her from him. "We'll get through this. I'll stay, and we'll get through this. You don't even know these things will actually happen."

"And if they don't, you'll come home. And everything will be as it was. But I can't manage this and fear for you at the same time."

"You don't need to fear—"

"I'm breaking!"

She stilled as he gripped her.

"I'm breaking," he whispered. "And I know I have your love. I know that now. I know you choose me. But it's not enough—I need to know you're safe. Go to the North. Let me focus on Gregor and Cyrus. Will you do this?"

She couldn't answer.

"Salara, please. Help me." He cupped her face in his hands, begging. "Salara. Please."

Norah drew in a ragged breath, and she nodded, relenting.

He pulled her close to him, then drew her face up to look at him again. His eyes glistened. "I need you," he whispered.

The sudden need to escape their clothes overtook them. Fabric tore as Mikael shucked his newly donned tunic and breeches, and Norah clawed off her dress, but neither of them cared.

They didn't come together in a sudden heat. It wasn't a wanton need. It was the need of touch, of the warmth of skin against skin. Mikael carried her to the bed and lowered himself to bury his face in the corner of her neck and breathe in her being. He simply held her. Tightly. And she held him, clinging to him like life, scared she might not be able to again.

Chapter Fifty-Four

Calla's face wore a firm frown. She wasn't one to hide her feelings. Norah knew she wanted to come to Mercia, and so did Cohen, although he was much more discreet with his disappointment. And Norah had wanted to bring them, but they would remain at the castle with their grandparents, who had finally come, at Norah's insistence, until threats against Kharav had passed. Norah needed them all safe.

The Crest stood in the courtyard, all of them ready and prepared to depart. Mikael would keep none of the warriors for himself or the castle, despite Norah's insistence. And, of course, Soren would go with her, as would Adrian. Norah had wanted Adrian to stay with his son and Sevina, but Mikael was firm. He even sent the dogs.

"You send too much," she told him as he placed a gentle kiss on her head. "You'll at least need the commander of your armies."

He feigned offense. "You think I don't know how to command an army?"

But she wasn't in the mind for jokes. Emotion overwhelmed her.

His face grew more serious when he saw it. "I need him to protect what's most important to me," he said.

Norah reached up and clasped the side of his face. "And who will protect what's important to me?" she said through her tears.

He pulled her hand to his lips and kissed her palm. "We've both seen my end, and it's not here. You don't need to fear for me."

"I still do." She stood up on her toes and kissed him. Then she climbed atop Sephir under the warm rays of the sun.

"Keep her well," he said to Soren as the commander mounted his destrier.

Soren nodded his oath.

Norah looked back at Mikael as they rode out of the courtyard. She felt like she would fall apart in the wind, like this was the last time she would see him. What if it was the last time?

The journey to Mercia was longer than she remembered. They traveled slower with so many men. The time was agonizing.

They passed through the Uru. Norah tried to enjoy her visit with Tahla, but all she could think about was Mikael. So many times she almost turned back. It wasn't too late, she told herself. She was so afraid—afraid she wouldn't see him again, afraid she wouldn't hold him again. She desperately wanted to run back to him, but she knew Soren wouldn't let her.

She tried to focus her mind on something else.

Adrian traveled silently, which was unlike him. He had started their journey with excitement at returning home again, but as they drew nearer to Mercia, he became quieter, worried even.

"Are you all right?" she asked him one evening after they had set camp.

He gave a stiff nod. They sat under the stars, and he rubbed the marking on his forearm. "He's going to be upset with me," he said quietly. He was worried about Alexander's reaction to the ink on his skin. It would be a challenging conversation, no doubt.

"Wait for the right time," she said. "Then explain it to him, privately. You just need to help him understand."

He nodded again, but her words obviously did little to allay his fears.

"He loves you, Adrian, and he'll be proud of you. He just needs you to talk to him."

Her own heart broke for him, but she knew the brothers loved each other deeply, and she was glad they would be together again. Alexander would be surprised when he saw him. Adrian didn't look like the same man that had come to Kharav. He was even taller now, broad shouldered, and cloaked in strength. He had the hardened look of a warrior. It was easy to forget he was so young. He'd taken on the lord commander's solemn countenance. Or perhaps it was Alexander's, she mused.

Adrian had become close friends with Cohen, she noticed. The two were inseparable, often exchanging silent words between them. Norah had worried about them both, that they might find life in Ashan difficult. But they seemed to thrive with every challenge, every trial—to relish them even. And with their resilience came the respect of the earlies and even the lord commander, although he didn't show it.

Calla had proven herself as well. Norah loved to watch her on the sparring field. While proficient in combat, the girl was quick-witted and clever and made up in intellect for what she lacked in physical strength. And she was a master with a bow. Norah was excited to one day take her to Mercia—home to the greatest bowmen in the world—to hone her skill even more.

Finally, after almost three weeks of travel, Mercia came into view, white and radiant in the light of the sun. Its towered turrets and spires rose high against the sky, adorned with arched clerestories and elegant tracery. It really was beautiful. But seeing her kingdom brought a deep and growing angst within Norah. With the news of Japheth breaking from Kharav, everyone would be looking to see what she would do now. Her grandmother, the council, Alexander—they would be waiting, watching, judging how she would handle Japheth and Rael, if she would drive Mercia to support a king they didn't even recognize as king. And she worried about how she would manage them, because that's exactly what she planned to do.

Norah looked at Adrian as they drew nearer. "Are you ready?"

He smiled, but she could see his anxiousness underneath.

She shifted her gaze to Soren. "Behave yourself," she told him. Then she eyed the dogs that trotted alongside the horses. "And don't let them eat the cat."

They crossed the bridge, then continued through the gates and into the courtyard of the castle. Norah saw Catherine waiting for her by the fountain, and a smile came to her lips. She had missed her grandmother. She had last parted Mercia with a rift between them, a rift she hoped had been forgiven.

Had she been forgiven?

Norah slid down from Sephir and paused just before she reached Catherine. She couldn't read her grandmother's expression, and angst twisted in her stomach.

But Catherine's eyes welled, and she smiled, then she stepped forward and hugged Norah tightly. "Welcome home, child," she said through her tears. She pulled back. "Oh, let me look at you." Her eyes were misted in happiness, her lips pursed to hold them from trembling. "I'm so glad you're home."

But this wasn't home. Still, Norah smiled as she stepped back, until another caught her eyes, and her smile fell.

Alexander. Her heart quickened in her chest. To see him again brought a heartache she'd thought long gone.

He approached with a gentle smile. "Queen Norah," he said softly.

"Lord Justice."

His eyes burned a brilliant blue, eyes that still held her.

"Lord Justice," came Adrian's voice from behind her. He grinned as he stepped forward and bowed his head.

"Brother," Alexander said in surprise. He let out a hearty laugh as he reached out and clasped his shoulder, then pulled him into an embrace. His face filled with emotion. They were the same height, but Adrian was larger now. Alexander still held him close, his hand on the back of his head as he embraced him, like he would a small boy. Pushing Adrian back slightly to look at him, Alexander scoffed, "What are you eating? And what have you done with your hair?"

Norah shifted. The Northmen kept their hair cut short, one of the many things they did differently than those in Kharav—as Alexander would surely find out.

"I'm letting it grow," Adrian replied with a grin.

Alexander's brow creased. "Why?"

Adrian shrugged. "Because I like the way it looks."

"His training is coming along well," Norah interrupted. "I know he's excited to tell you about it."

"I've earned my sword entitlement. And a blade," Adrian grinned, pulling the sword from his scabbard and holding it for his brother.

"It's a high achievement," Soren spoke out, surprising everyone around them. "One of the highest in the Kharavian army."

Catherine gaped at the lord commander and then looked back at Alexander.

Alexander stiffened at Soren speaking for his brother, but his pride was evident, and he gave a nod to Adrian. "Well done, brother."

Adrian let out an excited breath.

But then Alexander paused. "What's that?" he asked, his eyes on Adrian's forearm peeking out from under his sleeve.

Adrian glanced at Norah, and she gave a small shake of her head. But it wasn't unnoticed. Alexander grabbed Adrian's arm.

"Alec," Adrian pleaded as Alexander pushed back his sleeve to reveal the patterned black ink.

"You marked your skin?" Alexander asked, pained.

"By the gods," Catherine breathed.

Norah blinked slowly as a murmur rippled through the people around them.

"I told you, I earned my entitlement," Adrian said quickly.

"You're Mercian." Alexander's voice was low but tinged with anger. "We don't mark our skin."

"Alexander," Norah said quietly, trying to calm him.

"Did you know about this?" Catherine asked her.

Norah eyed her sharply. Her grandmother wasn't helping. She turned back to Alexander. "We'll discuss this privately."

"How could you allow him?" he said angrily. He turned to Soren. "This was you. This was your influence," he seethed.

"That marking is one of honor," Soren cut back. "Men die trying to achieve it. And he's not a boy; he can make his own choices."

Alexander's rage pushed him forward, but Norah stepped in front of him. "That's enough," she told him. "Walk with me. Alone." She needed to get him away, right now.

Alexander's eyes burned with anger, but she knew he would follow. Norah headed for the library. She felt Alexander's wrath behind her, but she didn't dare turn before they were away from prying ears, for fear of an argument. Once inside the library, she turned to face him.

"How could you allow this?" he seethed. "My own brother?"

Norah let out a long breath. "I wasn't aware until after."

"And you didn't want him to tell me?"

This was exactly what she had feared. "I wanted him to wait for a more opportune time, a more private time. It wasn't fair to you to find out that way."

His voice came sharp. "You should have written me."

She shook her head. "That's not the kind of thing I'd write to you about." She sighed. "Don't be angry at him."

Alexander's eyes stared right through her. "He would have known it was against Mercian custom and how I would feel about it, and he still did it."

"No," she argued. She couldn't let him think that. "He got carried away in the excitement. No other Northman, and very few Kharavian men, have accomplished what he has. It wasn't until he saw my reaction afterward that he thought of what it would mean when he came home, what it would mean to you." She let out a saddened breath. "The whole journey, he's been consumed with the fear of your disappointment. I'm surprised he didn't flay the skin from his arm to be rid of it."

Alexander sank onto a bench along the hallway of stone and glass. She could see it pained him to hear that, and she sat down beside him. "All he wants is for you to be proud of him." She could tell he was listening to her words, and she let him sit for a moment and soak them in. "He drew the lord commander's ire, showing off what you had taught him."

Alexander let out a faint snort.

"It made Soren hard on him. Perhaps too hard. There were days I feared for him. But he was strong, determined. Relentless." She smiled, remembering. "And then he began to rise." She paused. "Alexander, I wish you could have been there. I wish you could have seen him. There must have been a hundred soldiers beating their swords on their shields, calling for his entitlement. They were cheering him, they were *all* cheering him. He's respected by those who were once enemies. He's finding his way in two opposite worlds where most struggle in one. You should be proud, incredibly proud."

He was quiet for a long time. Then he said, "I am proud."

She put her hand on his arm. "Then let him embrace all that Kharav offers him. Think of what he can accomplish between our two kingdoms."

His blue eyes stared up at her, piercing. "When did you become so wise?" he asked.

She smiled.

He gave a small sigh. "I suppose you're also going to tell me to leave him alone about his hair."

"I think it looks good on him. You might want to consider it yourself."

He snorted.

"You should go talk to him," she urged.

"I will."

Norah stood to leave.

"Norah," he said, stopping her. "I don't ever want him to be anxious about returning home."

"Then you should tell him that."

Alexander found Adrian in his chamber, settling back in. His brother turned in surprise when he knocked on the doorframe.

"You didn't bring your son?" Alexander asked.

"Sevina wants to wait until he's a little older, and when we aren't on the brink of war."

Alexander could understand that, although he would've liked to have seen the child. It was hard to imagine Adrian, who was still so young himself, with a son. Alexander had been upset by the news of Adrian marrying a Kharavian woman, extremely upset. But not of the news of the child. Far from it, all he felt was... joy.

"How is the child?" he asked.

Adrian grinned, nodding. "He's good. Strong. Fat."

Alexander chuckled. Adrian had been a fat baby. "How is your wife?" Adrian's eyes lit up at the mention of her.

"She's well. You'd like her. She's smart and thoughtful. She cares for me a great deal." His grin grew wider. "She tells me not to do stupid things. Sometimes I hear you in her voice."

"Does it keep you from doing them?"

Adrian shook his head with a smiling frown. "No."

He laughed.

Adrian's face grew serious. "I know you're disappointed."

Alexander let out a long breath. "I had thought that you would hold our customs, hold our values. I'm disappointed you marked your skin."

Adrian nodded, his eyes falling to the floor.

"But I'm also proud," Alexander continued.

Adrian's head jerked up in surprise.

"You're the son of Beurnat the Bear, and you have the respect of the Destroyer and the army of the Shadowlands. You bring our kingdoms together. I'm proud that you're my brother." Adrian's lip trembled, and Alexander clasped the side of his neck affectionately. "Now get your sword. I want to see what you've learned."

Adrian nodded, smiling through his tears.

Norah knocked lightly on Adrian's chamber door. After the reunion with Alexander, she wanted to make sure he was all right.

She heard a small shuffle, but there was no reply. She knocked again.

"Not now, please," he called.

"Adrian?" she replied. "It's Norah."

More shuffling came, then the latch released and the door opened slowly, revealing Adrian with a half-cut head of hair.

"Norah," he greeted her as she gaped at him in surprise.

"What... what happened to your head?" she asked.

He smiled sheepishly. "You've caught me in the middle of cutting my hair."

She shook her head in confusion. "Why? I thought you were letting it grow long?"

He shrugged. "I was, but..." His words trailed off.

She sighed. The conversation with Alexander must have gone poorly, and by the looks of it—very poorly.

He opened the door wider, inviting her in, and she winced at his handiwork as she got a better look at his head.

"Thank you," he said, surprising her further. "I know you talked to him. He found me after, and he was... different. Understanding."

"Then why are you cutting your hair?"

Adrian inhaled deeply. "I'll continue to get ink markings if I earn them. It's who I am now." He paused for a moment. "But my hair, it means nothing to me. It means something to him, though, so I'll cut it to show that he's still in my heart and what's important to him is important to me."

Norah smiled through the emotion that had so suddenly overtaken her. "You're a good brother, Adrian."

He smiled bashfully.

"Would you like some help?" she asked.

"Very much so." He sighed in relief, and she laughed as he handed her the shears.

Chapter Fifty-Five

Time passed quickly in Mercia, more quickly than Norah thought it would. While the nights were long without Mikael beside her, the days were filled with challenges that kept her on her toes.

The first thing she'd done when she reached Mercia was redirect steel-good shipments to Kharav, much to the council's dismay. They had somewhat valid arguments: promised shipments to trade partners, low inventories, slow mining times. But promises to Kharav were most important—Mikael came first.

Getting settled into Mercia's affairs proved more difficult than she'd expected. She was surprised at how much the council had so freely taken upon themselves to adjudicate things—things well within her authority, within Catherine's authority as regent in her absence. She tried not to jump to judgment. She'd been away in Kharav for quite some time, and Mercia needed strong leadership.

The attacks on the villages in the outer reaches had mostly stopped, thanks to the coverage the Aleon legions provided. Norah was thankful. Phillip wrote to her often, mostly with updates for Alexander and her forces, for which she was also thankful.

The days came easier as she gained her footing, but she still fought the unease of returning to the North. She did love Mercia. It just wasn't her home anymore.

Norah walked briskly to the judisaept, with Cusco and Cavaatsa trailing behind. She took the dogs everywhere, even to address state matters, under the council's disapproving eye. But they said nothing. She dared them to.

Another letter had come from Phillip. She hoped it brought news of his plans to advance on Japheth. He'd been moving his forces to the southern border of Eilor and stretching them across to Bahoul.

Mikael had sent the Kharavian forces northeast to the Canyonlands, heavily manning the eastern pass, and was doubling armies at Kharav's only two seaports. She worried for him. Not because she thought Kharav was unsafe but because he was alone. And she loved him.

Norah stepped into the judisaept. As usual, the council had already arrived and was waiting. Did they ever leave? Sometimes she thought they slept there.

Soren took his usual place beside her, resting his axe between his feet. Catherine had urged her to keep him from bringing weapons, but Norah would save her arguments with Soren for things that really mattered.

Alexander handed her the sealed letter and then took his place at the opposite head of the table. She broke the wax and opened it.

"Queen Norah," she read Phillip's words aloud. "I trust you remain well and safe in Mercia. I write with urgency, for I've discovered the army of Rael is larger than we understood before. Much larger, in fact..."

She couldn't speak the words anymore, she only read. Her heart hammered in her chest. She handed the letter to Soren, who read it over.

"What does it say?" Edward asked.

"Aleon's not going to march on Japheth," she said breathlessly.

Soren tossed the letter onto the table for Alexander, who picked it up.

"So, a delay in war," Councilman Alastair said. "That's not necessarily a bad thing."

Norah snapped her head up with fire on her lips. "It most certainly is a bad thing. Mikael needs Aleon to attack, before Gregor acts against Kharav. It's what we were counting on."

The letter passed around the council, each member reading its news.

"The largest army they've ever seen," Councilman Henricus read with a frown. "Even larger than Aleon's."

"That's not possible," Edward scoffed.

"The Aleon king admits it with his own pen," Soren said with a slight snarl, his patience clearly gone. "It should come as no surprise. Cyrus's army has the freed slaves of Serra. Now others flock to him, fleeing their own kingdoms to join him."

"Slaves are not warriors," Alastair countered.

"What about the thousands used as blood sport fighters?" Soren snapped back. "Each one would kill ten of your Northmen."

Norah swallowed the bile building in her throat. "Kharav needs us," she said. "We'll send more Mercian steel—swords, shields, polearms."

"This will take time," Edward argued.

"Then send the mined iron. We'll build a Mercian forge in Kharav, with smiths."

"Queen Norah," he gasped. "You cannot give the Shadowlands the ability to forge Mercian steel. They could dilute our trade value in the market, forge weapons against us."

"They *are* us!" she snapped. "I am queen of Mercia *and* Kharav, and I'll use all means to protect both. And no more talk of delay. If it's not ready, I'll have every man mining until it is, including everyone in this room."

Her councilmen stiffened but offered no further argument.

"We need more to show Japheth that Mikael's not alone." She looked at Alexander. "We'll send an army of five thousand."

"You cannot send our forces when we battle unknown attacks on our own lands," Henricus argued.

But Norah ignored him. Still looking at Alexander, she said, "The lord justice will take the legion himself. I want Gregor to know how serious I am."

Edward gaped at his fellow councilmen around the room. "Queen Norah, you cannot send our forces *and* our justice to fight the Shadowland's war!"

"It's *our* war!" she said angrily. She looked back at Alexander. "We still have Phillip's ten thousand men?"

He nodded.

"Take five thousand of them as well," she added.

"If Rael's army is larger than Aleon's, ten thousand men won't matter," James said, finally speaking.

"I'm not trying to match their number," she countered. "But if we show that Mercia and Aleon stand with Kharav, it makes for a strong deterrence."

"And how do you know Phillip will agree to sending his men to aid the Shadow King?" Edward questioned.

"I'll write to him and ask," she replied.

Henricus snorted. "After you've already sent his army?"

"I only return the favor," she said shortly.

Crossing into the Shadowlands brought a rare air of excitement, a much different feel than the loathing that normally pulsed through Alexander as he made his way through the lands of his enemy. Perhaps it was because the Shadowlands were starting to feel less like the enemy. They were now home to his infant nephew, whom he would soon meet for the first time.

Adrian's face carried a broad grin, as it had ever since they'd passed through the Canyonlands. Alexander couldn't help a smile of his own. He'd been angry before—angry that Adrian had been so excited to leave Mercia, like he no longer belonged to his own kingdom. But as Alexander let his brother take the lead in driving the legions south, he could only watch with pride.

Adrian moved between the ranks with confidence and command. He checked on the forge equipment often, their precious cargo, knowing it was even more important than the ten thousand men they brought. He moved them along at a fast pace, but not too fast to exhaust them. Mercia, Aleon—it didn't matter—the men listened to him, respected him. All of them, even the Crest guards that Norah had sent with them.

While Adrian's charismatic grin could make any heart feel light, Alexander realized he was no longer a boy. He was a gentle soul, yes, full of fun and adventure. But he was also a natural leader, skilled in all the ways Alexander had taught him. And although Alexander loathed to admit it, Adrian was made even stronger by his time with the Destroyer.

Adrian exceeded what either kingdom alone could have made him, and he belonged to so much more than just Mercia—he was destined for even greater things beyond.

"What?" Adrian said, pulling him from his thoughts.

Alexander hadn't realized he'd been staring at him. He shook his head. "Nothing."

They marched through the capital city, rounding the legions toward the soldiers' barracks and into the provisioned overflow housing. After turning command over to the field captains to settle the army, Alexander and Adrian broke away to the courtyard, where Alexander knew the Shadow King would be waiting. He'd seen him on the wall.

His core didn't roil as it usually did on the way to the king, perhaps because his hatred for him had died somewhere along the way. Alexander wasn't sure when. Perhaps it was when he realized how Adrian had grown in the Shadowlands. Or maybe it was well before the journey, when the king had sent Norah to the safety of Mercia. He could have kept her, forcing Mercia and Aleon to his side to help him stand against the threat of Japheth and Rael. But he didn't.

Alexander still didn't like him, but he no longer hated him.

They entered the courtyard, where the Shadow King now stood, and brought their horses to a halt. Alexander slid down from his mount and gave a stiff bow of his head.

"You bring forces of Aleon to aid me?" the king asked, his voice laced with disbelief.

"They were given to the queen," Alexander said, "and she gives them to you."

"They will follow Kharavian command?"

Hardly. "They'll follow Mercian command. I also bring forge equipment, with smiths. We'll teach you how to work Mercian steel. If you can do the ironmaking and casting here, it will quicken the time it takes for us to get it to you."

The king shifted in surprise. He hadn't expected that either. This man didn't know how fortunate he was.

"She sends you everything she can," Alexander told him.

"Including you."

Alexander stilled. Was he rubbing it in? His blood heated under his skin.

"I'm grateful," the king said. "I know she wouldn't take sending you lightly."

Alexander eased.

The king pushed his gaze to Adrian. "The lord commander remains with her?"

Adrian bowed his head and pulled a letter from his jacket. "He does. And he sends this for you."

The Destroyer had entrusted Adrian with a letter to the king? Adrian had said nothing of it.

The Shadow King took it but didn't open it. His eyes met Alexander's again. "I need you to return to her."

Alexander straightened. He'd half expected the Shadow King to cast him from the Shadowlands, and he imagined it in all forms—ordering him to leave, driving him out, or even just killing him. But never had he imagined the king would tell him to *return* to her.

"You'll depart tomorrow."

Tomorrow? *Tomorrow?* "She sent me with two armies to aid you. I can't just leave."

"You can and you will."

Alexander stumbled over his words, caught between astonishment and disbelief. "You *need* me. There are ten thousand men who await my orders." Was he really arguing with the Shadow King to stay in the Shadowlands?

"Take them back with you."

Alexander snorted. Was this man mad? He needed all the help he could get.

The Shadow King stepped closer. "You and the lord commander are the only ones I trust with her safety. You have to return to her."

Alexander stilled, sobering. This king would deny himself aid to keep Norah safe. He'd send the man he hated most in the world safely home, to protect the woman they both loved. Alexander glanced down, gathering his thoughts. Norah expected him to keep this man safe too. "I'll go then. But I'll leave my brother in my stead."

From the corner of his eye, he saw Adrian's head jerk toward him in surprise. But this was what Adrian had prepared for his whole life—to serve, to lead. And the men would follow him.

The Shadow King nodded. "Depart before dawn." The king glanced at Adrian and gave him a small nod, then he turned and strode into the castle.

Alexander turned to Adrian. "Are you ready for this?"

"Ready as I can be. I won't disappoint you."

Alexander gave a small smile. "I know." He drew in a long breath. "There's only a little left of the day. Take me to my nephew."

The grin returned to Adrian's face, and they turned from the courtyard and strode toward the city.

Evening had turned into the full of night as Alexander stepped from the grand statehouse. Adrian followed him out. The hours had passed too quickly.

Adrian's son, Theisen, was everything Alexander had imagined him to be, and more. With a head full of black hair and blue eyes, the child was beautiful. He could steal a heart at first glance. This child was family, immediately loved. As Alexander held him in his arms, he felt what every man feels for those he loves—he'd give his life for this child.

And Sevina—Alexander knew instantly she was perfect for his brother. While she was the image of quiet beauty, Adrian responded to her every touch and followed every gentle word. Alexander watched in shock as his brother minded things that Catherine had never been able to get him to do: not setting his sword on the table and using his silverware properly at dinner. And Sevina looked at Adrian with eyes of a pure heart. Alexander found himself grateful his brother had found such a love.

As the evening drew to a close, Alexander said his goodbyes. He'd be leaving before the sun rose to return to Mercia, and he wasn't sure when he'd return. Adrian walked him to the door, then down the stairs and to the gate of the walk, where they paused.

His brother shifted uneasily. "There is something I wanted to talk to you about."

They'd just spent two weeks traveling together, what had not already been said?

"Mercia will always be in my heart," Adrian said. "But Kharav is where my son is, where my wife is. Where my home is."

Alexander took a step back.

Adrian swallowed. "And I'd like to provide for my family here." He paused as he looked back over his shoulder at the statehouse. "Sevina is accustomed to a very different life than that of a mere soldier's wife. And her father can and will provide, but... I'm her husband..."

Alexander knew what he was asking, and he didn't hesitate. "I'll sell the manor in Mercia, and you can use the money to establish a life for yourself here."

"No, not the manor." Adrian shook his head. "It's too much. The city house on the isle is sufficient. And you should keep the manor for your son one day."

Alexander smiled sadly. "You know I'll have no need of it."

"The manor was our home."

The manor had been *Adrian's* home, with their mother. But to Alexander, it was only a memory of the pain. Still, it was the house of his father, and his father's father. But this was the dawn of a new era, a new generation, and if Norah had taught him anything, it was that some things had to change to move forward. His next generation would be in Kharav, and Alexander would see them provided for.

He nodded. "The city house then. I'll arrange it and send the proceeds for you to purchase a home here."

Adrian's eyes welled. "Thank you, brother."

Alexander pulled him close and embraced him. "Stay well. Until we see each other again." He gave his brother a final cuff on the shoulder, then pushed open the gate and started back toward the castle.

When Alexander reached the mainway, a familiar face was waiting for him. He couldn't help but smile.

Katya was leaning against a gas lamp post. She wasn't wearing her wrap, and her long hair hung around her shoulders. She was beautiful.

"When they told me the Bear had brought the Aleon army to join us, I almost didn't believe them," she said.

He smirked. "I like to be beyond belief."

"As you always have been."

They stood in the light of the lamp post.

"Can I offer you a drink?" she asked.

It was late, but this wasn't an offer he could refuse. He glanced around for a tavern.

"My house is just a few streets up," she added.

He paused. "Ah." Her eyes held a welcome smile, and he smiled back. "I'd love a drink."

They walked the cobbled streets under the gas lamps. Alexander had never realized how peaceful Kharav was at night.

"You saw your nephew?" she asked.

"I did. He's beautiful."

"Not surprising. Look at his family."

Alexander chuckled, and a warmth came to his cheeks.

They reached a well-kept rowhome, and Katya led him through the front door and foyer and back into a kitchen.

Alexander glanced around. It was a nice home—nicer than he'd expect a soldier's home to be, even for a captain. Kharav paid its army well, and it showed. The high ceilings had simple but elegant trim, and the furniture, while not lavish, was beautifully made and well situated. The kitchen was large, with enough space to employ a castle's staff.

"You live here by yourself?"

She smiled as his eyes wandered around the massive kitchen. "With my mother. She loves to cook and always wanted a big kitchen. When I made captain and was able to buy her one, I did. She's at her sister's now. I would have liked for her to have met you."

Alexander would have liked to have met Katya's mother.

She pulled out a pitcher of ale and poured two glasses. Then she led him to a round table, and they sat.

"It's good to see you, Bear."

He chuckled.

Her brows dipped. "What?"

"I like to think we know each other. Perhaps we might move to a first-name basis." He stared at her: her eyes, her nose, her lips. He'd almost forgotten how beautiful she was. *Almost.* "Katya."

She pressed her lips to hold her smile as she stared back at him. "Alexander." She took another drink of her ale. "I've thought a lot about when I might see you again."

He had too. "And what did you think about?"

"How I'd invite you for a drink." She stilled as her eyes caught his, and they sat in the quiet of the moment. "And then I'd invite you to stay."

His pulse quickened, and the groin of his leathers grew tighter, but he settled himself. He couldn't give in to the wants of his body. It wouldn't be fair to her. "I wouldn't take advantage of you this way. I can give neither my hand nor my heart."

"*You?* Take advantage of *me?*" She gave a light laugh, then her face grew more serious. "I don't ask for your heart, and I don't want your hand." She tilted her head to the side. "But I do want you to stay."

Stay. And be with her. Gods, he wanted to. He'd thought about Katya a great deal since he'd last seen her. He'd thought about her eyes, and the line of her jaw, and the fullness of her lips. He'd thought about her skin, and the feel of it against his. But he couldn't stay. While she'd said he wouldn't be taking advantage, he couldn't help but feel...

She leaned back slightly. "I'm sorry. I've misread you, misread what's between us."

He caught her hand, stilling them both. "Katya." Her eyes stared at him, dark and deep. He felt like he could fall into them. "You've misread nothing." He shook his head. "But I leave tomorrow. What if we never see each other again?"

"Exactly," she whispered. "What if we never have the chance to be with each other again? To take peace in each other, enjoy each other. Is this time not precious?" She leaned closer. "Stay."

She was beautiful, but it was more than her beauty. Katya had come to know him well over the past months. He'd come to know her. Slowly, he brought his hand to her cheek, brushing her skin with his thumb, and he pulled her lips to his.

And he stayed.

CHAPTER FIFTY-SIX

Norah walked through the courtyard. Nearly a month had passed since Alexander had taken the legions to Kharav. She knew she was pushing her council to their limits. Even Catherine urged her to bring him back, but she couldn't. Mikael needed the best men. There were only two best men, and Soren wouldn't leave her.

It had been Alexander's idea to take Adrian with him. He and Soren had agreed, to her astonishment. But she supposed she wasn't too surprised. Adrian was perhaps the rarest of gems—as a Northman for their Mercian forces to follow, as brother to Alexander, who the forces of Aleon were committed to, and as an accepted warrior of the Kharavian army. Norah missed him, but she was happy for him to help Mikael, and she knew Sevina was happy to have her husband home. And Norah was happy Alexander would have the opportunity to meet his nephew while he was there.

Footfalls interrupted her thoughts, and she looked up to see Soren and Caspian approaching.

"Queen Norah," Caspian said, "you need to come to the judisaept. Urgently."

"What's happened?"

"It's the lord justice. He's been taken."

A weight hit Norah in her chest. "What do you mean *taken?*"

Caspian waved to a soldier behind him to come forward. The man's armor was crusted in dirt and blood. He bowed. "Regal High," he said. "We'd just left the Shadowlands to return to Mercia. But they were waiting for us."

Her pulse rose in her throat. "Why would you be leaving the Shadowlands, and who was waiting for you?"

"The Shadow King ordered the lord justice to return to you."

Mikael had sent Alexander back to her?

"But as we left the Canyonlands, the Horsemen were waiting. Their king—he said his name was King Abilash and that you have something that belongs to him."

Her eyes widened, and she looked at Soren. He returned her gaze, dark and angry. And it hit her—*the mare*. Mikael had taken the mare from the Horseman king at her asking. And now Abilash sought to get it back. It shouldn't have surprised her—Tahla had told her that anyone with mastery over a horse of the Wild could draw other tribes to follow them, and Abilash was an ambitious king. He could grow his power with the horse, grow his kingdom. A deep and burning fury grew inside her.

His ambition would cost him.

"The councilmen are assembling in the judisaept," Caspian said. "You need to come."

Norah strode quickly toward the castle, her anger building as she went, with Caspian and Soren following behind.

When she reached the chamber, the councilmen were already there. They surrounded the table but didn't sit, and their voices rang over one another with the details. Catherine stood to the side. When she saw Norah, she moved to her.

But Norah didn't waste time with greetings. "As I'm sure you've heard, the lord justice has been taken," she called out, drawing the room quiet.

Edward was the first to speak. "I knew it was a mistake to send him," he said angrily.

"What are the Horseman's demands?" James asked. "What is it that belongs to him?"

"He means the horse of the Wild," she said. "And she does *not* belong to him."

"This is over a horse?" Edward's voice was shrill, and it only angered her further. "By the gods, just send it!"

Just send it? Norah pushed out a furious breath between her teeth. Abilash had made a devastating mistake. And now she'd take everything from him. She turned to the messenger, who stood behind Soren and Caspian. "Where is he?" she demanded. "Where is he keeping the lord justice?"

"King Abilash has taken the ruins of Aviron for his own. They've somewhat rebuilt the destroyed castle. The lord justice and three other Northmen are being held in the dungeon as he awaits your reply."

"Get the horse," Edward said. "Send it to him."

"He'll get nothing!" Norah snapped, drawing all eyes to her. Her skin was on fire. This man dared to take something from her, something very dear. He thought he had power over her—the Shadow Queen. She looked at Soren. "Ready an army, one large enough to bring Aviron to the ground."

"You would march against Aviron?" Edward gasped.

Aviron—the kingdom that had tried to kill Mikael so long ago, the kingdom that Soren had destroyed.

"There is no Aviron!" she spat back. "Abilash is a pretender king in the bones of what used to be a wretched and wicked kingdom!"

Edward shook his finger at her. "You've already sent five thousand of our Northmen to the Shadowlands, as well as half our forces from Aleon. It's well within this council's authority to veto a march to war, which I recommend we—"

Surprisingly graceful for his size, Soren leapt onto the table, interrupting the councilman and forcing the room silent. He walked the table's length, toward Edward, dragging the edge of his axe along the wood and carving a trail of warning.

How she loved this brute. "If there's any councilman who doesn't support the retrieval of my lord justice, let him speak now," she challenged.

"Norah," James said. "You cannot mean to influence this council by force."

She looked around the room, her eyes ablaze. "Does anyone feel forced?"

Soren rolled his gaze over each one of them, awaiting the smallest objection. The room was silent. Even James.

"Norah!" Catherine whispered harshly. "I want Alexander back as much as you do."

Norah caught her with a look that silenced her. "That's not possible."

Soren dropped down from the table, shaking the room like thunder, and stood before her.

"If he's been harmed…" she let her words drop off, her silence speaking for her. She raised her eyes to his. "Go, Destroyer."

Water dripped from the stone of the ceilings to the stone of the floors. Alexander sat with his men in the cold, dark dungeon cell. They were starving. They'd been given two loaves of bread and a bucket of water a day for four men. It had been three weeks since the Horseman king had sent his demands to Norah. The horse of the Wild was what he wanted. It shouldn't be long now. Norah would send the mare, he was sure of it—she wouldn't accept his capture, but she'd resolve this diplomatically. He was grateful she was in Mercia, not the Shadowlands. Otherwise, she might be convinced to use more violent measures.

The Shadowlands. He didn't know what to feel about the kingdom anymore. He'd hated it. With every fiber of his being, he'd hated it. *Had* hated it. It had taken Norah from him, taken his brother. It had upheaved Mercia's political safeties and spit in the faces of tradition. But now it was home to his nephew, the small joy he'd been able to hold in his arms just a few weeks ago. It was where Adrian would build his life. Alexander had decided to sell both the city house and the manor when he returned to Mercia. He didn't have need for either of them and would see his brother had everything to support his wife and child.

His mind shifted to Katya. He'd almost lingered longer in the Shadowlands, for more time with her. He wished he had. It had been hard to leave her, even to return to Mercia. Even to return to Norah.

Outside the cell, footsteps approached. "Open it," a voice demanded—the Horseman king.

The heavy door swung open, and Alexander stood quickly. Relief rolled through him. His Northmen must have arrived with the horse of the Wild.

But instead of removing the chains around his wrists, a guard struck Alexander across the face, knocking him against the wall. Others held his men at bay with swords. Alexander spit blood as he tried to regain his senses.

The king's lips peeled back in a rage, flashing his decaying teeth. "Bring him."

The guards grabbed Alexander's arms and pulled him from the cell, down the dark and mildewy hall, and up a set of stairs to the outside. As he stepped into the light, the glare of the sun blinded him. He struggled to keep up and was forcefully pushed along. They took him up to the castle wall to look out to the east.

Leaning over the rampart, the Horseman king pointed in the distance. "You said she'd send the horse!"

Alexander squinted, still struggling to see. His eyes finally adjusted, and he could make out figures along the outer hills. But as he looked closer, he realized there were more men than required to bring a horse—many more. His pulse quickened. The council would have never sent an army. Then Alexander knew—he scanned the ranks and found him.

The Destroyer.

"Why is *he* here?" the king seethed.

Alexander pushed out a disappointed breath. "He serves my queen."

The color drained from the Horseman's face. "He is supposed to be in Kharav, with Salar!"

The Horseman king was expecting to capitalize on the separation of Norah and the Shadow King, Alexander realized, and on Kharav being distracted by war.

Alexander shook his head. "No, the Destroyer has joined the queen in Mercia." He looked out at the soldiers on the hills. "And he brings his methods of resolution with him. You need to release us."

"Do I?" the king sneered.

"If you know who he is, then you know he'll tear this castle to the ground," Alexander warned. "Not for me—he'll happily see me dead. He merely wants a reason. Don't give him one." Alexander looked out at the army, then back to the king. "I'm trying to help you save your people. You have families here."

The king ignored him.

Alexander sighed in exasperation. "If you care about your people, you'll let me meet him before he even reaches this castle, before he advances farther. He hasn't come to negotiate."

The king shook with anger. He turned to one of his warriors. "Ride out. Tell the commander all I want is the horse."

The Horseman warrior nodded and left.

Alexander shook his head again. "Why? Why do you provoke him? You know who he is. He's not going to talk. He's the *Destroyer*, and he's come to *destroy*."

The king glared at him. "I'm in here. He's out there. We'll see what he has to say." The Horsemen thought they had repaired the castle walls, but they knew nothing of stone foundations. They knew nothing of how to construct walls fit for battle.

"This is the man who originally destroyed this kingdom," Alexander pressed. "He's come to do it again."

The king said nothing.

"Are you mad?"

The king jerked his head back to Alexander. "I'm mad enough to throw you over this wall if you say another word."

Alexander's heart sank. He looked out over the wall as the Horseman messenger rode out to meet the army.

As the warrior neared the approaching army, the Destroyer dismounted and started walking toward him. The king smirked at Alexander. "Looks like he's willing to say a few words after all."

They waited. As the rider drew up his horse beside the commander, he appeared to relay the message. The commander stood for a moment, then faster than the warrior could react, he reached up and pulled the man from his horse. In a singular motion, the commander swung his battle-axe high and cleaved the man's head from his body. Then he shouted back to the army behind him.

Behind the ranks, a catapult was brought forward.

The Horseman king looked on in horror.

The army quickly readied the catapult, and the commander pushed the head of the man into the sling. With the catapult loaded, he released it, sending his message over the castle wall, amidst the screams of horrified people inside.

The commander turned and loosed his axe again, methodically loading pieces of the man's body into the catapult and sending them over the castle wall one at a time. After he sent over the body, the army loaded a boulder and took aim for the wall the Horsemen had repaired. It struck the stone with force that crumpled a large section to the ground.

Then the Destroyer mounted his destrier, and the army advanced.

"Do you understand now?" Alexander pressed the king. "Release us!"

Horrified and shocked, the king nodded his head, waving his men to release the Northmen. Soldiers removed the chains around Alexander's wrists and pushed him down the stairs and to the gates of the castle.

"If we release you, he will leave?" the king asked.

Alexander couldn't answer that, but... "If you don't release me, he'll kill you all."

The king swayed, seemingly unsure of what to do to stop the looming army. "Go!" he snapped finally.

Alexander and his men stumbled out of the gates and hurried toward the advancing army. He prayed he could stop the commander. The Horsemen had taken over the ruins, restoring much of Aviron and settling their families. Despite his anger at the king, Alexander didn't want harm to come to those families, a moral consideration he knew wouldn't concern the Destroyer.

When Alexander reached the army, he stopped to catch his breath, eyeing the commander before looking back at the castle. "Was that necessary?" he asked.

"Are you not released?" the Destroyer taunted, sitting on top of his horse and looking down at him. "You don't look as bad as I thought you would."

"Not as bad as you'd hoped?" Alexander cut back.

"There's still time."

Alexander ignored the jab and eyed the army. "What is your intent?"

A wrap covered the commander's face, but his eyes revealed his smile. "What Salara sent me here for—to see Aviron no more."

"Why didn't she send the horse, or at least a ransom?"

"Because then everyone would be trying to steal you away, with how easy it is."

Alexander shook his head. "What did you say to her? She wouldn't have been willing to destroy an entire tribe to release me."

"Had I said anything, it would have been for her to have left you," he snarled. "No, Bear, you're wrong. I don't imagine there's anything she wouldn't do to get you back."

Alexander stepped closer to his destrier, speaking low. "There are children in there. Families. If Norah has truly sent you, it's out of rash anger, but she wouldn't want them hurt. She wouldn't be able to bear it. If you care for her at all, you'll let them live."

The commander didn't answer. He simply urged his horse forward, closer to the walls of Aviron. "Abilash!" he bellowed, then waited. "Abilash!" he thundered again.

The king appeared on the top of the wall, looking down at them. Alexander knew the Horseman would be shaking in his boots.

"You are no longer king!" the commander roared. "I take from you your title, your lands, this very castle you try to squat yourself in, hiding like a coward. Everything you have is now Salara's. And you are no more!" He paused, letting his message sink in. "Anyone who seeks to leave will be given safe passage, but come tomorrow, Aviron and anyone in it will be destroyed."

The commander reined back his horse, toward the army. "Satisfied?" he sneered at Alexander.

Surprisingly, he was. It was more than he had hoped for.

"Where's your horse?" the commander asked him.

"Lost."

"That was a good horse," the Destroyer said angrily.

Of course the commander was more concerned with his horse. A soldier brought him another destrier, and Alexander mounted. He swept his eyes across the masses of Mercian forces that the commander had brought. He truly was prepared to destroy Aviron, and Norah had given him Northmen to do it. Alexander's attention shifted back to the commander, who growled out to the men, "I'll start back with the Bear. They have one day to leave the castle, then I want it torn to the ground. Every stone."

These were Mercian forces. Alexander's forces. But they looked to the Destroyer and nodded. Alexander's stomach turned.

"Every stone," the Shadow commander emphasized. Then he urged his mount north.

Anger knifed through Alexander, but he knew he couldn't stay. He knew he couldn't alter the task, not if Norah had sent the army. He cursed as he followed after.

The Destroyer looked back at the castle as they rode away. "I don't know which I despise more," he said to Alexander, "traveling all the way out here and being denied a battle, or seeing Salara absolutely consumed with your return."

"Is she well?" he asked.

"No, she's not well," the commander spat. "She had me march five thousand men to retrieve you. We lost more on the journey than we rescued from that flea-bitten castle. Now eat something. The only thing that could make this worse is having to explain to her how you died on the way back."

Norah paced her study as the sun set over the snow-packed mountains in the distance. She wrung her clammy hands, trying to force back the sickness bubbling in her stomach.

What had she done?

She had threatened her council with the very man they viewed as their enemy; sent Kharav all the steel trade bound for markets, even that in reserve; and stripped forces from a vulnerable Mercia to aid the Shadowlands. She'd sent an Aleon legion to Kharav, essentially forcing them to a side she wasn't sure Phillip would choose, and now her lord justice had been taken.

But all of that paled in comparison to the fact that she had sent Soren to Aviron. No, not Soren—*the Destroyer*. In her anger toward Abilash, she sent hell upon his people. She should have sent the horse of the Wild. She loved Sephir, but she would have sent a thousand horses. Ten thousand. She would have traded most anything for Alexander. But her rage hadn't let her. Soren would have no mercy, and now she'd have blood on her hands.

There was a shuffle outside. A guard's voice came. "You can't go—"

The door to her study swung open, and Soren stepped inside, followed by a few Mercian soldiers guarding the hall. Any other time, she'd have been amused. Some of the guards less acquainted with Soren still tried to stop him from going where he pleased.

But it wasn't the time for amusement. Norah stared at him, her mouth dry, her skin cold, her heart hammering so hard she thought it might burst from her chest. She was desperate to hear his news but feared what he'd tell her. She waved the guards away.

"I've brought him back," he said after they stepped out.

Her eyes welled. Alexander was safe.

"And I've removed Abilash as king."

"What about his people?" she breathed.

"Given safe passage to join another tribe, or form a separate one, I don't care, so long as it's not under Abilash."

Norah rushed forward and threw her arms around him. He hadn't killed them. *She* hadn't killed them.

He stiffened but let her cling to him until her emotion passed. Then he pushed her back so he could look her in the eye. "The Bear's cleaning up, then he's coming here. Don't let him see you like this. Pull yourself together."

She nodded. "Thank—"

"Don't," he said as he stepped back from her.

Norah swallowed back the rest of her words. She only nodded again, and he took his leave. She wiped her face and raked her fingers through her hair, then set back to pacing the room. Alexander was safe. Her relief threatened her with emotion again.

Years seemed to pass before a knock came to the door, and it opened. Alexander stepped inside. She could only look at him. It hadn't even been two months since he'd last left Mercia, but he looked older. He looked tired.

"Queen Norah," he said finally.

She crossed the space between them. His eyes were filled with an emotion she couldn't read—worry? Sadness? She wanted to hug him, she wanted to touch him, but she didn't. His eyes didn't hold the same softness toward her, they didn't beg her nearness the way they usually did.

"You sent the Destroyer?" he asked. There was judgment in his tone. His expression was clear now—disapproval. And it angered her. "Why didn't you send the horse?" he asked. "Or the ransom?"

"I sent what was required. And I will *not* negotiate with someone who tries to force my hand."

"This isn't who you are." His voice was softer now, but it still held the sting of a cut.

"Then perhaps you don't know me," she knifed back.

"There were families there, and you sent the Destroyer and a legion! For a few men!"

Anger radiated through her. "Who are you to judge me? You marched the entire Mercian army across the Tribelands, for one!"

"You're queen!" he thundered. "I'm nothing!"

But he wasn't nothing.

"And I would do things very differently now," he added.

What did that mean? He'd do things differently... He was different... now.

Silence came again. They stood in the quiet of the candlelit room, with only the sound of their hearts beating. What was this strangeness between them? Was it only his anger?

She let out a long exhale. She couldn't resolve it tonight. "The council will want to speak with you in the morning," she said, shifting the conversation away from one of emotion. "They're not very happy with me."

The air between them calmed, and the heat dissipated. His lips tightened in frustration still, but he nodded. "I'll help smooth things out."

It wouldn't be an easy task, to settle things with the council, but Alexander held their respect. Norah would talk to her grandmother too.

"Then I'll see you tomorrow," she said. What else could she say?

"Of course."

"Goodnight, Alexander."

"Goodnight."

CHAPTER FIFTY-SEVEN

With Alexander's political savvy, the council seemed to calm over the next few days. Norah kept Soren away, busy with what she was sure he felt were trivial tasks—assessing arrivals and risks from the ports, combing the isle for weaknesses—but there was nothing trivial about keeping busy and keeping the peace.

She walked the great hall with the dogs trailing behind her, her frustration growing. She felt chained, unable to move, just waiting for war. How long would it be like this?

Footfalls sounded from her left, and she turned to see a Kharavian soldier approaching—a messenger—with a letter in his hand. When she saw the black seal, she smiled—a letter from Mikael.

"Thank you," she said as she took it and broke the seal.

Mikael's words came as they usually did, wanting to make sure she was well. She had a small painted portrait that she planned to send with her next letter. Her smile widened as she thought of him receiving it. But as she read his letter, her thoughts of the portrait fell away.

Mikael wrote that Aleon had sent him a warning, advising him to close his ports. A fever was rumored to be sweeping through Nestrana, along the port cities, and down to Pryam—the kingdoms across the Aged Sea from Kharav.

Phillip hadn't responded to the matter of her sending Aleon forces to Kharav. She assumed he wasn't happy about it, but he hadn't called to withdraw them. Now, with his helpful warning of potential danger, she hoped she was seeing the beginnings of cooperation, even if reluctant.

With Phillip's letter to Mikael, there would have been one sent to Mercia as well. She caught a nearby servant. "Have the council meet me in the judisaept."

She made her way through the halls to the council chamber. Surely Aleon's amicable actions toward Kharav would help with the council's own feelings toward Mikael, or so she hoped.

For once, she was the first to arrive, and she waited as her councilmen each reached the judisaept. They filed in stiffly. Soren came with Alexander.

"Any news from Aleon?" she asked when they had all gathered.

"Not recently," James said.

She held up the letter from Mikael. "Phillip sent a warning for Kharav to close its ports. A fever spreads from Nestrana to Pryam. We should do the same."

Henricus scoffed. "James and I have just come from Damask. The ports are fine."

"Perhaps for now," Alexander said. "But if the fever travels from Nestrana, it will likely reach Tarsus, which means it could be in our harbors now."

"Unless there is no fever," Alastair said. "We've heard no word of this from anyone else."

"Then why would Phillip send a message to Kharav?" Norah asked, her irritation growing. "There's absolutely no benefit to Aleon for Kharav closing its ports, and no hardship to Kharav for doing so. It has only two, and other means to export trade."

"Why wouldn't Phillip send word to Mercia, then?" James asked.

That didn't make sense to Norah either, but there could be a number of reasons. "Still, we should be cautious, and close our ports as well."

"That's no small feat," Edward said. "We'd be closing trade to thousands—tens of thousands—on the basis of nothing. We don't even know how serious this fever is, if it even *is* at all."

Norah couldn't argue with that. She didn't know the consequences of the fever, although she couldn't imagine Aleon advising Kharav to close its ports if it wasn't serious. And while she didn't trust that her council would put the well-being of the people over profit or political gain, she also couldn't overrule them on everything.

"We'll leave them open, then," she said, relenting. "But have guards ready to close them down at the first sign of sickness."

The council grudgingly agreed.

Morning came, and the port situation still needled in Norah's mind. She'd write to Phillip and ask him what was happening. Serene helped her dress, and she made her way to the dining room for breakfast. Caspian picked up alongside her as she walked, like he usually did in the morning, briefing her of news and activities.

As she passed through the great hall, she saw Catherine and Edward in a seemingly heated conversation.

"What's going on?" she asked as she approached.

"Henricus has fallen ill," Catherine said.

Norah darted her eyes between her grandmother and Edward. "Does he have the fever?"

Edward held up his hands. "We can't jump to conclusions."

"He was just in Damask at the ports," Norah said, her pulse quickening.

"So was James," he argued, "who's perfectly well. This could be anything."

Norah shook her head. "But it's not just anything. I knew it." She turned to Caspian. "Send word—close the ports."

"We must assemble the council first," Edward stressed.

"The council has already agreed—the first sign of sickness."

"*At the ports,*" he said, his tone rising. "For all we know, Henricus might have eaten something that didn't agree with his stomach."

But Norah wasn't willing to take that risk. "Go," she told Caspian.

Edward's voice pitched higher. "You cannot make unilateral decisions that affect Mercia's trade and economy."

"Why not?" she snapped back. She was near breaking with this man. "Am I not queen?"

"You have a council—"

"Who's failing! If you were doing your job, you'd put aside your differences and help me build a stronger alliance between Mercia and Kharav, and stand beside your king! You would help me help our people. You wouldn't undermine me at every turn—don't think I haven't noticed." Her cheeks were hot with anger. "We'll stop all trade until we know just how serious this is. Lives mean more than money. We close the ports."

Things went from bad to worse. The sickness was as Norah had feared, and two days later, more men were showing signs of illness. They had all visited the ports or interacted with those who had done so.

She stood in her study, looking out the window over the castle. Caspian knocked on the door and entered.

"Norah," he said gently. His reluctant tone brought a chill to her spine.

She turned.

"Henricus is dead."

Her blood ran cold. "What?" she breathed.

"He died this morning."

"Of the fever?"

He nodded solemnly. "It appears so. Deaths are being reported through Damask and into the markets of the Free Cities."

Deaths. It was like a blow to the stomach. Her mind shifted to Mikael. Had he closed the ports of Kharav in time?

"There's more," Caspian said. "The lord commander has taken ill."

Norah's chest tightened. "What? How?" She needed to see him. She darted from the chamber before Caspian could answer.

"Norah, you can't see him."

"How is he sick? He didn't even go to the ports! He—" she stopped, and bile rose in the back of the throat. She'd sent him on miscellaneous tasks to keep him busy, which included assessing risks at the ports. And now he'd caught the fever. She turned and raced toward his chamber.

"Norah, you can't," Caspian called after her. But she ignored him.

As she neared Soren's chamber and reached for the latch, Caspian caught her arm. "Norah, you can't see him."

"Soren," she called from outside the door.

"Leave!" he called angrily from inside. "You can't be here."

She rattled the handle, but it didn't give. "The door's locked."

"Because I knew you'd be foolish enough to open it," Soren hurled back.

"You can't go in," Caspian told her. "You can't risk catching the fever. The healer says it can be passed easily: through touch, eating after one who has it, through the air when you cough."

She stepped backward, the devastation of the situation creeping in. It could pass so easily from one to another? That meant it would spread through Mercia like fire. How many would catch it? She turned her focus back to Soren. "I need to know you're all right."

"I'll be all right when you leave," he rumbled back.

"I'll be back to check on you," she said.

"Don't let her come back!" he bellowed, speaking to Caspian now.

"Queen Norah, you have to leave. Serene and Vitalia are preparing an isolation chamber for you now. You'll remain there with them, and I'll personally serve as your guard at all times to reduce your contact with anyone. Alexander will be down the hall from you, and members of the council will each stay in isolation in their separate chambers. The same with your grandmother."

"How long?" she asked.

He shook his head. "I don't know exactly, but it appears that as it spreads quickly, it also leaves quickly. For those who are surviving, they seem to recover after three days."

"How many recover?"

He grew quiet. "About half."

Serene stepped inside Norah's chamber with a tray of hot soup. It was the only food approved throughout Mercia—food that could be boiled. No bread, no fresh fruits or vegetables.

Norah was surprised at how quickly Caspian had put together a plan. Everyone was ordered to their chambers, and citizens were required to remain in their homes.

The castle worked at half staff, with each person contained within a specific area at all times. Caspian left food in the hall for Serene to bring inside after he stepped away. Messages were delivered through doors. Caspian kept her updated throughout the day. Alexander, her grandmother, the remaining members of the council—they were all keeping well, even James, despite his previous visit to the ports. Soren was still with fever, but Caspian said he continued to answer through the door, and the servants still found he was taking the food into his chamber after they left it for him.

Two days passed, with Norah's worry stretching the time even longer. She wished she had more books in her chamber. Had she been smarter, she would have asked to have been isolated in the library.

A knock on the door told her Caspian had brought dinner. Soup. Again.

"How is my grandmother?" she asked through the door.

"She says if she's served soup one more time, she'll throw it at me when she sees me next."

Norah smiled.

"The lord justice says to hold on. Hopefully this won't be for much longer."

"And Soren?" she asked.

He was quiet.

"Caspian?"

Still, he did not answer.

"Caspian?" she said, more urgently.

"I don't know."

"What do you mean, you don't know?"

"He hasn't taken his food, and he's not answering the servants at his door."

Her stomach twisted. *Half did not recover.* Soren had to recover—he was strong, he was the Destroyer. Why didn't he answer? Fear flooded her, and she swung the door to her chamber open.

Caspian stepped back, raising his arm to her. "Don't come out here."

But she wasn't listening. She tore from the room and down the hall.

"Norah!" he yelled, and tried to grab her, but he wasn't fast enough.

She ran by Alexander's door and to the hall of Soren's chamber. Two servants stood outside, and she pushed through them. "Soren!" she called, but there was no answer. "Soren!" She jerked at the iron handle, but it wouldn't open. "Soren!" she cried.

"Norah!" Alexander's voice came from behind.

She turned, her panic building. "He's not answering!"

"You can't be here," he told her.

Fear coursed through her. Why didn't Soren answer? She jerked the handle again. "Soren!"

Alexander caught her and pulled her back. "I'll see if he's all right and send word to you. But you need to go back to your chamber."

She shook her head. She couldn't. She wouldn't.

"You can't expose yourself."

Norah struggled to hold in her sob. She couldn't leave Soren.

"I'll make sure he's all right," he promised.

But she still couldn't go.

He gripped her shoulders and pulled her eyes to his. "I'll make sure he's all right. You have my word. Go."

Finally, she relented and backed away. Then she reluctantly turned and headed back to her chamber.

Alexander stood in front of the door to the Shadow commander's chamber. He looked at Caspian beside him. "You go too. You need to look after Norah."

"You can't go in there," Caspian argued. "I'll do it."

"No, you'll look after Norah. That's an order."

Caspian stood in the hallway.

"Go!" Alexander snapped.

Finally, the captain yielded and headed back to the hall of the queen's chamber. When he had gone, Alexander turned back to the door.

"Destroyer," he called.

There still came no answer. He put his ear against the door and listened. No movement inside. If this bastard was dead... he'd kill him.

Alexander pulled his sword and angled its tip into the crevice of the door. The latches were well-made and strong, but Mercian steel was stronger. He strained as he put his weight against it, prying it, forcing it. Finally, the latch broke, and the door swung open.

Soren lay on the floor near the window, stripped of his clothing. No doubt he'd been trying to pull the heat from his body with the cold stone. He lay still, his eyes closed, unmoving.

"Destroyer," Alexander called to him.

He didn't respond.

"Soren," he called again, stepping to the window and dropping down beside him. The commander's chest shuddered as a small gurgle escaped his lips—he was alive. He tried to cough, but only a choking noise came from his throat. He couldn't breathe. Alexander pulled him up to a sitting position. By the gods, he was a heavy beast.

"Breathe!" he ordered, giving Soren's back a hearty beat with the heel of his hand. The commander's body heaved and then let out a drowning cough. The thick warmth of blood ran over his own arm and down the commander's chest. Alexander hit Soren's back again.

The commander took a desperate breath and his body relaxed in relief. Alexander positioned himself against the wall behind Soren, leaning the weight of the commander against him and holding his body upright. The Shadow beast couldn't hold himself, and his head fell back against Alexander's shoulder. But he was able to breathe.

"Death is near," Soren's voice came in barely a whisper. "Let it come." His body shook with another cough, and Alexander held him forward as he purged more blood from his lungs.

"They say this is the worst—the third day," Alexander told him. "You need to stay upright. If you lie down, you'll drown in your blood."

"I don't have the strength."

Alexander shifted and positioned himself more firmly against the commander's back. "I know," he said.

And they sat.

Chapter Fifty-Eight

Nothing. Norah paced her chamber. There had been nothing—no word about Soren. Three times Serene had talked her out of leaving the room again, but she couldn't shake the crushing fear inside her.

She couldn't lose him.

Mikael needed him. She needed him. And he deserved to die in glory on a battlefield or ascend the earth as an immortal warrior of the gods, not broken by a port fever in a kingdom that wouldn't even speak his name. She'd never seen a vision of his end. Is that how it was for people with wretched deaths? Was their end not powerful enough to show their greatness to the seers?

He deserved so much more than this.

A knock on the door made her jump, and she raced over to it.

"Queen Norah," Caspian called.

"Tell me! Is Soren all right?"

"He's alive."

Norah leaned against the door and let out a shaking breath. She covered her face in her hands as tears came.

"The lord justice stays with him," he said. "He's keeping him upright and breathing."

Norah's heart stopped. "Alexander?" Alexander was with him, *inside*?

"Yes."

She heard the gravity in his voice; she felt the weight of his worry, because it was her own. Alexander would surely have the sickness within a day or two. With only half those afflicted surviving, what were the chances of both of them making it through safely?

Norah cursed herself. She knew she should have closed the ports, and she hadn't. She was queen, and she was responsible for the suffering of her people.

Two more days went by, with Caspian delivering the news that Soren was recovering. The danger of death had passed. Alexander had been confined to a far chamber in the castle to quarantine while he waited for the sickness to come. Norah was desperate to see him, but of course, she couldn't.

It wrecked the heart—waiting to see if death would come for a loved one, or if it would mercifully pass over. Did she deserve mercy? Did the gods still curse her?

After several more days, the sickness appeared to have left the castle. Slowly, Caspian executed plans for a return to normality. Sections of the castle were opened, with only those that had quarantined allowed to associate with one another. To Catherine's horror, they still ate soup.

At last free from her chamber, Norah strolled between the great hall and her study. The library was still closed. On her return walk, Caspian was waiting for her. He held a letter in his hand. Two letters, actually. She saw Mikael's seal, and she tore it open. Her eyes welled with relief as she read his words.

All was well in Kharav. Mikael had closed the ports immediately after Phillip's warning, and they had no reports of sickness. He'd sent food to the Uru and ordered them confined to the canyons—no contact with the outside world. They, too, had fared well. Of course, he asked about Mercia, and Soren. She was relieved she had good news to share, at least concerning Soren.

Her attention shifted to the second letter. It was a letter from Phillip. She would normally assemble the council before reading his letters, but she broke the seal and opened it.

Dear Norah,

I hope this letter finds you safe and in good health, and pray you received my last letter in time to close your ports. May you have fared the fever better than Aleon. It's with great regret I share that I've lost nearly one quarter of my men, with Tarsus hit hardest—I fear beyond recovery.

I'm grateful I didn't heed the words of your council and withdraw my forces from Kharav, for not a single man was lost there. If I'd not been so selfish, I would have sent more, and so saved more. Another lesson in humility from the gods.

Norah stopped. The council had written Phillip and told him to pull back the forces she had sent to Kharav? Anger pulsed through her.

But within the darkness, there comes a light. I've received reports that the armies of Japheth and Rael have suffered losses of almost half. And while I can't jump to war so soon after such devastation, I know that victory over Japheth is now within my grasp.

Write to me urgently, so I know you are well and safe.

Most anxiously, I wait,

Phillip

Phillip would be able to march against a weakened Japheth soon, and for that, she was grateful. But her face still burned with a rising anger. "I want to see the council in the judisaept," she said. "Now."

"I'll assemble them," Caspian replied.

"Where's Soren?"

"In his chamber still, resting."

"Time for rest is done," she said. "Tell him to come, and dress for blood. I may need it."

Caspian's brows dipped in concern. "Norah—"

"Do as I say."

Reluctantly, he nodded and left her in the hall, and she turned toward the judisaept.

Soren arrived before the councilmen, much sooner than she'd expected. She'd thought he would appear a little more just-coming-back-from-the-brink-of-death-like, not at all the full Destroyer that stood before her now. Perhaps the potential call for blood had breathed new life into him. It was the first she had seen him since he'd fallen sick, and she desperately wanted to hug him, but there would be time for merriment and thanksgiving later. Right now, she had things to address.

The councilmen came quickly. Of course, they expected her call would be in response to a letter. She doubted they expected what she had in store for them.

When Alexander stepped into the room, he surprised everyone, including Norah.

"Lord Justice," she said. She swallowed back her emotion at seeing him. Did this mean he was well?

"Queen Norah," he greeted back with a nod of his head. "The healer has said I'm beyond the window of danger. If I had the fever, I would have displayed symptoms already."

She let out a breath of relief, and the councilmen clapped. Even Soren gave him an indebted nod.

"Good news, Lord Justice," Edward said. "Praise the gods; they're merciful to their faithful subjects."

Norah's eyes narrowed. No doubt it was a jab at Soren. "Was Henricus not faithful?" she asked.

The room fell silent.

But she wasn't here to discuss the gods' mercy, or Henricus. "Where is the last letter from the king of Aleon?" she asked.

"Surely you have it," Edward said.

She eyed him suspiciously. "No, I don't. It never reached me."

"Then what makes you think there was a letter?"

"Because I know its contents. Phillip sent a warning to close our ports, the same warning he sent to Kharav." She kept her eyes on Edward. "But you didn't want to close the ports, Councilman Edward."

"I didn't take the letter, if that's what you are insinuating," he said, with an edge to his voice.

"I don't believe you," she challenged.

"That's a bold statement," Councilman Alastair warned.

"Not as bold as writing the king of Aleon and asking him to withdraw the forces your queen sent to Kharav."

Alastair looked around the table. "You cannot think anyone here would do such a thing."

She raised Phillip's letter. "I have the proof in my hand. Phillip shares how grateful he is that he didn't heed this council's advice and withdraw his forces, for not a single man was lost in Kharav. Meanwhile, the fever has taken nearly a quarter of his men across Aleon."

The council let out an audible gasp.

"I know you're not happy with my decision to close the ports and halt our trade," she continued. "I know you're not happy with many of my decisions, but perhaps you shouldn't have been so eager to put this crown on my head and call me queen. Well, now I *am* queen. I've forged an alliance that brings Mercia strength, one that's kept us from war. I've brought our people peace, provisions, security. But you don't want peace, do you? You work against me."

Her eyes moved around the table from councilman to councilman. "Do you know what that is?" she asked them. "*Treason.*"

"This is your council," Edward said with wide eyes. "It's our duty to protect the ways of Mercia."

"The old ways are dead," she said firmly. "I'll bring a new Mercia—a Mercia that thrives on unity and peace and strength with Kharav. It's what's best for the people. That is *my* duty. It's yours. And I will find who betrayed that duty."

And she meant every word.

Norah paced the side hall that ran the length of the west wing. She didn't know what she would do when she found out who'd written Phillip to withdraw his forces in Kharav. What if it was more than one person? What if it came from her collective council? She didn't want to rule Mercia with an iron hand. She didn't want to rule by force, but she couldn't tolerate divisive measures from her own council. She had condemned Mikael for his violence; she couldn't do the same. Nor could she show lenience. Expulsion perhaps. Was she able to do that? She cursed herself—she didn't even know the laws of her own kingdom. Alexander would know.

She found him in the courtyard, talking with a group of men. They wore leather armor and open-faced helms. They weren't from Mercia.

When he saw her, he excused them and crossed the distance to meet her.

"Who are those men?" she asked.

"The council has brought in mercenaries to augment our forces," he explained.

"Mercenaries? Without me knowing?"

"Yes, I've already addressed that. I wasn't aware either."

"They can't do that. Send these mercenaries on their way."

He extended a hand to calm her. "They've stepped beyond their bounds, certainly, but hiring mercenaries isn't a far-fetched idea. Especially when we've sent so many men to Kharav, and the attacks on our villages could start again at any time."

Anger swelled inside her. "They should have discussed it with me."

"Yes, they should have. And with me, as lord justice. But"—he paused—"give some leniency. You are... bringing a wave of change that's difficult for them, all of them, even Catherine. Give a little."

Give a little. She'd already given. But maybe he was right—she was pushing the council hard. Perhaps now wasn't the best time to bring up expulsion, but when she found out who had written Phillip, there would be consequences. Severe ones.

They turned and walked through the gardens together.

"Has it been difficult for you?" she asked softly.

He was quiet for a time, but she could see his mind churning. "Do you love the Shadow King?" he asked finally.

"Yes," she answered. She had no hesitation, no reservation. She did love him.

"I see it in you," he said.

Good. He should. Everyone should see it.

"His darkness," he added.

She stopped as she drew her brows together. "What?"

"You're not yourself, Norah. He's changed you."

Anger burned inside her. "Or perhaps I *am* myself, I'm just not who you want me to be."

He halted, and his face dropped in sadness. "I know you better than anyone. This isn't you. The Shadow King, he's made you harsh, and dark."

"If you really believe that, then you don't know me at all. Mikael has made me strong—stronger than I ever thought I could be, strong enough to be a queen."

He stepped back at her words, whether surprised or upset—she didn't care. She remembered so long ago, seeing the vision of herself on the Shadow throne. She hadn't thought she could be that woman, that woman who sat so tall amid the darkness. Now she couldn't imagine herself as anything else. It was where she belonged. It was who she was. And she wouldn't let anyone tell her different, even Alexander.

"And you've changed too," she said.

He quieted. He cast his eyes down and swallowed. "Yes, I suppose we both have," he said finally as he looked back up at her.

And when two people changed, what was left between them? She drew in a long breath and let it out slowly. She nodded solemnly, then turned back to the castle, leaving him alone in the courtyard.

Alexander walked through the castle without intention, lost in his mind. His chest felt it would cave under an invisible weight—a weight that forced the air from his lungs and crushed his heart.

"Alexander," a man's voice called.

He stopped, not sure from where it had come.

"Alexander," it called again.

He turned around to see Councilmen Edward and Alastair walking toward him. He frowned. Edward had called him by his name only a handful of times over his life, usually when he was trying to convince him of something.

"Are you well?" Edward said with a worried brow.

He wasn't well. He would never be well. But he didn't answer. What did Edward want from him now?

"Will you join us?" Edward asked him, motioning toward a small side hall.

Alexander didn't want to join them. He didn't want to hear whatever it was Edward was going to peddle, but one didn't simply ignore an elder councilman, even a lord justice. And he knew where they were headed. The councilmen had a small library in the east wing, more of a shared study, not large—a good place for talking and thinking. He didn't want to talk or think right now, but still he followed.

"Perhaps you're concerned, as we are, regarding this morning's council meeting?" Alastair said as they walked.

The council meeting. He'd almost forgotten—add it to the list of things that weighed on his shoulders.

When they reached the council's library, Alexander unbuckled his sword belt and set the blade at the foot of the oversize chair by the bookshelf that stretched to the ceiling. He forgot all proprieties and sank down into the soft leather. He just needed to sit.

"Here." Edward poured wine into a chalice and held it for him. "Have a drink. Ease your mind."

Norah closed the door of her chamber and leaned back against it. Her heart started to slow as she tried to cool her anger. Everyone wanted to tell her who she should be, who she shouldn't, even Alexander. But she knew who she was.

She knew now.

"Salara, are you all right?" Vitalia said, coming quickly to her side.

She nodded.

"You don't look all right." Vitalia knew her well. She pulled Norah to the chair by the small table and sat down across from her, pouring them both a cup of wine. She pushed Norah's cup in front of her. "Is it those old bastards again?" she asked as she took a drink from her own cup.

Norah smiled appreciatively. "They are old bastards, aren't they?"

Vitalia smiled.

Norah let out a long breath. "I've decided to return to Kharav."

Her maid's face grew serious, and she swallowed. "Surely it's not safe, Salara."

"I don't know why it wouldn't be," Norah countered. "Mikael still has a full army. He lost nothing to the sickness, and he has the additional forces of Mercia and Aleon. The armies of Japheth and Rael have been devastated by the fever. They can't move against us, at least not now. I should return. And I want to go home."

Vitalia swayed slightly in her chair.

Norah knew the news would disappoint her. Vitalia would be upset to leave if Serene stayed, which was likely. They had become very close friends. "I'll ask Serene to return with us," she said, "but I'll leave it her choice."

Vitalia didn't respond. She *was* disappointed, Norah was sure. But Norah hadn't expected her silence.

"Would you... want to stay in Mercia?" Norah hadn't thought Vitalia would want to stay, given Mercia's narrow moral views and constant judgment. She didn't know what she'd do for a maid, but if Vitalia wanted to stay in Mercia with Serene, she'd allow her to.

Still, Vitalia didn't answer.

Suddenly, the chalice dropped from the maid's hands, but she didn't move to catch it. "Vitalia, are you all right?"

Her maid swayed again and then fell forward out of the chair, hitting the table before collapsing to the floor.

"Vitalia!" Norah cried as she sprang down to her side.

Vitalia's eyes were open, but they stared blankly back at her. Norah clutched her face. "Vitalia!" Then her gaze moved to the chalice on the floor with spilled wine around it.

Beside her, Cusco whined.

Norah staggered to her feet. "Guards!" she screamed. But when she ripped the door to the hall open, it wasn't her guards looking back at her. They lay on the stone floor of the hall, dead.

The council's mercenaries blocked her way, their swords drawn.

Alexander took the chalice of wine from Edward and drank deeply.

"Lord Justice," the councilman said. "I'm sure you would agree that the queen's words and actions are quite troubling."

Yes, the council was troubled. And if he was honest with himself, Alexander was too. Not of Norah's intentions; in her heart, she truly wanted the best for both Mercia and Kharav, but things with the council were escalating. He took another drink.

"What she has done," the councilman continued, "what she continues to do—it will inflict great harm on Mercia." He refilled Alexander's chalice from the glass carafe of wine.

"Our values, our customs, our way of life, everything we believe and everything we stand for. I'm sure you can agree, she is not the woman who left us those years ago."

No, she was not. What he wouldn't give to have that woman back. He grieved her, the loss.

"She's been corrupted by the darkness," the councilman said.

Alexander found himself nodding. There was a darkness. But Norah couldn't see it, and he didn't know how to make her see. And to make it more complicated, he didn't entirely despise the king who brought this darkness. Alexander's head hurt, and he drew up his hand and pressed his fingers to his temples. He was just so tired.

He took another drink.

"So, again, we appear in agreement," Edward said.

Perhaps. He lauded Norah's effort for peace, her relentless struggle to bring two opposite worlds together, but they were two worlds that should remain opposite. He set the chalice down on the side table, and Edward promptly refilled it again.

"This is why she must be removed," the councilman said.

Removed. Alexander's head snapped up. Edward's words seemed to sink in for the first time. "What?"

"She must be removed," Edward repeated.

Alexander surged to his feet. A rush of fog filled his mind, but he blinked it back. What was happening? His hand moved to where the hilt of his sword normally sat against his hip, but he'd taken it off. He struggled to remember where he'd set it. "She's queen. You can't just remove her."

"We have another with royal blood, the queen's second cousin, Evangeline, and Catherine will continue as regent until the girl is of age. As before, we are here to guide her."

His breaths came harder now. The room swirled around him, and he parted his stance slightly to keep his balance. "Those are treasonous words," he warned. Catherine would never accept that. He'd never accept it. He blinked again to focus his failing vision. What was happening to him?

The wine.

Alexander spotted his sword on the floor by the foot of the chair, but he wasn't sure he'd stay on his feet if he reached for it.

"We have done everything in the name of Mercia," Edward said. "Our consciences are clear."

Alexander's heartbeat grew in his ears, thrumming with the heat of fight. What did that mean? "Where's the queen?"

"Alexander," Edward said. "Your family has safeguarded Mercia for generations upon generations. Your blood can be traced back to the original protector of the crown. Your father sacrificed for this great kingdom. And now so must you."

"Where's Norah?" he demanded again.

"You should sit down, Lord Justice."

Alexander had no intention of sitting down. His eyes dropped again to his sword.

"Sit down, Alexander," James said, stepping into the doorway.

He whirled around. *Even James?* "Where is Norah?" he asked again, more desperate now.

James stepped closer to him, with his eyes full of sorrow. "We had no choice."

Alexander shook with a fury seeping into his heart at the man he trusted most in the world—the man who'd guided him his whole life, mentored him, believed in him. He lunged toward his sword, but his body failed him, and he dropped to his knees.

James caught him, softening his fall.

"We had no choice," came the words again, as the darkness closed around him.

Norah stared at the mercenaries looking back at her with intentions of death in their eyes. But Cusco and Cavaatsa growled and leapt forward, each downing a man, and she darted out of her chamber.

The sound of steel rang through the air. Suddenly, Soren crashed into the hall with a half-dozen mercenaries around him. "Salara!" he roared as he fought them back.

Norah desperately searched for a weapon, but there was nothing close around her.

Soren cut down another man, then he grabbed her and barreled down the hall to the side door as the dogs took down another two mercenaries. "We need to get out of here!" he snarled.

"No! Vitalia's back there! She's been poisoned!"

"You can't help her now."

"I'm not leaving her!" she screamed as she fought him. He pulled her closer for a better hold. She caught his chin with her elbow, briefly stopping their flight, but he grabbed her as she tried to jerk away.

"Let me go!" she cried.

Soren pulled her back to him and clutched her close under his arm, covering her mouth and stifling her screams with his hand. He pulled her into a connecting hall and down a stair. The dogs followed.

From behind, she heard the wisp of an arrow. A dog yelped. Then only Cavaatsa was beside them.

She managed to pull Soren's hand free. "Cusco!" she screamed.

But the dog didn't come. And Soren didn't stop.

More footsteps came behind them. Soren called out in the Shadow tongue, and Cavaatsa turned back to slow their pursuers.

Soren dragged her down another hall and to a small side room, where they nearly collided with Caspian.

"Caspian!" she cried. "You have to save Vitalia!"

Caspian stepped forward and gripped her in Soren's hold. "Norah, listen to me. The council—they're trying to kill you."

"I can't leave her!"

"She's gone," Soren said firmly.

But she shook her head. She couldn't accept that.

Caspian clutched her firmly, looking into her eyes. "Norah, we have to get you out of here."

A sob escaped her throat.

Caspian rapidly led them down another stair and through the tunnels under the city. They came up through a row building, out the back, and to a small side street on the mainland, where they found a public stable. Caspian quickly set to saddling a horse.

Soren shoved her up and then mounted behind her.

She looked down at Caspian in horror. "You're not coming too?"

He shook his head. "You have a better chance of making it out alone."

"You can't stay here!"

"Don't you worry about me. Keep yourself safe." He looked up at her, his eyes full of sorrow. "I'm sorry, Norah."

But she didn't have time to respond before Soren urged the horse forward and into the night.

CHAPTER FIFTY-NINE

The journey back to Kharav was the longest Norah had ever known. She rode in the silence of defeat. She didn't sleep when they stopped to rest. Soren didn't either.

Their mount wasn't a destrier, and when they reached the Horsemen tribes, Soren traded it for a larger beast that could better carry them both.

He caught rabbits and a few birds as they went. Despite their fleeing and his aversion to fires while traveling, he built a small campfire for her each time they stopped.

Her cheeks were constantly wet with tears, her stomach sick.

"Why didn't Alexander come?" she whispered on the fifth night. It was the first she'd spoken since they left Mercia. "What if they killed him too?"

"That's not possible."

Her lip trembled. "But he would have come. He would have come for me."

Soren clasped her by the arm. "Look at me."

She couldn't.

He near shook her. "Look at me!"

She lifted her tear-filled eyes to his.

"That bastard won't die. I know. I've tried. He'll be all right."

But she couldn't stop the tears.

"Come here," he said, and pulled her close, wrapping his arm around her.

Days passed in a blur. Even visiting the Uru, Norah didn't remember much, only a little of Tahla taking care of her—helping her clean up, braiding her hair, giving her another knife. She had left Alexander's dagger back in her chamber in Mercia.

Once they cleared the Canyonlands, the Kharavian border patrol joined them. Soren spoke to them in Kharavian tongue, and two soldiers split off and away to the capital, to Mikael. She still couldn't speak the Kharavian language well, but she understood a large amount now. They rode to tell Mikael of the Mercian council's takeover, of the attempt against her life, and that Soren was bringing her home.

Mikael stood outside in the courtyard as they rode in, waiting. Soren slipped her down off the horse. The tears came again, and she let out a sob as Mikael swept her into his arms. She clung to him as she cried.

He held her tight. Then he picked her up and carried her into the safety of the Shadows.

Norah sat on her throne in stoic silence, with Mikael beside her on his own throne, as the nobles entered. They didn't sit close enough to touch, their chairs too far apart for her to do what she needed most—to simply hold his hand. But she could feel his rage. He hadn't even given her arrival a full day before he urgently summoned all his nobles. At least she'd had time to wash and look put together, even if just for appearances.

Soren stood to Mikael's right, and Salara-Mae stood to Norah's left, back just into the shadows. As the nobles took their places, Mikael rose.

"I've called you here to discuss an urgent matter," he said. "A march against the North."

Norah's head snapped up, and she gaped at him. That wasn't what she'd expected. She thought he'd only inform them of the circumstance. They hadn't discussed going to war against her council. Murmurs rippled through the nobles, and even Soren shifted in surprise.

"We can't march against the North," Lord Narsing said. "We have no allies and are on the brink of war ourselves."

"I'll remove the North's council." Mikael's words came with venom. *Punish them*, he had meant. He glanced at Norah and then back out to his nobles. "And I'll reestablish the alliance."

"The North was never an ally," Narsing argued. "Not a true one. And if Aleon decides to stand with them after this?"

"We can get there before Aleon mobilizes, but we'd have to march now."

Narsing scoffed. "You can't be serious."

"Salar," Soren said quietly. "We should discuss this."

Mikael shot him a look in surprise. Soren never spoke against him publicly. "There's nothing to discuss."

"Apparently there is," Narsing said. "Even your lord commander thinks it's a foolish idea." Another murmur rumbled through nobles in agreement. "What do you say, Lord Commander?"

But Soren didn't answer. He only looked at Mikael.

Norah caught Mikael's eyes. She silently prayed that he'd relent. He couldn't march to war against Mercia, not when his nobles, and even Soren, were unsupportive. And certainly not before Norah could get her mind around it. Perhaps there would come the time when she wanted revenge, but that time wasn't now. Now she was just trying to get her mind right about what had happened. She begged him with her eyes.

"Get out," Mikael told the room.

They stared at him for a moment.

"Now!" he demanded. And they slowly filed out.

The room emptied, and relief filled her. But the conversation wasn't done. Mikael's eyes bore into Soren. "You don't agree with me?" His voice was cold and calm—the deepest of anger.

But Soren held his own calm reply. "I wish you would have discussed it with me before bringing it to the nobles."

"I don't need your permission," Mikael snarled.

Soren's eyes were dark, darker than the midnight they normally were. "I'm lord commander. I lead our army."

Mikael bristled. "*My* army! *I* am Salar!" He was too far from Norah for her to reach out to him, to touch him, to try to calm him.

"This is just what you wanted," Salara-Mae hissed as she stepped out of the shadows, making them all stop. Norah jerked her head toward the woman in astonishment. But then she realized Salara-Mae wasn't talking to her. The woman's eyes were on Soren. "You supported this marriage when you knew it would be his downfall. Then you broke us from Japheth by murdering Gregor's nephew." Her words dripped with hatred. She looked at Mikael. "He provokes your enemies to rise against you! And now even your nobles."

"He's had nothing to do with anything that's happened," Mikael said shortly, his anger at Soren now switching to defense. "How can you even blame him?"

Salara-Mae snorted in rage and disbelief, wrinkling her face in disgust. "No," she said bitterly. "Get out!" She spoke to Soren directly. "Get out!" she seethed again.

"Mother!" Mikael tried to quiet her.

"Salara-Mae," Norah breathed.

"No!" The woman pointed at Soren, peeling her lips back in rage. "I've watched you plot and scheme and claw your way closer to the crown. This is just what you wanted! Salar on the cusp of defeat! You wanted this!"

Norah gaped at the woman in horror. "How can you say this?"

Salara-Mae's breath came ragged, her anger taking all her energy. "He knows," she seethed.

Norah looked at Soren, who stood bewildered.

"Bastard son of Rhalstad," the woman spat.

Rhalstad, *Mikael's father?*

Mikael leaned back on his heel, with his brow creased in confusion. He stared at his mother.

"He knows," Salara-Mae said again. "He knows who he is."

Mikael shifted his gaze to Soren.

Soren shook his head. "You're mistaken. My father was Tyrhar Nazim, captain of the Crest and lord of Bahoul."

Her rage sparked through the air. "Rhalstad thought he could hide you away, his son of a whore! She wasn't even a wife! When he had his captain of the Crest take you both to Bahoul, I knew. I knew!"

"That's not true," Soren said, but Norah could see the fear on his face.

Salara-Mae stepped forward, pointing a long, thin finger at him. "I watched you!" she seethed. "Always watching him! Always close! You were always scheming, just looking for your opportunity."

Norah's mind raced. Soren's claim to the throne wouldn't be a strong one if his mother *was* a concubine, but he would have one nonetheless, and an even stronger claim if the nobles didn't support the current king.

Soren stumbled backward, shaking his head. "No, that's not true," he said again.

"I saw the way you looked at him. You envied him! You envied what he had! You wanted it for yourself."

But Soren would never betray Mikael.

"Enough!" Norah cried, finally gathering the strength to stand.

Soren backed up, toward the ash-wood doors, his eyes filled with sorrow and disbelief, then he turned and staggered out into the side hall.

"Soren," Mikael called after him, but the commander didn't stop. "Soren!" he called again. He looked back at his mother.

Salara-Mae stood smugly, with her face covered in hate.

"You have no idea your ignorance," Mikael snarled at her.

"My ignorance!" she snapped back. "You defend a man with a claim to your throne, who your army follows. He can take everything from you!"

"He's *given* everything to me!" he thundered.

"You're a fool," she said, and stormed from the hall.

Norah looked to the open doors of the hall, and her blood ran cold. Several of the nobles stood, watching them. They turned and left quickly.

Norah's mind reeled from the exchange she had just witnessed and the events of the past several weeks. What had just happened? Soren was Mikael's half brother? And now the nobles knew—on top of everything else—*they knew.*

Mikael stood. Lost.

Finally, he sank down onto his throne. She crossed the space between them and stepped between his knees, taking his face in her hands and drawing his eyes up to look at her.

"Do you think she speaks the truth?" he asked hoarsely.

Norah was hesitant. She didn't know. "I think... *she* thinks it's the truth," she said finally.

"But do you?" he asked. "Do you think Soren's the son of my father?"

She pulled her bottom lip between her teeth. "We don't know that."

He let out a breath, his eyes rimmed red. "Don't we? Even *you* said a child of Soren could pass for my own. I didn't see it before, but..." His voice fell.

"We don't know that," she repeated softly.

"Why else would she hate him the way she does? Why else would she think he was after power? Even as the son of a concubine, he'd have a claim to the throne, a claim he could use to challenge me—a challenge that grows stronger with no heir." He looked up at her. "Why would she lie?" he whispered. "Do you think she lies?"

She ran her gaze over the darkness of his eyes and the strength of his jaw. The line of his nose and the shape of his brow. His black hair, dark like the night, with a faint curl. And his stature—how he stood, how he walked. All like Soren. She couldn't deny it, and she shook her head slowly.

Mikael squeezed his eyes shut and let out a shaking breath, and she pulled him to her.

Norah stood in front of Soren's chamber door. She raised her hand to knock. And stopped. She spread her palm against it. This news would have devastated him.

Finally, she knocked, but there was no answer. Slowly, she pushed open the door. Glass scraped against the floor underneath. She drew in a breath as she surveyed the room.

Everything was broken. Furniture, the mirror, the basin. Broken like Soren. Like Mikael. Like her.

"He's gone," a voice said behind her.

She turned to see Adrian—one of the few people helping her keep her sanity. Of course he'd been shocked and distraught over the news of Mercia, but he had jumped to support her and had promptly pledged himself, to which all five thousand Mercian soldiers in Kharav followed.

"I saw him as he was leaving the stables," he told her.

"When will he return?"

Adrian hesitated before shaking his head. "He's not coming back, Norah."

Not coming back? How could he just not come back? "Where did he go?"

He shook his head again. "I don't know. He said to tell Katya, and she would know what to do until Salar could appoint a new commander."

Her breath caught in her throat. A new commander? There could never be another.

"I'm on my way to find her now," he said. "I just wanted to make sure you knew first." He stood quietly for a moment. "Will you tell me if I can do anything?"

What could he do? What could anyone do? Her lip trembled.

He let out a sorrowful sigh and left her alone to the broken room.

Norah let herself sink down onto the edge of the bed, her legs weak beneath her. She covered her mouth as a sobbing breath escaped.

Alexander.

Vitalia.

Serene.

Her grandmother.

Mercia.

Cusco. Cavaatsa. Sephir.

They were all lost to her. And now Soren.

And once Mikael discovered he was gone, she'd lose him too. Soren's leaving would destroy him, like it was destroying her. They needed him. He couldn't leave.

Her silent cries turned to breathless rage—rage at the circumstance, her council, at the gods themselves.

She needed Soren back.

She needed her kingdom back.

And she needed blood.

Norah sat up as an icy fire burned over her skin. She'd get back what belonged to her, with the blood of recompense now owed. She'd take back what was hers. The Shadow Queen.

WAR QUEEN

CHAPTER ONE

Again. They were here again.

Norah's eyes drifted around the empty Kharavian throne room. It wouldn't be empty in a few moments. She sat in her chair on the dais and tried to push down the unease creeping in as Mikael took his own seat. She watched her husband and the calm that sat over him—not the calm of peace, but the calm that comes before battle.

"I hate this room," she muttered.

He turned to her. "Why?"

So many reasons. It was the coldest room in the castle; even in the warmth of summer, she practically needed a cloak. It was the room where they received bad news. And it was where the Kharavian nobles incessantly judged them, judged Mikael. She didn't say those things, not when they were about to face another slew of judgments—judgments that threatened Mikael's crown—and not when he worked so hard to protect her from the worry of it all.

"Because you're too far." She reached out her arm, unable to stretch even half the distance between them. It wasn't a petty complaint. They could face anything together, but here it didn't feel like they were together. She couldn't touch him, couldn't get strength from simply putting her hand in his. When he faced challenges from his nobles, she couldn't put her hand on his arm to help settle him as she usually would, to remind him he wasn't alone.

Norah looked down at the bottom of her chair. "And these gods-damned things were built into the floor. I can't even scooch over."

He raised a brow. "Scooch?"

"Yes." She frowned. "I can't move to come closer."

The corners of his mouth turned up ever so slightly. "Ah. Well, scooch just your body here then."

"What?"

"Come here."

She glanced at the closed double doors at the end of the hall. The nobles would arrive soon, but she rose and moved to him anyway. He reached out his hand, and she took it, and they threaded their fingers together as he pulled her closer. His lips held a smile she hadn't seen in months.

"Why are you smiling?" she asked. He shouldn't be smiling with what was coming in the next moments.

He brought her hand up and kissed the backs of her fingers. "Because I have you."

His words brought a wave of emotion as she caressed the side of his cheek. "I love you."

"I know," he whispered. "And I love you." He pulled her into his lap, and she laughed.

"This is a good compromise," she said, grinning. "Yes, I like this much better."

Mikael shrugged. "This is how we'll sit, then."

She laughed again. "You can't address your nobles with me sitting on your lap."

"Why not?"

Norah drew her brows together. "It's not... kingly."

"I don't care about being kingly; I care about making my salara happy." He pursed his lips through a small smile. "Which also makes me happy."

"Well, I don't want them seeing me like this—they already view me as a distraction to you."

"The most beautiful of distractions."

His body responded underneath her, and she swatted him. "Stop it!" she warned with a grin. Then she rested her hand on his chest. "I should start my journey back to my chair now if I'm going to make it there by nightfall. I'll miss you." And she kissed him deeply.

His body hardened more, and she smiled as she pulled away and walked back to her throne. He protested with a rumble in his chest.

Norah took her chair just as Salara-Mae entered. As soon as she saw the woman, the smile fell from her lips. For a fleeting moment, she'd forgotten what they were facing, and the woman's hard countenance pulled her back to the reality of their situation. Mikael's mother rarely joined them in the throne room, but she did now, no doubt to support her son.

The nobles were displeased. More than displeased. Kharav's alliance with Japheth was broken, and a new enemy—Rael—was on the horizon, an enemy they felt Mikael had underestimated. He had. They all had. Who would have thought a kingdom of freed slaves would be such a threat?

As if that weren't enough cause for concern, Kharav's alliance with Mercia had crumbled—an alliance the nobles had always doubted. If Mercia united once again with their old ally, Aleon, they'd have the advantage if they attacked.

With no allies, Kharav stood alone.

And now another had a claim to the Kharavian throne—one who held the respect and loyalty of their great armies as much as Mikael did, one that no longer stood by Mikael's side. Soren. After learning he was Mikael's half brother, he'd disappeared, and his absence was a gaping void.

Mikael was alone.

Norah glanced at him as he set his eyes on the heavy ashen doors, all traces of play now gone from his face. He wasn't Mikael now. He was salar. And this was the fight for his throne.

On her right, her Crest guard Bhastian stepped between their thrones, his spear in one hand and his other hand resting on the hilt of the sword around his waist. The Crest protected the king and royal family. Bhastian's place was to Mikael's right, on the side of the dais, but Mikael had wanted him closer to Norah. She caught movement to her left out of the corner of her eye and looked to see Adrian beside her as well. She hadn't noticed when either of them had entered, but she was glad they were there now. Her stomach turned at the thought that she might need them.

The doors swung open with a deep boom, startling her, and she forced herself to settle. She always forgot they did that—another reason she hated this room.

The nobles filed in. She lost count as they came through the doors. There were perhaps a hundred. Or a little less? And although they were nobles, they still embodied every aspect of Kharav's essence. These weren't like the nobles of Mercia—elevated and fattened solely on the backs of others. They were warriors, protectors of their people. Some of them were warlords with vast lands and armies of their own.

They had called for an audience to show their continued concern over the increasing threats to Kharav and press for Soren's return—neither of which Mikael had control over. She folded her clammy hands in her lap to keep from wringing them together. She wanted to look at Mikael, to draw in some of the power that radiated from him as he sat so calmly looking out across the nobles, but she didn't dare look away. Instead, she did her best to fake the same.

"Salar," Lord Narsing greeted, polite yet cold. "This is an unfortunate state in which we continue to find ourselves."

Norah hated this man. He reminded her of Edward, the elder Mercian councilman who'd no doubt been the one to orchestrate the coup against her—only he was a larger, more intimidating version of Edward. Unlike the other Kharavian nobles, there was an air of scheming about him, and when he spoke, he spoke only in challenge.

"It is," Mikael replied.

The noble's eyes narrowed. "We'd like to understand your plans to salvage the alliance with Japheth."

"There isn't one," Mikael replied, matter-of-factly.

Murmurs rippled through the nobles. Narsing puffed a small breath of incredulity.

Another noble stepped forward. Unlike most of the nobles, he covered his face like a warrior. But Norah knew who he was. Lord Jarik. This was a man who could plant seeds of fear in even the bravest of men. He was an influential lord, not just in status but by his pure embodiment of blood and battle. Jarik was a man of war, and the markings of his bravery covered almost his whole body. He was one of the few nobles to lead battle charges from the front. And he looked like he might lead a charge against Mikael now. "You plan for Kharav to stand alone?" he asked.

But Mikael wasn't shaken. "And what would you propose otherwise?"

"Gregor—"

Mikael cut him off. "Gregor is now an enemy of Kharav and has allied himself with Rael's King Cyrus."

"Is he an enemy of Kharav, or an enemy of Salara?" Narsing pressed.

Gregor. Norah tried to hold her repulsive shudder at the sound of his name. She knew they'd use her previous confrontation with Japheth's king against Mikael. They saw it as a deliberate attempt by her to fracture the alliance between Japheth and Kharav, with Mikael doing nothing to mend it. Heat radiated from Mikael, and her pulse quickened. He couldn't let his anger drive him. Not here. Not now. But she was too far to touch him, too far to pull him back.

"When will the lord commander be returning?" Narsing asked—a question with an indirect threat.

Mikael continued to sit on his throne, calm on the outside. "Why?"

"Would you not expect Kharavian nobles to want to keep track of those with a claim to the throne?" Jarik said.

"We must continue to assess options for Kharav," Narsing added, clearly emboldened by Jarik. A direct threat.

Another ripple of whispers moved through the crowd.

Mikael rose, and the murmurs in the room fell silent. He slowly stepped down the stairs.

Bhastian and Adrian shifted even closer to Norah. Her other Crest guard, Kiran, made his presence known as well. She gripped the arms of her chair, her fingernails biting into the ornately carved wood.

Mikael stopped in the center of the hall, in the center of what looked like a potential battlefield, only a few paces from Narsing. It was a move of challenge, daring them to act against him. Norah's heart pounded in her chest. She breathed prayers to every god she could remember for Mikael not to react with blood. The Crest and Adrian would be focused on her protection and wouldn't be able to help him, not with the nobles now surrounding him.

Salara-Mae stood to the right of the dais like a statue, but Norah knew she was beside herself. Soren's bloodline had been a secret the woman had harbored for so long, and in her moment of anger, she'd released it. Salara-Mae had brought this added threat to Mikael, and no doubt she blamed herself. As she should.

"Where is the lord commander now?" Lord Narsing asked.

"He's not here," Mikael replied stiffly.

"When will he return?"

"Again, why?" Mikael demanded. "*I* am salar. If you have a grievance, you'll address it with me, not the commander of *my* armies that he leads with the power given *by me.*" He loomed closer to Narsing, daring the noble to challenge him further.

Narsing's eyes flicked to Jarik. The large warlord put his hand on the hilt of his sword. Faster than Norah could blink, Narsing whipped his hand to his own sword. But Mikael was faster. Before Narsing had fully drawn his blade from the scabbard, Mikael had buried his own blade in the lord, to the hilt—so clean that blood had yet to spill.

Norah jumped to her feet. Adrian and Bhastian bumped against her shoulders on either side, their swords out. But no one else moved. The hall was silent.

Mikael leaned even closer to Narsing, who still hung on his sword. "I accept your challenge," he snarled. Then he shoved Narsing back off his blade. The lord fell to the floor of the hall and didn't get up. Blood pooled under his body, spidering along the lines where the patterned stone joined together.

Mikael roved his eyes over the nobles around him. "Anyone else?" His stare landed on Jarik, who stared back. The warlord's hand was still curled around the hilt of the sword at his side.

The air in the room was suffocating. Norah couldn't breathe. She had no doubt of Mikael's ability to fight, especially in defending what was his. But Jarik wasn't a man she wanted to see against him. He was a man even Soren respected. That meant he was dangerous.

"Anyone else?" Mikael pressed again, not taking his eyes from Jarik.

Norah couldn't see his face under his head wrap, but Jarik's eyes held enough of a message that one didn't need to see his face to understand—a warning.

Finally, after an eternity, the lord said, "No, Salar." But he didn't drop his hand from the hilt of his sword.

Norah didn't dare let relief settle her. This wasn't over.

Mikael looked around the room. "We're done here," he said. Then he turned his back—another invitation for violence that made bile rise in the back of Norah's throat—as he strode and took the stairs back to his throne.

It was perhaps the shortest, although seemingly the longest, exchange with the nobles Norah had seen. She shakily lowered herself back to her seat as Mikael took his own chair, and they watched everyone start to filter out. Two men grabbed Narsing's body and carried him from the room, leaving a trail of blood along the stone.

They waited until the last of the nobles had departed and the doors had closed. Even Salara-Mae wordlessly disappeared into the wings and down the side hall from where she'd come.

When they were alone, Norah turned to him. But she couldn't speak. Her heart still hadn't slowed.

He held out his hand for her. "Come, journey back to me from that ridiculously far chair." His words were said in jest, but there was no happiness in them, no play in his voice. Still, she was too eager to be back to him and moved quickly to his side. He caught her hand in his and brought her palm to his lips, planting a reassuring kiss. Whether he was reassuring himself or her, she wasn't sure.

"Are you all right?" he asked.

She nodded. "Are you?"

Heat still pulsed off him. He didn't answer.

She threaded her fingers into his hair, messing up the tie that bound it back, but she didn't care. She drew her fingertips gently across the back of his head, as she often did to help him relax.

"I need to appoint someone." His voice was empty. Hollow.

"For what?"

He didn't answer.

Norah cupped his cheek and pulled his face to look at her. "Appoint someone for what?" she asked again.

"Lord commander," he said finally.

She swallowed. "You have a lord commander."

He said nothing in reply.

She tightened her fingers against his skin. "Mikael, you have a lord commander."

"And he left me!" he raged suddenly.

But she didn't react to his explosion of hurt. It had been over three months since Soren had left, and his absence was felt every day, by both of them. Norah softened her touch but still held his face as she moved to his front and stepped between his knees. She pulled him to look at her again.

His brows dipped in sadness as he sucked in a heavy breath. "He left me," he said hoarsely. Emotion filled his face, and she pulled him to her, wrapping her arms around him.

"He'll be back," she tried to assure him.

"He's not welcome back."

She pulled back so that his eyes met hers again. "Don't say that."

"He's supposed to be by my side. But he left me when I need him most."

"No," she countered. "Did you not hear Narsing and Jarik? Soren knows he's seen as a threat to you—he would have wanted to remove that threat."

"He could have rejected his right. He didn't need to leave."

She shook her head. "You know it wouldn't have been that simple, not with the nobles. They're not happy. They'd use him to pressure you."

"And did he fear he'd so easily allow them?"

Norah sighed. He knew the answer to that foolish question. She ran her nails gently through his short-cut beard. "The news about your father—his father—had to have hurt him. Deeply. And to reconcile the feelings he had... around you... These things aren't easy."

"Why not? We would have been what we've always called each other—brothers—what I've always felt we were." He shook his head. "But I was wrong. He's not my brother."

"Mikael," she breathed. "You can't mean that."

"I mean it," he said coldly, his emotion gone. "Don't speak to me about him again. I no longer know him."

It was his pain talking. But she couldn't deny the deep, aching worry that seeped into her heart.

Chapter Two

The sun had started to sink under the horizon, and the sound of Salara-Mae's teacup clinking as she set it on the saucer echoed through the dining hall. Norah chewed her food slowly. That probably echoed too. Hardly any words were spoken as they ate, much like the last two days had been since the confrontation with the nobles. Mikael took drinks from his chalice, staring blankly at his plate of untouched food.

She knew what was on his mind. Her eyes drifted to Soren's empty chair, as they did every meal since he'd left. But Mikael never looked at the chair, or his mother. He had raged at Salara-Mae after first learning the secret that had rocked their kingdom. Now he only simmered in silent anger.

Norah had blamed her too, for a time, but as the months passed, she found her anger fading. Despite the turmoil it had caused, there was a relief to be living in truth, no matter the challenges it presented or how raw it rubbed the heart.

But she didn't like this, the way they were now. This wasn't how they healed—by not talking. But she couldn't force a conversation about Soren. Not with either of them. Not yet.

"I was going to take a walk in the gardens in the morning," Norah said in an effort to break the perpetual silence. "To try to take advantage of what's left of summer."

Mikael lifted his eyes to hers, and he nodded. "You should."

She shifted her gaze to the king's mother. "Will you join me, Salara-Mae?"

The woman paused her chewing, then swallowed. "Very well."

Norah had expected to have to work harder to convince her and was pleasantly surprised. "All right then," she said with a small smile.

Salara-Mae put her dinner cloth on her plate and rose with a nod. "But for tonight, I'll retire."

"Good night," Norah told her.

Mikael remained silent.

Salara-Mae left the dining hall, and Norah looked back to Mikael to find him watching her.

"You can't stay angry at her forever," she said softly.

He took another drink from his chalice.

Norah rose and moved to the chair beside him, then reached across the corner of the table and took his hand. "Mikael. She spoke in a moment of anger that she's deeply regretted ever since."

"I'm not angry with her for speaking the truth. I'm angry with her for not speaking it sooner."

"And when would she have done that? The longer you carry a secret, the harder it is to tell."

"It should never have been a secret!"

Norah sighed. She didn't disagree, but these things were never that simple. "It's a mother's job to protect her children. To love them." She squeezed his hand. "And she loves you fiercely. Whether what she did was right, whether you agree with her choices, she made those choices with your well-being in her heart."

His continued objection flashed in his eyes but remained unspoken on his lips. He pushed out a breath and covered her hand with his. "We don't need to talk about me. You've endured so much more."

"It's not a competition."

The muscle tightened along his jaw. "I haven't even asked you how you've been. I'm sorry."

She shook her head. "It's okay."

"No, it's not." He rested his weight on his elbows and cupped her hand in his. "Tell me how you are."

How she was—such a simple question, yet so complicated. She wanted to smile and tell him she was all right, mainly because if she spoke of what she was really feeling, it would bring a wave of emotion she couldn't control.

"Tell me," he said softly.

They had spoken of Mercia before, speculating on what might have happened after the coup, but only to a point and only of best-case scenarios—assuming that her grandmother was unharmed and that Alexander was all right.

Alexander.

Her heart still dropped like a rock every time she thought of him. Despite the harsh words between them when they last spoke, he would have never stood idle while Norah was attacked. And unlike her grandmother, an aged royal of Mercia easily overpowered, Alexander was a soldier. He would have fought. He would have come for her.

But he didn't.

"I'm scared," she whispered.

He nodded but didn't speak. He only waited for her to continue.

"We know nothing. The council has surely crowned my cousin, Evangeline, logically. But I know nothing of my grandmother, if she's well." She paused as her voice caught in her throat. "If she's even alive. And..." Her voice dropped off. She didn't want to raise her fears for Alexander. Of course Mikael would know she had them, but she didn't want to so openly lay them out before him.

He squeezed her hand tighter. "The Bear is alive," he said, as if reading her mind, "and he'll watch over your grandmother."

"But what if he can't?" Even if he hadn't been killed in the coup, he was only one man, and a man in danger at that. He might be lord justice, but the balance of power had shifted. The council was in control now. Even if he'd made it through the takeover alive, he wouldn't have stayed silent. He would have acted, with devastating consequences. The fact that she hadn't heard from him made that scenario all the more likely.

"If the Bear had fallen, we would have heard," Mikael said, trying to reassure her.

She'd like to think that, but her mind wouldn't let her take comfort so easily. Instead, it lingered on the worst-case scenario—the most likely scenario.

Something had happened to him.

Norah swallowed. "I was thinking of writing to King Phillip." She paused and waited for the reaction she knew was coming.

Mikael shifted his weight back.

"He would know what happened," she added. "The council would have written him."

"Salara, you cannot write the Aleon king."

"Why not? Phillip hasn't shown himself to be an enemy."

"He hasn't shown himself to be a friend," he argued. "He doesn't come to your aid against treason, and he still occupies Bahoul."

That was mostly true. She hadn't heard from him after the coup, and the forces of Aleon still remained in Bahoul, the Kharavian stronghold that Phillip had occupied without her consent first. But they'd come to what she thought were friendly terms in the months leading to the council overthrowing her. She thought he *had* shown himself to be a friend. "True, he has no duty to me; he's not an official ally. But he didn't recall his forces when I sent them to aid you against the threat of Japheth and Rael. And he did warn you to close your ports, saving Kharav from fever."

"That was when he thought the North was united with Kharav," he argued, "which quite obviously isn't the case anymore."

She pushed out a frustrated breath. "It's worth a try."

"Salara. Do *not* write the Aleon king," he warned. "If you haven't heard from him yet, he stands with your council. Don't show them your weakness."

Dearest Alexander.

Norah drew her bottom lip between her teeth, biting it raw. She crumpled the parchment into a ball and tossed it into the fire. Tapping the pen into the inkwell again, she brought the tip to another blank parchment.

Dear Alexander.

She stared at the words. His name. She'd started this letter a hundred times over the months, but she could never get past his name. What would she say? Their last words to each other had been harsh. She wanted to say she was sorry—sorry for the distance between them, sorry for the state in which they now found themselves. How did he find himself? Was he safe? Was he well?

The chamber door opened and closed, and Mikael's footfalls traveled around the hanging panel and into the room. Her breath hitched. She didn't move. His warmth seeped into her back as he came behind her, but she didn't try to hide what she was doing. His hand rested on her shoulder.

Norah swallowed. "I'm not going to send anything. I just..." Heat rushed to her cheeks. She was just what? Writing to the man she still deeply cared for? Writing to the man who was still foretold to bring her husband's end, wishing him unharmed and well?

Mikael's left hand came to her other shoulder, and he squeezed gently as he leaned forward to see. She held her breath.

"Tell him not to die," he said.

Her head jerked back to look up at him. "What?"

"Tell him not to die."

It took a moment for her words to come. "W-Why?"

"Because he listens to you."

She looked back at the parchment, bewildered. "But I'm not going to send it."

He gave her shoulders another light squeeze. "Just write it, and he'll know." He placed a kiss on top of her head, releasing her, then withdrew and stepped out of the chamber.

Norah looked back at the parchment and drew her fingertip across Alexander's name. *Don't die*, she wrote.

The mornings were turning colder, and Norah pulled her wrap tighter around her as she walked beside Salara-Mae through the late-summer gardens. Most of the flowers were spent now and had been trimmed back, but the evergreen topiaries still made for an impressive sight.

Their morning walk had started as quiet as their breakfast had been with Mikael, and their dinner the evening before. Salara-Mae walked with a stoic countenance. While Salara-Mae was still the model of regal poise, Norah knew below the surface she was tormented by what she'd done. And she felt for the woman in her silent suffering.

"He won't be angry forever," Norah said—no use avoiding the topic. "He just needs time."

"I know you talk to him."

Norah nibbled the inside of her lip. As in good talk or bad talk? The woman wasn't scowling. That was a good sign.

"You're the only one he listens to," Salara-Mae said, "and I know you try to talk reason into him."

Norah breathed out, smiling. *Progress*. She raised a brow and dipped her head. "Well, he's actually quite reasonable. He's just hurt. And matters of the heart aren't as simple as alliances and battle plans."

To her astonishment, the king's mother actually laughed. It occurred to her she had never heard Salara-Mae laugh. It was beautiful.

"No truer words have ever been spoken," the woman told her.

The morning was starting to warm, and Norah welcomed it.

"I'm glad that you invited me on your walk this morning," Salara-Mae said. "There's something I've been meaning to raise with you."

Oh. Her stomach started to tumble. No doubt there was something that needed correction, or it was perhaps again about a child. Salara-Mae hadn't broached the topic in a few months. Norah had thought she'd given up, but now that seemed foolish. Salara-Mae wasn't a woman who gave up easily. Would a child even matter anymore? Now that Norah was without a kingdom and Kharav was on the brink of rebellion, perhaps it was better she wasn't with child. All the easier when she and Mikael had to fight for their thrones, and possibly their lives. Or run. She wrinkled her nose. Mikael would never run. And she would never leave him to face it alone. It would be a fight, and if Mikael didn't make it through, she wouldn't either.

"Salara." Salara-Mae's voice brought her back to the present, and she turned to see the woman had stopped a few paces back, where Norah had simply continued on.

"Oh, I'm sorry," she said quickly.

"What were you thinking about?"

What had she been thinking about? "Oh, um... not being with child and hopefully not dying." She grimaced as she said the words. Sometimes her mind failed her. As she saw Salara-Mae's face, she knew this was clearly one of those times.

"I'd rather not follow that thought process," Salara-Mae said slowly.

Norah nodded, heat beginning to flush her cheeks.

Salara-Mae stepped to her side once again. "I don't always understand you."

Not unexpected. "Well..." Norah tilted her head slightly to the side. "In fairness, I don't always understand myself."

"But I have come to respect you."

Norah stopped. Now *that* was unexpected.

"I used to think Kharav was the only kingdom with great warriors. But you, North Queen, have rivaled them all." She looked down at her hand as she pulled a ring from the center finger on her left hand. "My mother gave me this ring. It was given to her by her mother before, and her mother before. It's a ring passed down generations, from a line of strong women. I had planned to give it to my own daughter one day. Fate took that opportunity from me."

A wave of sadness ran through her. Mikael's sister had passed from an illness. Norah had never met her, but Mikael had told her that his sister was a lot like him, and Norah knew she would have loved her.

"But fate has given me a new opportunity," Salara-Mae said. "Another daughter."

Norah locked eyes with her in surprise.

"You're a strong woman, a strong salara, and I want you to have this ring." She took Norah's hand and pushed the ring over her center finger. Then she reached up and clasped Norah's cheek, her eyes glistening. Norah's own emotion choked back any words that may have been in her throat. She glanced down at her hand, stretching her fingers out and admiring the smooth-cut black stone set deep in silver. Norah had never been one for jewelry, but this meant something. And that made it even more beautiful. All she could do was nod.

Salara-Mae let out a long breath. "Now I think I'd like to go sit and read awhile," she said, as if the short emotional exchange had completely drained her.

"Of course," Norah said.

The king's mother turned to leave, but Norah caught her.

"Salara-Mae, thank you. This means a lot to me."

The woman nodded. "Me too." Then she turned and walked back toward the castle.

Norah watched her go before heading to the strip of garden between the parallel windowed halls leading to the library. Breathing in the late-summer air, she closed her eyes as the sun kissed her face. Hope stirred within her. This was what she needed—light, warmth, healing.

She *was* a strong queen, she told herself. She wasn't perfect, but she forgave herself for that. And she wasn't without a kingdom, as she'd felt only moments ago. It had been temporarily taken from her, and she would take it back and see those she loved were safe.

Norah reached into the pocket of her gown and clutched the folded parchment inside—a letter she'd written but battled whether to send.

A letter to Phillip.

She turned on her heel and strode inside. She needed to find Adrian. As she stepped through the doors, she almost collided with a woman coming from the hall of the Circle's chamber. The Circle was Kharav's council.

"Forgive me, Salara," the woman said.

Norah stared at her for a moment. The woman's long, black hair hung loose over her shoulders, and her face was one Norah had seen uncovered only a couple of times. "Katya," she said in surprise. "I didn't recognize you for a moment. I hardly ever see you."

The Kharavian captain was rarely at the castle and rarely without her face wrap.

Katya smiled. "You'll likely see me a bit more, now that I've been assigned to matters at home. Until the child comes."

Child? Norah looked down to see her swelling belly and grinned with a gasp. "Katya! I didn't know you were with child!" She didn't even know she was married. Was she married? She supposed it didn't matter. Not in Kharav.

The captain nodded. "It was a surprise, but a welcome one."

"I'm so happy for you!" Norah meant it. To be blessed with a child was nothing short of a gift from the gods.

Katya's smile widened. "Thank you, Salara. It means a lot that you'd find joy for me in times like this."

"How soon are you expecting?" Just looking at her, it couldn't be terribly long now.

"Only a couple more months."

Children were a blessing. "If you need anything," Norah said, "anything at all."

The captain nodded appreciatively. "Thank you, Salara."

Norah watched as she disappeared down the adjoining hall, and pushed down the pang of jealousy. This was a good thing, and she was happy for Katya. She wondered if she'd see the child around the castle—she'd like that. Surely Adrian and Sevina were tired of her constant doting over their little boy, Theisen, and would welcome another child to occupy her attention. Thoughts of Adrian pulled her mind back to her task at hand, and she continued her course to find him.

Adrian had been in Kharav during the Mercian council's takeover and had stayed with Norah since. She knew he had to be sick with worry for Alexander—his brother was the person he loved most in the world. And Soren's absence had hit him hard as well, but he didn't show it. He always wore a brave face, for her benefit, no doubt.

She made her way through the castle, out the east door, and across the courtyard, and he was at the first place she'd guessed—the sparring field with Cohen. Adrian had become close with Calla and Cohen, the young siblings that had helped Norah travel to the seer, and whom she'd brought to Kharav to formally train. She watched as they worked through their movements. Fast. Precise. Deadly. Yet poetic.

Adrian and Cohen had become master swordsmen. Their dance was beautiful, their ease of movement deceiving. When Cohen noticed her, he signaled them to stop.

Adrian turned, and a grin spread across his face. "Norah."

Salara, Cohen greeted with his hands. Norah hadn't picked up the silent language entirely, but she could follow most of what the deaf boy said.

"Adrian, Cohen," she greeted back. "Where's Calla?"

Adrian smirked. "Where do you think?"

The archery field, Cohen answered. Where the girl always was.

Norah smiled. "Of course."

Cohen gave a small bow of his head, then signed, *I'll leave you.* He was always so perceptive, reading people like a book, and he left her and Adrian to speak privately.

"What do you need?" Adrian asked.

Glancing around, she pulled the letter from her pocket. "I need to get this to Phillip. In Bahoul."

Adrian shifted as the muscle tightened along his jaw. "Do you think that's wise?"

"I have to know what's happened in Mercia. What's happened to Grandmother, to Alexander. I'm calling on Phillip's friendship that he himself has proclaimed. And I'll see where he stands."

He stood taller at the mention of Alexander. She knew he was as desperate as she was to know how he fared. "And you think he'll tell you?"

She shook her head slowly. "I don't know, but I have to try." She put the letter in his hands.

Kharavian forces patrolled the border at the eastern pass. She couldn't send just any Northman without exposing her intention, but Adrian had influence with the Kharavian army. She needed him to help get her letter past them and to the stronghold, where she hoped Phillip still remained.

"All right," he said as he nodded in support. As she knew he would.

CHAPTER THREE

Mikael took another drink from his chalice. He leaned back in the desk chair of his study, staring at the parchments in front of him. War was coming. The armies of Japheth and Rael had been ravaged by fever, but they were rebuilding and growing stronger than before and faster than expected.

News flooded in that slaves from kingdoms all over the world were escaping to join Rael's cause, even slaves from Kharav. It was a compelling purpose—the fight for freedom. This Raelean king, Cyrus, had grown quite a name for himself. He had an impressive story, even to Mikael. He had been a bloodsport fighter, his origins unknown. It was said that he started the slave rebellion by attacking the onlooking Raelean king directly during a bloodsport match in the grand arena.

Rael was famed for their blood games. There would have been thousands of fighters—thousands of men to join him, and bloodsport fighters were the ultimate warriors. They rivaled even the warriors of Kharav. These men were raised in blood and battled for their lives daily.

Once he'd taken Rael, Cyrus turned to those who had enslaved him—the neighboring slaver kingdom of Serra. Within four days, he had taken all the port cities, and by the sixth, he had taken the kingdom.

Six days to take a kingdom.

It was an accomplishment unheard of. While Serra was primarily a wasteland island kingdom, it was larger than Kharav, and it would have required a large army to overtake it. Cyrus took it merely with the slaves from within.

Mikael took another drink of wine. It was rumored Cyrus had his sights on Kharav now. This puzzled him. *Why?* Yes, Kharav had slaves, but many other kingdoms did as well. Perhaps it was Kharav's proximity. Mikael's only consolation was that he wasn't the only enemy. With Rael allied with Japheth, Japheth's enemies were Rael's enemies. And Phillip, king of Aleon, was Japheth's greatest enemy. Japheth's King Gregor had tried to overtake his brother many times. No doubt it still consumed him.

So, the question was, would a united Japheth and Rael attack Aleon, which was Japheth's obsession? Or would they go after Kharav, which was Rael's target?

Rael's focus on Kharav didn't seem like a circumstance of convenience. Yes, the kingdoms were close, with only the Aged Sea between them, and yes, Kharav was a kingdom that had slaves. But it felt more personal, somehow.

Salara had tried to change the slaving norms in Kharav, but that change wasn't easy. Not one of his nobles would approve, and he couldn't risk even more of their dissatisfaction. Tensions were rising, as was the risk to his crown, especially since the confrontation with Narsing and Jarik. His anger surfaced again. Did they really think they could threaten him with Soren? His lord commander wouldn't usurp him. Soren didn't want power, but that wasn't enough to stop the nobles from taking dangerous action. And he was weak without Soren by his side.

Soren had left him weak.

His mind shifted back to Salara. It wouldn't be long before Kharav was no longer safe for her, but he had nowhere to send her, no place to keep her from harm. Soren's leaving stung. Not only had he abandoned his friend and brother in his time of need but he'd abandoned Salara, to whom he was sworn.

And Mikael would not forgive him.

Norah walked through the courtyard, a book in her hand. She'd thought she'd sit in the garden and read a bit, but she couldn't focus her mind. It had been two weeks since she'd sent Phillip her letter, and he still hadn't responded. With each day that passed, her worry grew. Was Phillip allied with Mercia? Had he been involved in her removal? Had he told her council of her letter? If not, why hadn't he answered?

She'd give anything to go for a ride on Sephir—to clear her mind—but she hadn't been able to get the mare before fleeing from Mercia. What had happened to her? Like all of those she loved and had left, the question remained. Adrian fell in step casually beside her, and she forced a smile. "Adrian," she greeted. She had stopped asking every other moment if news had come, resigned that he would tell her when it did. It was hard to hold back the question yet again.

"Nothing has come," he told her, as if reading her mind.

She pulled her bottom lip in between her teeth.

"Don't think the worst," he said.

"How can I not?" How could *he* not?

"There are many reasons you might not have heard. Maybe the message didn't reach him."

"Did the messenger not confirm he delivered it to Bahoul?"

"But not to Phillip's own hand," he countered. "We don't know if it made it to him. Maybe Phillip's not in Bahoul."

She took little comfort in that. A message from the queen of Mercia, even the overthrown queen, would have been treated urgently.

"And I'm sure he has his own worries," he added. "I hear Japheth and Rael are rebuilding their armies at a surprising rate."

More news that wasn't favorable for Kharav—as everything seemed to be. And what could she do? What could anyone do?

"I wish Soren were here," she found herself saying.

"Me too," he answered softly. Loss peppered his voice, and she glanced to see it written on his face as well. But he quickly stowed his emotion and straightened.

Her heart broke for him. She almost forgot sometimes how much this affected him too. Soren didn't just train him, he believed in Adrian, cared for him. Soren secured Adrian's marriage to a Kharavian nobleman's daughter with his own name and his own seal, as the head of a family would do. That was what Soren was to Adrian—family. Like he was to her and Mikael.

"I'll let you know if I hear of anything else," Adrian said.

"Thank you."

He nodded, and she watched him disappear toward the stables.

Norah made her way past the garden topiaries, trying to breathe calmness back into her body. But calmness wouldn't come. Day after day they remained in this hold. When would it end?

The flutter of a small bird drew her gaze. It lighted close by on a manicured laurel, looking at her curiously. She smiled.

Then the hair on the back of her neck stood on end.

She knew this kind of bird. A small brown bird with black eyes, watching. Watching her. And on its head—a smeared marking.

It was *him*. The man who had sent the assassins. The man who wanted her dead.

"Have you returned?" she called bitterly. She always knew he would. Eventually. "What do you want?" How long had he been watching her, waiting? Why now, after so long? He was obviously sending her a message in letting her see him. Did he think himself clever? Dangerous?

Well, she was dangerous too. "Have the courage to come yourself, coward!" she yelled as she hurled the book at him. He took flight and disappeared into the gardens.

Norah turned on her heel and stormed toward the armory. As she walked briskly through the courtyard, Kiran fell in close behind her.

"Is everything all right, Salara?" he asked.

Everything was not all right.

The guards bowed their heads as she entered the armory and swept past them. She had been here enough times with Soren; she knew exactly what she was looking for.

Norah tore open the cabinets lining the far wall and pulled a crossbow from its pegs. Soren's words echoed in her mind. She'd show this man how the Shadow Queen welcomed him.

Norah swung open the door to Mikael's study, followed closely by Calla and Kiran. In her hand, she held the shaft of an arrow that was speared through a small brown bird. Breathlessly, she smacked it on the desk in front of Mikael.

"He's back."

Mikael looked at the bird a moment before lifting his eyes to hers. His brows drew together in question. "Who?"

"*Him*," she said.

His face darkened. "The one who sent the assassins?"

"This is his bird. Look at the blood on its head." In the time that had passed since the assassination attempt against her, since her suspecting of being spied on by a bird, she'd almost convinced herself she'd imagined that detail, or misremembered. It sounded like lunacy—being watched by animals with blood markings. But lunacy or not, here it was in front of her, and she was sure now. The blood had to be part of his sorcery somehow.

Mikael stood and picked up the arrow, staring at the dead bird impaled on the end. "So, he's returned."

He didn't even question her mind. He believed her, no matter how absurd it sounded, and she loved him for it.

His brow dipped. "Did *you* hit this bird?"

Calla snorted behind her. "Are you serious?"

Mikael looked at the girl.

"Apologies, Salar," Calla said quickly.

Norah shot her a chastising glance to hide her own smile. For a moment, the air lightened. "I might have made a fool of myself with a crossbow before Calla stepped in," she admitted.

"With a longbow?" he asked.

"Yes, Salar," Calla answered.

He looked back at the bird and frowned. "An impressive shot."

She gave an appreciative bow of her head. "Thank you, Salar."

Mikael looked back to Norah. "I know you're not going to like this, but I'm going to double your guard."

He was right. She didn't like it, but she nodded.

Mikael turned to Kiran. "Find Bhastian." Of course, he'd rely on Soren's most trusted man.

Kiran bowed. "Yes, Salar." And he left to his task.

"I want him with you," he told her. "Always."

She wanted to object, but she didn't. This man unnerved her, whoever and whatever he was. What was this power? Was he a sorcerer? She hadn't thought sorcery or magic were real, but what does one call embodying another person using blood? Watching through birds—what was that if not magic?

Mikael looked back to Calla. "Take down every bird you see."

Norah held up her hand. "We're not going to start shooting all the birds from the sky."

"Perhaps just the birds that aren't of Kharav," Calla suggested.

Mikael paused. "What do you know about these birds?"

Calla shrugged. "Nothing, only they aren't native to Kharav."

"Where are they from?"

"I just said I don't know anything about them."

"Calla," Norah whispered.

"I'm sorry," the girl said quickly. "I mean, I don't know. *Again.*"

Norah shot her another daggered look. Despite being at the castle for over a year now, the girl was still oblivious to courtesies and societal norms. Mikael tolerated her, for Norah's benefit, but she had less desire to push his patience lately. "Wait for me in the hall," she said to Calla.

"Yes, Salara." The girl turned and stepped into the hall.

Norah looked back to Mikael. "She's young."

"It's not an excuse, but it's not the girl I'm concerned about right now." He tossed the arrow with the dead bird back onto his desk. "I'll find who's behind this," he promised.

She knew he already felt the sting of failure for not finding who was responsible for the assassins. Every path he'd chased led to a dead end. And things had quieted for a time—it was as if her enemy had forgotten about her, or no longer cared. Until today. She didn't want this to be yet another thing for him to worry about, but here they were.

And in the spirit of additional unpleasant things to deal with—

"There's something else I wanted to talk to you about," she told him. Something else that made her stomach knot.

"And what's that?"

"I've written Phillip for news," she confessed abruptly, and not as smoothly as she would have liked. She waited for his anger.

The line of his jaw tightened. "I told you not to do that." His voice came low and calm—the voice that made her squirm the most.

Yes, he had. He had told her. She said nothing.

"He stands with the North," he said as he stepped even closer.

"You don't know that," she countered.

His voice came more pressing now. "You shouldn't have written him."

"I have to know," she argued. "I have to know if my grandmother's all right." She stopped herself from the mention of Alexander. "I have to know where Phillip stands."

"You show your weakness."

"It's not weak to ask about those I love! And if it is, I don't care. I would ask my council directly if I could. I have to know."

"It's no longer your council! They're your enemy. And if they know what you care about, they'll use it against you."

"I think it's quite obvious I would care about my grandmother," she cut back, her own anger rising.

"And what about those not as obvious to them?"

Norah stopped. *Alexander.* She swallowed.

His voice dropped lower. "Did you ask about the Bear, Salara?"

A chill ran up her spine. "I asked Phillip if he'd heard from him," she answered finally.

"And?" he pressed. "What else did you ask?"

"If he knew whether Alexander was all right."

"Your grandmother and the Bear. That's all you asked about?"

She nodded.

Mikael pushed out a long breath as his jaw tightened again. "They'll be working to find those still loyal to you. Your actions put him in danger."

Her heart seized in her chest. She hadn't thought of that. If she was inquiring about Alexander, it would show she worried for him. If the council didn't know before, they'd know now—if Phillip told them. Would Phillip tell them, though? She felt like such a fool. She hadn't even realized.

Her lip trembled. "I didn't think. I was so desperate to know. I needed to know." What had she done?

Mikael sighed as he pulled her close and put his arms around her, but it brought little comfort now.

Chapter Four

"Salara?"

Norah snapped her attention to the maid that had been calling her. How many times had she said her name? Had she asked something? "I'm sorry, what?"

"Would you like me to make up the bed?"

Norah realized she had the quilt from the bed wrapped around her as she sat at the small table by the window. She wasn't ready to give it up yet. "No, I might... need to crawl back into it and hide." Her worry over her letter to Phillip still sat like a weight in her stomach.

Her maid smiled warmly. Salara-Mae had assigned her to Norah—not as a slave—when Norah returned from Mercia without Vitalia, and the girl had taken kindly to her. Amara was her name. She was no Vitalia, but Norah liked her. She was quiet but friendly, and reminded her a bit of her Mercian maid, Serene.

"You haven't even had breakfast yet," Amara said, "and it's getting late. You might feel better after you eat."

That was true. Mikael had risen early to tend some things. She knew he wouldn't take his breakfast in the dining hall, and she'd skipped it herself, but a little food might help, or just getting out and walking, perhaps. *Fine.*

Norah gave her maid a yielding smile and reluctantly gave up the quilt. She took the parchment and walked to the fireplace. Lighting the corner, she watched the flame eat her words until she could no longer hold on to it. Then she released it into the fire, willing the Aether to carry her words to Alexander. Or at least to Samuel, the Mercian seer who could paint them for him.

That wasn't how it worked, she told herself. Still, she wished it all the same.

Washed and dressed, Norah stepped out into the hall. Bhastian picked up behind her but gave her space. He was vigilant under the new threat of the blood-bird assassin.

The chill in the air reminded her that the last of summer was fading—gone too soon, just like everything else. The days came long and endless, but the months were gone in an instant.

Suddenly, Norah found herself at Soren's chamber door. She hadn't been paying attention to where she was walking in her blind thoughts.

She pushed it open.

After Soren had left, she'd put the room back together herself. She had set the furniture back in place, swept up the broken glass, and had the mirrors replaced. Clean linens covered the bed. It was ready for his return, whenever he decided to return. *If* he ever decided to return. The worrisome thought tried to snake its way into her mind, but she pushed it back. Soren *would* return. He wouldn't abandon them.

Norah imagined him sitting inside, angry at her disturbance. And she smiled. She came here a lot. Her best thinking, calm thinking, seemed to come here.

She let herself fall backward onto the bed, and she stared up at the ceiling as her mind took over. She worried for Mikael—not whether he could stay strong in the face of mounting threats, but for his heart and his happiness. Soren's leaving crushed him. It wasn't that Mikael needed his presence. He'd managed quite well without him when Norah had taken the commander to Mercia. But Mikael felt abandoned now, betrayed by the one closest to him, and it was eroding his spirit. She couldn't talk to him about it. She couldn't talk to anyone.

Norah missed Vitalia. She'd been a true friend and deserved so much more than what fate had given her. What had been done with her body? She didn't even know what Vitalia believed. Would she have wanted to be buried, as they did in Kharav? Or be sent by fire to the next life? Did Vitalia even believe in the next life? Norah cursed herself—how did she not know? Not that it would have changed anything, but she should know. Vitalia was her friend. Her eyes welled.

Her mind turned to Catherine. Had they killed her too? Surely not. The council had the authority to strip her of the regency, unlike with Norah and the crown. They wouldn't have needed to kill her grandmother, but that alone didn't ensure her safety. Catherine wouldn't have gone quietly, and she wasn't sure how much patience the council would have with her. Norah's stomach twisted.

And Alexander. What had her letter done to him? She tried to push it from her mind—it was breaking her.

The door of the chamber opened, and her heart nearly leapt out of her chest as she bolted upright. Then Norah let out a sigh of relief as she recognized Adrian. "Hammel's hell," she said breathlessly. "You scared me."

"I saw Bhastian and knew you must be in here."

She had forgotten about Bhastian. He must think it strange she'd be in Soren's room. She frowned.

Adrian looked around the room. "What *are* you doing in here?"

Heat rose in her cheeks. "I just come here to think sometimes," she confessed.

He eyed her skeptically. "Does it help?"

She paused for a moment, and shrugged. Then she let herself fall back on the bed again and reached over and patted the space beside her. She felt his hesitancy but smiled as his weight fell beside her, shaking the frame of the bed. They lay quietly, looking up at the ceiling.

"Mikael thinks I've put Alexander in danger by writing Phillip, by asking about his welfare." She turned her head to face him. "I fear he's right. I've shown he's important to me."

"Of course your lord justice would be important to you. It doesn't take a letter to know that." He turned his head toward her and met her eyes. "You don't need to worry about Alec. They won't kill him. They can't." He smiled. "Better men have tried and failed."

She wished she had his optimism. Perhaps they wouldn't kill him, but there were things worse than death. *No*—she couldn't think like that. Adrian was right. Alexander was no stranger to peril. And better men *had* stood against him—Mikael. And Soren. She gave a small laugh.

Adrian's brow creased. "What?"

"Soren *really* tried."

He smiled. "I know. But Alec holds the gods' favor. If the lord commander can't kill him, no one can."

Gods, she loved him for saying that, and for settling the gnawing worry in her stomach. She felt herself favored by the gods to have a friend like Adrian. He was the only one she could truly talk to now.

"What if Soren doesn't return?" she whispered. "I'm scared, Adrian. I can't lose him too."

"You won't," he promised. He rocked up to sit, then rose from the bed. "I have to go. Katya will be expecting me." Since Soren's departure, Katya had stepped in to fill a lot of his responsibilities, including monitoring the development of the earlies, the men in training for the Crest.

Norah sat up and raised a brow. "Don't keep her waiting, then."

He turned but stopped. "Oh, and, uh, I'd appreciate if you didn't tell the lord commander I was on his bed. When he does come back. Because he will."

She smiled as he winked and slipped out the door. Then she rose and straightened the furs and linens. She didn't want Soren knowing *she'd* lain on his bed either. Norah gave the room a final check, ensuring everything looked in its place, and then stepped back out into the hall. Bhastian acted like nothing was unusual, and she was appreciative. He missed the lord commander too.

Her stomach grumbled. She supposed she should get something to eat.

The sound of birds chirping gave the morning a song, but her spirit fell as they reminded her of *him*. Her unknown enemy. The man who wanted her dead. Was he watching her? What if he was? She tried not to dwell on it. She couldn't be paranoid. And surely a possessed bird wouldn't be singing. She glanced back at Bhastian, who followed at a respectful distance, and he nodded to her.

As she turned the corner into the mainway, she caught sight of Mikael at the end of the hall leading to the throne room. He was talking to a man—not a soldier or an adviser—a man in working clothes, uncommon around the castle. He nodded to the man, who bowed back and departed. Mikael held a smile on his lips as she approached, so whatever he was tending hadn't added to his burdens. That was good.

"Where are you headed?" he asked her.

"Just going to get some breakfast."

His brow dipped. "You haven't eaten yet?"

She shook her head. "I wasn't very hungry."

"I haven't had anything either. I'll eat with you." He held out his hand, and a light gleamed in the darks of his eyes. "But first, walk with me."

He seemed to be in a good mood, and she smiled. "All right." She put her hand in his, and he led her down the hall, toward the throne room. "Where are we going?" she asked.

"I just feel like walking with my wife."

Very suspicious. "Hmm," she said through a pursed smile as she looked up at him out of the corners of her eyes.

When they reached the throne room, he stopped. And waited.

She looked at him quizzically, then glanced around. The room was empty. No one was there...

Then she saw it. Her mouth fell open.

"What have you done?" she whispered.

Norah stared at the ornately carved thrones that had been cut from their foundations and placed side by side. While the old bases had been sanded down to be even with the stone floor, the remnants still showed where the chairs had spent many generations.

"What... Why... Mikael..." She stood, speechless.

"Now, perhaps you won't hate this room so much."

"I was joking!" *Kind of.* "I didn't think you'd rip up your throne room."

He smiled as he pulled her closer. "I didn't rip it up. I made improvements."

As much as she absolutely loved him right now, she shook her head. "Mikael, people are going to be upset by this. Those chairs were beautiful."

He shrugged. "They still are."

"But you've changed something that's been a certain way for generations. Like it was nothing."

"It wasn't nothing. It was a problem—a problem I've solved."

She tried to purse back her smile. "Your mother's going to die."

"Well, she's selected where she means to be buried, so I feel prepared."

She shouldn't have, but she laughed. "I'm serious! When she finds out..." Norah covered her mouth and then glanced at her hand. "I'll tell you what she's going to do, she's going to rip this ring back off my finger. She was just starting to *like* me."

He clasped her chin and forced her to look up at him. "Stop," he said softly. "I'm the first salar to have a salara that loves him so much that even the distance between our thrones is too great. Having to... resolve this issue... makes me proud. And anyone who objects, well..." He tilted his head in indifference.

She shook her head, grinning. "I love you."

He smiled back. "And I love you," he replied, and he kissed her.

Days passed slowly. Two, or three. Or four. Norah forgot how many.

"Another one," Calla said as she held up an arrow with a small dead bird pierced on the end.

Norah's attention popped back to the present, and her jaw tightened. *Another one.*

"What on earth?" Salara-Mae gasped.

They stood in the gardens where Norah and Salara-Mae had picked up a regular cadence after breakfast. It had been a challenge to explain the increased guard without alarming the king's mother. They hadn't told her about *him*—how the blood-bird man had returned. She rolled her eyes in her mind. She had to think of a better name.

Blood-bird man. Sender of her assassins. The birdman. Blood sorcerer. Everything she thought to call him sounded too silly or too reverent of his power—whatever inexplicable power he had. He was back, and he was watching her.

"Diseased birds," Norah said quickly. "We've been culling them to stop the spread."

Salara-Mae winced and gave a disgusted frown.

Norah picked up their walk again. They'd have to tell his mother at some point. Mikael had said he didn't want to worry her. More likely, he didn't want to face questions he couldn't answer from a person he was trying not to speak to. She silently chastised herself. She should give him the benefit of the doubt. It was true that burdening her wouldn't be of any benefit. They didn't know who was behind the birds, or what he would do next. The information would likely only make Salara-Mae paranoid of every bird she saw, as it did Norah. Or Salara-Mae would think they'd gone mad, which also wouldn't be helpful. They needed to find out more.

"Have you stopped trying for a child?" Salara-Mae asked as they continued.

Norah stopped, speechless for a moment. She'd raise this topic now? Now, of all times? "Ummm... now's perhaps not the best time for a child."

"On the contrary, it's the perfect time."

Perhaps it was Salara-Mae who had gone mad.

"My council has usurped my throne. We're on the brink of war with Japheth and Rael, perhaps Mercia and Aleon as well. How is this the perfect time?"

"So you *aren't* trying."

"It's not a choice!" she cut back, sharper than she'd intended. She drew in a deep breath to calm her anger. "It's not a choice," she said again, softer.

It wasn't that they hadn't been trying. They just hadn't come to expect anything. At least, not Mikael. He seemed happy without, as if Norah alone were enough. He placed the fault on himself, which might be true. Or perhaps it was her failure. There was no way to know for sure. Either way, something died a little more inside her every time her blood cycle came.

"We should get back," Norah said. She couldn't have this conversation again.

Salara-Mae didn't object, but as they turned toward the castle, a servant ran to meet them.

"Salara!" he called before he even reached them. "There's a messenger from the North."

Her breath caught in her throat, and she struggled to pull a breath. "A messenger?"

"They've escorted him through the western pass," he said, breathless. "They're bringing him to the castle now. Salar waits for you in the throne room."

Norah glanced at Salara-Mae, who held an equally shocked expression on her face. Norah turned back to the servant. "Send for Adrian as well. Have him meet me there." Then both she and Salara-Mae picked up quickly toward the throne room.

A messenger from Mercia—what news would he bring? Would Alexander have sent him? Or her council? What could they possibly have to say?

Mikael stood in the center of the room, waiting. They didn't spend much time in the throne room, but he always waited for her before taking his seat. He held out his hand as she walked toward him, and she took it. His warmth thawed her icy fingers, seeping up her arm and calming her racing heart. She forced a smile. He'd stood solid beside her through Mercia's betrayal. She feared he would waver with the pressures of his own kingdom, but when she needed him, he was there, as if nothing else mattered.

"What has happened in here?" Salara-Mae gasped.

Norah followed her horrified gaze to the two thrones cut from their elevated bases and set side by side. She bit her lip; she'd forgotten about that. Norah glanced at Mikael, and he shrugged.

"I like them better this way," he said.

And she loved him even more.

They took their seats. Norah waited impatiently. Months had passed since she'd fled Mercia. It felt like years and days at the same time. So much could have happened by now. What *had* happened? Now she would know. Suddenly, she didn't want to know. She glanced around. Where was Adrian?

Mikael's hand wrapped around hers, and she looked up at him. He brought her fingers to his lips and kissed her skin, and a calm returned.

"You settle me so easily," she told him.

He smiled. "You do the same. I didn't move these chairs together only for you, you know."

Gods, she loved this man.

Finally, the doors to the throne room swung open, and a small army of the Crest entered with a Northman at their center. Her heart pulsed so hard in her throat that she thought she might choke on it.

He stopped before her and bowed. "Queen Norah," he said as he pulled off his helm. He was younger than she'd expected. She didn't recognize him and glanced around again for Adrian, but he was strangely still absent.

"I bring a message from the lord justice," he said.

She froze. *Alexander.* Slowly, she stood. "Alexander sent you?" She didn't feel steady on her feet. "He's alive?"

He stood with his mouth open, as if confused. What was confusing about her question?

"He's alive, and he's well?" she asked again, more urgently this time.

He bobbed his head. "Yes, Regal High. Alive, anyway. *Well* is relative, yeah?"

What did *that* mean?

"And he sends me," the man added.

She clenched her hands to keep them from shaking. "You have a letter?"

He bowed his head again. "No, not a letter. Only his words." And he stood.

It was all she could do to not clamber down the steps and shake him. "Well, what does he say?" she pressed.

The soldier looked around uneasily. "Um, I'm to deliver it to the Destroyer."

"What?" *What?* Alexander would send a message to Soren and not her? "What's the message?" Her patience was now gone.

He hesitated.

Mikael rose from his throne and stepped beside her. "What is the message?" he demanded.

The soldier shifted back. "To prepare for war."

Her heart leapt into her throat. She couldn't breathe. "Alexander sends a threat?"

"No," the Mercian soldier said quickly as he eyed Mikael. "Not war against him. To join him in taking back Mercia. The lord justice holds the loyalty of the North in the queen's name."

"So why a call to war?" Mikael asked him shortly. "If the lord justice commands the army of the North, why doesn't he just give it back?"

"Well, because he's not lord justice anymore, I guess."

Norah's heart stopped. The council had removed him.

"And even if he was," the soldier continued, "the council holds control with mercenaries. He can't take the kingdom back alone, and so he's been waiting in silent opposition."

"And what of Aleon?" Mikael asked.

The soldier shook his head. "I don't know. I'm not privy to such information."

Norah narrowed her eyes at the man. "Yet you've been sent here with this message. Why would Alexander send someone I don't know?" And why to Soren?

"He and those close to you are watched by the council. And... he said the Destroyer would know I come truly."

"How would he know?"

"I don't know. I don't ask questions. I only come with the message."

"What of my grandmother?"

"She's well." Then his face twisted slightly. "Well, maybe not *well*. She's confined to the castle, and angry. All the time. She yells a lot. We can hear her over the wall."

Her body shook with relief. She looked at Mikael and could see the doubt on his face. "What's your name?" she asked the man.

"Colb, Regal High. Colb Matheson."

Norah let her eyes run over the man. He was dressed in Mercian armor, but he was missing the polish of a trained soldier, both in stance and in words. *Strange.* "You don't seem like a soldier."

"Because I'm not a soldier, Regal High. I work the mines."

Very strange indeed.

"The Bear sends a miner?" Mikael's voice was edged with skepticism.

The young man shifted again.

"Does Alexander say anything else?" Norah asked.

He shook his head. "No, Regal High. Only to bring the Shadow army, and he'll be waiting."

Mikael gave a slight wave of his hand, and the Crest ushered the man back out, leaving him and Norah alone. She watched him as he sank down on his throne and crossed his arms, bringing his fist to his lips. Her heart still thrummed in her throat. Was this her opportunity to take back Mercia?

"It could be a trick," he said, as if reading her thoughts. "If we marched on the North and Aleon was waiting with them, we'd be easily taken."

"It's possible," she admitted, "although if the council was trying to trick us, I don't think they'd send a miner to do it."

"Or it's exactly who they'd send. A disarming cover. And someone you wouldn't be familiar with. Perhaps they don't know who in your army is loyal to you."

"I can't help but be inclined to believe him. His knees were practically knocking together."

"A scared man isn't necessarily an innocent man. Or perhaps he does believe he comes with a message from the Bear, but he's been fooled himself."

True. Norah sighed. It was a very real possibility that the council was trying to trick her into marching to war. And Mikael was right. Together with Aleon, the council would be able to overtake Kharav. But if it wasn't a trick, then this was perhaps her only opportunity to take back Mercia—to take back what was rightfully hers.

She looked at Mikael. Could she really ask this of him now?

Chapter Five

The dining hall was quiet. Shocking. Norah kept herself from rolling her eyes as she chewed her food slowly. She shifted her gaze between Mikael and Salara-Mae, wagering which topic would first be broached—the call to war from Mercia or Mikael's choice to redecorate the throne room. One she was desperate to talk about, and one she wasn't.

Mikael mulled over a small stack of parchments as he ate, which wasn't unusual. He sometimes brought work to the dining hall instead of taking breakfast in his study. While it annoyed Salara-Mae, Norah didn't mind. He'd drop it in an instant if she mentioned it.

Mikael paused, perplexed at one letter in particular.

"What is it?" she asked.

"Outsiders. Possibly."

A chill ran down her spine. Could it be *him*, the man who'd sent the assassins? Had he sent more? She had been bolder in facing the blood birds, but now that he might be back, she couldn't shake the pang of fear that turned her stomach. "Possibly?"

"There are signs inside the Canyonlands, but no outsiders have been seen." His eyes met hers. "I don't want you to worry. You're safe."

"I know," she said quickly. But did she really believe that?

Mikael put down the letters. She pushed her breakfast across her plate with her fork.

"Salara," he said, calling her attention back to him. "I'll get to the bottom of this."

She nodded.

The hall grew quiet again. They ate the rest of their breakfast in silence, and Mikael left his remaining letters unread. She felt his eyes on her.

"Are we going to pretend there's nothing else to discuss?" Salara-Mae said as they neared finishing. "That you didn't uproot a keystone of this castle?"

Norah pursed her lips. She should have wagered more than a glass of wine in the bathtub that *that* would be the topic Salara-Mae broached. She motioned to the servant, who refilled her chalice—she'd take that wine right now.

"The throne room isn't a keystone," he replied calmly.

"Of course it is. It's what everyone sees. It represents your strength, your legacy, your family's legacy."

"A legacy of lies?" he cut back. "Secrets?"

"Oh, Mikael," Salara-Mae said with a sigh. It was the first time Norah had heard her call him by his name. And it was the call of a worried mother. "Now you're going to host your nobles to discuss this matter of the North, and they'll see how you focus your attention."

Norah knew what she meant, that he focused his attention on her more than his own kingdom. True or not, this was how the nobles felt.

"Are you not already under enough scrutiny?" Salara-Mae asked him.

He didn't answer.

"And I fear your answer for them," she added. "You know they won't support marching against the North." Her face turned bitter. "Even your commander didn't support it. *Publicly.* You know his voice will still be in their ears."

Slowly, he took a drink from his chalice. "They have a right to be concerned," he said finally. "It's a great risk."

She huffed a small breath. "Of course it's a great risk! Japheth and Rael are at our door, waiting for the moment to strike, and you would leave to go to war with the North? With no allies? No one by your side?"

Still, he said nothing. He only rested his gaze on Norah. She twisted inside.

"And don't be a fool to think the North is alone," Salara-Mae stressed. "Aleon will be lying in wait. This would be it—the vision of your end. The Bear lures you to it."

Mikael's eyes turned to his mother. "My fate comes when Salara rides beside the king of Aleon. Now is not my time." He looked at Norah. "And the Bear wouldn't betray his queen. The question is, did *he* send the messenger? Or is this a plot from the council?"

Salara-Mae gaped at Norah. "Talk him out of this madness."

But Norah wasn't sure she could do that. This could very well be an opportunity to take back Mercia. Perhaps the *only* opportunity.

Salara-Mae's voice came more urgently now, pleading Norah. "You would let him walk right into a trap?"

Of course she wouldn't. But was it a trap? The miner had been believable. A skilled deceiver, if that's what he was. But if Alexander *was* alive, he'd be working to take back her throne. If he wasn't and this was a trick from the council, she'd lose more than what she already had. But could they afford to do nothing? If they didn't win back Mercia, they'd have to stand alone against Rael and Japheth. She wasn't sure they'd survive that either.

It was a gamble of life and death, and she didn't know what to do.

Damn Adrian. Where was he? Norah stalked out of the army field office and toward the castle. He was nowhere to be found. Calla and Cohen hadn't seen him. She'd even checked with Katya, who'd told her she hadn't seen him in days and was livid about it. So was Norah, although perhaps she was more worried than livid. She just wanted to make sure he was all right. And she wanted to ask him about this Colb Matheson. Adrian would be able to help decipher anything suspicious and give her his thoughts on marching on Mercia. How would he feel about it? If he believed Alexander called them, no doubt he'd go. But to march against one's home, it was hard. Even for Norah.

Yells from soldiers on the sparring field caught her attention, and she turned. Men on the north side waved their arms toward her, signaling... something. She stood, staring at them. What were they saying? She swept her eyes around her but saw nothing. What did they see? She looked back to them and caught a man pointing north. Her gaze followed.

She squinted her eyes against the horizon. To the movement.

The ripple of white and silver.

And she gasped.

Tears sprang to her eyes, and she let out an emotional laugh. *Sephir.*

The mare galloped straight toward her. Norah ran to meet her, not able to wait for the animal to reach her.

Sephir skidded to a stop in front of her and reared before tossing her head with a squeal. Norah threw her arms around her neck. Her laughs turned to cries as she clung to the mare, her tears falling into the animal's thick mane. She smelled like mountain air and fresh forest pine.

The last time she'd seen Sephir, she'd been queen of Mercia. She'd had Alexander and Soren and her grandmother. And Vitalia. She'd had Cusco and Cavaatsa. Sephir smelled like family, like happiness and rich memories lost.

Norah cried.

The heartache turned to joy that she'd gotten something back. And she cried some more. Not just for Sephir's return, but for everything. All of it. It all came to the surface—her fear, her hope, her exhaustion, her loss. And now her joy.

And she needed this joy.

Norah held on to the mare until her tears ran dry. Then she held her longer. The animal's warmth seeped into her skin, the Wild spirit feeding her own. She'd known she needed Sephir back. She just hadn't known how much. It was like the gods had given her back a piece of herself.

Norah wiped her cheeks before stepping back. "You missed me, did you?" She smiled at the mare as she wiped her eyes again and patted the animal's neck.

Sephir snorted and tossed her head again.

Norah laughed. "Gods, I've missed you too." She grew more serious. "I was so worried something had happened to you."

Bhastian's voice came from behind her. "She's returned!"

She grinned back at him but didn't take her hand from the mare for fear it was only a dream.

Kiran came forward, his eyes smiling under his wrap. "She escaped the North and traveled all the way to Kharav to find you."

Norah hugged the mare again. "Maybe she heard my heart calling to her."

Kiran shook his head, still in disbelief. "The men can take her back to the stables, give her a good rub down and feed."

The stables. Right. Norah longed to jump atop the mare and feel the wind of a gallop again, but she had to find Mikael and talk to him about Adrian. Not to mention, galloping off alone with rumors of intruders wasn't the wisest idea.

Norah hugged the mare once more, scratching her neck affectionately. "You've journeyed a long way to get home, friend. How does a brush down and a bucket full of grain sound?"

The mare tossed her head, and Norah laughed. "All right then, go with them, and I'll come visit you later." She gave Sephir a pat, and the animal let two approaching stable hands lead her toward the stables.

"I almost thought you were going to jump on her and take off," Bhastian told her as she watched Sephir be led away.

"You know she thought about it," Calla added, coming up behind them.

Kiran and Bhastian chuckled.

"Of course she did," Kiran said.

Norah smiled at them both. They knew her well. "But I have something more important," she added as she turned her mind back to Adrian. She needed to find Mikael. "Where's my husband?"

Bhastian nodded toward the castle. "I last saw him in his study."

He was likely still there. She nodded and picked up her pace toward the castle. As expected, Mikael *was* in his study, where he'd been spending more and more of his time. *Plotting* is what Norah usually told him he was doing, but she knew it was more like thinking, and worrying, and searching for solutions.

He looked up from where he sat at his desk as she entered.

"What are you doing?" she asked as she moved behind him and wrapped her arms around his neck.

"Plotting," he said, putting his hand over hers and leaning back against her.

Her lips pulled into a smile. *Plotting*. She bent and nestled into his warmth and brushed her lips across his cheek. "You're always plotting."

"Well, that's how one becomes a master plotter."

Or it was how one lost their mind. "Sephir's returned."

He straightened and pulled her around in front of him. His eyes were large with surprise, and bright. "That's good news."

She nodded. "I'm so relieved and glad to have her back. I can't believe it, that she traveled all that way on her own to find me again."

"She's a special horse, Salara."

That she was.

His brows dipped. "But something's wrong?"

Yes. Something was wrong. "Have you sent Adrian on a task?"

He frowned and then shook his head. "No, why?"

She pushed out a breath, her worry returning. "He's gone. And no one knows where. Not Cohen or Calla. Not anyone. It's as if he's disappeared."

"Well, I'm sure he'll turn up."

"This isn't like him. I'm really worried. You were just talking about possible intruders again. What if something happened to him? What if he needs help? What if he's needed help and we've just been—"

"Hey," he said, pulling her closer and quieting her. "Adrian's a warrior. One of the best there is. And he's smart. He's fine. He'll show up."

"How do you know?" She could hear the desperation in her own voice.

"My master plotting senses."

That almost made her laugh. *Almost.*

He pulled her between his knees and looked up at her from his chair. "I'll send men out. We'll find him."

She nodded, feeling a little better.

His eyes lingered on her, and she knew his mind had drifted back to Mercia.

Norah held his face with her hands, lightly grazing his short-cut beard with her fingertips. "Talk to me," she whispered. "What are you in here thinking about?"

"Do you believe the Bear sends this miner?"

Such a difficult question. "I don't know."

"Not what you know. What do you *believe*?"

She swallowed. Such a subtle change of words, yet so significantly different. What did she believe? "I believe that if Alexander's well—even if he's not well, if he's simply alive—he'll stop at nothing to give me back my throne. He will have been... plotting himself." Despite the risks, despite the odds—any odds—Alexander would try. More than try. He would be compelled. And her lord justice compelled was a powerful thing.

"I don't believe the miner lies," she added. Then she swallowed again. "And I believe that if what he says is true, it may be our only opportunity to take back Mercia. And to gain back an alliance. To not stand alone."

Mikael drew in a long breath and then let it out slowly. He settled his arms around her more firmly, then nodded.

"Then tomorrow I'll tell the nobles we go to war," he said. "We'll march to join the Bear. And take back the North."

CHAPTER SIX

Kharavian nobles filled the throne room. There were more than Norah expected. More than last time. Their eyes shifted between her and Mikael as murmurs rippled through them. Their whispers and judgments, she'd expected that, but something was different today.

Kharavian nobles of the court bore the markings of fighting men, but unlike warriors of the army, they generally wore more clothing. Not substantially more—maybe a wrap of fine silk over a shoulder; an open, sleeveless tunic; or other accents and pieces that displayed their wealth. But today brought a throne room of bare chests and prominent battle markings. A message.

Norah's heart beat faster as her eyes traveled over their bodies laden with weapons. True, Kharavians loved their blades, and many wore them when they came before Mikael. But today, there seemed to be more. *Were* there more? More swords? More daggers?

Would there be more blood?

The prior confrontation between Mikael and the nobles that had left Narsing dead was still fresh in her mind. As it was for them all, she was sure. Did this display mean that they were well prepared to challenge the crown now?

And they didn't even know yet about Mikael's news.

Bile rose in the back of her throat.

The nobles wouldn't support a march to war with Mercia, especially to reseat a queen they didn't want from a kingdom they had warred with for ten years—a queen who'd failed to bring a true alliance with the marriage and who failed to give an heir. And judging from their stares, now a queen who influenced unwanted changes to their throne room.

The air hung heavy, leaving her lungs unfed despite her breaths. Sweat beaded across the nape of her neck. With no room now between the thrones, Bhastian stood to her left, close, where Adrian normally stood. Adrian still hadn't returned.

Kiran stood to Mikael's right, and the rest of the Crest lined the wall behind them. On the surface, they looked prepared for a confrontation. But truly, if a battle for the crown broke out, the Crest would take her and flee.

Norah's argument with Mikael had gone late into the night before, but it did nothing to change his position. She had refused to leave him, but it wasn't a choice anymore. Bhastian had his orders, and he'd follow them—if the nobles rose against them, he and the Crest would take her to the only place safe for her in the world now. Back to the Wild.

But Norah had no intention of going back to the Wild. The dagger strapped to her calf chafed her skin as she crossed her ankles, but she wanted the reminder it was there. She refused to lose two kingdoms. She refused to lose her king. There would be no leaving this throne room unless it was to march to take back Mercia.

She shifted in her chair as she cast a quick glance at Mikael. He sat calmly, his face giving no indication of worry, but his eyes held the threat of blood if things went poorly with his nobles. Mikael was a formidable man and a strong king, but even he couldn't stand alone against them—not all of them, and not without Soren. But the gods have mercy on the first man to oppose him.

Bhastian beat the floor with the butt of his spear, and a hush fell over the room. Norah's stomach turned.

"I've gathered you on the matter of the North," Mikael started. "We've received word that the Bear prepares to retake the throne in Salara's name and calls us to join him."

Yasir, an imposing lord, stepped forward. "You mean you have received word from a man who claims to be sent by the Bear." Several nobles were members of the Circle. Yasir was one of them and, as such, had already been briefed on the circumstance and all its details.

"Yes," Mikael answered.

"So, the North would draw us out from the protections of the Canyonlands to take back the throne of the queen they unseated?"

Norah hated how he spun the story.

"The council took the throne by mercenaries, not with the Northern army," Mikael countered.

Jarik stepped forward now. The sight of the warlord made Norah shudder. He was definitely wearing more blades than he had before. Her heart hammered against her chest.

"The time for the Northern army to have fought would have been during the coup," Yasir said.

"The attack came suddenly," Norah interjected. "No one knew it was happening. You know this."

Yasir ignored her, as did Jarik. Their eyes stayed leveled on Mikael.

Despite the cold of autumn creeping in, the air was suddenly stifling. Whether it was from her own anger or Mikael's as his patience started to burn to ash, she didn't know.

"How do we know Aleon hasn't joined the North and isn't merely lying in wait?" Jarik asked. "How do we know this isn't a trick?"

Mikael was silent for a moment. "We don't," he said finally.

A wave of murmurs bubbled through the hall again.

"And how will you respond to this call, Salar?" Yasir and the Circle had been pressing for an answer for days—an answer Mikael would not give.

Until now.

All eyes were on Mikael, and he answered, "We march."

Immediate objections rang through the hall, voices of disbelief and condemnation, calls for refusal, questions of intent. But Mikael sat firmly, unwavering.

Bhastian struck the floor with the butt of his spear again, bringing quiet back to the room.

"This is my decision," Mikael boomed out.

"And we should so blindly follow?" Jarik challenged. "Kharav is already weakened against our enemies, and you would bring us closer to fall?"

"Even the lord commander didn't support war," another noble spoke up angrily. Lord Arminar—another member of Mikael's Circle. It was true; Mikael had sought war after Norah fled Mercia, and Soren had spoken against it. In front of the nobles, it was the equivalent of denying him. And now the nobles knew of his blood right. As a bastard son, Soren held a weaker claim to the throne, but it was a claim nonetheless. And now he had the power to deny Mikael so much more than war—he had the power to deny him everything.

Mikael's gaze shifted to Lord Arminar. "Circumstances have changed, and the lord commander's not here."

"You don't know circumstances have changed," Jarik challenged.

The nobles crowded closer, and from the corner of her eye, Norah saw Bhastian step closer too, his hand clenching his spear. The hair on her arms stood on end, and her breaths came faster.

The nobles couldn't petition the Circle to override Mikael because the Circle couldn't veto a regal decision like Mercia's council. A noble could challenge him. Or they could collectively remove him. They would have to do it by force, and it was becoming increasingly likely they would try now.

Norah reached out and rested her hand on Mikael's arm. The fight of rage radiated from his skin, but he needed to calm. Violence would solve nothing here. She desperately searched her mind for anything that could sway them to see this was the only way to strengthen Kharav. They needed to take back Mercia. The kingdoms needed to be united again.

"Once again," Arminar said, still needling, "you put the North Queen before Kharav. And I see it comes on the heels of your decision to uproot our throne room at her whim."

"*My* throne room. Your *salara*," Mikael snarled as he rose. Norah still held on to him. "And would you rather our chairs parted?" he added. "As her hand on mine is the only thing keeping me from striking your head from your shoulders."

Jarik's hand moved to the hilt of his sword. "You continue to threaten your nobles?"

"Warn," Mikael corrected him.

Yasir stiffened. "A warning for you, Salar—when the lord commander returns, there will be much you'll be held accountable for."

Mikael laughed. "You'll challenge me? You think you can so easily give my crown to another? You think you can take it from me?" He bared his teeth and ripped his arm from Norah's grip as he pulled his sword. "If any man thinks he can, come forward!" he bellowed.

The hall fell silent, and all eyes were locked on Mikael. Then their gazes shifted to Jarik. In a challenge, the warlord was perhaps the only one who could rival Mikael; he was almost equal in size and covered in markings, noting his skill. If it would be a collective takedown, the nobles would look to Jarik to lead the effort.

Norah clenched her hands so tight her nails dug into her palms. Jarik pulled his sword, and Bhastian's hand wrapped around her arm.

Just then, the ash wood doors of the throne room swung open, booming an echo through the hall. All heads jerked toward the sound. Norah's heart leapt into her throat, and she staggered up from her chair.

Gods' mercy.

Through the threshold stepped Soren, axe in one hand, his sword in the other.

Norah's heartbeat pulsed loud in her ears, so loud she could hear nothing else. She glanced at Mikael, but he stood, unmoving. The muscle corded under his skin as he clutched his sword tighter—he was ready to use it.

The air hung thick with tension. The nobles on either side of the hall bounced their gazes between Jarik and Mikael, then Jarik and Soren. But no one spoke.

Soren's gaze swept over the room. His eyes held the night, darker than she'd ever seen, and they locked on Mikael as he strode forward.

Heat pulsed through Soren's veins. He kept his eyes on Mikael. He saw it now—the likeness between them. The same darkness. The same fire.

They had the same blood—the blood of salar.

The eyes of the nobles followed him down the center of the hall and toward the throne. They were eager to have him back, their disapproval of Mikael rich on their faces.

And they waited. They waited for him to make his claim. He had their support. His gaze shifted to Jarik, and their stares locked. The warlord had followed him into battle countless times. Jarik gave a small bow of his head. He'd follow Soren as salar.

But Soren wasn't salar. Salar of war, yes. But there was only one true salar of Kharav, and Soren had returned to make sure it stayed that way. He'd kill every man in this room if he had to, and by the looks of how the nobles were armed, he might just have to. But first, a message for them...

He strode to the edge of the dais, where Mikael stood with his sword ready. And Soren dropped to his knees, his head hung low.

This was his brother. His salar. Husband to the woman who had wormed her way into his heart. This was his family that he loved and would give anything for. He'd let there be no doubt of where his loyalties sat. He'd left because he was a threat to Mikael's crown, but then he realized—with some help—he didn't weaken Mikael's power. He made him stronger by standing at his side.

He felt his brother's eyes on him, but he didn't raise his gaze. Mikael would be upset by his leaving, hurt even, as Soren himself had been. But he would understand.

Mikael stepped down the stairs.

The cold steel of a sword pricked his chin as Mikael used its tip to draw up his face to look at him. Soren let his head fall back, offering his neck. Out of the corner of his eye, he saw Salara draw closer. How he missed that annoying woman.

"You've returned," Mikael said.

"I should have never left."

"But you did." Mikael's words were dipped in venom, each one delivering a sting. He was angry. Soren knew he would be.

Mikael stepped slowly to his right shoulder, his eyes burning into Soren. Soren knew his gaze was on the matching ink marking they both bore, the sun encircled by a ring of mountains—the marking of how they'd become brothers.

Suddenly, Mikael sliced his blade through the encircled sun, and the warmth of blood poured down Soren's arm. Soren gritted his teeth through the pain, but he didn't move.

"You are no longer lord commander," Mikael said.

A weight crushed him. He couldn't breathe. He knew Mikael would be upset, hurt at his leaving, but he never thought he would strip him of his place. The pain stung more than any pain of the flesh.

"Mikael," Salara whispered with a faint breath.

Mikael held his arms wide. "I asked you before, is there a challenge?" he bellowed across the hall. He looked directly at Jarik and pointed his sword. The warlord stood for a moment, his eyes moving to Soren, then back to Mikael. Then he sheathed his sword and bowed his head.

Soren's submission carried a message for the rest of the nobles as well. Now to remove Mikael, they'd face Soren too. They'd be victorious with their numbers, yes, but how many would live? Soren and Mikael together would spill the blood of at least half. Would they wager their lives? As the nobles drew back, Soren knew the answer.

"We march in a week's time," Mikael thundered, seizing control of the moment and keeping control of the crown. "Now get out."

Soren didn't move as the nobles shuffled out of the throne room. He didn't rise to his feet. He only waited for Mikael. He waited for him to say something—perhaps when the nobles all departed. But Mikael didn't wait. He left Soren on his knees and strode from the throne room himself. Soren's heart fell to his stomach.

Only Salara remained. He didn't look up, but he knew her eyes were on him. Did she feel he'd betrayed her too? She stepped in front of him, but he still couldn't look at her. He couldn't bear it.

She reached a hand and brought her fingers to his chin, pulling his face up to look at her. There were tears in her eyes, and it broke him. He sucked in an emotional breath, ready for her anger, her hatred for him now.

But she only dropped down and threw her arms around his neck, hugging him tightly. She clung to him, stripping him of the rest of his composure. Soren let himself fall apart. He wrapped his left arm around her and held her close as the emotion took over.

They stayed on the floor for a long time, until Soren could breathe again.

As they broke, she smiled through her tears. "You came back," she whispered.

It took a moment for him to answer. "I didn't have a choice. Adrian found me. Told me I had to come." Adrian had tracked him down all the way to the Stone Forest, talked some sense into him, told him he was needed. Of course he had to come.

"Adrian!" She let out a breath. "I've been worried sick about him. Gods, I'm going to kill him." She gave him a tear-filled smile. "But, Soren, I'm so glad you're home."

He was glad to be home. Even under the current circumstances.

"We have so much to catch up on." She stood and pulled him to rise. "But first, let's get you to the healer."

She led him to the healer's chamber, but the old man was gone. Soren moved to a narrow hutch with thin stacked drawers against the wall. He knew where to find what he needed and pulled a curved needle from a small dish and a string of silk from a separate drawer.

"Here, let me," Salara said as she moved to take it from him.

He pulled back. "I've seen your needlepoint."

She pursed her lips at him with an angry brow, but he shook his head. He did allow her to help thread the needle and clip the silk length, but he sat and stitched his skin together himself, as he'd done so many times before.

Except this time, it was different.

He paused on the last stitch, his breath catching on the broken image of the sun.

Salara put her hand on his knee. "Give him time, Soren," she said softly. "He loves you. He just needs time."

Chapter Seven

Hope came with the sun. Norah lay awake in bed but didn't move to rise. Soren had returned. Yes, the reunion wasn't quite as she had hoped—slightly more soul crushing. But still, he was home, and she had Sephir back, and Adrian was safe. That reminded her: she still needed to kill him for worrying her as he did, although he had brought Soren home, so he might escape with a mild bodily injury and a hug. A smile came to her lips as she nestled against Mikael under the quilts and furs.

"Come closer," he murmured.

Her smile grew as she wriggled nearer to him, soaking in his warmth.

"Closer," he said, and pulled her on top of him.

Norah laughed.

They lay in the quiet of the morning, her head on his chest. She felt the thrum of his heart under her cheek, in time with her own.

"Will you talk to him today?" she whispered.

His chest tightened underneath her, but he didn't answer. She couldn't feel his heart anymore, but she knew it was there. Angry, hurting, hiding.

Norah crossed her arms over his chest and rested her chin on them. "Will you not talk to me?"

She didn't think he'd answer her, but finally he said, "Not yet." But the anger in him was fading. *Progress.*

"Okay," she said softly, and gave him a small smile. The air became lighter with her acceptance, and he relaxed again.

She swirled her fingertips over his chest. "Will you eat breakfast with me?"

Mikael brushed her cheek, and a mischievousness came to his eyes. He drew her up and closer. "I want breakfast in bed," he said with a smirk, and pulled her to meet his kiss.

Norah laughed as he twisted and turned them, moving her underneath him. It wasn't unusual for him to wake with a hunger, one she was happy to satiate.

Morning Mikael, she called this side of him.

She loved Morning Mikael.

Norah frowned. Everything in Soren's chamber remained untouched. He hadn't been there. If he hadn't returned to his chamber, where had he stayed? She rolled her eyes. If this was some gods-damned humble acceptance of his discharge, she'd scream.

She turned on her heel and stalked out of the castle and toward the sparring fields. When she spotted him, anger rippled through her. He was on the field with the warriors, calling moves, as he usually did. Except now he was among them, participating. What in the nine hells?

She stormed onto the field toward him. He stopped when he saw her. They all stopped.

"What are you doing?" she demanded when she reached him.

Soren's brows creased in confusion. "What?"

She waved her hand at the field. "This. What's this? And why didn't you sleep in your chamber?"

"It's no longer my chamber."

What? "What do you mean it's no longer your chamber?"

"I'm no longer lord commander."

What complete and utter nonsense. "Wasn't it your chamber before you were lord commander?"

He shifted. "Kind of."

"What does that mean?"

He said nothing.

"Well?" she pressed.

"Well, we were like brothers then. I had more privilege."

"You're still brothers, dummy. It's still your chamber." She pulled the spear from his hands. "And you're still commander." Norah shoved the shaft of the spear against the warrior he'd been sparring with, who clasped on to it in surprise. "Take this," she said angrily.

She grabbed Soren's arm and pulled him toward the castle. "Come on." This was absolutely not the way things would be now. "He's still commander!" she shouted back to the men over her shoulder.

Norah practically dragged him into the castle and down the halls. He was a heavy beast, but her anger fueled her. Gods-damned men and their gods-damned sensitivity. And who did Soren think he was with his drivel of assumptions? He was the gods-damned lord commander of Kharav. She pulled him along as she cursed the gods for not having more curse words.

When she reached his chamber door, she swung it open. "Go on, then."

"What are you doing?"

"I'm reminding you of your place. *Someone* has to. And at least compliment me on your chamber not being the complete wreck you left it."

He snorted, then looked around. "It looks very nice," he said finally, but too forced for her taste, and she narrowed her eyes at him.

"Good," she snapped. "Glad you like it. Settle in."

"You can't just say it and have everything return to normal."

Norah pursed her lips. "Why not? I'm salara."

He paused, and the crease between his brow eased. "That you are," he said softly. He drew in a breath as he looked around.

Her anger dissipated and was replaced by the happiness in just having him home again. Gods, she'd missed him. She really wanted to hug him again, but they were past all the emotional homecoming energy that had allowed her to get away with it in the throne room.

"Have you been in my chamber often?" he asked her.

Norah raised a brow. "Oh, *now* it's your chamber?"

His eyes darkened.

"Maybe." She shifted. "Why?"

"It smells like you."

She frowned. "You say that like it's bad."

"Not bad," he said quickly. "Just... woman-y."

Whatever *that* meant.

He sat down on the bed. There was still a sadness in him. It would pass, she told herself. They'd get past this. She took a seat beside him, and they sat in the quiet.

"Where did you go?" she asked after a time.

"The Stone Forest of Khalakhan."

She hadn't heard of it before. "Is it in Kharav?"

"It is."

Norah waited, but that was all he said. She pursed her lips. "You're as bad as Caspian in telling a story. What is Khalakhan? Why did you go there? What have you been doing? How did Adrian find you?"

He grumbled at all her questions. "It's the place of dead gods. Back when Kharav had gods."

"Kharav had gods?"

He nodded. "Many generations ago, Kharav had many gods. There are ruins in Khalakhan, with their symbols still carved in the stone. It's where the gods were born. And where they died."

She stared at him. "So, they just all... died?"

Soren shrugged. "Well, that's what happens when men stop believing in gods. They die."

Norah drew her brows together. That made no sense. "Or... they continue living, because what do they care? They're gods."

"You wanted me to tell the story, and I'm telling it," he said between his teeth.

She shifted. "Fine. Sorry."

Soren set his eyes forward again but didn't pick back up. She squirmed inside. She hadn't meant to shut him down.

"Did you go to ask for wisdom from these gods?" she jested with a smile, trying to stir some lightness. "Because you obviously didn't have any of it when you left."

His brows dipped. "Why would I ask them for anything? I just said they were dead."

"Oh. Right."

He gave a faint shake of his head. "I went there because I was sad, and I wanted to be with dead things."

That wasn't the admission she was expecting, and she stilled. "Oh," she said softly.

"And I knew it was a place no one goes," he added. "No one would bother me."

"Except Adrian?"

"I should have known," he grumbled in agreement. "I thought if it was anyone it would be you, but I forgot how annoyingly persistent he can be too."

Her smile returned.

His brow creased again. "Did you lay on my bed?"

"No." She bit her bottom lip. *Not today.*

He pulled a long hair from the side of the bed as he glared at her. Then another.

Norah swayed as she looked around the room innocently. "I would come in here to think," she confessed. She grew more serious and turned back to him. "I missed you, Soren."

Surprisingly, she wasn't met with a snarky reply. He only looked at her. He wouldn't say it back, but his silence spoke for him.

"You're the only one," he said finally.

"Mikael's missed you too. Your leaving hurt him, but he'll come around." She reached out and clasped his forearm and gave him a reassuring squeeze.

Soren ran his fingers over the scabbed gash on his shoulder.

"It'll heal," she told him.

"But there will always be a scar."

In more ways than one, she knew. "Life is like the supreme Salta Tau," she told him, thinking of the ink mastera. "And scars are the markings of your story. They're a testament to what you've survived. You'll heal. *Both* of you."

Chapter Eight

The rump of Mikael's horse was quite large, like the rest of the beast. Dust faded the midnight-black coat that lay underneath. Why was she watching a horse's rump? They'd been riding for two days, having departed Kharav for Mercia with the full army, and her mind was all over the place. They were holding on to the nobles by a thread, headed toward a battle where they weren't sure whether they'd find an ally or a foe, and praying their other enemies wouldn't notice and take advantage of an undefended Kharav while they were gone. And then there was Soren's return. Norah blew out a breath and urged Sephir up beside her husband.

He rode quietly.

"You have to talk to him at some point, you know," she said.

He kept his eyes forward. "No, I don't."

She looked back over her shoulder at Soren riding at the end of their company. His wrap covered his face, and he was too far for her to see his eyes, but she knew he still wasn't himself.

"Yes, you do," she pressed. She smiled wryly. "It's not possible for you to hate him. I know—I've tried."

But his face held no reaction. "He betrayed us."

Norah stiffened and cast all joking aside now. "He didn't betray us. Knock it off with that absurdity."

"It's not absurd, he—"

"No more!" she snapped in a sudden flash of anger.

His head jerked toward her, and his eyes blazed. "You can't be serious."

She'd never been more serious. She'd tried continuously to help him move forward with Soren. She'd tried in all the ways of kindness, but her patience was gone, replaced by a sudden defensiveness. "I mean it," she hissed. "That is your brother, both of blood and heart. You need to sort out the mess between you two." She was done with this conversation and done with this ridiculousness altogether. Norah urged Sephir forward and away. "And don't come back to me until you do," she called over her shoulder.

Time passed slowly. They reached the eastern pass of the Canyonlands and then wove west, toward the Uru. It was a longer route, but easier and faster to navigate the whole of the Kharavian army through. The ride already felt like an eternity, and Mercia still seemed lifetimes away, especially with Mikael keeping his distance. As he should. She'd been serious—she was done with him until he mended things with Soren. He needed to do it soon, though. She missed him, especially at night alone in their tent, which he respectfully stayed out of.

They neared the Uru lands toward early evening on the fifth day, and she slipped down from Sephir with an exaggerated slump. They weren't quite to the village, but walking would breathe some life back into her.

Strange—Tahla hadn't come to greet her yet, but she would see her at the village. Norah was excited. She hadn't seen Tahla since fleeing Mercia so many months before, and even that time was a blur. Norah chided herself—she should have visited, or at least written. Why hadn't she? She'd been so caught up in her own wallowing. She hoped her friend had stayed well. They had a lot to catch up on.

They reached the ridge, and Norah smiled at the beautiful view of the sprawling terraced stone houses of the Uru. It had been too long since she'd been there.

"This sight never ceases to amaze me," Adrian said, drawing up and dismounting beside her.

She loved how he saw its beauty too. "Same." And she was happy he was with her again. Norah glanced at him. She had given him a good berating for the worry he'd caused when he left to find Soren without telling her, and she threw in a couple of threats for good measure before breaking down in tears of thanks. Now that he was by her side again, as was Soren and Sephir, and now that Mercia was potentially so close to being retaken, things seemed like they could be set right.

As she neared the center house leading Sephir, she stopped.

Tahla emerged from inside, smiling.

With a very swollen belly.

Mikael chuckled as he shifted in his saddle. Seeing Tahla with child was the last thing he'd expected. She was a woman who'd just as soon cut off one's manhood than allow herself to be wooed.

"Tahla!" Salara exclaimed, and Mikael watched as his wife swept forward and pulled the chief's daughter into a warm embrace. "What a surprise—congratulations!"

A pain daggered his heart. Salara put on a brave face, but she had to be thinking of their own failure for a child. Of his failure to give her one. He desperately wanted to put his arms around her now, to hold her. She'd want his touch. It comforted her like hers comforted him. But he wasn't allowed to do that. Not yet.

Mikael slid down from his destrier and made his way toward them. "Tahla," he greeted with a smile, putting on a brave face of his own.

She bowed her head with a grin. "Salar."

He glanced around the village. "Do you have a man tied up around here, or have you properly chosen a mate?"

She laughed.

"Good luck getting an answer from her," Coca Otay said in the Urun tongue, coming out of the center house. "She won't speak of him. I don't know if I'm welcoming a son or need to bury a body."

Mikael smiled at the Urun chief as the old man stepped to him and clasped his shoulder.

"It's good to see you," Coca said, but his eyes held concern. "You bring your army. And your anger."

"I go to war."

Coca nodded as he looked at Salara. "You go to put the North Queen back on the North throne?"

"Of course."

"You are a very different man now."

Yes. Yes, he was. He watched his wife fondly as she still talked with Tahla. His heart swelled. "She's made me a different man."

Coca nodded. "It suits you."

Mikael chuckled.

"Go settle, get food to eat. Rest, my son. You have quite a task ahead of you."

Mikael nodded as Coca left him to settle in. He glanced around. Tahla had led Salara away in a rush of conversation. It was good to see them together again, and happy.

Coca had been right. Salara had changed him—had changed how he saw the world, what he wanted. She was kind and smart and brave. She was compassionate and forgiving. She was strong, and she made him strong. And she was right. He needed to mend things with Soren. Not simply so he could go back to her, but because she knew what he needed. And he needed his brother.

Adrian approached. "The army's settled, Salar. I'll be with them."

Mikael nodded. "Where's Soren?"

"He's checking rations and weapons."

"Have him come."

"Yes, Salar." And the young bear turned on his heel and headed back to the army outside the village.

Mikael took a seat on a log by the large fire. He had always loved this about the Uru—that they grouped around the fire. Dancing. Celebrating. Celebrating wins, even in the face of loss. Celebrating life.

Obeweta brought him a large bowl of stew. He'd known the elder woman since he was a boy, and he smiled appreciatively at her. Coca was very much like a father figure to him, and the Uru were his family. And he was fortunate for his family.

All of them.

A silent presence stepped beside him.

"Salar," Soren said quietly.

They hadn't spoken since Mikael had stripped him of his title nearly a week and a half ago. The heat of anger at his betrayal came rushing back, but also the pain of loss. Soren's leaving had hurt him, more than he had thought he could ever be hurt. Yet there was still something that hurt worse. Missing him. Without Soren by his side, a piece was gone from him. And he needed to be whole again.

"Sit."

Soren took a seat on the log beside him.

Mikael handed him his bowl of stew. "Eat, brother. We've wounds to mend and battles to win."

Their eyes locked.

"Lord Commander," Mikael added.

Soren took it slowly, and his eyes glistened in the firelight.

They sat in silence. Soren pulled down his head wrap and drained the bowl before setting it down beside him.

Then Mikael held out his dagger.

Soren stared at him as his brows dipped in question.

"They need to match," Mikael said. The story of their brotherhood, the markings they both bore—except for the coloring of the sun, they were the same, and they needed to remain the same.

Soren was a little too accepting of the task, but at least he made it quick as he ripped a slice across Mikael's shoulder.

Mikael gritted his teeth. "Fuck, I didn't cut you that deep," he said angrily. He'd cut Soren only deep enough to leave a scar.

"Fuck, you did," Soren growled back. "Deeper. You got me with a damned sword."

Mikael gripped his shoulder as blood streamed down his arm. Well, now they'd both certainly have a scar.

Soren eyed him a moment. "Are you all right?" he asked finally.

He pushed out a breath between his teeth. "I'll have Salara stitch it."

"I'll stitch it."

Mikael nodded. "That would be better. Have you seen her needlework?"

Soren snorted. "Why do you think I didn't let her stitch mine?"

And just like that, they were well again.

With a stitched and aching arm, Mikael made his way toward the house where he knew Salara would be. He pushed open the door and stepped inside. She sat on the edge of the bed but rose when he entered.

She pursed her lips. "I told you not to come until you've settled things with Soren."

"We're settled," he said.

Her eyes narrowed at him.

He showed her his shoulder. Her mouth opened but no words came out. "We're settled," he said again.

"Oh." Then her eyes narrowed again. "Wait, did you really just willingly injure yourself to the point of stitches right before we walk into battle?"

He frowned. He hadn't thought of that, but no matter. "I'll be healed enough by the time we reach the North."

She eyed him skeptically.

He could only look at her, all beautiful in her admonition, but there was something more. Something else that troubled her.

She smiled. "I'm glad, then. I needed the two of you back." But it wasn't an easy smile.

He stepped closer. "Are you all right, Salara?"

She shook her head. "I'm fine."

But she wasn't fine, and he knew why. "Salara."

"Really," she insisted.

Ever so gently, he pulled her to him and drew his hand to her stomach, where there was no child and likely never would be. She sucked in a breath.

"I'm sorry," he said softly.

"I'm happy for her, I really am," she said, her voice tinged with emotion.

He nodded. "I know."

"I just—"

"You don't need to explain yourself. You can long for something and be sad when you're reminded of it." He pulled her chin up to make her look at him. "And I'll be here, sad with you."

She wrapped her arms around him and smiled with the most beautiful of sad smiles. "I love you."

"I love you." And nothing had ever been more true.

Chapter Nine

The Kharavian army reached the borders of the North, silently and undetected. As expected. They hadn't earned the name of Shadowmen without merit. Now the challenge would be making it to the capital.

Soren had ridden mostly in silence, his mind not entirely focused, which frustrated him. It was good to be back where he belonged, fighting for those he loved. Salar's forgiveness brought a joy that he struggled to push aside to keep his mind on the task at hand—the North.

Adrian rode beside him. He eyed the young bear. How strange it must feel to lead an army against one's home kingdom, but Salara was the North's true queen. Adrian believed this, and Soren had faith in him. And Adrian would see his brother again, a day Soren knew he longed for.

Salara worried for the Bear, and if he was honest with himself, Soren did too. The Bear would never stand idle as his kingdom was overthrown. And he'd certainly never stand for his queen being attacked. He'd die first. Soren prayed it hadn't come to that. He wasn't sure what he'd do if something had happened to the Bear—an enemy he'd fought for so long, yet a man he could never imagine himself without. So, he told himself what he told Salara time and time again—the bastard prick wouldn't die.

And Soren worried for Caspian. If he didn't deliver the Northman back to Tahla alive, back to his child that he knew nothing of yet, Tahla would never forgive him. Before departing the Uru, Soren had promised her. He needed to keep that promise.

The task before them was a dangerous gamble. For the first time, Soren wasn't completely confident in the outcome. If this was a ruse, if something had happened to the Bear and it was Aleon that awaited them, united with the North, the Kharavian army would be overtaken. Not easily, or so Soren preferred to think, but Aleon had one of the largest armies in the world, and the North not only had their own forces but mercenary armies as well.

And these were no ordinary mercenaries the council had obtained. The Holy Knights were the most sought after of mercenaries and came at the greatest cost, but unlike ordinary mercenaries, they didn't fight for gold alone. They fought only what they considered to be holy wars—battles of good and evil—and the council would have definitely made this a holy war.

Men fought most fiercely for that which they believed, and the Holy Knights fought only for what they believed. It made them near invincible.

The Kharavian army made their way through the outer reaches, spreading ranks out and weaving in and out of villages, using every tool of stealth to pass through the Northern lands in secret. The army had now made it farther than they ever had before. Soren would have liked to boast it as skill, but in truth, in their years of war, the Bear would have never let them get this far. He would have known the moment they stepped inside the borders. Someone was letting them draw near, but whether it was the Bear who called them to join him, or the North and Aleon luring them into a trap, he didn't know.

When they reached the midlands, Soren called for a group to break off, mitigating the risk if they were, in fact, walking into a trap. He and Mikael would covertly lead a smaller army through the mainland toward the isle, assessing possible routes across the channel to the castle and ensuring Aleon was not in wait. If all went well, they'd cross the channel and launch a surprise attack to divert attention. If the Northmen were on their side, they'd open the gates of the main bridge, where Adrian would lead the army across to join them. It was a solid plan.

That was, if the Northmen were loyal to Salara.

And if they weren't, if it was a trap, the army would retreat and get Salara to safety. Despite her vehement objections, he and Mikael were able to convince her to stay with the broader army. Soren ordered Adrian to keep behind as well, to make sure she followed the plan.

Night hung heavy over the mainland, the perfect cover, and the Kharavian army slipped quietly through the darkness. They followed the messenger who had brought the news to Kharav. Soren could practically hear the man shaking in his boots, and he gritted his teeth in annoyance.

Cohen followed after the messenger. Soren was glad to once again have him in his service. He watched the boy closely. Cohen's eyes and mind were sharp; he saw things others missed. If there were warnings to see, he'd be the one to catch them. But all was quiet, and Cohen motioned the small army forward.

There was no sign of Aleon—no sign that anyone knew they were there.

Good.

Or bad.

They slipped through the dark alleys of the city, and when they reached the channel, they scanned the banks, looking for the best way across. In all his time in Mercia, crossing the water to the capital isle was the one challenge Soren still didn't have a solution for. He knew there was a tunnel that ran underneath, one that Caspian had led him through when he'd fled with Salara. But his mind had been on escaping and keeping Salara safe. He couldn't remember his way back to it, and they didn't have time to find it.

The bridge was the only way across, although with summer now gone and winter approaching, the forming ice provided a possible alternative.

"There," Soren said to Mikael as he pointed to a strip of ice stretching across the still water between the mainland and the castle isle.

"It hasn't hardened enough to carry the weight of a man," the messenger said, his voice still lacking confidence. "And if you fall into the water, that cold will have you dead within moments."

"Then how do we get across?" Mikael asked.

The man shook his head. "The only way I know is the main bridge. But I'm supposed to bring you to the Narrows—the market stall side streets."

Soren snorted. "That sounds exactly like what we're *not* going to do."

"What's there?" Mikael asked him. "Why the side streets?"

The Northman shook his head. "I don't know. It's just what I was told."

"By the lord justice?"

"Yes," the Northman said nervously.

Mikael frowned. "And how does that get us to the castle?"

"I-I don't know."

"What *do* you know about the castle?" Soren growled impatiently.

"I've never even been in the castle. So nothing."

Soren forced himself to not dagger the man in the throat as he ripped an annoyed gaze toward Mikael.

Mikael cast his eyes out across the channel and over the castle, thinking. "We'll go to the side streets," he said finally.

"You can't be serious," Soren hissed. "Does a back alley not scream 'trap' to you?"

"We'll go," Mikael said again.

Soren clutched the messenger by the collar of his jacket. "If you're lying—"

"I know, you'll kill me," he finished quickly.

"No," Soren snarled. "You'll wish I would've killed you." He shoved the man forward, and they followed him into the dark.

The Narrows were just as their name implied—narrow market streets made even smaller by the covered merchant stalls. The men weaved in between the stations and carts, taking cover from shadow to shadow.

The messenger walked down the center. Like an idiot.

When he reached the end, he stopped.

They all stopped.

Soren scanned the street. All was quiet. They lifted their eyes to rooftops, searching for movement. But there was nothing. Soren looked at Mikael, who only looked back at him. They waited.

"We're here!" the man called.

Soren winced and gritted his teeth again. He'd kill him. This was definitely a trap.

A side door swung open from the end building, and Northmen poured out. The Kharavian soldiers fell back, surrounding Mikael, and Soren brought up his axe to strike.

"It *is* a trap," Mikael hissed beside him.

But then Soren stopped. His eyes trailed the person who stepped out behind the Northmen, and he snorted as he shook his head. He knew that frigid grace. "No. It's not. It's the grandmother."

"Destroyer," the foul woman said icily as she stood in the center of the street. "What took you so long?"

Irritation rippled through him. "We marched the entire Kharavian army across the Tribelands and through the North, in just over two weeks' time."

"Did anyone see you?"

Was she serious? "Of course not." *Insulting.* Curse the North gods, he hated this woman.

Her gaze moved past him to Mikael, and she stiffened. "Shadow King," she said. It was the first time they'd met.

"Lady Catherine," Mikael greeted her back, as politely as Soren had ever heard him speak—trying to make a good impression, no doubt.

Soren rolled his eyes. "What are you doing here?" he asked her.

"What do you mean *what am I doing here?* How do you think you're going to get in?"

"Across the bridge."

"I thought you Shadowmen were smarter at this battle thing."

Soren scowled at her.

"Come," she called to them, and stepped through the door from which she'd come. Soren snorted—she was taking them through the tunnel. He glanced at Mikael, who looked back at him with the flat want of refusal written all over his face. But Soren gave him an encouraging nod, and they followed after.

She led them down a steep staircase, into darkness that was dark even for the Shadowmen. Their way was lit only by the lantern the old woman carried.

"Are you sure about this?" Mikael said quietly to Soren.

"The old woman's annoying," Soren said, "but she's loyal to her granddaughter."

"This annoying old woman can hear you," she called out in front of them.

They poured into a larger tunnel, and she took them through a series of turns to a staircase leading upward, which Soren guessed came out somewhere in the main castle.

"This will bring you out inside the temple," she told them. "It's as close as I can get you to the bridge."

"Where's the Bear?" Mikael asked.

"He waits by the keep, at the north end, where the council will seek refuge when the battle starts."

The Bear was alive. A small wave a relief passed through Soren, and he thought he might have seen the same from Mikael. Likely not. But maybe.

"He plans to cut them off?" Mikael asked.

The old woman nodded in the lantern light. "But the mercenaries will be with them. It won't be an easy task."

Mikael looked at Soren. "I'll take half the men, clear the bridge for our army to enter. You join the Bear."

Soren nodded.

"There's a young girl, Norah's cousin, Evangeline," the grandmother told them. "She's a pawn in all of this. She's not to be harmed. Do you understand?"

Mikael nodded.

"But the council—show them no mercy," she said. "I want them destroyed for what they have done."

Soren snorted. "Do you not know who I am?"

And for the first time, the old woman smiled at him. "Then the gods go with you, Destroyer."

CHAPTER TEN

Soren ascended the staircase in the darkness, into the castle he'd dreamed of taking since he was a boy. But never had he imagined taking it in the name of the North Queen, who he was now sworn to, and never by the Bear's side. Five hundred of his men followed behind him—men who had followed him into the hells of battle again and again. And they would yet again. Not all of them would make it through this night, and if they died, then they died for the North's cause. Surely, they, too, had never dreamed this was their path, but still they followed him.

They silently spilled out into the darkness of the sleeping temple. Mikael split off and headed toward the bridge, taking Cohen and half their men with him, and Soren drove for the north side, toward the keep. He'd memorized the isle from his time before—every building, every structure, especially the keep—and knew exactly where he was going.

He thought about Mikael making his way toward the bridge, and he quickened his pace. He wanted to reach the Bear before—

Shouts rang out, and a horn sounded. The mercenaries knew they were there, and the night came alive.

Too late.

He pushed faster. Torches sprang up down the mainways, lighting up the night. As he rounded the corner of the massive library, almost to the keep, Soren spotted him.

The Bear.

The justice fought in his signature battle dress with the head of the great Northern bear on his shoulder. Flames from the torchlit city gleamed off his armor. Soren hated it—the Bear always looking so fucking majestic.

A small group of Northmen fought by his side against a troupe of mercenary Holy Knights as even more mercenaries poured out of the keep. Curse the North gods—they'd be slaughtered. Soren and his men surged toward them. These hired swords were the best there were, and the Northmen were no match.

A mercenary lunged at a Northman with his spear, and the soldier spun sideways, using the momentum to grab it and arc around, ripping it from the mercenary's hands.

Soren snorted. *Not bad.* Quite good, actually. Better than he'd remembered. Training in Kharav had turned the Northmen into respectable soldiers. Perhaps they'd last a little longer than he'd thought.

But now the Northmen were outnumbered and falling one by one. Three mercenaries swept around, attacking the Bear at all sides and knocking him to the ground. One advanced and swung his sword over his head to deliver a deathly blow. Soren let out a snarl as he barreled through, cleaving his massive battle-axe into the man's back and felling him midswing. The two Kharavian warriors by his side took up the others.

The Bear lay on his back, and Soren held out his hand. The justice gaped up at him for a moment before clasping his forearm and letting Soren pull him to his feet.

"What took you so long?" the Bear panted.

Soren cursed. "As I told the old woman, I got here in just over two weeks' time, with my *entire* army."

More mercenaries joined the ranks against them, and the two men defensively positioned themselves back-to-back.

"And we weren't sure the message wasn't a ruse," Soren added.

A mercenary attacked with a series of maneuvers that pushed Soren back, against the Bear. These soldiers were good—too good.

"What do you mean a ruse?" Alexander snapped over his shoulder as he worked his own defense. "I sent you a miner, so you'd know it was from me."

What? Why? Soren snorted in utter confusion. "Why would you send a *miner*?"

Alexander ran a man through on his sword and paused. "Are you serious?" he asked incredulously before kicking the dead man off his blade. "You told me Northmen soldiers were shit, that you'd rather have our miners because you'd only trust a man who could properly swing an axe." He panted between swings. "I sent you a miner."

Soren landed a fatal wound on the mercenary in front of him. "I never said that," he argued.

"You definitely said that."

And suddenly, he did remember telling the Bear those words. "Am I supposed to remember everything I say?" He kicked back another soldier. "And there was nothing else you could send? You know—a letter with a seal, something meaningful, other than a stupid reference to a comment I might have made years ago?"

"Something the council would have traced back to me should they have caught him?" the Bear cut back through labored breaths. "And it wasn't years ago. It was right before you left Mercia. You were supposed to know what it meant."

"Well, I didn't," Soren spat. "You should have sent something meaningful to Salara."

Alexander stopped. "But I needed *you*. The message was for *you*."

Soren spilled the entrails of another man and paused. The Bear had needed him. "Oh." He should have gotten the reference. He should have driven the army to the North faster. "Well, it was a stupid fucking message."

Soren glanced across the city, which was now lit up in battle. He could see that the tall gates of the bridge were open, which meant the Kharavian army was in. He looked back to Alexander. "Your brother leads my army across the bridge. Your queen comes for her throne."

The faintest of smiles pulled at the corners of the Bear's mouth. "To the keep, then? The council's there."

Soren gave a nod. "To the keep."

The clang of sword strikes rang through the air as she charged over the bridge atop Sephir. Norah held her own sword in her hand, although she hardly needed it. The Shadow army protectively surrounded her like a thick fog—she could barely see through them. It wasn't entirely as she'd imagined when she thought of herself riding into battle to take back her kingdom. Not that she wanted to fight, or kill, but she'd been prepared to.

In the distance, she heard Mikael's booming voice, giving orders to his army in the Kharavian tongue. Somewhere just ahead of her, Adrian echoed, and the ranks around her pushed forward.

Her eyes combed the sea of battling men... Where was Alexander?

As they pressed deeper into the capital and through the courtyard, more men flocked around her, and she noticed it wasn't just her Kharavian warriors. The gleam of silver armor blended into the black of shadows—her loyal Northmen, joining her at her side.

But this would not be an easy win. The castle was filled with mercenaries—the best in the world—and their numbers were greater than she'd imagined.

A *sip* flew past her, and she didn't need to see it to know it was an arrow. Her gaze shot to the turret's walls, where mercenaries fired down on them.

Bhastian grabbed her, pulling her off Sephir. "Keep down, Salara," he ordered as he raised his shield over her. Kiran pressed close on her other side.

She kept herself smartly under Bhastian's shield but still scanned the battle-strewn courtyard around them. "I have to find Alexander."

"He'll be going after the council, who are likely in the keep," Bhastian said. "But, Salara, the fighting will be strongest there."

"I have to find him," she insisted. She had to see him, see him with her own eyes, and know he was all right. Then they would face her council together.

The corners of her Crest guard's eyes creased with objection.

"Bhastian. I have to find him. Please."

Reluctantly, he nodded. Then he and Kiran shouldered closer, and they moved with her army as a unit toward the keep.

The ranks thinned as more mercenaries flooded them, and the fighting pressed closer. How were there so many of them? The Kharavian warriors and her Northmen fought shoulder to shoulder, working tirelessly to push them back.

Suddenly, to her right, the gleam of a sword caught her eye. Kiran spun and struck it to the side with his own blade before sinking his second short sword into the mercenary.

Bhastian swore. "Salara, we should fall back. It's not safe."

She hadn't come for safety. "We keep going," she said.

Another onslaught of arrows rained from the sky, taking some of the men down around her. Kiran and Bhastian pressed her between them with their shields held high. She glanced up at the walls lined with mercenaries, and her heart fell. There were so many of them.

Then she noticed a darkness snaking in from both ends, pressing the mercenaries toward the center, and hope sprang within her. The Kharavian army was closing in—her men were gaining ground. The arrows falling from the wall turned into falling bodies of the enemy.

She urged her men on toward the keep.

The fighting thickened, and the smell of blood filled her nose. Kiran drove back another attack to the right, and Bhastian felled a man who broke through on the left.

Norah heard her name, but she couldn't place where it had come from or who called it. The clang of battle was near deafening now, drowning out everything around her. Bhastian yelled something, but she couldn't make out what it was.

A mercenary broke through in front of her and drove a sharp swing from above. She countered with her own blade and then followed with a quick series of defensive moves. But he was good—too good—and pressed her back. He let out a roar as he launched a lethal sequence and swung again for her neck. But both Kiran and Bhastian crossed their swords to block him, and Kiran followed with a thrust to the mercenary's gut with his short sword. The man fell to his knees, and Bhastian took his head.

A hand grabbed her arm from behind, and she twisted, whipping her dagger from her waist and driving it into the man's side. It was a punishing blow, but his armor kept it from being a kill strike.

And Norah gasped.

Caspian stared back at her, still holding her arm, with a dagger jutting from his side.

He was alive. Or, he was...

No!

"Caspian!" She let go of the dagger.

He winced. "Queen Norah," he managed between his teeth. They both looked down at the hilt protruding from between his plates of armor just above his hip.

"Caspian!" she cried again.

"It's not a fatal wound," Bhastian said. "He'll live. But we can't just stand here."

Caspian curled his hand around the dagger and pulled the bloody blade from his side.

"Oh gods, Caspian! I'm so sorry!"

"No, it's all right. I'm all right." He grimaced through panting breaths. He didn't look all right. "We have to get you away from here until this is all over," he said. "It's not safe for you here."

She shook her head; she wasn't going anywhere. "I have to find Alexander."

"He's going after the council now," he told her.

"He's here?"

He nodded, still panting. "Yes, with the lord commander."

"Soren's with him?" Her eyes welled.

"They really work quite well together when they're not trying to kill each other."

She laughed through her emotion.

Swords rang behind her, and she glanced back to see Kiran and her Northmen fighting off another wave of mercenaries.

"Salara," Bhastian pressed. "You see? He says the Bear is well. We should fall back until the commander takes the council and secures the castle."

She shook her head again. "I can't *fall back* in the fight for my own kingdom."

Caspian wavered and dropped to a knee. Norah and Kiran both jumped forward and caught him.

She raked her eyes around them. "We need to get him somewhere safe."

"This way," Bhastian said, and they fell back toward the library.

Away from the thick of the fighting, Caspian sank to the ground along the arched stone. Their men formed a protective wall around them under the direction of Bhastian and Kiran.

"We'll get you a healer," Norah said as she dropped down beside him. "Just rest for a moment. You'll be okay."

"It's not feeling that way," Caspian said between labored breaths. He gripped his side tightly and grimaced again.

Her heart beat faster. "What do you mean? You said you were all right."

"Help me hold the bleeding," he said.

Norah's hands shook as she fumbled along the ridges of where the armor split. The tunic was stained with blood underneath, but she wasn't exactly sure where she had hurt him.

"It's a side wound," Bhastian said, "he's perfectly fine. He's not even bleeding that much."

"Shut up, Bhash," Kiran said.

She paused and glanced back at Bhastian, then at Kiran. "Wait, is this your way to keep me out of the battle?" she asked.

Kiran puffed an angry snort and cut Bhastian a glare. Bhastian shifted, just catching on.

She scowled back at Caspian and swatted him. "I can't believe you! I was actually worried!"

"Ow!" He winced. "In fairness, I didn't expect to get stabbed. I'm just trying to make it worth it. And it really does hurt."

"I should stab you again."

He gave a slight smile. "Welcome home, Norah."

Soren cut through the battle at Alexander's side as they raced toward the keep, with the Kharavian warriors at their heels. The mercenaries grew thick as they drew closer, but the Kharavian men were skilled swordsmen, and they kept the small team moving forward. Alexander and Soren charged the hold at the doors, bringing down the defense and bursting inside. Both men took the stairs at a run. Mercenaries met them in force, but Soren and Alexander shouldered them over the railing or cut them down. Bodies on the stairs slowed their advance, but they battled through. The sting of a blade ripped across Soren's arm, but it was only a surface wound, and he delivered a deadly blow back, ripping open his opponent's neck and sending him tumbling down the staircase.

The councilmen had already fallen back, deeper into the keep.

"We have to catch them before they reach the tunnels," Alexander told him.

They raced by a large hall and skidded to a stop. Inside stood a man with a dagger in his hand. Soren recognized him as a councilman—the one called James. He was thinner than Soren remembered, his frame now gaunt and his eyes, hollow.

The Bear held up his hand as he approached slowly. "James," he said, but instead of the warning or threat Soren expected, there was a pleading in his voice.

"I knew it was only a matter of time," the old councilman said, clutching the dagger and bringing the tip to his own chest. "The gods send their judgment for our sins. I'm sorry, Alexander. I've failed you."

The Bear shook his head. "James, don't do this."

Soren glared at Alexander. "That's exactly what you want him to do."

"Shut up," Alexander snapped back. "James," he called to the man. "Put the dagger down."

"I've failed you," the councilman said again. "I've failed Norah. But most of all I've failed Mercia."

Soren clenched his jaw. They didn't have time for this.

James plunged the dagger into his stomach.

Soren rolled his eyes. *Finally.*

"No!" Alexander shouted as the councilman fell forward to his knees. He caught the old man and eased him down. "No! James!"

"I'm sorry, Alexander. Forgive me."

"James!"

"Forgive me," he said as his last breath left him.

The Bear sat clutching the councilman.

Soren gaped at him. "Are you going to be able to do this? We have"—he counted on his fingers—"five more to go." Or more... He didn't remember how many councilmen there were. No matter—everyone in a robe would die today.

Alexander stood slowly. "James was like a father to me."

"Yeah, well, a coward, traitor father who tried to kill Salara. Come on."

The Bear grabbed Soren's arm. "It's not my intention to kill the council. These men need to be brought to trial for their crimes against the crown."

Soren stopped, speechless. He shook his head in confusion. "Trial?"

"This is the way things are done in Mercia."

Was it? "Are you not literally called the justice of the queen? Is it not you who judges their innocence?"

The Bear shifted his weight back on his heel. There was a pause before he said, "I am, and I do."

Soren stepped closer, his eyes burning into the Bear's. "Have you personally not witnessed their treason?"

Alexander's eyes burned back. "I have."

Soren gripped his breastplate. "And how do you find them?"

The Bear's breath deepened, and Soren soaked up the fury radiating from his armor. "I find them guilty," Alexander said.

He pounded his fist against the Bear's breastplate in solidarity. "Consider this your trial, then. Come the fuck on."

But Alexander grabbed him. "They *will* die for what they've done. But they'll stand before their queen and answer, after they've watched her retake her throne. I won't take that away from her."

Noble shit. Soren growled his protest. "Fine," he said between his teeth.

"Now come the fuck on," Alexander said to him, and Soren smiled.

They made it to the back of the keep. Despite the skill of the Holy Knights, there was now only a small group of soldiers providing a final defense. The rest of the mercenaries had made for the bridge to meet the Kharavian army coming through.

An elder Mercian councilman clutched a small satchel and cowered behind several men. Yes... Soren remembered this one. *Edward.*

"Attack!" Edward screamed at the mercenaries as he backed toward the wall. "Think of your souls. You would let this darkness defeat you?"

A knight rushed forward, and Alexander threw his dagger, catching him squarely in the base of the neck. The man fell backward, choking on his blood.

"The tunnels!" Alexander shouted at Soren, and he turned to see another councilman hurrying through a side door and down a stairwell.

Soren took after him. Austair? Alastair? He couldn't remember, and he didn't really care. As he caught up with him, the councilman pulled a vial from his pocket.

What—

His eyes widened as the old man quickly pulled off its topper and swallowed the contents. *Poison.* "No!" Soren shouted, springing forward. He grabbed the councilman by his robes, holding him against the wall, but within moments, foam sprang from the man's mouth, and his legs gave out from under him. There was nothing Soren could do, and he let the dying man sink to the ground.

Another one dead. Soren swore.

He took the stairs back to the keep, cursing himself again. Alexander would be angry with him for losing another councilman, and as much as he disagreed with the Bear, he respected what he wanted.

By the time he made it back, the Kharavian soldiers had bound the rest of the councilmen and were escorting them from the keep. Alexander stood at the window, looking out. Soren could hear cheering down below, in what could only be the calls of triumph in winning back the North. *Good*, it would soften his message.

"Unfortunate news," Soren said as he stepped back through the doorway. "Or you could look at it optimistically—you have one less councilman to hang."

But as Alexander turned, Soren's eyes locked on him and on the stream of blood pouring down the front of the Bear's armor.

Soren stopped in his step.

It was too much blood.

Alexander swayed, and Soren lunged forward to catch him.

"What happened?" he demanded.

Alexander scoffed. "Before or after I caught a blade to the stomach?"

"Damn you, man, this isn't a joke." He pulled the Bear's arm over his shoulder to support him. "We need to get you to the healer."

Alexander shook his head. "No, Destroyer," he said, breathing heavily. "This is my end."

The Bear's words knifed him. "If you say that again, I'll end you myself." Soren pulled him toward the stair.

Alexander grunted in pain. "I always thought you'd be the one to do it."

"There's still time," Soren cut back. "Hold yourself together." Where was Salara? He set his eyes on a nearby soldier. "Get Salara!" The soldier darted away.

Soren started forward again, but Alexander pulled him back.

"Soren," he gasped. "Stop."

There was a finality to his tone. The way he said his name—*no, no, no*. Soren shook his head. "You can't die now, Bear. Not now."

Alexander grew heavier as he weakened. "Let me down," he said.

Soren sank slowly to his knees, lowering the justice to the floor. He shifted behind him, holding him upright. "You have to hold on," Soren said. If he could just hold on...

The justice shook his head faintly.

"You have to hold on."

The Bear's body grew even heavier.

"You can't die," Soren told him. "They'll memorialize you, you bastard. Kids will be cursed with your name. And it's a fucking terrible name."

Alexander chuckled weakly.

"Of course you'd love that." Soren's lip trembled.

Alexander's breathing became labored. His face was pale now. Ghostly pale. Soren ripped off his armor to the blood-soaked shirt underneath. Alexander coughed, and more blood seeped from the wound in his stomach, tiding over his sides and puddling underneath them. It was dark blood. Life blood.

Soren bared his teeth, holding back the emotion. Death didn't deserve the Bear—the only worthy opponent he'd ever had. Soren had hated him for so long. He loved hating him. He wanted to keep hating him, to keep fighting him. He needed him.

"Don't even think about leaving yet," he said between his teeth. "You know she's coming."

"How do I look?" Alexander joked.

Soren grimaced. "Like a gutted pig."

He motioned to a soldier nearby. "Your cloak," he commanded. The soldier pulled it off quickly and covered the justice.

Soren nodded. "Now a little less gutted."

The justice's breaths came shallower. "Don't you pine after me when I'm gone."

Soren turned his head away, fighting the tears that stung his eyes. He had always planned to kill the Bear, but this...

"Soren." Alexander clutched him. "Norah, Adrian—watch over them." He squeezed Soren's arm, gasping for another breath. "I beg you. Brother."

Soren nodded, unable to speak.

Alexander's breath grew fainter, and the blink of his eyes slowed.

"Not yet." Soren shook him. "Not yet—Salara's coming." He looked around. Where was she? Shouts rang outside, with a shuffling below. "Salara!" he bellowed. He gripped the justice tightly. "She's coming. Norah's coming!"

Alexander drew in a breath, and Soren knew it was the last one. The last breath. The last of life.

The Bear stilled in his arms.

Soren slumped forward over the justice. He'd done everything in his power to kill this man all these years, and now he'd give anything to save him.

Salara's voice rang out below. "Alexander!"

Soren clung to him, unable to respond.

Footfalls hit the stairs. "Alexander!" she called again.

Soren leaned back, still holding the Bear up, and waited. He could do nothing more—he couldn't call to her; he couldn't even breathe.

She reached the top of the stair and stopped, horror flooding her face. "No!" she screamed, running to them and dropping to the floor. "Alexander!" she cried. She clutched his face and pulled it toward her. "Alexander!"

Soren watched her, his vision blurry. "He's gone," he said hoarsely.

"No!" she screamed. "No!" She clutched on to the Bear's shirt, shaking him. "Alexander! I'm here, come back. I'm here!"

Soren reached out a bloodied hand and grabbed her arm, pulling her still. She stopped, looking up at him, and he shook his head.

"Please," she begged him, like he had the power, like he could give the Bear back to her. But he didn't, and he couldn't. And it killed him.

A wail broke from her lips, a raw anguish that shook him to his soul. All the battles he'd fought, all the death he'd seen, but her cry—a long, keening wail—broke him. He'd never forget the sound.

Slowly, he eased out from behind the justice and laid him down gently.

She let out another sob and collapsed over him.

Soren waved out the remaining few soldiers. He stood and stretched his arm to the wall, leaning against it. He couldn't draw in a breath. The ache of loss in his chest was suffocating. He moved to the edge of the stair, looking back at his weeping queen.

He didn't know how he made it out. His legs felt like they might not hold him, but once outside the castle, he staggered through the carnage of the North. The weight of the air crushed him, but he turned his mind away from himself to someone more important. Soldiers called out to him, but he ignored them as he scanned the masses. He had to find him—where was he? A warrior trotted up to him, but Soren pushed him back, not hearing his words.

Where was he?

Then he saw him.

Although bloodstained and weary, Adrian's face held a wide grin. "Victory!" the young bear bellowed. He looked across the soldiers as they cheered around him.

Soren lingered, letting him reap the joy, if only for a moment.

Adrian spotted him and lifted his sword in triumph.

Soren moved toward him, slowly. Then he stopped, and Adrian's grin faded slightly. He pulled down the wrap from his face. Their stares locked.

The young bear stilled. "Where's Alec?" he called.

Soren hesitated.

Adrian's brows drew together. "Where's Alec?" he asked again.

Faintly, Soren shook his head.

His face twisted. "Where's Alec?" he asked more urgently. "Where is he?" Soren stepped toward him, but Adrian drew up his sword to halt him. "No. No! Where is he?" he demanded.

"Adrian." His voice cracked. "He's gone."

Adrian bared his teeth as he shook his head. "No." He shook his head again. "You're lying. Where is he?" he raged in desperation.

Soren let out a ragged breath. "He's gone."

Adrian shook his head again, refusing his answer. "Alec!" he cried out as he staggered back. He turned and stumbled in a circle, looking around for his brother. His eyes desperately combed the soldiers around him. "Alec!"

But there would be no answer.

Adrian dropped his sword from his hand and wavered as he stopped. "Alec!"

Soren caught him and pulled him close. Adrian was a large man now, not easily embraced, but Soren held him.

"Alec!" Adrian screamed into him.

Soren held him until his screams gave way to sobs, and then he held him longer. His own tears fell as he hugged him tightly. It wasn't right. The Bear should be the one alive—here. He had family, people who loved him, people who needed him. In that moment, Soren would have given anything to take his place. He held him tighter.

Adrian's body shook as he sobbed in the courtyard of death.

A slight breeze rippled over the carnage of the North, carrying the smell of blood and victory. Mikael stared down at the fallen mercenary commander of the Holy Knights.

Pity—they truly were a magnificent army. He surveyed the city. So many good soldiers lost, and the loss of good soldiers saddened him, even when they weren't his own. The mainway ran red with blood—blood of mercenaries, Northmen, and Kharavian warriors. But they'd taken back the North, and that was worth the cost.

He'd never stepped inside the kingdom of Mercia. Many times he'd imagined it, imagined the death-littered streets of the North that he'd hated for so long. But never like this. Never had he thought he'd fight to reclaim the throne for its queen—the woman he loved.

A mercenary stirred to his right and pushed himself to sit. He sputtered a broken cough, spitting blood down his chin, but he didn't seem fatally wounded.

Mikael stepped toward him. The soldier would be taken with the other survivors, made slaves—a tragic end for such men.

The soldier looked up at him, no fear in his eyes. "Shadow King," he panted with a hateful breath. "Come closer, that I might fight you with what little strength I have left."

Mikael snorted. Resilient bastards, he'd give them that. "Are you not afraid to die?"

The man took a raspy inhale. "What is death? I'll bask in the glory of the gods and be rewarded for my courage against evil."

"Evil," Mikael repeated. He stooped down beside the man. "Is that what you think I am?"

"What do you think you are?"

Mikael frowned. No one had ever asked him that. "A man." A salar. A husband.

The soldier chuckled before coughing and sputtering more blood down his chin. "If you're a man, have mercy as a man. Send me to my gods."

"Not all men have mercy."

"Honorable men do."

Mikael clasped the side of the soldier's neck, locking him with his gaze. "I'm not an honorable man." He pulled the soldier closer. "But you did fight with courage. Go to your gods." And he plunged his dagger into the soldier's chest, giving him a quick journey. For this man, he'd give mercy.

He laid the expired soldier back against the ground and wiped the blood from his dagger before sheathing it again at his waist.

"Salar!" Soren's voice came urgently from behind him.

Mikael turned.

The commander stopped, silent, as if words wouldn't come. It was the first time Mikael had seen him on the battlefield without his wrap. Anguish covered him. "The Bear," was all he said.

Mikael cast his eyes toward the castle. "What about the Bear?" Was he coming?

"He's dead."

A weight struck him. *No.* He couldn't have heard correctly. "What?"

"The Bear's dead."

Mikael shook his head. "No. That's not possible." He couldn't be dead. The Bear would be the one to bring his end. Mikael had seen it with his own eyes. This wasn't possible.

"You need to come. Now."

Mikael followed Soren through the field of the dead, to the castle, up the stairs, and down the marble halls darkening with the fading sun. Soren led him to the private mortium, where he stopped.

In the center of the room stood a stone slab table, where the body of the lord justice lay.

Salara sat beside him, leaning forward with her forehead against his shoulder as she wept. Mikael stepped into the room, and she looked up. Her eyes were swollen and red, her cheeks wet with tears. Blood stained her hands and arms, the blood of the Bear, no doubt.

The crimson saturating the front of his battle clothes told the story of his death—a weakness in the ornate Northern armor, where the breastplate met the waist piece.

And now the justice was dead.

The Bear was *dead*.

But this wasn't possible.

Mikael drew closer, looking down at him. He wasn't convinced this was real. This couldn't be real. He moved even closer to the side of the table. Slowly, he reached out, then stopped. To touch the Bear...

It was a violation of some kind.

The Bear had always been beyond his reach. This man, who had haunted him for so long. The only man he'd ever feared. Hated. Cursed. Resented.

Yet a man he now respected.

He dropped his hand to his side. The Bear would stay beyond his touch.

The head of the Northern Bear, its white fur splattered red, had been removed from the justice's shoulder and laid on the ground under the slab table. Perhaps it was best that it die too, for no one else was worthy of it.

His gaze shifted to Salara, who only watched Mikael as he stood there. Her eyes were the bluest they'd ever been, against her red-rimmed eyelids overflowing with sorrow. The initial anguish had passed, and now she sat in the quiet shock of grief, watching. Was she looking for something within him? Pleasure? Victory? Relief, even?

She would find none of it. He felt none of those things.

Her lip trembled. It was the slightest of movements, but it called him. Quickly he stepped around the table to her side, pulling her up and wrapping his arms around her. She let out a sob and clung to him. He said nothing. There were no words. He only held her. Tightly.

They stood for a long time, until the dark of night came and he felt her weight heavy against him. Keepers stepped into the mortium—those responsible for preparing the bodies of the dead to pass their souls to the next life. They lit candles throughout the room to chase back the night, then stood quietly, waiting to care for the body of the justice.

"Let me take you to your chamber," Mikael said softly. "You need to rest."

"I can't." Her voice was barely a bird's breath. "I can't leave him."

"The keepers are here. They'll take care of him."

Her head snapped up, and her eyes found them. She hadn't realized they'd come in. "No, they can't have him." Her eyes pleaded as she shook her head. "They can't take him."

Mikael gripped her shoulders, making her look at him. "They won't take him. I won't allow it." Then he softened his voice. "But don't let him lie like this, in his own blood. Let them clean him. And we'll stay."

She looked at the justice on the table and wiped her face with her hand. Her breaths still filled the silence of the room. Finally, she nodded.

Mikael led her to a bench against the wall and sat, gently guiding her down beside him and putting his arm around her. He nodded to the three men in gray robes, who silently stepped forward. They pulled off the rest of the justice's armor and cut away his clothing. A breathy cry escaped Salara as they stripped off the red-stained linen, revealing the deep wound to his stomach. Mikael pulled her closer to him. Two of the men brought a basin and started sponging the body clean, and one of the keepers prepared a needle and set to stitching the wound closed.

They worked with the care and reverence befitting a hero; that's what the Bear was to the North. And now Salara would have to find a way to fill his void. Mikael would have to find a way to help her.

When the keepers finished, they draped a white cloth over his body and bowed to Salara before leaving in silence.

He looked down at Salara but didn't dare suggest she leave again. "Has Adrian come?" he asked softly.

She nodded weakly. "Earlier, with my grandmother," she whispered. "He's not of right mind. Soren had to take him away."

The brother of the Bear would be devastated, as he knew Salara was. "Do you want to stay longer?"

Her red-rimmed eyes met his, and she nodded again.

He pulled her closer and kissed the top of her head. "I'll give you some space. Take all the time you need."

Mikael stood, squeezing her arm tenderly before leaving her the privacy to grieve.

CHAPTER ELEVEN

Norah sat beside the stone slab table that held Alexander. She didn't know how much time had passed. She could only stare at him. With his pallid skin and blue-tinged lips, she couldn't pretend he was only sleeping. His skin was cold to the touch.

How could this have happened?

She shouldn't have come. She'd been safe in Kharav. She'd had Mikael and Soren. She'd had Alexander. Even if she'd have never seen him again, he'd still be alive.

But she'd wanted her throne back. She'd wanted vengeance.

And this was what it cost her.

The tears came again, and she lay her head on his cold shoulder. Cold like the room. Like tomorrow, and every day after now. She'd brought this. She'd done this to him. To herself. To Adrian—*oh gods, Adrian*. And Catherine. How could she even face them again? She wanted their anger, their wrath. She needed it. She deserved no kindness, even in the bitter depths of her grief and loss.

There was a tremor in her mind, and she brought her fingers to her temples. She was exhausted, but she knew sleep wouldn't come. Not that it mattered—she didn't deserve sleep either.

A stirring rippled through the room, and Norah felt eyes on her. Her skin prickled. She lifted her head to see a man standing at the other end of the mortium, between two pillars in the shadows.

Just standing.

Watching.

She narrowed her eyes to focus better. And her breath left her as her chest seized.

Alexander.

She shook as she glanced down at his lifeless body under her hands, then looked back up at him on the other side of the room. Alexander was dead, right in front of her.

Yet his exact likeness stood at the edge of the room, as in life.

How?

"Alexander?" she breathed.

He was different—his hair was clipped shorter, and he was dressed in dark breeches with a gray tunic. His eyes were fierce, his face full of anger as he looked upon his body.

"Alexander?" she called again.

His attention jerked, his stare moving up from the body on the table slab to find her, as if just noticing her for the first time, and he took a step back.

"Is it really you?" she asked him.

His brow relaxed from its hold of anger, but his eyes gave way to alarm. No recognition came from him, no warmth. He backed farther into the shadows, and she feared she'd lose him.

"Wait!" she cried. "Don't go! Please."

He paused as she staggered up and drew around the table, closer to him.

"How is this possible?" she whispered. "How are you here?" She swallowed back a cry.

He shifted, leaning back on his heel, still on the verge of flight.

"Do you not know me?" Is this what death did to a man's spirit?

Alexander neither moved nor spoke, but he watched her apprehensively as she came closer—close enough to touch him.

She brought her hand up hesitantly to his face, but he pulled back. His eyes didn't know her. "It's me," she whispered, crying softly. "It's me, Norah."

He didn't respond, but his stance eased ever so slightly.

Markings on his neck caught her eye. Ink markings—different from the markings Mikael and Soren wore, yet they seemed familiar. When he noticed her gaze on them, he reached up to cover them and pulled back, his alarm returning. He retreated farther into the shadows.

"Wait!" she called to him. "Alexander!"

But he stepped backward, into the darkness, and disappeared.

"Wait! Don't go!" She ran past the columns and into the shadowed hall, looking desperately for him. "Alexander!"

The darkness swirled around her, and she woke abruptly, sitting up at the table beside Alexander's body once again. She jerked her head to her right, and then her left, scanning the room. She was alone. A cold sweat beaded on her brow, and her heart thundered in her chest. She forced herself to take deep breaths, willing back the calm.

She'd been dreaming.

But it had felt so real.

She wiped her face. Mikael's cloak lay around her. He must have come back to check on her. How long had she been there? It was still night.

"Norah."

She jumped at the voice behind her and turned. "Adrian," she said breathlessly.

His face was pale and hollowed from grieving, his eyes without the light they normally held. Her heart broke for him. She rose from the bench beside Alexander, ignoring the stiff ache in her muscles from sitting all night.

His eyes traveled over Alexander's body, then back to her, and his nostrils flared. The ache in her heart grew to a pain as her pulse quickened. She tried to form some kind of apology—where could she even start? But as her mouth struggled to shape the words that didn't exist, his face twisted in a silent grief, and he swept forward and pulled her close, embracing her tightly. Her body shook, or maybe it was his. She didn't know.

They stood, holding each other in their loss. She didn't know for how long. She didn't care. That he would embrace her at all brought another wave of emotion—she hadn't lost him too.

When their tears ran dry, they both sat on the bench by the table, clasping each other's hands. Silence filled the room. She was glad the keepers had cleaned Alexander—glad that Adrian didn't have to see him again in that state. But she'd never be able to clean the memory from her mind.

Adrian finally spoke. "You can't let them take him," he whispered.

She looked at him, but his eyes were fixed on Alexander. "What?"

"You can't let them take him to the pyre. You can't send him to the gods. He needs to stay here—he belongs in Mercia."

"Adrian," she said softly. "You would chain his spirit here?"

"He would want to stay, to watch over Mercia. To watch over you." His lip trembled slightly. "And he wouldn't leave me." He clutched her hands. "Don't send him," he begged as he turned to her. His eyes welled again. "Don't send him."

Norah didn't want to send Alexander to the gods, but she couldn't make that decision right now. She only clutched Adrian's hand tighter, and they both surrendered to the silence.

Adrian left just as the faint light of morning peeked over the horizon. Norah knew she needed to go clean up; she still had Alexander's blood on her skin.

She could only stare at him lying on the table. What would she do now? She'd never imagined her life without him. A life apart from him, yes, but never a life without him. Adrian's ask came back to her. Would she send him to the gods? Would Alexander want to go?

"What do you want me to do?" she whispered.

He'd always been a man of faith.

"Surely you want to join the gods. You deserve to join them, to bask in glory."

But Alexander had never been a man for glory. He was a man of duty, of sacrifice. He wouldn't want to leave Mercia, but could she really keep him from the gods? And what would she do otherwise? Mercia didn't bury their dead. She couldn't put him in the Hall of Souls—the tomb of Mercia's kings and queens.

How could she decide? That she needed to decide at all made anger flash through her.

"Damn you," she whispered. "I'll never forgive you for this."

Tears threatened again, and she laid her head forward onto his shoulder. This couldn't be real. He couldn't be gone. The bewilderment of grief was overwhelming, and exhaustion still pervaded her. All of it was too much, and she couldn't be there anymore.

Norah walked out of the mortium and into the rising sun, her legs numb. She kept her head down, shielding her eyes from the brightness. Bhastian and Kiran were at her side in a moment, but she waved them back.

"Please," she said softly. Space. She needed space and quiet and stillness. And darkness. It was too bright outside.

She didn't remember the walk to her chamber, only that when she reached it, it was empty. No one would have expected her there.

Norah stood. It was the first time she'd been back in her chamber since she'd returned to Mercia. When she'd been there last, it was before she'd fled. When she'd been there last, Alexander had been alive. She pressed her eyes closed—she couldn't think about that right now. She needed to hold herself together.

Norah glanced around the chamber and the adjoining bathroom. She desperately needed a bath, but the energy escaped her. The bed was too inviting, and she let herself fall back onto it. Just for a moment. She closed her eyes and gave in to her sorrow again.

A whisper stirred in her spirit, and she opened her eyes. She blinked, focusing. She lay in her bed in the middle of a tree-lined path. Slowly, she sat up. It was summer. Norah loved the summer. Was it summer already? She couldn't remember.

She dropped her legs over the edge of the bed and stood. Her mind was in a haze. Was she dreaming? Where was she? Flowers of all colors surrounded her. She closed her eyes and breathed in, but she couldn't smell their fragrance. Almost, but not quite. Puzzled, she opened her eyes again, and she saw him.

He stood at the end of the path between the rows of trees.

Alexander. She smiled.

She hadn't seen him since she'd left Mercia. No, that wasn't right... The haze in her mind cleared.

Alexander.

Her breath seized in her chest. Alexander was dead. *Dead*. And she was in Mercia. But where? And where was the mortium? Where was his body? Was this his body, alive again somehow? She swept her eyes around her. The bed she'd risen from was gone. Only the tree-lined path remained, and Alexander stood at the end of it. Another dream?

It didn't feel like a dream.

She started slowly toward him, not daring to take her eyes from him for fear that he would disappear again. This time, he waited for her. As she came close, he shifted uncomfortably, but he didn't step away.

"Please," she said softly. She feared her emotion might choke her. "Please don't leave."

He let her step closer. He looked... not like in the dream before, but more like himself now. He was dressed in his Mercian battle armor, everything but the head of the Northern bear, and his hair wasn't clipped quite so short. The markings on his skin were gone.

She searched his face for the affection he'd held in life, but she found none. Tears threatened. "Am I a stranger to you now?" she whispered.

He watched her curiously but didn't answer.

"Say something. How are you here?"

His silence crushed her.

"Say something," she begged him.

But there was only emptiness. Norah stepped closer. He wasn't really there, she told herself. She reached out. He leaned back but didn't completely avoid her, letting her touch find him.

She sucked in a breath as her fingers met the hardness of his body. How was this possible? How could she feel him? She spread her hand wide against his chest. But his eyes still held no knowing, no recognition.

Alexander reached up and caught her wrist. His message was clear: *Enough.* He brought her hand down but didn't release her as he pulled something from his pocket.

A vial of a red tonic.

No, not tonic. *Blood.*

He removed the top of the vial, then spread her hand wide and smeared a drop across her palm. His eyes burned a brilliant blue as he closed her hand in his. Her breath came faster, and he leaned closer, then closer still. He reached up and brushed his fingers over her eyes, bidding her to close them. And she did.

Her mind shuddered.

Norah woke with a start, and again found herself on her bed inside her chamber. Her breaths came fast, her lungs struggling for air. Had she been dreaming? She opened her hand and glanced at her palm, but there was no blood smear. No tree-lined path. No summer. No life in Alexander's body.

But she'd *felt* him. No, that was the madness coming through, the lack of sleep. She clutched her hands to her chest. Her grief was playing tricks on her. She took a deep inhale to focus herself.

She heard footfalls, and she sat up, but she didn't need to look to know who it was. Mikael. She knew his sound and welcomed the comfort that came with it. He'd help calm her mind. She pushed herself to stand.

He stepped from around the hanging panels to the bed and met her before she could find the strength to move to him. The warmth of his arms came around her, pulling her close. She reached up and held on to him. Gods, she needed him.

"Salara," he said softly. "You should eat something. Bathe. Rest."

There would be no rest. "I can't."

"You have to take care of yourself."

But there were so many other things she had to do first. "I have to figure out what I'm going to do with Alexander."

"Caspian is looking after him. You have time."

Caspian. She hadn't seen him since she'd left him wounded by the library. If he was tending Alexander, then he was doing better. And she could trust him, until she could think. Until she could figure out what to do.

"You need to eat."

"I'm not hungry."

He held her tightly. "Let's at least get you in the bath."

Finally, she nodded.

The door opened again, and Serene stepped inside. Her Mercian maid greeted her with tears in her eyes before moving quickly to prepare a bath. It was the first time she'd seen Serene since returning, and while she was happy to see her, she couldn't muster the energy of joy. Serene said something, but Norah wasn't sure what, and she couldn't bring herself to answer.

Norah stood numbly as Mikael pulled the tie from her hair and gently worked out the braid. Then he loosened the back of her gown and helped her step out of it.

Serene returned, but Mikael said, "I'll tend her." Then he led Norah to the bath.

She sank into the tub and tinged the water rust and brown. She couldn't move, she couldn't speak. She could only sit as Mikael washed her hair and scrubbed the last traces of blood and battle from her skin. Then she let him pull her out and dress her for sleep.

The overwhelming ache of loss left Norah exhausted, and she sank heavily onto the bed. She let her eyes close, but she knew sleep wouldn't come. There were no distractions from her grief in the darkness. Mikael crawled into bed beside her and held her as she wept long into the night. And when she thought she had no more tears, she wept some more.

CHAPTER TWELVE

Norah's legs felt like they might not hold her as she walked to the courtyard. The sun had risen, and it shined its warmth down through the crisp fall morning, but it wasn't enough warmth to stop the shaking inside her. She knew what was to come. She'd been here before—had seen it before—and she wasn't sure she could face it. But she had to.

The Kharavian warriors parted for her. She was glad they were here. It was easier to accept the darkness when it supported her. And despite the sun, this morning would be dark. Mikael walked behind her, giving her the lead to show a re-risen queen, but stayed close and occasionally brushed her back to remind her he was there.

She paused when she saw the gallows in the center of the courtyard. They'd been temporarily erected, but they seemed so sturdy. So permanent. She pushed out a breath—she'd have them broken down as soon as they were finished.

Three ropes hung from the beam above. There would have been five, but James and Alastair were already dead. She breathed a prayer of thanks that she didn't have to watch James hang. Despite his betrayal, she knew how much he'd meant to Alexander.

Norah took her place. Mikael once again brushed her back, and she slipped her hand behind her to lace her fingers into his. She skimmed the growing crowd. Not far to her left, she spotted Evangeline, who gave a small curtsy when their gazes caught. Norah nodded back. She didn't fault her for the circumstance, or anything that had happened. The girl had been a pawn of the council, as Norah had once been. Norah had welcomed her to stay at the castle, but with the death of her father, Lord Allan, during the battle to take back the kingdom, Evangeline had asked to return to her home city of Damask to live with her aunt. It was an understandable request, and one that Norah was happy to grant, and she also ensured Evangeline was provided everything fitting of a royal. It was the right thing to do. Evangeline would stay in the line of succession, should Norah have no heir.

So Evangeline would be queen one day.

The soldiers parted on the opposite side of the courtyard, both Kharavian and Mercian soldiers, and Soren pushed three men forward. Three councilmen. One man cowered behind the other two—Edward, unsurprisingly. Soren prodded them forward with the eye spear on his battle-axe, and they staggered to the gallows.

Edward's panicked eyes found Norah. Her fingers clutched Mikael's hand tighter, but she didn't waver. These men deserved death. And they'd receive it.

"The gods strike you all!" Edward screamed. "Be damned! You'll be damned by Hammel himself, in the darkest depths of the hells!"

The corners of Soren's eyes turned up. He was smiling underneath his wrap. "Good," he replied. "Then I'll see you there, where I can kill you again—but the way that I truly want to."

Edward gasped.

Soren pushed them under each rope, looping the noose and tightening it around each of their necks. The other two councilmen stood silently, but the eyes of all three were wide with terror.

Soren didn't look at her as he worked. After the battle, she had expected she'd have to restrain him from slaying the councilmen on sight, but he'd taken the laws of Mercia seriously, not just allowing a trial but requiring it—albeit a short trial. He brought the councilmen before her in the throne room, and he judged them in the name of Alexander—judged them as guilty and sentenced them to death.

He stood now, all preparations made, and finally looked to Norah. Her heart pounded in her chest. Faster. Then faster still. He turned and nodded to a man on the side of the gallows.

The floor fell out from underneath the feet of the councilmen, and even though she knew what was coming, she flinched. Mikael leaned into her back, ever so slightly, giving her the power of his body behind her. Two of the councilmen hung limply, their necks immediately broken, but Edward squirmed at the end of his rope. A sickening groan escaped his lips. Death was necessary, yes, but it was supposed to be quick. She needed it to be quick.

"Soren," she gasped.

He pulled a dagger and ran Edward through with the blade. The councilman stilled, then swung from his rope with the hilt of the dagger from his ribs. Soren turned back to her, his dark eyes burning.

Norah swallowed the bile building in her throat, and he dropped his head with a hint of apology. She leaned against Mikael, and let his warmth calm her.

It was over, and she could breathe.

Salara only stared at her breakfast as Mikael watched her. She put nothing in her mouth. She just stared at it. But he knew she wasn't looking at the food, wasn't seeing it.

The councilmen had been executed the day before, but no doubt it was still fresh in her mind, as it was in his. It had been too quick a death, too kind, but neither he nor Soren intervened to change it. Salara had needed it to be over, and he'd given her that.

He wished he could give her more. He wished he could give her the Bear. It was a strange feeling, watching one's wife grieve so deeply over another man, but he couldn't muster any jealousy, not anymore. He'd come to accept that the Bear held a piece of her heart. Mikael had the assurance she loved him—he knew she was faithful to him, and she chose him over and over again. And maybe he'd also come to accept that the Bear deserved her love. Maybe it was a combination of those things that let him be at peace with it.

Mikael had foregone his seat at the opposite end of the table in order to sit next to her. He knew she needed him near.

Her eyes closed, and it was a long moment before she opened them again. She swallowed cautiously, as if her own tongue might choke her. Mikael reached across the corner of the table and took her hand. He didn't try to make her eat. He didn't ask her questions or prompt her to speak. He just sat in the silence, letting her know he was there by his touch.

The grandmother sat stoically to Salara's left, across the table from him. Her face was pale, and her lined eyes were trenched in grief. She'd spent the early morning in the mortium with the Bear. This woman had seen a lot of death over her years, had lost many she'd cared about. But Mikael knew she loved the Bear as her own blood and the loss cut her deeply. It was a wound he wasn't sure her heart would ever fully recover from.

Catherine's voice came barely above a whisper, but it broke the quiet of the hall. "When are we sending him to the gods?" she asked.

Salara swallowed again, and her eyes drifted slowly up from her plate to her grandmother. It had been three days since the Bear's death. Mikael hadn't pressed her, but she'd have to make a decision soon.

For a moment, he wasn't sure she'd answer.

Then she said, "Adrian thinks he would have wanted to remain here, to watch over Mercia."

Catherine drew in an even breath as she stared at her granddaughter. "Are you thinking of not sending him?"

Salara didn't answer. Mikael knew she didn't want to talk about this right now. But she would have to, eventually.

"You would keep him from his glory? Give him no rest?" Her grandmother looked at Mikael, but he offered no reaction, no support. This wasn't his decision. The old woman shook her head. "Norah, you cannot."

Mikael didn't necessarily agree with that.

"I haven't decided," Salara replied.

"What is there to decide?" her grandmother pressed her. "You have to send him to the life beyond."

Yes, that was how things were done in the North, but as someone who didn't believe in a life beyond, Mikael deemed a body all the more sacred—it was all that was left of a person. And for a person so loved... He'd laid his father into the earth, and his sister. To have burned what was left—he wondered if he could've done that. It was hard to imagine.

"I'm just not sure that's what he would want," Salara said.

"Not what he would want?" the old woman asked sharply. "Or not what *you* want?"

Salara fell quiet. Anger coiled inside him. He didn't think this was about what Salara wanted—she didn't want any of this—and he didn't like that assumption placed on her.

"And where would you put him?" her grandmother asked. "Are you going to keep him in the mortium?"

Salara leaned forward with her elbow on the table and rubbed her temple. "I don't know. In the Hall of Souls, maybe."

"You can't put him in the Hall of Souls. There's no place for him!"

"I've been in there, I've seen it. There are lots of places." She was close to breaking; he could hear it in her voice.

"For future kings and queens, as they are bound to watch over Mercia. But you must relieve Alexander of his duty."

"He wouldn't want to be relieved!" Salara cried, her grief rising to the surface again and spilling down her cheeks.

The room quieted.

Still, Mikael said nothing.

Salara rested her forehead against her palm. She wasn't in a state to decide this now.

"Norah," her grandmother said, softly now. "You have to let him go."

She cut the old woman a fierce gaze. "How can you say that so easily? You love him too!"

"I say this *because* I love him. He should go to the gods. There's no place for him here."

Salara shook her head. "How can there not be a place for him?" she cried. "He is my lord justice! He gave his life for Mercia!"

"He can have my place," Mikael said, silencing them both.

Catherine and Norah both stopped and gaped at him in surprise.

"What?" the grandmother said breathlessly.

"Am I not king of Mercia?" he asked.

Her grandmother gave a faint nod. "Yes."

"Do I have a place?" It was likely not a place planned for him, but he'd claim it all the same.

The old woman pressed out a breath. "Well... I... I suppose, but..."

He took Salara's hand and his eyes locked with hers. "When I die, I'll return to Kharav, to the earth from which I came. You can give him my place."

Her lower lip trembled, and she brought his hand up and kissed it.

He looked at the untouched plate in front of her. "Are you finished?"

She nodded.

He stood and pulled her up. "Lady Catherine," he said with a polite nod to her grandmother, and led Salara from the dining hall.

She clung to him as they walked.

"Are you all right?" he asked.

She nodded and wiped her face. "I shouldn't have been so harsh with her. She does love Alexander. And she truly believes I'm keeping him from his glory."

"I know," he said.

She stopped them. "What do you think?"

He'd been hesitant to weigh in on this matter. He cast his gaze around and let out a long exhale. He hoped he didn't come to regret this, but... "The Bear doesn't care about glory. He would have wanted whatever you wanted."

"I love you, Mikael. This isn't... This doesn't mean—"

"I know," he said, quieting her.

Her breath came easier. "And you?" she asked. "Is it really what you want—to return to the earth of Kharav when you die?"

He gave a frown. "It's what I've always expected. But... I also want whatever you want."

She threaded her fingers between his. "I want us to never be parted."

He tilted his head to one side and then the other. "Well, we may have to share an eternal bed then, as I've just given mine away."

A laugh escaped through her tears. "I'd love to share an eternal bed with you."

He smiled, and they picked their walk back up again. "Does this mean I have to deal with the Bear in the afterlife as well?"

"You don't even believe in the afterlife."

"Thank the North gods. But if I'm wrong and there *is* a life beyond, I'd want to make sure I was with you."

She held his arm tighter, but she was smiling.

The ceremony had been short and private. Only those closest to Alexander were there to see him placed in the tomb of the king in the Hall of Souls. Soren and Mikael had helped seal it. Adrian had stood silently beside Norah, still mourning his brother. Catherine had given no more objections to Alexander taking a place in the Hall of Souls. Surely she, too, couldn't bring herself to let him go.

After, Norah sat in the gardens. Had she made the right decision? There was comfort in knowing Alexander was still with her, that his spirit was still watching over. Was he watching her now? If she spoke to him, would he hear her?

"Queen Norah," Caspian's voice came from behind. It held an urgency that made her stiffen. "You need to come," he said. "A letter has arrived from Kharav."

Who would have sent a letter? "Has something happened?"

"Katya writes of Rael amassing forces at the border. She thinks they're preparing to attack."

"Where is my husband now?"

"In the judisaept, with most of the others."

The others—those who had become her de facto council—Soren, Adrian, Caspian, and three of several nobles who had been loyal to Norah through the coup: Lord Bosley, Lord Branton, and Lord Semaine.

Norah hurried toward the judisaept. Catherine joined her in the hall and hurried along beside her.

"Have you heard?" Norah said breathlessly.

"Just now."

Mikael was waiting when they arrived. He held a letter in his hand and gave it to Norah as she neared him.

"I have to return," he said. "Their numbers near the eastern pass double each day. I brought the entire Kharavian army to take back the North. Now there's no one to protect Kharav other than the border forces and the Uru. The Canyonlands provide natural protection, but even if a small army gets through, they could take the kingdom."

"And what about you?" she countered. "If they move to confront you on your journey back—alone against Japheth and Rael, you can't take them both."

"I'll march the army back through the Tribelands and through the western pass, then move north so the eastern Canyonlands will be between us. It will take longer to get the army through, but we should be able to clear it before anyone knows."

Her stomach turned at the thought of him leaving her. "I'm going with you."

He shook his head. "No. You just got your kingdom back. You'll stay here."

"We have to leave today," Soren said.

Mikael drew in a long breath, and his eyes met his commander's. "Brother," he said softly. "I don't want to deny you a good fight should it come to that with Rael, but you know what's most important to me."

Soren glanced at Norah and then back at Mikael. He gave a stiff nod.

No, he needed Soren. "You need a commander," Norah insisted.

The corner of his mouth gave the hint of a smile. "I've told you this before, but I'm beginning to think you don't believe me—I *can* command an army."

Norah took his hand. "Of course you can, but I don't like the thought of you going alone."

"I won't be alone. I have the entire Kharavian army. And I'll take Adrian."

Adrian gave a nod.

Mikael reached up and brushed Norah's cheek, giving her a soft kiss on her forehead, then he led Adrian out to prepare the forces for departure. Soren followed after with Caspian and the lords, leaving Norah and Catherine.

Norah glanced at Catherine, but the woman said nothing. She narrowed her eyes. "No objections to him taking Adrian?"

Her grandmother frowned. "Why would I?"

Why *wouldn't* she?

"You've brought Mercia a strong king, Norah," Catherine said. "A fiendish king, with his... fiendlings... but a protector of the North. We should make an effort to keep him."

An emotional smile worked its way along her mouth. "You'd like Kharav, you know."

Catherine scowled. "Don't push it."

CHAPTER THIRTEEN

The fog of her breath lingered as Norah stood in the courtyard in the cold of morning. Winter was almost upon them. Mikael and his warriors readied to depart. The Kharavian army waited on the mainland outside the castle isle. It would take them two weeks to reach the Canyonlands and pass through its maze on the western side as Japheth and Rael amassed their forces in the east.

The Canyonlands posed fatal threats to those who didn't know them. Most who tried to pass got lost, then died of hunger or dehydration. Deep trenches funneled large armies into smaller groups, who could be picked off by arrows from the top. The smaller Kharavian army could defend against one three times its size, or more. But if they didn't reach the Canyonlands, they'd be overwhelmed and defeated with Rael's numbers.

It was a significant risk, but Mikael had left Kharav undefended in order to retake Mercia, and he had no choice—he had to return, and he had to return now.

The Kharavian army was feared by many, but these men were not the monsters of stories told. Regardless of how skilled they were, they were only men. Norah worried for them, and for her Shadow King husband. They needed to reach the safety of the Canyonlands, and Kharav beyond.

Soren stood beside her, no worry in his eyes. How was he so calm? As if they were marching to dinner.

Adrian checked the saddle on his horse, then turned to Norah. He gave her a respectful bow of his head, but she reached out and pulled him into a hug.

"Stay safe," she told him. "The gods watch over you."

"And Alec," he said.

"And Alec," she whispered back.

He mounted his horse.

Soren stepped up, waving him close, and Adrian leaned down. Soren clutched him by the breastplate and pulled him even closer. "This is what you've trained for, Little Bear. Protect your king."

Norah smiled at Soren's nickname for him. She'd heard it a few times now. *Little Bear*. Adrian was anything but little. He was larger than Alexander, larger than most Northmen, almost as large as Mikael. But to Soren he was the little Bear.

Adrian nodded.

"Keep your shield up. You get markings for kills, not wounds. Salta Tau will see them all." Soren released him and gave an affectionate beat on his breastplate with his fist. "Keep well, brother."

When they were ready to depart, Mikael stepped to her. His face was long, and shadows hung from his brow.

"Why do you look worried?" she asked him. "I'm the one who should be worried."

"Don't worry for me. I'll be safe as soon as I reach the Canyonlands."

"I know you won't listen, but I still think you should take a Northern legion as well."

He shook his head. "No. If things go poorly, I want the entire Northern army here with you. We still don't know Aleon's intentions."

"Well, Phillip's not going to attack Mercia with Japheth and Rael still threatening."

He clasped the side of her neck warmly. "I take no chances when it comes to you." He dropped his head and kissed her. "I love you."

"I love you," she whispered.

He looked to the castle at the top of the stair, where her grandmother stood, and gave the woman a nod before mounting his destrier.

Norah watched as they rode out of the courtyard and across the bridge to the mainland and beyond. She stood there, her cloak pulled tight around her, until long after they were gone. And as Mikael disappeared from her sight, she couldn't shake the sweeping feeling of loss, that she was all alone now. *No*. She wasn't alone, she reminded herself, and looked at Soren, who stood beside her.

"I want to start dining together again in the evenings," she told him. "Like we did in Kharav."

"Is your grandmother all right with that?"

"She told me to tell you to come."

His brow raised in surprise. "Did she?"

Damn. She pulled her lip between her teeth. "No. But she probably would."

"Would she?"

Damn. "No." She swallowed. "I just want you there."

"Then I'll be there."

She gave him a relieved smile. "Thank you," she whispered, and turned toward the castle.

Mercia was beautiful in the beams of the morning sun. Even in the cold. It was easy to pretend that everything was the way it had always been, that nothing had changed—no battle, no blood, no loss. Alexander could still be in his study, as he usually was in the mornings.

Alexander.

She could pretend, if only for a moment, Alexander was still there.

But he wasn't.

Norah paused on the stair and gripped the railing. She thought she'd battled the worst of the grief, but it swelled inside her again and threatened to cripple her.

"Salara," Bhastian called from behind. "Are you all right?"

She nodded. "I just want to go to my chamber."

"Do you need help?"

"No, I'm fine," she said quickly. She just needed to get to her chamber and catch her breath. Norah waved him off and forced herself up the rest of the stairs and into the castle. She took the halls as quickly as she could, trying to bite back her emotion. As she reached her own hall and turned the corner, the free fall of her mind momentarily stopped. She spotted a familiar face standing guard outside her door.

"Titus!"

The large guard bowed his head, respectfully formal, but Norah didn't care about formalities. She crossed the distance between them, leapt up, and threw her arms around his shoulders.

"I'm so glad you're here, and well!"

She hadn't seen the Northman since she'd fled Mercia. Or had she? Perhaps he'd been near, she just hadn't noticed him in the chaos of her return. A pang of guilt needled her that he hadn't crossed her mind in the days she'd been back, that she hadn't sought him out.

He patted the back of her shoulder but refrained from hugging her back. Still, she let herself hold on to him a little longer before releasing him. She couldn't handle any more loss, and seeing Titus walked her back from the sorrow's edge that had threatened her composure just moments before.

He cleared his throat, and she finally pulled back.

"Queen Norah, it's very important to me that you know I would have given my life to stop the council. But I wasn't on guard, and I didn't know what had happened until after you'd fled."

"I know." She clutched his arm in reassurance. "Titus, I never doubted you. Not for a moment. I only worried that those I cared about had suffered or been harmed in some way, including you. I'm so relieved to see you well, and back in my service."

A slight smile touched his lips. "I'm glad to be back in your service. And to see you back on your throne."

"How's your wife?"

He nodded. "She's well. As is my daughter."

"A daughter!" Norah grinned. "Titus, congratulations!"

The guardsman smiled. "Thank you, Regal High."

She squeezed his arm again. "I really needed some good news. Thank *you*." She smiled again, and he bowed his head as she stepped into her chamber and closed the door behind her.

Serene was straightening the room when she entered. Norah hadn't said much to her since she'd been back. She hadn't had the chance, or the mental wherewithal. But now, alone in the quiet... she was so happy to see her. She stared at her maid for a moment.

"Are you all right, Regal High?"

Norah nodded. "I've really missed you, Serene."

The maid's eyes glistened, and she smiled. "I've missed you too."

They both gave an emotional laugh as they embraced and held each other. Things would never feel right again, but they were starting to feel better.

"What happened to Vitalia?" Norah asked softly. Her maid had died when she fled Mercia during the coup. "What did they do with her?"

Serene held her hands. "The lord justice sent her body to the sea, as is the custom where she was from."

The sea. Vitalia was sent to the next life in the way she would have wanted. Norah nodded as tears came; she was so grateful that Alexander had known what to do and had seen it done. And here she was, still uncovering his mercies even after he was gone.

"I'm so sorry," Serene whispered. "I know you loved him. We all did."

Yes, Alexander was loved by many. She could only nod.

Norah looked around her chamber, trying to avoid the next wave of emotion that would come at any moment. On the vanity, a small box wrapped with a ribbon caught her attention.

"What's that?" she asked Serene.

"Oh, I don't know. But it was sitting on the balcony."

Odd. Who would have sent her something? Norah stepped to the vanity and picked up the box. She pulled the ribbon free and opened the lid. Inside sat a small glass vial.

A vial of blood...

The same vial of blood from her dream of Alexander.

Chapter Fourteen

Red.

Back and forth. Rolling like an ocean wave. A blood ocean.

Norah sat alone at her vanity, tilting the vial back and forth between her thumb and forefinger, rolling the blood within. The vial was small, no larger than her smallest finger, and tapered to its base. Where had it come from? *Who* had it come from? This was the same vial Alexander had held in her dream. Had he sent it to her?

That would be impossible.

Alexander was gone. She'd only dreamed of him.

Hadn't she?

She set it down on the polished wood and sat back in the chair, wishing for Mikael. She wished she could show him, talk to him. Grief made it hard to think. He'd calm the wildness of her mind and help her make sense of everything. But Mikael was gone, tending concerns far greater than dream trickeries. She'd need to figure this out on her own.

Norah poked at the vial, moving it from one side of the vanity to the other. What was she supposed to do with it? In the dream, Alexander had brushed a drop onto her skin. Across the palm of her hand. Seemingly, that was the appropriate action, but what would happen?

She could ask Soren what he thought.

No. He would make her throw it out. And there was a purpose here.

Alexander had given it to her in the dream. And blood... Seers used blood. Or rather, traveler seers did. Her hand curled around the vial. They had to be related somehow. Her mind spun through her memories—through everything she knew.

When they'd gone to the Wild, both Wild women had thought Alexander was a seer. They'd been sure of it. And he did have some kind of power—a power strong enough to keep the women from entering his mind. What if he'd been a seer and didn't know? Or maybe he'd been something entirely different. If he had power that let him bridge the void between the living and the dead...

Before she could talk herself out of it, she pulled the stopper from the top and touched it to her finger, turning it. Then she brushed a stroke of blood across her palm and curled her fingers closed.

And she waited.

Her heart raced in her chest.

She glanced around the room, still waiting. This was what she was supposed to do. This was what Alexander had shown her. Hadn't he? Or had she imagined it all?

Either way, she wasn't imagining the vial in her hands right now. It was very real, and very... full of blood. The vial and the dream had to be connected.

But all was quiet.

"Well, that's... strangely disappointing," she whispered to herself. Heat flushed her cheeks from the embarrassment that she'd expected anything at all from merely dabbing blood onto her skin. At least she was alone in her embarrassment—thank the gods she hadn't involved Soren. He would have thought she'd lost her mind completely.

Norah opened her palm and stared down at the blood smeared across her skin. Whose blood was this anyway? A small flutter whispered in her mind, like a bird's breath. When she looked back at her reflection in the vanity mirror, she jumped out of her chair, knocking it back and overturning it.

Just behind her stood Alexander.

She whirled to face him.

But the room was empty. He wasn't there.

No one was.

Shakily, she turned back to the mirror and sucked in a breath as he stood looking back at her again.

"How is this possible?" she whispered. She spun back to where he should have been standing behind her, but again, no one was there.

Norah turned back to the mirror. His image crushed her heart. "How are you here?" she whispered. Everything came all at once: sadness, happiness, relief, confusion. It was overwhelming. She forced herself to breathe. "Is it really you?"

He didn't speak. Could he not? Or did he just not want to?

She finally found words. "Does the blood bring you?"

He gave no answer.

Of course it did. She glanced down at the vial of blood. This didn't make sense. It was as if he were a traveler. But not.

"How? I didn't consume it, I only..." She looked down at her palm again. "Is this how you came to me in the mortium? Your blood on my skin?"

He still said nothing, but the slight tightening under his eyes told her she was right. He'd come while his blood had been on her skin. Like his blood was on her skin now.

"I wasn't really dreaming then. And I'm not dreaming now. Are you in my mind?"

The corners of his lips turned up slightly. Then he relaxed his face and closed his eyes. And waited.

Slowly, she followed suit and closed her eyes. And in the depths of her mind, he stood in front of her.

"How are you here?" she whispered as she stepped closer to him. "Is it really you?"

But he still didn't answer.

"Can you not speak?"

Again, no answer.

She knew he was just a vision in her mind. She couldn't touch him, couldn't feel him. And yet she couldn't help herself—she reached out her hand. But where she expected nothing, her fingers met the firmness of his body.

Norah let out a ragged breath. She *could* feel him. This wasn't just a vision.

And then she remembered, she'd felt him in her dream as well.

"How is this possible?" But she didn't care how it was possible, she only cared that he was there. He wasn't gone—not completely.

She pulled back and looked up at him. He was different, somehow. He seemed to recognize her... but not *know* her.

"Is this what happens when you leave life?"

His expression changed, but she couldn't read it. The wall of her chamber fell away to reveal the tree-lined walk that had been in her dream. He gave a slight motion toward it with his hand.

A walk? So... strange, yet not. So seemingly familiar, yet not. Like him. Slowly, she started forward, and they made their way down the path.

"Please, talk to me."

He glanced down at her for a moment, then looked ahead again. How she wished he would speak.

"I miss you, Alexander." The sudden sorrow returned, and she had to stop. Stupid emotion. She hated it. It crippled her. She clutched her chest. "It hurts," she breathed.

But the hurt turned to anger. It wasn't anger at him, or maybe it was. Maybe it was anger at herself, at the gods, at the world. He'd been taken from her.

"I need you." She needed her lord justice. He knew her, knew her heart. He'd always been someone who knew what to do, someone she trusted, someone who listened. She needed someone to listen now.

He took her hand. She stared at it a moment before looking up at him. His eyes moved back and forth between hers, their blue so settling. He was listening.

"I feel so lost. And scared." Just talking to him made her feel better. "Mikael went back to Kharav. And, of course, he's made Soren stay with me. He's all alone."

Alexander stilled. It was as if words were trapped inside his lips. He didn't speak.

"I'm worried for him. If Japheth and Rael attack before he makes it through the Canyonlands, it could be disastrous. He'll try to make it through the western pass. If he does, he'll be safe. But until then..."

Until then, she'd be sick with worry. Should she have done something different? Should she have sent a legion of Northmen? She still could. They'd be only a few days behind the Kharavian army.

"Should I send a legion?"

But he didn't seem to be listening anymore. The garden path around them flickered.

She caught his arm. "Alexander." He stiffened and leaned back, pulling away. A darkness crept around them, and once again they were back in her chamber. Their walk was over.

"Alexander," she said softly, but he stepped back farther. Why was he so distant, so cold? "I don't understand. Have you only returned to take silent walks with me? Why have you come?"

He stepped back, farther into the shadows.

"Are you leaving?"

His eyes held a stone gaze.

"Wait. Will you come back?"

And he disappeared into the darkness.

Norah paced the floor of her chamber. Her hands were sweaty, but chills prickled her skin. She clasped the vial tightly. She still didn't understand it.

A rough knock sounded at the door, and then it swung open. Soren stepped inside. "What's wrong?" he said as he swept the door closed behind him. "Bhastian said it was urgent."

"It is." She swallowed and clenched her hands around the vial. It had taken her two days to gather the nerve to tell him, but *now* it was urgent. "I need to tell you something, and it's going to sound completely mad."

His eyes narrowed.

"Sit down."

He shook his head. "I don't think so."

No matter. Either way he'd think she'd lost her mind. Might as well get it out. "Alexander's still here," she said. "Somehow. His spirit."

Soren frowned. "Did you expect something different? Did you not trap him here?"

"No—" She stopped. Is that why he had come to her? Had she trapped him by not sending him to the gods? No... She shook her head. It had to be something more. "He came to me. I've seen him."

Soren only stood, staring at her. Yes, she knew it sounded mad.

"It first happened in the mortium," she continued. "I had Alexander's blood on me, and he came to me, as the seer did in Odepeth. I mean, not exactly like the seer. With Bhasim, I had to drink the blood—"

Soren's eyes narrowed.

Speed it along, she told herself. "Anyway, I thought it was a dream, but he came back, again, here in my chamber after I left the mortium. Which makes sense because I still had his blood on me. Then, in the dream, or the vision, or whatever it was, he showed me a vial of blood and smeared a drop on my hand."

The lines at the corners of his eyes deepened, but still he said nothing.

"And two days ago, I received this." Her hands shook as she showed him the vial.

Soren stepped closer.

"Just like the one Alexander gave me in the dream."

His breath came with a deep vibration. "Whatever you think that dream is telling you to do, it's a lie. Don't do it."

Norah swallowed. "That's... the thing I wanted to talk to you about. I thought about it, and I was thinking..." Her words came all over the place. "I thought—"

"Don't do it. That's not the Bear's blood."

"But it was Alexander's blood in the mortium—"

"Salara, don't do it."

"I kind of already have," she blurted.

Soren's eyes blazed.

"He came back!"

"Salara," he said through his teeth. "Why would you do such a stupid thing?"

"Because he's trying to talk to me!"

"And what did he say?" he demanded.

Nothing. Her breath left her. "Nothing. I don't think... he can speak. It's like a... a vision, where you see but can't hear."

"That is *not* Alexander," he said angrily. "It's a trick, and a cruel trick at that."

"No." She shook her head. "Soren, I saw him. It's Alexander. I felt him!"

"It's not Alexander." He grabbed the vial from her hand and flung it into the fireplace.

"No!" she cried as it shattered into pieces.

He grabbed her arm and pulled her to look at him. "That is not Alexander," he said firmly, his eyes burning into her. "Don't let someone use your grief to trick you."

Her lip trembled. "Soren," she pleaded.

He softened, and his grip on her arm relaxed. But he didn't release her. He only pulled her closer. "Salara," he said softly. "He's gone. And whatever you think you see, it's not real. Do you understand?"

No. It *was* real. It was very real.

He caught her chin and forced her to look at him. "It's not the Bear."

She yielded, nodding. He squeezed her arm, as much of a consolation she would get from the Destroyer, and he left her to the quiet of the afternoon.

Norah sank to the stone floor beside the fireplace and wiped the tears from her face. No fire burned inside, but the small shards of glass lay in the ash at the bottom.

If this was a trick, who would do such a thing? Who could? They'd have to possess the power of a traveler, or something like it.

But...

Alexander *did* have power. Nothing she could define, or explain; Alexander hadn't understood it himself. But he had *something*. The Wild hadn't been able to see him.

The Wild sisters hadn't been able to enter his mind. He was strong, Naavi had told Norah—strong enough that his shield had covered them all while they escaped.

Was he strong enough to deny death?

She needed to see him again. She needed to ask him. But what remained of the blood had soaked into the logs and ash.

All but one drop, which had splattered on the metal andirons.

Her breath came faster, and her hand shook as she ran her forefinger up the iron and scooped the last of the blood. Then she curled it in her palm, closed her eyes, and waited, praying it was enough.

She imagined herself sitting on the bench in the garden in the light of the sun and waited for him to return.

And he did.

She didn't turn when she felt his presence. She didn't look; she didn't want to drive him away again. But she knew he was there.

Alexander.

He sat down beside her.

"Is it your power that allows you to come to me?" she asked, finally looking at him. "The same power that kept the Wild from entering your mind, kept them from seeing you?"

His eyes flashed with surprise, yet he still didn't speak. But he could hear her. And understand her.

"How do you come through the blood? Are you a traveler?"

The corners of his mouth twitched slightly. Was it the hint of a smile? Was she right?

"How did you get the vial to me?"

He leaned back against the bench. She wasn't sure whether he didn't want to give her an answer or just didn't have one for her. Was she pressing him too much?

"Soren tells me this is a trick." But her eyes ran over every detail of his face, his body. Everything about him was just as she knew him to be. Exactly. An impossible trick, surely.

His hands lay still in his lap. Her eye snagged on his wrist and a small bracelet of tiny shells. She sucked in a breath. It was the bracelet she'd woven for him so long ago. No one else would have known about it—*except Alexander.*

This couldn't be a trick, but how was he here? And why?

"Are you here because I haven't sent you to the gods?" she whispered. "Do you want to go?"

His lips formed, as if to speak, but he remained silent. Then he gave a slow, faint shake of his head.

Her heart leapt. An answer from him. Finally. It was the bare minimum of communication, but she'd take it. She forced her breath calm. "I... I didn't know what you would have wanted. I feared I'd trapped you." She stopped. Her eyes welled. Why was this making her so emotional? "But this is the last time I can bring you back. I don't have any more blood."

His brows drew together, and the garden fell into nothingness around them. She felt unsteady as he pulled forward her memories in front of them and reeled through to the one of Soren throwing the vial into the fireplace. His ability to pull it so easily surprised her. How much freedom did he have of her mind? What else was he able to do?

Anger lined his face.

"Don't be angry with him," she said. "He cares for me. And worries."

His brow creased in confusion.

"He took your death hard. He won't admit it, but I see it in him. Adrian did too. He was devastated. Still is." She sucked in a breath. "Are you able to go to others—"

He stood. She *was* pressing him too hard.

"All right," she said quickly, and she stood too. "I just thought, at least Adrian."

Adrian's name brought no reaction from him, no semblance of recognition.

"Do you not remember your brother?" she asked him.

He stilled, and his eyes widened.

"He misses you. Terribly."

His expression was still one of surprise, but his eyes shifted down as sadness moved over him. How cruel fate was. All Alexander had known was loss—loss of family, of love. Of life.

And she owned a piece of that. What she wouldn't do to go back and give him a different life...

She reached out and placed her hand on his arm. He didn't balk. "I'm sorry," she whispered. "For everything. For any pain I've ever caused you, I'm sorry." Tears sprung from her eyes. "You deserved so much more, so much better than me, and so much better than what fate gave you."

His eyes softened as they met hers, and his lips parted slightly. He covered her hand with his.

"Alexander," she breathed.

Suddenly his expression changed, hardened, and he pulled back.

"Alexander," she said again, and she stepped forward, following him as the darkness closed around her. "Alexander!"

But he was gone.

Norah opened her eyes and found herself again on the floor of her chamber, near the fireplace. She crossed her arms and hugged herself to ease her shaking.

This was no madness of the mind.

Alexander wasn't dead.

CHAPTER FIFTEEN

The young bear rode ahead of him. Soren had charged him with protecting his king, and Mikael knew it was a charge Adrian took as seriously as life. In such a short time, he'd grown from a boy to man, from simple soldier to warrior. Mikael had noted a change in Soren toward him too—a shift from enemy to friend. To brother.

It was good. Soren needed more brothers.

They traveled with only the sound of their horses' hoofbeats. Adrian's eyes swept the horizon diligently—assessing every ridge, every rock, every detail—as they made their way through the flats of the Tribelands. They stayed wary through their grueling pace, with good reason. They had to reach the Canyonlands to protect Kharav, and to protect themselves. Only with the canyons could they defend against the combined armies of Japheth and Rael. Although, even with the canyons...

Mikael pushed the thought from his mind. Kharav had never been conquered. He wouldn't allow it now.

Adrian glanced over his shoulder, and their gazes met. Each day he looked more like his brother—more serious, more determined, more purposeful.

Fearless and loyal.

The Bear brothers were nothing if not fearless and loyal. Caution to the man who fought against them, and fortune to the man with one by his side. Mikael reached up and brushed the scar on his face that the Bear had given him so long ago. It was faint now, barely noticeable, but a reminder, as if he'd ever forget. He'd been fortunate that day to keep his life, and in looking at the young bear now, he considered himself fortunate still.

Adrian's armor bore the winterhawk crest of the North, but the dark color of Kharav, the only armor of its kind. Adrian had it made after Soren had mentioned him taking up his brother's armor, the armor that had once belonged to their father. Adrian had flatly refused. Mikael could understand. There were two ways to honor fallen blood: wear the armor or display it.

The Bear's armor now hung in the judisaept of the North, where his shield hung as well. Although it was a chamber frequently used by Salara and the council for matters of rule, the judisaept was a sacred place. Mikael had known it the moment he'd set foot in it. Along the high walls hung shields of bravery past. He had recognized the shield of the North King, Aamon. The Bear's now hung beside it, the only shield not a king's, just like his body was the only body not a royal's to lay in the Hall of Souls. But he was worthy.

Mikael turned his thoughts home. When he'd left Kharav, he couldn't shake the feeling he wouldn't return. He'd been so sure that the battle to win back the North would be the battle that sealed his fate. Yet he hadn't feared it. Mikael had never been one to fear death, but he did fear failure. He had feared not winning back the North for Salara. Now he feared not protecting Kharav from Japheth and Rael. If he didn't make it to the canyons, that's exactly what would happen, and the stakes were higher now. The North needed Kharav. Salara needed Kharav, especially without the Bear.

Mikael still couldn't believe he was gone. He hadn't wanted to leave Salara so soon after his death, with her still so raw and broken, but time was against him and there was nothing he could do. It would be a grief she would always carry, as would Adrian. The young bear's signature smile hadn't shown itself since the justice's death. All his youth seemed gone. That's what grief did—it stole one's youth.

And Mikael carried a grief of his own—not just the loss of a great man, but also the loss of knowing his fate. He'd always thought it was a curse knowing he'd die, and how. But now with that knowing gone, he realized it had given him confidence and security. To be at a distance from the Bear—at a distance from his fate—had made him feel invincible. To know what his end was going to be meant that he'd known what wasn't. It made him all the bolder. But now... his new fate could come at any moment. It could come now, with Rael and Japheth.

When he'd first left the North, he set his intention on visiting the seer as soon as he reached Kharav. But now, as the journey allowed his mind to think, he wasn't so sure he would. When a man knew his fate, it became an obsession. And Mikael had obsessed for so long.

Their urgency to reach the Canyonlands pushed them to travel both night and day, resting only a few hours at a time, to sleep, and leaving them all the weaker if they did face a battle.

They had traveled rapidly to the North, warred a battle that had tested the limits of their skill and determination, and now they traveled rapidly home. Weary. Worn. It wasn't a state the Kharavian army was accustomed to. Yes, they were warriors—the greatest of warriors—but their strength was the lowest it had ever been. Even the great warlord, Jarik, nodded off as he rode. Still, they pressed on. They needed to make it to the Canyonlands.

On the tenth day, the army's spirit started to lift. Only two more days and they'd reach the pass. Mikael's hope grew with each hour, but he dared not call it a victory yet. It would take time to get the army through. The western pass was narrower than the eastern pass, and it was the less favored of the two. But it was closest.

The sun broke through the clouds. The day was beautiful. Absent the circumstance, Salara would have loved being out for a ride. Only ten days had passed since he'd left her, but it was ten days too long, and an eternity longer before he'd see her again.

A shout rang out.

Adrian pulled up his horse abruptly. Mikael broke from his thoughts and straightened, following his gaze east to see movement on the horizon.

A single rider galloped toward them. Dust plumed behind him.

It was a Kharavian rider, driving his mount faster than a horse should go.

"Rael!" he bellowed as he drew closer. "Rael!"

Adrian cast Mikael a quick glance and reigned his horse closer. Jarik urged his destrier to Mikael's other side.

The rider pulled up his mount, which was lathered with sweat and mud. Blood streaked the animal's legs.

"Rael is coming," the scout panted. His horse stumbled in exhaustion, and the warrior slid to the ground. His legs gave way underneath him, and he dropped to a knee, but he didn't let it keep him from delivering the news. "They come with numbers much greater than ours." He gasped for breath between words. "Twofold at least."

A warrior close by grabbed the scout and helped him stand.

"How far?" Mikael asked him.

"A day's ride at most."

Two days it would take to reach the Canyonlands. One day until Rael reached them. Mikael's army wouldn't make it.

"Water," the scout begged.

Another warrior stepped forward with a water skin, and the scout drank deeply, coughing between swallows.

"And Japheth is with them?" Adrian asked.

The scout shook his head. "Not that I saw. Only the banner of Rael."

Mikael and Adrian looked at each other in surprise. "That doesn't mean Cyrus comes alone," Mikael said.

"We should rest the army," Jarik said. "Prepare to meet him."

"Or we could still get as close as we can to the Canyonlands," Yassar, a field captain, said.

Jarik cut him a disapproving glance. "But that would leave our men without the strength for battle," he argued. "This is an army of freed slaves—many have never held a weapon in their lives. Even if their numbers are three times our size, we can prevail, so long as we're rested."

"Unless they have the bloodsport fighters," Yassar countered. "Or if Japheth is with them. Then it won't matter how rested we are."

"Being closer to the Canyonlands only matters if you plan on retreating," Jarik quipped back.

"No one is planning on retreating," Yassar replied, his tone rising, "but if Japheth is with Rael, and it would be stupid if they weren't, we all know this is a battle we cannot win."

"Unless we split the army," Adrian said, finally speaking.

Everyone stopped and stared at him.

Adrian's eyes burned with a determination that reminded Mikael so much of the Bear.

"I can stay, with half our forces, and hold them long enough for you and Jarik to take the other half and reach the Canyonlands," Adrian told him. "Once there, you'll be able to defend the pass, and protect Kharav."

"Defend Kharav with half an army?" Yassar asked.

"It's better than no army," Adrian said. "And their numbers will be less, too, by the time they reach you. We'll launch a defensive here, and take as many as we can."

Jarik snorted. "You think I'm going to let a Northman hold off our enemy while I retreat?"

"Not retreating," Adrian countered. "Kharav needs you to defend her. I'm only buying you time to get there."

Mikael stared at Adrian, someone he knew so well and yet a man who never ceased to surprise him. This was a solid plan—a plan that could save Kharav. A plan by a Northman.

"All who stay will be lost," Mikael said.

Adrian gave a somber nod. "Yet if you reach the Canyonlands, all will be won."

Perhaps. It was a gamble. But what other choice did they have? Mikael sighed and looked to Jarik, who nodded his reluctant agreement.

"I still have to think on it," Mikael said. "Rest the men for now, and I'll let you know my answer."

The army slept under the last bit of warmth of the setting sun. It was a developed skill of a good warrior—to sleep anywhere, at any time. Mikael's eyes found Adrian, who lay awake, fidgeting with something instead of sleeping—sometimes he was not a good warrior. As Mikael drew near, he saw there was a small parchment and pen in Adrian's hands.

"What are you writing?" Mikael asked.

Adrian looked up, then back at the parchment. He hesitated, pulling his dry lips between his teeth, then said, "Instructions."

Mikael dropped down to sit beside him. "For what?"

Adrian scribbled the last of his writing, then put down the pen and folded the piece of parchment before tucking it into a small pouch that hung around his neck under his armor. "For when I die. If my body is recovered, I don't want to be sent to the pyre."

The words struck him, and Mikael needed a moment. He looked out at the resting army, gathering his words. "You don't want to be sent to your gods?" he asked finally.

Adrian looked down. "I want to see my brother again."

Mikael could only sit in silence. The Kharavians would recover their dead, and honor Adrian's wishes. They'd put him into the earth. Mikael would do it himself, just as he himself had laid the Bear to rest.

Adrian reached into his pocket and pulled out a piece of polished wood. He handed it to Mikael. "Will you give this to my son?"

Mikael turned it over in his hand, and he immediately recognized the small metal plate set into the bottom with the image of a bear. A seal.

"It's my family seal. I don't know if Theisen will ever want to use it, but… I want him to have it."

Curse this Northman. Mikael had become quite fond of him. He pursed his lips as he clutched the seal in his fist, then he held it for Adrian to take back. "You'll give it to him yourself. You're going to Kharav with Jarik."

Adrian's brows dipped. "What?" He leaned back and away. "No. I'm staying. It's what the lord commander would expect."

"Your salar orders you to go."

"My queen would say different," Adrian argued.

"She would not have you die!"

"She'd have her husband live!"

Norah wouldn't let either of them stay. And Kharav would fall.

"I'm staying," Mikael said.

Adrian's face held firm. "Then I'm staying with you."

Mikael knew there was nothing he could say to convince him. This bear wouldn't listen to him. Just like his brother.

It was almost night as Mikael watched Jarik prepare to depart. The warlord would lead half the army under the cover of darkness, getting as far as they could toward the Canyonlands before the sun rose. With luck, Rael would keep their attention fixed on Mikael and not notice them.

Mikael selected his best to send. He needed the confidence that they'd be able to defend Kharav, and Salara, if the need arose. He walked the legions of men, ensuring everything was set. He stopped when he reached Jarik.

"The army is ready, Salar," the warlord said. "But you should be leading them. I should be the one staying."

Mikael shook his head. "Cyrus won't waste his time on a distraction. To hold him from Kharav, to buy you enough time, it must be me."

The lines around the warlord's eyes deepened. Reluctantly, Jarik nodded.

Mikael sighed. He wasn't one for goodbyes, but words needed to be said. "Jarik. We haven't always agreed, but I know you've always had Kharav's best interest at heart."

"After today," Jarik said, "I can't say you haven't." He paused. "I hope the North gods are with you, Salar."

Mikael nodded. He did too.

"I'll await word from the lord commander, and you have my promise—I'll follow his order and ensure the others do the same."

Mikael extended his arm, and Jarik grasped it.

"For Kharav," Jarik said.

"For Kharav."

Adrian stood beside Mikael. Jarik extended his hand, and Adrian clasped his arm in return.

"For Salar," Jarik said.

The line between Adrian's brow creased in confusion, and Jarik held him tighter. Adrian moved to pull back, but Jarik didn't let him go. Three other warriors quickly stepped behind the young bear—two grabbed his arms, and one locked a grip around his shoulders.

"What—" Adrian struggled, but they held him.

Jarik pulled out a cord.

Adrian fought, but with three seasoned warriors holding him, there wasn't anything he could do. Jarik bound his hands.

"What are you doing?" Adrian raged.

Mikael stepped in front of him. It didn't give him pleasure to see Adrian this way, but it was for his own good. For Salara. And Soren.

Adrian's face twisted in anger.

Mikael reached out and gripped his shoulder. "I'm sorry. You'll have to wait a little longer to see your brother. Salara needs you alive." He pulled the seal from his own pocket and pushed it into Adrian's. "So does your son."

Mikael nodded to Jarik and the warriors, and they pushed Adrian onto a horse and tied his hands to the saddle pommel.

"No, Salar—"

"Goodbye, Adrian," Mikael said somberly.

"Salar!"

Jarik mounted his destrier and the army started out.

"Salar!" Adrian bellowed.

They disappeared into the night.

"Mikael!" Adrian's voice carried back.

Mikael watched them leave. Then he turned to wait for his enemy.

Chapter Sixteen

Norah held out her hand for the most delicate of flakes to land. It melted the moment it touched her skin. It was the first snow of the season. It had been almost three weeks since Mikael had left, but it felt like months. She stood on a terrace in the southern tower. She came here often to watch the sky and wait impatiently for word. A bird should have come already to tell her he'd made it to the Canyonlands safely. Why hadn't it come? He would know she'd be waiting.

"Tell me about your daughter," she said over her shoulder to Titus, who stood with Bhastian by the doors leading inside, to the upper south halls. She needed something to occupy her mind between her worry for Mikael and her thoughts of Alexander—*gods,* she couldn't fall back into thinking of Alexander right now.

"She's three months old now," Titus said.

She could hear the smile in his voice and turned to face him.

"Sarah is her name."

Norah smiled. "That's beautiful."

His own smile grew. "She is too. She looks like her mother."

"Thank your gods," Bhastian said with a smirk.

They all laughed.

"I never thought of having a daughter, of wanting one," Titus said. "But she has my heart. We're still praying for a son, though. To carry the legacy."

"What do you mean?" Bhastian asked.

"My family's served the crown for generations. I want it to continue."

Bhastian frowned. "Why can't it?"

"What?" Titus asked.

"Your daughter. She carries your name, no?"

Titus looked at him in confusion. "She can't be a soldier, though. She's a woman."

Bhastian snorted. "Tell that to Katya. See if she doesn't make you a woman."

Norah laughed. If Titus were wise, he most certainly wouldn't say that to the Kharavian captain.

Just then, Bhastian's eyes darted to the sky. "Salara."

She followed his gaze to the horizon. And the bird it carried.

Her heart leapt to her throat. She raced back into the castle and down the stairs. Bhastian and Titus followed close behind. Damn the avian tower—it had to be all the way across the courtyard, above the library. It took an eternity to reach it. She pushed against the large oaken doors of the library, not waiting for them to fully open before sliding inside and bounding up the stairs of the tower to where Rector Tusten would have received the bird.

"Did he make it?" she asked breathlessly as she burst in.

The rector stood by the window, a bird in his hands. He turned abruptly at her entrance. "Regal High," he greeted in surprise, then he glanced down at the bird in his hands. He pulled the capsule tied around its leg and held it out for her.

Norah reached for it eagerly, breaking it open and fumbling with the tightly rolled parchment.

And she sucked in a breath.

Soren burst into the room, obviously seeking the same news. Her hands shook as she held it for him.

"What does he say?" he asked.

"Cyrus moved to attack before he was able to reach the western pass."

Soren grabbed the small piece of parchment.

"But Aleon forces moved south and stopped Rael's advance," she said. "He made it. Mikael made it through the pass." Her eyes stung as she said the words. *He'd made it.*

The note was short. Word that traveled by bird was always short. More would follow by messenger, she knew. She would have to wait. But she couldn't.

Her heart raced at the thought of what could have happened had Aleon not moved to stop Rael. But why? She hadn't heard from King Phillip since her council had tried to kill her. "Why would Phillip help Mikael?" she asked.

But Soren seemed distracted.

"What's wrong?" she asked him.

"How did Cyrus know Salar would be headed for the western pass? The eastern pass is more favorable; the canyons are wider, allowing an army to move through more quickly. If I were him, I would have anticipated Salar returning through the eastern pass."

Norah shook her head. "You said it yourself. Mikael's moving an entire army. I'm sure they've been seen."

"Kharavian warriors aren't seen."

Norah sighed. "I know you have pride in your army, but we're talking tens of thousands of warriors. You don't move an army that size in complete secrecy."

The shadow darkened under his brow. "It's how we marched to Mercia. The Holy Knights didn't know we were coming, and they were some of the greatest mercenaries in the world."

"I'd like to think Alexander had a hand in that."

"That he did," Soren admitted. "But Cyrus knew Salar would go through the western pass. How?"

Norah shook her head. There was so much she didn't have answers for.

The dining hall was quiet, save the *tick tick tick* of their forks against their plates as they ate. Soren had started joining for dinner, as Norah had asked, with surprisingly little objection from her grandmother. Catherine absolutely refused him having a blood bowl, and Norah found herself speechless that Soren obliged her. He did, however, continue to take bites of food from his knife instead of his fork, for which Catherine cast him a constant judging eye.

A week had passed since the news had come of Mikael safely making it through the Canyonlands, but she still awaited a messenger with more detail. Couldn't he have just sent more birds? He'd taken several with him, couldn't he have sent them all?

Things seemed to be settling, yet Norah didn't feel settled. Cyrus had pulled back his forces at the sight of Aleon's army, which was still a mystery, as was the fact that Japheth hadn't joined the initial move on Kharav.

The doors to the dining hall opened, and a servant entered with a letter. "This just arrived for you, Salara," he said with a bow.

Finally. Thank the gods. A message from Mikael.

Norah took it eagerly, but as she flipped it over, she stopped. On the back wasn't the black seal of Kharav but the royal-blue seal of Aleon. She looked up at her grandmother, then Soren. "It's from King Phillip."

Catherine set down her fork, and they stared at each other for a moment.

Then Norah looked at Soren.

"Well, read it," he said impatiently.

Right. Read it. She broke the seal and unfolded the parchment to find the words. "Dearest Norah," she started. She swallowed. Why was reading so hard right now? "I've never celebrated another kingdom as I've celebrated your retaking of Mercia. It was a victory I personally felt."

"Interesting," Soren said sourly, "as he played no part in helping."

"Nor did he help the Mercian council," Catherine countered.

"Perhaps he's a coward all around," Soren quipped.

Catherine scoffed. "King Phillip is no coward."

Norah rolled her eyes and continued. "As you're aware, the situation with Japheth and Rael is escalating, and I have decided to expedite my marriage to the princess of Osan."

"What?" Catherine gasped. "He plans to marry the princess of Osan?"

Norah paused. The princess of Osan? She read the line again as she tried to wrap her mind around it herself. "Osan has a formidable naval fleet, and King Tagasi has agreed to join our cause."

"We have a fleet," Catherine said. "Mercian ships are world renowned."

"Unsinkable ships, yes," Soren cut in. "But Osan has warships with cannons. They would be an asset against Gregor and Cyrus, to stop the route along the channel between Japheth and Rael. To stop them from moving forces. That's excellent."

Catherine straightened. "Finally, something positive from you about Aleon."

Soren's brows dipped. "It's not about Aleon, it's about Osan."

Norah pursed her lips. She was already regretting reading aloud. "I extend a warm invitation that you might attend the wedding here in the capital city of Valour, for Mercia has always been the closest of friends with Aleon. It's important to me that you're here."

Soren snorted.

"What?" Catherine challenged him. "Mercia and Aleon have ruled side by side for generations. It's proper Phillip would have her attend."

"Salara does not come to his call."

"It's an invitation," her grandmother said, "not a demand."

"Given the growing threat against our kingdoms," Norah said, speaking over them, "I pray you'll forgive the short notice. The wedding will be held in the upcoming fourth septimana."

"That's hardly any time!" Catherine said. "Even if you leave tomorrow, you might not make it."

"You can't seriously be considering going," Soren pressed.

"I don't know what I'm considering!" Norah snapped. "Let me finish the gods-damned letter!"

Catherine and Soren quieted, and she drew her eyes back to the parchment.

"I understand if you hesitate, but I hope Mercia and Kharav recognize the recent actions of Aleon as that of a friend and have faith in future intentions. The northern kingdoms are united, as they've always been and always will be. Your support would honor my marriage, and I most look forward to seeing you again, Norah. Please come. I eagerly await your reply. Most sincerely, I am, Phillip."

Soren's eyes burned into her as she folded back the letter.

"Say what you're going to say," she told him.

"You don't find this highly suspicious? You hear nothing from him when you need his friendship most, when you're trying to take back your kingdom. But now that Salar has returned to Kharav, now that you're alone, he calls you to Aleon?"

"He does not *call* me. And I'm not alone. You're here."

Soren's lips thinned. "Well, how does the Osan princess get to Valour so quickly? It would have taken more than three weeks to travel from Osan to Aleon."

"He said *expedite* his marriage. She's probably already there."

His nostrils flared. "Don't be so quick to take him for an ally, or one to be trusted. Sharing a common foe doesn't make one a friend."

"The kingdoms of Aleon and Mercia have been allies and friends for generations," Catherine interjected.

Soren locked eyes with Norah. "Until you set the North on a different course with an alliance with Kharav."

She leaned back in her chair. "But I feel like not going to his marriage would be a slight."

"That's if he's really getting married," Soren countered.

Norah sighed. She didn't know what to believe. "I do think Phillip has shown himself to be a friend. He gave me forces to defend Mercia against the attacks on our villages—"

"In exchange for Bahoul," he countered, "which he'd already taken, by the way."

"He warned Mikael to close his ports, which saved Kharav from fever."

He tilted his head. "Yes, people are capable of doing nice things while still having an agenda."

"Then why would he defend Kharav against Rael?"

"If he's also facing war with Japheth and Rael, he has a joint interest in Kharav not falling."

She shook her head. "Soren, any one of these individually, I agree with you. But together, they're compelling. Phillip presents himself as a friend, and I believe him. I think I should attend the wedding. And I want to see him—meet him face-to-face. I'll determine if this is truly an alliance we can trust."

"That's the worst idea you've had yet," he insisted.

She shrugged. "Well, I'm still going."

His jaw tightened. "Then I'm going with you."

"I don't think—"

"Take him, Norah," Catherine said. "He might be a fiend, but he's a fiend that will see you safe. I don't doubt Phillip's intentions, but I do fear your journey, and would see you back to Mercia as quickly as possible."

Norah shifted her eyes between the both of them, then sighed. "Fine. We'll leave tomorrow."

CHAPTER SEVENTEEN

The late afternoon sun gleamed off the bright city of Valour, the capital of Aleon. It was breathtakingly beautiful. The architecture shone white, like Mercia, but rather than the tall spires and turrets of the Northern kingdom, Valour was topped with patinated copper domes. And unlike Mercia, green scapes and fountains layered the city, creating a garden paradise. Autumn hung in the air, but there was no sign of winter yet.

The journey had been uneventful. Norah supposed that was the best kind of journey, although she would have given anything to keep her roaming mind from the worries of Mikael and Rael. And from Alexander, whose being still haunted her. Her only relief—and it was a painful relief—had been the distraction of Soren's unending attempts to talk her out of going to Phillip's wedding. She didn't think it was possible, but he talked more than Calla along the way. Calla took Soren's side, only fueling him more. Norah almost wished she'd left the girl back with Cohen and Catherine. Her grandmother had already taken to the siblings, pecking them around the castle like her new adoptees.

But Norah wouldn't be talked out of this. She needed to go—this, she was certain, although it didn't settle the gnawing angst in her stomach.

She wished she remembered Phillip. Would it make this easier? Of course it would, she told herself. Did they have a friendship? His letter sounded like they did. How well did he know her? She wasn't sure if she'd tell him about the loss of her memories. Would he know something was different now? She'd have to determine all that when she arrived.

Bells chimed with their entry through the gates, and they rode down the mainway toward the center citadel. The Crest rode close to her in tight formation, but nothing seemed sinister—quite the opposite. People lined the street, throwing flower petals into the air.

"Quite the welcome," Calla said.

Norah raised a brow to Soren riding beside her. "Do they know who I am? Do you think they've confused me with the princess of Osan?"

"If they think the princess of Osan rides with the Destroyer under the flags of the North, you're lucky you didn't marry the Aleon king and have to rule these idiots."

She couldn't help a laugh.

"But really, I think they see a beautiful queen worthy of a rose-petal welcome," he added.

She looked over at him with a smile on her lips. "I think that's one of the nicest things you've ever said to me."

He rolled his eyes. "I'm already regretting it."

As they neared the citadel, an entourage emerged and made their way down the steps, led by a man that could be no other than Phillip, king of Aleon. He was a tall man, lean but well muscled, which was apparent even through a tunic and vest.

"The fuck," Soren breathed beside her, and she glanced to see his eyes on the king. He seemed shaken, but she didn't have time to try to understand as Phillip stepped toward her.

"Queen Norah." He greeted her with a smile. "Welcome to Aleon."

Norah slipped down from Sephir, and Phillip took her hand and brought it to his lips. He paused after planting a kiss against her skin, still holding her, as his eyes locked with hers. The painted portrait she remembered didn't do him justice. Of course, he looked even better having shaved the small animal off his top lip. She judged him to be the same age as Mikael and Soren, but unlike the darkness they carried, Phillip had an air of light. His blue eyes smiled with a boyish enchantment, and his tousled bronze locks fell over his brow. A glow of wild spirit hung around him. He was warm. Likable.

"It's been a long time," he said. "I'm so happy you've come. I honestly... didn't know if I would ever see you again. This is a fortunate day." He stared at her. She stood frozen, not expecting this warmth. He stepped even closer, almost like he might embrace her. Was he going to? His eyes were happy, but they held something else too—a sadness, something still unsaid.

She moved back slightly. "King Phillip." Her voice cracked as she spoke, and she hoped he hadn't noticed. His brow twitched.

He released her hand, and she took a breath—she hadn't realized she'd been holding it in. His eyes stayed locked on her, as if trying to figure her out. Perhaps he'd known her well in the past, perhaps well enough to know there was something off about her now.

But he only smiled politely. "Well, let me show you—"

His words cut off as his eyes moved past her and stopped. She turned to see they'd landed on Soren.

"You bring the Destroyer," he said.

Soren wasn't generally a welcomed presence, and she cursed herself that she hadn't even thought that bringing him might feel more of a threat than a friendly visit.

But Phillip gave a small smile. "A fortunate day indeed."

Norah raised a brow. Wait, what? Most people avoided Soren. At all costs.

"And how do you find Aleon, Destroyer?" Phillip asked Soren as the commander swung down from his destrier.

Soren didn't answer. He only stood with the look of war in his eye and the rigidity of restraint. She pursed her lips. He'd had this entire journey to resolve his feelings of coming to Aleon, of meeting King Phillip. Could he not at least pretend to be civil?

Phillip was a tall man. Not as tall as Soren, and certainly leaner, but he didn't shy from the mountain of a man in front of him. It was bold. Or stupid.

"The demon of war," the king said, not taking his eyes from him. "Or so they say."

Norah frowned. *Partly* true, perhaps.

Phillip stepped nearer to him.

That was close enough, really. She clamped her clammy hands together.

"But you don't look like a demon," he added.

Did he not? Soren could look very scary when he wanted to. Still, her commander didn't answer.

"I want to see his face," Phillip told her, seemingly unbothered with Soren's refusal to converse with him.

Norah's eyes locked with Soren's, and his silent warning scorched the air between them.

She forced a calm breath and a steady voice. "Kharav believes the markings of accomplishment show a man's true self, not his face."

Phillip cast his gaze over the markings covering Soren's bare arms and torso. "And if I require it?" he pressed.

"That's how you lose yourself an Aleon king," Soren snarled to Norah.

Phillip rocked back slightly on his heel. But then he gave a light chuckle, as if more amused than threatened.

"I'd rather you not try to require it," Norah told Phillip with her sweetest voice. And it would certainly be a *try* because there would be no requiring Soren to do anything. Not by the king of Aleon, and not on this matter.

Phillip shifted his gaze back to her. There was an intensity in his eye that made her stomach clench. There was no fear in him. Again, it was bold, or stupid. But then he shifted back, and a warm smile broke across his lips. "Then I'll refrain, as you wish."

She let out an appreciative breath. Excellent. Aleon might see its king live yet another day.

Phillip held his arm out for Norah. "Shall we?"

Here we go, she thought. She glanced back at Soren with a scowl before accepting and letting Phillip lead her into the castle.

"I have to admit, I was starting to worry you might not make it, with the wedding in two days' time," Phillip told her as he led them through the high-arched halls dripping in golden sunlight. "But I'm grateful you're here. The journey wasn't too uncomfortable, I hope."

"The journey was fine, thank you." It really had been, despite its boredom. It had given her a chance to think, to question herself, to convince herself she was still sane, and to question herself again. And now she was here, in Aleon. It all felt so strange.

"How long will you stay?" he asked.

"Oh, um... a few days past the wedding, I suppose." She glanced around them. "Is Princess Daiyona here?"

"She is, and I would love to introduce you."

So it appeared there *was* to be a wedding, and the princess was here. A relief.

"There is a pre-celebration dinner tomorrow evening," he said, "although I'll arrange something for us tonight."

"No, that's all right," she said quickly. "It's late, and I'm quite tired, actually. Tomorrow is perfect. It will give me some time to put myself back together and look somewhat presentable."

He chuckled. "Norah." His hand clasped warmly over hers on his arm. "It's hard to imagine you any more beautiful than you are now."

"Oh, he's a charmer," came Calla's voice behind her.

Norah cut the girl a daggered glance to hush her. Calla shrugged innocently. Norah looked back at Phillip, whose lips held a smile. She feigned one of her own.

But it wasn't lost on her that he called her by her name. And the way he held her hand. So casually. So freely. As if they were close.

Soren was up before the sun, unable to sleep, unable to quiet his mind. The Aleon king. *The Aleon king.* His skin burned with anger. He felt... betrayed, but no one had betrayed him. Deceived, but no one had deceived him. He didn't know what he was feeling, only that he needed to get ahold of himself, of his anger. He needed to get his senses back.

He left Titus and Kiran at Salara's door and headed out to have a look around, not bothering to take Caspian either. He didn't want conversation. He hadn't told the captain about Tahla and the child. And he wouldn't. Not yet. He needed Caspian sharp and focused.

The morning light peeked over the horizon as he stepped out onto the polished cobblestone mainway. Salara had been impressed by the sight of the city. It was beautiful, he'd give her that, with its celestial gardens and utopian aura. Absolutely beautiful. And it made him even more angry.

The morning air was cool, but not cool enough to pull the heat radiating from his body. Why had he come here? To this entitled kingdom with this entitled king. This man was the enemy, not to be trusted. And if this king expected anything other than a fight, he'd be sorely disappointed.

He walked the mainway, toward what was clearly the war office and army sector of the city. Men of arms stopped and gave respectful bows of their heads as he passed. *Bastards.* Niceties wouldn't win him over. He ignored them. Behind the war office, he found the sparring fields and training arena. Beautiful, like the city. Too beautiful. Too perfect. Not used enough, and empty now.

Soren ran his hand along the side of the weapons' hold. The polished wood was smooth to the touch. He pulled open a locker to find a row of swords hanging in a perfect line. Running his finger down a blade, he snorted. Mercian steel. Of course. Kings would kill for a sword of Mercian steel, and Aleon had practice arms of it.

He turned his attention to the perfectly parallel posts lining the field and their colorful archery target markings. Fancy. But no matter. Aleon's archers weren't as good as his Northmen, or even as good as his Kharavian warriors. He cursed himself for leaving Calla back at the castle. His farm girl would show the shit out of these pretentious pricks.

Soren pulled the small battle-axe from his side and flung it down the field, burying it into one of the closer pole targets. *Not bad*.

"Impressive," a voice called from behind him, and he whipped around to see a man approaching.

His pulse thrummed faster. It couldn't be. But it was.

The Aleon king. No guard—unprotected. A careless decision.

"How are you with a sword?" the king asked with a friendly smile.

But Soren didn't like friendly people. And he didn't like Aleon kings.

"Are you up for a spar? It would be an honor to try my hand with the great Destroyer."

Soren eyed the king. He wore only light armor. Pretty armor. Too pretty to have experienced the hardship of battle. And his invitation to test blades—*another* careless decision.

The king pulled his sword from its scabbard and swept his arms out with an amicable bow of his head. Soren could crucify him against the field rail like that. Perhaps he might. He pulled his own sword and looked around the field again. They were alone, and Soren stepped forward to the challenge.

They circled one another, each waiting for the other to strike. The Aleon king was calm, steady.

Interesting.

Soren launched the first attack with a lunge and a powerful swing. He could already tell the king had some skill just by his fluidity of movement. But not enough skill to save him. Soren chuckled silently to himself—he would flay this man.

The king was quick and met his sword with a firm counter before launching an attack of his own. Soren had to shift swiftly to keep from being driven back.

Very interesting.

They broke and circled again, but the Aleon king didn't give Soren much time before launching another attack. He arced a series of swings, and Soren had no choice but to take defense. As they broke, the king shot him a grin.

What was even happening? Anger coursed through him.

Soren shifted his mind. For blood. He leapt forward in a lethal sequence, each strike carrying with it the power of death. The Aleon king met each one with a skilled counter but slowly gave up ground. Soren refused to relent. He wielded his blade with more speed, more power, driving the king back farther, toward the rail. He would pin him to it, soak the wood in his blood. Soren was stronger, but the king was faster, and as they drew nearer to the rail, the king twisted in another counter and spun right, repositioning himself toward the field and out of the path of Soren's drive toward death.

The king gave another grin, seemingly unrattled. "I think you're even better than the stories," he said. He took another step back and paused, a call to end, and slid his sword back in its scabbard. Their spar was finished, and Soren silently cursed his missed opportunity. But he couldn't bring himself to sheath his own blade.

"You're impressive, Destroyer. But I'm not surprised. I know I don't match your skill. Or your power." He gave a sly smile. "And I do appreciate your restraint."

Restraint. Soren could still kill him. He wanted to kill him, more than anything. For what he'd done. For who he was—Soren hated him for who he was. But Salara wouldn't be pleased. The opposite, in fact. Yes, not killing him now required restraint.

The king drew nearer to him. "Do you ever show your face?" he asked. He stepped even closer, but Soren brought the tip of his blade to the king's chest, stopping him.

The act would have earned him a lashing in Kharav. Salar would have flayed any man who raised a sword to him, but this king wasn't Salar.

The Aleon king only looked down at the sword against his chest. Then he gave a light chuckle with a smiling frown. "I hope you'll entertain a conversation with me while you're here. I'd really like to know—and see—the great Destroyer." Then he gave a nod, turned, and headed back toward the castle.

Soren could only watch as the king disappeared back into the safety of the citadel. He let him go, and he cursed himself. What was he even doing? He cursed again. Then, he stalked back himself, his sword still in hand, unable to sheath it. Unable to sheath his anger.

His mind reeled. He'd tried to temper his reaction to this man, tried to act as though seeing him—meeting him—hadn't possessed him with an all-consuming fury. Soren tried to act like he didn't know who and what this man was.

But he did.

Chapter Eighteen

The castle buzzed with activity. Norah stepped out into the hall from her chamber, feeling the excitement in the air, and headed toward the sound of celebration. It was the night before the wedding of King Phillip and Princess Daiyona of Osan.

Cascades of vining flowers draped the hall's arches and flowed down the pillars to the ground, and bright silk swags with colorful bouquets crested every door. White-clothed tables hosted assortments of sweet treats and wine, and she hadn't even reached the great hall yet.

Norah looked back at Titus behind her. "Fancy."

She stepped into the great hall, and a hush fell over the room as all heads turned toward her. Then the crowd brought their hands together and clapped. Heat sprang to her cheeks, and she resisted the urge to crawl under a table. She glanced back at Titus, who was also not one for attention and was doing his best to conceal a scowl. Kiran, beside him, raised his brow.

As she turned her focus back, Phillip appeared before her, taking her hand and lifting it to his lips.

"Queen Norah," he said with a smile.

"You certainly know how to make someone feel like a guest of honor."

"As you should. You were almost queen of Aleon."

She wasn't sure if it was a jest or a jab, or simply a genuine statement. She supposed they would talk about their failed alliance at some point, how she broke their betrothal. Preferably that point wouldn't be here. Or now.

Phillip pulled her hand around his arm assumingly and led her toward the center banquet table. As they approached, a petite woman stood. Her skin was dark, like the people of Kharav, and her hair was black as night. But her eyes slanted back like trails of teardrops. Elegant. Beautiful.

"Queen Norah, may I present my betrothed, Princess Daiyona."

The Osan princess curtsied respectfully with a warm smile and a bow of her head. "Queen Norah. It's an honor." She bowed again. "And I've not forgotten the kindness you showed my brother when he so foolishly crossed the border into the Shadowlands."

"Oh," Norah breathed. She *had* almost forgotten. Not long after she'd first arrived in Kharav, the Osan prince had crossed the border with several of his friends, and Norah had sent him home. Only he encountered Soren on the return, and barely made it back alive. His friends were not so fortunate.

She glanced around the room, looking for the lord commander. If Daiyona knew about Norah trying to send the trespassing prince home, she'd surely know about the lord commander so savagely killing the men accompanying him. It was a memory she had tried to forget, and hopefully it wasn't something that would come back to haunt her now. "Well, thank you," she managed to get out. "And I'm looking forward to us becoming fast friends."

Norah glanced around the hall again, hoping Soren had decided not to come, which was likely. He hated socials. She spotted Caspian, but he stood alone.

The princess smiled. "Absolutely, Your Majesty."

Past their easy pleasantries, Princess Daiyona was swept away with other guests, and Phillip took a place beside Norah.

"She's very beautiful," she said.

Phillip glanced out at the Osan princess and frowned. "Yes, I suppose she is."

Not the response she'd expected. *All right, then.*

"And where is your Destroyer?" he asked.

"My lord commander?" Not here, hopefully, but she wished she knew. "He had something to tend to."

He paused. "Lord commander. Is that what he wishes to be called?"

"It's his title, and what *I* would like him to be called."

He gave a smiling nod. "Very well then."

They stood together, looking out over the festivities. People gathered around tables of tiered food, and more filled the dance floor.

"Why didn't you marry me, Norah?"

Here it was. Did he really want to have this conversation now? *Fine.* "You know why. I wanted peace. Kharav was the only one who could offer that."

"But did you really get peace? You just finished waging a war to take back your own kingdom, and a war with Japheth and Rael waits for us still."

Norah glanced down at her hands clasped at her waist in front of her. Heat flushed her cheeks.

No. She wouldn't let him do this.

She straightened and met his gaze. "Are you trying to rub my naivety in my face? Should a queen not expect her council to support her sacrifice for peace and her kingdom's prosperity, and not try to overthrow her for their own subversive agenda?"

"Our marriage would have given us what we both wanted."

She shook her head. "I didn't want war. An alliance with Kharav brought the real *possibility* for peace, even if I didn't achieve it."

He was silent a moment. "Is that what you've reduced us to? Mere war partners?"

She wasn't sure how to answer that. "Is that not what we were?"

His brow creased, and he pulled his eyes from her and roved his gaze back across the great hall. His face held steady, but his throat moved with a hurt swallow. Then he gave her a polite nod. "Enjoy the evening, Queen Norah." And he stepped away, in the direction of his betrothed.

Her mind swirled around her as she tried to piece together this puzzle of the past. Why was he acting so strangely? What had been between them?

Norah stared into the mirror as Serene pulled tight the lacing on the back of her dress. In a few hours, Phillip would be wed to the Osan princess, and in a few days, Norah would be on her way back to Mercia. And she was very much looking forward to that. However, she couldn't shake the sinking feeling in her gut from her conversation with Phillip the evening before. Her refusal of marriage had more than hurt his pride. There was something else.

But what?

And why?

Her chamber door opened, and Soren stalked inside.

Her brows drew together. "I could have not been dressed yet, you know."

"Well, then you would've been late, and it would've been your own fault," he said shortly, not caring. "Everyone is assembling. It's time to go."

Norah pushed a stray lock of hair behind her ear and turned to him with a frown. "About that. I was thinking you could find something else to do while I go to the wedding."

His face wrinkled in disapproval. "Why?"

"You don't even want to go."

His eyes narrowed. "Maybe I do."

"No, you don't."

"Well, I don't want you to not want me to go."

She sighed. "It's not that I don't *want* you to go. Princess Daiyora remembers—and brought up—what happened to her brother when he foolishly crossed the border into Kharav. You know, when you killed his friends like a manic fiend? I just don't want to stir up ill feelings. We're guests, and it's her wedding day."

"Well, what am I supposed to do?"

She shrugged. "I don't know, whatever you did yesterday. Or take Calla to the sparring field because she *really* doesn't want to go to the wedding either."

"I don't," chimed Calla from the corner chair she sat in. She'd been so quiet Norah had almost forgotten she was there.

He grumbled. "I already saw the sparring field, and tested swords against the Aleon king."

"Wait... what?" Her heart quickened. "Did you hurt him?"

"He made it to the celebration last night, didn't he?" He pushed out an irritated breath. "He's… very good with a sword. Unfortunately."

Curse the gods. She just wanted to get through this wedding and back to Mercia with everyone alive. Specifically Phillip. Things hadn't started off as well as she would've liked, and she feared them going even more poorly.

"Just stay here, or at least out of sight," she said.

He scowled at her.

"Watch him," she told Calla.

The girl gave a smile, happy to be out of going to the wedding, and Norah stepped out of the chamber. Titus and Caspian picked up behind her, followed by the rest of the Crest.

After a series of awkward wrong turns, she made it to the great hall. Soren was right—everyone had assembled.

"I hope they don't do the clapping thing," Titus muttered.

No one clapped, thankfully, and Norah made her way to the front right of the hall as the guest of honor and took her seat. Titus, Caspian, and the rest of the Crest took their posts against the wall.

Phillip stood at the front of the room and gave her a small smile. Despite the awkward end to their conversation the night before, he seemed to hold no personal animosity now. Suddenly, everyone rose. Norah turned around to see Princess Daiyona entering through the double iron doors at the back of the hall.

The Osan princess walked the mainway, toward Phillip. This was what Norah's wedding would have been. This is what her future would have been—queen of an empire, living in a beautiful city in wealth and extravagance.

But all she could think about was how much she missed Mikael. As beautiful as Valour was, she'd give anything to slip back into the comfort of the shadows and find warmth in the arms of the man she loved. They were too far apart, and she needed to get back to him.

The wedding passed as weddings typically do—meaningful words spoken, people smiling… and waiting for the end. They exchanged rings, and the priest wrapped a ribbon around their joined hands and pronounced them married. Daiyona looked at Phillip with a broad smile on her face. She was happy about this wedding.

And Norah was happy for her.

The celebration followed in normal fare and fashion, with no expense spared. Norah stood contently at the side of the floor, watching the dancing as she shoved another shrimp into her mouth. The food was delicious.

"You seem to be enjoying yourself," Caspian said beside her.

She shrugged. "Why shouldn't I? It's not *my* wedding."

He chuckled.

Phillip approached, and Caspian gave her a small bow and left them to take a position against the far wall.

"Congratulations," she said warmly as Phillip stepped beside her.

He glanced sideways at her with a slight smile. "Thank you."

"You're a married man now."

"And everyone is finally happy," he added.

She looked at him, his face pleasant and kind as usual, yet a sadness seemed to linger. One that unsettled her.

"But you're not happy?" she asked.

Her words seemed to hit him strangely, but she couldn't decipher why.

His blue eyes caught hers. "I'm as happy as I'll ever be," he said finally. He gave a respectful bow. "Enjoy the evening, Queen Norah." Then he stepped away to other guests who came to offer their congratulations.

She watched him go.

What did *that* mean?

"I think Phillip is in love with me."

Soren snorted as they stood in her chamber. "Not everyone just falls in love with you."

Norah puffed a breath of annoyance. "This isn't my ego speaking. He's acting very strange. He still seems bothered I broke off our marriage."

"You did promise him an alliance that would help him get revenge against his brother, and then you ran off and married his brother's ally."

"I didn't *run off*," she cut back. "I was abducted. You know this, you were there."

Soren shrugged. "You still dumped him and married his brother's ally."

She shook her head. "No, there's something else there. It's like I've personally wounded him." Norah pushed open the doors of her balcony and breathed in the morning air as the sun warmed her face. "I think we were close. I feel like there was some kind of connection between us. I just can't remember."

She gazed across the city. Norah liked the buildings of Aleon: the tall arched windows that let the sun spill in, the airy colors that bounced the light. Everywhere around her seemed bright and beautiful.

As she looked down, a sight caught her eye. Princess Daiyona's army had assembled—Phillip's new bride was preparing to depart, the day after her wedding. How strange. Was something wrong? Why was she leaving?

"Soren," she called back to him.

He stepped out beside her.

"The queen's leaving." She leaned slightly over the railing, as if it would give her a better view. "Already."

"Are you sure?"

She waved to the scene below. "Well, what does it look like?"

He gave a yielding shrug. "Like she's leaving."

She stepped back into her chamber and pulled her cloak over her shoulders. "I have to go find Phillip. I have to find out what's happening. You stay here."

"All I've been doing is staying here," he protested.

"Except when you tried to kill Phillip on the sparring field."

He threw out his hands. "That was one time."

"Where's Calla?"

"I don't need to be watched."

She pursed her lips. "Stay here."

Norah walked quickly from her chamber, with Titus close behind, through the side hall and then down the curved stair. When she reached the bottom, she hurried down the main hall and through to the front.

Phillip walked in from the outside just as she reached the door. He smiled when he saw her, and everything seemed... perfectly normal. "Queen Norah," he greeted her. "Good morning."

"King Phillip," she greeted him back, trying to hide her breathlessness. "Is everything all right?"

"Why wouldn't it be?"

She gave a small shrug. "It's just... a little unusual for your new wife to depart the morning after her wedding, before even the guests."

The corner of his mouth twitched as he stood in silence for a moment. He paused, before saying, "I gave her the same choice I gave you."

Unhelpful. "And what choice would that be?"

His eyes narrowed. He glanced at Titus and then back to her. "Will you walk with me? Privately?"

She looked back at Titus, then nodded and waved him to stay. Phillip offered his arm. She hesitated, then took it and let him lead her outside and into the gardens. They watched the tail end of Daiyona's army leaving until the red-and-yellow banners disappeared through the gates.

"We had a plan, Norah." He stopped when they reached a fountain in the center of the scrolling topiary and turned to her. "Why do you act as though it meant nothing? Did your love mean nothing?"

She stood speechless for a moment. "Ummm... I don't know what you think you and I had, but—"

"We had an arrangement," he said, cutting her off. There was a sharpness in his voice now.

"Things change."

"Did your love change?" he asked.

Oh gods. "Phillip, I don't love you. I don't think I ever did."

His brow dipped as he took a step back. "Me? Of course you didn't."

Oh gods, oh gods... She didn't know what to say.

"Wait..." He raised a brow. "Did you think I'd fallen in love with you?"

Soren was going to enjoy hearing how this conversation went. Immensely. She swallowed and cursed in her mind again. "Ummm... I think I may have read this entire situation wrong."

His mouth moved to form words, but nothing came out.

There was no way to redirect the conversation. Norah sighed, taking his hand and pulling him toward a bench. "Come, sit down with me." She let him go and wiped her face with her hands as she drew in a deep breath. Where to begin?

First, sit. She sat. And he sat beside her.

"Phillip, this is going to sound a bit incredulous and strange, but I have to tell you something."

He only waited for her to speak.

"The reason I was missing for three years was because my father took me away to keep me safe from the Shadow King."

"Yes, I know. Although you've still not told me where you were."

"That's... a small detail... but, to truly keep me hidden, my memories were taken from me."

His brow dipped. "What?"

"Everything was taken from me to hide me, erasing everything I was before. And when I returned to Mercia, I remembered nothing." She watched as he seemed to absorb the information. "I quickly learned that I was betrothed to you, with the plan to go to war against Japheth and Kharav, save Mercia, help avenge the death of your younger brother, take the throne of the Shadow King, and banish his so-called evil from this world."

He still only watched her. Not speaking.

"And I know my decision to... marry the Shadow King instead did nothing for your cause," she continued. "But I found that Kharav was not the evil kingdom it was made out to be, and I saw a real opportunity for peace. So I took it. And Mikael..." She smiled. "He's a good man. I think you'd like him."

His brow twitched in surprise. "You love him?"

More than loved him. "I do," she said, but sometimes words just weren't enough. "I'm sorry, Phillip, for how things turned out for you. But I hope you can understand."

He crossed his arms and sat back against the bench, staring out at the fountain. Then he gave a chuckle. But it wasn't an amused chuckle. His face held a sadness.

"And you don't remember? Still?" he asked.

She shook her head. "No."

"Then you don't remember our friendship?"

So they did have a friendship. "No," she whispered.

"Or our circumstance?"

What was their *circumstance*? She shook her head again, slowly, and resisted the urge to ask. It was coming. She waited.

He stared into the fountain for a long time. When he finally spoke, his voice came soft. "You must have asked yourself, why the princess of Osan for my queen?"

Yes, that was true.

"Well, first and foremost, it's because Osan will make an effective ally. But equally important, to me anyway, it's because she doesn't want to be married. She wants freedom."

Norah scoffed. "And so you decided to marry her?" Well, that was cruel.

"We made the same arrangement as you and I once had—giving ourselves the freedom to love who we chose, while keeping our kingdoms relatively happy. You were to return to your love in Mercia, as Daiyona returned to hers in Osan this morning."

What? Her mouth fell open, but she couldn't speak. *That* was the arrangement he was talking about. She would have returned to Mercia after wedding Phillip. She would have returned to her love.

To Alexander.

Norah couldn't breathe. She swallowed back the choking sensation in her throat. Her mind swirled around her as she forced the words to come.

"How much did you know about..." She didn't want to say Alexander's name. "How much did you know?"

He gave a thoughtful frown. "Not who he was. Only that you loved another. As I did."

His words hit her like a physical strike, and she swayed slightly. If she had married Phillip, she could have stayed with Alexander. She struggled to pull her mind back. She couldn't let herself think about that. Not now.

"Do you remember him?" he asked. "The one you left?"

Tears threatened, but she blinked them back. "He's gone," she whispered. "He died in taking back Mercia."

He gave the moment silence. "I'm sorry."

She couldn't talk about Alexander. Not now. Maybe not ever, but especially not now. Norah swallowed, forcing herself to speak. "With Daiyona returning to Osan, at least you can finally be with your love."

He sat quietly, but then shook his head. "No. He died too. When I took Tarsus."

He. "Oh," she breathed. Her heart hurt for him. "Phillip, I'm so sorry."

He smiled sadly. "It was a good plan we had, though, wasn't it? A good effort?"

She nodded.

They sat in silence.

"Why did you take Tarsus?" she asked finally. Mikael and Soren had been so sure Phillip was driven to accomplish what his grandfather could not—taking the island trading nation and further building his empire. It fueled their suspicion he would do the same to Kharav.

"Because it was Gregor's primary source of trade revenues. When I heard rumors that he was pressing the Shadowlands for a change in trade terms and that the alliance was souring, I saw it as an opportunity for him to lose it all. It would have been a significant blow to him financially, and perhaps a fatal blow in my favor, as he employs mercenaries and must keep paying them to wage war against me. So I took Tarsus. But with heavy losses."

Norah started to piece everything together. Gregor had been pressing Mikael for new terms and had even ventured so far as to skip due trade. Gregor had been so confident with Tarsus to fall back on, but Phillip had taken that away from him. Gregor needed a new alliance, and he must have found that in the Raelean king.

"Taking Tarsus was necessary," he added. "But I still question if it was worth it. Had I known... what would happen to Jonah... I wouldn't have."

"His name was Jonah?"

Phillip nodded as he stared into the fountain. He let out a heavy sigh and turned his gaze back to her. Gently, he took her hand. "I'm not angry with you, Norah. I thought I'd brought the gods' disfavor with the shame of my sin in whom I loved."

Norah shook her head. "Don't say that. There is no sin in love."

His eyes glistened, and he gave an emotional smile. "I would feel favored once more to be considered a friend again, both to you and this Shadow King you speak so highly of."

She put her hand over his and smiled. "I would love that."

"And I'd like to invite your lord commander hunting with me tomorrow."

She wrinkled her nose. "I don't know if that's a good idea."

"He doesn't like hunting?"

Soren liked hunting. "He doesn't like people."

He chuckled. "Well, will you ask him?"

She pursed her lips into a polite smile and forced a nod.

Chapter Nineteen

Soren's eyes blazed. "If I go hunting with that bastard, he'll end up gutted."

Norah shot him a disapproving look. "Soren, this is a diplomatic visit; can you try to be a little more... you know... diplomatic?"

"I'm not a diplomatic man."

"Then pretend," she snapped, her patience waning. "You insisted on coming. And perhaps no one's ever told you this before, but being a commander is more than war and hate and wanting to kill people."

"Alexander was the diplomat."

"Alexander's gone!" She sucked in a breath. "He's gone. And I need more from you."

Norah moved to the edge of the bed and sat down, struggling against the emotion that threatened. She waited for the calm to return.

"Phillip's not an enemy," she said as she gained back control. "He and I knew each other before I lost my memories. Surprisingly well, actually." She looked down at her hands. "I found out we had an agreement, a long time ago: to wed and let each other be free. I was going to return to Alexander, and Phillip would have been free to be with his own love."

Soren shifted. Quiet came, and they let it hang between them awhile. Then he sat on the edge of the bed beside her. "I'm sorry," he said softly.

"Me too," she whispered.

"Do you regret things now?" he asked. "Not marrying him?"

Her lip trembled. It was the question that she feared asking herself. One that she'd avoided asking, but one she couldn't keep avoiding. "What kind of person would I be if I said I wouldn't change my choice to wed Mikael?" She covered her face in her hands.

Soren sighed. "It doesn't mean you would have chosen the Bear's fate, or that you wanted it for him."

She sniffed and looked up at him. Sometimes Soren was a beautiful person.

"In fact," he added, "even if your arrangement would have played out, he still would have died. I would have killed him. More horribly."

And the beauty rapidly left. She shook her head and grimaced. "I know you're trying to make me feel better."

He nodded. "Yeah."

"Stop," she whispered.

"Okay."

It grew quiet between them again.

"Is the Aleon king with his love now?" he asked. "Is that why the princess of Osan departed?"

She pulled herself from her emotion and wiped her cheeks. "They made the same arrangement, yes. But Phillip's love is gone too. He died when taking Tarsus."

Soren's weight shifted back, as surprised at Phillip's news as she had been, she was sure.

Norah let out a breath. "But now he's making a valiant effort to bring together our three kingdoms in friendship, and I really want that. So, you'll go hunting tomorrow morning, and not bring back a dead king of Aleon."

He stared at her a moment, as if about to say something, then stopped.

"Will you go?" she asked. "Please?"

A protest rumbled from his chest.

"Please, Soren?"

Finally, he nodded. "Fine."

She gave a tired smile. "Thank you."

Soren sat on his destrier, struggling against the impatience twisting through him—he had thought *Salar* took too long departing places. Curse the North gods. They could have been well on the hunt by now, but this Aleon king took an eternity. And this man defined hunting as riding along with an army of men and a pack of noisy dogs. What was this madness?

"Are you ready?" the Aleon king asked him as he finally mounted his horse.

Was he serious? Soren cursed under his breath again. He should have made Caspian come. At least then he'd have someone else to witness this lunacy. And to complain to. Or Calla. He cursed himself again. He'd have loved to see his farm girl outshoot these cowards. But this was better, he supposed. If he wasn't with Salara, he wanted people he trusted with her.

They urged their mounts through the gates, toward the forested hills, surrounded by hound vocals that could surely be heard across the four kingdoms.

Soren let the Aleon king lead, silently judging him from behind.

The lands of Aleon were breathtaking, much like the capital city. Everything seemed perfect. They passed a grove of autumn-laden aspens that made Soren want to stop and stare, but he pushed himself on. Over dreams of rolling hills they rode, then through wheaten grass so tall it brushed the calves of his boots. When they reached the edge of the pine forest, the Aleon king grinned back at him. "Beautiful, isn't it?"

Of course it was beautiful—the curse of this place. It could draw a man in, make him not want to leave. But Soren wanted to leave.

The hounds let out a series of howling barks and raced deeper ahead, into the wood.

"They've got a scent!" Phillip called out, and they all kicked their mounts into a gallop to follow.

They chased the hounds to the base of a sprawling tree, where the dogs barked up at their catch. Soren shifted his eyes upward to find a large mountain lion in the far branches.

"Look at that beauty!" Phillip exclaimed excitedly. He dropped down from his mount and pulled his crossbow.

Wait, wait, wait. "You're going to kill it?" Soren asked.

"Of course I am."

Was this man serious? "Are you going to eat it?"

Phillip chuckled. "I'm going to stuff it."

"And for that, you'll kill this animal?" Soren reached down to settle his destrier, who moved under the rage of its master.

The Aleon king eyed him in surprise. "I thought you enjoyed hunting."

Soren did enjoy hunting, but... "This isn't hunting. There's no need. If you're going to waste a life, let it be your own."

Phillip's smile fell from his face. "I see."

Soren shifted his shoulder, readying to pull the sword from his back. Surely this would be the start of battle—where he would have to kill this king. He glanced around at the surrounding men. He definitely should have brought Calla with her bow. It would be hard getting out of this alone.

"What would you rather?" the king asked.

His question took Soren by surprise, and it made him pause. "What?"

"The morning's still early."

Soren snorted. *Barely.*

"What would you rather?" Phillip asked again. "Duck? Deer? What do you want to eat tonight?"

"Deer need to hang. You can't eat them the same day you hunt."

Phillip stepped closer to Soren's mount, looking up at him. "Do you not see my effort?" he asked so that only Soren could hear. "Can you not manage a little of your own?"

No. He couldn't. He didn't want to. But Soren did promise Salara he'd hunt. He sighed. "How's your grouse hunting?"

The corners of the king's mouth turned up. "Did you see the aspens to the south?"

Obviously. "That's why I ask."

"Back to the castle with the dogs," Phillip ordered out. "The lord commander and I will keep out."

They would go alone?

"Majesty," a fair-haired man beside the king said to him, a not-so-subtle warning—the only man of intelligence among them.

The king met Soren's stare and gave a smile. "Let Queen Norah know that the lord commander and I will be out awhile longer," he said to his men. "We'll return later this afternoon."

Soren clenched his jaw. If the Aleon bastard thought that reminding him about Salara would protect him... Damn the North gods, he might be right. *Might.*

The king's men reluctantly started back toward the castle, surrounded by the flurry of barking hounds. Phillip swung up onto his horse, and then they turned and urged their mounts south, toward the aspens.

Norah stood on the balcony of her chamber, watching the mainway toward the gates of the city. She hadn't been able to sit still since receiving the message that Soren and Phillip were hunting alone.

"Watching for them will only make them take longer," Calla said.

Norah groaned and stepped back inside to pace the room. She stretched out her fingers to stop wringing them.

Alone. Phillip would be alone... without his guard... with Soren... and with weapons. Which would be perfectly safe, she told herself.

"They're going to be fine," Norah said aloud. Yes, they'd been enemies for ten years, at war for ten years. And Phillip had given men to her father to help capture Bahoul from Kharav—the battle where Soren lost his family. But... "The war is behind us," she said, more to herself than to Calla. "And Soren knows the importance of a relationship with Aleon now." She bit her lip. "Surely he can put aside old animosities, now that the opportunity for peace and friendship is within our grasp."

Calla snorted. "Because the lord commander is so good at peace and friendship."

Norah cursed under her breath, and her stomach twisted. Calla was right. Why had she made him go? She should have known.

No. She had to think positively. Soren would be fine with Phillip. He loved hunting. He would love...

Nine hells. He'd love to kill the king of Aleon.

She wrung her hands, her worry growing as the afternoon waned. Where were they?

Movement caught her eye, and she nearly tripped as she stumbled out to the balcony. As she squinted, she made out Soren walking toward the castle from the south. He hadn't come through the gates and down the mainway? Why not? "Where's Phillip?"

"Uh-oh," Calla said. "That doesn't seem good."

"You're not helping. Stay here." She turned and walked quickly from her chamber, down the hall, and to the stairs. If anything had happened... she'd kill him herself.

She reached the entry hall, just as Soren entered.

"Where have you been?" she demanded. "Where's Phillip? And—"

The sight of dried blood down his front stopped her in her steps.

"What have you done?" she asked breathlessly.

"He killed a charging boar that we startled while hunting," Phillip's voice called, and she whipped her head past Soren to see Phillip. She let out a sigh of relief.

"Were you worried, Salara?" Soren asked. His eyes smiled. He knew exactly what she'd been thinking.

She feigned a scowl. "Well, you look like you enjoyed yourself. So yes."

Phillip chuckled as he clapped Soren on the shoulder. "I venture to say he did, as did I."

Soren's eyes darkened at Phillip's touch, and Norah saw the warning. She stepped forward.

"I have to admit," Phillip added with a grin, "if one would have told me a few months ago I'd strike up a friendship with the Destroyer, I would have called them a liar."

Before Norah could react, Soren spun, snatching Phillip's wrist from his shoulder and clutching him by his leathers. "Do not mistake my tolerance for friendship," he snarled. "And touch me again only if you no longer value your life."

Norah's heart leapt into her throat as four door sentries pulled their swords. "Soren!" she cried. What was wrong with him? Behind her, Caspian and Titus pulled their own swords. She hadn't even realized they'd trailed her.

She held out her hand, desperate to settle everyone. "Soren," she said again.

Soren released his grip, and Phillip held out his own hand to stay his guards. Phillip's face was serious now as both men faced each other, poised with fight. Norah's heart pulsed in her ears. This would not end well. Soren had crossed the line of no return, so boldly threatening a king in his own kingdom, but she didn't know how to bring them back to the floor of reason.

They all stood frozen in the silence.

Then Phillip straightened as he dropped his hand, and the tension settled ever so slightly. "I know it takes time to heal from the damages of war," he said, "but I've been a patient man, Lord Commander, and a friend to both Mercia and the Shadowlands. You'll find my patience waning now."

Was Phillip giving him a warning? Was that all? She begged the gods that Soren would take it and keep his mouth shut, but she knew him better.

"I'm so sorry, Phillip," she interjected as she cut Soren a daggered eye. "You've given the lord commander a great deal to reflect on. Thank you for that."

Phillip looked to Norah. "I know you journey back to Mercia tomorrow. I invite you to dine with me this evening." He glanced back at Soren. "Both of you, if you can find the civility within you." Then he gave a short nod and left them in the quiet of the hall.

Soren didn't look at Norah before he turned toward his own chamber.

"Soren," she called after him, but he didn't stop. By the gods, she'd murder this man with her bare hands. "Soren," she called again. She picked up after him, needing almost the full length of the hall to catch up.

When they reached the end, she grabbed his arm. "Soren! Are you going to tell me what happened back there? What was that?"

"He takes too many freedoms," he said angrily.

"He is king!"

"Not over me! Not over you."

Norah hushed him as she pushed him inside his chamber and closed the door behind them. She grabbed him again and made him look at her. She was done with this nonsense.

"What's the matter with you?" she hissed. "Phillip's done nothing but extend the hand of friendship since we got here, and you spit on it."

"I don't want his friendship!" he thundered.

"It's not about what you want. Phillip is the king of Aleon, he—"

"It's *him*! The man in the vision, it's *him*." He pulled down his wrap and roughly wiped his face. "He's the one the seer showed me."

Norah stopped. They hadn't talked about Soren's vision for a long time—the vision of a man he didn't know. A lover.

A quiet came between them.

Slowly, he moved to the bed and sat down on the edge. He pulled the wrap from his head, as if he needed to escape it, as if he couldn't breathe. Then he just sat. Lost.

Norah sat down beside him. But she didn't know what to say.

His breaths were shallow. His voice wavered slightly. "I'd never seen the Aleon king before. But I recognized him from the vision the moment he greeted us."

"Why didn't you tell me?" she whispered.

He shook his head. "I don't know. I was upset. And... ashamed."

"But I already knew about the vision."

His eyes glistened with anger. "It wasn't just a vision," he said through his teeth. "Once it was in my mind, once he was in my mind, he stayed. And when something occupies your mind long enough, it becomes real, it feels real. And he's occupied my mind for a long time."

"But why are you so angry?"

"Because he's taken that from me! I know who he is now." He drew in a breath. "And I'm angry because I let myself..."

He had let himself dream. And he let himself feel for a dream. She had no place to judge him for that; she'd fallen in love with dreams. She sighed. "You haven't even tried to know him."

"I don't want to know him. He's the Aleon king."

"Uh, you're the one they call the Destroyer. Talk about *perceptions*."

He snorted, and it brought a small smile to her own lips.

"Soren, if you want to hate him, then hate him. But you have to control yourself. We need this alliance. And for gods' sakes, stop trying to kill him."

"I didn't try to kill him today."

"Then stop threatening to kill him. I know it's hard, what's happened in the past, and I know you don't trust him, but you have to at least pretend civility. Phillip is deeply offended, and you have to help me smooth things over."

He gave a reluctant nod.

"And, Soren, I don't want you to feel shame. Even now that you know who he is, if he... continues to occupy your mind, that's okay. And if you ever find yourself... wanting to get to know him, that's okay too. You deserve to be happy."

"No one deserves to be happy. We're all wretched creatures."

She put her hand on his arm, making him look at her. "Well, deserved or not, I want you to be happy. I love you, Soren."

His eyes glistened, and his nostrils flared. "Then you're the most wretched of us all."

She smiled as she leaned her head against his shoulder.

Evening had set over Aleon. Norah looked forward to the morning, for when they'd start the journey back to Mercia, but first, dinner with Phillip. She searched her mind for how to mend things after what had happened with Soren. Of course, she'd apologize, and she'd explain... What would she explain? She couldn't tell him about Soren's vision, or his struggles. She shook her head. She'd just have to rely on her own rapport with him and try to build their friendship further. It shouldn't be terribly hard, with just the two of them. She stepped into her silk slippers and opened the door to her chamber, then stopped abruptly.

Soren stood in the hall. Without his head wrap. She could only gape at him.

"What?" he said irritably.

She shook her head, raising her brows in surprise. "I almost didn't recognize you."

"You know what I look like." He missed her jest completely.

"I just didn't expect to see you like this. Or to see you at all."

He creased his brow. "I was invited."

"I know," she answered quickly. "I... I just didn't think you'd come."

He hesitated, glancing to the floor. Then he swallowed. "I wanted to come."

"Oh," she said. Then her breath caught. *Oh.*

"Stop grinning like a fat-fed hound."

Was she grinning? She pulled her lips between her teeth.

They started their walk toward the dining hall.

Norah glanced at him. "You look nice."

"It's not my intention to look nice," he replied, annoyed.

"Really?" He'd washed and trimmed his beard... and was actually wearing a tunic. *Really?*

"What?" he asked shortly.

She smiled. "Nothing."

His brow etched deeper, and a shadow hung over his eyes. "What?" he asked again.

She wouldn't say it. "Nothing," she said again, and kept toward the dining hall.

They reached the hall, where Phillip was waiting. He turned when they entered. "Queen Norah," he greeted her politely, but his eyes widened when he saw Soren. "Lord Commander," he said in surprise.

Soren didn't answer, but he gave an ever-so-slight, stiff bow of his head.

Phillip drew closer. Norah clenched her hands so tightly her nails dug into her palms. He was close enough. But Soren didn't balk. He stood silently, giving himself to be looked upon. Phillip stepped even closer. His eyes traveled over Soren's face—his pulled-back hair, his jaw, his lips—and back to lock their stare.

Norah pulled her gaze away. It felt... too intimate to watch.

"Thank you for coming," Phillip told him. He waved his hand toward the dining table, then said to both of them, "Please."

Norah stepped to the table and sat down. Soren seated himself to her right as Phillip took his chair at the opposite end.

"I am sure you're eager to get back to Mercia," Phillip started as the servants busied themselves filling their plates with food.

She smiled. "I've quite enjoyed the time here, but it'll be good to return."

"You're welcome back anytime." He turned his gaze to Soren. "As are you, Lord Commander."

She smiled at Soren and raised a brow, and he cut her back a daggered glance.

Time passed quickly, and conversation came easier. Norah couldn't help but notice Phillip's gaze roll back to Soren as he talked. His smile was natural and warm, and his laugh light and infectious. And she almost thought she saw the corners of Soren's mouth curve slightly upward once. Maybe.

Norah watched her friend with her heart full, and for his wounds of the past, she felt the beginnings of healing. For them both.

CHAPTER TWENTY

Morning came quickly. Norah was happy to be on her way back to Mercia but sad to be departing Aleon so soon. Dinner the evening before had set them on the course of friendship with Phillip, and leaving now seemed to cut it too short.

She had penned a letter to Mikael in the early hours, telling him of her decision to go to Aleon, of the wedding, of this new friendship, and of her safe journey home—well, by the time it reached him, she would be safely home. Soren had pressed her to write him before going to Aleon, but she knew that would have drawn Mikael in full force back to Mercia, no matter what threats lay before Kharav. She had no intention of keeping the visit from him, but she wanted to make sure she had a good-news message that wouldn't take his attention away from Kharav and drive him to return.

Looking back, it was a risky decision, but one she was right about and glad she had made. Mikael would still be angry, of course, but he would come around to understanding, she was sure.

Soren gave Sephir a pat on the neck as Norah mounted in the courtyard of the citadel. The mare tolerated him now—she seemed to like him even. Two kind stable hands and the commander were all she permitted to touch her. Norah smiled. Soren had a way of growing on a person, even on the spirit of the Wild.

Phillip stepped forward from where he had been waiting while the company readied in the mainway. He looked up at Norah with a warm smile. "Thank you for coming, Norah. And for trusting me. I can see why you wouldn't have, but I'm glad you did." His eyes moved to Soren and then back to her. "Let's not wait so long to see one another again."

"I'm glad I came too. And I'm thankful for your friendship and hospitality. You're welcome to visit Mercia anytime."

"I'd like that." He looked back to Soren, who had mounted his destrier. "Lord Commander. It was an honor to meet you, and I hope... I hope we meet again. And not on opposite sides of the battlefield."

Soren hesitated a moment, then gave a nod of his head.

Phillip's gaze met hers again. "Goodbye, Norah."

"Goodbye, Phillip." First names, because this time, they really did feel like friends.

She gave a final smile, and they urged their mounts down the mainway with the rest of their party behind them. Crowds had lined to see them off, waving them through.

"They're happy to see us leaving," she said to Soren in jest.

"They were happy when we came," he said. "I think they're just generally happy people."

"Did he really just say that?" Calla said.

Norah laughed. "Look at you, being all positive," she teased him.

"I didn't say I liked it," he cut back. When they reached the main gates, he cast a glance back at the castle.

She pulled Sephir closer, dropping her voice for more privacy. "Did you enjoy yesterday evening? Phillip seemed—"

"Stop."

"I'm just—"

"No," he said firmly, with his eyes forward and avoiding hers. "I want you to forget yesterday."

Wait, what? "Soren—"

"I don't want to talk about it," he said sharply.

He was obviously still battling the demons in his own mind. She puffed out a breath between her lips. He wore more armor on the inside than out.

An autumn blanket of red, orange, and yellow covered the hills as they rode through the morning. Norah tried to soak in as much of it as she could. In only a short time, they'd reach the snow of the North, and winter would be long. Longer without Mikael. How long would he have to be in Kharav? As long as Japheth and Rael posed a threat, she supposed. But now with Aleon and Osan joining them, there was hope in seeing him again soon.

"You were right about something, though," Soren said after a while, breaking the quiet.

She cast him a playful scowl. "You say that like I'm never right."

He shrugged, and she rolled her eyes.

"Well, what was I right about?"

"I'm not a diplomat. Nor can I be."

Where was this coming from? And where was it headed? "I think you managed all right."

He pulled the wrap down from his face, and her stomach dipped slightly. He was Serious Soren when he took down his wrap to speak—more serious than usual. He had a hard message.

"You need to name a new lord justice."

A knot formed at the base of her throat at the mention. She shook her head. "No."

"You have to."

"No, I don't," she argued. "I have you. I don't need another."

"Salara, I'm your agent of war. But for the North, for peace, you need another." He paused and looked back at Caspian trailing their unit. "And there is a ready and capable man. The Bear named him his second. Will you not trust that?"

Of course she trusted Alexander's endorsement, although it wasn't his decision. She trusted Caspian, but she wasn't ready to name another. And—she turned her mind back to what the visit to Aleon had almost distracted her from—Alexander wasn't gone.

Snow covered the ground. Norah wished she'd spent just a few more days in Aleon's autumnal beauty, but it was still good to be back in Mercia. Catherine had made her recount each detail of the wedding. Norah stuck *only* to the wedding, keeping her discovery of her and Phillip's arrangement, and other private matters, to herself. She found she remembered more about the food than the ceremony, drawing her grandmother's ire.

Late into the evening, Norah found herself in Alexander's study. Everything was just as he'd left it. No one entered this room. It wasn't a room she'd been in often, but it was one she imagined he'd spent quite a lot of time in. She trailed her fingers the length of his desk as she moved by it. How many hours had he sat here? Her eyes traveled over the shelves of books and ledgers. Caspian would know what to make of all this, and what needed to be done. Why did she hesitate to name him justice?

She sank into the oversize chair by the window. The cold leather prickled her skin through her gown. Had Alexander sat here, mulling hard decisions? She stared out the windowpanes and into the courtyard below.

No.

She stood and moved back to his desk, easing herself into the chair behind it. This was where he'd done his work. She brushed her hands across the top of the desk, over the parchments and maps strewn across the wood.

"Norah!" Catherine's voice came urgently as she burst in. "There you are. What are you even doing in here? I've been looking all over for you."

She silently cursed herself. Now what? "Why? What's wrong?"

"You have to come."

"Where?" What was so urgent? Her stomach knotted as her mind turned to Mikael. "Has something happened?"

"Samuel's had a vision." Catherine waved her up. "Quickly!"

The seer? "What is it?" she asked as she followed her grandmother out of Alexander's study, through the castle, into the courtyard, and around to the seer's gallery.

"You have to see."

Norah wanted to shake her. Why couldn't she just tell her?

They reached the gallery, and Catherine maneuvered through the narrow walkway and the stacks of paintings as if she'd done so a hundred times. Norah bumped a few trying to keep up as she followed her to the back room.

Samuel looked up as they entered, his face pale, his lips pressed in silent worry. He held a paintbrush in his hand—he hadn't even finished. What had been so urgent? As Norah stepped around it, her breath left her lungs.

In the center of the canvas stood Alexander.

In his hand, he held a horned helm, bloodied and separated from its wearer. Her stomach twisted. She thought she might be sick.

She knew the dark, armored body that lay at his feet—a body she knew as well as her own.

Alexander's eyes blazed in triumphant hatred, staring off the canvas at her. A deep shudder gripped her spine. She reached out and clutched Samuel's chair for balance.

No.

"This isn't possible," she whispered. Tears stung her eyes. How had this vision not perished with Alexander? Was Mikael still in danger? Had his fate not changed? "Maybe... maybe it's an old vision?"

Samuel shook his head. "The power that carries this vision is still very much alive. And with its detail... it's very strong. Stronger than it's ever been."

Norah couldn't stop her shaking. "Get the lord commander," she whispered.

Samuel stood frozen.

"Get him!" she cried.

He quickly shuffled from the room, still holding his brush.

Norah shook her head. "This can't be," she said. Even if Alexander still lived, he wouldn't do this. He wouldn't take Mikael from her. Would he? But if he wasn't himself...

And there was something strange about this vision. Alexander's hair was cut shorter than how he'd normally worn it. And he wasn't wearing his signature battle armor with the pauldron of the great Northern bear. Instead, he was armored in black and red. Her eyes narrowed. Markings on the skin of his neck just above his breastplate caught her attention, as did those on his wrists peeking out from under the armor along his forearm. She'd seen these markings before...

Catherine had moved to the next room and was sifting feverishly through all the new paintings Samuel had done.

Soren charged in with Samuel close behind. He knocked back stacks of paintings along the narrow path as he made his way through the gallery, but when he reached Norah and saw the image, he stopped.

She gave him a moment to comprehend what he was looking at before asking, "How is this possible?"

He shook his head. "It's not. The Bear's dead."

"But what if he's not?" she whispered, wary of Catherine in the room nearby. "I know I saw him. I know he came to me."

"Salara," he said, low. His lips moved to protest more, but he said nothing else. He didn't believe her; he didn't believe she called Alexander with the blood.

"Then explain this," she pressed. "How can you not believe it now?"

"I don't believe that's the Bear."

"Because, as you like to remind me, he's dead?" she snapped.

He clasped her shoulders and made her look at him. "No," he said. "Because I know him. I would trust the Bear with Salar's life, as I would my own. That is not him." He looked back to the painting. "But I will find out who it is."

The day seemed to have gotten colder as Norah walked toward her chamber. Her mind and her stomach twisted all at once. She needed Mikael back. She needed to see him, hold him, keep him from this cursed fate that refused to release him.

She reached her chamber and pulled off her cloak before even fully getting through the door.

And stopped.

On her vanity was a small package with a ribbon. She didn't have to open it to know what was inside.

A vial of blood.

CHAPTER TWENTY-ONE

Norah clutched the vial in her hand, her thumb numb from pressing it against the decorative beveled point at its top. She lay on her back across the bed in her chamber as she stared up at the ceiling.

They were supposed to be past this, past the vision. Mikael was supposed to be safe.

The cool air sat stagnant around her. It was suffocating.

How could this be Mikael's fate still?

And Alexander. Soren was so certain there was someone else behind it all—someone tricking her. But the vision in the painting had been clear, as had the one in her mind. It was Alexander.

Norah sat up and looked at the vial in her hand. She tilted it to one side, then the other. She knew Alexander, more than anyone else. She would know if it was him, or if it wasn't. Wouldn't she?

She would.

Then why was she doubting?

She needed to see him again. She would know. She would know if it was him. Norah clutched the vial tighter. She would know, she told herself again.

Before she could talk herself out of it, she dabbed a smear of blood across her palm and closed her eyes.

Her skin prickled with nervousness. This was a stupid idea. Soren would rage through the floorboards if he found out.

No, it wasn't stupid. She had to see Alexander. She needed to know how he came to her, and if he truly posed a threat to Mikael.

She waited, but all was quiet.

This was a stupid idea.

Her pulse quickened. It wasn't too late. She could wipe off the blood.

But she didn't.

And then she felt him.

He entered her mind like a gentle breeze, not as invasive as the traveler seers Nemus and Bhasim. He entered softly, gracefully, as if it were natural. As if he'd done it a thousand times.

He stood in front of her, in normal attire—dark brown breeches with a white, long-sleeved tunic. He looked every bit the Alexander she knew.

Norah eyed him warily, then rose from where she had been sitting on the bed. She studied him—every part of him, every detail.

He seemed to know this was a different calling, a different visit. He didn't speak, but he waited patiently.

Norah stepped silently to him. Her eyes moved over his face, his hair, his eyes, his mouth. To his chest and down his front and back up. Around him, she walked, moving slowly. Every line, every detail—it was everything she knew. And yet something she didn't... Something wasn't quite right. She moved closer as she came back around in front of him.

Still, he waited.

Norah reached out and took his hand. She expected him to pull away, but he didn't. Unlike the previous visits, he was... amenable. She pushed up the sleeve of his tunic and searched his arm, looking for the markings she'd seen in the painting. There were none. Her eyes moved to his neck, and she reached and pulled down his collar. No markings were on his skin.

He stood, unmoving.

She released him. The Alexander in front of her was not the Alexander in the painting. His eyes didn't hold the same hatred, the same rage.

"How are you here?" she asked him.

A question he wouldn't answer.

Yes or no questions, she told herself. "Can you come whenever you want?"

He eyed her for a moment, then gave a single shake of his head. *No.*

Her pulse quickened. "You need the blood."

Only a single nod in reply. *Yes.*

He was talking to her. Two answers now. This was further than she'd gotten with him before. He was *talking*. Her heart beat faster. "But how did you send it to me? How can you... engage?"

No answer.

She sighed, frustrated. "Is it *your* blood?"

He pulled back slightly. His mouth opened, then closed. Then he stilled. He wasn't going to answer.

Of course he wouldn't. Because it wasn't his blood.

She brought her hand to her forehead, clutching her temples. She should have listened to Soren.

But his touch on her arm made her pause. He pulled her hand down for her to look at him.

Then he gave a nod.

Her eyes narrowed. Was he answering her? "Yes, it's your blood?"

He nodded again.

"That's not possible."

He only watched her.

"No," she insisted.

But the blues of his eyes looking back at her—they weren't lying. He nodded again.

She gritted her teeth. "Gods, why do I believe you?" she whispered. She stared at him. "But your body... How? How is that possible? I saw you sealed in the Hall of Souls. Your body is... there should be no blood to send. And even if there were..." She rubbed her hand over her face. This didn't make any sense. Alexander's dead body was sealed in a sarcophagus, in a hall under guard. How could he reach her?

Unless it wasn't Alexander. Soren was so sure. But as she looked at him, he couldn't be anyone else. There were details that lived only in her memories, things only she and Alexander would have known—the shell bracelet. Yet... there was something...

"Do you deceive me?"

His eyes—she couldn't read them now. They almost seemed... sad.

Just as she was about to ask him again, he reached behind him and pulled out a box. A navy velvet box. Her heart beat even faster.

She knew this box.

Gently, he placed it in her hands.

Norah couldn't breathe. Her fingers trembled as she stepped to the vanity and set it down. She could only stare at it.

Norah glanced back at him in disbelief, and the corners of his mouth turned up ever so slightly. He gave a small nod.

She turned back to the box, finally summoning the courage to open it, and blinked back her tears.

Her mother's crown.

"Where did you find this?" she whispered.

No. He couldn't have found it. This was a vision. It wasn't real. When she left this dream, she'd leave the crown too. But to hold it in her hands, see it, touch it—this was truly a gift, and only people who loved her would know how much it meant to her.

She stood and turned to him, and without even thinking, pulled him into an embrace. "Thank you," she whispered.

He wrapped his arms around her and embraced her back—an embrace Alexander would give, because somehow this was Alexander.

The table was quiet as dinner was served. Her grandmother hadn't said much since seeing the painting. Neither had Soren. But she knew what was on their minds, what was on all their minds.

"I'll head out in the morning," Soren said, breaking the silence.

Norah's head jerked up. "What? Why?"

"To get to the bottom of this. I'll take the pair." *The pair*—what he called Calla and Cohen, who had become somewhat of his little sidekicks. As if she hadn't noticed.

"And what are you expecting to find?" she asked.

"Who's behind this. Who's in your head."

Catherine looked at Norah with a bent brow. "What do you mean?"

Norah cut Soren a daggered glance. She hadn't told her grandmother about Alexander coming to her. She hadn't planned to. But Soren's chastising gaze told her he wouldn't let her keep it to herself.

"Norah," Catherine pressed.

How to explain this as sanely as possible... "I've been having visions."

Her grandmother's eyes widened. "You've seen what is to come? The future?"

"No, not like the seers." She shot Soren a frustrated scowl as she searched for words. Then turning back to her grandmother, she said, "They're not exactly visions, but more like... visits."

"Visits?" Catherine frowned. "From whom?"

"That's what I mean to get to the bottom of," Soren said.

Norah pursed her lips. "I know who it is."

Soren shifted back in his chair. "Salara."

He didn't believe her, but it didn't matter. "It's Alexander." Her heart pulsed in her throat as Catherine gaped at her.

Her grandmother looked at Soren, then back at her.

Norah could feel Soren's eyes on her, but she couldn't meet them.

"It's a trick," he said.

"It's Alexander," she argued, now looking at Catherine. Someone needed to believe her. "He's come to me, as only I would know. It sounds like madness, yes, but it's him." A desperation washed over her. She needed her grandmother to believe her. "He gave me back my mother's crown."

Catherine drew in a breath. "You have it?"

"No, I mean..." This was certainly sounding like madness. "He gave it back to me in a vision."

"You saw him again?" Soren asked angrily.

Curse the gods. This was getting worse. She finally faced him. "How could I not after Samuel's vision? I'm trying to get to the bottom of this too."

His nostrils flared, and the muscle along his jaw tightened.

"Don't you see?" she begged him. "He knows what would have been important to me—something only those close to me would know."

"Everyone knows that crown is important to you," he snapped back. "I've lit up half this cursed world searching for it."

Norah quieted. She'd forgotten about that, and a wave of guilt washed over her. Still, it changed nothing of how she felt. Soren hadn't been there—he hadn't seen Alexander like she had.

Catherine's face was hard to read. Did she believe her? Norah searched her eyes... and her heart sank. Oh gods, she didn't. Worse than that, her eyes were the eyes of pity. At least Soren believed she saw *someone*, even if he believed it wasn't Alexander.

She desperately missed Mikael. He would have believed her.

A servant entered the dining hall. "Regal High, this arrived for you," he said as he held out a crimson, fabric-wrapped box for her.

Norah glanced at Catherine and Soren. Who would have sent her something? Soren's eyes narrowed, annoyed. At least it was a distraction to break the tension. She took the box and set it on the table in front of her before pulling the thick satin ribbon from around it.

But on lifting the lid, she rose with a start.

Soren stood abruptly. "What is it?" he asked.

But Norah couldn't speak. She could only stare at the box in front of her. Inside of it was a smaller box—a navy velvet box.

But she didn't open it. She couldn't. If the crown was inside, Alexander wouldn't have just given it to her in the vision, but in life as well. How? How had he found it? And how had he sent it to her?

Soren moved to her side. Norah stepped back as he reached in and pulled out the velvet box. Catherine rose.

He opened it. And pulled out her mother's crown.

Catherine gasped, and Norah's own breath shook.

"The bastard's had it this entire time," he said.

Norah shook her head. "No, Alexander would have given it to me sooner if he'd had it. He must have found it."

He clenched the crown in his hand. "I'm telling you it wasn't to be found. It wasn't lost. He had it."

Just because Soren couldn't find the crown didn't mean Alexander couldn't.

He bared his teeth, his anger growing. "Salara, this didn't come from the Bear."

"You don't know that!"

"I watched him die!" he thundered. "I saw him gutted, the blood run out of him, and I watched him die! And I sealed him in that sarcophagus myself. Even if by some miracle he wasn't dead when I put him in, he's certainly dead and rotting now." His words and his tone were like knives—angry, searing knives.

Her lip trembled. "Get out," she whispered.

He let out a long breath as his shoulders dropped. His face sobered, and he shook his head apologetically. "Salara," he said softly.

"Get out!" she cried.

He hesitated a moment, then gave a small nod. Leaving the crown on the table beside the box, he stepped from the dining room.

Norah's eyes found Catherine's.

Her grandmother opened her mouth.

"Don't," Norah warned. She was in no mood to argue about this any longer. She would find out what was happening herself.

Soren beat on the thick oaken door. There was no answer, and he beat again. He knew she was in there. He wouldn't let her avoid him, even if *he* wanted to avoid *her*.

Finally, the door swung open, and the grandmother stood with a scathing scowl.

"By the gods, fiend, what's the matter with you?" she snapped at him. "Must you beat down the door?"

Irritation rumbled in his chest. "You weren't answering."

"I was walking to answer!"

"Too slowly."

She pursed her lips with a glare that would freeze the wind.

"Take me to him," he told her.

Loathing shadowed her eyes. "To whom?"

"The Bear. Your guards don't allow me to pass. Don't make me kill them."

She puffed a breath. "I'll have you know there are more civilized ways."

Soren gritted his teeth. "This is me being civilized. Now take me to him."

"Absolutely not—"

"Woman!" He was losing his patience. He culled his irritation. That would get him nowhere with her. He drew in a long breath and let it out slowly. "Please. Take me to him. Salara's not safe, and I have to find out what's going on."

She stared at him a moment. "Fine," she said finally. Then she stepped into the hall, and he followed.

He knew where the tombs were, where he had helped seal in the Bear, but he let the old woman lead him through a series of halls. When they reached the Hall of Souls, she waved the guards to step aside. They looked at Soren warily but did as they were bid and let them pass.

Bastards.

She led him down the wide, winding stair to the bottom. The glass of the high ceiling spilled light down to the floor. It had been night when he was here before, but now in the day, he realized how beautiful this place of death was.

Tombs lined the walls, generations of Northern rulers, each within a carved alcove of stone. The Northmen believed them to be watching over Mercia. Were they watching now? He almost smiled. Were their bones twisting in their beds of stone at a Shadowman among them?

He followed the woman to a side dais with a sarcophagus draped in silver-embroidered linen. It was just as he remembered. She put her hand on top.

Soren reached and pulled off the silver cloth.

"What are you doing?" she demanded.

"Hold this," he said, pushing the cloth into her arms.

"You have no right—"

He clasped the top of the sarcophagus.

"No, don't!" she cried—not the cry of anger, but one of pain. A plea. "You can't."

He stopped, then turned to her. With the greatest effort of compassion, he said, "Alexander would want me to find out what's happening. And see Salara safe."

"By wreaking havoc on his place of rest? Destroying it? Disturbing his body?"

"I'm not destroying it. And you burn bodies, by the way. Moving his around a bit won't make a difference."

Her face still held the look of horror. He probably could have handled that a little softer.

"And when did he ever care about rest?" he added, trying to change his approach. "Nothing as it relates to Salara could ever disturb him. He would be doing this himself if he could."

"This is the madness of grief," she argued. "Her thinking that he comes back to her even in death! She's not accepting that he's gone."

"She's not mad," he cut back. "She *does* see something. Someone is toying with her. And I'm going to find out who it is." He clutched the cover of the sarcophagus again.

"You won't be able to open it. It took four men to put it on."

Soren gritted his teeth again. Yes, he knew—he'd been one of them. He strained against the heavy stone and pushed the lid sideways. The stench of death filled the room, and the woman gasped. He looked into the sarcophagus, and there lay the body of the Bear, adorned in the colors of the North. His face was unrecognizable, but Soren knew the golden locks.

This was the Bear. A very dead Bear.

Relief filled him. Not that he actually believed him to be alive again, or to have cheated death. But Salara was a smart woman, and it would be very difficult to fool her, especially using the image of a man she knew so well—a man she loved. He'd been so sure it wasn't the Bear, but for her to believe so strongly, it had begun to eat away at his confidence. And she said she'd touched him, felt him. He ran his eyes over the remains—not this body, she hadn't.

"Sorry, brother," he said quietly. Then he pushed the top of the sarcophagus back into place.

Soren looked and found Salara's grandmother off to the side. She had lowered herself to sit on a bench along the wall. His opening of the tomb had shaken her. To breathe in the death of one lost, that would stay with her. And he pitied her.

Her lips were pursed, but he knew it was to control her emotion. Slowly, he approached and sat beside her.

They sat in silence for a long time.

"I raised him, you know," she said finally. "After his mother went mad. His father... Well, the work of a justice is unending, and so I saw to the boys. I raised Alexander to be a proper lord. He was a sweet child. Kind, loyal. He was easy to love, and I did so like he was my own. Both of them." A tear escaped down her cheek, and she wiped it back.

"You raised good men," he told her. He looked back at the sarcophagus. "The Bear was the only adversary I've ever grieved. And in the end, one of the few men who ever truly knew me." He stopped. Curse the North gods, he was starting to feel emotional himself.

The woman leaned back slightly. "You are surprisingly gracious for one so fiendish in nature."

Soren snorted. From her, he'd take that as a compliment.

She looked across the room. "And you care for Norah, I can tell."

He did. And it was annoying.

"What are you going to do now?" she asked.

"I'm going to take her back to Kharav."

The woman stood abruptly. "Have you lost your mind? Closer to Rael and Japheth? Closer to war? Is that not why you brought her to Mercia in the first place?"

He stood too. "She's in danger here."

"This is her home! This is where she's protected!"

"Yet this trickster of the mind is reaching her here. Do you know how she sees him? He can't just come to her. He needs his blood to touch her skin, and she finds the vials in her chamber. He's getting *into her chamber* somehow."

Catherine's eyes widened, and her breath quickened. "Then we'll increase the guard."

"I already have." Was she really going to try to tell him how to protect Salara?

She shook her head. "And you think her being in Mercia is more dangerous than the Shadowlands? I think not!"

"Circumstances have changed, now that we've confirmed our alliance with Aleon and Osan. And I can protect her better in Kharav."

"Like you protected her from the assassins?"

He grew quiet. "That was a failure I take very personally." He softened toward the woman. He understood her hesitance. "Salara's not safe here. And yes, there are dangers in Kharav, but these are dangers I know, dangers I can fight and defend against. I don't know what's happening here." He sighed. "And I think it will be better for her mind to get away from the things that constantly remind her of him, to get back to the one person who can help her heal."

She stood quietly, uncertainty still on her face.

He needed the grandmother's help in convincing Salara to appoint a justice; she couldn't leave Mercia without one. He clenched his jaw. The woman needed more convincing herself, but what else did he have?

"Lady grandmother," he said as respectfully as he could. "She needs to set up the North so she can return to Kharav. She needs to name another lord justice. I'm sworn to her. I wouldn't press this if I didn't believe it was best. And I know you don't trust my king, but you would be sending her back to the man who loves her above all else."

Her lip twitched slightly as she looked around the hall again. Finally, she nodded. "I'll talk to Norah about a justice," she said. "There are a few lords—"

"Caspian. The Bear trusted Caspian. As do I."

She hesitated, but then nodded. "All right."

Uncurse the North gods. *Finally.*

"And about your king," she added. "I don't like him. But he's a good king, and I do trust him."

Soren gave a faint smile under his wrap. "Perhaps one day you'll feel the same about me."

"No, Destroyer," she said. "I actually like you."

He looked at her from the corner of his eye with a hidden smirk. He might actually like her too.

Chapter Twenty-Two

It smelled like shit—not of the animals as he passed the stables, but of the chaos that fouled the air around them all. Soren knew he'd spoken harshly to Salara, and undeservedly so. She truly thought she'd seen the Bear. Clever bastard—whoever was behind the elaborate scheme. He'd find them. And gut them.

He carried the crimson box that had held Salara's crown as he strode toward the sparring field where he knew he'd find the pair of raven-haired siblings. He'd come to rely on them. Often. Soren trusted very few—select members of the Crest, the young bear, Caspian, and the pair.

Cohen saw him first as he approached, but both came immediately to meet him.

Soren pulled down his wrap from his face. "I've a task for you," he told them as they neared, and he held out the box. "Salara received a gift yesterday. It came in this. I want to know if anyone saw anything."

"What was in it?" Calla asked.

He eyed her in annoyance. Always so many questions. At least they weren't stupid questions. "Her crown."

The girl's mouth popped open. "Her mother's crown? The one you lost when you first took her and haven't been able to find?"

Well, most of her questions weren't stupid questions. "I didn't lose—" He looked at the boy in disbelief. Cohen shrugged.

Curse the North gods. Soren didn't have time for this. "I want to know who sent it."

Where was it delivered? Cohen asked.

Soren liked the boy's silent language. He wished the girl would use it more. He wished everyone would use it more.

"The servant who brought it in said it had been left in the entry of the main doors," he told them. "Someone had to have seen something."

Cohen frowned. *Do you think the sender means harm to Salara?*

"I do."

Calla took the box. "Do you think it's a Northman?"

He let out a long breath. "I want to say no. But I don't know how an outsider's getting through to her here."

She nodded, with her normal determination coming to her eyes—that determination that Soren needed. "We'll see what we can find."

Norah stared at the crown in front of her as she sat at her vanity under the light of morning. She clenched the blood vial in her hand and thumbed the top as she mulled.

How had Alexander found her crown? Where had it been? And how had he gotten it to her? Here. Now. Perhaps it was the same way as he'd gotten her the vials.

When he'd given her the crown in the vision, she'd thought it was a symbol—something he knew would be important to her to show her he was real. But it wasn't a symbol. He had truly given it to her, and now even more questions flooded her mind.

She wanted to call him back, but how many answers would he give her? And how long could she keep calling him? Perhaps indefinitely, so long as she had the blood. But where was the blood coming from?

The door to her chamber opened, and she jumped, quickly shoving the vial into the pocket of her gown and turning.

Her grandmother swept in, with Serene carrying a plate of fruit and cheese behind her. "I thought we could take breakfast in here together this morning," Catherine said as she pushed the draperies wider, letting in more light.

Norah forced a smile. *Great*—a private conversation. No doubt to question her sanity after learning of her visions of Alexander. She rose from the vanity with a sigh and joined Catherine at the small table by the window. Serene poured a hot cup of tea for both of them. Her grandmother flicked her hand, and Serene added a chalice of wine. Then the maid saw herself out, closing the door behind her.

Norah sat. Where would they start? Would she be made to recount everything she'd seen in the visions? Likely. All the while being told it was a product of her grief, a lapse in her sanity.

"It's time, Norah," Catherine said directly. "Mercia needs a justice."

Norah stiffened. That wasn't what she'd expected. She would have rather talked about her sanity. Her grandmother let the silence sit between them, waiting for her to respond. And she'd have to respond. Eventually. She took Catherine's chalice and swallowed a large swig of wine.

"I don't need a lord justice, I have the lord commander," she said finally.

"Yes, well, as pleasant as he is, he's a beast of the Shadowlands. That's where he belongs."

"I'm not sending him back—"

"You'll need him by your side when *you* go back."

Norah jerked her head up. "What?"

"With Aleon and Osan now, you don't need to hide away in Mercia. And I'll not play ignorant, I know your heart is in the Shadowlands."

Her pulse raced. She could go back to Kharav? Back to Mikael?

"However, Mercia needs a proper justice, and a proper council."

But Mercia didn't deserve anything less than Alexander. "I'm sure you've already prepared a recommendation?" Most likely one of the elder lords—

"Caspian."

Norah sat back. That, too, was unexpected.

Catherine took a drink from their now-shared wine chalice. "You and I both know he was Alexander's choice, not that it was or is his choice to make. But I trust it's the right decision."

Caspian. Soren had felt the same. If she didn't know him and her grandmother better, she would have thought them to be colluding. She drew in a long breath. Caspian had been Alexander's choice. If she were to name *anyone*, it should be him.

"Of course, then you'll have to name a new captain," Catherine added.

Or let Soren do it. Or Caspian. That sounded like a justice's task anyway.

"Norah, you can continue to mourn for as long as you need, but see Mercia well. Don't forget your duty, or your people. They look to you."

The thought of seeing Mikael again, and so soon, filled her with a rush of emotion. She needed him. She needed to be home again. He could help make things right, if ever things could truly be right again.

Norah turned her mind to Mercia—she did need to move her kingdom forward, both with a justice and a council. Especially if she would be returning to Kharav. And she most certainly would be returning to Kharav. She nodded. "All right."

Catherine gave a sad smile, then reached across the table and clasped her hand. "I love you, my darling. I don't say those words enough."

Norah clutched her hand through her tears. They were exactly the words she needed to hear.

Soren sat at the large desk in the Bear's study. He'd been using it as his own quite a bit lately. At first it seemed sacrilegious, but thoughts came easier here—in the place where the Bear had planned and strategized. Maybe his spirit lingered, watching over and helping him, like Norah and the Northmen believed. More likely the Bear was annoyed by Soren's complete disregard for how everything had been meticulously situated. Soren had moved the larger chair from the window to the desk—it was more comfortable—and he'd pushed the desk forward to create more room from the shelves behind. Yes, that was more likely—he was sitting in the Bear's irritation. Soren gave a small chuckle. *Good.* "That's what you get for dying, you bastard."

He looked up from his thoughts to see the pair as they stepped inside from the hall. "What have you found?" he asked.

"No one has seen outsiders that seem suspicious," Calla said. "But there was a man who saw this box." The siblings looked at each other hesitantly.

"And?" Soren prompted them.

"He said a dog was carrying it."

"A dog?"

"Large dog, big jowls, short hair, black. No ears and no tail."

Soren frowned. "A dog with no ears and no tail?"

Calla's face twisted. "He said it looked like they'd been removed."

Men were disgusting animals. "He said this dog was carrying the box?"

She nodded.

"You believe him?"

No one has lied to us, Cohen said.

Cohen's read on people was absolute. Soren nodded. It was a dog then. But how had the blood vial been delivered to Salara's chamber? A dog wouldn't have been able to do that. So much remained unanswered. But they had a start.

"Find that dog," he told him. "And we'll find its master."

"Caspian Frey. Come forward."

Norah stood in the throne room filled with the nobles of Mercia. Her grandmother and the members of her newly formed council stood in front, watching the appointment of their new lord justice. It had been six weeks since she'd retaken her kingdom.

Six weeks since Alexander had died.

It felt even longer that she'd been without Mikael. She needed to get back to him. And this was the first step.

But all morning, she'd felt in a daze, like this reality wasn't real. Like she was there, but she wasn't. Why was it so hard? This was the right thing to do. It was the obvious thing to do. It's what would get her back to Mikael. And it was Caspian—a man she trusted with her life and her kingdom.

Caspian stepped forward, coming in front of her.

"Kneel," she told him.

He dropped to his knees and held out his hands, palms up, as Alexander had once knelt in front of her.

"Caspian Frey." Her voice broke as she spoke. "I appoint you…"

A knot formed in her throat. This shouldn't be this hard. It was the right decision. She had no doubt. She tried to start again. "I appoint you…"

Why couldn't she speak? Why couldn't she breathe?

"Norah," Caspian whispered as she stood frozen.

But she couldn't answer. She couldn't move.

"Norah," he whispered again, and she looked down and locked eyes with his. "I'm not here to replace him," he said softly. "I'm here to join him by your side." He nodded his reassurance, and she found herself nodding in return. The gods bless this man—the only man who could get her through this.

"I appoint you," she continued, "lord justice of Mercia"—those words were the hardest—"high commander, proxy of the queen, and protector of the North and her people."

The priest held a bowl of oil beside her, and she dipped her fingers into it. Slowly, she drew her fingertips along his palms, as she had done with Alexander. "May your hands be my hands."

As she ran her thumb across his lips, her hands shook. "May your words be my words."

She reached and scribed a line on his breastplate with her fingers, just above the winterhawk. The same winterhawk that had marked Alexander's breastplate. But she couldn't say the words.

Caspian reached up and covered her hand with his against his chest. "Take your time," he said quietly. "There's no hurry. Although"—he grimaced—"it would be unfortunate, at this point, if you were having second thoughts and would rather choose someone different."

She didn't know why she laughed. But she did. It helped curb the threatening tears. She shook her head. "No. No one different."

He let out a breath. "Good," he said, nodding. "I don't consider myself a prideful man, but having come this far, it would be slightly embarrassing."

She laughed again. This was the justice she needed. She squeezed his hand and pulled hers free, then finished her mark across his breastplate. "May your heart be my heart."

And it was done.

Norah smiled down at him, her eyes blurry. "Thank you, Caspian," she whispered, then, louder, "Rise, Lord Justice."

Chapter Twenty-Three

Snow fell heavily on the northern castle isle, but nothing could frost her spirits. Her heart beat happily at the thought of returning to Kharav. It would be a cold journey, but it didn't matter. She missed Mikael terribly.

As she swept her eyes around her, she stopped on Bhastian. He stood to the side of the rest of the Crest, in a slightly different stance.

She narrowed her eyes as she stepped in front of him. "There's something different about you."

The slight creases at the corners of his eyes gave away the hidden smile underneath his wrap. "Yes, Salara."

"He's been promoted to Captain of the Crest," Caspian said, coming up beside her.

She popped her mouth open with a big grin. "Bhastian!" She laughed and swept him into an embrace. "Congratulations!"

He bent stiffly to receive it, but he didn't embrace her back. He just gave an awkward bow of his head as she squeezed him. "Thank you, Salara."

She pulled back. Bhastian would be the perfect captain. She wrinkled her nose as she cut him another grin and turned and mounted Sephir.

"Are you ready?" Soren asked her after she'd settled in the saddle.

"I've been ready."

His eyes smiled. He was happy to be heading back too.

Catherine stood at the top of the stair. They'd said their emotional goodbyes inside. As regent again, her grandmother would look after Mercia in Norah's absence, with the support of the newly formed council. Norah gave her a final wave before they urged their mounts out of the gates and across the bridge.

They traveled lightly, with the Crest and the siblings. Caspian also joined them. He'd see Norah back to Kharav, then return to Mercia to help manage things with her grandmother. It was the first time he was returning to Kharav since the council's coup, and he seemed in good spirits. Serene came as well. Norah was surprised the maid had decided to return with her, but was thankful to have her company again, although she still painfully missed Vitalia.

When they reached the outskirts of the city, Norah urged Sephir into a gallop. She stretched forward, giving the mare her head to run. The icy wind brought tears to her eyes and froze them across her temples. She smiled. This was the feeling of freedom, the feeling of going home.

They rode until the sun dipped below the horizon, and just as Norah thought she might turn to ice, they stopped and made camp. Serene laid out bedrolls for them in their tent, and Soren laid out one for himself. When Mikael wasn't with her, Soren slept inside, not trusting her safety with anyone else while they traveled, especially considering the situation with Alexander.

"It's going to be a cold night," Serene said. "I hope it doesn't storm. I'll get more furs for us." She darted back out of the tent.

"I remember the last time we were caught in a storm while traveling," Soren said as he pulled off his weapons strap and sank down onto his bedroll. A deep chuckle rumbled from him. "The look of horror on your face when you woke."

She rolled her eyes, remembering as well—losing consciousness in the cold and waking in the ruins of Aviron not long after she'd first been captured by Mikael. "You were completely naked after being quite mean to me, let me remind you, and I was a proper lady. Of course I was mortified. How did you expect me to feel?"

His chuckle grew to a hearty laugh. "That was exactly how I expected you'd feel—or hoped, anyway."

"You were absolutely terrible."

He laughed again. She hadn't heard him laugh in a long time, and it was nice. It prompted her own smile.

"And I don't know what's funnier," he added, "remembering that look, or you thinking you were a proper lady."

Norah pursed her lips. "Yeah, well, looking back, if I'd been smarter, I would have pretended to enjoy it. That would have scatted you away."

"Well, you weren't smarter."

She scowled at him.

Serene returned with more furs. Soren shook one out over him and held up the corner. "Come on," he said to Norah, nodding to the space beside him. "Get in here. Even the Crest are tented and sleeping back-to-back."

It wasn't an unwelcome invitation, and she sidled up against the heat of his body as he pulled the furs over them. The warmth was nice. Quite nice. She might actually be able to get some sleep.

"If you start snoring..." he warned.

"I don't snore." *The nerve.* But she would get more comfortable. She accidentally kneed him while slipping off her boots, and he grunted—served him right. Then she stuck her freezing toes under the warmth of his calves, eliciting a growl.

"What about Serene?" she asked as she got settled. Serene would be cold, too, although she doubted her Mercian maid would be keen on cozying up to the Destroyer.

His lips thinned in irritation "Fine," he hissed. "Come on." Surprisingly, Serene sidled in on his opposite side, shimmying close. "Curse the North gods!" he spat. "Are all women's feet made of ice?"

Serene gave a giggle, and Norah smiled as she tucked her frigid fingers in the fold of his arm, drawing another snarl.

Despite the cold, sleep came quickly.

They rode for two weeks, stopping late into the night to make camp and rest. It warmed as they traveled south, and Caspian was grateful. The first few nights he thought he might freeze to death, but thoughts of seeing Tahla again warmed him. He wondered how she was and if she missed him. Surely, she knew what had happened, what had kept him away. He prayed she knew he'd find a way to return to her.

Evening came again. They set up camp in the low of the rocky hills. Caspian laid out his bedroll bedside Bhastian's. They were far enough south that the air wasn't freezing, but it was still cold, and while they didn't use the tents anymore, the warriors still slept back-to-back for warmth. He checked on the men taking watch, then took off his sword to settle in, but he paused when he saw the lord commander walking toward him. Bhastian moved to give them some space to speak privately.

The commander swept his eyes around the camp as he drew near, and when he reached Caspian, he stepped close—uncomfortably close. "We'll reach the Uru tomorrow," the commander said quietly. "But circumstances have changed since you last saw Tahla."

Caspian's pulse quickened. What did that mean? "Changed how?"

The lord commander let out a long sigh and pulled down his wrap. "This isn't my news to tell, but I don't want you caught unaware, and I need you to remember your duty." He clasped Caspian's shoulder. "You have a child, Caspian."

Caspian sucked in a breath. His mind swirled around him, and he swayed. A child. *A child.*

The commander's hand gripped his shoulder tighter. "I wanted to tell you sooner, but I needed your mind clear in the North."

His mind clear. Yes, this would have certainly muddied it. As it did now. *A child.* "Does Norah know?" he asked finally, his voice barely a whisper.

"She knows of the babe, but not that it's yours. No one knows. Tahla hasn't shared who the father is, but she was heavy with child when we last passed through."

He couldn't imagine Tahla with child. "And you're sure it's mine?"

The commander's eyes blazed with anger. "Who else's would it be, you dumb fuck?"

"No, that's not..." He didn't mean it like that. "I want it to be my child." It would crush him if it weren't his. "I want it to be mine."

The commander settled and finally nodded. "Well, I'm telling you because you need to remember your duty. You're lord justice now. Salara needs you more than ever. Take tonight before we get there. Steep your mind in it, figure out a way to manage yourself."

Caspian nodded.

The commander cuffed him on the shoulder and left him alone in the dark.

The night passed without bringing sleep. Caspian didn't know if he was warm or cold, happy or sad. Did Tahla want a child? Surely this made her life harder now. It would make things between them harder. Would she deny him still?

Caspian rose well before the sun, while the rest of the warriors slept. He joined Kiran, who stood watch.

"Can't sleep?" the warrior asked.

Caspian smiled weakly. "Just a lot on my mind." He nodded back toward the camp. "Go get some rest before we leave. I'll take over."

Kiran nodded his thanks and headed to where the other men slept.

Caspian breathed in the sharp air. In a day's time, he would see Tahla. What would he say when he saw her? What would she say to him? The possibilities swirled around him—ones that made him smile, ones that gutted him. But deep inside, fear sprouted, and that fear gnawed at his soul.

Footfalls behind him made him turn. The lord commander approached. Caspian shifted his gaze back over the hills. He hadn't realized the sun had started to peek over the horizon.

"Did you sleep?" the commander asked.

He shook his head. "No."

"Is your mind right?"

What was *right*? Claiming the child? Loving it? Pretending it didn't exist for the sake of his duty? But he nodded.

The commander gripped the top of Caspian's breastplate and pulled him close. The dark pools of his eyes searched Caspian's. Weakness—he was looking for weakness. "Is your mind right?" he asked again.

Caspian would have to figure it out. And quickly. He nodded again. "Yes."

"Get something to eat," the commander said, releasing him. "We're leaving."

Before the sun had fully risen, they were on their way. Norah seemed in high spirits as she rode; no doubt excitement was coursing through her in returning home. Caspian was happy for her. She deserved it, especially after everything she'd been through.

After the endless day, the sun set too soon, and they reached the Uru. Caspian's heart pulsed in his chest. They dismounted, and he followed closely behind Norah into the village.

As they neared the center house, he almost stumbled as he caught sight of Tahla approaching. Behind her, an Urun woman followed holding a small bundle in her arms.

"Tahla!" Norah exclaimed.

The daughter of the chief smiled. "Salara."

Norah hurried forward in excitement. "Let me see!"

Tahla laughed as she turned to the woman who held the infant. She took the child from the woman's arms and held it to Norah. "His name is Katakah."

Caspian's chest tightened. Tahla had borne a son. He had a son. *Katakah.*

Norah smiled as she took the boy into her arms. "Hello, Katakah Otay," she cooed. Then she glanced up at Tahla. "He's got your eyes."

Tahla smiled. "Yes, he does. Come, let's get something for you to eat."

The words between the women blurred together. All Caspian could think about was the child. His child. He stepped forward but a hand gripped his arm, stopping him.

The lord commander. "You'll wait," the commander told him.

Caspian watched the women, his head spinning. Suddenly, Tahla's eyes locked with his. And she smiled. Then she turned and walked toward the center house with Norah.

He stood in a daze. He couldn't move, he couldn't breathe. The lord commander said something to him, but he didn't understand.

"Caspian," the lord commander's voice came more sternly.

Caspian looked at him.

"Settle the men and go to your accommodations."

He nodded.

"Are you well, Lord Justice?" Bhastian asked as Caspian walked back toward the men.

Lord Justice. Caspian had almost forgotten. He felt so unworthy of the name. So unworthy of the title Alexander had once held. Unworthy of the title of father. He nodded, but he wasn't well.

He never imagined himself a father. Of course, he had dreamed, but it was never a life he'd dared to expect. Most soldiers married. Lord justices married. But there was only one woman he wanted, and she was beyond his reach. Now he had a son. And while joy sprang from every fiber of his being, so did an overwhelming sadness. Would he be able to be a father to the boy? Would the child even know him?

He worked numbly through his duties. He found himself in the house the Uru had provided without remembering the activity. Had he done everything? Food had been left on the table, but he couldn't eat. He paced the room. Would Tahla come to him? Would she bring the boy? He had to see him.

Night came, and Tahla didn't. He finally sat on the edge of the bed. But he knew he wouldn't sleep.

A knock on the door made him jump to his feet, and he swung it open. Only it wasn't Tahla. His heart fell. It was the lord commander.

"Come with me," the commander said.

Caspian, his pulse racing, followed Soren through the darkness to a large house off the mainway. The commander opened the door, but he didn't enter. He only waited for Caspian to step inside, then closed it behind him, leaving Caspian alone in the house.

"Northman," Tahla's voice came, and he whirled to see her step from behind a hanging panel that separated the adjoining room.

She was more beautiful than the day he'd met her, if that was even possible. Her skin glowed in the candlelight like sparkling sands under the sun. Her dark hair hung long and wavy from its loosened braids.

Caspian couldn't speak. He could only step closer. He reached up and brushed her cheek with his fingertips, and she smiled as she brought her hand over his.

"Tahla," he whispered.

"After Salara fled the North, I feared I wouldn't see you again," she told him. "I thought something had happened to you. But Soren told me you lived, and I knew you'd come again." She held his hand and looked down at their entwined fingers. "I've missed you, Northman. And I'm glad you're here." She stepped closer. "We have so much to talk about. With the child."

With the child. She had to be considering their lives together now. Surely.

She gave a warm smile. "Do you want to see him?"

His heart stopped. Of course he wanted to see him. But he couldn't speak. All he could do was nod. She pulled his hand and led him behind the panel to the adjoining room. Inside sat a small crib with the sleeping child. His breath shook as he drew closer to look at him—he was the most beautiful thing he'd ever seen.

"Can I hold him?" he whispered.

"Of course."

Tahla reached into the crib and gently lifted the child without waking him. Ever so carefully, she placed him in Caspian's arms.

Caspian moved and sat down on the edge of the bed. He couldn't take his eyes from the boy. He drew the infant's small hand between his fingers—the skin was so soft and warm. He moved his fingertips to the roundness of his plump cheeks, grazing them lovingly. The child opened his eyes and let out a large yawn.

Caspian chuckled as tears came to his eyes. This was his child. His son.

"Katakah," Tahla said. "His name means golden light."

He chuckled again, looking at the boy's dark hair and brown eyes now staring back up at him. "I don't think there's any gold about him."

"He's filled with it. From his father."

Caspian looked up at her. This woman in front him, his child in his arms—never had his heart felt so full. He stood and stepped to her, holding the child between them. "Tahla," he said softly as he reached his hand and pulled them together. "Marry me. I know I'm not worthy, but I would be a good husband, a good father."

But sadness filled her eyes. "Caspian." The way his name sat on her lips crushed him. "No one is more worthy," she said. "But it's not about being worthy."

She took the child back and gently laid him in his crib, and Katakah promptly closed his eyes and fell back asleep.

"I can't," she said.

It was as he feared. "Why?" His voice broke to match his heart.

Tahla sat on the edge of the bed and pulled him down beside her. She smiled, but there were tears in her eyes.

"Are you betrothed to another?" he asked.

She shook her head. "No, of course not."

"Then why?"

"You know why. I will be chieftess. I belong to the Uru, and so must Katakah. And you belong to Salara and the North. We can't pull each other from our duties."

"I would never pull you away from the Uru, nor will I abandon Salara. I only want to know you as my wife, and for my son to know his father."

"Katakah will be chief one day. I can't have him torn between the North and the Uru."

What did that mean? "So you would keep him from his father altogether?"

"There will be strong men in his life. My father. Salar. Soren." She looked at him. "And you—lord justice of the North, a role model for any man. But I want him to know he is Urun, and only Urun, and his duty is to the Urun people."

Caspian's heart shattered. He watched the sleeping child—he already loved him. He would give his own life for him, betray everything for him, and for Tahla, which meant she was right. Blood ties weakened the pull of duty. They already weakened his own, and he didn't want that for his son. He didn't want that for Tahla. "I respect your wishes," he said finally. "But I want to be a part of his life as much as I can."

"I want you to as well. But as Caspian, lord justice. Not Caspian, his father."

It wasn't enough. But it would have to be.

She curved her hand around the back of his neck and pulled him close. "Will you stay with me tonight, Northman?" She ran her fingers up the back of his head and threaded them into his hair. "I've missed you."

"Is this how we're to be, then? Together but forever apart?"

"Or just together, as fate allows." Her eyes drew him in and held him. "Kiss me, Northman."

He couldn't deny her his love, and he lowered his mouth to hers.

Chapter Twenty-Four

The Canyonlands—a dark and twisted labyrinth of rock and trench that swallowed men caught unaware—marked the entry to Kharav. Many had died in these folds of earth, lost and abandoned or picked off from the top ridges by those who called Kharav home. Norah followed Soren through. It would take many more times before she knew the way, but she floated through the arms of darkness with a joy building in her heart. On the other side, Mikael would be waiting.

They emerged from the Canyonlands and made their way up the ridge to where the breathtaking scape of rice terraces rolled as far as the eye could see. In a month or two, they'd be steeped in snow, creating a whole new magical world. Winter was almost to Kharav, bringing frosted mornings and light afternoon snows that melted as they touched the ground. Norah hated winter, but in Kharav, it didn't matter. She loved all seasons here. Gods, she missed this place.

They reached the capital city of Ashan the following day. She hadn't slept at all the night before, and her stomach tumbled as they rode through the gates. The city bustled with a familiarity that she'd missed. The wind brought smells of home, and when she saw the castle, her heart leapt. This was where she belonged.

"You'll tell him?" Soren said, pushing his destrier up beside hers as they rode.

It was the one thing she wasn't looking forward to. She nodded. "Yes, I'll tell him what we saw in the painting."

"And about the blood. And the visions."

Right. "Of course." That would be equally as difficult.

When they reached the courtyard, Mikael was waiting. Before she even fully came to a stop, he was beside her, reaching up and bringing his hands to her sides to ease her down from the mare. He kissed her, deeply.

When he pulled back, he still held her tightly. "I only received your letter a few days ago that you were returning. I almost came to meet you partway. You should have stayed in the North." He glanced at Soren, clearly displeased at him for bringing her back. Then he looked down to her. "It's safer for you there."

"Don't look at him like that," she chided. "I wanted to come home. I'll be apart from you only in dire circumstances, and now with Aleon and Osan, things are no longer dire."

"We don't hold a formal alliance with Aleon. There's still risk."

"Not enough to keep me from you. Say what you want. I've never been so happy to be home, and I'm *not* leaving."

He held her cheek in his palm. "I don't want you to leave," he said softly.

Her smile widened. "Then take me inside, husband."

Mikael swept her up in his arms and carried her into the castle. The feel of his body drew a new wave of longing through her, and she spread her hand against the hardness of his chest. Too long it had been, and she needed him. But there was so much she needed to tell him first.

"Salar," a voice called from behind them, and she looked over Mikael's shoulder to see a messenger approaching.

"No," Mikael called out to the messenger, not turning, not slowing his step.

Wait... "What if it's important?" she pressed, as much as she hated to. She had her own important things to tell him.

"It's not," he said firmly, and continued to their chamber.

"How do you know?"

He carried her inside and kicked the door closed behind them. Setting her down, he still held her close. "Nothing else is important right now."

She raised a brow. "What if Rael is marching against us again?"

From around her waist, his hands ran up her back and then down again, curving around her buttocks through her riding gown as he walked her backward toward the bed. "It will take them some time to get here."

Gods, she missed this man. Perhaps her own important things could wait just a little longer. "They could be at our gates," she warned playfully.

He didn't stop his movement toward the bed. "Did you see them when you came through?"

She bit her bottom lip and shook her head.

"Then we have some time yet." His voice came lower now. "Kiss me before I go to battle."

Hunger radiated off him, and the muscle tightened under his skin, but before they reached the bed, she put a hand on his chest to still him. "I need to clean up." And calm things down to tell him about the visions of Alexander.

He slowed but didn't stop. "I'm not waiting."

"Mikael, I'm so dirty."

"Then we'll both be dirty." They reached the bed, and he pushed her back onto it with his frame, but his arms supported her, and he lowered her gently to the furs.

"I smell like... I've been on a horse for weeks—"

"I like horses." He lowered himself over her.

Norah couldn't help a laugh. He moved his hips between her thighs.

"I need to talk to you," she said.

"After."

The air changed, and she quieted. The dark pools of his eyes traced her face, moving from her eyes to her hair, then back down to her lips.

He was quiet.

And then he wasn't.

An urgency came to him, and he reached underneath her skirts. Need trembled through him. She shifted her weight, helping him free her of the riding breeches and undergarments. Mikael stripped them both of everything that kept their skin from touching, everything that kept them apart. Grasping, pulling, tearing. He moved with a feral need, violent but not hurtful, and they became one as he sank inside her.

A calm returned, and he stilled. He buried his face into her neck, and the heat of his breath licked her skin. As they lay quietly, he trailed kisses along her jaw.

Her eyes narrowed. "You'd better not be finished."

He chuckled. "No," he said softly. His flesh pulsed inside her, hard and thick, offering proof. He lifted himself to look at her again, and his eyes shone bright, but there was a seriousness to them. "I just needed to be close to you right now."

She tightened her thighs around him. "Is this close enough?"

But he shook his head slowly. "Nothing with you is ever enough."

Norah reached up and softly scored her fingertips through the short cut of his beard. "I've missed you," she whispered. She had missed everything about him—his touch, his voice, his love, the way he needed her.

"I've missed you too." And he lowered himself back to her waiting lips.

Morning brought the sun, and Norah walked to the dining hall. Mikael had left early to see what unimportant news the messenger from the day before had delivered. It gave her a moment to get her thoughts in order. She reached her hand inside the pocket of her gown and clutched the small vial. She'd show it to Mikael today. Or maybe she shouldn't. Maybe she should just tell him about it, and not show him. What if he told her to call Alexander? What if he wanted to see for himself? Would it work this far from Mercia? It had been a month since she'd received the vial and had last seen Alexander. Would it work at all? Or would its power fade with time? It wasn't like normal blood—it didn't clot or separate. Perhaps something had been mixed with it. Or perhaps it wasn't normal blood. She mocked herself. Obviously it wasn't normal blood.

Soren fell into step beside her, and she jerked her hand from her pocket.

"Did you tell him?" he asked.

About the visions. She glanced at him out of the corner of her eye as she kept walking. "Not yet."

His eyes burned into her, but she avoided them. "Why not?" he demanded.

She pursed her lips. "It wasn't the right time."

"What do you mean 'it wasn't the right time'?"

"Not while we're getting reacquainted."

"You had all night."

She didn't have the energy for this. "I said not while we're getting reacquainted."

He grimaced. "You rutted all night?"

"Soren!" She stopped abruptly and smacked his arm. "Do you have to be so foul? And that's none of your business."

The corners of his lips turned up slightly. "Are you going to tell me you're a proper lady again?"

She scowled at him. "I hate you."

"I don't believe that."

Gods help her.

They reached the dining hall, and Soren stopped at the door. She'd almost forgotten. In Kharav, he respected the mornings as Salara-Mae's time and didn't eat breakfast with them. With Catherine's tolerance in Mercia, Norah had grown used to sharing nearly every meal with him over the past several months. Being without him now seemed... amiss. She'd have to talk to Salara-Mae, but one thing at a time.

"You have to tell him," he pressed.

"I will. Today."

He gave a short nod, doubt still filling his eyes, and then left her at the door. She stepped inside and moved to the table where Salara-Mae sat sipping her morning tea.

Norah took her place at the end.

Mikael's mother set down her cup and smiled at her. It was the most warmth she had ever shown. "It's good to have you back."

Norah smiled back at her. "It's good to be home." The woman seemed in high spirits. Maybe now *was* a good time to talk about Soren. "Salara-Mae, there's something I'd like to talk to you about."

The woman gave an agreeable lift to her brow.

Mikael entered and stopped by her chair. He gently clasped under her jaw and pulled her lips up as he leaned down to kiss her. His kiss was hungry and left her completely forgetting her train of thought. She blushed as they broke, all too aware of his mother's nearness. But Salara-Mae said nothing. She took another drink of her tea as if she hadn't even noticed. Norah smiled at him with chastising eyes, and he moved to take his seat at the opposite end.

What had she been thinking about? *Oh right*—Soren at breakfast, but she didn't want to have that conversation in front of Mikael.

"Maybe we could resume our walks after breakfast again, this morning even, if you'd like," she said, picking back up her conversation with Mikael's mother.

Salara-Mae nodded. "I would like that, although I can't this morning, I have new gown fittings." She took another sip of her tea. "You should come; you need more gowns yourself."

Absolutely not. "Oh... uh, no, I can't, I—"

"You were just going to go for a walk."

Damn. She wasn't getting out of this one.

Norah glanced at Mikael, and he smiled at her. She sighed. Well, she wasn't making any progress on either of her tasks at the moment: talking to Mikael or getting Soren back to the table. Time spent in dress fittings wouldn't get her any further, and time with Salara-Mae meant time away from Mikael. Later, she promised herself.

"What news came yesterday?" she asked Mikael, remembering the messenger.

He swallowed his bite of food and took a drink. "There are rumors that the alliance between Gregor and Cyrus is weakening."

"What?" That was great news. "Are you sure?"

"One is never sure of gossip. But it appears Rael is focused on Kharav, and Japheth on Aleon."

"It would explain why Gregor didn't join Cyrus when Rael moved against you." She frowned. "But they're bickering over who to go to war with? Surely now they know Aleon, Mercia, and Kharav stand together, so what would it matter? And, if anything, the threat should strengthen their alliance."

He nodded. "As I said, one can never be sure of gossip." He took another drink from his cup. "I would like you to come with me to Salta Tau. Tonight."

Salta Tau was the ink mastera who marked the stories on his skin. "Oh," she breathed. His comment caught her by surprise.

"For the story of taking the North," he said.

Taking the North. The idea knifed her and left her breathless—it hurt. Why? Of course he'd want to get the markings of victory for taking Mercia, and why shouldn't he?

Because it wasn't an accomplishment. It wasn't something to celebrate. Having to march against her own kingdom was a great tragedy, and with everything she'd lost in the process... for him to want it proudly displayed on his skin felt like a slap in the face.

She couldn't speak. She only found herself nodding, but why? Why was she nodding? She didn't want to see the markings. She didn't want them on his skin. Forever. But after everything he'd done for her, she couldn't bring herself to tell him not to.

He rose from the table and stopped beside her, leaning down to kiss her as he had done when he arrived. "I'll see you this evening."

"This evening," she echoed blankly.

Salara-Mae stood as well. "Be at my chamber within the hour. I'll have the seamstresses ready a fitting space for you." Then she whisked out of the room, leaving Norah to herself.

Norah sat at the table in silence. She tried to shake off the misgiving growing in her stomach. Don't be ridiculous, she scolded herself. Why shouldn't Mikael be proud? It was a significant feat to take back Mercia from the council, which had been defended by some of the most renowned mercenaries in the world, and it was to put her back on the throne. But no matter how logical she made it sound to herself, she still couldn't shake the emotion against it.

She pushed a breath out. She still needed to tell him of the visions—that his fate still remained—and how Alexander had come to her. In Mercia, she'd been desperate to tell him, to have him help her make sense of it all, but now it seemed an impossible task. Why was it so hard?

Because she'd loved Alexander.

A dress fitting was the opposite of what she wanted to be doing right now. She leaned forward against the table and rested her cheek against her palm. There was really no avoiding it. She stood and headed to Salara-Mae's chamber.

As she walked down the hall, she spotted Katya outside through the glass. A woman stood beside her, holding a small child. Norah's heart beat with happiness. Of course Katya would have had her baby by now. She made her way quickly to the doors at the end and out to catch them.

"Katya!" she called as she approached.

"Salara," Katya bowed her head in greeting.

"Is this your little one?"

Katya nodded. "Yes. I'm sorry, Salara. My mother only brought him by to say hello."

"Don't be sorry! I'm so happy to see you." She stepped closer to the child.

Katya smiled as she presented him. "My son, Araseth. And my mother, Delina."

"Lovely to meet you," Norah told the older woman, who smiled with a bow of her head. Then she turned her attention to the boy. He was a plump child with a full head of black hair. But his eyes were a deep cerulean blue. A Northman's eyes, no doubt. "Katya. He's beautiful."

The captain's smile grew. "That he is." She looked to the ground, her smile fading and her pain showing through. "His father fell taking back Mercia."

Norah reached out and clasped her arm. "Oh, Katya, I'm so sorry." Norah knew loss, yes, but to lose the father of a child, she couldn't imagine. To raise a child alone... Then she remembered: "Katya, Mercia grants provisions for children of fallen heroes. If you only record the child—"

"No," Katya said quickly. "I know that Kharav and the North view intimacy and marriage differently. And a child out of wedlock... I won't dishonor his father's legacy."

Norah stared at her, speechless. Then she shook her head. "You know what, it's perfectly fine. You don't even need to record the child. I'll make sure—"

"No, Salara. Really. I want for nothing here. I have everything I need."

Norah's heart broke. She wanted to do more, to offer more, but Katya would refuse, she knew. She nodded. "All right. Well, if there's ever anything..."

"I'll let you know."

Norah nodded again. "Well, bring Araseth to the castle anytime. It would be wonderful to have a child around."

Katya's smile returned. "You're too kind, Salara."

Norah meant every word.

CHAPTER TWENTY-FIVE

It was late afternoon before Norah could escape to her chamber. She sat at her vanity, staring at her own image, yet her mind wasn't on herself. Her stomach twisted. She still hadn't told Mikael his fate remained. Or that Alexander had come to her with the blood. She needed to. It was important. But their brief time alone together had been spent in each other's arms—poor timing to share this news.

And now the evening ahead would be special for Mikael; she couldn't tell him tonight. *Tomorrow*. It would have to be tomorrow.

Soren would be furious.

Her mind turned to the evening ahead—something else that turned her stomach—when Mikael would get his markings for taking Mercia.

For her, taking back Mercia was the correction of a great wrong, but still the stain remained, and the loss suffered in doing so made her question if it was even worth it. But for Mikael, it was an accomplishment. He'd always wanted to take Mercia, and while it had been in a different form and under very different circumstances, he'd finally done it. It was now a significant part of his story—his story that she would have to look at every day, and be reminded of...

No, she didn't have to look at it. She wouldn't look at it.

What if it was on his neck? Or on his face? She groaned to herself. Did Kharavian warriors mark their faces? Master archers bore fletching-patterned marks on their bow-side eye. Other than that, she hadn't seen any others—which was a small relief, but one that brought little comfort. This would be Mikael's greatest accomplishment, and surely it would be bold and prominent across his body.

Norah moved her gaze over her reflection. She wore a gown the color of night, the color of Kharav. And right now, it was the color of her heart.

"Are you all right?" Mikael asked, coming up behind her.

She gave a small start; she hadn't realized he'd come in. Her eyes met his in the mirror, and she nodded. Why did she nod? Of course she wasn't all right. She should just say something. But she couldn't. It was only a marking. She should let him have it—for all he had done for her, and all he had done for Mercia.

"Are you ready?" he asked.

No. She nodded again and rose.

Mikael took her hand, and they walked through the castle, into the courtyard, and across the gardens to the temple of Salta Tau.

It was just as she remembered from the last time she'd been there, when Mikael had gotten the marking of her crown.

The crown that she'd lost.

The crown that was now hidden in its velvet box in her vanity drawer.

They walked a series of halls back to a large open chamber. Salara-Mae and Soren were already there, just as they had been before. They stood on opposite sides of the chamber from each other, as they had before.

Salta Tau stood in the room's center, wearing a cream linen gown and her hair pulled back in a braid. She bowed as they drew near. "Salar. Salara."

"Salta Tau," Mikael replied, and both he and Norah bowed their heads in return.

The old woman spoke in the Kharavian tongue, which Norah understood now. "What do you seek to record?" Her voice was gravelly from age, but there was a smoothness to it still.

Norah cursed herself silently. She should have said something, told him how she felt about the marking. Now it was too late.

"I come for the story of taking the North," Mikael said.

Norah hated those words—*taking the North.*

Salta Tau took Mikael's hands before closing her eyes and speaking her spell into the air. She swayed in her chant, her voice drifting in and out, echoing through the chamber. Then she stopped. The old woman opened her eyes and stood for a moment, silent, looking forward but at nothing in particular.

What did she see?

Salta Tau's words made Norah freeze. "The story of the North, it brings you sorrow," she said to Mikael in the Kharavian tongue.

Sorrow? Not pride? Not accomplishment? But sorrow?

Mikael nodded.

The old woman frowned. "And you still want this story on your skin?"

He looked at Norah, then back to Salta Tau. "I do."

Norah's eyes welled. He wasn't celebrating Mercia. He felt her loss with her. Even in his triumph, even in the happiness of having believed he'd changed his fate, he felt sorrow.

Salta Tau motioned for him to lie down on the mat.

No. No, *no.* He couldn't do this. "Wait!" she cried.

Mikael's brows drew together as he shifted his weight back. "Wha-?"

"You wouldn't feel sorrow if you knew the truth." Her words came before they could stop them. "Alexander's not gone, and your fate's still unchanged. I saw it."

Salara-Mae covered her mouth with her hand.

A line spread deep across his brow. "What do you mean? My fate? You saw it?"

"Samuel painted it again. It hasn't changed." She shook her head. "Mikael, I'm sorry. I've been trying to tell you, but..."

"The Bear is dead."

Norah winced. "Yes. And no."

"What do you mean *no*?" Then his stare shifted from confusion to anger. "You saw this in the North? Why didn't you send word?"

"Because... I needed to tell you in person."

"But you didn't."

Norah cursed herself for it not being the first words off her lips when she saw him. She looked at Soren, and he gave a small nod of encouragement for her to tell him the rest.

Mikael twisted his head toward him. "You knew about this?"

"Don't blame Soren," she said quickly. "I told him I would tell you. I should have already, but I was waiting for the right time."

"Now would be the right time." His words simmered in anger.

The right time would have been sooner. This was a very wrong time, but she had no choice. She drew in a breath. "He's shown himself to me. Even after death. Visions, or his spirit, I don't know how to explain it, but he comes to me."

"The Bear is dead," he said again.

"I know, which is why I said I can't explain it."

His nostrils flared, and light caught the white of his teeth between his partially parted lips. "Who else has seen him?"

"He's come only to me."

The darks of his eyes were the darkest they'd ever been.

"Tell him how," said Soren.

She tried to swallow the growing lump in her throat. Her hand shook as she reached into her pocket and pulled out the blood vial. She felt Soren's searing gaze, but she didn't look at him. He hadn't known she had more. "I receive these," she told Mikael as she held it out for him. "When the blood touches my skin, he comes to me."

Mikael took the vial from her hand, looking at it closely. He was calm now. Too calm—the calm that came when he shifted to battle. "And you invite him?" he asked. "You call him to you?"

The perception was damning. "I'm trying to find out what's going on."

"And have you?"

She glanced at the floor. Of course she hadn't.

"What does he tell you?"

"He can't speak in the vision. But he finds other ways to show me he's real." She swallowed again and paused. "When he came to me in my mind, he gave me a gift. My mother's crown." She glanced at Soren. "The next day, it arrived at the castle."

The corners of Mikael's eyes creased, and he glanced down at its image on his chest. Then he looked back at Norah.

"He found it," she said.

"Or had it all along," Soren added.

"Alexander wouldn't have done that," she argued. "He wouldn't have kept it from me."

"It's not Alexander," Soren countered.

Norah reached out and clasped Mikael's hand. He had to believe her. "Mikael, it *is* Alexander I see. Everything about him, every detail of things only he would know." *The shell bracelet.* "Things only *I* would know."

"You should have made them things I know," he said. He was angry, and he had every right to be. Still, his cold gaze crushed her. He pulled his hand from hers, then turned and strode from the room.

Norah stood in silence as Salara-Mae followed her son. She couldn't bring herself to look at Soren, who stood for a moment, then left as well.

Only Salta Tau remained. She stared at Norah, but not with eyes of judgment.

Norah glanced around the empty chamber, trying to keep herself together. Then to Salta Tau, she said, "I think I'm just going to sit here awhile," she whispered. "If that's okay."

The old woman bowed and left her to the cold of the empty room.

It was morning. Norah sat on the edge of the bed. Mikael hadn't returned to their chamber through the night. She didn't fault him. He'd been hit with two blows: The first was the false relief his fate had changed. To be struck with its truth again would surely be defeating. Second, Mikael thought himself free of Alexander. He would see him as a threat again, both to his crown and her heart. And she had willingly called Alexander back to her. Even with her pure intentions, she couldn't deny it looked damning.

The creak of the door opening made her look up, and Mikael stepped inside. She hadn't expected him to come, not so soon, not now, but she was glad he had. They could talk it out now, she could try to explain. She rose, her heart pounding in her ears.

He stepped toward her.

"Mikael, I—"

"Don't." He stood in front of her, the pools of his eyes dark and drowning.

Norah pulled her bottom lip between her teeth. She was desperate to set things right between them.

He pulled off his tunic, and she stepped back slightly. What was he doing? Her breath left her as she saw a wrap around his torso just under his chest—the kind of wrap one gets after visiting Salta Tau. Slowly, he removed the side pins and rolled back the linen strip that held the pads of healing mixture over the marking.

And she saw it.

It wasn't as she had imagined Salta Tau's marking would be. *Taking the North*, Mikael had called it. She'd expected a broken banner, perhaps a falling winterhawk or a castle in ruin. Not the glorious bird with wings spread wide against the sun. Mikael's sun. The same as the one on his shoulder. It was beautiful, so bold against his skin.

"You got it anyway?" she whispered.

"Nothing you've said makes me feel differently." He stepped closer to her and brought his hand to her face. "I don't know what's happening right now, or what you're seeing, but I know I sealed in the sarcophagus the body of the Bear—a great warrior, a man the North needs and lost. I saw a great kingdom taken from her queen, and that brings me sadness. All of it. Sadness for the North." He tipped her chin up. "Sadness for you. But we've set things right, you and I. And now we're the strongest we've ever been. Together. So yes, I got the marking."

He reached into his pocket and pulled out the vial he'd taken from her.

Her heart stopped.

It was empty.

Why was it empty?

"What have you done?" she breathed.

He held it out for her. "He didn't come."

Her eyes dropped in a long blink as she curled her hand around the vial. He had used it. But Alexander hadn't come. Relief washed over her. Then that relief turned to anger, and her eyes blazed back open.

"It wasn't meant for you," she snapped.

The shadow under his brow grew. "You're angry at *me*?"

Was he serious? "To have taken the liberty, yes! To give no thought of what this means to me."

"What this means to you?" His own voice was laced with anger now.

"You *know* what Alexander means to me!"

"So you wanted for me to just accept this?"

"I don't know!" she cried. "I wanted you not to have used it! So readily, without even speaking to me about it, and on top of that, to have no regard for yourself!"

"What am I to fear for myself?"

Gods, this man was an idiot sometimes. "I don't know what his power is. I don't know what he's capable of."

"Yet you call him to you?" he challenged.

"Because he's not here to harm me."

"You don't know that."

"No!" She pushed him back from her. "*You* don't know!" A tear escaped down her cheek, and her voice dropped to a whisper. "You don't understand." He wasn't even trying to understand.

Norah shouldered past him, out of the room, taking the empty vial with her.

CHAPTER TWENTY-SIX

Norah finished scanning the letter Soren had given her—a letter from Aleon. Communications flowed freely now between the two kingdoms. Phillip wrote to Soren directly even, sending him scout updates and military reports. In return, Soren sent information their own armies had collected on Japheth and Rael.

Mikael remained wary of the empire, as she expected, but he also realized the value of friendship between the kingdoms. He hadn't been happy about her attending Phillip's wedding, feeling it had been too great a risk, but it had been a risk she'd had to take. These Shadowmen might know war, but they didn't know the art of diplomacy, the power of politics.

She held the letter out for Mikael. A tension still hung between them. He'd apologized after their argument, and so had she, but the weight, the heaviness, of the circumstance lingered.

Norah watched him as he read the letter, and he nodded.

"It's not a surprise," he said.

Rael's forces were heavy in number and just inside Japheth's border, no doubt preparing to launch a joint attack. Following the rumors, if there *had* been a rift between the two kingdoms, clearly it wasn't enough to dissolve their pact.

"You don't find the numbers surprising?" she asked.

"We know slaves have been flocking to the army of Rael for months, from all kingdoms. Their numbers will continue to grow." He turned to Soren. "You'll go to Aleon, devise our joint strategy."

Soren shifted uneasily. "You need me in Kharav."

"No." Mikael shook his head. "I need you to figure out how to win this war when it comes." He handed the letter back to Norah and leaned to kiss her on the cheek. His eyes were somber. "I'll see you tonight."

She nodded. Then he left them to the quiet of the room.

"Did you put him up to this?" Soren asked after he'd gone, pulling her attention.

"Up to what?"

"Sending me to Aleon?"

"No, of course not." She didn't entirely trust that Soren wouldn't still try to kill Phillip. While it did seem like something she would do—creating opportunity for a budding relationship—there was no budding relationship. Soren learning that Phillip was the man in his vision had severely affected him, hurt him even, and he was still angry. She knew he felt like Phillip had taken something from him. Now she worried he might take something from Phillip. Like his life.

"You have to talk to him," he pressed. "I can't leave Kharav. I have matters to tend here. I have things to look after."

"You mean me?"

He stilled.

"Soren, you've done a fine job looking after me ever since... well, ever since I met you, but you're lord commander. You have to get back to... lord commanding. War is coming. I don't want you to have to go to Aleon—I know what it means for you. But Mikael's right, we need you to go. I'll send word for Caspian to meet you there, and after you confer with him and Phillip, you'll decide our collective approach."

The muscle along his temple tightened. "You assume the Aleon king will follow my plan."

"I assume he'll appreciate the counsel of a renowned commander and will want a unified effort." As they all did.

"I can determine that from here."

"I also want you to determine how to better fortify Aleon. That you can't do from here."

"That's the responsibility of his own commander," he argued.

"Soren. You know your value. This is a completely appropriate duty."

He sighed. "Fine. I'll go. Just don't do anything stupid while I'm gone."

She narrowed her eyes. "When have I ever done anything stupid?"

Aleon was as Soren remembered—glorious, beautiful, welcoming.

Complete shit.

He wrestled with his mind the whole journey from Kharav. Memories of what the seer had shown him haunted his thoughts. Shame still hung around him, for the nameless face he'd thought about so often. But it was nameless no more, and he had to see things for what they were. This king had become an informal ally of the North and Kharav, that was true.

But he was not a friend.

In the Great War, the Aleon king had given the North King the forces to take Bahoul—the battle in which Kharav had lost its mountain stronghold and Soren had lost his family. And even if this king hadn't wielded the sword himself, he was still complicit, still to blame. He would continue to grow his empire, remaining an ally only so long as his and Salara's interests aligned. He couldn't be trusted, even if he *had* recently come to Mikael's aid when Rael moved against him.

Soren had made good time in traveling alone to Aleon's capital city of Valour, arriving even before the Northmen. He wanted to finish and return to Kharav as soon as possible. Return to... *looking after* Salara. That was what she had called it, but he wasn't only looking after her. Rael would move against Kharav soon, and he was needed at home. The faster he could finish with this Aleon king, the faster he could get back. It wasn't necessary to have traveled all this way. He knew what needed to be done; Norah could have sent a letter, giving the Aleon king instruction. He only needed to do as he was told. Soren ran his eyes over the brilliance of the mainway, its opulent splendor. This kingdom was built on pride. He hoped that pride wouldn't stand in his way.

People lined the street with his arrival, as they had done when he had come before with Salara. Only this time, they threw no flowers. Should he be offended? He almost chuckled. But they welcomed him with smiling faces. Like they knew him. Now that was *truly* offensive.

As he reached the citadel, the Aleon king was waiting, as he had been before. Was there nothing else for him to do? Did he just stare out his window waiting for visitors to arrive?

He was as Soren remembered him—bronze hair, messy, but in a perfect kind of way. He wore a stupid smile that made Soren want to gut him. But Soren was prepared this time. At least, he had thought he was prepared, but seeing Phillip struck something within, and a flash of anger swept through him. He pushed it down—he was here with a purpose, and he wouldn't let himself be distracted.

"Lord Commander," the king greeted as Soren slid down from his destrier. "I trust you journeyed well."

Journeyed unnecessarily. Diplomacy, Soren reminded himself. "Aleon King," he replied.

The king's smile widened, flashing a row of perfect teeth. "You're welcome to call me by my name. Phillip."

Soren would *not* be calling him by his name, and if this king was looking for reciprocation, he wouldn't get it. "Have the Northmen arrived?" Of course they hadn't.

"Not yet. But I received a message yesterday. They're yet another day or two out."

What was taking so long? Was Caspian fucking *walking*?

"I'll show you inside," the king said.

"I've seen inside." Soren knew what he meant, but he didn't want an escort.

"Then you'll act surprised."

Oh. Some wit, then. Soren narrowed his eyes.

Phillip's face still held a smile, was still friendly, only a little more serious now. Firm. The king turned and strode up the stairs to the castle.

Who did this man think he was? Did he think Soren would just follow? Like he could be commanded? Soren stood for a moment in his surprise. Curse this Aleon king. Then he pushed a snarl between his teeth and followed him inside.

The king looked over his shoulder as they entered. "I trust the chamber you stayed in before was suitable. I've had it prepared again."

It had been more than suitable—it had been excessive. It was the equivalent to the royal guest chambers in Kharav. "It's unnecessary." As were most things in Aleon. "Soldiers' quarters are suitable enough."

"I want your comfort."

Soren almost laughed. *Comfort.* This wasn't about comfort. It was a display of wealth and power.

They moved down a side hall to the guest chamber, where the king stopped in front of the door. "I'll send someone to make sure you have everything you need."

"I don't need anything." And he certainly didn't need someone else bothering him.

The king's expression changed, although not of annoyance, or frustration. His brow softened, and his lips parted slightly. "I am honored to host you again, Lord Commander."

His words felt... genuine, and the fight inside Soren ebbed slightly. But only for a moment.

"Please, settle in and make yourself comfortable." Then the king gave a friendly nod, left, and headed toward the main hall. Soren watched him go, his irritation returning. This man was infuriatingly pleasant.

Soren found his chamber to be as over-the-top as it had been before. An assortment of food sat on the table by the balcony door. Large windows let in the sight of the capital and all its beauty. He let himself fall back onto the bed. This was the bed he'd slept in during his last visit. It was ridiculous and overindulgent, so plush that he couldn't feel the frame underneath.

And he could easily sleep for a week.

Back in Kharav, he had thought about how he might recreate it, but he pushed it from his mind and forced himself up. That would have to wait. He wasn't here for his enjoyment. He looked around the room. *Settle*, Phillip had told him. There was nothing to settle. And he struck back out to explore things once again on his own.

Even with winter creeping in, the gardens of Kharav were beautiful. Their year-round green contrasted sharply against the light dusting of snow that now covered the earth. Norah sat on a bench between two topiaries, soaking in the false promise of warmth from the sun. She was grateful to not be in the North—she'd be bundled in layers and pausing by each fireplace in the castle every moment she got the chance.

And she was glad to be away from everything that reminded her of what she'd lost. Had it not been enough for fate to take her childhood, her memories, her parents? Everything she'd ever loved? Then to take Alexander from her too—a second time—was just cruel.

But just as much as she wanted to distance herself from the pain, she wanted to hang on—to not let go of any scrap of what she'd fought so hard to gain back. She wanted to cling to every piece of her shredded heart.

But Mikael didn't understand. He didn't know the pain of loss like this. He didn't know the fight to endure. He'd have her put Alexander behind her. But she couldn't. She wouldn't.

If there was something still remaining of him, she'd track it to the ends of the earth. If he was trying to speak to her, she'd listen.

She breathed in the cold winter air, then froze.

Her pulse quickened.

She hadn't even noticed the small white box on the end of the bench that was blending with the light layer of snow. Her hands shook as she placed it in her lap and opened the lid to what she knew she'd find inside—a vial of blood.

His legs burned. There were so many cursed stairs in this city. Soren grumbled as he cleared the last run of them to the top of a hill where there stood a temple larger than any he had ever seen. But he wasn't here for the temple—he'd come for the view. He ran his eyes over the city to the horizon. He would have given anything for this sight years ago in the height of the Great War. It was a sight he'd never dreamed he'd see. At least not in friendship. Still not in friendship, he reminded himself.

"And how are you finding Valour?" a voice called to his right. *The Aleon king.*

Did this man not relent? Could he not just leave him in peace until Caspian arrived? What did he want? Soren's honest opinion? *Doubtful.* He turned to look at him, and the king smiled.

"Well?" Phillip pressed, not even out of breath from walking up all the cursed stairs.

Fine. "Had I known there were no obstacles to your capital, I would have taken Aleon in the Great War."

The king chuckled. "You think you could have?"

Soren tightened his fist. The heat of challenge rose in his chest as he turned to him. "I know I could have."

Phillip raised a brow. "Gregor has tried with fervor and failed."

"Gregor's an idiot. He confronted your forces openly. Few armies can match your numbers."

The king stepped closer to him with an amused smile—a disarming smile, and Soren hated it.

"And what would you have done differently?" Phillip asked him.

"I would come in the night. Slaughter everyone in their sleep." He didn't use past tense. It wasn't a threat that had passed.

The king's smile fell. "Where's the honor in that?"

"There is no honor in war." Soren looked out across the city. "Rolling forestland surrounding the city, no walls, no barriers. So many places for an attacking army to hide, so many opportunities to create distraction—this is the perfect city to take by surprise. If only I had known. I could have brought your empire to the ground."

"You're quite confident."

Soren snorted. "I didn't name *myself* the Destroyer." He could tell his words troubled the king.

"Then why didn't you try to take Aleon?"

A great regret, now that he knew. "I expected more from an empire. A mistake on my part—Mercia was the goal, and I thought the path to victory was a direct one." Soren shook his head. "If only I had known. You were the North's weakness—they needed you. I could have just taken Aleon. Cut off the sword arm, cut off the ability to fight."

"They would have still been on the isle, behind their impenetrable walls, with their archers. What would you have done then?"

Soren shrugged. "Nothing. The starvation of winter would have finished them for me."

The king eyed him. "Why are you telling me this?"

"Because I've been tasked with a collective strategy, which means I must also look for the protection of Aleon."

"And you share with me the weakness of Mercia?"

"If you were a smart king, you would have already known this. In any regard, it's no longer true. The North's weakness is no longer Aleon. The North has Kharav. Salara has me."

A smile returned to the king's lips. "I would very much like to know... how does one *get* you, Lord Commander?"

The question caught Soren by surprise, but the answer was simple. Especially for this man. "One doesn't."

The king looked at him a moment, still smiling. "Well, as I've arranged with Norah and your king, you'll help determine our collective approach, so I look forward to your counsel."

Counsel. Soren snorted again. No, he would not simply give counsel. He would tell this king what he would do. And he would do it. There was so much to be done.

"Are you hungry?" Phillip asked.

He was practically starved. Soren hadn't eaten anything since the day before, but he had food in his chamber, where he'd rather be. Alone. "No."

"I am. We'll eat. Come." The king turned and headed down the steps toward the central castle.

Come? Soren watched him descend the stairs of the temple in disbelief. Had he just told him to *come*? Like a dog? So casual Phillip was, so smug in his confidence. Well, curse him. Curse the North gods. He hated this king. He hated this place. Perhaps he'd take Aleon after all. But he hadn't brought an army. Where were Caspian and his Northmen?

Curse everything. He stood as he stewed, his fists clenched. Then he sucked in a breath through his teeth and blew it out slowly.

There was nothing he could do.

Except follow after Phillip.

The dining hall was as he remembered—too big with too much... stuff. He wanted to break away, return to his chamber, but he was committed now. He had followed the king this far. He had followed *the Aleon king.* He clenched his teeth so tightly they ached. He should have left him to walk back on his own. Eat on his own. Fuck off on his own. Now it was too late.

Now he was here, expected to eat. Expected to show his face. He had shown his face to the Aleon king before. Why had he done that? He had felt... What had he felt? An obligation to Salara to smooth the tension, yes, but something more...

He had wanted to show his face.

It had been a mistake.

"What would you like?" the king asked as they neared the table being prepared by servants.

Blood.

"Anything you want," Phillip added, "I'll have it made for you."

Enough. He couldn't bear it any longer. "Do you expect me to be impressed? Bow at your feet in thanks?"

The king whirled around, stopping them both abruptly. He didn't match Soren in size, but he certainly met his challenge. "I do want you to be impressed. *Destroyer.*" His eyes locked with Soren's boldly, unafraid. More than unafraid. Angry. "I'm the king of Aleon. I've defeated those undefeated. When I kill the man that I'm ashamed to call my brother, I'll have the largest empire in the world, riches unmeasurable. But you're not impressed, are you? And I know you're the last man who will bow to me."

Soren bristled at the king's sudden anger. "But that's what you want, isn't it?" he snarled back. "And you'll carry on with your riches, pursuing your glory, as you continue to take, continue to conquer and build your empire, as will the next Aleon king after."

Phillip's shoulders fell, and a calm returned. His anger seemed to dissipate as quickly as it came. "No," he said softly. He walked to the chair at the table's end and leaned against it, as if he suddenly didn't have the strength to stand. "No," he said again. "I'll have no heir."

What? Soren could only stare at him.

The king sat down and motioned for Soren to take the chair at the other end. "Please."

Still Soren stood.

Phillip sighed. He waved to the servants waiting near the door, and they disappeared into an adjoining room. Then he said, "When I take my final rest, I'll give the empire to the people."

What?

"I've been planning it, setting in place the laws that will govern and those who will enforce them and carry out the will of the people through elected officials."

Soren didn't understand, or if he did, he didn't believe it. "Aleon will no longer have a king?"

Phillip motioned again to the chair at the end of the table. "Please."

Finally, Soren moved to it and sat.

"Men are not meant to be ruled." Phillip let out a long breath. "And power... power corrupts everything it touches. It's taken everything and everyone I love."

Soren didn't agree. Men needed the strength of a ruler. And not everyone with power was corrupt. Not Salara. Not Salar. But he didn't offer an argument. "What do you want, then?" he asked instead.

Phillip frowned, ever so slightly leaning back in his chair. "To structure Aleon for the future. And to kill Gregor." He paused. "After that, I don't know. Perhaps then I'll feel complete." He raised his eyes to Soren's. "Do you feel complete, Lord Commander?"

Of course he was complete. He had everything he could ever ask for. He had Salara, and Salar. But why did the question hit him so heavily?

Mercifully, the servants reappeared with trays of assorted meats and vegetables, redirecting their attention and rescuing him from answering. A large platter was laid to Soren's right, and his stomach growled at the heavenly smell of herbs and spices.

"I don't go after Gregor with the lust of power," Phillip said. "I go to avenge my younger brother."

Soren knew the history. As Phillips's father lay on his deathbed, he split the empire between his three sons. Gregor, the oldest, was furious, and killed his youngest brother, joining the kingdom of Hetahl with his own kingdom of Japheth. He had tried to take Aleon and the lesser kingdoms from Phillip, but Salara's father stood as his ally, and that had been the beginning of the Great War.

"Aston was fourteen," Phillip said, staring at his chalice, but Soren knew he was staring into his memories. "Fourteen when Gregor slit his throat. He was just a boy."

Soren had always hated Gregor. Crowns in general were not kind to those who wore them, especially the young. But he didn't feel pity. "My brother was twelve when he died," he said. "My sister, nine." He had never spoken about them. Not since it happened. Only Mikael knew, and Salara. The words on his lips brought back the rage long buried.

Phillip's face grimaced slightly, and he nodded. "So, you understand. You understand the need."

Soren's fingers tightened around the knife beside his plate. "I understand."

The king nodded again and picked up his chalice of wine. "Did you lose them in the war?"

Everything within Soren tightened and coiled to strike. "I lost them when you gave the North King an army to take Bahoul."

Phillip paused, then set his chalice down. His face paled. They locked in their stare, frozen. Then his eyes moved to Soren's grip on his knife.

"Is this why you're truly here?" Phillip challenged.

Soren didn't want to think about why he was truly here. He didn't want to think about his obligations, his duty. "Have you nothing to say for yourself?" he hissed.

The king sat, unmoving, and then shook his head. "I didn't know about your family, but that's not an excuse. The truth is I would've done whatever Aamon asked of me."

Aamon. The North King. Soren clutched the knife tighter.

"I'm sorry for your family. I am. But if you'd have me recant my course, I won't."

"You continue this charade of loyalty to the North." This fakery.

Phillip's brow dipped. "Charade?" He straightened. "My father didn't prepare me for the crown. I was never meant to wear it. He saw what Gregor was becoming, the evil inside him, and decided to split the empire in his final days. He thought he'd given me enough to stand on my own, with Aleon and the smaller kingdoms. But I had no idea how to be king." He swallowed as he looked down at his plate, then back to Soren. "Aston... Well, Gregor went for him first. He didn't even make it to his coronation. I would have fallen, too, if not for King Aamon."

Phillip paused, and a quiet fell over the room. "Aamon spent a lot of time in Aleon," he continued. "And I in Mercia. He looked after me, became like a second father. He taught me things I should've learned early on, but never did. I thought I was a man at the time, but I was just a boy. He stood by my side against Gregor. Aamon taught me how to survive, how to lead a kingdom. I know you've seen devastation at his hand, but he was a good king, and he made me the man—the king—I am today. And I'm loyal to him still."

Soren didn't want to believe him. "Then why didn't you help Salara when the council took her throne?"

Phillip clasped his hands in front of him and rested them on the table. "It's a great regret, one I'll always live with. I would have harbored her, protected her, kept her safe, but she fled to the Shadowlands before I'd even learned what had happened. And then I was torn. I couldn't march against Mercia. It felt so wrong."

"So you did nothing."

"And I regret that now." He drew in a long breath and let it out. "If I could go back, change the past, I would." He finally took a drink of his chalice. "The council wrote to me. They wanted to reestablish the alliance. They offered me her cousin's hand."

Of course they had. Soren would forever be grateful he'd been able to see them hang. "What did you say to them?"

"Nothing. I didn't respond. Evangeline's a child, for gods' sakes, and she wasn't Mercia's true queen. Of course I wouldn't have agreed to that. But I said nothing. It's the only time in my life I felt like a coward. And then Norah's letter came. She didn't even ask me for help, she only asked if I knew how the people she cared about fared." Phillip's eyes welled. "But I said nothing." His face twisted in self-loathing. "To this day, I'm ashamed. I'm grateful to your king for stepping up in my failing. Grateful to you."

The room grew quiet again, and Phillip straightened. His eyes met Soren's. "And I'm grateful you're here now, Lord Commander."

Soren shifted back in his chair. He knew lies when he saw them, but this king carried no lies. This was perhaps the realest anyone had ever been with him, other than Salara and Salar. And not under threat of death or pain. This king laid himself open, willingly, and Soren didn't know what to do with him.

Slowly, he reached up and pulled down the wrap from his face. Then he stabbed a chunk of meat with his knife and pulled it to his plate and took a bite.

Curse the North gods. The food was delicious.

CHAPTER TWENTY-SEVEN

Mikael stripped off his tunic. Yes, it was winter, but Salara had a fire lit in every room of the castle. For a North queen, she certainly liked the warmth. He stared at their bed for a moment, with its heaping mounds of quilts and furs. When he'd been alone, he'd only used a sheet. This woman would sweat him out of his own castle. It was a small price, though.

The truth was, he'd give anything to make her happy, would pay any price. He'd burn his castle to the ground for her.

Yet he was losing her.

He could feel it—this distance between them, her grief and her pain; she was spiraling further away from him. Even in death, the Bear had the power to take her from him, regardless of whether this ghost was real or not. And the more Mikael fought against it, the more he pushed her away.

She was the furthest from him she'd ever been, even when she was right beside him. Mikael had used the blood, and it had upset her. He'd tried to call the ghost to him, to see what Salara had seen. She had seen *something*.

The blood only needed to touch Salara's skin for her to call the Bear, Soren had said. Mikael had poured it into his hand and waited. But no one came. He felt nothing, saw nothing. He went so far as to smear it up his arms and across his chest. All of it.

"Show yourself!" he'd snarled.

But nothing came of it.

Except Salara's unraveling.

He hadn't meant to upset her; he hadn't meant to hurt her. She was right—he hadn't thought of what it would mean to her. In his anger, he hadn't thought at all. Perhaps he was too desperate to know what it meant for himself. If the Bear still remained, so did his fate.

Or perhaps he was jealous that she still clung to another man. She'd always protected the Bear from Mikael. She'd loved the Bear, and still did. And Mikael wasn't a fool. If this was the Bear, he knew he wouldn't be able to keep her from him.

But nor would he try to.

No. It was neither of those things.

He was angry, yes, but not because he feared his fate or sharing her love. He feared this vision was a trickster that meant to do Salara harm. He feared not being able to keep her safe, and it was an ever-increasing fear.

They still had no heir. They didn't talk about it anymore—he'd told her they'd manage without—but it was no less a concern. It still haunted the shadows of his mind.

After his death, Salara would have to fight to keep Kharav. This had always been known, but things had been different before. She'd had Soren, and the Bear, and a formal offer of alliance from Aleon to fall back on. She'd been safely behind the impenetrable walls of the North. Now the Bear was gone, and the Aleon king had wed. She was deep within a kingdom surrounded by a growing enemy, and the political powers within would not be ruled by an outsider. She still had Soren and had gained the loyalty of a few other Kharavian nobles, but it wasn't enough. She wouldn't be able to keep the crown. Not without a child.

But there would be no child.

That left her with only one other option—one Mikael wasn't sure he could convince her of.

CHAPTER TWENTY-EIGHT

The Northmen arrived with the sun, and Soren was waiting. The Aleon king stood beside him at the top of the citadel stairs. Bells had chimed in the castle, alerting the arrival through the main gates, and they'd gone out to meet them.

"I love this," Phillip said.

Soren wrinkled his brow and looked at the smiling king—such a peculiar man. Was he always this happy? But it wasn't entirely annoying.

Phillip tilted his head back in question. "Don't you enjoy people arriving?"

Soren grimaced. "No."

The king chuckled.

Why was that funny? Soren shifted his gaze back to the approaching Northmen, and they both took the stairs to the bottom.

Caspian brought his horse to a halt and slid down. "Lord Commander," he said with a small bow of his head.

"What took you so long?" Soren rumbled.

Caspian's brows drew together. "I came immediately once I got the message."

"Lord Justice," the king greeted.

Caspian shifted his attention to the Aleon king and bowed his head. "King Phillip."

"Welcome back to Aleon, and congratulations on your position."

"Thank you. I appreciate that. And it's good to be back."

"How is the queen regent?"

"Well," Caspian said. "Very much herself."

Phillip chuckled.

Soren held back the impatience growing in his chest. There was work to be done, and they were standing here chatting.

The king motioned for a servant. "Prato will show you to your chamber," he told Caspian. "Freshen up. Get something to eat, then meet us in my study. He'll show you the way."

"Thank you," Caspian said. He gave another nod to Soren and then followed the servant to his chambers.

Phillip turned to Soren. "Shall we?"

Finally. "Lead the way," he replied irritably.

Soren followed the king down a series of halls. They reached a back study, and his eyes widened as he caught sight of a large table map of Aleon and the lands beyond. He stepped slowly to the table and ran his hands along the smooth edging of polished wood. Now this—this was a work of art. Kharav was exhaustive in planning, and Soren considered his own maps to be some of the best in the world, but this in front of him... he could only admire. The line topography was meticulous. Moveable figures in polished iron marked the placement of forces, both those of Aleon and of Mercia, as well as those of Japheth and Rael. And this Aleon king was well informed.

"Does it meet your expectations?" Phillip asked him.

Soren glanced at him, and the king smiled. Distractingly so. Soren forced his eyes back to the table. "It isn't disappointing."

He set his mind on the task at hand, staring at the figures of enemy forces along the inside border of Japheth. Rael would likely make the first move, and there were two options. Cyrus could advance north against Eilor, the southernmost kingdom of the Aleon Empire. This was the least-favored option to Soren, as Kharavian forces would have to give up the advantage of the Canyonlands to join the battle. But Soren had a hunch: Gregor wanted Aleon, and Cyrus wanted Kharav—they would attack Kharav. Rael was the more powerful force, Gregor the weaker in both strength and courage. Cyrus would get what he wanted. And Soren planned to make it a more appealing option as well.

Phillip stepped to the table map beside Soren. "What do you think, Lord Commander?"

Soren tapped on Aleon's southern kingdom of Eilor. "Put your forces on your southern border and show Aleon as a less desirable option. Push Rael and Japheth toward Kharav, and when they take the pass, you'll move south and keep pressure on them to stay along the canyons."

"And then?"

Soren drew his finger along the map and stopped at the central Canyonlands—the land he knew like his own flesh. "Once they reach here, you'll push them back into the canyons, where my men will finish them."

Phillip leaned across the table and clasped two of Aleon's battalion figurines. Soren's eyes caught on the lines of his lean-muscled arm, but he quickly pulled his gaze away. Phillip moved them on the map just north of the Canyonlands. "Two or three?"

Forcing his attention on the map, Soren said, "All of your forces."

Phillip looked at Soren in surprise. "All?"

"You have to come with enough power that they won't consider moving north."

He stared at Soren a moment. "All?"

"All."

"Even my forces in Bahoul?"

Especially his forces in Bahoul. "My Northmen will keep the stronghold."

Phillip chuckled. "And how do I know this isn't your strategy to get me out of there?"

Perhaps it was. The stronghold belonged to Kharav and the North, not to Aleon. "Even so, it's still the right move. I need your cavalry and swordsmen at the southern border of Eilor."

"You *need*?" Phillip's eyes were a piercing blue, challenging. "Are you commandeering my army, Lord Commander?"

"Is that not why I'm here?" Soren said shortly. Diplomacy, he reminded himself. He drew in a breath. "Forgive my overreach. It's not my intention to take command."

The corner of Phillip's mouth curved up ever so slightly. "Perhaps I want you to."

Their stares locked, and Soren froze. Was the king giving him the Aleon army? His pulse quickened. Was there another meaning to his words? *No.* He swallowed and tore his eyes away, looking back to the map. The army—the king meant the army. But when he raised his gaze again, he caught Phillip's smile, and the glint in his eye—

The doors to the study opened, and Caspian stepped in. *Thank the North gods.*

"Lord Justice," Phillip said, motioning to the map. "We were just talking about positioning."

Soren shifted.

Caspian stepped to the table and eyed the setup. "Impressive," he said.

Phillip smiled proudly as he looked back down at it. A bronze lock fell over his brow, and he brushed it back. He glanced up at Soren, his blue eyes shining. Soren hated blue eyes. But these blue eyes...

"The lord commander believes the best course is for me to move the entirety of my forces south to Eilor," Phillip said. "Push Japheth and Rael back into the Canyonlands."

Caspian nodded. "It makes sense, but it's a great risk. Your advantage before was your overwhelming numbers, but that's not in our favor now, not with Rael. It's essentially a bluff, and if they break through, you've no defenses to stop them from moving up through Aleon."

Phillip nodded, mulling. "I'd rather position my forces farther north, in Songs."

Caspian's brow creased. "You'd give up Eilor?"

"Temporarily, yes. For more advantageous ground. If I put all my forces south in Eilor and am overwhelmed, I would have to trust the Shadowlands to come to my defense."

"Do you not?" Soren quipped.

Phillip's eyes met Soren's again, locking them into a stare once more. "I want to."

The king's reply stole whatever smart response sat on his tongue.

Phillip looked back down at the table, pausing. "I've never shied from a risk, if the reward is worth it." Then he brought his gaze back to Soren's. "This is a dangerous path for me." He gave a faint smile. "But I'm willing."

That smile wasn't about the battle. Soren shook his head—of course he was talking about the battle. What else would he be talking about? Soren's pulse thrummed faster, and he clenched the edges of the table.

Phillip stepped around to where Soren stood, reaching across and taking Aleon's figurine from Bahoul. Their shoulders brushed. Soren tensed as a jolt of electricity ran through him. Their eyes locked again as Phillip moved the figurine to the border of Eilor.

"Together, or spread along the border?" Phillip asked.

Soren swallowed the fire that was building in his throat. He tried to push it down. "Together," he said. "Moving together as Rael progresses." A strange grip held him. He needed to get away from this man.

Phillip moved the rest of the Aleon figurines to Eilor. Their shoulders still touched as they both leaned on the table over the map.

Never had someone stood so casually close to him before. Never had someone dared to touch him. Still, Soren couldn't bring himself to move away.

"I'm choosing to trust you," Phillip said. He turned and his eyes found Soren's again.

Fire rippled across Soren's skin. Phillip was talking about the battle. Nothing else. But the way he looked at him...

"Let's think on it," Caspian said. "For now, I want to see if my men have settled in the barracks."

"Go," Phillip said, "we'll think more on it and reconvene."

Caspian gave a small nod and departed.

Soren moved to leave, but Phillip caught him.

"You own the next move, Lord Commander." The corners of his mouth turned upward, and he left out the door and disappeared down the hall.

The battle. He was talking about the battle. Soren pulled down his wrap and wiped his face. He pushed out a long breath. He needed to get his mind back.

The afternoon passed too slowly, and too quickly. Soren found himself back at the map with Phillip. They'd already met with Caspian again and confirmed the plan from before. Phillip would move the entirety of his forces south, putting pressure on Japheth and Rael to keep them along the Canyonlands and giving the advantage to Kharav. If they were lucky, they'd contain the war there, and finish it.

Caspian left to write orders for the legions.

It was a bold plan, and a risky one for Phillip, Soren knew. The Aleon king would be placing his trust in an enemy he had warred against for ten years, an enemy who had dreamed of his death many times over, who still dreamed of it. Although Soren had to admit, he dreamed of it a little less now. This king puzzled him, both in mind and... He didn't know how to describe it. Phillip was different from what he'd thought. It cooled Soren's anger toward him.

And the way Phillip looked at him...

Soren sucked in a breath. It was all in his head. He needed to get out of this kingdom. It was messing with his mind. He turned his thoughts to something he could think about more rationally—war. War was coming. He felt solid with this plan he'd devised with Phillip and Caspian.

That reminded him... "Where's your commander?" he asked Phillip as they stood at the table.

Phillip shifted back, hesitating before he answered. "I lost him when I took Tarsus. But I have my generals."

Wait... "You have the largest empire in the world, and you have no commander?"

"*I* am commander."

Soren could only stare at him in surprise. Was this man mad? "Who devises your strategies?"

Phillip frowned with a shrug. "I devise my own strategies."

"Who executes them?"

"As I said, I have my generals."

Even with generals, being both king and commander was too much for one person. "Do you not have a trusted man?"

Phillip sighed. "I'm working to dissolve the absolute power of an empire. As you can imagine, for those who reap the benefits of status, it's an unpopular plan." He looked back to the table. "I trust my enemies more than I trust my own heads of state." He raised his eyes to Soren's again. "Am I making a mistake by trusting *you*, Lord Commander?"

Absolutely. Soren would just as soon run him through than... he cursed himself silently. He hated the North gods more than he ever had. Because he wouldn't harm this man. "Maybe," he said simply.

Phillip nodded. "Yet I find myself doing just that." His voice dropped. "Perhaps because I see you, Soren."

Soren shifted back on his heel. For the king to so boldly call him by his name...

And the way he'd said it—all play gone, stripped and open, completely genuine. Soren's breath seized in his chest. He searched his mind for something—anything—to redirect the conversation. "You need a commander. You can't do this on your own."

A hint of a smile returned to Phillip's lips. "You sound... concerned for me."

"If you fail, we all fail."

Phillip nodded as he stepped closer. "Is that all?"

Was that all? What kind of question was that? What answer did he want? Soren shifted. It wasn't all. His heart hammered faster at the answer he didn't dare give.

The king gave a small chuckle. Did he notice? "Have I improved my standing with you, Lord Commander? Or do you still think of killing me?" Phillip stepped even closer. "I know you've thought about it. Killing me, that is. I've seen it in your eyes."

Soren swallowed. He wouldn't deny it, although it wasn't exactly true now—but *that* he would deny.

"Strange it doesn't make me wary of you." The king was so close now, close enough to touch. Too close. "Perhaps that's foolish of me," he added.

It was.

Phillip reached up and brought his hand to Soren's wrap. Soren didn't move to stop him. Perhaps it was the shock of it. Or perhaps he didn't want to. Ever so carefully, Phillip pulled the cloth down to reveal his face. No one had ever been so bold before.

"Am I foolish, Soren?"

Only a foolish man would touch him. "Very." But perhaps Soren was foolish for letting him.

Phillip leaned forward, lifting his face. His lips parted slightly. He was a beautiful man—a beautiful and powerful man. And something told Soren he was a very dangerous man...

Soren leaned forward, an invisible force drawing him closer. Then closer still. He couldn't breathe as the air conspired against him.

But suddenly his will broke through and something splintered within, freeing him. He jerked back.

The king drew back with a start as well.

Soren shook his head, but more at himself than Phillip. Had he lost his mind completely? The heat of embarrassment flushed across his skin, then a rush of anger. What was he doing? His hand wrapped around the dagger at his waist. His focus should be on the war at hand. Not... whatever this was.

It was nothing.

But it wasn't nothing.

And where did this leave them now?

"I'm sorry," said Phillip. "I shouldn't have done that." His eyes caught Soren's again, but it wasn't a reciprocation of shame Soren saw. The king's eyes gleamed with a hint of mischief. "I did say it was your move."

The shock still gripped him. Soren couldn't speak. He couldn't move.

The king turned to leave, but paused and looked back at him. His smile grew. "And, Lord Commander, when we become better friends, I'll tell you about a vision I've seen." Then he left Soren standing alone in the study.

Soren's heart pounded in his ears.

Phillip knew.

CHAPTER TWENTY-NINE

Adrian's nostrils flared. "The Aleon king needs a trusted man, and he can't pick one from the hundred thousand he already has?" He shook his head. "I can't go to Aleon."

Norah sighed. She didn't blame him. He didn't want to serve Aleon. He wanted to serve Kharav. He wanted to serve Mercia. She reached out and clasped his arm. "Phillip has given the lord commander control of his army. Think of it as Soren needing a trusted man, and he trusts you."

"What about Katya?" he argued. "She'd do far better than I would."

"The lord commander is a purposeful man, and he's called for *you*," Norah said. "He has a reason. And Katya's just had a child."

"You'll go," Mikael told him.

Adrian cut Mikael a sharp glance, one that would have normally garnered a swift and harsh punishment. Something had happened between them—she wasn't sure what. Whatever it was, it fueled Adrian with an anger rarely seen, and drew from Mikael a tolerance rarely given. Norah told herself to pry later.

"I belong here," Adrian said to Norah. "The Aleon king doesn't even know me."

"Adrian—"

"Norah, you need me here—"

Mikael's eyes blazed, and he grabbed Adrian's breastplate. "Your salar commands you. Your salara commands you. But that aside, if the lord commander has called you, you'll go. Do you understand?"

Adrian stilled, but he didn't respond.

"You leave tomorrow," Mikael said.

Adrian glanced back at Norah and, finally, gave a reluctant bow of his head. Then he left to prepare without further protest.

"Don't be angry with him," she said after Adrian was gone. "He's still young, unsure of himself."

"He knows exactly what he's capable of." He reached down and took her hand. "He just wants to stay with his queen. He worries for you here."

"He doesn't need to worry." She squeezed his hand. "I have you."

He lifted her chin to him. "I'm worried too, Salara. I want you to think about returning to the North."

She pulled back. "What?"

"It's safer for you there."

She shook her head. "No, I'm not leaving you. I've only been back a few weeks. And it's perfectly safe here, safer than traveling."

"You're only thinking about today. You need to think about tomorrow."

She paused, and her eyes narrowed. "What's that supposed to mean?"

"It means you have to think of the future, and about your strategy."

She only stared at him. Where was he going with this?

"You have to fortify yourself in the North," he said, "and continue to grow your friendship with Aleon and Osan." Then he paused and swallowed. "And you have to marry Soren after I'm gone."

Her mouth dropped open. "Have you lost your mind?" she hissed.

"He has claim to the throne. The nobles will support him."

She shook her head. "No. We've been through this. I won't bed him, and I certainly won't marry him."

"You'd have the same relationship you have now. He'll give you freedom. He'll protect you."

"He protects me now."

"You know what I mean!" His voice came thick with frustration. "I'm not talking about his strength or his fortitude. When I'm gone, you'll need his name."

His frustration fueled her own. "Because you don't think I'm strong enough without you?"

"That's not what I said."

"But it's what you meant. You think I'm weak. Because I'm a woman? Because I love? Because I grieve?" She stepped closer, seething. "I'm queen of Mercia and salara of Kharav, with or without a husband. If someone wants my crown, they'll have to pry it from my dead fingers, if they still have a head to wear it."

A deep horn sounded through the air, and Norah looked through the window from where she sat at her vanity.

"The lord commander must be returning," her maid Amara said as she finished pinning back a lock in Norah's hair.

Norah knew what the horn meant. She'd been waiting for it. "Send for him," she said. "Tell him I need to speak to him immediately."

Amara nodded and left to do as she was bid.

No doubt Mikael would be eager to speak to Soren too. But Norah couldn't wait. She hoped Soren would seek her out first.

Not long after, two knocks on the door gave her answer, and it swung open before she could even rise.

"What?" Soren said as he stepped inside. He looked like he'd been riding for weeks. And he smelled like he'd been riding for weeks. But Norah didn't care about his look or his smell, she was just grateful he was there.

"Is there still a king of Aleon?" she asked him. While she trusted Soren implicitly, she also knew he was confined to few boundaries, and wanted to make sure their new ally still had his head.

"He lives."

That was a miracle in itself. She nodded appreciatively. "I was surprised you called Adrian to go." And she was surprised Soren had left him there. Not that she worried for Adrian in Aleon, he was just still so young, and to be serving on his own in another kingdom...

Soren shifted slightly. "You wanted me to have asked you first?"

She shook her head. "No, you're making decisions for all our armies now, and I trust those decisions. I'm just saying I'm surprised, that's all."

He seemed to mull over her words, then he said, "The Aleon king has no commander."

Her brows drew together. Was that an explanation? "Adrian isn't a commander." Gods, he wasn't even a captain. He had no status, other than a Crest sword entitlement.

"Not yet. But he doesn't need to be. The Aleon king is a smart man, but he needs someone to challenge his thinking, someone who doesn't have his own agenda. And yes, surprisingly, this Aleon king is accepting of Kharav, but some of those around him are still wary."

She understood. "You couldn't send a Kharavian."

"So I sent him a Kharavian Northman." His eyes smiled.

She couldn't help a smile of her own. No doubt Adrian's being the brother of Mercia's former lord justice also helped. And he was right, Adrian was extremely clever and knew Kharavian battle standards and strategies, and he wouldn't shy away from challenging one's thinking—even a king's.

Soren gave a quick nod and then turned for the door. "Salar wants to see me."

"There is one more thing," she said, stopping him. He paused and looked at her, a wariness immediately coming to him. She didn't say anything else; she only turned her eyes to the small vial that sat on top of her vanity, waiting for him to react.

And he did. "You received that here? Just now?"

She shook her head. "No, while you were in Aleon."

"What did Salar say?"

Damn it. She rocked forward as she searched for the words.

"You *did* tell Salar. Didn't you?"

"I wanted to, but—"

"How could you not?" His voice was thick with anger.

Norah stood. "I panicked! Mikael used the last vial, and we're lucky nothing happened. We don't know what power we're dealing with. I didn't know how he'd react, or how

Alexander would react. And when I didn't tell him the first day, the second day was even harder. Then the third, then the fourth." She looked down at her hands. "I can't tell him now. Now he'll think I'm hiding something."

"Well, you are," he snapped.

"You know what I mean," she cut back. Her stomach twisted, and she moved and sat on the edge of the bed. "Soren," she breathed. "Please. I don't know what to do."

He lingered by the vanity before picking up the vial. She couldn't look at him. She only waited for the lecture she knew would come.

But it didn't.

The bed sank under his weight as he sat beside her, and they let the quiet lay between them for a while.

"You truly believe this is the Bear?" he asked.

She didn't know what to believe anymore. "I don't know." Her lip trembled as her eyes welled. "I want it to be."

"And that's why you didn't tell Salar."

"He doesn't understand. He doesn't *try* to understand. But it's not what it appears, it's not like that—"

"I know." He stared at the vial in his hand. "Let's say it is Alexander." He looked at her. "There is a time where we all say goodbye."

The breath left her lungs. She knew this. But still...

"We have to move forward," he continued.

"It's easy for you to say," she whispered. "You hated him."

He sighed. Then he stood and slowly unclipped his cloak from his shoulders and pulled it off.

She gasped as she stood. Covering the broad stretch of skin across the center of his back was the image of a shield. But it wasn't just any shield—it was Alexander's shield.

She reached out and brushed her fingertips over the patterns that together formed a greater picture.

"I asked Salta Tau for the marking," he said, "for the loss of my greatest adversary. And she gave me his shield upon my back." He turned, and his eyes found hers again. "I carry him with me now. And so will you. But you have to say goodbye."

Say goodbye? She couldn't do that. "I'm still figuring things out."

He shook his head. "You're not figuring things out. There's no information he gives you. He doesn't speak. There's no purpose to seeing him, other than comfort. But that comfort will keep you from moving forward. You have to let him go." His brows drew together. "And he's supposed to be watching over the North, not visiting you in visions. Tell him to do his job, or I'll pull his worthless body from the Hall of Souls and send him to your gods."

His jest broke the tension, and she gave a small laugh through the tears that were threatening.

He held the vial for her, and she took it back, but he didn't release it immediately. A seriousness returned to him. "Say goodbye. Then that will be the end of this."

He let it go, and with a final nod, left her to the quiet of the room.

Norah watched him leave before looking back at the vial in her hands. *Say goodbye.* How simple, yet not. How could she say goodbye? But Soren was right. She needed to put an end to this and move forward. For herself, for Mikael, and for Alexander.

She inhaled deeply as she opened the vial and drew a line of blood across her palm. Then she closed her eyes and waited.

All was quiet.

Then he came.

Alexander stood in front of her in the depths of her mind and gave a small smile. Gods, she missed that smile. She had last called him when she had been in Mercia, and to see him now, again... A wave of emotion hit her.

His brows dipped, and he stepped closer.

"I wasn't sure you'd come, after Mikael..." She paused. "I'm sorry about that. I didn't know he'd use the blood. I'm sure that was a surprise."

His face showed no reaction.

"I... I thought about it a lot, him calling you. At first I thought it would have helped him understand if he'd seen you." She paused again, looking down at her hands. "But now"—she shook her head—"I think it would have made it worse, knowing you really are here. So thank you, for not engaging." And not doing anything else that this strange power allowed him to do.

She stared at him, chained by the blue eyes staring back at her. Gods, this was hard. "But Soren says it's time for me to say goodbye." She pulled her bottom lip between her teeth. "And he's right." She gave a sad smile and let out a laughing breath through her tears. "He said you need to start doing your job looking over Mercia and stop haunting me."

But Alexander's smile was gone, his face dark. He obviously didn't appreciate the humor as much as she had.

She cleared her throat and became serious again. "I know you're not yourself, at least not exactly, but I think it's what the old you would have wanted—for me to be able to move forward."

His face grew sharper and more shadowed. He stepped closer, shaking his head. Her words were upsetting him.

"I want you to know that I'm all right. That I'm cared for and looked after."

He shook his head again as he reached up and clasped her cheek. It broke her. She hadn't expected him to object. She thought this would bring closure.

"I'm all right, Alexander," she tried to encourage him again. And then she hugged him. Tightly. She gave herself only a moment.

Then she had to go. With tears in her eyes, she stepped up on her toes and brought her lips to his cheek.

"Goodbye," she whispered.

Norah opened her eyes to her empty chamber. She drew in a tear-laden breath and wiped off her hand, then looked down at the vial, at the blood still within. She sank to the floor of the fireplace and sat. She just sat.

The hours passed in a blur.

The day faded into evening.

Finally, she picked herself up off the floor and dropped the vial into the letter box on the vanity before leaving the chamber.

The sun had already set as she walked across the courtyard, but its colors still painted the sky. Through a window, she spotted Soren inside speaking to one of the nobles, but when he saw her, he excused himself and stepped outside. Norah picked up her walk along the castle toward the gardens, and he fell in step beside her.

"He didn't understand," she said, not looking at him as she spoke. "He didn't want to say goodbye."

"You did the right thing."

She shook her head. "What if he had a purpose, and I just cut him off?"

"It's not a pure purpose, I assure you."

Norah stopped abruptly by the wall of the tower. "You still don't think it's Alexander?"

He sighed.

"So all those heartfelt words of saying goodbye were a cart full of rubbish?"

"If it were Alexander, every word I said holds true. You can't keep him, Salara."

"I'm not trying to keep him!" she cried.

"Then what are you trying to do?"

The question left her speechless.

A noise in the distance caught her attention, and she turned toward it. She squinted and saw a large flock of birds flying toward the castle. Their multitudes created a giant swarm, twisting and floating through the painted sky.

"What's that?" she asked.

"Looks like a massive flock of starlings."

There were hundreds, maybe thousands of them. "It's amazing," she whispered, temporarily forgetting everything else in the moment.

The birds drew closer, and the collective sound of their wings grew louder. She stood mesmerized. The swarm moved as one, weaving in and out in a meticulously coordinated dance, like chaos through the halls of air but with beautiful purpose.

"Have you ever seen anything like it?"

Soren shook his head. "Farther south, but not this large."

Suddenly, the flock swarmed downward, and Norah let out a sharp cry as they plummeted into the side walls of the tower above her and then fell to the ground from overhead. Carcasses poured down like rain. She dropped to her knees with her hands over her head, and Soren covered her. He held her tightly, protecting her from the falling creatures. The Crest swept around them, their shields up. The sickening blows of death rang out as the birds dropped down over top of them. Norah covered her ears to muffle the sound.

When the last bird had fallen, a haunting silence came. The Crest drew back, and Soren rose slowly, pulling Norah up with him. The guard stood in a circle around her, their swords out, but equally as confused as to what had just happened. She covered her mouth in horror as she looked at the dead birds blanketing the earth around them.

"Get inside," Soren said to her as the Crest quickly made a path through the dead birds back to the entry hall.

Norah stumbled back to the castle in a daze. Inside, she let out a ragged breath, trying to keep herself calm. Caspian appeared beside her. Where had he come from? He was supposed to be in Mercia. But she couldn't think straight right now.

"I saw what happened," he said. "Are you all right?"

"No, I'm not all right!" she cried. She looked at Soren, who had followed her. "It's him, I know it's him."

Soren's brows drew together. "The Bear?"

She nodded, clutching her arms around her. "He's angry."

"Alexander?" Caspian asked, his face etched in confusion.

"Salara." Soren reached out and clasped her arms, making her look at him. "Angry or no, the Bear would never do this. You know him. He had respect for life and all things. I don't know what happened here, but whoever comes to you in these visions, if he is linked to this, it's not the Bear. I need to tell Salar."

She grabbed his hand. "No! Soren, no! Please!"

"You have to tell him what's going on!"

"He'll send me back to Mercia."

"Queen Norah," Caspian said, stepping forward. "You *have* to come back to Mercia. It's why I'm here."

She stopped and stared at him. "What? Why?"

He hesitated a moment, then said, "It's your grandmother. She's sick. Very sick."

She forgot about the birds. "How sick?"

"She's dying, Norah."

The cold had settled in her core, but she didn't have the energy to pull more blankets over her. Norah lay in her bed, staring blankly out the window, unseeing. Mikael had stayed with her for a time as the news about her grandmother sank in, then he had gone to prepare for the journey back to Mercia. As she had expected, the birds sparked a fury in him, as did the news about Alexander and the vial of blood, and he insisted on returning with her. It was nonsensical that both he and Soren would accompany her back, but he wouldn't hear of anything else. She tried to talk him out of it, but only half-heartedly. The truth was she was glad he'd stay with her. She needed him.

Her mind raced and stumbled all at once. The news of Catherine took the air from her lungs. She was all Norah had left. And despite her callousness at times, she was the matriarch that had held Mercia together, had made Norah strong, and Norah loved her. What would life be like without her? What would she even do with Mercia? Catherine took care of everything—Norah didn't even have to think about it. How was she going to run a kingdom on her own? Catherine couldn't leave her.

Like Alexander had.

Alexander.

Alexander had left her. More than left her—he was supposed to be watching over her, watching over Mercia, helping her, helping Catherine. Her face twisted as the emotion washed over her. She ripped back the furs and stumbled to the vanity, clawing off the lid and finding the vial. She poured the blood out across her palm.

She demanded him to come. "Alexander!"

But there was no answer.

She tried to calm herself as she closed her eyes. "Where are you?" She heard the anger in her own voice. Anger at him. At her grandmother. At fate.

"Alexander!"

But she stood alone in the darkness of her mind. Would he not come? Was this what had become of them? She sank into the chair of the vanity. Even in her mind she didn't have the strength to stand.

"Alexander," she whispered.

Then... the faintest of stirring.

"I know you're there."

He stepped forward from the darkness, but she didn't stand.

"Did you send the birds?" she asked. Her voice cracked. "Did you do that?"

He drew closer, his eyes apologetic, sad.

She shook her head as emotion built in her throat. "Why?"

He stepped even closer, his mouth opening as if about to speak, but he stopped.

"Why would you do that to me?" she whispered. "How could you do that?"

In front of her, slowly, he sank to his knees. Asking forgiveness. A deep sorrow hung across his brow. Her anger dissipated.

"What happened to you?" she whispered. She leaned forward slightly and brought her hand to his cheek. "Is there anything left of the Alexander I knew?"

His eyes shifted down. Ever so slowly, he shook his head.

A cry rose in her throat, and she swallowed it down as she pulled back. "Then you're not Alexander. If you were, you aren't anymore. Not truly."

His chest rose and fell, and a pain etched his face. Again, he shook his head, but he took her hand and pulled it back to his cheek.

Her lip trembled. The tears came freely now. She needed him—not just the Alexander she once loved, not just her lord justice, but the man who had shared a bond with Catherine, the man who would have mourned her grandmother as his own, so that Norah wouldn't mourn her alone.

"Grandmother's dying." Her voice broke as she said it.

His brow dipped, and he clutched her hands tightly.

"Without her, I don't know what to do." She shook her head. "And without you too." Her voice dropped to a whisper. "I'm trying not to hate you for leaving me, but I do. I do sometimes."

Norah pulled her hands from his and wiped her face. "Mikael is taking me back to Mercia tomorrow." She paused. "This is the last time I'll call you."

He shook his head, and it knifed her heart. She brought her hands back to his face, tracing the lines she knew so well. His eyes pleaded to her.

"Goodbye, Alexander," she whispered, and opened her eyes to the living.

The room was quiet.

Norah sat for a time, staring at her lap where Alexander had knelt in front of her in her mind. She pulled a small handkerchief from the vanity and wiped the blood from her hand, then rose unsteadily.

Move forward. That was what she needed to do.

She threw the vial into the fireplace.

Chapter Thirty

Most of the Kharavian army stayed in Kharav, with only one legion accompanying Norah and the king back to Mercia. Caspian rode near the back as they traveled north. He was happy to be headed back to the Uru, where he'd been the week prior in coming to Kharav, but too soon he'd be leaving Tahla and his son again, and he didn't know when he'd see them next.

Caspian accepted this life, welcomed it even. He'd never imagined himself finding love or having a son. Now he had both, and he was grateful. Men wasted their joy on seeking perfection in it, but he'd relish every moment. He had to. He had to find joy where he could.

Alexander's death had hit him harder than he could have ever imagined. He missed the man he'd known his entire life, the man that was like a brother to him. Caspian had always expected himself to be the first between them to leave this world. To him, Alexander had been... invincible, his death impossible. Caspian would have given his life for him, and it's what he always thought he would do. When Alexander died, it had shaken everything within him, rocked his very foundation. And now he found himself in a role he wasn't worthy of, praying that he could fill it half as well as his friend had.

He'd worried for Adrian, but the young man had surprised him. Adrian had shown himself to be every part Alexander's brother, every part the son of the great Beurnat the Bear. He'd grieved deeply, but then he'd risen.

The lord commander had a hand in it, no doubt. And the king. They treated Adrian as if he were their own man—they had faith in him, and expectations of him—and he rose to those expectations. Now under the lord commander's watch, Adrian served beside King Phillip—a seemingly impossible circumstance. Yet here they were in seemingly impossible times—Mercia and Kharav united with Aleon, with Caspian as lord justice. Although months had passed, it still hadn't taken hold in his heart, but he'd give his everything to it.

His pulse raced as they neared the Canyonlands. It had only been a week, but he couldn't wait to hold his son in his arms again, to hold Tahla.

When they reached the tribe, he worked quickly to settle the legion outside. Then he made his way inside, to the village's center fire, where Norah and the others had settled among the Urun people, visiting. Norah sat on a large rock by the warmth of the fire, laughing and holding Katakah in her lap.

Caspian took a seat close by. He couldn't take his eyes from the infant. The child sat contently, bundled in furs, looking like a bedroll. He had to hold back his chuckle. He glanced up to see Norah looking back at him.

"Sorry," he murmured as he shifted his gaze to the fire.

The center of her brows twitched. "Why?"

He only shook his head. "I don't know. I didn't mean to stare."

She grinned. "How can you not?" She looked back down at the infant in her lap and scrunched her nose at him. "He's the most adorable thing."

Caspian couldn't help a smile as he looked at the child. "That he is."

"Do you want to hold him?"

Yes. Yes, he did. "No," he said quickly. "No." It would be awkward for the Mercian lord justice to hold an Urun baby. Norah never thought about what was awkward, only about sharing things that brought joy. This baby certainly brought joy, but Caspian had to decline. Still, he watched as she adjusted Katakah's cover more snugly over his head and around his cheeks to keep him warm. But there was no covering the plump rounds on the babe's face, and a chuckle escaped Caspian as Norah's attempts only squished the fat and puffed out the child's lips more.

Norah laughed too. "Did you see Katya's son?" she asked.

He nodded with a smile. "I did."

She laughed again. "These chub babies just melt my heart." She looked over at him. "Fatherhood would look good on you too, Caspian."

His smile died, and he had to force himself to keep it.

She must have noticed, as she stammered, "I-I mean... you should just know if it's what you wanted... I'd want it for you, that's all."

It was what he wanted. More than anything.

"Not that it's my business," she added. "I just, I, uh"—she smiled as she shook her head—"or maybe it is my business because Titus asked me. But I don't think you'd ask, so you should just know that you'd have my blessing if it was what you wanted."

He swallowed the lump forming in his throat. "Thank you."

While his heart leapt at her words, they didn't matter. He couldn't let them matter. This was Tahla's decision, and he respected it, regardless of how much it hurt. And it was the right decision. Whether Caspian had an heir was of no consequence—there was nothing to pass down, nothing to inherit. There was nothing at stake. But Tahla had a duty to her people. Katakah would be chief one day, and the Uru depended on that identity, that loyalty. He knew Tahla loved him, but he also knew duty. And for duty, they'd sacrifice.

Tahla appeared and stepped around the fire, and both Norah and Caspian shifted their attention to her. She paused when she saw him and gave a warm smile. "Lord Justice," she said.

He loved the sound of her voice, no matter what she said. He gave a respectful nod, as anyone would, grateful he didn't have to speak, because he didn't think he could.

"I think he's ready for bed," Norah said as she passed the child back to Tahla. "His eyes are sleepy."

"He most certainly is." Tahla scooped the baby into her arms, looking down at him. "I have to feed him and put him down. I'll see you off in the morning, Salara."

Norah clasped her arm with a smile. "I'll see you in the morning."

Tahla left with the child, and Caspian had to force himself not to watch her go. He waited until he had finished his soup and until Norah left for her own bed. Then he could wait no more.

He trailed the shadows of the village streets, moving quietly, back to where he knew Tahla resided with the child. He wasn't sure how she'd feel about him coming on his own. She'd always come to his dwelling, or invited him to her. But he couldn't wait for that. He didn't know when he'd see her or Katakah again, and he wanted every moment.

When he reached the house, he was surprised to find the door ajar. He paused, swaying to eye the candlelit room inside through the crack, but it seemed empty. Slowly, he pushed the door open and stepped inside.

"Back here," came Tahla's voice from the room behind a hanging panel.

Caspian closed the door behind him and moved toward the back room. Stepping around the panel, he drew in a breath as his eyes caught Tahla sitting in the center of the bed, cross-legged, with Katakah at her breast. Never had he seen her more beautiful.

She smiled at him. "I was hoping you wouldn't make me come get you."

He smiled back. "If I'm welcome, I'll come directly from now on."

She held out a hand for him. He closed the gap between them and took it, letting her pull him onto the bed beside her.

"You're always welcome," she said.

Caspian clasped her cheek and leaned in to kiss her. Her lips were warm and sweet. When he pulled back, he looked down at the child. "He's growing," he said softly.

"He is."

"He looks like you." He cupped the top of the child's head. The boy's dark hair was thick but soft, and there was a lot of it. Caspian could already see he'd have his mother's mane.

She smiled as she grazed the child's cheeks with her fingertips. "I still see you when I look at him." Her face turned serious. "I'm sorry, Caspian. For tonight. I know it's hard, and I know this isn't what you want."

He shook his head. "You don't have to apologize. You're making the right decision for Katakah and your people. I only want to share this life with you as much as I can. I love you, Tahla."

Her smile returned. "I love you," she whispered.

"There is something, though." He sat for a moment, swallowing the lump rising in his throat. Then he pulled the ring off his smallest finger and placed it in her hand.

"What's this?" she asked.

"It's customary in Mercia for a man to give a woman a ring when they're wed, to remind her of his love for her."

"Caspian," she breathed.

"I know," he said quickly as he shifted closer to her, being careful not to bump Katakah. "And I won't speak of it again after this. I won't ask you anymore. I only want you to know there will be no other in my heart but you. I make you this vow. I love you, Tahla. I love our child. And I want you to remember that every day." He paused and swallowed again. "And if you should ever find in your heart that you think of me as your husband, just wear this ring, and it will be so."

"Caspian, I—"

"Don't answer," he stopped her. "Don't answer. I say this only for you to know."

Her eyes glistened as she curled her fingers around the ring, and he brought his lips to hers.

Chapter Thirty-One

The open markets smelled of cooking meat, and Norah's stomach grumbled. She followed the scent of smoke and spice through the streets of Redding, one of the Free Cities just beyond the outer reaches of Mercia. Mikael and Soren weren't keen on stopping in the Free Cities when traveling between Mercia and Kharav—they weren't keen on any city not in Kharav—but Mikael had surprised her with the idea, and Norah had quickly accepted. She needed a break, something to distract her mind.

She walked freely. The city was so used to travelers and merchants passing through that no one took notice of her, no one recognized her. She loved it. Only a few of the Crest moved through the crowds around her, at a distance, not close enough to draw attention to her, as she had asked of them. However, there was no convincing Mikael and Soren, who paid no mind to blending in and followed ridiculously close.

She finally found the source of the wonderful smell and stopped at the stall of the culprit.

"What'll ya 'ave?" asked a pot-bellied man without looking up. He stood over a grate along a pit fire, turning meats as they cooked.

"One of those sausages," she said, pointing to a steaming plate on the side.

"Two sum."

Norah puffed a breath through her lips. She had forgotten they dealt in a separate currency here. She pulled a gold coin from her pouch. "I think this will suffice?"

The man grinned and held out his hand, and she dropped it into his palm. Then he offered her the plate to take her pick. Norah pulled her dagger and speared the one on the end, and then smiled as she turned to continue walking. But she stopped when she saw Mikael and Soren staring at her in surprise.

"Did you just pay a gold coin for a sausage?" Soren asked with a snaked brow.

She looked at Mikael, then back at Soren. "No."

"I saw you."

She pursed her lips. "I was hungry."

"You could have at least gotten more than one then."

She eyed him directly as she took a bite of the sausage.

Mikael brushed her arm. "Do you want to stay longer?"

She shook her head and swallowed. "No, we should get going. It was nice to stop for a little while, though."

"We'll still reach the Fork by nightfall, so no time lost."

He was trying to keep pressure off her, and she appreciated that. "I'm good," she assured him, and looped her arm in his. She took another bite of her sausage as they headed out of the city and back to where the rest of the men waited.

"Do you want a bite?" she asked, holding the daggered meat up toward his lips.

Mikael leaned forward and bit the sausage, but instead of taking a piece, he polished off the rest.

She gasped. "I said a bite! Not my whole sausage!"

He chuckled and then swallowed the meat. Norah put on her best attempt at a mad face, but she couldn't keep it. It had been a while since she'd heard him laugh or seen him smile, and she'd missed it. She gazed up at him, and the air lightened. She'd missed that too. He grazed her cheek with his hand—she knew he missed the closeness between them as well.

He pulled her into a kiss. "I'll get you another," he said, and turned back to the market stall not far behind them.

She pursed her lips at Soren, who stood with a scowl. "Go get yourself one; I know you want to. I'll wait."

He mumbled what could only be curses under his wrap, but he followed after Mikael. She knew it—who could resist a sausage?

She caught sight of Bhastian across the way to her right, keeping his eye on her, and he shook his head in amusement.

Norah couldn't help a smile. Despite the heaviness of the circumstances, her heart was lighter than it had been in a while. Maybe it was this place. Freedom hung all around from her insignificance in the hustle and bustle of the city, and she simply stood and closed her eyes in its noisy peacefulness. A slight breeze danced around her, cold but refreshing, and the weight of everything fell away. The coming war, Japheth and Rael, Alexander, her grandmother—she dropped them from her mind, just for a moment. She didn't allow herself to enjoy these fleeting moments often. This one, she would. And soon she'd have another delicious sausage, so it would be even better.

Norah opened her eyes again and glanced back at Mikael, who was paying the merchant for the whole plate of sausages, and she laughed.

A faint wind swept through again, but colder this time.

It carried with it the feeling of being watched.

Her laugh quieted on her lips, and she stilled. Prickles rose across her skin underneath her cloak.

Norah turned and cast her gaze around the market: the cobbled mainway with its centered merchant stalls, the side shops and their open doors.

But all around her the market bustled; sellers continued on with their wares.

"Salara," Kiran called out from her left. "Are you all right?"

Was she all right?

Mikael appeared beside her. "Another sausage?" her offered, breaking her thought. He looked at her a moment, and then his brows stitched together. "Is something wrong?"

She glanced around one last time. There was nothing, and no one. "Um, no." She shook her head and gave a smile. "Of course not. Just waiting on my sausage."

He daggered one and held it out for her, and she gladly accepted. "Anything else you want to get here?" he asked.

She noticed Soren eyeing the plate of meat, but he wouldn't eat in the market. He wouldn't uncover his face until they were away from public view.

"No, we can go," she said. "This was a nice break, but I'm ready."

Mikael nodded, and they headed back to their horses outside the gates to rejoin the army and continue on their way.

Norah lay awake in the darkness. They'd stopped in Hanset for the night, the last of the Free Cities just before the Mercian border. The Fork was shortly beyond, where they'd planned to make camp, but the temperature had dipped low. The army continued on to make camp there, but Mikael suggested Norah stay at the town castle that had been converted into a merchant house and inn. She didn't need much convincing. She hadn't had a proper bath since she'd left Kharav, and she allowed herself a long soak in the tub—with a glass or two or three of wine—before collapsing onto the feather bed. It was more comfortable than she'd expected from an inn. Much more comfortable.

But despite the comfort and her weariness, and the effects of the wine, sleep wouldn't come. Her thoughts turned to her grandmother. Catherine was sick. She was dying. Norah had tried to deny it, push it from her mind, as if not accepting it would make it not true. But it *was* true, and she'd have to face that truth in only a few days. At least she had Mikael with her. She didn't know how long he'd be able to stay in Mercia. Perhaps with Katya remaining with the army in Kharav and overseeing things, he wouldn't have to go back immediately. Unlikely, she told herself. But she still hoped for it.

Norah sat up and took the chalice from the table beside the bed and polished off the last of the wine. She thought she could chase away the swirling thoughts from her mind, but instead she brought on a swirling room as well. She wiped her face with her hands, her cheeks flush, and she let herself sink back against the pillows.

Soren had gone to check the horses, and Mikael to bring back a hot meal. Mikael wasn't keen on her eating in the tavern on the far side of the castle. She didn't blame him. Even from a little distance, its rowdiness carried through the air. She also wasn't going to complain about being served a warm meal in a plush feather bed or being able to enjoy eating in the comforts of a nightgown instead of a stiff-fitted riding dress.

Muffled voices sounded in the hall—Bhastian and Kiran at their posts outside the door. Although Bhastian was captain now, he still took shifts accompanying her guard, and the men seemed to respect him even more for it. She hoped they'd get some rest; they had to be tired as well. Her eyelids grew heavy, and she let them fall. Time passed slowly. Maybe it was the wine. Everything always seemed longer with wine.

Cold air swept over her skin, and she opened her eyes. The side window was cracked open to the icy air outside.

Strange. It hadn't been open before. Had it?

She sat up slowly and blinked, pushing back the grogginess. Had she fallen asleep? *No.* The sounds of the tavern still lingered in the air, and the candle that had been burning was still tall. But its flame had been snuffed—recently—its fresh smoky coils still rising in the moonlight.

From the corner of her eye, a shadow moved in the darkness.

"Mikael?" she called softly.

All was quiet.

But she wasn't alone.

And it wasn't Mikael.

Her mind roiled through the effects of the alcohol, struggling for clarity. Where was her knife? She had peeled off her dress in the far corner, where it still lay in a pile, before changing into her nightgown. But where had she put her calf sheath and blade?

The air stirred again.

"I know you're there," she said into the darkness.

A shadow stepped forward and loomed into the moonlight beaming through the window. Her pulse quickened, but she wasn't afraid. Not of one man. She wasn't the weak woman she once was. Knife or no, she was salara. This man would do well to take care.

Norah remembered now—her calf strapping and blade lay on the tufted bench at the end of the bed. She rose to her knees and moved to the edge. Slowly, she stepped down onto the floor, putting the bed between her and this stranger. The hooded figure waited, unmoving.

"What do you want?" she demanded. She moved carefully around the far edge of the bed, to the end, until her thigh touched the bench. *Just a little more.* She took another step. The flow of her nightgown concealed her reach, and she exhaled a thankful breath as she found her knife and curled her hand around the hilt.

He didn't answer her. His silhouette held no weapon—a mistake.

She moved closer, her knife now in hand and hidden in the hanging folds of her nightgown. "Why are you here?"

Still, he didn't answer.

Norah cocked her head to the side. "I should tell you about the last time I woke to a strange man in my room." She tightened her grip on her blade. "I hate to spoil a good story, but it didn't end well for him. For any of them."

She drew closer—she was right in front of him now, but still he made no move. Was he not here to harm her? That didn't mean she wouldn't harm him. Foolish man.

She whipped the dagger to his throat. "Final words?" she hissed.

He held his hands up, showing her they were empty in the pale light of the moon. Then, ever so slowly, he reached up and pulled back his hood.

Norah sucked in a breath. The knife in her hand clambered to the floor as she lost her grip on it.

Alexander stood, looking back at her.

The moonlight showed only half of his face, but there was no mistaking him—the high of his cheekbones, the line of his jaw.

She stumbled back. "What magic is this?" she whispered. No blood. No calling him. No going to the depths of her mind to see him. He was here. In front of her.

No. She had to be dreaming.

He didn't answer, the same as before. But he stood, waiting patiently.

She stepped forward again, reaching out. Her hands shook as she tested her fingertips against his chest, and they met the hardness of muscle through his tunic. She spread her hand flat against him. Warmth seeped into her—the warmth of life. In the visions she could touch him, but she couldn't feel warmth. Not like this.

She couldn't be dreaming. He was really here.

"How is this possible?" she whispered.

Norah ran her gaze from her hand on his chest to his face. Tears sprang to her eyes as the emotion flooded back—the pain, the loss.

"How are you here?" All she could do was ask him the same question over and over again. But its answer still escaped her.

Still, he said nothing.

He raised a hand to her cheek, and she closed her eyes against his warmth. Life—it was life she felt in him now. He had a beating heart, blood coursing through his veins. This was more than a spirit.

And before she could stop herself, she threw her arms around him and pulled him tightly against her. He was really here. And just to embrace him—truly—she couldn't do anything but simply hold on to him. She'd never gotten to tell him goodbye in life, not the way she wanted. But he was here now. He was here, and she clung to him.

Alexander hugged her back, his arms warm around her. There was a strength to him, and it permeated to her core. She needed this strength, and she soaked it in.

They finally broke, and she stepped back, but still held on to his hands. There were so many things she wanted to say, but no words would come.

He brought his hand to her cheek again and brushed her skin softly with the back of his fingers. She tilted her head into his touch.

Then he stepped forward and caught her mouth with his. Surprise jolted through her, and her eyes flashed open. His lips were firm—not harsh, but they weren't tender.

He used his body to walk her backward. She tried to blink back the still-swirling fog of her mind.

He smelled like smoky pear, deliciously sweet, but not like Alexander. And Alexander wouldn't kiss her like this; he wouldn't be here like this. Alexander knew her heart.

She spread her palms against his chest and pushed him to stop. "No," she breathed as she broke from him.

The shadow of his brows drew together, confused. Did he really not remember? He paused a moment, then dropped his head to hers again.

"No," she said more firmly, pushing him back farther. "This isn't who you are, or who I am. This isn't what we were."

He stopped, seeming to study her. Was he still confused?

"My heart belongs to another," she said. "You can't be here. Not like this."

He only stared at her.

"Alexander," she whispered.

Even in the darkness, his face grew more shadowed, and he pulled himself from her. How was he even here? Her mind swirled around her. The wine didn't help.

She wiped her face, drawing in a breath, but when she looked up again, she was alone in the night.

He was gone.

Her breath started to shake. Had that really just happened? She couldn't have imagined it all. Perhaps it was the wine. But... *No.* She brought her fingertips to her lips where she still felt him, tasted him. She knew it had all been real.

The chamber door opened, and she jumped.

"Salara," Mikael's voice came. In his hand he held a covered plate of food. When he saw her, he set it down on the small side table.

She let out a breath as emotion flooded her.

"Are you all right?" he asked, glancing around the room.

But she couldn't speak. She couldn't tell him what had happened. She couldn't explain it without sounding like she'd lost her mind. And what had just happened... how he would react...

The wind swept through the open window, pulling his attention, and he moved to close it. But when he turned back, he stopped. He stared at her in her nightgown in the moonlight, then he looked around the room again, as if recognizing something. He moved toward her slowly, his breaths coming heavier now.

"Salara," he said, his voice low. "Was the Bear here?"

How did he know? Had he seen him too? Her heart raced in her chest. Slowly, she nodded.

His eyes combed the room again, and he moved quickly back to the window and threw it open, leaning to look out from their second-story room.

Finding nothing, he turned back to her. Then his eyes found the knife on the floor. He picked it up. "Did he hurt you?"

She shook her head.

"Did he—" He stopped, and his breaths came faster. His voice came lower. "Did he take you?"

She shook her head again. "No," she said quickly, "but he..." She drew her fingers back up to her lips.

He clutched the knife in his hand, and his teeth flashed. "I've seen this moment before."

Oh gods, the vision from the seer. He'd told her he'd seen Alexander come to her bed, that he'd seen her take him. This had to be the moment. She shook her head again. "Mikael, I promise you nothing happened. He kissed me, and I stopped him. I told him that's not how we were. I promise you."

His face hardened. "Did you call him to you?"

Her heart pulsed quicker. "Of course not."

But his eyes betrayed his doubt.

She stepped forward and grasped his arm, squeezing it tightly. "No. I promise you. Mikael."

His stance didn't soften.

"Mikael," she said again. "I didn't call him. Please. You have to believe this."

But she wasn't sure he did.

Salara was asleep. Her breaths came deep and rhythmic as Mikael held her in his arms in the bed at the inn. But anger coursed through him. He shouldn't have brought her here. The plan had been to make camp at the Fork, that's where the army was now. Yes, it was cold, but they could have made do with a tent.

He cursed himself again. He'd been lax with her safety, knowing the happiness it would bring her to walk through the markets of the Free Cities, and how she'd enjoy a bath and bed as a break from the travel. He'd wanted to take her mind from the pressures that weighted her spirit.

But they were so close to the North; they could have waited. She hadn't even asked him to stop in the Free Cities. He'd done it simply for her enjoyment. As much as it killed him to admit it, he shouldn't have stopped here.

He couldn't shake the doubt that lingered. She'd said she hadn't called the Bear. Everything in him wanted to believe that, was desperate to believe it... Why couldn't he?

She'd had no blood on her, no vial. So why couldn't he believe?

Because the Bear could take her from him. She'd lied for the Bear before, had kept things from Mikael. Given a worthy enough cause, Mikael knew, she'd do it again. He didn't doubt her heart; he knew she loved him. But they both had drastically different ideas on the best way to handle things.

If the Bear was in her mind, he would have needed the blood—she had to have called him.

Suddenly, Mikael stiffened. *If* the Bear was in her mind. *If.*

If he wasn't in her mind, it meant he had come in person. And she wouldn't have called his person...

Carefully, he slipped his arm out from underneath Salara and rose. He pulled on his boots and jacket and quietly opened the door to Bhastian, who stood right outside. Mikael waved the Crest captain in. He wouldn't risk leaving her alone again while he went to find Soren.

Bhastian took his post just inside the door, and Mikael closed it behind him as he stepped into the hall.

His anger built—for Salara, not at her. He'd long since accepted the Bear's place in her heart, understood it even, but continuing to see him wasn't allowing her the space to heal. With her grandmother now dying, could she handle both?

Mikael tried not to think about what the Bear's continued presence meant for his own fate, although the thought haunted him still. The Bear would bring his end. From the dead, apparently.

No—this man wasn't the Bear. He couldn't be. And if this wasn't a ghost in her mind, someone was toying with her, and doing it by getting dangerously close to her.

Mikael strode outside, toward a few of the Crest standing together with Soren. They hadn't captured anyone, as he'd hoped. Perhaps no one had truly been there.

Mikael had thought the worst case would be her calling the Bear back to her mind. That would have hurt the most. But even so, he found himself wishing it were what had happened. For if she didn't call him, this man now had the power to visit her without the blood, which was alarming. Worse yet, if he came in person, he had the ability to hurt her. Mikael prayed to gods he didn't believe in that she'd called him.

"We even swept the tavern," Soren said as he approached.

"So, he's in her mind."

"I thought the same," Soren replied. "But come here." He led Mikael to the wall of the castle, under the window of the room in which Salara slept on the second story. Soren crouched down, holding out the lantern in his hand. "What do you make of these?" he asked as he motioned to the ground in front of him, and Mikael shifted his eyes to boot prints in the dirt.

Chapter Thirty-Two

Mercia stood exactly as it had the day she'd left it, but it seemed a little darker now. The white of the castle seemed more gray, and even the stained glass windows didn't hold the same shine. Maybe it was the winter skies, or maybe it was the darkness hanging over her heart.

She tried not to think about the journey, or Alexander, but the memory of the night before kept creeping back into her mind. Why had he come to her? How had he come?

And just when she thought things were settling with Mikael, this brought back the distance between them. She'd seen it—the doubt in his eyes when she'd told him she hadn't called Alexander. She couldn't be angry with him; she hadn't been entirely honest with him in the past when it had come to Alexander. But his doubt still hurt.

When they crossed the bridge to the castle isle and reached the courtyard, Catherine was waiting for them. She sat in a wheeled chair with a fur draped over her lap. Her cheekbones seemed a little higher on her face, or perhaps the recesses of her eyes had dipped farther, making them look that way. She was so thin.

Norah stopped, then slowly slid down from Sephir.

Catherine stood shakily, but steadied and reached out her hand.

Norah wavered. Caspian had told her Catherine had a terminal sickness, but that she was still active and somewhat herself. Norah hadn't known it was this bad yet. Her eyes welled as she took Catherine's hand.

"Took you long enough to get here," her grandmother said, hiding her own emotion in jest.

Norah looked over her frail body and glanced at the wheeled chair. Hold it together, she told herself. But her lip trembled.

"Oh, my dear," Catherine said softly, and she pulled Norah closer. "Come here."

Norah stepped forward and hugged her grandmother. Tightly. She smelled of oranges, her grandmother's favorite fruit from her home kingdom of Eilor, and Norah breathed it in.

"I'm glad you came," Catherine said into her ear.

"Of course I came." Norah pulled back and looked at her. "Although if you wanted me to come back, you could have just asked." She sniffed. "You didn't need to be so dramatic and start dying."

Catherine gave a weak laugh, and her eyes glistened. "Come inside, child. There's so much to talk about."

Norah nodded.

Shakily, her grandmother sat back down in her wheeled chair, and the guard turned it and started her toward the castle.

Norah turned to Mikael, looking to take his arm, but his attention was fixed on the sky. She followed his gaze to the Mercian banner on one of the turrets. His eyes found hers again in surprise.

She couldn't help a smile. It had been over a month since she'd sent the changes of her sigil back to Mercia, and it was the first time she'd seen it on something other than a parchment drawing. She let herself take it in, in all its glory against the sky. It was the same image that was marked on Mikael's skin. A winterhawk rising with the sun, as she had risen with him. The original symbol had never truly felt like her own. Now it did, because it had a piece of him in it.

He gave a smile of his own. And that made her happy.

Mercia almost felt like home with Mikael there. He seemed more and more like he belonged, and Soren seemed... less Destroyer-like, especially when he pushed her grandmother around in her wheeled chair.

And, of course, Catherine loved it.

As evening fell, they entered the dining hall. Soren pushed Catherine to her place at the table and then took his own seat as Norah and Mikael took theirs. Mikael raised a brow at Soren's joining, then looked at Catherine. But her grandmother only took another large swig from her wineglass as if nothing was amiss. Because it wasn't.

Norah looked at Mikael and smiled at him. She'd forgotten to fill him in that Soren had a place at the table with Catherine for all meals. Her grandmother had even stopped scowling at the commander for eating with his knife.

It was nice—their being together. She wondered how long Mikael would stay. Katya had sent a quarter of the Kharavian army to Bahoul and held the rest along the Canyonlands, ready, and Phillip had his forces in Eilor, all according to plan. But Mikael couldn't be away from Kharav for long, especially if things escalated with Japheth and Rael. He shouldn't have come at all, but he'd have things no other way. And she loved him for it.

Catherine took another deep drink of wine. "We must discuss the regency," she said, rather abruptly.

Norah stopped and stared at her. "What... what about it?"

"We need to discuss who's to be named regent."

Why was she raising this now? That wasn't—no, they didn't need to talk about this now. Catherine still had plenty of time. They could talk about this later. They had time. *She* had time.

"Norah?"

She glanced back up to find her grandmother looking back at her. But she just shook her head. "No, we should talk about this with the council. Later."

Catherine frowned. "I want us to talk about it now, before there's pressure to make a decision quickly."

"We still have plenty of time," Norah argued. And she wasn't ready.

"There isn't as much time as you think."

Norah clenched her fork in her hand to force down the rise of emotion. "I said I don't want to talk about it right now." She couldn't. She needed her mind calm to talk about this, and right now... it wasn't. And this conversation was so sudden. Too sudden.

"Norah, I know it's a difficult—"

"No!"

"We don't have to talk about it now," Mikael said, interrupting and quieting the room.

Norah inhaled and pushed her breath out slowly. Under the table, she relaxed her fist, where her fingernails were digging into her palm. When she raised her gaze, Mikael was watching her. She couldn't read his expression.

They finished dinner quietly, and after, Mikael walked her back to their chamber.

"Thank you," she said softly as they stepped inside.

Mikael waved out Serene and closed the door behind her.

She pushed out another breath. "I just... I can't even think about the regency right now."

He pulled her close and gently smoothed her hair back over her shoulder. Hesitation sat on his lips. "Salara," he said softly, "I don't think the North needs a regent."

It was true the collective council could look after Mercia. She could take her time to make a decision. That made her feel a little better.

"Not if her queen is here," he added.

She stopped. "What?" What was that supposed to mean?

He clasped her hands in his and held them to his chest. "Salara. Your place is here now."

She shook her head. Was he serious? "No, it's not. My place is in Kharav."

"You're the North Queen."

"I'm salara!" She pulled her hands from his. "I'm going back to Kharav with you."

Pain etched across his brow. His lips parted, but he paused before saying, "I'm not going back to Kharav again."

The finality of his words shook her. She couldn't speak.

His eyes were heavy with his own emotion. "You and I both know my fate. You must be prepared... to rule alone. And you should be here. Whatever is left of the Kharavian army, if Kharav still stands at the end of all this—"

"Stop." She shook her head.

"Listen to me—"

"No."

"Salara," he pressed.

"No!"

He clutched her firmly by the arms. "Listen!"

Tears streamed down her cheeks as she quieted.

Mikael brought his hand up to her face and held her to look at him. "When I fall, it's likely Kharav will as well. Even if it doesn't, it won't be safe for you there."

"I'm not marrying Soren—"

"I'm not asking you to again."

He dropped his head for a moment and then looked back at her. "Soren will stay in the North. With you. What's left of the army will follow him and add to your defenses. With Soren and Adrian and Caspian, and this king of Aleon, you'll have most of what you need."

But that wasn't what she needed.

"But you have to stay in the North," he said. "Do you understand?"

No.

"I know you're a strong queen, the strongest there's ever been. And you'll stay strong. Here." He clutched her tighter. "Promise me."

She wouldn't.

"Promise me!" he demanded.

Another tear escaped down her cheek. She shook her head.

"Norah," he said softly. It broke her. "Promise me," he said again.

She let out a trembling breath through her tears. "I promise."

He gave a sad smile as he brushed her face with his fingertips. Then he pulled her close and wrapped his arms around her. She breathed him in—his scent, his nearness, his being. No, she told herself. If he thought he was just going to traipse off to war and kill himself, he was wrong. They'd find a way to get through this, and they'd go back to Kharav together.

She couldn't lose him. She wouldn't.

He nuzzled the top of her head. "Can I make love to you, wife?" he whispered.

She looked up at him and ran her hand around the back of his neck and pulled him down to kiss her. Then he picked her up and carried her to the bed.

Two days passed, but tears threatened every time she thought about the conversation between her and Mikael, every time she thought about his fate and about the possibility of never returning to Kharav again.

Then she resolved herself. She'd find a way to stop it. How, she didn't know. All she knew is that she'd keep Mikael. Or join him in death in the pursuit of trying. Either way, Mercia would need someone, and it gave her the strength to talk about the regency.

Norah knocked on Catherine's door. She'd take her grandmother for a walk outside for some fresh air, then talk about options. She was sure Catherine had already put together some recommendations.

"Come back later," came Catherine's voice.

Norah almost smiled and opened the door.

"Oh, it's you," her grandmother said as she stepped inside.

"You sound disappointed."

"No, no. You can get my robe."

This time Norah did smile. "Glad I can be of help."

"Well, I sent the maid away because I actually wanted to rest awhile longer, but then I couldn't."

"That explains why you're not dressed yet." Catherine was always put together, no matter the circumstance. It probably bothered her that she wasn't right now.

Norah walked into the side chamber and pulled out a dress. "Here, I'll help you."

"I don't like that one," her grandmother said as Norah stepped back to the bed and held it up.

Norah pushed a breath between her lips and pulled another. As she stepped back to the bed, Catherine moved to rise, then lost her balance.

"Grandmother!" Norah dropped the dress and caught her in her fall. They landed awkwardly but were otherwise fine.

Catherine gripped her arm tightly, then resigned to sit. She waved her back. "I don't think I'm going to go."

"It's all right. It was just a misstep. Here, let's get you dressed."

"I said no."

Norah stopped. She sighed and moved to pick up the dropped dress from the floor. "All right. We can go later."

"No, Norah. I don't think I'm going out again."

Wait... *again*? "Why not again?"

"I just don't have the energy anymore."

Norah stared at her.

"Plus, being outside is overrated. I hate the cold." Catherine shifted back. "Just help me get situated back in bed, and I'd like that book over there on the cabinet."

Norah looked over and stared at the book. Not go out again? How could she say it so casually? She got the book and slowly handed it to her grandmother.

Settled back in her bed with her book, Catherine asked, "Did you want to stay for a while, my dear?"

Norah only stared at her. Catherine talked like everything was so normal... so... fine. But it wasn't fine. She was dying. And she was perfectly accepting of it—planning a new regent, reading her book, deciding she just wouldn't go outside anymore.

Just like Mikael was so accepting of his fate.

Why were they so accepting?

She couldn't breathe.

"Norah? Are you going to stay?"

"Um…" She couldn't. She needed to breathe, to think, just for a moment. "Maybe I'll come back in a little bit? I was just going to tend to some things."

"Very well." Catherine opened her book. To read. Dying.

Norah walked numbly down the hall. It wouldn't be long now. Catherine had been right—she didn't have as much time as Norah had thought. Her world was caving in around her, and what could she do? She stepped outside but didn't feel the cold.

She did need to see to one thing, though. She found Soren with Caspian on the bridge, discussing more fortifications and defensive efforts.

"We'll keep the ships moving through the channel," Caspian was saying. "It's cold enough for ice to form, and we'll keep it clear."

"Let it form in the areas where it won't support weight. If someone is stupid enough to attack the North, let them venture out onto it. We'll let winter help us."

Not a pleasant thought—men being swallowed by the icy waters—but effective, she supposed. The benefits of having a man of war plan war strategies.

Soren stopped when he saw her. "What do you want?" he asked in his normal gruff voice, but she knew it wasn't a gruff question. He genuinely wanted to know what she wanted, and he'd make sure she got it. He wouldn't like this request, though…

"I need Adrian to come home."

He shifted his weight back. He definitely didn't like the request.

"There's not much time now, and…" She closed her eyes and shook her head as she gathered herself again. "And he needs to be able to say goodbye. If even for a short time."

Catherine had raised Adrian, loved him, and he loved her. He hadn't gotten the chance to say goodbye to Alexander, but she could bring him home for Catherine. Of course, Soren would be against the idea. Adrian was in service to Phillip in Aleon, where he was helping prepare for war—an important task. But this was important too.

"All right," he said.

She snapped her gaze up in surprise. Not even an argument?

"I'll send a message and tell him to come with urgency," he added.

She stood, still frozen in her surprise. "O-Okay, thank you." The thought of Adrian coming home made her heart suddenly feel not quite so heavy.

Chapter Thirty-Three

Soren hammered the last nail into the iron shoe around his destrier's hoof before clipping and smoothing the outer edges. When it came to the care of the animal he depended so much on, he trusted only himself, as with Salar's destrier as well. Salara's mare, the horse of the Wild, didn't need shoes or maintaining, but he checked on her regularly regardless.

He released the animal's leg and patted the stallion on the shoulder—a horse he'd trained himself, the best he'd had yet. It was a strong beast, black as night, smart and fearless; he earned every bit of his noble name, Khalel al'Dakar V. Of course, he followed Khalel IV—the horse Soren had been forced to fell at the base of Bahoul to prevent Salara from escaping those years ago. It had been a great loss.

The original Khalel had been the famed destrier of his father—well, the father that had raised Soren—captain of the Crest, Tyrhar Nazim. And Khalel al'Dakar became the name of every destrier Soren trusted to carry him into battle.

When he'd fled with Salara back to Kharav after the council had tried to kill her, he'd left the animal behind. He didn't think he'd find him again in returning to the North, but when he did, he nearly wept. Soren didn't have many things. Besides his father's sword, this horse was the most important thing to him.

Soren's eye caught on the small braid in the animal's mane, and he scowled.

Salara.

Kal, she called him. Kal sounded like a packhorse name, but the animal came to it nonetheless, much to Soren's dismay. She was always giving him sugar and fruit, spoiling him, as she had the dogs. He missed the dogs. Brave beasts. If there were gods, and if anyone or anything deserved to be among them, it was the selfless animals that had given their all.

Soren pulled off his leather farrier's apron and draped it over the rail, then unclipped the animal's halter from the wall. "Come on, Kal," he said as he led the great destrier back to his stall.

The light of morning brought little warmth as he stepped into the frigid air, but Soren was in high spirits, and that was enough to warm him. Adrian would be arriving soon, something he was looking forward to. He'd never been a proud man, but he was proud now. Adrian had grown into a warrior, a leader, and a man respected by three of the greatest kingdoms in the world, and Soren loved him like his own blood. But it was under sad circumstances he was returning. Death would come soon for the grandmother. This was the woman who had raised Salara, and the Bear, and Adrian. She was a woman greatly respected, and she'd be a woman greatly mourned.

It shouldn't take Adrian too long to reach the castle. Last Soren had received word from him, he'd been on his way to Praetoria, the westernmost kingdom of the Aleon Empire. *Aleon.*

Soren tried not to think about Aleon. He'd left the king with an awkwardness between them. Phillip had told him it was his move. And he'd simply left.

The bells rang out, and Soren's lips curved into a smile under his wrap. Adrian had arrived. He pulled his cloak around him, clipped it in place, and started toward the castle. The stables sat on the lower west bank, and it was a long walk for such a small isle. He reached the west doors and wove through the halls, but when he stepped into the great hall, it was empty. Unusual.

"Where's the arrival?" he called to a servant.

"Queen Norah is in the throne room, my lord."

The throne room? That was a bit much to receive Adrian, but this was the North, and they were strange here. He picked up toward the throne room and entered from a side hall to see Salara and Salar both on their thrones. Mikael didn't like the Northern throne; he didn't like to sit on it. Strange that he would take it now. Perhaps this place was turning him strange too.

Adrian stood with a small cluster of Aleon soldiers, his helm under his arm. A smile broke across his face when he saw Soren. "Lord Commander," he greeted.

Soren crossed the space between them and clasped Adrian's shoulder in warm welcome. "Little Bear."

"Soren!" Salara exclaimed as she stood. "Where were you? I've been looking all over for you." There was urgency in her voice, and Soren jerked his head toward her in surprise. Why would—

The doors of the throne room opened, quieting the hall, and another group of Aleon soldiers entered.

And leading them—*the Aleon king.*

Soren froze. The king swept forward with a graceful strength, his movement sure and fluid. His long strides covered the length of the throne room faster than Soren could wrap his mind around his arrival.

The king stopped a short distance from him, his eyes on Salar and Salara.

"King Phillip," Salara said, "welcome to Mercia."

He'd come to the North. *Why?*

"Queen Norah," Phillip greeted in return. "I know I come on little notice, but when I heard about Lady Catherine, and given your invitation when last in Aleon, I couldn't not."

"I'm glad you did," she said. "My grandmother will be very happy to see you." Salara stood and held out her hand.

Phillip stepped forward and took it, bringing it to his lips with a slight dip of his head. As he released Salara's hand, he locked stares with Salar. They stood in silence, taking each other in.

Mikael stood as well. His face remained fixed, showing nothing, but this was the first time he'd met the Aleon king face-to-face. Surely this surprise visit wouldn't come easily.

Salara reached back and looped her hand under Mikael's arm. "Let me present my husband, Mikael Ratha Shal, salar of Kharav and king of Mercia."

"Salar Mikael," Phillip greeted, dipping his head respectfully.

Mikael stood for a moment, then did the same. "King Phillip," he said, and the air lightened. But only ever so slightly.

The Aleon king turned his head, and his eyes found Soren's. Their stares caught, perhaps a little too long. Soren knew the other eyes in the room were on them, but he couldn't pull his gaze from the king. "Lord Commander," Phillip greeted finally.

But Soren was lost for words. He said nothing.

Salara stepped to Phillip's side with an uneasy smile. "I'm sure you'd like to freshen up. I know it's been a long journey. Let me show you to your chamber, and then we can catch up on everything at dinner."

"That would be wonderful," he said. He gave a nod to Mikael and glanced once more at Soren before letting Salara lead him away.

Soren numbly stepped beside Mikael, and they both watched the Aleon king leave. When Phillip was out of sight, he could finally breathe, and he turned to Mikael. "Did you know about this?"

"We received word earlier this morning. Salara had given him an open invitation when she was in Aleon, but I didn't think he'd actually come."

"And now that he has?"

Mikael turned to him. "You'll not harm him. Let him stay. And let him leave."

But Soren's mind wasn't on harming the Aleon king.

Norah smoothed the front of her gown and drew in a deep breath before she dared to step into the great hall. It had taken Adrian a little less than a week to arrive in Mercia after receiving the message. She was surprised he'd come so quickly. And with Phillip. And although a week seemed no time at all, it did give her some space to wrap her mind around the circumstance and come to terms with the things she *had* to accept—rationally, at least. Catherine would be with her for only a short while longer. There was nothing she could do to stop it, and this she'd come to accept.

But Mikael... Mikael—*no*. Nothing would make her accept that. Nothing would make her accept his fate. They'd find a way through. *She'd* find a way through. But for now, she'd focus on tonight.

Music carried from inside the great hall and out through the castle—merry music—but she wasn't in the spirit for merrymaking. She and Phillip had spent the afternoon with Catherine, who was certainly thrilled about the visit of a king in her name, and in seeing Adrian. Her grandmother properly enjoyed every bit of attention she could manage. Even though Catherine was confined to her bed, it was good to see her enjoying herself. She was so frail now, so weak, a shell of what she once was. But with Phillip's charm and Adrian's smile, Catherine had color in her cheeks and even managed a few laughs.

Now with her grandmother tended to and resting for the night, Norah turned her attention to the evening. While it was proper to host a dinner for Phillip, and despite being happy to see him again, she wasn't exactly looking forward to the social. Tonight would be about brokering relations between Aleon and Kharav, between Phillip and Mikael: enemies-forced-allies now together for the first time. It was complicated by Soren, who no doubt would be facing struggles of his own. She wasn't entirely sure where the lord commander now sat on the spectrum of complete hatred and cautious interest. She'd thought she'd seen a glimmer of something when they'd had dinner with Phillip in Aleon. And Soren had since traveled to Aleon, and not only did Phillip still live but Soren had sent Adrian to his service. Did Phillip hold an importance to Soren beyond pure duty now?

Norah pushed out a breath. It was none of her business, she scolded herself. But curse the gods, who was she kidding? The wonder was killing her.

With another deep breath, she stepped inside. The hall was alive with conversation and laughter. A few nobles from Aleon were in attendance, and they stood among the Mercian nobles as old friends. She spotted Mikael at the front, with Caspian and two Mercian councilmen beside him. Conversation passed easily between them, and she paused. It was a sight she thought she'd never see, and it brought a smile to her face.

Mikael caught sight of her and smiled as she approached. His thick, dark hair was tied back as it usually was, and his beard was cut short, almost to the skin. But unlike his normal attire, he wore an embellished black doublet over a long-sleeved black tunic, covering his markings. The Kharavians took care for modesty in Mercia, and the effort wasn't lost on her. He held his hand out for her, and she took it. "You look beautiful," he said.

Caspian and the councilmen gave a small bow and left them some space.

"You're quite handsome yourself," she said, squeezing his hand. "People might actually start believing you're king of Mercia now."

He chuckled. But then he quieted as his eyes drifted across the room, and his smile fell.

"What's wrong?" She followed his gaze to see Soren at the end of the hall, and beside him stood Phillip. Her pulse quickened, and her smile widened. Perhaps she'd get an answer to her wonderings sooner than she'd thought.

Phillip spoke with a genuine smile, clearly engaged with whatever he was saying. Soren didn't appear like he was on the brink of murder—which was always a good sign. Was he actually enjoying himself?

"What are they doing?" Mikael asked.

His voice brought her back; she'd almost forgotten he was standing there. "It looks like they're talking." *Miraculously.*

"I'm going over there."

She tightened her hand around his. "Soren's perfectly capable of taking care of himself."

"I didn't say he wasn't." He started again toward his commander, but she pulled him back.

"If you interrupt them, I'll properly cut you," she warned.

He gaped at her in surprise. "What?"

"You heard me. Leave them alone." She threaded her fingers in his for a better hold on him and set her eyes back on Soren. "Just stand here and spy on them with me," she whispered.

"Why are you spying on them?"

"Hush, I'm trying to hear." She strained her ears. "Is Soren smiling?" *Damn the wrap.* She wasn't close enough to see his eyes to tell.

"Why would he be smiling?"

Well, she didn't know if the lord commander *was* actually smiling. She squinted, trying to focus on the telltale creases of his eyes. She hated not being able to see his face right now.

"Why would he be smiling?" Mikael asked again. His voice was different now, and Norah glanced up to see his expression had changed.

She held on to his hand. Mikael knew who Soren was. Now the question would be if he could support Soren in his happiness. She watched him closely as the realization came to him. His nostrils flared, and his breath came slightly uneven.

"Don't get weird," she said.

His lips tightened. "I'm not getting weird," he quipped back, as he stood, getting weird.

She kept her hold on him and leaned into him softly. "He deserves this."

He glanced down at her. "This?" he said angrily.

"Yes, whatever you call the happiness of being with another. Soren deserves it."

"But not with..." He stifled a snarl as he looked back out at Soren and Phillip.

"Not with a man?"

"That's not what I was going to say." The hard line of his lips turned into a slight frown. "Not with that one." His frown deepened. "A better one."

"Better than the ruler of an empire?"

"When has that mattered?"

The corner of her mouth tugged down. *True.* But Phillip was more. "Phillip's beautiful and smart, and makes you feel happy, and he's good with a sword. And you know that sword part has always mattered to Soren."

He grimaced and looked down at her. "You think the Aleon king is beautiful?"

"Are we not looking at the same man?"

He puffed a breath between his teeth as he looked back across the floor. "Soren can do better."

Was he serious? "Fine. Name your match."

His brows drew together. "I'm not going to mate-match my lord commander."

"Ha!" She grinned triumphantly. "Because you don't have a match." He crossed his arms. She wedged her hand between them and tugged at him to open up. "Phillip's shown himself to be a good king and friend. If Soren sees your disapproval, he won't allow himself that happiness. But he deserves to. Would you keep him from that?"

He was quiet for a time, then said finally, "I want him to be happy."

"Then you should let him know. But take care. I never told him you knew about him." And she pulled him down and kissed his cheek.

Soren drew in a deep breath of winter air out on the terrace. The music and laughing carried from the inside out into the night. He needed a moment of quiet, but he supposed this would do. He typically skipped socials; he didn't know what had made him come to this one.

That was a lie—yes, he did. He cursed the Aleon king under his breath.

Back in Aleon, Phillip had made his interest quite clear. Of course, Soren's interest had been in killing the man who wore the face of a dream he'd carried for some time. Of all the people, why did it have to be the Aleon king? He had hated Phillip for ruining it.

And then something changed. Soren started to like the ruin. The man in his dream hadn't smiled, but Phillip smiled. Often. And he laughed—something Soren despised. Until he found himself not despising it anymore.

Something felt different now, and he wasn't sure if it frightened him or excited him. He wasn't sure of anything anymore with this man. Only that he wanted more.

But that wasn't possible. He couldn't face Mikael with this ask. Mikael wouldn't understand. No one would, except for Salara.

A presence came beside him. He didn't need to look to know who it was.

"Salara is dancing with the Aleon king," Mikael said, breaking the quiet.

"I'm sure she's being polite," Soren assured him.

"Oh, she's quite enjoying herself. She says he's a beautiful man."

Soren chuckled. That he was. "You know she means nothing by it."

"No, I know. And I don't mind. Especially as she's trying to convince me that he's good enough for you."

Soren's heart stopped, and he struggled to force his breath calm and silent. He looked across the torchlit city. Had he heard him correctly?

"She says he's beautiful and smart and makes people happy, and he's good with a sword." Mikael turned and looked at him. "But you don't even like happy."

Soren turned, and their eyes locked. He knew. *Mikael knew.* Soren searched his face for judgment, disapproval—disgust, even. He found none of those things. Emotion breached the walls he fought so desperately to hold in place, and he broke away to blink it back. He looked back out at the city, gripping the balcony railing. "Maybe I'm starting to," he said hoarsely.

Mikael turned and leaned his back against the rail. Their eyes locked again. His gaze was penetrating, and Soren could barely hold it. Just as he was about to break, Mikael said, "He better make you pretty damned happy, then." He cuffed the top of Soren's shoulder and left to return inside.

Soren gripped the rail so tight his knuckles whitened. He couldn't breathe. He reached up and ripped the wrap from his face and sucked in the icy air. Mikael knew. He knew about Phillip.

More—he knew about Soren; he knew who he was.

Soren cursed under panting breaths. He had to pull himself together. He wiped his face with his hands.

"Are you going to stand out here all night?" Salara said, coming up behind him.

He straightened and sucked in another breath of winter. Wiping his face again, he quickly composed himself and pulled up his wrap. "Aren't you supposed to be dancing?" he asked as coolly as he could manage.

"Phillip's free now if you'd like a twirl about."

He snorted.

She clasped the railing beside him and rocked against it. "I saw Mikael out here."

Of course she had. "You told him about me."

She shook her head. "He's always known."

His pulse picked back up, and their stares locked. "How much?" he asked.

She didn't answer.

Soren grabbed her arm, pulling her still. "How much does he know?"

Her eyes darted back and forth between his, and ever so slightly, she winced. But he saw it. "Everything," she whispered.

He could barely speak. "How I felt before?"

Silently, she nodded.

All this time?

He released her and leaned heavily against the rail, returning his gaze across the city. Mikael knew. He had known all along.

"But he loves you," she said. "And he wants you to be happy. Like I do."

He couldn't reply. They only stood. Salara leaned against him—whether to steal some of his warmth or to comfort him, he didn't care. He was glad she was there.

They stayed on the terrace awhile, until Salara squeezed his arm and then left him for the warmth inside. He stayed long after the activities died down inside, and after most had retired for the evening.

He only stood, breathing in the night. Mikael's judgment, his disappointment, his rejection as his friend and now brother—these things had been Soren's greatest fears—to lose Mikael's love. But that hadn't happened. And now something felt new. For the first time, he felt... free.

There was something he needed to do.

He turned and strode back through the empty halls, his heart thrumming. The surge of the hunt raced through his veins. He reached the royal guest chamber and pushed open the door without knocking.

Phillip stood in the center of the room, his back to the door, reading a letter in his hands. He turned as Soren latched the lock behind him. Their stares locked, and Phillip's lips parted, yet he didn't speak.

His scent was faint—an autumn breeze—but one that Soren knew. One that he'd dreamed about.

Soren crossed the room, ripping his wrap down from his face as he closed the space between them. He caught Phillip just under his jaw and pushed him to the wall, covering his mouth with his own. To taste him was even better than he'd imagined, and it threatened his control—his very small scrap of control.

Soren was a larger man than the king, and he held him to the wall with a force. But Phillip wasn't a man to be forced. He yielded willingly. Still, Soren felt the power of his body, and he slid his hand down and tightened it around Phillip's neck. That power—held in his grip.

They broke from their kiss, and their eyes locked. Phillip reached his hand to Soren's chest, spreading it wide across his skin, then ran it up toward his face. But Soren caught it. It was too intimate, too close. Too much.

"Do you not want me to touch you?" Phillip asked.

This man didn't know him to touch him this way.

Phillip's eyes moved back and forth between his. "Take what you want, then."

Soren's breath faltered. He would just give himself?

Phillip reached up and clasped the weapons strap across Soren's chest and pulled Soren to him, bringing their mouths back together.

Then Soren's control was gone. He spun Phillip to face the wall and stripped his vest and shirt from him. Linen tore, and buttons fell to the floor. Not that Soren cared. He pushed him hard against the stone. The muscle across Phillip's back bulged. Soren let his eyes take in the beauty. Unlike his own back, marred by scars of battle and scars of the whip, Phillip's skin was smooth. Perfection. Soren raked the pads of his fingertips down it, and red marks sprang to the surface. Phillip writhed under his bruising hold, and Soren gripped him harder.

"Do you want my pain?" Phillip panted.

Soren paused. *Pain.*

"Is that what you like?"

He frowned. There were times Soren liked pain—liked inflicting it, sometimes even receiving it. But he didn't want Phillip's pain. He loosened his grip. "No." His voice came softer than what he'd expected. "I don't want to hurt you."

Phillip turned to face him, and the corners of his mouth turned up. "I'm glad to hear it, although..." His lips parted slightly. "You don't have to be gentle." And the Aleon king sank to the floor in front of him.

Soren's breaths came faster. Phillip unlaced Soren's breeches and pulled them down, releasing his flesh and wrapping his hand around him. Soren let his head fall back. It felt... so good. Too good. And when Phillip's mouth found him, he worried he might not be able to keep standing. He panted as he reached out and caught himself against the wall.

Never had he let someone be so free with him, so free in touching him. And never had someone made him want to relinquish control. He forced himself to keep it. "Get on the bed," he rasped.

Phillip looked up at him, his lips still around his head. He took Soren all the way into his throat before pulling his mouth away, leaving a string of saliva between them. It was almost Soren's undoing.

It took all his control to wait for Phillip to move to the bed before he came behind him. He gripped the nape of his neck and pushed the king forward onto his stomach. Slower, he told himself. He slid his length down Phillip's center and positioned himself, but Phillip was tight against him. Too tight. Phillip had had a male lover before, but it was clear to Soren now with the king beneath him, he wasn't a man accustomed to being taken. Soren was still wet from Phillip's mouth, but not enough. He glanced around the room. On the small table near the bed was a tray of bread and cheese, with a side bowl of olive oil. Soren pulled back and took it. Then he dropped a trail of the oil between them and spread it with his fingers.

Soren repositioned. Lowering himself over the king again, he brought his mouth to Phillip's ear and breathed, "Let me inside you." Phillip's body eased. Soren pushed against him, testing, and Phillip gave. Soren pushed harder, and they both gasped as he sank fully inside him. Then he stilled, giving them both a moment.

Soren had been with women before, but he'd never had the strength of a man. He'd dreamed about it, craved it—the hard steel of a masculine body, a body that could handle his own strength. With the softness of a woman, it took effort for pleasure to come. But here, with Phillip—pure power underneath him—it took effort to not lose himself completely.

He moved slowly to start, then faster. Harder. Phillip didn't quail underneath him. Instead, he pushed back against him, asking for more. And Soren gave it to him.

Phillip's body called to him—called him to own it, to relish it, to touch it. So he did. He curled his arm around Phillip's hips and pulled him back hard, driving himself deeper. Phillip arched against him, reaching back and gripping Soren to pull him even deeper.

The king's arousal fueled his own. He took Phillip's flesh in his hand and stroked his length as he drove harder. They were both close now, their breaths shorter and faster. The heat built between them until he feared they would both catch fire. And then Phillip's body tightened under him. Liquid warmth pulsed into Soren's hand and onto the bed underneath them. It was too much to keep control, and he let out a growl as he shattered in his own release. He pushed himself deeper, then deeper still. He pushed until he was completely spent and empty, completely enraptured by this man.

They collapsed, still joined, both panting. The air smelled of male and sex and power, and Soren breathed it in. Everything about this king was intoxicating.

Phillip chuckled under Soren's weight. "I'll call for new bedding."

Soren bared his teeth against his neck. "You say that like I'm finished with you."

Phillip chuckled again.

The hours passed quickly. Soren took him two more times, not able to get enough, not able to pull himself away from Phillip's body. Then finally, exhausted, they both lay in the quiet of the candlelight, facing each other.

Phillip's eyes burned blue, blue like the brightest gems. He stretched his hand wide against Soren's skin, just under his shoulder. Their stares remained locked as he drew his fingers softly down the dell of his chest. Soren's mind told him to pull back, but he didn't. He kept his eyes on the Aleon king and let himself stay, let the king touch him. He wanted his touch.

Phillip's mouth moved to speak, but he hesitated. Soren waited. Almost fearing it. He knew what he'd ask. It was what everyone who he'd ever taken to bed asked—about the future. And his answer would be offensive. It wasn't meant to be offensive. He wanted this man. But want wasn't enough. And Phillip wouldn't understand. No one did.

The Aleon king gave a small smile. He grazed his fingers across Soren's skin again. "I know you don't belong to me," he said softly. "Your loyalty, your devotion to Norah and your king—I would never ask you to betray that. And when you let me touch you, when you let me have you, I see it for exactly what it is. A gift." He drew Soren's hand up to his lips and kissed his palm. "Thank you for this gift."

Soren's breath shook. This man understood him. He saw him.

And that was a dangerous thing.

CHAPTER THIRTY-FOUR

Soren lay in the quiet of the rising sun. He watched the Aleon king sleep—inhaling deeply and then releasing—the rise of his chest, the glow of his skin under the morning rays.

Phillip was a beautiful man, sculpted of strength and light. His nose sat straight between the thick, dark lashes of his eyelids. The square of his jaw tapered gently to his chin, just underneath the perfection of his lips. Hints of copper in his bronze locks begged the touch of fingers, and Soren couldn't help himself.

It hurt. Phillip had said he would never pull him from his duty, but any pull at all was a pull away from duty. Soren couldn't allow it. He clenched his jaw until it ached to match the ache in his chest as he drew his fingers through Phillip's hair.

The king's eyes opened slowly, and he smiled. He looked like an Aleon god. Soren loved how he smiled. He hated that he loved it. It made it all the harder. He cursed himself—he shouldn't have come.

"I have to go," Soren said.

"Will you come later, then—"

"No. I can't come back to you."

Phillip stilled, and his brows drew together. "I don't understand."

Soren didn't expect him to. "This can't happen again. I shouldn't have come."

Phillip pushed himself up and reached for him. "Soren, I—"

He pulled back and moved to stand, but Phillip caught him.

"Soren, wait."

Soren pulled against his hold, but Phillip tightened his grasp. Soren wanted to wait, wanted to stay, but he couldn't. "Let me go," he warned.

"I said wait."

"Let me go," he said again.

"No."

The longer Soren waited, the more he might stay. But he couldn't stay. So he couldn't wait. Soren twisted against Phillip's hold, but Phillip was a powerful man, and fast, and he jerked Soren forward. Soren's balance gave way, and he fell back onto the bed. Phillip sprung over him, pinning him down.

"Stop!" Phillip demanded. "You'll stop. And talk to me."

Soren could have fought back, overpowered him. But there was a heartbroken ferocity in Phillip's eyes that stole his strength. So he stopped.

Phillip's voice came softer now. "Why? I told you I would never ask you to betray your duty. Why can't you return? Can we not simply enjoy each other?"

It was such a simple question, yet such a difficult answer. It was more than simply enjoying each other now, more than just sating the needs of the flesh. "Because you're a distraction," Soren said. *A dangerous distraction.*

"A distraction?" Phillip nodded, but it wasn't a nod of agreement. "You see me as a weakness?"

"Love makes one weak."

"Is that so?" Phillip's grip softened, but he didn't release him. His eyes dipped in sorrow. No, not sorrow—pity, as if Soren didn't understand. What didn't he understand?

"Did you not become lord commander because the king loves you?" Phillip asked.

What was his point?

"And Norah, she has a lord justice, but you control Mercia's army because she loves you and trusts you above all others. And now..." Phillip leaned closer. "Now, you control the king of Aleon, who will submit to your every ask. You think that love makes you weak, but has it not made you the most powerful man in the world?"

Soren blinked back his emotion. How did this man affect him like this? He couldn't let him, no matter how convincing his words. "I'm not a man who can love." He shoved Phillip back and off him. "I'm not a man who can be loved."

Then Soren left before he lost the power to do so.

He kept his eyes on the map stretched out on the table. His wrap was suffocating. Soren had never felt that way about it in all the years he'd worn it, but over the past few days, he'd felt it often. Mikael stood beside him, with Caspian across from him, next to Phillip. They'd just run through the battle strategy for a sixth time, making sure they missed nothing, forgot nothing. It was a solid plan. Yet Soren felt anything but solid.

After he'd left Phillip's chamber, the king let him be, as if Soren were in control. Except standing here now, with only a table between them, Soren was certainly not in control.

Phillip pulled the battalion figurines back to their original position. Soren's eyes followed his hands. Strong hands. He knew those hands—they were hands that had touched him. So softly, and not so softly. He closed his eyes and sucked in a breath. *Control.*

"It's a great risk," Mikael said, helping break through the fog in Soren's head.

Soren focused his mind back on the battle. This plan *was* a great risk for Phillip. It was one that turned his own stomach.

"As I've told the lord commander, I'm willing," Phillip said. His eyes were on him. Soren took care not to look, not to get caught in their snare, but he felt them—the eyes that knew him so intimately.

"And I understand the risk," Phillip added, "but this alliance promises me something greater, and I'm willing to take it."

Soren's inhale stuttered in his chest. Was he still talking about the battle?

"This is unconventional, this alliance," Mikael said.

Phillip gave a soft chuckle, and Soren could almost feel the puffs of breath on his skin, where he'd felt Phillip's chuckle the night before. On his hip, on his thighs—

He sucked in another breath.

"I'm an unconventional man," Phillip said. "And I'm sure you agree that convention holds us back. This is about knowing the opportunity and taking it. Doing the most with what we have and what we're given."

Soren lifted his gaze. Phillip's eyes were fixed on him, as he knew they had been, and he was caught. But his mind was on Phillip's words. This was no longer a conversation about battle. Or maybe it was, just not the battle against Rael.

"I agree," Mikael said.

"And if we respect one another, we can hold true to our values," Phillip said. "Hold what's important to each of us."

"I think that's possible," Mikael answered.

But it wasn't possible. Soren remained pinned under Phillip's gaze—the gaze that laid him open and bare and vulnerable, that tested his heart against his duty. He couldn't shoulder them separately. It wasn't possible. His heart *was* his duty. Salar and Salara were his heart. Salar and Salara were his duty. Phillip was...

Phillip was...

It wasn't possible. Just like it wasn't possible for Soren to stay in this room any longer. Without air. He ripped himself free of those eyes and pushed off the table. But as he headed to the door, Mikael caught his arm.

Mikael's brow dipped. "Where are you going?"

Soren had nothing in answer. To think? He couldn't think. He'd forgotten how. He needed to... He didn't know what he needed to do, other than get away. "Let me go," he said quietly, so that only Mikael could hear. "Please." He was practically begging.

Mikael's eyes moved back and forth between his. He didn't press. He knew something was wrong. Soren prayed he wouldn't keep him longer. And Mikael didn't. He only nodded and let him go.

He stood in the day's fading light, his back against the wall in the room's quiet. Soren wasn't sure what had come over him earlier that afternoon. He'd lost himself, lost his mind, and he'd had to walk nearly the entire city before he could get it back.

Now, he could breathe again, think again.

Even so, a tempest still raged.

This man. *Phillip.* Just the thought of him stirred Soren's arousal. The smoothness of his skin, the hardness of his muscle. His touch, his scent, his taste. Soren pulled off his wrap and wiped his face. Fire rippled through him, but he forced it down. This wasn't about desire. It was about what pulled him from deep within—that was the danger.

But Soren knew his duty, and nothing could pull him from it.

So now he waited in Phillip's chamber, his dagger in hand.

The door to the chamber opened, then closed.

Soren stilled, silent, hidden in the small recess of the wall. Then he moved quickly. He had his blade to Phillip's throat before Phillip even knew he was there. The king stopped. His mouth moved to speak, but when his eyes met Soren's, he quieted. Soren pressed the blade more firmly against his skin.

Phillip didn't react. He said nothing. He simply dropped his head back slightly, offering more of his neck. Was that submission? Or a challenge?

It didn't matter. Soren's voice came low, thick with his purpose. "If you move against Salara, against Salar, I won't hesitate to kill you."

Phillip's face stayed fixed, but his eyes smiled. "From anyone else, that's a threat. From you, Destroyer... Well, this feels strangely like courtship."

"I need to make sure you understand."

Faster than Soren thought possible, Phillip slammed against his forearm with a stinging force that made him drop the blade. Phillip snatched it and turned it back on him. He dug the tip into Soren's throat. And smiled. That smile—beautiful and disarming. It had the power to make Soren forget how strong this king actually was. How deadly. Like he'd forgotten just now.

Phillip's voice came in a whisper, but it held the weight of a roar. "There may come a day that we find ourselves on opposite sides of the battlefield. And I welcome you to try to kill me. If you can."

Soren's body flamed. This king was skilled *and* bold. His breeches grew tight against him. He felt the trickle of blood down his neck from where Phillip broke the skin with his own blade, and it made him even harder.

"But I told you," Phillip said, "I'll never ask you to betray your duty. I don't ask for your loyalty. Your heart, maybe, in time. But never your loyalty."

Those eyes pierced him more than any blade could. Soren couldn't hold his gaze, yet he couldn't look away. "What do you ask for now, then?"

"You. Your body. Your pleasure." Phillip pressed the blade harder against him. A tremor ran up Soren's spine, but not from fear. Phillip's eyes danced. "And just to make sure *you* understand," he added, "I'm not asking."

Soren snorted. "You should know me well enough to know I don't respond to demands."

"Take off your clothes."

Soren didn't *think* he responded to demands, but his body said otherwise. He shifted—he was painfully hard now. His hands betrayed him and unbuckled his strappings and unlaced his breeches. He kicked them off with his boots before he realized what he was doing. The tip of the dagger cut deeper into his skin with his movements, but there was something thrilling about the pain, something exquisite. And there was something exquisite about the gleam in Phillip's eye as he watched him.

Without his clothing, there was no hiding his arousal, no hiding his want. Naked, Soren waited for the next demand.

Phillip still held the dagger. Soren didn't try to take it back. He knew he couldn't. While he was larger than Phillip, and stronger, he wasn't faster. His mind flashed back to sparring on the practice field with the king in Aleon. Phillip had matched him in skill with a sword; he should have guessed he'd be keen with a dagger as well. Soren couldn't take it back. And he didn't want to.

So close they stood.

A small trickle of blood ran down Soren's chest, and Phillip leaned forward and caught it with his tongue. Soren quivered under what was surely the most erotic and arousing thing he'd ever experienced. This man was... He didn't know what this man was. And he didn't know how to react. So, he stood, unmoving. Slowly, Phillip followed the trickle, his tongue lapping tormenting caresses upward. Soren's body threatened to burst from the confines of his skin.

When Phillip reached his neck, he pulled the blade away and covered the cut he'd made with his mouth. He sucked gently, bringing back memories of what his mouth had done to other parts of Soren's body. Soren clung to control. By a thread.

Pulling back, Phillip met Soren's eyes again, blood on his bottom lip. He flicked out his tongue across it and smiled.

Soren lost himself. He surged forward and caught Phillip's lips with his. He tasted his blood—blood mixed with desire—and he chased it with his tongue. Phillip opened his mouth to him, and Soren drank him in. This man knew what Soren wanted, what he needed, what he didn't even know he needed. Phillip knew where there were limits, but right now, there were no limits.

He ripped Phillip's clothing from him as the king pushed him backward toward the bed. Phillip flung the dagger and lodged it into the headboard. He grinned. "In case I need it later."

Soren couldn't help a smile of his own.

Then Phillip's hands were on him—roaming, feeling, gripping, driving him mad with want. Soren slid his hand down between Phillip's muscled thighs to feel if he wanted this as much as Soren.

Phillip groaned—he did.

The backs of Soren's legs brushed against the bed, and he shifted to move behind the king. But Phillip caught him.

"No."

Soren paused.

"I want to see you," Phillip said. He moved onto the bed, and slowly lay back on the pillows. Soren edged over him, leading but following, prowling but caught. He wasn't sure whether he was predator or prey.

He didn't care. He seized Phillip's mouth again with his. Soren had never liked kissing. Kissing was too intimate, too much. But with this man, he couldn't get enough.

He needed more.

Soren stopped and glanced around the room. His eyes found a small bowl of oil on the table by the bed, and he stopped. *Convenient.*

Phillip gave a wry smile. "I knew you'd come back."

"You say that like you know me." Soren had meant his words to be playful, but they didn't come out that way.

Phillip's face grew serious, and Soren searched his mind for how to bring them back.

"I want to know you," Phillip said softly. He reached his hand around the nape of Soren's neck. "Will you let me know you?"

Soren studied his face. He'd let this man do almost anything. "Do I make it difficult?"

Phillip chuckled. "Where's that dagger?" He pulled Soren down, and their mouths found each other again. He tasted of sweet and citrus, like something to be devoured, and Soren wanted to devour him.

Soren broke away to coat himself with oil, then moved between Phillip's thighs, positioning them both. Skin against skin, hard muscle brushing either side of his hips, male power underneath him—he had to work to keep control. Phillip blinked slowly, his breaths long and heavy. Soren gripped Phillip's thigh and watched him as he pushed inside. Phillip surrendered to him, panting a breath that made Soren almost lose himself. Soren pushed deeper and stilled. He needed to be inside him—to claim him, to be close. To be part of him.

He forced himself to be slow, trying to deny the fever of urgency. But Phillip's body rocked against him and drove him faster. It drove him harder. He clasped Phillip's hands and pushed them above his head and dipped his head to drink from his mouth again. The want was so intense it hurt. The storm grew between them—building, roiling—threatening to consume them both.

Then Phillip's body pulsed underneath him, tightening, and warmth spurted up between their stomachs. He groaned into Soren's mouth, and Soren unraveled. He drove himself deeper, erupting within and seeding his claim.

This man was his.

They both stilled, panting. Soren let himself collapse. Phillip was a large enough man that he could hold his weight. It was bliss to simply lay.

Soft fingers trailed through Soren's hair, raising prickles across his skin. "Stay," Phillip whispered.

Soren lifted his head to the piercing blue eyes staring back at him. He'd given himself permission to love this man, and permission to kill him.

He had no intention of going anywhere.

The soft silk of Norah's shoes fell silently through the hall as she made her way to the dining room for dinner. She was late, having lost track of time. She didn't even have a reason—she'd been sitting in the side chair of her chamber, wrapped in her thoughts: of Soren and whatever was happening between him and Phillip, of the impending war, and of Catherine, who drifted further and further from her with each day.

Mikael would wait for her, but she didn't want him to, and she picked up her pace even more. As she swept past the drawing room, she paused. Soren stood by the window, looking across the isle. Why wasn't he in the dining room?

"Are you coming to eat?" she asked him, and he turned with a start. "I didn't mean to startle you," she added.

"You didn't startle me," he replied quickly.

The corners of her mouth turned up. "Okay." But Soren wasn't in a light mood, and her smile fell. "What's wrong?"

He was silent for a moment, then he said, "A message arrived this morning. The full Aleon army has amassed in Eilor. They're prepared for when Japheth and Rael march."

She nodded slowly. That *was* the plan... "Sounds like a good thing."

"The Aleon king has decided to join his army."

While typically kings—and queens—remained safely back from the front lines of war, it also wasn't unusual for them to be with their army. And although this was something she had expected Soren to praise, it clearly wasn't a decision he was pleased with.

"He wanted to position his army in the mountains of Songs," he told her. "He'd give up Eilor temporarily but hold more favorable ground in the mountains. I told him I needed his forces in Eilor to push Rael into the Canyonlands."

"Was it the wrong decision? For him to move his forces to Eilor?"

He shook his head. "No. Not for the overall strategy. But it's dangerous for Aleon. Our plan assumes Rael will be more inclined to drive the war to Kharav. If they strike Aleon up through Eilor, Phillip's army isn't at an advantage, and they could be broken."

And then she realized. "You worry for him." It wasn't a question.

They stood quietly.

"It's different," he said after a while.

She looked up at him. "What is?"

"With Salar, I felt like... together we could conquer the world. And simply standing beside him, being loved by him was enough. Enough to be content. Happy." He glanced down at his hands. "But Phillip—Phillip is different. There's... a wanting. A hunger that can't be sated, a thirst that can't be quenched, like nothing will ever be enough. I don't want..." He drew in a deep breath and let it out slowly. "I don't want him to go."

"Phillip is a very competent king," she assured him, "with one of the largest armies in the world surrounding him. And you yourself have tested his skills. He can certainly take care of himself."

"It's not enough."

She understood that feeling—she felt it with Mikael. So, she offered him the choice she had wanted: "Do you want to go with him? Do you want to go to Eilor?" With Phillip and the guarantee of blood and battle, she was certain he would take her up the suggestion.

But his brows drew together. "My place is here. With you."

"Just because you're sworn to me doesn't mean you have to stay in Mercia."

He shook his head. "I promised to watch over you."

"Mikael understands that Eilor—"

"Not Salar. I promised the Bear. If Eilor falls and Rael advances north, you'll need me. My place is here."

"Soren—"

"Stop," he said sharply, and she quieted. He sighed. "This is where my family is—you and Salar. Where my duty is. I don't want to go. I won't."

"Okay," she said, softer now. "But we can't let Aleon fall. If Phillip needs you, you'll have to go. I'd want you to go."

Finally, he nodded. "If he needs me."

"Now come on, we're late for dinner. Phillip will be by himself with Mikael, and while things have been going well so far, I'd like to not push it."

Soren snorted, and they headed toward the dining room.

Despite the army of men in the courtyard preparing to take the Aleon king to Eilor, the halls of the castle were eerily silent. Soren reached Phillip's chamber and raised his fist to the door, but paused. He cursed himself. He'd told Salara he didn't want to go, but he did. It had been a long time since he'd quenched his thirst for battle, but that wasn't what called him. Eilor would be dangerous, even for a king like Phillip. Soren would send Adrian back to Phillip after the grandmother passed, sooner if Rael attacked. But even with Adrian by his side, Phillip wouldn't be safe enough. He pulled down his wrap and drew in a breath.

Suddenly the door opened, and he jerked up to find the king looking back at him.

Phillip took a step back in surprise. Then he smiled—that smile. "Lord Commander." He stepped back farther, opening the door, and Soren swept inside.

"The army's ready," Soren told him. "Are you?"

Phillip nodded. "I was just headed down."

They stood, staring at each other.

Phillip stepped closer to him. "I wish I didn't have to go."

"Then don't."

"Would you not? If you were me?"

Soren couldn't answer that, because his answer would be different from what he wanted the king to do.

Phillip moved even closer. His voice came softly, almost a whisper. "These past couple days have been... I didn't think it was possible. To feel this way again. But..." Then he smiled that smile again.

Soren grabbed the king at the top of his breastplate and pressed him against the wall, catching him in a kiss. Phillip tasted of honey and sunlight and summer, and everything he never knew he needed. But now he knew.

They broke, but Soren still clutched Phillip's breastplate firmly. "Do *not* fucking die. Do you understand me?"

Phillip smiled. "Very clearly."

"I'll send Adrian to you soon. Listen to him and take no risks. If Rael attacks and your forces are failing, ride for Mercia."

"I can't abandon Aleon."

Spoken like a noble king. Soren hated it. "Then fall back to the mountains of Songs. I'll come to you."

Phillip smiled again, but not the smile of sunlight. It was the smile of sorrow, of not believing. "If you don't, I understand."

He clutched Phillip tighter. "I *will* come for you," he promised.

CHAPTER THIRTY-FIVE

Norah sat at the dining table, barely breathing, staring at the letter in her hand. Phillip had departed for Eilor the day before, and she already found herself wanting to call him back. Not that he'd provide anything Mikael or Soren couldn't, but they were all one team now—friends, allies—and a collective thought around the morning's situation would certainly help.

She hadn't recognized the letter's seal—red with a short sword sigil—until the messenger had announced his master.

From King Cyrus of Rael and Serra, he had said. Caspian stood beside him, having escorted him in.

She sent the messenger away to read the letter privately, or as privately as she could in front of Mikael, Soren, and her justice. Why would Cyrus write to *her*?

Norah stared at the words and read them for a third time.

Queen Norah,

Is this not an unexpected world in which we find ourselves? Gregor's cause is not my own. Yet we've advanced directly to the commitment of war, without even a conversation between us.

I wish to remedy that.

Are we not rational people? As I've come to learn more about you, I wonder if we're not as different as I once thought. I would like us to meet, on neutral terms, if only even to grant each other the respect of acknowledgment.

I await your reply,

Cyrus

She passed the note down to Mikael and didn't take her eyes from his face as he read it. Strangely, he seemed unbothered. When he was finished, he passed it to Soren.

"He only wants to meet Salara?" Soren asked.

"It's a trick," Mikael said.

Soren shrugged. "Or he thinks Salara's the only one who won't knife him." Mikael looked at Soren and they both chuckled.

"What's so funny?" Norah asked. "I'm the most peaceful person here."

"You've literally stabbed everyone in this room," Soren said.

Norah's mouth dropped open, and she scoffed. "First, Caspian was an accident." She cast him a glance. "Sorry again."

Her justice smiled. "It's all right."

"And Mikael"—she eyed her husband accusatively—"in fairness, you were kidnapping me." She looked back at Soren. "As were you."

Soren's deep, rumbling chuckle came again.

Norah narrowed her eyes at him. "Keep it up and I might give you another scar to reminisce about."

The smile still didn't leave his face.

"What if his intentions are true?" she asked, shifting them back to the matter at hand. "What if he wants to talk about a possible treaty?" Didn't they see? This was an opportunity to change the course of war—perhaps a very small opportunity, but an opportunity nonetheless.

"His intentions aren't true, Salara," Mikael said.

"You don't know that."

"I know," he said firmly.

She could only stare at him with her mouth slightly agape. "I'm just to tell him no?"

"You'll tell him nothing."

"So... I'm to send his messenger back with *nothing*? That's the same thing as telling him no."

"You won't send his messenger back."

"I'll take care of him," Soren said.

She dropped her napkin down beside her plate. "Absolutely not. I won't respond to a letter of peace with blood." That certainly wouldn't help prevent war.

"I can do it without blood," Soren said.

She scowled at him. "I said no." She needed to buy more time to talk to Mikael, to get him to see reason and to convince him of the value of diplomacy. "Put him somewhere until we can decide what to do with him. Not the cells. Somewhere comfortable."

The center of Mikael's brow creased. "You would put our enemy's messenger somewhere comfortable?"

Soren snorted. "Is that a rhetorical question?" he asked, drawing a sharp glance from Mikael.

Caspian shifted his gaze from Norah to Mikael, then back to Norah again. "I will put him in a guest chamber."

Norah kept her eyes on her husband. He had an objection—she could see it. But he only took a drink from his chalice, yielding. It was a start.

Norah pulled her fingers from between Mikael's and balled her fist against his palm to get more of his warmth. They walked the long hall of the castle, toward the study, and she was cold. She was always cold, it seemed. Castles were cold. He chuckled and pulled her hand over his arm and covered it with his own. Gods, she loved his warmth. She shuffled closer to him.

"Any word from Soren's Aleon king?" he asked.

"They're almost to Songs. Making good progress." The corners of her mouth turned up. *Soren's Aleon king.* She hadn't been sure that Mikael would accept Phillip, and in many ways he hadn't. As a no-choice ally, yes, but not as someone he trusted, and certainly not as a friend. But he accepted him as Soren's, and so accepted him as a man that needed to remain alive and well. Soren loved Phillip, and Mikael loved Soren. Perhaps that protected Phillip more than any alliance.

As they neared the end of the hall, Caspian and Soren came around the corner, their strides full of purpose.

"A letter," Soren said as they reached them. "Another one. From Cyrus." Caspian held it for Norah.

She broke the seal and found the words. Her heart beat faster.

Queen Norah,

My letter goes unanswered, but as my messenger has been treated kindly, I don't believe this to be a complete refusal. Perhaps it's not a refusal at all; perhaps it's only hesitation, which I understand. To show my intent, I'll come meet you in the outer reaches of Mercia, on your terms. Let's meet and speak, for I'm sure we'll find common ground.

Cyrus.

She gave it to Mikael. His face hardened as he read it. "Bold that he assumes we don't have intention to answer when only two days have passed since his first letter," he said, and he passed the letter to Soren.

"Well, he's not wrong," Norah pointed out.

Soren's eyes scanned the parchment. "And how does he know his messenger's been treated kindly?"

"I don't know," Norah answered, "but we have two of them now. For a second message to come this quickly, he has to be close. What if he's already in Mercia?"

"He wouldn't be so foolish," Mikael said. "It has to be a trick."

"We should hear what he has to say," she urged. Cyrus wanted to talk, and talking brought the real opportunity for peace. "Mikael, this is an invitation to potentially avoid war. If I can just speak to him—"

"You're not going alone to meet this man," he said firmly.

"Soren will go with me." She wasn't sure if she was closer or further from convincing him, and it made her all the more desperate. "And you and Caspian can be ready with the army close by," she added. "It's a big risk for Cyrus to meet in Mercia. If he comes alone, we could take him. But Mikael, if we can reach an agreement, gain an ally, we could bring an end to this threat. We could end it all."

"Only blood can end it all."

She shook her head. "I don't believe that," she said. "You know his army is at Japheth's border, too far to be an immediate threat, and we could make sure he comes alone. It's but a small risk."

His lips thinned.

She took his hand. "Mikael, we have to try. *Please.* I have to try."

He glanced at Soren, who returned a skeptical stare of his own. Then Soren shrugged. Mikael sighed. "Fine. We'll meet him in the valley in the outer reaches."

Her heart leapt. This was it—this was their chance. And she knew the valley he spoke about. It dipped low and was surrounded by the ridges of the highlands. It was a perfect place to meet; it was out in the open and they'd be able to see everything around them.

"I'll bring the Northern army to the ridge," he said. "Should Cyrus try anything, anything at all, then you must be prepared it will start this war."

To that, she could agree. "And I'll know I'll have done everything I could to prevent it."

The same day they released the messengers back to Cyrus, they received another message—to meet in two days.

Two days.

She didn't know how word could have reached him so quickly—no bird could have carried it that fast. Nor did she know how he was prepared to meet her so soon. It would be difficult even for her to make it to the valley with the army in two days' time.

But they'd go. They had to. They had to stop this war.

Chapter Thirty-Six

The Raelean king, or who she assumed was the Raelean king, waited atop his horse on the far ridge. He sat tall, confident. Behind him was another group of riders, not large enough to be an army. Norah glanced over her shoulder at the ridge where Mikael waited with Caspian, the Crest, and half of the Mercian army. Adrian stayed with Calla and Cohen and the remaining half of the army closer to the capital, at the risk the meeting might be a distraction.

Norah looked at Soren beside her. Hopefully seeing Cyrus with no army settled him and Mikael slightly, but it didn't necessarily settle her. This day would be the start of peace or the start of war. Her stomach turned at not knowing which.

Cyrus advanced his horse down the ridge toward them with only one rider beside him, and Norah and Soren did the same. As they drew closer to each other, Norah could make out more of his appearance. He wore black-plated armor with accents of earthy red, like blood. Black and blood. A sharp helm covered his face, with a daggered crown fused on top. Across his back he wore a sword, accented in gold, with a large red stone in the hilt that reflected the light.

The rider beside him wasn't a soldier, but a woman. Her dark, curly hair hung long down the breast of her winter riding dress, but her face was hidden by the hood of her cloak.

They stopped a few lengths from each other. Soren gripped the hilt of his sword, but no one moved. All was quiet.

Norah couldn't see Cyrus's face, but she was certain he was smiling behind his helm. He sat like he was smiling. Cold needled down her spine, and suddenly, she felt like Mikael might have been right. Was this a trick? She forced herself calm.

"King Cyrus," she greeted him.

He didn't reply. And no one moved. Her heart beat faster. She glanced at Soren, who was tense and coiled, waiting for a reason to spring for blood. She turned her eyes back to the king.

Slowly, Cyrus reached up and pulled his helm from his head.

Norah gasped. The face that looked back at her nearly broke her.

The blond hair.

The square jaw.

The blue eyes.

"Alexander?" she breathed. Her mind had to be fooling her. She glanced at Soren for validation that he saw the same, and his dark stare told her he did. Her eyes darted back to Alexander. She could only sit with her mouth agape, unable to speak, unable to breathe.

How was this possible? It wasn't. As she looked closer, she saw this wasn't Alexander. He had the same face, the same hair, the same eyes, but he was different. An imposter—Cyrus was an imposter.

Suddenly the air shook. Cyrus jerked up his shield as two bolts from Soren's crossbow buried themselves into the black metal.

Soren was attacking.

"No!" she cried.

But it was too late. His horse charged.

The woman beside Cyrus raised her arms and whispered foreign words into the air. A stinging wind swept through. Soren's destrier reared and lashed out with its front hooves, as if fighting an invisible enemy, but it didn't continue its charge.

Sephir tossed her head and reared. Norah clutched the mare to keep from falling off and dropped a hand to the animal's neck to calm her.

Soren twisted atop his mount, his hand straining for the small battle-axe at his side, but he couldn't grab it, and Norah realized he was being held by an unseen force. A growl of pain ripped from his lips.

"Stop!" she screamed as she reached for him, but she wasn't close enough to touch him. And there was nothing she could do to help. Soren bellowed again.

"Stop!" She shot a glance at the ridge where Mikael was waiting. Was he seeing this? Why wasn't he coming? She needed him.

"The Shadow King cannot see." Cyrus said calmly, answering. "Nothing looks amiss for him." The voice was Alexander's, but this couldn't be Alexander.

Norah glanced at the woman beside him, who continued to mouth silent words into the air. She turned her eyes back to the ridge, where Mikael still waited. He had no idea what was really happening. She was on her own.

Soren groaned again, and Norah looked back to Cyrus. "Please," she said, forcing her voice steady. "Stop. You're hurting him."

The corners of his mouth turned up ever so slightly, then he cut a look to the woman beside him.

Soren's body sagged in relief, but he still sat unnaturally, held by the unseen force.

Norah stared back at the Raelean king. She knew this wasn't Alexander, but she couldn't take her eyes from all his familiar features. Her lip trembled. "Who are you?"

"Perhaps the name Lucien may be more familiar to you," he said.

Lucien? "Alexander's brother?" she asked. Alexander had a brother who'd died as a child. Only, this man was very much alive.

His eyes gave a cruel smirk as he watched the realization hit her.

"You're his exact likeness," she whispered.

"As many twins are."

Twins. She hadn't known they were twins. Apparently, there was a lot she hadn't known. Norah shook her head in disbelief. "You're supposed to be dead."

Lucien gave a slight tilt of his head. "Yes, I am. At least that was the intent of my mother."

"But now you're king of Rael?"

"Now I'm king of Rael and Serra."

She knew now—this was the man she'd been seeing. Not Alexander. The loss flooded back. The realization ripped her chest open again. She'd taken comfort that he was still with her somehow. But now she knew.

Alexander was gone.

Norah wavered, then caught herself. She couldn't let grief take her, not now. Her kingdoms were depending on her. Mikael was depending on her. She drew in a breath and released it slowly.

He was an imposter, a pretender, but he still held the crown. Regardless of her emotions, this man was king, she was queen, and together they had the ability to stop this war. She forced her mind to focus on her purpose. No one was dying today.

She kept her voice steady and her eyes on Lucien. "I did *not* come here for blood."

Lucien looked at Soren. "He seems to have other intentions."

"He doesn't respond well to deception," she said coldly. "Neither do I." She could hear the sharpness of her own voice, and she exhaled another breath to soften her stance. "But I have come to talk."

Lucien's eyes moved to the ridge where Mikael waited. "With an army?" Then his gaze found Soren again. "And the Destroyer."

"Well, you didn't come alone either, with your..." She looked at the woman and paused.

"Witch?" the woman said as a cruel smile touched her lips. "You can say it."

But Norah didn't want to say it. She hadn't even thought witches were real.

Soren strained again, but the witch's power held. This wasn't going well, and Norah desperately needed it to go well. If she could just speak to Lucien alone...

"Can we take a walk?" she asked him. "Just you and me?"

"Salara," Soren hissed, but she ignored him.

"I would love a walk," Lucien said.

Norah looked back at the ridge. "Will he see?" No doubt a walk alone beside the Raelean king would bring Mikael in full force.

Lucien shook his head. "No."

Norah slid down from Sephir, and Lucien did the same.

Soren snarled and wrenched against his hold again. She hated this for him, but he was a liability.

"You won't hurt him?" she asked.

"Not too much," the witch said with a wry smile.

"She won't hurt him," Lucien assured her. Norah believed him.

"Salara," Soren growled, thrashing again. But she ignored him. She was the only one who could manage a civil conversation right now.

She let her gaze travel over Lucien. He held up his hands, showing them empty, but she wasn't a fool. She knew who he was and that he had power beyond weapons. Still, there was something that told her she could trust him, at least for today. She stepped toward him, and he motioned for them to continue together away from Soren and the witch. Away from listening ears.

A calm settled between them as they walked.

"It was you," she said finally. "It was you who came to me."

He didn't answer.

"All this time. The visions, the dreams, it was all you."

He still didn't answer, but she knew she was right.

"You're a seer? No, not just a seer, a traveler."

A small smile came to his lips. "You continue to surprise me, Norah."

A faint memory flickered. Had he told her that before?

Norah spotted something on his neck and stopped. He stopped too. She stepped closer, not that she trusted him, but she had to see... She eyed the ink that marked his skin, just above his armor. Her pulse quickened. She knew these markings. He'd had them when she'd first seen him in the mortium.

As she studied him, all the pieces fell into place. When he'd returned to her, he must have modified his image, like the traveler Nemus had been able to do in Mercia. He'd made himself as Alexander.

Lucien stood quietly, giving himself to her questioning eyes and roving mind.

"It was your blood," she said. And it was his blood that allowed him into her mind.

Then another thought came to her. Her chest tightened as her heart pounded in her ears. "But in the Free Cities, in the inn, that wasn't a vision," she said. "You really were there." Her pulse was racing now.

He didn't deny it.

"You came to my bed," she whispered. Her heart ached as she looked into the same eyes as Alexander's. "I let you close," she said. "An enemy of Mercia and Kharav, you could have killed me then. Why didn't you?"

He held the same expressions as Alexander did, the same mannerisms. Her question bothered him. Or perhaps he didn't favor his answer. Why didn't he say something?

Anger flashed through her. "Is this all you wanted?" she snapped. "We came all this way to meet only so that I could see your face?"

"No," he said finally. "I came to give you this, in person this time." He pulled out a small vial and held it for her. *Blood*.

She stared at him. "What's that?"

"You know what it is. Invite me back, and I'll tell you everything."

The audacity. "You've told me nothing!"

"I will," he promised. "I need more time, time we don't have here. Let me come to you."

She shook her head. "Absolutely not."

"Did you really think we'd settle things so quickly? With your army on the ridge and a few fleeting moments?"

Norah swallowed. She didn't know what she'd thought. But reality hit her that it wouldn't be that simple.

He held the vial for her. "Take it," he said. "And then decide."

Norah glanced back at Soren, who was still held by the witch's magic. He continued to fight with everything he had, to no avail. There was no way he and Mikael would let her take the blood again.

Lucien closed his empty hand into a fist, and when he opened it again, a small necklace lay across his palm. He reached out and put the vial and necklace into her hand.

"What's this for?" she asked of the necklace.

His eyes moved back to Soren. "A small gift. To use."

What did *that* mean?

The corners of his mouth curved up, and he turned back toward his own horse, leaving her standing alone.

Norah could only watch him as he walked back and mounted his destrier before departing with his witch. When they reached the base of the ridge and started up, Soren's body jolted as the hold released him. Freed, he thundered to the ground and started toward her as she made her own way back.

"What did he say?" he snarled with a raging brow. "What did he give you?"

She hesitated.

His eyes burned into her. "How can you walk with him and be so trusting?" he seethed. "Now that you know what he's done! How he's deceived you!"

Her own anger simmered at his tone. She wasn't an idiot.

"What did he give you?" he demanded.

She ignored his question. "I came here to talk, and that's what I did."

"You walk with him like he's a friend. He's not the Bear!"

"I know he's not!" she snapped back.

"That makes it even worse."

His words were like knives; they stung. His eyes still blazed. "What did he give you?" he demanded again. But he was in no mind for her to show him the vial yet. Not with the want for battle radiating from his skin and Lucien still so close.

To use, Lucien had said. She pulled the necklace from her pocket and shoved it into his hand. "A customary greeting gift," she said shortly. Then she pushed past him to Sephir.

The short ride back up the ridge to Mikael and the waiting Mercian army with Soren beside her took an eternity. Soren boiled in a pool of anger as he rode. Well, he could be angry at himself. He was the one who chose violence at a meeting meant for peace. She'd come to talk to Cyrus—Lucien—and they'd talked.

They reached the top of the ridge, and Mikael and Caspian urged their mounts to meet them.

"What happened?" Mikael asked when they reached them. "What did he say? It didn't even look like you were talking."

She hesitated as she glanced at Soren.

"Oh, they were talking, and walking, and having a great conversation," Soren said angrily.

Mikael's forehead creased. "What?"

"He put some trickery in place to keep you from seeing, and bound me so I couldn't move."

This wasn't helping. "It's Lucien," she said.

Caspian shifted back on his horse, and his mouth opened in surprise. He knew who Lucien was and was obviously just as shocked at the news he still lived.

"Who's Lucien?" Mikael asked.

She swallowed. "Alexander's brother."

Mikael glanced at Soren, then back to Norah. "Then where's Cyrus?"

"No." She shook her head. "There is no Cyrus. I mean, there is, but he's one and the same. Lucien *is* Cyrus."

Mikael only stared at her as it sank in. Then he looked out over the valley from which Lucien had long since left.

She looked at Caspian. Her voice dropped to almost a whisper. "He's Alexander's exact likeness."

Caspian let out a long exhale. "As he was when they were children."

Mikael's eyes jerked back to her, and the shadow under his brow darkened. "It was him coming to you all this time? Cyrus? Lucien?"

She nodded reluctantly. "He's a seer."

"A powerful one," Soren added. "And he's got a fucking witch, on top of everything else."

A quiet came, and they all sat, letting the realization settle. Where did they go from here?

"Are you going to tell Adrian?" Caspian asked her after a time.

She hesitated. "I want to, but..." She shook her head. "Not yet. I just have to... I don't know, I just need to think. It's all so much."

Mikael's expression changed, but she wasn't sure to what. He dropped down from his horse and stepped to the ridge, away from them. Something was wrong. Or rather, something was *more* wrong...

Norah slipped off Sephir and followed. She waited for more of his anger.

But it didn't come.

Instead, he turned and held out his hand. She took it, and he pulled her close and drew her chin up to look at him. "He looks just like the Bear?"

She nodded.

His voice dropped to just above a whisper. "I know that must be hard for you. I'm sorry."

Gods, she loved this man, and she hugged him tightly. "Thank you. For us coming. For just being here."

"Always." And he held her closer.

As she pulled back, her eye caught something, and she froze. In a tree not far away sat a small bird—a small, brown bird, with a blood mark on its head. She clutched Mikael's arm.

"Are you all right?" he asked.

"The bird," she whispered.

Both Mikael and Soren, who was dropping down from his own mount, looked to where she stared.

"It's his," she said, realizing. "The birds are his." It all fell into place. Her pulse beat faster as her mind swirled. "That means he's the one who sent the assassins."

She flinched as Soren grabbed his crossbow from the back of his saddle and loosed an arrow, dropping the bird to the ground.

Mikael pulled her back to look at him, his face gravely serious. "Salara, you understand there can be no peace with this man."

She jerked back. "Wait, what?"

"He tried to take your life."

"That was quite a while ago. Circumstances can change. People can change."

His eyes grew darker. "You defend him?"

"No, I just don't want to throw away the possibility for peace based on something he did before he even knew me!"

"He doesn't know you!" he said, louder now. "And you don't know him. He's violated your mind and deceived you, and you can't trust him."

She wouldn't deny that, but she couldn't skip so quickly to war for actions of the past. She needed to let her mind calm and talk it through when the tension faded.

"Can we just go home?" she asked. "And talk about this then?"

He quieted and sighed. "Of course."

They mounted their horses and started back north.

Chapter Thirty-Seven

Calm.

Calm, she told herself.

But Norah was anything but calm. The journey back hadn't brought her to a rational place; it had only allowed her mind the space to rehash everything Lucien had done. And it made her angry.

Back at the castle in her chamber, she clutched the vial of blood in her hand as that anger grew. He'd lied to her. She clenched her teeth until they hurt—*so stupid*—she was so stupid. All this time she'd thought it could be Alexander somehow. Of course it wasn't Alexander. She should have known. He wore Alexander's face, but everything about him was wrong. She should have known. Even Soren knew it wasn't him. And Mikael. How could she not have known? How could she have been so blind?

She stood in front of the fireplace in her chamber.

Throw it in, her anger told her.

He had said he'd explain everything, if she'd only call him back. That he'd even have the audacity to ask her to invite his return...

Throw it into the fire.

He didn't deserve to explain. He'd used her pain to get close to her. He'd used her most private thoughts, her most private weaknesses. He had used *her*. He'd let her talk to him, tell him things.

Throw it in.

It was Lucien—not Alexander—who she had told that Mikael would be traveling through the western pass when he had first returned to Kharav, and Lucien had used it to advance his army and attack. Thank the gods Phillip had moved his army to stop them.

And she'd told Lucien she was traveling back to Mercia after Catherine had fallen ill. He came to her because he knew where she'd be, and because he could. But not to harm her. Why? It would have been so easy for him. What did he want?

Well, she wanted to tell him a thing or two...

She fumed with fury.

She needed answers.

Before she could talk herself out of it, she drew the blood across her palm and closed her fist over it. Then she closed her eyes and stood in her chamber in her mind.

Norah knew he was here. She could feel him.

The door of her chamber opened, but no one entered. Cautiously, she walked toward it. As she stepped into the hall, it was no longer a hall but a bright grassy knoll atop a large cliff, overlooking the sea.

And she saw him. Lucien.

He sat on a rock near the edge of the cliff, staring out over the water.

Norah walked slowly toward him. He was different now. His hair was cropped short, and he wore dark breeches and a loose-fitting gray shirt. Ink marked his skin, just above the neck of his tunic. He looked as he had the first time she saw him in the mortium.

"This is my favorite place," he said, not turning as she approached. His voice surprised her.

"You speak? Have you been able to speak this entire time?"

He didn't answer her.

Of course he wouldn't. "Why?" she demanded. "Why didn't you?"

"I didn't know his sound. Only his image."

What did that mean? "What?"

He pulled a long blade of grass from in front of him. "I didn't know his voice, his words. I couldn't speak as he did."

Then it occurred to her—the limitations of the gift of sight—he could only see the memories in her mind, not hear them. Alexander's speech was the only thing he couldn't copy. Her blood boiled. "So to keep up your charade, you said nothing?"

"I didn't intend to deceive you."

"Yes, you did," she snapped back. "Otherwise, you would have told me exactly who you were."

He stood, and the vision of the coast fell away. "You asked me if I was Alexander, and I told you no."

"You knew my context! I thought death had changed you!"

"I never lied to you."

"That's all you've done! Deception is a lie, whether you spoke the words directly or not. And you"—she sucked in a breath—"you made yourself him. You showed yourself as Alexander." The worst lie of all.

He quieted. The earth changed below her feet, and they stood in a sun-filled forest. These visions were not from her memory. He was choosing the locations. He was creating the vision around them.

"I'm sorry," he said softly.

His apology surprised her, but it wasn't enough. "You're sorry you tried to kill me?"

He shifted his weight back.

"That's right, I know. I know it was you who sent the assassins. It was you who spoke through them."

He eyed her before answering. "I've done many terrible things I should probably be sorry for. Many I'm not, but"—he paused—"that has become one."

"Why did you do it?"

"To break the Shadow King from his alliance with Mercia. And you were Alexander's queen—I knew it would destroy him."

"You did it to hurt Alexander?"

"I did it to hurt them both," he snapped. His eyes blazed, and the forest around them darkened.

Yes—he'd come for vengeance. She remembered. "Why?"

He drew in a long breath, and the sun returned. But he didn't answer.

"You said you would explain everything." That was why she'd called him. "Explain."

He swept his eyes to the trees in hesitation, then back to her. "Where do you want me to start?"

Norah sat on a fallen tree. "From the beginning," she said as she crossed her arms. "What are you?" She had already guessed a traveler seer, but he hadn't actually acknowledged it.

He nodded slowly and sat on the opposite end of the tree. He took his time, wiping his hand over the bottom half of his face. "The Evil is what my mother called it. I didn't know how I was able to do it, get inside her mind, but I could. Not Alexander's, but I could hers."

Caspian had said their mother had gone mad. Was it madness? Or was it Lucien?

"I would have dreams," he continued. "Some were... terrible things. The worst was when I was scared. I just wanted to be near her, but she cast me out. I tried to show her."

Norah's chest tightened. To be a child...

He leaned forward with his forearms on his knees and his hands clasped. The landscape around them turned to winter. "I was so young, but I remember. I remember how she took me away. And left me in the forest." Snow blanketed the ground around them now. The trees stood like skeletons, stripped of their leaves. "I ran after her as she rode away. I ran until my legs wouldn't work and I couldn't feel my face for the cold." His voice was stoic, unemotional. "I fell, and I lay there, looking up at the tops of the trees, calling out for her. For my father. Calling out for Alexander. And that's how I was found."

Caspian said Lucien had died of a sickness. That must have been what his mother had told everyone. A pain seeped deeper into her heart.

"Who found you?" she asked, softer now.

He seemed to snap back to the present, and the corner of his mouth turned up. "By fate or by luck, the man who came upon me had a wife. They had for a long time tried to conceive a child but couldn't." Lucien smiled to himself. "And they raised me as their own."

Norah exhaled out a small breath of relief.

But then Lucien chuckled darkly and shook his head. "No. That's not what happened. It's what I imagined had happened many times over in my life. How... different... things would have been. But that's not what happened."

Norah's stomach twisted.

He stood, and the earth swirled under her feet again. Everything went dark. She staggered up but couldn't see.

When his voice came, it was all around her. "I was found by a demon in the night, and he took me to his hell."

Norah almost screamed as the darkness broke, and cages came down around her. Men filled the cages, stripped of their armor and most of their clothing, even though it was the dead of winter. Some were bloodied, as though they'd just seen war. Others were emaciated, as if they'd been in the cages for some time. She couldn't hear them, but terror still filled her. A man to her right retched his stomach contents through the bars of the cage onto the wheel of the wagon that carried them. Another man was hunched in a corner. His uncovered toes were black as death. Perhaps he *was* dead.

"This isn't real," she whispered to herself, trying to quell the panic. *It's just a vision.*

"Oh, it's real," he hissed. "It's very real."

The wagon stopped, and all the men around her were dragged from their cage. The vision shifted, and she was now among them. She gasped as she saw their captors. Their faces were wrapped in black like the night, and ink marked their skin. Shadowmen. Darkness loomed over her, and she jerked her head up. Her heart stopped. She knew this man, this horn-helmed giant. *Mikael.*

He spoke to a tall man with a shaved head beside him.

Norah was afraid to ask, but she forced herself to anyway. "Who's he talking to? What are they saying?"

"A Serran slaver. And he's deciding whether a small boy is worth any price at all, or if I should just be killed."

Oh gods. He was just a child.

Mikael gave a short nod and left the slaver to his cargo, but she didn't take her eyes from him. His movements were heavier, slower. And he was older. This wasn't Mikael. This was long ago, and she would have been a child herself. This wasn't Mikael—it was his father.

"Everyone I loved abandoned me," Lucien said, "including Alexander."

No. No, that wasn't true. "He didn't abandon you! Your brother loved you."

The cages and men in chains fell away, and Lucien and Norah stood again in the winter forest.

Lucien snorted, shaking his head. "No. If he loved me, he would have looked for me. He would have tried to find me."

"He was only a boy! He thought you were dead."

"He would have felt me!" he thundered. "The way I have felt him all these years."

"He didn't have your gift!"

"He did," he insisted. "He had a shield. I couldn't see him."

"No, it wasn't the same. It was... different."

He paused, and his face sobered. "How?"

How could she explain it? She couldn't, and she shook her head. "I... We don't know. He was only starting to uncover it when he died. But I swear to you, he didn't know you were alive. He would have gone to the ends of the world to find you."

He stared at her, not believing.

"I mean it," she said. "If he had any idea you were still alive, he would have come for you."

The anger on his skin cooled slightly.

"He would have come," she said again, "as soon as he was able."

His face softened, and his shoulders slumped forward. "I spent my entire life hating him. I followed the news of his rise, planning how I'd kill him too."

Too? Had he killed someone else? Someone else close to him... Her pulse quickened. "What happened to your mother?"

His eyes locked with hers, dark blue like stormy seas.

"I told you. I've done terrible things," he said. He didn't look like Alexander anymore. She could see the differences now. The lines between his eyes were more pronounced. His face was... harsher.

She swallowed. This man was not Alexander. But she could see him—she could see the pain. And this wasn't wholly who he was.

She stepped closer to him. "Lucien, your brother loved you. Family was so important to him. And to Adrian—do you know what it would mean to him to learn that you're alive?"

For the first time, a sense of heart flickered across his face. His eyes glistened. "I never knew I had another brother. Not until you told me."

He hadn't known? Her heart hurt. "He's such a beautiful person."

"Is he... like... us? Alexander and me?" He rested his hand on his chest.

She shook her head. "No, there's nothing weird about him. He's perfectly normal." *Wait.* She bit her lip as she squirmed. "That didn't come out right."

He gave a small smile, a genuine one, and her heart leapt—the beginnings of goodness. This was what they needed. She knew if they could just connect and talk and work through things—

Suddenly, Norah was ripped from the vision. Her eyes flew open to being shaken abruptly.

"Salara!"

She gasped. Where was she? On the floor in her chamber. Mikael stared down at her as he clutched her shoulders. Soren knelt beside him. *Wait...*

No. No, no, no...

"Salara," Mikael called again, an urgency in his voice.

Soren gripped her hand, peeling open her fingers and wiping Lucien's blood away with a cloth.

"No," she cried as she tried to jerk it away. "No! I have to go back."

Mikael's eyes were dark and angry. And something else—scared. "What are you doing?" he raged. "You called him to you?"

"Mikael, please! He's there. I have to go back!"

The look in his eyes killed her—the look of betrayal.

"No. Mikael, he's talking to me. I'm getting through to him! His anger's built on perceptions that... that aren't true. And those he seeks vengeance against, they're all gone. It's not you he holds ill will for, it's your father. And he's learned about Adrian. I can see it—I'm getting through to him!"

"Salara," he said between his teeth as he shook his head.

She had to get him to understand. "Do you see what this means? What if I can convince him? Break his alliance with Gregor? Mikael, I could stop all of this. I could stop this war!"

He shook his head again.

"Please! I have to go back."

He clutched her tightly. "This man is deceiving you."

"Not anymore, he's not!"

He held up the vial. "Where did you get this?"

Damn it. She couldn't answer.

"Where did you get it?" he demanded again.

"He gave it to me," she confessed finally, "when I met him in the valley." She avoided Soren's burning glare.

Mikael stood. "You kept this from me?" he asked angrily.

"Because I knew you'd take it from me."

"So you lied?"

"I didn't lie. I just didn't tell you."

"That's lying!" he thundered.

She wanted to yell back, but—gods damn it... *Fair*.

He started toward the door, but he still had the blood.

"Wait!" she called, scrambling to her feet. "I need that!"

With a final look of insult, he stepped from the chamber.

"Mikael!" she called after him.

Her eyes found Soren staring back at her, but not with the anger she expected. Disappointment. That was worse.

"Soren—"

But he turned and followed Mikael from the room.

Gods damn it all. She sank into the chair at her vanity and covered her face with her hands. She breathed. In and out.

The calm returned. She couldn't be angry at Mikael. Of course he'd be upset. He didn't understand. He didn't see what she saw in Lucien. He thought she was being naive, and maybe she was before. But not now. She had to get him to understand.

Everything depended on it.

Dinner was quiet. Quieter than usual. Catherine ate in her chamber. She never left her room now.

At the end of the table in the dining hall, Mikael hardly touched his food. He was angry with her, Norah knew. As was Soren. She'd lied to him. He'd asked her what Lucien gave her, and she had only given him the necklace. Guilt ate at her, but she couldn't make herself regret it. If she had told either of them about the vial, she would have never been able to connect with Lucien at all.

After dinner, Mikael walked her back to their chamber. He still looped her arm through his, even in his anger. Her heart beat steadier. They were okay. He was still angry, but they were okay. When they reached the chamber, he pulled her to look at him, and brushed her cheek softly.

She needed to get him to understand. "Mikael. I need you to trust me."

He sighed. "I know. And I do."

She smiled up at him. *Finally.*

"But I know your weakness for his face," he said.

She rocked back on her heel in surprise. "I'm sorry, what?" Was he serious? "My *weakness for his face?*" Her voice came stronger with her own anger now. "I know you fear he's using my heart—"

"No," he said heatedly, responding to her anger with his own. "I fear he holds a piece of your heart, and he's not even the Bear."

Norah stopped. Did he really think that? Her anger dissipated. She shook her head. "No. That's not true." She reached up and brought a hand to his cheek. "That's not true. I need you to believe this if nothing else."

His anger evaporated, and he let out a long exhale. "I believe you," he said softly. "It was a fear in the moment, when you wanted the blood back."

She nodded. That she could understand. "Now you know." She leaned closer and ran her hand down to his chest, over his heart. He covered it with his own. "But I do need the blood back," she said. "I have to talk to him."

The muscle tightened under her hand. Heat grew across his body. "You won't. I know you're doing what you think is right—"

She pulled her hand away. "It *is* right! If it's a chance to prevent war, we have to try!"

"I said no."

"You won't tell me what I won't do." She was queen. And nothing would stop her from trying to keep her husband. Not even Mikael himself.

He stepped back from her. "Then you'll do this and continue to lie to me?"

"No lies," she snapped back. "I'm telling you right now—I *will* talk to him."

His eyes burned. "That's not going to happen."

Nine hells it wouldn't.

Mikael rumbled with anger, then turned and left their chamber in a storm.

Norah clenched her fists in frustration. She let herself fall back onto the bed and threw her arm over her face. She wanted to scream. It might make her feel better. But things wouldn't actually be better. No—she needed to find a way to get the vial back.

But when she sat up, she froze. Outside the window on her balcony sat a small bird on the railing. She rose and walked to the doors, opening them.

It was *him*.

Lucien.

She knew it was.

"Can you hear me too?" This wasn't a vision—she hoped he was able to.

The bird cocked its head to the side.

"I need more blood," she said.

And it flew off into the sky.

Chapter Thirty-Eight

Norah sat in the dark. No one would find her in the hidden stairwell leading to the tunnels under the castle. The cold seeped through to her skin, and she tucked more of her skirts under her thighs. She should have brought her cloak, but no matter.

She held the vial of blood in her hand that she'd found on her terrace that morning. In the dim light of her lantern, it looked black as the night. Her heart beat heavily in her chest. She'd told Mikael she would speak to Lucien again. She hated to do it in secret, but she would do whatever it took to stop this war.

She pulled the top off the vial and smeared a streak across her palm, curling her fingers closed. And she let her eyelids fall shut.

He came immediately, as if he'd been waiting, and stood at the bottom of the short stairwell.

She couldn't see his face in the darkness of her mind, but she knew it was him.

"An interesting place to call me to," he said.

Norah couldn't help an amused smile. Perhaps she could have imagined a room in the castle, something more pleasant. She didn't put much thought into the space around her when she'd called him, she'd only imagined herself in her current surroundings.

"We won't be interrupted here," she told him.

He lit up the passageway around them, and she was able to see his face—harsh, but not unfriendly.

"I take it that's what happened before?" he asked. "Why you left so suddenly?"

"I'm sorry about that. But there's still so much more to talk about. I wanted to see you again. I hope you don't mind."

He gave her a small smile. "I don't mind."

The nervous racing of her heart eased.

"Will you walk with me?" he asked.

She nodded and stood and stepped down the remaining few stairs to the tunnels. The light grew brighter around them, bright as the outside day, and she glanced around to see tunnels no longer of stone but of wisteria and vining flowers. The cobbled walk under her feet turned to a pathway lined with ferns.

He motioned them forward. "Shall we?" he asked, and she fell in step beside him.

"I've been thinking, a lot, just about everything," she started.

He nodded. "I have too."

Promising. "I still have questions."

"Ask them."

It was a genuine invitation, but it didn't make it easier. "Why didn't you try to kill me again? Why only come after me once?"

"I came twice, actually."

She stopped. "What?"

"I came once before, when you traveled to marry the king of Aleon "

Her pulse beat faster.

"But by the time I arrived, someone had beaten me to you."

The tunnel of vining flowers fell away, and darkness surrounded them, but moonlight painted the scene. They stood in a travel camp off the road she had journeyed on her way to wed Phillip in Aleon. The remains of her army lay around them, all dead.

Yes, Mikael had reached her first. Her stomach twisted at the sight.

"It's when I found this," he said, opening his hand and revealing her mother's crown.

She gaped back at him. "You had my crown all that time?" Her mind swirled around her. If Mikael hadn't taken her, she still wouldn't have made it to Aleon.

"Then came news of your marriage to the Shadow King," he continued. "*That...* was a surprise."

It had been to her as well, she remembered.

Lucien looked back at the crown. Then he dropped his hand, and it vanished into the night. "It was never really about you, though, Norah. I wanted Alexander. I thought he'd accompany you to Aleon, and he didn't. But, when his blood touched your skin in the Shadowlands, I knew he was there with you. He was so close; I couldn't not come."

"So it was never *about* me, but you came to *kill* me?"

His eyes were harsh and piercing now. "I came to kill the both of you."

It still didn't make sense to her. Alexander, yes... "But why me?"

"Because Alexander was sworn to protect you, and I wanted to show him he had no power to do so. And you weren't innocent—you so willingly allied yourself with a monster, the Shadow King. To turn a blind eye to everything he's done, that makes you complicit!"

She quieted. She wouldn't deny that—she'd been guilted by it many times over. But she was working to change things. Mikael was changing.

"And the Shadow King loved you," he added.

Compelling reasons. He certainly had motive. "Why didn't you try again?" she asked.

He paused, and his anger seemed to fade. "Because... you were not as I'd expected. And... I didn't want to, after that."

His words left her speechless. The tone had shifted between them. She hadn't forgotten that he'd kissed her in the Free Cities. A far leap to make, from trying to kill her to kissing her. She'd get to that. Eventually.

"How did you get into Kharav?" she asked.

"You ask me my secrets?"

"Do they really still need to be secrets?"

He'd said he would tell her everything, and if he shared this with her, it could mean a budding trust and that they were on a path toward friendship. If they were on a path toward friendship, it was a path away from war.

The darkness of night around them brightened to day, and the scene of death faded and opened to a landscape of rolling rocky hills. A flock of birds flew overhead, and he lifted his eyes to them.

"They show me," he said.

She followed his gaze up to the birds.

"They show me the landscape, how to get through, if danger is near. They are my eyes."

His birds. "You control them with your blood?"

Lucien gave a small acknowledging smile.

"So, you just go around dripping blood on creatures, having them do your will?"

He chuckled. "Something like that."

"Does it hurt? You have to... cut yourself?"

He nodded. "It did, but I'm used to it now."

"I'm sorry," she said, softer. "That still sounds terrible." He had to hurt himself to give the blood. He had to cut himself to talk to her like they were now.

"You don't need to feel sorry for me." He pulled his dagger from his belt and drew the blade across his palm, opening the skin and spilling his blood to the floor.

She gasped. But before her eyes, the edges of the skin closed themselves, and the wound healed. Her mouth fell open. "You can heal yourself?"

He watched her a moment before saying, "No. I have a healer. A true healer."

"Your witch?"

"No. Another, not a witch."

The fact that he would tell her that surprised her. She was gaining his trust, and her heart leapt. Would he tell her more?

"How do you control someone's mind?" she asked him.

He hesitated, then said, "I can't. Humans are too intelligent, too strong."

"But the men you sent to kill me—"

"They willingly yielded their minds to me."

"And died for you," she added.

"They're all willing to die for me, for our cause."

"And what cause is that?"

But he didn't answer. She blew out a breath. So much death. And for what? They continued their walk through the rocky hills, although the birds had disappeared.

She had so many more questions for him but was wary of it being too much, too soon. This was so much more progress than she'd expected, and she wanted to protect it.

"I should return, before I'm missed," she said.

The scene around them changed back to the tunnels of woven greenery and flowers. He walked her to the short stair that led back up to her dressing room.

"I'd like to talk again," she said.

The sharpness of his face softened, and he gave a small nod. "I'd like that too."

"Goodbye, Lucien."

She opened her eyes back to the darkness of the stairwell.

Winter chilled the long main hall of the castle, but the light of the sun made it seem not so cold. Still, Norah pulled her shawl tighter around her shoulders. As she neared Catherine's room, she slowed to see Soren coming from the opposite direction. What was he doing here? Only Catherine's chamber and the music room were in the far east wing, neither of which she expected Soren to be anywhere near.

Norah eyed him suspiciously, waiting for him to explain himself. He didn't. He simply eyed her back and said nothing as he passed. She scoffed as she looked back to Catherine's chamber, then back to Soren, who disappeared into an adjoining hall. What was going on?

Stepping into Catherine's chamber, she saw her grandmother propped up and sitting against the tufted headboard of her bed. A needlepoint hoop lay in her lap, although she wasn't working on it.

"Good morning," Norah said sweetly. "A few visitors already?"

Catherine drew in a breath and gave a proper smile. "Not particularly."

Norah narrowed her eyes. Did she just lie? "Hmmm." Norah sat down on the chair beside the bed. It was warm... from someone else. Recently. "Are you sure?"

"Stop beating around the bush, what are you getting at?"

"Was the lord commander sitting in this chair?"

"So what if he was?"

Norah gasped. "I knew it!"

Catherine puffed a breath. "What?"

"Are you two becoming friends?" she goaded with a mischievous smile.

Catherine's lip twitched. "Nothing of the sort."

Norah's smile widened.

Catherine gave a weak harrumph. "He says you're still trying to broker peace with this king Cyrus."

That was probably a nicer version of what Soren had actually said. "*Trying*." And had he not told her Cyrus was Lucien? Apparently not by the way she was acting. Norah wouldn't tell her either. It would only upset her, and her health couldn't take it.

"You can't be afraid to fight, Norah."

"I'm not afraid to fight, but this war will bring tragedy and suffering, to all sides, and I need to stop it before it starts."

Catherine gave a small smile. "You're a strong queen, Norah. I know you'll do what you think is right and best." Catherine paused, her eyes tearing. "And everything you've done has all been right and best." She shifted slightly and winced, bringing her hand to her side.

Norah moved quickly to the bed and sat down on the edge. Catherine's pain had been growing worse.

"I don't have much time left," her grandmother said. "But I wanted you to know that even when I'm gone, I'll never be gone from you. I'll be with you always."

Norah nodded, her emotion keeping her from speaking.

"I have one thing left to ask of you, though."

Norah's heart was breaking—Catherine was preparing for her end, and Norah didn't think she could handle it. But she nodded again.

"Send Alexander to the gods."

Norah stilled. Then she looked down at the patterned quilt on the bed. She couldn't have this conversation now.

"I've told the fiend to hound you until you do," Catherine said. "He's promised me."

"So that was your conversation with Soren this morning?" Norah asked. No surprise.

"That and Sophia."

Norah frowned as she looked at the gray feline on the foot of the bed.

"Your cat?"

"Mmm," Catherine pursed her lips in simple acknowledgement as she reached for her cup of tea on the bedside table.

Norah picked up the cup and handed it to her. "What about your cat?"

Catherine shrugged. "Nothing. I only want to make sure she's cared for after I'm gone."

Norah sat back, looking squarely at her grandmother. "Wait. You've asked the lord commander of a four-nation army to look after your cat?"

"Oh, Norah, he's the only one who pays her any mind at all."

Norah scoffed. "I do too!"

"When? You don't so much as look at her."

Because she was a *cat*. Norah wasn't too keen on cats, but she would have taken care of her grandmother's cat.

Catherine's eyes taunted her. "He pets her every time he comes in."

Norah wrinkled her face. "How many times has he come?"

"More than you!"

"I come here every day!"

"So does he, sometimes twice a day!"

Soren came regularly to see her grandmother? Well—"I'm running two kingdoms!"

"He's leading a four-nation army to war!"

Norah gasped. "You got that from me."

Catherine pursed her lips, looking quite pleased with herself.

Norah stood. She couldn't believe this. "Fine. I don't want your cat anyway."

"That's why I'm giving her to the Destroyer."

She wanted to scream. "Well, I hope you're *all* happy together!"

"*They* will be," her grandmother replied shortly. "*I'll* be dead!"

Norah turned and stalked out of the chamber, her mind fuming. What was even happening? When she reached the main hall, she stopped and sank down onto a side bench, covering her face in her hands.

"Salara," came Mikael's voice, and she looked up as he sat down beside her. "Are you all right? What's happened?"

She sat back against the bench and shook her head. "I'm losing my mind. I just"—she paused and took a breath—"I just got into an argument with my grandmother about not giving me her cat." She covered her face with her hands again. "I don't even want her cat."

He put his arm around her and pulled her to him. "You're under a lot of stress right now."

"We all are." She put her hand on his thigh. "Including you."

He covered her hand with his. "Are we all right?" he asked softly.

Oh, right. They were supposed to be angry at each other. But she didn't want to be angry at him anymore. She sighed. "Of course."

He pulled up her fingers to his lips to kiss them. "Good."

In the dimly lit stairwell, Norah held the vial of blood in her hand. She'd have to tell Mikael she was talking to Lucien eventually. But when? She sighed.

After she brokered peace, she told herself.

That was her purpose, after all, and she was close—she could feel it. She drew a deep breath and called Lucien back.

She knew he was there when the room changed around her. Her seat on the stair turned to a seat on a garden bench. It was summertime. A bird lighted on a fountain in front of her, and then flew away, and she felt his presence on the bench beside her. She still had so many questions. She hoped they might be able to pick up where they left off before.

She pulled the vial from her pocket. "So, your birds bring me these?"

He nodded. A good start.

"And my crown?"

"I have larger friends." From between the topiaries in the garden, two dogs emerged, but they weren't like any dogs she'd seen before. They were black dogs, large—almost as big as Cusco and Cavaatsa had been, except they had no ears and no tails.

Norah shuddered. "Did you do that to them?"

He shook his head. "No. With me, they have a very different life than the one they had before."

A different life than before... Lucien had had a different life too. Mikael had told her how he'd been a bloodsport fighter and led the rebellion against the old king of Rael.

He watched her watching him. "You have more questions?"

She pulled her mind back; she did have more questions. "You said something, before, both the last time we spoke and when you came as the assassins. You knew Alexander's blood had touched my skin in Kharav. How?" It felt strange to be talking so casually about the attempt on her life with the one who had tried to claim it.

He nodded. "His blood allowed me to travel the same as my own. When it touched your skin, I saw you. And I knew he was with you."

"And that's how you came to me in the mortium after he died."

He sat for a time before speaking. "I knew something had happened. A searing pain came to me, greater than I'd ever felt before. When I woke, his weight—the weight I'd carried inside for my entire life—it was just gone. And his blood touched so many. So many minds, so loud—his blood was on all their skins. And I knew."

She could only watch him.

"All those years, I wanted him dead," he continued, "and then for him to be snuffed from me in an instant... I wasn't ready. I couldn't believe it."

Lucien paused. "I wanted him back," he whispered. "And so I searched, but the weight was gone. I sought his blood, reaching out to everyone it had touched. And it brought me to the mortium. To you." He paused, his eyes now staring through her. "I saw him," he whispered, "in your mind, for the first time in our adult lives."

Norah swallowed. All the pieces were falling into place.

He smiled sadly. "You saw me as I am, before I realized where I was, before I realized I was in *your* mind. It was too late to change my projection."

"The markings on your neck," she remembered.

He nodded.

Norah pressed her knuckles to her lips, trying to make sense of the chaos in her mind. "And then you came back; you came as Alexander."

He gave another nod, seemingly ashamed. "I wanted you to let me back in," he said. "You still had his blood on your skin, and so I returned. I could project everything: his dress, his hair"—he paused—"everything but his voice and his words."

"So, you came back for my secrets."

"I saw it as an opportunity against my enemy, yes," he admitted. He hesitated before saying, "But as I got to know you"—he stopped again—"it didn't make me happy to deceive you."

They sat in the quiet for a long time.

"And now?" she asked. "Now that you know things are different, that things have changed—"

"Nothing's changed."

She shook her head. "How can you say that? You would still move against Mercia?"

"Norah, Mercia was never the target of my wrath. Only those who've oppressed my people." He sighed. "For Alexander I felt a personal vengeance, yes, but you and I have never truly been enemies. And I'm sorry you've been caught in the middle."

And she believed him. Her hope grew. He was being completely open with her. This was exactly what she needed—what they all needed. "No one wants this war."

But his eyes blazed back at her. "I want this war."

His sudden change in demeanor rattled her, and she stumbled over her thoughts for a moment. She shook her head in confusion. "What? No—why?"

"Because that's what change requires. And that's the price owed."

He *wanted* war? "Lucien, thousands of people will die, your own people included."

"All of us are willing to sacrifice."

"For what?"

"For justice! The Shadowlands must pay." His eyes flamed with a frightening fury. And it was growing.

Where was all this hate coming from? She desperately searched her mind for anything to help ease the tension. "Kharav is not the only kingdom who has slaves."

"The Shadowlands fuel it. They sell the spoils of their wars; the slavers use Shadow rice to support their trade. There are others, it's true—Etreus, Persus, Elam, Lorys—and they'll all pay. Every single one of them. But I'll take the Shadowlands first."

The tension was escalating, and not in the right direction. She needed to get them back to where they were before. But she wouldn't be able to do that now; she needed to let him calm.

She steadied her voice the best she could. "I think we're both tired and have a lot to think on. Can we talk more later?"

He rose from the bench. For a moment, she thought he might not answer. Then he nodded. The world fell away, and they stood where they had started, at the stairwell.

"You'll return to me?" she asked.

"When you call me." It was a small reassurance. It wasn't broken between them.

"Good night, Lucien."

"Good night," he said with a stiff bow of his head.

A new day came with the sun, one Norah was determined to make the most of. She swept into Catherine's room. "I've decided that I'm perfectly fine that you'd rather have the Destroyer of the Shadowlands, known for his brutality and complete unpleasantness, look after your beloved Sophia, instead of your one and only endearing granddaughter—your own flesh and blood."

Where she'd expected a snarky reply, there was none.

She'd take it as forgiveness. She walked to the window and pulled open the draperies.

Catherine was still sleeping on the bed. She was growing more and more tired. *Great,* now she was going to have to repeat that all over again when she woke.

"I never thought I'd see the day you'd sleep longer than me. Time to stir. Serene's bringing breakfast."

But her grandmother didn't move.

She slowed. "Grandmother?"

Silence.

She approached the bed. "Grandmother?" Her breath wavered. Catherine looked so pale. Why was she so pale? She swallowed. Ever so slowly, she drew closer.

"Grandmother," she whispered.

Norah reached out and took Catherine's hand. But it was cold, void of spirit. Void of life.

She dropped it as she sucked in a breath. A cry escaped her lips, and she covered her mouth with her hand.

No, not yet. She wasn't ready.

She sank down onto the bed beside Catherine's body as sobs shook her.

She wasn't ready.

Chapter Thirty-Nine

Norah lay across her bed, staring up at the ceiling. Three days had passed, but it felt like both an hour and a year. Time had fallen apart. That morning she'd watched as her grandmother was sealed in the Hall of Souls. As important as it was, everything was a blur. All she could remember was Catherine's face: pale and hollow, a shell of the spirit she'd been. How did one so strong just waste away? The image would haunt her.

She couldn't believe her grandmother was gone. Now what would she do? She couldn't be queen without her. She didn't want to be queen without her. And now what? How was she supposed to do everything on her own—look after Mercia, be salara of Kharav, stop this war...

She bolted up.

Lucien.

They left their last conversation on a somewhat uneasy note, and she hadn't called him since. In the chaos, she'd completely forgotten. He must think... What must he think? She jumped off the bed. She was in no mind for conversation, but she couldn't let all the progress with Lucien fall apart.

Down in the stairwell, she stopped a moment to catch her breath. *Calmly. Calmly.* She didn't want to show up to a conversation with Lucien unsettled, and she forced in a deep inhale before pushing it out of her lungs completely. She hadn't brought a lantern in her hurry, and she fumbled with the top of the vial. With shaky hands, she drew a smear of blood across her palm.

Be calm, she told herself again, and she clenched her fist closed.

Her mind was quiet.

"I thought you might not invite me again," came his voice all around her.

He didn't light the darkness, and she couldn't see him.

"I thought you might be angry," he said, "but now... I see. I see your sorrow."

She hadn't planned to tell him about Catherine, but she supposed she couldn't keep it from him. Not when he was inside her mind. Did he see everything?

The darkness faded, and he stood at the foot of the stair. "I'm sorry for your loss."

She felt sorry too, but for what? For her own sorrow? For the time it took to call him again? Her mind churned for words, and still she found herself without them.

He offered his hand. She stared at it for a moment, then took it and stepped down beside him. He didn't release her. Instead, he pulled her hand into the fold of his arm and led them down the darkness of the tunnel. The stone walls fell away, and they walked through a field in the night. Around them flashed the luminescence of fireflies.

He led her to a bench beside a bubbling stream. The dark gave way to light, like the dawn before the sun, and they sat.

Perhaps it was against the laws of nature to share one's sorrow with the enemy, but here, it felt... not wrong.

"I can't believe she's gone," she whispered.

Lucien looked at her, his eyes carrying a sorrow in return. He didn't reply.

"How cruel death is," she said, her voice shaking. "I spoke harshly to her before, over something... so *stupid*, and I didn't even get a chance to make it right." She sniffed. "Death took the chance to tell her I was sorry, the chance to tell her goodbye."

He sat quietly, simply listening.

"She looked so fragile in her bed," she told him. "And I tried to remember her as she was before, but even that seems to be taken from me." Everything was being taken from her.

"I can show her to you," he said softly. "As she was. I can help you remember."

"No." She shook her head. "I would know it would be you under her face."

"And if I stay right here?" he asked. "I can simply show her to you."

She stared at him. Could he really do that? "Like a vision, or a memory?"

"Something like that, yes."

Just the thought of seeing Catherine well again knotted a cry in her throat. She couldn't speak; she only nodded through her tears.

The sky brightened, and he looked past her shoulder.

Norah turned and followed his gaze. Her breath caught as she saw her grandmother standing by the stream. She glanced at Lucien in disbelief, then back to Catherine.

Her grandmother's face was bright, healthy. She held out her arms to Norah.

Norah glanced back at Lucien, her eyes wide. "It's not a memory, it's..." She looked back to Catherine. "It's like she's there."

"You can touch her," he said softly.

She gripped his hand tightly as she stared at him in astonishment. He gave her a nod, and Norah stumbled up from the bench and rushed to her. She cried as her grandmother's arms swept around her, and she buried her face into the softness of her fur-shouldered gown.

Warmth. She felt warmth.

This wasn't a normal vision. Yes, she could feel Lucien when he came to her, but not his warmth. Norah didn't understand how it was possible, but she didn't care. She only clung to Catherine.

Finally, her grandmother pulled her back, looking into her eyes. Norah wanted to remember her just like this—smiling, happy. Catherine wiped a tear from Norah's face and pushed her hair back over her shoulder. Ever so softly, she leaned forward and gave Norah a kiss on her cheek. With a final smile and soft squeeze of her hands, she slipped back into the light and was gone.

Norah wept, smiling through her tears. She stared at the light long after Catherine had left.

Finally, she turned back to Lucien, but something was wrong. Blood ran from his right nostril.

"Lucien!" she cried, and ran to him. She dropped down on the bench beside him and pulled his face so that he looked at her. "Lucien, are you all right?"

"I don't have the strength to stay with you much longer," he said weakly. "It's the seemingly simplest things that are sometimes the hardest."

"What do you mean?"

He gave a weak smile and squeezed her hand. Blood spilled now from his left nostril. It grew dark around them.

"Lucien! Whatever you're doing, you have to stop! Go. Rest."

"Will you call me back, Norah?" he asked, wavering.

His image faded, and her hand pushed through him as though he were only a shadow. She gasped. She could no longer feel him. He slumped to the side, barely able to keep himself up, but Norah couldn't help him.

"Yes, but go," she urged him. "You're hurting yourself."

He gave her another weak smile and faded until he was gone.

She sat alone in the darkness of the stairwell, her pulse racing. What had just happened? Showing Catherine to her had obviously done something to him, had hurt him somehow. Why had he done that, at his own expense?

Her racing heart warmed.

It was a kindness. He'd given her a kindness.

She was getting through to him.

Norah closed her eyes and brought back her grandmother's smiling face.

"Queen Norah?"

Norah snapped her head up at the sound of her name. Around the table in the judisaept, the eyes of her council stared back at her. Her mind had wandered again. Two times she had tried to call Lucien back since he'd showed her Catherine, but he hadn't come, and she was worried. But she tried to push that from her mind as she struggled to focus on her council.

She swallowed. "I'm sorry, what was the question?"

"What are your thoughts?" Lord Semaine asked.

Not helpful.

She looked at Mikael at the opposite end of the table. His brow quirked. He knew something was off with her.

"She thinks we should wait," Soren interjected. "As I said."

"Yes." She nodded. "I agree with the lord commander. We should wait." What were they talking about?

"If Rael attacks within the next two weeks, we run the risk of not having our forces in position in time," Lord Branton said.

And she realized—they were talking about when to move the Mercian army to the stronghold in Bahoul.

Norah liked Lord Branton. He'd been a field general under her father; he was a man adept at war. He was thoughtful and honest, and she didn't take his concerns lightly.

"But if we move them too soon," Soren said, "we won't be able to sustain them."

It was in Soren's interest to move sooner, for Phillip's sake. But he said to wait. He would choose what was best for Mercia and Kharav.

"We wait," she said.

The councilmen bowed their heads, and they all rose from the table. Her thoughts turned back to Lucien. She suspected he'd overexerted himself, as Alexander once had, but it had been two days, and he still hadn't come.

She didn't have much blood left, perhaps enough to call him one, maybe two more times.

Norah brushed the wrinkles from her gown as she stepped out of the judisaept. A warm hand caught her arm.

Mikael. She cursed herself. She should have waited for him before stepping out. Her mind was failing her.

"Are you all right?" he asked.

She forced a nod. "Yes. I'm sorry. There's just a lot on my mind."

His brow dipped in concern, and he brushed her cheek. "Are you sure?"

She nodded again. "Yes." She spied Soren waiting in the hall for Mikael to join him. "Soren's waiting. Go. I'm perfectly fine."

"All right," he said. Then he kissed her forehead and went to join Soren.

Norah watched them disappear down the adjoining walk, then she turned and quickly made her way toward her chamber. Not too quickly. Not quickly enough to draw notice, or the suspicion of her guard. They'd tell Bhastian, and Bhastian's attention was like Soren's: hawkeyed for anything amiss. She loved her Crest captain, but that didn't mean she wouldn't avoid him like the fever when she was trying to hide something.

Safely in the privacy of her chamber, she lit a lantern. Then she fumbled with the access door under the hastily thrown-back rug and ducked into the stairwell.

Sparingly, she drew the blood across her palm and closed her hand over it. She prayed as she waited.

A flutter touched her mind, and she let out a relieved breath.

"I was worried for you," she said. She couldn't see him, but she knew he was there.

A shadow in front of her appeared, and the tunnel lit around them until she could finally see him. His brow dipped. "You were worried?"

"Of course. Two times I called you and you didn't come. I thought something might have happened."

The faint trace of a smile crossed his lips. "My last visit pulled a lot of strength. My healer can only repair the flesh, so I had to recover the old-fashioned way—sleep."

She smiled. He was so open with her now, his defenses gone. He trusted her. And she was beginning to trust him. "Thank you," she said softly.

He gave a small nod.

"What happened to you?" she asked.

He offered her his arm, like a proper man of court. "Walk with me."

She slipped her arm underneath, and they started down the tunnel. As they went, the walls fell away to reveal a walk along a cliff overlooking the sea. She loved some of the places he took her.

"How did you show me my grandmother like that?" she asked. "That wasn't a memory, or a vision. I know it wan't real, but how could I feel her warmth?"

"Don't break the magic," he told her.

"But it was difficult for you."

"It's the most difficult. More than anything else. As I said, it's the seemingly smallest of things."

"Well, thank you," she said softly. "For that." She watched him as they walked. "You're a very powerful traveler, aren't you?"

"I suppose."

"Are those staves on your neck?"

His brows drew together. "How do you know about staves?"

"All travelers have them." Well... all the travelers she knew. Which was two, now three. *Close enough.* "Are they?"

Slowly, he nodded.

"Can I see them?" She resisted the urge to pull down the neck of his tunic and look closer at them herself.

He paused a moment, then reached between his shoulders and pulled his tunic forward, over his head and off.

Oh, all right then. She hadn't expected he'd take the whole tunic off, but here they were.

Then he reached down and pulled off his boots. *Wait*, what was happening? He loosened the ties on his breeches and stripped down to his braies.

"Oh... uh... I didn't mean—"

But she stopped when she saw him. There were hundreds of them, all over his body—smaller staves grouped together to form even larger ones. He held his arms open, giving himself for her study. Then he turned and showed her his back.

All bashfulness forgotten, she stepped closer, mesmerized. The markings weren't the same as those the Kharavian warriors bore. Instinctively, she put her hand out to him, but stopped herself.

"You can touch them," he said.

She refrained.

"What do you know of staves?" he asked her.

She shrugged. "Not much. Only that they protect your body from the strain of your power. And that the more power you have, the more staves you need." She paused for a moment. "You have more than I've ever seen."

"Alexander didn't have them?"

She shook her head. "He didn't... use power like you do. It was more like... he was immune to others', or something. He didn't really need staves." Her mind drifted back to the pool of the Wild where Alexander had overexerted himself. Maybe he did, and he just didn't know about them. But whatever Alexander was, whatever power he had, she'd never know...

She looked up to see Lucien watching her. And looking at her the way that he was, he looked so much like Alexander...

"I could give him to you, Norah. I could give you Alexander."

Her heart stopped. *Alexander*. She could see him again. Be near him. She could hug him again, feel his warmth.

But Alexander was gone. Her chest tightened, and emotion rose in her throat. "It wouldn't be real," she whispered.

"You could let it be real."

She smiled sadly. "No, Lucien."

They stood quietly for a time.

"Would you let me see Adrian?" he asked. "Will you let him come to see me? I've looked at him in your mind, but... to see him in his person, in life. I'd like that."

She hesitated, searching for words. "Things are... complicated." She licked her lips. "I haven't even told him you're alive."

His eyes gave a flash of surprise, but he nodded. "I understand," he said softly.

"Can I think about things?"

"Yes, of course."

Her eyes moved back over his body. So many markings. Everything she asked, he so freely answered, so freely gave to her. "Thank you, for sharing this with me," she said. "For sharing everything with me."

He nodded.

"I should go."

"Do you have enough blood to call me back?"

She had enough for one more visit, and she nodded.

"Goodbye, Norah."

"Goodbye."

She opened her eyes to the darkness of the stairwell and wiped the blood from her palm with her handkerchief. She was about to step back up into her dressing chamber, but she paused and leaned against the railing, trying to get a hold of the sudden swell of emotion.

He could give her Alexander.

No. He couldn't.

Alexander was gone.

Gone.

She turned back toward the tunnels and took the right narrow passage to the end before turning left. The lantern provided little light, but she knew where she was going. She followed the tunnel to the end and pushed out the door to a small cobbled street outside the castle. She glanced around as she hurried to the cliffs, making sure she wasn't seen.

Norah lowered herself down the center crag and toward the cave. She hadn't visited for some time, but the nostalgia that settled over her as she stepped inside brought a wave of tears. She didn't try to hold them. She felt her way along the cave until she reached the caverns.

Clouds choked out the sky, but the opening above still provided enough light to fill the cavern. She sucked in a breath, simply letting the emotion come. All of it. The sorrow in losing Catherine, in missing Alexander, the crushing weight of threatening war—everything.

Everything.

And she wept.

She stumbled into the pool and let the water's warmth envelope her. Her skirts billowed up around her. She wanted them off, she wanted it all off, and she clawed at the lacing on her back. Fabric tore as she pushed the gown down and over her hips, but she didn't care. She needed to get out of it. She stripped it away, until she stood only in her shift in the pool.

And she sank deep into the water.

Its warmth took her in its arms, holding her, rocking her. The pool drank her tears, became her tears, and she emptied her sorrow into its depths.

And then there were no more tears. She floated on her back in the water, looking up at the clouded sky through the opening in the top of the cavern, and a ray of sun broke through. She closed her eyes, feeling its warmth on her face. She didn't move as the light kissed her skin.

Alexander had called this a magical place. And it was. She felt him here.

As she opened her eyes, she splashed up abruptly. There was something she needed to do.

She waded back to the edge of the pool and clambered out, not bothering with her dress, and wove back through the tunnel of the cave, up the crag, and toward the castle. As she strode through the courtyard, Bhastian came running to meet her, with Titus close behind.

"Salara," he said breathlessly. "What happened?"

Oh, right. She glanced down at herself. She supposed she did look a mess in her chemise and sopping hair in the snow. She hadn't even felt the cold.

"I just want to get back to my chamber," she said.

Titus handed Bhastian his cloak, and Bhastian swept it around her. "But are you all right? Where were you? What happened to you?"

"Bhastian, I'm fine. In fact, I'm better than I've been in a long while. Can you just see me back to my chamber?"

He nodded with his eyes still full of concern. "Of course."

Norah took a bite of meat from her plate as they sat quietly at the table in the dining hall. Mikael and Soren watched her closely. Neither brought up the fact she'd shown up to the castle soaking wet in her undergarments, although they were quite aware.

She took another bite, giving herself time to chew and swallow before setting down her fork.

Then she took a drink of her wine.

"I'm going to send Alexander to the gods," she said.

Mikael's eyes locked with hers, and Soren set down his knife.

"Are you sure?" Mikael asked her.

She nodded.

"You don't have to if you don't want to."

"But she *should*," Soren said, casting a hard eye at Mikael.

Mikael shot a daggered glance back at him.

"I'm sure," she said, bringing their attention back to her. "And I do want to."

Slowly, Mikael nodded.

"I need to tell Adrian," she said.

"Of course."

"About Alexander *and* about Lucien," she added.

Both Soren and Mikael leaned back in their chairs and cast worrisome glances at each other.

"I don't think that's a good idea," Soren said.

"I can't keep this from him. He deserves to know."

"What if he wants to see him?" Mikael asked.

"Then he'll see him," she said firmly.

The shadow under Mikael's brow grew darker, but he didn't argue.

Chapter Forty

The pyre burned brightly. Heat tinged her face, but she didn't move. She only stood, hypnotized by the flame. Norah thought she'd been ready, but as Caspian had lit the base, it was all she could do not to stop him. She needed this, she reminded herself. They all needed this. Alexander too.

She also thought she'd have tears. The gods knew how much she missed him—how she would give almost anything in the world to have him back again. And her heart still hurt and grieved, but the tears didn't come. Maybe it was a sign she truly was ready. Or maybe it was because she knew she needed to be strong for Adrian, who stood beside her.

When she'd told him she was going to send Alexander to the gods, he hadn't said anything, hadn't objected. Perhaps he accepted it now too. That's what she hoped. This would help them both heal.

They stood silently, watching the pyre being consumed by the flame. She hadn't told him about Lucien yet. She wasn't sure whether to deliver the news all at once or separately. And how would she find the words?

Her eyes drifted to him as he watched the flame. His face was fixed, stoic. Normally so full of expression, so full of light, he wore a mask now. Norah reached out her hand and took his. He didn't look at her but tightened his fingers around hers.

And they stood.

They stood until the fire ebbed and faded. Until everyone finally took their leave to give them space. They stood until they were the last two, and then they stood some more.

She looked up at him, watching his unmoving sorrow.

"He was all I had left," he whispered when only embers remained.

Well, if she didn't take that as an opportunity, she was a fool. But her stomach still dipped in apprehension. "There's something else I have to tell you," she said softly.

Finally, he broke his gaze from what remained of the pyre and looked down at her by his side.

"Adrian, Lucien's alive."

His brow came down slightly, and he leaned back on his heel. Then he shook his head. "No, that's not possible. He died. A long time ago."

"No," she whispered. "He didn't. He lives."

He shook his head again. "Alexander wouldn't have lied to me."

"He didn't know."

His breaths came faster and shallower. "My mother wouldn't have lied to me. Or my father."

As lord justice, his father would have been occupied by the needs of the kingdom. He would have known whatever his wife had wanted him to know. And Adrian remembered his mother fondly—very differently from Lucien.

"He's dead," he said firmly. He nodded as he trembled. "He's dead."

"I've seen him."

He stepped back, pulling his hand from hers. "When? Where?" His breath became ragged.

"When I went to meet Cyrus."

Confusion flooded his face.

"He *is* Cyrus," she said.

He shook his head again, and his nostrils flared. "No, that's not possible."

"He was captured as a child and taken as a slave to Rael. As a man, he led a rebellion and overthrew the king. Then he took the kingdom of Serra from those who had put him into slavery."

"And now he marches against us? Against Mercia?"

She left out Lucien's quest for vengeance against Alexander. That wouldn't help anything. And it didn't really matter now. "He marches against Kharav. Mikael's father is the one who gave him to the Serran slavers."

"The Shadow King is dead," he argued.

"I know, but Lucien still holds Mikael accountable. Kharav still has slaves and is still a primary supporter of slave trade."

He shook his head again but said nothing as he looked back to the pyre. His eyes glistened.

"I told Lucien about you," she said softly. "He didn't know."

His head snapped back to her.

"All this time, he didn't know about you. He wants to meet you."

His breath faltered. "You talk to him?"

She nodded.

"Does Salar know? The lord commander?"

She bit the side of her cheek and shook her head.

His eyes blazed back at her. "You've been talking to him without Salar knowing?"

"I've been trying to broker peace and stop this war. Lucien—he has a heart in him. It's broken and damaged, but I think it's possible to get through to him."

Adrian looked back at the fading embers of the pyre, his breaths uneven. Nothing remained of Alexander now. Adrian wiped his face with his hand.

She reached out her hand to his arm, but he pulled away. "Adrian," she said.

He shook his head and didn't answer. Then he turned and started back toward the castle.

"Adrian," she called after him. But he didn't stop.

A new day came with the sun. Norah drew in a deep breath as she stepped out of her chamber and down the hall to the stairs. The night had been quiet. Mikael had lain silently, leaving space for her to talk if she wanted, but she didn't. She did want the comfort of his touch, though, and buried herself in his warmth and refuge.

He had risen with the morning and kissed her before leaving, lingering just long enough to make sure she didn't want him to stay—to make sure that she didn't need him, that she wasn't going to fall apart in delayed sorrow. The scars still remained, but time had healed the sharpest of her pain, and she really was doing better. She kissed him back and waved him off.

Norah hadn't talked to Adrian again after she'd sent Alexander to the gods. She wanted to give him time to absorb everything, time to think.

She walked alone down the main hall and out through the courtyard, breathing in the winter air. As her eyes settled on Samuel's gallery, she paused. She hadn't seen the seer or his painted visions since she last went with Catherine, when Mikael's fate still remained—even after Alexander was gone.

Now she knew. They all knew. It wasn't Alexander.

And she froze. It had *never* been Alexander in the paintings with Mikael—what about the others? Were there others?

She found herself in front of the door, about to knock, but she stopped. Should she knock? Catherine never knocked. But just like with Soren, that wasn't indicative. She glanced back at Kiran and Titus. "Wait here," she told them.

Slowly, she pushed open the door. "Hello?" she called out.

No one answered.

She stepped inside. Paintings stacked in piles littered the gallery floor, just as they had before. But today she had a new eye, a new understanding. She moved through the piles, looking for images of Alexander.

"Queen Norah!"

She turned at the sound of her name as the old seer hobbled in from a back room. "Forgive me, I didn't know you were coming. Is there something I can help you with?"

"Yes, actually. I was wondering—could you show me all the paintings of Alexander?"

His face grew serious, and he hesitated.

"Is something wrong?" she asked.

The ball of his throat bobbed. "*All* of them?"

She opened her mouth, then stopped. Then she glanced around. Looking back at Samuel, she said, "How many are there?"

His throat bobbed again. Then he gave a jerky nod and waved her to follow him.

Norah stepped into the hall and followed the old seer to the back room. She'd been there with Catherine before, although she hadn't remembered a lot of paintings with Alexander then. In the room, he moved to the far wall and pulled away some of the larger paintings. Behind them sat a door, and he opened it.

Her pulse quickened.

It was a small door, perhaps for a storage closet, but as they ducked inside, she saw it opened into a room as large as the one before.

And all around them—paintings of Alexander.

She moved through them, her mouth open. "You saw all of these?" she asked.

"Yes, Regal High."

"How are there so many?"

He shrugged. "The life force that draws the attention of the Eye—it must be very powerful."

She wasn't exactly sure what that meant, but she got the idea. Lucien was powerful—that wasn't news. Her eyes traveled over the paintings, not looking for anything specific, just... looking.

She stopped on one.

Alexander stood, sword in hand, facing another man armed with two. *No*—not Alexander. *Lucien.* He had only a battle garb around his waist, no tunic. No markings showed on his skin. Was this an old vision? Maybe he hadn't gotten them yet? She stared at him. It was so easy to think this was Alexander. But it wasn't. She could see it now.

Her eyes swept the details around him: sand under his feet, and in the near distance, a curved wall with grated gates evenly spaced.

Where was this?

She moved on through the paintings, noting others that were similar, and more of the background for her to put together that he was in an arena. An arena in Rael? Mikael said Lucien had been a bloodsport fighter before he'd led the rebellion. Is that what she was looking at now?

Another painting made her stop.

It was a sprawling landscape of blood and battle, with Lucien at its center. A flag lay on the ground, nearly trampled into the mud. Red and yellow—so familiar. Had she seen it before?

"What kingdom has these colors?" she asked.

"I don't know, Regal High. I'll have Rector Tusten research it."

Was this an old vision or was it yet to come? Her heart beat faster as she focused her attention back on Lucien. He rode a black horse, dressed in armor of black and blood. He had the markings on his neck in this one.

Norah moved to another painting, then another. She pulled back the canvases and looked at the ones underneath. Then she moved to the wall and flipped through the ones standing on their side.

Lucien—they were all Lucien. In fact, nothing she saw was Alexander. But Lucien was a seer, and seers couldn't be seen by other seers. None of this made sense. "Did Alexander ever see these?"

Samuel shrugged. "Some. Not all. Visions of the lord justice never came to be, so we stopped paying mind to them."

Because they were never Alexander. All this time, they were seeing Lucien, and they didn't even know.

The door to the room swung open, and she jumped.

"Hammel's hell," she said.

Adrian.

His eyes traveled around the room, and he stepped through the small doorway inside. He stopped when he saw the paintings. Norah only stood and waited. He made his way slowly, looking at each one, taking them in as she had done.

"It's him, isn't it?" he asked her. "Lucien?"

She nodded.

His gaze locked with hers. "I want to see him."

Chapter Forty-One

A tent stood in the distance. Norah drew in a deep breath. She'd used the last of the blood to call Lucien, to tell him she was bringing Adrian to meet him. He'd been surprised. She'd surprised herself. But if there was one thing that might temper Lucien's thirst for vengeance, it might be a connection with his brother. Adrian held a deep respect for Mikael and Kharav, a belonging and love. Kharav was a part of him now, a part of who Adrian was, and if Lucien could see that...

She glanced at Adrian as he sat on his horse beside her. It had been easier than she'd thought to take the tunnels and slip out of the castle. After a couple wrong turns, they'd found themselves near a city bakery, but they'd quickly been able to find the stables and leave without drawing attention. Bhastian and Soren would be looking for her now. She tried to push it from her mind and focused on the tent in the distance. There was a singular horse outside.

"Looks like he's quite trusting," Adrian said.

She combed her eyes across the empty terrain. "Well, he's confirmed we've come alone too, no doubt." She glanced up at the sky for birds.

Adrian followed her eyes and looked at the sky. "And you're sure we can trust *him*?"

She had told him of Lucien's ability, and how she'd been able to communicate with him. She wasn't sure he believed her or not.

"I don't know." She wanted to believe they could. "I do think there's good in him, though. There's a lot of pain... but kindness too."

He nodded.

"Are you ready?" she asked.

"I think so," he whispered.

They made their way toward the tent. As they neared, two dogs stepped out from around the sides. They were the same dogs Lucien had shown her before—the dogs used in bloodsport that he'd taken for his own. A low growl emanated from them.

Just then, Lucien ducked outside, and the dogs dropped back and disappeared once more behind the tent. Lucien paused when he saw Norah and Adrian, then he started toward them. There was no sign of his witch.

Adrian pulled up his horse, and Norah brought Sephir to a halt as well. He slid down, and she followed suit.

Lucien wore no armor. He was dressed simply in a dark fitted tunic and breeches. His hair had grown slightly since the last time she'd seen him in person—it was still short, but it was long enough to show a slight curl, like Alexander's.

When he saw them, he smiled. Except for the staves reaching up his neck above the top of his tunic, he looked more like Alexander than he ever had.

Norah glanced up at Adrian, who only stared at him. His eyes welled. No doubt he felt the same shock she had when she'd first seen Alexander's exact likeness.

Lucien's eyes stayed locked on Adrian as he neared. His smile faded as he was caught in his own emotion. While Adrian wasn't a twin, there was no denying the similarity, no denying the blood relation. Lucien stepped slowly in front of him. They could only stare at each other.

Adrian was slightly taller and more heavily built, as he had been compared with Alexander, but somehow, now, he seemed smaller. He reached up his hand, trembling, and touched Lucien's face. A tear escaped down his cheek.

Lucien stood motionless—patient, or perhaps caught in his own wonder.

Adrian drew his hand down to Lucien's shoulder, as if testing that he was real. Then he abruptly pulled Lucien to him in an embrace. Whether he was hugging Lucien or Alexander, she didn't know.

But Lucien hugged him back. They held one another.

Curse the gods. Tears came to her own eyes.

Finally, they broke and stared at each other for another moment.

Then Lucien cuffed Adrian's shoulder. "Come inside," he said, with a slight crack in his own voice, and led them toward the tent.

Norah and Adrian followed and ducked inside. It was bare, save a small seating roll, but it was warm, like a fire was near. It felt nice to be out of the cold.

Finally finding his voice, Adrian said, "Mother told me you'd died."

Lucien's eyes found Norah's, and her stomach twisted. Adrian remembered his mother differently. She prayed he wouldn't take that from him too. What their mother had done to Lucien, and what Lucien had done in return to their mother, was something she wanted to protect Adrian from.

Lucien said simply, "She thought I did. I was taken away."

She let out a silent breath of relief.

Adrian gave an uneasy nod. "Norah told me."

Lucien glanced again at Norah, then back to Adrian. "Then you know my story."

Part of it. She clenched her hands together.

Adrian nodded again. "You were taken as a slave, led a rebellion... and now you're a king."

The corner of Lucien's mouth turned up, and his eyes narrowed slightly. "And now I'm a king."

Adrian stood, still staring at him in disbelief—disbelief that he was still looking at his very-much-alive brother or that Lucien had risen to hold two kingdoms. Maybe both.

"Do you want to see?" Lucien asked. "I can show you."

And there was *that* too.

Adrian's brows dipped, and he drew in an air of hesitation, but he nodded.

Lucien pulled his dagger and slipped his thumb along the edge, drawing blood. "Close your eyes."

Adrian looked at Norah. Her heart raced, but she nodded. He closed his eyes. Lucien took Adrian's hand, pressing his blood to his skin, then closed his own eyes.

Norah's heart beat in her throat. She didn't dare breathe.

Adrian jerked in surprise but didn't open his eyes. His breath came faster. He moved his head, as if looking around, but kept his eyes closed. "Where is this?" he said aloud.

"Rael," Lucien answered. He opened his eyes and looked at Norah, then pulled his hand from Adrian's and held it out to her.

Adrian's eyes remained closed as he stood, completely enthralled. She couldn't deny she was curious herself. Slowly, she stepped forward.

He touched his blood to her skin as he took her hand and closed his eyes again. And she closed hers.

Norah gasped as the sight of a massive city lay before her. But she wasn't walking, she was... flying. Cobbled market streets full of people passed underneath her. The city sprawled as large as Valour in Aleon—larger even—and just as beautiful. It was different than she'd imagined. Tall buildings—sets of stacked sandstone adorned with carved apertures and intricately latticed partitions—lined narrow streets. The golden stone glowed in the light of the sun and held an ethereal beauty.

"You can fly?" Adrian asked Lucien as they all looked down on the Raelean city.

Lucien chuckled. "No. Now *that* would be power."

Norah found herself suddenly standing on the cobbled street, now empty of people, and looking up at the sky. A flock of birds flew overhead.

"I see it through them," he said.

Norah swallowed. His birds.

"You control them?" Adrian asked.

"I can."

Norah couldn't see Adrian in the vision, but she could hear him next to her.

"Can you control all animals?" he asked.

"Most, I can. With blood."

"Did Alexander have power?"

The vision faded to dark, and they all opened their eyes. Norah opened hers to find Lucien looking back at her.

"He had power, yes," he said, "but it was different. What it was—I don't know."

"You"—Adrian's words caught in his throat—"you look just like him." He could only stare. "Just like him."

A sympathetic line etched across Lucien's brow. "Norah said you two were close."

Adrian nodded, and his eyes welled again.

Lucien's gaze fell to the ground as the line of his lips tightened. "I like to think we would have been close."

Adrian shifted as he swallowed. "We could be."

Lucien smiled sadly. "If I had known... about you... things might have been very different. I'm sorry, Adrian."

"Things don't have to be this way," Norah said. "Mercia's not your enemy."

"I don't see Mercia as an enemy."

He'd already told her that, but she wanted him to remember. "And Kharav isn't the same kingdom as it was," she added.

But his face sobered, and he took a step back.

"The king you knew is dead," she told him. "Everything has changed."

"Does the Shadowlands still force people into slavery?" he challenged back. "Still buy them? Still sell them?"

The answer was damning, and she couldn't bring herself to answer.

"Then nothing has changed," he said with steel in his voice.

"Lucien, change takes time," she pleaded. "Mikael is a good king."

"A good king?" he snarled back. "I've been in his mind, seen his memories. You think he's innocent?"

Norah stopped. Mikael had called Lucien with the blood he took from her. *He hadn't come*, he'd told her. "He said you didn't come."

"I didn't show myself to him. That doesn't mean I didn't see."

Adrian stepped forward. "Then you would have seen the good as well, unless you chose not to."

Lucien's gaze darted to his brother, and the corners of his eyes creased. "You defend the Shadow King?"

"I defend *my* king," Adrian said firmly.

Lucien took another step back.

Adrian's face softened, and he took another step forward, extending his hand. "Brother, things aren't as they were, and they can be different still."

Lucien's eyes moved to Adrian's hand and the sword entitlement marking that extended out from under his sleeve. Disgust flashed across his face. "You're one of them?"

"Mercia and Kharav are united," Norah said.

Lucien's face twisted, and any likeness of Alexander vanished. "Then Mercia will share the same fate."

She could feel his anger building. "Lucien, change doesn't always require war. Mikael works for things to be different; he just needs time. Even as king, he has people that he's accountable to."

"I do too!" he thundered.

Norah startled at his burst of anger but held her ground.

The darkness around him ebbed ever so slightly. "Even if I didn't want to take the Shadowlands, I have no choice," he said.

"There is always a choice," she pressed.

"Then you'll just have to accept the fact that I want to." His eyes turned cold and cruel.

She didn't know this man. She needed to bring back the man she'd come to know over the past few weeks, and she reached out and took his arm. "Lucien, please. I beg you. Help me change fate. I can't lose him. I can't."

His expression changed, then changed again—from realization to surprise and a myriad in between. Thoughts swirled within him, she only wished she knew what they were.

"The Shadow King falls?" he asked.

"By your hand," Adrian said.

Lucien's head jerked toward him. "What?"

"All this time, we thought it was Alexander," Adrian explained, "but it's you who will kill Salar."

"Me?"

Adrian snorted. "You're a seer, and you haven't seen this?"

"I can't see myself." He looked back at Norah. "I kill the Shadow King?" Then he froze. "Wait, you *saw* me?" His face twisted in confusion. "I can be seen?"

Silently, she nodded.

Lucien shook his head. "You're not supposed to see me. I'm not supposed to be seen." He pulled away and ran a hand over his face. "I can be seen?" He turned away from them.

Norah glanced at Adrian, but his eyes were on Lucien. She turned back and watched as the Raelean king slowly paced the length of the tent, then turned back.

When he reached them again, he stopped. "So, you can see me in the visions. And I succeed?"

Adrian shot her a troubled eye. Her pulse quickened. "Lucien," she whispered, "I'm begging you to help me create a different future. You're the only one who can." She reached out and took his hand. "Lucien. Please."

His eyes saddened, and his shoulders sank. "I'm sorry, Norah. I can't."

She fought the emotion building in her chest. *No.* No, she couldn't accept that. Her fingers tightened around his. He had to help her. He cared about her, she knew. And there was good inside him. He had to help her.

But he shook his head. "It's fate, Norah. If it's been seen, there's nothing you can do. And that means this is my fate too."

"No. *No.* We can change it."

He shook his head again. "I don't want to change it. It's my fate. I have to do it."

"No," she gripped him tighter. "I won't let you."

"As I've said, there's nothing you can do."

Her lip trembled, and her eyes welled—not tears of sadness, but tears of anger. Tears of hopelessness.

Fate, he'd said.

Well, curse fate, and curse the gods, and curse this king who thought he could take Mikael from her.

Norah ripped her dagger from her waist and let out a cry as she plunged it forward, but he caught it and twisted her wrist outward, and she dropped the blade.

Adrian pulled his sword and lunged to her aid, but Lucien bared his teeth, and suddenly Adrian sank to his knees, screaming as he held his head in his hands.

Lucien was still in his mind. He couldn't control him, but he could make Adrian feel pain. Norah delivered a hard kick to Lucien's inside thigh, almost dropping him.

Adrian fell forward in relief and struggled to stand.

But Lucien still held her. She clawed at his eyes, and when he raised his arm to shield himself, she reached for the dagger at his waist. He stunned her with an elbow to her face, making her stumble back. As she lost her balance, he grabbed her again. He held her by the throat, but not tight enough to choke her.

Blood trickled from her lip, and the taste of metal filled her mouth.

"I don't want to hurt you," he said angrily.

"Then don't do this," she hissed.

"I don't have a choice," he snarled back. "Fate is fate, Norah."

"I won't let you," she said between her teeth.

"How will you stop me? With the Destroyer?" He looked at her curiously, and his expression changed. "No. He'll do nothing. Neither will your king." Then he kissed her.

She froze, too stunned to fight him. It wasn't the kiss of affection, or even dominance. It was... strangely transactional.

Lucien pulled back with her blood on his lips. Then he closed his eyes and whispered into the air. She felt light-headed, but it passed quickly. He released her.

Adrian staggered and picked up his sword.

Lucien spun. "You don't want to do that," he said.

Adrian bared his teeth. "Brother or not, I think I do," he spat.

Lucien stepped back from the both of them. Then he pulled the blade of his dagger from his waist and sliced it across his own hand.

A searing pain cut across Norah's palm, and it pulled a cry from her lips. She gaped down in horror to see Lucien's wound on her own hand.

"We're bound now, you and I," he said. "Tethered through blood. What happens to me also happens to you."

She looked at Adrian, and he stopped his advance. Horror set across his brow. He could do nothing now. She glared back at Lucien. *Bastard.* He sought to protect himself by linking them together.

But if he thought this would give him power over Mikael and Soren, he was wrong. She wouldn't let that happen. "I won't tell them. So, all you've done is made me share your fate."

He gave a cruel smile. "You might not"—he looked at Adrian—"but he will."

Adrian trembled in rage.

"Do your duty, brother," Lucien told Adrian. "Protect your queen."

Lucien looked back at Norah, and the smile dropped from his lips. "I'm sorry, Norah," he said, and stepped out of the tent, leaving them in the quiet of defeat.

CHAPTER FORTY-TWO

Norah sat on the edge of her bed, her eyes swollen from her tears, her cheek swollen from the blow of Lucien's elbow. She hated that she was crying. Why was she crying? The pain had ebbed—it wasn't enough to be emotional. She wasn't sad, just... angry. And overwhelmed. She cursed herself for being so *very* foolish.

She clutched her hands together, rubbing her thumb over her palm where Lucien had sliced his own flesh. It had healed on the return ride, no doubt from the help of his healer. If only she could get the same benefit to her face, but that wasn't a shared injury between them.

Adrian sat beside her. He took her chin gently and tilted her face up to the light, wincing as he eyed her.

"Is it bad?" she asked.

He grimaced. "No."

"Your face says it is."

"My face lies."

"Well, your face is the one I believe." She sighed. "I'm so stupid. I should have never gone."

"It's my fault. I wanted to see him."

She shook her head, but Adrian took her hand.

"I mean it," he said. "You gave me the choice, and I chose this. I'm so sorry."

"You didn't make me do anything I wouldn't have done eventually." She shook her head again as she let out an emotional breath. "I wanted so badly to believe I could stop this war." But she couldn't—just as Mikael had told her, just as Soren had. She couldn't bring herself to face them now, but she didn't have a choice as they barged through the door.

Adrian stood abruptly as they surged toward them.

"What happened?" Mikael demanded. His eyes traveled over her, and his face twisted in anger. And fear.

Her breath shook. "Mikael, I'm sorry."

"What happened?" he asked again, his voice deeper. "Where were you?"

Might as well get it out. "I went to go see Lucien."

Mikael's nostrils flared. "You did *what*?" he thundered.

"I told you I would!"

"What's the matter with you?"

Lots of things, at this point...

The lines of his jaw, bold even under the short cut of his beard, tightened. "Do you forget he tried to kill you?"

Yes, there was *that*.

"He deceived you, came to our bed under the guise of a ghost."

And that.

"He conspires to destroy me. And you go to him—unprotected and trusting."

Not her finest decision. She couldn't argue with any of it. Not anymore.

"It was my doing," Adrian interjected. "I wanted to go."

Mikael and Soren ripped their gazes to Adrian.

"I wanted to see my brother." He stood for their judgment.

"As I told him he could," Norah added, "if he wanted to."

Mikael turned back to Norah, and his shoulders sank. He sighed. Then he took her hand and pulled her up and held her to him. "You're an infuriating woman sometimes," he said as he held her tight. He turned her face up to get a better look at her. "I'll kill him for this," he said softly as he brushed the swelling on her cheek.

She bit her lip. *About that...*

"Are you all right otherwise?" Mikael asked.

Norah could only nod.

"Not exactly," Adrian said.

She cut him a daggered warning. "Adrian."

"I'm sorry, Norah." He looked back to Mikael and Soren. "He tethered himself to her."

Mikael shifted his stance, and his hold on her tightened. "What does that mean?"

"Whatever injury he suffers, she'll suffer the same. You can't kill him. You can't harm him at all." He nodded back at Norah. "Not unless you want the same to happen to her."

"Perhaps it's another trick," Soren said.

"I've seen it with my own eyes," Adrian told him.

Mikael forced her to look at him. "Is this true?"

She swallowed. "He did it to protect himself. From you and Soren."

Mikael bared his teeth with a growling curse and released her. Then he lumbered backward and sank down into the side chair. Defeat hung over him. He leaned forward with his elbows on his knees and rested his forehead against his fists, thinking.

They sat in silence.

"He's clever, isn't he?" he said finally.

"What do you want to do?" Soren asked him.

Mikael drew in a deep breath and let it out again. "The only thing I can do." He raised his head and looked at Soren. "He's not to be harmed. No one's to touch him."

Norah bolted upright in the darkness of the night with a sharp pain across her left hand. A scream ripped from her lips.

Mikael jumped up beside her. "What is it?"

She clenched her fist to her chest as blood ran down the length of her forearm to her elbow. What was happening?

The Crest burst through the chamber door.

She let out another scream as the pain attacked her right hand now.

Mikael grabbed her shoulders. "What is it!"

But she couldn't answer.

Bhastian held a torch that lit the room, making them all gasp. Norah sobbed as blood poured from her hands, staining her nightgown red.

Mikael gaped at her in horror, then he moved into action. "Salara," he said, grabbing her hands and holding them tightly. "Look at me."

But she could only stare at the blood. Her blood. *So much blood.*

"Look at me!" he commanded, and finally she lifted her eyes to his.

"You're going to be all right," he promised as he pressed his palms against hers. "Hold through the pain, you'll be all right." He turned back over his shoulder. "Get the healer!" he raged.

Dizziness caught her, and she wavered.

"Look at me," he called her back, and her tear-filled eyes met his again. "You're going to be all right."

Suddenly, the burn subsided, and she gasped as she looked back at her hands to see the flesh bonding back together, healing as if the wounds had never existed. The pain faded altogether.

Her sobs calmed, and she quieted. Mikael's brows drew together in confusion as he stared at her hands. He wiped back the blood and gaped at her flawless palms.

"What..." He stopped, his mouth slightly open. "What happened? How is this possible?"

Her heart slowed as her terror subsided. She ran her thumb over the flesh. "He has a healer," she finally managed to get out. "A special healer."

"He did this to himself?"

Then she knew. "He's drawing his blood. So he can use it."

The pounding echoed through the darkness. Norah stood beside Mikael as he beat his fist against the door of the row home on a cobbled side street. They were looking for Nemus, the Mercian traveler seer, to see if he knew how to break the tether.

Norah's breath shook as they waited.

"Are you sure this is the one?" Soren asked from behind them.

Mikael beat the door again, harder this time.

She bit her bottom lip. "Ummm... yes." *Maybe*. She'd only been here once with Catherine... in the dark... after being led through a maze of tunnels. But this door looked like the one from before.

"Really?" Adrian asked. "Because it looks like all the others."

She glanced down the street at the rest of the houses. It did look like every other door.

"Perhaps it's a different one?" Caspian asked.

She pursed her lips. There were too many men here with too many opinions. This was the door.

Just as Mikael was about to beat again, it opened.

Norah let out a sigh of relief as a familiar face looked back at them. Esther, Nemus's wife. Norah had first met her when Catherine had brought Norah to see if Nemus could unlock her memory.

But Norah's relief was short-lived. Esther stood horror stricken, her eyes red and swollen, her breaths short and gasping.

Something was wrong, and it wasn't their midnight visit.

"Esther, what's wrong?" she asked.

Esther stepped backward.

"Where's Nemus?" Norah asked.

The woman shook her head, still overcome with emotion.

"Esther, where's Nemus?" she asked again. Her stomach twisted. Something was *very* wrong.

Slowly, the woman pointed back into the house, her hand shaking.

Mikael and Soren pushed past, drawing their swords. Norah followed. Adrian reached and grabbed her hand, ready to pull her back, but she shook him off. She needed to find out what was happening.

They reached the back room where a modest bed was centered on the wall. But Nemus lay unnaturally on the floor in the corner of the chamber, unmoving. A cushion had been flung against the foot of the bedpost—the same kind of cushion he and Norah had sat on when he'd done the blood spell to enter her mind.

They approached slowly.

The old seer was the color of death, his mouth open in a silent scream, his eyes wide with horror but unseeing. Black veins spidered under the icy hue of his skin, stretching from his fingers up his arms.

Soren dropped down and reached out to his neck.

Norah jerked up her hand. "Don't—"

But Soren paid her no mind and brought his fingers to feel the old man's pulse. Nothing happened, but it didn't keep her heart from nearly beating out of her chest.

"He's dead," Soren said.

Norah glanced at Mikael, but his eyes were fixed on the dead seer.

"It was a serpent," came a shaking voice from behind them, and they turned to find Esther.

A serpent? Norah drew her brows together. "A what?"

"In the Aether. He screamed for it to be gone. I couldn't wake him from it." Tears streamed down her face as she gave a small sob. "I couldn't wake him."

Soren stood, looking at Mikael. "We should take Salara to Kharav, to our seer. He can help us understand what's going on here."

"No!" Esther cried. "The serpent in the Aether—it would have come for him too."

Serpent in the Aether? Norah's heart stopped.

Samuel. The Mercian seer. He wasn't a traveler like Nemus, but he still entered the Aether to see visions and create his paintings.

"Samuel! I have to get to Samuel!" she cried, and she fled from the small home and out into the night.

Mikael and Soren were quick to follow, with Caspian, Adrian and the Crest in tow. Her side stitched as she ran, but she didn't stop. Racing back across the bridge, she barreled through the courtyard to Samuel's gallery. She nearly collided with the door when she couldn't open it fast enough but managed to swing it clear and maneuvered through the narrow aisle of paintings, knocking some over as she went.

"Samuel!" she called.

The rooms were lit by dim candles, and they moved farther back. When they reached the far room, she gasped as she saw Samuel lying facedown on the floor.

"Samuel!"

Norah ran to his side and turned him over. Like Nemus, black veins showed from under his skin. His hands caught her eye, and she jumped. They were covered in blood.

No, not blood. Paint. Wet, red paint. As if he'd dipped them in a can of it. She stared at them. Why did he have paint on his hands?

"Salara," Mikael said, and she looked up. A canvas sat on the easel, still glistening with wet paint and a new image.

The image of a red serpent.

Chapter Forty-Three

Norah lay in the bed in her chamber, curled under the quilts with her legs folded to her chest and her hands around her knees. She waited the long, agonizing wait for the pain of when her hands would rip open again and blood would pour from her open flesh. It had been nearly two weeks since Lucien had placed the tether. The cuts came more often now, but irregularly and without warning. Sometimes it was only her hands, and sometimes, perhaps when a lot of blood was needed, her forearm would open—a long cut from the center of the arm to her wrist. Sometimes she would grow faint, the energy draining from her. But as soon as the wound closed, the pain would leave as quickly as it came, as if it had never happened.

Each time it took a piece of her, of her hope. The loss of control eroded her spirit and the resilience of her mind.

Now she could only wait.

A message from Phillip had arrived a week prior. Two of Aleon's three seers had mysteriously died. It was a short message—delivered by bird—and likely followed by a messenger that would soon arrive with a more detailed one, perhaps with assumptions about how they'd died. But she knew how.

Lucien.

The door to her chamber opened quietly, followed by the clinks of a tray being set on the side table. Even though it was midday, Serene didn't say anything to her, didn't disturb her. For the past four days, Norah woke to dress and minimally tend herself. Sometimes she'd eat, then give herself to the solitude of her bed. Mikael came often, checking on her, kissing her palms, and nuzzling her cheek, then he'd leave her to the quiet. He was gentle, sweet, but underneath she could feel his silent rage, his hating anger, and his own suffering that there was nothing he could do to help her.

Bells rang out. She wasn't entirely sure she wasn't dreaming.

"Regal High," Serene said.

Norah didn't move.

"Regal High," her maid said again.

Slowly, Norah turned to Serene, who was standing at the window and looking down into the courtyard.

"You might want to come," Serene said.

Norah pushed herself up and ambled from the bed. She blinked her eyes into focus as she stared down at the group of riders who had arrived. Who were they?

She squinted against the light. Why was it so bright? Didn't the sun know it was a time of darkness?

Norah focused again on the riders. A smaller man slid from his horse, hooded with an oversize cloak. Suddenly, her heart picked up. She recognized the bright red garb of the men surrounding him—guards of the seer's temple in Kharav. The seer had come to Mercia.

The Kharavian seer had left his temple. And had come to Mercia.

Finding a burst of energy, she turned on her heel and sprang for the door. She raced down the hall and the stairs with her guards Titus and Kiran picking up behind her.

When she reached the courtyard, Soren and Mikael were already there. They stood with the seer, their large frames towering over him.

"Bhasim!" she called as she raced toward them.

Mikael and Soren turned in surprise, and when she saw the seer, she stopped in her step.

He stood solemnly, his left hand holding the wrapped stub of where his right hand used to be.

She gaped at him. "Bhasim," she said with a gasp, and drew closer. "Are you all right? What happened?"

"This is best suited as a private conversation," he said weakly. "Do you mind if we go inside?"

"Of course," she said quickly.

A guard of the seer stepped beside the old man, and Bhasim took his arm to steady himself, then followed them into the castle.

They swept into the dining room, and Caspian and Adrian joined them as they took seats around the large table.

Norah waved in water and hot tea.

"I'm going to need something a little stronger," Bhasim said.

Despite the seriousness of the situation, the corners of her mouth turned up ever so slightly. "Wine," she called.

"What happened?" Mikael asked as the doors closed behind the departing servants.

"There resides a great evil in the Aether now," he said finally. "A dark-magic serpent, attacking those who step in to touch the Eye."

"The what?" Soren asked.

"What's the Eye?" Mikael added.

Norah frowned. All those visits to the seer and they'd never bothered to ask how the visions actually worked?

"The Eye," Bhasim said. Then he sighed. He'd been annoyed at Norah for knowing about the Eye when she went to see him at the temple. Now he seemed annoyed he had to explain its existence. "There exists the Aether—the space through which the energy from all beings flows. It's here that the Eye sits. This is how seers see the visions, by stepping into the Aether and touching the Eye."

Norah glanced around the table. Excellent, everyone was caught up. "So what's happening with it?" she prompted Bhasim for more.

"The Aether has been infected with dark magic. A serpent guards the Eye, seeking to poison anyone who steps inside. It attacked me." He motioned to his absent hand. "Bit me, but I was able to escape the Aether, and"—he paused and looked at his guard—"cut the poison off before it traveled to the rest of my body."

Norah glanced at his guard who held a bladed staff in his hand. He'd cut off Bhasim's arm before it could spread. She shuddered at the thought. "If it bites you in the Aether, then it harms you in this world?" she asked.

"As I said, it's dark magic."

She lifted her eyes to Mikael. "It's Lucien. Now that he knows he can be seen, he seeks to prevent others from using the Eye."

"Who is Lucien?" Bhasim asked.

"The King of Rael and Serra," she explained. "He's a traveler. He's tethered himself to me, so that if anything harms him, then it also harms me."

The old seer's eyes widened as he looked at Mikael and then back to Norah. "A traveler that can be seen?"

"It's him in your visions," Mikael said. "Not the Bear." He was quite for a moment, then he said softer, "It was never the Bear." His stare locked with Norah's, and he held it.

"A traveler that can be seen by the Eye," Bhasim echoed again, still surprised, forcing Norah's attention back. "But this serpent is not the work of a seer," he said. "Seers have the gift to touch the Eye, but not the gift of magic. They can't create tethers. Or infect the Aether."

"He has a witch," said Soren.

"He'd need more than a witch," Bhasim said. "He'd need an entire coven."

Mikael watched the seer as the old man took a long drink from his wine chalice. "What do we do to stop him and break the tether?"

Bhasim shook his head. "The serpent is too powerful. A seer can't even step into the Aether, much less try to break a tether."

"There was a seer that survived in Aleon as well," Soren said. "Perhaps he has an answer."

"I am the strongest of the four kingdoms!" Bhasim said angrily. "And you're not listening. No seer can enter the Aether now, not while the serpent is there. And you must understand, the one who tethers you does so through the Aether. Perhaps a mind worker not of the Aether can help you, can go into your mind and break the tether from the other side."

"Get into my mind without using the Aether?" Norah asked. "So not a seer?"

The traveler gave a single nod.

"But who else can get into my mind if not a seer?" she asked.

"The Wild," Mikael said.

Norah jerked her head to meet his gaze. "We can't go back to the Wild." They'd barely made it out the last time they went.

"Their mind magic works outside the realms of the Aether, it's true," Bhasim said.

Mikael looked at Soren. "We go to the Wild."

"You can't go back there," she told him. "Naavi said they won't show you mercy if you return."

"I'll go," Soren said.

She shook her head. "They like you even less."

Soren didn't seem bothered, he only looked at Mikael. "You stay here. We *are* at war, or about to be, and the North at least needs her king. I'll take Salara and return when we've broken the tether."

Mikael nodded.

"Soren," she persisted.

"He's taking you," Mikael said.

And that was final.

Chapter Forty-Four

The Wild was as Norah remembered—quite ordinary, but beautiful. Chilled wind whispered through the trees, billowing back the hood of her cloak. She glanced over at Soren riding beside her, who'd come with little more than a winter tunic even though it was freezing. *Idiot.*

"Let me do the talking," she told him. "I don't know how eager they'll be to help, considering how we left things last." Not that he remembered; Naavi had stripped him of his memories of the Wild, except the memory of him nearly being forced to kill Mikael. "It's important this goes well. They're the only ones who can help. I just hope they know how. They should. They have a magical pool that should be able to show them. And even if it can't, they have a great library of magic that might have other options."

He said nothing as his eyes combed the trees around them. She sighed—he wasn't even listening. She'd made him leave his weapons at the tree line. All of them. And he wasn't happy. A twitch in his eye told her his mind was turning in thought—no doubt with something very unpleasant, something she wouldn't like hearing, but she couldn't help herself.

"What are you thinking about?" she asked.

"How I'd kill myself without a weapon."

She knew it—something unpleasant. She rolled her eyes. "You could be thinking of how beautiful the forest is."

"Why would I be thinking about that?"

She scrunched her face at him. "Why would you be thinking about killing yourself?"

"Because if the Wild is to kill me, they'll make me do it myself. That's likely. So I'm thinking about it."

Well, she *didn't* want to think about it. She puffed a small breath through her lips; she shouldn't have asked.

"I think I'd rip out my throat," he said.

Norah gaped at him, her eyes wide. "Gods, what? *Why?*"

"Were you not listening?"

She sputtered formless words. What was wrong with this man? "I mean, why would you pick that? That's terrible!"

"It's not what I'd pick for myself. It's what I would pick if I were *them*."

Norah shook her head, her mouth still open in silent disgust.

"What?" he asked with a shrug. "I couldn't choke myself. I'd pass out, continue breathing. I don't think I could rip out my heart." He looked down at his forearms. "I could probably open my veins, I'm not sure with what, though. This is why you should've at least let me keep the dagger. I could have killed myself quickly. Now you'll make me suffer."

"Can you stop? Gods, Soren." She shook her head again. "You're not going to rip out your throat, or open your veins, or whatever your twisted mind can come up with."

He gave her an annoyed scowl but said no more.

Something had changed in the forest around them. Even the wind seemed to disappear. Sephir shook her head.

"Soren," she said as her pulse quickened.

They brought their horses to a stop and slid down. She looked at him, and he tapped his fingers to his throat, as if placing a bet.

"Shut up," she whispered.

He chuckled.

But it wasn't funny.

"Norah," sung a voice from the forest, and Naavi stepped out from between the trees.

Norah smiled. "Naavi!" A wave of emotion hit her. She wanted to go to her, hug her, but that seemed... perhaps too forward. She was happy to see the Wild woman again, though.

As if in answer, Naavi swept forward and pulled her into an embrace. "I knew I'd see you again, but I didn't expect so soon." She pulled back with a smile, but that smile fell when she saw Soren. The Wild woman glared at him. "You weren't welcome to return."

He shrugged. "I get that a lot."

"Naavi, I need your help again," Norah said, trying to pull her attention off Soren. "I need to know how to break a tether."

Naavi's focus snapped to Norah, forgetting Soren. Her eyes widened. "You've been tethered?"

That reaction didn't seem promising. Norah swallowed and nodded.

"Your Northman did this?"

"Alexander..." She glanced down at the ground. "Alexander's dead. It was his brother."

Naavi drew in a breath. Her eyes swept their gaze from one side to another, unseeing. "He had a brother?"

Norah nodded. "Yes."

"Is this brother a twin?" her voice came more urgent now, more concerned.

Norah's heart beat faster. "Yes, why?"

"Of course," Naavi said breathlessly to herself. "Why didn't we see it?"

Norah glanced at Soren, and then back to the Wild woman. "What didn't you see?"

"It's so obvious," the Wild woman mumbled to herself.

Soren frowned. "It's the opposite of obvious."

Naavi grabbed Norah's hand and pulled her toward the forest. "Come with me. Quickly!"

Norah let out a surprised gasp, but she let herself be led, hurrying along with Soren close behind. "We have to stop him," Norah said as they went. "Not only has he tethered himself to me, but he's killing seers."

"What do you mean he's killing seers?"

"As in, they're dying," Soren said irritably.

Norah glared back at him.

"Yes, but how?" Naavi pressed, not breaking her stride.

Norah almost had to run to keep up with her. "He's put some kind of dark magic into the Aether, a serpent, and it attacks anyone who enters to touch the Eye." She couldn't deny the small bit of pride in properly recounting Bhasim's explanation.

"How did he put dark magic into the Aether?"

Soren snorted. "Aren't *you* supposed to know things?"

"This is how you get forced to rip out your throat," Norah whispered back at him.

"Why?" he cut back. "Isn't there supposed to be a magical library somewhere with all these answers?"

Naavi stopped abruptly, and Norah almost ran into her. "How do you know about our library?" she hissed at Soren.

"I might... have told him that," Norah said quickly. The one time she wished he hadn't been listening.

Soren looked at her. "You *did* tell me that. And that they have a magic pool."

She pursed her lips at him. "Can you just... hush?"

Naavi sighed and pulled Norah forward again. "Don't repeat that if you know what's good for you. I have to take you to Sana."

"At the pool?" Norah asked.

"Yes."

"Wait"—she pulled the Wild woman to pause—"can we use the door?"

Naavi gave an exasperated sigh. "Fine."

Norah glanced back at Soren. "You're welcome."

"For what?"

She rolled her eyes; he remembered nothing of this place. "Never mind."

Norah was no stranger to the Wild, but it took her breath away nonetheless. The forest cathedral was still one of the most beautiful sights she'd ever seen. The high walls of trees and woven medallions of vine and stained glass stood like dreams from the gods. Hanging stars floated above, kissing the rooms with their light.

"I've been here?" Soren asked.

She smiled at him. "You were a little grumpier back then. Didn't appreciate the full beauty of things. That, and you were also coming off almost killing Mikael, so..."

"That I remember."

And that reminded Norah—"Is Sana still... mad? About how we parted last?"

"Yes," Naavi answered shortly.

And... "Do you think she'll help me?"

"I don't know."

Well... that didn't inspire confidence.

As if on cue, Sana stepped into the hall. "You return," she said to Norah coldly. Then her eyes moved to Soren. "Very foolish."

"He's a twin," Naavi said, as if there was no underlying threat to Sana's comment. "The Northman has a twin."

Sana's scowl turned to surprise, and her lips parted slightly. "Of course."

Norah glanced at Soren and then back to the Wild women. "Can someone explain what that means?"

Naavi drew an uneasy breath. "Twin travelers are the most powerful of seers. One carries the sight, and one carries the shield. Their bodies individually are not burdened with both sight and shield, so they're able to grow the gift more, handle more of its power. Think of it as... double the power"—she shook her head—"more than double, it's exponential."

Norah nodded slowly, absorbing the information. "So that's why you couldn't see Alexander? Because he carried the shield?"

Naavi nodded. "And it explains why his shield was so strong. It was meant to cover them both."

"But Lucien was still seen in visions."

"If they were far apart... A shield is not infinite. At least not while both twins are alive."

"What does that mean?" Soren interjected.

Naavi sighed. "Together, they remain balanced, but when one twin dies, there is nothing to balance the power, and the remaining force will only grow."

"Grow to what?" Norah asked.

"There is only one record in our library of twin travelers. They lived a thousand years ago. The twin with the sight perished in a fire. The twin with the shield survived. His power grew, encompassing the earth, shielding all the world and blinding all seers for eleven years until his death."

That's what would have happened if Lucien had died and Alexander had lived. "But it's Lucien who lives, and he has the sight. What does that mean? What will happen?"

Naavi shook her head. "I don't know."

Soren snorted, but Norah shot him a daggered gaze, and he kept silent.

"Perhaps he might eventually become powerful enough to break the confines of the blood spell," Sana said, "travel into the minds of others without their consent. Take control of them, even."

Norah's mind drifted to the birds. "He already does this with animals. But he still needs the blood."

"Probably not for much longer. He needs to be stopped."

"Can't have him being like you?" Soren snarked.

"Our power is bound by the forest," Sana cut back. "Even *we* have limits. But he would not. He would have more power than any one man should hold. And if he has ill intent, there will be no one able to stand against him. You have to stop him before he reaches that point."

"How?"

"You have to kill him."

Norah looked at Soren in desperation. "Mikael will never let that happen while we're still tethered." She turned back to Sana. "Do you know how to break it?"

"I do."

She sighed in relief. *Thank the gods.* "How?"

"The same way Naavi broke the seers' ability to see you when your father brought you here."

Norah's heart caught in her throat. "I would lose my memories again?"

Naavi nodded. "Yes."

"You are tethered through the Aether," Sana said. "We would break your connection to the Aether again, and thus break the tether."

She needed to sit down, but there was no chair. Her lungs called for air, but there wasn't enough of it. She couldn't get a breath. To break the tether, she'd have to lose herself again. She'd lose everything. She shook her head. *No*, there had to be another way.

"There is no other way," Sana said.

Norah looked back to Soren. How could there be no other way?

He stepped closer to her. His voice came softly. "You probably wouldn't come to like me again, but I'd understand."

"What?" she breathed.

"But with Salar, you'd come to love him again. I know you would."

She shook her head. "No. Soren. No. I'm not losing my memories again. It's all I have left of those I've lost: my grandmother, Alexander, Vitalia. And my memories with Mikael, I won't have them taken from me."

He stepped closer. "You don't have a choice."

"Yes, I do."

"If Lucien dies, you'll die. And you know Salar won't let that happen. We need to kill him. This is the only way to stop him."

Norah shook her head again. No. She wouldn't. She couldn't. "I'll find another way."

"The only other way is if the traveler breaks the tether himself," Sana said.

"Then that's what I'll have to get Lucien to do."

"Have you lost your mind?" Soren asked her.

"He's not a bad person! He's just... wrong. And he's angry. But if I see him again, if I talk to him... I do think he cares about me."

"Salara, did you just hear them?" Soren asked. "We have to kill him. He's not going to help us do that, no matter how much you think he cares." He looked to Naavi and Sana. "Do it. Break the tether."

"No," Norah said, stepping back.

His eyes grew dark and serious, burning into the sisters. "A threat you described is a universal threat. You think he'll stop with the world of men? Do it!"

"No!" Norah cried. "Soren! I can't lose everything. I can't lose Alexander. Or Mikael. I can't lose you!"

"You won't lose us."

She turned to Naavi. "No," she begged.

"Do it," Soren demanded.

Naavi stared at Norah for a moment, and her eyes welled. "I can't," she said, shaking her head. "I can't if it's not what she wants. I can't do it again."

Soren let out a snarl. "As long as he's tethered to her, no one will kill him. And you know what will come. You have to stop him. Break it!"

Sana stepped forward. "Hold her."

Norah shook her head again. Fear coursed through her as Soren moved toward her. "Soren, no." She took a step backward, but her back hit the wall. "No," she begged. "Soren, please! No!"

He brought his hands to cup the sides of her face. "I'm sorry, Salara."

"Soren!" she sobbed.

The gentleness of his hands hardened, and he gripped her still. "Do it!" he said between his teeth.

"No!" Norah screamed as she clawed at him, but he held her. Panic flooded her, and she lashed out. This couldn't be happening. They couldn't do this to her. Not again.

His eyes welled. Still, he held her.

Sana put her hands atop Norah's head.

But Norah fought. With everything she had, she fought. Pain seared through her mind, melting her from the inside. It was unbearable. But still she fought.

Burning, ripping, tearing.

She fought.

It was agony. Claws of destruction mauled her mind, breaking her. Erasing her.

And then thunder boomed, and suddenly the pain stopped.

A cloak of darkness swept around her.

Soren's hands fell away. Cool soothed the burn. What was happening? Was it over? But she could still remember...

When she opened her eyes, she was still standing, but leaning against the wall, doubled over. Soren stood against the far wall, steadying himself and holding his head, and Sana lay a few paces away, picking herself up from the floor.

Naavi rushed to Sana's side. "What happened?"

"It's him," Sana panted. "He's fighting back."

Him? Lucien?

"How's that possible?" Naavi asked.

Sana stood and straightened, breathless. "I don't know. But I felt him breaking through into my own mind. I can't go back. He's too strong."

"How was he able to hit me?" Soren asked, still recovering. They stared at him.

"You felt him?" Sana asked.

"Like a bolt of lightning."

"The limits of the blood are weakening. He's growing more powerful."

"How did he know what we were doing?" Soren asked.

"If his pain hurts her, then her pain hurts him as well." Sana shook her head. "But I can't go back in. There's nothing else we can do."

Norah only stood, half listening. Never had she felt so betrayed, so violated.

Soren's eyes met hers. "Salara," he said softly. He stepped forward and reached for her. "Don't touch me," she seethed.

She stumbled down the hall the way she had come. She needed to get out of this cursed Wild, and away from those who had almost stolen that which she held most dear.

They rode in silence, Norah on Sephir and Soren on his destrier beside her. Her anger had left her. All she felt now was hurt. She'd trusted Soren. She'd trusted him not to hurt her, and this was the worst kind of hurt—the hurt of betrayal. Of course, he thought he was protecting her, and protecting Mikael, and he didn't know what it was like to lose himself. Regardless, it would stay with her. For a long time.

Pain ripped across her left hand, and she sucked in the cold air through her teeth as she doubled over, clutching her palms together tightly. The other cut would soon follow... and it did.

Soren reined his horse closer. "Salara!"

"I'm fine," she panted. "It'll pass."

She'd come to appreciate that she didn't know when she'd be cut. At first, she thought it was a curse, and it stole her spirit, but then she'd come to believe it would have been worse to know when it was coming and wait each time for it. And to know the healing would come shortly, somehow that soothed her.

Norah stopped and slid off Sephir. She waited for the healing.

"Are you all right?" he asked.

She only nodded with her eyes closed. The sharp pain dulled to an ache, then disappeared altogether, and her palms became smooth again, as if nothing had ever happened. Finally. She straightened.

He offered her the waterskin for a drink, but she didn't take it. She didn't look at him. She couldn't.

He sighed. "What would you do if someone you loved was choosing to hurt themselves?"

She didn't respond to him.

"Look what this does to you! And Lucien has to die. You're choosing to die with him."

"It's my choice!" she cried. "You would have taken everything from me!"

"Your life is everything!"

"I'll die before I lose myself again."

"Then you'll let Salar die too. He won't raise a sword to Lucien if he thinks it will harm you. He won't even fight. And Lucien will kill him, as the seer has shown us."

She knew the vision. She'd seen it a thousand times over in her mind, lived it a thousand times, mourned it a thousand times. Lucien would kill Mikael. And Mikael would let him. Because of her.

"He doesn't even lift his sword," Soren said, his voice cracking.

"But you will," she told him.

His head jerked up, and she met his tormented eyes. He shook his head.

"You'll kill him, Soren. The opportunity will come, and you'll take it." It was so quiet she could almost hear their hearts beating.

"No," he said softly. "I won't. I can't."

"You will. It's the last thing I'll ask of you."

He shook his head.

"I need you to do it."

His eyes welled.

"Swear to me," she said.

His breaths came uneven underneath his wrap.

"Swear to me, Soren. You'll kill him."

For a moment, she thought he might not.

"I swear," he said finally.

Relief washed over her. It was done. Her heart filled with sadness—not for her death, but for what she was asking her friend to do.

"It's okay if it hurts," she told him. She was getting used to pain.

"You won't feel a thing," he whispered.

And she believed him. Soren could be trusted with how to end a life.

CHAPTER FORTY-FIVE

The sound of metal and horses hung in the air as the Mercian army readied to depart. They would march to Bahoul to join part of the Kharavian army, in line with their battle plans. Then the forces from Bahoul, with Mikael and Soren, would be ready to help Phillip drive Rael and Japheth south into the Canyonlands where Katya and the remaining Kharavian army would be waiting.

Norah felt uneasy; timing was critical. They couldn't sustain a large army in Bahoul for long; moving too early could work against them. But not being positioned in time would leave them without a full force if they fell under attack. The question was—when to go?

Word had come from Osan, thanks to Phillip's new alliance, that no more ships had sailed between Rael and Japheth—they weren't moving more forces between the two kingdoms. But the Raelean army had sat just inside the Japheth border for weeks. So if they weren't moving more of their army, what were they waiting for? That had been the question for some time. Soren suspected something wasn't right and didn't want to wait any longer. He wanted to move now, and Mikael agreed.

Norah would accompany them as far as Sandor, a Mercian stronghold just north of the Tribelands. Mikael had wanted Norah to stay in Mercia, but there was no way she'd stay in the safety of the North while everyone she loved marched to war. He reluctantly agreed she could join them as far as Sandor and then return to Mercia while he continued on to Bahoul.

The ride to Sandor was shorter than she'd expected. It took five days moving with the army, as planned, but time was in short supply, and it felt like barely a day. They didn't talk about what had happened in the Wild. Norah had told Mikael they couldn't break the tether, and they left it at that. She didn't tell him about almost losing her memories again. It didn't matter—it hadn't worked anyway. And she wouldn't let the end to come haunt him like it haunted her.

She wished Adrian was still with her. She could have talked to him. Soren had sent him back to Phillip before they left for the Wild. He'd have arrived by now. She hoped he was doing well. Of course he was doing well. He was tasked with helping Aleon build up their defenses and prepare Phillip's army to drive Japheth and Rael to the Canyonlands. And he had been taught by the best.

They reached Sandor, and the gates of the stronghold opened. It was the first time she'd been to this fortress, or rather, the first time that she remembered. It was smaller than the castle of Mercia, and smaller than the stronghold in Bahoul, but it was surprisingly beautiful. There were trees all around and throughout, and a garden in the center. It was interesting to have something so serene in a place meant as a stronghold of war.

She found herself in the garden as Mikael and Soren worked through final plans with Caspian and sent messages to Phillip and Katya. She'd imagined things differently when she had thought about accompanying Mikael. She didn't know what—just not sitting to herself. She wouldn't complain; she'd take every moment she could get, just knowing Mikael was near.

Sorrow sat heavy in her heart. Each day took them closer to war, closer to Mikael's fate. The sorrow grew to desperation as she watched everyone working toward the future that had been foretold—Mikael's future. Everyone was so accepting. Had she become accepting too?

Soren had sworn he'd kill Lucien, no matter the cost. While she trusted him completely, trusted him to do everything in his power to save Mikael, not everything was within his power. She couldn't rely on his promise.

Snow covered the ground. Norah sat on the bench in the middle of the evergreen gardens with quiet all around her. It was a deceiving peace. A flutter caught her eye, and she paused as a butterfly danced through the air. In the middle of winter—*how beautifully strange.*

It floated closer, dipping and rising around her, and she held out her hand. With a flit of its wings, it landed on her palm. She couldn't help an amazed laugh. For a butterfly to land on her hand—

She stopped.

She'd been here before.

Her lip trembled as she looked at the butterfly, and the world stood still. Even the light froze.

She clenched her hand and crushed it.

Her mouth opened in a silent scream, but she didn't make a noise. Not a noise. She could only sit, with the crushed butterfly in her hand.

She had crushed it. Not let it fly off again. *Crushed it.*

Hopelessness fell away, and air filled her lungs, and for the first time in months... she could breathe.

Norah sprang from the bench and ran back through the gardens, still clutching the butterfly. She tore into the war office, where Mikael stood with Caspian over a series of maps. "Fate can be changed!" she cried. She held the crushed butterfly in her hand, breathless. "Look!"

Mikael stared at her. Caspian gave a polite nod and left to give them privacy. She didn't wait for Mikael to react.

"Look," she said again as she held the butterfly closer. "Bhasim showed me a vision, when I went to the temple, where I held a butterfly in my hand in the garden, and then it flew away. But I changed it."

He brought his hand under hers, pulling it up to look closer. But he said nothing.

"Don't you see what this means?" she said. "Fate can be changed!"

He reached and cupped her cheek, giving a sad smile. "You never give up."

She drew her brows together. "What does that mean?"

"I've tried to change my fate long enough to know what the seer says is true."

He didn't believe her, and her pulse raced faster. He had to. "It's not! Look!"

"The fate of a butterfly isn't the fate of a king."

"It doesn't matter. It *can* be changed. No matter how small it is, this proves that change can happen."

He nodded, but didn't seem to accept what she was saying.

"Mikael, please."

"What does this matter? Being able to change fate or not, what would you have me do differently now? Everything's been set in motion."

She didn't have an answer for him.

"It's too late, Salara."

"How is it too late? I literally changed this vision in the moment! We have to keep trying."

He frowned and swayed away from her, but she caught his arm.

"Mikael. Mikael, listen to me. Don't go to battle." Desperation filled her voice because it filled her heart. "Let these days pass. We can change it."

"You want me to... just not show up for my fate?"

"Yes! Yes, I do." That's exactly what she wanted.

"If it were only that simple. Would men not have done that already?" He paused and pulled her closer with a deep sigh. "The curse of fate isn't truly one's actual fate. The curse is being consumed with changing it. And I've wasted enough with this obsession." He smiled sadly.

She shook her head. He was accepting his fate. He couldn't. She wouldn't let him. "No. Mikael—"

"You're a strong queen, Salara. I know you'll stay strong, no matter what happens." He locked his eyes with hers. "I don't want to speak about fate again. Ever again. I want to take each day as it comes." He brought his lips to hers in a tender kiss. As he pulled back, he smiled. "I love you, Salara." Then he turned and followed after Caspian.

She stood alone, astonished. It was like he didn't believe her. He didn't even want to try. No—he wasn't allowed to do that. She wouldn't let him. She raced through halls, almost tripping, bumping into random people and not caring at all.

She finally found Soren in the armory. "Soren!" The poor soldier she interrupted gave a startled bow and backed away before leaving. "Soren! Fate can be changed!"

He turned toward her with a crease in his brow. "What?"

She held up the butterfly to him. By now, it was barely recognizable in her clammy hand.

His eyes moved to the crushed remains in her palm, and his brow creased more. "You killed a butterfly."

"No." She shook her head, stepping closer and clasping his arm as she held the dead creature nearer to his face. "I mean, yes, I did, but I saw it fly away."

He glanced at the butterfly again, and his eyes narrowed. "It doesn't look like it flew away."

She wanted to scream. Her conversation with Mikael had shaken her. She knew she wasn't making sense, but she couldn't get her words out. "No! In the temple of the seer, Bhasim showed me a vision. It was of me in the garden and a butterfly landing on my hand. And I let it fly away. But look!" She shoved the butterfly closer to his face. "I *changed* the vision."

He lifted his chin to avoid her smacking him with the dead insect. "Changing the fate of a butterfly doesn't mean you can change the fate of a king."

Did Soren and Mikael both inherit the same blindness? "Why not? Bhasim said visions can't be changed, but they can! If something small can be changed, why not something more significant?"

"It's not that simple."

"But what if it is?"

"If it were that easy, we would have changed it by now." Irritation grew in his voice. "But look at everything that's happened—everything has unfolded as it was seen. No matter what we've done to stop it."

"Because we didn't recognize the moments, or what they meant! My father couldn't stop my capture because he didn't know it was *Mikael* who would take me, not the senior Shadow King. Mikael didn't know that the vision of me on his throne was as his wife and not his enemy. We thought Lucien was Alexander. Don't you see? We couldn't stop them because of our ignorance, not because it was impossible. But this vision of Mikael's death, it's here now. I know it. And we have the chance to stop it."

"And how do you know that everything you do won't take us one step closer to that vision?"

"We have to remove Mikael. We have to get him away and let this moment pass. We can save him." It sounded weak, she knew, but it was the only thing left she could think of.

He shook his head. "I can't do that."

"Soren, why won't you even try?"

"Do you think I haven't given everything to trying!" His voice shook in anger. "Do you not think I've spent my life trying to find ways to save him? Fate is always one step ahead. And it toys with us, teases us, gives us hope when there is none."

"I don't believe there's no hope!" she cried. "I don't accept that." She wiped the smear of butterfly on her dress. "Soren," she begged, "please."

"Have you shown him this? Have you told him what you're telling me now?"

"Yes! But he refuses the idea."

"Then what would you have me do?"

"You can force him away. You control the army; you can force him to return to Mercia where he'll be safe."

"You would have me usurp his power?"

"Just until this is over."

He reached out and clasped both sides of her face and held her. "Do you hear what you're saying? You would have me take his choice?" He shook his head. "I've done that once, Salara, and you above all others should know what it takes from you. I won't do it again. It's his decision to stay. I stand by his side. And you can't change fate. It's shown us time and time again." He released her, and with a final look of sadness, he left her to the room alone.

The room they'd taken for their chamber was quiet. Mikael sat on the edge of the bed in the dim candlelight, his hair loose around his shoulders. He was beautiful. She tried to capture this image of him, tried to burn it into her mind to remember forever. In the morning, he'd be gone. So she just stood, looking at him.

He returned her gaze. "Can I see you, Salara?" he asked softly.

He wanted to see her, to remember her, the way she wanted to remember him. Slowly, she reached behind her and loosened the ties of her gown. She pulled the shoulders down, slipping one arm from its sleeve and then the other before pushing it over her hips and letting it fall to the floor. Her corset, her shift, the silks—she removed them one at a time and discarded them to the side until she stood naked in front of him. Her skin prickled in the cool air, but she stood as he looked at her. She let him take his time.

He held his hand out for her, and she took it. Slowly, he pulled her to him. She stood between his knees as his eyes traveled her face and then ran back and forth between hers. He didn't speak. He only reached up and flattened his hand against her chest. Her heart beat under his palm.

"Of all the things this life has given me, you're the most precious."

She took his face in her hands. "Come away with me," she begged.

"Where?"

"Anywhere. We'll go where no one knows us. We'll have nothing, but we'll have each other. I'll learn... how to cook, and you'll... do everything else."

He smiled. "I would even do the cooking."

She laughed, but her laugh turned to tears, and she couldn't keep them back. Because she knew she couldn't keep him back.

"No, no, no," he whispered. "Don't be sad."

"You can't leave me."

He shook his head. "I'll never leave you. If I should go anywhere, I only go to our eternal bed. And when you're tired of this world and ready for sleep, I'll be waiting."

"You won't wait long."
He clutched her tighter. "Don't say that. Don't ever say that."
"I don't want to be in this world without you," she whispered.
He smiled, but his eyes glistened. "Kiss me, wife."
And she did.

CHAPTER FORTY-SIX

It was almost morning. Norah stretched along Mikael's warmth. They'd spent the hours of darkness making love and drifting in and out of dreams—dreams she never wanted to leave. She let her hands travel over his skin, etching each line of his body, each curve of his muscle, into her memory. The way he moved. The way he wrapped himself around her. His taste, his smell. His touch. Everything about him.

A horn sounded outside. Footsteps in the hall and a bang at the door jarred them awake. Soren swung it open without giving a hair's width of time.

"A messenger," he said brusquely, and left as quickly as he had come. The door slammed closed behind him.

Mikael was up in an instant, pulling on his breeches, and Norah rose quickly.

"Do you think it's from Aleon?" Her heart raced. She wasn't ready. She wasn't ready to get up, or for this day. She wasn't ready for him to leave.

"Likely," he said as he pulled on his boots. "Meet us in the courtyard."

"Wait, I'm coming too." She pulled on a thick robe over her nightdress and her cloak over the top and stepped into her bed slippers—hardly proper attire, but it was still dark out, and she didn't care. She followed Mikael, her hand in his, down to the courtyard.

Soren and Caspian were already there, waiting impatiently as the iron gate of the stronghold was raised. A soldier on a horse swept in, and his mount skidded on the cobblestone as he came to a halt and slid down. Despite the mud coating his armor, hints of blue peeked from underneath—a soldier of Aleon. He bowed his head to Soren and held out a letter. "Japheth and Rael are marching on Eilor."

Eilor—the southernmost kingdom of Aleon and Catherine's home kingdom—where Phillip was with his army.

"What?" Norah gasped. They had been so sure Rael would move against Kharav first.

Bhastian stepped closer with a torchlight as Soren broke the seal and scanned the parchment.

"Japheth *and* Rael?" Mikael asked.

Soren nodded and handed him the letter. "It's what he writes."

Phillip.

"How long do they have?" Mikael asked.

The lord commander looked back to the messenger. "How long did it take you to get here?"

"Three days."

"Then Phillip has another day before they reach him, maybe two given the size of Rael's army and how slowly they'll be moving." He shook his head, and Norah watched as his concern built. "Even if I diverted the Northern army and took them now, I wouldn't get there in time." He cursed.

"Do it," Mikael told him. "Take them. He'll hold until you get there."

Soren pulled down his wrap, his face the palest Norah had ever seen. "Phillip can't stand against both Japheth *and* Rael."

"He has a hundred thousand men," Mikael assured him. "He can hold until you get there."

"You ride ahead," Caspian told Soren. "I'll follow as quickly as I can with the army, but you go now."

Soren looked at Mikael. "You need the Northmen in Bahoul."

Mikael shook his head. "They're needed in Aleon more now. Take the Northern army, join with Aleon, push Rael and Japheth down toward the Canyonlands. I'll be ready with the forces in Bahoul to join you." He clasped Soren's shoulder. "Now go get your Aleon king."

Soren reached out and gripped him, pulling their foreheads together. "You'll keep yourself well until we meet again."

"Until we meet again," Mikael said. "Goodbye, brother."

They broke, and Soren looked at Norah. He gave her the faintest of nods, then turned to leave.

"What was that?" she demanded.

Soren stopped. "It was... goodbye."

"That's not a proper goodbye." She crossed the space between them and threw her arms around him, gripping him fiercely. "Keep yourself well," she whispered.

For once, he returned her hug. "I'll come back."

"You'd better."

He nodded. Then he moved to get his horse, and Caspian followed after.

Mikael's face was somber as he looked at her, and their stares locked. The time had come. He had to leave. Wordlessly, he took her hand, and they walked back to their chamber.

Neither of them spoke as she helped him dress. She knew his departure was urgent, but she took her time, pulling each tie tight on his clothing, each strap straight on his armor. His eyes watched her as she worked. On the last vambrace, the last fastening, she stopped. She couldn't close it. Once it was fastened, he'd be ready.

But he couldn't be ready, because she wasn't ready. So, she stood, her fingers frozen.

Slowly, he put his hand over hers and pressed it closed. The click of the metal rang in her ears—a sound that would forever stay in her mind. He pulled her close and drew his eyes over her face before bringing his lips to hers. His kiss trailed from her lips to her cheeks, over each eye, to her forehead, and back to her lips again. She tried to capture each touch in her mind—to remember, to never forget.

"Stay strong, Salara," he said.

Then he turned and left for Bahoul.

Soren urged his mount relentlessly toward Aleon's southern kingdom of Eilor. He'd only taken Cohen with him, because the boy wouldn't slow him down, and Soren could use him. Caspian would follow behind with the Northern army.

They traveled quickly. Phillip could hold until he got there, he told himself. And if he couldn't, he'd fall back to the mountains of Songs—that was the plan. He cursed himself. The plan had been that Rael would attack Kharav. Now he had to shift, change the strategy. Aleon could fall because of his mistake. He couldn't let that happen.

They journeyed for what seemed like an eternity, stopping only to rest their horses. They could swap mounts in the Tribelands, but then he'd be left without a proper warhorse when he reached Eilor. He needed his destrier, Khalel al'Dakar, for the battle he would bring to this pretend Bear and the coward king of Japheth.

Cohen didn't speak, not even using his silent language. Soren knew he sensed his worry and chose to remain quiet. And Soren was grateful.

The lowlands turned into highlands, then to hills, and he pushed his destrier on. His body tired but his mind raged, and he pushed himself on. He had to get to Phillip.

Suddenly, Cohen reined his horse to a sliding stop. Soren didn't have time to snap his head to see before he was falling.

The ground quaked underneath him as he hit the earth. Pain shot up his back and into his neck, and the world spun around him. He groaned as he rolled onto his side, then struggled to his knees. A few paces back, his mount flailed in a hidden trench.

"Kal!" He staggered up and toward the animal as Cohen jumped down from his own horse. As Soren neared, the destrier managed to get back on its feet. He let out a pant of relief. Curse the North gods if he'd lost this horse.

A stir behind him made him spin around and reach for the short sword at his back.

He was met with a grinning face. Adrian chuckled from atop his horse. "Looks like you found our defenses."

Soren hissed out a breath but couldn't help a small smile. "Little Bear."

Adrian dropped down from his mount and reached for him. They clasped arms, cuffing each other on the shoulders.

"Where's the king?" Soren asked.

"Not far. He'll be glad to see you."

Soren exhaled the fear that had been consuming him. Phillip was all right. He could breathe again. He tightened his grip and jerked Adrian closer. "You almost hurt my horse."

Adrian still wore his grin. "Yeah, well, I didn't expect you to come tearing across the hills and get caught in our own traps. It was a good set, though, right?" He looked past Soren to Cohen. "Didn't drop *you*, though."

Soren glanced over his shoulder, and the boy smiled. Of course Cohen had seen it. He had an eye. And while Soren had admittedly been distracted, he couldn't deny the handiwork. "It was a good set." At least Aleon had some defenses now. *Wait*—"What's going on? Where is everyone?" He'd expected to arrive straight into a full-fledged battle.

"That's a good question," Adrian answered. "Japheth and Rael stopped just short of our borders. They wait."

That didn't make any sense. "For what?"

Adrian shook his head. "We don't know. Come on, I'll take you to King Phillip."

Soren and Cohen followed Adrian through the hills and across the river to the army camp of Aleon. Before they even reached Phillip, Soren could already see what Adrian had been talking about. Across the flatlands to the south, from horizon to horizon, spanned the largest army he'd ever seen. But they waited, just short of the border. The armies were split in two: part of the army, presumably Japheth, lay to the east, and Rael just to the west.

"Why are they split?" Soren asked.

Adrian shrugged. "We have suspicions. It's best to show you."

Interesting...

"This way." Adrian led him to a large center tent and ducked between the flaps.

Soren followed, and when he stepped inside, he stopped.

Phillip sat, pouring over letters. When he looked up, he stood in surprise, and a smile came to his face. That beautiful smile that made Soren's chest hurt—the smile he'd feared he wouldn't see again.

Phillip wore only a few pieces of armor. The lion surrounded by four stars, representing the four kingdoms of the empire, shone proudly on his breastplate. He stepped to Soren and stared at him for a moment. Then he reached up and clutched him by the shoulders and pulled him into a tight embrace.

Soren stiffened. Adrian and Cohen's presence ate into his mind. Soren wasn't one for affection, and certainly not so publicly, and not so openly with the Aleon king.

"I didn't think you'd come," Phillip said as he clutched him even tighter.

How could he think he wouldn't come? Soren forgot all thoughts of watching eyes. He leaned back and caught Phillip's eyes with his own. "You didn't think I'd come? I told you I would."

"I know where your duty lies."

Soren gripped the nape of Phillip's neck, holding him close. "I told you I'd come for you."

Phillip's eyes glistened, and Soren felt his own rush of emotion. Remembering himself, he stepped back and glanced at Adrian and Cohen, but they looked at him as though nothing were amiss, as if they hadn't just seen his heart in his hands. And he loved them all the more. The battle, he reminded himself. "Caspian follows with the Northern army; they're another day behind, maybe two."

Phillip smiled, emotion still in his eyes. "You bring the Mercian army?"

"Salar and Salara send them for you."

Phillip shook his head. "No, they send them for you. And I'm grateful."

Soren's own emotion still lingered. "I was so certain Rael would march on Kharav first. I'm sorry."

Phillip's hand gripped him reassuringly. "We need to show you something." He led Soren out of the tent to where the enemy armies spanned the horizon.

Adrian pointed to the far right of the Raelean army. "Look at that tent. The one with the large red banner."

Soren saw it. "All right."

"And now look at the one in the center. Look at their banners."

"All right." What was he looking for?

"Do you see how they move exactly the same with the wind?"

Banners flying in the wind. "All right?"

Adrian's brows creased. "Isn't that interesting?"

Was it?

"Keep following," Adrian said. He pointed back to the far right of the army. "Do you see that man, on the end, with a can-looking helm?"

Soren squinted. The army was far, and he could barely make out one man from another. Damn getting old. But then he spotted the man Adrian referred to. "Okay."

"Now look." Adrian swung his finger to the left a little.

It took Soren a moment, but then he spotted him. The same man. But standing in a different place.

Adrian pointed a little more to the left, at another. "And again."

And Soren saw the same man yet again.

"Pick another man," Phillip said, "any other Raelean man, and it's all the same. Replicated across."

Replicated across... Soren's mind turned. What did that mean? How was an army replicated—

"I think they're fake," Adrian said.

A fake army...

Why would Rael have a fake army?

Norah stood in the courtyard of the stronghold, eyeing Titus with frustration as she readied to depart. Mikael had made him swear to take her back to Mercia, even if he had to drag her. She promised to go, but she couldn't. She stalled for two days, until Titus wouldn't let her delay anymore and threatened to make good on his promise, and it infuriated her.

Calla sat on her horse quietly, which was out of character. It was better that way. Norah didn't need anything else fueling her fire. She was already two heartbeats away from knifing Titus in the heel and making a run for Bahoul, to Mikael. But what would she do after? She had nothing that would help him. In fact, she'd be a hindrance more than anything else. But she couldn't go back to Mercia.

A horn blew in the distance, and she turned.

"Messenger!" the watchman called, and her pulse quickened.

From where? Who would send a messenger?

The iron gate raised, and a messenger swept in on a heavily lathered horse, pulling it up abruptly. He'd driven the animal hard. "I've a message for King Mikael of Kharav," he announced.

Norah frowned. The title sounded strange to her ears. "He departed already," she said, "but I'm salara of Kharav and queen of Mercia. What's your message?"

He slid from his horse and held the letter for her with a bow. "From King Tagasi of Osan."

Why would King Tagasi be sending Mikael a letter? Yes, he was now allied with Phillip and had joined their cause, but she hadn't thought them friendly enough to be exchanging letters directly. Norah broke the red-and-yellow seal, then stopped suddenly.

Red and yellow. Red and yellow were the colors of Osan.

And the colors of the flag of the kingdom that had fallen to Lucien in the vision.

Her heart jumped to her throat, and she ripped open the parchment to find the words she feared.

"I thought the Aleon messenger brought word that Rael was marching to attack Eilor," she said to Bhastian, her voice shaking.

He nodded. "That's right. And your Northmen are headed there now."

She shook her head. "King Tagasi says that Rael just marched a path of destruction through Osan. Osan has fallen. Now Rael is headed toward Bahoul and will attack from the west." The opposite direction of Aleon.

She clutched the letter tightly in her hand, a horror washing over her. "Lucien's marching on Bahoul. And Mikael's all alone."

Bhastian shifted. "Salar only has a quarter of the Kharavian army in Bahoul. Katya holds the rest in the Canyonlands, waiting."

Her heart jumped to her throat. They'd been tricked. She swallowed as sickness filled her stomach. "Lucien *is* attacking Kharav first. And tricked us into leaving Mikael vulnerable."

"Bahoul is a fortress," Bhastian tried to assure her. "Salar can hold against a much larger army."

"Against the entire army of Rael?" For months escaped slaves from all kingdoms had been flocking to Rael. It was now the largest army in the world. Larger than Phillip's legendary hundred thousand.

He didn't need to say it. She saw her answer in his eyes.

"We need to get you to Mercia," Titus said.

Her eyes blazed. "I'm not going to Mercia. I'm going to get my army. Then I'm going get my husband."

Soren drew his brows together as he stood beside Phillip and Adrian and looked out across the waiting ranks of Japheth and Rael. "A fake army?"

"At least Rael's," Adrian said. "We haven't seen the same on the Japheth side."

Cohen stepped up beside him. *Something's not right about Rael*, he said.

Soren pulled down his wrap so the boy could read his mouth. "That's what we're talking about."

Adrian chuckled. "He's good. Took me two days before I noticed it."

Soren turned his eyes back to the horizon. A fake army? How was that possible? Adrian was a clever man—perhaps the cleverest he'd ever known. He wanted to trust him, but it just sounded like madness, like... *witchcraft*.

Soren stilled. "He has a witch."

Phillip's brows creased. "What?"

"The Blood King. He has a witch. That has to be how he's doing it."

Phillip stared back out at the armies. "Why would Rael show up with a fake army?"

"It would explain why they haven't attacked yet," Adrian said.

A worrisome thought came to Soren. "I'd show up with a fake army if I wanted to create a diversion." His worry pitted itself deeper. A diversion that would take him away from Mikael. His pulse quickened.

Phillip frowned. "Gregor's army seems real enough, though. And he'd never show up on his own against me with a fake ally."

"Unless he doesn't know," Adrian said. "Maybe that's why they're separate. Easier to keep the ruse."

Phillip lifted a brow and tipped his head to the side in agreement with the possibility.

Soren's heart beat faster. "If this is a diversion, I need to know *now*. It would mean Rael isn't here, and I'd need to get the Northern army back to Salar as quickly as I can."

"We could attack," Adrian said. "If it's witchery, and not real, it will only be Gregor. We could take Japheth. That could leave Rael to stand alone and us with more of an advantage."

Possibly—if they could make it back to Mikael in time for all their armies to stand together.

"And if the Raelean army *is* real?" Phillip asked.

They all knew what would happen if it was real and they attacked—even at a hundred thousand strong, Aleon would be decimated, especially since Caspian and the Northern army still hadn't arrived to join them.

But Soren couldn't wait for the Northern army to arrive to find out. That would be too late for Mikael—if it wasn't too late already. He turned to Adrian. "Do you think it's real?"

Adrian swept his eyes across the line that stretched horizon to horizon. He pursed his lips together, then shook his head. "No. I don't."

Soren looked at Cohen. "You?"

Cohen shook his head. *I don't think it's real*, he answered.

Soren didn't either, but was he sure enough to risk it all? If he didn't, he risked Mikael. "Today's a day for blood then."

It was just a matter of whose.

Chapter Forty-Seven

The earth shook as Soren thundered forward with the Aleon army behind him. He'd always loved the charge to battle, but this battle was different. He'd always fought to take. Now he fought to keep, and he had more to lose than he ever had before.

If he'd decided wrong, if the Raelean forces *were* real, he'd be damning both Phillip and Mikael. The Aleon army would be overwhelmed and defeated. Then Rael and Japheth would rest a day or two and easily take the Northern army when they arrived late. And then Mikael would stand alone.

Mikael would fall alone.

But it was too late to turn back. Soren's eyes locked on the enemy as he led the charge; he had to push out the doubt. He had to focus on what he did best—killing. He'd kill as many as he could. And then he'd kill more.

Japheth's army reacted in surprise, with a delayed start of their return charge. *Unprepared.* Or cowards. Or both. Of course, it helped that they assumed only fools would attack their joint armies. But they finally did return the charge and drove their forces to meet the attack.

Rael waited, although its army seemed ready. The army waited with intention, but just what was the intention? Finally, the army of the Blood King swept forward like an ocean wave—massive, with the speed of the tide. It would be Rael that met him first, and Soren welcomed it—fortune or foolishness, he would know now.

Cohen rode at his side, his sword drawn. Soren wasn't ashamed to wager the boy might claim more kills than he did. He was fast—faster than Soren—and precise. And Soren realized that other than Adrian, there wasn't a better man beside him in battle. He should have given him a proper place in the army. If they survived this, he would.

Three legions of the Aleon army followed closely behind him. He'd only led the army of Kharav into battle, never another, and he was sure the soldiers of Aleon had never followed a commander like him. For a brief moment, he smiled. They were about to find out exactly what it was like.

Adrian and Phillip took the left flank with the majority of the Aleon army, driving straight for Japheth and Gregor. If the decision to attack was wrong, Soren hoped Phillip would at least get his brother's head. With Adrian by his side, it was likely.

The armies came together like mountains colliding. Soren let go of Kal's reins—the destrier knew what to do—and he swung his battle-axe high above his head. The Raelean army rushed forward to meet him. He let out a raging roar and gave all of himself to the clash. His horse leapt high, kicking out its cleated ironclad hooves at the enemy as Soren brought his axe down to collect the first strike of heads.

And his blade cut through like it was an army of air.

No flesh.

No bone.

No blood.

The Raelean army was a false image—a ruse. Soren's destrier landed with a jerk, and he reached his hand down to steady the beast. Soren was a bit unnerved himself as the image of the army charged through him. The chaos threatened his senses. He gave his mind a moment to process the state around him and regain his balance. Then he twisted around to find Cohen. The boy was just behind him, with the Aleon legions. Even with the image still moving through them, they gave a ready signal.

Relief hit him, but only for a moment. Still the clash of battle rang in the air. Japheth's army was very much real, and the battle hadn't been won yet. Gregor still had a significant army, and not only that but if there was a witch on the battlefield, she could bring more trouble than just a ruse.

"Find the witch!" Soren bellowed, and he pushed his Aleon legions deeper into the sea of spirits. Even though the images didn't harm them, it was hard to find their way through the madness. They still used their weapons, not willing to take the risk of a threat being real. Soren drove his men deeper.

More spirits flooded through them, their numbers growing. He was getting closer, and the witch was throwing chaos at him. He pressed on. He could feel her desperation in the growing masses, and it gave him strength. Desperation meant fear. Fear meant victory.

Suddenly, the sky darkened and the spirits of men turned to spirits of monsters. Scaled-serpent bodies broke from the ground and shot into the sky, sprouting webbed wings and claws that threatened to snatch a man to the hells. They gained height and swooped back down toward the army, their mouths open for blood.

"They're not real!" Soren bellowed back to his men. "Press on!"

But the Aleon army wasn't the Kharavian army, and they wavered.

"Forward!" he ordered.

Waves of soldiers flung their shields up over them and ducked down. The horses panicked, throwing their riders. Cohen's mount reared but settled under the boy's hand. Soren's destrier held steady. The Aleon army's advance stopped. But they couldn't stop. Soren needed to find the witch, then lead his legions back to help Phillip take Gregor. He glanced at Cohen, and the boy drove his mount forward alone. Cohen was right—forget the army—and Soren pressed his destrier forward after him.

They ripped through the horror-filled void, ignoring the winged serpents that turned to writhing, rotting carcasses of terror dropping from the sky.

Suddenly, the ground split open in front of them, and their horses came to a grinding halt. Cohen's mount cut sideways, nearly throwing the boy to the ground, but he recovered. Total pandemonium surrounded them. Behind them, Aleon soldiers still swung their weapons at ghosts of the enemy; they still cowered at the monsters of the sky. It was like nothing he'd ever seen.

A low whistle sounded, and Soren threw his attention back to Cohen. The boy pointed his blade to the south, and Soren focused his eyes through the chaos to a small group of soldiers. Forty to fifty Raelean men stood defensively in a circle, and at their center Soren caught glimpses of a blonde-haired woman.

He glanced back at Cohen.

The witch, the boy said.

He saw her. Her eyes were closed, and her hands lifted as she breathed silent words into the air. It was a different woman from the one that had been with the Blood King before. *Curse the North gods.* How many witches did he have? It didn't matter. There would be one less. He looked back at Cohen, and the boy clutched his sword and gave him a ready nod.

Soren hated to rob him of a good charge, especially one that would give him a score of more kills, but it wasn't necessary. He held out his hand for Cohen to throw him his spear, and he did.

Soren circled his destrier. The witch was far, but he could hit farther. He coiled back, his eyes locking on his target, his body aligning to his intent. He ignored the turmoil around him and drowned out the sound of battle. Then he hurled the spear at the circle's center.

His aim was true. He knew it the moment the spear left his hand.

The witch's eyes flew open as she stopped abruptly, the spear protruding from her chest. She staggered backward. Her eyes met Soren's in surprise, and she pointed at him, but she couldn't speak before she collapsed to the ground.

The vast Raelean army evaporated into nothing, and the winged serpents disappeared from the sky. The soldiers that had surrounded the witch pulled the spear from her body and grabbed her from the ground. Then they leapt onto horses and retreated toward Japheth.

Soren's legions looked around, confused by the sudden absence of an enemy, but battle still rang in the air. Japheth remained—now alone against Phillip's hundred thousand men.

Soren turned his attention on them.

He pulled up his large battle-axe and circled his destrier back to his legions. Then, with a haunting call to battle, he led the charge to join Phillip against Gregor.

The second clash came like thunder; this time weapons met flesh and bone. Now attacked by both the north and west sides, the Japheth army fell back in surprise. Bellows rippled through them of Rael's disappearance. And realizing their situation, they started to flee.

Soren smiled. That was the problem with mercenary armies—they were the first to desert. He looked across the Aleon ranks and spotted Phillip in the distance—his Aleon-blue forces pushing back Japheth's sea of green. Soren could only watch him.

Phillip led his own men, deep in the front lines of battle. He wielded his sword like it was a part of his own body. He was fluid. Graceful. Beautiful. His armor gleamed under the sun as he moved. Soren usually hated armor, generally considering it protection for cowards. But Phillip didn't need protecting. And there was nothing about him Soren hated. Even his armor.

A death cry rang to his right, and he jerked as a sword came for his head. But Cohen's blade caught the man, dropping him to the ground.

Soren cursed. That had been close. Maybe *he* should start wearing armor. This distraction of an Aleon king was going to get him killed.

Cohen's eyes locked with his. *Pay attention*, the boy told him.

Soren snorted at Cohen's reprimand but snapped his attention back to the battle. They needed to find Gregor.

"Hold! Hold, you cowards!" a man's voice screamed from a distance. "Cyrus! You fucking traitor! Fucking coward!"

Soren chuckled. He thought it would've been harder. His eyes followed the screams of desperation to the rear of the dispersing Japheth army, where Gregor sat atop his horse. *The back of the army*. Who was the coward now?

Soren scanned the horizon and found Phillip's legions pressing in from the east, toward Gregor. He needed to bring around the west side and surround the Japheth king and trap him.

He drove his destrier back to realign his legions. "With me!" he bellowed to them. And they followed.

The remaining forces of Japheth fought with panic, and Soren cleaved a trail of blood to the king as he thundered through, mercilessly dropping men clad in green before they could scream. The Aleon army swarmed them. All one hundred thousand.

And then there was no Japheth army.

Gregor held a small force around him, a force already wavering. When he saw Soren, his eyes widened, rimmed with fear. He froze.

Soren smiled.

It was a good day to kill a king.

Soren pressed his mount toward him as the last of the Japheth king's forces were cut down.

"Come on!" Gregor screamed at him.

Oh, he was coming.

"And, Cyrus!" Gregor screamed out into the sky. "Fuck you and your witch, you coward! The gods will curse you!"

Soren's smile grew. Too bad Gregor couldn't see it underneath his wrap. He pulled it down. It was rare he wanted to show his face, but this king would see him as he died.

Gregor tried to rein his horse around to flee, and he struck its flank with the flat of his sword. But instead of jumping to a gallop back toward Japheth, the beast reared, dropping Gregor to the ground before taking flight.

Poetic.

When Soren reached him, he dropped down from his destrier. "Looks like even your horse abandoned you," he said to Gregor as he lumbered nearer. "Along with your ally."

Gregor stumbled to his feet and clutched his sword, holding it out, threatening. "I'm not afraid of you, Destroyer!"

Soren chuckled. "Yes, you are." And he swung and severed Gregor's sword arm.

Gregor screamed. He gaped in terror at Soren as he held the stump that had once been connected to his hand. Blood pulsed from the wound, feeding the battlefield. "Don't kill me!" he cried.

Soren delivered a sharp blow to Gregor's stomach, and the king fell to the ground. "I'm not going to kill you," he said as he knocked off Gregor's helmet. He grabbed the king by his thinning hair and pulled him to his knees, stepping behind him and holding him still. "I've saved that for someone who wants your head even more."

Phillip stepped in front of Gregor.

"You!" the Japheth king seethed with spittle around his mouth.

Phillip only stared at him. Soren knew that stare—the realization of a moment long dreamed.

"I'm the rightful king of Aleon!" Gregor spat at him. "You don't have what it takes to be the king of an empire!"

Phillip's eyes brimmed full of emotion. "I'll be the last king of Aleon. When I'm gone, I'll give the empire to democracy. But not before I erase you from history."

"You can't erase me!" Gregor screamed. "I'm the firstborn of Horath, and the rightful heir! Japheth, Hetahl, and Aleon are my birthright!"

Phillip said nothing. He only pulled his dagger and held it to Gregor's throat.

Gregor choked on a raging sob. "You would destroy the empire our family has worked so hard to build?"

Phillip's eyes met Soren's. His voice softened. "Sometimes those feared for destroying things... actually make them better." His eyes locked back on Gregor. "I'll make Aleon better. Greater than it ever was."

Gregor seethed under Soren's hold. "You think this war is done?" he snapped. He looked back at Soren over his shoulder. "Well, I'm not the only one fooled today. Ask yourself, where is Cyrus?"

Soren stared down at the pitiful excuse for a king. "He'll join you soon." He glanced back at Phillip and nodded.

Phillip drew the blade along Gregor's throat, spilling blood down the Japheth king's front. Gregor gurgled and sputtered, and Soren held him as he flailed weakly. Phillip only stood, watching him, clenching the bloodied dagger in his hand. When Gregor's body stilled, Soren pushed him forward to the ground.

And it was done.

Phillip stood frozen. Then his lip quivered. His lips parted in a silent cry, and his body shook. He started to sink. Soren surged forward over Gregor and caught him, stopping him from dropping to his knees. He gripped Phillip's face, pulling him to meet his eyes.

"Stand," Soren commanded. "High King."

It was a title that hadn't been used in thirteen years. Phillip wept.

"High King," Soren told him again, and he pulled him into a tight embrace.

Phillip held on to him, letting the emotion ripple through him. "It's over," he finally whispered. "Thirteen years, and it's finally over." He pulled back and looked up at Soren with tears in his eyes. Soren saw it—his release, the release that vengeance brought. The relief.

But Phillip was wrong, and Soren didn't share his relief. It wasn't over.

Phillip stilled, and his face sobered. "What's wrong?" he asked.

Soren's gut turned as his mind recovered from battle, seeding horror with his next question. "Gregor's right. He wasn't the only one fooled. This *was* a diversion. If that was Cyrus's fake army, where's his real one?"

Mikael walked the corridor of the mountain stronghold of Bahoul. He grazed his fingers along its stone walls, felt its foundation under his step. His bloodline had built this stronghold. Had lost it. And now he held it again. Being back in this place drew emotion from him that he wasn't accustomed to, and hadn't expected.

The last time he'd been here was with his father. The senior king had made sure he knew every defense, every strength, every weakness. Mikael ran through them now. He'd thought it likely not much had changed since he'd last been there. Of course, the Northmen had repaired the wall they'd crushed in taking it, and as much as he hated to admit it, they'd rebuilt it even stronger.

But he'd been wrong. A lot had changed.

The North was good at building things. Their isle capital had near impenetrable walls. They may not be a kingdom of warriors, for which he judged them harshly, but they were a kingdom of scholars. Their architectural calculations and tools made for the strongest of structures, and when reinforced with Mercian steel, no other kingdom could compare. Perhaps he should be happy Bahoul had fallen into their hands for a time. The structural improvements—improvements he would never have been able to make—weren't lost on him.

The double doors at the entry had been replaced and were now Mercian steel, as were the side doors and defensive gates. No man would get through there. The rock foundations had all been reinforced and sealed, and battlements added to the walls. Impressive, it was. Perhaps when all this was over, he'd invite more Northmen to Kharav.

Mikael smiled sadly to himself. He knew he wouldn't live to see that day. But still, it was nice to dream about. It was nice to dream about Salara—being with her. Happy. Their two kingdoms united, fortifying each other. Her dream had become his dream.

Salara.

He likely wouldn't see her again. The thought brought him to a stop, and he let himself lean back against the wall. It gutted him.

No. He wiped his hand over his face and tried to push the crushing weight off. The past three years of his life had been the best he'd ever had. Even if it was all that fate would give him, he considered himself fortunate.

Mikael pushed himself off the wall and continued on. He needed to focus on the plan. The Northern army had diverted from Bahoul to join Aleon, where they'd meet the armies of Japheth and Rael. With luck, they'd push them down and progress them toward Kharav. He held a quarter of his army in the mountains, and when Soren and Phillip drew close enough, he'd join them to push the enemy armies back into the Canyonlands, where the rest of the Kharavian army would finish them.

It was a solid plan, even though they'd miscalculated the offensive. He hadn't thought Rael would attack Aleon first. Neither had Soren. It had been a terrible time to be wrong, but hopefully they'd recover. Now he just needed to prepare. And wait. There wasn't much else he could do anyway with only a quarter of an army.

Bells rang, and he paused. A messenger must have arrived. He strode to the stairs and took them up, two at a time, to the wall. He squinted as he stepped into the light, temporarily blinded. A group of soldiers were gathered.

"What is it?" he asked. They looked at him with eyes wide, then motioned past the base of the mountains. He shielded his eyes as he looked out, then stopped.

There was movement on the horizon, not singular, not small. A wave, like an ocean wave, spanned from sky to sky. It was an army—the largest he'd ever seen—headed toward him. A warrior stepped beside him, and his eyes widened.

Kiran. He was supposed to be with Salara.

"What are you doing here?" Mikael demanded.

The guard of the Crest held out a rolled parchment. "From Salara."

Mikael glanced back at the sea of approaching men as he unrolled the message to find Salara's words inside. But he didn't need to read them to know her warning.

Rael wasn't east. Cyrus wasn't in Aleon. They came from the west to march on Bahoul.

Cyrus was coming for him.

Norah pressed the small group hard toward Aleon, after the Mercian army. She'd sent Kiran and the Crest to Mikael before leaving the stronghold, all except Bhastian and Titus, who'd flat out refused to leave her. Calla stayed with her as well, but everyone else she sent. With only a small portion of the Kharavian army, Mikael needed every man he could get, but she knew it wasn't enough. Rael's numbers threatened Aleon, Mercia, and Kharav combined. He couldn't possibly stand against Lucien by himself, but she tried not to let panic take over.

Focused now on catching up to her army, she'd intended to set a fast but sustainable pace, but as her mind turned, she pushed them even faster. Cuts marred her hands twice while they rode, but she kept linen wrapped tightly around her palms and continued on. As evening fell, Titus pulled them up. "We have to slow, Regal High. We're going to exhaust the horses."

She forgot sometimes; Sephir didn't tire as a normal horse. But they couldn't slow. Mikael only had days before Lucien reached him.

Norah sat at the fire, clutching her arms. Days, he had. If Lucien hadn't reached him already.

It could be days before they reached the Mercian army, and that meant even more days to bring them back. Her desperation grew. Mikael needed help. She couldn't lose him. Panic threatened again, but she pushed it down, inhaling deeply. She had to be smart.

What else could she do? She stilled, then turned to Bhastian. "You have to get to the eastern pass, where Katya waits, and tell her Mikael needs her in Bahoul. By the time he gets the messenger that we sent, then sends one of his own to her, he'll lose at least a day."

Bhastian looked uneasily at Titus. He'd already refused to leave her, but they had no choice. They needed Katya to bring the rest of the army to Bahoul. Reluctantly, he nodded. "I'll rest my horse another hour or so, and I'll go." He looked back to Titus. "But you'll stay. Regardless the task she tries to send you on."

Titus nodded. When Bhastian was appointed captain of the Crest, she wasn't sure how her Mercian guard would take answering to a Kharavian warrior. But the two held a mutual respect for each other and seemed to view managing her safety as more than a one-man job. When Bhastian was away, the Crest answered to Titus.

Her focus turned back to Mikael. It was only a small relief that Katya would bring the Kharavian army. He needed more. But Norah was at a loss for other options. The wheels of her mind turned as her desperation grew.

Her eyes landed on Sephir. That was it—

She jumped up and turned to Calla. "I need you to go to the Uru. To Tahla. The Kharavian army won't be enough, and I don't even know if they'll make it in time." She pulled the girl to the mare. "Take Sephir. You don't need to wait. Go now!"

"But you're the only one who can ride her," Calla protested.

"Get on!"

The girl looked at the mare with her eyes wide, but she obeyed, and Sephir stood quietly as she mounted.

Norah clutched Calla's knee. "Tell her to come and bring everything she has. Mikael needs her. I need her." Then she drew to the front of the horse and put her hands on each side of the mare's face, pressing their foreheads together. "Get her to Tahla. I beg you." The animal gave a snort. Norah released her, and the mare tossed her head. Then she kicked up in a gallop toward the western pass.

Norah turned back to Titus. "We keep going. Now." They pressed on after her army.

Chapter Forty-Eight

Rael came like a curse of locusts, with more bodies than could be counted. They charged the stronghold of Bahoul. There were so many that Mikael couldn't see the ground underneath them. Fifteen thousand men he had in the fortress. A quarter of his army—fifteen thousand men. Rael's army had to be twenty times that size. At least.

And they swarmed.

But this wasn't a seasoned army. These men of Rael weren't soldiers. They'd been slaves, and now they were free. And while they fought with heart, heart wouldn't protect them. Heart wouldn't give them the experience they needed to survive.

They started their charge too early, and fatigue slowed them before they even reached the walls. His archers loosed arrows as they came into range, dropping them almost as quickly as they passed the threshold of reach. Mikael put the rest of his men along the walls to rain down arrows on those who got through. Not all his men were archers, but even the worst of them would hit a body down below in the masses.

The numbers kept coming. They reached the base of the fortress and started to lean ladders up against it. Mikael signaled the counter—another Mercian defense blessing. Large boulders with chains drilled through them were released off the battlements, swinging like a ball on a string. They arced across the stone face of the stronghold, sweeping anything clear from their path. Then they were hoisted back and released again. All along the wall these defenses were positioned. And his men could do this all day, and all night, as the bodies piled below.

But he wasn't encouraged. It was a cruel strategy, but a common one—use the weak forces first to drain the enemy—use up arrows, spears, and energy. Cyrus had bloodsport fighters from the Raelean arenas, like Cyrus himself. They'd be his best warriors. He'd bring them in the end. But right now, they were nowhere in sight. Which meant the end was nowhere in sight.

Her pace felt slower without Sephir, but Norah pushed on. It was another day without the Mercian army on the horizon, and she was on the verge of breaking. Each day it took to reach them meant a day more in returning. Mikael didn't have that long.

And what had happened in Aleon? Adrian's message had said they were being attacked. But who was attacking if not Rael? Japheth? She prayed they fared all right.

Titus urged her to slow, to rest, but she couldn't. She hadn't slept since they left the stronghold. Two days? Three days? More? She didn't know what time was anymore. Her body ached, and she could barely feel her legs, but she drove them on. They couldn't stop. She had to get to her army. Mikael needed them.

They took a rocky ridge to the top, but when they dropped down the other side, her horse stumbled, dropping to its knees.

Norah jumped off, almost falling herself. "No! No, no, no," she begged. The horse moved to rise again, but its knees buckled, and it resigned to lie down. "No!" she pleaded.

"Regal High," Titus called to her, "we have to stop."

She ignored him, and petted the animal's face, trying to coax it up again. "Please get up!"

"Regal High."

"We have to keep going!" she snapped.

"Let's rest for just a few hours, then we can pick up again."

She couldn't just... pause. She didn't have time. Mikael didn't have time. She stumbled the rest of the way down the ridge, continuing on foot.

"Regal High!"

But she kept going. She had to keep going.

"Norah!"

Her legs were numb. She ignored them too. Another small ridge rose in front of her, and she charged up it.

Titus's arms came around her. "Norah!"

"No!" she cried. "We have to keep going. I have to get the army!"

"You have to stop!"

"Let me go!" she screamed.

"Stop!"

Norah threw back her elbow, catching him in the chin and dropping him to a knee, and he released her. She ripped away from him, but he caught her calf, and she fell forward. They moved slowly from exhaustion, but still she managed to kick him off and took the ridge again. She stumbled once, then again. Days of travel, days without sleep. Without much food. Her body was failing her, but still she pushed on.

"Norah!"

No! But she didn't have the energy to scream it back. She focused everything she had on just reaching the top. And as she did, she stopped.

And let out a cry.

Before her stretched the Mercian army—marching toward them.

Norah staggered down the ridge toward the army. She wanted to cry, to laugh, but the only thing she had energy for was keeping herself upright. She saw a rider break toward her, and she knew it was Soren. She cried in relief as she ran, not trusting herself not to fall, but not caring.

When he reached her, he dropped from his mount and caught her in his arms. "Salara!"

She clutched him. "Soren!"

He held her tightly. "What happened?"

Tears threatened, but she swallowed them back. *Stupid emotion*—not now! "Lucien's launching an attack from the west. Aleon was a trick!" She gasped between breaths. "We have to get the Mercian army to Bahoul."

He nodded. "I know—we're headed there now."

"We're not going to reach him in time. Osan's fallen. I've sent word to both Katya and Tahla to come, but it won't be enough."

"You called Katya and Tahla?"

She nodded.

"And you came to retrieve the North army to take back to Bahoul?"

Her brows dipped. "Of course I did."

The corners of his eyes smiled slightly.

She shook her head. Her mind wasn't even working to draw anything from what he was saying. "What?"

"You're a proper war queen now."

She'd be amused later. "We have to go to Bahoul. Right now."

"We're going," he assured her.

Relief flooded, and suddenly, she didn't have the strength to stand.

"Come on," he said, and scooped her up.

She let him carry her. She couldn't do anything else. "Where's Phillip?" she mumbled as her eyes grew heavy.

But she didn't hear his answer.

Enemy bodies continued to pile at the base of the stronghold walls, but Mikael urged his warriors on. They took shifts, using arrows less and less to conserve them and relying on the boulders to sweep the walls free of climbing men. He'd lost three hundred of his own to attacking arrows and spears between the battlements. He couldn't lose any more—he needed every man he had for when Cyrus launched his real attack.

But the first wave kept coming. Their bodies covered the ground. There were so many that it broke the fall of those cast down, only for them to be able to attack again. Mikael knew they couldn't sustain with these volumes. It was only a matter of time before they breached the walls.

"Salar," Rahim, one of his captains, called.

Mikael turned. "How many more have we lost?"

"A hundred and eighty-four."

Mikael swore. Fifteen thousand men sounded like a lot, but he couldn't lose one more.

"And they've calculated where the arcs of the boulders don't clear. We've had to move back to arrows for those areas."

Mikael swore again. They'd run out of arrows before Rael ran out of men.

"It's only a matter of time," the captain said.

Mikael wanted to grab him by the weapons strap fastened tight across his chest and shove him against the wall, but he couldn't be angry with the captain for saying what he'd been thinking only a moment earlier. And it was the truth. They couldn't hold for much longer.

"It's time to think of the tunnel," Rahim said.

The tunnel was a narrow passage under the stronghold that ran below the mountains and up into the hills toward the Canyonlands, coming out not far from the abandoned manor where Soren had grown up. It wasn't meant for more than a handful of men at a time; it was designed for a king to escape.

"The tunnel was sealed when the North took Bahoul," Mikael said. He knew. He'd tried to use it to retake the stronghold himself in the Great War.

"The Bear had it unsealed when Aleon came, so we had a way to sneak back in should the Aleon king prove to be untrustworthy."

Mikael stared at him, realizing. "That cunning bastard." He chuckled to himself. The Bear was still helping him beyond the grave. But it didn't matter. He had no plans to use the tunnel. "I can't leave, Rahim. I'll stay with the men and hold this fortress. Plus, my fate is with Cyrus."

The captain nodded. "We fight on, then."

"We fight on."

To the end. It wouldn't be a long wait.

Chapter Forty-Nine

Her body ached, still steeped in exhaustion, and her muscles complained as she stirred awake. Wait—was she on a horse? Suddenly, Norah's mind came reeling back.

Mikael.

The Mercian army.

She startled awake at the unfamiliar arms wrapped around her and was about to push herself off the horse.

"Easy," Adrian calmed her as she twisted against him. "It's just me."

She let out a panting breath. "Hammel's hell." Despite the scare, she was happy to see him.

He chuckled. "I was beginning to wonder if you'd ever wake up."

She frowned. "How long have I been asleep?"

"All day," said Soren, riding beside them. "After sleeping all night."

"All night and all day!" She brought her fingertips to her head. She *had* been exhausted. She glanced back at Adrian, and he flashed her a grin. "Have you been carrying me this whole time?" she asked him.

Soren snorted.

"Uh, no," Adrian said. "I... we... just, uh—"

"We passed you around a bit," Soren finished.

If she wasn't awake before, she was now. "What?"

He shrugged. "You're heavy."

"Excuse me?"

"Just the lord commander and I," Adrian said. "Oh, and Caspian."

"Cohen," Soren added.

"Oh, right. Cohen. Titus, for a little while, although he fell asleep too, and you both almost fell off his horse. You didn't wake for any of it."

She rubbed her temples again. Gods, help her.

"She drooled on Phillip too," Soren added. "I almost forgot."

"Right, Phillip too. Okay, so a few."

Gods, take her now. She covered her face with her hands. "I drooled?"

"Well, you bled on me," Soren said.

The cuts. She looked at her hands. Dried blood stained her sleeves and parts of her shirt and breeches. She didn't even wake for that?

"You were really out of it," Adrian said. "How are you feeling now?"

"Better, actually. Hungry. Thirsty. But a lot better."

"Here." Soren held out a waterskin, and she took it and drank deeply until she coughed.

"How far are we from Bahoul?" she asked.

"Another day and a half yet."

Any relief she'd previously garnered quickly left her. Norah felt like she couldn't breathe. "Lucien's reached Mikael by now."

Soren's face was somber. "A small army can hold Bahoul."

She closed her eyes. She wished she could believe that.

"Salara."

She looked back at him.

"He'll hold till we get there."

So she prayed.

"We're out of arrows."

Mikael slowly nodded as one of his captains delivered the news. It had only been a matter of time. And still Rael came—unending waves of bodies.

"We'll keep using the boulders," Rahim said, "but we're down to hand-to-hand fighting to hold from a breach where the boulders don't reach."

"How many men have we lost?"

"Over a thousand now. We've taken nearly ten times that of the enemy, but it hasn't seemed to have fazed them."

Mikael searched his mind for additional options.

"Salar," Rahim said, "please. Take the tunnel, fall back. We'll hold them here, distract them."

Mikael reached out and clasped the captain's shoulder. "No. I stay. We kill as many as we can and give the lord commander the best chance to defeat them when he comes." He *would* come. Mikael didn't know what had happened with Aleon. But if Kharav fell, Soren and the Mercian army might be the only thing that remained between Rael and the North—between Cyrus and Salara. Mikael would give Soren the best chance he could.

A bell rang out.

A warning bell.

Something was wrong.

Mikael and Rahim ran along the walls of the stronghold, looking down at the attacking Raelean army. They were still coming strong but hadn't yet breached. Still the Kharavian soldiers held.

The bell came again, and Mikael looked at Rahim in confusion. "Where is it coming from? Rael hasn't breached the outside."

Rahim shook his head, then he stopped and his face paled. "Not an outside breach. One within."

Mikael's pulse thrummed. A breach within. Which could only mean... the tunnel. *Curse the North gods*, the Blood King's army had found the tunnel.

They raced down the stairs, deep into the stronghold, gathering men as they went. If the Raelean army breached through the tunnel, it would be over. Bahoul would be lost.

They reached the door of the tunnel where a half dozen Kharavian warriors stood with their blades drawn. Mikael pulled his own sword, ready. He cursed the North—the one door that hadn't been replaced with Mercian steel. The Bear had kept one way to break in.

Behind it—the scrape of metal, the sounds of an army. He waited. When they broke through the door, he would attack with everything he had. He'd kill as many as he could. They all would. His only consolation: he wouldn't die here. He'd seen the vision. He'd die outside. By Cyrus's hand.

Until then, he'd fight. He clutched his sword tighter.

But it wasn't the banging of a metal ram trying to break down the doors that they heard.

It was a key.

A key.

Mikael glanced at Rahim, and the captain glanced back at him, his own sword ready.

Then the door swung open.

It wasn't the Raelean army looking back at him.

It was the eyes of someone he hadn't expected to see again.

Katya.

"Salara sent a message, said you boys could use some help," she said wryly as she stepped aside and Kharavian warriors poured out of the tunnel and into the stronghold.

It took a moment for him to fully understand what was happening. Then Mikael straightened, giving a chuckle laced with relief, and he sheathed his sword. The captain's eyes smiled as she stepped in front of him. He reached out and clutched her shoulder, simply holding her. Grateful.

"Don't get emotional, Salar."

He laughed.

"I bring two thousand through the tunnel to help reinforce from within," she said. "The rest of the army will wait until the cover of night, then attack the enemy from the outside."

Mikael nodded. A fair approach. She wouldn't have been able to bring all forty-five thousand through the tunnel anyway. Warriors poured into the stronghold. Hundreds. "To the wall!" Katya ordered, and they raced to join their brothers-in-arms against the attack on the wall.

Mikael spotted Bhastian, captain of the Crest. He'd been with Salara, and now he stood beside Katya. "Salara sent you to get the army?" Mikael asked him.

Bhastian nodded. "Yes, Salar."

His heart nearly burst with pride. He was just grateful she was safe now. "And she's returned to Mercia?"

Bhastian stiffened. His hesitation sent a wave of dread through Mikael.

"She's returned to Mercia?" he asked again.

"No, Salar. She's gone to call the Northern army back to you."

Mikael's chest seized. He should be happy about the possibility of aid from the Northern army. But that meant Salara would be with them. Not in Mercia. Not away from the battle. Not safe.

No.

But before he could protest, shouting rang through the tunnel, and they all spun toward it.

"What's that?" Katya asked to no one in particular.

"Rael!" came shouts from the men in the tunnel.

Mikael ripped his sword from his scabbard again. "Rael's in the tunnel!" A weakness—the entry from the outside to the tunnel, while far from the stronghold, wasn't well hidden. It came out among the barren rocks in the low of the hills. Rael must have spotted them enter—two thousand men were hard to hide, even for the Shadowmen—and followed.

His blood pulsed hot, ready for the battle that was coming. His Kharavian warriors were still inside the tunnel, but instead of continuing into the stronghold, they turned back to face the enemy.

Katya scanned her eyes around the room, then back to the tunnel. "This door won't hold them out, even if we bar it." The darkness of worry filled her eyes. "If they get inside, Bahoul will fall."

"We have to collapse the tunnel," Bhastian said.

They snapped their gazes to him.

"Our men are still in there," Katya said.

"And they'll help me do it." Bhastian pulled up his battle-axe. "It's the only way. We can't let them through." He barreled back into the tunnel. Bhastian—Soren's trusted man.

"No!" Katya yelled as he raced to the thick wooden beam that framed the sides and swung his axe against it.

"Bring it down!" Bhastian bellowed. Another warrior with an axe struck another beam.

She tried to go after him, but Mikael grabbed her. As painful as it was, it was worth the lives of fifteen hundred men for Bahoul to remain strong. It was worth Bhastian's sacrifice. The rest of the Kharavian army still remained just beyond the battle and would attack at nightfall. They had to hold until then. It was these decisions that crushed him the most.

It took Bhastian four body swings for the beam to cave and fall. The warriors beside him took out two more beams. Some dirt and small rocks fell from the top. It wasn't enough.

"Bhastian!" Katya cried.

He moved to the next beam and swung with everything he had, again and again. Then he gave one last look back to them, his fist to his chest, before the rush of rock collapsed on top of him.

A tear streamed down Katya's cheek.

Mikael panted back the pain of the loss. They would all fall. Even him. And he accepted this. He had to make the most of the time he had left.

He had to focus on the battle. The war.

It would be a long day, and an even longer night.

Despite the exhaustion that still lingered, Norah couldn't sleep. How could she when Mikael was under attack? She knew Lucien would have made it to him by now. He would have reached Mikael days ago. How long could Mikael hold?

He had to hold.

They started their march again before dawn. The time it took to move an army was excruciatingly slow. It was all Norah could do to not break from them and race alone the rest of the way.

She rode with her hand wrapped around the hilt of her sword. Adrian had given the weapon to her, and being able to clutch it brought her an inkling of comfort. Soren had also strategically stowed a short sword and two additional daggers in the folds of her saddle. She carried a crossbow fastened to the back of her seat, although she'd always struggled with the strength it took to pull back the cord. Still, having it made her feel slightly better.

The Aleon army had come with them, aside from two legions that had stayed behind to finish the takeover of Japheth. The ranks traveled in file, Mercia in the front, led by Soren and Caspian, trailed by Aleon with Adrian and Phillip. As they drew nearer to the mountains, they moved to stretch across horizontally. Phillip and Adrian joined beside her.

They reached the final ridge, and the mountains of Bahoul came into view. They seemed darker now than they had before—her mind was playing tricks on her. She squinted, and a sickening chill went through her.

The mountains seemed darker because they were covered in men—the men of the Raelean army.

Had they taken the stronghold? Had Lucien gotten to Mikael?

The urgency now cut to her soul. "Soren!"

His horse quickened, but he said, "We can't start the charge from this far. We need to save strength for the battle."

The wave of their armies moved faster, but not fast enough. Rael's numbers were staggering. *So many*—there were so many men that she couldn't see the snow that blanketed the ground of the mountains. But—

They were fighting...

The Kharavian army was still fighting. Hope seeded inside her. They hadn't taken the stronghold yet.

Hold on, she begged Mikael. She couldn't breathe.

The time it took to bridge the gap felt longer than the entire journey, but their pace quickened as they neared.

"Fall to the back," Soren told Norah as they got closer.

As if he could make her...

Phillip pulled his sword as he rode beside her. The horses of the cavalry around them picked up to a trot, then a canter.

"Fall back!" Soren demanded of her.

But the army picked up more speed, and she pulled her own sword as she pushed her horse to a gallop. She wasn't here to fall back.

"Salara!"

Horns sounded from the enemy, and the Raelean army poured out to meet them.

Norah charged with Phillip riding beside her. Their men followed, bellowing their cries of attack. The ground shook underneath her. Time slowed in the thunder. She cast her eyes down the sweeping line of Mercia and Aleon. For as long as she could remember, she'd fought the notion of war. She'd rejected its violence, its death. But now she came for Mikael, and she'd bring death to save him.

The initial clash was deafening. Metal rang in her ears. Soren veered his destrier toward her, but she cut her horse left and away. She hadn't come to watch—she'd come to fight for what she loved. To the end. She screamed as she charged into the masses of black and blood.

Her blade met armor and bone, and she tore through with a fury, but no one tried to strike her back. As the enemy attacked her army, they only parted around her.

And she realized—she was linked to their king—they wouldn't hurt her.

That didn't mean she'd give them mercy.

Norah pushed her horse forward, toward the stronghold, striking down anyone that couldn't get out of the way of her blade. To her right, Soren swung his axe like he was skinning the earth, arcing blood through the air. He'd stopped yelling at her, understanding, too, why the Raelean army steered clear of her.

Phillip fought to her left, bellowing commands as they tried to push forward.

But they weren't moving forward. They were being pushed back. The armies of Mercia and Aleon were formidable, but as the sea of Rael swept through them, the realization hit her that it wouldn't be enough. Rael came in floods, and the northern kingdoms were now losing ground. She set her eyes on the stronghold in desperation. She had to make it to Mikael. Where was he?

She couldn't see through the battle; she only felt herself being driven backward. A Raelean soldier leapt at Adrian, and she caught him midair with her sword.

"That was luck!" Adrian shouted with the hint of a smile.

But she couldn't smile back. They needed more. They weren't enough. They needed the rest of the Kharavian army. "We have to hold until Katya gets here with the army!" she yelled over the deafening clash of battle.

"They're already here!" Adrian yelled back. "No one else is coming."

What? The rest of the Kharavian army was already there? She scanned the bloody scene around them. The Raelean forces were so many that Kharav seemed so few. But they were all here. They were all dying.

No one else was coming. That wasn't entirely true—Tahla hadn't reached them yet, but the forces of Rael were too overwhelming. The numbers of the Uru wouldn't matter.

She swept her eyes desperately around her. And she froze.

The north wall of the stronghold had crumbled. How had they brought down the wall? It was breached. Bahoul was *breached*. Rael was both outside and within.

Panic threatened. Where was Mikael?

A pain sliced through her hand—*no!* Not now! But it was just the left hand that bore the cut. The right didn't come.

She tried to ignore it and focus on the chaos around her. They were falling. Mercia and Aleon were falling to Rael.

She turned her mind to the only thing that mattered now. "Where's Mikael?" The stronghold was overrun. "Where's Mikael?" she screamed.

Chapter Fifty

Mercia and Aleon were falling. Kharav was falling. Soren had been hit and knocked from his horse. He stood shoulder to shoulder with Adrian now, desperately trying to hold the line and keep Rael from driving them away from the stronghold—away from Mikael. Caspian worked on the north side to keep Rael from flanking them, and Phillip cut south with the Aleon army, but they were slowly losing ground.

Salara fought with a vengeance, striking down man after man. He realized they weren't trying to kill her. She did, too, and used it. Soren had thought he'd be focused on keeping her protected, but she'd saved even him a time or two. If they lived through this, he had every intention of dragging her to Salta Tau for the markings.

The Northmen loosed arrows as fast as they could draw them, but it merely dented the waves of Rael. The enemy numbers were staggering. Slaves had flocked to the army of the Blood King, but no one could have imagined how many. Most of them weren't warriors, but they didn't have to be. Their numbers alone were overwhelming.

Salara's scream stopped him cold, and he whirled to see her dragged off her horse by two Raelean soldiers. Soren snarled and tried to cut through the wave of men that had rushed between them, but a sharp pain sliced across his side, dropping him. He took the head of the man who did it before he paused to check himself. Blood poured from his side, but it looked worse than it was. It would make for a painful continuation, but he'd be all right.

Soren pushed forward and shaved the field with his battle-axe, showering the Raelean soldiers in their own blood. But it didn't stop them. They kept coming. He tried to push through to Salara, who had been dragged farther from him now. "Salara!" he bellowed. But he couldn't see her.

He swept his axe for blood again, only this time, it was met with the strength of steel—that had equal power behind it. Around him moved soldiers of Rael. Not slaves. He knew fighting men when he saw them. These were the bloodsport fighters freed from the arenas of Rael, men who lived battle every day. The Blood King's trusted—his best, saved for the end.

Because the end was near.

His eyes flicked between them. Four, five, six. But one in particular caught his attention. A man with skin of night, not like the others, and almost as large as Soren. The way the other men's eyes flicked between him and Soren—he was clearly a man of authority. Their leader. A thumb's smear of dark crimson marked his forehead. *Blood.* Purposeful blood. Soren's mind turned. That was how the Blood King talked to him, how he coordinated his army. How many men bore the king's blood? How many men could send messages?

Soren dropped his axe and pulled his two short swords from his back. He bared his teeth. Well, he had a message for the Blood King.

Their dance was a battle within the battle, a tempest of steel and blood. All around him they swarmed. Just as he kicked one back, he had to spin to face another. Each of their blows carried the strength of death.

Another sting bit his thigh, almost sending him to the ground, but miraculously he stayed upright, fighting on. Soren dropped two of them, he wasn't sure how.

A blow hit his stomach, and he doubled over, only to catch a knee to the face. He blocked the second and sliced through his opponent's leg, severing it.

Behind him came another, and he spun again.

He almost didn't feel the blade as it pierced through the low of his left shoulder, just narrowly missing his heart.

Their leader.

The bloodsport soldier pushed the sword through Soren all the way to the hilt. Face-to-face, they stopped, close enough to feel each other's breath. And they both looked down between them.

Soren's blades sat buried in the man's gut, to the hilt as well. Their eyes locked, the man's realization sinking in. In a final effort, with his final breaths, the bloodsport fighter tried to twist his weapon in Soren's shoulder, but Soren butted his head forward, knocking him with a *crack*, and shoved the man off his swords. The fighter pulled his blade with him as he fell backward, and Soren bellowed in pain.

"Everan!" another soldier cried out.

The rest of the men were on him in an instant. A searing burn ripped across his arm, but he ignored it. Soren drove his exhausted body purely from muscle memory, from instinct. He let his rage fuel him. He didn't know where Salara was. He'd lost her. Adrian was missing from his side. Had death claimed him? He forced it from his mind—he couldn't let his desperation take over.

Only two of the bloodsport fighters were left now, but there was no relief. His left arm could no longer hold a weapon. Something struck him in the back of his head, and he fell to his knees. Another blow to his stomach took the wind from him, and he fell forward. He struggled to raise his head.

Was this how it ended?

Phillip's horse galloped by, riderless. He couldn't draw a breath.

All around him Rael swarmed, drowning him. Darkness closed around him.

He fought blindly now. Blood ran down his face. He wasn't sure if it was even his own, but it didn't matter—he'd fight until the life ran out of him.

And it was running out.

The earth shook underneath him. Was it coming to swallow him in eternal sleep? No—not yet. *Salara. Mikael. Phillip.* He couldn't leave them yet...

The vibration underneath him felt like thunder.

He wiped back the blood from his eyes, but it still clouded his vision. A sword came for his head, and he knocked it from the air—the sword and the arm that held it dropped to the ground. Screams rang around him.

The thunder—another Raelean wave of attack.

He wiped his face again and turned to meet the clash of battle he heard coming from behind. He turned to meet his end.

But it wasn't the rush of Rael.

A wave of Horsemen crashed into the sea of carnage.

They came in the thousands. More warriors than the Uru—so many. *So many Horsemen.* Not just the Uru, he realized. All of them. All the tribes. Some he recognized, some not. Some were friends of Kharav. Some weren't. But they all came and launched themselves against Rael.

And leading them—*Tahla.*

Riding Sephir.

Her sword gleamed under the blood-misted rays of the sun. She charged high in the saddle, her blade in the air, her lips peeled back in a snarling scream that he didn't need to hear to feel—the scream of battle.

Soren struggled to keep his footing as the masses rushed past him.

A distance away, he spotted Adrian. Emotion swept through him, but he managed a nod as their eyes met. Adrian gaped at the tidal wave of Horsemen sweeping around them and locked eyes back with Soren in disbelief.

With a newfound energy, Soren charged into action. He needed to find Salara. He cut down men as he went, but froze as his eyes caught a fallen body on the field.

No...

He raced to Cohen and dropped down beside the boy. Blood poured from his partially severed arm.

But the boy pushed him off. *No, I'm fine*, he said. *Go! Salara needs you!*

"Cohen!" Adrian yelled and was beside him in a moment. He stripped linen from his undertunic to bind his arm.

Cohen struck Soren in the shoulder. The injured one. Hard. *Go!*

"I've got him," Adrian said. "Go!"

Soren pushed on and dodged through the battle, looking for Salara. Where had they taken her? The small consolation he carried was that they wouldn't kill her. But it was a *very small* consolation.

He swept his eyes over the screams and sound of steel, but the battle raged around him, blocking his view. What direction had they taken her in? He couldn't see her through the fighting. He couldn't find her. Defeat washed over him.

He'd lost her. The one person he was supposed to protect, the one person he was supposed to keep. He'd lost her.

"Soren!" Her cry rang above the sound of battle, and he spun. Through the fighting, Salara rode toward him on his own horse. *Kal*. Phillip rode beside her.

He almost wept.

She reined his destrier up beside him, kicking her foot out of the stirrup so he could swing up behind her. "We have to find Mikael!"

He noticed her left hand dripping with blood, and he pulled it to look. Across her palm were two cuts. Deep.

"They're not healing," she said. "I think he's lost his healer."

A terrifying thought.

"It's fine," she said. "My right's fine. I don't know why, but he hasn't cut it."

Soren knew why—if he'd lost his healer, he wouldn't cut his sword hand.

Together they charged back through the Horsemen to where the Kharavian army was locked with Rael. The fortress was overrun, with all armies both inside and outside its walls.

Rael's numbers seemed less now. He looked across the Raelean forces and noticed some of them fleeing. Despite that, Rael still held strong, although the Horseman joining had turned the tide, and they started losing ground.

"There!" Salara cried.

And then he saw him.

Mikael fought from atop his horse surrounded by his Kharavian soldiers. They battled against a thick ring of the Raelean army around them. Soren was still too far to help him, and he drove his horse toward him.

His destrier plowed through, catching the enemy under his heavy hooves and driving forward. Salara fought as they went. She leaned far to reach as many heads as she could, even one handed, and Soren struggled to keep hold of her. The wind caught her winter mane, and it whipped him in the face. He cursed. Just what he needed—to be blinded by blood *and* hair.

And then they were falling.

Soren hit the ground with a force that tore his left shoulder from the socket. As if it didn't hurt enough. He staggered up. Salara slowly rose beside him. The wind had been knocked out of her, but she was seemingly unhurt. He looked back in horror to see his destrier felled with a spear to the chest.

Phillip rushed to beat back the enemy that swarmed them. Another horse leapt forward, and Soren's eye caught sight of his farm girl.

Calla loosed arrows at men as they rushed toward them, taking them down before they reached him and Salara. Not a single miss. Soren gritted his teeth and jerked his shoulder back into place. He looked back at Mikael, who was still battling.

"Soren!" Salara cried, and he snapped to see the Blood King bearing down on Mikael on a horse of night. But Soren was still too far to do anything.

"I'm out of arrows!" Calla cried.

Soren sliced through another Raelean soldier, and they raced toward Mikael on foot. Fear rippled through him. They weren't going to make it in time. They were too far.

Suddenly, an arrow wisped through the air and hit Mikael in the side.

"No!" Soren bellowed, and Salara screamed from behind him.

Mikael stayed for a moment, wavering in his saddle, then slowly dropped from his horse.

Soren barreled forward with a snarl, swinging his sword wide and laying a path of blood and destruction as he tried to bridge the eternity of space between them. He jerked up a spear from a fallen man as he went.

The Blood King stopped just short of reaching Mikael and slid down from his horse, sword in his right hand. Mikael dragged himself back. He didn't try to stand. He wouldn't. He wouldn't fight Cyrus, just like the vision.

"Soren!" Salara cried from behind him.

Soren stopped and coiled back with the spear in his hand. The Blood King was within range. He could hit him. He could kill him.

Cyrus struck Mikael's sword from his hand, and Mikael dragged himself farther backward, the arrow still protruding from his side.

Soren settled his sight on the Raelean king and steadied his breath to steady his hand.

"What are you waiting for?" she screamed from behind him.

He'd promised Salara he'd take the opportunity when he had it. And he had it. But he couldn't. He couldn't do it.

It gutted him.

"Stop him!" The terror in her voice was another dagger to his heart.

His hand burned to release the spear—the spear that would save his brother, the spear that would end it all. But it would also end Salara. He couldn't do it.

"Soren!" she screamed. "Do it!"

Cyrus swung his sword above his head, and Soren bared his teeth as he wept, but he still couldn't throw it. Anguish ripped from his throat.

Cyrus's sword gleamed, as if celebrating its want for blood—celebrating that it was about to take the head of a king.

The Blood King held it high.

But it didn't come down.

Cyrus wavered. Then he stumbled sideways, swaying.

Soren's brows dipped. What was happening?

Then the Blood King staggered backward as he let go of his raised sword, and it fell to the ground behind him. He clawed at his chest, looking down as blood poured from underneath his ribbed breastplate. But there was no weapon. Nothing had struck him.

Cyrus sank to his knees.

Soren could only stare as confusion flooded him. There was nothing—

His heart stopped, and he glanced back at Salara.

He gaped in horror.

She stood unsteadily, with her hand wrapped around the hilt of a dagger protruding from just below her breast.

"No," he mouthed as he dropped his spear and raced toward her. Then his voice broke with a thunder. "No!"

"Norah!" Phillip yelled, but he was still fighting back Raelean soldiers in the thick of the battle around them.

Soren reached her just as she fell forward to her knees, and he caught her in his arms. "Salara!"

Her mouth moved, but no words came out.

Stupid woman. Stupid, stupid woman. "What did you do!" he raged at her. "What did you fucking do?"

She frowned as tears stippled the corners of her eyes, and then she tried to smile. "I think you're getting blind as you age," she answered between gasps.

"I'm sorry," he begged. "I couldn't do it. I'm so sorry."

She shook her head. "I should have never asked you to."

Soren wept as he pulled her into his arms, ignoring the searing pain in his shoulder. He had to get her to Mikael.

"I'm sorry," she whispered.

He shook his head as he picked her up and rose to his feet, but he couldn't speak. He didn't want her apology. Not when it was for taking the most important person in the world from him, taking herself from Mikael and from Adrian. From everyone who loved her—everyone who needed her.

Her breaths came labored, and he moved faster.

"Salara!" Mikael's bellow rang out when he saw them. He struggled up and toward them, limping as he clasped the arrow in his side.

Soren laid her down on the ground as gently as he could. Mikael sank down on her other side, his hands shaking as he hovered them over the hilt of the dagger just under her breast.

Mikael's voice shook. "Salara."

She reached up and grazed his face with her fingertips. "I told you fate can be changed." She smiled weakly.

Mikael wept as he looked around them in desperation. The battle still waged as far as the eye could see, but then his eyes stopped, spotting something. Soren followed his gaze to Tahla in the far distance, still on top of Sephir and battling back the Raelean army.

"The Wild," he said.

Soren creased his brow. "What?"

Mikael reached up and palmed his scarred shoulder where Soren had once hit him with an arrow. "The Wild. How far are we from the Wild?"

What difference did that make? Soren shook his head. "Three days' ride? Likely more."

"We have to get her to the Wild. They can heal her."

Soren glanced down at Norah. Her eyelids fell. "We'll never make it in time. She won't last the hour." His words shook as he said them.

Mikael grabbed him. "Don't say that!" He looked back down at her as tears fell from his eyes. "We have to."

Picking up Salara carefully, Mikael moved to a nearby horse and mounted with her in his arms. Calla gave Soren her own mount, and grabbed another nearby for herself, and they urged the animals through the carnage and west.

To the Wild they'd never reach in time.

Chapter Fifty-One

Adrian stepped through the bodies on the battlefield. Pockets of fighting still remained, but the army of Rael had largely scattered, retreating back as the news of their dead king rippled through. The Mercian soldiers had helped him with Cohen—his friend would lose his arm but keep his life.

He'd caught up to Phillip, who told him what had happened to Norah, and the high of victory came crashing down. He could do nothing—nothing but wait to see if they made it. But in his heart, he knew they wouldn't. The Wild was too far.

Adrian stumbled through the carnage, numb. In a way, he was glad Alexander had gone to the gods—that he wasn't there to suffer the loss of Norah. Again. Tears streamed down his face. Adrian would suffer it for the both of them.

There was a rustle to his right, and he looked to see Katya. She was checking the battlefield for survivors. When she saw him, she approached.

"You look like shit," she said when she reached him. She pulled down her wrap and took a swig of water from the goatskin at her hip.

He knew it was a jest, but he couldn't bring himself to smile. She offered him the water. He declined.

Her face sobered. "You fought well today."

"Not well enough."

She looked out across the battlefield. "Is it ever enough?"

No. No, it wasn't.

She sighed and looked back to him. "Will you be going back to the North?" she asked.

He shook his head. "No. To Kharav. I need to get back to Sevina and Theisen. They're... they're all I have left."

Her eyes glistened, and her lips parted slightly. She stepped closer to him. "Adrian... I need to tell you something..." She paused.

His brows dipped. She seemed nervous. He'd never seen Katya nervous before. They'd just finished a war for gods' sakes.

She only stared at him.

"Katya?"

She swallowed. "We're all your family," she said finally. "You have us all."

That wasn't... what he'd expected. He opened his mouth to speak, then closed it again. She clasped his shoulder and then continued her work across the battlefield looking for survivors.

Adrian turned his own attention back to the battlefield. The injured had been carried off, but Bahoul still looked like a mountain of bodies, and the hills around it a rolling sea of death. He recognized a Crest warrior half buried and hurried toward him. Dropping down beside him, he reached a hand to the man's neck to feel for a pulse.

He was gone.

Adrian stood again, his eyes still on the warrior. So many were gone—so many he knew, so many he loved.

He continued, sweeping side to side, searching.

Then, in the hallow of a hill, he saw something that made him stop.

Lucien.

He lay on his back. Blood seeped from underneath the armor on his chest, down his sides and into the ground. His face was turned up toward the sky, staring blankly.

Adrian drew closer, and Lucien's hand moved ever so slightly.

He still lived.

He stepped even closer, his shadow falling over him, and Lucien's eyes found him.

"Adrian," he said weakly, so quiet he almost didn't hear.

Slowly, Adrian sank down beside him.

Lucien opened his mouth to speak, but no words came. He reached his bloodied hand along the ground toward him.

Adrian stared at it. If he took it, Lucien could come to him, enter his mind.

"Adrian," Lucien struggled again. Pleading.

Adrian's lip trembled as Alexander's face looked back at him—the face that tore his heart in two, the face that he missed more than anything in the world. He looked down at Lucien's outstretched hand, then took it and closed his eyes.

In the depths of his mind, they were still in the battlefield. But now, Lucien stood in front of him, whole and well.

"Brother," Lucien said.

Adrian looked at him warily.

"I broke the tether," Lucien told him.

"But it won't help her now, will it?" It wouldn't heal her.

Lucien's eyes tightened, as if filled with guilt. Did he feel guilty? He was. "I've sent someone to help her. A friend."

The faintest of hope flickered in him. "A healer?"

Lucien shook his head. "I lost my healer."

Adrian shifted. "Will this friend save her?" Did he dare to hope?

"I don't know if she can." Lucien swallowed. "I didn't mean to hurt Norah. I didn't think she'd sacrifice herself."

"Because you don't know her at all," he snapped back.

Lucien nodded, accepting the guilt, accepting Adrian's anger. "I don't have much time, but I wanted you to know that I wish things could have been different between us. I like to think they could have been, if we'd have lived in a different world, in a different time." He smiled sadly. "I don't dare ask your forgiveness, but I do want to give you something."

Lucien looked to his right, and Adrian followed his gaze to see Alexander walking toward them. He wore a warm smile.

Adrian trembled as his breath left him. "Is it really him?"

Lucien nodded.

"I don't understand. You can link with the dead?"

Slowly, Lucien nodded again. "Something like that."

But Adrian didn't really care how. He stumbled toward Alexander, and his brother held his arms wide. He fell into them with a sob. Alexander's arms came around him and embraced him tightly. Warmth from his body surrounded him. He was there. *He was really there.* Adrian clung to him.

He pulled back, blinking back his tears. "How are you here?"

But Alexander only smiled. Everything about him was as he remembered. His eyes, his face, his smile. He'd never gotten to see him one last time, to say goodbye. But now, he was here. And he could feel him—feel his warmth.

Adrian glanced back at Lucien. "Can he not speak?"

"I don't have enough power to let him speak, but he wants you to know that he loves you." His voice tightened in emotion. "He's proud of you and the man you've become. He says our father's proud."

"I love you, Alec," Adrian said through his tears. "I'll hold everything you taught me. I'll honor our father, and our family. I love you."

Alexander clasped the side of his neck and gripped him tightly. He nodded. With a final smile, he faded.

"Our time's come," Lucien told him.

Adrian looked back at him.

"Goodbye, brother," Lucien said softly, and Adrian's mind faded into darkness.

He opened his eyes. Lucien still lay in front of him. But he was gone. Blood trailed from his nose and down his cheeks. Adrian leaned over the body of his brother and wept.

Soren and Mikael drove their mounts hard, with Calla close behind them. The girl had picked up a few more arrow quivers that lay with fallen archers on the field, but they didn't need much now. They weren't met with resistance. Most of the Raelean army had begun to flee. Soren was grateful. He wasn't sure he could get another fight out of his body. He could barely hold his sword.

Mikael wasn't faring well either. He'd broken the arrow off in his side, unable to pull it out. He still carried Salara in his arms. Soren feared they'd already lost her. *No*—he couldn't think about that—it would break him.

Suddenly, their horses reared and skidded to a grinding halt as a woman appeared before them. She wore a cloak the color of burnt blood, with her long, dark curls loose down her front. She pulled back her hood.

Although Soren hadn't seen her face the last time they'd met, he knew exactly who she was. "It's the Blood King's witch," he called to Mikael. He pulled his sword, having to use all his strength now to wield it.

She turned her eyes on him. "That didn't get you very far before, and it won't get you far now."

"Get out of our way," Mikael snarled between his teeth.

"My king has sent me to help the North Queen."

Soren snorted. "Your king is dead."

The faintest of emotion flashed across her face. Surprise? No. Blood marked her forehead. She knew he was dead. It was pain. "I'll still keep my promise," she said.

A promise to kill Salara, more likely. Soren clutched his sword tighter, ready to take her head.

"Are you a healer?" Mikael demanded.

"If you wanted a healer, your army shouldn't have killed the only one in this world," she snapped back.

"It's *your* king that started this war," Soren snarled.

"Enough," Mikael hissed at him. He turned back to the witch. "How can you help her?"

Soren looked at him in astonishment. "You can't be serious."

"I'm not a healer," she said, "but I can give you more time to get to someone who might be able to help you."

"Or you could kill her," Soren growled. "Kill us all."

The witch gave a cruel smile. "She's already dying. I needn't do anything. And yes, I brought down the wall of your mighty fortress. I could kill you. Right now."

Soren spat in frustration. Why didn't she, then?

"Make your decision quickly," she snapped as she looked at Norah. "She only has moments left."

Mikael slid down from his horse with Salara in his arms. Soren gaped at him. He couldn't believe he was trusting her. "Take caution, witch," Mikael warned.

Slowly, the woman looked over Norah and put a hand on her head. Then she reached out and touched Mikael, whispering words Soren didn't understand. He clutched his sword tighter. A slight wind swept over them, and then the air calmed.

"What did you do?" Mikael asked.

"This won't save her, but so long as she touches you, she can draw life from you, until you get to where you're going. Don't let her go—if you break the touch, you break the bond."

Mikael let out an emotional breath and nodded. "Why do you do this?"

"I already told you," she snapped. "For my king."

Why would the Blood King help Salara?

Mikael mounted his horse again, with Salara in his arms.

"This magic comes with a price," she warned. "It gives you time, yes, but it's limited. So long as the bond isn't broken, she'll draw life from you. But she'll draw it until she drains it all, and then both of you will die. So I suggest you get to wherever you're going quickly."

Death sat everywhere around him, death from every kingdom—Mercia, Kharav, Rael, and the Horsemen. So many were dead. Caspian stumbled through the sea of bodies.

They'd been victorious, although this didn't feel victorious. The fighting had stopped, and everyone who remained seemed to be collecting their wounded. Everyone except Rael, who'd fled. His eyes found a soldier in the carnage, carrying the body of another. They were covered in blood. He couldn't tell whether they were from Mercia or Aleon.

"Hang on, you're going to be all right," the soldier said to the man he carried as he staggered by. But his friend was already gone. Caspian could only watch as they faded into the fog of death.

His own weariness was on him now. He hadn't slept in two days, and he'd fought until his arms couldn't lift his sword. But he needed to turn his attention to anyone who might be alive. With the battle now over, he started sifting through the bodies of the fallen.

Caspian's eye caught movement, and he stooped down beside a soldier. It was a man of Rael. He was young, and his eyes were wide with fear.

"Please," the young man begged. "I don't want to die."

Caspian's eyes drifted to his blood-soaked midsection, where he'd taken a blade. There was no escaping death for this one. Caspian moved to stand.

"Please," the soldier said, his eyes filling with tears. "Don't leave me." He reached out, and Caspian dropped back down and took his hand. "Don't leave me," he begged again.

"I won't," Caspian said gently.

The man clung to his hand, pulling him closer. "I don't want to die," he pleaded again.

"You're going to be all right," he lied, echoing the soldier carrying his dead friend. But he could still see the man's fear. "What's your name?"

The soldier drew a labored breath. "Brandon."

"Brandon." Caspian looked at him. The man was young, too young to die. "I'm here with you, Brandon."

The soldier clasped his hand and seemed to calm. "I have a son," he said.

Caspian smiled sadly. "I do too."

"I haven't met him yet. I need to get home."

It was all Caspian could do to keep his emotion in. "You will."

Brandon nodded, but his eyes grew heavier, and his breathing became shallow.

"Rest awhile first," Caspian said softly. "Then you'll go home."

He nodded faintly. "All right. Maybe just a little while."

The soldier let his eyes close but kept hold of Caspian's hand. Then his grip relaxed, and the rise and fall of his chest slowed to a stop.

Caspian's lip trembled, and he wiped back the tears from his face. Curse the gods and curse this wretched fate. He released the soldier's hand and fell onto his back on the ground, looking up at the sky.

Curse this world. Was this all there was to life? Pain and death and heartbreak? And for what? It was all for nothing. Everything had been taken from him. Alexander. Norah. There was only one thing left that he wanted in this world—the one thing he couldn't have—Tahla and Katakah. He wanted them so badly he could almost see them as he looked up at the clouds. He could almost feel Tahla in his arms. He could almost hear her.

"Caspian," she seemed to call.

He clutched on to everything in his mind, everything he remembered of her—her touch, her taste, her sound. He closed his eyes. Maybe he'd rest awhile too.

"Caspian!" came her voice, and he opened his eyes. "Caspian!"

He bolted up to sit and looked out across the field of fallen battle.

"Caspian!"

It came from his right, and he jerked toward her sound. And there she was, running toward him.

Tahla.

He staggered to his feet just as she launched herself and threw her arms around him. He clung to her.

"I saw you," she cried. "I saw you, and..." She couldn't finish. She'd seen him on the ground.

"I'm all right," he assured her. "I'm all right."

She wept into his neck.

"I'm all right," he said again.

Finally, she pulled back to look at him, but still clutched him tightly. "I was so scared."

"I'm here," he assured her. Then he stopped. "*You're* here. Tahla, you saved us. You saved us all." He was still astonished at the sheer number of Horsemen that had come to their aid. "How did you get them all?"

"I called them with Savantahla. And they followed."

Norah's mare. The mare of the Wild.

This woman—this woman had united all the tribes of the Horsemen to turn the tide of war against Rael. He held her in his arms, then pulled her hands up to his lips and kissed them. Then he stopped. On her forefinger was a ring.

His ring.

His eyes locked with hers, and she smiled through her tears. "I put it on the night you gave it to me."

Tears came freely now, and he couldn't speak.
"I haven't told anyone what it means," she whispered.
"It's okay. It was only for you to know."
She smiled through her tears. "But now it's for you to know too. Husband."
He pulled her closer—his love, his wife.

Chapter Fifty-Two

The ride to the Wild was the longest Soren had ever known. Mikael carried Salara like he carried his heart in his arms, watching it fade. And he was fading with her. Soren worried neither of them would last the journey, but still they rode. They stopped only for a few hours each night to rest their horses before continuing. Then on they went—not eating, not speaking, just desperately riding.

They reached the tree line of the Wild on the third day, their horses staggering in exhaustion.

"You stay with the horses," Soren told Calla as he slid down from his mount. There was a chance no one would return from the Wild alive, and he didn't want her pulled into that.

Mikael dropped down from his horse, but he couldn't catch himself and fell to his knees. He tried to stand again but stumbled and dropped back to the ground.

Soren cursed. He was losing them both. He hooked an arm around Mikael and pulled him to stand, but Mikael was almost as large as he was, and almost as heavy. With his own injuries, Soren couldn't hold them both. Mikael fell again, and Soren spewed another slew of curses. They'd never make it.

"Let me carry her," he said.

"I have to stay connected."

"Hold her damned hand!" He pulled Salara from his arms, despite the nauseating pain in his shoulder, and gave Mikael a moment to get to his feet. "We have to go. Quickly."

They were anything but quick. Soren carried Salara, but slowly, so Mikael could hold on to her as they went. The pain in his shoulder was excruciating, but he ignored it. He was the least injured of them all. Blood soaked Mikael's side from the arrow still within—too much blood. Soren tried not to think of how close death was to them.

The forest fell quiet around them. Eerily quiet. Were the Wild women here?

"Naavi!" Soren bellowed. "Sana!" But neither of the sisters showed themselves.

Mikael stumbled. He fell to the ground and broke his hold from Salara. "No!" he cried.

Soren's breath caught. *No.* The bond, they had to get back the bond. He dropped to his knees beside Mikael, and Mikael clasped hold of her again.

"Salara!" Mikael called to her, holding her hand tightly. But her breath was fading. "No. No! Salara!" Mikael clutched her tightly. "I'm here. I'm here!"

But as she exhaled, she didn't draw in another breath.

Soren shook as he held her. *No*—they were so close. They were practically here. She couldn't leave them yet. But she didn't draw a breath. She had to breathe.

She had to *breathe*.

"Naavi!" Soren bellowed.

"What have you done?" a voice came behind them, and they spun to see the green Wild woman.

"Please," Mikael begged. "I know you have the power to heal. You have to heal her!"

Naavi's eyes widened as she looked over Norah, and she stepped to them. Her hands shook as she dropped down to brush Salara's cheek. She held her face. "No," the Wild woman whispered. Her lips pulled back in a silent sob, then she screamed, "Sana!"

A second Wild woman appeared from between the trees, and quickly came to them. No smart remarks about Mikael or Soren, just her eyes on Salara. She reached out and touched Salara's pale skin, and her face twisted. Then she looked at her sister with a great sadness in her eyes. "Sister," she whispered. "She's gone."

Soren's chest seized. She couldn't be gone.

"No," Naavi pleaded. "We have to try."

Sana's frown deepened. "Even with the power of the pool, you know we can't bring life back after it's completely gone."

"We have to try," Naavi pressed.

"But it's not possible."

"Try!" Mikael and Soren raged together. Soren would burn this forest to the ground if they didn't at least try to help her.

Sana looked at her sister, and then gave a reluctant nod. "Quickly, bring her to the pool."

Naavi scooped Salara from Soren's arms like she weighed nothing at all and followed her sister. Soren pulled Mikael to his feet and, with Mikael's arm wrapped around his shoulder, they followed after.

The Wild held all the beauty and amazement Soren remembered, but he didn't pay attention now. He only followed the sisters to the pool. When they reached it, they splashed into the water. Soren and Mikael followed, surprisingly with no objections. The sisters weren't focused on Soren and Mikael—they were focused on Salara. They placed their hands on her and closed their eyes.

Soren locked eyes with Mikael. He could see his fear and felt his own fear swelling. If Salara died...

The women broke from their concentration and looked at each other, their eyes wide. "We don't have enough strength," Sana panted. "We need to pull more."

"Can you use me?" Soren asked. He considered himself pretty damned strong.

"You don't have power, you idiot," Sana snapped.

Soren didn't even know how to respond to that. He was about to argue that the witch had used power from Mikael, but a small, horned creature appeared and put her hand on Sana's shoulder, and his argument left him as he realized they were surrounded by creatures. So many of them—where had they come from?

Another creature followed suit, reaching out to Sana. All the creatures of the Wild around them drew forward, placing their hands on one another, linking their strength.

Naavi and Sana closed their eyes again. Sweat beaded on their brows. Everything was quiet. *Eternity in the quiet.*

Tears streamed down Naavi's face. That couldn't be good. Soren's heart pulsed faster. He looked at Mikael, whose own eyes were rimmed red.

And then they all stopped.

Warmth. Warmth flooded her senses.

Norah's eyes opened as she sucked in a breath. Was she in water? She focused her eyes to see Naavi looking back at her, smiling with tears in her eyes. She smiled back. *Naavi?*

And then Mikael pulled her to him, holding her tight. How was Mikael here? A splash sounded beside her, and Soren leaned closer. What was happening?

And then the memories flooded her.

The war.

The battle.

How she'd used the dagger on herself to stop Cyrus.

She twisted as she clutched her chest.

Mikael gripped her hand to calm her. "You're all right," he said through his tears. "You're all right."

She stopped, and her breaths started to calm. *He* was all right. And he was here, with her.

"You came back," he whispered.

"There was life still in her," Naavi said.

Norah reached up and touched his face. She couldn't take her eyes from him. He was alive, and with her. She smiled through her tears at him. "I was so scared," she whispered. "I thought you were going to die."

He held her tighter. "I thought you *had* died."

"She did," Naavi said. "But there was still life inside." The woman gestured to her stomach, smiling at Norah. "We used it to keep you."

Life inside. Norah looked at her stomach and then to Mikael, then back to Naavi. "What?" She didn't dare to hope their meaning.

"You carry a life inside you," Naavi said. "A child."

"A child?" Norah breathed, tears springing from her eyes. "I'm with child?" A sob rose in her throat. After all this time, after all the wanting and the disappointment and the heartache. Finally. *A child.*

Naavi nodded.

Norah let out a laugh through her sob. Mikael pulled her to him and shook as he buried his face in the fold of her neck. All she could do was hold on to him. *A child.* Mikael was all right, they were together, and they were going to have a child. Her heart was so happy it hurt.

Suddenly, Mikael pulled back and looked at the Wild women. "You used the child to save her?"

Naavi nodded again. "Yes."

His brow creased in worry. "Is he all right?"

"She." Naavi's smile widened. "She's perfectly fine."

Soren sat in wet clothes. He didn't care, but he still grumbled about it. It was the only thing that kept him from losing himself to the emotion he struggled so hard to keep down. He wished he had his wrap to hide his face, to hide the emotion brimming. He'd lost it somewhere on the ride to the Wild.

Salara had done it—she'd changed fate. Mikael was safe, and for that Soren wanted to cling on to her, hold her, hug her.

Then she'd almost died and, in doing so, had ripped his heart from his chest. This wretched woman, the thought had destroyed him. And now... she and Mikael had what they'd wanted for so long—a child. His heart swelled to near bursting.

A movement to his right caught his eye, and he turned to see the two Wild women approaching. Finally, something to be annoyed about to distract his mind from feelings.

"Destroyer," Sana said as they neared. They really liked calling him that, but he didn't mind too much. It reminded him of Salara's grandmother—feisty wench. Death didn't deserve her.

His attention shifted back to the women, and he stood. "Come to take my memories?" he said with an edge of challenge. Not that he could stop them, but he'd still give them the nine hells if they tried. They hadn't taken them the last time he was here with Salara—they had a lot to catch up for.

The Wild women stopped in front of him and stared at him for a moment.

He stood and shifted uncomfortably.

"We saw you in the water."

How observant. "Yes, I was in the water." Maybe he shouldn't have jumped in the pool—the magical pool—but he hadn't even cared. Salara was all he could think about.

"No, we *saw* you," Naavi said. "We saw who you are."

He raised a brow. "I've been here three times, and you're just now seeing?"

Sana rolled her eyes. "We didn't care before. And to be very clear, we don't care now. But the pool showed us regardless." She reached out and gripped his shoulder.

He stiffened, and a groan escaped him as pain shot through him. It almost brought him to his knees. When she pulled back her hand, he gaped down at his shoulder. The sword wound was stitched with an earthy binding. She'd healed him. He drew his fingers over it as he stared back at them in surprise.

"And we have something else we want to give you," Naavi said. "A gift."

Soren didn't like gifts. They were generally in poor taste and expected to be reciprocated. But he stilled as he saw two wolves step out from between the trees—large wolves, the largest he'd ever seen. Both wore coats of black, and their eyes burned a deep gold.

Naavi's eyes changed from green to bright gold, and she stepped in front him. Her hands reached up and cupped his cheeks, and she pulled his face down to hers. Ever so softly, she pushed herself up on her toes and planted a kiss on his forehead.

He gasped as visions rippled through him, and he realized—he was looking through the eyes of the wolves. His eyes flew open, and he stumbled backward, almost falling, but he managed to catch himself.

"You've made me a seer?"

Sana looked at Naavi. "He really is an idiot sometimes."

Naavi smiled. "No. Not a seer. But these wolves are bonded to you now. They're loyal to you, and they'll give you a greater power to do what you've always done."

He snorted. "Destroy?"

Naavi shook her head. "Protect."

He stilled and stood wordlessly. He looked at the wolves and then back at the sisters. Naavi nodded to him.

Then he knelt down and willed the wolves to him. And they came, knowing his mind. His hands trembled as he reached out to run his fingers through their thick fur. They were beautiful beasts. Strong. Fearless. They would do nicely. He looked back at the sisters.

"Now get out of our forest," Sana said.

Soren smiled.

The morning air was frigid as they prepared to leave the Wild and head back to the North. The rising sun spilled its rays down on them, but they held no warmth. Soren scowled out at the snow-laden sky in the distance. It would turn colder as they traveled. He hated the cold.

The Wild women had offered them to stay longer, to wait out the small storm approaching, but Salara was eager to get back and show their people that their queen was alive and well—a little snow wouldn't keep her. Soren was eager too. He needed to return to what was left after the battle. Caspian and Adrian would be waiting for him.

Phillip would be waiting for him. The thought warmed him.

Soren sat on his horse, his wolves standing beside him, and rolled his eyes as he waited the eternity it took for Salara to say goodbye to the Wild women and mount up behind Mikael. Calla sat on her own horse, smiling. The girl was in a perky mood, which meant he'd have to listen to her incessant chatter all the way back. The journey already felt long, and they hadn't even started yet.

Soren glanced around impatiently and found Mikael looking back at him with a smile on his lips. Never had he seen his brother so happy.

Happy was different.

Many things would be different now. Their kingdoms were united with the new Aleon Empire. A lot would change. Kharav would change. They were already abandoning their slaving norms, which had fallen apart through the course of the war. Salara would make sure it stayed that way.

The united kingdoms would no longer be constantly on the brink of battle. Soren wasn't quite sure what he'd do with himself. He thought of Phillip again. He'd figure it out.

Finally, to his relief, they started on their way, urging their mounts past the tree line of the Wild and north.

A stinging wind swept through with the faint beginnings of snow.

"Curse the North gods," he muttered.

Calla wrinkled her brow. "Why the North gods?"

"Because we don't have gods, so you curse the North ones."

"But... why the North ones? Elam has gods, and Persus. And Lorys."

Soren shot the girl an annoyed glance. "Because everything that makes your life hard comes from the North."

"Not me," Salara said sweetly as she leaned against Mikael's back with her arms wrapped around him.

Mikael chuckled.

Soren dipped his brow. "Especially you." He glanced at her belly and then rolled his eyes again. "And now there's going to be two of you."

"Ah, Soren," she teased him, "what are you going to do with another girl around?"

Soren snorted as he looked out at the rising sun. He'd do the only thing to be done with a girl—

Make her a warrior.

THE BLOOD DUOLOGY

Continue the journey with:

Blood King I

He doesn't want the throne. He wants revenge.
A new crown. An old wound.
And a reckoning written in blood.

ABOUT THE AUTHOR

Nicola Tyche is a romantic fantasy author, weaving stories full of twisty suspense, fierce heroines, villains you can't help but root for, and lovers who kiss *and* kill.

She lives in the Pacific Northwest with her husband and three daughters. When she isn't writing, she enjoys tacos, traveling, gardening, exploring the great outdoors, and other creative projects.

Visit her website at www.nicolatyche.com, join her reader communities on Facebook or Discord, and find her on your favorite social platforms through the link below!